The tallest stones, reaching twice a woman's height, had thrust up from the earth in a rough circle, like a fort or crown. For the first time since she had left her brother's body, Caribou felt afraid. Her people called such rings of rock trolls' hedges, for here the *daimons* of the earth gathered to smoke and play dice. . . .

She stared at the rocks, and knew she should not go in. To enter a trolls' hedge, even by day, was dangerous, and to sleep in one, certainly death.

But she was very cold still, and night was drawing on, and it was into the trolls' hedge that the golden trail disappeared. She was dead anyway. So Caribou clambered up over the lower rocks and between two taller ones where the golden spatters led. . . .

Tor Books by Meredith Ann Pierce

The Dark Angel
A Gathering of Gargoyles
The Woman Who Loved Reindeer

The Woman Who Loved Reindeer

Meredith Ann Pierce

A TOM DOHERTY ASSOCIATES BOOK
NEW YORK

THE WOMAN WHO LOVED REINDEER

Reprinted by arrangement with Atlantic Monthly Press

A TOR Book
Published by Tom Doherty Associates, Inc.
49 West 24 Street
New York, NY 10010

Cover art by Dennis Nolan

ISBN: 0-812-50305-8   Can. ISBN: 0-812-50306-6

Library of Congress Catalog Card Number: 87-80291

First Tor edition: December 1989

Printed in the United States of America

0 9 8 7 6 5 4 3 2 1

With heartfelt thanks to Nancy Willard who,
at the Bread Loaf Writers' Conference (August 1984),
asked all the right questions

NOTE TO THE READER

"J" is pronounced like the consonant "y." (Branja rhymes with Tanya.) "Sj" sounds almost like "sh" (*pisjlak* = PISH-lahk) and "tj" almost like "ch" (Tjaalsénji = chăl-SEN-yee).

Contents

The Woman Who Loved Reindeer

I

Branja

CARIBOU was not yet thirteen summers when Branja brought to her the child. The sun, silver and haze-obscured, had nearly topped the sky. The moons, both in their first quarter, hung side by side above the far horizon. Caribou stood in the doorway of her *ntula,* gazing out over the mixed forest and tundra just beginning to lose color and come into fruit as brief summer hurried to its end.

She had known her fair-sister would come. The night before, she had dreamed a snow-bunting alighted on her windowsill with a sprig of bloodthorn in its bill. It had left the berries and flown away, crying its own name: "*branja! branja!*" This was always the way of it. Snow-birds were the messengers of the ancestors, and Caribou was a dreamer of dreams.

The figure of her brother's wife, lapped in traveling furs, emerged from the woods many paces from Caribou and struggled slowly toward her up the barren rise. She looked weighted with weariness.

It was two days' journey in summer from Branja's house to Caribou's, and although she was unwed, not yet in womanhood, Caribou lived alone in her father's house — because she could read things in flurries of falling snow, hear words in wind, knew all the old tales by heart, and sometimes dreamed. The villagers were afraid of her.

No one had offered to take her in when her father had died, last summer's end, though by custom she was a child still, barely woman-shaped. Not even Visjna, her brother — for he had been newly married then, to a woman outside the Tribe. His wife had not wanted to share their house with someone little more than a stranger.

Caribou watched as Branja struggled up the gentle slope. She was bearing two burdens, Caribou saw, one a bundle cradled in her arm, the other a deep sack dragging along the ground. Caribou did not go to her. Her dream had not told her what her sister-in-law would want.

As Branja staggered up to where Caribou stood, dropping her heavy sack upon the ground, Caribou realized that the bundle Branja cradled so clumsily was a child, just lately come into the world. One bone-and-leather fasten at the throat of Branja's *lanlan* had come undone, and Caribou glimpsed her fair-sister's smock, stained in two places from the milk in her breasts.

"Caribou," her brother's wife said, panting, not even bothering with the proper greetings, "you take this child."

She held the bundle out. Caribou looked at the tiny thing, golden-haired, fair-skinned, and flush-cheeked with cold, but sleeping peacefully. Her hands did not move from her sides.

"What child is this?"

"My child," said Branja. She was dark-haired like Caribou, but with the tan-shaded skin of the River-Valley People. Warily, Caribou eyed the other's jutting cheekbones and little eyes. They told her nothing. Her fair-sister held the bundle out still.

"Why do you and Visjna give it to me?" Caribou began.

"No." Branja shook her head, still breathless. "He does not give it. I give it."

Caribou frowned and was silent for a while. She did not understand. And then she felt a little thump of surprise as, all at once, she did. "It is not his child."

The realization unnerved her. She did not like Branja, but she would never have thought her unfaithful. Branja's face crumpled. Blinking, she struggled, her voice tight.

"It . . ." she said. "It is not his concern what I do with this child."

Caribou studied the infant's fair, well-fashioned features — so unlike her brother's lean, olive ones. She could not get over her astonishment.

"How old?" she managed.

"Midsummer," her brother's wife told her. "He was born two months ago."

While Visjna was away with the caribou at the calving grounds, thought Caribou acidly. Outrage was beginning to replace her numb surprise. Branja chewed her lip, picked at the edge of the fur wrapping the child. It sighed in sleep and did not wake.

"I have kept him as long as I could" — her voice

was low, a nervous whisper — "that he might be strong when I brought him to you."

She glanced about suddenly, as if fearing somehow to be overheard. Caribou, too, looked up. The vastness of the Wilderland surrounded them, empty — completely empty but for the two of them and the sleeping infant. Even so, Branja's voice hushed lower.

"But Visjna will be returning soon with the herd, and I cannot hide him any longer from the village — I cannot keep this child!" Desperation made her voice tremble.

Caribou tried to rein her own emotions in, to keep her voice steady and calm. "Did Visjna know you were with child when he went north this spring?"

Branja looked down, shook her head. "No. I do not know. I did not tell him." She looked at Caribou again, eyes bright, almost pleading. "If he guessed, I will tell him I lost the child."

Caribou stood silent. She was thinking of Visjna, defying their father and dismaying the village to marry this foreigner, this woman from outside the Tribe. *And you betrayed him,* thought Caribou, still looking at Branja. *Within a year you took a lover.* She could feel no pity either for Branja or the child.

"Why not tell him the child is his?" said Caribou quietly, full of contempt. "How could he know?"

The other shook her head. "He would know."

"He would not care." It was almost the truth. Caribou sighed. Visjna would care. Branja's betrayal would cut him to the bone — but it would make no difference in the end. Caribou closed her eyes, desperately wishing that Branja's faithlessness could matter.

She pictured Visjna disowning his wife, sending her back to the River-Valley People with her babe. She could not help the wish. With Branja gone, Visjna could leave the village and come back to the Wilderland. *Back to me,* thought Caribou.

She opened her eyes and sighed again shortly. Hoping was useless. Visjna loved Branja. He would never cast her off. Caribou wished angrily that the other woman would go away.

"Show him the child," she told her. "He will forgive you. He must."

But Branja only dropped her voice again, her whisper growing frantic. "I am afraid."

Caribou drew back from her, surprised. "My brother will not harm you."

Her fair-sister's eyes implored her. "Not of Visjna," she said. She glanced at the golden infant in her arms. "Of the child's father."

"Who is the father?" said Caribou sharply.

The other hesitated. "A stranger," she said at last. "He . . . came through, passing southward, last fall."

A stranger. Caribou sighed, relieved. *And one long gone.* If it had been one of the village men, Visjna would have had to kill him. Then Caribou frowned as the last of Branja's words caught up with her.

"Passing *southward?*" she said. "Toward the Pole — in fall?"

That was strange. Only the wild herds, the reindeer, ran southward over the Burning Plain in winter. No one knew why they went there, or how they survived the cold. But always they returned in spring, surging northward toward the warmer lands to calve.

"Was this stranger a lone one," asked Caribou, "a tracker following the wild herds?"

Branja shook her head. "No. I . . . He did not say."

She drew breath, gazing at the child, her face contorted with indecision, or grief. Caribou waited impatiently. Branja seemed about to speak again, then halted, swallowed, shook her head and would not look at Caribou.

"Why are you afraid of him?" she asked.

"I fear for the child," the other murmured.

"What is the child to him?"

Branja's eyes flashed up. "He said that he would *take* the child!"

Caribou tightened her lips. "Why give him to me then?" she snapped. "Let the father have him if you do not want him."

Her sister-in-law's green eyes welled up with tears. Her full breasts heaved against the clasps of the too-tight *lanlan*. "You do not . . . you do not understand. This stranger — he is not as we are, Cari."

"*You* are not as we are, Branja," breathed Caribou.

Fury was choking her. She hated Branja — for coming, for daring. For using the familiar form of her name. Now that her father was gone, only Visjna could do that. For trying to foist on her this bantling, some stranger's, not even her brother's child. The woman across from her bowed her head. The infant in her arms kicked beneath the furs, slept on. Caribou's fury subsided.

"And how did this stranger know that you would bear a child?" she asked after a moment.

Branja shook her head, her eyes cast down. "I do not know. He said so afterward — just as he left me."

Caribou shrugged. "Perhaps he will not come back."

"No," cried Branja. Her eyes met Caribou's again. "I saw him. I saw him in the spring."

When the reindeer herds came back from the Pole, thought Caribou. Her jaw hurt from clenching it. Surely her fair-sister's lover must be a hunter, following the herds.

"Did you speak?" she asked her brother's wife.

The tears in Branja's eyes spilled over now. "No. He stood at a distance. But I saw his eyes." Her glance darted to the child, then back to Caribou. "He knew. And I knew he meant to return and take the child."

Caribou looked at her sister-in-law. Branja held the bundle out to her again.

"Here, Cari, you take this child — for Visjna's sake, not mine."

Caribou twitched. Once more Branja had called her Cari. Her blood was burning. *As if I could be cajoled into helping her. As if I owed her something — for Visjna's sake!* Anyone with eyes could see the child looked nothing like him. *So now I am to take the evidence off her hands and spare my brother the shame of being known a cuckold.* Caribou felt her heart close tight then, like a little fist.

"What would I do with a child?" she said, very quietly. She did not trust herself to say more.

"Raise it," cried Branja. "Care for it."

"For my brother's sake." Branja fell silent. Caribou let anger come into her voice now for the first time. "And how if your lover comes to me, demanding his child?"

Branja shook her head. "He will not come. He will not know I came here. I was careful. I told no one where I was going — I left no trail."

Caribou considered the other's heavy burdens, her staggering steps, her childhood spent among the Barge People of the River — not among the woodcrafters and trackers of the Wilds — and doubted she could have left no trail. Anyone could follow Branja. Caribou crossed her arms, her patience flayed.

"Why should I ruin myself for you?" she demanded at last. "How do I say to anyone who asks where the infant came from?"

Tears spilled again, streaking the Valley woman's cheeks. "Because you have nothing to lose. You live alone, far from any village."

Yes, alone, thought Caribou. The cold wind off the tundra breathed and sighed through her. Alone since her father had died. Alone since Branja had refused to allow Visjna to take her in. She glared at her fair-sister, but the other woman took no notice.

"No one cares if you have a child without a man," Branja wept. "Say the child is yours, or that you found it. Say that someone gave it to you — only do not say it came from me."

Caribou said nothing. There was nothing more to say. She uncrossed her arms, gazing off across the tundra, the woods, wondering what she must do to make Branja go away.

And the moment Caribou dropped her guard, her sister-in-law sprang, pressing the bundle to her. She closed her arms about the fur-wrapped load reflexively, to keep it from falling, and Branja hastily stepped back.

Caribou stared at the thing in her arms. Within its furs, still sleeping, the infant sighed and turned to her. Freeing one tiny fist from the folds, it closed its fingers about one of the long, dark braids falling over her breast.

"Here, Cari, you take this, too," Branja was saying, grasping at the sack she had set down upon first arriving. She twitched open the neck. "You see, I have brought you *pisjlak* — how do you say it? — provisions: caribou meat and snow hares, cheese, berries, sweet syrup, and *jaaro* stalks . . ."

She rummaged in the sack, half drawing out packets of this and that.

"I have ample *pisjlak* of my own," snapped Caribou, struggling to support the heavy child and free her braid. "More than I need. What I do *not* need is this child."

Branja jerked upright, dropping the sack. She backed away. "But these things will help you, help you with him."

"How could such things help me feed a child?" demanded Caribou. The infant's grasp upon her braid was like a hawk's. Still he slept. "A child needs milk. I have no goats or caribou —"

"There's *mmoli* . . ." Branja's words hardly carried now, but as she backed farther away they seemed to gain strength. "Oh, he will be no trouble. He is the perfect child. He sleeps and sleeps and never cries. He will be no burden."

Branja was now paces from the house, still edging backward and wringing her hands. Caribou wanted to follow — seize Branja and shake her — but the weight of the child was so awkward in her arms, she could only stand clutching it. She feared to move lest it slip from her. She had never held a child before.

"And these provisions," her brother's wife was saying. "They are a gift, a little peace-offering from me to you." A timid smile flitted now across her lips. "We are sisters-in-law, Cari. We should do such things for one another."

Caribou made to protest, scream, but all at once she found her throat was stopped. She had gotten better hold of the child now. His weight was still comfortable in her arms, his warm breath light against her breast, and the tug of his tiny fists upon her braid almost . . . agreeable.

"What name does he have?" she managed at last.

Her brother's wife stood watching her. "No name."

For a moment, it seemed that Branja would say more, but suddenly she let her breath out as though she had been holding it. It was an outbreath of relief. Caribou realized that she had lifted the child to lay its little body against her breast.

Branja whirled, like a milch-goat suddenly untethered, and hurried away, almost running. Caribou stood mute, unable to move, watching until the other disappeared into the woods at the foot of the slope.

A sudden panic seized her. She could not believe she had been stupid enough to let Branja thrust this child into her care. Perhaps, perhaps if she ran, she could still catch her, force her to take back the child . . . But then she heard the infant sigh, just as Branja had done, and looking down she saw the little gold-haired creature gazing at her. The child had golden eyes.

A hot dart went through her, some feeling she had never felt before. He breathed again and closed his eyes, sighing in sleep. All at once her wildly beating heart grew still, the racing in her blood subsided. Absently, almost without realizing it, Caribou smiled. It had been a long time since she had smiled. She was no longer alone.

His tiny hand released her braid, and Caribou tucked the little arm back beneath the fur. Then she knelt and laid him gently beside the doorsill. Rising, she caught hold of the *pisjlak* sack and heaved it over the threshold, dragged it in to lean against the wall. Then she returned to the infant and, carefully lifting him, carried him into the house.

2

The Child

So Caribou took the golden-eyed child that had no name into her hut. That evening, until dusk, she left him beside the fire and ranged through the woods, covering Branja's tracks against discovery — she wanted no meddlesome villager trailing the Valley woman to her door — and searching the brown, crisping undergrowth for bitter, green-leafed *mmoli*, that brings the milk to any woman's breast, even to a grandmother aged half a hundred summers or a young girl who has never known a man.

The milk came into Caribou's breasts in three days' time. Until then she kept the child alive on caribou butter, hare's blood, and a paste of powdered marrow root, which the child laughed and smiled to suck.

Caribou tried to think of a name for him. At first she tried calling him Goldeneye, but he would not answer to it. Yet he laughed and cooed when she called him "child," so "child" it was, with the golden eyes, that slept and slept like some tiny sage, dreaming wise little dreams.

Caribou fashioned for him three *bela* — sacks of rabbit fur that could be layered one inside another — for she had once seen a woman use such a garment for her babe-in-arms. Then she set the child to sleep in a box beside the fire. He never cried, and when he woke, he smiled and took her long brown braids in his fists.

And sometimes as she dandled him, she found herself wondering, *What am I doing? What have I done, taking in this little creature that is no kith to me at all, only my fair-sister's child?* Had it been loneliness — only that — which had caused her sudden change of heart? The memory of that strange, hot dart when first she had seen the child's eyes came back to her. It troubled her sometimes.

But in truth he was so quiet that most days she almost forgot he was there, until her breasts grew full and she went to suckle him: at first light and midmorning, noon, midafternoon and dusk, then again in the evening and just before bed. He never cried in the night for warmth or nourishment, sleeping in his box beside the fire while Caribou slept apart from him beneath her caribou skins.

Fleeting summer passed away. The autumnal equinox came and went, and the days grew briefer than the nights. Caribou dreamed of the return of the herders with their caribou from the summer calving grounds. Laying in the last of her winter stores, she dreamed of the wild deer returning as well, streaming south from the warm northern places where they summered. Soon they would pass Poleward in a great thundering train, beyond the Burning Plain, which only they knew how to cross.

It was the morning after her dream of the reindeer

that Caribou went to the hot spring in the high country. Hard frost was already on the ground. Soon, she knew, the heavy snows would begin to fall, shutting the passes and snowing everything under.

After that, it would be spring again before she might visit the pool. Caribou wanted to bathe there one last time before the snowfall, and because it would be a day's journey there and back, she took the child with her.

The water of the spring was warm and steamy, melting the crust of frost on the nearby ground. Caribou laid the child upon the banks, then stripped off her boots and leggings, her shirt and smock of skins, and swam naked in the hot mineral pool.

Leaning over the half-thawed bank, she freed the child from his *bela* and brought him, too, into the water, towing him along after her by his little white arms, flushed pink as a wolf's tongue now from the heat. He kicked and splashed in the steaming pool, under the pale far sun in the ice-chill air, grinning and gurgling. Then she dried him with a soft, scraped rabbitskin and laid him among his wrappings again.

At noon, Caribou emerged, dried herself, and dressed. She nursed the child and ate the small packet of pemmican she had brought, and left an offering of honeycake for the water-daimon. Then, setting the child on her hip, she wrapped her traveling cloak about them both and started down from the high country.

She had not been traveling more than an hour when she knew by the slope of the ground that she was nearing the narrow glacier-trough that rambled north-south between two rills of high country: the Reindeer's Path. She would have to descend and cross, then climb again through sloping woodlands to reach home.

A strange rushing sound met her ears as she drew near the Path. It seemed muffled at first, but grew louder the nearer she came to the slender valley. She could not think what it was at first and began to hurry, for the sky had clouded over and she feared suddenly some storm.

But when she emerged from the trees on the slope above the ravine, she saw what made the sound: not wind. She laughed at her own misgivings then, for below her thundered the reindeer, the vast wild herds sweeping like a river of living silver — all heads and antlers and backs, the tendons in their limbs snapping like willow flicks. They paced along, faster than human legs could run, southward toward the Pole.

The ground on which Caribou stood trembled. In her alarm a few moments past, she had completely forgotten her dream of the reindeer the night before. Gazing south, she glimpsed their rumbling train filling the narrow channel as far as she could see.

They must have been passing for hours, she realized, must have begun to come through just after she had crossed the valley that morning. Still smiling, she walked along the slope above the herd until she found a place where the hillside was not too steep, and sat down.

While she sat waiting for the herd to pass, she took

the child out from beneath her *lanlan* into the open air. The infant cried out with delight, his little mouth agape, laughing. Caribou laughed with him as he stretched his tiny hands out to the running deer as they hurtled by.

After a little, the rush began to thin, then to dwindle. When at length the last of the wild deer, even the stragglers, had passed, Caribou rose. Keeping the child still outside her cloak, she began descending toward the valley floor.

Halfway across the barren, uneven terrain of the narrow trough, she saw two figures on the far slope, one very tall and long of limb, dark-haired and olive-skinned: a man. The other, a woman in a bright-embroidered skirt of the River-Valley People, had the black hair and tan complexion of that tribe.

The man waved with his free arm — in his other hand he held a bow, the quiver slung from his hip — and Caribou recognized him then: her brother, Visjna. The woman beside him must be Branja. Caribou halted, apprehensive suddenly, feeling the weight of the child in her arms.

Just as she did so, before she could think what to do or say, she heard a sound: a long bawling like someone in great grief. It came from the north, the direction from which the reindeer had come. Caribou turned, but could see nothing beyond a rill in the floor of the valley where she was standing.

Before her on the slope she saw Visjna and his wife also turn, and she heard her brother give a shout. Her sister-in-law uttered a little scream and covered her mouth. The loud lowing sounded again, nearer this time.

Caribou felt the child on her hip wake with a start, his little body suddenly rigid against her. He gave a high, keening wail like no sound she had ever heard — it echoed the lower, louder cry that had wakened him — and began to struggle.

His tiny fists thrashed free of the swaddling clothes; his little legs kicked and churned inside the rabbit's-fur bundling. Caribou gripped him tighter, lifted him from her hip. Then her unease shivered into alarm, for all this time the child's small, round face was screwed into a curiously adult expression: not infant's squalling, but some deep-felt sorrow, his loud, piercing wail slitting the air.

Caribou shushed at him, tried the soft chattering of lips and tongue her father had used to quiet caribou calves — to no avail. The child wailed on and struggled even as Caribou bounced him gently, crooning to him, until his thrashing grew so vigorous she had to clutch him tight to keep from dropping him.

Without warning, his keening halted, so abruptly Caribou knew that nothing she had done could have stilled it. The child had fallen silent, half-turned in her hands, his eyes cast toward the rise in the middle of the gorge where they stood. Just then, Caribou heard Branja's second scream.

Suddenly she saw what it was that had caught the child's eye. On the crest of the rise, bright-lit, in sharp relief against the stark hills behind, stood a great reindeer stag of tawny gold. Taller he was than even the biggest stag she had ever seen. His rack of horns rose from his brow like a nest of golden arms and hands, webbed fingers wide-spread to the gray-bright sky.

He pawed the earth, stamped once with his great splay hoof, and the tendons clacked. The plumes of breath that shot from his nostrils made little clouds. His great, expressionless eyes as they studied the child in Caribou's arms were deep, pure gold.

The child reached out to him with a delighted cry, so much like one of recognition that Caribou was baffled. The great deer circled, pawing the earth again. His breath spurted and steamed.

The child laughed, and the reindeer started forward, then halted suddenly, stiff-legged. His eyes, as they settled on Caribou, grew dark and dangerous. She grasped the bundled infant tighter and stepped back. The golden stag lifted his head and belled — long, deep: a challenge.

Caribou backed away from him, toward the sloping hillside of the trough. From the corner of her eye, she saw her brother and his wife start down the slope toward her, Visjna running. The reindeer stared at Caribou, his head high, half turned.

The child began to struggle in her arms again, more violently than before. Caribou was hard pressed to keep her hold. Crying, he twisted toward the deer, opening his tiny hands, and reached out to him. The stag let go an answering cry, strangely mournful, and launched his great golden form toward them.

Caribou stumbled into a run. Her limbs felt light. Her breath came harsh and hard. Before her she saw her brother halt as he neared the bottom of the slope. His wife dashed past him.

Branja shouted something, interposing herself between Caribou and the charging deer, but the golden stag only dodged, lowering his horns, and feinted toward her. The Valley woman threw up her arms with a cry and fell back as the great deer sprang by.

Caribou lost her balance, her foot skidding on a stone. The child slipped, and Caribou clutched at him. She heard the dull smarting of reindeer hooves upon the frozen turf. Wailing, the child writhed in his padded *bela*. Caribou's foot slid again on the slick, icebound ground, and she lost her grip. The bundled child slipped free.

She lunged, trying to catch him. But before the child could touch the earth, before her hands could reach the child, a wall of gold passed before her, almost touching. The reindeer had dropped his head in passing, catching the infant in his nested horns.

Caribou heard a whistling, felt an arrow pass over her left shoulder, and saw it just miss the back ridge of the gold stag's lowered neck. Whirling, Caribou saw her brother reaching for another arrow from the quiver at his hip.

She spun again. The bending stag sprang up, snapping the antler-cradle high, out of her reach. Caribou cried out, her arms outstretched after the child, but the wild deer was already vaulting away over the frozen ground.

She heard screaming, and realized dazedly that it came from behind her: Branja. Caribou stood unmoving, her lips parted and the wind blowing into her mouth. Wind blew between the wide-spread fingers of her hands.

Visjna was running full tilt after the stag that held the child overhead, unharmed, in his horns. Her brother still clutched his longbow in one hand, and in the other, a long, slim arrow, double-barbed. His narrow quiver banged against his thigh.

Caribou felt her wrist grabbed suddenly, and jerked around to find herself facing Branja. The Valley woman clung to her, her wide green eyes beseeching, her words a breathless shriek.

"He came back, Cari," she panted. "Two nights ago, just as he said he would. Visjna was there. I had told him, told him everything, just the day before . . ."

Caribou stared at her sister-in-law. Words seemed to be falling from the other's mouth of their own accord.

"He came back . . ." Branja gasped.

"Turn me loose," hissed Caribou. "What are you talking of?"

"The father — the father of the child!" the Valley woman cried. "But he did not care, my husband, about the child. Cari, it was just as you said. Visjna told him to go away, stood in the doorway with his longbow. He told him the child was not with us, was far away where he would never find him . . ."

Sobs choked Branja. Caribou stared after her brother, the stag, and the child, and tried to drag her sleeve from Branja's grasp.

"We spoke; we discussed it," her fair-sister sobbed. "Visjna said we must bring the child and you to live with us. We were coming to find you! But the stag, the stag —"

Caribou tugged her sleeve harder. "Let me go, Branja," she said frantically. "So your lover returned — how does that matter now?"

But Branja was already speaking. "Oh, help me, Cari. Help me." The words ran and tumbled. Branja moaned, then cried aloud, "The stag! The golden stag . . . carrying off the child."

Caribou stared after the shrinking figures, now dwindled finger-small. She had no idea what Branja was trying to say to her. She cried out, "Let go!" and managed to break free at last. She sped away at a dead run.

Branja did not follow; Caribou heard her behind, crying and moaning. A long way ahead, she saw the great stag spring up one side of the trough and bolt away into the trees.

For an instant, her brother halted, fitted the arrow he held to the cord of his bow, and shot. He climbed on then, not even waiting to see whether the shaft found its mark. It fell short, striking the slope behind the reindeer's heels.

Caribou had nearly reached the slope herself now. Before her, the stag vanished into the trees, and a moment later, her brother as well. She struggled up the steep hillside, bent, catching at the frost-caked stub-grass for a better purchase. She reached the woods' edge.

And the last she heard of those she followed, above the harshness of her own breathing, above the soughing of wind and Branja's bitten-off cries, was the crashing of the golden reindeer and her brother through the brush, and also — could she be hearing right? — strangely, occasionally, cries from the child: no longer wails and screaming now, but laughing gurgles of delight.

3

The Golden Stag

CARIBOU plunged into the dark woods after her brother, the golden reindeer, and the child. She followed their trail of broken frost among the barren trees. But presently the trees grew so thick no frost had formed, and the ground itself was too hard to show any track.

The close-spaced boles threw vague shadows, and the day grew grayer as the clouds thickened overhead. She had long since lost all sound of those she pursued, and had no idea of where she was or how late the afternoon had grown. The black, wind-gnarled branches bent over her.

At last, she fell against a tree-trunk and leaned there panting; she did not know how long. When her breath came back, she staggered on. Her limbs felt thick and clumsy, heavy as iron. She struggled over the rough ground, half trotting when she could. A stitch had grown into her side, and her breasts felt tight because she had not suckled the child since noon. Thinking of him, she forced herself forward.

The trees gave out, turning to scrub. She came to a rocky place where the ground felt hot underfoot. The frost formed a thin crust, inches above the ground;

it broke beneath her step. Here and there plumes of steam rose through cracks in the earth.

She knew she must be nearing the Burning Plain, which her people also called the Land of Broken Snow. No one knew what lay beyond; only the reindeer passed over, every autumn at this time, seeking the Pole.

Then, all at once, the rocky country fell away before her in a graded cliff of steep stair-runs and blocks of stone. Caribou saw a vast plain lying below, faulted in places. Great expanses lay covered with unfrozen water, while fountains of pale steam spurted and gushed along the faults.

The earth, where she could see it through the frost, was in some parts grayish-brown, in others white as salt. There were pits of what seemed to be bubbling mud, and a line of dark, jagged peaks lay on the far horizon.

She heard rumbling then, and felt a trembling in the ground. Off to her left, the cliffside was fissured in a wide groove. From this trough, suddenly, issued a stream of white and gray, thundering, like a forest of deadwood buoyed along on a torrent.

Her dulled vision refused to focus for a moment, and then she realized with a start that it was the reindeer. They streamed from the glacier-canyon and fanned out over the Broken Plain, flying south. How had she outrun them? She could not guess, and was too tired to care.

As Caribou watched the galloping deer, small and far below her, the weariness in her welled into despair.

She thought of the golden stag, lost somewhere in that teeming tide, and the child bundled in his horns. Her breasts ached; her throat felt tense and sore. Her breath came in short, bitten gasps.

The child, the child. I have lost him — her mind nattered on without her conscious thought. She had never known she could feel such bitterness. Not since her father's death had she felt such a loss. *I never wanted him in the first place!* she tried to tell herself, clenching her teeth, but it did no good.

She wanted him now. In the short month since she had taken him in, she had grown so accustomed to the care and tending of him, to the weight of him in her arms, to his constant presence, that she could no longer imagine living without him.

Now he was gone — hopelessly lost. She would never find him, never touch or nurse him again. How long before he would slip from the golden reindeer's horns? He would be trampled to death beneath the drumming heels! Or what if he never fell — remained trapped in the antlers until he starved to death, or the cold killed him?

She could not bear to think of it, and yet she could not turn away. She scanned the surging torrent of silver until the afternoon darkened and the last fleet stragglers bolted from the trough. But not one speck of gold did she glimpse in all that time in all that river of gray.

As the vast herd of reindeer dwindled into the southern distance of the Plain, Caribou turned numbly from the rocks, back toward the woods. The autumn afternoon was very late, and she knew herself to be a half-day's walking journey from her *ntula,* at least.

She felt badly chilled from long standing, and she had no heavy, fur-stuffed *grimmul* to wrap around her against the cold, no flint for making fire, no food, no strength or spirit left, and she knew of no one living so near the Burning Plain with whom she might seek shelter.

Dazed, Caribou gazed at the sky. A thin, bitter breeze had sprung up. She spotted cloud-banks in the south and west. Dark, heavy, they looked as though they carried snow. Greatmoon hung very low over the hills, and Littlemoon was not yet rising. She quickened her pace as she reached the woods, chafing her arms.

Scanning about her, she called out her brother's name. But she saw no one, nothing but lifeless branches and trunks. No answer came. Her legs were aching. She called again, at intervals, until her voice was hoarse.

Caribou wandered through the close, barren trees. As dark clouds rolled overhead and Greatmoon slipped away, the afternoon grew grayer still. She skirted the edge of the warm, treeless ground she had passed before, still calling her brother's name.

"Visjna!"

Even in their fur-lined mitts, the hands she cupped to her mouth were numb. No sound replied. The soft, biting wind lifted her words away until, when she came across her brother's body not far from there, she was too tired even to weep. She halted dead. Her ribs seemed to fold in around her lungs so that she could hardly breathe, only gasp at the air: dry sobs. No tears would come.

Visjna lay prone, and must have been dead some hours, she guessed, for he was frozen to the ground. She could not budge the body to turn it over. Her eyes stung fiercely. They felt windburned, cold. "Visjna," she tried to say, but her voice was gone. Her lips formed the words and made no sound. She knelt beside him for a long time then, simply staring.

Her brother's clothes were torn and scuffed across the back and shoulders — bloody there, as though he had been struck several times by something both heavy and sharp. She remembered the huge stag's great, splay hooves.

At last, when she could breathe again and felt her voice once more in her throat, Caribou laid her hands upon her brother's shoulders and sang the dead-song for him as the long, southern twilight began. Afterwards, she crossed her hands and laid them upon her own shoulders and sang again, for herself this time, for she knew she would be joining her brother's *wajn* very soon on its journey across the skybridge into the Land of Everlasting Night.

Visjna's parka was frozen to his body, but even if she could have cut it free, it was too stiff with blood and cold to give her any warmth. She managed to work his *ca'xat* out of its sheath at the side of his belt, and used the blade to slit the leather food-pouch that hung beside it.

Opening it, she found the little bag half full of travel fare, all frozen: pemmican, dried berries, nuts. She chipped at them with the *ca'xat*, working off a few slivers. But they were hard and tasteless as bits of bone. They chilled her teeth and gave her no nourishment.

So she spat them out and stared at her brother. A flash of desperation warmed her. He had no right to be dead! His flints and tinder would be in another pouch, sewn to his belt near the buckle, and there was no way she could get to them. *Wake up,* she wanted to tell him. *Wake up and help me . . .* The warmth faded. She was shuddering with cold. Nothing seemed to matter anymore. Surely she would soon be dead.

Then Caribou noticed a thing she had not seen before, as she eyed the blood frozen brown on her brother's parka: spatters of something else, little smears upon the body and the ground. Some liquid, now frozen dry — it was pale and it was bright, like purest gold.

Caribou stared at it, studied it, but could not figure out what it was. Turning, following the drops of gold with her eyes, she saw that they led off through the woods in the direction her brother lay facing, nearly the direction from which she had just come.

If she sat there any longer, she would freeze to death. Despite the leaden fatigue that filled her, her tearing hunger, and the bitter cold that clenched her bones, Caribou rose, stiffly, gritting her teeth against the rigor in her joints. She set out to follow the trail of gold.

The trail led her back to the clearing of tumbled rock and warm steam-vents, the place she had crossed going toward the cliffs and skirted coming back. The warmth of the earth rose through the soles of her boots. Her toes ached, burning at the gentle heat. She stared stupidly. She had forgotten the warmth of this place.

Pausing now, Caribou pulled off her gloves with her teeth and put her hands to the hard, barren earth to warm them. After a little while, rising, she followed the trail of gold to an outcropping of rock near the center of the clearing.

The tallest stones, reaching twice a woman's height, had thrust up from the earth in a rough circle, like a fort or crown. For the first time since she had left her brother's body, Caribou felt afraid. Her people called such rings of rocks trolls' hedges, for here the daimons of the earth gathered to smoke and play at dice.

She stared at the rocks, and knew that she should not go in. To enter a trolls' hedge, even by day, was dangerous, and to sleep in one, certainly death — so her father's tales had always said.

But she was very cold still, and night was drawing on, and it was into the trolls' hedge that the golden trail disappeared. She was dead anyway. So Caribou clambered up over the lower rocks and between two taller ones where the golden spatters led.

She glanced around nervously, but it looked like any other place: rocks and ground, and sky overhead. Taking another step, she came suddenly upon the stag, fallen forward on his knees, an arrow fletched with Visjna's colors buried in his ribs. He had been so close she had not noticed him.

His proud neck lay stretched forward, his throat and jaw resting on the ground, the cradle-like antlers balanced upon his brow — as though he had fallen to earth with the greatest care, to avoid spilling the burden he bore. No breath steamed from the reindeer's nostrils. His golden blood spattered the ground.

And there upon his rack rested the struggling bundle of the child, crying feebly, as though he had been doing so for hours and his strength was nearly gone. Caribou felt a pang of wild joy. She forgot all thought of trolls and dying, and ran to him, lifting him from the dead stag's horns. The ground was very much warmer here, within the rocks. She had stopped shivering. Steam-vents, closely spaced, were misting hot, humid air.

The child struggled in her arms, flushed, alive, his spent voice making more of a hiss than an angry scream. Kneeling, Caribou dandled him, cooed to him, laughing, unfastened her smock from the shoulder and gave him the breast.

The child ceased his crying and nursed eagerly. Caribou felt the pain in her breasts easing, and let him suckle as long as he liked. He closed his golden eyes at last, drifted sighing toward sleep. Caribou stroked and patted him upon her shoulder until he gave up his air, then laid him down upon the warm ground.

What was she to do? She refastened her smock, her elation dissolving. Her teeth were chattering again, for though the ground was warm, the air was fast chilling and the light was fading with the coming of night. Worriedly, she glanced around.

The enclosure of stones seemed completely natural. There was no disturbance of the ground or rocks to indicate that anyone had ever come there. She shivered and muttered a charm against the anger of the earth-daimons, then shoved the fear of them out of her mind and tried to think.

Caribou gazed at the fallen reindeer and ran her hands over his heavy winter coat. His body was warm still, unfrozen from the heat of the ground. Caribou took her brother's *ca'xat* and knelt beside the golden stag.

She put her shoulder to the body to shift it onto its side, then slipped the knife through the skin of the chest, drawing a long slit down the belly. The hide parted easily. Though heavier and much thicker-furred, it was as supple as rabbitskin. The pelt came away smoothly, bloodless from the fair white flesh.

She did not stop to wonder at it. Darkness was settling down. She pulled the hide from the carcass and swaddled it about her, fur-side in, laying the sleeping child upon her lap. Then she cut some of the flank meat from the fallen stag to quiet the tearing hunger in her belly.

The flesh was white as breast of ptarmigan, and tasted as though it had been basted in butter — though she knew it had had no heat sufficient to have cooked it, only the faint warmth of the ground, and the deer but lately dead. But this was a daimon place. Anything might happen here.

Presently, Caribou sensed her spirit returning. She felt strangely rested and well, immensely strong. Then, just before the dark was completely upon them, she cut the reindeer carcass into quarters and dragged each piece beyond the rocks and into the frozen woods near her brother's body, where the heated earth would not spoil the meat.

Returning to the child, she took off her travel clothing and spread it in layers upon the ground to be her mattress. Darkness had fallen. Littlemoon hung hidden behind the clouds. A light snow had begun to fall; she felt the feathery flakes touching her body, heard them hissing to steam when they touched the heated earth.

She unwrapped the child from his rabbitskin *bela* and gathered him into her arms. Lying down, she pulled the soft reindeer hide over them both, fur-side against the skin for warmth. No sound disturbed their sleep. No daimons troubled them.

That night, in dreams, she beheld no child, but a reindeer calf suckling all night at her breast.

4

Wisewoman

So Caribou brought the child into her home a second time, and afterward he no longer slept in the box beside the hearth, but with Caribou in her own bed beneath the golden reindeer pelt. As she had that first night, she turned it underside out, for the fur was clean and very soft. She loved its touch against her skin.

She rested all the next day, regaining her strength. The following morning, she strapped willow *binnakai* to her feet and returned over the fresh-fallen snow to the warm, barren place. She searched first for the trolls' hedge, to leave a thank-offering — but she could not find it, though she searched the better part of an hour and covered every pace of that bare, steaming stretch.

Her inability to find it left her baffled and ill at ease. Everything looked different in the snow. At last she gave up searching and left the loaf of tree-sugar on a flat, gray rock, saying a charm over it to draw the daimons. Then she returned to the woods where she had stowed the fallen stag, to build a drag-sled of branches and bring home as much of the carcass as she could carry in several trips.

The child came with her on the first of these, but he wept and fretted so when they came upon the stag, and would not be stilled all the long trek back, that afterward she left him in the hut.

Another thing puzzled her as well: she found that her brother's arrow, which had pierced the fallen reindeer's side, had turned itself all golden, like the blood. It felt heavy now and hard, and seemed to want to turn in her hand, pointing southward, in the direction the reindeer had run.

But what puzzled her most was that during all the time she was dragging the carcass back to her lodge, though she often heard the wild wolves crying like *waijen* in the hills all around, none ever came near the reindeer's body or harassed her in the slightest.

At the end of a week's time, when she had all the carcass of the wild deer safely stowed in the deep pit cut into the ground beside the house, covered with turf and weighted with stones, she returned at last to the woods to light a smoldering fire around her brother's body, to thaw the earth to which he lay frozen and cut him free.

She dragged him out onto open ground and burned him there upon a pyre of deadwood, with the proper laments and offerings. Then scoring her palms with a fox's tooth, she clapped them like a shaman and sang, "Let the skybridge be smooth; let it not be too narrow," because that was what her father had done when their mother had died, a long time ago.

This time the tears welled up, and Caribou let them

come. With Visjna gone, she was the last of her house: no aunts or cousins, no friends or kith. Of Branja she had found no trace. *I have only the child now,* she told herself. At last the fire died down to coals.

Of the ashes of that pyre and the fat of the fallen stag, Caribou made funeral soap, golden and smooth. She wondered whether her fair-sister, being ignorant of the ways of the hinterland, might have frozen to death that night in the snow.

Or, she reasoned doubtfully, as she washed death from the cabin with the tallow soap, perhaps the green-eyed woman had managed to make her way back to her own people. Caribou shrugged restlessly as she swabbed the close-grained wood with clear water, then dried it. She hoped so. She never wanted to see her brother's wife again.

Caribou made many things from the golden stag. The remainder of his fat she rendered into tallow, which formed many long, very thin candles, each of which burned longer than a whole lamp of oil. From the toes of his hooves, she fashioned cups for salt and condiments.

His bones she sawed and ground into buttons and counters and cuff-clasps and fishing weights, slivered into birks and needles, hollowed into candlesticks, fashioned into the handles of knives and the hafts of other tools.

But none of these would the child touch. Nor would he consent to be fed from the little hoof-bowls. He would not eat the meat of the golden stag when Caribou offered it to him finely ground, well mixed with fat and honey, though he easily took cheese and caribou butter or the flesh of hare and ptarmigan.

Indeed, the only gleanings of the wild deer the child would touch were the necklace of reindeer teeth Caribou now wore, which he handled and played with for long stretches; the golden pelt that was their blanket at night; and the golden stag's antlers, which she had lined with felt and furs to be the child's day-cradle beside the fire.

The child grew rapidly that winter, while Caribou fashioned things upon the hearth. He learned to creep and crawl about, well bundled, upon the reindeer hide on Caribou's bed or the furs on the floor. Gradually his infant's quips changed to more articulate babbling, though his cries could still sound uncannily like a reindeer lowing and he was a long time learning the sounds for speech.

His eyes never darkened to anything deeper than yellow gold, nor did his curls turn from their pure, pale blond. Caribou suckled him till he was fully two years old, that he might be well-fleshed and strong. And she called him Reindeer, in remembrance of the golden stag.

It was during the dark of that first, long winter season with the child that Caribou, eating of the reindeer's flesh and sleeping beneath his golden pelt, felt her dreams growing deeper, more vivid and prophetic. She had begun to bleed, in time with the moons, and so counted herself a woman now, no longer a girl.

One morning in early spring a drover stopped at her lodge to ask if she had seen his little herd of milch-caribou, which had started at the cries of wolves and fled away from him the evening before. Caribou told the astonished man that he would find the whole herd safe, grazing on a hillside above the falling stream on the other slope of the mountain, with a new calf among them, for she had seen it in a dream, drowsing by the hearth the night before.

Later, not ten days after the drover passed through, while Caribou was out hunting, she came upon a woman gathering red fool's cap in a basket. Without thinking, Caribou told her that adder's bark was much better for childbirth pangs than fool's cap, and that she would find some only a little farther on.

The woman, very taken aback, demanded, "How did you know I wanted this wort for childbirth pangs?"

Caribou blushed, realizing what she had done. "I dreamed it," she stammered, and glimpsed the woman making the sign against evil behind the basket.

"You're Visjna's sister, aren't you?" the woman said nervously. She was holding the basket in front of her as if to keep Caribou away. "The one who sees things."

Caribou felt her blush deepening. Her hands on the bow shaft tightened. So the village people were still afraid of her. She nodded, saying nothing. The village woman was edging away.

"No one's seen Visjna, nor his wife — that Valley woman — since the fall," she started.

"Visjna's dead." Caribou made herself say it. The words came out harsh. She was not used to talking to strangers, and if she said much of Visjna she was afraid she might weep. "One of the wild deer killed him. I found him and burned him." She blinked hard and bit her lip. "I didn't find Branja."

The village woman came no nearer, but her stance seemed to relax a little. Her tone, when she spoke, had softened. "You're . . . you're younger than I thought," she said at last. "I've a girl about your age."

Caribou's eyes flashed up. "I'm a woman," she hissed. The other flinched but did not run. She fingered the basket uncertainly. She seemed at a loss. Caribou shouldered her bow and started upslope past her. "Do your gathering and get home quickly," she added, more softly now. "Your sister will be in labor before her time — before moonrise."

The woman was staring at her again. "Visjna's sister —" she began.

Caribou halted. "My name is Caribou," she said.

The other nodded. "My thanks for your help, Visj — Caribou." She sounded sincere.

Caribou felt something tugging at the corner of her mouth. In a moment, she realized, surprised, that it was a smile. The village woman managed a smile in return. Caribou turned and continued through the trees. Oddly, her heart felt lighter than it had in days.

There had been no fear on the other's face just then, at the last, only curiosity. *Or pity?* Caribou sighed. The villagers were strange to her, their lives as far away from hers as the unseen moons. She despaired of ever touching them. She sighed again. The day was late, and she had not found so much as a ptarmigan yet. She shoved the thought of the woman with the basket from her mind and hurried on in search of game.

After that, people sometimes sought Caribou out to ask advice — only a few from the nearby villages at first, but gradually more and more, until she began to earn for herself the name of wisewoman. In the beginning it was difficult, meeting so many strangers and deciding what they should do, but after a time she caught the knack of it.

When they came, she gave them food and drink, then sat upon the doorstep of her *ntula,* with the child beside her and the golden arrow on her lap, listening to their concerns. After much thinking and running of her fingers along the smooth yellow shaft, she would tell them what they wanted to know: why it was their nannies would not bring forth live kids, or where lost articles were to be found, or which would be the better man to wed.

They went away, back to their farms and villages, thanking her with smiles and gifts. Sometimes they came a second time, either for themselves or bringing someone else who needed help. Always those who came again said Caribou's advice on the other matter had been good and that things had been as she had said.

Sometimes it was things she remembered seeing in her dreams, and other times it was her own weighing of their words that determined what she told them; but always, when they went away, they seemed satisfied. Caribou found her heart opening out a little at last, to see people grateful to her and not so much afraid anymore.

She felt happier, less of an outcast from her Tribe. She had been alone a long time, with only the golden child to comfort her. Now, before two or three years had gone by, not a fortnight passed without some traveler footing the new-worn path to her lonely hut to ask the wisewoman's advice.

Only one thing troubled her, and that was Reindeer. While still she suckled him, he usually sat on her lap when she answered those who came, and later, when he was older, on the step beside her, listening to her and watching the others with his great, still, luminous eyes.

Later, when they had gone, he would question her about them, who they were and where they came from, how they lived, why they needed her advice and why she had told them what she had. The strangers fascinated him.

"They are not like us, are they, Cari?" he asked her once, a question that puzzled her.

"No," she answered, "for they live together in villages, or on farms outside of villages, and we live here in the Wilderland, alone."

She answered his other questions as best she could. Although he was brighter and quicker than other children she saw, even children older than he, he did not always seem to understand.

"You told that man who came to you this morning to marry the woman who loved him," the child said to her one afternoon, "and forget the one who would cause him sorrow."

Sitting upon her lap beside the cutting table outside, he was using a broad-bladed chop with laborious care to dice the red rushes for their dinner. Caribou guided his small, square hands.

"Why?" Reindeer asked her. "Why did you say those things to him?"

Caribou laughed, squeezing his cool fingers. "Did that not seem sound advice to you?"

The sun was bright. The metal blade went chop, and chop. "What's love?" the child said. "What's sorrow?"

Caribou frowned, puzzled. She did not know what to make of the questions. "Love is . . ." she said. "Love is what I feel for you — and you for me, I hope."

Reindeer had laid the square blade down. All the rushes were cut and oozing clear, sweet juice. His face was blank. "I don't understand."

Caribou pursed her lips, perturbed, and swept the

rushes into a clay pot to be steamed. She found his questions very odd. How could a person, even a child, not know what love was?

"I take care of you," she began, "because I love you . . ."

The boy on her lap shifted, turning to look at her. "I don't take care of *you*."

Caribou sighed. "No, but you love me just the same — because I love you."

Reindeer did not say anything. Caribou laid the pot of rushes down and drew breath to try again, but the boy spoke first, getting down from her lap. His golden eyes looked deep into hers.

"And sorrow?"

Caribou despaired. "Sorrow is," she began. "It is what you feel if someone hurts you, or if someone you love is hurt — or is gone from you." She felt ridiculous trying to put it into words. No one had ever explained such things to her. She simply knew.

Reindeer nodded then, very thoughtfully — though she had an eerie feeling that even now he had no inkling what she meant. The people from the villages called her wisewoman because she could see things in dreams. But she never dreamed about Reindeer. He was a mystery to her.

5

Reindeer

TIME PASSED. Reindeer grew a year older, and Caribou came no closer to understanding him. Sometimes she saw people who came to her murmuring behind their hands and looking at him. They whispered that he was odd, with his yellow hair and fair, white skin, though to her face they said he was a fine boy, strapping and strong, very comely to look at.

And Caribou, who knew nothing of beauty that was not in the lay of the land, or in livestock or household things, gazed at the fine-planed features of her growing boy, and was not sure. But when they asked who he was, she answered always, "My brother's child, not mine."

She had never thought of him as hers somehow, even after so long. No tie of blood bound them, and the older he grew, the less he seemed like her or the others of her Tribe. He was a strange child, very solemn now, who neither laughed nor cried anymore, and rarely spoke.

He sat beside her in the evenings on the hearthstone, listening to some tale she might be telling, half to herself and half to him, and playing with the necklace of reindeer teeth upon her breast.

Tales of *iff*s and *ont*s and other kinds of daimons — trolls that played at dice, and cave-boggles, sea-maidens with gray-green hair, and halflings that could change their skins. Tales of ghostly *waijen,* the ancestors, who lived beyond the skybridge in the Land of Everlasting Night, and could be seen dancing in the southern sky on winter evenings in shimmering trains of red and green.

Reindeer never tired of them — all the tales Caribou's father had told her before his death. She hardly missed him now that Reindeer had come. One evening he turned to her as they sat upon the hearth. He was very small still, but seemed far older than his age.

He asked her, "Cari, what is a *trangl?*"

Caribou looked up from the basket she was mending and frowned. She knew the word, but could not remember what it meant. "Why do you ask?" she said. "Where did you hear of it?"

The boy replied, "I overheard the people who came to see you today using it. Do they lie with men?"

"What?"

"The *traangol.* Do they lie with men? The people were saying one of the men of their village had been charmed by one." Reindeer shifted upon the hearth. "What is one? Is it a daimon?"

Caribou nodded and picked up her basket again. She remembered now. "Yes. A kind of daimon that can walk in human shape."

Reindeer watched her. "Why have you told me no tales of them?" he asked.

"I don't know any," Caribou replied, deftly teasing out the broken strip of basket-bark from the others. "My brother Visjna would have known." She sighed. Even four years after, her breast still tightened at the thought of Visjna. "He tended my father's caribou and sometimes spoke to *kaaluwati,* who track the wild deer and tell tales of such things — but he is dead."

She shook her head, trying to banish the painful memory, and began paring a new strip of bark very carefully. Just then a log in the fire burst, in a rain of sparks, and the knife slipped in her hand. A line of blood welled up from her thumb, and Caribou dropped blade and basket with a curse.

"What's that?" said Reindeer suddenly, staring at her hand. "Cari, what's that?"

Caribou bit down on her thumb to make the bleeding stop, and glanced at him. "It's blood," she said, puzzled, reaching to show him. "Don't you know?"

He took her hand on his lap and gazed at the dark trickle there, intrigued.

"It's red," he said.

"Of course." She took her hand back, went to get a clean strip of woven cloth. "Like animals' blood. Like the hares I bring home." She wrapped the linen around her thumb. "What color did you think it would be?"

Reindeer never took his eyes from her, but scratched the back of his neck meditatively. Caribou sat back down on the hearth.

"Will I ever bleed like that, Cari?"

He asked it so solemnly that Caribou laughed.

"Not if you don't cut yourself," she replied, and picked the basket up again.

For a moment, she thought he might say more, but he only nodded. Already he was turning back toward the fire — indeed, sometimes he sat, hands on lap, and stared into the coals so long and so still that Caribou was sure he had fallen asleep with his eyes open. But whenever she spoke, he turned and answered her without starting.

He was restless in spring when the reindeer were running, and seemed to know to the moment when they had returned. Caribou often found him, at the end of the day in the twilight, gazing off toward the chilly southlands until the wild herds had passed north to the warmer calving grounds. Then he gazed northward for the rest of the season.

He was like the golden arrow, she thought, which, no matter how she laid it upon the shelf above the hearth, always seemed to have turned itself northward after a little, in spring. It was the same in winter, though then the arrow pointed Poleward, and Reindeer too gazed southward again, to where the reindeer had passed beyond the Burning Plain.

And sometimes at day's end, when she saw him sitting at hearthside or staring off into the twilight, wholly absorbed, oblivious to her, more still than any creature she had ever seen, she found herself marveling, lost in a dream that he was no human child at all, but some strange other thing that had no human heart.

Yet, for all his strangeness, he was her only joy. Caribou could not say how, before he came, she had borne the solitude. He was her companion in the day-chores of the lodge — building and mending and splitting wood for the fire — and he shared the reindeer coverlet with her at night.

As soon as he was old enough, he accompanied her wood-gathering, or berry-picking, or checking her snares. And before much longer, she could send him out by himself on one errand while she herself attended to another.

There was no greater happiness for her than to await his homecoming of an evening, or to come home to him at dusk on those days when it had been her turn to check the traps, to find him waiting on the doorsill and have him come out to meet her, put his arms about her waist, and gaze at her with his great gold eyes and ask her solemnly what luck the traps had had that day.

Then one day when Reindeer was nearly five summers old, something happened that troubled Caribou more than she could say. It was springtime, the ice of winter gone and the rush of melting snow now past. Caribou had taken him with her fishing for salmon in the quiet stream that wended past the rise on which their *ntula* stood.

She had been sitting a long time on the stony bank

with her fishing line wrapped around a shuttle that lay in her lap. Reindeer had wandered away, but she felt no alarm. He was a remarkably safe child, and seemed never to lose or injure himself. She had never seen him bruised or scraped. He would be back in his own time, when it suited him. Dozing, she dreamed a fish stole the bait from her line.

Something startled her awake, and she sat very still, listening, but heard nothing. Then after a moment, she realized that in the water before her, beside her own reflection, was the image of a reindeer calf.

She made no sound, not wanting to frighten it, and wondered what calf this could be, so well grown so early in the season, and so far south of the calving grounds — unless it were the calf of someone's milch-caribou, wandered off from its dam.

The calf was watching her and not its own reflection. She did not move or turn, was just preparing to cluck softly, in hopes of coaxing it close enough to catch, when Reindeer's voice sounded, so near it made her jump.

"There's a fish nibbling your line, Cari."

Caribou caught in her breath, started to her feet and whirled. Reindeer stood upon the bank and no caribou calf.

"Where is it?" she stammered. "Did you chase it away?"

"Chase what," the boy replied, "the fish? No, it's still on the line."

"The calf," cried Caribou, glancing into the woods behind him, trying to spot it.

"What calf?" said Reindeer. "You've dropped your framework, and the fish is pulling it into the water."

Caribou gave an exasperated sigh, turned back to the stream to retrieve the line — and halted dead. Beside her own reflection in the water still stood that of the reindeer calf. She whirled. Nothing stood there but Reindeer, her boy.

Reindeer moved one hand slightly, scratching his wrist. A gasp caught in Caribou's throat as she gazed at the image of the calf in the water, scratching one foreleg with its hoof. She turned and stared at Reindeer.

"What is it?" he murmured, frowning, then gestured beyond her. "You're going to lose it, the fishing line."

Caribou backed away from him on the bank, bent down to fish the framework from the water without looking at it. The stream was icy on her hand. Reindeer still looked at her; he had taken no notice yet of his own reflection.

"Get . . . get back from the water," she stammered. She must not let him see. The water held something unearthly, so strange she could not understand it. Some trick of the water-daimon? Hurriedly, she searched her memory, but could remember no tale that spoke of such a thing. "You're standing too near," she told Reindeer. "You might fall."

The boy retreated a few paces from the bank. Caribou got hold of the fishing line and straightened, pulling too hard. She felt the fish slip from the hook.

"What is it?" said Reindeer, coming a pace closer to her. "Cari, what's frightened you?"

"Nothing," she said, coming toward him lest he draw near enough to the water again to see himself. She wound the draggled fishline about the framework nervously. "You came upon me so silently, I didn't know you were there. You startled me. I wasn't awake."

"I'm sorry," he began, as if by rote — and all at once she had the strange feeling that he had no notion still what sorrow meant. "I made you lose your fish."

"It doesn't matter," said Caribou. "We have enough fish." She knelt to pull the line of caught fish from the water, then started past him up the bank. "Let's go home."

"But it's not yet twilight."

Caribou did not answer, strode on toward the lodge not daring to look behind. Relief flooded her as she heard the boy was following, hurrying to keep up. But as they cleaned and dried the fish that afternoon, Reindeer was even more silent than usual, and Caribou did not try to draw him out. She stared down at her work and said nothing.

That evening after supper, when the boy sat on the hearthstone staring into the fire, Caribou took out the little disk of silver glass that had been her father's wedding present to her mother, and which she had not looked in for many years.

Holding it aslant so that it showed the hearth across the room, she looked at it now. With her own eyes she saw Reindeer, the boy, but the mirror showed no boy — only a reindeer calf lounging beside the fire.

A tremor passed through her. Her hands shook. So it had not been the water-sprite at all. She closed her eyes against the terror that rose in her, and tried desperately to think. *Am I going mad?* No. She shook her head. Not madness, but a terrible mystery, and she wanted no part of it.

Caribou tightened her fingers around the glass. She would not let this strange riddle into her house. She would not seek to answer it. She would not let it touch either her or Reindeer. Quietly, she put the mirror away. The next day she sent Reindeer off through the woods to a far-off slope to gather medicine-flower, and broke the mirror into slivers, then buried them between two roots of a tree.

Afterward, she told Reindeer no more tales. She herself did all their fishing in the quiet pools, though Reindeer fished the foaming rapids. Caribou painted the bottoms of all her water vessels white with bone enamel so that they would be too pale to show an image.

Her *mar long,* the only blade she had burnished bright enough to reflect images, she kept firmly in its sheath when Reindeer was with her, and she warned him away from still, standing water, telling him that it was treacherous. They still went to the hot pool to bathe, but those waters were always milky with steam, so she did not fear.

Reindeer seemed to take no notice of these changes. She had watched him at first for any reaction, but his great unchanging eyes seemed unable to evidence any mood. He did not complain. Only once did he reveal that he had noticed a difference: one morning when he was ten summers old and she was warning him for the second time to stay away from clear, dark water while hunting.

"Why is that?" he asked her. "Why are you so afraid? There is something, Cari, that you are not telling me."

Caribou felt the inexplicable terror sweeping over her again. She shook her head. "No. No, there is nothing," and pretended to be busy with the birchroot she was paring. "It is only . . ."

He said nothing, so that she had to look at him. The fear had changed to a kind of rigor. She did not think she could have stood if she had tried. Her eyes, she knew, entreated him, though she doubted he could understand.

"Reindeer, I . . ." She almost told him. "It is only that I do not want to lose you."

He stared at her intently then, for a space of several breaths, with his golden eyes. Caribou dropped her gaze. She could not tell him. She had only a terrifying suspicion buried so deep down that she herself scarcely knew what it was she feared.

Reindeer took his bow from the table then and went off into the forest to hunt, while Caribou dropped her face to her hands and moaned. She sat a long time, motionless, before the trembling passed.

6

Trangl

THE BOY came to her one day in early fall. He
had seen his thirteenth summer and was nearly
as tall as Caribou now. He had been restless for many
days, so she knew the reindeer were running — though
they had not yet returned from their summer calving
grounds, for the arrow pointed away from the Pole
and still Reindeer stared off northward in the evenings. But they were coming. She could tell from his
manner that they would pass by soon.

"Cari," he said, "there is something I must tell
you." His voice was changing, cracked unexpectedly
now and again.

Caribou looked up from the candles she was dipping. "What thing, Reindeer?" she asked.

"Cari," he said quietly, "I want to go away."

Tallow spattered on Caribou's hand as she dropped
the wooden candleframe into the heated kettle, and
she winced. Reindeer took the iron tong from beside
the hearth and fished the framework out for her.

"Go away?" she exclaimed.

Reindeer handed her the wax-coated frame; she took
it gingerly. He gazed off across the room, breathed
restlessly.

"Because the reindeer are running. I want to follow them and see what lies beyond the Burning Plain."

"Beyond?" cried Caribou, gripping the waxy frame till her knuckles whitened and her fingers made impressions in the soft tallow. "There lies only death beyond the Burning Plain."

The boy shook his head, still looking off. "Not for the reindeer, and not for me."

Caribou clapped the framework to the hearth-stones, shoved it away. "Why do you say that? How do you know?"

He turned to look at her now, his pale eyes burning in the firelight. "Because they have told me, Cari."

Caribou's heart shrank. She stared at him, and drew back from him, and was afraid.

"Every year at their running they call to me and tell me of sweet pastures beyond the Land of Broken Snow, and beg me to come with them."

The breath in Caribou's breast grew still then, and for a long time she could not answer him. Her thoughts spun. She felt feverish. What was he talking of — speaking with the wild deer? "Why do you want to leave me?" she whispered at last.

He shook his head and knelt upon the hearthstone by her. "I do not *want* to leave you. Each year I have refused them, till now."

"Then why now?" she whispered. She scarcely grasped what he was saying.

His tone grew warmer. "Because now I am grown tall enough and strong enough to make the trek." He laid his hands upon her hands. They felt cool against her skin. "Cari, I would ask you to come with me, but the reindeer will not let you come. I have asked them. They do not want you. Only me."

Caribou's hands curled into fists. "But you cannot go!" she burst out, gazing at him, both angry and beseeching at once. "You are just a boy, not yet a man . . ."

Reindeer took his hands from her, stood back and looked away. "Cari, I will never be a *man*. We both know it."

None of this could be happening. She clenched her teeth against the fear thickening her throat. It was a dream. "Why do you say that? What do you mean?"

He looked at her again, with his great gold eyes. "Cari, I am not like you. I am not like the others, the people who come to you and ask advice."

"Them!" cried Caribou. "Why do you listen to them, their muttering — what do they know?"

He looked at her. "More than you, in some things," he said softly.

Caribou caught in her breath. "We . . . we are not different," she stammered, stumbling on the words. "You are not different — not from *me*. I suckled you." Her hands were fists. "We are the same."

Reindeer shook his head and knelt beside her again, took up her hand in both of his. "How can you say that — why deny it? It is the difference you have been hiding from me since that day beside the stream."

Caribou felt her throat closing tight. It was no dream.

"I have seen my shadow," said the boy. "Have you never noticed it?" She shook her head, mute, staring at him. His shadow! She had not once thought of it. "It isn't like yours, a human shape. Mine is different."

Caribou blanched and closed her eyes, leaned back against the mantel stones. Her body felt wavery, thin as water. She did not want to hear any more.

"And when I listen and talk to the birds and the animals," Reindeer was saying, "you act as though you do not hear it. So many things are different between us. You laugh and you cry, and I don't understand."

Caribou's breast heaved, but she could get no air.

"And Caribou, look at this," said Reindeer. "Cari, look."

His hands left hers and her fear suddenly sharpened. She sat up quickly, snapped open her eyes, half expecting to find him vanished. But he was still beside her, had drawn his *ca'xat* from his belt and pressed its edge to the fleshy part of his palm. Caribou saw a line of gold well up. He wiped and sheathed the knife again, held up his hand to her.

"See, Cari; it's not like yours," said Reindeer. "It's gold."

Caribou felt her body slipping. The room grew dark and distorted. The firelight to the right of her tipped far away and vanished. A brief rush of cooler air brushed her. Her left arm and shoulder struck something hard. Then her cheek. She closed her eyes, because she did not want to see anymore.

"Cari," she heard him saying. "Caribou."

She found herself laid upon the hearth, the wax kettle pushed out of the way on its swinging arm, back over the coals. The heat of the close fire made her sweat. The stones against her back were uneven and hard.

She saw Reindeer above her dimly. He was bending over her, shaking her. The shaking made her gasp, and the air coming suddenly into her throat again made things grow sharper and steadier. She pushed away from Reindeer, swinging her legs to the floor, and sat up. Then she put one hand to her head and leaned against him.

"What happened?" he asked her. "Why did you do that?"

"I don't know," she muttered. She felt dizzy. Her tongue and lips were slow. "I don't understand."

"You looked like a hare that has been frightened to death," said Reindeer. His tone, oddly flat, seemed to express neither worry nor distress.

He is like a comet, or a running stream, she thought, *that has no thought for anything but itself and its own path.*

Reindeer said, "You looked like something dead in the snow. I laid you on the hearthstone to warm you."

Caribou straightened and took several quick, deep breaths. The room steadied. Her head grew clearer. "I fainted," she told him, "because I forgot to breathe."

"Did I make you do that?" he asked her. "Did I frighten you?"

She did not answer, did not look at him. She took his wounded hand that still bled slightly, drops of gold, and stared at it.

"There is something I have not told you," she said quietly. "There is something I have never told you."

She held his hand in her lap and gazed off across the twilit room.

"You are the child of my fair-sister, but not my brother's child. She brought you to me when you were newly born, just two months old, and gave you to me for safekeeping. But a great golden stag caught you out of my arms — that fall, when the reindeer were running — and carried you away in his horns. My brother killed the stag, but died himself to do it. When I came upon the two of you, the stag was bleeding drops of gold."

The boy beside her nodded. "Yes, I remember that."

Caribou turned to stare at him, his fine, fair features catching the firelight. Reindeer nodded again.

"I remember from the time the other, that other woman, brought me to you. She was my mother, I think, but she was afraid of me. And I remember when the reindeer came and bore me away. He was my father, he told me, and would carry me beyond the Land of Broken Snow. But then he stumbled, and wheeled about, and struck down the man who had been chasing us. Then we went on a little way, as far as the rocks, before he lay down, saying no more to me. And then you came."

Caribou gazed at him, unmoving. "Daimon," she whispered. "Halfling. I don't know what you are."

But she did know; she understood now — as she let herself understand at last what it was she had reared, and the thing that she had feared so long: he was a *trangl*, one of the *traangol*, the golden deer-men and deer-women that ran with the wild deer.

Reindeer took his hand from hers. "Cari," he said, "I am going away to follow the reindeer."

She looked at him, drew breath. "Will you come back?"

The boy rose, shaking his head a little, shrugged. "I don't know."

Oh, he is; he is, she thought, *a daimon, a thing I cannot understand. He is beyond my grasp. I can no more hold him than I can halt the running of water, or the turning of stars.* She tried to smile then, but her face felt crusted, crushed and set like drying clay.

"Come back," she said. "I will use the time you are away to make beautiful things for you."

Reindeer said nothing. He turned from her, going to the door, and when he opened it Caribou saw that outside the sunset was burning down the whole sky to glowing coals.

"Wait," Caribou cried. "You'll take no *pisjlak,* provisions for the journey?"

The boy stepped over the threshold and said without turning, "The reindeer will show me where good forage lies. I will need no other."

"But wait," cried Caribou again, bolting to her feet, her mind racing. Desperately, she searched the room. She had to find some way to bind him, to bring him back to her. Her eye settled on the golden reindeer hide. She ran to their bed and tore it off. *He will wear this,* she told herself, *and think of me.* She went to him outside. "Take this, at least, against the cold."

But as he took it from her, with hardly a glance,

she had suddenly the odd feeling that he had never meant to leave without it. He stroked the fur.

"My thanks," the *trangl* said.

He spoke without human inflection or emotion. He had lived in her house all these dozen years and more as a guest, nothing other, and was no kith to her at all. She felt a sudden stab of something that was almost envy. What could it be like to be like him: a daimon, untouchable by love or sorrow? Without a word, he kissed her lips.

Caribou drew back, surprised, for she had never kissed him, even as a baby, nor he her. Her people were not like the River-Valley Folk, always kissing one another's mouths. His tone grew softer then, so much so that if she had not known him for a daimon that had no use for mortal cares she would have said he spoke gently.

"Perhaps I will see you again," said Reindeer, and turned away.

Caribou stood by the house door, watching him go. Her face crumpled in despair. It was useless. She could not have held him. He had never been hers to hold. The sky above was burning gold.

She saw him take the reindeer pelt from his arm as he reached the woods' edge. He threw it about his shoulders, skin-side to him, fur-side out. Then all the woods for an instant grew bright as fire, and when Caribou could see again, she could no longer find Reindeer among the trees.

She started forward with a cry and darted down the hard, frozen slope to the woods' edge below. But the woods were empty, silent, still, all the trees black and barren, as if burnt. Nothing caught her eye but a wild stag, very far off, bounding through the trees in great strides, a young rack of antlers crowning his head. The setting sun upon his pelt made it shimmer, fire-gold.

7

The Bad Year

CARIBOU took the day-cradle of the golden stag's antlers that had lain beside the fire these many years unused and began to dismantle it with a hack-blade and saw, to fashion into beautiful things for Reindeer's return. *He will come back to me,* she told herself. *He must.* That desperate hope was the only thing that kept her moving.

She made him a horn-handled knife with intricate carvings upon the haft, spoons and little prongs for spearing food. From the spatulate antler tips she made him brooches: silhouettes of falcons and running wolves. Some of the shafts she cut into buttons, or beads, or other small things.

The last thing she started to make, from the longest and heaviest shaft of either of the antlers, was a baton such as herders used to prod their caribou. But she could not bring herself to finish it, somehow. Some impulse stopped her hand.

The rest of the autumn and all winter long, she worked on these things, hardly stirring from her cabin, for there were *waijen* all around, walking and wandering, whispering — not just dancing in the distant southern sky. It was as though the fabric between the worlds had rent, and the ancestors could now pass freely across the skybridge into the land of the living again.

Whenever Caribou did go outside, she could see them. Sometimes she thought she saw her brother in the distance, walking, his bow in hand, or her father tending his caribou — they never turned when she called. She knew they must be *waijen* and not living flesh, for there was no one in these parts who owned any caribou, and the reindeer had all run away.

Caribou did not want to see them, so mostly she stayed inside, working, scarcely pausing except to build up the fire, eat a little, and sleep. But by night or by day, whenever she slept — on the hearthstone now, for warmth, since the reindeer hide was gone — she dreamed of the wild deer rushing away from her in unstoppable torrents toward the southern Pole.

And ever as she worked — sometimes hardly knowing what it was she carved — she felt a great tightness beneath her breastbone, as though her heart had been torn out, the wound now clenching and closing over, stiff and sore. Sometimes she noticed drops of water falling onto her handiwork, as she rasped and whittled, polished and hacked, though she was barely aware that she wept.

One morning her father's *wajn* came to her. Though she did not look up, she could feel its presence filling the *ntula*, and though it did not speak, she could hear its thoughts.

You did not love him enough, my girl. That is why he has gone away.

Caribou stared down, clenching the bit of bone that she was carving. "I loved him," she whispered, then almost shouted, "I love him!"

Not enough, the *wajn*'s thoughts replied. But when she looked up with a start that felt oddly like waking, no one and nothing was there.

The cold season dragged on. By day, the wan sun seemed barely to clear the horizon. The nights were interminably long. Winter storms blew in, lasting for many days. Occasionally, when the tearing wind outside her cabin dropped to eerie stillness, she could hear her own voice muttering, sometimes gasping.

"He has left me. He has left me. He will never come back."

But always the fragments of antler in her lap clicked and clattered, as clearly as if someone had spoken to her, "He will come back."

"Oh, so you think he will return to you?" someone else's voice said to her one day. "Don't believe a *trangl*'s bones. All daimons are capricious, and they lie."

Caribou sat up with a start, staring. A ghostly *wajn* stood across the room. *Branja.*

"It wasn't my fault I bore a *trangl*'s child," Branja's *wajn* said. "The *trangl* charmed me. One look into his golden eyes and I was powerless. Now my son has done the same to you. Look at you. You are in the same state I was in when my *trangl* left me."

"That is not so; that is not so," whispered Caribou.

"Don't lie," the *wajn* said. "You love him."

"He is like my own kith." A lie. A lie. He was nothing like a son or brother to her.

"He was never yours," the *wajn* spat. "He is *my* son, and no blood kith to you at all. You only raised him."

"I suckled him," choked Caribou.

"But could not keep him."

"Go away!" shouted Caribou, lunging to her feet. She hurled the little box she had been carving at the laughing *wajn*. The golden rectangle of horn shattered against the wall across the room. Branja was no longer there.

Spring came. The fabric of the world mended and the *waijen* went home to their Land of Endless Night. The snow about the *ntula* turned to slush. Ice upon the tree limbs cracked and fell away. Caribou finished her carving and came out to look at the world again. All around her the winter was melting in a warm, storming rush.

When the first month of spring had passed, and flowers lay strewn like broken garlands on every hill, Caribou dreamed that the reindeer were coming northward again, back from the far, southern Pole. She awoke long before dawn in a passion of desperate hope and fear. As soon as there was light enough outside to see, she left her *ntula* and hurried to the hillside beside the Reindeer's Path to wait for them.

Caribou sat trembling upon the slope green with fragrant grass. She had put on her finest clothes: a shirt and smock of white caribou skin stitched with threads of blue, wine, and green. Her boots were of golden calf's hide, and her cap, of snow-owl feathers.

The weather was unseasonably warm. Her hands plucked and worried at the shoots of grass. Time passed, endlessly, until morning was just edging into noon.

She felt the tremor in the earth and heard the far thunder of their coming long before she saw. They came in a surge, thick as gray dark water, filling the bed of the glacier-trough like a sudden flood. Caribou bolted to her feet and stood scanning the sweep of silver and gray for some glint of gold.

She saw it! *Something,* still far off — a flash of tawny yellow in the sunlight peering uncertainly through the woolen clouds. The torrent swept by her. It was a stag, golden, she could see that now, though it was difficult for her to keep him in sight amid that shifting mass. He seemed to be holding to the center of the stream.

"Reindeer! Reindeer!"

She did not understand why he did not make his way toward her, toward the edge. Surely he could see her. Caribou cupped her hands to her mouth and shouted again. The clacking thunder of the herd stole her words, trampled them to nothing. She waved her arms.

The golden reindeer turned his head. He was almost level with her now, but half the width of the channel separated them. She saw his gold eyes glance through her without thought or recognition, like a hawk's eyes, like two burning stones. Caribou dropped her arms, and the golden stag rushed by her, vanished among the stampeding forms. Gray clouds swallowed up the sun.

She could not stand. She fell forward, onto her forearms, and put her forehead to the soft, cool grass. Not even desperation held her upright anymore. The earth beneath her trembled, as she herself lay trembling.

"I have lost him; I have lost him," she whispered. She could hear nothing but the pounding of the wild deer's passing, shaking the world apart. "He has forgotten me. He will not come back."

But the necklace of reindeer teeth that bit against her breast clattered softly. Strange how she could hear them still, even above the thunder of the wild deer. "He has not forgotten you. He will come back."

The cool of evening woke her, and when she rose, stiff from having lain so long, and trembling with fatigue, she saw that the herd had passed, the earth again grown still. Dusk was drawing on, the air fast giving up its heat.

Numbly, Caribou went home, and wept no more — she was worn out with it; there was nothing she could do. She locked the things she had made of the golden stag's horns away in a wooden chest, and slept that night on her own bed again, not the hearth, beneath an old coverlet of gray caribou hide, and thought no more of Reindeer.

I should never have loved him, she told herself bitterly. *I will never love anyone again.*

That was the year the people from the villages began

bringing their disputes to her, because of the reputation that had sprung up around her in the last years as a wisewoman. The chieftain over the whole Tribe had died that winter, and his children were bickering over who should succeed him. The elder-councils were deadlocked as well.

So slowly at first, then more and more frequently, the people came to her with their cases to be settled, because they could get no satisfaction from the councils and had no tribal head to lay down for them the Law.

Caribou heard them, and passed judgments, which she insisted both parties agree to honor before she would consent to hear them. Sometimes more than one group came on a day, so that the opponents of the first party presented their cases while those of the other watched and listened. Always it was agreed that her decisions were just and fair. She did not mind the time it took. It kept her from being alone.

People still came to her for advice, or information, or help finding lost articles as well, for still she dreamed wise dreams of prophecy. She turned no one unanswered away, till word began to spread that the wisewoman who lived near the Broken Lands had grown more sage and deep than ever, though rather sad now that her nephew, or son, or younger brother — the golden boy — had gone away to become a *kaluwak*, a tracker who followed the wild deer.

Such was the way of things for a long year's time. Then came the Bad Year. It started in spring, growing worse as the months wore into summer. Caribou saw some of it for herself, and the people who came for her judgments brought tales of it with them.

It began with tremors in the earth — though this was not unusual, in the cold country of geysers and mud-springs, for the earth to tremble now and again; at first no one had thought anything of it. But soon the shocks began to come more frequently, and were more violent, so that by the end of summer scarcely a day went by that Caribou did not feel at least a mild shudder pass through the earth.

In early fall, before the snows blocked off the passages, when people still came with their troubles and their news, she heard of worse things yet. Great cracks had been found, thirty els deep in the earth. Certain geysers had ceased to spout, others begun spouting erratically. Landslides sheared off whole sides of hills, and rivers flowed muddy, thick with debris.

Then, at mid-autumn, after the reindeer had run, Caribou made her way across the glacier-trough and through the woods to bathe in the hot pool one last time before the snows. She had not been there all summer, so often had the villagers been coming to her.

On her way to the pool, to her surprise, she found that the barren patch of warm ground in the forest had grown hotter, expanding and killing the trees that had formerly ringed it. The earth was almost too hot for her to travel across, and noxious fumes now rose from vents in the crust.

When she neared the hot spring, she discovered that it had turned a soupy yellow, with great streams of particulated sulfur extending far over the rocky ground where wind had blown the spray of geysers. Animal tracks — all fleeing — showed here and there in the thick, pollen-colored dust.

Suddenly as she approached, crunching over the hardened crust, she realized that what she had thought were mineral mounds beside the spring were really the carcasses of animals, covered with sulfur, those that had been caught drinking from the spring and had not had time to flee.

Caribou stood staring at them, horrified. What could have become of the water-daimon to have allowed this to happen? She muttered a propitiation under her breath — but before she had even half finished, she heard a rumbling from across the little pond. A great plume of yellow steam jetted up from a fissure in the rock, with a spitting hiss and a stink like rotting eggs.

Caribou gasped and fell back, nearly overcome by the heat. Surely the water-sprite was dead or driven away, and no daimon protected this place anymore. A gust of wind began blowing spray from the hot, churning plume. Caribou turned and fled away over the sulfurous earth, that crunched like yellow salt beneath her heels.

All that winter, Caribou stayed close to the lodge but for brief forays into the near woods for hunting or checking her traps. Sometimes during the stillness of the night, she heard avalanches tearing apart the mountains many miles to the east.

One morning, while she sat mending a broken snare

by the hearthside, she heard a distant booming. Rushing outside, she saw above the low slopes far to the west a dark cloud welling up from beyond the horizon's edge, mounting and spreading into the sky like a swarm of black birds. That evening, ash fell, graying the leafless trees and dirtying the snow.

It was as if all order and balance had left the world — nothing could be predicted anymore. Whereas the winter before, the earth had seemed crowded with unearthly *waijen,* now it seemed deserted, empty. Game had grown scarce. Butter would not come in the churn. There seemed to be no magic in any of the charms.

It was as if every sprite and *ont* and troll that kept the mountains and the geysers, the paths and streams, had abruptly vanished, leaving the world without keeper or guide. There was no appealing to them for luck or appeasement. The offerings Caribou left along the paths and the streams remained untouched.

Still she dreamed, but her dreams were no help. They remained blank of these things, telling her nothing. Though sometimes she felt as if she knew where every lost article lay in all the sixteen villages of her Tribe, she had no inkling why the world should be so restless and intractable.

It was at the first of spring, as soon as the passages were open again, that the elders came to her.

"We are a special council," their spokesman said, "formed of an elder from each of the sixteen villages."

They sat on blankets spread on the barren ground outside her hut. Caribou had served them honeycakes and bitter tea. She sat facing them from the threshold, the golden arrow across her lap. She liked to run her hands over its hard, cool surface while she listened. It pointed south, for the wild deer had not yet returned.

"Have the elder-councils chosen a new chieftain yet?" she inquired, sipping her tea.

The speaker shook his head. He was a man late in middle age, with hair like a silver cap upon his head and a drooping gray moustache. He came from nearby Vlad. "No, wisewoman," he told her. "Our late chieftain's children and the village councils are all quarreling still, and the events of the past winter have thrown us all into confusion."

Caribou was silent then, wondering why they had come. At length one man among the group laid down his tea-flask and brushed the crumbs from his beard.

"My name is Ksistan," he said to Caribou, "and I come from the village of Bintuk, several leagues north of here. There the shaking of the earth has been most violent — sometimes so severe it throws people to the ground and pitches down fences so our caribou run wild-eyed and screaming till the shaking stops."

A woman spoke. She was from the village of Bora, she said. Caribou could tell that even before she spoke, by the red *pistra*-shawl about her shoulders.

"Our water-sprites are dead, wisewoman. All the wells of our villages have been poisoned with red rust," she told her. "Even the river is fouled. We have to climb the mountain every day for water, to the high springs where the hot jets have grown unpredictable. Already three of our people have been killed, and many more spattered and scalded.''

She held out her wrist so Caribou could see the burn-welt across the palm and forearm.

Another woman came forward, with thick gray hair that had once been black, plaited into braids with beads in them, like the River-Valley People wore, but her skin was olive, not tan, and her eyes were dark, not green.

"I am Brikka," she told Caribou, "and my village lies on the high slopes, steep above the Huëndl River. A village of Valley Folk used to lie below us. But when the great mountain to the west of us burst apart — you saw the smoke? Cinders fell on us."

"Here, too," Caribou answered, lifting a palmful of soil from the ground beside her, made grayer by fine ash. "But what happened to the Valley Folk?"

"The ashfall did no great damage," the woman Brikka continued, "either to our own village or to theirs. No one was killed. But the shock of the explosion shook free the cliffs beside the Forbidden Caves, below our village and to the south of us. Again, no one was harmed.

"But during the night, we surmise, some heavy ether — tasteless, odorless — seeped from the broken slope and down into the valley below us, poisoning the air. In the morning we saw Valley People stagger from their houses and fall dead. We were afraid to go to them. Some of our cattle wandered too far down the slopes and also died."

Caribou's skin prickled as she listened. She gripped

the arrow in her lap. She had never heard of such a thing before. The elder with the beads in her hair went on.

"This was two months ago. We have tried offerings and propitiations to every daimon we know, but nothing avails. The valley below us is sheltered, but sometimes when a strong wind sweeps through from the southeast, blowing hard for half a day, the valley is safe to venture into for a few hours' time.

"But as soon as the wind stills, we must climb the slopes at once, or perish. We have floated messages of warning to villages downstream, but as yet no one has brought any reply. We think the river-daimons have stolen our messages, or else the Valley People have already fled in their barges to the sea."

One by one the council members came forward, each in turn telling Caribou his or her tale of disaster. When they were done, Caribou sat speechless. Alone all winter in her *ntula,* cut off from the rest of her Tribe, she had had no idea of the extent of the calamity. She gazed at the drawn and worried faces of the councillors.

"Surely all of this is horrible," she managed at last. "But . . . why come to me? What am I to do?"

"We have come to you," their spokesman Djenret said, "O wisest of women, to ask what daimons are angry with us. Or is it our *waijen* we must propitiate? And how? You are a seer and a dreamer of dreams. Surely you must know."

But Caribou only shook her head. She felt as puzzled as he. "No daimons are angry with you, as far as I can see. Nor is it your ancestors who protest some slight. You have offended no one."

"Is it the earth, then?" ventured a woman with the pleated smock of a mountain goatherd. "Have we ill-used the earth somehow, that it heaves and groans to snuff us out?"

Again Caribou shook her head. "I have had no dreams of that." She had had no dreams of any of it, or none that she could recall.

"Is it . . . ?" a man near the back of the group began. "Is it then, truly, the end of the world, as our village shaman has said — there is no escaping the destruction?"

Caribou sighed deeply and said to him, "I cannot believe the earth is dying. Fire and steam are part of the earth and do it no damage. They only harm people and animals, and green growing things."

She paused a moment, frowning and thinking. There must be an answer to it, somehow, somewhere.

"But as for why this trembling of the earth has come, or where the magic and the daimons have gone, I have no answer yet."

She sighed, glancing toward the western horizon, which was smoldering to dusk. Never before had anyone laid such a task upon her. She was keenly aware that whatever answer she gave would affect the whole of her Tribe.

"Will you give me one night to dream on it?" she asked of them. "In the morning, I will tell you what I can recommend."

She rose. The elders bowed their heads respectfully,

accepting her words, but she could see they were surprised, and not at all satisfied that she would not answer them at once. She herself felt pained and weary.

"Very well, *i'dris*," their leader told her — it was a name they had begun to call her, for they considered her a seer. "We will camp away from your *ntula*, at wood's edge, so that our campfires and our councils will not disturb you."

She offered them food for the night, but they said they had brought their own. They gathered up their blankets and went away, and Caribou went inside the hut. She was troubled still. Not in all her years as a wisewoman had she turned anyone away unanswered, even for a night.

And thinking now, very deep, she began to recall the barest edges of dreams, dreams that she had forgotten immediately upon waking: of the upheavals in the earth and the raining destruction, and all the daimons moving off southward in a great troup, toward the Pole and the spirit world, the Land of Everlasting Night.

She concentrated deeply, desperately. But not one dream, now only fleetingly recalled, gave her any inkling of what was causing the disorder, or how to bring the daimons back or halt the rending of the world.

Caribou shook herself. Her head was aching now, and she had achieved nothing. Slowly, she took off her smock and shirt and set her boots and leggings at the foot of her bed. She was very tired, and would doubtless dream truer sleeping than awake. At last she crawled beneath the coverlet of gray caribou skins and, though restless and uneasy still, soon drifted into sleep.

A soft scratching at the door awakened her in the dark. The night was still. She could hear someone's impatient breathing, short snorts, just outside the door. Caribou got up from the bed and wrapped the caribou skins around her, shaking with cold.

What could the councillors want at such an hour? She had not dreamed yet, even one dream that night, and they had said that they would not disturb her. Caribou sighed and relented a little then. Perhaps they had let their coals die, and needed fire.

She padded barefoot across the soft, cool skins on the floor, and laid her hand upon the latch. As she did so, a brilliant light shone for an instant outside. Its brightness dazzled her, even through the cracks. Caribou started, shielding her eyes. She had seen such a brightness only once before.

Heaving up the latch, she hauled open the door. A fair-skinned youth stood on the threshold, not more than sixteen summers old. He had wheat-colored hair and golden eyes. A robe of golden reindeer pelt lay over his arm. He did not tremble with the cold, only gazed on her, his eyes revealing neither joy nor sorrow.

8

The Wild Deer

CARIBOU stood in her doorway, clutching the caribou robe about her, and stared at Reindeer. It had been two years and a half since he had gone away. She could hardly believe the change in him. He was no longer a boy . . . But what was he doing here? The question panged in her suddenly. Why had he returned to her now, after all this time?

"They wanted me to stay with them," he told her, speaking without hesitation — as though he had never been away — "the wild deer. They wanted me to run with them forever over the frozen plain." The night was dark and chill. She shivered again. The *trangl* shook his head. "But I could not. I have wanted to return for many months. And so at last, this season, I came away."

Caribou could say nothing, could only gaze at him. He was taller than she was now, his golden hair longer and untrimmed, his voice deeper. A few silk strands of unshaven beard pricked the smooth skin of his cheeks, but that was all. Somehow she knew he would never have more beard than that. He was not a man. His golden eyes were exactly as she remembered them.

"There are some people camped near here, at the

woods' edge," he said after a moment. "I saw their fires, and waited until they were asleep."

Caribou nodded and found that she, too, could speak now, almost naturally. "Yes, I know. They came about the failing geysers, the trembling ground, and the great upheavals in the earth."

"What trembling?" Reindeer asked. "What upheavals in the earth?"

"Come inside," she told him, shaking, "and I will say."

She held back the door, and when he had entered, she shut it. Reindeer knelt beside the hearth, made up the fire with kindling and an iron tong while Caribou took a sash to tie the caribou robe. Then she brought him food, which he ate willingly, almost ravenously.

"I have not tasted human food these many months," he said, "since I was gone from you."

Caribou knelt beside the hearth as well, partly for warmth, but mostly to be near him. She was shivering still. "You leapt away from me," she said softly, "that first spring when the reindeer came back. I stood on the hillside of the Reindeer's Path and watched for you, but you rushed on with the others. Why? After that, I never looked for you."

The youth laid down his bowl, and now, it seemed, he hesitated. "I did not want to remain away from you," he said at last. His fathomless eyes sometimes looked at her, and sometimes down. "The others urged me to it. They said the pain would pass — but it did not pass."

His fingers touched hers upon the hearth.

"You told me once, Cari, that you feared I had no human heart. Perhaps that is so. I am not a man. But heart I have; that much I know, for it ached after that, very sorely, like a wound. Sometimes it eased a little, or I forgot the pain, but always it returned, more and more strongly."

Caribou smiled then, a little smile. Her fingers closed over his. It had been a long time since she had touched him. The joy in her was so great it was almost pain.

"My eyes stung," the young man said.

He looked off across the darkened room as if puzzled. Then he caught her hand suddenly, and his golden eyes catching the firelight, burned bright as meteors.

"How can I tell you what it was like, Cari? Running with the wild deer over the Burning Plain and beyond the southern Pole. That season, that first season, was the only time I truly forgot you here, this house, and the people of this land. There were . . . such things, so *much* to see and learn."

The heat of him warmed Caribou's hand. His breath quickened. Then abruptly his expression darkened.

"They are very different from your people, are the wild deer. They know nothing of laughing and weeping, Cari, only a fierce, wild freedom in coursing the Broken Plain. They did not want to accept me at first, saying I was too old to join them, had worn a human shape too long. They said that though I now wore a reindeer's hide, I was still a man beneath the skin — too cautious and trembling and tiring, not fearsome as they are, and free."

His eyes were fixed on some far point across the room. Caribou watched him.

"They debated long. But at last I persuaded them, for my father's sake, to take me in. I told them I would never be happy among humankind, which is the truth."

He glanced at Caribou. Her fingers tightened, and her heart grew cold, hearing him, but she did not speak. He looked away.

"So they said I must forget love and sorrow, all human things, and ride with them all day without resting, over the Burning Plain, beyond the broken snow."

A little silence followed, filling the room, sifting into the cracks, like darkness falling. They sat a time, not looking or speaking to one another.

"Are they," said Caribou at last, softly, "are all of them like you — able to throw off their hides and walk in human shape?"

He shook his head. "Only the golden ones," he said. "There is a legend — a legend that our kind were human once, outcasts from your people: *kaaluwati,* who followed the reindeer. But one day they stood in a golden shower that spouts beside the Forge of the Fireking, a geyser of burning gold that transfigured them into stags and hinds."

"The Fireking," murmured Caribou. She had never heard of such a one. "Who is the Fireking?"

"The king of the firelords, the lords of the earth," Reindeer replied. "They mine deep below the ground, hunting for gold and precious silver. They came here long ago, and that is when the earth first began to be restless." He glanced at her. "They work at their forge, sweating and smelting, all night and all day."

"What do they make?" whispered Caribou, but Reindeer only shrugged.

"Who knows?"

His expression grew more solemn still. Caribou eased her grip upon his hand. Again he looked away.

"I have seen that shower," Reindeer said, "and stood in its spray. All *traangol* must bathe in it at least once, early in life — else their reindeer selves begin to fade, and die away."

Caribou felt a little twinge, thinking, *if only I could have held him a little longer, perhaps, perhaps* . . . But it was no use wishing. She said instead, "And why is that — does not the line of the golden ones breed true?"

"It does not breed at all," said Reindeer suddenly. His brusqueness startled her. "The halflings cannot conceive with one another's seed, but must return here to the country of their ancestors to lie with human women and men."

Caribou listened to him, frowning.

"The hinds carry their calves to the calving grounds to bear them in spring. Then in fall, when we pass by the Fount of Gold, they bathe them in its rain to loosen their reindeer skins so they may lay them aside at will. The stags carry off their children from their human mothers in the fall, before they have been long suckled and grown too human. Then they bathe them in the Fount to give them reindeer skins and let them run with the wild deer beyond the Burning Plain."

The youth sat looking down as he said that, picking absently at a rough place on the hearth. Caribou stirred. She was frowning still. "But it is wrong to lie with men only for the getting of children," she began.

Memory of Branja came to her, for the first time since the winter of the *waijen* and of Reindeer's leaving her. But it was not the taunting *wajn* she pictured now. Rather it was Branja as she had been in life — flinging herself before the golden stag, and clutching at Caribou's arm. Hapless Branja. Caribou's voice gained strength.

"And it is wrong to steal a woman's child when she does not want to give it up."

Reindeer shrugged and shook his head. "The *traangol* are a proud race, august and cold. They do not understand the warmer hearts of mortal creatures." He looked at her. "They bear your people no malice, Cari, and take from you only what they need."

Caribou drew back from him. His flat, dispassionate tone still had the power to surprise her. "Perhaps," she answered softly, "but still they *take* from my people what is not freely offered. And that is wrong."

He sighed, and stubbed his thumb and forefinger against the roughened stone. Almost, it seemed, he was smiling at her with his golden eyes, till she wondered, How human was he — or did she only imagine it? He took her hand again.

"Come tell them so yourself, then, Cari," he told her. "You are very wise. I have no doubt you could find words to make the wild deer listen."

For a moment she could not speak. "What are you saying?" she whispered. She had not intended the words to be so soft.

"I want you to come back with me," said the golden-eyed young man, "when the reindeer run southward in the fall. I will carry you upon my back as far as the Fount. There you can bathe in its spray and become a *trangl*, like me, and run with me among the wild deer by winter and spring."

Caribou gazed at him dismayed. She saw the fire that had come into his face, heard the expectation with which he spoke, as though already certain what her answer would be. But what he wanted filled her with fear. She was a mortal woman, and had no *trangl*'s blood in her, like Reindeer, yearning to join the wild deer.

She said nothing. A space of silence then. The room grew very still. No wind, no wolf, no *wajn* whispered at the door. The fire was dying down. Caribou took her hand from his and threw another piece of kindling on the fire. She sighed.

"If you had come last night," she began, "but one day earlier, perhaps . . . perhaps I could have gone with you. But now — now I cannot."

She glanced at him and saw that his face had paled and fallen. Did she detect somehow upon those unearthly features a sadness? She could not be sure. The sense of desperation and futility that had gripped her only hours before returned. She thought of the councillors outside, dozing beside their campfires at the woods' edge.

"Those people you saw camped below," she told him, unable to keep the urgency from her voice anymore, "they have asked my aid, not only for themselves, but for all the villages of my Tribe. There have been great changes in the earth since you left, great geysers of fire and the hotlands spreading."

Briefly, she told him what she knew.

"I am afraid. All my people will perish if I do not help them." *But how?* Fatigue nibbled at her. She could not think. "Is the earth dying? Why have the daimons gone away?"

And Reindeer replied, almost indifferently, "The firelords are turning the earth, for they have mined all the gold and precious silver they can find here. The daimons know this. That is why they have gone."

Caribou stared at him. "Turning the earth — what do you mean?"

"They are making it new," he told her, "reshaping it, like a *trangl* throwing its skin, so that in time it will make new gold and silver for them."

Whatever she thought she had seen in his face a moment before had vanished. She could not fathom his calm. That he could speak of such things, such incomprehensible things, so easily! Surely he was a daimon — how could she ever have mistaken him for a man?

"But what are my people to do?" Caribou said desperately. "How may we live where the earth is changing, without our daimons to protect us?"

Again she thought of the councillors. She had promised to dream on it and give them their answer at dawn. But she had had no dreams that night, or none she could recall.

Reindeer said, "I know of a place where the firelords do not come, where the earth is not restless."

Caribou turned, her weariness once more overcome by surprise. Something seemed to have rekindled in him.

"It is the wintering ground of the wild deer," the golden young man told her, "and lies beyond the Pole."

Then Caribou's heart closed up, and she tore her gaze away, certain suddenly that he was mocking her. "Beyond the Pole?" she hissed. "That is the way the *waijen* go, to their Country of Endless Night."

"Not so," the *trangl* said. "Sweet lands of forest lie there, and green grass growing."

"But none may pass so far south," she said. "The cold . . ."

He shook his head. "The reindeer pass."

"And how may one follow the reindeer?" she asked bitterly, hardly listening, angry at his mocking her, "that run more swiftly than a bird can fly?"

"The caribou may follow," the young man upon the hearthstone said. "They are near cousins of the wild deer, and almost as fleet. And your people may follow, too, if they will, for I can build you a thing, a kind of boat that skates upon the land. It is drawn by another kind of deer than reindeer, though caribou could draw it."

Caribou stood listening.

Reindeer said, "I have seen such a thing on the other side of the world. I put off my *trangl*-skin at the edge of our wintering grounds this winter past, to help a girl and her brother repair their boat, whose runner had broken. They showed me how to guide it."

She searched his face, but it told her nothing. Could her people use such things as he described to escape the fire and storm of the firelords' turning of the earth? He was a daimon. He would know such things. But what had Branja's *wajn* said? *All daimons are capricious, and they lie*.

Could she trust him? In all his years with her, Reindeer had never done anything to cause her to doubt him — yet he had been with the wild deer since then, and learned their ways. Caribou shoved such thoughts aside and made up her mind. She had no choice.

"What is needed for the building of these boats that skate upon the land?" she asked.

"Not much," he said. "Only wood, and sinew for binding, and reins."

"Are they difficult to build or hard to sail?"

Again he shook his head, and she swore that in another moment he would smile. She had come to stand very near him, less than an arm's reach away. She could feel his breath upon the air.

"Then I will tell the councillors tomorrow," she answered. "And we will build our landships to be away across the southern Pole as soon as may be."

He put his hands on her arms to draw her closer. "Not quite so soon. We must wait until fall. Only then is the Burning Plain solid enough to bear the weight of our passage. Landships must have hard, frozen ground to skate upon."

"Fall?" whispered Caribou, suddenly fearful. She thought of the worsening fury of the earth all that winter past and shuddered. "Do we have so long?"

Reindeer nodded, but she wondered if even a daimon could know such a thing with certainty. She avoided his eyes, and managed to draw away from him. She went to her storing chest.

"Let me show you the things I made for you from your cradle-antlers," she said, and brought some of them to him beside the fire: the horn-hafted knife, the brooches and buttons, cuff-clasps and needles, the unfinished baton.

He knelt and looked at them all very carefully in the firelight, picking each up and fingering it before laying it down. Finally he looked at her, saying solemnly, "These are all very fine, beautifully made. But I have no use for them. I am a *trangl*."

Caribou closed her eyes, for her eyelids stung fiercely. She refused to think of it — refused to think of his putting on his *trangl*-skin and going away from her again. "But you may use them while you remain with me, and wear your man-shape," she whispered, beseeching. "Take them."

He nodded, and then just for a moment his unreadable expression seemed to soften, to change. Could she be seeing him right? The flickering of the embers was dim and full of shadows. He took his hand from the carved things on the hearth and hesitated, then reached to touch her face.

"If I take your people to a safe land," he asked her, very gently, "far from burning earth and spouting fire, will you then come with me, and run beside me with the wild deer?"

She wanted to shake her head or turn away from him, but she could not. His flesh was warm against the bone of her cheek, and her own hands very cold. His golden eyes were searching hers. She felt a flash of something hot darting through her then, and thought of Branja's *wajn* again, for she found that at that moment she could neither say nor do anything Reindeer did not want.

She told him, "Yes."

He drew her to him, and kissed her forehead and eyes. The heat of him, and the strength of his arms encircling her made Caribou's knees weak. She put her own arms about his neck to keep from falling.

"My people will not welcome you," he whispered, "but I do not fear for you at all. They do not understand why I long for the company of a human creature. But in the end they will admire you, as I do. I know it."

His breath had a sweet taste, like new grass growing. She gasped for breath.

"If they so disapprove of me already," she managed, "why ever did they let you go?"

"I told them," he answered — did his eyes laugh? Did they smile? — "that I must go among my mother's people again to find me a mate and get me a child."

Her hands upon his shoulders tightened. "Is that the reason you have returned to me?" she wondered, and did not realize she had spoken aloud until he answered, "Yes."

Caribou's heart grew cold then, even as he kissed her mouth. *I know beyond all hope of saving that I love you,* she thought, *but do you love me? You are not mortal. Can you love?* It made not the slightest bit of difference, for she had looked into his daimon's eyes.

9

Boats That Skate
upon the Land

THAT DAWN Caribou rose, put on her shirt and
smock and boots, wrapped her heavy *lanlan* about
her, and walked down to the camp of the elders to
speak with them. She found them already awake and
looking as if they, too, had not slept much the night
before.

They eyed her strangely, and seemed much more
reticent than they had been the previous day. Now
and again, their glances strayed to her *ntula*. Caribou
told them of the firelords, letting them believe she
had learned of them in a dream. Then she told them
to go back to their villages and be of good heart, for
very soon — within the month — she would come
down from the Wilderland with a means to save them
from the changing of the earth.

The councillors rose, gathering their possessions,
and went away — but with much soft murmuring
among themselves and much furtive glancing back
through the trees toward Caribou and the cabin on
the bare rise behind her. Some of them whispered that
they had dreamed of a golden light shining through
the woods the night before. Some said the wise-

woman had called a *trangl* to consult with her, while others said the *trangl* always came.

She overheard a little of their talk and almost laughed, for she felt lightheaded with lack of sleep and with joy at Reindeer's return. She loved him. Nothing else mattered. When at last the elders were gone, Caribou turned and went back to lie the rest of the morning with her golden daimon, dozing and talking with him.

He built the landboat, as he had promised her, hewing the hard-grained ash trees down with the antlerhafted ax she had made him. He split the timbers and planed them smooth, shaping them, then fitted them with dovetailing and pegs.

She, meanwhile, on his instruction, slit out and braided cords and cords of leather thong. These he used to reinforce the joints and lash the runners underneath the belly, after he had shod them with gold by running a little of his blood all down their length.

"Why have you done that?" Caribou asked him, coming out of the house to bring him more thong. Reindeer nodded toward the gold-smeared runners already drying in the cool spring breeze.

"To point them always toward where the reindeer are," he replied, "like that arrow that you keep."

And when the landboat at last was done and the gilded runners lashed into place, he called it a *gristal*, for that was the name the two young strangers he had rescued had called theirs. It rode low to the ground and was narrow, less than a woman's arm-span across, with a substantial hold in front, deceptively shallow-seeming, in which gear and supplies could be packed.

Near the back was space for one or more passengers to sit, one behind the other on top of the baggage, and behind that, a running board for one to stand upon and drive the sledge, using a willow switch and a pair of thongs, called reins, for guiding.

Once the *gristal* itself was made, Reindeer set about fashioning a padded collar of strong, supple leather stuffed with fur, that a draft-deer might pull the sledge, while Caribou braided more strips and stitched together bands of leather for making what Reindeer told her would form the harness and traces.

Each thing he did, he showed her carefully how it was done and let her try it, so that she would know exactly how it had been accomplished and could instruct the others of her Tribe.

She and Reindeer worked hard each day outside while the light lasted and late into the evenings by the hearthside at night, then lay in each other's arms beneath the fur of the reindeer robe, till dawn. The spring moons dwindled and grew fat, and by day Caribou felt that she had never been more happy. No people came at all that month to trouble them. She and her *trangl* were left alone.

The earth still trembled beneath their feet, often violently, and sometimes in the west they saw dark haze that turned the sunset sepia. But it all seemed very distant from her now, and at times Caribou felt her heart swell nearly to bursting with contentment as she worked beside her golden young man.

At night, though, her sense of well-being faded. Sometimes she and Reindeer heard the crash of mountains falling far away, and felt the tremors. She dreamed then, terrible dreams that made her toss, moaning and muttering, until Reindeer shook her awake, saying, "What is it? What is it — are you in pain?"

"No," Caribou told him once, sitting up beneath the reindeer robe. The cold night air rushed in around her. "No, I had a nightmare."

She put the heel of one hand to her eye to scrub the sleep away, brushed back a loose strand of hair. Sleep drained from her in a pungent prickle. She glanced at Reindeer, but he seemed puzzled still.

"A . . . kind of vision," she murmured. "All smoke and burning."

"Tell me," he said, putting his arms around her and lying back down with her against him. The reindeer fur settled on top of them again.

"I saw," she sighed, remembering, "that it was evening; all the air was filled with choking smoke. I saw you standing in your man-shape. Your hair was a golden fire that lit up the night and did not harm you. Then you vanished, and all was darkness again.

"Suddenly there were people all around me, running and screaming. I could hear the caribou snorting, stampeding, and I could hear bells. Dimly, I saw people trying to flee through the woods, but the trees were all alight. Some of the people were trying to escape over a bare rocky place, away from the trees, but the earth broke apart, and the rocks melted into a slow liquid fire."

She shook her head, shuddering. Her voice was shuddering as well.

"Still others were poling in barges downriver toward the sea. I have never seen the sea, but in the dream it looked like open tundra, flat and gray — save that when the barges reached it, the water began to heave and boil, sending up great gouts of steam like white plumes into the air. They swamped the boats, and the people pitched into the water and drowned.

"And the last people I saw had run to the tops of the highest hills to pray to the moons to succor them. But Greatmoon floated above them, dull copper in the heavens, stripped of its brightness, and Littlemoon lay pale and thin upon the far horizon. Only those people who had followed the sound of the bells got safe away."

She did not realize that she had begun to weep until she felt Reindeer touching her damp cheeks, then saw him holding his fingers up to look at the tears there in the dull glow of the hearth. His face bore the same impassive, perplexed look he always wore whenever she laughed or wept. She held him closer, and he put his arms around her once again.

"We will go down to the first of the villages tomorrow," he told her, "and you can show them how to build *gristaal* and how to drive them."

"Tomorrow?" Caribou asked him. "But . . . what will I say to them? I have had no time to prepare —"

Reindeer took her hand. "When have you ever needed more than a moment to consider your words?" he asked, in a tone that, if he had been human, would have sounded chiding. "You will speak to your people as you always have, telling them all they need to know. And they will listen."

She was not so sure. Uncertainty nagged at her. Would her people trust her tale of the firelords — strange beings they had never heard of before? Would they follow her advice to build sledges and flee? Another thought occurred to her.

"But how can we go tomorrow?" she asked. "We haven't any caribou to pull the sledge, and no *pisjlak* laid in."

"Never mind about supplies," Reindeer replied. "The villagers will supply you with all."

Caribou looked at him, more puzzled now. His face had no expression, like a *wajn*'s, like an owl's. She did not question him.

"And do not worry about the caribou. I will pull your sledge."

Caribou felt her heart grow small. She laid her head against his shoulder. "You'll not come down in man-shape to the villages?"

He shook his head. "Let them wonder who and what I am." He ran his hand along her shoulder a moment, absently. "Besides, if I go man-disguised, who will teach the caribou to draw the sledges?"

She put her hand on his and closed her eyes, telling herself his distance was not strange to her. He had always been so — and after so many months without him, his presence alone should comfort her. She would not think of anything else. Soon sleep welled up around her in his arms, and she dreamed no more until morning.

At first light, they rose and loaded the sledge with what little food was on hand. There were hardly any of the winter stores left, and they had both been too busy to lay in new. Then they shut up the house.

The sledge rode light. Even Caribou, who had not driven the *gristal* before, could tell as she stood upon the driver's step, bundled in her *lanlan* against the wind, how easily the craft bucked and skipped across the slick, muddy ground, through the last of the slushy snow, the runners sparking when they hit a stone.

Reindeer had thrown off the new man-clothes Caribou had made him, thrown on his golden deer-pelt, skin-side to his skin, and now ran between the traces, drawing the sledge behind him. Caribou was dazzled at their downhill speed. Not even in dreams had she ever flown so swift.

They ran through noon, into the afternoon, coming into the first village just at dusk. People ran to them and cried in wonder, reaching to touch — yet not quite touch — the sleek wooden craft, the strange golden deer.

"What marvel is this," they cried, "that skims over land light as a bird through air, *i'dris?*"

Caribou reined in her Reindeer — gently, gently — let the landboat slide to a stop before the main hall of the village just as the village elders emerged and stood, wide-eyed, upon the porch. *They are more speechless than I,* she thought, relieved, and felt her confidence beginning to return.

Amid the crowd of their strange faces, she noted one that was familiar, the spokesman of the special council that had come to her. Caribou searched her memory, then smiled.

"Hail, Djenret of Vlad," she called. "Why so amazed? Did I not say I would come within the month with the means to rescue us from this unsettled place?"

"Welcome, *i'dris,*" the councillor replied, regaining himself a little after his surprise. "Will you come into our council hall and tell us of this thing?"

He and the rest of the elders fell back then as Caribou brought Reindeer and the *gristal* right up the steps and into the hall. Her nervousness had vanished now. Inside, she talked to the elders and as many of the villagers as could crowd into the room. She spoke of the firelords' changing of the earth, which had driven all the daimons away.

As darkness fell, bonfires were lit in the streets outside and the great hearths stoked within. Meat and drink were brought to refresh the wisewoman, and sweet hay for her golden stag. Those villagers who could not fit into the hall crowded about the unshuttered windows, wrapped in furs, or gossiped and sipped hot ale about the bonfires or upon the porch, wondering about the wisewoman and her godlike car, and the wild golden deer that drew it.

Caribou explained the workings of the sledge and the means for its construction. She described the felling and splitting of the wood, the shaping and shaving, the fitting of joints to be both strong and flexible, the lashing of runners and their waxing with beeswax.

She told them of the land beyond the Burning Plain, that she had dreamed of and been told of by one who had followed the wild deer there and back again — she let them think what they would of that — and how, come fall, they must follow the wild herds across the Pole to the other side of the world, or perish.

When at last the evening had grown so late and still that none felt they could hold open their eyes a moment more, people within the hall stretched out where they were and huddled beneath their *lanlani* beside the great fireplaces. Those outside who had gotten places beside the bonfires sat nodding by the warmth, while those who had not retreated to the shelter of their houses for the few hours till dawn.

The day broke — too soon, it seemed to Caribou. She awakened, astonished to hear the ring of axes and the fall of timber through the woods as people, already up, were even now felling trees for the construction of sledges. All day, while the wood-shapers and carpenters worked, Caribou showed the others how to braid and stitch the harness-lines, how to fashion them into halters and bridles, how to pad the harness-straps with fur.

That night, exhausted again, she slept in the best guesthouse, quartered there at the villagers' insistence — and nothing half so fine had she ever seen in all her life. The walls of her chamber were paneled and decorated with carvings, and there were candles of beeswax and soap that foamed like beer yet bore the strong, sweet scent of roses.

Reindeer they had corraled with the village caribou, where he waited patiently until late evening when every soul, or nearly, was asleep; then he leapt the high-railed fence in a bound and pawed softly at Caribou's window. She opened the shutters, and he threw off his deerskin, coming in to lie the night with her.

They stayed six days in Vlad, till Littlemoon was new again. Caribou showed the people how to pack the landboats properly, wedging the stores in, lashing them down, laying the weight evenly and taking care not to overload the hold. She showed many of them how to drive a sledge, using her own, letting them handle the reins and guide Reindeer — gently, always gently — where they wished to go.

"You must train your teams for stamina," she said to Djenret, "for by fall they must be able to run for hours at a stretch."

While Caribou helped the people fashion their sledges, Reindeer mingled with their caribou, singing them the songs the golden ones had taught him, teaching them all they would need to know to draw the sledges across the Burning Plain and follow the reindeer over the Pole.

On the seventh day, she and Reindeer left Vlad. The building of the *gristaal* was well underway, and she knew by the growing number of strangers coming into town to stare at her and the building that word of her landboat was spreading.

She had to give back most of the provisions and

thank-offerings the villagers had pressed on her, for she could not have used them up in a year's time, much less fit them all into her sledge. She bade the councillors good working and farewell, and told them to meet her upon the Open Hills beside the Plain of Providences that fall at reindeer time.

She went to Lasjmar next, the nearest village to Vlad and the second of the sixteen of her Tribe. Once more she was welcomed. After that, she went to Baslak and Insfélo, and each of the other lesser villages in turn. The task invigorated her, gave her a sense of urgency and purpose she had never known before.

Always, in every village, when she first arrived everyone came running and was curious, listening eagerly to her description of the *gristal* and the country beyond the Pole. But invariably when it came time to begin to build, some held back, watching still, and some shortly drifted away from the work. Others stood by, openly jeering.

When she questioned them, they often said, "We do not believe there is a land beyond the Plain of Broken Snow. All this effort will be for nothing."

"Then where do you think the reindeer go in winter?" she asked them.

At that they would shake their heads, still laughing. "We do not know, but it is no land where we may follow."

Others told her, "The world will not end. We do not believe in your Fireking. Your dreams are false."

"I have never said the world was ending," Caribou

replied. "It is changing. That is all that I have said."

Then sometimes they laughed again, or went away. Still others told her, "There is no escaping doom. Why try? If these firelords you speak of are angry with us, then we are meant to die." That puzzled her, for she had never told anyone that the firelords were angry.

They baffled her and troubled her, these people who would not join the work. She asked Reindeer one night about them when the two of them lay beside their campfire in the forest. The road between the village of Lukasj, which they had just departed, and Prino, where they were bound, was too long to travel — even by *gristal* — in a day.

Reindeer turned at her question to look at her, his golden eyes expressionless. "Why will they not build sledges — Cari, have you not asked them that yourself?"

She nodded, yawning, throwing another piece of deadwood on the fire. "Yes, but I find their answers very strange. Why will they not see the danger, and flee it while they can?"

She glanced at Reindeer and saw him gazing at her with the closest thing to amusement in his eyes that she had ever seen. But his tone was neutral still.

"Your people are indeed very strange," he said, "and have always puzzled me. But if even you, Cari, who are the wisest of them, do not understand them, how is it you hope that I, who am not even human, ever could?"

10

Tjaalsénji

T HE LAST SETTLEMENT they went to was Tjaalsénji, the High City, where the chieftain of the
whole Tribe had lived before his death and where his
children still dwelled and quarreled. The village lay
in a high meadow that caught the morning sun. It
was late summer now, barely a month before the
autumnal equinox.

Caribou saw workers tilling the ripening fields as
she and Reindeer drew near, the landboat bucking and
sledding over the hard, slick road. Some of the workers looked up as she skimmed past, but none of them
paused from their tilling or pointed, shouting to their
companions, or dropped their tools and ran toward
her.

Instead, those that looked up turned back quickly
to their task, some going at it even more deter-
minedly. Caribou gazed at them, frowning. Never
before had she approached a town and not had people
cry out and run to meet her.

As they passed a woman weeding near the roadside,
Caribou reined in Reindeer.

"Is this the road to Tjaalsénji," she called, though
she did not doubt it, "and am I very far?"

The woman looked up, eyeing her resentfully, and answered curtly, "Yes and no," then turned back to her work.

Caribou stood a moment, not understanding, until she realized the woman had simply answered each of her questions in turn. She had shown no interest in the sledge.

"But —" Caribou began. The woman's head snapped up again, so swiftly that Caribou was startled. The field-worker's eyes were bright with loathing.

"Do not question me," she cried. "Vasli has told us of your coming. You are the false prophet from the Wildlands by the Waste, you with your talk of Firekings and your 'divine car' — divine indeed! — and your painted deer, spreading false rumors of the end of the world."

"He isn't —" Caribou started.

"*What?*" the woman shrieked.

"He isn't painted," Caribou repeated. This woman seemed almost a raver. The ties of her blouse were haphazardly looped, and dark circles curved beneath her eyes. "Gold is his own color," Caribou told her. "I have not gilded him."

"More lies," the woman spat. "Vasli has told us. You are in league with our foes. They set fire to the forests to blacken the sky, and shove rubble down the mountainsides to cause the earth to shake."

The woman had thrown down her spade and risen, wringing her hands. She glared at Caribou.

"Well, we are not frightened. Foes do not frighten us! You wish us to panic and lay ourselves open. Well, let others panic. Vasli protects us. What are a little smoke and trembling to us?"

She threw back her head then and gave a laugh, short and wild, then bit it off quickly and stared at Caribou.

"Who are these foes?" Caribou asked her, certain she could not mean the firelords. "The River-Valley People have fled away, and our villages are all one Tribe."

Reindeer was tugging at the reins, but Caribou held him.

"Renegades, then," the woman snapped, glancing off and shrugging frantically. "Or strangers. How should I know? I'm not Vasli. But Vasli has told us. Vasli says . . ."

"Who is Vasli?"

Reindeer stamped.

"Our leader!" The woman's eyes snapped back to Caribou. "The youngest, the only true son of Bhesjti, our late chief. Vasli knows — Vasli knows how things truly are."

Caribou studied the circles like berry-stains under the other's eyes. "How much sleep do you get . . . ?" she began.

"We *don't sleep*," the woman growled, snatching up her digging tool again. "We work — day and night. It is the only way we can keep ourselves ready."

Caribou stayed silent a moment. She glanced at Reindeer. He stood watching the woman digging. His golden eyes met Caribou's, but they told her nothing.

"Suppose I offered you an escape from this place,

these foes you fear," Caribou said to her. "Would you take it?"

"No!" the woman cried, spading furiously and tearing up the ripening crops as well as weeds now in her grubby fingers. "This is our land, *our* land. We will not leave it — not leave it, though the earth itself open and swallow us . . ."

Her words grew ragged, trailing off. Caribou saw the other's lips tremble, her breast heave and fall. Sweat or tears, Caribou could not tell which, made tracks along the woman's face. Her spade threw jets of soil into the air.

Caribou clucked to Reindeer and drove on.

The woman had been right; they were not far from the town. As they entered the outskirts, Caribou heard snatches of what sounded like singing — some near, some distant — and drunken revelry, though it was only late morning, and no feast-day.

Litter lay about the streets — broken drinking mugs, bread-heels, and half-picked bones. Household possessions lay strewn here and there, most dirtied or broken. The houses looked abandoned, many with a door or window staved in. More than once, in the distance, she heard shouts and the sound of splintering wood.

Three youths staggered out of an alleyway onto the main street ahead of her. One bore on his back a small chest and a sack. Another held an earthenware jug in each hand, and the third, a round of bread and a haunch of venison.

They were singing a drinking tune, but the words straggled off as they squinted and stared. Caribou and Reindeer glided by, but a little distance down the street Caribou pulled Reindeer to a halt, and turned to look at them over one shoulder.

"Ho, what says Vasli to this?" she cried. "Do not his followers hereabouts believe in work before there's war?"

The two youths with the chest and the bread blinked at her again, obviously baffled. But the other youth, the one with the wine jugs, who appeared younger and drunker than the other two, burst into laughter.

"Vasli?" he cried, hooted, almost unintelligible: "That no-name. *Vasli?* And war?" He roared. "There'll be no war. The world's about to end! And where . . . and just where . . . ?"

He staggered, trying to focus on her.

"May that . . . that is, may I . . ." He took a deep breath, got it sorted out. "And just where, may I ask, is it you've been this last twelvemonth, my young fine . . . fine young dame?"

His companions nudged him to silence then, eyeing her with some unease. They clearly took her for a person of importance. One of them hissed something at their companion. Caribou called to the other one, the one carrying bread and venison.

"Where may I find the town council?"

"Council hall's in the middle of town, Honor," the one she had addressed called. He seemed reluctant to approach. "Just follow the street."

"No councillors in it, though," the one with the

wine jugs called, over his companions' shushing. "All gone — driven away. Council hall's gone, too. Burnt. Brakla burnt it — all down."

"Who is Brakla?" Caribou asked.

The one with the chest and bag on his back brightened. "Our leader, Worship," he called, beaming. "Bhesjti's son."

Caribou nodded. "The only true child of the late chieftain, I daresay."

"The truth!" the wine-jug lad cried with a hiccough and a laugh. He had a dark, rather comely face, made silly by drink. He reminded her vaguely of someone she knew.

"And what does Brakla say?" Caribou inquired.

The one with the loaf and meat replied. "He says, 'be gay,' Honor! Be happy while you can. The world's about to end. Why not? Eat, drink, live well — who cares? None of it matters, and it's over too soon."

His companion with the wine jugs began a sort of jig, accompanying himself with an off-key ditty, one Caribou had not heard before:

> "*The end is near:*
>   *Soon falls the sky.*
> *I want to live*
>   *Before I die.*
>
> *So revel, feast —*
>   *Why let or stop?*
> *And foot the dance*
>   *Before we drop.*

> Let mountains fall
> > And fountains churn.
> To sing's the thing
> > Before we burn . . . !"

He lost his footing then and sprawled upon the cobbles, breaking one drinking jug with a crash. His companions snatched the other before he could do it damage. The one holding the chest set down his loot and began wrestling the fallen youth to his feet. The youth looked up at Caribou, still watching from a little distance.

"Join our . . . merry revel, Worship?" he managed.

Caribou turned to Reindeer and lifted the reins, let him draw her and their *gristal* away down the street.

As Caribou and Reindeer drew nearer to the center of town, the buildings began to look less disordered and deserted. Less rubbish lay about the streets. The houses were all shut tight.

As she neared the village square, she became aware of people, a long line, each group with a caribou calf that they were leading by the ear. Now and then, when the wind swung in the right direction, Caribou caught the scent of burning, and the sweet stench of the slaughterhouse. People turned to stare at her as she and Reindeer passed by.

When they reached the square, Caribou saw more villagers — though not really so many for such a great town as this. They were crowded about a great heap of ashes and charred timbers — the remains of the council hall, Caribou guessed.

As she got closer, she saw one knot of people with a caribou calf go forward. A tall woman wearing a white *mbolap* that fell to her knees and a headdress of caribou antlers stood upon the ashes, the fabric of her clothes spattered with wet red and drier brown. She held a long-bladed *ca'xat* in one hand.

The people brought the calf to the woman. She took it by the ear and cried out some garbled words toward the noon sky, which shone faint blue above the strands of gray smoke hanging in the air. Then she slashed the calf's throat with the blade. It fell struggling to the ash, and after a moment lay still. Two people, also in white, came forward and carried the carcass away as the woman carefully wiped the blade.

Caribou, shocked and alarmed, drew the sledge to a halt before the ashes of the council hall. The people there seemed to take note of her for the first time. They fell back, murmuring. The woman with the antlers looked up from her meticulous cleaning of the knife. She started, seeing Caribou, and her face, already hard, grew harder.

"Why have you come?" She lowered the blade, letting the white rag slip from her hand. "You who call yourself *i'dris* and wisewoman."

"I call myself neither," Caribou replied. Reindeer shook himself. The leather traces rattled and creaked.

"Why have you come?"

"I have come to offer safety to any who would have

it," Caribou answered, raising her voice enough for the others in the square to hear. "I come to warn you of the firelords' doing, how they are turning the earth to make it new again. I have come to show you how to build *gristaal,* that you may follow the reindeer with me beyond the Land of Broken Snow, and escape the changing of the earth."

"Go back," the woman in the horns spat. "We do not want you. We laugh at your firelords. You will die upon the Burning Plain if you try to follow the reindeer. I have heard of you and what you preach."

"I preach nothing," Caribou told her. "I am no godspeaker."

"All lies," the other shouted. "Emptiness and air!"

Caribou laid the reins of the sledge on the board in front of her and considered the woman across from her. "Since you already know my name," she said at last, "do me the kindness of telling me yours."

The other, in her bloodstained smock, drew herself up very straight. "I am Nilsa, first and only daughter of Bhesjti. I wear the horns of leadership now."

Caribou eyed her, and wondered that the people of the square stood so quiet, so lifeless, so cowed. "You have two brothers, so I have heard, who say similarly," she observed.

"I spit on those mice!" the antlered woman shouted, clutching her knife. "*I* am the eldest-born. It is I who am best-suited to lead the Tribe." She gestured, smiling now. "And, as you see, the people follow me. Not them — or you."

Caribou glanced around her, dismayed, at the silent, meager crowd in the square. "Why are you slaughtering your caribou calves?"

"Hah!" the eldest-born of Bhesjti cried. "Wise-woman indeed — you fraud. We sacrifice them to the ancestors. The daimons, too, are angry with us. We had forgotten them and turned away. They shake the ground and boil the blood of the earth to remind us how we have failed them with our faithlessness."

"The *waijen* live across the sky in the Land of End-less Night," said Caribou, "and the daimons have all gone away. What good does the blood of caribou do such as they?"

The other woman shouted with laughter, but the crowd about them remained motionless, quiet. "Why, it satisfies them, propitiates them. They drink it up" — she gestured — "like wine."

"The earth drinks it," Caribou told her, "and trem-bles still."

The antlered woman did not reply, but nodded curtly, right and left. A knot of white-robed assistants on either side of her started forward. Caribou felt a surge of alarm.

"Enough of these words," the daughter of Bhesjti hissed. A little smile twisted her lips. "Let us see how the gods like the blood of your painted deer — or *your* blood, seeing-woman, if it comes to that."

Reindeer snorted, wheeling in the traces. Caribou hastily gathered the reins and held him back. He would have fallen on Nilsa's henchmen if she had let him. Reindeer struck the cobbles with his hooves and danced. The assistants halted in confusion. Some of them held cudgels of black, charred wood. Nilsa stood furious, with folded arms.

Reindeer did not fight Caribou as she turned him, but sprang away, drawing the sledge behind him in a swift, smooth sweep. She circled the square once, crying to the people who yet stood still, like stone, holding their caribou calves and watching her with dull, hopeless eyes.

"Any of you who would follow me, any of you who would learn to build a landboat such as this one and escape with me across the Burning Plain, come now, come soon, to the nearby villages: Fusklaf, or Kiord, or Ersk. They are building sledges there and will welcome you."

Behind her, she heard Nilsa speaking harshly to her servants, urging them after the sledge. Caribou kept Reindeer moving in a wide arc, and cried out once more to the people in the square.

"But if you stay here past our departure in the autumn, when the reindeer are running, surely you will all perish, for the firelords here are changing the earth, like a *trangl* throwing its skin — without a thought that mortal creatures such as we may not survive the flash. Come away with me and save yourselves!"

The sparse crowd neither moved nor spoke. She glimpsed the assistants of the chieftain's daughter following her now, trotting half-heartedly after the sledge. Reindeer completed his circuit of the square and sprang off down the side-street by which he and she had come.

Glancing back, Caribou spotted the assistants standing at the square's edge, gazing after her now less with anger than with apathy. Again she heard their leader crying out, her words unintelligible. Caribou shuddered and clapped the reins for more speed from her golden Reindeer, so eager was she to be gone from that place.

II

The Plain of Providences

AFTER the High City of Tjaalsénji, Reindeer and Caribou returned home. They spent the last days of summer laying in their provisions and awaiting the cooler weather that would bring the wild deer. When the time arrived, in the midst of fall, Reindeer came to her in his man-shape as she sat upon the hearth, brewing berries into sweet jam.

"Cari," he told her, "the reindeer are running. I feel it. My blood flows quicker with their running, and I am restless. Their snorting and stamping and their wild cries call me."

Caribou nodded without looking up and laid down the sticky spoon with which she ladled off the dross.

"I know it," she answered. "I dreamed of it last night."

And the golden arrow had turned very strongly in her hand this morning, when she had held it, as it always did when the wild herd was near. Reindeer sat beside her at the hearth's edge. She sighed.

"We must pack the sledge tomorrow," she said, "and shut up the house. You must throw on your reindeer skin again and don the traces. Then we will go down the Open Hills, where they meet the Plain of Providences, which the wild deer must cross to reach their Path which funnels them on to the Burning Plain. There we will meet those who would come with us to the world's other side, and await the reindeer."

He nodded, still not speaking, seeming at once both restive and weary. Caribou poured the hot, bubbling jam, smelling of mint and stewed berries, into earthen pots, and melted wax over them to seal the lids. Then she laid them along the wall in the coldest part of the lodge.

Reindeer meanwhile went to their bed and threw off his man-clothes. He crawled beneath the fur of the golden deer-pelt. Caribou came back to the hearth but did not bank the fire. He watched her for a little while, sleepy-seeming, and held out his hand to her at last.

"Are you not coming?"

"You sleep," she bade him, rising and going to lift the lid of the chest where she stored her birks and needles. "I will come in a little while."

The next morning they rose before first light and laid all the stores they would need in the hold of the sledge: dried meat and bread, preserves of fruit and fat bitternuts, fish roe in pots and honey, soap and tallow candles, oil for burning, tinder, wicks, and many kinds of tools, all wrapped in woven cloth and furs, wedged tight and laced firmly down.

It was still the earliest part of the day, just past dawn, when they finished. Reindeer came to where she stood in her travel furs, and asked, "Where are the traces? I cannot find them. How shall I pull the sledge without them — have you seen them? Did you bring them into the house last night?"

Caribou went into the dark, shut-up *ntula* for the last time and opened the chest where she had kept her birks and sewing things. She brought out the tack and harness she had laid there the evening before and carried them out to Reindeer, jingling and tinkling like a thousand bits of glass.

"Bells," he cried, astonished, fingering them. "You have sewn them all with bells."

She nodded. "Last night, while you slept. It came to me that our sledge might well be lost from sight at times, hidden by fog or smoke. These bells will sound above the clack and thunder of the wild deer's running, and our followers will know where we are."

He ran his hands over the traces then, examining the bells. "You carved these of my father's bones."

Again, her nod. "A long time past, when first you went away. I did not know why at the time. I forgot about them afterward, till now."

Reindeer dropped the traces suddenly, took her face in his hands. He cradled it a moment, then bent and kissed her. She clung to him and did not want to let him go. But he drew away from her, gently, and threw off the man-clothes she had made for him. He donned the golden reindeer pelt, skin-side to his skin.

Caribou hid her eyes from the brilliant light. She told herself she must not weep. *He is not really leaving me. The transformation is necessary. He must be a stag for a little while now, so that he may pull the sledge.* But that did not ease the ache in her heart. Already she was longing for him in his man-shape again — but when she looked up, her fair-skinned youth was a deer again, just shrugging into the belled traces.

Sighing, she buckled them, then took the reins and climbed into the driver's box, dropping the bar across the open space behind her so that she might lean back against it if she liked. Then she clucked to Reindeer and let him take her — bounding and leaping as though the sledge's weight were nothing to him, his tendons snapping and the harness singing — away toward their meeting with the others of her Tribe.

From the hilly Wilds that bordered on the Broken Plain, they came down and inland toward the rolling, treeless tableland her people called the Open Hills. The sky hung lower now, gray with clouds and smoke. The Spouting Springs, a low range of geysers off to the west, were breathing cinders and steam. From time to time, as she and Reindeer drew near the flatter tundra called the Plain of Providences, Caribou heard the distant crash of geysers splitting rock.

They came upon the others almost before she was aware, nearly stumbling into the midst of their encampment before the ragged veil of fog parted, revealing them. Reindeer snorted, and Caribou reined in. The jingling of his bells abruptly ceased.

She stared at the group of sledges before her. Teams of four and six caribou lounged in their traces. Off to one side, a common herd milled about a makeshift enclosure of sledges and campfires. Caribou looked around in dismay. The people standing among the sledges stared back at her.

"Is this all," she cried at last, "all that came?" The meager crowd before her would scarcely have peopled two of the sixteen villages of the Tribe. Caribou glanced about. "Or are the others late?"

Reindeer shook himself. The bells whirred and jingled like cricket-song. The people before her were shaking their heads. She recognized a face, one of the elders who had come to her in spring.

"No more than this, *i'dris*," the woman said, her worn fingers playing with the beads in one braid. "They laughed us out of town in most of our villages, for many have turned away from the work and against you since you came. Though the daimons are gone and the charms no longer work, though the earth trembles still, most no longer take heed." She bowed her head. "No more are coming, *i'dris*."

Caribou shook her head, appalled, for the tremors of the earth and the black cinder-clouds had grown even more frequent, more violent since spring. Reindeer stood in the traces before her, golden and unperturbed. Her mouth felt dry.

"The councillors," she said at length. "How many of them came?"

She spotted others now, moving among the crowd. Her voice carried well over the open, rolling hills. The ragged fog had begun to lift; a faint breeze fanned her cheek. She saw the councilwoman glancing at the others.

"All of us," she said, and other voices echoed, "All of us came, *i'dris*."

Caribou's heart grew warmer then. For the first time she was able to smile. At least the elders had not lost faith in her. She sighed. It was too late to do anything about the rest. The people before her stood waiting, expectant.

"Well, so be it," said Caribou. "If this is our number, we must be content."

She felt her blood beginning to quicken. From far in the northern distance, coming over the Plain from beyond the horizon's edge, she could hear the reindeer running. She did not see them yet, but they made the ground tremble even here, even so far.

The caribou were growing restless in their pen. Reindeer stamped one hoof and champed. Others of her people had caught sound of the thunder now. She saw them turning their heads, scanning — and then the vast wild herd hove into sight over the rim of the world. They closed rapidly, until soon the ground was trembling so violently that Caribou half believed the rumble must be the earth itself, and not the wild deer.

From their vantage point on the last of the hills, she and her people watched the tide of silver thundering past. Far ahead, to the south, where the tundra rose to meet the Wilderlands, they could see the living river narrow, bunching as the reindeer reached the glacier-trough and plunged into its bottleneck, which channeled them toward the Land of Broken Snow. The caribou within the enclosure circled restively, while those in the traces strained and bawled so the people could scarcely hold them. Caribou kept her arm raised to keep her people back — the golden arrow held in one hand — for she dared not let them brave that headlong, trampling rush.

At last the great flood had swept by them and, as if at some unspoken signal, the caribou in the enclosure stampeded, leaping the barricades to follow. "Let them go; let them go," Caribou cried to those trying frantically to re-corral them. "It is time we were away ourselves."

She let her hand fall forward, southward, pointing.

"Let us run across the Land of Broken Snow," she shouted, "chasing the wild deer — to the Pole, and beyond, to the other side of the world."

Reindeer sprang away at Caribou's word. With a shout, the others scrambled to their sledges, the drivers leaping onto the back-end step, passengers bundling themselves onto the baggage hold in front and lapping their furs.

Caribou saw all this in a rush as Reindeer bounded away, dragging her sledge more easily and swiftly than the teams of four and six caribou behind them pulled theirs. The bells settled themselves into a chanting rhythm in time with Reindeer's pacing stride. Glancing back, she saw the rest fanning out behind, their draft-caribou beginning to find their strides and the last few unhitched caribou running alongside and among them.

They ran until they neared the tundra's edge, where

the ground rose and funneled into the glacier trough. Caribou could see the dark, moving mass that was the last of the reindeer passing into the funnel ahead, and heard their distant thunder, more faintly now, above the clacking of her own Tribe's caribou and the singing of Reindeer's bells.

As they drew near the tundra's narrowing, near the low, wooded slopes that formed the northern extreme of the Wilderlands through which the funnel traveled, Caribou suddenly spotted people — Tribeswomen, and men, a few children — most of them ragged and exhausted, standing among the trees.

A few staggered down the short hillside toward the sledges. Caribou had swept past the first of them almost before she saw them. They held out their hands to the passing *gristaal*. Caribou could hear some of their cries.

"Help us!" someone shouted. "Take us with you!"

"The mountain," another voice, a woman's, called. "The mountain by Aba Barkán has fallen. We saw it from across the valley at Davín — all firefall and killing smoke. We ran, but most could not escape."

"It is the end of the world!" an old woman screamed.

"Take us with you; take us with you, *i'dris*," Caribou heard someone pleading. "You were right. Oh, save us. We must get away!"

Caribou tried to slow Reindeer then, but he had taken the bit in his teeth. He ran on faster than before. Caribou shouted for him to stop, and when he would not, she turned to call back over her shoulder to the others in sledges behind her, "Have you room to take some of these people with you?"

Those on the landboats shook their heads. One of them, a man with two children on a heavily burdened *gristal,* cried back, "We've neither space nor weight to spare, *i'dris.* We are loaded as much as may be."

Another man called out; Caribou thought she recognized him as one of the council members. "We cannot take on any more load without killing our caribou or falling behind — and if we lose the reindeer, how will we find our way across the Burning Plain?"

Caribou tugged at the useless reins. The ground shuddered suddenly underfoot; the sledge lurched. Caribou pitched painfully against the rail. She heard a roar like shifting earth, saw those on foot by the hillside stagger.

She heard the wild snorts and whistles of frightened caribou. Reindeer sprang into a faster lope. Behind her, more people came running over the crest of the hill. Smoke billowed up from beyond the trees.

"The geyser has flung itself apart!" a fleeing woman cried. "The earth has split and is spouting fire. The woods are burning! The woods —"

Screaming followed and shouts of dismay from those driving the sledges. People on foot fled the hillside, dashing onto the plain. The earth shuddered again with a terrible groaning. Caribou clung to the rail of her *gristal,* and this time she saw spouts of fire beyond the crest of the wooded hill. Smoke roiled up. Before her and behind, people rushed for the landboats, seized hold of the sides, tried to drag out their occupants.

Caribou heard curses, shouting, moans, and prayers from both the sledge-drivers and those grappling with them. The free caribou dashed wildly among the *gristaal* now. Some of the people who had rushed to the sledges managed to cling for a few moments, only to fall at last — sometimes beneath some caribou's heels. Caribou watched, horrified and helpless.

Someone, a youth, seized hold of the side of her *gristal* suddenly. He clutched her arm, and she tried to pull him up, but he fought her clumsily — and she realized, astonished, that he was trying to fling her from the landboat. Terror surged in her. She fended him off. Gritting her teeth, she kicked him hard in the chest. He fell. She clung to the rail of the *gristal*, gasping, and did not look behind.

Up ahead she saw Reindeer lower his horns and toss aside a man who had planted himself squarely in their path, his *ca'xat* drawn. Caribou bit back a cry. She fumbled with the dangling reins and managed to catch hold of them, lift them up so they could not tangle Reindeer's heels.

The ground shuddered for a third time, most violently. She saw the surface of the tundra pull apart like rent cloth. In places the cracks were an el across. Reindeer vaulted over these, and the sledge bucked roughly. The people on foot were falling behind them now. The sledges had all swept past. Caribou saw bodies lying scattered on the cracked tundra.

Sparks of fire gusted over the hillcrest. Flames appeared in the crowns of the trees; more cries came from those who fled on foot behind, curses and wails of despair. Smoke billowed down as the wind whipped over the hill. Some of it smelled like burning pine, and the rest like poison stench. Caribou held a flap of her *lanlan* over her face.

"More speed!" she cried. "We must get past. There is death in this smoke — it comes of burning rock!"

The drivers following her whipped their caribou into a hurtling run. Though swifter than all of them, Reindeer was keeping his pace in check so as not to outdistance the others. His bells chanted above the sound of caribou hooves, clacking tendons, sliding runners, and the commotion of forest and earth behind.

The unharnessed caribou had begun to outstrip the sledges now. Reindeer let them pull past him and run on ahead after the wild deer. Moments later, Caribou started as the walls of a canyon loomed suddenly and swallowed them. *The glacier-trough.*

They were running the Path of the reindeer now, tracing their passage through the Wilderland. Caribou cast her eyes behind her one last time, but what little she could see through the canyon's mouth was a dismal haze of fire and smoke.

12

The Land of
Broken Snow

THEY RAN and twisted, sledding through the great glacier-trough, following their own deer as they chased the even greater thunder of the wild deer, invisible now beyond the closer caribou.

Gazing back, Caribou saw the other sledges bunched in the turning meanders of the trough. The ground was shaking under the sledge-runners from the reindeer's passing. Caribou rested the reins on the rail and let Reindeer run as he pleased.

Sometime later they neared the end of the narrow gorge. Caribou glimpsed ahead of them the last of the reindeer, fanning out over the snowy plain like a gray torrent. The caribou, like a much smaller rivulet, did the same, spreading and running southward after the wild deer.

Caribou reined her golden stag in a little as they left the canyon's steep, high walls behind, looked back over her shoulder at their little band. She circled as the last of them emerged from the canyon, raising her golden arrow high.

"Follow," she cried. "The reindeer run far ahead of us now. Quickly! We must catch them."

Reindeer wheeled, sped off across the Broken Plain,

and Caribou let him run for a few moments before pulling back gently to remind him that the others had not his speed. Her *trangl* dropped to a rapid trot; his belled harness chanted and sang.

The ground over which they sledded now was hard and hot. Caribou felt its warmth rising moist against her unmuffled face. Some places seemed warmer than others, though, and she saw great swatches where snow had formed, interspersed with patches of exposed, sometimes steaming ground.

The vast herd ahead of them had trampled down much of the snow, but here and there whole stretches lay undisturbed. Reindeer, too, refused to tread them, even when Caribou tried guiding him toward one. He only clamped the bit more firmly in his teeth and tossed his head from side to side.

Not long after, she realized that some of the sledges forming the leading edge of the fan had begun to pull ahead of her. They were driven by maidens and youths mostly, lashing their teams to greater speed, laughing and racing. Caribou only glanced at them at first, shaking her head. She decided to let them run a bit till their hot heads cooled.

"Snow!" she heard one of the young women call out suddenly. "Fresh snow!"

Another voice took up the cry.

Then, "A race! Come, Val, Tor. We'll race!"

Looking ahead, Caribou saw the snow — a broad, soft expanse of white, unusually deep, perhaps knee-high. At the same moment she felt a change in Reindeer's stride.

Three sledges were veering toward the snow blanket, the drivers tapping their caribou into a gallop with their willow flicks. They cut across Caribou's path, laughing and shouting, ignoring the cries of their elders. Caribou shouted a warning, too, but they only lashed their teams and swept by.

Caribou gathered in the reins, but before she could so much as clap them, Reindeer had sprung into a gallop on his own. Their sledge bolted in pursuit, passing two of the three *gristaal* in a moment.

Reindeer gave a bell-like cry. The caribou teams of those two sledges flicked their ears to the sound, then wheeled, galloping back to rejoin the others despite their drivers' dismayed and angry cries.

The third sledge had a much greater lead and was by this time almost to the snow. Reindeer redoubled his speed, but just as he drew even with it, that sledge's team vaulted up onto the snowbed. The landboat bucked up behind — they were running along the snow's edge now, Caribou and Reindeer along the flat.

"Hah!" cried the youth at the reins of the other *gristal*, "so you'd race with us, wisewoman? Let us see if six earthly caribou can outrun your golden stag!"

He lashed his team with his long willow wand and his landboat leapt ahead. For a moment, Caribou could only stare, for she had recognized him — one of the three youths she had seen in Tjaalsénji, the one who had been carrying the chest. Were those his two companions on the sledge with him?

Caribou shoved useless wondering away and clapped

the reins to Reindeer, but he was already lengthening his stride. Pulling even again with the sledge on the snow, he gave a long, belling cry, and the caribou in the other teams faltered, falling back. Their driver leaned forward and lashed them again.

"Ho, no magic from your golden deer, wise-woman," he cried. "Let the race be fair!"

One of his companions urged him on. Caribou could see them better now, and recognized them both. The younger, darker one did not join in the hying. He seemed sober enough now, a little pale, and not half so exhilarated as his fellows. For a moment, his eyes met Caribou's.

"Rein in, you fool," she cried at the driver. "This is treacherous ground. Why do you think the reindeer have not —"

The phrase died on her lips as, abruptly, she felt Reindeer shorten his stride. Glancing ahead, she saw where the snow blanket suddenly widened. If the two sledges held course, both would be up on the snow soon, and in the middle of it, no longer on the edge.

Reindeer bolted forward, and Caribou had to clutch the rail to keep from falling. Her golden stag drew ahead of the other sledge till Caribou herself was opposite the lead team. Then Reindeer veered hard toward the team, within an arm's length of them.

Caribou stood mystified. Why did Reindeer not turn, away from the snow? They would be on it themselves in another minute if they did not veer. Reindeer gave out a long, bawling cry. The caribou of the other team lifted their heads, swerving toward Caribou.

The other driver lashed and cursed his team, fighting to pull them away, but the caribou strained toward her still, leaning out their necks — and all at once she understood. Dropping her own reins, she reached as far as she could across the rail to grasp the cheek strap of the nearest caribou. They were almost to the snow.

"I have it," she shouted. "Reindeer, I have it in hand!"

With a cry, the golden stag shied, very hard. Caribou was thrown to her knees on the driver's step, but she clung tight to the rail and managed to keep her grip on the team's bridle. Then the caribou came down off the snow, and the violence of their descent jerked the cheek strap from her hand.

She saw the other *gristal*, still on the snow, break through a sort of crust underneath. The rear half of the sledge's near runner fell through with a muffled crunch. The whole landboat tilted. Driver and passengers cried out, clung to the sledge. Thick, gray water spattered up, and Caribou heard shouts of pain, surprise, as droplets touched faces and hands.

The caribou struggled forward, bawling. Caribou managed to get hold again, this time of the strap linking the bits of the lead pair. She braced herself. The sledge behind her came free of the snowbank, crashing down on the hard ground — and the runners held.

Caribou let go of the strap. Shaking, she got to her feet. Her chest above the breasts felt bruised where it had met the rail, and her fingers and knees were gashed. Panting, trying to regain her breath, she caught up the dangling reins of the six-caribou sledge and led it back to rejoin the others. Neither the young driver nor his passengers protested now, but instead sat clinging to their *gristal*.

Caribou flung them their reins, then circled the other sledges to shout: "This is the Burning Plain, the Land of Broken Snow. There is fire in the earth here, and hidden pools of caustic water. Who dare forget that now? Run only where the reindeer have run, and follow my golden stag. Only he has run this path before. Only he can lead the way."

She let Reindeer take her to the front of the band then, drawing out well ahead so that all might see her, yet still hear the chanting of his bells.

They ran on, beneath a hidden sun that skulked behind the high, gray clouds. The reindeer had become no more than a dark mass on the far horizon, and the caribou were only a little less far ahead. They ran past places where rocks littered the ground. They skated vast flats where the earth was cracked and level.

For long stretches they passed over only trampled snow. The going was smoother there, and at such times Caribou felt both herself and her people grow easier. Other times they wove through great fields of shallow water, patched with algae and mineral scum, dull gray, reflecting the duller sky.

Sometimes, when the ground was hard and hot, the heat rose so intensely that Caribou felt her armpits growing slick and had to open the throat and sleeves of her *lanlan* to let in enough wind to cool her.

Time passed. The sun, hidden behind the clouds, declined, and the afternoon grew late. Often when the terrain ahead looked regular and safe, Caribou circled back to survey her band. Their going had grown much slower now.

Though she trusted that they had been training their teams to run long stretches without tiring as she had bade them, she could see that the caribou were finding the pace hard going. They could barely keep up a ragged trot. And with the unharnessed caribou now far ahead, there would be no changing spent animals for fresh.

The people themselves looked weary and dispirited. They no longer shouted and called to one another as they drove, or laughed with giddy release at the dizzying speed. They talked to her sometimes, as she circled them, working her way back up through their ranks.

"*I'dris,* when will we get there?" a young girl cried, and then her brother, even younger, yawning, echoed, "Aren't we there yet, wisewoman?"

"*I'dris,* I'm so hungry. Can't we stop and eat?"

"I have to rest! I'm so tired I can hardly stand."

"The trace-caribou, *i'dris,* look at them. They're staggering."

"It's so hot here, it's like a spring."

"Take heart," called Caribou. "I cannot say how long we must run, for the wild deer run this trek without resting, and we must do the best we can. If you are hungry, eat of your stores. Have you not kept them close at hand as I instructed you? If you are warm, unlatch your *lanlani*. If you are tired, those of you who are not minding the reins pillow your heads and sleep. The Burning Plain cannot last forever. When we are past it, we will stop."

Caribou clucked to her golden stag and let Reindeer take her up to the head of the band. Dusk fell, grayly; it hung a long time in the sky. The air grew cooler, though gusts of steam still rose from the warm, flat earth.

The character of the land had begun to change — it was still flat where they traveled now, but the horizon ahead seemed elevated, uneven, like a low ridge of hills. Then Caribou discovered with a start that she could no longer see the dark tide of reindeer before them. It was only the smaller, lighter band of caribou that she could make out, far on the limit of her vision.

As she watched, she saw them, too, beginning to dwindle and disappear over the horizon's rim. Her skin grew cold, and her heart sank like a stone. Her dreams had not shown her any of this — nor indeed anything of what lay beyond the Plain of Providences, she realized. She had come on Reindeer's word alone, with blind trust in him and in his tales of sweet pastures beyond the snows.

A momentary panic gripped her. *Should I have placed my faith in a daimon?* she wondered. *What do I really know of him now, of what he has become? Does he love me — does he truly care what happens to my people, or is he just using me, using us all somehow, for some unfathomable purpose of his own?*

She fought the icy terror down. *No. I trust Reindeer;*

I must *trust him. For he loves me. He must.* But she shivered still. She had no more definite idea of where they were going, of how to get there, or of how long they must go than the people who followed her.

Night settled, deepening from pale gray through charcoal toward black. When there was yet the barest trace of light left to see by, Caribou reined gently, and Reindeer slowed, coming at last to a stop.

She had felt the land beginning to change again beneath the sledge's runners, growing hillier and cooler. Though she wanted to get beyond the worst of the Burning Plain before halting, now she feared to leave it entirely and so lose its warmth.

She stepped down from the halted sledge, feeling the slight heat rising through the soles of her boots, and managed a smile. She had gauged it right. Though warm, the ground here was cool enough to camp upon. She waved and shouted to the others. The dozing drivers gliding past her jerked awake, reining in their teams. Exhausted caribou collapsed in their traces.

With the cessation of the bells and the cracking of caribou tendons, with no more dull thud of hooves or hissing grind of runners on the hard earth, all the world seemed suddenly, oddly, utterly still. Caribou stood beside Reindeer and gazed at the tired people around them, stumbling down from their sledges.

"Let lamps be lit," she told them, "and fires made. Prepare food and skins for sleeping. Tend your caribou. We will travel again at first light."

The people turned and followed her instructions —

numbly, like sleepwalkers. Fires were struck up. She saw food and bedding being unpacked. No one answered her. No one spoke to anyone else. Their silence niggled at her, like an itch between the shoulder blades, but she shook it off. *I am weary myself,* she thought. She unharnessed Reindeer and walked with him through the silent others to the edge of the camp.

She could see little of their surroundings for the dark, but the terrain was more hilly now than it had been. Lichens and reindeer moss crunched with the pebbles underfoot. She stood with her golden stag beyond the light of the nearest fire. They both stared toward the midnight Pole.

"Reindeer, do you know where we are?" she asked him quietly.

The gold deer snorted and lifted his head. Pensive, she fingered the thick, golden hairs of his hide, frustrated that he could not throw off his deer-shape even for a little — but there was no cover here to conceal the brilliance of the light his transformation always made, and he was shy of people. She remembered his words from before their departure: *The route changes a little every year as the Burning Plain shifts itself and changes*.

"What lies ahead —" she began again, and was startled at the sound of her own voice in the stillness. She dropped it to a murmur: "the Fount of Gold?"

The *trangl* bowed his head and stamped.

She sighed, resting her head against him a moment. "Aye, that and more, I suppose."

She gazed at the last of the dusklight abandoning

the sky, and was aware for the first time of a dim glow in the south, red above the low, near hills. She had thought all this while that it was some reflection of the smoldering sun, but she saw now that it could not be, must be instead the reflection of some other, reddish light beyond the horizon's edge.

"What is it?" she asked Reindeer. "Do you know?"

She felt the golden stag tense beneath her hand. Again he snorted, stamped. She could not tell whether he meant that as an affirmation or denial.

"Can you tell me?"

He shook his head, great gold eyes gazing into hers with no expression. She held his head in her hands and gazed in return. Her voice was more hushed when at last she spoke. Her dreams had told her nothing of this.

"It is something wondrous," she asked him, "is it not? And terrible."

But his deer's eyes could not answer her. He leaned forward and touched his nose to her cheek, then pulled away. He was leaving her. She sensed it suddenly and struggled to be calm.

"Will you go and scout the way for us?" she asked.

The stag half turned, eyeing her over one shoulder. Her voice rose.

"Will you be back by morning?"

Her *trangl* bowed his head, then leapt away into the dark. With a little cry, Caribou reached after him, but he was already gone. Unbidden tears sprang to her eyes, but she shook her head angrily and brushed them away. *I am behaving like a frightened child*, she told herself. *He will return. Of course he will.* She sighed and worked her shoulders then. Her body felt knotted with fatigue. She stared into the dark a little while longer, then at last turned wearily and started back toward the camp.

13

Tor

CARIBOU NOTICED that the people had grouped their burning oil-pots into rings and drawn their teams and sledges into rough circles around their fires — more for light and companionship, she guessed, than for warmth. The night was not yet truly cold. Still no one spoke as she passed, though now it seemed that quiet conversations broke off at her approach, and the people watched her.

She found that a circle of oil-pots had formed alongside her *gristal*. Caribou unpacked her own oil-pot, placing it among the rest, and set a bowl of frozen lard and rabbit's meat over the flame, as others had done, to thaw the meat.

Some of the faces around the fire she recognized. Three of them were members of the embassy that had come to her in spring. She glanced at Djenret of Vlad, but he quickly looked down and seemed uncomfortable. There was little speaking, and all of that in low murmurs. The food in the pots bubbled, giving off savory smells.

Caribou lifted her coal-hot bowl from the flame with a rabbitskin, set it in its muffler, and ate. Others about the campfire were doing the same. With the warmth of food in her, a little of her weariness left her, but still no one spoke, and the silence weighed on her.

At last Djenret, sitting across from her, laid down his bowl. Caribou heard others in the ring draw breath, their eyes darting between her and the councilman. Uneasily, Caribou laid down her own dish. She felt those around other fire-rings turning to watch as well.

"Wisewoman," the gray-haired elder began, gazing at his lined and craggy hands, and not at her. "It has been decided . . . That is, we have discussed among ourselves . . ."

Words failed him. He groped, still looking down — at the firepots now. Then he glanced up, his eyes barely brushing hers before springing away.

"While you stood with your reindeer at camp's edge," the councilman told her, "some people came to me, a number of people — many of us. And we fear . . ."

He glanced at her again, but Caribou would not help him. The unease in her had grown very sharp. She said nothing, moved not at all, only waited.

"*I'dris*, we fear that we are lost."

Caribou's eyes widened. She drew breath in surprise, but the councilman hurried on.

"Wisewoman, we have lost the reindeer — can you deny it? Brikka and many others saw them disappearing over the horizon's edge before dusk — our caribou as well."

Caribou clenched her teeth against the bitter taste that had come into her mouth. She kept her voice steady. "Aye."

The councilman looked up, his own frustration clear. "Well, how shall we catch them, then? You told us we must run behind the reindeer, but the reindeer run without resting — and our caribou seem to have done the same."

"They have stolen our caribou," she heard an old woman from another circle cry. "The wild deer have."

The councilman said, "Without our herds, we cannot change our sledge-teams. And we ourselves must stop to rest as well. How will we ever find the wild deer now? We are lost."

Caribou folded her arms across her drawn-up knees, for she was cold. Djenret of Vlad spoke more truth than she would have wished — all except for that last. They had indeed lost their own herd and the wild deer. She had not anticipated that — nor, she guessed, had Reindeer.

But she refused to believe they were lost, not while her *trangl* was with them. Despite her alarm when she had seen the caribou vanish, and again when Reindeer had bounded away into the dark, Caribou gritted her teeth against despair and answered Djenret and the others as openly and encouragingly as she could.

"The wild deer we will never catch, but our caribou we will find awaiting us when we have reached the other side of the world. I am certain of it."

"And when will that be?" she heard a man's voice demand. She fought the urge to snap back at him.

"Who can say?" she replied evenly. "Only the reindeer have run this path before, and they run without resting, as we cannot. We must simply go on, as long as we must, until we are there."

"But we are so tired!" someone cried.

"And what lies ahead of us?" exclaimed a woman in Caribou's own circle. "Exhaustion and hunger — more hardship and pain? The earth here is strange and treacherous, worse than our homeland. We may all die . . ."

Her last words were drowned out by some man's angry shout: "And what is that red glow in the sky to the south of us? Answer us that."

Murmurs and cries of approval followed — angry, cutting. Their ugliness astonished her. Caribou was on her feet before she knew it. The blood came to her face, though her body still shivered and felt cold. Her hands clenched into fists, but with an effort, she held herself in check. She answered the man behind her without turning; her words were for them all.

"You speak of the red glow ahead. But how many of you have heeded that even fiercer glow to the north, whence we came?"

She pointed, hardly looking herself, felt people all around her turning. She heard gasps, and murmurs of fear.

"Two things only make such a glow," she told them, "Brimming rock spilling from the earth and forests rabid with fire. Do you wish to return, to that?"

She fell silent a moment and let them think. She

looked at Djenret. The councilman sat tugging nervously on his moustache. Then she looked at each one of her own ring in turn before casting her voice out onto the stillness again for all to hear.

"One thing is certain: we cannot go back. Our homes are no more! The firelords have awakened the earth. Already it is changing its skin. Nothing remains of what we left behind. Have you forgotten the terror in which you sent your embassy to me last spring? 'Save us from the quaking of the earth and the fountains of fire, O *i'dris!*' "

She stood, breathing hard. Anger made her breathless.

"You call me wisewoman. Do you think then that I am not wise? That I do not, now and again, dream dreams that speak the truth?"

She pierced them once again with her gaze, and fought to be calm. Where was Reindeer? She wanted him. Why had he not stayed with her — why had she let him go? But she had no time for useless thoughts, and shoved them angrily away. Facing her people, she made her voice sure and strong.

"How many of you have I helped through my judgments and dreams? And I tell you now that not long after your council came to me, I dreamed a dream that spoke of burning brush and running firestone, streaming sea and a moon of blood. I would not have dreamed these things if they were not to come to pass. Which of you would go home now?"

Silence greeted her. No one spoke, though there were murmurs, mutters, and shifting glances among the people. Caribou eyed the councilman across from her and the woman who had cried out. Neither of them would look at her.

Someone spoke. "But we are lost, *i'dris*." It was a boy's voice, afraid. "The reindeer have run away."

Caribou sighed, letting some of the fierceness fade from her. "We will not see them again," she replied, more gently now, "until we have reached the land we seek, but we can follow their footsteps."

"And where the ground is hard, where there is no snow?" A woman's voice.

"Where no tracks show, my golden Reindeer will lead us," said Caribou. "He knows the way."

"Your golden reindeer has deserted you," she heard another woman crying out. The accusation cut her to the bone, but Caribou only shook her head.

"He will return by morning. He has but gone to scout the way."

"Lies!" the same voice replied. "Nilsa was right. I should have stayed in Tjaalsénji! You are a false prophetess . . ."

The nails of Caribou's fingers bit into her palms. She wanted to fly at the follower of Nilsa and scratch her eyes. She wanted to weep. Reindeer, Reindeer — where was Reindeer? She held herself back.

"You have led us here but to leave us to die," a man was saying.

"That is not so!" answered Caribou, with such force that she cut the other short.

"Then perhaps, *i'dris*, you are misled," the councilman's voice began, "your reindeer false . . ."

"Nor is that so," spat Caribou, taking a step toward Djenret. She stopped herself, unclenched her fists, and drew deep breaths, remembering Reindeer's words to her once, when he had been a child.

Cari, your sudden fits of anger or of tears startle me and serve no purpose that I can see.

She made herself outwardly calm. Carefully, she reached behind her and lifted her golden arrow from where it lay close at hand on her sledge. She held it up so that it glinted in the yellow oil-light.

"But even were that so," she said, pitching her voice to carry, but less angry now, "even were it so that my Reindeer had left me, it would make no matter. This arrow that I carry points ever toward the wild deer, wherever they may be."

She threw the arrow down. It fell within the ring of oil-pots of her own circle. The arrow lay golden upon the ground, pointing due south. The crowd was silent.

"And the runners of my sledge," said Caribou, "are shod with the self-same gold."

Djenret was leaning forward between the flaring oil-pots. He held a stick in his hand. Using it, he turned the golden shaft upon the ground. The crowd murmured. Then suddenly the arrow twitched and turned itself Poleward again. The councilman dropped his stick, starting back with a cry. The others gasped. Caribou watched them.

"And these teeth," she said, touching the necklace about her neck. It rattled. "I wear them upon my breast by night and noon, and never take them off.

They speak to me, telling me always and ever the way. Just as my dreams speak to me. They will tell me surely the safe way to go."

She heard more murmurs, but they had lost their ugliness. The people still eyed her, but no longer in anger and wariness. The councilman was looking at her almost in awe. Here and there she saw a head nodding. Some of the children slept.

"We have already reached the Burning Plain's edge," she said to them, "which formerly it was said no one could ever cross. I have brought you safe so far. Will you not come with me the rest of the way?"

Again the murmurs, more of them this time, quieter now, no longer restless with fear. The stillness around her began to seem less ominous, the darkness now less wholly dark. Her body's warmth returned to Caribou. She knew they waited for some last word from her, to end it. Finally, she said:

"Who will sledge with me tomorrow along the reindeer's track?"

Slowly Djenret before her stirred. He glanced at her, then quickly about him as if gauging the others' thoughts. When he spoke, it was for all of them.

"We will sledge with you at daybreak, *i'dris.*"

The rest of the ring nodded silently, and those of the other rings as well.

"All of us will come." It was a young man's voice.

Turning, Caribou saw who had spoken: one of the youths on the sledge she and Reindeer had saved, the one who had been falling-down drunk on wine in Tjaalsénji, though today he had seemed sober enough.

He was not with his companions now. He could not have been much older than seventeen.

He sat just on the edge of her own circle, partly behind another traveler, his face mostly in shadow. She had not noticed him before. There was a red mark on his cheek where the gray water had burned him.

He did not seem to want to meet her eyes, but he had spoken with sincerity. For no reason, Caribou felt the hint of a smile edging the corner of her lips. Without thinking, she said something to cover it, but the youth had caught her smile. She saw him smiling a little in return.

"Eat, then," Caribou said, half over one shoulder at the others, but still looking at the youth. "Rest yourselves and sleep. Put out some of your fires once you have had done cooking. We must conserve our stores."

Caribou went back to her sledge and sat down. The people turned away, back to their own fires and food. Caribou cleaned out her cooled baking-bowl with moss. When she looked up, she saw the Tjaalsénji youth still watching her.

"Come here," she said. "I have a salve that will help your cheek."

He rose and came to her, knelt down again. Caribou did not search for the salve at once.

· "Why did you come," she asked him, "you and your companions? I thought you followed Brakla in Tjaalsénji."

The youth blushed and looked down, away. His

hair and eyes were dark, his complexion olive. She had glimpsed shame on his face.

"You recognized us," he muttered.

Caribou put her cooking pot away. "Yes."

She waited then, let him realize she still wanted to know why he had come. The youth chafed his arms. He wore no *lanlan*, and was not very warmly dressed. Now that the flush had faded, his face seemed pale beneath its olive cast.

"We found the sledge," he murmured, "my friends and I. We didn't build it. The caribou, too. We found them. I think their owner must have gone to follow Nilsa or Vasli." He shook his head.

"Why did you come?" Caribou said again.

He looked back at her, his gaze full of pain suddenly.

"Val said we should go to the Open Hills, to see what the wisewoman would do, and the people there — for sport." He looked away again. "So we did, and watched your meeting, and ran with you a little way. Then the geyser split, and the woods were on fire. The caribou stampeded. The people on foot rushed for our sledge. So we fled with you into the canyon and came away."

The young man's voice had fallen to a whisper. Caribou rose and rummaged in the sledge to find the pot of salve she carried. "Why are you not with your friends now?"

The Tjaalsénji youth was standing now as well. He shook his head, put his hands beneath his armpits and shivered, shrugged. "When we halted tonight, they told me to go and not to come back." His voice tightened. "I had told them they could have killed us today — or you — racing on the snow. They are angry with me."

"You have foolish companions," Caribou said.

The young man breathed on his fingers, still looking away. She saw that he glanced back toward the oil fires, toward the people still eating from their pits.

"*I'dris*, I'm hungry," he said suddenly, so softly Caribou barely heard him.

She stared at him. "Did the three of you bring no food or supplies?"

He shook his head. "We weren't intending to come with you. We only meant to laugh at you on the Open Hills, and then go home."

His face crumpled for a moment, as though he might weep. But then he straightened and breathed deep, a little raggedly, still not looking at her. He was just a boy, really, Caribou found herself thinking. Only a boy.

"Here," she said, and handed him another of her cookpots from the sledge. "Put that on the fire." He would not take it from her at first, till she told him, "Don't worry. I brought enough."

He took it then, his face relaxing first into a look of relief, then gratitude.

"Did you bring anything to sleep on?" she asked him.

Blushing again, he shook his head.

"Well," she said. "I brought more skins than I need. Use these." She gave him some.

He simply stood there, holding the things she had given him. He looked up at last and gazed at her, and she at him. He had a beautiful, open face. She could not think who he reminded her of. He was tall for a youth, and would make a tall man in time.

"What is your name?" she asked him.

He answered, "Tor."

Caribou put her thumb in the pot of salve and touched it to the burn welt on his cheek. The hairs of his light, boy's beard were hardly sprung.

"Sledge with me tomorrow, Tor," she told him. "Don't go back to your friends."

The Tjaalsénji youth looked at her a moment more. He was of a slender build, his fingers long-made and strong-looking. It seemed to her that he wanted to say something more then, but after a moment, tongue-tied, he turned away and went back to the fire. He huddled over it, putting the cookpot on.

Caribou laid out her bedding on the ground. One by one she saw the oil-pots damped and taken up, until only a few in each circle remained. She let hers burn, for her lamp was filled with oil from the golden stag her brother had slain so long ago. In all this time it had never spoiled or been used up.

It seemed to burn without being consumed, a clear white flame, very hot. The salve she had put on Tor's cheek had been of the same stuff. The Tjaalsénji youth had finished his meal now, gone off somewhere to sleep. She searched but could not find him in the dark.

Caribou undressed in the flickering darkness, pulled off her boots and outer clothes, lay down upon her sleeping skins, and pillowed her head on her arm. By the dim light of the remaining oil-pots, she saw the others undressing and rolling into their sleeping skins, backs to the fire.

Caribou herself lay facing the fire. She did not sleep, but lay waking, longing for Reindeer and waiting for him to return. But now and again her thoughts wandered to Tor and his dark eyes that were not at all like Reindeer's eyes. Not expressionless at all.

14

Land's End

CARIBOU awakened the next morning before day-break to dress, roll up her bed, and pack the skins away. By the stray light of the few remaining oil-pots, she saw others doing the same. She had dreamed of Reindeer in his man-shape again, his yellow hair blazing.

In her dream, he was walking, leading a long file of caribou down a smooth, steep slope before striking out across a narrow bridge of land that spanned the black, watery sky. Lost in thought, Caribou stowed her bedroll in the *gristal*, feeling a sharp ache in her breast for Reindeer in his man-shape. She had no idea what the vision meant.

The people had gotten out their oil-pots again, arranging them in a circle and setting their long-legged bowls above them to cook the morning meal. She saw Tor huddled in the skins she had given him, beside a family from another sledge. He seemed to have begged his food from them this time, for he did not come to her. Caribou left him to himself.

She cooked her own meal and ate it in silence. Draft-caribou browsed on the reindeer moss. People sat on their heels about the flickering oil-pots, warming their hands and waiting for dawn. When daybreak came at last, all ash-gray light and cloud spread out in a long bar above the east horizon, Reindeer returned to the camp — as fresh and limber as if he had rested a week.

He vaulted the ring of *gristaal* effortlessly, and came on toward Caribou, shaking his golden pelt. The people fell back from him, murmuring. The caribou lifted their heads and looked. Caribou put her arms about her Reindeer's neck and leaned against him, laughing.

"So you are returned then, from your scouting," she said. "I never doubted, but some others among us did."

She felt his nose touching her shoulder and the hot cloud of his breath. Then he pulled free of her and went to stand before the sledge. Caribou scrubbed out her eating-bowl and put it up, blew out the oil-pot and stored that, too, then went to her golden stag to begin buckling the traces on.

"What did you see in your scouting?" she asked him.

He looked at her, but his great eyes told her nothing.

She lowered her voice and leaned nearer. "Can you give me no inkling?"

Frustration bit at her. How she wanted him in his man-shape again! Before her, the golden stag snorted, his breath twin jets of steam, and shook his head. Caribou sighed shortly and fastened the halter about his head, set the bit between his teeth, and brought the reins back to the sledge. He could speak no human words to her as he was.

When she reached the rear of the *gristal*, she found Tor standing there. He smiled at her shyly. He had scraped out the bowl she had given him the night before. Caribou smiled back as she took it. She pointed to a spot in the sledge-bed just before the driver's step.

"Sit there," she told him, "and muffle those skins about you. We will soon be past the Burning Plain, and your own light clothes will not be enough to keep you warm."

The youth obeyed, using the thongs she handed him to lash himself to the sledge beneath the skins. Reindeer had turned and now stood looking at them with his great golden eyes. He cavaled, but Caribou only clacked the reins at him, clicking her tongue and calling, "Oh, why do you caval? He is only a boy that has no *gristal* to ride on. Would you begrudge him that?"

Tor stared at Reindeer, his dark eyes uncertain, his face a little pale, till Caribou touched her passenger's shoulder. He flushed as she murmured for him to be easy. After that he gazed only at Caribou. All around them, the others were breaking camp.

Reindeer watched both of them a moment more, then turned and stood still, save for a furious shaking of his hide in the traces — till the bells sang like a shower of gold — and after that, a slow, measured picking at the turf with one great, splay hoof.

They set off southward toward the Pole, in the direction the reindeer had run, toward the dim horizon over which that silver hoard had disappeared, toward the point where the red glow, now invisible, had hung in the darkness the night before.

As on the previous day, the sledges fanned out behind Caribou's lead, Reindeer drawing their own *gristal* far to the fore. They went swiftly and steadily, but with none of the wild rush of their first day's running. All was gray silence, which the chanting of the bells in Reindeer's harness only seemed to magnify.

As the hidden sun came up, the day growing gradually light enough to distinguish gray land from gray-colored sky, Caribou could see that indeed the land had changed. The terrain was hillier, frost-dry, and barren but for the reindeer moss and some lichen. The land spread in wrinkled tundra, and it was cold. No warmth seeped up in steam from beneath these hills. They had passed beyond the Burning Plain.

People latched their *lanlani* about their throats and tightened the wrists of their sleeves, muffled their faces with wool-woven scarfs. Gradually, they approached the low line of black hills they had seen by the last of yesterday's light.

They were loose drifts, their surface tiny bits of brittle cinders, black as burnt sugar, though here and there dusted with white snow like crumbled tallow. Their sledges moved sluggishly over the soft, sifting stuff, the caribou struggling to keep their footing.

From time to time, passengers had to spring down to shoulder their landboats over the rough places. Only Reindeer seemed able to pick his way over the black dunes with ease. They slogged for hours, the land rising gradually and the air growing drier and thin as a knife. The caribou labored getting up the slopes, their breath thick, white clouds.

At length, near noon, Caribou perceived an edge to the Cinderlands ahead, a point beyond which she saw only sky marking the high point of the dunes, beyond which the land must slope downward again. She did not guess how steeply till Reindeer drew even with the crest of the hill.

Caribou started, and heard her passenger draw breath. She reined in, reflexively, though Reindeer had already stopped. Lifting her golden arrow, she motioned for the *gristaal* behind to come on, slowly. They halted in a long line on either side.

The land before them fell sharply away, as steeply as the crisp, sliding cinders would allow. What lay beyond was a great, level reach of land — the same black grit — while far in the distance on either side lay the flat, silvery sea. Cold, foaming, and salt, it battered itself in white breakers against the black beachhead.

A long river of calmer water reached from the cliffs directly below toward the horizon straight ahead. No ultimate sea was visible there. The river-course steamed, hissing like boiling broth. Geysers of white cloud spouted and subsided; their spray hung in the air. The end of the narrow neck of land was obscured by fog.

Caribou heard a woman behind her exclaim, "Is that what we must cross, that skinny arm of land between two seas, with a hot ditch down the middle of it?"

"No other way south unless you'd swim," a man's voice called.

Caribou drew breath to speak.

"But how shall we even get down to it?" she heard a youth's voice saying quietly, very near. She realized it was Tor. He sat shaking his head. "The reindeer made their way down, and the caribou — see their tracks? — but they were not encumbered by sleds."

He glanced at her, his dark eyes frowning. Caribou laid her hand on his shoulder for the second time that day and smiled. Her dream of the night before was beginning to come clear. She turned, her golden arrow raised, to address the others.

"Follow me," she bade them, "in a single file, slowly. We will descend in long switchbacks, doubling back on our course, but lower down the slope each time. Be not dismayed. My golden stag will lead you. Everything proceeds as I have dreamed."

At her signal, Reindeer started down the steep, slippery slope. He picked his way carefully, mindful of the heavier sledges behind. Drivers tied up their reins and walked beside their teams, but Caribou stayed on the driver's stand, letting Reindeer choose his own pace and way.

When at last they reached the bottom of the black cinder slope, Caribou called a halt to allow the others to catch up. Here the long black arm of land stretched out into the sea, and the long reach of water swirled in a wide pool under the cliffs. Caribou gazed at the shallow cave in the rock — hardly more than an overhang — and felt a sudden puzzlement, for she could see no hollow deep enough for any underground water-source.

Before her, Tor knelt upon the black shingle bank. He held his hand above the steaming water a moment, then swiftly dipped one finger in. When he touched its tip to his tongue, Caribou saw his eyes widen. He raised his head to glance at her, then dipped his hand again and rose. Coming to her, he let her taste.

"This water is neither sweet nor mineral," she exclaimed, "but salt."

Caribou gazed out to sea. Suddenly she understood: the water in the trough did not run outward, oceanward, from the land, but inland from the horizon toward the hills with an ebb and flow of crestless waves that had carved out the underside of the cliff. She turned to Tor again.

"This channel is no river-course, but a long firth of the sea."

Before her, in the traces, Reindeer snorted and stamped. His silent breath came in rapid little bursts, so that if she had not known he had no human heart, she would have sworn he was laughing at them — that they had taken so long in puzzling it out, and seemed so taken with wonder at the discovery.

Caribou pursed her lips with a twinge of vexation, but she let it go. She would not quarrel with her *trangl* now. When all the sledges had assembled at the foot of the slope, she motioned Tor aboard and whistled

Reindeer into a trot. He went docilely enough, following the reindeer tracks southward along the left bank of the boiling firth.

They traveled at a rapid pace until the early afternoon, the broad stretch of land on which they fared growing gradually narrower, until a heavy bank of fog enveloped them. Caribou did not slow; rather, she called out over one shoulder, "My bells! Follow the chant of my Reindeer's bells."

Behind her she heard cries of assent, and thereafter she heard the drivers of the other sledges talking and calling to one another. Caribou smiled, for their voices told her that her people had once more taken heart.

By midafternoon the fog had passed. The sky overhead arched high and clear, with scarves of cold, white cloud scudding the blue. The wind was crisp and salt and chill, the sun poised halfway down the sky, white as flame. The land ran on and on.

Then all at once ahead of them lay the end of the land. The firth opened and shallowed, joining the sea. The bank on the right seemed to fall away steeply; their own leftward bank, much more gradually. She saw the uncountable reindeer tracks on the black shingle shore disappearing into the waves.

Reindeer stopped at the water's edge. Caribou heard the others pulling up behind. The cold sun shone brilliant in her eyes as she studied the water. The currents ran swift and treacherous over the shoal. Her people were not like the River-Valley Folk; they knew nothing of boats.

No shore lay in sight beyond the waves, only a

little promontory of standing stones jutting from the water a few score paces down the beach. Herds of sea-beasts that barked like dogs glided in flocks through the shallows. Small, ice-encrusted islands rose from the sea to east and west — and then Caribou saw they were not rock at all.

They were moving: floating chunks of ice that gleamed beneath the sun like palaces of polished bone. She stared at them, at all of it, astonished — until all at once she realized that the people behind her were arguing, had been arguing for some time now while she had gazed. Caribou turned to face them.

"And what do we do now?" one driver was demanding of another, older woman, a council member. Caribou remembered her: Brikka, the one with beads in her hair.

"You see?" another driver interjected, gesturing with his willow whip. "I was right. They are all *traangol*, the reindeer, and can run upon the waves."

"Or swim the running sea, like those seadogs there," an old man cried.

Caribou glanced back at the bright, breaking waves. Some of the seadogs had stopped their frolic, hung upright in the water, their sleek, dark heads turned toward the shore, their black eyes curious.

Caribou sighed and turned toward her people again. More drivers and passengers had come down from their sledges to approach the councilwoman. Above the general clamor, Caribou finally heard Brikka exclaim, "Enough, enough! Let us hear what our wisewoman says."

"Yes," Djenret of Vlad called. "Our *i'dris* will know."

But Caribou did not know. Her heart felt tight with fear. She had no idea why the land had ended. Her dreams had shown her nothing of this, only Reindeer crossing a landbridge that stretched the length of the sky to the other side of the world.

She glanced at her *trangl*, but he only gazed back and chivied at the water's edge. Though his gold eyes were as expressionless as ever, telling her nothing, she sensed he was as baffled as she. All eyes had turned to Caribou. On her own sledge, Tor had turned to her as well.

"*I'dris*," the young man said, "what must we do?"

Other voices echoed his. Caribou tasted the salt breeze on her lips, eyeing the little promontory of rock standing out from shore.

"I must think on it," she answered. "We must wait."

15

Trolls' Hedge

CARIBOU got down from her sledge and bade Tor and the others do the same. She told them to stretch their legs, or rest, or eat if they felt hungry, or tend to their caribou. Then she unbuckled Reindeer from his bells and walked with him a little way down the beach that she might speak with him alone.

"You know nothing of this, do you?" she asked him, stroking his neck and ears as he stood before her.

Reindeer snorted and tossed his head, gazing out to sea where the reindeer tracks led. Caribou, too, gazed.

"Can you not speak?" she whispered, unable to keep the urgency from her voice. She nodded toward the cluster of rocks that stood off from shore a little way. "We could go out to that promontory there. You could put on your man-shape and tell me what you know."

Her fingers in his thick golden fur tightened, but Reindeer pulled away from her and pawed at the beach, glancing back toward the others and their *gristaal*. Tor had just climbed down from their own sledge and was stretching. Caribou sighed.

"I must dream on it, then. But not here. I will go out to the rocks." She held out her hand to Reindeer, although in his deer-shape he could not take it. "Come with me."

The golden *trangl* only shook himself and did not look at her. He stood watching the others. Far away, Tor was kneeling to pick up a stone from the beach. Rising, he threw it into the sea. Caribou bit her lip in frustration and turned back to Reindeer. She sighed again.

"Well," she said at last. "You know best whether you can help me in this or not. I see it is my turn, now, to scout the way."

Reluctantly, Caribou walked away from her *trangl*. She followed a sandbar across the chill, shallow salt water toward the tiny island of rock. Approaching, she saw with a little start that it was a trolls' hedge, a circle of standing stones shaped like a fort or crown.

The rocks looked oddly familiar somehow. The sandbar's path led to a low place between two taller rocks, and she realized that she must either enter the hedge or remain standing in the shallow sea. There was no beach at all about the stones. So, reciting under her breath a charm against offending the daimons, Caribou climbed between the stones.

The interior was exactly as she recalled that other trolls' hedge, the one that had sheltered her and Reindeer the night his father had borne him away. Little steam-vents in the bare, flat ground misted up warm wisps of cloud. Caribou sat down. After the bracing sea-breeze and the motion of the sledge all morning long, the warmth and stillness of this sheltered air made her suddenly sleepy. She let her eyelids slip shut.

After a little time, she heard all around her a rustling and a sighing. Opening her eyes, she found that the stones of the hedge seemed to be shifting, jostling where they stood. A moment later, when her vision had cleared, she saw that she was surrounded not by stones at all anymore, but by a dozen great crouching trolls.

Or rather, she realized in panic, the stones had always been trolls, only they had been sitting so still in their drab gray garb, their heads nodded and their eyelids closed, as if napping, that she had not been able to tell till now what they were.

They had great, coarse hands and long noses, and little eyes. But they smiled at her with their huge stonelike teeth, and seemed to be at pains not to frighten her. Caribou sat very still.

"Do you remember us?" one of them said. She held a squat clay pipe in her teeth like a shaman, and smoked. "We are hedgewives."

Caribou realized with a start that they were all women.

"We remember you," one sitting beside the first one said. Her voice sounded very like the sighing of a steam-vent, or sea-surf, or wind. "You are the little one who stayed with us before, a long time ago, and suckled the *trangl*'s child."

"I meant no trespass," said Caribou hastily, "then or now." She had to swallow, her throat was so dry.

The hedgewives nodded. One of them answered, "We did not begrudge you your stay." She spoke slowly, as though not familiar with mortal speech. "Though your presence that night did keep us from gambling —"

"We are very fond of gambling," the hedgewife with the clay pipe said.

"In any case, we had already dined for the day," her sister continued, "and saw no need to trouble you."

"Besides, you had the little *trangl* with you," another said, "whose father had died. The *traangol* are daimons, as we are, and so for his sake we did not disturb you."

She put her teeth together with the crushing sound of rock rubbing rock, and smiled. Caribou shivered, and wondered if the hedgewives had dined yet *this* day, and whether or not they would be so kindly disposed toward her now that her *trangl* was no longer with her.

"But what has brought you back to us?" one of the trolls behind her asked, so that Caribou started and turned around — she had forgotten they surrounded her.

Before she could answer, the troll continued, "We were on our way across the landbridge, away from the troubled country where we used to dwell — but we stopped to take our rest and gamble a little, and the reindeer passed us by. So now it will be spring before we can get across."

Caribou felt her heartbeat beginning to quicken,

but it was from hope now, not fear. "Daimons," she said, "my people, too, are on their way across, away from the troubled earth. But what has happened to the land? How did the reindeer get across?"

"Ah." The hedgewives nodded. "The firelords have lowered the bridge so that the sea covers it, for the reindeer have already passed, and the *waijen* must not be allowed to get back across."

"Every year a few *waijen* manage it," one of the trollwomen put in, "to wander again in their old country and haunt the people they do not love. But not many. The firelords guard their landbridge well."

"Except three winters back," another hedgewife cried, laughing and jabbing her sister with the stem of her pipe. "When the sea-maidens sang the bridge-man to sleep before he had lowered the bridge again — and as many of the *waijen* as pleased flocked back across into the land of the living again. Such a ghostly winter we had!"

Caribou remembered the first winter after Reindeer had left her, and all the *waijen* that had roamed about her *ntula,* and those of her father and Branja that had spoken to her. She turned back from her thoughts to the trollwomen sitting around her.

"Then I must go to the firelords and ask them to raise the bridge again," Caribou said, "so that I and my people may cross. Can you tell me where I may find them?"

At that the hedgewives shifted and grumbled among themselves, and she heard some of them grinding their teeth.

"We could," one of them said. "We know where they dwell. But perhaps —" She leaned closer to Caribou. "But perhaps you could give us something in return?"

Though the hedgewives still smiled, they had all leaned closer now, looming over Caribou.

"We have not dined for the day," one of them said.

Caribou started quickly to her feet — she knew well enough from the stories her father had told her, what food such daimons were fondest of. But seeing her alarm, the trollwomen all leaned back a little, and Caribou's panic eased. She made herself breathe deep.

"We have no *pisjlak* to spare," she said firmly.

"Well, a few of your caribou, then?" one of the hedgewives suggested.

"We have no spare caribou," Caribou answered. "They all ran on the heels of the reindeer."

The hedgewives grumbled.

"Perhaps a few of your people . . . ?" the one holding the pipe began, but Caribou quickly cut her off.

"No, they would not consent. I promised to bring them all safe away, all of them."

The thought of these trollwomen feasting on the marrow of her people's bones chilled her. The hedgewives muttered and consulted among themselves. Caribou stood taut, straining, but could not distinguish what they said. Their great brows frowned above their little eyes. Unease gripped her. Then, all at once, one of the trollwomen said to another, "Perhaps the mortal woman will gamble for it."

"Ah," the others all said, beginning to smile again. "Perhaps she will gamble for it." They turned back to Caribou. "Take the dice out of your sash, little one, and we will all have a throw. If you win, we will tell you the way to the firelords and ask nothing in return."

Caribou's hand went to her sash, and there, to her surprise, she felt the hard lumps of the three dice she had carved from the golden stag's horns. She drew them out, unable to fathom it, for she did not remember having put them in her sash that morning when she dressed. She turned the little forms over in her hand.

"And if I lose?" she asked them softly.

"Then you must give us your bones," the hedgewives said.

Caribou shuddered, her stomach knotting. The sour taste of bile rose in her throat. The hedgewives nodded cheerfully, expectantly. Caribou swallowed and fought her revulsion down. *I must do this,* she told herself. *There is no other way.* Her fingers closed around the dice. *If I do not find my way to the firelords and persuade them to raise the bridge, we are all dead in any case.*

So Caribou played the trollwomen at dice. Shaking the cube, the flattened cylinder, and the many-sided piece in her hands, she called out what marks she hoped for — foxpaws, or pigeons' wings, or snakes' tongues, or one of each — and then the hedgewives each in turn did the same.

Every time Caribou shook the dice, she listened to

the rattle of the golden stag's teeth against her breast, for they whispered to her how the throw would fall. By the time the dice had passed once around the circle, Caribou had won every throw and the hedgewives not a one. They grumbled even louder then, and one of them cried, "Those dice are weighted."

"They are not," Caribou replied, "else they would have fallen the same on every throw, and the same for you as they did for me. In any case, you chose the dice, not I."

The first of the hedgewives, the one who held the pipe, nodded with a sigh. "Aye. Sisters, she has spoke the truth. Fair is fair, and we agreed. Here, little one. Here is the way to the firelords. We have been sitting at the gate all along."

She leaned down and touched the earth with her pipe, and suddenly, soundlessly — without so much as a rumble or a tremor — the ground opened before Caribou like the mouth of a sack. A long tunnel led down into the dimness, its under-surface cut into steps.

"Just follow the stair," the trollwoman said. "It will take you straight to the firelords' hall."

"The way forks once," another hedgewife added, "but take the right-hand fork, and you will not go wrong."

Then the trollwomen all smiled and nodded at her, seeming suddenly much happier than they had been, so that Caribou was suspicious. But she could do no other than follow their advice. She turned and stepped into the darkness of the tunnel, and started down the stair.

Caribou descended — for a long time, it seemed. She quickly lost count of the steps. The way was lit, dimly, by a reddish-yellow glow, though she could not tell the source. The deeper she went, the warmer the air became, so that she had to unfasten her *lanlan*, and then remove it entirely, take off her cap and mitts, and finally her leggings. She loosened the laces at the throat of her smock and rolled up the sleeves.

At first she tried to carry all her garments with her, but since there were so many they were very cumbersome. At length she left them on the steps, along with her smock and boots. By the time she came to the fork in the stair, she wore only the inner slippers of her boots and her shift.

She stood a long moment at the fork, listening, for it seemed that far below them, to the left, she could hear faint noises of laughter and merriment. But she took the right-hand branch in the end, as the hedge-wives had instructed, though its passage seemed darker than the left-hand one, and very silent, too.

Again Caribou descended for a very long time, but at last, reaching the bottom of the steps, she found herself within a few paces of a great square arch made of carved whalebone, such as the chieftain of the whole Tribe might have set before his house.

Beyond the archway stood a great winch and tackle of wood, such as workers might raise a roof beam with, the cable for which, thick as a child's body, rose away into the darkness above. Near it rose a vast building like a chieftain's house or a meeting hall, save that it was made of chiseled stone and not of wood. Though she craned her neck, Caribou could not see any roof topping the walls.

So intent was she on these things as she approached that she did not notice the figure dozing against the arch until she was almost upon him. He awoke with a start and sat up sputtering. Caribou swallowed her own surprise.

"Good greetings," she told him courteously.

He only blinked and stared at her. "Hie," he huffed at last, "I didn't think to be disturbed till spring, when the reindeer come again. What right have you —" He lumbered to his feet suddenly, peering at her. "You're not a sea-maid, are you?"

Caribou shook her head. "No, I am a mortal woman who has come to beg a boon of the Fireking. Are you one of his lords?"

She asked this uncertainly, for there was nothing fiery about the one who stood before her. He was of no great height — barely as tall as Caribou — but he had legs thick as tree boles and was twice as broad across the ribs and shoulders as any mortal man, with great blunt hands, no hair on his pate at all, and long, slanting eyes. He appeared immensely strong, strong enough to turn the enormous winch beyond the gate.

"A firelord?" the other boomed, and his laughter sounded like a great tree creaking. "I'm only the bridgeman, mortal, their gatekeeper."

"The bridgeman?" Caribou exclaimed. The hedge-wives had not told her that her path would lead to the bridgeman himself, only that it would take her to the Fireking. Her heart leapt with hope. Perhaps she need go no farther. "I and my people are fleeing the country where the firelords have wakened the earth," she told him. "We wish to pass across to the land beyond, where the reindeer winter. Will you raise the bridge?"

The bridgeman, peering at her again with his long, narrow eyes, gave a disgruntled sigh. "You come from the land north of here? Yes, I see now you are not a sea-maid. Slippery thieves! They made a fool of me once."

He folded his powerful arms.

"My masters would never pardon me a second time if I kept the bridge up out of season. I will not raise it. The bridge cannot go up again till spring. You will have to wait." He closed his eyes and settled himself back down to doze.

"But we cannot wait," cried Caribou. "The cold will kill us. We will starve."

The bridgeman shrugged. "It is none of my affair. I can do nothing for you without my masters' word."

"Where are your masters, then, that I may speak with them?" demanded Caribou. "How may I find them?"

"They are in the hall," the bridgeman replied, nodding over one shoulder. But when Caribou came forward to pass through the arch, he held up one large square hand. "Not so swiftly, mortalwoman. There is the matter of my toll. None enter the hall of the Fireking without paying."

Caribou stopped short. She had never heard of such a thing, and she had nothing to pay with now but her slippers and shift. "What must I pay?"

"Oh, anything you please," the gatekeeper replied, "so long as it is to my liking."

Caribou knelt down on the stone path, frowning hard, trying to think what lay in her power to offer the bridgeman.

"I can tell you a tale," she began, "for my father taught me many before he died . . ."

The gateman only laughed. "Oh, tales. I have heard more tales than time can count, as many as there ever were in the world, for that is what the *waijen* pay me with when they cross the bridge." He settled himself a little more comfortably. "There was such a crowd of them clamoring at my gate not long ago!"

For a moment Caribou thought of the rest of her Tribe, all the people that had been left behind in the land where she had dwelled. Had they all perished and become *waijen*? Her stomach clenched.

The same thing will happen to the people in my care, those who wait on the beach above, she thought, *if I do not find a toll to pay this bridgeman. Then how many more* waijen *will be clamoring at his gate?*

The gatekeeper sighed. "I can tell you the ending of any tale that has ever been told," he grunted, "before you have said a dozen words."

Caribou thought again, determined. "Have you a

dream to be interpreted?" she asked. "I have done that, too, in the country from which I come."

The firelords' bridgeman only shook his head. "I am a daimon, mortal. I do not dream."

She grimaced. Frustration made her ribs feel tight. "Then have you lost anything? I can tell you where to look for it."

But again, no. "Oh, I own next to nothing," he said, "and it is all safe in my keeping still."

Caribou racked her brains. "Do you need advice?" she asked. "I can advise you whom best to marry, or which of your children to leave your goods to . . ."

The bridgeman shrugged. "Those are mortal concerns, all of them, and have no meaning for me. You will have to do better."

Caribou bit her lip, nearly frantic. She had no idea how long she had been away from her people, gambling with the hedgewives above, then descending the steps and arguing with the bridgeman here below. There were stories she had heard of mortals who had come into the company of daimons. Sometimes such mortals were gone for years, though it had seemed only moments to them, or for only moments, though it had seemed years and years.

A sudden image came to her of her people many seasons dead, and their bones rotting on the sand — but then she realized it must be only fear that made her think of that, and not true vision, for the reindeer had not yet returned to cross the bridge again. Relief overwhelmed her. She felt weak. No, it could not be spring yet, for the reindeer had not returned. The teeth on her breast rattled and clicked, and all at once Caribou felt her desperation subside.

"You say you know every tale that is," she said to the bridgeman, "but I know one you have not heard — and you are in the tale."

The bridgeman sat up abruptly and ceased his yawning. "I have never heard a tale wherein I played a part," he told her, then grinned with teeth that looked like white ash wood. "Tell on."

So Caribou told him the tale of the *trangl*'s child that she had raised, and how he had gone away, then returned to lead her people away from the restless earth; how they had crossed the Burning Plain and come to Land's End, how she had gambled with the hedgewives, then descended toward the Fireking's hall, and had spoken with the gateman there, and begun to tell him a tale . . .

"But why have you stopped?" the square-shouldered daimon cried out. He had been listening, rapt, with all appearance of delight, until Caribou reached that point and ceased to speak. "What happens next? I do not know the ending of this tale."

Caribou sighed. "Nor do I. Nor will it have an end, unless you let me pass your gate into the Fireking's hall. This tale is not finished yet."

The gatekeeper frowned, gnashing his wooden teeth, but at last he answered. "So. Aye. I suppose I must let you through. *Hmpf.* But you must promise to give me the ending when you come out again."

Caribou rose, almost laughing with relief. "When

next I pass through your gate," she promised, "I will tell you the rest."

He allowed her to walk by him then, under the whalebone arch, beside the great winch governing the landbridge, which no mortal hand could ever have turned, and on through the doorway of the great gray stone building, into the hall of the Fireking.

16

The Fireking

T HE HALL was vast, bright-lit, all one great room, with the roof beams so high in the shadows above that Caribou could not see them, the walls so far away on either hand that she could scarcely discern them, and the other end ahead of her so distant she could barely make it out. Caribou stood wonderstruck.

At last she set out across the great stone hall, her feet making no echo at all upon the floor, toward those who must be the firelords. They stood in council at the far end. One of their number sat in a chair upon a platform with steps, and Caribou guessed he must be the Fireking.

She passed without a word among the other daimons that stood about the hall conversing, or sat at table, or made music: tall, willowy *iffs*, and squat, prickly *onts*, yellow pool-sprites steaming and smelling of sulfur, fire-daimons, and other creatures so strange she could not put a name to them. Uncertain how they might take her curiosity, Caribou tried not to stare. But none of them paid her any attention.

She felt uneasy in their midst, ragged, almost a beggar, and she wished keenly that Reindeer had consented to come with her. He was a daimon, and would know how to carry himself among such as these. But Reindeer was not here. She would have to deal with the firelords on her own — *as I have dealt with the hedgewives and the bridgekeeper,* she told herself. Even so, as she crossed the seemingly endless hall, she was trembling.

She drew near the firelords at last. They stood twice her height and more, their fine garb all black and umber, a fiery reddish glow about their skin and hair, like dying coals. Caribou knelt, but they were deeply absorbed in some debate, arguing before their chief, and took no note of her.

"O firelords," Caribou cried, loudly. The great hall surrounded her words and swallowed them. "O Fireking, I have come to ask a mercy of you."

The firelords who had been debating with their king upon his chair turned and looked at her, surprised.

"And what has the gateman let in this time?" one of them said.

"I daresay he was asleep, and this slipped past," the other mused.

Caribou shook her head and tried to keep her voice steady. "I gave him a toll that was to his liking, and so he let me through."

Some of the firelords murmured then, and the two who had been debating crossed their arms in displeasure, but the man on the great, raised chair waved them all to silence.

"We will continue what we were arguing once we have seen to this." He leaned toward Caribou. "What are you, little one?"

His skin was black and hard-looking as cooled earthrock, glowing red along the creases and seams. His eyes were yellow, like an oil lamp's flame, and his hair and his beard were like burning fire. Caribou's mouth was dry.

"Lord, I am a mortal woman," she whispered.

"Mortal?" the Fireking asked. "What is that? I have not heard of that race."

Caribou sat a moment, frowning, and a little of her fear subsided into puzzlement. Though she had never heard of the firelords before Reindeer had told her, it had never occurred to her that the firelords might not have heard of her Tribe.

"Our kind pass over the landbridge after death," she began, but the Fireking murmured, "Death," as though he did not know what it meant.

Caribou tried again. "They come this way and tell your gateman tales to let them cross the bridge."

"Oh, *waijen*," the Fireking said. "But they are gaunt and ghostly things. You do not look like a *wajn* to me."

Caribou shook her head. "Not *waijen*, lord. We are . . ." She struggled. "We are what the *waijen* are before they become the *waijen*."

"Strange."

"We come from the country north of here, beyond the Burning Plain."

"Ah." The Fireking smiled. "I know your country. Where the *traangol* summer and calve."

Relief made Caribou flush. She nodded. "Lord, the *traangol* say your people have wakened the earth there."

The other answered, "Yes. I have sent my workmen there to stir the earth, and turn it, for it is time for the land there to change its mantle. We have mined all the gold and precious silver from it that we can, and now must make it new again."

Caribou's uneasiness returned, for she understood no more of this than when she had heard the same from Reindeer, but she continued, "My lord, your turning of the earth has forced my people to flee our homeland."

"I know nothing of that."

"Lord, we wish to go where the *traangol* winter, beyond the Pole to another country where the earth rests peaceful still. We wish to cross the bridge."

She waited then, expectant, hanging on his silence. Surely no ruler could refuse so worthy a request. She thought of her people waiting on the beach. How long had she been gone? She must get back to them . . . All at once dismay filled her. The Fireking was shaking his head.

"That cannot be," he said. "The gateman has already lowered the bridge. It may not be raised again until spring."

Desperation brought Caribou to her feet. "But we will die if you make us wait until spring," she cried. "The cold will kill us. My people will starve."

"Cold?" the Fireking said. "You find the world above us cold?"

"It is cold to *us*, my lord . . ."

"And starve?" the Fireking asked. "How may you starve in the midst of so much earth and snow?"

"We do not eat that, lord."

The Fireking did not seem to hear. "But what is 'die'?" he said, frowning. "I do not understand what you mean by that."

Caribou wrung her hands. The lives of her people depended on her being able to persuade the Fireking.

"Become *waijen*," she exclaimed, barely able to contain her frustration now.

"Why do you not become *waijen*?" he asked her. "Then you would not mind the wait, or the cold and starving."

"But we do not *wish* to become *waijen*," Caribou insisted, groping. "It . . . it is not the time."

"Hmm," the Fireking said, running his stone-black fingers through his beard of fire, "very strange. You are fragile creatures indeed if you do not like the cold and must eat other things besides earth and snow."

"We cannot help that, lord," said Caribou softly.

"Why did you not come when the reindeer passed?"

"We tried, lord, but the reindeer outran us."

"The reindeer?" the Fireking exclaimed. "They are hardly even as swift as the wind. If even the reindeer outpaced you, then your people are very slow."

"Lord," Caribou told him, feeling a helplessness bordering on despair, "we go as quickly as we can."

"Hmm," the Fireking said, musing, "well — what would you have me do?"

"Command the gatekeeper to raise the bridge and let us pass!" she cried.

But the Fireking only laughed. "Oh, I could command him, mortalwoman, but I doubt that he would follow my command."

"What, how do you mean?" exclaimed Caribou, gathering courage to go closer to him. Her people's need made her bold. "Are you not his master? Must he not obey when you command?"

The king of the firelords shrugged. "His master? More or less. As much as any of us is master of another. But I tell you, he will not raise the bridge till spring, no matter what I ask. He cannot."

Caribou stared at him.

"It is a mighty task even for one so square and strong as he," the Fireking said, "and the bridgeman can manage it only once every season, winter and spring, and then must rest the next half-year until he has grown strong enough again."

"But . . . the sea-maidens . . ." Caribou stammered.

The Fireking snorted. "Them. Oh, they sang him to sleep one year before he could lower the bridge after the reindeer had passed. He had not raised it especially for them."

Caribou's heart grew very still. Her ribs tightened, and she could get no air. "But why . . ." she began, "why did he not tell me this when I spoke with him?"

The Fireking smiled. "I imagine he wanted your toll."

Daimons, said Caribou to herself, furious, thinking of the bridgeman, of the hedgewives, of the golden stag that had been Reindeer's father — charming Branja and stealing her child. *And Reindeer,* she thought suddenly, with a pulse of fear, *is he, too, treacherous — a deceiver, as Branja's wajn said?* The old tales of her father always spoke of the daimons as perilous. Caribou's legs felt weak.

"But," she said all at once, observing once more the Fireking's size and strength, "are *you* not strong enough, my lord — might *you* not turn the winch? Your kind have the power to shake mountains and rend the earth. Surely you have might enough —"

Sudden hope had brought the vigor back into her voice. The Fireking rose, coming down from his chair, and drew near Caribou. She felt the terrible heat of him, and flinched, afraid. Kneeling, he showed her his hands. The backs of them were crusted and cool, but the palms blazed red as liquid stone.

"Mortalwoman," he said, "were I to touch the Winch of Wood, it would be destroyed, and then the bridge might never be raised or lowered again. None but the gateman may turn that wheel, for it is of a stuff very like himself and responds to him alone. No other daimon has this power."

He sighed then, and seemed to shrug — the burning air about him shimmered so that it was hard for Caribou to be certain. Rising, he turned and went back to his chair. Hope died in Caribou. She felt sick and faint from the heat.

"I wish that I might help you, mortalwoman," the Fireking remarked, "but there is nothing I can do."

Slowly, Caribou turned away from the Fireking. She could scarcely see, blinded by heat and tears. She heard the firelords behind her resuming their debate as she stumbled away toward the far entrance of the hall.

What more could she do? The landbridge could not be raised until spring. Her people would perish. *Better,* she raged bitterly, *better to have left them all to perish — to have perished with them at the start — than to have held out to them this hope of rescue, now destroyed.*

As she neared the wide entrance to the hall, she passed a little crowd of women she had not noticed before. They were not much taller than she, though very long and slender. Their hair was wet and yellow-green, and they were clothed all in some dripping, filmy stuff that was neither of skin nor of woven cloth.

It clung to them and hid their legs, so that Caribou, blinking and staring, was not able to tell whether they had legs at all, or fishes' tails. Their garb left pools of water where they stood. One of them caught Caribou's hand as she went by. Her touch was damp and very cold. Another touched her arm.

"Mortalwoman," one of them said, and another: "*I'dris.* Caribou."

Caribou stopped and looked at them. "You know my name."

"Yes," they answered. "We know of you. Even so far away in our home in the sea, there are tales of you, for all rivers flow there, and everything comes down to the sea in the end. We are the sea-maidens, and we have heard of you."

"You are the one who suckled the *trangl*'s child,"

another said, "and brought him back to you after he had gone away."

"And have kept him beside you for a whole season, not just for a night."

"How lucky you are," the sea-women sighed. "We envy you."

"What do you want?" said Caribou curtly. She did not trust any of the daimons anymore. *Except Reindeer,* she told herself fiercely: *Reindeer, whom I love.*

"We want to help you," all the women-of-the-sea replied. "Only that, and no deceit. We heard your petition to the Fireking."

Caribou turned away. "You know my people's plight is hopeless, then."

"No, no," the sea-women cried. "Not hopeless. We can help."

"Why?" demanded Caribou, taking her hand from the sea-maiden's cool, wet clasp. "Why should daimons wish to help me?"

"Because we know what it is to crave another so much that it is hard to bear, and yet have the one we crave remain indifferent."

Caribou frowned, uncertain what they meant.

"We crave the firelords," another sea-maiden said, "though they will not come to us. Each night we sing to them and woo them, but all in vain. They say we long only to quench and devour them."

"It is not so," her sister beside her said. "They burn so hot it is we, not they, who would be consumed in a flash if ever they allowed us to embrace them and kiss them."

"But they will not. And so we crave them still, and sigh."

"But you," one of the sea-women said, "you have succeeded where we have failed. We see how you have bound the young *trangl* to you . . ."

"But . . . I do not bind him," Caribou said, surprised. "I love him. He came back to me because he wanted to."

"Love?" the sea-maidens asked her. "What is love?"

And Caribou remembered how Reindeer had asked her the same question once, a long time ago. Could she answer any better now?

"It is . . ." she began, then sighed. How to tell them? They were not mortal. Would they understand her any more than Reindeer had? "It is a longing — but true love has no wish to bind. I know that I can never hold Reindeer against his will. I tried to once." She blushed with shame. "But never again. That was not love."

The sea-maidens listened, rapt, saying nothing. Caribou groped. She had no idea how to express to them what she felt for Reindeer. She tried again.

"When I am with him, though I may be sad, my sadness seems lighter. His presence brings me happiness. And I want never to cause him sorrow, only joy . . ."

There she stopped herself, realizing. *But see how I think of him still*, still *as though he were a mortal man. And what does he think*, she wondered. *How does he think of me? He is a daimon, as these sea-maidens are. Does he understand anything of what*

I feel for him? Does he return it? How can I ever know?

"Joy?" the women-of-the-sea replied. "Sorrow? We know nothing of these things."

Caribou looked down. The way they echoed Reindeer's words made her feel oddly, incongruously like laughing. It came out almost a sob. "Nor does he." She feared that was the truth.

"He does not feel this love, this sorrow, as you do?" the one who had taken her hand asked Caribou.

She shook her head, at a loss. What did she really know of Reindeer? "I think . . . I think that he can know only a feeling of loss, never sorrow — no sort of love, only desire." Did she really believe that? The sea-women watched her. She looked at them bitterly. "He is a daimon. Like you. He cannot."

She was weeping again. The sea-maidens stood silent, lost in their own thoughts. After a time, the tears stopped and Caribou sighed. She felt very tired.

"How can you help me?" she asked them at last. "The Fireking said the landbridge cannot be raised."

"Oh, it cannot," one of the maidens replied. "That is not what we propose. Even now the bridge does not lie so very deep beneath the waves."

The sea-maid who had touched Caribou's arm said, "We can sing the sea away from the bridge for a little while, leaving the way dry, or nearly so."

"Then you could cross," another broke in. "We have seen the sledges that your people use."

Caribou stared at them. "Can you, can you do this thing?" she whispered, then stopped herself, remembering the bridgeman, the hedgewives. "I have nothing to pay you with."

"You have already paid us," the fairest of the sea-maidens said. She was the one who had taken Caribou's hand, and she wore a comb of red coral in her sea-green hair. She was holding a bundle in her arms. She offered it to Caribou now. "For you have given us hope, hope that the firelords may someday come to us, if only we can learn to love."

Caribou frowned, looking at the bundle the sea-maiden held.

"Dress, dress," another standing beside the first urged then, and Caribou realized that what the other held out to her was her *lanlan* and other clothes, those she had discarded on the way down into the Fireking's realm.

"We gathered them up for you, that you might lose no time."

Numbly, she put on her clothes again, smock and leggings and outer boots, cap and *lanlan* and mitts. She did not feel overburdened with heat now; the presence of the sea-maidens kept the air around her pleasantly cool.

"We will take you up another stair," they said, motioning her to follow, "so that you will not need to pass the gateman again."

Caribou stopped short. "The gateman," she murmured. She had forgotten all about him. "I promised to return and tell him what befell me in the Fireking's hall . . ."

"No fear," the sea-maid with the comb in her hair

replied, smiling, "we will tell him the ending of your tale. He has already fallen asleep again by this time, and if you went back the other way, you would only wake him. Come."

Caribou allowed herself to be led away from the hall's entrance then, toward one of the long side walls. Into the stone of this wall, she saw, had been chiseled a stair which the sea-maidens motioned her to climb. They themselves came behind her so the sea water they trailed would not make the steps slippery.

As they climbed, higher and higher, the stone of the hall seemed to change into the earth itself. Caribou knew that they had left the hall of the Fireking then, though looking back she could still see it, far below, growing smaller.

The stair curved around and joined another, and Caribou guessed that the steps the sea-maidens had put her on must be the left-hand fork of the one she had taken down, the one the hedgewives had told her not to take. Caribou clenched her teeth.

"If I had taken this stair at the first," she exclaimed, "I would have come directly into the Fireking's hall, and avoided the gateman altogether."

The sea-maidens behind her said, "Yes, you should have come directly to us and not to those ugly troll-wives at all."

"They sent you down the other stair, most likely, because you beat them gambling. They hoped the bridgeman would not let you through. They do not like to lose."

Caribou felt a sudden twinge of apprehension. "But

what shall I do when I reach the top?" she asked. The hedgewives would be there. Already she could see daylight above. "I do not trust them now."

"All is well," the sea-maidens said. "We sang them to sleep while you were below. They will not stir again till spring."

Caribou's breath came easier then.

"Hurry," another maiden was saying now. "Already our sisters are singing back the sea."

"But how will I know when it is safe to begin to cross?" Caribou asked them, climbing, climbing the stair toward daylight and the upper air.

"Wait a little," they replied, "an hour or two — until the sun further declines and you begin to see the land. Then go."

"The sea will continue to fall," another maiden added, "until the sun is set and Greatmoon just barely risen. From then on the water will start to return, slowly."

"Do not delay, for you must be across by the time Greatmoon hangs at zenith in the sky and Littlemoon is just coming over the horizon's edge — for we cannot hold the sea back any longer than that."

The daylight was streaming into the tunnel now, nearly blinding her. Caribou blinked and climbed, feeling the crisp, cold sea air against her face.

"How will I know when we are safe?" she asked.

"You will have reached the landbridge's end, where it joins the snow-covered shore," the sea-maidens whispered. "You will have passed beside the Forge of the Fireking."

"Forge?" Caribou said. She had heard the word before, from Reindeer, once. "What is —?"

But the sea-maids were already shoving her through the tunnel's entrance, out into the world again.

"Haste, haste," they said. "Do not delay."

The sky above was very blue, the sun overhead just coming down from its height. Caribou tasted the sting of salt breeze on her lips. The circle of hedgewives all around was once more stone.

When she looked back over her shoulder, there were no sea-maids anymore in the tunnel's entrance, only puddles of sea water on the stairs, and here and there a draggle of kelp. Then the earth drew together again in a smooth, soundless snap like the closing of a drawstring bag, and Caribou stood alone.

17

The Song of
the Sea-Maidens

WHEN CARIBOU EMERGED from the trolls' hedge, she saw that the sea had grown shallower. The sandbar seemed wider now, with more of its surface exposed. She walked along it, back toward the crowd of sledges and people on the beach.

As she neared, she sensed an odd commotion, and realized that none of the people had taken any note of her. They all faced inward, toward her *gristal* not far from shore. Frowning, Caribou hurried closer — then saw with a start what had drawn her people's eyes.

Reindeer stood before her sledge, his head up, his eyes very wide and golden, as if daring any of her people to approach it. The breath from his nostrils made little spurts of steam. He pawed the shingle of the beach.

Tor stood facing him, as far away from the golden stag as he could get without stepping into the sea. From the tracks in the sand, Caribou could see how Reindeer had driven him away from her sledge, away from the others. The gold stag dodged, feinting at Tor, but the Tjaalsénji youth had stopped running.

He stood watching the *trangl*. His back was straight,

his face very pale, and though he had no weapon and nothing at hand that he might use for one, he did not look as if he meant to run from the golden daimon again. Tor cried out to him, "Why do you come at me and try to do me harm when I have done you no offense that I can see?"

Reindeer stamped and wheeled. Tor tensed, but held his ground. The gray waves licked at his heels.

"If you mean to drive me from your *gristal*, very well, I will not go there again — but I have ridden with you at the *i'dris*'s bidding, not on my own."

Caribou saw Reindeer give a great snort at the mention of her and come toward the tall youth suddenly, so that Tor fell back a pace. The sea-water splashed beneath his step. She hastened toward them along the beach.

The people stood silent, motionless, as if watching some storyteller. Their eyes were all fixed on Tor and Reindeer; no one seemed aware of her. Tor called out to the golden stag, "Why do you hesitate? You are a *trangl*, and I am unarmed. The *i'dris* has given me her protection — though I do not claim to deserve it — but I can see her wishes mean little to you when she is not here. Is she not your mistress, or is it you who . . . ?"

Without warning, Reindeer dropped his head and rushed at Tor. The young man had not yet finished speaking. There was nowhere for him to run. Caribou dashed along the beach and sprang between him and the charging stag. Flinging her arms out to keep Tor behind, she shouted, "Stop!" and heard people in the crowd cry out, dismayed.

Reindeer pulled up as quickly as he could, shying sharply away, but even so, one tine of his golden horns grazed her breast, tearing the soft leather of her *lanlan.* Caribou stared at him, more surprised than she had ever been, for her *trangl* had never offered her any harm in all his life. And though she knew those hooves, those horns had been meant for Tor, not for her, still she stared.

She could sense the young man standing motionless behind her. His breathing was shallow, and she could feel him shaking. She was shaking as well. She came away from him a few steps, her eyes on Reindeer.

"What are you doing?" she cried. "Why have you fallen on one of my people?"

Reindeer dropped his head a little, then raised it suddenly. She could not tell what he meant by that, only that he no longer seemed ready to spring at Tor. She kept herself between the two of them.

"*I'dris.*" It was Tor's voice behind her. She only half turned, afraid to take her eyes for long from Reindeer. Tor had knelt down at the water's edge. He seemed very weary suddenly. "*I'dris,* my companions tried to steal from your *gristal.*"

He pointed, and the crowd that still stood silent, transfixed, now drew back a bit. Caribou was hardly aware of them, only of Reindeer and Tor. For the first time she saw the two figures sprawled on the sand beside the sledge. One lay with her golden arrow in his hand. She was too astonished at first to speak.

"What happened?" she managed.

"I went . . . back to my companions," Tor told her. His voice was tight. "To see if I might sledge with them again."

"I told you not to do that," Caribou cried. Tor nodded.

"I know. But I did not wish to burden you any-more."

"You are no burden."

He had stopped then, looking at Reindeer. He spoke more softly. "And I know your *trangl* does not like me."

Reindeer snorted and stamped, so that Caribou glared at him.

"But my companions said — they said they would not take me back unless I helped them steal your golden arrow."

Caribou wheeled on Tor. She felt a hot flush of anger flooding her, and saw surprise mirrored in his eyes.

"Val had it in his head that this was the source of your magic, your dreams," he told her quickly. "He said if he could steal it, he could command your golden *trangl* and lead the people instead of you."

"Your companions are idiots," Caribou snapped. "I have always dreamed my dreams, and the only magic in that golden arrow is that it points toward where the reindeer are."

The crowd murmured then, protesting her words. Still they stood watching. Reindeer stamped.

"What happened then?" said Caribou to Tor. "What did you say to your companions?"

"I told them they were mad," exclaimed Tor, as if suddenly uncertain whether she believed him. "I said I would not help them."

Reindeer cavaled, pawing the sand.

"And then?"

"They shoved me aside and started for your sledge. I shouted at them to stop; I ran after — I shouted for others to help me stop them. But Orin already had the arrow in his hand."

"Why did none of you stop them?" Caribou demanded of the people around her. "Would you let two young thieves pillage your own sledges so?"

The crowd shifted and murmured. "We were afraid, *i'dris*," one woman said.

"Of them?" cried Caribou, with a glance at the fallen pair. She saw people shaking their heads.

"Of the arrow, *i'dris*," a man replied.

Caribou let out her breath. "It is only an arrow," she told them, "made golden by a *trangl*'s blood."

But the people cast down their eyes and would not look at her. Where were the councillors, Caribou wondered. She could not find Djenret or Brikka among the crowd. Were they hiding from her gaze? She clenched her teeth. Tor continued.

"When your *trangl* saw them, he rushed forward, and Val cried, 'You see! We have only to touch the arrow and he comes.' Orin held up the arrow before him and commanded, 'Halt,' as though certain your *trangl* would obey. But . . . your *trangl* . . ."

Tor paused there, fighting for breath.

". . . smote him down with his hooves," he said at last. "And when Val tried to flee, he tossed him with his horns. They lay still then — neither of them has moved since. They are dead. I am sure of it."

Caribou looked at the two lying on the strand. "But why did my *trangl* then come after you?" she said softly. "I thought you said you were not with them."

Tor shook his head. "I was not. I tried to go to them. I bent to take the arrow from Orin's hand."

"That was not wise," said Caribou.

"I meant no harm," cried Tor. "I meant only to put it back upon your sledge. I did not like to leave him holding it. But your *trangl* . . ."

"Yes," said Caribou. "Yes, I see. Go do it now. Go take the arrow from your companion's hand and stow it in my sledge."

The young man rose, then hesitated, eyeing Reindeer. Caribou said, not looking at him, still watching the golden stag, "Go on. My *trangl* will not harm you or any of my people ever again for no cause. I promise you that."

Tor went. Caribou listened to his footfalls crunching away across the shingle. She walked toward Reindeer, but he backed away from her, then wheeled and trotted. She followed, not running. They were half a hundred paces down the strand when at last he stopped and let her draw alongside him. And Caribou, who had never struck Reindeer a blow in all her life, felt very near doing so now.

"Why have you done that?" she hissed. "What is

the matter with you? Is this why you would not come with me when I asked, but left me to do it all alone — because you had another thing in mind to do while I was gone?"

Reindeer gazed down on her, motionless. She stood near enough to feel his breath. Her eyes narrowed.

"You may be able to guile others — even Tor, perhaps — into thinking you meant to kill him for touching some talisman of mine, but it is only an arrow, which you know as well as I. I have not weighed the hearts of men and sat in judgment, offering counsel, for as many years as you have been alive that you might guile *me* so. By the *waijen!* If I did not know you for a daimon that has no human heart, I would believe you are jealous of that boy because he has sledged with me."

Reindeer shook himself, very hard, and turned away from her — but Caribou grasped his antler in one hand so that he turned again, not because she had the strength to compel him, but from surprise. She had never touched him in anger before. Her breast ached where the tine of his horn had bruised her. She let go of his antler and took his head in her hands.

"What manner of daimon are you," she whispered, "that you can feel such a thing — regarding a stranger I have known only a handful of days? Do you not know, can you not see with your great gold eyes that seem to take in everything and tell me nothing, that it is only you I love — that I have loved you all your life?"

Her voice broke.

"Would you murder a boy, for nothing? Are you so treacherous — like the hedgewives, like the gateman of the Fireking? Can I not trust you? You promised that you would lead my people, *all* my people, safe into your winter land. And have I not said that I will come away with you, as soon as that is done?"

Reindeer stopped his snorting. The little spurts of steam from his nostrils grew calmer and less fierce. The pulse in his throat that had been beating wildly against her hand was quieting now. He touched his great, square nose to her breast and knelt down on the beach.

Caribou, kneeling as well, put her arms about his neck. He lay down and she leaned against him, stroking her fingers through his dense golden fur. She was so weary she could not stand. She wanted Reindeer in his man-shape again, if only for a moment, for an hour. She felt lost and desperate, for the sound of his voice, for the touch of his hand. But it was only a great golden stag that she held.

After a time, she rose and went back to tell her people what had befallen her in the trolls' hedge, and in the Fireking's realm below. While they waited for the sun to fall, she instructed them to see to their caribou, feed them lightly and check their hooves.

"Tend to your *gristaal* as well," she bade them. "Inspect the runners and see that your provisions are securely lashed down. Then tend to yourselves. Let all eat enough to sustain them, for we may be sledging half the night or more, and hard going."

She sought out Tor and spoke with him concerning his companions. They had neither fuel nor time to burn them properly, so she helped the young man scoop out a shallow trench for them on the beach and sing the dirge. Caribou wondered what tales their *waijen* would tell the bridgeman next spring when he raised the bridge and they crossed over into the Land of Everlasting Night. She and Tor covered them over with sand.

"I will take my companions' *gristal*," he told her then, "and not trouble you further."

Caribou rose, brushing the wet black grit from her hands and leggings. She eyed the young man a moment. His face was drawn but determined. Caribou nodded.

"Very well," she said. "I will give you half of what I carry." He made to protest, but she told him, "Peace. I brought enough, three times enough to keep me, and your sledge must have some weight, or it will run too light."

She and Tor unpacked her *gristal*, moving furs and foodstuffs to the hold of his, and lashing them down. As they worked, he told her a little of his life as it had been in Tjaalsénji. He was the son of a merchant, he said. Others, seeing how the *i'dris* favored the youth, seemed more kindly disposed toward him now, and gave him a little of their own *pisjlak* as well.

Caribou in turn told Tor of living alone, far from any town, on the edges of the Wilderland, offering judgments and counsel to people who came. She had never spoken of such to anyone before, not even Reindeer. Doing so now made her feel strangely bashful. She found herself blushing. The boy from Tjaalsénji had a beautiful, shy smile.

Reindeer watched the pair of them in silence from a little way down the beach. When at last the sun was languishing low in the sky, Caribou rose and went to him, put her arms around him and led him back to the sledge. As she buckled on the chinkling bells, she saw others around her putting up the last of their cooking pots, securing the lashings, and hurrying their draft-caribou into the traces.

Tor stood well away from Reindeer and a little behind Caribou as she regarded the sea. It had fallen at last. The shore before them stretched a long way into the sun-glared distance, and the water lay shallower off to either side. Caribou turned and walked back along the landboat toward the driver's step.

"*I'dris*," said Tor, "the sun will be down in another hour, and Greatmoon will not rise till an hour after that. How will we see to follow you? How will you see the way?"

Caribou took her oil-pot from the sledge. She opened it. "That, too, I have dreamed," she said, and found herself able to smile again now, just a trace — for the reindeer's teeth upon her breast at last were whispering to her the meaning of one of her most troubling dreams.

She walked with the pot back toward Reindeer. Tor followed, careful still to remain well back — but the *trangl* hardly gave him a glance.

"The landbridge is narrow," Caribou told Tor. "So

the others cannot go far wrong. There will be moonlight, and the sound of my *trangl*'s bells."

She grasped Reindeer's harness then and shook it. The bells tinkled like crystal ice.

"Still . . ." the youth replied.

Caribou nodded, smiling. "I know." She put her hand into the pot until her fingers were covered with the soft, slurry stuff — it did not solidify, even in the cold. Then she smeared the yellow oil along the tips of Reindeer's horns. He bowed his head that she might reach them, ignoring Tor.

The Tjaalsénji youth stood watching her, no less baffled, while Caribou scrubbed her hand clean with some of the black grit from the beach. Then she fetched her golden arrow from the sledge and dipped the point of it into the oil. She closed the pot and stored it. Tor continued to watch her.

"*I'dris* . . ." he said.

Caribou handed him the arrow. He started violently as she pressed it into his hand. He glanced at Reindeer, but the *trangl* stood gazing off. Caribou kept her hand on Tor's a moment to steady him.

"Go to Brikka," she said, "that woman there who has not yet covered her fire. Light the tip of this arrow, and bring it back to me. Then we will go."

Caribou went and took the driver's step while Tor did as she had told him. He brought the golden arrow with its burning point back to her, and she tied it to the railing with a thong, the burning tip upright and well away from the wood of the sledge.

The fire on the arrow had almost no color, seemed

only a rippling in the air about the arrow's head and a thread of smoke. The young man watched her a moment more, then went to take his place on the step of his own *gristal*. Caribou turned to her waiting people.

"We must be off," she cried, "for the sea-maidens have sung the waves back from the land, and we must pass while we may."

"But *i'dris*," someone cried, "how shall we see you in the dark?"

"You will see me," answered Caribou. "Have no fear."

"But wisewoman," another man called, "how long will the landbridge last?"

"The water will fall," answered Caribou, "until Greatmoon begins to rise. The sea will then be at its lowest point. From moonrise on, the waves will begin to return — slowly. So let us make what speed we can."

She clapped the reins and Reindeer sprang away. With a shout, the others in their *gristaal* followed. The seadogs that had lounged upon the dry land in their path fled before them, humping away across the shallows toward the retreating waves. The landbridge lay before them like the backbone of the sea.

The sun fell down the western sky like a great, burning bird. At last it rolled gently into the sea, dousing itself amid clouds of low-lying steam. Caribou listened for the hiss, or for some hint of the sea-maidens' song, but she could hear nothing above the plangent surf and the singing of Reindeer's bells.

Night fell. Shade by shade the sky darkened. The stars overhead reflected in the waves, so that the landbridge seemed surrounded by stars. At last Caribou took the burning arrow from the rail. The tip blazed in the blackness now with a brilliant, white-yellow light that hardly seemed to flicker.

Far ahead of the others, she pulled Reindeer to a halt and darted forward along the sledge's length, then sprang from the landboat's toe onto Reindeer's back. He stood still without flinching, steady as a house as Caribou touched the flaring arrow to his oil-smeared horns.

They caught, all the tips in a wreath of light, blazed up in a white glow that danced like summer lightning — it hardly seemed to be flame at all. She heard Tor, heard others behind her crying out in surprise.

Caribou leapt lightly back to the sledge and back to the driver's box. The other *gristaal* had almost drawn even with her now. Still holding the golden arrow, she gathered the reins in her other hand. Reindeer sprang, and they were off again, into the utter blackness of the night.

The fierce red glow in the west that had been the sunset gradually faded. The stars seemed very many and far away, while the flame in Caribou's hand and upon Reindeer's horns barely guttered in the chill, evening wind. Their brightness lit the dark.

The shingle beach was slick and smooth, the going swift. The sea continued to retreat, exposing more and more of the black beachhead. Greatmoon rose, a ghostly face, pale and glaring, silver-white.

The tide was at its lowest ebb. The moon floated above the flat rim of the world beside them, scarcely an arm's reach away, it seemed. The landbridge spread before them, black and gleaming.

The polar cluster of stars burned like a fistful of jewels directly overhead, and the only sound in the stillness was the gusting of the cold, light sea-breeze, the crash and wash of distant breakers, and the high, clear singing of the bells.

They sledded for hours over the left-hand bank. The firth had now opened out into a vast bay that stretched to their right. By moonlight, she could barely spot the other side. As they sped, Caribou saw sea-beasts that leapt in graceful arcs, frolicking in the shallow sea.

Square, flat animals with many legs — hard-bodied like spiders — danced sideways under the moonlight in the shallow tide-pools. A flock of great birds, larger than fish hawks, skimmed barely a hand's breadth above the combers with the moon in their wings. The ice-mountains, like crystal houses, drifted serenely along the horizon's edge, back-lighted by the low, rising moon.

As Greatmoon began to rise higher, the beach beneath their runners became more slick, the sea water slowly welling up. It seeped through the cinder-like sand — only a few fingers deep at first, then in little running ripples that swept from the eastern sea toward the firth.

"Haste!" Caribou cried, above the jangled burring of the bells. "We must make haste. The sea returns!"

How long this spine of black cinders would continue she did not know. The sea-maidens had given them only a handful of hours. She wondered how long it took the reindeer to cross. *We are slower than they.* She knew — all her people knew — if they had not reached higher ground by the time Greatmoon had reached its zenith and Littlemoon was just beginning to rise, they were lost.

She felt Reindeer's pace becoming swifter. The bells chanted more loudly, in quicker rhythm. She held the burning arrow high, heard the others clapping their reins and tapping their willows across the backs of their teams. The beach beneath their runners sloshed and ground, awash with shallow waves, as Greatmoon slowly mounted the dark blue, star-pitted sky.

18

The Forge of
the Fireking

THE SMOOTHNESS of the fine-grained cinders beneath the runners began to change. The surface grew rocky, seamed and slippery, still of that same black stone. The right-hand bank of the firth had long since fallen away, and a single high peak rose against the stars in the distance before them.

Caribou peered, trying to make out the shadowy peak beyond the flare of Reindeer's burning. The peak seemed oddly conical, like a potter's kiln, plunging steeply away into the sea on either side. It spanned the whole width of the landbridge they traveled.

Caribou's heart contracted violently — they would never get their sledges over those plunging slopes . . . ! And then she made out faintly, by moonlight, a long line of shallow breakers foaming landward, never quite reaching the cliffs: a narrow beachhead allowing passage around the mountain on one side.

But the tightness beneath her breastbone did not ease. How long would it take them to reach the strand? The night was so dark; she could not judge. How long to skirt the mountain, and how far beyond it lay the landbridge's end? Greatmoon was more than halfway to its zenith: the draft-caribou were in water midway to their knees, and the broad sledge-runners were nearly submerged beneath the shallow waves.

If the water rises much further, she realized, *if we do not reach the mountain soon, there will be no beachhead at all to cross, leaving us trapped between that black peak and the sea.* Caribou shoved the thought away. She dared not clap the reins to Reindeer. If he ran any swifter, he would outdistance the others.

They came at last to a place where the land began to rise, and Caribou heard her people shouting with relief. The water around them fell away by degrees. The closer to the dark mountain they drew, the higher and drier the ground beneath their *gristal*-runners became.

But Caribou could not join in her people's rejoicing, for the surface of the beach was hilly and pitted here, no longer smooth, as though the earth had been much disturbed. Great rills extended from the mountain's foot like long toes into the sea, their ups and downs impeding the progress of the gristaal.

Glancing back, Caribou glimpsed drivers and passengers leaping down now and again to help shoulder their sledges along. Some of the troughs between the rills went down very deep. Her golden *trangl* avoided these, and the echoes thrown back from their darkness had an eerie sound.

Taps and groans and sometimes creakings came to her ears — like the blows of smiths' hammers or the workings of a great bellows. What had Reindeer told her once, about the firelords' mining of the earth? *Are they below us now*, she wondered, *forging their precious silver and their gold?*

The speculation alarmed her somehow. She tried to shut her mind, but the image persisted, vivid and bright, of the firelords with their beards of fire, shaping the burning metal with hammer and tongs.

The teeth upon her breast chattered and clicked, unintelligibly. The bells of Reindeer's harness ranted and chimed. Caribou flinched as sometimes a fierce heat drafted up from the troughs, as though their depths plumbed for leagues, straight down into the fiery heart of the world.

Their *gristaal* had reached the slopes of the mountain now and were skirting along toward the low, curving beach. A mere ribbon of sand still showed between the cliffs and the incoming waves. All at once, Caribou noticed a dull glow shining between cracks in the mountainside, a reddish light that grew brighter and stronger with each crevice they passed.

Others among the band had seen it as well. She listened to their cries of bewilderment, wonder, alarm. Then someone called out something new, his voice harsh with surprise. Other voices caught up the cry. Caribou cast about her, trying to see what they saw. She spotted Tor on the driver's step of his *gristal*, only a few paces behind her. He raised one arm toward the summit overhead.

"*I'dris*, look!"

Caribou stared. As they rounded one bend of the conical slope, shoving over the last of the long fingers down to the beachhead below, she saw that the peak above had fallen away, like the rim of a broken bowl. Through the gap, she beheld a sea of glowing stone.

Smoking, it churned, the steam roiling dull red into a black, starry sky. Within the crater, little fountains spewed like spurting stars. Littlemoon, a wan blue eye, was just peering over the rim of the sea to the east of them. Greatmoon hung suspended at its zenith above.

The mount erupted with a roar. It started as a trembling in the earth, then thundered suddenly to a rumbling shout, like a geyser bursting. Bits of fire, like flocks of birds, leapt into the dark night-sky, and the white moon overhead turned coppery, like blood.

The caribou brayed and bolted then. Caribou saw one *gristal* overturned and dragged into the sea. She shouted, tried to call out to her people, but the mountain's blast carried her words away. Reindeer gave out a belling cry. Caribou heard it clearly through the haze of other noise, the mountain's thunder and her people's screams.

The caribou quieted at the sound, slowing their frenzied flight. She saw one group with an overturned sledge manage to right it again. The earth trembled, but less violently now. Fire continued to spew from the mouth of the mount, but none of it was falling far enough downslope to reach them.

Caribou signaled with her burning arrow for her people to hasten, to guide their *gristaal* after her along the black ribbon of beach. Reindeer's horns were a white wreath of fire. He called again to the teams, and they followed him. Gazing up, Caribou saw liquid firestone spilling over the crater's rim like spattered broth.

Glowing, feverish red, the fiery river crept down the mountain's slope. Caribou felt a sickening jolt — *if it reaches the beach before we do, if it flows across and blocks our path, we will be trapped, cut off from the white snowy plains just coming into view ahead, drowned in the rising waves.*

Caribou slapped the reins and called. Reindeer quickened his pace effortlessly. They flew over the smooth, wet, black beachhead. The incoming tide had made it so narrow in places that two sledges could scarcely run abreast. Caribou and her people made their way halfway around the mountain's side, and then further, nearly three-quarters of the way.

The tremors and deafening rumbles of the mountain grew more violent. Fountains of brimstone spouted into the sky. Smoking ash and cinders began to fall. She heard screams of caribou and people touched by the particles. She glimpsed Tor behind her, crouching and holding a skin over his head. Caribou ducked down as far as she could into her *lanlan*, smelling the stench of scorched leather and hair.

The fireflood crept down the mountainside like the bright blood of the earth. It loomed just ahead; it had nearly reached the strand. The air above it shivered and burned. Caribou cried out to her people: words, anything. She pointed forward with her arrow at the fields of snow beyond,

They were on the beach. All around her, teams of

caribou shied and balked. Caribou pulled back, trying to slow Reindeer. She would not leave her people, and she would not let them stop. Using her willow switch, she hied the balking teams. Shouting, she dragged them by the bit. Reindeer belled out his golden cry, and the caribou came on.

The heat grew fierce, gusting and billowing. All Caribou could see was red. She felt flushed, drenched in her heavy *lanlan,* and clawed at its latches to open the throat. Her knees weakened. She felt herself fainting against the rail.

Then, all at once, they were past. The slowly advancing river of firestone fell behind. A blast of frigid air brought her awake again, invaded her *lanlan,* chilled her to the bone. She latched the throat closed again. Turning, she watched the other sledges behind her coming, and felt a stab of fear until she saw Tor's among them, passing the narrow point and flying out onto the wide, open beach beyond.

The last ones got by. Their caribou were staggering. Caribou saw passengers and several drivers swooned upon their sledges, but the caribou ran on, following Reindeer's cry. Further back, well behind the last *gristal,* with a howling hiss and towering plumes of steam, the fireflood merged into the sea.

The broad cinder beach ground flat and loose beneath her sledge's runners now. Another half mile and they would reach the snow. She looked back just once more before they came upon that white expanse.

Beneath the red violence of the flaring mountain, in a recess on the southwestern face of the peak, near its foot, all seemed quiet — strangely so. In the recess lay a pool, where a fountain gushed, its color visible even in the pale leaching light of Greatmoon: pure gold.

As golden as her *trangl*'s coat, his golden eyes, his spattered blood — as golden as Reindeer's hair in his man-shape, that fountain rose. Caribou felt her sledge leap up behind Reindeer onto the deep-packed snow. Still looking back, wonderstruck, she kept her eyes on the Forge of the Fireking, beside which stood spouting the Fount of Gold.

Their sledges sped over the plain of snow, deep clean white snow that showed the passage of a vast herd of deer before them. They followed the wide cut of that passage, fleeing the burning mountain and the Firth of Fire.

And after the moons set on them that night, very low in the north, they never rose again, nor did their companion the sun, until Caribou and her people had neared their journey's end, though they traveled many sleeps over the Country of Unbroken Snow.

The people were much afraid, fearing that they had passed into the Land of Everlasting Night, for often, directly above them as they camped, the ghostly *wai-jen* danced, long shimmering ribbons of blue, violet, and green.

But Caribou spoke words of comfort to her folk beside their fires, telling old tales to ease their minds and new tales, to give them heart, of the land beyond.

They followed her grimly, without complaint. They had no choice, she realized. They could not go back.

At last they left the Plain of Endless Snow, and the *waijen*'s dance fell away in the darkness behind. The sun rose again, hanging low and bright in the sky, and the moons as well. Once again they had the day to travel by and the night for sleep. Reindeer's horns and Caribou's arrow finally burned themselves out.

Caribou and her people found themselves passing over tundra again, as flat and featureless as the frozen plains they had known in the country they had left behind. In a few days' time, the tundra gave way to hills, and trees covered with late-autumn snow.

Eventually they passed down out of the high country, into sheltered valleys of dry, yellow grass, where snow had not yet fallen. Wearily, Caribou led them past the first such valley, and the second as well.

Her people were angry then, crying out that they longed to rest, to settle and build their winter shelters. But Caribou refused to call a permanent halt, insisting, "We have not yet found the place that I have spoken of, the place that is to be our home."

"How is it we will know it, *i'dris?*" Djenret asked her.

But Caribou, her brow wrinkled with determination, would only say, "I will know it, and so will you."

They drove on, until they had passed into the third valley. At last Caribou called a halt. She was utterly spent. She ached from all the days they had sledged and all the nights she had spent sleepless, reassuring her disspirited followers, from all the cold and hardship. But she was smiling now.

"Here we will settle," she declared.

A moment of startled silence, then a ragged cheer rose from the sledges behind.

"But why here?" asked Brikka softly, her *gristal* drawn alongside Caribou's. "*I'dris,* how is this valley different from the others we passed through?"

With her arrow, Caribou pointed down the slope toward the meadow below them. "What do you see there?" she asked.

The councilwoman looked, staring at the gray specks dotting the sides of the far-off meadow. The air was crisp and clear.

"The wild deer!" Caribou heard Tor's voice behind her exclaim.

She only laughed and shook her head. "Not the wild deer," she answered, clapping the reins to Reindeer to bear her downslope toward the meadow. "Our caribou."

19

Strangers

I T WAS SIX WEEKS still to the solstice when they reached their journey's end, and the first snows long overdue. Caribou felt a sense of wonder. Was it only a month they had traveled in their sledges — four short littlemoons? She had lost all sense of time in the sunless Region of Endless Snow. It had seemed much longer. She was weary to the bone.

Jubilation overshadowed her weariness though, as she watched her people settle into the broad, protected valley, building hasty enclosures for their caribou and felling trees to make shelters for themselves before snowfall. The weather continued sunny and mild.

Nuts, fish, wild fruits and game were all abundant. Families began laying in their stores. There were daimons in every tree and rock, it seemed, accepting the offerings left for them. The little charms people said — against ill-luck or to help untangle a cord or plane a board — began to work again, and there was magic once more in the shamans' talismans and bones.

Caribou's people had been in their new land scarcely two littlemoons when the elders of the council called for a feast in honor of Caribou. Bonfires were set in the sandy clearing between the two streams wending through the vale, and there was much carousing and toasting of the *i'dris* with draughts of herbal tea and berry cider.

Both moons were full and high in the sky. Tor sang his silly song about the end of the world and the falling sky till the company roared, stamping in time. Then all of them tossed their guest of honor in a blanket, higher and higher, until Caribou thought she might touch the moons. They shouted, "*I'dris! I'dris!*" tossing, until Caribou grew dizzy and made them stop. She had never laughed so hard in her life.

But when she staggered back to her sledge at last, long after midnight, Reindeer was not there. She had been so busy overseeing her people's settling in that she had not had time even to choose a place for building her own *ntula*. The aportioning of land was the council's job, but they could not do it all, and the people trusted Caribou's judgment. Besides, she enjoyed the work. It exhilarated her.

Reindeer had remained with her. By day he drifted through the trees, never far from her sight but unwilling to join her among her people. By night he lay beside the sledge where she slept — but always in deer-shape. He would not change. And Caribou, impatient, felt even more frustrated that she could not ask him why.

This was the first night he had ever left her alone. Caribou stood beside the sledge in the moonlight, vexed and bewildered. She called for him once, but got no answer. He did not come. Caribou undressed and climbed beneath the caribou skins on her sledge.

he was too muzzy-headed to go looking for him.

Perhaps it is just as well that he is not here and in his man-shape, she found herself thinking uncertainly as she drifted into sleep. *I have fallen asleep the moment I lay down every night since we came here.* She dreamed of Tor and the others toasting her, and not drawing away or making the sign against evil when she approached. She dreamed of touching the moons.

By morning Reindeer had not returned. Caribou woke late, feeling strained and cross. Her joints were stiff. She dressed with a growing feeling of panic, casting about her through the trees, searching their brown and red and black for a glimpse of gold. *No more of this,* she told herself finally. *He cannot be far. He would not leave me.*

She did not go into the settlement that day. Instead, she climbed high up one rocky slope to a spot overlooking the vale. Her head still ached a little from the revel the night before. The morning light made her wince. From below, the sound of ax and mallet rang out sharply in the crisp, cool air, and the shouts of workers calling to one another. She thought she might even have caught a faint snatch of Tor's song, from far away, sung by someone else.

Below, most of the half-finished houses clustered along the streams, but others were scattered here and there about the slopes. She stood higher than them all. Soon, she knew, there would not be one family or group that had sledged together that did not have at least a low roof over their heads.

Except for me, thought Caribou, and sighed. *I have been minding my people's lives so long I have forgotten my own. Dying-summer will not last forever. I must set to work. I have delayed too long.*

"Is this the spot where we shall build your *ntula?*" a voice behind her asked.

Caribou spun around. She had not heard that voice since they had left the Wilderland, forever ago, on the other side of the world. Reindeer in his man-shape was coming toward her out of the trees. With a cry of joy, she ran to him.

"I thought you would never come away from the others," he said. His face had no expression. His eyes were just the same. She clung to him, laughing, all her aches vanished. He put his arms around her and kissed her, and she knew then, beyond all doubt, that he had longed for her these past weeks as urgently as she had longed for him.

"Stay now," she told him. "Stay in your man-shape with me."

He pulled her down to the grassy ground with him. "I will stay in my man-shape all winter with you."

Reindeer and Caribou built their *ntula,* felling trees, raising the roof and caulking the walls. After the building, there was much to be done in the way of gathering, preserving, and storing. Caribou's provisions were nearly exhausted. She went down daily into the settlement to arbitrate disputes and advise the council. No one came to her *ntula* to trouble her and Reindeer.

At last the snows of winter came. With their *gristaal,* Caribou's people ranged far afield in search of stores: wood, game, fodder for their caribou. They saw no sign of other people, no track or trap, no house or smoke, tamed beast or bird. The land seemed completely virgin, untrespassed by any — until a few days before solstice, when Djenret and Brikka sought Caribou out in her hut.

"*I'dris,*" they told her, "we have seen strangers. They have come to us in the village below, two of them, a boy and a woman, driving a sledge drawn by a troika of strange beasts."

Caribou served her guests flat cakes of acorn meal and elder tea upon the doorstep of her hut. She spotted Tor among the little group that had come with the two elders. Seeing him, she felt an unexpected twinge, part plain happiness at seeing him and finding him well, part an odd uneasiness in his presence. Behind her, Reindeer lingered in his man-shape within the darkness of the hut, reluctant to show himself, she knew, but listening.

"These deer —" the youth from Tjaalsénji was telling her. The two elders stepped back, acknowledging the special place that he held with their wisewoman. "These deer that draw the strangers' sledge," he said, "they are larger than our caribou, rounder of body and coarser of head. I saw them close. Their hooves are not divided, but solid, a single toe."

Caribou sat listening, trying not to smile. The young man's face was alive, his fascination clear. He gestured as he spoke.

"They have long tails, too, of silky hair, and a fringe of the same running along their necks. Little ears, no horns — like calves. But they wear bridles and tack, and seem as docile as caribou."

"Tell me of the strangers themselves," murmured Caribou, sipping her tea.

"They are odd." Brikka spoke now. "Their garments are of woven cloth, in bright colors, like the River-Valley Folk. Their hair is brown, but of a lighter color than our hair. The boy's has a red cast to it. Their skin is not olive like ours, but the color of cream. The woman's eyes are brown — but again, a lighter brown. The boy's eyes are oddly pale, as gray as glass."

Caribou ground the dense, coarse acorn cake between her teeth and thought a moment, not smiling now. Tor was watching her from the group. His gaze upon her made her restless.

"You have greeted them?" she asked.

The others nodded.

"Made them welcome?"

"Aye."

Caribou set down her cup, fingered the golden arrow on her lap. Across from her, Djenret of Vlad stood tugging on his moustache.

"We want you to come look at them, *i'dris*," he told her. "Talk to them and discover what they want."

Caribou scratched her arm, eyeing the councillor. Intrigued as she was by the news of these strangers, her people's expectation puzzled her. She had led them safe into a new land, as she had promised, but she was not their chieftain. They had no chieftain. The council ruled.

"These strangers," she inquired, "do they refuse to talk to the council?"

Brikka came forward now. "They are ready and willing to talk to the council, *i'dris*. We want them to talk to you."

Caribou frowned, keenly aware now for the first time how much the elders relied on her in making their decisions. She thought of Reindeer suddenly, in the dark of her hut, listening. *I must not let them become too dependent on me,* she thought suddenly, worried, *for I will not be here after the spring.* A few paces away she saw Tor studying her. She turned back to the councilman again.

"Djenret," she exclaimed, "you head the council of elders. I am only a wisewoman —"

Tor's words cut her off. "You are our *i'dris!*" He stopped, disconcerted at his own outburst, but recovered quickly. "You led us across the Land of Everlasting Night. Of course we have come to you." His voice had a different timbre from Reindeer's: darker, full of emotion. He came forward and knelt before Caribou. "Please come, *i'dris*," he said.

His perfect seriousness — as if he truly thought she did not mean to come — made Caribou laugh. Rising, she took his empty cup from him, and those from the others standing before her. "Very well," she told them. "I will come."

Going back into the hut, she laid the teacups by the firepit and spoke to Reindeer, sitting far from the coals' heat and light. The beauty of his goldenness seemed diminished somehow, lost in shadow. She went to him.

"I am going down into the valley to see these strangers," she said. "Will you come with me?"

He shook his head.

"Not even in deer-shape?"

Again he shook his head.

"What is it?" she asked, drawing near. "You seem . . . melancholy." She had to search for the word. She had never thought to use such a word for him. He looked at her then, with that fathomless expression that had come to seem almost a smile — gone rueful now?

"I am a *trangl*," he told her, removing his hand gently from hers, "and *traangol* can be neither melancholy nor glad."

She eyed him for a long moment, but could not read him. She almost wished that she might stay then, or that he would come, but she had no time to coax him further. Tor and the others waited. Reluctantly, she rose.

"I will tell you of these strangers when I return."

Caribou went with the townspeople down the steep, rocky slope to see the two strangers in the village below. She spotted them, the woman and the boy, beside their *gristal* drawn by the peculiar, undeerlike deer, in the sandy clearing between the two streams.

"Greetings, strangers; our guests, and be welcome," Caribou said, as was fitting, while the council members stood looking on from a few paces back, and other townsfolk clustered about the clearing's edge. "I am Caribou, whom my people call their *i'dris*. Tell me your names, if you will, and why you have come."

The woman stepped forward, all grace and self-possession. She was older than Caribou, and she wore ornaments of carved amber, like a shaman.

"Greetings, seer," she said, smiling. "I am called Olwen. I, too, am priestess to my people, who live north of here. This is Sigl" — she gestured to the boy — "my son and acolyte. We came to gather gold-berry for our celebration of the winter solstice, before the hard snows come and cut us off from here. But from afar we saw the smoke of your fires. We did not know that any tribe lived here. We have always called these the Unclaimed Lands."

Caribou smiled a little then, to herself, and gestured around her at the rude hovels surrounding the square. "As you see, Olwen, we are but lately arrived and newly settled. Great upheavals in the earth of our homeland drove us away. We sought new country to settle in."

Watching Olwen's cream-colored face, Caribou saw surprise there, but the priestess's manner remained gracious.

"Where do you come from?" Olwen asked.

Caribou forgave the baldness of it. Perhaps, like the River-Valley People, Olwen's tribe did not consider such questions forward. Caribou gestured.

"We come from there, beyond the Pole. Over the Burning Plain and the Cinderlands we came, passing beside the Firth of Fire, over the Backbone of the Sea, beside the Forge of the Fireking, and over the Plain of Unbroken Snow, where neither moon nor sun ever shine. We sledged, following the wild deer from the other side of the world."

Caribou saw growing astonishment in Olwen's face, in the boy's, open-mouthed awe that was almost fear. He stared at Caribou.

"From the other side of the world?" whispered Olwen. "From beyond the Pole? Then you are . . . you are from the Golden Lands."

She seemed at a loss for the first time, and sought Caribou's eyes, as if to reassure herself that the other truly stood there.

"Our legends tell of a people who dwell there," Olwen breathed. "And just this autumn past, a year ago, two of my acolytes met in these hills a golden man who said he had come from there . . ."

Caribou remembered Reindeer telling her how he had learned the workings of a *gristal* by helping two children repair theirs. She smiled and nodded. "He brought word of your country back to us and led us here. But we have never called the lands where we used to dwell golden —"

Just at that moment, one of the village sledges pulled into the clearing. Caribou realized in surprise that it was Tor upon the driver's step — when had he slipped away? A great pile of branches laden with yellow waxbud lay lashed on the prow.

At the sight of the sledge, Olwen cried out, "Oh,

surely you must be they — for your *gristaal* are drawn
by the great deer, tame as any horses or kine!"

Tor guided his team near, reined to a halt, and leapt
down. He lifted a bundle of branches from the hold.

"*I'dris*," he said, "I heard these strangers say they
had come searching for goldberry, but I saw none in
their sledge. I went to cut some."

Caribou nodded and answered, "You did well."

He handed a bundle to the acolyte. The gray-eyed
boy took the branches reverently, staring at Tor as if
the young man might suddenly change into a bird
before his eyes.

Olwen turned back to Caribou with a similar look,
and seemed about to speak, when across the stream
appeared the village's caribou, driven by young children on foot with long willow switches. They were
bringing the herd down from the high pastures, for
the sun had already fallen low enough to shade the
best slopes.

Some of the caribou bent to drink, and the children
halted, gazing at the crowd across the stream. Djenret
started to shoo them away, but Caribou took his arm
and said, "Let them be."

Olwen had ceased staring. She folded her wrists
across her breast and made a deep obeisance to Caribou.

"Surely you are they, the divine ones from the Golden
Lands, great *i'dris*," she murmured. "You have clothed
yourselves in mortal shape, but who could fail to
recognize you? For the wild deer run meekly before
the swats of your children."

Caribou shook her head and knelt down beside Olwen.

"These are not the wild deer," she answered, "but caribou, their tame cousins. The wild deer have run on before us to their wintering grounds north of here."

"Oh, yes," Olwen replied, her head still bowed, not looking at Caribou. "They winter on the verges of our country, and roam wherever they will. We do not molest them, for they belong to you. The herdbeasts of the gods are sacred to us."

Caribou laid her hand upon the other woman's arm.

"Olwen," she said, "my people are no gods — not even little ones — but flesh. We are a Tribe, villagers and woodfolk, like you."

The strange priestess raised her eyes slowly. At last she uncrossed her hands. Her face was very pale, her skin like ice, but Caribou's touch seemed to reassure her. When Caribou rose, Olwen rose with her.

"You have said so much, and I have seen such things," she said uncertainly, "that my head aches with it. I must think on all of this."

She glanced toward her son. Caribou saw that Tor and the boy had loaded all of the waxbud into the strangers' *gristal*.

"Sigl and I must start homeward now," Olwen said, "or we will not reach our village before the heavy snows." She glanced at Caribou again, still half in puzzlement and half in awe.

"Will you come again," said Caribou, "in spring, Olwen, when the rains have gone? Then the leaders of your people and our leaders, the council, may confer."

She felt oddly uneasy as she said that — not at the thought of Olwen or her people, but because she was speaking of her Tribe's future, which she would not be present to share. She thought of her promise to Reindeer and felt a stab of bitter regret.

She would miss her people, very sorely. They had accepted her, and she had learned to live among them at last. Angrily, she shoved regret away. Her promise to the *trangl* had saved all their lives. *And I love him. I need him. I want to be with him. I have given my word; now I must be content.*

With an effort, Caribou turned her thoughts back to Olwen. What had they just spoken of? Oh yes, of the leaders of Olwen's people coming in the spring. The pale-skinned woman nodded to Caribou. She seemed uncertain, but determined to act.

She shooed her son up into the sledge before her. Caribou saw with fascination that it was driven from a bench mounted high in the forepart, not at the rear, as with their own *gristaal*. The boy sat on the bench.

Olwen turned and bowed to Caribou before climbing to take her place beside the boy. Caribou, unsure whether the priestess's gesture had been meant simply as a politeness upon parting or as a reverence, carefully returned it.

The priestess caught up the reins of her strange,

long-faced beasts and whistled to them, turning them, and glided out of the settlement, away over the hilly terrain. Caribou watched with the others until the sledge was lost among the trees on the northern slope, then turned to go back to her hut.

20

The People of Caribou

WHEN SHE REACHED HOME, Caribou told Reindeer of the meeting, of the strangers' words, of their new kind of *gristal,* and of their promise to come again in springtime with their chieftains — but all the while she spoke, her golden youth remained pensive and silent.

"I know what is troubling you," she told him at last. "You are weary of your man-shape and restless to run with the reindeer again. Why do you not go?"

She spoke quietly, touching his arm, but her teeth were clenched. She had to force herself to say the words — not because she wanted him to leave her, but because she knew she had no power to hold him if he wished to be gone.

"My hut here is built and my stores all laid in. I would not starve to death or freeze this winter, if you were to go away."

Evening outside was dark, and within the hut only firelight illuminated him. As she spoke, she felt him shiver. He turned to her quickly, taking her hands, and gazed at her very intently.

"No, Cari," he whispered. "I will stay with you.

The reindeer will not die of longing for me, either, if I stay away a little more."

She leaned against him then, so glad she could scarcely speak, and felt his strong arms about her. "Stay with me till springtime," she said. "My people will be settled by then, and have no more need of me."

No more need of me. She willed away the sudden sharp ache that the thought caused her. She willed it to be the truth. He stroked her hair.

"Then when the reindeer run southward again,' he murmured, "back to the other side of the world where your people used to dwell, you will go with me as you promised, and bathe in the Fount of Gold."

Reindeer stayed with her that winter, casting off his deer-shape all through the months of snow. Caribou tried to be happy, to think only of the present. She did not want to think about the spring. She clung to him almost desperately now and could hardly bear to be parted from him, but he seemed to have no wish to be anywhere but at her side.

It troubled her, though, that they were not undisturbed. Despite the distance and the hard climb to her hovel, people from the settlement below often made the steep journey to receive her judgment or ask for advice. Though she knew she ought not to encourage them — for she would not be among them much longer — Caribou could not turn any of them away.

Reindeer always sat within when her people came, listening from the darkness of the hut and not emerging until they had gone, even if the consultation took all morning or all afternoon. Or else he went away into the woods when he saw them climbing toward the house — returning only after sunset at the end of the day.

The best days were the ones they spent alone together, when no one came. Then Caribou could forget her people, forget all obligations to any but herself, and think only of Reindeer. Even so, her golden youth was often silent.

When she tried to discover why, he answered none of her gentle questions, or answered distantly. More than once, he was gone from the hut when she awoke at dawn, staying away long hours, and would say nothing of where he had been. Her dreams did not help her understand him. They never had.

Spring came. The snow upon the slopes grew soft, trickling down to swell the streams. Caribou had hoped that the return of warmth and sun would lighten her golden *trangl*'s mood, but Reindeer only seemed to become more troubled.

She felt his restlessness, and the golden arrow's twitch, and knew the reindeer would be running soon. The prospect filled her with dread. Soon Reindeer would hold her to her promise. Putting on his deer-shape again, he would carry her away.

She tried to resign herself to it, to feel glad. The running of the wild deer would mean that she might leave behind this life with all its mortal cares, and these people, from whom she had always felt so different.

But I am not an outcast anymore! she found herself

thinking desperately one night. *I want to stay here with my people. They need me. We are just beginning here.* And yet she loved Reindeer with all her heart and did not know how she could live without him. She felt as if she were being torn in two.

Then one day when Reindeer was away, the sixteen elders made the difficult climb to her hovel. Tor came with them, and the elders all stood back to let the young man speak. He made their supplication eloquently, speaking of the people's great love for her.

Caribou felt cold with surprise. Her belly clenched. She answered very shortly and sent the astonished councillors away. Tor stayed behind, without her bidding, but she refused to meet his concerned, inquiring eyes.

"*I'dris,* what is it?" he asked at last. "Surely you knew we would ask you this?"

She sat on the threshold of her hut, half turned away from him. She shook her head. "My mind has been on other things this winter past," she said. "I did not guess."

"Have we angered you?" His words were soft.

She almost laughed — not from mirth. She felt like weeping instead. "The council *honors* me," she whispered.

He came and knelt beside her. "But you are sad, *i'dris.* Why?"

She turned to look at him. "I owe a debt," she said, "a debt to my *trangl.*" She had not meant to speak of it, but now that she had started, she found she could not stop. "In exchange for his leading us safe to this new land, I have promised to go away with him."

She saw the young man's eyes widen. "Go?" he whispered. "Go where, when?"

"*Now*, soon, when the reindeer are running." She was angry at Tor suddenly for no reason. The golden arrow twitched in her hand. She had begun to shake. Then she blurted out, "I do not want to go."

She felt a sudden pressure on her wrist. Tor had reached to take hold of it. "*I'dris*, don't," he said. "Don't go with him." She shook her head and tried to pull away, but Tor held on. "Tell him you wish to stay with us," the young man said urgently. "He will release you. If he loves you, he must."

And she remembered how she had said almost the same thing once, to Branja, a very long time ago. She stopped struggling and gazed at Tor's very young and human face. She realized whom he reminded her of suddenly: of Visjna, her brother. She put her fingers to the spot on his cheek where the gray water had burned him. The skin was pale there still. Of Reindeer, she said:

"But you speak as though he were a man. He is not a man. Did you think the *traangol* do anything for love?" *Even though I love* him, she added silently. To Tor she said, "And I have given him my word."

He seemed to realize only then that he had taken hold of her. He dropped her wrist. She saw him blushing. Caribou drew away from him and rose.

"Go back to the village," she told him. "I must treat with my *trangl* now."

"*I'dris,*" he began, his dark eyes beseeching her, but she shook her head.

"Go," she told him gently. "These things are between my *trangl* and me."

Tor did not rise at first, but she turned away and after a little she heard him go. After he had gone, she went inside the hut. She felt as though she were dying inside. Her abdomen knotted and cramped. A great weight oppressed her heart. She sat by the firepit till evening and wept.

Reindeer came into the hut. His figure blocked the twilight in the doorway. He threw off his reindeer cape, which he wore fur-side in so that the skin of the pelt would not cleave to him and make him a reindeer. He stood pinning shut the flap of stitched hide that was their door; then turning, he seemed to see for the first time that she was weeping. He came to her, and knelt.

"Why are you doing that?" he said, touching her cheek.

Caribou brushed at the tears impatiently. "Where did you go?" she cried. "Where were you all day — why weren't you here?"

"What has happened?" he asked.

"The elders came."

"What of them?"

Caribou's throat was too tight to speak. She swallowed. "They have chosen a new chieftain for the Tribe."

"You weep for that?"

She looked at him, into his changeless, fathomless golden eyes that she could never understand. "They have chosen *me*."

He showed no surprise. "But you told them no."

She looked away. "I . . . told them I would think on it." She felt fresh tears hot upon her cheeks. Reindeer, she knew, was still watching her.

"Why did you not tell them you were going away?"

Caribou bit her lip. "I don't know. I don't know." Her voice was a whisper. She had told Tor — but he was not a member of the council.

A little silence then.

"You promised to come away with me in the spring."

She shut her eyes, shook her head, put both hands to her face. Her belly felt like a wound that had healed drawn and sore. She bent over. "I know that," she whispered. "I know."

She felt the young man's hard arms fold about her then, drawing her up. She put her own arms about his neck and pressed her face to his shoulder, but holding him was no comfort to her.

"How can I leave now?" she gasped. "My people need me. The chieftains of the milk-skinned strangers will be coming, and who will treat with them if I am gone? Then the planting must be begun — the villagers have asked me to allot the land for their fields. They trust me. They want me to stay."

She struggled and could hardly find the words.

"The People of Caribou. That is what they are calling themselves now — did you know it? And they make no distinction between the term we call our herdbeasts and the word which is my name. How may I go with you now? How may I go? It isn't finished yet, what I have begun."

His face never changed, but she felt a tremor pass through his arms. She had never seen him flinch before. Suddenly, she could not look at him. Her voice deserted her. And Reindeer held her still, gently, almost absently, his gaze expressionless.

When at last her weeping ceased, he said, "Tomorrow, go down to the settlement and call your sixteen elders to you. Tell them that you accept their offer. Tell them you will be their chief."

The words startled her. She tried to pull away, but the band of his arms neither tightened nor yielded.

"But . . ." She shook her head. "I promised you."

His voice grew even softer then, as though something stopped his throat. He could only breathe, "I forgive you your promise to me."

She felt something burning splash down the side of her face, and then another drop of fire upon her neck. She leaned back a little, saw Reindeer touch each of his eyes, bewildered, and stand staring at the golden liquid on his fingertips.

"Are these tears?" he said. "I have never wept before."

She touched the gold on his cheeks. It burned her fingers, hot as tallow. He looked up at the touch.

"You used to tell me, Cari, that I had no human heart. But I think that it has become human — or more human — now, because of you. Or perhaps it was only that that side of me deeply slept, and you have wakened it, for knowing that I must run with the wild deer without you a while is making a great pain in my breast."

She wiped the gold tears from his cheeks. She remembered the strange, hot dart she had felt the very first time she had taken him into her house, and on the night of his return from the wild deer. She said to him, "You have the power to compel me to come."

His breath caught strangely. He answered, "No. I will not bind you. I do not wish to take from you what is not freely offered." He touched his breast. "I do not want you to feel this pain that I am feeling now. And I know that you will feel it if you come with me before you have finished here."

He shook his head, as if to clear it, with a kind of grimace — and then she saw that he was trying to smile. It came easier on the second try. The unearthly fair features of his face became near-human suddenly. He looked almost mortal then. She had never seen him more beautiful. He cradled her face between his hands.

"But I will come to you each autumn and spring, to ask you if you are finished yet."

He turned and went to the little chest where she kept his things — man-clothes and boots, traces and bells, and the gifts she had once carved him from the golden stag's bones. Reindeer lifted the lid and took out the long haft of reindeer horn — the only piece Caribou had never finished. He returned with it to the firepit, held out the haft to her.

"I have known since autumn," he sighed, "that you

would not come with me. All winter I have been making this."

Taking it, she saw that it was wondrously carved, beyond all human skill, with tiny figures that told the story of his life and Caribou's: how Branja had brought to her the babe; how his father had stolen him away and then fallen beneath her brother's arrow; how he himself had gone away to join the wild deer — and then returned to help Caribou lead her people beyond the Burning Plain. The lower end of the haft was left uncarved.

"What is it?" she asked softly.

"A chieftain's wand. Your people brought none of the old one's things with them when they came away." Caribou knelt, holding the bone wand in both her hands. "The other half," he said, "is for you to carve. Show it to me when I come to you every winter and spring, and I will see if you have finished it."

Reindeer rose, pulling off his man-clothes and laying them aside.

"Keep these for me," he said, "till I return. And promise me —" He touched her belly lightly with one hand. She looked at him, but did not draw away. "I promise you that I will not bear our child away, as my father tried to do with me."

His golden eyes looked into hers.

"But promise me in return that you will send our son to me when he is old enough."

She stared at him, and felt cold with wonder suddenly, though the room was warm. "How did you know?" she whispered. "I was not even sure myself. I did not want to tell you until I was sure."

He looked at her. His golden eyes lightened. "I am a *trangl*," he said, kissing her. "We always know."

She felt her breath catch in her throat, and clung to him. All at once she felt light: no sorrow anymore. It was as if a great stone had been lifted from her. She wanted to laugh, and found she was weeping again. He took her hands in his.

"One day," he said, looking deep into her with his golden eyes. "One day you will come with me."

He stood away from her and turned, reaching to catch up the golden pelt.

"Wait," she cried. "Wait." She could not bear to let him go. "I trust you," she found herself saying, "and know that you will keep your word to me concerning our child — but how if others of your kind come among my people again, to charm them, and lie with them, and steal their children?"

Reindeer turned to her. "Once I had hoped you would come among us and bring the *traangol* to your understanding. But since you cannot come with me yet, it is I who must speak to my people now, and dissuade them."

"Will they listen?" she asked.

He pressed her hands. "They will listen. They must — I will tell them the People of Caribou forbid such things. And if any *trangl* shall come among your people," he said, "and seek to charm them against their will, I will put a stop to it."

She touched his cheek — but he pulled free of her and stepped away. He threw his golden pelt around him, skin-side to his skin. Caribou fell back, but did not hide her eyes from the change, as she always had before.

What she saw was a golden light leaping from the pelt to edge Reindeer round in a sharp line, like the sun behind a cloud. Then, instantly, his form collapsed from that of a man into that of an antlered stag. The light faded. Caribou stood dazzled.

She heard a rush and the clatter of hooves, felt a moment's cold air. Silence then. Presently, she heard one of the great deer belling, off down the slope across the valley somewhere, and the thunder of many heels. She stood, still starstruck, the drum of running reindeer filling the night. Her senses returned only gradually. The chieftain's wand in her hand felt heavy and cool.

When at last she could see again, she was aware of the dim glow of the firepit behind her, the hut door unpinned and flapping in the gaunt night breeze, and beyond that, by moonlight, far away, the wild deer streaming through the valley below. Southward, Poleward, they ran. Her golden Reindeer was with them.

THE BEST IN FANTASY

☐ 53954-0 SPIRAL OF FIRE by Deborah Turner Harris $3.95
  53955-9   Canada $4.95

☐ 53401-8 NEMESIS by Louise Cooper (U.S. only) $3.95

☐ 53382-8 SHADOW GAMES by Glen Cook $3.95
  53381-X   Canada $4.95

☐ 53815-5 CASTING FORTUNE by John M. Ford $3.95
  53826-1   Canada $4.95

☐ 53351-8 HART'S HOPE by Orson Scott Card $3.95
  53352-6   Canada $4.95

☐ 53397-6 MIRAGE by Louise Cooper (U.S. only) $3.95

☐ 53671-1 THE DOOR INTO FIRE by Diane Duane $2.95
  53672-X   Canada $3.50

☐ 54902-3 A GATHERING OF GARGOYLES by Meredith Ann Pierce $2.95
  54903-1   Canada $3.50

☐ 55614-3 JINIAN STAR-EYE by Sheri S. Tepper $2.95
  55615-1   Canada $3.75

Buy them at your local bookstore or use this handy coupon:
Clip and mail this page with your order.

Publishers Book and Audio Mailing Service
P.O. Box 120159, Staten Island, NY 10312-0004

Please send me the book(s) I have checked above. I am enclosing $_____
(please add $1.25 for the first book, and $.25 for each additional book to
cover postage and handling. Send check or money order only — no CODs.)

Name _____

Address _____

City _____ State/Zip _____

Please allow six weeks for delivery. Prices subject to change without notice.

THE TOR DOUBLES

Two complete short science fiction novels in one volume!

THE BEST IN SCIENCE FICTION

BESTSELLING BOOKS FROM TOR

CONTENTS

EDITORIAL STAFF

Editor in Chief
Michael Agnes

Project Editor
Jonathan L. Goldman

Editor and Database Administrator
Donald Stewart

Editorial Staff
James E. Naso   Katherine Soltis
Andrew N. Sparks   Stephen P. Teresi
Laura Borovac Walker

Administrative, Data Processing, and Clerical Staff
Cynthia M. Sadonick   Betty Dziedzic Thompson

Citation Readers
Batya Jundef
Joan Komic

Production Coordinator
Barbara Apanites

PRONUNCIATION KEY

	as in		*as in*
a	cat	ou	out
ā	ape	u	up
ä	cot	u	fur
e	ten	ə	*a* in ago, *o* in atom
ē	me	'	fertile (furt"l)
i	fit	ch	chin
ī	ice	ŋ	ring
ō	go	sh	she
ô	fall	th	thin
oi	oil	th	then
oo	look	zh	measure
oo	tool	n	Indicates nasal quality of preceding vowel

Note: Pronunciations, using the symbols above, are given selectively in this dictionary. Proper pronunciation can be derived by using the stress markings on the boldface entry words—primary stress (') for syllables spoken with the most force and secondary stress (') for syllables spoken with relatively less force. Unmarked (unstressed) syllables are spoken with the least force and tend to have a lessening of their vowel sounds.

ABBREVIATIONS USED

a.	adjective	n.	noun
abbrev.	abbreviation	Naut.	nautical
adv.	adverb	Obs.	obsolete
alt.	alternate	orig.	originally
Ar.	archaic	pl.	plural
Biol.	biology	Poet.	poetic
Br.	British	pp.	past participle
c.	century	pref.	prefix
Chem.	chemistry	prep.	preposition
con.	conjunction	pres.	present
Dial.	dialectal	pron.	pronoun
esp.	especially	prp.	present participle
etc.	et cetera	pt.	past tense
fem.	feminine	R.C.Ch.	Roman Catholic Church
Fr.	French	Rom.	Roman
Gr.	Greek	Scot.	Scottish
Gram.	grammar	sing.	singular
Heb.	Hebrew	Sl.	slang
Inf.	informal	sp.	spelling; spelled
int.	interjection	Sp.	Spanish
It.	Italian	spec.	specifically
L.	Latin	suf.	suffix
Math.	mathematics	t.	tense
Mil.	military	Theol.	theology
Mus.	music	v.	verb
myth.	mythology		

A

a *a.*, *indefinite article* **1** one **2** each; any one

a *abbrev.* adjective

A *abbrev. Baseball, Basketball* assist(s)

a- *pref.* not

AA *abbrev.* **1** Alcoholics Anonymous **2** Associate in (or of) Arts

aard'vark' (ärd'-) *n.* African mammal that eats ants

AB *abbrev.* **1** Alberta **2** Bachelor of Arts: also **A.B.**

ab- *pref.* away; from; down

ABA *abbrev.* American Bar Association

a·back' *adv.* used only in **taken aback,** surprised

ab'a·cus *n.* frame with beads for doing arithmetic

ab'a·lo'ne *n.* sea mollusk

a·ban'don *v.* **1** give up entirely **2** to desert **—n.** lack of restraint

a·ban'doned *a.* **1** deserted **2** shamefully wicked **3** unrestrained

a·base' *v.* to humble

a·bash' *v.* embarrass

a·bate' *v.* lessen **—a·bate'ment** *n.*

ab·at·toir' (-ə twär') *n.* slaughterhouse

ab·bé (a'bā) *n.* priest's title in France

ab'bess *n.* woman who is head of a convent

ab'bey *n.* monastery or convent

ab'bot *n.* man who is head of a monastery

abbr, abbrev *abbrev.* **1** abbreviated **2** abbreviation

ab·bre'vi·ate' *v.* shorten, as a word **— ab·bre'vi·a'tion** *n.*

ABC *n.*, *pl.* **ABC's 1** *pl.* the alphabet **2** basics; rudiments

ab'di·cate' *v.* give up, as a throne **—ab' di·ca'tion** *n.*

ab'do·men (or ab dō'-) *n.* part of the body between chest and pelvis **—ab· dom'i·nal** (-däm'-) *a.*

ab·duct' *v.* kidnap **—ab·duc'tion** *n.* **— ab·duc'tor** *n.*

a·bed' *adv.*, *a.* in bed

ab'er·ra'tion *n.* deviation from normal, right, etc.

a·bet' *v.* **a·bet'ted, a·bet'ting** to help, esp. in crime **—a·bet'tor, a·bet'ter** *n.*

a·bey'ance (-bā'-) *n.* temporary suspension

ab·hor' *v.* **-horred', -hor'ring** shun in disgust, hatred, etc. **—ab·hor'rence** *n.*

ab·hor'rent *a.* detestable

a·bide' *v.* **a·bode'** or **a·bid'ed, a·bid' ing 1** remain **2** [Ar.] reside **3** await **4** endure **—abide by** keep (a promise) or obey (rules)

a·bid'ing *a.* enduring

a·bil'i·ty *n.*, *pl.* **-ties 1** a being able **2** talent

ab'ject' *a.* miserable

ab·jure' (-joor') *v.* renounce on oath

a·blaze' *a.* on fire

a'ble *a.* **1** having power to do something **2** talented; skilled **—a'bly** *adv.*

-able *suf.* **1** that can or should be **2** tending to

a'ble-bod'ied *a.* healthy

able-bodied seaman *n.* skilled seaman: also **able seaman**

ab·lu'tions *pl.n.* washing of the body, esp. as a rite

ab'ne·gate' *v.* renounce; give up **—ab' ne·ga'tion** *n.*

ab·nor'mal *a.* not normal **—ab'nor· mal'i·ty** *n.*, *pl.* **-ties —ab·nor'mal·ly** *adv.*

a·board' *adv.*, *prep.* on or in (a train, ship, etc.)

a·bode' *n.* home

a·bol'ish *v.* do away with

ab'o·li'tion *n.* an abolishing, spec. [*occas.* **A-**] of slavery in the U.S. **— ab'o·li'tion·ist** *n.*

A'-bomb' *n.* atomic bomb

a·bom'i·na·ble *a.* **1** disgusting **2** very bad **—a·bom'i·na·bly** *adv.*

a·bom'i·nate' *v.* loathe **—a·bom'i·na' tion** *n.*

ab'o·rig'i·ne' (-rij'ə nē') *n.* first known inhabitant **—ab'o·rig'i·nal** *a.*, *n.*

a·bort' *v.* **1** have a miscarriage **2** cause to have an abortion **3** cut short (a flight, etc.), as because of equipment failure

a·bor'tion *n.* deliberate expulsion of a fetus **—a·bor'tive** *a.*

a·bound' *v.* be plentiful

a·bout' *adv.* **1** around **2** near **3** in an opposite direction **4** nearly **—a.** astir **—prep. 1** around **2** near to **3** just starting **4** concerning

a·bout'-face' *n.* a reversal

a·bove' *adv.* **1** higher **2** earlier on a page **—prep. 1** over **2** higher than **— a.** mentioned above

a·bove'board' *a.*, *adv.* in plain view; honest(ly)

a·bove'ground' *a.* **1** above the surface of the earth **2** not secret

a·brade' *v.* scrape away **—a·bra'sive** *a.*, *n.*

a·bra'sion *n.* **1** an abrading **2**

abraded spot

a·breast' *adv., a.* **1** side by side **2** informed (*of*)

a·bridge' *v.* shorten, as in wording; lessen —**a·bridg'ment, a·bridge'ment** *n.*

a·broad' *adv.* **1** far and wide **2** outdoors **3** to or in foreign lands

ab'ro·gate *v.* abolish; repeal —**ab'ro·ga'tion** *n.*

a·brupt' *a.* **1** sudden **2** brusque; curt **3** steep —**a·brupt'ly** *adv.*

abs *pl.n.* [Sl.] abdominal muscles

ABS *abbrev.* anti-lock braking system

ab'scess (-ses') *n.* inflamed, pus-filled area in body

ab·scond' (-skänd') *v.* flee and hide to escape the law

ab'sent (*v.:* ab sent') *a.* **1** not present; away **2** lacking —*v.* keep (oneself) away —**ab'sence** *n.*

ab'sen·tee' *n.* absent person —*a.* of, by, or from one who is absent —**ab'sen·tee'ism'** *n.*

absentee ballot *n.* ballot marked and sent to a board of elections by a voter (**absentee voter**) who cannot be present to vote in an election

ab'sent-mind'ed, ab'sent·mind'ed *a.* **1** not attentive **2** forgetful

absent without leave *a. Mil.* absent from duty without official permission

ab'sinthe', ab'sinth' (-sinth') *n.* green, bitter liqueur

ab'so·lute' *a.* **1** perfect **2** complete **3** not mixed; pure **4** certain; positive **5** real —**ab'so·lute'ly** *adv.*

ab'so·lu'tion *n.* **1** forgiveness **2** remission (*of* sin)

ab·solve' *v.* to free from guilt, a duty, etc.

ab·sorb' *v.* **1** suck up **2** engulf wholly **3** interest greatly —**ab·sorp'tion** *n.* —**ab·sorp'tive** *a.*

ab·sorb'ent *a.* able to absorb moisture, etc. —**ab·sorb'en·cy** *n.*

ab·stain' *v.* do without; refrain —**ab·sten'tion** *n.*

ab·ste'mi·ous *a.* not eating or drinking too much

ab'sti·nence *n.* an abstaining from food, liquor, etc.

ab'stract (*a.: also* ab strakt') *a.* **1** apart from material objects; not concrete **2** theoretical —*v.* summarize —*n.* summary —**ab·strac'tion** *n.*

ab·stract'ed *a.* preoccupied

ab·struse' *a.* hard to understand

ab·surd' *a.* ridiculous —**ab·surd'i·ty** *n., pl.* -**ties**

a·bun'dance *n.* more than is needed —

a·bun'dant *a.*

a·buse' (-by $\overline{oo}$ z'; *n.:* -by $\overline{oo}$ s') *v.* **1** use wrongly **2** mistreat **3** berate —*n.* **1** wrong use **2** mistreatment **3** vile language —**a·bu'sive** *a.*

a·but' *v.* **a·but'ted, a·but'ting** to border (*on* or *upon*)

a·but'ment *n.* part supporting an arch, strut, etc.

a·bys'mal (-biz'-) *a.* very bad; wretched

a·byss' (-bis') *n.* deep or bottomless gulf

AC, ac *abbrev.* **1** air conditioning **2** alternating current

a·ca'cia (-kā'shə) *n.* tree with yellow or white flowers

ac'a·dem'ic *a.* **1** of schools or colleges **2** of liberal arts **3** theoretical —**ac'a·dem'i·cal·ly** *adv.*

a·cad'e·my *n., pl.* -**mies 1** private high school **2** school for special study **3** society of scholars, etc.

a·can'thus *n.* plant with large, graceful leaves

a cap·pel·la (ä kə pel'ə) *a., adv.* with no instruments accompanying: said of choral singing: also sp. **a ca·pel'la**

ac·cede' (ak sēd') *v.* **1** agree (*to*) **2** enter upon the duties (of an office)

ac·cel'er·ate' *v.* **1** increase in speed **2** make happen sooner —**ac·cel'er·a'tion** *n.* —**ac·cel'er·a'tor** *n.*

ac'cent *n.* **1** stress on a syllable in speaking **2** mark showing this **3** distinctive way of pronouncing **4** rhythmic stress —*v.* emphasize

ac·cen'tu·ate' (-ch $\overline{oo}$ -) *v.* to accent; emphasize; stress

ac·cept' *v.* **1** receive willingly **2** approve **3** agree to **4** believe in —**ac·cept'ance** *n.*

ac·cept'a·ble *a.* satisfactory —**ac·cept'a·bly** *adv.*

ac·cept'ed *a.* generally regarded as true, proper, etc.; conventional; approved

ac'cess' *n.* **1** right to enter, use, etc. **2** means of approach —*v.* gain access to

ac·ces'si·ble *a.* **1** easy to enter, etc. **2** obtainable

ac·ces'sion *n.* **1** an attaining (the throne, etc.) **2** an addition or increase

ac·ces'so·ry *n., pl.* -**ries 1** thing added for decoration **2** helper in a crime

ac'ci·dent *n.* **1** unexpected happening **2** mishap **3** chance —**ac'ci·den'tal** *a.*

ac'ci·dent-prone' *a.* likely or tending to be in or have accidents

ac·claim' *v.* greet with applause —*n.* great approval

ac·cla·ma'tion n. **1** strong approval or loud applause **2** spoken vote of "yes" by many

ac·cli·mate (ak'lə māt') v. get used to a new climate or situation: also **ac·cli'ma·tize'**

ac'co·lade' n. high praise

ac·com'mo·date' v. **1** adjust **2** do a favor for **3** have room for; lodge —**ac·com'mo·da'tion** n.

ac·com'mo·dat·ing a. obliging

ac·com'pa·ny v. **-nied, -ny·ing 1** add to **2** go with **3** play music supporting a soloist —**ac·com'pa·ni·ment** n. —**ac·com'pa·nist** n.

ac·com'plice (-plis) n. partner in crime

ac·com'plish v. do; complete —**ac·com'plish·ment** n.

ac·com'plished a. skilled

ac·cord' v. **1** agree **2** grant —n. agreement —**according to 1** consistent with **2** as stated by —**of one's own accord** voluntarily —**ac·cord'ance** n.

ac·cord'ing·ly adv. **1** in a fitting way **2** therefore

ac·cor'di·on n. musical instrument with a bellows

ac·cost' v. approach and speak to intrusively

ac·count' v. **1** give reasons (*for*) **2** judge to be —n. **1** *often pl.* record of business dealings **2** worth **3** explanation **4** report —**on account** as part payment —**on account of** because of —**on no account** never —**take into account** consider

ac·count'a·ble a. **1** responsible **2** explainable

ac·count'ing n. the keeping of business records —**ac·count'ant** n.

ac·cou'ter·ments, ac·cou'tre·ments (-kōōt'ər-, -kōō'trə-) pl.n. personal outfit; clothes

ac·cred'it v. authorize; certify —**ac·cred'i·ta'tion** n.

ac·cre'tion n. **1** growth in size **2** accumulated matter

ac·crue' v. be added, as interest on money —**ac·cru'al** n.

acct abbrev. account

ac·cu'mu·late' v. pile up; collect —**ac·cu'mu·la'tion** n.

ac'cu·rate a. exactly correct —**ac'cu·ra·cy** n. —**ac'cu·rate·ly** adv.

ac·curs'ed a. damnable

ac·cuse' v. **1** to blame **2** charge with doing wrong —**ac'cu·sa'tion** n.

ac·cus'tom v. make familiar by habit or use

ac·cus'tomed a. **1** usual; customary **2** used (*to*)

ace n. **1** playing card with one spot **2** expert —a. [Inf.] first-rate

ace in the hole n. [Sl.] any advantage held in reserve

a·cer'bi·ty (-sur'-) n. sourness; sharpness —**a·cer'bic** a.

ac·e·ta·min'o·phen (ə sēt'ə-) n. drug used to lessen fever or pain

ac·et·an·i·lide (as'ə tan'ə lid') n. drug used to lessen pain and fever

ac'e·tate' n. **1** salt or ester of an acid (**a·ce'tic acid**) found in vinegar **2** fabric made of an acetate of cellulose

ac'e·tone' n. liquid solvent for certain oils, etc.

a·cet'y·lene' (ə set''l ēn') n. gas used in a blowtorch

ache (āk) n. dull, steady pain —v. have such pain

a·chieve' v. **1** do; accomplish **2** get by effort —**a·chieve'ment** n.

achievement test n. standardized test to measure mastery of a school subject

A·chil'les' heel (ə kil'ēz') n. vulnerable spot

Achilles tendon n. tendon from heel to calf

a·choo' int. sound imitating a sneeze

ac'id n. **1** sour substance **2** chemical that reacts with a base to form a salt —a. **1** sour; sharp **2** of an acid —**a·cid'ic** a. —**a·cid'i·ty** n.

acid rain n. rain containing acids from pollution

acid test n. crucial, final test

a·cid'u·lous (-sij'ōō-) a. somewhat acid or sour

ac·knowl'edge v. **1** admit or recognize **2** to respond to (a greeting, etc.) **3** express thanks for —**ac·knowl'edg·ment, ac·knowl'edge·ment** n.

ac'me (-mē) n. highest point

ac'ne (-nē) n. pimply skin

ac'o·lyte' n. one who helps a priest at services, esp. at Mass

ac'o·nite' n. poisonous plant with hoodlike flowers

a'corn' n. nut of the oak

acorn squash n. winter squash, acorn-shaped with green skin

a·cous'tics (-kōōs'-) pl.n. qualities of a room that affect sound —n. science of sound —**a·cous'tic, a·cous'ti·cal** a. —**a·cous'ti·cal·ly** adv.

ac·quaint' v. **1** make familiar (*with*) **2** inform

ac·quaint'ance n. **1** personal knowledge **2** person one knows slightly

ac·qui·esce (ak'wē es') v. consent without protest —**ac'qui·es'cence** n.

—ac·qui·es·cent *a.*

ac·quire' *v.* get as one's own —ac·quire'ment *n.*

ac·qui·si·tion (-zish'ən) *n.* 1 an acquiring 2 something or someone acquired —ac·quis'i·tive (-kwiz'-) *a.*

ac·quit' *v.* -quit'ted, -quit'ting 1 declare not guilty 2 conduct (oneself) —ac·quit'tal *n.*

a·cre (ā'kər) *n.* measure of land, 43,560 square feet —a'cre·age *n.*

ac'rid *a.* sharp or bitter

ac'ri·mo·ny *n.* bitterness, as of manner or speech —ac·ri·mo'ni·ous *a.*

ac'ro·bat *n.* performer on the trapeze, tightrope, etc. —ac·ro·bat'ic *a.*

ac'ro·bat'ics *pl.n.* acrobat's tricks

ac'ro·nym' (-nim') *n.* a word formed from the first letters of several words

ac'ro·pho'bi·a *n.* fear of being in high places

a·cross' *adv.* from one side to the other —*prep.* 1 from one side to the other of 2 on the other side of 3 into contact with

a·cross'-the-board' *a.* affecting every group

a·cros'tic *n.* arrangement of words in which certain letters spell something

a·cryl'ic (-kril'-) *a.* of certain synthetic fibers or resins used to make fabrics, paints, etc.

act *n.* 1 thing done 2 a doing 3 a law 4 division of a play or opera —*v.* 1 perform in a play, etc. 2 behave 3 function 4 have an effect (on)

act'ing *a.* substitute

ac·tin'ic *a.* designating rays causing chemical change

ac'tion *n.* 1 a doing of something 2 thing done 3 *pl.* behavior 4 way of working 5 lawsuit 6 combat

ac'ti·vate' *v.* make active —ac'ti·va'tion *n.*

ac'tive *a.* 1 acting; working 2 busy; lively; agile —ac·tiv'i·ty *n., pl.* -ties

ac'tiv·ist *n., a.* (person) active in political protests, etc.

ac'tor *n.* one who acts in plays —ac'tress *n.fem.*

ac'tu·al (-chōo-) *a.* existing; real —ac'tu·al'i·ty *n.*

ac'tu·al·ize' *v.* make actual or real

ac'tu·al·ly *adv.* really

ac'tu·ar·y *n., pl.* -ies insurance statistician —ac·tu·ar'i·al *a.*

ac'tu·ate' *v.* 1 put into action 2 impel to action

a·cu'i·ty (-kyōō'-) *n.* keenness of thought or vision

a·cu'men (ə kyōō'-, ak'yə-) *n.* keenness of mind

ac'u·punc'ture (ak'yōō-) *n.* the practice of piercing the body with needles to treat disease or pain

a·cute' *a.* 1 sharp-pointed 2 shrewd 3 keen 4 severe 5 critical 6 less than 90°: said of angles

ad *n.* [Inf.] advertisement

AD, A.D. *abbrev.* of the Christian era

ad'age *n.* proverb

a·da'gio (-dä'jō) *a., adv. Mus.* slow(ly)

ad'a·mant *a.* unyielding

Ad'am's apple *n.* bulge in the front of a person's throat: seen chiefly in men

a·dapt' *v.* fit or adjust as needed —a·dapt'a·ble *a.* —ad·ap·ta'tion *n.* —a·dapt'er, a·dapt'or *n.*

add *v.* 1 join (*to*) so as to increase 2 increase 3 find the sum of 4 say further —add up seem reasonable —add up to signify

ad·den'dum *n., pl.* -da thing added, as an appendix

ad'der *n.* small snake, sometimes poisonous

ad·dict (ə dikt'; *n.:* ad'ikt) *v.* give (oneself) up (*to* a habit) —*n.* one addicted, as to a drug —ad·dic'tion *n.* —ad·dic'tive *a.*

ad·di'tion *n.* 1 an adding 2 part added —ad·di'tion·al *a.*

ad'di·tive *n.* something added

ad'dle *v.* make or become confused —ad'dled *a.*

ad·dress' (ə dres'; *n.: also* a'dres') *v.* 1 speak or write to 2 write the destination on (mail, etc.) 3 apply (oneself *to*) —*n.* 1 a speech 2 place where one lives 3 *Comput.* location on the Internet, etc. —ad·dress·ee' *n.*

ad·duce' *v.* give as proof

-ade *suf.* 1 the act of 2 participants in 3 drink made from

ad'e·noids' *pl.n.* growths in the throat behind the nose

a·dept' (*n.:* ad'ept') *a.* highly skilled —*n.* an expert

ad'e·quate (-kwət) *a.* enough or good enough —ad'e·qua·cy *n.*

ad·here' *v.* 1 stick fast 2 give support (*to*) —ad·her'ence *n.* —ad·her'ent *n.*

ad·he'sive *a.* sticking —*n.* sticky substance, as glue —ad·he'sion *n.*

ad hoc' *a., adv.* for a specific purpose

a·dieu (ə dyōō') *int.* goodbye

ad in·fi·ni'tum (-nīt'əm) *adv.* endlessly

a·di·os' (ä'dē ōs') *int.* goodbye

ad'i·pose' (-pōs') *a.* fatty

adj *abbrev.* adjective

ad·ja·cent (ə jā'sənt) *a.* near or next

ad·jec·tive (aj'ik tiv) *n.* word that

qualifies a noun —**ad'jec·ti'val** (-tī'-) *a.*

ad·join' *v.* be next to

ad·journ' (-jurn') *v.* suspend (a meeting, etc.) for a time —**ad·journ'ment** *n.*

ad·judge' *v.* judge, declare, or award

ad·ju'di·cate' *v.* act as judge (*in* or *on*)

ad·junct' *n.* a nonessential addition

ad·jure' (-joor') *n.* **1** order solemnly **2** ask earnestly

ad·just' *v.* **1** alter to make fit **2** regulate **3** settle rightly —**ad·just'a·ble** *a.* —**ad·just'ment** *n.*

ad·ju'tant (aj'ə tant) *n.* assistant, esp. to a commanding officer

ad'-lib' [Inf.] *v.* **-libbed', -lib'bing** improvise (words, etc.) —*n.* ad-libbed remark: also **ad lib**

adm, admin *abbrev.* administration

Adm *abbrev.* Admiral

ad'man' *n., pl.* **-men'** man whose work is advertising

ad·min'is·ter *v.* **1** manage; direct: also **ad·min'is·trate' 2** give; attend (*to*) —**ad·min'is·tra'tor** *n.*

ad·min'is·tra'tion *n.* **1** an administering **2** executive officials; management —**ad·min'is·tra'tive** *a.*

ad·mi'ra·ble *a.* worth admiring —**ad'mi·ra·bly** *adv.*

ad·mi·ral *n.* high-ranking naval officer

ad'mi·ral·ty *n.* department of naval affairs

ad·mire' *v.* have high regard for —**ad'mi·ra'tion** *n.*

ad·mis'si·ble *a.* acceptable

ad·mis'sion *n.* **1** an admitting **2** entrance fee **3** confession or concession

ad·mit' *v.* **-mit'ted, -mit'ting 1** let enter **2** concede or confess —**ad·mit'tance** *n.* —**ad·mit'ted·ly** *adv.*

ad·mix'ture *n.* mixture

ad·mon'ish *v.* **1** warn or advise **2** reprove mildly —**ad·mo·ni'tion** *v.* —**ad·mon'i·to·ry** *a.*

ad nau'se·am (-nô'zē-) *adv.* to the point of disgust

a·do' *n.* fuss; trouble

a·do'be (-dō'bē) *n.* unburnt, sun-dried brick

ad'o·les'cence *n.* time between childhood and adulthood; youth —**ad'o·les'cent** *a., n.*

A·don'is *n.* Gr. myth. handsome young man

a·dopt' *v.* **1** take legally as one's child **2** take as one's own —**a·dop'tion** *n.* —**a·dop'tive** *a.*

a·dore' *v.* **1** worship **2** love greatly —

a·dor'a·ble *a.* —**ad'o·ra'tion** *n.*

a·dorn' *v.* decorate; ornament —**a·dorn'ment** *n.*

a·dre'nal (ə drē'-) *a.* of two ductless glands (**adrenal glands**) just above the kidneys

a·dren'a·line' (-lin') *n.* hormone secreted by the adrenal glands, which increases strength, etc.

a·drift' *adv., a.* floating aimlessly

a·droit' *a.* skillful and clever —**a·droit'ly** *adv.*

ad'u·late' (aj'ə-) *v.* admire intensely —**ad'u·la'tion** *n.* —**ad'u·la·to·ry** *a.*

a·dult' *a.* grown-up; mature —*n.* mature person, animal, or plant —**a·dult'hood** *n.*

a·dul'ter·ate' *v.* make impure by adding things —**a·dul'ter·ant** *n., a.* —**a·dul'ter·a'tion** *n.*

a·dul'ter·y *n.* sexual unfaithfulness in marriage —**a·dul'ter·er** *n.* —**a·dul'ter·ess** *n.fem.* —**a·dul'ter·ous** *a.*

adv *abbrev.* adverb

ad·vance' *v.* **1** bring or go forward **2** pay before due **3** rise or raise in rank —*n.* **1** a move forward **2** *pl.* approaches to get favor —**in advance** ahead of time —**ad·vance'ment** *n.*

ad·vanced' *a.* **1** in front **2** old **3** ahead or higher in progress, price, etc.

ad·van'tage *n.* **1** superiority **2** gain; benefit —**take advantage of** use for one's own benefit —**ad'van·ta'geous** *a.*

Ad'vent' *n.* **1** period before Christmas **2** [a-] arrival

ad·ven·ti'tious (-tish'əs) *a.* not inherent; accidental

ad·ven'ture *n.* **1** dangerous undertaking **2** exciting experience —**ad·ven'tur·er** *n.* —**ad·ven'ture·some** *a.* —**ad·ven'tur·ous** *a.*

ad'verb' *n.* word that modifies a verb, adjective, or other adverb —**ad·ver'bi·al** *a.*

ad'ver·sar'y *n., pl.* **-ies** foe; opponent —**ad'ver·sar'i·al** *a.*

ad·verse' (or ad'vurs) *a.* **1** opposed **2** harmful

ad·ver'si·ty *n., pl.* **-ties** misfortune

ad'ver·tise' *v.* tell about publicly to promote sales, etc. —**ad'ver·tis'ing** *n.*

ad'ver·tise'ment (or -vur'tiz-) *n.* public notice, usually paid for

ad·vice' *n.* opinion on what to do

ad·vis'a·ble (-vīz'-) *a.* being good advice; wise —**ad·vis'a·bil'i·ty** *n.*

ad·vise' *v.* **1** give advice (to) **2** offer as advice **3** inform —**ad·vi'sor, ad·vis'er**

n. —**ad·vi'so·ry** *a.*

ad·vis'ed·ly *adv.* with due consideration

ad·vise'ment *n.* careful consideration

ad·vi'so·ry *a.* advising or empowered to advise —*n.*, *pl.* **-ries** a report, esp. about weather conditions

ad'vo·cate' (-kāt'; *n.:* -kət) *v.* support or urge —*n.* one who supports another or a cause —**ad'vo·ca·cy** *n.*

adz, adze *n.* axlike tool for trimming wood

ae·gis (ē'jis) *n.* sponsorship

ae·on (ē'ən) *n.* eon

aer'ate' (er'-) *v.* expose to air —**aer·a'tion** *n.*

aer'i·al *a.* **1** of or like air **2** of flying —*n.* radio or TV antenna

aero- *pref.* **1** air; of air **2** of aircraft

aer·o'bic *a.* of exercise that conditions heart and lungs —*n.* [*pl.*, *sing.* or *pl. v.*] aerobic exercise(s)

aer'o·dy·nam'ics *n.* science dealing with force of air in motion —*pl.n.* vehicle body qualities affecting movement through air

aer'o·nau'tics *n.* aviation —**aer'o·nau'ti·cal** *a.*

aer'o·sol' *a.* using gas under pressure to dispense liquid or foam

aer'o·space' *n.* earth's atmosphere and outer space

aes·thet'ic (es thet'-) *a.* **1** of beauty or aesthetics **2** sensitive to art and beauty —**aes'thete'** (-thēt') *n.*

aes·thet'ics *n.* philosophy of beauty

a·far' *adv.* used only in **from afar**, from a distance

AFDC *abbrev.* Aid to Families with Dependent Children

af·fa·ble *a.* pleasant; sociable —**af'fa·bil'i·ty** *n.*

af·fair' *n.* **1** matter; event **2** *pl.* business matters **3** amorous relationship of two people not married to each other

af·fect' *v.* **1** act on; influence **2** stir emotionally **3** like to wear, use, etc. **4** pretend to be or feel

af'fec·ta'tion *n.* **1** pretense **2** artificial behavior

af·fect'ed *a.* **1** artificial **2** influenced **3** emotionally moved

af·fect'ing *a.* emotionally moving

af·fec'tion *n.* fond feeling

af·fec'tion·ate *a.* tender and loving

af'fi·da'vit *n.* sworn statement in writing

af·fil'i·ate' (-āt'; *n.:* -ət) *v.* join as a member; associate —*n.* affiliated member —**af·fil'i·a'tion** *n.*

af·fin'i·ty *n.*, *pl.* **-ties 1** close relationship or kinship **2** attraction

af·firm' *v.* assert or confirm —**af'fir·ma'tion** *n.*

af·firm'a·tive *a.* assenting; agreeing —*n.* assent

affirmative action *n.* policy for remedying past racial, etc. discrimination

af·fix' (ə fiks'; *n.:* af'iks) *v.* attach —*n.* thing affixed, as a prefix

af·flict' *v.* cause pain to; distress —**af·flic'tion** *n.*

af'flu·ence *n.* wealth —**af'flu·ent** *a.*

af·ford' *v.* **1** have money enough for **2** provide

af'front' *v.*, *n.* insult

af'ghan' (-gan') *n.* crocheted or knitted blanket

a·fi·cio·na·do (ə fish'ə nä'dō) *n.* enthusiastic supporter

a·field' *adv.* away; astray

a·fire' *adv.*, *a.* on fire

a·flame' *adv.*, *a.* in flames

AFL-CIO *abbrev.* American Federation of Labor and Congress of Industrial Organizations: a labor union

a·float' *a.* **1** floating **2** current

a·flut'ter *adv.*, *a.* in a flutter

a·foot' *adv.*, *a.* **1** on foot **2** in motion; astir

a·fore'men'tioned *a.* mentioned before

a·fore'said' *a.* said before

a·fore'thought' *a.* thought out beforehand; premeditated

a·foul' *adv.*, *a.* used chiefly in **afoul of**, into trouble with

a·fraid' *a.* **1** frightened **2** regretful

a·fresh' *adv.* anew; again

Af'ri·can *a.* of Africa —*n.* native of Africa

Af'ri·can-A·mer'i·can *a.*, *n.* (of) a black American of African ancestry

aft *adv.* near the stern

af'ter *adv.* **1** behind **2** later —*prep.* **1** behind **2** in search of **3** later than **4** because of **5** in spite of **6** in imitation of **7** for —*con.* later than —*a.* later

af'ter·birth' *n.* placenta, etc. expelled after childbirth

af'ter·ef·fect' *n.* an effect coming later, or as a secondary result

af'ter·life' *n.* life after death

af'ter·math' *n.* (bad) result

af'ter·noon' *n.* time from noon to evening

af'ter-tax' *a.* after taxes are deducted

af'ter·thought' *n.* thought coming later or too late

af'ter·ward *adv.* later: also **af'ter·**

wards

a·gain' *adv.* **1** once more **2** besides

a·gainst' *prep.* **1** opposed to **2** so as to hit **3** in preparation for

a·gape' *adv., a.* wide open

ag'ate *n.* hard semiprecious stone, often striped

a·ga've (-gä'vē) *n.* desert plant with thick leaves

agcy *abbrev.* agency

age *n.* **1** length of time of existence **2** stage of life **3** old age **4** historical period —*v.* grow old or make old —**of age** having reached the age of full legal rights

-age *suf.* act or state of; amount of; place of or for

a·ged (ā'jid; 2: ājd) *a.* **1** old **2** of the age of

age'less *a.* **1** seemingly not older **2** eternal

a'gen·cy *n., pl.* **-cies 1** action or means **2** firm acting for another

a·gen'da *n.* list of things to be dealt with

a'gent *n.* **1** force, or cause of an effect **2** one that acts for another

age'-old' *a.* ancient

ag·gran'dize *v.* to increase in power, riches, etc. —**ag·gran'dize·ment** *n.*

ag'gra·vate' *v.* **1** make worse **2** [Inf.] vex; annoy —**ag'gra·va'tion** *n.*

ag'gre·gate (-gət; *v.:* -gāt') *a., n., v.* total; mass —**ag'gre·ga'tion** *n.*

ag·gres'sion *n.* unprovoked attack —**ag·gres'sor** *n.*

ag·gres'sive *a.* **1** quarrelsome **2** bold and active —**ag·gres'sive·ly** *adv.*

ag·grieve' *v.* offend

a·ghast' (-gast') *a.* horrified

ag·ile (aj'əl) *a.* quick; nimble —**a·gil'i·ty** (-jil'-) *n.*

a·glow' *adv., a.* in a glow

ag·nos'tic *n.* one who doubts the existence of God —**ag·nos'ti·cism** *n.*

a·go' *adv., a.* (in the) past

a·gog' *a.* eager; excited

ag'o·nize' *v.* cause or be in agony

ag'o·ny *n.* great suffering

a·go'ra·pho'bi·a *n.* fear of being in public places

a·grar'i·an *a.* of land and farming

a·gree' *v.* **1** to consent **2** be in harmony or accord —**a·gree'ment** *n.*

a·gree'a·ble *a.* **1** pleasing **2** willing to consent

ag'ri·cul'ture *n.* farming —**ag'ri·cul'tur·al** *a.*

a·gron'o·my *n.* science, etc. of crop production —**a·gron'o·mist** *n.*

a·ground' *adv., a.* on or onto the shore, a reef, etc.

a·gue (ā'gyōō) *n.* fever with chills

ah *int.* cry of pain, delight, etc.

a·ha' *int.* cry of satisfaction, triumph, etc.

a·head' *adv., a.* in front; forward; in advance

a·hoy' *int. Naut.* hailing call

aid *v., n.* help

aide *n.* **1** assistant **2** military officer assisting a superior: also **aide'-de-camp'**, *pl.* **aides'-**

AIDS *n.* viral condition resulting in infections, cancer, etc.

ail *v.* **1** to pain **2** be ill

ai'le·ron' (ā'-) *n.* hinged flap of an airplane wing

ail'ment *n.* chronic illness

aim *v.* **1** direct (a gun, blow, etc.) **2** intend —*n.* **1** an aiming **2** direction of aiming **3** intention; goal —**aim'less** *a.*

ain't *contr.* **1** [Inf.] am not **2** [Dial.] is not; are not; has not; have not

air *n.* **1** mixture of gases around the earth **2** appearance **3** *pl.* haughty manners **4** song or tune —*v.* **1** let air into **2** publicize —*a.* of aviation —**on the air** broadcasting on TV or radio

air bag *n.* inflatable bag to protect passenger in auto accident

air base *n.* base for military aircraft

air'borne' *a.* **1** carried in the air **2** aloft

air conditioning *n.* controlling of humidity and temperature of air in a room, etc. —**air'-con·di'tion** *v.* —**air conditioner** *n.*

air'craft' *n., pl.* **-craft'** machine or machines for flying

Aire'dale (er'-) *n.* large terrier with a wiry coat

air'fare' *n.* transportation charge on airplane

air'field' *n.* field where aircraft can take off and land

air force *n.* aviation branch of a country's armed forces

air'freight' *n.* airplane freight

air'head' *n.* [Sl.] silly, ignorant person

air lane *n.* route for air travel

air'lift' *n.* the transporting of troops, supplies, etc. by aircraft —*v.* transport by airlift

air'line' *n.* air transport system or company

air'lin'er *n.* large, passenger aircraft of an airline

air'mail' n. mail transported by aircraft

air'man n., pl. **-men** 1 aviator 2 enlisted person in U.S. Air Force

air'plane' n. motor-driven or jet-propelled aircraft

air'play' n. broadcast of a recording

air'port' n. airfield with facilities for repair, etc.

air pressure n. pressure of the atmosphere or of compressed air

air raid n. attack by aircraft

air rifle n. rifle operated by compressed air

air'ship' n. steerable aircraft that is lighter than air

air'sick' a. nauseated because of air travel

air'tight' a. too tight for air to enter or escape

air'way' n. air lane

air'y a. **-i·er, -i·est** 1 open to the air 2 flimsy as air 3 light; graceful 4 light-hearted —**air'i·ly** adv.

aisle (īl) n. passageway between rows of seats

a·jar' adv., a. slightly open

AK abbrev. Alaska

aka abbrev. also known as

a·kim'bo adv., a. with hands on hips

a·kin' a. similar; alike

AL abbrev. Alabama

-al suf. 1 of; like; fit for 2 act or process of

al'a·bas'ter n. whitish, translucent gypsum

a' la carte' adv., a. with a separate price for each dish

a·lac'ri·ty n. quick willingness; readiness

a' la mode' adv., a. 1 in fashion 2 served with ice cream

a·larm' n. 1 signal or device to warn or waken 2 fear —v. to frighten

alarm clock n. clock with a device that sounds at a set time

a·larm'ist n. one who expresses needless alarm

a·las' int. cry of sorrow, etc.

alb n. priest's white robe

al'ba·core' n. kind of tuna

al'ba·tross' n. large, web-footed seabird

al·be'it (ôl-) con. although

al·bi'no (-bī'-) n., pl. **-nos** individual lacking normal coloration

al'bum n. blank book for photographs, stamps, etc.

al·bu'men (-byōō'-) n. white of an egg

al·bu'min n. protein in egg, milk, muscle, etc.

al'che·my (-kə-) n. chemistry of the Middle Ages —**al'che·mist** n.

al'co·hol' n. colorless, intoxicating liquid obtained from fermented grain, fruit, etc.

al'co·hol'ic a. of alcohol —n. one addicted to alcohol

al'co·hol·ism' n. addiction to alcohol

al'cove' n. recess; nook

al'der (ôl'-) n. small tree of the birch family

al'der·man n., pl. **-men** member of a city council

ale n. kind of beer

a·lert' a. watchful; ready —n. an alarm —v. warn to be ready —**a·lert'ness** n.

al·fal'fa n. plant used for fodder, etc.

al'gae (-jē') pl.n. primitive water plants

al'ge·bra n. mathematics using letters and numbers in equations —**al'ge·bra'ic** a.

a'li·as n. assumed name —adv. otherwise named

al'i·bi' (-bī') n., pl. **-bis'** 1 plea that the accused was not at the scene of the crime 2 [Inf.] any excuse —v. [Inf.] give an excuse

al'ien (āl'yən, ā'lē ən) a. foreign —n. 1 foreigner 2 creature from another planet

al'ien·ate' v. make unfriendly —**al'ien·a'tion** n.

a·light' v. 1 dismount 2 land after flight —a. lighted up

a·lign' (-līn') v. 1 line up 2 make agree —**a·lign'ment** n.

a·like' a. similar —adv. 1 similarly 2 equally

al'i·men'ta·ry canal n. the passage in the body that food goes through

al'i·mo'ny n. money paid to support one's former spouse

a·live' a. 1 living; in existence 2 lively —**alive with** teeming with

al·ka·li' (-lī') n., pl. **-lies'** or **-lis'** substance that neutralizes acids —**al'ka·line'** a. —**al'ka·lin'i·ty** n. —**al'ka·lize'** v.

al'ka·loid n. alkaline drug from plants

al'kyd (-kid') n. synthetic resin used in paints, etc.

all a. 1 the whole of 2 every one of 3 complete —pron. 1 [pl. v.] everyone 2 everything 3 every bit —n. 1 everything one has 2 the whole amount —adv. entirely —**after all** nevertheless —**at all** in any way

all- pref. 1 entirely 2 for every 3 of everything

Al·lah (ä′lə) *n.* God: Muslim name

all′-A·mer′i·can *a.* chosen as the best in the U.S. —*n.* all-American team player

all′-a·round′ *a.* having many abilities, uses, etc.

al·lay′ *v.* to calm; quiet

all′-clear′ *n.* siren or signal that an air raid is over

al·lege′ *v.* declare, esp. without proof —**al′le·ga′tion** *n.* —**al·leg′ed·ly** *adv.*

al·le′giance (-lē′jəns) *n.* loyalty, as to one's country

al·le·go′ry *n., pl.* **-ries** story in which things, actions, etc. are symbolic —**al′le·gor′i·cal** *a.*

al·le·gret′to *a., adv. Mus.* moderately fast

al·le·gro (-lě′-) *a., adv. Mus.* fast

al·le·lu′ia (- yə) *int., n.* hallelujah

al′ler·gen *n.* allergy-causing substance —**al′ler·gen′ic** *a.*

al′ler·gy *n., pl.* **-gies** sensitive reaction to certain food, pollen, etc. —**al·ler′gic** *a.*

al·le′vi·ate′ *v.* relieve; ease —**al·le′vi·a′tion** *n.*

al′ley *n., pl.* **-leys** 1 narrow street 2 bowling lane

al·li′ance (-lī′-) *n.* 1 an allying 2 association; league

al·lied′ *a.* 1 united by treaty, etc. 2 related

al′li·ga′tor *n.* large lizard like a crocodile

alligator clip *n.* fastening device with spring-loaded jaws

alligator pear *n.* avocado

all′-im·por′tant *a.* necessary

all′-in·clu′sive *a.* comprehensive

al·lit·er·a′tion *n.* use of the same initial sound in a series of words

al′lo·cate′ *v.* allot —**al′lo·ca′tion** *n.*

al·lot′ *v.* **-lot′ted, -lot′ting** 1 distribute in shares 2 assign —**al·lot′ment** *n.*

all′-out′ *a.* thorough

all′o′ver *a.* over the whole surface

al·low′ *v.* 1 to permit 2 let have 3 grant —**allow for** leave room, time, etc. for —**al·low′a·ble** *a.*

al·low′ance *n.* 1 thing allowed 2 amount given regularly

al′loy (*v.*: ə loi′) *n.* metal mixture —*v.* mix (metals)

all′-pur′pose *a.* useful in many ways

all right *a.* 1 satisfactory 2 unhurt 3 correct —*adv.* yes

all′spice′ *n.* pungent spice from a berry

all′-star′ *a.* made up of star performers —*n.* member of an all-star team

all′-time′ *a.* unsurpassed up to the present time

al·lude′ *v.* refer (*to*)

al·lure′ *v.* tempt; attract —*n.* fascination —**al·lur′ing** *a.*

al·lu′sion *n.* indirect or casual mention —**al·lu′sive** *a.*

al·ly (ə lī′; *n.*: al′ī) *v.* **-lied′, -ly′ing** unite; join —*n., pl.* **-lies** country or person joined with another

al′ma ma′ter (mät′ər) *n.* college or school that one attended

al′ma·nac′ *n.* 1 calendar with miscellaneous data 2 book published annually, with statistical information

al·might′y *a.* all-powerful —**the Almighty** God

al·mond (ä′mənd, ôl′-) *n.* edible, nutlike, oval seed of a tree of the rose family

al′most′ *adv.* very nearly

alms (ämz) *n.* money, food, etc. given to the poor

al·oe′ (-ō′) *n.* African plant whose juice is used in ointments, etc.

a·loft′ *adv.* high up

a·lo·ha (ä lō′hä) *n., int.* love: Hawaiian "hello" or "goodbye"

a·lone′ *a., adv.* with no other —**let alone** not to mention

a·long′ *prep.* on or beside the length of —*adv.* 1 onward 2 together (*with*) 3 with one —**all along** from the beginning —**get along** manage

a·long′side′ *adv.* at the side —*prep.* beside

a·loof′ (-loof′) *adv.* apart —*a.* cool and reserved

a·loud′ *adv.* loudly

al·pac′a *n.* 1 kind of llama 2 cloth from its long, silky wool

al′pha *n.* first letter of the Greek alphabet

al′pha·bet′ *n.* letters of a language, in the regular order —**al′pha·bet′i·cal** *a.*

al′pha·bet·ize′ *v.* arrange in alphabetical order

al′pha·nu·mer′ic *a.* having numbers and letters

alpha particle *n.* a positively charged particle given off by a radioactive substance

alpha ray *n.* stream of alpha particles

al·read′y *adv.* by or before the given time; previously

al′so *adv.* in addition; too

al′so-ran′ *n.* [Inf.] defeated contestant in a race, etc.

alt *abbrev.* 1 alternate 2 altitude

al′tar *n.* table, etc. for sacred rites, as in a church

altar boy n. boy or man who helps a priest at religious services, esp. at Mass

al'ter v. change; modify —**al'ter·a'tion** n.

al·ter·ca'tion n. a quarrel

alter ego n. 1 one's other self 2 constant companion

al'ter·nate (-nət; v.: -nāt') a. 1 succeeding each other 2 every other —n. a substitute —v. do, use, act, etc. by turns —**al'ter·na'tion** n.

alternating current n. electric current that reverses its direction

al·ter'na·tive n. choice between two or more —a. giving such a choice

al'ter·na'tor n. generator producing alternating current

al·though' con. in spite of the fact that

al·tim'e·ter (al-) n. instrument for measuring altitude

al'ti·tude' n. height, esp. above sea level

al'to n., pl. **-tos** lowest female voice

al'to·geth'er adv. wholly

al'tru·ism' (al'-) n. unselfish concern for others —**al'tru·ist** n. —**al'tru·is'tic** a.

al'um n. astringent salt

a·lu'mi·num n. silvery, lightweight metal, a chemical element: also [Br.] **al'u·min'i·um**

a·lum'nus n., pl. **-ni** (-nī') former student of a certain school or college —**a·lum'na** n.fem., pl. **-nae** (-nē)

al'ways adv. 1 at all times 2 continually

Alz·hei·mer's disease (älts'hī'mərz) n. disease causing degeneration of brain cells

am v. pres. t. of BE: used with I

Am abbrev. America(n)

AM n. long-distance broadcasting by amplitude modulation

AM abbrev. 1 before noon: also **A.M.**, **a.m.**, **am** 2 amplitude modulation 3 Master of Arts: also **A.M.**

AMA abbrev. American Medical Association

a·mal'gam (-gəm) n. alloy of mercury and another metal

a·mal'ga·mate' v. unite —**a·mal'ga·ma'tion** n.

a·man·u·en'sis (-yoo͞-) n., pl. **-ses** (-sēz) a secretary: now used jokingly

am'a·ranth' n. plant with showy flowers

am'a·ryl'lis (-ril'-) n. bulb plant with lilylike flowers

a·mass' v. pile up; collect

am'a·teur (-chər, -tər) n. 1 one who does something for pleasure, not pay 2 unskillful person —**am'a·teur·ish** a.

am'a·to'ry a. of love

a·maze' v. astonish; surprise —**a·maze'ment** n.

am'a·zon' n. strong woman

am·bas'sa·dor n. top-ranking diplomatic official —**am·bas'sa·dor·ship'** n.

am'ber n. 1 yellowish fossil resin 2 its color

am'ber·gris' (-grēs') n. waxy secretion of certain whales, used in perfumes

am·bi·dex'trous a. using both hands with equal ease

am'bi·ence n. milieu; environment: also **am'bi·ance**

am'bi·ent a. surrounding

am·big'u·ous a. having two or more meanings; vague —**am·bi·gu'i·ty** n., pl. **-ties**

am·bi'tion n. 1 desire to succeed 2 success desired —**am·bi'tious** a.

am·biv'a·lence n. simultaneous conflicting feelings —**am·biv'a·lent** a.

am'ble v. move at an easy gait —n. easy gait

am·bro'sia (-zhə) n. Gr. & Rom. myth. food of the gods

am'bu·lance n. vehicle to carry sick or wounded

am'bu·late' v. walk

am'bu·la·to'ry a. 1 of walking 2 able to walk

am'bus·cade' n., v. ambush

am'bush' n. 1 a hiding for a surprise attack 2 the hiding place or group 3 surprise attack —v. to attack from hiding

a·me'ba n., pl. **-bas** or **-bae** (-bē) amoeba

a·mel'io·rate' (-mēl'yə-) v. improve —**a·mel'io·ra'tion** n.

a'men' int. may it be so

a·me'na·ble (-mē'nə-, -men'ə-) a. willing to obey or heed advice; responsive —**a·me'na·bly** adv.

a·mend' v. 1 to correct 2 improve 3 revise, as a law —**a·mend'ment** n.

a·mends' pl.n. a making up for injury, loss, etc.

a·men'i·ty n., pl. **-ties** 1 pleasantness 2 pl. courtesies 3 convenience

a·ment' n. spike of small flowers, as on a willow; catkin

A·mer'i·can a. 1 of America 2 of the U.S. —n. 1 native of America 2 U.S. citizen

American Indian n., a. INDIAN (sense 2)

A·mer'i·can·ism' n. 1 U.S. custom 2 word or idiom originating in American English **3** devotion to the U.S.

A·mer'i·can·ize' v. make or become American

American plan n. hotel billing in which the rate covers room and meals

am'e·thyst (-thist) n. purple quartz for jewelry

a'mi·a·ble a. good-natured; friendly

am'i·ca·ble a. friendly; peaceable — **am'i·ca·bly** adv.

a·mid', a·midst' prep. among

a·mid'ships adv., a. in or toward the middle of a ship

a·mi'go n., pl. **-gos** friend

a·mi'no acid (-mē'-) n. any of several basic building blocks of protein

Am'ish (äm'-) a., n. (of) a Christian sect favoring plain living

a·miss' adv., a. wrong

am'i·ty n. friendship

am·me'ter n. instrument for measuring amperes

am'mo n. [Sl.] ammunition

am·mo'ni·a n. **1** acrid gas **2** water solution of it

am'mu·ni'tion n. bullets, gunpowder, bombs, etc.

am·ne'sia (-zhə) n. loss of memory

am'nes·ty n. general pardon for political offenses

am'ni·o·cen·te'sis n. extracting fluid (**am'ni·ot'ic fluid**) from a pregnant woman

a·moe'ba (-mē-) n., pl. **-bas** or **-bae** (-bē) one-celled animal — **a·moe'bic** a.

a·mok' (-muk') a., adv. used chiefly in **run amok**, lose control and behave violently

a·mong', a·mongst' prep. **1** surrounded by **2** in the group of **3** to or for each of

a·mon·til·la'do (-lä'-) n. pale, rather dry sherry

a·mor'al (ā-) a. with no moral sense or standards

am'o·rous a. **1** fond of making love **2** full of love

a·mor'phous a. **1** shapeless **2** of no definite type

am'or·tize' v. provide for gradual payment of — **am'or·ti·za'tion** n.

a·mount' v. **1** add up (to) **2** be equal (to) — n. **1** sum **2** quantity

a·mour' (-mōor') n. love affair

am'per·age n. strength of an electric current in amperes

am'pere (-pir') n. unit of electric current

am'per·sand' n. sign (&) meaning and

am·phet'a·mine (-mēn', min) n. drug used as a stimulant and to lessen

appetite

am·phib'i·an n. **1** land-and-water animal, as the frog **2** land-and-water vehicle — a. amphibious

am·phib'i·ous a. adapted to both land and water

am'phi·the'a·ter, am'phi·the'a·tre n. open theater with central space circled by tiers of seats

am'ple a. **1** large **2** adequate — **am'ply** adv.

am'pli·fy' v. **-fied', -fy'ing** make stronger, louder, or fuller — **am'pli·fi·ca'tion** n. — **am'pli·fi'er** n.

am'pli·tude' n. **1** extent or breadth **2** abundance

amplitude modulation n. changing of the amplitude of the radio wave according to the signal being broadcast

am'pul' n. small container for a dose of medicine to be injected: also **am'pule'** or **am'poule'**

am'pu·tate' v. to cut off, esp. by surgery — **am'pu·ta'tion** n.

am'pu·tee' n. one who has had a limb amputated

a·muck' n. amok

am'u·let (-yə-) n. charm worn against evil

a·muse' v. **1** entertain **2** make laugh — **a·mus'ing** a. — **a·muse'ment** n.

amusement park n. entertainment area with rides, food, etc.

am'yl·ase' (-ə lās') n. enzyme that helps change starch into sugar, found in saliva

an a., indefinite article **1** one **2** each; any one

-an suf. **1** of **2** born in; living in **3** believing in

a·nach'ro·nism' (-nak'-) n. thing out of proper historical time — **a·nach'ro·nis'tic** a.

an'a·con'da n. large South American boa snake

an·aer·o'bic (-ər-) a. able to live without air or free oxygen, as some bacteria

an'a·gram' n. word made by rearranging the letters of another word

a'nal a. of the anus

an'al·ge'sic (-jē'zik) n., a. (drug) that eases pain

an'a·log' a. **1** of electronic equipment, recordings, etc. in which the signal corresponds to physical change **2** using hands, dials, etc. to show number amounts

an'a·logue' n. something analogous

a·nal'o·gy n., pl. **-gies** similarity in

some ways —a·nal'o·gous (-gəs) a.

a·nal'y·sis n., pl. -ses' (-sēz') 1 separation of a whole into its parts to find out their nature, etc. 2 psychoanalysis —an'a·lyst (-list) n. —an'a·lyt'ic, an'a·lyt'i·cal a. —an'a·lyze' v.

an'ar·chism' (-kiz'əm) n. opposition to all government —an'ar·chist' n.

an'ar·chy n. 1 absence of government and law 2 great disorder —an·ar'chic a.

a·nath'e·ma n. 1 person or thing accursed or detested 2 ritual curse —a·nath'e·ma·tize' v.

a·nat'o·mize' v. 1 dissect, as animals 2 analyze

a·nat'o·my n. 1 science of plant or animal structure 2 structure of an organism —an'a·tom'i·cal a.

-ance suf. 1 action or state of 2 a thing that (is)

an'ces·tor n. person from whom one is descended —an'ces·tress n.fem.

an'ces·try n. 1 family descent 2 all one's ancestors —an·ces'tral a.

an'chor n. 1 metal weight lowered from a ship to prevent drifting 2 one who anchors a newscast: also an'chor·man', pl. -men', or an'chor·wom·an', pl. -wom·en, or an'chor·per·son —v. 1 hold secure 2 coordinate and report (a newscast) —at anchor anchored —an'chor·age n.

an'cho·rite' (-kə-) n. hermit

an'cho·vy (-chō'-) n., pl. -vies tiny fish used as a relish

an·cient (ān'chənt, -shənt) a. 1 of times long past 2 very old —the ancients people of ancient times

an'cil·lar·y a. auxiliary

and con. 1 also 2 plus 3 as a result

an·dan·te (än dän'tā) a., adv. Mus. moderately slow

and'i·ron n. either of a pair of metal supports for logs in a fireplace

an'dro·gen n. male sex hormone

an·drog'y·nous (-dräj'ə-) a. 1 blending male and female characteristics 2 unisex

an'droid' n. fictional, human-looking robot

an'ec·dot'al a. based on personal experience

an'ec·dote' n. brief story

a·ne'mi·a n. deficiency of red blood cells —a·ne'mic a.

an·e·mom'e·ter n. gauge measuring wind velocity

a·nem'o·ne' (-nē') n. plant with cup-shaped flowers

a·nent' prep. [Now Rare] concerning

an·es·the'si·a (-zhə) n. loss of the sense of pain, touch, etc.

an·es·the'si·ol'o·gist (-zē-) n. doctor specializing in giving anesthetics

an·es·thet'ic n., a. (drug, gas, etc.) that produces anesthesia —an·es'the·tist n. —an·es'the·tize' v.

an'eu·rysm', an'eu·rism' (-yōō riz'əm) n. sac formed by swelling in an artery wall

a·new' adv. 1 once more 2 in a new way

an·gel (ān'jəl) n. messenger of God, pictured with wings and halo —an·gel'ic (an-) a.

an'gel·fish' n. spiny-finned, bright-colored tropical fish

angel (food) cake n. light, spongy white cake

an'ger n. hostile feeling; wrath —v. make angry

an·gi'na pec'to·ris (-jī'-) n. heart disease with chest pains

an'gi·o·plas'ty (-jē-) n. technique for repairing blood vessels

an'gle n. 1 space formed by two lines or surfaces that meet 2 point of view —v. 1 bend at an angle 2 fish with hook and line 3 use tricks to get something —an'gler n.

angle iron n. piece of iron bent at a right angle, for joining two beams, etc.

an'gle·worm' n. earthworm

An'gli·can n., a. (member) of the Church of England

An'gli·cize' v. make English in form, sound, customs, etc.

Anglo- pref. English (and)

An'glo–Sax'on n. 1 native of England before 12th c. 2 person of English descent 3 Old English

An·go'ra n. wool from longhaired goat or rabbit

an'gry a. -gri·er, -gri·est 1 feeling anger; enraged 2 stormy —an'gri·ly adv.

ang'strom n. unit for measuring length of light waves: also angstrom unit

an'guish n. great pain, worry, etc. —v. feel or make feel anguish

an'gu·lar a. having angles —an'gu·lar'i·ty n.

an'i·line (-lin) n. oily liquid made from benzene, used in dyes, etc.

an'i·mad·ver'sion n. criticism

an'i·mal n. 1 living organism able to move about 2 any four-footed creature —a. 1 of an animal 2 bestial

an'i·mate' (-māt'; a.: -mət) v. 1 give

life to **2** make lively —*a.* **1** living **2** lively —**an'i·mat·ed** *a.* —**an'i·ma'tion** *n.* —**an'i·ma'tor** *n.*

animated cartoon *n.* movie made by filming a series of cartoons

an'i·mism *n.* belief that all things in nature have souls —**an'i·mis'tic** *a.*

an·i·mos'i·ty *n.* strong hatred; ill will

an'i·mus *n.* ill will

an'ise (-is) *n.* plant whose seed is used as flavoring

an'i·sette' (-zet', -set') *n.* a sweet, anise-flavored liqueur

ankh (aŋk, äŋk) *n.* cross with a loop at the top, ancient Egyptian symbol of life

an'kle *n.* joint connecting foot and leg

an'klet *n.* short sock

an'nals *pl.n.* historical records, year by year

an·neal' *v.* toughen (glass or metal) by heating and then cooling slowly

an'ne·lid *n.* any worm with a body of joined segments, as the earthworm

an·nex' (ə neks'; *n.*: an'eks) *v.* attach or join to a larger unit —*n.* something annexed —**an'nex·a'tion** *n.*

an·ni'hi·late' (-nī'ə-) *v.* destroy —**an·ni·hi·la'tion** *n.*

an'ni·ver'sa·ry *n., pl.* **-ries** yearly return of the date of some event

an'no·tate' *v.* provide explanatory notes for —**an'no·ta'tion** *n.*

an·nounce' *v.* make known; tell about —**an·nounce'ment** *n.* —**an·nounc'er** *n.*

an·noy' *v.* to bother or anger —**an·noy'ance** *n.*

an'nu·al *a.* yearly —*n.* **1** plant living one year **2** yearbook —**an'nu·al·ly** *adv.*

an·nu'i·ty *n., pl.* **-ties** investment yielding fixed annual payments

an·nul' *v.* **-nulled', -nul'ling** make null and void —**an·nul'ment** *n.*

an·nun·ci·a'tion *n.* **1** an announcing **2** [A-] announcement to Mary, mother of Jesus, that she would bear Jesus

an'ode *n.* positive electrode

an'o·dize *v.* put a protective oxide film on (a metal) by an electrolytic process

an'o·dyne' (-dīn') *n.* anything that relieves pain

a·noint' *v.* put oil on, as in consecrating

a·nom'a·ly *n., pl.* **-lies** unusual or irregular thing —**a·nom'a·lous** *a.*

a·non' *adv.* [Ar.] **1** soon **2** at another time

Anon, anon *abbrev.* anonymous

a·non'y·mous (-ə məs) *a.* with name unknown or withheld; unidentified —**an'o·nym'i·ty** (-nim'-) *n.*

a·noph'e·les' (-lēz') *n.* mosquito that can transmit malaria

an'o·rex'i·a *n.* ailment characterized by aversion to food —**an'o·rex'ic** *a.*

an·oth'er *a., pron.* **1** one more **2** a different (one)

an'swer (-sər) *n.* **1** thing said or done in return; reply **2** solution to a problem —*v.* **1** reply (to) **2** serve or fulfill **3** suit **4** be responsible —**an'swer·a·ble** *a.*

ant *n.* small insect living in colonies

-ant *suf.* **1** that has, shows, or does **2** one that

ant·ac'id *n., a.* (substance) counteracting acids

an·tag'o·nism' *n.* hostility —**an·tag'o·nis'tic** *a.*

an·tag'o·nist *n.* opponent

an·tag'o·nize' *v.* incur the dislike of

ant·arc'tic *a.* of or near the South Pole —*n.* [A-] antarctic region

an'te (-tē) *n.* player's stake in poker —*v.* **-ted** or **-teed, -te·ing** put in one's stake

ante- *pref.* before

ant'eat'er *n.* long-snouted mammal that feeds on ants

an'te·bel'lum *a.* before the war

an'te·ce'dent *a.* coming before; prior —*n.* **1** thing prior to another **2** word or phrase to which a pronoun refers

an'te·cham'ber *n.* room leading to larger room

an'te·date' *v.* occur before

an'te·di·lu'vi·an *a.* **1** before the Biblical Flood **2** outmoded

an'te·lope' *n.* horned animal like the deer

an·ten'na *n., pl.* **-nae** (-ē) or **-nas 1** feeler on the head of an insect, etc. **2** *pl.* **-nas** device of wires, etc. for sending and receiving radio waves

an·te'ri·or *a.* **1** toward the front **2** earlier

an'te·room' *n.* room leading to another room

an'them *n.* religious or patriotic choral song

an'ther *n.* pollen-bearing part of a stamen

an·thol'o·gize' *v.* include in an anthology

an·thol'o·gy *n., pl.* **-gies** collection of poems, stories, etc. —**an·thol'o·gist** *n.*

an'thra·cite' *n.* hard coal

an'thrax' *n.* disease of cattle

an'thro·poid' *a.* resembling a human

—*n.* an anthropoid ape

an·thro·pol·o·gy *n.* study of the human race, including physical types, cultures, customs, etc. —**an'thro·pol·o·gist** *n.*

an·thro·po·mor'phism' *n.* an attributing of human qualities to animals or things —**an'thro·po·mor'phic** *a.*

an'ti *n., pl.* **-tis** [Inf.] a person opposed to something —*prep.* [Inf.] opposed to

anti- *pref.* **1** against **2** that acts against

an'ti·air'craft' *a.* used against hostile aircraft

an'ti·bal·lis'tic missile *n.* ballistic missile for stopping enemy ballistic missile

an'ti·bi·ot'ic *n.* substance produced by some microorganisms, able to kill or weaken bacteria

an'ti·bod·y *n., pl.* **-ies** substance produced in the body to act against toxins, etc.

an'tic *n.* silly act; prank

an·tic'i·pate (-tis'-) *v.* **1** expect **2** act on before —**an·tic'i·pa'tion** *n.*

an'ti·cli'max' *n.* sudden drop from the important to the trivial —**an'ti·cli·mac'tic** *a.*

an'ti·co·ag'u·lant *n.* drug that delays or prevents the clotting of blood

an'ti·de·pres'sant *n.* drug that lessens emotional depression

an'ti·dote' *n.* remedy to counteract a poison or evil

an'ti·freeze' *n.* substance used to prevent freezing

an'ti·gen *n.* substance to which the body reacts by producing antibodies

an'ti·he'ro *n.* unheroic protagonist of a novel, etc.

an'ti·his'ta·mine' (-mēn') *n.* drug used to treat allergies

an'ti·knock' *n.* substance added to fuel of internal-combustion engines to do away with noise of too rapid combustion

an'ti·ma·cas'sar (-mə kas'ər) *n.* small cover for the back of a chair, etc.

an'ti·mat·ter *n.* matter in which the electrical charge of each particle is the reverse of that in usual matter

an'ti·mo'ny *n.* silvery metal in alloys, a chemical element

an'ti·par'ti·cle *n.* any particle of antimatter

an'ti·pas'to (-päs'-) *n.* appetizer of spicy meat, fish, etc.

an·tip'a·thy *n., pl.* **-thies** strong dislike

an'ti·per·son·nel' *a.* meant to destroy

people rather than buildings or objects

an'ti·per'spi·rant *n.* skin lotion, cream, etc. for reducing perspiration

an·tiph'o·nal *a.* sung in responsive, alternating parts

an·tip'o·des' (-dēz') *pl.n.* opposite places on the earth

an'ti·quar'i·an (-kwer'-) *a.* of antiques or antiquaries —*n.* antiquary

an'ti·quar·y *n., pl.* **-ies** collector or student of antiquities

an'ti·quat'ed *a.* obsolete, old-fashioned, etc.

an·tique' (-tēk') *a.* **1** of a former period **2** out-of-date —*n.* piece of furniture, etc. from earlier times

an·tiq'ui·ty (-tik'wə-) *n.* **1** ancient times **2** great age **3** *pl.* **-ties** ancient relic, etc.

an'ti·Sem'i·tism' *n.* prejudice against Jews —**an'ti·Sem'ite'** *n.* —**an'ti·Se·mit'ic** *a.*

an'ti·sep'tic *a.* preventing infection by killing germs —*n.* antiseptic substance

an'ti·slav'er·y *a.* against slavery

an'ti·so'cial *a.* **1** not sociable **2** harmful to society

an'ti·tank' *a.* for use against tanks in war

an·tith'e·sis *n., pl.* **-ses** (-sēz') exact opposite —**an'ti·thet'i·cal** *a.*

an'ti·tox'in *n.* serum that counteracts a disease

an'ti·trust' *a.* regulating business trusts

an'ti·viv'i·sec'tion·ist *n.* one opposing vivisection

ant'ler *n.* branched horn of a deer, elk, etc.

an'to·nym' (-nim') *n.* word opposite in meaning to another

a'nus *n.* opening at lower end of the alimentary canal

an'vil *n.* block on which metal objects are hammered

anx·i'e·ty (aŋ zī'-) *n., pl.* **-ties** worry about what may happen

anx·ious (aŋk'shəs) *a.* **1** worried **2** eagerly wishing —**anx'ious·ly** *adv.*

an'y *a.* **1** one of more than two **2** some **3** every —*pron.* [*sing. or pl. v.*] any person(s) or amount —*adv.* at all

an'y·bod'y *pron.* any person; anyone

an'y·how' *adv.* **1** in any way **2** in any case

an'y·one' *pron.* any person; anybody

an'y·thing' *pron.* any thing — anything but not at all

an'y·time' *adv.* at any time —*con.*

whenever

an'y·way' *adv.* anyhow

an'y·where' *adv.* in, at, or to any place

A-OK *a.* [Inf.] excellent, fine, etc.: also **A'-O·kay'**

A one *a.* [Inf.] superior; first-class: also **A1, A number 1**

a·or'ta (ā-) *n.* main artery leading from the heart

a·pace' *adv.* swiftly

A·pach'e (-ē) *n.* member of an Indian people of SW U.S.

a·part' *adv.* 1 aside 2 away from (one) another 3 into pieces —*a.* separated

a·part'heid' (-pär'tāt', -tīt') *n.* strict racial segregation as formerly practiced in South Africa

a·part'ment *n.* room or set of rooms to live in

ap'a·thy *n.* lack of feeling or interest —**ap·a·thet'ic** *a.*

ape *n.* large, tailless monkey —*v.* imitate

a·pe'ri·tif' (-tēf') *n.* alcoholic drink before a meal

ap'er·ture (-chər) *n.* opening

a'pex *n.* highest point

a·pha'si·a (-zhə) *n.* loss of power to use or understand words

a·phid (ā'fid, af'id) *n.* insect that sucks the juices of plants

aph'o·rism' *n.* wise saying

aph'ro·dis'i·ac' (-de'zē-, -diz'ē-) *n., a.* (drug, etc.) arousing sexual desire

a'pi·ar·y *n., pl.* **-ies** collection of beehives

a·piece' *adv.* for each one

a·plen'ty *a., adv.* [Inf.] in abundance

a·plomb' (ə pläm') *n.* poise

a·poc'a·lypse' (-lips') *n.* total devastation, as doomsday —**a·poc'a·lyp'tic** *a.*

a·poc'ry·phal (-rə fəl) *a.* of doubtful authenticity

ap'o·gee' *n.* point farthest from earth in a satellite's orbit

a'po·lit'i·cal (ā'-) *a.* not concerned with political matters —**a'po·lit'i·cal·ly** *adv.*

A·pol'lo *n.* 1 Gr. and Rom. god of music, etc. 2 handsome young man

a·pol'o·gist *n.* defender of a doctrine, action, etc.

a·pol'o·gy *n., pl.* **-gies** 1 expression of regret for a fault, etc. 2 defense of an idea, etc. —**a·pol'o·get'ic** *a.* —**a·pol'o·gize'** *v.*

ap'o·plex'y *n.* a stroke, or injury to the brain: old-fashioned term —**ap'o·plec'tic** *a.*

a·pos'tate' *n.* one who abandons one's

faith, principles, etc. —**a·pos'ta·sy** *n.*

A·pos'tle (-päs'əl) *n.* 1 any of the disciples of Jesus 2 [a-] leader of a new movement —**ap'os·tol'ic** *a.*

a·pos'tro·phe (-fē) *n.* sign (') indicating omission of letter(s) from a word or the possessive case

a·poth'e·car·y *n., pl.* **-ies** druggist: old-fashioned term

a·poth'e·o'sis *n.* 1 deifying of a person 2 glorification of a person or thing 3 glorified ideal

ap·pall', ap·pal' *v.* **-palled', -pall'ing** to shock or dismay —**ap·pall'ing** *a.*

ap'pa·ra'tus (-rat'əs, -rāt'əs) *n.* 1 tools, etc. for a specific use 2 complex device

ap·par'el *n.* clothes —*v.* clothe; dress

ap·par'ent *a.* 1 obvious; plain 2 seeming —**ap·par'ent·ly** *adv.*

ap'pa·ri'tion *n.* ghost

ap·peal' *n.* 1 request for help 2 attraction 3 request for rehearing by a higher court —*v.* 1 make an appeal 2 be attractive

ap·pear' *v.* 1 come into sight 2 seem 3 come before the public —**ap·pear' ance** *n.*

ap·pease' (-pēz') *v.* to quiet by satisfying —**ap·pease'ment** *n.*

ap·pel'lant *n.* one who appeals to a higher court

ap·pel'late court (-pel'ət) *n.* court handling appeals

ap'pel·la'tion *n.* a name

ap·pend' *v.* add or attach

ap·pend'age *n.* an attached part, as a tail

ap'pen·dec'to·my *n., pl.* **-mies** surgical removal of the appendix

ap·pen·di·ci'tis (-sī'-) *n.* inflammation of the appendix

ap·pen'dix *n., pl.* **-dix·es** or **-di·ces'** (-də sēz') 1 extra material at the end of a book 2 small, closed tube attached to large intestine

ap'per·tain' *v.* pertain

ap'pe·ten·cy *n., pl.* **-cies** appetite

ap'pe·tite' *n.* desire, esp. for food

ap'pe·tiz'ing *a.* stimulating the appetite; savory —**ap'pe·tiz'er** *n.*

ap·plaud' *v.* show approval, esp. by clapping the hands; praise

ap·plause' *n.* approval, esp. by clapping

ap'ple *n.* round, fleshy fruit —**ap'ple·sauce'** *n.*

apple butter *n.* jam made of stewed apples

ap'ple·jack' *n.* brandy distilled from apple cider

ap′ple-pie′ *a.* [Inf.] **1** orderly **2** wholesome

ap·pli′ance *n.* device or machine, esp. for home use

ap′pli·ca·ble *a.* appropriate —**ap′pli·ca·bil′i·ty** *n.*

ap′pli·cant *n.* one who applies, as for a job

ap′pli·ca′tion *n.* **1** an applying **2** thing applied **3** formal request

ap′pli·ca′tor *n.* device for applying medicine, paint, etc.

ap′pli·qué′ (-kā′) *n.* decoration made by attaching one fabric to another

ap·ply′ *v.* **-plied′, -ply′ing 1** to put on **2** put into use **3** devote (oneself) diligently **4** ask formally **5** be relevant —**ap′pli·ca·ble** *a.*

ap·point′ *v.* **1** set (a time, etc.) **2** name to an office —**ap·point·ee′** *n.* —**ap·point′ive** *a.* —**ap·point′ment** *n.*

ap·por′tion *v.* portion out —**ap·por′tion·ment** *n.*

ap′po·site (-zit) *a.* fitting; appropriate

ap′po·si′tion *n.* placing of a word or phrase beside another in explanation —**ap·pos′i·tive** *a.*, *n.*

ap·praise′ *v.* estimate the value of —**ap·prais′al** *n.* —**ap·prais′er** *n.*

ap·pre′ci·a·ble (-shə bəl) *a.* enough to be noticed —**ap·pre′ci·a·bly** *adv.*

ap·pre′ci·ate′ (-shē-) *v.* **1** value; enjoy **2** recognize rightly or gratefully —**ap·pre′ci·a′tion** *n.* —**ap·pre′ci·a·tive** *a.*

ap′pre·hend′ *v.* **1** arrest **2** understand —**ap′pre·hen′sion** *n.*

ap′pre·hen′sive *a.* anxious; uneasy

ap·pren′tice *n.* helper who is being taught a trade —*v.* to place or serve as apprentice —**ap·pren′tice·ship′** *n.*

ap·prise′, ap·prize′ (-prīz′) *v.* inform; notify

ap·proach′ *v.* **1** come nearer (to) **2** speak to —*n.* **1** a coming near **2** way of beginning **3** access

ap′pro·ba′tion *n.* approval

ap·pro′pri·ate′ (-āt′; *a.:* -ət) *v.* **1** take for one's own use **2** set (money) aside for some use —*a.* suitable —**ap·pro′pri·ate·ly** *adv.* —**ap·pro′pri·a′tion** *n.*

ap·prove′ *v.* **1** consent to **2** have a favorable opinion (*of*) —**ap·prov′al** *n.*

ap·prox′i·mate′ (-māt′; *a.:* -mət) *v.* be about the same as —*a.* nearly exact or correct —**ap·prox′i·ma′tion** *n.*

ap·pur′te·nance (-pur′-) *n.* **1** adjunct **2** additional right

Apr *abbrev.* April

APR *abbrev.* annual percentage rate

ap′ri·cot′ (ap′rə-, ā′prə-) *a.* small peachlike fruit

A′pril *n.* fourth month

a′pron *n.* garment worn to protect the front of one's clothing

ap′ro·pos′ (-pō′) *a.* appropriate —*prep.* regarding —**apropos of** regarding

apse (aps) *n.* domed or vaulted projection of a church

apt *a.* **1** fitting; suitable **2** likely (*to*) **3** quick to learn

apt *abbrev.* apartment

ap′ti·tude′ *n.* **1** ability **2** quickness to learn

aq′ua·cul′ture *n.* cultivation of water plants and animals for human use

Aq′ua-Lung′ *trademark* an older type of apparatus for breathing under water —*n.* [*usually* **aqualung**] similar apparatus

aq′ua·ma·rine′ (ak′wə-, äk′wə-) *n.*, *a.* bluish green: also **aq′ua**

aq′ua·naut′ *n.* one who does undersea experiments in a watertight chamber

a·quar′i·um (-kwer′-) *n.* tank, etc. for keeping fish or other water animals

A·quar′i·us *n.* 11th sign of the zodiac

a·quat′ic (-kwat′-, -kwät′-) *a.* **1** living in water **2** taking place in water

aq′ue·duct′ (ak′wə-) *n.* large pipe or channel bringing water from a distance

a′que·ous (ā′kwē-) *a.* of or like water

aqueous humor *n.* watery fluid between the cornea and the lens of the eye

aq′ui·line′ (-līn′, -lin) *a.* curved like an eagle's beak

AR *abbrev.* Arkansas

Ar′ab *n.*, *a.* **1** (native) of Arabia **2** (one) of a people now scattered through lands around Arabia

A·ra′bi·an *a.* of Arabia or the Arabs —*n.* ARAB (*n.* 1)

Ar′a·bic *a.* of the people or language of Arabia, etc. —*n.* this language

Arabic numerals *n.* figures 1, 2, 3, 4, 5, 6, 7, 8, 9, and 0

ar′a·ble *a.* fit for producing crops

a·rach′nid (-rak′-) *n.* small, eight-legged animal, as the spider or mite

ar′bi·ter *n.* one who judges; umpire

ar′bi·trage′ (-träzh′) *n.* simultaneous purchase and sale in two markets

ar′bi·trar′y *a.* using only one's own wishes or whim —**ar′bi·trar′i·ly** *adv.*

ar′bi·trate′ *v.* settle (a dispute) by using or being an arbiter —**ar′bi·tra′tion** *n.* —**ar′bi·tra′tor** *n.*

ar′bor *n.* place shaded by trees, shrubs, or vines

ar·bo′re·al *a.* of, like, or living in trees

ar′bo·re′tum *n.*, *pl.* **-tums** or **-ta** place

where many kinds of trees are grown

ar'bor·vi'tae (-vī'tē) *n.* evergreen tree or shrub

ar·bu'tus (-byoo'-) *n.* evergreen trailing plant

arc *n.* **1** curved line, as part of a circle **2** band of light made by electricity leaping a gap

ar·cade' *n.* **1** covered passage, esp. one lined with shops **2** row of arches or columns

ar·cane' *a.* secret or esoteric

arch *n.* curved support over an opening —*v.* form (as) an arch —*a.* **1** chief **2** mischievous; coy

arch- *pref.* main; principal

ar'chae·ol'o·gy (-kē-) *n.* study of ancient peoples, as by excavation of ruins: also sp. **ar'che·ol'o·gy** — **ar'chae·o·log'i·cal** *a.* —**ar'chae·ol'o·gist** *n.*

ar·cha'ic (-kā'-) *a.* **1** out-of-date **2** now seldom used

arch'an'gel (ärk'-) *n.* angel of high rank

arch'bish'op (ärch'-) *n.* bishop of the highest rank

arch'dea'con *n.* church official ranking just below a bishop

arch'di'o·cese (-sis, -sēz') *n.* diocese headed by an archbishop

arch'duke' *n.* ruling prince

arch'en'e·my *n.* chief enemy

arch'er·y *n.* practice or sport of shooting with bow and arrow —**arch'er** *n.*

ar'che·type' (-kə-) *n.* original model — **ar'che·typ'al, ar'che·typ'i·cal** *a.*

ar'chi·pel'a·go' (-kə-) *n., pl.* **-goes'** or **-gos'** chain of islands in a sea

ar'chi·tect' *n.* one who designs buildings

ar'chi·tec'ture *n.* science of designing and constructing buildings —**ar'chi·tec'tur·al** *a.*

ar'chive' (-kīv') *n. usually pl.* public records or place to store them —**ar'chi·vist** *n.*

arch'way' *n.* passage under an arch

arc lamp *n.* lamp in which light is made by an arc between electrodes

arc'tic *a.* of or near the North Pole —*n.* [A-] arctic region

ar'dent *a.* passionate; enthusiastic — **ar'dent·ly** *adv.*

ar'dor *n.* passion; zeal

ar'du·ous (-jōō-) *a.* laborious or strenuous

are *v. pres. t. of* BE: used with *you*, *we*, or *they*

ar'e·a (er'ē-) *n.* **1** region **2** total surface, measured in square units **3** scope

area code *n.* telephone code number for any of the areas into which U.S. and Canada are divided

a·re'na *n.* **1** center of amphitheater, for contests, shows, etc. **2** area of struggle

arena theater *n.* theater with a central stage surrounded by seats

aren't *contr.* are not

ar'gon *n.* chemical element, gas used in light bulbs, etc.

ar'go·sy *n., pl.* **-sies** [Poet.] large merchant ship or fleet

ar'got (-gō, -gət) *n.* special vocabulary, as of those in the same work

ar'gu·a·ble *a.* supportable by argument —**ar'gu·a·bly** *adv.*

ar·gue *v.* **1** give reasons (*for* or *against*) **2** dispute; debate —**ar'gu·ment** *n.* —**ar'gu·men·ta'tion** *n.* —**ar'gu·men'ta·tive** *a.*

ar'gyle' (-gīl') *a.* knitted or woven in a diamond-shaped pattern

a'ri·a (ä'rē-) *n.* solo in an opera, etc.

-arian *suf.* one of a specified age, belief, work, etc.

ar'id *a.* **1** dry **2** dull —**a·rid'i·ty** *n.*

Ar·ies (er'ēz) *n.* first sign of the zodiac

a·right' *adv.* correctly

a·rise' *v.* **a·rose', a·ris'en** (-riz'-), **a·ris'ing 1** get up; rise **2** come into being

ar·is·toc'ra·cy *n.* **1** government by an upper class minority **2** *pl.* **-cies** upper class —**a·ris'to·crat'** *n.* —**a·ris'to·crat'ic** *a.*

a·rith'me·tic (*a.:* ar'ith met'ik) *n.* science of computing by numbers —*a.* of arithmetic: also **ar'ith·met'i·cal** *a.*

ark *n. Bible* boat in which Noah, etc. survived the Flood

arm *n.* **1** one of two upper limbs of the human body **2** anything like this **3** weapon: *usually used in pl.* **4** branch of the military **5** *pl.* coat of arms —*v.* provide with weapons —**arm in arm** with arms interlocked —**up in arms** indignant —**with open arms** cordially

ar·ma'da (-mä'-) *n.* fleet of warships

ar·ma·dil'lo *n., pl.* **-los** tropical mammal covered with bony plates

Ar'ma·ged'don *n.* (place of) the great battle at doomsday

ar'ma·ments *pl.n.* military forces and equipment

ar'ma·ture *n.* revolving coil in an electric motor or dynamo

arm'chair' *n.* chair with supports for one's arms

armed forces *pl.n.* all the military, naval, and air forces of a country

arm'ful *n.*, *pl.* **-fuls** as much as the arms or one arm can hold

arm'hole' *n.* opening for the arm in a garment

ar'mi·stice (-stis) *n.* truce

arm'let *n.* ornamental band worn on the upper arm

arm'load' *n.* as much as the arms or one arm can hold

ar'mor *n.* protective covering —**ar'mored** *a.*

armored car *n.* vehicle with armor plate, as a truck carrying money to or from a bank

armor plate *n.* protective covering of steel plates

ar'mor·y *n.*, *pl.* **-ies** 1 arsenal 2 military drill hall

arm'pit' *n.* the hollow under the arm at the shoulder

arm'rest' *n.* support for the arm as on inside of car door

ar'my *n.*, *pl.* **-mies** 1 large body of soldiers 2 any very large group

a·ro'ma *n.* pleasant odor —**ar'o·mat'ic** *a.*

a·rose' *v.* pt. of ARISE

a·round' *adv.*, *prep.* 1 in a circle (about) 2 on all sides (of) 3 to the opposite direction (about) [Inf.] near

a·rouse' *v.* wake; stir up

ar·peg'gi·o (-pej'ō) *n.*, *pl.* **-os** chord with notes played in quick succession

ar·raign' (-rān') *v.* 1 bring to court to answer charges 2 accuse —**ar·raign'ment** *n.*

ar·range' *v.* 1 put in a certain order 2 plan 3 adapt (a musical composition) —**ar·range'ment** *n.*

ar'rant (ar'-) *a.* out-and-out

ar'ras (ar'-) *n.* tapestry wall hanging

ar·ray' *v.* 1 place in order 2 dress finely —*n.* 1 an orderly grouping 2 impressive display 3 fine clothes

ar·rears' *pl.n.* overdue debts —**in arrears** behind in payment

ar·rest' *v.* 1 stop or check 2 seize and hold by law 3 catch and keep —*n.* an arresting

ar·rest'ing *a.* interesting

ar·rhyth'mi·a (-rith'-) *n.* irregular heart beat

ar·rive' *v.* 1 reach one's destination 2 come —**ar·riv'al** *n.*

ar'ro·gant *a.* haughty; overbearing —**ar'ro·gance** *n.*

ar'ro·gate' *v.* seize arrogantly

ar'row *n.* 1 pointed shaft shot from a bow 2 sign (←) to show direction

ar'row·head' *n.* pointed tip of an arrow

ar'row·root' *n.* starch from a tropical plant root

ar·roy'o *n.*, *pl.* **-os** 1 dry gully 2 stream

ar'se·nal *n.* place for making or storing weapons

ar'se·nic *n.* silvery-white, poisonous chemical element

ar'son *n.* crime of purposely setting fire to property —**ar'son·ist** *n.*

art *n.* 1 skill; craft 2 aesthetic work, as painting, sculpture, or music 3 *pl.* academic studies 4 cunning; wile —*v.* [Ar.] form of ARE: used with *thou*

art dec'o *n.* decorative style of the 1920s and 1930s

ar·te'ri·o·scle·ro'sis (-tir'ē-) *n.* hardening of the arteries

ar'ter·y *n.*, *pl.* **-ies** 1 blood vessel coming from the heart 2 a main road —**ar·te'ri·al** (-tir'ē-) *a.*

ar·te'sian well (-tē'zhən) *n.* deep well with water forced up by underground water pressure

art film *n.* artistic film not made to appeal to popular tastes

art'ful *a.* 1 skillful; clever 2 crafty; cunning

art house *n.* theater specializing in art films

ar·thri'tis *n.* inflammation of joints —**ar·thrit'ic** *a.*

ar'thro·pod' *n.* invertebrate animal with jointed legs and segmented body

ar'thro·scope' *n.* surgical device for use inside a joint —**ar·thro·scop'ic** *a.*

ar'ti·choke' *n.* 1 thistlelike plant 2 its flower head, cooked as a vegetable

ar'ti·cle *n.* 1 single item 2 separate piece of writing, as in a magazine 3 section of a document 4 any of the words *a*, *an*, or *the*

ar·tic'u·late' (-lāt'; *a.*: -lət) *v.* 1 speak clearly 2 put together by joints —*a.* 1 clear in speech 2 jointed: usually **ar·tic'u·lat'ed** —**ar·tic'u·la'tion** *n.*

ar'ti·fact' *n.* any object made by human work

ar·ti·fice (-fis) *n.* 1 trick or trickery 2 clever skill

ar·ti·fi'cial *a.* 1 made by human work; not natural 2 not genuine; affected —**ar·ti·fi'ci·al'i·ty** *n.*

artificial intelligence *n.* (science of) computer intelligence

artificial respiration *n.* artificial maintenance of breathing

ar·til'ler·y *n.* 1 mounted guns, as cannon 2 military branch using these

ar'ti·san (-zən) *n.* skilled worker

art'ist *n.* person with skill, esp. in any

of the fine arts

ar·tis'tic a. 1 of art or artists 2 skill-ful —**art'ist·ry** n.

art'less a. simple; natural

art'y a. **-i·er, -i·est** [Inf.] affectedly artistic: also **art'sy, -si·er, -si·est**

ar'um (er'-) n. plant with flowers inside hooded leaf

as adv. 1 equally 2 for instance —con. 1 in the way that 2 while 3 because 4 though —pron. that —prep. in the role of —**as for** (or **to**) concerning —**as is** [Inf.] just as it is: said of damaged merchandise —**as of** on or up to (a certain time)

ASAP abbrev. as soon as possible: also **a.s.a.p.**

as·bes'tos n. fibrous mineral used formerly in fireproofing

as·cend' (-send') v. go up; climb —**as·cen'sion** n.

as·cend'an·cy, as·cend'en·cy n. domination —**as·cend'ant, as·cend'ent** a.

as·cent' n. 1 an ascending 2 upward slope

as·cer·tain' v. find out with certainty

as·cet'ic (-set'-) a. self-denying —n. one who denies pleasures to himself or herself —**as·cet'i·cism** n.

ASCII (as'kē) n. Comput. American Standard Code for Information Interchange

a·scor'bic acid n. vitamin C

as'cot n. scarflike necktie

as·cribe' v. assign or attribute —**as·crip'tion** n.

a·sep'tic (ā-) a. free from disease germs

a·sex'u·al (ā-) a. sexless

ash n. 1 often pl. grayish powder left from something burned 2 shade tree —**ash'en** a. —**ash'y** a., **-i·er, -i·est**

a·shamed' a. feeling shame

a·shore' adv. 1 to the shore 2 on land

ash'tray n. container for smokers' tobacco ashes: also **ash tray**

A'sian (-zhən) n., a. (native) of the continent of Asia: also, now less preferred, **A'si·at'ic** (-zhē at')

a·side' adv. 1 on or to one side 2 away 3 apart —n. an actor's words spoken aside from except for

as'i·nine' (-nīn') a. stupid; silly —**as'i·nin'i·ty** (-nin'-) n.

ask v. 1 call for an answer to 2 inquire of or about 3 request 4 invite

a·skance' adv. 1 sideways 2 with suspicion

a·skew' (-skyoo') adv., a. awry

ask'ing price n. price asked by a seller, to begin bargaining

a·slant' adv., a. on a slant —prep. on a slant across

a·sleep' a. 1 sleeping 2 numb —adv. into sleep

a·so'cial (ā-) a. not social; avoiding others

asp n. poisonous snake

as·par'a·gus n. plant with edible green shoots

as'par·tame' n. artificial, low-calorie sweetener

as'pect' n. 1 look or appearance 2 side or facet

as'pen n. poplar tree with fluttering leaves

as·per'i·ty (ə sper'-) n., pl. **-ties** harshness; sharpness

as·per'sion (ə spur'-) n. a slur; slander

as'phalt' n. tarlike substance used for paving, etc.

as'pho·del' n. plant like a lily, with white or yellow flowers

as·phyx'i·ate' (-fik'sē-) v. suffocate —**as·phyx'i·a'tion** n.

as'pic' n. jelly of meat juice, tomato juice, etc.

as'pi·rate' v. 1 begin (a syllable, etc.) with sound of English h 2 suck in or suck up

as'pi·ra'tion n. ambition

as'pi·ra'tor n. apparatus using suction to remove air, fluids, etc.

as·pire' v. be ambitious (to) —**as'pi·rant** n. —**as·pir'ing** a.

as'pi·rin' (or -prin') n. drug that relieves pain or fever

ass n. 1 donkey 2 fool

as·sail' v. attack

as·sail'ant n. attacker

as·sas'sin n. murderer

as·sas'si·nate' v. murder, esp. for political reasons —**as·sas'si·na'tion** n.

as·sault' (-sôlt') n., v. attack

assault and battery n. Law the carrying out of threatened physical harm

as'say n., v. test; attempt

as·sem'ble v. 1 gather in a group 2 fit or put together —**as·sem'blage** (-blij') n.

as·sem'bly n., pl. **-blies** 1 an assembling 2 group 3 [A-] legislative body

assembly line n. line of workers in a factory who assemble a product as it passes along

as·sem'bly·man n., pl. **-men** member of a legislative assembly —**as·sem'bly·wom'an** n.fem., pl. **-wom'en**

as·sent' v., n. consent

as·sert' v. 1 declare 2 defend (rights, etc.) —**as·ser'tion** n. —**as·ser'tive** a.

as·sess' v. 1 set a value on for taxes 2

impose a fine, tax, etc. —**as·sess'ment** n. —**as·ses'sor** n.

as'set n. **1** valuable thing **2** pl. property, cash, etc.

as·sev'er·ate' v. declare

as·sid'u·ous (-sij'⁞-) a. diligent

as·sign' v. **1** designate **2** appoint **3** allot; give —**as·sign'ment** n.

as·sig·na'tion n. lovers' secret meeting

as·sim'i·late' v. merge; absorb —**as·sim·i·la'tion** n.

as·sist' v., n. help; aid —**as·sist'ance** n. —**as·sist'ant** a., n.

assisted living n. living arrangement providing assistance to elderly or disabled persons

assn abbrev. association

assoc abbrev. associate(s)

as·so'ci·ate' (-āt'; n., a.: -ət) v. **1** join **2** connect in the mind **3** join (with) as a partner, colleague, etc. —a. associated —**as·so'ci·a'tion** n.

association football n. soccer

as'so·nance n. likeness of sound

as·sort'ed a. miscellaneous

as·sort'ment n. variety

asst abbrev. assistant

as·suage' (-swāj') v. ease (pain, hunger, etc.)

as·sume' v. **1** take on (a role, look, etc.) **2** undertake **3** take for granted **4** pretend to have —**as·sump'tion** n.

as·sure' v. **1** make sure; convince **2** give confidence to **3** promise **4** guarantee —**as·sur'ance** n. —**as·sured'** a.

as'ter n. daisylike flower

as'ter·isk' n. sign (*) used to mark footnotes, etc.

a·stern' adv. at or toward the rear of a ship

as'ter·oid n. any of the small planets between Mars and Jupiter

asth'ma (az'-) n. chronic disorder characterized by coughing, hard breathing, etc. —**asth·mat'ic** a.

a·stig'ma·tism' n. eye defect that keeps light rays from focusing at one point

a·stil'be (-bē) n. plant with flower spikes

a·stir' adv., a. in motion

as·ton'ish v. fill with sudden surprise —**as·ton'ish·ing** a. —**as·ton'ish·ment** n.

as·tound' v. astonish greatly —**as·tound'ing** a.

a·strad'dle adv. in a straddling position

as'tra·khan (-kən) n. curled fur from young lamb pelts

as'tral a. of, from, or like the stars

a·stray' adv., a. off the right path

a·stride' adv., prep. with a leg on either side (of)

as·trin'gent n., a. (substance) contracting body tissue and blood vessels

as·trol'o·gy n. system based on the belief that the stars, etc. affect human affairs —**as·trol'o·ger** n. —**as'tro·log'i·cal** a.

as'tro·naut' n. traveler in outer space

as'tro·nau'tics n. science of spacecraft and space travel —**as'tro·nau'ti·cal** a.

as'tro·nom'i·cal a. **1** of astronomy **2** huge: said of numbers Also **as'tro·nom'ic**

as·tron'o·my n. science of the stars, planets, etc. —**as·tron'o·mer** n.

as'tro·phys'ics n. study of the physics of astronomy

as·tute' a. shrewd; keen

a·sun'der adv. into parts or pieces

a·sy'lum n. **1** place of safety **2** institution for the mentally ill, aged, etc.: old-fashioned term

a·sym'me·try (ā sim'-) n. lack of symmetry —**a·sym·met'ri·cal** a.

at prep. **1** on; in; near **2** to or toward **3** busy with **4** in the state of **5** because of

at'a·vism' n. a throwback

ate v. pt. of EAT

-ate suf. **1** make, become, or form **2** to treat with **3** of or like

at·el·ier' (at''l ā') n. studio

a'the·ism' n. belief that there is no God —**a'the·ist'** n. —**a'the·is'tic** a.

ath'er·o·scle·ro'sis n. formation of nodules on hardening artery walls

a·thirst' a. eager

ath'lete' n. one skilled at sports requiring strength, speed, etc. —**ath·let'ic** a. —**ath·let'i·cism'** n. —**ath·let'ics** pl.n.

athlete's foot n. ringworm of the feet

a·thwart' prep., adv. across

a·tilt' a., adv. in a tilted position

a·tin'gle a. tingling

-ation suf. act, condition, or result of

-ative suf. of or relating to; serving to

At·lan'tis n. Gr. myth. ancient sunken island

at'las n. book of maps

ATM n. computer terminal for automatic deposit, withdrawal, etc. of bank funds

at'mos·phere' (-fir') n. **1** the air surrounding the earth **2** general feeling or spirit **3** [Inf.] interesting effect produced by decoration, etc. —**at'mos·pher'ic** a.

at·oll (a'tôl') n. coral island surrounding a lagoon

at·om *n.* smallest particle of a chemical element, made up of electrons, protons, etc. —**a·tom'ic** *a.*

atomic (or **atom**) **bomb** *n.* bomb whose immense power derives from nuclear fission

atomic energy *n.* energy released from an atom in nuclear reactions

at·om·iz·er *n.* device for spraying liquid in a mist

a·to·nal'i·ty (ā'-) *n. Mus.* organization of tones without relation to a key —**a·ton'al** *a.*

a·tone' *v.* make amends (*for*) —**a·tone' ment** *n.*

a·top' *adv., prep.* on the top (of)

a'tri·um *n.* hall or lobby rising up through several stories

a·tro'cious (-shəs) *a.* **1** cruel or evil **2** very bad —**a·troc'i·ty** (-träs'-) *n., pl.* -ties

at'ro·phy (-fē) *v.* -phied, -phy·ing waste away or shrink up —*n.* an atrophying

at'ro·pine' (-pēn') *n.* alkaloid used to relieve spasms

at·tach' *v.* **1** fasten; join **2** tie by devotion **3** seize by legal order —**at·tach' ment** *n.*

at·ta·ché' (-shā') *n.* member of a diplomatic staff

attaché case *n.* flat, rectangular case for carrying papers

at·tack' *v.* **1** to fight or work against **2** undertake vigorously —*n.* **1** an attacking **2** fit of illness

at·tain' *v.* **1** to gain; achieve **2** arrive at —**at·tain'a·ble** *a.* —**at·tain'ment** *n.*

at·tain'der *n.* loss of civil rights and property by one sentenced to death or outlawed

at'tar (-ər) *n.* perfume made from flower petals

at·tempt' *v., n.* try

at·tend' *v.* **1** be present at **2** pay attention **3** accompany —**attend to** take care of —**at·tend'ant** *n.*

at·tend'ance *n.* **1** an attending **2** number present

at·ten'tion *n.* **1** a giving heed **2** heed; notice **3** *pl.* kind acts —**at·ten'tive** *a.*

at·ten'u·ate' *v.* thin out; weaken —**at· ten'u·a'tion** *n.*

at·test' *v.* **1** declare to be true **2** be proof of

at'tic *n.* space just below the roof; garret

at·tire' *v.* clothe; dress up —*n.* clothes

at'ti·tude' *n.* **1** bodily posture **2** way of looking at things, or manner

at·ti·tu'di·nize' *v.* to pose for effect

Attn, attn *abbrev.* attention

at·tor'ney (-tur'-) *n., pl.* -neys lawyer: also **attorney at law**

attorney general *n.* chief law officer of a government

at·tract' *v.* **1** draw to itself **2** make notice or like one —**at·trac'tion** *n.* —**at·trac'tive** *a.*

at·trib·ute (ə trib'yoot; *n.:* a'trə byoot') *v.* think of as belonging or owing (*to*) —*n.* a characteristic —**at·trib'ut·a·ble** *a.* —**at'tri·bu'tion** *n.*

at·tri'tion (-trish'ən) *n.* **1** a wearing down bit by bit **2** loss of staff as by retirement

at·tune' *v.* bring into harmony or agreement

atty *abbrev.* attorney

ATV *n., pl.* **ATVs** small motor vehicle for rough ground, snow, ice, and shallow water

a·twit'ter *a.* twittering

a·typ'i·cal (ā-) *a.* not typical

au'burn *a., n.* reddish-brown

auc'tion *n.* public sale in which items go to the highest bidder —*v.* sell at an auction —**auc'tion·eer'** *n., v.*

au·da'cious (-shəs) *a.* **1** bold; reckless **2** insolent —**au·dac'i·ty** (-das'-) *n.*

au'di·ble *a.* loud enough to be heard —**au'di·bly** *adv.*

au'di·ence *n.* **1** group seeing or hearing a play, concert, radio or TV show, etc. **2** formal interview

au'di·o' *a.* of the sound portion of a TV broadcast

au'di·o·book' *n.* a recording of a reading of a book as by the author

au'di·o·phile' *n.* devotee of hi-fi sound reproduction

au'di·o·vis'u·al *a.* involving both hearing and sight

au'dit *v.* examine and check (accounts) —*n.* an auditing —**au'di·tor** *n.*

au·di'tion *n.* a hearing to try out a singer, actor, etc. —*v.* try out in an audition

au'di·to'ri·um *n.* a hall for speeches, concerts, etc.

au'di·to·ry *a.* of hearing

Aug *abbrev.* August

au'ger *n.* tool for boring holes in wood

aught (ôt) *n.* zero

aug·ment' *v.* increase —**aug'men·ta' tion** *n.*

au gra·tin (ō grät'n) *a.* with browned cheese crust

au'gur (-gər) *v.* foretell —**augur ill** (or **well**) be a bad (or good) omen —**au' gu·ry** (-gyə rē) *n.*

Au′gust *n.* eighth month

au·gust′ *a.* imposing; venerable

au jus (ō zhōō′) *a.* in its natural gravy

auk *n.* diving seabird

aunt (ant, änt) *n.* **1** sister of one's parent **2** uncle's wife

au′ra *n.* radiance or special atmosphere about a person or thing

au′ral *a.* of hearing

au·re·ole′ *n.* halo

Au′re·o·my′cin *trademark* antibiotic drug

au re·voir (ō′rə vwär′) *int.* goodbye

au′ri·cle *n.* outer part of the ear

au·ro′ra *n.* dawn

aurora bo·re·al′is *n.* luminous bands in the northern night sky

aus·cul·ta′tion *n.* a listening to chest sounds with a stethoscope

aus′pi·ces (-siz) *pl.n.* patronage

aus·pi′cious (-pish′əs) *a.* favorable; of good omen —**aus·pi′cious·ly** *adv.*

aus·tere (ô stir′) *a.* **1** strict **2** very plain; severe —**aus·ter′i·ty** (ô ster′-) *n., pl.* -**ties**

Aus·tral′i·an *n., a.* (native) of the continent or country of Australia

Aus′tri·an *n., a.* (native) of Austria

au·then′tic *a.* true, real, genuine, etc. —**au·then·tic′i·ty** (-tis′-) *n.*

au·then′ti·cate′ *v.* **1** verify **2** prove to be genuine —**au·then′ti·ca′tion** *n.*

au′thor *n.* writer or originator —**au′thor·ship′** *n.*

au·thor′i·tar′i·an *a.* enforcing or favoring strict obedience to authority

au·thor′i·ta′tive *a.* having or showing authority

au·thor′i·ty *n., pl.* -**ties 1** power to command **2** *pl.* persons with such power **3** expert; reliable source

au′thor·ize′ *v.* give official approval to —**au′thor·i·za′tion** *n.*

au′tism′ *n.* mental state marked by disregard of external reality —**au·tis′tic** *a.*

au′to *n., pl.* -**tos** automobile

auto- *pref.* self

au′to·bi·og′ra·phy *n., pl.* -**phies** one's own life story written by oneself —**au′to·bi′o·graph′i·cal** *a.*

au′to·crat′ *n.* ruler with unlimited power —**au·toc′ra·cy** *n.* —**au′to·crat′ic** *a.*

au′to·di·dact′ *n.* person who is self-taught

au′to·graph′ *n.* signature —*v.* write one's signature on

au′to·mat′ *n.* restaurant dispensing food from coin-operated compartments

au′to·mate′ *v.* convert to automation

au′to·mat′ic *a.* **1** done without conscious effort **2** operating by itself —**au′to·mat′i·cal·ly** *adv.*

automatic pilot *n.* gyroscopic instrument for piloting an aircraft, missile, etc.: also **au′to·pi′lot**

au′to·ma′tion *n.* automatic system of manufacture, as by electronic devices

au′tom′a·ton′ *n.* robot

au′to·mo·bile′ *n.* passenger vehicle propelled by an engine, for use on streets and roads —**au′to·mo′tive** *a.*

au′to·nom′ic *a.* of the nervous system regulating the heart, lungs, etc.

au·ton′o·my *n.* self-government —**au·ton′o·mous** *a.*

au′top′sy *n., pl.* -**sies** examination of a corpse to find cause of death

au·tumn (ôt′əm) *n.* season after summer, when leaves fall —*a.* of, for, or in autumn —**au·tum′nal** *a.*

aux·il·ia·ry (ôg zil′yə rē) *a.* **1** helping **2** subsidiary —*n., pl.* -**ries** auxiliary group, etc.

auxiliary verb *v.* verb used to help form tenses, etc., as *will, have, do, be,* or *must*

av *abbrev.* **1** average: also **avg 2** avoirdupois

Av *abbrev.* **1** Avenue **2** avoirdupois

a·vail′ *v.* be of use or help (to) —*n.* use or help —**avail oneself of** make use of

a·vail′a·ble *a.* that can be gotten or had —**a·vail′a·bil′i·ty** *n.*

av′a·lanche′ *n.* great fall of rock, snow, etc. down a hill

a·vant-garde (ä′vänt-gärd′) *n.* vanguard

av′a·rice (-ris) *n.* greed for money —**av′a·ri′cious** (-rish′əs) *a.*

a·vast′ *int. Naut.* stop; halt

Ave *abbrev.* Avenue

a·venge′ *v.* get revenge for —**a·veng′er** *n.*

av′e·nue′ *n.* **1** street **2** way to something; approach

a·ver′ (-vur′) *v.* **a·verred′, a·ver′ring** declare to be true

av′er·age *n.* **1** sum divided by the number of quantities added **2** usual kind, amount, etc. —*a.* being the average —*v.* **1** figure the average of **2** do, take, etc. on the average —**on the average** as an average amount, rate, etc.

a·verse′ *a.* unwilling

a·ver′sion *n.* strong dislike

a·vert′ *v.* **1** turn away **2** prevent

a′vi·ar·y *n., pl.* -**ies** large cage for many birds

a·vi·a'tion *n.* science or work of flying airplanes —**a'vi·a'tor** *n.*

av'id *a.* eager or greedy

a·vi·on·ics *n.* electronics applied in aviation and astronautics

av·o·ca'do (-kä'-) *n.*, *pl.* **-dos** thick-skinned tropical fruit with buttery flesh

av·o·ca'tion *n.* hobby

a·void' *v.* 1 keep away from; shun 2 prevent —**a·void'a·ble** *a.* —**a·void'ance** *n.*

av·oir·du·pois (av'ər də poiz') *n.* weight system in which 16 ounces = 1 pound

a·vouch' *v.* assert; affirm

a·vow' *v.* declare openly —**a·vow'al** *n.*

a·vun'cu·lar *a.* typical of an uncle

aw *int.* sound of protest or sympathy

a·wait' *v.* wait for

a·wake' *v.* **a·woke'** or **a·waked'**, **a·waked'** or **a·wok'en**, **a·wak'ing** rouse from sleep —*a.* 1 not asleep 2 alert

a·wak'en *v.* rouse; awake —**a·wak'en·ing** *n.*, *a.*

a·ward' *v.* give after judging —*n.* 1 decision, as by judges 2 prize

a·ware' *a.* conscious; knowing —**a·ware'ness** *n.*

a·wash' *a.* 1 with water washing over the surface 2 flooded

a·way' *adv.* 1 from a place 2 aside 3 from one's keeping —*a.* 1 absent 2 at a distance —**do away with** 1 get rid of 2 kill

awe *n.* reverent fear and wonder —*v.* inspire awe in

a·weigh' *a.* just clear of the bottom: said of an anchor

awe'some *a.* causing awe

awe'-struck' *a.* filled with awe: also **awe'-strick'en**

aw'ful *a.* 1 terrifying; dreadful 2 bad —*adv.* [Inf.] very —**aw'ful·ly** *adv.*

a·while' *adv.* for a short time

awk'ward *a.* 1 clumsy 2 uncomfortable 3 embarrassing —**awk'ward·ly** *adv.*

awl *n.* pointed tool for making holes in wood, etc.

awn *n.* bristly fibers on a head of barley, oats, etc.

awn'ing *n.* overhanging shade of canvas, metal, etc.

AWOL, awol (ā'wôl) *a.* absent without leave

a·wry (ə rī') *adv.*, *a.* 1 with a twist to a side 2 amiss

ax, axe *n.*, *pl.* **ax'es** tool for chopping wood, etc.

ax'i·om *n.* an evident truth —**ax'i·o·**

mat'ic *a.*

ax'is *n.*, *pl.* **ax'es** (-ēz') straight line around which a thing rotates —**ax'i·al** *a.*

ax'le *n.* rod on which a wheel revolves

ax'le·tree' *n.* axle of a wagon, carriage, etc.

ax'o·lotl' (-lät'l) *n.* dark salamander of Mexico and western U.S.

a·ya·tol·lah (ī'ə tō'lə) *n.* Muslim religious and governmental leader

aye (ā) *adv.* [Ar.] always

aye (ī) *adv.*, *n.* yes

AZ *abbrev.* Arizona

a·za'lea (-zāl'yə) *n.* shrub with brightly colored flowers

Az'tec' *a.*, *n.* (of) a member of an Indian people of Mexico

az'ure (azh'-) *a.*, *n.* sky blue

B

B, b *abbrev.* born

BA *abbrev.* Bachelor of Arts: also **B.A.**

baa (bä) *n.*, *v.* bleat

bab'ble *v.* 1 talk in a foolish or jumbled way 2 murmur —*n.* babbling talk or sound —**bab'bler** *n.*

babe *n.* baby

ba'bel *n.* confusion; tumult

ba·boon' *n.* ape with doglike snout

ba·bush'ka *n.* woman's scarf worn on the head

ba'by *n.*, *pl.* **-bies** very young child; infant —*a.* 1 of, for, or like a baby 2 small or young —*v.* **-bied, -by·ing** pamper —**ba'by·hood'** *n.* —**ba'by·ish** *a.*

baby carriage *n.* light carriage for wheeling a baby about: also **baby buggy**

baby grand *n.* small grand piano

baby's breath *n.* plant with small white or pink flowers

ba'by-sit' *v.* **-sat', -sit'ting** take care of children when parents are away — **baby sitter** *n.*

bac·ca·lau're·ate (-lôr'ē ət) *n.* 1 bachelor's degree 2 a talk to graduating class

bac·cha·nal (bak'ə nal') *n.* drunken orgy —**bac'cha·na'li·an** (-nā'-) *a.*

bach'e·lor *n.* unmarried man —**bach'e·lor·hood'** *n.*

Bachelor of Arts (or **Science**, etc.) *n.* four-year college degree

bachelor's button *n.* plant with showy white, pink, or blue flowers

ba·cil'lus (-sil'-) *n.*, *pl.* **-li** (-ī) kind of bacteria

back *n.* **1** rear or hind part **2** backbone **3** the reverse **4** football player behind the line —*a.* **1** at the rear **2** of the past **3** backward —*adv.* **1** at or to the rear **2** to a former time, place, etc. **3** in return —*v.* **1** move backward **2** support **3** provide a back for —**back down** retract an opinion, etc. —**back up 1** accumulate **2** make a copy of (data) —**back'er** *n.* —**back'ing** *n.*

back'ache' *n.* an ache in the back

back'bite' *v.* to slander

back'board' *n. Basketball* board behind the basket

back'bone' *n.* **1** spinal column **2** courage; firmness

back'break'ing *a.* very tiring

back'coun'try *n.* remote area

back'drop' *n.* curtain at the back of a stage

back'field' *n. Football* players behind the line

back'fire' *n.* faulty ignition in an engine —*v.* **1** have a backfire **2** go awry, as plans

back'gam'mon *n.* game played by moving pieces on a special board

back'ground' *n.* **1** the part behind, more distant, etc. **2** past events, causes, etc.

back'hand' *n.* a backhanded stroke, as in tennis

back'hand'ed *a.* **1** with the back of the hand forward **2** insincere

back'lash' *n.* sharp reaction

back'log' *n.* piling up, as of work to be done

back'-of'fice *a.* of the routine functions of an office

back order *n.* order not yet filled

back'pack' *n.* knapsack —*v.* hike wearing a backpack

back'ped'al *v.* **1** to step backward **2** retract an opinion, etc.

back'rest' *n.* support for the back

back'side' *n.* **1** back part **2** rump

back'slap'per *n.* [Inf.] effusively friendly person

back'slide' *v.* become less virtuous, less pious, etc.

back'splash' *n.* protective surface behind a sink, etc.

back'stage' *adv.* in theater dressing rooms, etc.

back'stretch' *n.* part of a racetrack opposite the homestretch

back'stroke' *n.* swimming stroke made while lying face upward

back talk *n.* [Inf.] insolence

back'-to-back' *a.* [Inf.] consecutive

back'track' *v.* to retreat

back'ward *adv.* **1** toward the back **2** with the back foremost **3** into the past Also **back'wards** —*a.* **1** turned to the rear or away **2** shy **3** slow or retarded —**back'ward·ness** *n.*

back'woods' *pl.n.* remote, wooded areas —**back'woods'man** *n., pl.* **-men**

ba'con *n.* cured meat from hog's back or sides

bac·te'ri·a *pl.n., sing.* **-ri·um** microorganisms causing diseases, fermentation, etc. —**bac·te'ri·al** *a.*

bac·te'ri·ol'o·gy *n.* study of bacteria

bad *a.* **worse, worst 1** not good **2** spoiled **3** incorrect **4** wicked **5** severe —*adv.* [Inf.] badly —*n.* anything bad —**bad'ly** *adv.* —**bad'ness** *n.*

bad blood *n.* (mutual) ill will

bade (bad) *v.* pt. of BID (*v.* **1** & **2**)

badge *n.* pin or emblem worn to show rank, membership, etc.

badg'er *n.* furry burrowing animal —*v.* to nag; pester

bad'man *n., pl.* **-men'** desperado, cattle thief, etc. of the old West

bad'min'ton *n.* game using rackets and a shuttlecock

bad'-mouth' *v.* [Sl.] find fault (with)

bad'-tem'pered *a.* irritable

baf'fle *v.* puzzle; bewilder —*n.* deflecting screen —**baf'fling** *a.*

bag *n.* **1** container made of fabric, paper, etc. **2** suitcase **3** purse —*v.* **bagged, bag'ging 1** hang loosely **2** kill or capture **3** put into a bag —**in the bag** [Sl.] certain —**bag'gy** *a.*

bag·a·telle' *n.* a trifle

ba'gel (-gəl) *n.* hard bread roll like a small doughnut

bag'gage *n.* luggage

bag'pipe' *n. often pl.* musical instrument with a bag from which air is forced into pipes

bah (bä) *int.* shout of scorn

bail *n.* money left as security to free a prisoner until trial —*v.* **1** get freed by giving bail **2** dip out (water) from (a boat) —**bail out 1** to help **2** to parachute

bail'iff *n.* **1** court officer guarding prisoners and jurors **2** sheriff's deputy

bail'i·wick' (bāl'ē-) *n.* one's field of interest or authority

bait *v.* **1** torment, as by insults **2** put food on (a hook, etc.) as a lure —*n.* anything used as a lure

baize (bāz) *n.* coarse, feltlike cloth

bake *v.* **1** cook by dry heat in an oven **2** harden by heat —**bak'er** *n.*

baker's dozen *n.* thirteen

bak'er·y n., pl. **-ies** place where bread, etc. is baked

baking powder n. leavening powder

baking soda n. sodium bicarbonate, powder used as leavening and as an antacid

bal'a·lai'ka (-lī'-) n. Russian instrument like a guitar

bal'ance n. **1** instrument for weighing, with two pans **2** equilibrium **3** harmonious proportion **4** equality of or difference between credits and debits **5** remainder —v. **1** compare **2** offset; counteract **3** put, keep, or be in equilibrium **4** be equal **5** sum up or equalize the debits and credits of (an account) —**in the balance** not yet settled

balance sheet n. statement of financial status of a business

bal'co·ny n., pl. **-nies 1** platform projecting from an upper story **2** tier of theater seats above main floor

bald a. **1** lacking hair on the head **2** plain and frank —**bald'ness** n.

bald eagle n. large eagle of North America, with white-feathered head

bal'der·dash' (bôl'-) n. nonsense

bald'faced' a. shameless

bald'ing a. becoming bald

bal'dric (bôl'-) n. belt over the shoulder to support a sword

bale n. large bundle, as of raw cotton —v. make into bales

ba·leen' n. whalebone

bale'ful a. harmful; evil

balk v. **1** stop and refuse to move **2** obstruct —n. **1** hindrance; obstruction **2** *Baseball* illegal motion by pitcher —**balk'y** a., **-i·er, -i·est**

ball n. **1** round object; sphere **2** round or oval object used in games **3** formal social dance **4** *Baseball* pitched baseball that is not a strike **5** [Sl.] good time —v. form into a ball —**be on the ball** [Sl.] be alert

bal'lad n. **1** popular love song **2** folk song or poem telling a story

ball'-and-sock'et joint n. joint, as the hip, like a ball in a socket

bal'last (-əst) n. heavy matter put in a ship, etc. to keep it steady —v. to furnish with ballast

ball bearing n. **1** bearing in which the parts turn on rolling metal balls **2** one of these balls

bal·le·ri'na n. woman ballet dancer

bal·let (ba lā') n. intricate, formalized group dance

bal·lis'tic missile n. long-range guided missile that falls free as it nears its target

bal·lis'tics n. science of the motion of projectiles

bal·loon' n. bag that rises when filled with light gas —v. swell; expand

bal'lot n. **1** paper marked in voting **2** voting —v. to vote

ball'park' n. baseball stadium

ball'play'er n. baseball player

ball'point' (pen) n. pen with ink cartridge and small ball bearing for a point

ball'room' n. large room for social dances

bal'ly·hoo' n. exaggerated or sensational advertising or propaganda

balm (bäm) n. fragrant healing ointment or oil

balm'y a. **-i·er, -i·est** soothing, mild, etc.

ba·lo'ney n. **1** bologna **2** [Sl.] nonsense

bal'sa (bôl'-) n. lightweight wood of a tropical tree

bal'sam (bôl'-) n. **1** aromatic resin **2** tree yielding it

bal·sam'ic vinegar n. dark-brown vinegar used in salad dressing, etc.

bal'us·ter n. railing post

bal'us·trade' n. row of balusters supporting a rail

bam·boo' n. tropical grass with hollow, treelike stems

bam·boo'zle v. **1** trick **2** confuse

ban v. **banned, ban'ning** forbid —n. formal forbidding by authorities

ba·nal' (bā'nəl, bə nal') a. trite —**ba·nal'i·ty** n., pl. **-ties**

ba·nan'a n. long tropical fruit with creamy flesh

band n. **1** strip of cloth, etc. as for binding **2** stripe **3** range of radio wavelengths **4** group of people **5** group of performing musicians —v. **1** mark or tie with a band **2** join (together)

band'age n. cloth strip to bind an injury —v. bind with a bandage

Band'-Aid' trademark small bandage of gauze and adhesive tape —n. [b-a-] such a bandage: also **band'aid'**

ban·dan'na, ban·dan'a n. large, colored handkerchief

band'box' n. light, round box for hats, etc.

ban'dit n. robber; brigand —**ban'dit·ry** n.

ban·do·leer', ban·do·lier' n. belt holding bullets, worn over one shoulder

band saw n. power saw that is an endless, toothed steel belt

band'stand' *n.* (outdoor) platform for an orchestra

band'wag'on *n.* winning or popular side

ban'dy *v.* **-died, -dy·ing** toss or pass back and forth —*a.* curved outward —**ban'dy·leg'ged** *a.*

bane *n.* cause of harm or ruin —**bane'ful** *a.*

bang *v.*, *n.* (make, or hit with) a loud noise

ban'gle *n.* bracelet

bangs *pl.n.* short hair worn across the forehead

ban'ish *v.* **1** to exile **2** dismiss —**ban'ish·ment** *n.*

ban'is·ter *n.* handrail along a staircase

ban'jo *n.*, *pl.* **-jos** or **-joes** stringed musical instrument with a circular body

bank *n.* **1** mound; heap **2** rising land, as along a river **3** row; tier **4** business handling savings, loans, etc. —*v.* **1** form a bank **2** put (money) in a bank **3** cover (a fire) to make last —**bank on** [Inf.] rely on —**bank'er** *n.*

bank account *n.* money deposited in a bank and credited to the depositor

bank'book' *n.* booklet recording depositor's bank account

bank card *n.* encoded plastic card for use at a bank ATM

bank'ing *n.* business of a bank

bank note *n.* piece of paper money

bank'roll' *n.* supply of money —*v.* [Inf.] supply with money

bank'rupt' *a.* **1** legally declared unable to pay one's debts **2** lacking —*n.* bankrupt person —*v.* make bankrupt —**bank'rupt·cy** *n.*

ban'ner *n.* **1** flag **2** long strip of cloth with writing, etc. —*a.* foremost; leading

banns *pl.n.* church notice of an upcoming marriage

ban'quet (-kwət) *n.* formal dinner

ban·quette' (-ket') *n.* padded bench

ban'shee *n.* *Folklore* wailing female spirit

ban'tam (-təm) *n.* breed of small chickens —*a.* small

ban'ter *v.* tease playfully —*n.* genial teasing

ban'yan (-yən) *n.* Asian fig tree with many trunks

bap'tism' *n.* rite of admission into a Christian church by dipping in or sprinkling with water —**bap·tis'mal** *a.* —**bap'tize** *v.*

Bap'tist *n.* member of Protestant church practicing baptism of believers by immersion

bap'tis·ter·y (*or* -tis trē) *n.*, *pl.* **-ies** place in a church used for baptizing: also **bap'tis·try**, *pl.* **-tries**

bar *n.* **1** long, narrow piece of wood, metal, etc. **2** oblong piece, as of soap **3** obstruction **4** band or strip **5** law court **6** legal profession **7** counter or place for serving liquor **8** *Mus.* a measure or vertical line marking it off —*v.* **barred, bar'ring 1** obstruct; close **2** oppose **3** exclude —*prep.* excluding

barb *n.* sharp, back-curving point —**barbed** *a.*

bar·bar'i·an (-ber'-) *n.* uncivilized person; savage —*a.* uncivilized —**bar·bar'ic** *a.*

bar'ba·rize' *v.* make or become barbarous

bar'ba·rous *a.* **1** uncivilized **2** crude; coarse **3** brutal —**bar'ba·rism'** *n.*

bar'be·cue' *n.* **1** meat roasted over open fire **2** picnic at which such meat is served **3** structure or device for outdoor roasting —*v.* **1** roast outdoors **2** broil in spicy sauce (**barbecue sauce**)

barbed wire *n.* twisted strands of wire with barbs at close intervals: also **barb'wire'** *n.*

bar'bel (-bəl) *n.* threadlike growth from lip or jaw of a fish

bar'bell' *n.* metal bar with weights at each end, used in weight lifting

bar'ber *n.* one who cuts hair, shaves beards, etc.

bar'ber·ry (*or* -bə rē) *n.*, *pl.* **-ries 1** spiny shrub with red berries **2** the berry

bar·bi'tu·rate (-bich'ər it) *n.* drug used as a sedative

bar·ca·role', **bar·ca·rolle'** *n.* Venetian gondolier song, or such music

bar code *n.* *Comput.* set of printed lines containing coded information

bard *n.* poet

bare *a.* **1** naked **2** exposed **3** empty **4** mere —*v.* uncover —**bare'foot', bare'foot·ed** *a.*, *adv.* —**bare'head'ed** *a.*, *adv.*

bare'back' *adv.*, *a.* on a horse with no saddle

bare'-bones' *a.* simple; basic

bare'faced *a.* shameless

bare'ly *adv.* only just

bar'gain (-gən) *n.* **1** agreement or contract **2** item bought at a favorable price —*v.* haggle —**bargain for** (or **on**) expect — **into** (or **in**) **the bargain** besides

barge n. flat-bottomed freight boat —
v. enter abruptly (*into*)

bar'i·tone' n. male voice, or instrument, between tenor and bass

bar'i·um n. silver-white metallic chemical element

bark n. 1 outside covering of trees 2 sharp cry of a dog 3 sailing vessel —
v. 1 utter a bark 2 scrape off the skin of

bark'keep'er n. 1 owner of a barroom 2 bartender Also **bar'keep'**

bark'er n. announcer at a carnival sideshow

bar'ley n. cereal grain

bar'maid n. waitress in a bar

bar mitz'vah n. religious ceremony for a Jewish boy at the age of 13 years

barn n. farm building for livestock, storage, etc. —**barn'yard'** n.

bar'na·cle n. shellfish that clings to ships, etc.

barn'storm' v. tour small towns, acting plays, etc.

ba·rom'e·ter n. instrument to measure atmospheric pressure —**bar'o·met'ric a.**

bar'on n. nobleman of lowest rank —
bar'on·ess n.fem. —**ba·ro'ni·al a.**

bar'on·et' n. Br. man with hereditary rank of honor

ba·roque' (-rōk') a. having elaborate decoration

bar'racks pl.n. building(s) for housing soldiers

bar·ra·cu'da n., pl. **-da** or **-das** fierce tropical fish

bar·rage' (bə räzh') n. curtain of artillery fire

barred a. 1 having bars or stripes 2 closed off with bars 3 not allowed

bar'rel n. 1 round, wooden container with bulging sides 2 unit of measure, as of petroleum 3 tube of a gun —
bar'rel·ful n.

barrel organ n. musical instrument played by turning a crank

bar'ren a. 1 sterile 2 unproductive

bar·rette' (bə ret') n. clasp for a girl's hair

bar'ri·cade' n. barrier for defense —v. block with a barricade

bar'ri·er n. fence, wall, or other obstruction

bar'ring prep. excepting

bar'ris·ter n. in England, courtroom lawyer

bar'room' n. room with a BAR (n. 7)

bar'row n. traylike frame for carrying loads

bar'tend'er n. person serving drinks

at a BAR (n. 7)

bar'ter v. exchange (goods) —n. a bartering

ba'sal a. basic

basal metabolism n. quantity of energy used by any organism at rest

ba·salt' n. dark volcanic rock

base n. 1 part that a thing rests on 2 basis 3 goal in some games 4 headquarters or a source of supply 5 substance reacting with an acid to form a salt —v. put on a base —a. 1 morally low 2 inferior —**base'ly** adv.

base'ball' n. 1 team game played with a bat and ball 2 the ball used

base'board' n. molding along the bottom of a wall

base hit n. Baseball batted ball that is a single, double, triple, or home run

base'less a. unfounded

base line n. 1 Baseball lane from one base to the next 2 back line on a tennis court

base'man n., pl. **-men** Baseball infielder at first, second, or third base

base'ment n. story just below the main floor

base on balls n. Baseball walk

base pay n. basic rate of pay, not counting overtime pay

base runner n. Baseball player at or trying to reach a base

bash v. [Inf.] hit or attack hard

bash'ful a. socially timid; shy —**bash'ful·ly** adv. —**bash'ful·ness** n.

bas'ic a. of or at the base; fundamental —**bas'i·cal·ly** adv.

bas'il (bāz'-, baz'-) n. an herb

ba·sil'i·ca n. church with broad nave and columned aisles

bas'i·lisk' (bas'-) n. mythical, lizardlike monster whose glance could kill

ba'sin n. 1 wide, shallow container for liquid 2 a sink 3 bay, cove, etc. 4 area drained by a river

ba'sis n., pl. **-ses'** (-sēz') 1 base or foundation 2 main constituent

bask v. warm oneself

bas'ket n. 1 container made of interwoven strips 2 goal in basketball

bas'ket·ball' n. 1 team game with raised open nets through which a large ball must be tossed 2 this ball

bas'-re·lief' (bä'-, bas'-) n. sculpture with figures projecting a little from a flat background

bass (bās) n. 1 lowest male singing voice 2 singer or instrument with low range

bass (bas) n. perchlike fish

bas'set n. short-legged hound

bas'si·net' n. baby's bed like a large basket

bas·so (bas'ō, bäs'ō) n., pl. **-sos** bass voice or singer

bas·soon' n. double-reed, bass woodwind instrument

bass vi·ol (vī'əl) n. double bass

bast n. plant fiber used for ropes, mats, etc.

bas'tard n. illegitimate child —a. **1** illegitimate **2** sham, not standard, etc. —**bas'tard·ize'** v.

baste v. **1** sew with loose, temporary stitches **2** moisten (a roast) with drippings, etc. —**bast'ing** n.

bas'tion (-chən) n. **1** part of a fort that juts out **2** any strong defense

bat n. **1** a club to hit a ball, as in baseball **2** nocturnal, mouselike, flying mammal —v. **bat'ted, bat'ting 1** hit as with a bat **2** [Inf.] blink

batch n. quantity taken, made, etc. in one lot

bat'ed a. held in, as the breath in fear

bath n. **1** a washing of the body **2** water, etc. for bathing or soaking something **3** bathtub **4** bathroom

bathe (bāth) v. **1** give a bath to, or take a bath **2** put into a liquid **3** cover as with liquid —**bath'er** n.

bath'ing suit n. swimsuit

bath'mat' n. mat used in or next to a bathtub

ba·thos (bā'thäs') n. **1** a shift from noble to trivial **2** sentimentality or triteness

bath'robe' n. loose robe worn to or from the bath

bath'room' n. room with a bathtub, toilet, etc.

bath'tub' n. tub to bathe in

bath'y·scaph' (-ə skaf') n. small vessel that submerges deep into the sea

ba·tik' (-tēk') n. cloth with design dyed only on parts not coated with wax

ba·tiste' (-tēst') n. fine, thin cotton fabric

bat mitz'vah (bät-) n. religious ceremony for a Jewish girl similar to bar mitzvah: also **bas mitz'vah** (bäs-)

ba·ton' n. **1** stick used in leading an orchestra, etc. **2** staff serving as a symbol of office

bat·tal'ion n. subdivision of a regiment

bat'ten n. strip of wood —v. **1** fasten with battens **2** fatten; thrive

bat'ter v. **1** strike repeatedly **2** injure by hard use —n. **1** player at bat in baseball **2** mixture of flour, milk, etc. for making cakes

bat'ter·ing ram n. heavy beam, etc. to batter down gates, etc.

bat'ter·y n., pl. **-ies 1** cell or cells providing electric current **2** set of artillery guns **3** pitcher and catcher in baseball **4** illegal beating of a person

bat'ting n. wadded fiber

bat'tle n., v. fight, esp. between armies —**bat'tler** n.

bat'tle-ax', bat'tle-axe' n. heavy ax formerly used as a weapon

bat'tle-dore' n. racket for a game like badminton

bat'tle-field' n. place of battle: also **bat'tle-ground'**

bat'tle-ment n. low wall on a tower with open spaces for shooting

battle royal n., pl. **battles royal 1** a brawl **2** heated dispute

bat'tle-ship' n. large warship with big guns

bat'ty a. **-ti·er, -ti·est** [Sl.] crazy, odd, etc.

bau'ble n. trinket

baud (bôd) n. the number of bits per second transmitted in a computer system

baux'ite' (-īt) n. claylike aluminum ore

bawd n. [Rare] a prostitute

bawd'y a. **-i·er, -i·est** lewd yet humorous —**bawd'i·ness** n.

bawl v. **1** to shout **2** to weep noisily —**bawl out** [Sl.] scold angrily

bay n. **1** wide inlet of a sea or lake **2** alcove **3** recess in a wall, as for a window (**bay window**) **4** laurel tree **5** reddish brown **6** horse of this color —v. bark or howl in long, deep tones —**at bay 1** with escape cut off **2** held off —**bring to bay** cut off escape of

bay'ber·ry n., pl. **-ries 1** wax myrtle **2** its berry

bay leaf n. laurel leaf, dried and used as spice in cooking

bay'o·net' n. blade attached to a rifle barrel —v. to stab with a bayonet

bay·ou (bī'o͞o) n. marshy inlet or outlet, as a lake

ba·zaar' (-zär') n. **1** market place with shops, stalls, etc. **2** benefit sale for a club, etc.

ba·zoo'ka n. portable tubelike weapon for firing rockets as at tanks

bbl abbrev. barrel(s)

BBQ (bär'bə kyo͞o') n. barbecue

BB (shot) n. tiny metal shot for an air rifle (**BB gun**)

BC abbrev. **1** before Christ: also **B.C. 2** British Columbia

be v. was or were, been, be'ing **1** exist; live **2** occur **3** remain; continue

Be is also an important auxiliary verb

be- *pref.* **1** around **2** completely **3** away **4** about

beach *n.* stretch of sandy shore —*v.* ground (a boat)

beach′comb′er *n.* one who scavenges along beaches

beach′head′ *n.* shore area taken by invading troops

beach′wear′ *n.* clothing for the beach

bea′con *n.* guiding light

bead *n.* **1** small ball of glass, etc., pierced for stringing **2** *pl.* string of beads **3** drop or bubble —**draw a bead on** take careful aim at —**bead′ed** *a.* —**bead′y** *a.*

bea′dle *n.* [Hist.] minor officer who keeps order in church

bea′gle *n.* small, short-legged hound

beak *n.* **1** bird's bill **2** any beaklike mouth part

beak′er *n.* glass container used in a laboratory

beam *n.* **1** long, thick piece of timber, etc. **2** ship's greatest breadth **3** shaft of light **4** radiant look or smile **5** guiding radio signal —*v.* **1** radiate in a beam **2** smile warmly

bean *n.* **1** edible seed of some plants **2** pod of these

bean counter *n.* [Inf.] accountant

bear *n.* **1** large, heavy mammal with shaggy fur **2** rough, rude person —*v.* bore, borne or born, bear′ing **1** carry **2** have or show **3** give birth to **4** produce **5** permit of **6** endure —**bear down** exert pressure —**bear on** relate to —**bear out** confirm —**bear up** endure —**bear with** tolerate —**bear′a·ble** *a.* —**bear′er** *n.*

beard *n.* **1** hair on a man's face **2** awn —**beard′ed** *a.*

bear′ing *n.* **1** way one carries oneself **2** relative position or direction **3** relation **4** ball, roller, etc. on which something turns or slides

bear′ish *a.* **1** bearlike **2** pessimistic

bear′skin′ *n.* **1** furry hide of a bear **2** rug, coat, etc. made from this

beast *n.* **1** any large animal **2** brutal, gross person —**beast′ly** *a.*

beast of burden *n.* any animal used for carrying things

beast of prey *n.* any animal that hunts and kills other animals for food

beat *v.* beat, beat′en, beat′ing **1** strike repeatedly **2** punish by striking **3** mix by stirring **4** defeat **5** throb **6** flap (wings) **7** make (a path) by tramping —*n.* **1** a throbbing **2** habitual route **3** unit of musical

rhythm —*a.* [Inf.] tired —**beat back** (or **off**) drive back —**beat it** [Sl.] go away —**beat up** (**on**) [Sl.] thrash —**beat′er** *n.*

be′a·tif′ic *a.* blissful

be·at′i·fy *v.* -fied′, -fy′ing *R.C.Ch.* declare one who has died to be among the blessed in heaven

be·at′i·tude′ *n.* bliss

beat′nik *n.* bohemian of the 1950s

beat′-up′ *a.* [Sl.] worn-out, shabby, etc.

beau (bō) *n.*, *pl.* beaus or beaux (bōz) woman's sweetheart: old-fashioned

beau·ti′cian (-tish′ən) *n.* one who works styling hair, etc.

beau′ti·ful *a.* having beauty: also **beau′te·ous** —**beau′ti·ful·ly** *adv.*

beau′ti·fy′ *v.* -fied′, -fy′ing make beautiful

beau′ty *n.*, *pl.* -ties **1** pleasing quality as in looks, sound, etc. **2** person or thing of beauty

beauty salon (or **shop** or **parlor**) *n.* business that does hair styling, etc.

bea′ver *n.* **1** amphibious animal with webbed hind feet **2** its brown fur

be·calm′ *v.* **1** make calm **2** make (a ship) motionless from lack of wind

be·cause′ *con.* for the reason that —**because of** on account of

beck *n.* beckoning gesture

beck′on *v.* call by gesture

be·cloud′ *v.* to obscure

be·come′ *v.* -came′, -come′, -com′ing **1** come to be **2** suit —**become of** happen to

be·com′ing *a.* right or suitable; attractive

bed *n.* **1** piece of furniture to sleep on **2** plot of soil for plants **3** flat bottom or foundation **4** layer —*v.* bed′ded, bed′ding put or go to bed

be·daz′zle *v.* dazzle thoroughly

bed′bug′ *n.* small, wingless, biting insect

bed′clothes′ *pl.n.* sheets, blankets, etc.

bed′cov′er *n.* bedspread

bed′ding *n.* mattresses and bedclothes

be·deck′ *v.* adorn

be·dev′il *v.* to torment or worry —**be·dev′il·ment** *n.*

bed′fel′low *n.* ally, comrade, etc.

bed′lam (-ləm) *n.* noisy confusion

bed liner *n.* lining for cargo area of a pickup truck

bed of roses *n.* [Inf.] situation of ease and luxury

Bed′ou·in′ (-ōō-) *n.* Arab nomad

bed′pan′ *n.* shallow pan used as a toilet by a bedridden person

be·drag′gled *a.* wet and dirty; messy

bed·rid′den *a.* confined to bed, as by long illness

bed′rock′ *n.* **1** solid rock under soil **2** base or bottom

bed′roll′ *n.* portable roll of bedding, used by campers

bed′room′ *n.* sleeping room

bed′sore′ *n.* sore on a bedridden person

bed′spread′ *n.* ornamental cover for a bed

bed′spring′ *n.* framework of springs under a mattress

bed′stead′ *n.* frame of a bed

bed′time′ *n.* one's usual time for going to bed

bee *n.* **1** winged insect that makes honey **2** meeting of group, as to work together

beech *n.* hardwood tree with gray bark

beech′nut′ *n.* small, edible, three-cornered nut of the beech

beef *n., pl.* **beeves** or **beefs 1** cow, bull, or steer **2** its meat —*v.* [Sl.] complain

beef′steak′ *n.* thick slice of beef

beef′y *a.* **-i·er, -i·est** brawny

bee′hive′ *n.* hive for bees

bee′keep′er *n.* one who keeps bees to make honey —**bee′keep′ing** *n.*

bee′line′ *n.* straight course

been *v.* pp. of BE

beep *n.* brief, shrill sound of a horn or electronic signal —*v.* make this sound

beep′er *n.* portable electronic device for contacting people

beer *n.* mildly alcoholic drink brewed from malt, hops, etc.

bees′wax′ *n.* wax from bees, used in their honeycomb

beet *n.* plant with edible red or white root

bee′tle *n.* insect with hard front wings —*v.* jut out

bee′tle-browed′ *a.* **1** having bushy eyebrows **2** frowning

be·fall′ *v.* **-fell′, -fall′en, -fall′ing** happen (to)

be·fit′ *v.* **-fit′ted, -fit′ting** be fitting for

be·fog′ *v.* **-fogged′, -fog′ging** confuse

be·fore′ *adv.* **1** in front **2** till now **3** earlier —*prep.* **1** ahead of **2** in sight of **3** earlier than **4** rather than — *con.* earlier or sooner than

be·fore′hand′ *adv., a.* ahead of time

be·foul′ *v.* **1** to soil **2** to slander

be·friend′ *v.* be a friend to

be·fud′dle *v.* confuse

beg *v.* **begged, beg′ging 1** ask for

(alms) **2** entreat —**go begging** be unwanted

be·get′ *v.* **-got′** or [Ar.] **-gat′, -got′ten** or **-got′, -get′ting 1** to father **2** to cause

beg′gar *n.* one who lives by begging

beg′gar·ly *a.* poor; mean

be·gin′ *v.* **-gan′, -gun′, -gin′ning 1** to start **2** originate —**be·gin′ner** *n.*

be·gin′ning *n.* **1** start **2** origin **3** first part

be·gone′ *int., v.* go away

be·gon′ia (-gōn′yə) *n.* plant with showy flowers

be·grudge′ *v.* **1** envy the possession of **2** give reluctantly —**be·grudg′ing·ly** *adv.*

be·guile′ (-gīl′) *v.* **1** deceive or trick **2** charm **3** pass (time) pleasantly

be·half′ *n.* support, side, etc. —**in** (or **on**) **behalf of** in the interest of

be·have′ *v.* conduct (oneself) properly or in a specified way

be·hav′ior *n.* conduct —**be·hav′ior·al** *a.*

be·head′ *v.* cut off the head of

be·he′moth *n.* huge animal

be·hest′ *n.* a command or request

be·hind′ *adv.* **1** in the rear **2** slow; late **3** to the back —*prep.* **1** in back of **2** later or slower than **3** supporting —*a.* **1** that follows **2** in arrears

be·hold′ *v.* **-held′, -hold′ing** see; look at —*int.* look; see

be·hold′en *a.* indebted

be·hoove′ *v.* be necessary or fitting (for)

beige (bāzh) *n.* grayish tan

be′ing *n.* **1** existence; life **2** one that lives

be·la′bor *v.* spend too much time on

be·lat′ed *a.* too late

be·lay′ *v.* **-layed′, -lay′ing 1** secure (a rope) around a cleat **2** [Inf.] *Naut.* to stop

bel can′to (kän′-) *n.* brilliant singing style with purity of tone

belch *v.* **1** expel stomach gas orally **2** eject with force —*n.* a belching

be·lea′guer (-lē′gər) *v.* **1** besiege **2** beset

bel′fry (-frē) *n., pl.* **-fries** bell tower

Bel′gian *n., a.* (native) of Belgium

be·lie′ *v.* **-lied′, -ly′ing 1** misrepresent **2** prove false

be·lief′ *n.* **1** conviction; faith **2** trust **3** opinion

be·lieve′ *v.* **1** take as true **2** have faith (in) **3** suppose; guess —**be·liev′a·ble** *a.* —**be·liev′er** *n.*

be·lit′tle *v.* make seem little or unimportant

bell *n.* **1** hollow metal object that rings when struck **2** sound of a bell

bel'la·don'na *n.* **1** poisonous plant yielding a drug that relieves spasms **2** the drug

bell'-bot'tom *a.* flared at the bottom, as trousers

belle (bel) *n.* pretty girl

belles-let·tres (bel le'tr') *pl.n.* fiction, poetry, drama, etc.; literature

bell'hop' *n.* one who does errands at a hotel: also **bell'boy'**

bel'li·cose' *a.* quarrelsome —**bel'li·cos'i·ty** (-käs'-) *n.*

bel·lig'er·ent *a.* warlike —*n.* nation or person at war —**bel·lig'er·ence** *n.*

bell jar *n.* glass, bell-shaped container, used to keep air, moisture, etc. in or out: also **bell glass**

bel'low *v., n.* roar or shout

bel'lows' *n., pl.* **-lows'** collapsible device for producing a stream of air

bell pepper *n.* large, sweet red pepper

bell'weth·er *n.* **1** male sheep that leads a flock **2** indicator of a trend, style, etc.

bel'ly *n., pl.* **-lies 1** abdomen **2** stomach —*v.* **-lied, -ly·ing** to bulge

bel'ly·ache' *n.* pain in the belly —*v.* [Sl.] complain

bel'ly·but'ton *n.* [Inf.] the navel

bel'ly·ful' *n.* **1** more than enough to eat **2** [Sl.] all that one can bear

belly laugh *n.* [Inf.] hearty laugh

be·long' *v.* have a proper place —**belong to 1** be a part of **2** be owned by **3** be a member of

be·long'ings *pl.n.* possessions

be·lov'ed (-luv'id, -luvd') *a., n.* dearly loved (person)

be·low' *adv., a.* in or to a lower place; beneath —*prep.* lower than; beneath

belt *n.* **1** encircling band, as around the waist **2** distinct area —*v.* strike as with a belt —**below the belt** unfair(ly)

belt'-tight·en·ing *n.* reduction of expenditures

belt'way' *n.* expressway around urban area

be·moan' *v.* lament

be·mused' *a.* preoccupied

bench *n.* **1** long seat **2** worktable **3** seat for judges **4** status of a judge —*v.* remove (a player) from a game

bench mark *n.* standard or model: also **bench'mark'**

bench warrant *n.* order by judge or law court for an arrest

bend *v.* **bent, bend'ing 1** to curve, as

by pressure **2** (make) yield **3** stoop —*n.* **1** a bending **2** bent part

be·neath' *adv., a.* below; underneath —*prep.* **1** below; under **2** unworthy of

ben·e·dic'tion *n.* blessing

ben'e·fac'tor *n.* one who has given money or aid —**ben·e·fac'tion** *n.* —**ben'e·fac'tress** *n.fem.*

ben'e·fice (-fis) *n.* endowed church position

be·nef'i·cence *n.* **1** kindness **2** kindly act or gift —**be·nef'i·cent** *a.*

ben·e·fi'cial (-fish'əl) *a.* producing benefits

ben·e·fi'ci·ar·y (-fish'ər ē) *n., pl.* **-ies** one receiving benefits, as from insurance

ben'e·fit *n.* **1** help or advantage **2** a show, etc. to raise money for a cause —*v.* **1** to help **2** profit

be·nev'o·lence *n.* the wish to do good; kindness; generosity —**be·nev'o·lent** *a.* —**be·nev'o·lent·ly** *adv.*

be·night'ed *a.* ignorant

be·nign' (-nīn') *a.* **1** kindly **2** favorable **3** not malignant

be·nig'nant *a.* benign

ben'i·son *n.* blessing

bent *a.* **1** curved **2** determined (*on*) —*n.* inclination

bent'grass' *n.* low-growing grass that puts out runners, used for lawns

bent'wood' *a.* made of pieces of wood permanently bent

be·numb' *v.* make numb

Ben·ze·drine' (-drēn') *trademark* amphetamine —*n.* [**b-**] this drug

ben'zene *n.* coal-tar derivative used as a solvent

ben'zo·ate' *n.* chemical used to preserve food

be·queath' (-kwēth', -kwēth') *v.* **1** leave (property) to another by one's will **2** hand down —**be·quest'** *n.*

be·rate' *v.* scold severely

be·reave' *v.* **-reaved'** or **-reft', -reav'ing 1** deprive **2** leave forlorn, as by death —**be·reave'ment** *n.* —**be·reft'** *a.*

be·ret' (-rā') *n.* flat, round, soft cap

berg *n.* iceberg

beri·beri *n.* disease caused by lack of vitamin B₁

berm *n.* ledge along the edge of a paved road

ber'ry *n., pl.* **-ries** small, fleshy fruit with seeds

ber·serk' (-surk', -zurk') *a., adv.* in(to) a violent rage

berth *n.* **1** ship's place of anchorage **2**

built-in bed **3** position or job

ber′yl (-əl) *n.* hard, bright mineral, as the emerald

be·ryl′li·um (-ril′-) *n.* rare, metallic chemical element used in alloys

be·seech′ *v.* **-sought′** or **-seeched′** **-seech′ing** ask (for) earnestly; entreat —**be·seech′ing·ly** *adv.*

be·set′ *v.* **-set′, -set′ting** **1** attack from all sides **2** surround

be·set′ting *a.* always harassing

be·side′ *prep.* **1** at the side of; near **2** as compared with **3** besides **4** aside from —*adv.* besides —**beside oneself** wild, as with fear or anger

be·sides′ *adv.* **1** in addition **2** else **3** moreover —*prep.* in addition to

be·siege′ *v.* **1** lay siege to; hem in **2** overwhelm, harass, etc. **3** close in on

be·smirch′ *v.* to soil; sully

be·sot′ted *a.* stupefied, as with liquor

be·speak′ *v.* **1** speak for; reserve **2** indicate

best *a.* **1** most excellent **2** most suitable —*adv.* **1** in the best way **2** most —*n.* **1** best person, thing, etc. **2** the utmost —*v.* outdo; beat —**all for the best** turning out to be good —**at best** under the most favorable conditions —**get (or have) the best of** defeat or outwit —**had best** should —**make the best of** adjust to

bes′tial (-chəl) *a.* like a beast; brutal

be·stir′ *v.* stir up; busy

best man *n.* main attendant of a bridegroom

be·stow′ *v.* present as a gift (*on* or *upon*)

be·stride′ *v.* **-strode′, -strid′den, -strid′ing** sit, mount, or stand astride

bet *n.* **1** agreement that the one proved wrong will pay something **2** thing so staked —*v.* **bet** or **bet′ted, bet′ting** **1** make a bet **2** stake in a bet —**bet′tor, bet′ter** *n.*

be·ta (bā′tə) *n.* second letter of the Greek alphabet

be·take′ *v.* take (oneself); go

beta particle *n.* electron or positron ejected from an atomic nucleus during radioactive disintegration

beta ray *n.* stream of beta particles

be·tel nut (bēt′'l) *n.* fruit of a tree (**betel palm**), chewed with leaves of a plant (**betel pepper**) by some Asian peoples

be·think′ *v.* think of; remind (oneself)

be·tide′ *v.* happen (to)

be·to′ken *v.* be a sign of

be·tray′ *v.* **1** be disloyal to **2** deceive **3** seduce **4** reveal —**be·tray′al** *n.*

be·troth′ (-trōth′, -trôth′) *v.* promise in marriage —**be·troth′al** (-trōth′-) *n.* — **be·trothed′** (-trōt͟hd′) *a., n.*

bet′ter *a.* **1** more excellent **2** more suitable **3** improved —*adv.* **1** in a better way **2** more —*n.* **1** a superior **2** a better thing, etc. —*v.* to surpass or improve —**better off** in better circumstances —**get (or have) the better of** defeat or outwit —**had better** should

bet′ter·ment *n.* improvement

be·tween′ *prep.* **1** in the space or time separating **2** involving **3** joining **4** in the common possession of **5** one of — *adv.* in the middle

be·twixt′ *prep., adv.* [Ar.] between

bev′el *n.* **1** angled part or surface **2** tool for marking angles —*v.* cut or slope at an angle

bev′er·age *n.* drink

bev′y *n., pl.* **-ies 1** group, as of women **2** flock of quail

be·wail′ *v.* wail over

be·ware′ *v.* guard against

be·wil′der *v.* confuse —**be·wil′der· ment** *n.*

be·witch′ *v.* to enchant —**be·witch′ing** *a.* —**be·witch′ment** *n.*

bey (bā) *n.* Turkish title of respect

be·yond′ *prep.* **1** farther or later than; past **2** more than —*adv.* farther away —**the (great) beyond** whatever follows death

bez′el *n.* slanting faces of a cut jewel

bi- *pref.* two or twice

bi·an′nu·al *a.* twice a year

bi·as (bī′əs) *n.* **1** diagonal or slanting line **2** prejudice —*v.* to prejudice — **on the bias** diagonally

bib *n.* cloth tied under a child's chin at meals

bibb lettuce *n.* lettuce with loose, dark-green leaves

Bi′ble *n.* sacred book of Christians or Jews —**Bib′li·cal, Bib′li·cal** *a.*

bib·li·og′ra·phy *n., pl.* **-phies** list of writings on one subject or by one author

bib′li·o·phile′ *n.* one who loves or collects books

bib′u·lous *a.* fond of alcoholic liquor

bi·cam′er·al *a.* having two legislative branches

bi·car′bon·ate of soda *n.* baking soda

bi·cen·ten′ni·al *n.* 200th anniversary

bi′ceps′ *n., pl.* **-ceps′** large front muscle of the upper arm

bick′er *v., n.* quarrel

bi·cus′pid *n.* tooth with two-pointed crown

bi′cy·cle *n.* two-wheeled vehicle with pedals —*v.* ride a bicycle —**bi′cy·clist, bi′cy·cler** *n.*

bid *v.* **bade** (bad) or **bid, bid′den** or **bid, bid′ding 1** command or ask **2** tell **3 bid, bid′ding** offer as a price —*n.* **1** amount bid **2** attempt —**bid′der** *n.*

bide *v.* **bode** or **bid′ed, bid′ed, bid′ing 1** stay **2** dwell **3** wait —**bide one's time** wait patiently for a chance

bi·det′ (-dā′) *n.* bathroom fixture, for bathing the crotch

bi·en′ni·al *a.* **1** every two years **2** lasting two years —*n.* plant living two years

bier (bir) *n.* frame on which a coffin is put

bi′fo·cals *pl.n.* eyeglasses with lenses having two parts, for close and far focus

big *a.* **big′ger, big′gest 1** of great size **2** loud **3** important **4** noble —*adv.* [Inf.] **1** boastfully **2** impressively —**big′ness** *n.*

big′a·my *n.* crime of marrying again while still married —**big′a·mist** *n.* —**big′a·mous** *a.*

Big Dipper *n.* dipper-shaped group of stars

big game *n.* large wild animals hunted for sport, as lions

big′heart′ed *a.* generous

big′horn′ *n.* horned, wild sheep of Rocky Mountains

bight (bīt) *n.* **1** loop in a rope **2** curve in a coastline **3** a bay formed by such a curve

big′ot *n.* narrow-minded, intolerant person —**big′ot·ed** *a.* —**big′ot·ry** *n.*

big shot *n.* [Sl.] important person

big′-time′ *a., adv.* [Sl.] great(ly)

bike *n., v.* [Inf.] **1** bicycle **2** motorcycle

bi·ki′ni *n., pl.* **-nis 1** women's very brief, two-piece swimsuit **2** very brief underpants or trunks

bi·lat′er·al *a.* on, by, or having two sides

bile *n.* **1** bitter liver secretion **2** bad temper

bilge *n.* **1** lower part of a ship's hold **2** stale water that gathers there **3** [Sl.] nonsense

bi·lin′gual *a.* of, in, or speaking two languages

bil′ious (-yəs) *a.* bad-tempered

bilk *v.* to swindle

bill *n.* **1** statement of charges, as for goods **2** list of things offered **3** proposed law **4** piece of paper money **5** bird's beak —*v.* present a bill of

charges to

bill′board′ *n.* signboard

bil′let *n.* lodging, as for soldiers —*v.* assign to lodging

bill′fold′ *n.* wallet

bil′liards (-yərdz) *n.* game played with cue and three balls on a table with raised edges

bil′lion *n.* thousand millions —**bil′lionth** *a., n.*

bil′lion·aire′ *n.* one having at least a billion dollars

bill of fare *n.* menu

Bill of Rights *n.* first ten amendments to U.S. Constitution

bill of sale *n.* paper transferring ownership by sale

bil′low *n.* **1** large wave **2** swelling mass, as of smoke —*v.* surge or swell —**bil′low·y** *a.,* -**i·er,** -**i·est**

bil′ly *n., pl.* **-lies** club, esp. a policeman's stick

billy goat *n.* male goat

bi·month′ly *a., adv.* once every two months

bin *n.* box or enclosed space for storage

bi′na·ry *a.* **1** twofold **2** of a number system with only two digits

bin·au′ral (bīn-) *a.* stereophonic

bind *v.* **bound, bind′ing 1** tie together **2** to hold; restrain **3** encircle with (a belt, etc.) **4** bandage **5** put together pages and cover of (a book) **6** to obligate —**bind′er** *n.*

bind′er·y *n., pl.* **-ies** place where books are bound

bind′ing *n.* **1** anything that binds **2** covering of a book

binge *n.* [Inf.] spree

bin′go *n.* game played on cards with numbered squares

bin′na·cle *n.* case enclosing a ship's compass

bin·oc′u·lars (bī näk′-, bi-) *pl.n.* field glasses

bi′o·chem′is·try *n.* chemistry of living organisms

bi′o·cide′ *n.* poisonous chemical substance

bi′o·de·grad′a·ble (-grād′-) *a.* readily decomposed by bacteria

bi′o·di·ver′si·ty *n.* variety of living things in an area

bi′o·feed′back *n.* technique for controlling emotions

bi·og′ra·phy *n., pl.* **-phies** one's life story written by another —**bi·og′ra·pher** *n.* —**bi′o·graph′i·cal** *a.*

biol *abbrev.* biology

biological warfare *n.* use of deadly microorganisms, toxins, etc. in war

bi·ol'o·gy *n.* science of plants and animals —**bi·o·log'i·cal** *a.* —**bi·ol'o·gist** *n.*

bi·on'ics *n.* science of modeling instruments or systems after living organisms

bi'o·phys'ics *n.* study of the physics of biology

bi'op·sy *n., pl.* **-sies** removal of living body tissue for diagnosis

bi·par'ti·san (-zən) *a.* representing two parties

bi'ped' *n.* two-footed animal

bi·po'lar *a.* having alternating periods of mania and mental depression

birch *n.* **1** tree with smooth bark **2** its hard wood

bird *n.* warmblooded vertebrate with feathers and wings

bird'ie *n. Golf* score of one under par for a hole

bird'ing *n.* bird-watching as a hobby —**bird'er** *n.*

bird's'-eye' view *a.* **1** view from above or at a distance **2** general view

bird'-watch'ing *n.* observation of wild birds as a hobby

birth *n.* **1** a being born **2** descent or origin **3** beginning —**give birth (to)** bring into being —**birth'place'** *n.*

birth'day' *n.* day of birth or its anniversary

birth'ing *a., n.* (for) giving birth

birth'mark' *n.* skin blemish present at birth

birth'rate' *n.* number of births per year in an area

birth'right' *n.* rights a person has by birth

bis'cuit (-kit) *n.* **1** small bread roll **2** [Br.] cracker or cookie

bi·sect' *v.* divide into two equal parts —**bi·sec'tor** *n.*

bi·sex'u·al *a.* sexually attracted to both sexes —*n.* bisexual person

bish'op *n.* **1** clergyman heading a diocese **2** chessman moving diagonally

bish'op·ric *n.* diocese, rank, etc. of a bishop

bis'muth (biz'-) *n.* metallic chemical element used in medicine

bi'son *n., pl.* **bi'son** shaggy, oxlike animal of North America

bisque (bisk) *n.* thick, creamy soup made from shellfish, etc. or strained vegetables

bis'tro (bēs'-) *n., pl.* **-tros'** small cafe

bit *n.* **1** mouthpiece on a bridle, for control **2** cutting part of a drill **3** small piece or amount **4** single digit in a binary number system **5** short time —**bit by bit** gradually —**do one's bit** do one's share

bitch *n.* female dog, fox, etc. —*v.* [Sl.] complain

bite *v.* **bit, bit'ten** or **bit, bit'ing 1** seize or cut as with the teeth **2** sting, as an insect **3** cause to smart **4** seize a bait —*n.* **1** a biting **2** biting quality; sting **3** wound from biting **4** mouthful **5** light meal

bit'ing *a.* **1** cutting; sharp **2** sarcastic

bit'ter *a.* **1** sharp to the taste **2** sorrowful, painful, resentful, etc. **3** harsh —**bit'ter·ly** *adv.*

bit'tern *n.* heronlike bird

bit'ters *pl.n.* liquor containing bitter herbs, etc.

bit'ter·sweet' *a.* both bitter and sweet

bi·tu'men *n.* natural asphalt or similar substance made from coal, etc.

bi·tu'mi·nous coal *n.* soft coal, easy to burn but smoky

bi'valve' *n.* mollusk with two shells, as a clam

biv'ou·ac' (-wak', -ōō ak') *n.* temporary camp (of soldiers) —*v.* **-ou·acked', -ou·ack'ing** make such a camp

bi·week'ly *a., adv.* once every two weeks

bi·zarre (bi zär') *a.* odd; fantastic

blab *v.* **blabbed, blab'bing** to talk idly; gossip, etc.

black *a.* **1** of the color of coal; opposite to white **2** having dark skin **3** without light; dark **4** dirty **5** evil **6** sad —*n.* **1** black pigment **2** member of a dark-skinned people, or person having African ancestry —*v.* to blacken —**black out** lose consciousness —**black'ish** *a.* —**black'ness** *n.*

black'-and-blue' *a.* discolored by a bruise

black'ball' *n., v.* (a) vote against

black belt *n.* black belt awarded to an expert of the highest skill in judo or karate

black'ber'ry *v., pl.* **-ries 1** small, edible, dark fruit **2** bramble it grows on

black'bird' *n.* bird the male of which is all black

black'board' *n.* smooth surface for writing on with chalk

black'en *v.* **1** make or become black **2** slander

black eye *n.* discoloration of skin around the eye, as from a blow

black'-eyed' Su'san *n.* yellow flower like a daisy

black·guard (blag'ərd) *n.* scoundrel; villain

black'head' n. plug of dirt in a pore of the skin

black ice n. thin layer of ice on pavement

black'jack' n. **1** small bludgeon **2** a gambling game at cards

black light n. ultraviolet or infrared radiation

black'list' n. list of those to be punished, refused jobs, etc.

black lung (disease) n. lung disease from continual inhaling of coal dust

black magic n. evil magic; sorcery

black'mail' n. extortion by threatening to reveal disgraceful secret —v. (try to) get money by blackmail —**black'mail'er** n.

black market n. system for selling goods illegally during rationing, etc.

black'out' n. **1** concealing of light, facts, etc. **2** a faint **3** loss of electricity in an area

black sheep n. disgraceful member of a family, etc.

black'smith' n. one who forges iron and shoes horses

black'thorn' n. thorny shrub

black'top' n. asphalt mixture used to surface roads, etc.

black widow n. small, poisonous spider

blad'der n. sac that collects urine from the kidneys

blade n. **1** leaf of grass **2** cutting part of a knife, tool, etc. **3** flat surface, as of an oar

blame v. **1** accuse of being at fault **2** put the responsibility of (on) —n. **1** a blaming **2** responsibility for a fault —**be to blame** deserve blame —**blame'less** a. —**blame'wor'thy** a.

blanch v. **1** whiten **2** make or turn pale

bland a. **1** mild; soothing **2** dull; tasteless

blan'dish v. flatter; coax —**blan'dish·ment** n.

blank a. **1** not written on **2** empty **3** without expression —n. **1** (printed form with) space to be filled in **2** cartridge without a bullet —**draw a blank** [Inf.] be unable to remember something

blank check n. unconditional permission

blan'ket n. **1** wool spread used as bed cover, etc. **2** a covering, as of snow —a. all-inclusive —v. to cover

blare v. sound loudly —n. loud, trumpetlike sound

blar'ney (blär'-) n. flattery

bla·sé' (blä zā') a. bored

blas'phe·my' (-fə mē) n., pl. **-mies** profane abuse of God —**blas·pheme'** (-fēm') v. —**blas'phe·mous** a.

blast n. **1** strong rush of air **2** loud sound of horn, etc. **3** explosion —v. **1** explode **2** to blight; wither

blast furnace n. furnace for smelting iron ore

blast'off', blast'-off' n. launching of a rocket, etc.

bla'tant a. **1** loud and vulgar **2** glaringly obvious —**bla'tan·cy** n.

blaze n. **1** burst of flame **2** bright light **3** vivid display **4** outburst **5** white spot on an animal's face —v. **1** burn or shine brightly **2** mark (a trail)

blaz'er n. lightweight sports jacket in a solid color

bla'zon n. coat of arms —v. proclaim

bldg abbrev. building

bleach v. whiten —n. chemical that bleaches

bleach'ers pl.n. roofless stand where spectators sit

bleak a. **1** unsheltered; bare **2** cheerless; gloomy

blear (blir) v. to dim or blur, as with tears —**blear'y** a.

bleat n. cry of a sheep or goat —v. make this cry

bleed v. **bled, bleed'ing 1** lose blood **2** draw blood, air, etc. from **3** [Inf.] extort from

bleep n., v. beep

blem'ish v. mar; injure —n. defect; fault

blend v. **1** mix **2** shade into each other —n. **1** a blending **2** mixture

blend'er n. kitchen appliance for chopping, mixing, etc.

bless v. **blessed** or **blest, bless'ing 1** make holy **2** ask divine favor for **3** make happy —**bless·ed** (bles'əd, blest) a. —**bless'ing** n.

blew v. pt. of BLOW

blight n. **1** insect, disease, etc. that destroys plants **2** anything that destroys —v. destroy; ruin

blimp n. [Inf.] small airship like a dirigible

blind a. **1** without sight **2** lacking insight **3** having no outlet **4** not controlled by reason —n. **1** window shade **2** hiding place for hunter —v. make sightless —**blind'ly** adv. —**blind'ness** n.

blind date n. [Inf.] date with a stranger, arranged by a third person

blind'fold' v. cover the eyes of —n.

cloth used for this

blind'side' v. hit someone who is unprepared or looking away

blink v. **1** wink rapidly **2** flash on and off —n. **1** a blinking **2** twinkle —**blink at** ignore —**on the blink** [Sl.] malfunctioning

blink'er n. flashing light

blintz n. thin, rolled pancake

blip n. **1** image on radar **2** slight change or interruption

bliss n. great happiness —**bliss'ful** a.

blis'ter n. fluid-filled skin swelling caused by a burn, etc. —v. form blisters

blis'ter·ing a. **1** very hot **2** very intense, fast, etc.

blithe (blīth, blīth) a. carefree; cheerful

blitz n. sudden, overwhelming attack

bliz'zard n. severe snowstorm with high wind

bloat v. swell up

blob n. small drop or mass

bloc n. group united for a common purpose

block n. **1** solid piece **2** auction platform **3** obstruction **4** city square or street section **5** pulley in a frame **6** part taken as a unit —v. **1** obstruct **2** shape —**block out** sketch roughly —**on the block** for sale

block·ade' n. a shutting off of a place by warships, etc. —v. to subject to a blockade

block'bust'er n. an expensive movie, etc. intended to have wide appeal

block'bust'ing n. [Inf.] frightening owners into selling homes because minority group will become neighbors

block'head' n. stupid person

block'house' n. wooden fort

blond a. **1** having light-colored hair and skin **2** light-colored Also **blonde** —n. **1.** blond man or boy —**blonde** n.fem.

blood n. **1** red fluid in the arteries and veins **2** lineage **3** kinship —**in cold blood** deliberately —**blood'less** a.

blood bank n. supply of blood stored for transfusions

blood'cur'dling a. very frightening; terrifying

blood'hound' n. large, keen-scented tracking dog

blood'mo·bile' n. mobile unit for collecting blood for blood banks

blood'shed' n. killing

blood'shot' a. tinged with blood: said of the eyes

blood'thirst'y a. murderous

blood vessel n. artery, vein, or capillary

blood'y a. **-i·er, -i·est 1** of or covered with blood **2** involving bloodshed **3** bloodthirsty —v. **-ied, -y·ing** stain with blood

bloom n. **1** a flower **2** time of flowering **3** healthy glow —v. be in bloom

bloom'ers pl.n. women's baggy underpants

bloop'er n. [Sl.] stupid mistake

blos'som n., v. flower

blot n. spot or stain —v. **blot'ted, blot'ting 1** spot, as with ink **2** erase or cancel (out) **3** to dry with soft paper, etc. —**blot'ter** n.

blotch n. discolored spot —v. mark with blotches —**blotch'y** a., **-i·er, -i·est**

blouse (blous) n. shirtlike garment for girls

blow v. **blew, blown, blow'ing 1** move, as (by) wind **2** force air out, as with the mouth **3** sound by blowing —n. **1** a blowing **2** gale **3** a hit **4** shock —**blow out 1** extinguish **2** burst —**blow up 1** inflate **2** explode —**blow'er** n.

blow'gun' n. tubular weapon through which darts, etc. are blown

blow'out' n. bursting of a tire

blow'torch' n. small torch for welding

blow'up' n. **1** an explosion **2** enlarged photograph

blowz·y (blou'zē) a. **-i·er, -i·est** slovenly: also sp. **blows'y**

blub'ber n. whale fat —v. weep loudly

bludg·eon (bluj'ən) n. short, heavy club —v. to club

blue a. **1** of the color of the clear sky **2** gloomy —n. color of the clear sky —**the blues 1** [Inf.] depressed feeling **2** slow, sad jazz song

blue baby n. baby born with bluish skin, esp. because of a heart defect

blue'bell' n. plant with blue, bell-shaped flowers

blue'ber'ry n., pl. **-ries** small, edible, bluish berry

blue'bird' n. small bird with blue back and wings

blue blood n. aristocrat: also **blue' blood'** n.

blue'-col'lar a. of industrial workers

blue'fish' n. blue Atlantic food fish

blue'grass' n. **1** type of grass with bluish-green stems **2** S U.S. folk music

blue jay n. crested bird with a blue back

blue'jeans' pl.n. jeans of blue denim

blue law n. puritanical law, esp. one prohibiting certain activities on Sunday

blue moon n. a very long time

blue'-pen'cil v. edit

blue'print' n. **1** photographic copy, white on blue, of architectural plans, etc. **2** any detailed plan —v. make a blueprint of

bluff v. mislead by a fake, bold front —a. rough and frank —n. **1** a bluffing **2** one who bluffs **3** steep bank

blu'ing n. blue rinse for white fabrics

blu'ish a. somewhat blue: also sp. **blue'ish**

blun'der n. foolish mistake —v. **1** make a blunder **2** move clumsily

blun'der·buss' n. obsolete gun with a broad muzzle

blunt a. **1** dull-edged **2** plain-spoken —v. make dull

blur v. **blurred, blur'ring 1** to smudge **2** make or become indistinct —n. indistinct thing —**blur'ry** a., **-ri·er, -ri·est**

blurb n. advertisement, as on a book jacket

blurt v. say impulsively

blush v. redden, as from shame —n. a blushing

blus'ter v. **1** blow stormily **2** speak noisily or boastfully —n. swaggering talk —**blus'ter·y** a.

Blvd abbrev. Boulevard

bo·a (bō'ə) n. **1** large snake that suffocates its prey in its coils **2** scarf of feathers

boar n. wild hog

board n. **1** broad, flat piece of wood, etc. **2** meals provided regularly for pay **3** council —v. **1** cover (up) with boards **2** get on (a ship, train, etc.) **3** get meals regularly for pay —**on board** on a ship, etc. —**board'er** n.

board'ing·house' n. house where one can pay for a room and meals

board'walk' n. wooden walk along a beach

boast v. **1** talk with too much pride **2** take pride in —n. thing boasted of —**boast'er** n. —**boast'ful** a.

boat n. water craft, esp. a small one —**rock the boat** [Inf.] disturb the status quo —**boat'man** n., pl. **-men**

boat'ing n. rowing, sailing, etc.

boat'lift' n. a transporting of refugees by small boats, etc.

boat·swain (bō'sən) n. ship's petty officer directing deck work

boat'yard' n. place where boats are built, repaired, etc.

bob n. **1** small hanging weight **2** float on a fishing line —v. **bobbed, bob'bing 1** move jerkily **2** cut short, as hair

bob'bin n. spool for thread

bob'by n. [Inf.] Br. policeman

bob'by pin n. tight hairpin

bob'by socks (or **sox**) n. [Inf.] girls' short socks

bob'cat' n. American lynx

bob'o·link' n. songbird with a call like its name

bob'sled' n. racing sled

bob'white' n. small quail

bock (beer) n. a dark beer

bode v. **1** be an omen of **2** pt. of BIDE

bod·ice (bäd'is) n. snug upper part of a dress

bod'y n., pl. **-ies 1** whole physical structure **2** trunk of a man or animal **3** main part **4** distinct mass or group **5** [Inf.] person —**bod'i·ly** a., adv.

bod'y·guard' n. person(s) assigned to protect someone

body language n. unconscious bodily movements that communicate something

body stocking n. one-piece, tight-fitting garment

bod'y·suit' n. one-piece, tight-fitting garment for torso: also **body shirt**

bog n. small swamp —v. **bogged, bog'ging** sink (down) as in a bog —**bog'gy** a.

bog'gle v. **1** be startled or hesitate (at) **2** confuse

bo'gus a. not genuine

bo·gy (bō'gē) n., pl. **-gies** imaginary evil spirit; goblin: also sp. **bo'gey** or **bo'gie**

bo·he'mi·an n. one who lives unconventionally

boil v. **1** bubble up into vapor by being heated **2** be agitated **3** cook by boiling —n. **1** boiling state **2** pus-filled pimple —**boil down** condense

boil'er n. tank for making steam or storing hot water

boiler room n. room where a boiler is located

bois'ter·ous a. rough, noisy, lively, etc.

bold a. **1** daring; fearless **2** impudent **3** sharp and clear —**bold'ly** adv.

bo·le'ro (-ler'ō) n., pl. **-ros 1** Spanish dance **2** short, open vest

boll (bōl) n. pod of cotton or flax

boll weevil n. beetle that harms cotton pods

bo·lo'gna (-lō'nē) n. type of smoked sausage

Bol'she·vik (bōl'-) n. a communist during the Russian Revolution

bol'ster (bōl'-) *n.* long pillow —*v.* prop (*up*)

bolt *n.* 1 flash of lightning 2 sliding bar that locks a door, etc. 3 threaded metal rod used with a nut 4 roll of cloth —*v.* 1 gulp (food) 2 rush out 3 fasten with a bolt —**bolt upright** straight upright

bo'lus (bō'-) *n.* large pill

bomb (bäm) *n.* 1 explosive device or missile 2 [Inf.] complete failure —*v.* 1 attack with bombs 2 [Inf.] be a failure

bom·bard' *v.* attack as with artillery or bombs —**bom'bar·dier'** (-bər dir') *n.* —**bom·bard'ment** *n.*

bom'bast' *n.* pompous speech —**bom·bas'tic** *a.*

bomb'er *n.* airplane designed for dropping bombs

bomb'shell' *n.* 1 bomb 2 shocking surprise

bo·na fi·de (bō'nə fīd', bä'-) *a.* 1 sincere 2 genuine

bo·nan'za *n.* 1 rich vein of ore 2 any rich source

bon'bon' *n.* piece of candy

bond *n.* 1 thing that binds or unites 2 binding agreement 3 interest-bearing certificate 4 surety against theft, etc. —*v.* 1 bind 2 furnish a BOND (*n.* 4) for

bond'age *n.* slavery

bonds'man *n., pl.* **-men** one furnishing a BOND (*n.* 4)

bone *n.* material of the skeleton or piece of this —*v.* 1 remove the bones from 2 [Sl.] study hard: with *up* —**make no bones about** [Inf.] admit freely —**bone'less** *a.*

bone'-dry' *a.* [Inf.] very dry

bone meal *n.* crushed bones used as feed or fertilizer

bon'er (bōn'-) *n.* [Sl.] a blunder

bon'fire' *n.* large fire built outdoors

bong *n.* deep ringing sound —*v.* make this sound

bon'go *n., pl.* **-gos** either of a pair of small drums struck with the hands

bo·ni'to (-nē'tō) *n., pl.* **-tos** or **-toes** kind of tuna

bon·jour (bōn zhoor') *int., n.* [[Fr.]] good day; hello

bonk'ers *a.* [Sl.] crazy

bon'net *n.* hat

bon'ny *a., pl.* **-ni·er** or **-ni·est** 1 handsome; pretty 2 pleasant

bo·no'bo *n., pl.* **-bos** small chimpanzee

bon·sai' (-sī') *n., pl.* **-sai** dwarfed tree

or shrub

bo'nus *n.* payment over the usual or required amount

bon' voy·age' (-äzh') *int., n.* pleasant journey

bon'y *a.* **-i·er, -i·est** 1 (full) of bones 2 lean; thin —**bon'i·ness** *n.*

boo *int., n., pl.* **boos** sound made to show disapproval or to startle —*v.* shout "boo" at

boo'-boo', boo'boo' *n., pl.* **-boos** 1 [Sl.] stupid mistake 2 minor injury: child's word

boo'by *n., pl.* **-bies** a fool

booby trap *n.* device, etc. for tricking or injuring unexpectedly

book *n.* 1 set of printed or blank sheets bound together 2 a division of a long literary work 3 *pl.* business accounts —*v.* 1 to list in a book 2 to reserve, as rooms

book'case' *n.* set of shelves for holding books

book'end' *n.* support to hold a row of books upright

book'ie *n.* [Sl.] bookmaker

book'ish *a.* 1 inclined to read or study 2 pedantic

book'keep'ing *n.* work of recording business transactions —**book'keep'er** *n.*

book'let *n.* small book

book'mak'er *n.* one who takes bets, esp. on horse races

book'mark' *n.* slip, etc. for marking a place in a book

book'worm' *n.* one who reads or studies much

boom *v.* 1 make a deep, hollow sound 2 grow rapidly 3 promote —*n.* 1 deep sound 2 long beam on a derrick 3 spar at the foot of a sail 4 period of prosperity

boom'er·ang' *n.* Australian curved stick that returns to the thrower —*v.* go awry

boon *n.* benefit

boon'docks' *pl.n.* [Inf.] remote rural region

boon'dog'gle *n.* pointless work financed with public funds

boor *n.* rude person

boost *v., n.* [Inf.] 1 push upward; raise 2 support —**boost'er** *n.*

booster shot *n.* later injection of vaccine, to keep immunity

boot *n.* outer covering for the foot and leg —*v.* 1 to kick 2 [Inf.] dismiss 3 start *up* (a computer)

boot·ee, boot'ie *n.* baby's knitted or cloth shoe

booth *n.* small stall or enclosure

boot'leg' *n.* **-legged', -leg'ging** sell (liquor) illegally —*a.* sold illegally — **boot'leg'ger** *n.*

boot'less *a.* useless

boo'ty *n.* plunder; spoils

booze *n.* [Inf.] liquor —*v.* [Inf.] to drink too much liquor —**booz'er** *n.*

bo'rax' *n.* a white salt used in glass, soaps, etc.

bor'der *n.* **1** edge; margin **2** boundary —*v.* put a border on —*a.* near a border —**border on** (or **upon**) be next to —**bor'der·land'** *n.*

bor'der·line' *n.* boundary —*a.* **1** on a boundary **2** indefinite

bore *v.* **1** drill a hole (in) **2** weary by being dull —*n.* **1** inside or diameter of a tube **2** dull person or thing — **bore'dom** *n.*

bore *v.* pt. of BEAR

bo'ric acid *n.* powder used in solution as an antiseptic

born *v.* pp. of BEAR (*v.* 3) —*a.* **1** brought into life **2** by nature

borne *v.* pp. of BEAR (*v.* 1)

bo'ron' *n.* nonmetallic chemical element

bor·ough (bur'ō) *n.* **1** in some U.S. states, self-governing town **2** division of New York City

bor'row *v.* **1** take on loan **2** adopt (an idea)

borscht, borsch (bôrsh) *n.* beet soup, often served with sour cream

bor'zoi' *n.* large dog with narrow head and long legs

bosh *n., int.* [Inf.] nonsense

bos'om (booz'-) *n.* breast —*a.* intimate, as a friend

boss *n.* **1** employer or supervisor **2** head politician —*v.* **1** supervise **2** [Inf.] order about —**boss'y** *a.*, **-i·er, -i·est** —**boss'i·ness** *n.*

bo'sun *n.* boatswain

bot'a·ny *n.* science of plants —**bo·tan'i·cal** *a.* —**bot'a·nist** *n.*

botch *v.* spoil; bungle —*n.* bungled work

both *a., pron.* the two —*con., adv.* equally

both'er (bäth'-) *v.* **1** annoy; worry **2** trouble (oneself) —*n.* annoying matter —**both'er·some** *a.*

bot'tle *n.* glass container for liquids — *v.* put into a bottle —**bottle up** hold in or suppress

bot'tle·neck' *n.* **1** narrow passage **2** any hindrance

bot'tom *n.* lowest part; base; underside

bottom line *n.* **1** [Inf.] profit or loss **2** [Sl.] main point

bot'u·lism' (bäch'ə-) *n.* food poisoning caused by bacteria

bou·doir' (bōō dwär') *n.* woman's private room

bouf·fant (bōō fänt') *a.* puffed out; full

bough (bou) *n.* tree branch

bought (bôt) *v.* pt. & pp. of BUY

bouil·lon (bool'yän') *n.* clear broth

boul'der (bōl'-) *n.* large rock

bou'le·vard' (bool'-) *n.* broad, treelined street

bounce *v.* **1** spring back on impact **2** make bounce **3** leap —*n.* a bouncing —**bounc'y** *a.*, **-i·er, -i·est**

bounc'er *n.* one hired to expel disorderly persons from nightclub, etc.

bounc'ing *a.* healthy

bound *v.* **1** pt. & pp. of BIND **2** leap or bounce **3** be a limit or boundary to — *a.* **1** tied **2** certain (*to*) **3** obliged **4** with a binding **5** headed (*for*) **6** [Inf.] determined —*n.* **1** a leap or bounce **2** boundary —**out of bounds** prohibited —**bound'less** *a.*

bound'a·ry *n., pl.* **-ries** anything marking a limit

boun'te·ous *a.* **1** generous **2** abundant

boun'ti·ful *a.* bounteous

boun'ty *n.* **1** *pl.* **-ties** generosity **2** gift or reward

bou·quet' (bō kā', bōō-) *n.* **1** bunch of flowers **2** aroma

bour·bon (bur'bən) *n.* corn whiskey

bour·geois (-zhwä') *a., n.* middle-class (person)

bour·geoi·sie (boor'zhwä zē') *n.* social middle class

bout (bout) *n.* **1** struggle; contest **2** spell or term

bou·tique' (bōō tēk', bō-) *n.* small shop selling costly articles

bou·ton·niere, bou·ton·nière (bōō'tə nir') *n.* flower worn in a buttonhole

bo'vine' *a.* of or like a cow or ox

bow (bou) *v.* **1** bend down in respect **2** submit **3** weigh (*down*) —*n.* **1** a bending of the head or body **2** front part of a ship —**take a bow** acknowledge applause

bow (bō) *n.* **1** curved stick strung with cord for shooting arrows **2** stick strung with horsehairs, for playing a violin, etc. **3** knot with broad loops — *a.* curved —*v.* play (a violin) with a bow

bow·els (bou'-) *pl.n.* **1** intestines **2** depths

bow'er (bou'-) *n.* arbor

bow·ie knife (bōō'ē, bō'-) *n.* long, single-edged hunting knife

bow'knot' (bō'-) *n.* knot usually with two loops and two ends

bowl *n.* 1 hollow, rounded dish or part 2 amphitheater —*v.* 1 roll (a ball) in bowling 2 move fast —**bowl over** knock over

bow'leg'ged (bō'-) *a.* with the legs curved out

bowl'ing *n.* game in which a ball is rolled along a wooden lane (**bowling alley**) at ten wooden pins

bowls *n.* bowling game played on a smooth lawn (**bowling green**)

bow'man (bō'-) *n., pl.* -men archer

bow'sprit' (bou'-, bō'-) *n.* tapered spar at bow of a ship

bow tie (bō) *n.* necktie tied in a bow

box *n.* 1 container made of wood, cardboard, etc. 2 enclosed group of seats 3 a blow with the hand 4 evergreen shrub: also **box'wood** —*v.* 1 put (*in*) or shut (*up*) as in a box 2 fight with the fists —**box'er** *n.* —**box'ing** *n.*

box'car' *n.* enclosed railroad freight car

box office *n.* place in a theater to buy tickets

box wrench *n.* wrench that wraps entirely around nut, etc.

boy *n.* male child —**boy'hood'** *n.* —**boy'ish** *n.*

boy'cott' *v.* refuse to deal with —*n.* a boycotting

boy'friend' *n.* [Inf.] 1 sweetheart who is a boy or man 2 friend who is a boy

boy scout *n.* member of the Boy Scouts, boys' club stressing outdoor life

boy'sen·ber·ry *n., pl.* -ries berry crossed from raspberry, loganberry, and blackberry

Br *abbrev.* British

bra *n.* woman's undergarment for supporting the breasts

brace *v.* 1 strengthen with supports 2 prepare for a shock 3 stimulate —*n.* 1 pair 2 clamp 3 supporting device 4 handle of a drilling tool (**brace and bit**) 5 either of the signs { }, used to connect words, etc.

brace'let *n.* decorative band for the arm

brack'et *n.* 1 projecting support 2 either of the signs [ ], for enclosing words 3 classification —*v.* 1 support with brackets 2 enclose in brackets 3 classify together

brack'ish *a.* salty or rank

bract *n.* leaf at the base of a flower or on its stalk

brad *n.* thin wire nail

brae (brā) *n.* [Scot.] hillside

brag *n., v.* **bragged**, **brag'ging** boast

brag'gart (-ərt) *n.* boaster

braid *v.* 1 interweave strands of 2 trim with braid —*n.* braided strip

Braille, braille (brāl) *n.* system of printing for the blind, using raised dots

brain *n.* 1 mass of nerve tissue in the head 2 *pl.* intelligence —*v.* dash out the brains of —[Inf.] **brain'y** *a.*, -i-er, -i-est

brain'child' *n.* [Inf.] one's own idea or plan

brain'less *a.* foolish or stupid

brain'storm' *n.* [Inf.] sudden idea

brain'wash' *v.* [Inf.] indoctrinate thoroughly

brain wave *n.* rhythmic electric impulses in the brain

braise (brāz) *v.* to brown, then simmer (meat, etc.)

brake *n.* 1 thicket 2 device to stop or slow a car, etc. —*v.* stop or slow as with a brake

brake'man *n., pl.* -men train conductor's assistant

bram'ble *n.* prickly shrub

bran *n.* husks separated from grains of wheat, etc.

branch *n.* 1 limb of a tree 2 offshoot or division 3 tributary stream 4 local unit of an organization —*v.* put forth branches —**branch off** diverge —**branch out** broaden one's activities, etc. —**branch'like'** *a.*

brand *n.* 1 burning stick 2 owner's mark burned on cattle 3 stigma 4 make or kind —*v.* mark with a brand

bran'dish *v.* wave about

brand'-new' *a.* entirely new

bran'dy *n., pl.* -dies liquor distilled from wine or fruit juice

brash *a.* rash or insolent

brass *n.* 1 alloy of copper and zinc 2 [often with pl. v.] coiled musical instruments made of metal, as the trumpet, tuba, etc. 3 [Inf.] rude boldness 4 [Sl.] military officers of high rank —**brass'y** *a.*, -i-er, -i-est

bras·siere (brə zir') *n.* bra

brass tacks *n.* [Inf.] basic facts

brat *n.* unruly child

brat'wurst' (brät'wurst') *n.* sausage of veal and pork

braun'schwei·ger (broun'shwī'-) *n.* smoked liverwurst

bra·va'do (-vä'-) n. pretended courage

brave a. full of courage —n. a North American Indian warrior —v. meet with courage —**brav'er·y** n.

bra·vo (brä'-) int., n., pl. **-vos** shout of approval

bra·vu'ra (-vyoor'ə) n. boldness

brawl v. quarrel or fight noisily —n. noisy fight

brawn n. muscular strength — **brawn'y** a., **-i·er**, **-i·est**

bray n. sound a donkey makes —v. make this sound

bra'zen a. 1 of or like brass 2 shameless —**brazen it out** act unashamed of

bra'zier (-zhər) n. pan for holding burning coals

Bra·zil' nut n. edible, three-sided, tropical nut

breach n. 1 a break in something; gap 2 violation of a promise, friendship, etc. —v. make a breach in

bread n. 1 baked food of flour dough 2 livelihood —v. cover with bread crumbs

breadth n. width or scope

bread'win'ner n. one who supports dependents by earning money

break v. **broke**, **bro'ken**, **break'ing** 1 split apart; smash 2 make or become unusable 3 tame by force 4 make penniless 5 surpass (a record) 6 violate (a law) 7 interrupt 8 stop 9 make or become known —n. 1 a breaking 2 broken place 3 interruption 4 beginning (of day) 5 sudden change 6 a piece of good luck —**break in** 1 enter forcibly 2 interrupt 3 train —**break off** stop abruptly — **break out** develop pimples —**break up** 1 to separate 2 to stop 3 [Inf.] (make) laugh —**break'a·ble** a.

break'age n. 1 a breaking 2 loss due to breaking

break'down' n. 1 mechanical failure 2 physical or mental collapse 3 analysis

break'er n. breaking wave

break'fast (brek'fəst) n. first meal of the day —v. eat breakfast

break'-in' n. forcible entering of a building, as to rob it

break'neck' a. very fast and dangerous

break'through' n. 1 act, place, etc. of breaking through resistance 2 important discovery

break'up' n. a going apart

break'wa'ter n. barrier to break the impact of waves

breast (brest) n. 1 milk-secreting gland on a woman's body 2 upper front of the body —v. to face bravely —**make a clean breast of** confess

breast'bone' n. sternum

breast stroke n. swimming stroke in which arms are extended sideways from the chest

breast'work' n. low barrier to protect gunners

breath (breth) n. 1 air taken into and let out of the lungs 2 power to breathe easily 3 life 4 slight breeze

breathe (brēth) v. 1 inhale and exhale 2 live 3 whisper —**breathe a word** say something or anything

breath·er (brē'thər) n. [Inf.] pause for rest

breath'less a. panting

breath'tak'ing a. exciting

breech n. 1 back part 2 gun part behind the barrel

breech'es (brich'-) pl.n. knickers or trousers

breed v. **bred**, **breed'ing** 1 bring forth (offspring) 2 produce 3 raise (animals) —n. 1 a race or stock 2 type

breeze n. gentle wind —v. [Inf.] move briskly —**breez'y** a., **-i·er**, **-i·est**

breeze'way' n. covered passageway, as from house to garage

breth'ren pl.n. brothers: chiefly in religious use

bre'vi·a·ry (brē'-) n. R.C.Ch. book of daily prayers

brev'i·ty n. briefness

brew v. 1 make (beer, etc.) 2 steep (tea, etc.) 3 form —n. beverage brewed —**brew'er** n.

brew'er·y n., pl. **-ies** place where beer is brewed

bri'ar n. tobacco pipe

bribe n. thing given or promised as an inducement, esp. to wrongdoing —v. offer or give a bribe to —**brib'er·y** n.

bric'-a-brac' n. figurines, curios, etc.

brick n. 1 building block of baked clay 2 any oblong piece —a. built of brick —v. to cover with bricks

brick'lay'ing n. work of building with bricks

bride n. woman just married or about to be married —**brid'al** a.

bride'groom' n. man just married or about to be married

brides'maid' n. any of the bride's wedding attendants

bridge n. 1 structure for crossing a river, etc. 2 thing like a bridge in shape or use 3 mounting for false teeth 4 card game for two pairs of players —v. build or be a bridge over

bridge'work' n. dental bridge(s)

bri'dle n. **1** head harness for a horse **2** thing that restrains —v. **1** put a bridle on **2** curb

bridle path n. path for horseback riding

brief a. short; concise —n. summary, as of a law case —v. summarize the facts for

brief'case' n. small case for carrying papers, books, etc.

bri'er n. **1** thorny bush **2** its root, used for making tobacco pipes

brig n. **1** two-masted ship with square sails **2** ship's prison

bri·gade' n. **1** military unit of several regiments **2** group organized for a task

brig'a·dier' general (-dir') n. officer just above a colonel

brig'and n. roving bandit

bright a. **1** shining; full of light **2** vivid **3** cheerful **4** mentally quick — **bright'en** v. **bright'ly** adv. **bright'ness** n.

bril'liant (-yont) a. **1** shining brightly **2** splendid **3** keenly intelligent —**bril'liance** n. —**bril'liant·ly** adv.

brim n. **1** top edge of a cup, etc. **2** projecting rim of a hat —v. brimmed, **brim'ming** be full to the brim — **brim'ful'** a.

brim'stone' n. sulfur

brin'dled a. having dark streaks, as a cow: also **brin'dle**

brine n. **1** water full of salt **2** ocean — **brin'y** a., **-i·er, -i·est**

bring v. brought, **bring'ing** cause to come or happen; fetch, get, lead to, etc. —**bring about** to cause —**bring forth** give birth to; produce —**bring off** accomplish —**bring out** reveal —**bring to** revive —**bring up 1** rear (a child) **2** mention

brink n. edge, as of a cliff

bri·quette', **bri·quet'** (-ket') n. small block of charcoal

brisk a. **1** quick; energetic **2** invigorating

bris'ket n. breast meat

bris'ling n. sprat canned as a sardine

bris·tle (bris'əl) n. short, stiff hair —v. **1** stiffen like bristles **2** stiffen with anger —**bris'tly** a.

Brit abbrev. British

britch'es pl.n. [Inf.] breeches

Brit'ish a. of Great Britain or its people

British thermal unit n. unit of heat, equal to about 252 calories

brit'tle a. hard but easily broken —

brit'tle·ness n.

broach n. tapered BIT (n. 2) —v. **1** make a hole in **2** start a discussion of

broad a. **1** wide **2** obvious **3** tolerant **4** extensive; general

broad'band' a. of cable communications devices carrying much data at high speeds

broad'cast' v. **-cast'** or **-cast'ed, -cast' ing 1** spread widely **2** send by radio, TV, etc. —n. radio, TV, etc. program —adv. far and wide —**broad'cast'er** n.

broad'cloth' n. a fine cloth

broad'en v. widen

broad jump n. long jump

broad'loom' a. woven on a wide loom, as a carpet

broad'-mind'ed a. liberal

broad'side' n. **1** firing of all guns on a ship's side **2** large sheet with advertising —adv. with the side facing

bro·cade' n. cloth of a richly patterned weave —v. weave a raised design in

broc'co·li n. green-headed cauliflower

bro·chette' (-shet') n. a skewer for broiling chunks of meat

bro·chure' (-shoor') n. pamphlet

bro'gan n. heavy work shoe, fitting high on the ankle

brogue (brōg) n. Irish accent

broil v. cook by direct heat

broil'er n. **1** pan or stove section for broiling **2** chicken fit for broiling

broke v. pt. of BREAK —a. [Inf.] without money

bro'ken v. pp. of BREAK —a. **1** fractured **2** not in working order **3** violated, as a vow **4** interrupted **5** imperfectly spoken **6** tamed

bro'ken-down' a. **1** sick or worn out **2** not in working order

bro'ken·heart'ed a. crushed by grief

bro'ker n. agent hired to buy and sell —**bro'ker·age** n.

bro'mide' (-mīd') n. sedative

bro'mine' (-mēn') n. corrosive liquid, a chemical element

bron'chi' (-kī') pl.n. the two main branches of the windpipe

bron'chi·al (-kē-) a. of the branches of the windpipe

bron·chi'tis (-kī'-) n. inflammation of the bronchial tubes

bron'co n., pl. **-cos** small, wild horse of the West

bron'to·saur' (-sôr') n. huge, plant-eating dinosaur: also **bron'to·saur'us**

bronze n. **1** alloy of copper and tin **2**

reddish brown —v. make bronze in color

brooch (brōch, brōōch) n. large ornamental pin with a clasp

brood n. 1 birds hatched at one time 2 offspring —v. dwell on moodily

brook n. a small stream —v. endure or tolerate

broom n. 1 long-handled brush for sweeping 2 kind of shrub

broom'stick' n. broom handle

Bros, bros abbrev. brothers

broth n. clear soup

broth'el n. house of prostitution

broth'er n. 1 male related to one by having the same parents 2 fellow member 3 [often B-] monk —**broth'er·hood'** n. —**broth'er·ly** a.

broth'er-in-law' n., pl. **broth'ers-** 1 brother of one's spouse 2 sister's husband

brought v. pt. & pp. of BRING

brou'ha·ha' (brōō'-) n. uproar

brow n. 1 eyebrow 2 forehead 3 edge of a cliff

brow'beat' v. -beat', -beat'en, -beat'ing to bully

brown a. 1 chocolate-colored 2 tanned; dark-skinned —n. brown color —v. make or become brown

brown'-bag' v. carry one's lunch to work, etc.

brown'ie n. square of flat chocolate cake

brown'out' n. a dimming of lights during a power shortage

brown rice n. rice retaining its outer coating

brown'stone' n. reddish-brown sandstone, used for building

brown sugar n. sugar with crystals coated with brown syrup

browse v. 1 feed on grass, etc. 2 to glance through books, the Internet, etc.

brows'er n. 1 one that browses 2 software for gaining access to the World Wide Web

bru'in n. a bear

bruise (brōōz) v. 1 injure and discolor (the skin) without breaking it —n. discolored injury of the skin

bruis'er n. [Inf.] pugnacious man

bruit (brōōt) v. spread (about) as a rumor

brunch n. combined breakfast and lunch

bru·net' a. having dark hair —n. brunet person

bru·nette' a. brunet —n. brunette woman or girl

brunt n. main impact

brush n. 1 device with bristles, wires, etc. for cleaning, painting, etc. 2 a brushing 3 skirmish 4 underbrush —v. 1 use a brush on 2 touch lightly 3 remove as with a brush —**brush off** [Sl.] dismiss rudely —**brush up** refresh one's memory

brush cut n. a crew cut

brush'off' n. [Sl.] rude dismissal

brusque (brusk) a. abrupt in manner —**brusque'ly** adv.

Brus'sels sprout n. 1 plant bearing small cabbage-like heads 2 one of these edible heads

bru'tal a. savage, cruel, etc. —**bru·tal'i·ty** n., pl. **-ties** —**bru'tal·ly** adv.

bru'tal·ize' v. 1 make brutal 2 treat brutally

brute a. of or like an animal; cruel, stupid, etc. —n. 1 animal 2 brutal person —**brut'ish** a.

BS abbrev. Bachelor of Science: also **B.S.**

Btu abbrev. British thermal unit(s): also **BTU** or **btu**

bu abbrev. bushel(s)

bub'ble n. globule of air or gas in a liquid or solid —v. 1 rise in bubbles 2 gurgle —**on the bubble** [Inf.] in an uncertain situation —**bub'bly** a.

bubble gum n. chewing gum for blowing into large bubbles

bub'ble·head' n. [Sl.] silly or ignorant person

bu·bon'ic plague (byōō-) n. deadly contagious disease

buc'ca·neer' n. pirate

buck n. 1 male deer, goat, etc. 2 a bucking 3 [Sl.] dollar —v. 1 rear up, as to throw off (a rider) 2 [Inf.] resist —**pass the buck** [Inf.] shift the blame

buck'et n. container with a handle, for water, etc.; pail —**buck'et·ful'** n.

bucket seat n. single contoured seat, as in sports cars

buck'eye' n. 1 horse chestnut with shiny, brown seeds 2 the seed

buck'le n. clasp for fastening a belt, etc. —v. 1 fasten with a buckle 2 bend or crumple —**buckle down** apply oneself

buck'ler n. round shield

buck'-pass'er n. [Inf.] one who puts the blame on someone else —**buck'-pass'ing** n.

buck'ram (-rəm) n. stiff cloth

buck'shot' n. large lead shot for a gun

buck'skin' n. leather from skins of deer or sheep

buck'tooth' n., pl. **-teeth'** projecting

tooth —**buck'toothed'** a.

buck'wheat' n. plant with seeds that are ground into dark flour

bu·col'ic (byōō-) a. rustic

bud n. small swelling on a plant, from which a leaf, shoot, or flower develops —v. **bud'ded, bud'ding** 1 put forth buds 2 begin to develop

Bud·dhism (bōō'diz'əm) n. a religion of Asia —**Bud'dhist** n., a.

bud'dy n., pl. **-dies** [Inf.] comrade

budge v. move slightly

budg'er·i·gar' n. Australian parakeet: also [Inf.] **budg'ie**

budg'et n. 1 plan adjusting expenses to income 2 estimated cost of operating, etc. —v. 1 put on a budget 2 to schedule

buff v. polish, as with soft leather —**buff'er** n.

buf'fa·lo' n., pl. **-loes, -lo,** or **-los** 1 wild ox 2 American bison —v. [Sl.] to bluff

Buffalo wings pl.n. spicy fried segments of chicken wings

buff'er n. anything that lessens shock

buf'fet (-ət) n. a blow —v. to slap

buf·fet' (-fā') n. 1 cabinet for dishes, silver, etc. 2 meal which guests serve themselves as from a buffet

buf·foon' n. a clown —**buf·foon'er·y** n.

bug n. 1 crawling insect, esp. when a pest 2 [Inf.] germ 3 defect 4 [Inf.] tiny, hidden microphone

bug'bear' n. imaginary terror: also **bug'a·boo'**, pl. **-boos'**

bug'gy n., pl. **-gies** 1 light, one-horse carriage 2 baby carriage —a. infested with bugs

bu'gle (byōō'-) n. small, valveless trumpet —**bu'gler** n.

build v. **built, build'ing** 1 make by putting together parts 2 create, develop, etc. —n. form or structure — **build up** make more attractive — **build'er** n.

build'ing n. structure

build'up', build'-up' n. [Inf.] 1 praise 2 gradual increase

built'-in' a. 1 made as part of the structure 2 inherent

built'-up' a. 1 made higher, etc. with added parts 2 with many buildings on or in it

bulb n. 1 underground bud, as the onion 2 bulblike electric LAMP (n. 1) —**bul'bous** a.

bulge n. outward swelling —v. swell out —**bulg'y** a.

bu·lim'i·a (byōō lē'-) n. an eating dis-

order —**bu·lim'ic** a.

bulk n. 1 size or mass, esp. if great 2 main part —v. have, or gain in, size or importance —a. not packaged — **bulk'y** a., **-i·er, -i·est**

bulk'head' n. vertical partition, as in a ship

bull n. 1 male bovine animal, or male seal, elephant, etc. 2 edict of the pope —a. male

bull'dog' n. heavily built dog with a stubborn grip

bull'doze' v. 1 [Inf.] to bully 2 move or level with a bulldozer

bull'doz'er n. tractor with a large shovel-like blade

bul'let n. shaped metal piece to be shot from a gun

bul'le·tin n. 1 brief news item 2 regular publication of a group

bulletin board n. board for posting bulletins or notices

bul'let-proof' a. that bullets cannot pierce

bull'fight' n. spectacle in which a bull is provoked, then killed —**bull'fighter** n.

bull'finch' n. small European songbird

bull'frog' n. large frog

bull'head'ed a. stubborn

bull'horn' n. portable electronic voice amplifier

bul·lion (bool'yən) n. gold or silver ingots

bull'ish a. 1 like a bull 2 having, causing, etc. a rise in stock exchange prices

bull'ock n. castrated bull

bull's'-eye' n. target center

bul'ly n., pl. **-lies** one who hurts or threatens weaker people —v. **-lied, -ly·ing** to behave like a bully toward

bul'rush' n. tall grasslike plant, in marshes, etc.

bul'wark n. rampart; defense

bum n. [Inf.] a vagrant —v. **bummed, bum'ming** 1 [Sl.] beg for 2 [Inf.] loaf —a. [Sl.] 1 poor in quality 2 false 3 lame

bum'ble v. to blunder or stumble — **bum'bler** n.

bum'ble·bee' n. large bee

bummed a. [Sl.] in a bad mood: usually used with *out*

bum'mer n. [Sl.] unpleasant experience

bump v. collide (with) —n. 1 light collision 2 swelling —**bump'y** a., **-i·er, -i·est**

bump'er n. device, as on a car, for easing collisions —a. unusually abundant

bumper sticker *n.* sticker with slogan, etc., for a car bumper

bump'kin *n.* awkward or simple person from the country

bun *n.* small bread roll

bunch *n.* cluster of similar things —*v.* gather; group

bun'dle *n.* **1** number of things bound together **2** package —*v.* **1** make into a bundle **2** send hastily —**bundle up** dress warmly

bun'ga·low *n.* small house

bun'gee cord *n.* strong, elastic cord

bun'gle *v.* do clumsily; spoil —**bun'gler** *n.*

bun'ion *n.* swelling at the base of the big toe

bunk *n.* **1** built-in bed **2** [Inf.] any narrow bed **3** [Sl.] empty talk —*v.* sleep in a bunk

bunk'er *n.* **1** large bin **2** underground fortification **3** obstacle on a golf course

bunk'house' *n.* barracks for ranch hands, etc.

bun'ny *n.*, *pl.* **-nies** rabbit: child's word

bunt *Baseball v.* to bat (a pitch) so it does not go beyond the infield —*n.* a bunted ball

bunt'ing *n.* **1** thin cloth for flags, etc. **2** baby's hooded blanket **3** small finch

buoy (boo'ē; *v.* 2 boi) *n.* floating marker —*v.* **1** keep afloat **2** lift up in spirits

buoy'an·cy (boi'-) *n.* **1** ability to float **2** cheerfulness —**buoy'ant** *a.*

bur *n.* prickly seedcase

bur'den *n.* **1** load carried **2** thing hard to bear —*v.* weigh down —**bur'den·some** *a.*

bur'dock' *n.* plant with prickly burs

bu·reau (byoor'ō) *n.*, *pl.* **-reaus'** or **-reaux** (-ōz') **1** chest of drawers **2** government department **3** office or agency

bu·reauc'ra·cy (-räk'-) *n.*, *pl.* **-cies** (government by) officials following rigid rules —**bu'reau·crat'** *n.* —**bu'reau·crat'ic** *a.*

burg *n.* [Inf.] quiet city or town

bur'geon (-jən) *v.* to sprout

bur'ger *n.* [Inf.] hamburger or cheeseburger

-burger *suf.* **1** sandwich of ground meat, etc. **2** hamburger and

bur'glar *n.* one who breaks into a building to steal —**bur'gla·ry** *n.*, *pl.* **-ries**

bur'glar·ize' *v.* commit burglary in

bur'gle *v.* [Inf.] burglarize

Bur'gun·dy *n.* **1** kind of wine **2** purplish red

bur'i·al (ber'-) *n.* the burying of a dead body

burl *n.* **1** knot on some tree trunks **2** veneer from wood with burls —**burled** *a.*

bur'lap' *n.* coarse cloth of hemp, etc., used for bags

bur·lesque' (-lesk') *n.* **1** broadly comic satire **2** type of vaudeville —*v.* imitate comically

bur'ly *a.* **-li·er, -li·est** big and strong

burn *v.* **burned** or **burnt, burn'ing** **1** be or set on fire **2** destroy or be destroyed by fire **3** hurt or be hurt by acid, friction, etc. **4** feel or make feel hot **5** be excited **6** [Sl.] cheat or trick —*n.* injury from fire, acid, etc.

burn'er *n.* part of a stove, etc. producing the flame

bur'nish *v.*, *n.* polish

bur·noose' *n.* hooded cloak worn by Arabs

burn'out' *n.* state of emotional exhaustion from stress, etc.

burp *v.*, *n.* belch

burr *n.* **1** rough edge left on metal **2** trilling of *r* **3** bur

bur'ro *n.*, *pl.* **-ros** donkey

bur'row *n.* hole dug by an animal —*v.* make a burrow

bur'sa *n.*, *pl.* **-sae** (-sē) or **-sas** body sac with fluid, as between tendon and bone

bur'sar (-sər) *n.* college treasurer

bur·si'tis *n.* inflammation of a bursa

burst *v.* **burst, burst'ing** **1** come apart suddenly; explode **2** appear, enter, etc. suddenly **3** be too full —*n.* a bursting

bur·y (ber'ē) *v.* **-ied, -y·ing** **1** put in a grave, tomb, etc. **2** cover; hide

bus *n.*, *pl.* **bus'es** or **bus'ses** large motor coach

bus'boy' *n.* assistant to waiter or waitress

bus·by (buz'bē) *n.*, *pl.* **-bies** tall fur hat, part of some full-dress uniforms

bush *n.* **1** low, woody plant **2** uncleared land

bushed *a.* [Inf.] exhausted

bush'el *n.* a dry measure equal to 4 pecks

bush'ing *n.* removable metal lining to reduce friction

bush league *n.* [Sl.] small or second-rate type of activity, etc.

bush'whack' *v.* ambush

bush'y *a.* **-i·er, -i·est** thick and spreading out

busi·ness (biz'nəs) *n.* **1** commerce **2** commercial or industrial establishment; store, factory, etc. **3** occupation **4** rightful concern **5** matter; affair —**busi'ness·man'** *n.,* *pl.* **-men'**

business administration *n.* college studies to prepare for a business career

business card *n.* small card identifying one's business connection

busi'ness·like' *a.* efficient

bus'ing, bus'sing *n.* a taking children by bus to a school out of their neighborhood so as to achieve racial balance

bust *n.* **1** sculpture of head and shoulders **2** woman's bosom **3** [Inf.] failure —*v.* [Inf.] break

bus·tle (bus'əl) *v.* hurry busily —*n.* **1** a bustling **2** padding for the back of a skirt

bus'y (biz'-) *a.* **-i·er, -i·est 1** active; at work **2** full of activity —*v.* **-ied, -y·ing** make busy —**bus'i·ly** *adv.* —**bus'y·ness** *n.*

bus'y·bod'y *n.,* *pl.* **-ies** meddler

but *prep.* except —*con.* **1** yet **2** on the contrary **3** unless —*adv.* **1** only **2** merely —**all but** almost —**but for** if it were not for

bu'tane' (byōō'-) *n.* a hydrocarbon used as fuel

butch (booch) *a.* [Sl.] masculine —*n.* buzz cut

butch'er *n.* **1** one who kills and dresses animals for meat **2** one who sells meat **3** killer —*v.* **1** slaughter **2** botch —**butch'er·y** *n.*

but'ler *n.* head manservant

butt *n.* **1** thick end **2** stub **3** object of ridicule **4** large cask —*v.* **1** join end to end **2** ram with the head —**butt in(to)** [Inf.] meddle (in)

butte (byōōt) *n.* small mesa

but'ter *n.* yellow fat churned from cream —*v.* spread with butter —**but'ter·y** *a.*

butter bean *n.* **1** lima bean **2** wax bean

but'ter·cup' *n.* bright-yellow flower

but'ter·fat' *n.* fatty part of milk

but'ter·fly' *n.,* *pl.* **-flies'** insect with four broad, colorful wings

but'ter·milk' *n.* sour milk left after churning butter

but'ter·nut' *n.* white walnut tree or its edible nut

but'ter·scotch' *n.* hard candy made with brown sugar, butter, etc.

but'tocks *pl.n.* fleshy, rounded parts of the hips

but'ton *n.* **1** small disk for fastening a garment, etc. **2** buttonlike part —*v.* to fasten with buttons —**on the button** [Sl.] precisely

but'ton·hole' *n.* slit for a button —*v.* detain in talk

but'tress *n.* **1** outer structure supporting a wall **2** a prop —*v.* prop up

bux'om *a.* shapely, with a full bosom

buy *v.* **bought, buy'ing 1** get by paying money, etc. **2** to bribe **3** accept as true or valid —*n.* [Inf.] a bargain —**buy into** [Sl.] BUY (*v.* 3) —**buy'er** *n.*

buy'out' *n.* the purchase of a business by employees, etc.

buzz *v.* hum like a bee —*n.* buzzing sound

buz'zard *n.* **1** kind of large hawk **2** kind of vulture

buzz cut *n.* [Inf.] man's very short haircut

buzz'er *n.* electrical device signaling with a buzz

buzz saw *n.* circular saw rotated by machinery

buzz'word' *n.* jargon word having little meaning, but sounding impressive

by *prep.* **1** near; beside **2** during **3** not later than **4** through **5** past **6** for **7** according to —*adv.* **1** near **2** past —**by and by** after a while —**by and large** in most respects —**by the by** incidentally

bye *n.* advancement to next round of tournament without having to compete

bye'-bye' *n.,* *int.* goodbye

by'gone' *a.* past —*n.* anything past

by'law' *n.* local law or rule

by'line' *n.* writer's name heading a newspaper article

BYO *abbrev.* bring your own (alcoholic beverages)

by'pass' *n.* **1** road, pipe, etc. that gets around the main way **2** surgery or passage to route blood around a diseased part —*v.* **1** to detour around **2** ignore

by'path' *n.* side path

by'prod'uct, by'-prod'uct *n.* secondary product or result

by'stand'er *n.* one standing near but not taking part

byte (bīt) *n.* string of bits: basic unit in computing

by'way' *n.* side road

by'word' *n.* **1** proverb **2** thing well-known for some quality

C

C *abbrev.* **1** Celsius (or centigrade) **2** centimeter(s) **3** century **4** circa (about): also **ca 5** copyright **6** cup(s) Also, for 2-6, **c**

CA *abbrev.* California

cab *n.* **1** taxicab **2** place in a truck, etc. where the operator sits

ca·bal (kə bäl′) *n.* **1** group of conspirators **2** plot

ca·bal·le·ro *n., pl.* **-ros** horseman

ca·ban′a *n.* **1** cabin **2** small shelter for swimmers, etc. to change clothes

cab·a·ret′ (-rā′) *n.* cafe with entertainment

cab′bage *n.* vegetable with round head of thick leaves

cab′by, cab′bie *n., pl.* **-bies** [Inf.] taxi driver

ca′ber·net′ (-nā′) *n.* dry red wine

cab′in *n.* **1** hut **2** a room on a ship, etc.

cab′i·net *n.* **1** case with drawers or shelves **2** [*often* C-] body of official advisers

cab′i·net·mak′er *n.* maker of fine furniture —**cab′i·net·work′, cab′i·net·ry** *n.*

ca′ble *n.* **1** thick rope, often of wire **2** cablegram **3** insulated wires carrying electric current, etc. **4** cable TV —*v.* send a cablegram (to)

cable car *n.* car drawn up an incline by a moving cable

ca′ble·gram′ *n.* telegram sent overseas by wire

cable TV *n.* TV system transmitting via cables to subscribers

ca·bo·chon (kab′ə shän′) *n.* precious stone cut in convex shape

ca·boo′dle *n.* [Inf.] lot; group —**the whole kit and caboodle** everything

ca·boose′ *n.* crew's car on a freight train

ca·ca·o (**bean**) (kə kā′ō) *n.* seed of tropical American tree: source of chocolate

cache (kash) *n.* **1** place for hiding food, supplies, etc. **2** anything so hidden —*v.* to place in a cache

cache·pot (kash′pät′, -pō′) *n.* jar to hold a potted plant

ca·chet′ (-shā′) *n.* (sign of) official approval or prestige

cack′le *v., n.* (make) the shrill sound of a hen

ca·coph′o·ny (-käf′-) *n., pl.* **-nies** harsh, jarring sound(s) —**ca·coph′o·nous** *a.*

cac′tus *n., pl.* **-tus·es** or **-ti′** (-tī′) spiny desert plant

cad *n.* ungentlemanly man

ca·dav′er (-dav′-) *n.* corpse —**ca·dav′er·ous** *a.*

cad′die, cad′dy *n., pl.* **-ies** attendant to a golfer —*v.* **-died, -dy·ing** be a caddy

cad′dy *n., pl.* **-dies** small container, as for tea

ca′dence *n.* **1** fall of the voice in speaking **2** rhythm; measured movement

ca·den′za *n.* elaborate passage for solo instrument in a concerto

ca·det′ *n.* student at a military or naval school

cadge *v.* beg —**cadg′er** *n.*

cad′mi·um *n.* metallic chemical element used in alloys, etc.

ca·dre (ka′drē, kä′drä) *n.* nucleus for a larger organization

Cae·sar (sē′zər) *n.* Roman emperor

Cae·sar′e·an (**section**) *n.* cesarean section

ca·fe (ka fā′) *n.* **1** restaurant **2** barroom

caf·e·te′ri·a (-tir′ē ə) *n.* self-service restaurant

caf′feine′ (-ēn′) *n.* stimulant in coffee, tea, etc.: also sp. **caf′fein′**

caf·tan′ *n.* long-sleeved robe, worn in E Mediterranean lands

cage *n.* structure with bars, wire mesh, etc., esp. for confining animals —*v.* put in a cage

cag′er *n.* [Sl.] basketball player

ca′gey, ca′gy *a.* **-gi·er, -gi·est** [Inf.] sly; cunning —**ca′gi·ly** *adv.*

ca·hoots′ *n.* [Sl.] scheming partnership

cais·son (kā′sən, -sän′) *n.* **1** ammunition wagon **2** watertight box for underwater construction work

ca·jole′ *v.* coax or wheedle —**ca·jol′er·y** *n.*

Ca′jun, Ca′jan *n.* Canadian French native of Louisiana

cake *n.* **1** baked dough or batter of flour, eggs, sugar, etc. **2** solid, formed, usually flat mass —*v.* form into a hard mass

cal *abbrev.* calorie(s)

cal′a·bash′ *n.* gourdlike fruit of a tropical tree

ca′la·ma′ri *n.* squid cooked as food

cal′a·mine *n.* zinc compound used in lotions, etc.

ca·lam′i·ty *n., pl.* **-ties** disaster —**ca·lam′i·tous** *a.*

cal·ci·fy' v. **-fied', -fy'ing** change into stony matter —**cal'ci·fi·ca'tion** n.

cal·ci·mine' n. thin, watery paint for covering plaster —v. to cover with calcimine

cal'ci·um n. chemical element in bone, limestone, etc.

calcium carbonate n. white compound found in limestone, bones, etc.

cal'cu·late' v. **1** figure by arithmetic **2** estimate —**cal'cu·la·ble** a. —**cal'cu·la'tion** n. —**cal'cu·la'tor** n.

cal'cu·lat'ed a. deliberately planned or intended

cal'cu·lat'ing a. **1** scheming **2** shrewd; cautious

cal'cu·lus n. branch of higher mathematics

cal·dron (kôl'drən) n. large kettle or boiler

cal'en·dar n. **1** table showing the days, weeks, and months of a year **2** schedule

cal'en·der n. machine with rollers for making paper, cloth, etc. smooth or glossy

calf n., pl. **calves 1** young cow or bull **2** young elephant, seal, etc. **3** fleshy part of leg below the knee

calf'skin' n. leather made from the skin of a calf

cal'i·ber n. **1** diameter of a bullet, bore of a gun, etc. **2** quality

cal'i·brate' v. mark or fix the graduations of (a measuring device) —**cal'i·bra'tion** n. —**cal'i·bra'tor** n.

cal'i·co' n., pl. **-coes'** or **-cos'** cotton cloth, usually printed

cal'i·pers pl.n. instrument for measuring diameter

ca'liph, ca'lif (kā'-) n. old title of Muslim rulers

cal·is·then'ics pl.n. simple athletic exercises

calk (kôk) v., n. caulk

call v. **1** say loudly; shout **2** summon **3** name **4** telephone **5** stop (a game) —n. **1** shout or cry **2** summons **3** demand **4** need **5** short visit —**call for 1** demand **2** come and get —**call off** cancel —**call on 1** visit briefly **2** ask to speak —**on call** available when called —**call'er** n.

cal'la (lily) (kal'ə) n. plant with yellow flower spike inside a large, white leaf

call girl n. prostitute hired by telephone

cal·lig'ra·phy n. artistic handwriting —**cal·lig'ra·pher** n.

call'-in' a. of a radio or TV program having an audience participating by telephone

call'ing n. vocation; trade

calling card n. **1** card with one's name and, sometimes, address **2** credit card for making long-distance telephone calls

cal·li'o·pe' (-lī'ə pē') n. organlike musical instrument with steam whistles

cal'lous a. **1** hardened **2** unfeeling —**cal'lous·ly** adv.

cal'low a. inexperienced

cal'lus n. hard, thickened place on the skin

calm n. stillness —a. still; tranquil —v. make or become calm: often with *down* —**calm'ly** adv. —**calm'ness** n.

cal·or'ic a. of heat or calories

cal'o·rie, cal'o·ry (-rē) n., pl. **-ries** unit of heat or of the energy from food

cal'o·rif'ic a. producing heat

cal'u·met' (-ya-) n. ceremonial pipe with long stem smoked by North American Indians

ca·lum'ni·ate' v. to slander —**ca·lum'ni·a'tion** n.

cal'um·ny n., pl. **-nies** slander

calve (kav) v. give birth to (a calf)

ca·lyp'so (-lip'-) n., pl. **-sos** improvised ballad sung in the West Indies

ca'lyx (kā'liks') n., pl. **-lyx·es** or **-ly·ces'** (-la sēz') sepals of a flower

cam n. projection on a wheel to give irregular motion, as to a shaft (**cam'shaft'**)

ca·ma·ra·de·rie (kä'mə räd'ə rē) n. comradeship

cam'ber n. slight convexity

cam'bi·um n. cell layer under bark of plants from which new wood and bark grow

cam'bric (kām'-) n. fine linen or cotton cloth

cam'cord'er n. portable videotape recorder and TV camera

came v. pt. of COME

cam'el n. beast of burden with a humped back

ca·mel'li·a (-mēl'yə) n. large, roselike flower

Cam'em·bert' (**cheese**) (-ber') n. soft, creamy, rich cheese

cam'e·o' n., pl. **-os' 1** gem, etc. with figure carved on it **2** small role for notable actor

cam'er·a n. **1** device for taking photographs **2** TV or video device that first receives the images for transmission or recording

cam'er·a·man' n., pl. **-men'** operator of a movie or TV camera

cam'i·sole' n. short negligee

cam′o·mile′ *n.* flower used in medicinal tea

cam′ou·flage′ (-ə fläzh′) *n.* a disguising of potential targets in wartime —*v.* conceal by disguising

camp *n.* **1** place with tents, huts, etc., as for vacationers or soldiers **2** supporters of a cause —*v.* set up a camp —**camp′er** *n.*

cam·paign′ (-pān′) *n.* series of planned actions, as in war, an election, etc. —*v.* wage a campaign

cam·pa·ni′le (-nē′lē) *n.* bell tower

camp′fire′ *n.* **1** outdoor fire at a camp **2** social gathering around such a fire

cam′phor (-fər) *n.* strong-smelling crystalline substance used in mothballs, medicine, etc.

camp′site′ *n.* place for camping

cam′pus *n.* school or college grounds —*a.* of students

camp′y *a.* **-i·er, -i·est** [Sl.] so artificial or trite as to amuse

can *v.* pt. **could** auxiliary verb showing: **1** ability **2** likelihood **3** [Inf.] permission

can *n.* metal container, as for foods —*v.* **canned, can′ning** preserve (food) in cans or jars —**can′ner** *n.*

Can *abbrev.* **1** Canada **2** Canadian

Ca·na′di·an *n., a.* (native) of Canada

ca·nal′ *n.* **1** artificial waterway **2** body duct

ca′na·pé′ (-pā′) *n.* appetizer on a cracker, etc.

ca·nard′ *n.* false rumor

ca·nar′y *n., pl.* **-ies** small, yellow songbird

ca·nas′ta *n.* double-deck card game

can′can′ *n.* lively dance with much high kicking

can′cel *v.* **1** cross out **2** make invalid **3** abolish —**can′cel·la′tion** *n.*

can′cer *n.* **1** malignant tumor **2** a spreading evil **3** [C-] fourth sign of the zodiac —**can′cer·ous** *a.*

can′de·la′brum (-lä′-, -lā′-) *n., pl.* **-bra** or **-brums** large, branched candlestick: also **can′de·la′bra,** *pl.* **-bras**

can′did *a.* **1** frank; honest **2** informal —**can′did·ly** *adv.*

can′di·date′ *n.* one seeking office, etc. —**can′di·da·cy** *n.*

can′died (-dēd) *a.* sugary

can′dle *n.* wax taper with a wick, burned for light

can′dle·pow′er *n.* unit for measuring light

can′dle·stick′ *n.* holder for a candle or candles

can′dor *n.* frankness

can′dy *n., pl.* **-dies** confection of sugar or syrup —*v.* **-died, -dy·ing** cook or preserve in sugar

cane *n.* **1** hollow, jointed stem, as of bamboo **2** walking stick **3** split rattan —*v.* to beat with a cane

cane′brake′ *n.* dense growth of cane plants

ca′nine′ *a.* of or like a dog —*n.* dog

canine tooth *n.* any of the four sharp-pointed teeth

can′is·ter *n.* box or can for coffee, tea, etc.

can′ker *n.* a sore, esp. in the mouth —**can′ker·ous** *a.*

can′na·bis′ *n.* **1** hemp **2** marijuana, etc. from the flowering tops of hemp

canned *a.* **1** preserved, as in cans **2** [Sl.] recorded for reproduction, as on TV

can′nel (**coal**) *n.* tough bituminous coal

can′ner·y *n., pl.* **-ies** factory for canning foods

can′ni·bal *n.* person who eats human flesh —**can′ni·bal·ism′** *n.* —**can′ni·bal·is′tic** *a.*

can′ni·bal·ize′ *v.* strip (old equipment) for usable parts

can′non *n., pl.* **-nons** or **-non** large mounted gun

can′non·ade′ *n.* continuous firing of artillery

can·not′ (or kə nät′) can not

can′ny *a.* **-ni·er, -ni·est 1** cautious **2** shrewd —**can′ni·ly** *adv.*

ca·noe′ (-nōō′) *n.* narrow, light boat moved with paddles —*v.* paddle or go in a canoe

ca·no′la (**oil**) *n.* cooking oil, from the seed of the rape plant

can′on *n.* **1** body of church laws **2** any law **3** official list **4** clergyman serving in a cathedral **5** musical round —**ca·non′i·cal, ca·non′ic** *a.*

ca′ñon *n.* canyon

can′on·ize′ *v.* declare as a saint —**can′on·i·za′tion** *n.*

can′o·py *n., pl.* **-pies** covering hung over a bed, throne, etc. —**can′o·pied** *a.*

cant *n.* **1** special vocabulary of a class; jargon **2** hypocritical talk —*v.* use cant

cant *n., v.* tilt; slant

can′t *contr.* cannot

can′ta·loupe′, can′ta·loup′ (-ə lōp′) *n.* sweet, juicy melon

can·tan′ker·ous *a.* bad-tempered; quarrelsome

can·ta′ta *n.* dramatic choral composition

can·teen' *n.* **1** general store at an army post **2** soldier's water flask

can'ter *n.* easy gallop —*v.* go at this pace

can'ti·cle *n.* hymn

can'ti·le'ver (-lĕ'vər, -lev'ər) *n.* structure that is anchored at only one end

can'to *n., pl.* **-tos** division of a long poem

can·ton (-tən, -tän') *n.* a state in the Swiss Republic

can·ton'ment (-tän'-, -tōn'-) *n.* temporary quarters for troops

can'tor *n.* liturgical singer in a synagogue

can'vas *n.* coarse cloth used for tents, sails, oil paintings, etc.

can'vas·back' *n.* wild duck with a grayish back

can'vass (-vəs) *v.* seek votes, opinions, etc. (from) —*n.* a canvassing —**can'vass·er** *n.*

can'yon *n.* narrow valley between high cliffs

cap *n.* **1** brimless hat, often with a visor **2** caplike cover **3** upper limit —*v.* **capped, cap'ping 1** put a cap on **2** to climax

cap *abbrev.* **1** capacity **2** capital(ize)

ca'pa·ble *a.* able; skilled —**capable of** able or likely to —**ca'pa·bil'i·ty** *n., pl.* **-ties** —**ca'pa·bly** *adv.*

ca·pa'cious (-shəs) *a.* roomy; wide

ca·pac'i·tor *n.* device for storing an electrical charge

ca·pac'i·ty *n.* **1** ability to contain or hold **2** volume **3** ability **4** position

cape *n.* **1** sleeveless coat fastened about the neck **2** land jutting into water

ca'per *v.* skip about playfully —*n.* **1** wild, foolish act **2** [Sl.] criminal act, esp. a robbery **3** tiny pickled bud used as seasoning

cap'il·lar'y *a.* having a tiny bore, as a tube —*n., pl.* **-ies** tiny blood vessel

cap'i·tal *a.* **1** bringing or punishable by death **2** chief; main **3** excellent —*n.* **1** capital letter **2** city from which a state is governed **3** money or property owned or used in business **4** top of a column

capital gain *n.* profit made from sale of stocks, etc.

cap'i·tal·ism' *n.* economic system in which the means of production and distribution are privately owned

cap'i·tal·ist *n.* owner of wealth used in business —**cap'i·tal·is'tic** *a.*

cap'i·tal·ize' *v.* **1** convert into capital **2** use to advantage: with *on* **3** supply

capital for **4** write with a capital letter —**cap'i·tal·i·za'tion** *n.*

capital letter *n.* large letter used to begin a sentence, name, etc.

cap'i·tal·ly *adv.* very well

capital punishment *n.* penalty of death for a crime

Cap'i·tol *n.* building where a legislature meets

ca·pit'u·late' (-pich'ə-) *v.* surrender —**ca·pit·u·la'tion** *n.*

cap'let *n.* medicinal tablet with a protective coating

ca'pon' *n.* castrated rooster

cap·puc·ci·no (kä'pə chē'nō, kap'ə-) *n.* steamed coffee mixed with steamed milk

ca·price' (-prēs') *n.* whim

ca·pri'cious (-prish'əs, -prē'shəs) *a.* unpredictable

Cap'ri·corn' *n.* tenth sign of the zodiac

cap'size' *v.* upset; overturn

cap'stan *n.* device around which cables are wound

cap'sule *n.* **1** small case, as for a dose of medicine **2** closed compartment, as in a rocket —**cap'sul·ize'** *v.*

Capt *abbrev.* Captain

cap'tain *n.* **1** leader **2** army officer above lieutenant **3** navy officer above commander **4** master of a ship —*v.* to head —**cap'tain·cy** *n.*

cap'tion *n.* **1** title, as under a newspaper picture **2** TV or film subtitle

cap'tious (-shəs) *a.* **1** made for the sake of argument **2** quick to find fault

cap'ti·vate' *v.* fascinate

cap'tive *a., n.* (held) prisoner —**cap·tiv'i·ty** *n.*

cap'tor *n.* one who captures

cap'ture *v.* take by force, by surprise, etc. —*n.* a capturing or the thing captured

car *n.* **1** wheeled vehicle; esp., an automobile **2** elevator

ca·rafe' (-raf') *n.* bottle for water, coffee, etc.

car'a·mel (*or* kär'məl) *n.* **1** burnt sugar used to flavor **2** chewy candy

car'at *n.* **1** unit of weight for jewels **2** karat

car'a·van' *n.* group traveling together, as through a desert

car'a·van'sa·ry *n., pl.* **-ries** in the Middle East, inn for caravans

car'a·way' *n.* spicy seeds used as flavoring

car'bide' *n.* compound of a metal with carbon

car'bine' (-bīn', -bēn') *n.* light, short-barreled rifle

carbo- *pref.* carbon

car'bo·hy'drate *n.* compound of carbon, hydrogen, and oxygen, as sugar or starch

car·bol'ic acid *n.* an acid used as an antiseptic, etc.

car'bon *n.* nonmetallic chemical element in all organic compounds: diamond and graphite are pure carbon

car'bon·ate' *v.* charge with carbon dioxide —**car'bo·na'tion** *n.*

carbon copy *n.* copy, spec. one made with carbon paper

carbon dating *n.* the finding of a fossil's age by measuring radioactive carbon in it

carbon dioxide *n.* odorless gas given off in breathing

car·bon·if'er·ous *a.* containing carbon or coal

carbon monoxide *n.* colorless, odorless, poisonous gas

carbon paper *n.* paper coated with a carbon preparation, used to make copies of letters, etc.

carbon tet'ra·chlo'ride' *n.* a cleaning fluid

Car·bo·run'dum *trademark* hard abrasive, esp. of carbon and silicon —*n.* [c-] such a substance

car'boy' *n.* large bottle to hold corrosive liquids

car'bun·cle *n.* painful inflammation below the skin

car·bu·ret'or (-bə rāt'ər) *n.* device in an engine for mixing air with gasoline

car'cass (-kəs) *n.* dead body of an animal

car·cin'o·gen (-sin'-) *n.* substance causing cancer —**car'ci·no·gen'ic** *a.*

car·ci·no'ma *n.* cancer of certain tissues, esp. the epidermis

car coat *n.* short overcoat

card *n.* **1** flat piece of stiff paper **2** postcard **3** playing card **4** *pl.* game played with cards **5** metal comb for wool, etc. —*v.* to comb with a card

card'board' *n.* stiff paper

car'di·ac' *a.* of the heart

car'di·gan *n.* knitted jacketlike sweater

car'di·nal *a.* **1** chief; main **2** bright-red —*n.* **1** high R.C. Church official **2** red American songbird

cardinal number *n.* number used in counting, as 7, 42, etc.

cardio- *pref.* of the heart

car'di·o·gram' *n.* electrocardiogram

car'di·o·graph' *n.* electrocardiograph

car'di·ol'o·gy *n.* branch of medicine dealing with the heart —**car'di·ol'o·gist** *n.*

car'di·o·pul'mo·nar·y *a.* involving the heart and lungs

car'di·o·vas'cu·lar *a.* of the heart and blood vessels

card'sharp' *n.* [Inf.] professional cheater at cards: also **card shark**

care *n.* **1** worry **2** watchfulness **3** charge; keeping —*v.* **1** be concerned **2** wish (to do) —**care for 1** love or like **2** look after —(in) care of at the address of —**take care of 1** look after **2** protect

ca·reen' *v.* tilt; lurch

ca·reer' *n.* profession or occupation —*v.* to rush wildly

care'free' *a.* without care

care'ful *a.* **1** cautious; wary **2** thoroughly done —**care'ful·ly** *adv.*

care'less *a.* **1** carefree **2** not paying enough attention or heed —**care'less·ness** *n.*

ca·ress' *v.* touch lovingly —*n.* affectionate touch

car'et *n.* mark (∧) to show where addition is to be made in a printed line

care'tak'er *n.* one who takes care of a building, etc.

care'worn' *a.* weary with care

car'fare' *n.* price of a ride on a bus, etc.

car'go *n., pl.* **-goes** or **-gos** load carried by a ship, etc.

Car·ib·be'an (or kə rib'ē ən) *a.* of the Caribbean Sea, its islands, etc.

car'i·bou' (-boo') *n., pl.* **-bous'** or **-bou'** North American reindeer

car·i·ca·ture (kar'i kə chər) *n.* distorted imitation or picture for satire —*v.* do a caricature of

car·ies (ker'ēz) *n.* decay of teeth, bones, etc.

car'il·lon' *n.* set of tuned bells

car'jack'ing *n.* the taking of a car from passengers by force

car'mine (-min, -mīn') *n.* red or purplish red

car'nage *n.* slaughter

car'nal *a.* bodily; sensual

car·na'tion *n.* **1** variety of the pink **2** its flower

car'ni·val *n.* **1** festivity **2** kind of fair, with rides, etc.

car·niv'o·rous *a.* flesh-eating —**car'ni·vore'** *n.*

car'ob *n.* tree with sweet pods used in candy, etc.

car'ol *n.* (Christmas) song of joy —*v.* sing —**car'ol·er, car'ol·ler** *n.*

car'om n., v. hit and rebound

ca·rot'id n. either of two main arteries in the neck

ca·rouse' (-rouz') v., n. (join in) a drinking party

car·ou·sel', car·rou·sel' n. merry-go-round

carp n. freshwater fish —v. find fault pettily

car'pal tunnel syndrome n. pain or numbness in wrist, etc. from repetitive hand movement

car'pel n. modified leaf forming a pistil

car'pen·ter n. construction worker who makes wooden parts —**car'pen·try** n.

carpenter ant n. large, black ant that gnaws at wood

car'pet n. heavy fabric for covering a floor —v. to cover as with a carpet

car'pet·bag' n. old-fashioned traveling bag of carpeting

car'pet·bag'ger n. politician, promoter, etc. from the outside whose influence is resented

car'pet·ing n. carpets or carpet fabric

car phone n. cellular phone in a car, etc.

car pool n. group plan to rotate cars, going to and from work —**car'pool'**, **car'-pool'** v.

car'port' n. roofed shelter for an automobile

car'rel, car'rell n. small enclosure for study in a library

car'riage n. 1 horse-drawn vehicle 2 posture 3 moving part that holds and shifts something

car'ri·er n. one that carries

car'ri·on n. decaying flesh of a dead body

car'rot n. an orange-red root, eaten as a vegetable

car'ry v. **-ried, -ry·ing** 1 take to another place 2 lead, transmit, etc. 3 win (an election, etc.) 4 hold; support 5 bear (oneself) 6 keep in stock 7 cover a range —**be (or get) carried away** to become very emotional or enthusiastic —**carry on** 1 do or continue 2 [Inf.] behave wildly —**carry out (or through)** to accomplish

car'ry·out' a. of prepared food sold to be eaten elsewhere

car seat n. portable seat fastened to a car's seat for securing a child

car'sick' a. nauseated from riding in a car, etc.

cart n. small wagon or vehicle with wheels, esp. one pushed or pulled by hand —v. carry as in a vehicle

cart'age n. 1 a carting 2 charge for this

carte' blanche' (blänsh') n. full authority

car·tel' n. national or international monopoly

car'ti·lage n. tough, elastic skeletal tissue

car·tog'ra·phy n. mapmaking —**car·tog'ra·pher** n.

car'ton n. cardboard box

car·toon' n. 1 drawing that is a caricature 2 comic strip 3 film of drawn figures that seem to move —**car·toon'ist** n.

car'tridge n. 1 cylinder holding the charge and bullet or shot for a firearm 2 small container for film, etc.

cart'wheel' n. a sideways turning, heels over head, with the legs extended

carve v. 1 make or shape by cutting 2 slice —**carv'er** n. —**carv'ing** n.

car'wash' n. business at which cars are washed

ca·sa'ba (-sä'-) n. melon with a yellow rind

Ca·sa·no'va n. man who has many love affairs

cas·cade' n. 1 waterfall 2 a shower —v. fall in a cascade

case n. 1 example or instance 2 situation 3 lawsuit 4 form of a noun, etc. showing its relation to neighboring words 5 container 6 protective cover —**in case** if —**in case of** in the event of

ca'se·in (-sē in, sēn') n. protein constituent of milk

case'load' n. number of cases being handled by a court, caseworker, etc.

case'ment n. hinged window that opens outward

case'work' n. social work dealing with cases of personal and family maladjustment —**case'work'er** n.

cash n. money on hand —v. give or get cash for: often with **in**

cash'ew n. kidney-shaped, edible nut

cash·ier' n. one in charge of cash transactions —v. dismiss in disgrace

cash'mere' (kash'-, kazh'-) n. soft, fine goat's wool, or a cloth of this

cash register n. device for showing the amount of a sale

cas'ing n. 1 outer covering 2 door frame

ca·si'no n., pl. **-nos** hall for dancing, gambling, etc.

cask n. barrel for liquid

cas′ket n. coffin

cas·sa′va (-sä′-) n. tropical plant with starchy roots

cas′se·role′ n. covered dish for baking and serving

cas·sette′ n. case with film or tape for a camera, tape recorder, VCR, etc.

cas′sia (kash′ə) n. 1 bark of an Asian tree, from which cinnamon comes 2 tropical plant whose leaves yield senna

cas′sock n. long vestment worn by clergy

cast v. **cast, cast′ing** 1 throw 2 deposit (a vote) 3 mold 4 select (an actor) —n. 1 a throw 2 plaster form for broken limb 3 the actors in a play 4 type or quality 5 tinge —**cast about** search —**cast aside** (or **away** or **off**) discard

cas′ta·nets′ pl.n. pair of small, hollowed pieces clicked together in one hand to keep musical rhythm

cast′a·way′ n. shipwrecked person

caste (kast) n. class (distinction) based on birth, etc.

cast′er n. small swiveled wheel as on a table leg

cas′ti·gate′ v. criticize severely —**cas′ti·ga′tion** n. —**cas′ti·ga′tor** n.

cast′ing n. metal cast in a mold

cast iron n. hard, brittle iron made by casting —**cast′-i′ron** a.

cas·tle (kas′əl) n. 1 large, fortified dwelling 2 *Chess* rook

cast′off′ a. discarded —n. person or thing abandoned

cas′tor oil n. oil used as a laxative

cas′trate′ v. remove the testicles of —**cas·tra′tion** n.

cas′u·al (kazh′ōō-) a. 1 by chance 2 careless 3 nonchalant 4 informal

cas′u·al·ty n., pl. **-ties** one hurt or killed in an accident or in war

cas′u·ist·ry n. subtle but false reasoning

cat n. 1 small, soft-furred animal kept as a pet 2 any related mammal, as the lion

cat′a·clysm′ (-kliz′əm) n. sudden, violent change —**cat′a·clys′mic** a.

cat′a·comb′ (-kōm′) n. tunnel-like burial place

cat′a·falque′ (-falk′, -fôlk′) n. wooden framework for holding a coffin

cat′a·lep′sy n. loss of consciousness, with body rigidity —**cat′a·lep′tic** a., n.

cat′a·log′, cat′a·logue′ n. 1 complete list, as of library books 2 booklet of articles for sale —v. to list

ca·tal′pa (-tal′-) n. tree with heart-shaped leaves

cat′a·lyst′ (-list) a. 1 substance that affects a chemical reaction but itself remains unchanged 2 stimulus —**cat′a·lyt′ic** a.

cat′a·mount′ n. 1 cougar 2 lynx

cat′a·pult′ n. device for throwing or launching —v. shoot as from a catapult

cat′a·ract′ n. 1 large waterfall 2 opaque condition of eye lens

ca·tarrh′ (-kä tär′) n. inflammation of the respiratory passages

ca·tas′tro·phe (-trə fē) n. sudden great disaster —**cat′a·stroph′ic** a.

cat′a·ton′ic a. being in a stupor in which the muscles are rigid

cat′bird′ n. songbird with a call like a cat's

cat′call′ n. derisive call

catch v. **caught, catch′ing** 1 capture 2 deceive 3 surprise 4 get 5 grab 6 understand 7 take or keep hold —n. 1 a catching 2 thing that catches or is caught —**catch on** 1 understand 2 become popular —**catch up** to overtake —**catch′er** n.

catch′all′ n. container for holding all sorts of things

catch′ing a. 1 contagious 2 attractive

catch′phrase′ n. expression meant to catch people's attention

catch′up n. ketchup

catch′y a. **-i·er, -i·est** 1 easily remembered 2 tricky

cat′e·chism′ (-kiz′əm) n. list of questions and answers to teach religious beliefs

cat′e·chize′ v. to question searchingly: also sp. **cat′e·chise′**

cat′e·gor′i·cal a. 1 of or in a category 2 positive

cat′e·go′ry n., pl. **-ries** any of a system of classes —**cat′e·go·rize′** v.

ca′ter v. provide food, etc. for a party —**ca′ter·er** n.

cat′er-cor′nered (kat′ə-, kat′ē-) a. diagonal —adv. diagonally Also **cat′er-cor′ner**

cat′er·pil′lar n. larva of a butterfly, moth, etc.

cat′er·waul′ (-wôl′) v., n. wail

cat′fight′ n. [Inf.] angry quarrel, esp. between women

cat′fish′ n. fish with long feelers about the mouth

cat′gut′ n. tough thread made from animal intestines

ca·thar′sis n. a relieving of emotional tension

ca·thar′tic a. purging —n. a laxative

ca·the′dral *n.* large church

cath′e·ter *n.* tube put in the bladder to remove urine

cath′ode′ *n.* **1** a negatively charged electrode **2** positive terminal of a battery

cathode rays *pl.n.* streams of electrons producing X-rays when striking solids

cath′ode′-ray′ tube *n.* vacuum tube, as in a TV set, sending electrons onto a fluorescent screen to form images

cath′o·lic *a.* **1** universal **2** liberal **3** [C-] Roman Catholic —*n.* [C-] member of the R.C. Church —**Ca·thol′i·cism′** *n.* —**cath′o·lic′i·ty** *n.*

cat′kin *n.* spike of clustered small flowers

cat′nap′ *n.* short sleep; doze —*v.* take a catnap

cat′nip′ *n.* plant like mint

cat′-o′-nine′-tails′ *n., pl.* **-tails′** whip of nine knotted cords attached to a handle

CAT scan (kat) *n.* CT scan

cat′s cradle *n.* game played by looping string over the fingers to make designs

cat′s′-paw′ *n.* a dupe

cat′sup (or kech′əp) *n.* ketchup

cat′tail′ *n.* marsh plant with long, brown spikes

cat′tle *pl.n.* **1** livestock **2** cows, bulls, steers, or oxen —**cat′tle·man** *n., pl.* **-men**

cat′ty *a.* **-ti·er, -ti·est** spiteful or mean

cat′ty-cor′nered *a., adv.* cater-cornered: also **cat′ty-cor′ner**

cat′walk′ *n.* high, narrow walk

Cau·ca·soid′ *n., a.* (member) of one of the major groups of human beings, loosely called the *white race*: also **Cau·ca′sian** (-kā′zhən)

cau′cus *n.* political meeting to choose party candidates, etc. —*v.* hold a caucus

cau′dal *a.* of the tail

caught *v.* pt. & pp. of CATCH

caul *n.* membrane enclosing the head of a fetus at birth

caul′dron *n.* caldron

cau′li·flow′er *n.* edible, hard, white head of a cabbagelike plant

caulk (kôk) *v.* make watertight or airtight by filling cracks with a puttylike sealant —*n.* this sealant

caus′al (kôz′-) *a.* of a cause or causes —**cau·sal′i·ty** *n.*

cau·sa′tion *n.* **1** a causing **2** anything producing an effect

cause *n.* **1** thing bringing a result **2** motive **3** group movement with an aim **4** lawsuit —*v.* bring about

cause′way′ *n.* raised road, as across a marsh

caus′tic (kôs′-) *a.* **1** corrosive **2** sarcastic —*n.* caustic substance

cau′ter·ize′ *v.* burn dead tissue off, as with a hot iron

cau′tion *n.* **1** warning **2** prudence —*v.* warn —**cau′tious** *a.*

cav′al·cade′ *n.* procession

cav′a·lier′ (-lir′) *n.* **1** knight **2** gallant gentleman —*a.* **1** casual **2** arrogant —**cav′a·lier′ly** *adv.*

cav′al·ry *n., pl.* **-ries** army troops on horses or in motorized vehicles —**cav′al·ry·man** *n., pl.* **-men**

cave *n.* hollow place in the earth —*v.* collapse (*in*)

cave′-in′ *n.* **1** a caving in **2** place where ground, etc. has caved in

cave man *n.* prehistoric human being who lived in caves

cav′ern *n.* large cave —**cav′ern·ous** *a.*

cav′i·ar′, cav′i·are′ *n.* fish eggs eaten as an appetizer

cav′il *v.* quibble

cav′i·ty *n., pl.* **-ties** hole or hollow place

ca·vort′ *v.* prance; caper

caw *n.* crow's harsh cry —*v.* make this sound

cay·enne′ (kī-, kā-) *n.* ground hot red pepper

cay·use (kī′yōōs) *n., pl.* **-us′es** small horse of the W U.S.

CB *a.* of radio frequencies for local use by private persons —*n.* CB radio

cc *abbrev.* **1** carbon copy (or copies) **2** cubic centimeter(s)

CD *n.* compact disc

Cdn *abbrev.* Canadian

CD-ROM *n.* compact disc for storing and retrieving computer data

cease (sēs) *v.* to end; stop

cease′-fire′ *n.* truce

cease′less *a.* unceasing

ce·cum (sē′kəm) *n., pl.* **-ca** pouch at the beginning of the large intestine

ce′dar *n.* evergreen tree with fragrant wood

cede (sēd) *v.* give up; transfer

ceil′ing *n.* **1** inner roof of a room **2** upper limit

cel′an·dine′ (-dīn′, -dēn′) *n.* **1** poppy **2** buttercup

cel′e·brate′ *v.* **1** perform (a ritual) **2** commemorate with festivity **3** to honor; praise —**cel′e·bra′tion** *n.*

cel′e·brat′ed *a.* famous

ce·leb′ri·ty *n.* **1** fame **2** *pl.* **-ties**

famous person

ce·ler'i·ty *n.* speed

cel'er·y *n.* plant with edible crisp stalks

ce·les'tial (-chəl) *a.* **1** of the heavens **2** divine

cel'i·ba·cy *n.* unmarried state **—cel'i·bate** (-bət) *a.*, *n.*

cell *n.* **1** small room as in a prison **2** small unit of protoplasm **3** device for generating electricity chemically **4** unit of an organization **—cel'lu·lar** *a.*

cel'lar *n.* room(s) below ground under a building

cel·lo (chel'ō) *n.*, *pl.* **-los** instrument like a large violin, held between the knees in playing **—cel'list** *n.*

cel'lo·phane (sel'ə-) *n.* thin, transparent cellulose material, used as a wrapping

cel'lu·lar phone *n.* mobile radio telephone: also [Inf.] **cell'phone'**

cel'lu·lite' *n.* fatty deposits on the hips and thighs

cel'lu·loid' *n.* flammable plastic substance of cellulose

cel'lu·lose' (-yōō lōs') *n.* substance in plant cell walls, used in making paper, etc.

Cel'si·us *a.* of a thermometer on which 0° is the freezing point and 100° the boiling point of water

ce·ment' *n.* **1** mixture of lime, clay, and water, used for paving, in mortar, etc. **2** any adhesive **—v.** join as with cement

cem'e·ter·y *n.*, *pl.* **-ies** place for burying the dead

cen'ser *n.* container in which incense is burned

cen'sor *n.* one who examines books, mail, etc. to remove things considered unsuitable **—v.** act as a censor of **—cen'sor·ship'** *n.*

cen·so'ri·ous (-sôr'ē-) *a.* critical

cen'sure *n.*, *v.* blame

cen'sus *n.* official count of population

cent *n.* 100th part of a dollar; penny

cent *abbrev.* **1** century **2** centuries

cen'taur (-tôr') *n.* Gr. myth. monster with a man's head and trunk and a horse's body

cen·ta'vo (-tä'-) *n.*, *pl.* **-vos** 100th part of a peso, etc.

cen·ten'ni·al *n.* 100th anniversary **—** *a.* of a centennial Also **cen'te·nar'y** (or sen ten'ər ē)

cen'ter *n.* **1** middle point, esp. of a circle or sphere **2** any central place, thing, or person **—v.** **1** put or be at the center **2** gather to one place

cen'ter·fold' *n.* center facing pages of a magazine

cen'ter·piece' *n.* ornament for the center of a table

centi- *pref.* **1** hundred **2** 100th part of

cen'ti·grade' *a.* Celsius

cen'ti·gram' *n.* 1/100 gram

cen·ti·li'ter *n.* 1/100 liter

cen·time (sän'tēm') *n.* 100th part of a franc

cen'ti·me'ter *n.* 1/100 meter

cen'ti·pede' *n.* wormlike animal with many pairs of legs

cen'tral *a.* **1** in or near the center **2** main; chief **—cen'tral·ly** *adv.*

cen'tral·ize' *v.* **1** bring to a center **2** organize under one control **—cen'tral·i·za'tion** *n.*

cen'tre *n.*, *v.* Br. sp. of CENTER

cen·trif'u·gal force *n.* force that makes rotating bodies move away from the center

cen'tri·fuge' (-fyōōj') *n.* machine using centrifugal force to separate particles

cen·trip'e·tal force *n.* force that makes rotating bodies move toward the center

cen'trist *n.* person with moderate political opinions

cen·tu'ri·on *n.* military commander in ancient Rome

cen'tu·ry (-chə-) *n.*, *pl.* **-ries** period of 100 years

CEO *abbrev.* chief executive officer

ce·phal'ic (-fal'-) *a.* of, in, or on the head or skull

ce·ram'ics *n.* the making of pottery, porcelain, etc. **—pl.n.** pottery, etc. **—ce·ram'ic** *a.*

ce're·al (sir'ē-) *n.* **1** grain used for food, as wheat, oats, etc. **2** (breakfast) food made from grain

cer·e·bel'lum (ser'ə-) *n.* lower rear part of the brain

cerebral palsy *n.* paralysis due to a lesion of the brain

cer'e·bral (or sə rē'-) *a.* of the brain

cer'e·brum (or sə rē'-) *n.* upper, main part of the brain

cer'e·ment *n.* shroud

cer·e·mo'ni·al *a.* ritual; formal **—n.** system of rites

cer·e·mo'ny *n.* **1** *pl.* **-nies** set of formal acts; rite **2** rigid etiquette; formality **—cer·e·mo'ni·ous** *a.*

ce·rise (sə rēz', -rēs') *a.* cherry-red

cert *abbrev.* **1** certificate **2** certified

cer'tain *a.* **1** fixed; settled **2** sure; positive **3** specific, but unnamed **4** some **—for certain** surely **—cer'tain·ly** *adv.* **—cer'tain·ty** *n.*

cer·tif'i·cate (-kət) *n.* written statement testifying to a fact, promise, etc.

cer'ti·fy' *v.* **-fied', -fy'ing 1** formally declare to be true, etc. **2** guarantee — **cer·ti·fi·ca'tion** *n.*

cer'ti·tude' *n.* assurance

ce·ru'le·an *a.* sky-blue

cer'vix' *n.* narrow portion of uterus — **cer'vi·cal** *a.*

ce·sar'e·an (section) *n.* surgery to deliver a baby

ces·sa'tion *n.* stop; pause

ces'sion *n.* a ceding

cess'pool' *n.* deep hole in the ground for sewage, etc.

cf *abbrev.* compare

CFO *abbrev.* chief financial officer

cg, cgm *abbrev.* centigram(s)

Ch *abbrev.* **1** chapter **2** church Also **ch**

Cha·blis (sha blē') *n.* dry white wine

chafe *v.* **1** make warm or sore by rubbing **2** be annoyed or impatient

chaff *n.* **1** threshed husks of grain **2** worthless stuff —*v.* to tease; banter

chaf'ing dish (chāf'-) *n.* pan for cooking food at the table

cha·grin' (sha-) *n.* disappointment, humiliation, etc. —*v.* to make feel chagrin

chain *n.* **1** flexible series of joined links **2** *pl.* fetters **3** connected series —*v.* restrain as with chains

chain reaction *n.* a series of (nuclear) reactions whose results cause new reactions

chain saw *n.* portable power saw with a chain loop of cutting teeth

chain store *n.* any of a group of retail stores owned by one company

chair *n.* **1** seat with a back **2** office of authority —*v.* preside at (a meeting)

chair'lift' *n.* seats on a cable for carrying skiers uphill

chair'man *n.*, *pl.* **-men** one who presides at a meeting —**chair'man·ship'** *n.* —**chair'per·son** *n.* —**chair'wom·an** *n.fem.*, *pl.* **-wom'en**

chaise longue (shāz' lôṇ') *n.*, *pl.* **chaise longues** couchlike chair with a long seat: also **chaise lounge**

chal·ced'o·ny (kal sed'-) *n.* colored waxlike quartz

cha·let (sha lā') *n.* cottage with overhanging eaves

chal·ice (chal'is) *n.* cup or goblet

chalk (chôk) *n.* soft limestone for writing on a blackboard —**chalk up** to record —**chalk'y** *a.*, **-i·er**, **-i·est**

chalk'board' *n.* blackboard

chal'lenge *n.* **1** demand for identification **2** a calling into question **3** call to a contest, etc. **4** anything calling for special effort —*v.* put a challenge to —**chal'leng·er** *n.*

chal'lenged *a.* disabled or handicapped

cham'ber (chām'-) *n.* **1** room **2** *pl.* judge's office **3** assembly or council **4** part of gun that holds a cartridge

cham'ber·maid' *n.* maid who keeps bedrooms neat

chamber music *n.* music for performance by a small group

cham'bray' (sham'-) *n.* smooth cotton fabric

cha·me'le·on (kə mē'-) *n.* lizard able to change its color

cham·ois (sham'ē) *n.*, *pl.* **-ois 1** small antelope **2** soft kind of leather

cham'o·mile' (kam'-) *n.* camomile

champ *v.* chew or bite noisily —*n.* [Inf.] champion —**champ at the bit** be impatient when held back

cham·pagne' (sham pān') *n.* effervescent white wine

cham·paign' (sham pān') *n.* flat, open country

cham'pi·on *n.* **1** one who fights for a cause **2** winner of first place —*a.* best —*v.* defend; support —**cham'pi·on·ship'** *n.*

chance *n.* **1** luck; fortune **2** risk **3** opportunity **4** possibility —*a.* accidental —*v.* **1** happen **2** to risk

chan'cel *n.* place around an altar for clergy and choir

chan'cel·lor *n.* **1** high state or church official **2** university head —**chan'cel·ler·y** *n.*, *pl.* **-ies**

chan·cre (shaṇ'kər) *n.* sore or ulcer of syphilis

chan'cy *a.* **-i·er**, **-i·est** risky

chan·de·lier (shan'də lir') *n.* hanging lighting fixture

chan'dler *n.* **1** candle maker **2** retailer of supplies, as for ships

change *v.* **1** to substitute **2** to exchange **3** alter; vary —*n.* **1** alteration or variation **2** variety **3** money returned as overpayment **4** small coins —**change'a·ble** *a.* —**change'less** *a.*

change of life *n.* menopause

change'o'ver *n.* a complete change

chan'nel *n.* **1** bed of a river, etc. **2** wide strait joining two seas **3** any passage **4** official course of action **5** assigned frequency band, esp. in TV —*v.* make, or send through, a channel

chant *n.* song with several words to each tone —*v.* to utter in a chant

chan·tey (shan'tē, chan'-) *n.* sailors' work song

chan'ti·cleer' *n.* rooster

Cha·nu·kah (khä'noo kä') *n.* Hanukkah

cha·os (kā'äs') *n.* complete disorder —**cha·ot'ic** *a.*

chap *n.* [Inf.] a fellow —*v.* **chapped, chap'ping** become rough and red as from the cold

chap *abbrev.* chapter

cha·peau (sha pō') *n., pl.* **-peaus'** or **-peaux'** (-pōz') hat

chap'el *n.* small church

chap·er·on, chap·er·one (shap'ə rōn') *n.* older person in charge of unmarried people at social affairs —*v.* be a chaperon to

chap'lain (-lən) *n.* clergyman in the armed forces

chap'let *n.* garland

chaps *pl.n.* leather trousers worn by cowboys

chap'ter *n.* 1 main division of a book 2 branch of an organization

chapter book *n.* children's book, divided into chapters

char *v.* **charred, char'ring** scorch

char·ac·ter (ker'-) *n.* 1 letter or symbol 2 characteristic 3 moral nature or strength 4 reputation 5 person in a play, novel, etc. 6 [Inf.] eccentric person

char·ac·ter·is'tic *a.* typical; distinctive —*n.* distinguishing quality

char·ac·ter·ize' *v.* 1 describe 2 be a quality of —**char·ac·ter·i·za'tion** *n.*

cha·rade' (sha-) *n.* 1 *pl.* word game in pantomime 2 transparent pretense

char·broil', char'-broil' *v.* broil over a charcoal fire

char'coal' *n.* pieces of incompletely burned wood

chard *n.* beet with edible leaves and stalks

char·don·nay' (shär'-) *n.* [*also* C-] dry white wine

charge *v.* 1 fill (*with*) 2 add electricity to 3 command 4 accuse 5 ask as a price 6 ask payment (*for*) 7 put as a debt 8 attack —*n.* 1 load 2 responsibility or care (*of*) 3 chemical energy in a battery 4 someone in one's care 5 command 6 accusation 7 a cost 8 debt or charge 9 attack —**in charge (of)** in control (*of*)

charge account *n.* arrangement to pay within some future period

charg'er *n.* 1 war horse 2 device that charges batteries

char'grill' *v.* to grill over a charcoal fire

char'i·ot *n.* ancient, horse-drawn, two-wheeled cart —**char'i·ot·eer'** *n.*

cha·ris'ma (kə riz'-) *n.* charming or inspiring quality —**char·is·mat'ic** *a.*

char'i·ty *n., pl.* **-ties** 1 leniency in judging others 2 a helping those in need 3 institution for so helping —**char'i·ta·ble** *a.*

char·la·tan (shär'lə tən) *n.* quack; impostor

char'ley horse *n.* [Inf.] muscle cramp in the thigh

charm *n.* 1 words or thing supposed to have magic power 2 trinket on a bracelet, etc. 3 fascination; allure —*v.* 1 to use a magical charm on 2 fascinate; delight —**charm'ing** *a.*

char'nel (house) *n.* place for corpses

chart *n.* 1 map, esp. for navigation 2 graph, table, etc. —*v.* make a chart of

char·ter *n.* official paper licensing a new company, society, chapter, etc. —*v.* 1 grant a charter to 2 hire

charter member *n.* original member of an organization

char·treuse (shär trooz') *n., a.* pale, yellowish green

char'wom·an *n., pl.* **-wom'en** cleaning woman

char·y (cher'ē) *a.* **-i·er, -i·est** careful; cautious —**char'i·ly** *adv.*

chase *v.* 1 follow in order to catch 2 drive away 3 decorate (metal) as by engraving —*n.* a chasing —**give chase** pursue

chas'er *n.* [Inf.] water, etc. taken after liquor

chasm (kaz'əm) *n.* deep crack in the earth's surface

chas·sis (chas'ē, shas'-) *n., pl.* **-sis** (-ēz) 1 frame, wheels, and motor of a car 2 frame, circuits, etc. of an electronic device

chaste *a.* 1 sexually virtuous 2 decent; modest 3 simple in style —**chas'ti·ty** *n.*

chas·ten (chās'ən) *v.* 1 punish so as to correct 2 subdue

chas·tise' (-tīz') *v.* 1 punish as by beating 2 scold sharply —**chas·tise'ment** *n.*

chat *v.* **chat'ted, chat'ting;** *n.* talk in a light, informal way —**chat'ty** *a.,* **-ti·er, -ti·est**

châ·teau (sha tō') *n., pl.* **-teaux'** (-tōz', tō') or **-teaus'** mansion

chat'tel *n.* piece of movable property

chat'ter *v.* 1 talk much and foolishly 2 click together rapidly —*n.* a chattering

chauf·feur (shō'fər) *n.* person hired to

drive one's car —v. act as chauffeur to

chau'vin·ism' (shō'-) n. 1 fanatical patriotism 2 unreasoning devotion to one's race, sex, etc. —**chau'vin·ist** a., n. —**chau'vin·is'tic** a.

cheap a. 1 low in price 2 of little value —adv. at a low cost —**cheap'ly** adv. —**cheap'ness** n.

cheap'en v. make cheaper

cheap'skate' n. [Sl.] stingy person

cheat n. 1 fraud 2 swindler —v. 1 deceive or practice fraud 2 escape

check n. 1 sudden stop 2 restraint or restrainer 3 test of accuracy, etc. 4 mark (✓) used to verify 5 identifying token to show ownership 6 bill, as at a restaurant 7 written order to a bank to pay money 8 pattern of squares 9 Chess threat to the king —int. [Inf.] right —v. 1 stop or restrain 2 test, verify, etc. 3 mark with a check 4 deposit temporarily in a checkroom, etc. —**check in** register at a hotel, etc. —**check out 1** officially leave a hotel, etc. 2 collect amount owed in a supermarket, etc. —**check'er** n.

check'book' n. booklet of bank checks

checked a. having a pattern of squares

check'er n. flat, round piece used in checkers

check'er·board' n. board for checkers, with 64 squares

check'ered a. 1 having a pattern of squares 2 varied

check'ers n. game like chess, for two players

check'ing account n. bank account for writing checks

check'list' n. list to be referred to: also **check list**

check'mate' n. Chess position from which king cannot escape, ending the game —v. to put in checkmate

check'out' n. place or time for checking out

check'point' n. place where road traffic is inspected

check'room' n. room for leaving hats, coats, etc.

check'up' n. medical examination

ched'dar (cheese) n. [often C-] a hard, smooth cheese

cheek n. 1 side of face below eye 2 [Inf.] impudence

cheep n. young bird's short, shrill sound —v. make this sound

cheer n. 1 joy; gladness 2 shout of excitement, welcome, etc. —v. 1 fill with cheer 2 urge on, praise, etc.

with cheers —**cheer up** make or become glad

cheer'ful a. 1 joyful 2 bright and attractive —**cheer'ful·ly** adv.

cheer·lead'er n. person who leads cheers for a team —**cheer'lead'** v.

cheer'less a. not cheerful

cheers int. good health: used as a toast

cheer'y a. **-i·er, -i·est** cheerful; bright

cheese n. solid food made from milk curds

cheese'burg'er n. hamburger with melted cheese

cheese'cloth' n. cotton cloth with a loose weave

chees'y a. **-i·er, -i·est** 1 like cheese 2 [Sl.] inferior; poor

chee'tah n. animal like the leopard

chef (shef) n. head cook

chem abbrev. chemistry

chem'i·cal (kem'-) a. of, in, or by chemistry —n. substance used in or obtained by chemistry —**chem'i·cal·ly** adv.

che·mise (shə mēz') n. woman's undergarment

chem'is·try n. 1 science dealing with the composition, reactions, etc. of substances 2 rapport —**chem'ist** n.

che'mo·ther'a·py (kē'mō-) n. use of drugs in treating disease: also [Inf.] **che'mo**

che·nille (shə nēl') n. fabric woven with tufted cord

cheque (chek) n. Br. sp. of CHECK (n. 7)

cher'ish v. 1 hold or treat tenderly 2 keep in mind

Cher·o·kee' n. member of an Indian people of the SE U.S.

cher'ry n., pl. **-ries** small, red fruit

cher'ub n., pl. **-ubs** or **-u·bim'** angel, pictured as a chubby child with wings —**che·ru'bic** (-roo'-) a.

chess n. checkerboard game for two players using various pieces (**chess' men**)

chest n. 1 box with a lid 2 piece of furniture with drawers 3 front part of the body above the abdomen

ches'ter·field' n. [Cdn.] a sofa

chest'nut' n. 1 edible nut of various beech trees 2 [Inf.] trite joke —a. reddish-brown

chev·i·ot (shev'ē ət) n. twilled wool fabric

chev'ron (shev'-) n. V-shaped sleeve insignia of rank

chew v. grind with the teeth —n. something for chewing —**chew'y** a., **-i·er, -i·est**

chew′ing gum n. flavored chicle, etc. for chewing

Chey·enne (shī an′) n. member of an Indian people of the N and central U.S.

chg(d) abbrev. charge(d)

Chi·an·ti (kē än′tē) n. [also **c-**] a dry red wine

chic (shēk) a. smartly stylish —**chic′ly** adv. —**chic′ness** n.

chi·can·er·y (shi kān′-) n., pl. **-ies** 1 trickery 2 trick

Chi·ca·no (chi kä′nō) n., pl. **-nos** Mexican-American —**Chi·ca′na** n.fem.

chick n. 1 young chicken 2 [Sl.] young woman

chick′a·dee′ n. small bird of the titmouse family

chick′en n. hen or rooster, or its edible flesh

chick′en·pox′ n. infectious disease with skin eruptions

chick′pea′ n. pealike plant with edible seeds

chic′le n. gummy substance from a tropical tree

chic′o·ry n. plant with leaf used in salads and root used as a coffee substitute

chide v. scold; rebuke

chief n. leader —a. main; most important —**chief′ly** adv.

chief′tain (-tən) n. chief of a clan or tribe

chif·fon (shi fän′) n. sheer silk cloth

chif·fo·nier, chif·fon·nier (shif′ə nir′) n. tall, narrow bureau

chig′ger n. a mite larva that causes itching

chi·gnon (shēn′yän′) n. coil of hair worn at the back of the neck by women

Chi·hua·hua (chi wä′wä) n. tiny dog with large, pointed ears

chil′blain′ n. inflamed sore caused by exposure to cold

child n., pl. **chil′dren** 1 infant 2 boy or girl before puberty 3 son or daughter —**with child** pregnant —**child′hood′** n. —**child′like′** a.

child′birth′ n. a giving birth to a child

child′ish a. silly; immature

chi·le re·lle′no (re yā′nō) n., pl. **chi·les re·lle′nos** a stuffed chili pepper

chil′i n., pl. **-ies** or **-is** 1 hot, dried pod of red pepper 2 spicy dish of beef, chilies, beans, etc.

chili sauce n. spiced sauce of chopped tomatoes, sweet peppers, onions, etc.

chill n. 1 moderate coldness 2 body coldness with shivering 3 sudden fear —a. uncomfortably cool —v. make or become cold —**chill′y** a., **-li·er, -li·est**

chill factor n. windchill factor

chime n. usually pl. set of tuned bells —v. to sound as a chime

chi·me·ra (ki mir′ə) n. impossible or foolish fancy

chim′ney n. passage for smoke from a furnace, etc.

chim·pan·zee′ n. medium-sized African ape: also [Inf.] **chimp**

chin n. face below the lips —v. **chinned, chin′ning** pull (oneself) up until the chin is above a bar being grasped

chi′na n. dishes, etc. of fine porcelain

chin·chil′la n. 1 small South American rodent 2 its costly fur

Chi·nese′ n., pl. **-nese′; a.** (native or language) of China

chink n. 1 crack 2 clinking sound —v. to clink

chi′no (chē′-, shē′-) n., pl. **-nos** 1 strong cotton cloth 2 pl. pants of chino

chintz n. glazed, printed cotton cloth

chintz′y a. **-i·er, -i′est** [Inf.] cheap, stingy, etc.

chip v. **chipped, chip′ping** break or cut off bits from —n. 1 fragment 2 place where bit is chipped off 3 small disk used in gambling 4 thin slice of food 5 electronic circuit on a tiny semiconductor —**chip in** [Inf.] contribute

chip′munk′ n. small, striped squirrel

chipped beef n. dried or smoked beef sliced into shavings

chip′per a. [Inf.] lively

chi·rop′o·dist (ki räp′-) n. podiatrist

chi·rop′o·dy (ki räp′-) n. podiatry

chi′ro·prac′tic (kī′rə-) n. treatment by manipulation of body joints, etc. —**chi′ro·prac′tor** n.

chirp v. make short, shrill sounds —n. such a sound

chir′rup v., n. chirp

chis′el (chiz′-) n. tool for chipping wood, stone, etc. —v. 1 chip with a chisel 2 [Inf.] swindle —**chis′el·er, chis′el·ler** n.

chit′chat′ n. small talk

chi′tin (kī′-) n. horny covering of insects, etc.

chit·ter·lings (chit′linz) pl.n. pig intestines, used for food: also **chit′lins** or **chit′lings**

chiv′al·ry (shiv′-) n. 1 medieval system of knighthood 2 courtesy, fairness, etc. —**chiv′al·rous** a.

chives pl.n. herb with slender leaves

with mild onion odor

chlo'ride' n. compound of chlorine

chlo'ri·nate' v. purify (water) with chlorine

chlo·rine (klôr'ēn) n. greenish gas, a chemical element

chlo'ro·form' n. colorless liquid solvent and former anesthetic —v. anesthetize or kill with this

chlo'ro·phyll', chlo'ro·phyl' (-fil') n. green coloring in plants

chock n., v. block; wedge

chock'-full' a. as full as possible

choc'o·late (usually chôk'lət) n. 1 ground cacao seeds 2 drink or candy made with this 3 reddish brown

choice n. 1 selection 2 right to choose 3 the one chosen —a. excellent

choir (kwīr) n. group of singers, esp. in a church —**choir'boy'** n.

choke v. 1 stop the breathing of; suffocate 2 obstruct; clog —n. a choking

choke collar n. dog collar that tightens when leash is taut: also **choke chain**

choke'hold' n. absolute control

chok'er n. closefitting necklace

chol'er (käl'-) n. [Now Rare] anger

chol'er·a n. infectious, often fatal, intestinal disease

chol'er·ic (or kə ler'-) a. having a quick temper

cho·les'ter·ol' (kə-) n. substance in animal fats, etc.

chomp v. chew or bite noisily —**chomp at the bit** be impatient when held back

choose v. **chose**, **cho'sen**, **choos'ing** 1 take; select 2 prefer; decide

choos'ey, choos'y a. **-i·er**, **-i·est** [Inf.] fussy in choosing

chop v. **chopped**, **chop'ping** 1 cut by blows of sharp tool 2 cut in bits —n. 1 sharp blow 2 a slice from the rib or loin

chop'per n. 1 pl. [Sl.] set of artificial teeth 2 [Inf.] helicopter

chop'py a. **-pi·er**, **-pi·est** with rough, abrupt waves or motions

chops pl.n. 1 jaws 2 flesh about the mouth

chop'sticks' pl.n. two sticks used as eating utensils in some Asian countries

chop su·ey (sōō'ē) n. American-Chinese stew served with rice

cho·ral (kôr'əl) a. of or for a choir or chorus

cho·rale, cho·ral (kə ral') n. simple hymn tune

chord (kôrd) n. 1 straight line joining two points on an arc 2 three or more

tones sounded together in harmony

chore n. daily task

chor·e·og'ra·phy (kôr'-) n. the devising of dances, esp. ballets —**chor'e·og'ra·pher** n.

chor'is·ter (kôr'-) n. choir member

chor·tle (chôrt'l) v., n. chuckle or snort

cho·rus (kôr'əs) n. 1 group of singers or of singers and dancers 2 music for group singing 3 refrain of a song —v. sing or recite in unison

chose v. pt. of CHOOSE

cho'sen v. pp. of CHOOSE —a. selected; choice

chow n. 1 medium-sized Chinese dog 2 [Sl.] food

chow'der n. fish or clam soup with vegetables

chow'hound' n. [Sl.] glutton

chow mein (mān) n. Chinese-American stew served on fried noodles

Christ Jesus as the Messiah

chris·ten (kris'ən) v. 1 baptize 2 name —**chris'ten·ing** n.

Chris'ten·dom (kris'ən-) n. Christians collectively

Chris·ti·an'i·ty n. religion based on teachings of Jesus —**Chris'tian** a., n.

Christ'mas n. celebration of Jesus' birth; December 25

chro·mat'ic a. 1 of color 2 Mus. in semitones

chrome n. alloy, etc. of chromium

chro'mi·um n. hard metal in alloys, a chemical element

chro'mo·some' n. any of the microscopic bodies carrying the genes of heredity

chron'ic a. long-lasting or recurring —**chron'i·cal·ly** adv.

chron'i·cle n. historical record —v. to tell the history of —**chron'i·cler** n.

chron·o·log'i·cal a. in order of occurrence —**chron'o·log'i·cal·ly** adv. —**chro·nol'o·gy** n.

chro·nom'e·ter n. very accurate clock or watch

chrys'a·lis (kris'-) n. pupa or its cocoon

chrys·an'the·mum n. plant with ball-shaped flowers

chub n. freshwater fish related to the carp

chub'by a. **-bi·er**, **-bi·est** plump

chuck v. 1 tap playfully 2 toss —n. 1 tap 2 toss 3 shoulder cut of beef 4 clamplike device as on a lathe

chuck'-full' a. chock-full

chuck'hole' n. rough hole in pavement

chuck·le v. laugh softly —n. soft laugh

chuck wagon n. wagon with kitchen for feeding cowboys

chug n. explosive sound —v. **chugged, chug'ging** make this sound

chuk'ka boot n. ankle-high boot

chum [Inf.] n. close friend —v. **chummed, chum'ming** be chums — **chum'my** a., **-mi·er, -mi·est**

chump n. [Inf.] fool

chunk n. thick piece

chunk'y a. **-i·er, -i·est** short and thickset

church n. **1** building for public worship **2** religion or religious sect

church'go'er n. one who attends church regularly —**church'go'ing** a.

church'yard' n. yard beside a church, often a cemetery

churl n. rude, surly person

churl'ish a. rude; surly

churn n. device for making butter —v. **1** shake (cream) in a churn to make butter **2** stir about vigorously

chute (shōōt) n. inclined passage for sliding things

chut'ney (chut'-) n., pl. **-neys** relish of fruits, spices, etc.

chutz'pah, chutz'pa (hōōts'-) n. [Inf.] impudence; audacity

CIA abbrev. Central Intelligence Agency

ci·ca'da (si kā'-) n. large flying insect making a shrill sound

ci'der n. juice from apples

ci·gar' n. roll of tobacco leaves for smoking

cig'a·rette', cig'a·ret' n. tobacco cut fine and rolled in paper for smoking

cig'a·ril'lo n., pl. **-los** small, thin cigar

cil'i·a pl.n. small hairlike growths

cinch n. **1** saddle girth **2** [Sl.] thing easy to do

cin·cho'na (sin kō'-) n. tree whose bark yields quinine

cinc'ture (sink'-) n. belt or girdle

cin'der n. **1** tiny charred piece of wood, etc. **2** pl. ashes

cin'e·ma n. used in the cinema, films collectively; the movies —**cin'e·mat'ic** a.

cin'e·ma·tog'ra·phy n. art of photography in making movies —**cin'e·ma·tog'ra·pher** n.

cin'na·mon n. brown spice from East Indian tree bark

ci·pher (sī'fər) n. **1** zero; 0 **2** code **3** key to a code

cir'ca prep. [also in italics] about; approximately

cir·ca'di·an a. of the body cycles associated with the earth's daily rotation

cir'cle n. **1** closed, curved line always equidistant from the center **2** cycle **3** group with interests in common **4** extent; scope —v. form or go in a circle around

cir'cuit (-kət) n. **1** boundary **2** regular, routine journey **3** theater chain **4** path for electric current

circuit breaker n. safety device that interrupts excess electric current

cir·cu'i·tous (-kyōō'-) a. roundabout; indirect

cir'cuit·ry n. electric circuit(s)

cir'cu·lar a. **1** round **2** roundabout — n. advertisement sent to many people

cir'cu·late' v. move or spread about — **cir'cu·la·to'ry** a.

cir'cu·la'tion n. **1** movement, as of blood through the body **2** distribution

cir'cum·cise' (-sīz') v. cut off the foreskin of —**cir'cum·ci'sion** (-sizh'ən) n.

cir·cum'fer·ence n. distance around a circle, etc.

cir'cum·flex' n. pronunciation mark (^)

cir'cum·lo·cu'tion n. roundabout way of talking

cir'cum·nav'i·gate' v. sail around (the earth, etc.)

cir'cum·scribe' v. **1** encircle **2** limit; confine

cir'cum·spect' a. cautious; discreet — **cir'cum·spec'tion** n.

cir'cum·stance' n. **1** connected fact or event **2** pl. financial condition **3** ceremony —**under no circumstances** never —**cir'cum·stan'tial** (-shəl) a.

cir'cum·vent' v. outwit or prevent by cleverness

cir'cus n. a show with acrobats, animals, clowns, etc.

cir·rho'sis (sə rō'-) n. disease, esp. of the liver

cir'rus (sir'əs) n. fleecy, white cloud formation

cis'tern n. large storage tank, esp. for rain water

cit'a·del n. fortress

cite v. **1** summon by law **2** quote **3** mention as example **4** mention in praise —**ci·ta'tion** n.

cit'i·zen n. member of a nation by birth or naturalization —**cit'i·zen·ry** n. —**cit'i·zen·ship'** n.

cit'ric a. of an acid in citrus fruits

cit'ron n. lemonlike fruit

cit'ron·el'la n. pungent oil that repels insects

cit'rus n. orange, lemon, etc. —a. of these trees or fruits

cit'y n., pl. **-ies** large town

civ'et n. fatty secretion of an animal (**civet cat**): used in perfume

civ'ic a. of a city or citizens

civ'ic-mind'ed *a.* showing concern for the welfare of one's community

civ'ics *n.* study of civic affairs and duties

civ'il *a.* **1** of citizens **2** polite **3** not military or religious —**civ'il·ly** *adv.*

civil disobedience *n.* nonviolent refusal to obey a law on grounds of one's conscience

civil engineering *n.* engineering that deals with the building of bridges, roads, etc.

ci·vil'ian *a., n.* (of a) person not in armed forces

ci·vil'i·ty *n.* **1** courtesy **2** *pl.* **-ties** polite act

civ'i·li·za'tion *n.* **1** high social and cultural development **2** culture of a certain time or place

civ'i·lize' *v.* bring out of savagery or barbarism

civil liberties *pl.n.* rights of free speech, assembly, etc.

civil rights *pl.n.* rights of all people to equal treatment

civil servant *n.* civil service employee

civil service *n.* government employees except soldiers, legislators, and judges

civil war *n.* war between factions of the same nation

civ'vies *pl.n.* [Inf.] civilian clothes: also sp. **civ'ies**

cl *abbrev.* centiliter

clack *v.* make an abrupt sharp sound —*n.* this sound

clad *v.* alt. pt. & pp. of CLOTHE

claim *v.* **1** demand as rightfully one's own **2** assert —*n.* **1** a claiming **2** right to something **3** thing claimed —**claim'ant** *n.*

clair·voy'ance *n.* supposed ability to perceive things not in sight —**clair·voy'ant** *a., n.*

clam *n.* hard-shelled, often edible, bivalve mollusk

clam'bake' *n.* picnic at which clams are served

clam'ber *v.* climb clumsily

clam'my *a.* **-mi·er, -mi·est** moist, cold, and sticky

clam'or *n.* **1** uproar **2** noisy demand —*v.* make a clamor —**clam'or·ous** *a.*

clamp *n.* device for clasping things together —*v.* fasten with a clamp

clan *n.* **1** group of related families **2** group with interests in common

clan·des'tine (-tin) *a.* secret

clang *v.* make a loud ringing sound —*n.* this sound

clang'or *n.* series of clangs

clank *v.* make a sharp metallic sound —*n.* this sound

clap *v.* **clapped, clap'ping 1** make the sound of flat surfaces struck together **2** to strike together, as the hands in applauding —*n.* sound or act of clapping —**clap'per** *n.*

clap·board (klab'ərd) *n.* tapered board, used as siding

clap'trap' *n.* insincere, empty talk, meant to get applause

claque (klak) *n.* group of fawning admirers

clar'et (klar'-) *n.* dry red wine

clar'i·fy' *v.* **-fied', -fy'ing** make or become clear —**clar·i·fi·ca'tion** *n.*

clar'i·net' *n.* single-reed woodwind —**clar·i·net'ist, clar·i·net'tist** *n.*

clar'i·on *a.* clear and shrill

clar'i·ty *n.* clearness

clash *v.* **1** collide noisily **2** disagree —*n.* a clashing

clasp *n.* **1** device to fasten things **2** an embrace **3** grip of the hand —*v.* **1** fasten **2** hold tightly

class *n.* **1** group of like people or things; sort **2** social rank **3** group of students in school **4** grade or quality **5** [Inf.] excellence —*v.* classify

class action (**suit**) *n.* lawsuit for a large group having the same cause for complaint

clas'sic *a.* **1** most excellent **2** in the style of ancient Greece or Rome —*n.* a book, work of art, etc. of highest excellence —**the classics** writings of ancient Greece and Rome

clas'si·cal *a.* **1** CLASSIC (*a.* 2) **2** of such music as symphonies, concertos, etc.

clas'si·cist *n.* specialist in ancient Greek and Roman literature

clas'si·fied' *a.* secret and only for authorized persons —*pl.n.* classified advertising

classified advertising *n.* advertising under such listings as *help wanted*

clas'si·fy' *v.* **-fied', -fy'ing 1** arrange in classes **2** designate as secret —**clas·si·fi·ca'tion** *n.*

class'mate' *n.* member of the same class at a school

class'room' *n.* room where a class is taught at a school

class'y *a.* **-i·er, -i·est** [Inf.] first-class; elegant

clat'ter *n.* series of sharp noises —*v.* make a clatter

clause *n.* **1** part of a sentence, with a subject and verb **2** provision in a document

claus'tro·pho'bi·a *n.* fear of being in

enclosed places

clav'i·chord' *n.* early kind of piano

clav'i·cle *n.* bone connecting the breastbone and shoulder

cla·vier (klə vir') *n.* **1** keyboard, as of a piano **2** any stringed keyboard instrument

claw *n.* **1** sharp nail of an animal's or bird's foot **2** pincers of a lobster, crab, etc. —*v.* scratch as with claws

clay *n.* firm, plastic earth, used for pottery, etc.

clean *a.* **1** free from dirt **2** sinless **3** free from flaws **4** complete —*adv.* completely —*v.* make clean —**clean'er** *n.* —**clean'ly** (klēn'-) *adv.*

clean'-cut' *a.* trim, neat, etc.

clean'ly (klen'-) *a.* **-li·er, -li·est 1** having clean habits **2** always kept clean —**clean'li·ness** *n.*

cleanse (klenz) *v.* make clean or pure —**cleans'er** *n.*

clear *a.* **1** free from clouds **2** transparent **3** distinct **4** obvious **5** free from charges, guilt, obstruction, debt, etc. —*adv.* **1** in a clear way **2** completely —*v.* **1** make or become clear **2** pass or leap over **3** make as profit **4** to empty or unload **5** rid (the throat) of phlegm —**clear away** (or **off**) remove —**in the clear** in the open —**clear'ly** *adv.* —**clear'ness** *n.*

clear'ance *n.* clear space between two objects

clear'ing *n.* plot of land cleared of trees

clear'ing·house' *n.* center for exchanging bank checks, collecting and disseminating information, etc.

cleat *n.* piece used to give firmness or secure footing

cleav'age *n.* a split, crack, division, etc.

cleave *v.* **cleaved** or **cleft, cleav'ing** split; sever

cleave *v.* adhere; cling

cleav'er *n.* butcher's tool

clef *n.* musical symbol to indicate pitch

cleft *a., n.* split

cleft lip *n.* congenital cleft of the upper lip often with a cleft of the palate (**cleft palate**)

clem'a·tis (*or* klə mat'is) *n.* vine with colorful flowers

clem'en·cy *n.* mercy

clem'ent *a.* **1** lenient **2** mild

clench *v.* close tightly

cler'gy *n., pl.* **-gies** ministers, priests, etc. collectively

cler'gy·man *n., pl.* **-men** minister, priest, etc. —**cler'gy·wom'an** *n.fem.,*

pl. **-wom'en**

cler'ic *n.* member of the clergy

cler'i·cal *a.* **1** of the clergy **2** of office clerks

clerk *n.* **1** office worker who keeps records, etc. **2** salesperson in a store —*v.* work as a clerk

clev'er *a.* **1** skillful **2** intelligent —**clev'er·ness** *n.*

clew *n.* **1** ball of thread, etc. **2** [Ar.] clue

cli·ché (klē shā') *n.* trite expression or idea —**cli·chéd'** *a.*

click *n.* slight, sharp sound —*v.* make a click

cli'ent *n.* **1** person or company for whom a lawyer, etc. acts **2** customer

cli'en·tele' (-tel') *n.* clients

cliff *n.* high, steep rock

cliff'hang'er, cliff'-hang'er *n.* highly suspenseful story, etc.

cli'mate *n.* average weather conditions —**cli·mat'ic** *a.*

cli'max' *n.* highest point, as of interest or excitement; culmination —*v.* bring to a climax —**cli·mac'tic** *a.*

climb *v.* **1** go up; ascend **2** move (*down, over,* etc.) —*n.* a climbing —**climb'er** *n.*

clinch *v.* **1** fasten (a nail) by bending the end **2** settle (an argument, etc.) **3** *Boxing* grip with the arms —*n.* a clinching in boxing

cling *v.* **clung, cling'ing 1** hold fast **2** stay near

clin'ic *n.* **1** outpatient department **2** intense session of group instruction —**cli·ni'cian** (-nish'ən) *n.*

clin'i·cal *a.* **1** of medical treatment, as in clinics **2** dispassionate

clink *n.* short, tinkling sound —*v.* make this sound

clink'er *n.* [Sl.] mistake or failure

clip *v.* **clipped, clip'ping 1** cut short **2** cut the hair of **3** [Inf.] hit sharply **4** fasten together —*n.* **1** a clipping **2** [Inf.] rapid pace **3** fastening device

clip'board' *n.* writing board with a hinged clip to hold papers

clip'per *n.* **1** clipping tool **2** fast sailing ship

clip'ping *n.* piece cut out, as an item from a newspaper

clique (klik, klēk) *n.* small, exclusive circle of people

clit'o·ris *n.* small, sensitive organ of the vulva

cloak *n.* **1** loose, sleeveless outer garment **2** thing that conceals —*v.* conceal; hide

clob'ber *v.* [Sl.] **1** to hit repeatedly **2**

defeat decisively

clock n. device for measuring and showing time

clock'wise adv., a. in the direction in which the hands of a clock rotate

clock'work n. mechanism of a clock —**like clockwork** very regularly

clod n. 1 lump of earth 2 dull, stupid person

clod'hop'per n. 1 clumsy, stupid fellow 2 coarse, heavy shoe

clog n. 1 thing that hinders 2 shoe with a thick sole —v. **clogged, clog'ging** 1 hinder 2 block up

clois'ter n. monastery or convent 2 covered walk along a wall —v. seclude

clomp v. walk heavily or noisily

clone n. exact genetic duplicate of an organism —v. produce as a clone

clop n. sound as of a hoofbeat —v. **clopped, clop'ping** make such sounds

close (klōs) a. 1 confined 2 secretive 3 stingy 4 humid; stuffy 5 near together 6 intimate 7 thorough 8 nearly alike; nearly equal —adv. in a close way or position —n. [Chiefly Br.] dead-end street —**close'ly** adv.

close (klōz) v. 1 shut or stop up 2 end 3 come close, as to attack —n. end —**close down** (or **up**) stop entirely —**close in** surround

close call (klōs) n. [Inf.] narrow escape from danger: also **close shave**

close'-cropped' a. clipped very short

closed circuit n. TV system only for receivers connected by cable to its circuit

close'fit'ting a. fitting tightly

close'-knit' a. closely united

close'out' n. final sale at a low price, as of goods no longer carried

clos'er (klōz'-) n. one adept at completing successfully

clos'et (kläz'-) n. small room for clothes, etc. —v. shut in a room for private talk

close'-up' n. photograph, etc. taken at very close range

clo'sure (-zhər) n. a closing, finish, etc.

clot n. coagulated mass, as of blood —v. **clot'ted, clot'ting** coagulate

cloth n. 1 fabric of cotton, wool, synthetics, etc. 2 tablecloth, dustcloth, etc.

clothe (klōth) v. **clothed** or **clad, cloth'ing** 1 to put clothes on 2 provide with clothes

clothes (klōthz, klōz) pl.n. clothing

cloth-ier (klōth'yər) n. dealer in clothes or cloth

cloth·ing (klō'thiŋ) n. wearing apparel; garments

clo'ture (-chər) n. end of debate by putting a bill to the vote

cloud n. 1 mass of vapor in the sky 2 mass of smoke, dust, etc. 3 thing that darkens, etc. —v. darken as with clouds, gloom, etc. —**cloud'y** a., -i-er, -i-est

cloud'burst' n. sudden heavy rain

clout n. [Inf.] 1 a hard hit 2 political power

clove n. 1 pungent spice 2 segment of a bulb

clo'ven a. split

clo'ver n. small forage plant with triple leaves

clo'ver-leaf' n. highway intersection with curving ramps to ease traffic

clown n. comic entertainer as in a circus —v. act like a clown

cloy v. surfeit by excess

cloy'ing a. too sweet, sentimental, etc.

club n. 1 stick used as a weapon, or in games 2 social group or its meeting place 3 playing card marked with a ♣ —v. **clubbed, club'bing** strike with a club

club'foot' n., pl. **-feet'** congenitally misshapen foot

club'house' n. room with lockers used by an athletic team

club soda n. soda water

cluck n. low, clicking sound made by a hen —v. make this sound

clue n. hint or fact that helps solve a mystery

clue'less a. [Inf.] 1 stupid 2 uninformed

clump n. 1 lump 2 cluster —v. tramp heavily

clum'sy (-zē) a. -si-er, -si-est lacking grace; awkward —**clum'si-ly** adv.

clung v. pt. & pp. of CLING

clunk'er n. [Sl.] old, noisy car, etc.

clus'ter n., v. group; bunch

cluster bomb n. bomb that explodes in the air and scatters smaller bombs

clutch v. 1 snatch (at) 2 hold tightly —n. 1 pl. control 2 grip 3 device for engaging and disengaging an engine

clut'ter n., v. disorder

cm abbrev. centimeter(s)

Cmdr abbrev. Commander

Co abbrev. 1 Company 2 County

CO abbrev. 1 Colorado 2 Commanding Officer

C/O, c/o abbrev. care of

co- pref. 1 together 2 joint 3 equally

coach n. 1 big, four-wheeled carriage 2 railroad passenger car 3 bus 4 trainer of athletes, singers, etc. —v. be a coach (for)

co·ad'ju·tor (-aj'ə tər, -ə jŏo'-) n. assistant, esp. to a bishop

co·ag'u·late' v. thicken; clot —**co·ag'u·la'tion** n.

coal n. 1 black mineral used as fuel 2 ember

co·a·lesce' (-les') v. unite into a single body —**co·a·les'cence** n.

co'a·li'tion n. union

coal oil n. kerosene

coal tar n. black, thick liquid made from coal, used in dyes, medicines, etc.

co'-an'chor n. one of usually two newscast anchors

coarse a. 1 made up of large particles 2 rough 3 vulgar —**coars'en** v.

coast n. seashore —v. 1 slide down an incline 2 continue moving on momentum —**coast'al** a.

coast'er n. small tray for a glass

coast guard n. group defending a nation's coasts, aiding ships, etc.

coast'line' n. contour of a coast

coat n. 1 sleeved outer garment 2 natural covering 3 layer, as of paint —v. cover with a layer

coat'ing n. surface layer

coat of arms n. heraldic symbols, as on a family escutcheon

coat'tail' n. either half of the lower back part of a coat

co'au'thor n. joint author

coax v. urge or get by soothing words, etc.

co·ax'i·al a. of a cable for sending telephone or TV impulses

cob n. corncob

co'balt' n. gray metallic chemical element

cob'ble v. mend (shoes)

cob'bler n. 1 shoemaker 2 fruit pie

cob'ble·stone' n. rounded stone once used for paving

co'bra n. poisonous snake of Asia and Africa

cob'web' n. spider web

co·caine' n. drug used as a narcotic or anesthetic

coc·cyx (käk'siks') n., pl. **coc·cy'ges'** (-sī'jēz') bone at base of spine

co-chair' (v.: kō'cher') n. person who chairs a meeting with one or more others —v. act as a co-chair of

coch·i·neal (käch'ə nēl') n. red dye from tropical insect

coch·le·a (käk'lē ə) n. spiral part of the inner ear

cock n. 1 rooster 2 any male bird 3

faucet —v. 1 tilt 2 set hammer of (a gun) to fire

cock·ade' n. badge on a hat

cock'a·too' n. crested Australian parrot

cocked hat n. three-cornered hat

cock'er n. [Sl.] an old man: a mocking term

cock'er·el n. young rooster

cock'er (spaniel) n. small spaniel with drooping ears

cock'eyed' a. 1 cross-eyed 2 [Sl.] awry 3 [Sl.] absurd

cock'le n. edible shellfish —**warm the cockles of someone's heart** to please or cheer

cock'pit' n. space for pilot in an airplane

cock'roach' n. flat-bodied, dark insect, a kitchen pest

cocks'comb' n. red, fleshy growth on a rooster's head

cock'sure' a. self-confident

cock'tail' n. 1 mixed alcoholic drink 2 appetizer

cock'y a. -i·er, -i·est [Inf.] conceited

co'co' n., pl. -cos' coconut palm or coconut

co'coa' (-kō', n. 1 powder made from roasted cacao seeds 2 drink made of this

cocoa butter n. fat from cacao seeds

co'co·nut', co'coa·nut' n. hard-shelled fruit of a palm tree, with edible white meat

co·coon' n. silky case of certain insect larvae

cod n. N Atlantic food fish: also **cod'fish'**

COD, cod abbrev. cash (or collect) on delivery

co'da n. Mus. end passage

cod'dle v. pamper

code n. 1 body of laws 2 set of principles 3 set of signals or symbols for messages —v. put or write in code

co'deine' (-dēn') n. sedative drug derived from opium

co'de·pend'ent, co'-de·pend'ent a. psychologically needing another who is addicted to alcohol, etc.

codg'er n. [Inf.] elderly man

cod'i·cil n. addition to a will

cod'i·fy' (or kō'də-) v. -fied', -fy'ing arrange (laws) in a code

co'ed', co'-ed' n. [Inf.] young woman at a coeducational college

co'ed·u·ca'tion n. education of both sexes in the same classes —**co'ed·u·ca'tion·al** a.

co·e'qual a., n. equal

co·erce' (-urs') v. force; compel —**co·er'cion** n. —**co·er'cive** a.

co·e'val a., n. contemporary

co·ex·ist' v. exist together —**co'ex·ist'ence** n.

cof'fee n. **1** drink made from roasted seeds of a tropical shrub **2** the seeds

coffee break n. brief respite from work for having coffee, etc.

cof'fee·cake' n. cake or roll to be eaten with coffee, etc.

cof'fee·pot' n. pot with a spout, for brewing or serving coffee

coffee table n. small, low table for serving refreshments

cof'fer n. **1** chest for money, etc. **2** pl. treasury

cof'fin n. case in which to bury a dead person

cog n. tooth on a cogwheel

co'gent a. convincing —**co'gen·cy** n.

cog'i·tate' (käj'-) v. think (about) —**cog'i·ta'tion** n.

co·gnac (kōn'yak') n. brandy

cog'nate' a. related; kindred

cog·ni'tion n. knowledge

cog'ni·zance n. awareness; notice —**cog'ni·zant** a.

cog·no'men n. surname

cog'wheel' n. wheel rimmed with teeth, as in a gear

co·hab'it v. live together, esp. as if legally married

co·here' (-hir') v. **1** to stick together **2** be connected logically

co·her'ent (-hir'-, -her'-) a. clear and intelligible —**co·her'ence** n.

co·he'sion (-hē'zhən) n. a sticking together —**co·he'sive** a.

co'ho' n., pl. **-ho'** or **-hos'** small salmon

co'hort' n. **1** group, esp. of soldiers **2** an associate

coif (koif, 2: kwäf) n. hair style —v. to style (hair)

coif·fure' (kwä fyoor') n. **1** headdress **2** hairstyle —v. to coif

coil v. to wind in a spiral —n. anything coiled

coin n. stamped metal piece, issued as money —v. **1** make into coins **2** make up (new word) —**coin'age** n.

co·in·cide' v. **1** occur at the same time **2** agree; match

co·in·ci·dence n. **1** a coinciding **2** accidental occurrence of events —**co·in·ci·den'tal** a. —**co·in·ci·den'tal·ly** adv.

co·i·tus (kō'it əs) n. sexual intercourse: also **co·i'tion** (-ish'ən)

coke n. **1** fuel made by removing

gases from coal **2** [Sl.] cocaine

Col abbrev. Colonel

co'la n. carbonated soft drink with flavoring from the nut of an African tree

col'an·der (kul'-, käl'-) n. perforated bowl used as a strainer

cold a. **1** low in temperature **2** feeling chilled **3** without feeling **4** unfriendly **5** [Inf.] unconscious —adv. [Inf.] **1** completely **2** without preparation —n. **1** absence of heat **2** common virus infection with sneezing, coughing, etc. —**catch cold** become ill with a cold

cold'blood'ed a. **1** having a body temperature that varies with the surroundings **2** cruel; callous

cold cream n. creamy cleanser for the skin

cold cuts n. variety of sliced cold meats and cheeses

cold shoulder n. [Inf.] snub

cold sore n. blisters about the mouth during a cold or fever

cold turkey adv. [Sl.] **1** by abrupt withdrawal **2** without preparation

cold war n. conflict between nations without actual war

cole'slaw' n. salad made of shredded raw cabbage

col'ic n. sharp abdominal pain from the bowels —**col'ick·y** a.

col'i·se'um n. large stadium

co·li'tis n. inflammation of the large intestine

col·lab'o·rate' v. **1** to work together **2** help the enemy —**col·lab'o·ra'tion** n. —**col·lab'o·ra'tor** n.

col·lage' (-läzh') n. bits of objects pasted onto a surface to make a work of art

col·lapse' v. **1** fall in or shrink **2** break down; fail **3** fold together —n. a collapsing —**col·laps'i·ble** a.

col'lar n. a band, or the part of a garment, around the neck —v. **1** put a collar on **2** seize by the collar

col'lar·bone' n. clavicle

col'lard n. kind of kale

col·late' (kō'-) v. compare, or sort (texts)

col·lat'er·al a. of the same descent but in a different line **2** secondary —n. thing pledged as security for a loan

col'league' n. fellow worker; associate

col·lect' v. **1** gather together **2** get payment for **3** regain control of (oneself) —a., adv. with the receiver paying —**col·lect'i·ble, col·lect'a·ble** a. —**col·lec'tion** n. —**col·lec'tor** n.

col·lect'ed a. **1** gathered together **2**

calm

col·lec'tive *a.* **1** of or as a group **2** singular in form, but referring to a group —*n.* **1** a collective enterprise **2** collective noun

col'lege *n.* **1** school of higher learning or special instruction **2** group with certain powers —**col·le'gian** *n.* —**col·le'giate** *a.*

col·lide' *v.* **1** come into violent contact **2** to conflict; clash

col'lie *n.* large, long-haired sheep dog

col·li'sion (-lizh'ən) *n.* **1** a colliding **2** conflict

col·lo'di·on *n.* solution that dries into tough, elastic film

col'loid' *n.* substance of insoluble particles suspended in a solid, liquid, or gas —**col·loi'dal** *a.*

col·lo'qui·al (-kwē-) *a.* used in informal talk and writing —**col·lo'qui·al·ism'** *n.*

col·lo'qui·um (-kwē-) *n., pl.* **-qui·a** or **-qui·ums** organized conference or seminar

col·lo·quy (käl'ə kwē) *n., pl.* **-quies** formal discussion; conference

col·lu'sion *n.* secret agreement for an illegal purpose

co·logne' (-lōn') *n.* scented liquid like diluted perfume

co'lon *n.* **1** mark of punctuation (:) **2** lower part of the large intestine

colo·nel (kur'nəl) *n.* officer above lieutenant colonel

co·lo'ni·al·ism' *n.* economic exploitation of colonies

col'on·nade' *n.* row of evenly spaced columns

col'o·ny *n., pl.* **-nies 1** group of settlers from a distant land **2** land ruled by a distant country **3** community with common interests —**co·lo'ni·al** *a.* —**col'o·nist** *n.* —**col'o·nize'** *v.*

col'or *n.* **1** effect on the eyes of light waves of different wavelengths **2** pigment **3** complexion **4** *pl.* a flag **5** outward appearance **6** picturesque quality —*v.* **1** paint or dye **2** alter or distort **3** blush —**of color** not Caucasoid; spec., black —**col'or·a'tion** *n.* —**col'or·ful** *a.* —**col'or·ing** *n.* —**col'or·less** *a.*

col'or·a·tu'ra (-toor'ə) *n.* soprano with high, flexible voice: in full **coloratura soprano**

col'or·blind' *a.* unable to distinguish (certain) colors

col'ored *a.* **1** not Caucasoid **2** of a person having African ancestry: an old-fashioned term

col'or·fast' *a.* with color that will not fade or run

co·los'sal *a.* huge; immense

co·los'sus *n.* huge or important person or thing

col'our *n., v.* Br. sp. of COLOR

colt *n.* young male horse

colt'ish *a.* frisky

col'um·bine' (-bīn') *n.* plant with showy, spurred flowers

col'umn (-əm) *n.* **1** slender upright structure **2** vertical section of printed matter **3** line of troops, etc. —**col'um·nist'** *n.*

com- *pref.* with; together

co'ma *n.* deep unconsciousness, as from injury —**co'ma·tose'** (-tōs') *a.*

comb (kōm) *n.* **1** flat, toothed object for grooming the hair **2** cockscomb **3** honeycomb —*v.* **1** groom with a comb **2** search

com'bat' (*v.: also* kəm bat') *v., n.* fight; struggle —**com·bat'ant** *n.*

com·bat'ive *a.* ready or eager to fight

com'bi·na'tion *n.* **1** a combining **2** combined things, groups, etc. **3** series of numbers dialed to open a lock

com·bine' (*n.:* käm'bīn') *v.* join; unite —*n.* **1** machine for harvesting and threshing grain **2** commercial or political alliance

com'bo' *n., pl.* **-bos'** **1** [Inf.] combination **2** a small jazz ensemble

com·bus'ti·ble *n., a.* flammable (thing)

com·bus'tion *n.* a burning

come *v.* **came, come, com'ing** **1** move from "there" to "here" **2** arrive or appear **3** happen **4** result **5** become **6** amount (*to*) **7** extend —**come about** to happen —**come around to 1** to recover **2** to yield —**come by** get —**come to** regain consciousness —**come up** arise in discussion

come'back' *n.* **1** a return, as to power **2** witty answer

co·me'di·an *n.* actor who plays comic parts —**co·me'di·enne'** (-en') *n.fem.*

come'down' *n.* loss of status

com'e·dy *n., pl.* **-dies** a humorous play, TV show, etc.

come'ly (kum'-) *a.* **-li·er, -li·est** attractive —**come'li·ness** *n.*

come'-on' *n.* [Sl.] inducement

co·mes'ti·bles *pl.n.* food

com'et *n.* mass of dust and gas in space, with a luminous tail

come'up'pance *n.* [Inf.] deserved punishment

com'fort *v.* soothe in distress; console —*n.* **1** relief from distress **2** one that comforts **3** ease —**com'fort·a·ble** *a.*

com'fort·er *n.* 1 one that comforts 2 a quilt

com'fy *a.* **-fi·er, -fi·est** [Inf.] comfortable

com'ic *a.* 1 of comedy 2 funny: also **com'i·cal** —*n.* 1 comedian 2 *pl.* comic strips

comic book *n.* booklet of comic strips

comic strip *n.* cartoon series, as in a newspaper

com'ing *a.* 1 approaching; next 2 promising success —*n.* arrival; approach

com'i·ty (käm'-) *n., pl.* **-ties** courtesy

com'ma *n.* punctuation mark (,)

com·mand' *v.* 1 to order 2 to control 3 deserve and get —*n.* 1 an order 2 control 3 military force, etc. under someone's control

com'man·dant' (-dant', -dänt') *n.* commanding officer

com'man·deer' *v.* seize for military or government use

com·mand'er *n.* 1 leader; officer 2 naval officer below a captain

commander in chief *n.* top commander of a nation's armed forces

com·mand'ing *a.* 1 having authority 2 impressive 3 very large

com·mand'ment *n.* command; law

com·man'do *n., pl.* **-dos** or **-does** member of a small force for raiding enemy territory

command post *n.* field headquarters of a military unit

com·mem'o·rate' *v.* honor the memory of —**com·mem'o·ra'tion** *n.*

com·mem'o·ra'tive *a.* commemorating —*n.* stamp or coin marking an event, etc.

com·mence' *v.* begin

com·mence'ment *n.* 1 beginning 2 graduation ceremony of a school, etc.

com·mend' *v.* 1 entrust 2 recommend 3 to praise —**com·mend'a·ble** *a.* —**com·men·da'tion** *n.*

com·mend'a·to·ry *a.* praising or recommending

com·men'su·ra·ble (-sha-) *a.* measurable by the same standard or measure

com·men'su·rate (-sə rət) *a.* equal or proportionate

com'ment' *n.* 1 explanatory note 2 remark 3 talk —*v.* make comments

com'men·tar'y *n., pl.* **-ies** series of explanatory notes or remarks

com'men·ta'tor *n.* radio or TV news analyst

com'merce *n.* trade on a large scale

com·mer'cial (-shəl) *a.* 1 connected with commerce 2 done for profit —*n.* *Radio & TV* paid advertisement

com·mer'cial·ize' *v.* put on a profit-making basis —**com·mer'cial·i·za'tion** *n.*

com·min'gle *v.* mix; blend

com·mis'er·ate' *v.* sympathize (*with*)

com'mis·sar' *n.* government official in the Soviet Union

com'mis·sar'y *n., pl.* **-ies** a store in an army camp for the sale of food, etc.

com·mis'sion *n.* 1 authority to act 2 group chosen to do something 3 percentage of a sale allotted to the agent 4 military officer's certificate of rank —*v.* 1 give a commission to 2 authorize —**in** (or **out of**) **commission** (not) usable

com·mis'sion·er *n.* governmental department head

com·mit' *v.* **-mit'ted, -mit'ting** 1 put in custody 2 do 3 pledge; bind —**com·mit'ment** *n.*

com·mit'tee *n.* group chosen to do something

com·mode' *n.* 1 chest of drawers 2 toilet

com·mod'i·fy *v.* **-fied', -fy'ing** treat like a mere commodity

com·mo'di·ous *a.* spacious

com·mod'i·ty *n., pl.* **-ties** anything bought and sold

com'mo·dore' *n.* former naval rank

com'mon *a.* 1 shared by all 2 general 3 usual; ordinary 4 vulgar 5 designating a noun that refers to any of a group —*n.* also *pl.* town's public land —**in common** shared by all

com'mon·al·ty *n.* common people; public

common carrier *n.* transportation company

common denominator *n.* a characteristic held in common

com'mon·er *n.* person not of the nobility

common law *n.* law based on custom, usage, etc.

common market *n.* association of countries in an economic union

com'mon·place' *n.* 1 trite or obvious remark 2 anything ordinary —*a.* ordinary

common pleas *n.* civil and criminal court in some U.S. states

common sense *n.* good sense or practical judgment

com'mon·weal' *n.* the public good

com'mon·wealth' *n.* 1 people of a state 2 democracy or republic

com·mo'tion *n.* turmoil

com·mu'nal a. of a community; public

com'mune' n. small group living together and sharing work, etc.

com·mune' v. be in close rapport

com·mu'ni·cate' v. 1 transmit 2 give or exchange (information) —**com·mu'ni·ca·ble** a. —**com·mu'ni·ca'tive** a. —**com·mu'ni·ca'tor** n.

com·mu'ni·ca'tion n. 1 a communicating or means of doing this 2 message, etc.

com·mun'ion n. 1 a sharing or being close 2 group of the same religious faith 3 [C-] Holy Communion

com·mu'ni·qué' (-kā') n. official communication

com'mu·nism' n. theory or system of ownership of all property by the community —**com'mu·nist** n., a.

com·mu'ni·ty n. 1 pl. **-ties** body of people living in the same place 2 a sharing in common

community college n. junior college for a certain community

community service n. unpaid work for the community

com·mute' v. 1 lessen (a punishment, etc.) 2 travel by train, etc. to and from work —**com·mut'er** n.

com·pact' (or käm'pakt'; n.: käm' pakt) a. 1 firmly packed 2 terse —n. 1 small case for face powder, etc. 2 an agreement

compact disc (or **disk**) n. digital disc for recording music, data, etc.

com·pac'tor n. device that compresses trash

com·pan'ion n. 1 comrade; associate 2 thing that matches or goes with another —**com·pan'ion·a·ble** a. —**com·pan'ion·ship'** n.

com·pan'ion·way' n. stairway from one deck of a ship to another

com'pa·ny n., pl. **-nies** 1 group of people associated for some purpose 2 [Inf.] guest(s) 3 military unit

com·par'a·tive a. by comparison —n. the second degree of comparison of adjectives and adverbs

com·pare' v. 1 liken (to) 2 examine for similarities or differences 3 form the positive, comparative, and superlative degrees of (adjective or adverb) —**beyond compare** without equal —**com'pa·ra·ble** a. —**com·par'i·son** n.

com·part'ment n. section partitioned off

com·pass (kum'pəs) n. 1 instrument for drawing circles, etc. 2 range; extent 3 instrument for showing direction

com·pas'sion n. pity —**com·pas'sion·ate** (-ət) a.

com·pat'i·ble a. capable of getting along well together

com·pa'tri·ot n. person of one's own country

com'peer' n. peer or comrade

com·pel' v. **-pelled', -pel'ling** to force

com·pen'di·um n., pl. **-ums** or **-a** comprehensive summary

com'pen·sate' v. 1 make up for 2 pay —**com·pen·sa'tion** n.

com·pete' v. take part in a contest

com'pe·tent a. 1 capable; able 2 adequate —**com'pe·tence, com'pe·ten·cy** n.

com'pe·ti'tion (-tish'ən) n. 1 a competing; rivalry 2 contest 3 those against whom one competes —**com·pet'i·tive** a. —**com·pet'i·tor** n.

com·pile' v. compose by collecting from various sources —**com'pi·la'tion** n.

com·pla'cen·cy, com·pla'cence n. smugness —**com·pla'cent** a.

com·plain' v. 1 express pain, dissatisfaction, etc. 2 make an accusation —**com·plain'er** n.

com·plain'ant n. plaintiff

com·plai'sant (-zənt, -sənt) a. obliging

com·plect'ed a. complexioned

com'ple·ment (-mənt; v.: -ment') n. 1 that which completes 2 complete set —v. make complete —**com'ple·men' ta·ry** a.

com·plete' a. 1 lacking no parts 2 finished 3 thorough; perfect —v. make complete —**com·plete'ly** adv. —**com·ple'tion** n.

com·plex' (or käm'pleks'; n.: käm' pleks') a. 1 having two or more parts 2 complicated —n. 1 complex whole 2 group of feelings and ideas about a thing that influences a person's behavior —**com·plex'i·ty** n., pl. **-ties**

com·plex'ion (-plek'shən) n. 1 color or texture of the skin 2 nature; aspect

com·plex'ioned a. having a (specified) complexion

com·pli'ance n. 1 a complying 2 tendency to give in —**com·pli'ant** a.

com'pli·cate' v. make difficult or involved —**com'pli·cat'ed** a. —**com' pli·ca'tion** n.

com·plic'i·ty (-plis'-) n. partnership in wrongdoing

com'pli·ment (-mənt; v.: -ment') n. 1 something said in praise 2 pl. regards —v. pay a compliment to

com'pli·men'ta·ry a. 1 giving praise 2 given free

com·ply' v. **-plied', -ply'ing** conform (*with* a request, rule, etc.)

com·po'nent a., n. (being) part of a whole

com·port' v. **1** conduct (oneself) **2** agree (*with*) —**com·port'ment** n.

com·pose' v. **1** make by combining **2** put in proper form **3** write (a song, poem, etc.) **4** make calm —**com·posed'** a. —**com·pos'er** n. —**com'po·si'tion** (-zish'ən) n.

com·pos'ite (-it) n., a. (thing) formed of distinct parts

com·pos'i·tor n. one who sets type

com'post' n. rotting vegetation, etc. used as fertilizer

com·po'sure n. calmness; self-possession

com'pote' (-pōt') n. **1** stewed fruit **2** dish with a long stem

com'pound' (v.: also kəm pound') v. combine —n. **1** substance with combined elements **2** enclosed place —a. with two or more parts

compound interest n. interest paid on both the principal and the accumulated unpaid interest

com'pre·hend' v. **1** understand **2** include —**com'pre·hen'si·ble** a. —**com'pre·hen'sion** n. —**com'pre·hen'sive** a.

com·press' (n.: käm'pres') v. press tight —n. moistened pad —**com·pres'sion** n. —**com·pres'sor** n.

com·prise' v. consist of; include

com'pro·mise' n. settlement made with concessions —v. **1** settle by compromise **2** make suspect

comp time n. paid time off from work in place of overtime pay

comp·trol'ler (kən-) n. controller

com·pul'sion n. a forcing or being forced —**com·pul'sive** a. —**com·pul'so·ry** a.

com·punc'tion n. slight regret for wrongdoing

com·pute' v. **1** calculate; figure **2** [Inf.] make sense —**com'pu·ta'tion** n.

com·put'er n. electronic machine that rapidly calculates or correlates data —**com·put'er·i·za'tion** n. —**com·put'er·ize'** v.

com'rade' (-rad') n. **1** close friend **2** an associate —**com'rade·ship'** n.

con adv. against —v. conned, con'ning **1** study carefully **2** [Sl.] swindle

con·cat·e·na'tion n. connected series, as of events

con·cave' (or kän'kāv') a. curved like the inside of a sphere —**con·cav'i·ty** n.

con·ceal' v. hide —**con·ceal'ment** n.

con·cede' v. **1** admit as true **2** grant as a right

con·ceit' n. **1** vanity; pride **2** fanciful notion —**con·ceit'ed** a.

con·ceive' v. **1** become pregnant **2** think of **3** understand —**con·ceiv'a·ble** a.

con·cen'trate' v. **1** fix one's attention, etc. (*on*) **2** increase, as in density —n. concentrated substance —**con'cen·tra'tion** n.

concentration camp n. prison camp for political foes, ethnic minorities, etc.

con·cen'tric a. having a common center: said of circles

con'cept' n. idea; notion

con·cep'tion n. **1** a conceiving **2** concept

con·cep'tu·al a. of concepts

con·cep'tu·al·ize' v. form a concept of

con·cern' v. be related to; involve —n. **1** business **2** interest **3** worry

con·cerned' a. **1** involved or interested **2** anxious; uneasy

con·cern'ing prep. relating to

con'cert n. **1** agreement **2** musical performance

con·cert'ed a. combined

con·cer·ti'na (-tē'-) n. small accordion

con·cert·ize' v. perform as a soloist in concerts on a tour

con·cer'to (-cher'-) n., pl. **-tos** or **-ti** (-tē) composition for solo instrument(s) and orchestra

con·ces'sion n. **1** a conceding **2** thing conceded **3** franchise, as for selling food

con·ces'sion·aire' n. holder of a CONCESSION (n. 3)

conch (käŋk, känch) n. large, spiral seashell

con'ci·erge' (-sē erzh') n. custodian or aide, as in an apartment house

con·cil'i·ate' v. make friendly —**con·cil'i·a'tion** n. —**con·cil'i·a'tor** n. —**con·cil'i·a·to'ry** a.

con·cise' (-sīs') a. short and clear; terse —**con·cise'ly** adv.

con'clave' n. private meeting

con·clude' v. **1** finish **2** decide **3** arrange —**con·clu'sion** n.

con·clu'sive a. decisive

con·coct' v. prepare or plan —**con·coc'tion** n.

con·com'i·tant a. accompanying —n. concomitant thing

con'cord' n. **1** agreement **2** peaceful relations

con·cord'ance n. **1** agreement **2** com-

con·cord'ant *a.*

con·cor'dat' *n.* formal agreement

con'course' *n.* open space for crowds

con'crete' (*or* kän krēt') *a.* **1** real; actual **2** specific —*n.* hard material made of cement, sand, and gravel — **con·crete'ly** *adv.* —**con·cre'tion** *n.*

con'cu·bine' (-kyōō-) *n.* wife of lesser status

con·cu'pis·cence (-kyōōp'ə-) *n.* lust — **con·cu'pis·cent** *a.*

con·cur' *v.* -**curred'**, -**cur'ring 1** occur together **2** agree —**con·cur'rence** *n.* —**con·cur'rent** *a.*

con·cus'sion *n.* **1** shock, as from impact **2** brain injury from a blow

con·demn' (-dem') *v.* **1** disapprove of **2** declare guilty **3** to doom **4** take for public use **5** declare unfit —**con'dem·na'tion** *n.*

con·dense' *v.* **1** make or become denser **2** express concisely —**con'den·sa'tion** *n.* —**con·dens'er** *n.*

con·densed' milk *n.* thickened milk with sugar added

con'de·scend' (-send') *v.* stoop; deign —**con'de·scen'sion** *n.*

con·dign' (-dīn') *a.* deserved; suitable

con'di·ment *n.* a seasoning

con·di'tion *n.* **1** prerequisite **2** state of being **3** healthy state **4** rank —*v.* **1** to make healthy **2** make accustomed (*to*) —**on condition that** provided that —**con·di'tion·er** *n.*

con·di'tion·al *a.* dependent on conditions —**con·di'tion·al·ly** *adv.*

con·di'tioned *a.* **1** in a desired condition **2** affected by conditioning **3** accustomed (*to*)

con·dole' *v.* show sympathy —**con·do'lence** *n.*

con'dom *n.* covering for the penis, worn during sexual intercourse

con'do·min'i·um *n.* separately owned unit in a multiple-unit dwelling: also **con'do'**

con·done' (-dōn') *v.* forgive or overlook

con'dor (-dər, -dôr') *n.* large vulture

con·duce' *v.* tend; lead (*to*) —**con·du'cive** *a.*

con'duct (*v.:* kən dukt') *n.* **1** management **2** behavior —*v.* **1** to lead **2** manage **3** to direct **4** behave (oneself) **5** transmit (electricity, etc.) — **con·duc'tion** *n.* —**con·duc'tive** *a.* —**con'duc·tiv'i·ty** *n.*

con·duct'ance *n.* ability to conduct electricity

con·duc'tor *n.* **1** orchestra leader **2** one in charge of passengers, etc. **3** thing that conducts heat, etc.

con'duit (-dōō it) *n.* pipe, tube, etc. for fluids or wires

cone *n.* **1** pointed, tapered figure with circular base **2** woody fruit of evergreens

co'ney *n., pl.* -**neys** rabbit or its fur

con·fec'tion *n.* candy, ice cream, etc. —**con·fec'tion·er** *n.*

con·fec'tion·er'y *n., pl.* -**ies** confectioner's shop

con·fed'er·a·cy *n., pl.* -**cies 1** league **2** [C-] South in the Civil War

con·fed'er·ate (-ət; *v.:* -āt') *a.* united; allied —*n.* **1** an ally **2** accomplice — *v.* unite; ally —**con·fed'er·a'tion** *n.*

con·fer' *v.* -**ferred'**, -**fer'ring 1** give **2** meet to discuss —**con'fer·ence** *n.*

con·fer'ral *n.* a giving of a degree, honor, etc.

con·fess' *v.* **1** admit (a crime) **2** affirm (a faith) **3** tell (one's sins) —**con·fes'sion** *n.*

con·fes'sion·al *n.* enclosed place where a priest hears confessions

con·fes'sor *n.* priest who hears confessions

con·fet'ti *n.* bits of colored paper thrown as at celebrations

con'fi·dant' (-dant', -dänt') *n.* trusted friend —**con'fi·dante'** *n.fem.*

con·fide' *v.* **1** tell about as a secret **2** entrust to someone

con'fi·dence *n.* **1** trust **2** assurance **3** self-reliance **4** belief that a secret will be kept **5** something told as a secret —**con'fi·dent** *a.*

confidence game *n.* swindle done by one (**confidence man**) who gains the victim's trust

con'fi·den'tial (-shəl) *a.* **1** secret **2** entrusted with private matters

con·fig'u·ra'tion *n.* contour

con·fine' (*v.:* kən fīn') *n. usually pl.* limit —*v.* **1** restrict **2** to keep shut up, as in prison —**con·fine'ment** *n.*

con·firm' *v.* **1** approve formally **2** prove to be true **3** admit to membership in a church —**con'fir·ma'tion** *n.*

con·firmed' *a.* firmly established; habitual

con'fis·cate' *v.* seize legally —**con'fis·ca'tion** *n.*

con·fis'ca·to'ry *a.* of or effecting confiscation

con'fla·gra'tion *n.* big, destructive fire

con·flict' (*n.:* kän'flikt') *v.* be in opposition —*n.* **1** a fight **2** sharp disagreement

conflict of interest *n.* conflict between public obligation and self-interest

con·flic'tu·al *a.* having to do with conflict

con'flu·ence *n.* place where streams flow together

con·form' *v.* **1** be in accord **2** act according to rules, customs, etc. —**con·form'ist** *n.* —**con·form'i·ty** *n.*

con'for·ma'tion *n.* **1** symmetrical arrangement **2** shape

con·found' *v.* confuse

con·found'ed *a.* **1** confused **2** damned

con·front' *v.* **1** face boldly **2** bring face to face —**con'fron·ta'tion** *n.* —**con'fron·ta'tion·al** *a.*

con·fuse' *v.* **1** mix up **2** bewilder —**con·fu'sion** *n.*

con·fute' *v.* prove wrong

Cong *abbrev.* Congress

con·geal' (-jēl') *v.* **1** freeze **2** thicken; jell

con·ge'nial (-jēn'yəl) *a.* friendly; agreeable —**con·ge'ni·al'i·ty** *n.*

con·gen'i·tal *a.* existing from birth —**con·gen'i·tal·ly** *adv.*

con'ger (eel) (-gər) *n.* large, edible saltwater eel

con'ge·ries (-jə rēz') *n., pl.* **-ries** heap or pile

con·gest' *v.* fill too full, as with blood —**con·ges'tion** *n.* —**con·ges'tive** *a.*

con·glom'er·ate (-ət) *n.* large corporation formed by merging many companies

con·glom'er·a'tion *n.* collection; mass

con·grat'u·late' (-grach'ə-) *v.* rejoice with (a fortunate person) —**con·grat'u·la·to'ry** *a.*

con·grat'u·la'tions *pl.n.* expressions of pleasure over another's good luck, etc.

con'gre·gate' *v.* gather into a crowd

con'gre·ga'tion *n.* assembly of people, esp. for worship

con'gress *n.* **1** assembly **2** legislature, esp. [C-] of the U.S. —**con·gres'sion·al** *a.* —**con'gress·man** *n., pl.* **-men** —**con'gress·per'son** *n.* —**con'gress·wom'an** *n.fem., pl.* **-wom·en**

con'gru·ent *a.* agreeing; corresponding

con'gru·ous *a.* suitable —**con·gru'i·ty** *n.*

con'i·cal (kän'-) *a.* of or like a cone: also **con'ic**

con'i·fer (kän'ə-, kō'nə-) *n.* cone-bearing tree

con·jec'ture *n., v.* guess —**con·jec'tur·al** *a.*

con·join' *v.* join together

con'ju·gal *a.* of marriage

con'ju·gate' *v.* give the inflected forms of (a verb) —**con'ju·ga'tion** *n.*

con·junc'tion *n.* **1** a joining together; union **2** an occurring together **3** word used to join words, clauses, etc. —**con·junc'tive** *a.*

con·junc·ti'va (-tī'-) *n., pl.* **-vas** or **-vae** (-vē) mucous membrane covering inner eyelids and the front of the eyeball

con·junc·ti·vi'tis (-vī'-) *n.* inflammation of the conjunctiva

con·junc'ture *n.* combination of events

con'jure *v.* **1** practice magic **2** entreat **3** cause to appear, etc., as by magic —**con'jur·er, con'ju·ror** *n.*

conk [Sl.] *n., v.* hit on the head —**conk out 1** fail suddenly **2** fall asleep from fatigue

con man *n.* [Sl.] confidence man

con·nect' *v.* **1** join; link **2** show or think of as related —**con·nec'tive** *a.*

con·nec'tion *n.* **1** a connecting or being connected **2** thing that connects **3** relation

con·nip'tion (fit) *n.* [Inf.] fit of anger, hysteria, etc.: also **con·nip'tions** *pl.n.*

con·nive' *v.* **1** pretend not to look (*at* crime, etc.) **2** cooperate secretly in wrongdoing —**con·niv'ance** *n.*

con·nois·seur' (kän'ə sur') *n.* expert, esp. in the fine arts

con·note' *v.* suggest in addition to the explicit meaning —**con'no·ta'tion** *n.*

con·nu'bi·al *a.* of marriage

con'quer (-kər) *v.* defeat; overcome —**con'quer·or** *n.*

con'quest' *n.* a conquering

con·quis·ta·dor' (kwis'-, -kēs'-) *n., pl.* **-dors'** or **-do'res'** (-dôr'ēz') 16th-c. Spanish conqueror of Mexico, Peru, etc.

con'science (-shəns) *n.* sense of right and wrong

con·sci·en'tious (-shē-) *a.* scrupulous; honest

conscientious objector *n.* person refusing to go to war for reasons of conscience

con'scious (-shəs) *a.* **1** aware (*of* or *that*) **2** able to feel and think; awake **3** intentional —**con'scious·ness** *n.*

con·script' (*n.:* kän'skript') *v.* to draft (into the armed services) —*n.* draftee —**con·scrip'tion** *n.*

con'se·crate' *v.* set apart as holy **2** devote —**con'se·cra'tion** *n.*

con·sec'u·tive *a.* following in order without a break —**con·sec'u·tive·ly** *adv.*

con·sen'sus *n.* general opinion

con·sent' *v.* agree —*n.* agreement or

approval

con·se·quence′ *n.* **1** a result **2** importance

con′se·quent *a.* resulting

con′se·quen′tial (-shəl) *a.* **1** consequent **2** important

con′se·quent·ly *adv.* as a result; therefore

con·ser′va·tive *a.* **1** opposed to change **2** cautious —*n.* conservative person

con·serv′a·to′ry *n., pl.* **-ries** school of music, art, etc.

con·serve′ *v.* keep from being damaged, lost, etc. —**con′ser·va′tion** *n.*

con·sid′er *v.* **1** think over **2** keep in mind **3** have regard for **4** believe to be —**con·sid′er·ate** (-ət) *a.* —**con·sid′er·a′tion** *n.*

con·sid′er·a·ble *a.* large or important —**con·sid′er·a·bly** *adv.*

con·sid′ered *a.* arrived at after careful thought

con·sid′er·ing *prep.* taking into account

con·sign′ *v.* **1** entrust **2** assign **3** deliver (goods) —**con·sign′ment** *n.*

con·sist′ *v.* be made up (*of*)

con·sis′ten·cy *n., pl.* **-cies** **1** thickness, as of a liquid **2** agreement **3** uniformity of action —**con·sis′tent** *a.*

con·sole′ *v.* comfort; cheer up —**con′so·la′tion** *n.*

con′sole′ *n.* floor cabinet of an organ, radio, TV, etc.

con·sol′i·date′ *v.* unite —**con·sol′i·da′tion** *n.*

con′som·mé′ (-sə mā′) *n.* clear meat soup

con′so·nant *n.* letter, as *p, t,* or *l,* representing a breath-blocked speech sound —*a.* in harmony —**con′so·nance** *n.*

con′sort′ (*v.:* kən sôrt′) *n.* spouse, esp. of a monarch —*v.* to associate (*with*)

con·sor′ti·um (*or* -sôr′shəm) *n., pl.* **-ti·a** international alliance, as of banks

con·spec′tus *n.* **1** general view **2** summary

con·spic′u·ous *a.* **1** easy to see **2** outstanding —**con·spic′u·ous·ly** *adv.*

con·spire′ *v.* join in a plot —**con·spir′a·cy** (-spir′-) *n., pl.* **-cies** —**con·spir′a·tor** *n.*

con′sta·ble *n.* police officer

con·stab′u·lar′y *n., pl.* **-ies** police force

con′stant *a.* **1** not changing **2** faithful **3** continual —*n.* unchanging thing —**con′stan·cy** *n.* —**con′stant·ly** *adv.*

con′stel·la′tion *n.* group of fixed stars

con′ster·na′tion *n.* great alarm or dismay

con′sti·pate′ *v.* make it difficult to move the bowels —**con′sti·pa′tion** *n.*

con·stit′u·en·cy (-stich′oo-) *n., pl.* **-cies** voters in a district

con·stit′u·ent *n.* **1** necessary part **2** voter —*a.* needed to form a whole

con′sti·tute′ *v.* form; set up

con′sti·tu′tion *n.* **1** structure; makeup **2** basic laws of a government, etc., esp. [C-] of the U.S. —**con′sti·tu′tion·al** *a.*

con·strain′ *v.* force or restrain —**con·straint′** *n.*

con·strict′ *v.* make smaller by squeezing, etc.; contract —**con·stric′tion** *n.*

con·struct′ *v.* build; devise

con·struc′tion *n.* **1** a constructing **2** structure **3** explanation **4** arrangement of words —**con·struc′tive** *a.*

con·strue′ *v.* interpret

con′sul *n.* government official in a foreign city looking after his or her country's business there —**con′su·lar** *a.* —**con′sul·ate** (-ət) *n.*

con·sult′ *v.* **1** talk things over; confer **2** ask the advice of **3** consider —**con·sult′ant** *n.* —**con′sul·ta′tion** *n.*

con·sume′ *v.* **1** destroy **2** use up **3** eat or drink up

con·sum′er *n.* buyer of goods for personal use

con·sum′er·ism′ *n.* movement to protect consumers against harmful products, etc.

con′sum·mate′ (*a.:* -mit) *v.* complete —*a.* complete —**con′sum·ma′tion** *n.*

con·sump′tion *n.* **1** a consuming **2** using up of goods **3** amount used up **4** tuberculosis of the lungs: term no longer used

con·sump′tive *n., a.* (one) having tuberculosis of the lungs

cont *abbrev.* continued

con′tact′ *n.* **1** a touching **2** a being in touch (*with*) **3** influential acquaintance **4** connection —*v.* **1** place in contact **2** get in touch with

contact lens *n.* tiny, thin lens worn on the eye to improve vision

con·ta′gion (-jən) *n.* a spreading of disease, an idea, etc. —**con·ta′gious** (-jəs) *a.*

con·tain′ *v.* **1** have in it **2** be able to hold **3** restrain —**con·tain′er** *n.*

con·tain′er·ize′ *v.* to ship (cargo) in huge, standardized containers

con·tam′i·nate′ *v.* make impure; pollute —**con·tam′i·nant** *n.* —**con·tam′i·na′tion** *n.*

con·tem·plate′ *v.* **1** to watch intently **2** meditate **3** intend —**con′tem·pla′**

tion *n.* —**con·tem'pla·tive'** *a.*

con·tem'po·rar·y *n.*, *pl.* **-ries**; *a.* (one) living in the same period —**con·tem'po·ra'ne·ous** *a.*

con·tempt' *n.* 1 scorn 2 disgrace 3 disrespect shown for a judge, etc.

con·tempt'i·ble *a.* deserving contempt

con·temp'tu·ous (-choo əs) *a.* scornful; disdainful

con·tend' *v.* 1 struggle 2 compete 3 assert

con·tent' *a.* satisfied: also **con·tent'ed** —*n.* satisfaction —**con·tent'ment** *n.*

con'tent' *n.* 1 *pl.* all that is contained 2 meaning 3 capacity

con·ten'tion *n.* argument or struggle —**con·ten'tious** *a.*

con·test' (*n.*: kän'test') *v.* 1 to dispute; question 2 fight for —*n.* 1 struggle 2 race, game, etc. —**con·test'ant** *n.*

con'text' *n.* 1 words surrounding a word or phrase that fix its meaning 2 whole background, etc., as of an event

con·tex'tu·al·ize' *v.* put into a context so as to understand

con·tig'u·ous *a.* in contact

con'ti·nence *n.* sexual self-restraint —**con'ti·nent** *a.*

con'ti·nent *n.* large landmass —**the Continent** Europe —**con'ti·nen'tal** *a.*

con·tin'gen·cy *n.*, *pl.* **-cies** uncertain event

con·tin'gent *a.* dependent (*on*); conditional —*n.* quota, as of troops

con·tin'u·al *a.* 1 repeated often 2 continuous

con·tin'ue *v.* 1 keep on; go on 2 endure; last 3 resume 4 extend 5 postpone —**con·tin'u·ance, con·tin'u·a'tion** *n.*

con·ti·nu'i·ty *n.*, *pl.* **-ties** continuous state or thing

con·tin'u·ous *a.* without interruption; unbroken

con·tin'u·um *n.*, *pl.* **-u·a** or **-u·ums** continuous whole, quantity, or series

con·tort' *v.* twist out of shape —**con·tor'tion** *n.*

con·tor'tion·ist *n.* one who can twist his or her body strangely

con'tour' (-toor) *n.* outline of a figure, land, etc. —*v.* shape to a contour —*a.* made to fit the contour of something

con'tra *prep.* against

contra- *pref.* against

con'tra·band' *n.* smuggled goods —*a.* prohibited

con'tra·cep'tion *n.* prevention of human conception —**con'tra·cep'tive** *a.*, *n.*

con·tract' (*v.* 2, 3: kən trakt') *n.* legally

valid agreement —*v.* 1 undertake by contract 2 get; incur 3 shrink —**con'trac'tor** *n.* —**con·trac'tu·al** (-choo əl) *a.*

con·trac'tile (-til) *a.* able to contract

con·trac'tion *n.* 1 a contracting 2 shortened form

con'tra·dict' *v.* say or be the opposite of —**con'tra·dic'tion** *n.* —**con'tra·dic'to·ry** *a.*

con'trail' *n.* white trail of condensed water vapor in an aircraft's wake

con'tra·in'di·cate' *v.* make (the indicated drug or treatment) inadvisable

con·tral'to *n.*, *pl.* **-tos** lowest female voice

con·trap'tion *n.* contrivance; gadget

con'tra·pun'tal *a.* of counterpoint

con'tra·ri·wise' *adv.* 1 on the contrary 2 in the opposite way, order, etc.

con'trar·y *a.* 1 opposed; different 2 perverse —*n.* the opposite —**on the contrary** as opposed to what has been said —**con'trar·i·ly** *adv.*

con·trast' (*n.*: kän'trast') *v.* 1 compare 2 show difference —*n.* striking difference when compared

con'tra·vene' *v.* go against

con·tre·temps (kän'trə tän') *n.*, *pl.* **-temps** (-tän') awkward mishap

con·trib'ute *v.* 1 give, esp. to a common fund 2 furnish (an idea, article, etc.) —**contribute to** help bring about —**con'tri·bu'tion** *n.* —**con·trib'u·tor** *n.*

con·trite' *a.* remorseful —**con·tri'tion** (-trish'ən) *n.*

con·trive' *v.* 1 devise; invent 2 manage; bring about —**con·triv'ance** *n.*

con·trol' *v.* **-trolled', -trol'ling** 1 regulate (finances) 2 direct 3 restrain —*n.* 1 authority 2 means of restraint 3 *pl.* regulating mechanism

control group *n.* group, in an experiment, not given the drug, etc. being tested

con·trol'ler *n.* one who regulates finances, as in a business

con'tro·ver·sy *n.* debate or dispute —**con'tro·ver'sial** (-shəl) *a.*

con'tro·vert' *v.* to dispute —**con'tro·vert'i·ble** *a.*

con'tu·ma·cy *n.* disobedience —**con·tu'ma'cious** (-shəs) *a.*

con'tu·me·ly *n.* haughty rudeness

con·tu'sion *n.* a bruise

co·nun'drum *n.* a puzzle

con·ur·ba'tion *n.* vast urban area made up of a large city and its environs

con'va·les'cence *n.* (period of) recovery after illness —**con'va·lesce'** *v.* —

con·va·les·cent *a.*, *n.*

con·vec·tion *n.* transmission of heat in currents

con·vene *v.* assemble; meet

con·ven·ience (-vēn´yəns) *n.* **1** a being convenient **2** comfort **3** thing that saves work, etc.

con·ven·ient *a.* easy to do, use, or get to; handy

con·vent *n.* community of nuns or their living place

con·ven·tion *n.* **1** an assembly **2** custom; usage

con·ven·tion·al *a.* **1** customary **2** conforming

con·verge *v.* come together —**con·ver´gence** *n.* —**con·ver´gent** *a.*

con·ver·sant *a.* familiar (*with*)

con·ver·sa·tion *n.* informal talk —**con´ver·sa·tion·al** *a.* —**con´ver·sa·tion·al·ist** *n.*

conversation piece *n.* something unusual, as a piece of furniture, that invites comment

con·verse´ (*n.:* kän´vʉrs) *v.* to talk — *a.* opposite —*n.* **1** conversation **2** the opposite —**con·verse´ly** *adv.*

con·vert (*n.:* kän´vʉrt) *v.* change in form, use, etc. or in religion —*n.* person who has converted —**con·ver´sion** *n.* —**con·vert´er, con·vert´or** *n.*

con·vert´i·ble *a.* that can be converted —*n.* automobile with a folding or removable top

con·vex´ *a.* curved outward like the outside of a sphere —**con·vex´i·ty** *n.*

con·vey´ (-vā´) *v.* **1** carry **2** transmit —**con·vey´or, con·vey´er** *n.*

con·vey´ance *n.* **1** a conveying **2** vehicle

con·vict (*n.:* kän´vikt´) *v.* find guilty — *n.* prisoner serving a sentence

con·vic´tion *n.* **1** a being convicted **2** strong belief

con·vince´ *v.* make feel sure —**con·vinc´ing** *a.*

con·viv´i·al *a.* sociable; jovial —**con·viv´i·al´i·ty** *n.*

con·voke´ *v.* call together —**con´vo·ca´tion** *n.*

con·vo·lu´tion *n.* a twist or twisting —**con´vo·lut´ed** *a.*

con·voy´ *v.* escort —*n.* ships, etc. being escorted

con·vulse´ *v.* shake as with violent spasms —**con·vul´sion** *n.* —**con·vul´sive** *a.*

coo *v.* make the soft sound of a pigeon or dove —*n.* this sound

COO *abbrev.* chief operating officer

cook *v.* boil, bake, fry, etc. —*n.* one who cooks —**cook´er·y** *n.*

cook´book´ *n.* book of recipes

cook´ie, cook´y *n.*, *pl.* **-ies** small, sweet, flat cake

cook´out´ *n.* party at which a meal is cooked and eaten outdoors

cook´top´ *n.* stove top, with burners, etc., or such a unit in a countertop

cool *a.* **1** moderately cold **2** not excited **3** unfriendly **4** [Sl.] very good —*n.* cool place, time, etc. —*v.* make or become cool —**cool´er** *n.* —**cool´ly** *adv.* —**cool´ness** *n.*

cool´ant *n.* fluid for cooling engines, etc.

coo´lie *n.*, *pl.* **-lies** Asian laborer

coon *n.* raccoon

coop *n.* pen for poultry —*v.* confine as in a coop: used with *up*

co´-op´ *n.* [Inf.] a cooperative

co·op´er·ate´, co-op´er·ate´ *v.* to work together: also **co·öp´er·ate´** —**co·op´er·a´tion, co-op´er·a´tion** *n.*

co·op´er·a·tive, co-op´er·a·tive *a.* cooperating —*n.* a collective, profit-sharing enterprise Also **co·öp´er·a·tive**

co·opt´ *v.* get (an opponent) to join one's side

co·or´di·nate, co-or´di·nate (-nət; *v.:* -nāt´) *a.* equally important —*v.* to harmonize; adjust Also **co·ör´di·nate** —**co·or´di·na´tion, co-or´di·na´tion** *n.* —**co·or´di·na´tor, co-or´di·na´tor** *n.*

coot (kōōt) *n.* water bird

cop *n.* [Sl.] policeman

co´-pay´ment *n.* part of a medical bill not covered by insurance

cope *v.* deal (*with*) successfully —*n.* priest's vestment

cop´i·er *n.* person who copies or machine that makes copies

co´pi´lot *n.* assistant pilot of an aircraft

cop·ing (kō´piŋ) *n.* top of masonry wall

co´pi·ous *a.* abundant

cop´per *n.* reddish-brown metal, a chemical element

cop´per·head´ *n.* a poisonous snake

co´pra (kä´-, kō´-) *n.* dried coconut meat

copse *n.* thicket

cop´ter *n.* [Inf.] helicopter

cop´u·late´ *v.* have sexual intercourse —**cop´u·la´tion** *n.*

cop´y *n.*, *pl.* **-ies** **1** thing made just like another **2** one of many books, etc. all alike —*v.* **-ied, -y·ing** **1** make a copy of **2** imitate

cop´y·cat´ *n.* imitator: chiefly child's term —*a.* imitating a recent event

cop'y·right' *n.* exclusive rights over a book, song, etc. —*v.* protect by copyright

co·quette' (-ket') *n.* female flirt —**co·quet'tish** *a.*

cor'al *n.* **1** hard mass of sea animal skeletons **2** yellowish red

cord *n.* **1** thick string **2** wood pile of 128 cubic feet **3** insulated electric wire —**cord'less** *a.*

cor'dial (-jol) *a.* friendly —*n.* syrupy alcoholic drink —**cor·di·al'i·ty** (-jē al'-) *n.* —**cor'dial·ly** *adv.*

cor'don *n.* line or circle of guards

cor'do·van *n.* soft leather

cor'du·roy' *n.* cotton fabric woven with raised parallel lines

core *n.* **1** central part, as of an apple **2** most important part —*v.* remove the core of

co're·spond'ent (kō'-) *n.* person in divorce suit charged with adultery with another's spouse

co'ri·an'der *n.* herb used for flavoring

cork *n.* **1** light, thick bark of a certain oak **2** a stopper —*v.* stop with a cork

cork'board' *n.* insulation material made with granulated cork

cork'screw' *n.* spiral device for removing corks from bottles

corm *n.* bulblike underground stem of certain plants

cor'mo·rant *n.* seabird

corn *n.* **1** grain that grows on large ears with a hard core (**corn'cob'**) **2** [Inf.] trite humor **3** hard, thick growth of skin —*v.* to pickle (meat, etc.)

cor'ne·a *n.* clear, outer layer of the eyeball —**cor'ne·al** *a.*

cor'ner *n.* **1** place where lines or surfaces meet **2** a region **3** monopoly —*v.* **1** put into a difficult position **2** get a monopoly on —**cut corners** cut down expenses, etc.

cor'ner·back' *n.* Football either of two defensive backs behind the line of scrimmage

cor'ner·stone' *n.* stone at a corner of a building

cor'net' *n.* brass instrument like a trumpet

corn'flow'er *n.* plant with small, showy flowers

cor'nice (-nis) *n.* molding along the top of a wall, etc.

corn'meal' *n.* meal made from corn (maize)

corn'starch' *n.* starchy flour made from corn, used in cooking

corn syrup *n.* sweet syrup made from

cornstarch

cor'nu·co'pi·a *n.* horn-shaped container overflowing with fruits, etc.

corn'y *a.* **-i·er, -i·est** [Inf.] trite or sentimental

co·rol'la (-rōl'-, -räl'-) *n.* petals of a flower

cor'ol·lar'y *n., pl.* **-ies** proposition following from one already proved

co·ro'na *n.* ring of light around the sun or moon

cor'o·nar'y *a.* of the arteries supplying the heart —*n., pl.* **-ies** thrombosis in a coronary artery: in full, **coronary thrombosis**

cor'o·na'tion *n.* crowning of a sovereign

cor'o·ner *n.* official who investigates deaths not due to natural causes

cor'o·net' *n.* small crown worn by nobility

Corp *abbrev.* **1** Corporal **2** Corporation: also **corp**

cor'po·ral (-pə rəl, -prəl) *n.* lowest ranking noncommissioned officer —*a.* of the body

corporal punishment *n.* bodily punishment, as flogging

cor'po·ra'tion *n.* group given legal status of an individual —**cor'po·rate** *a.*

cor·po're·al (-pôr'ē-) *a.* **1** of the body **2** material

corps (kôr) *n.* **1** organized group **2** large military unit

corpse *n.* dead body

cor'pu·lent *a.* fat; fleshy —**cor'pu·lence** *n.*

cor'pus *n.* body, as of laws

cor'pus·cle (-əl) *n.* cell in the blood, lymph, etc.

cor·ral' *n.* pen for horses, etc. —*v.* **-ralled', -ral'ling** confine in a corral

cor·rect' *v.* **1** make right **2** mark errors of **3** punish —*a.* right, true, etc. —**cor·rec'tion** *n.* —**cor·rec'tion·al** *a.* —**cor·rec'tive** *a., n.* —**cor·rect'ly** *adv.*

cor're·late' *v.* bring into mutual relation —**cor're·la'tion** *n.*

cor·rel'a·tive *n., a.* (conjunction) showing mutual relation, as *either ... or*

cor're·spond' *v.* **1** be similar or equal to **2** communicate as by letters —**cor're·spond'ence** *n.*

cor're·spond'ent *n.* **1** person exchanging letters with another **2** journalist providing news from a distant place

cor'ri·dor (-dər, -dôr') *n.* long hall

cor·rob'o·rate' *v.* confirm —**cor·rob'o·ra'tion** *n.* —**cor·rob'o·ra'tive** *a.*

cor·rode' v. wear away, as by rusting —**cor·ro'sion** n. —**cor·ro'sive** a., n.

cor·ru·gate' v. make parallel ridges or wrinkles in

cor·rupt' a. 1 evil 2 taking bribes —v. to make or become corrupt —**cor·rupt'i·ble** a. —**cor·rup'tion** n.

cor·sage' (-säzh') n. small bouquet worn by a woman

cor'set n. tight undergarment to support the torso

cor·tege' (-tezh') n. ceremonial procession

cor'tex' n., pl. **-ti·ces'** (-tə sēz') outer layer of the brain, kidney, etc. —**cor'ti·cal** a.

cor'ti·sone' (-sōn', -zōn') n. hormone used to treat allergies, inflammations, etc.

co·run'dum n. mineral used for grinding wheels, etc.

cor'us·cate' v. to glitter; sparkle —**cor'us·ca'tion** n.

co'sign' v. sign jointly —**co'sign'er** n.

cos·met'ic n., a. (preparation) for enhancing beauty —**cos·me·tol'o·gist** n. —**cos·me·tol'o·gy** n.

cos'mic a. 1 of the cosmos 2 vast; huge

cos'mo·naut' n. Russian astronaut

cos'mo·pol'i·tan a. at home all over the world; worldly —n. a worldly person

cos'mos (-məs, -mōs') n. the universe seen as an orderly system

co'spon'sor v., n. (be) a joint sponsor

cost v. cost, cost'ing require the payment, etc. of —n. 1 price 2 loss; sacrifice —**at all costs** by any means whatever

co'star' n. any of the actors or actresses who are stars in a movie or play —v. -starred', -star'ring make or be a costar

cost'-ef·fec'tive a. efficient or economical

cos'tive (käs'-, kôs'-) a. constipated or constipating

cost'ly a. -li·er, -li·est expensive —**cost'li·ness** n.

cost of living n. averge cost of necessities, as food, shelter, and clothes

cos'tume' n. 1 the dress of a people, period, etc. 2 set of outer clothes for some purpose

co'sy (-zē) a. -si·er, -si·est chiefly Br. sp. of COZY —**co'si·ly** adv.

cot n. folding bed

cote n. small shelter for sheep, doves, etc.

co·te·rie (kōt'ər ē) n. social set; clique

co·til'lion (-yən) n. formal dance

cot'tage n. small house

cottage cheese n. soft, white cheese made from sour milk

cot'ter pin n. pin with two stems that can be spread apart

cot'ton n. 1 plant with head of soft, white fibers 2 thread or cloth from this —**cot'ton·y** a.

cot'ton·mouth' n. water moccasin

cot'ton·seed' n. seed of the cotton plant, containing oil (**cottonseed oil**) used in margarine, soap, etc.

cot'ton·wood' n. poplar having seeds covered with cottony fibers

cot·y·le·don (kät'ə lēd''n) n. first leaf produced by a plant embryo

couch n. piece of furniture to sit or lie on —v. put in words

cou'gar (kōō'-) n. large American wildcat

cough (kôf) v. expel lung air in a loud burst —n. 1 a coughing 2 condition of frequent coughing

cough drop n. small tablet for relief of coughs

could v. pt. of CAN

could'n't contr. could not

coun'cil n. an advisory, administrative, or legislative body —**coun'cil·man** n., pl. **-men** —**coun'cil·per·son** n. —**coun'cil·wom·an** n.fem., pl. **-wom·en**

coun'ci·lor n. member of a council: also [Chiefly Br.] **coun'cil·lor**

coun'sel n. 1 advice 2 lawyer(s) —v. to advise —**coun'se·lor, coun'sel·lor** n.

count v. 1 add up to get a total 2 name numbers in order 3 include or be included 4 consider 5 be important —n. 1 a counting 2 total number 3 each charge in an indictment 4 nobleman —**count on** rely on

count'down' n. counting off of time units, in reverse order

coun'te·nance n. 1 a facial expression 2 face —v. to sanction

count'er n. long table, board, etc. for displaying goods, serving food, etc. —adv., a. (in a) contrary (way) —v. oppose

counter- pref. 1 opposite 2 against 3 in return

coun'ter·act' v. act against

coun'ter·at·tack' n., v. attack in return

coun'ter·bal'ance n. thing that balances or offsets another —v. offset

coun'ter·clock'wise' adv., a. like the hands of a clock moving in reverse

coun'ter·feit' (-fit') a. made in imitation with intent to defraud —n. fraudulent imitation —v. 1 make counterfeits 2 pretend

coun'ter·mand' v. cancel (a command)

coun'ter·mel'o·dy n. subordinate melody

coun'ter·pane' n. bedspread

coun'ter·part' n. matching or corresponding thing

coun'ter·point' n. harmonic interweaving of melodies

coun'ter·poise' n., v. counterbalance

coun'ter·pro·duc'tive a. producing the opposite of what is intended

coun'ter·sign' n. password —v. confirm another's signature by signing

coun'ter·sink' v. sink a bolt or screw into a hole large enough to receive its head

coun'ter·ten'or n. highest tenor voice

coun'ter·top' n. upper surface of a counter

count'ess n. wife or widow of a count or earl

count'less a. too many to count

coun'try (kun'-) n., pl. **-tries** 1 region 2 nation 3 rural area —a. rural — **coun'try·man** n., pl. **-men**

country club n. social club with a golf course, etc.

country music n. rural folk music, esp. of the South

coun'try·side' n. rural region

coun'try·wide' a., adv. throughout the whole nation

coun'ty n., pl. **-ties** subdivision of a U.S. state

coup (kōō) n., pl. **coups** (kōōz) 1 bold, successful stroke 2 coup d'état

coup d'é·tat (kōō'dā tä') n. sudden overthrow of a ruler

cou·ple (kup'əl) n. 1 a pair 2 engaged, married, etc. man and woman 3 [Inf.] a few —v. join together

cou'plet n. two successive rhyming lines of poetry

cou'pling n. device for joining things together

cou'pon (kōō'-, kyōō'-) n. certificate, ticket, etc. redeemable for cash or gifts

cour'age n. fearless or brave quality —**cou·ra'geous** a.

cou'ri·er (koor'ē-, kur'ē-) n. messenger

course n. 1 path or channel 2 direction taken 3 regular mode of action 4 series 5 separate part of a meal 6 unit of instruction in a subject —v. run —**in the course of** during —**of**

course 1 naturally 2 certainly

court n. 1 an open space surrounded by buildings or walls: also **court'yard'** 2 playing area 3 royal palace 4 family, advisers, etc. of a sovereign 5 respectful attention 6 Law judge(s) 7 Law place where trials are held: also **court'room'** —v. woo

cour·te·san (-zən) n. prostitute

cour'te·sy (kurt'ə-) n., pl. **-sies** polite behavior or act —a. free; complimentary —**cour'te·ous** a.

court'house' n. building housing the offices and courtrooms of a county

cour'ti·er n. attendant at a royal court

court'ly a. dignified

court'-mar'tial n., pl. **courts'-mar'tial** or **court'-mar'tials** trial by a military or naval court —v. try by such a court

court reporter n. person producing a verbatim record of a trial, etc.

court'ship' n. period or act of courting or wooing

court'side' n. area around a basketball, tennis, etc. court

cous'in (kuz'-) n. child of one's uncle or aunt

cous'in·age n. group of cousins

cou·tu·ri·er (kōō'toor ē ā') n. designer of women's clothing

cove n. small bay

cov'en (kuv'-) n. witches' meeting

cov'e·nant n. agreement; compact

cov'er v. 1 place something over 2 extend over 3 conceal 4 protect 5 include; deal with —n. thing that covers —**take cover** seek shelter —**cov'er·ing** n.

cov'er·age n. amount covered by something

cov'er·alls' pl.n. one-piece work garment with legs

cover charge n. fixed charge added to a nightclub or restaurant bill

covered wagon n. large wagon with an arched canvas cover

cov'er·let n. bedspread

cov'ert (kō'vərt, kuv'ərt) n. hidden

cov'er·up' n. an attempt to keep blunders, crimes, etc. undisclosed

cov'et (kuv'-) v. desire ardently (what belongs to another)

cov'et·ous a. greedy

cov'ey (kuv'ē) n. small flock, as of quail

cow n. mature female of cattle, or of the elephant, seal, etc. —v. make timid

cow'ard n. one lacking courage —**cow'ard·ice'** (-ər dis') n. —**cow'ard·ly** a., adv.

cow'boy' *n.* worker who herds cattle: also **cow'hand'**

cow'er *v.* cringe as in fear

cow'hide' *n.* leather made from the hide of a cow

cowl *n.* monk's hood

cow'lick' *n.* tuft of hair difficult to comb flat

cowl'ing *n.* metal covering for an airplane engine

co'-work'er *n.* fellow worker

cow'slip' *n.* plant with yellow flowers

cox'comb' (-kōm') *n.* fop

cox·swain (käk'sən, -swān') *n.* one who steers a boat

coy *a.* pretending to be shy —**coy'ly** *adv.*

coy·o·te (kī ōt'ē, kī'ōt') *n.* small prairie wolf

coz'en (kuz'-) *v.* to cheat

co'zy *a.* **-zi·er, -zi·est** warm and comfortable; snug

CPA *abbrev.* Certified Public Accountant

CPI *abbrev.* consumer price index

CPR *abbrev.* cardiopulmonary resuscitation

CPU *n.* central processing unit

crab *n.* **1** shellfish with eight legs and two pincers **2** irritable person

crab apple *n.* small, sour apple

crab'by *a.* **-bi·er, -bi·est** peevish; cross —**crab'bi·ness** *n.*

crab grass *n.* weedy grass that spreads rapidly

crack *v.* **1** make a sudden, sharp noise **2** break without separation of parts **3** [Sl.] make (a joke) **4** solve —*n.* **1** sudden, sharp noise **2** incomplete break **3** sharp blow **4** [Inf.] try **5** [Sl.] sharp remark **6** [Sl.] form of cocaine —*a.* [Inf.] first-rate —**crack down (on)** become strict (with)

crack'down' *n.* a resorting to strict discipline or rules

crack'er *n.* thin, crisp wafer

crack'head' *n.* [Sl.] crack cocaine addict

crack'le *v., n.* (make) a series of slight, sharp sounds

crack'pot' *n.* [Inf.] mentally unbalanced or eccentric person

crack'up' *n.* **1** crash **2** [Inf.] mental breakdown

cra'dle *n.* baby's bed on rockers —*v.* put as in a cradle

craft *n.* **1** occupation requiring special skills **2** slyness **3** *pl.* **craft** boat or aircraft

crafts'man *n., pl.* **-men** skilled worker —**crafts'man·ship'** *n.*

craft'y *a.* **-i·er, -i·est** sly; cunning —**craft'i·ly** *adv.*

crag *n.* steep, projecting rock —**crag'gy** *a.*, **-gi·er, -gi·est**

cram *v.* **crammed, cram'ming 1** to stuff **2** study hurriedly for a test

cramp *n.* **1** painful contraction of a muscle **2** *pl.* intestinal pain —*v.* to hamper

cramped *a.* confined

cran'ber·ry *n., pl.* **-ries** sour, edible, red berry

crane *n.* **1** long-legged wading bird **2** machine for lifting heavy weights —*v.* stretch (the neck)

cra'ni·um *n.* the skull —**cra'ni·al** *a.*

crank *n.* **1** handle for turning a shaft **2** [Inf.] eccentric person —*v.* start or work by a crank

crank'shaft' *n.* shaft for transferring motion in an engine, contained in a metal case (**crank'case'**)

crank'y *a.* **-i·er, -i·est** irritable; cross

cran'ny *n., pl.* **-nies** chink

crap *n.* [Sl.] **1** nonsense **2** junk

crape *n.* crepe

craps *pl.n.* dice game

crap'shoot' *n.* [Inf.] a gamble; risk

crash *v.* **1** fall, break, drop, etc. with a loud noise **2** fail **3** [Inf.] get into uninvited —*n.* **1** loud noise **2** a crashing **3** failure, as of business

crash'-land' *v.* bring (an airplane) down without landing gear —**crash landing** *n.*

crass *a.* showing poor taste or greed for money —**crass'ly** *adv.* —**crass'ness** *n.*

crate *n.* wooden packing case —*v.* pack in a crate

cra'ter *n.* bowl-shaped cavity or pit, as of a volcano —*v.* to form craters (in)

cra·vat' *n.* necktie

crave *v.* desire strongly

cra'ven *a.* cowardly —*n.* coward

crav'ing *n.* intense desire

craw *n.* bird's crop

crawl *v.* **1** move slowly while flat on the ground **2** creep **3** swarm with crawling things —*n.* **1** a crawling **2** swimming stroke

cray'fish' *n.* shellfish like a small lobster: also **craw'fish'**

cray'on *n.* small stick of chalk, wax, etc. for drawing

craze *v.* make or become insane —*n.* fad

cra'zy *a.* **-zi·er, -zi·est 1** insane **2** [Inf.] foolish, wild, etc. —*n., pl.* **-zies** [Sl.] an insane person —**cra'zi·ly** *adv.* —**cra'zi·ness** *n.*

crazy quilt *n.* quilt of odd patches in

no regular design

creak v., n. squeak

cream n. 1 oily part of milk 2 creamy cosmetic 3 best part —v. beat till smooth as cream —**cream** of purée of —**creamy** a., **-i-er, -i-est**

cream cheese n. soft, white cheese of cream and milk

cream'er n. cream pitcher

cream'er·y n., pl. **-ies** place where dairy products are made or sold

crease n. line made by folding —v. make a crease in

cre·ate' v. make; bring about —**cre·a' tion** n. —**cre·a'tive** a. —**cre·a'tor** n.

crea'ture n. living being, real or imaginary

cre'dence n. belief; trust

cre·den'tials (-shəlz) pl.n. document showing proof of one's position, etc.

cre·den'za n. buffet or sideboard

credibility gap n. disparity between a statement and the truth

cred'i·ble a. believable —**cred'i·bil'i·ty** n.

cred'it n. 1 belief; trust 2 reputation 3 praise 4 trust that one will pay later 5 completed unit of study —v. 1 believe; trust 2 give credit for —**cred'it·a·ble** a. —**cred'it·a·bly** adv.

credit card n. card entitling one to charge bills

cred'i·tor n. one to whom another owes a debt

cred'it·wor'thy a. seen as financially safe enough to be lent money

cre'do' (krē'-, krā'-) n., pl. **-dos'** creed

cred·u·lous (krej'ə ləs) a. believing too readily —**cre·du'li·ty** (krə dōō'-) n.

creed n. statement of belief

creek n. small stream

creel n. basket for fish

creep v. **crept, creep'ing** 1 go on hands and knees 2 go slowly or stealthily 3 grow along the ground, etc. —n. [Sl.] disgusting person —the **creeps** [Inf.] feeling of fear, disgust, etc.

creep'y a. **-i-er, -i-est** causing fear, disgust, etc.

cre'mate' v. burn (a dead body) —**cre·ma'tion** n.

cre·ma·to·ry n., pl. **-ries** furnace for cremating: also **cre·ma·to'ri·um**, pl. **-ums** or **-a**

Cre·ole' n. descendant of original French settlers of Louisiana, sometimes also having black ancestors

cre'o·sote' n. oily preservative distilled from tar

crepe, crêpe (krāp, n. 2: also krep) n.

1 thin, crinkled silk, rayon, etc. 2 thin pancake, rolled and filled

crept v. pt. & pp. of CREEP

cre·scen'do' (-shen'-) n., pl. **-dos'** Mus. a growing louder

cres'cent n. shape of a quarter moon

crest n. 1 tuft on an animal's head 2 heraldic device 3 top; summit

crest'fall'en a. dejected

cre'tin n. idiot

cre·tonne' (krē tän') n. printed linen or cotton cloth

cre·vasse' (krə vas') n. deep crack, as in a glacier

crev'ice n. narrow crack; fissure

crew n. group of workers, as the sailors on a ship

crew v. alt. pt. of CROW

crew cut n. man's very short haircut

crew'el n. yarn used in embroidery —**crew'el·work'** n.

crib n. 1 box for fodder 2 baby's small bed 3 wood shed for grain —v. **cribbed, crib'bing** 1 confine 2 [Inf.] steal or plagiarize

crib'bage' n. card game

crick n. painful cramp

crick'et n. 1 leaping insect 2 ball game played with bats and wickets

cried v. pt. & pp. of CRY

cri'er n. one who cries

crime n. 1 an act in violation of a law 2 sin

crim'i·nal a. of crime —n. person guilty of crime —**crim'i·nal'i·ty** n.

crim'i·nal·ist n. expert in using physical evidence to investigate crimes

crim'i·nol'o·gy n. study of crime and criminals

crimp v., n. pleat or curl

crim'son (-zən, -sən) n. deep red

cringe (krinj) v. 1 shrink back as in fear 2 to fawn

crin'kle v. to wrinkle or rustle —**crin' kly** a.

crin'o·line (-lin) n. 1 stiff cloth 2 hoop skirt

crip'ple n. disabled person —v. disable

cri'sis n., pl. **-ses'** (-sēz') 1 turning point 2 crucial situation

crisp a. 1 brittle 2 clear 3 fresh; bracing

criss'cross' n. crossed lines —v. 1 mark with crisscross 2 move to and fro across —adv. crosswise

cri·te'ri·on (-tir'ē-) n., pl. **-ri·a** or **-ri·ons** standard; rule

crit'ic n. 1 judge of books, art, etc. 2 faultfinder

crit'i·cal a. 1 finding fault 2 of critics or their work 3 being a crisis —**crit'i·**

cal·ly *adv.*

crit'i·cism *n.* **1** fault finding **2** analysis and evaluation

crit'i·cize *v.* **1** judge as a critic **2** find fault (with)

cri·tique' (-tēk') *n.* critical evaluation

crit'ter *n.* [Dial.] creature

croak *v., n.* (to make) a deep, hoarse sound

cro·chet' (-shā') *v.* knit with one hooked needle

crock *n.* earthenware jar

crocked *a.* [Sl.] drunk

crock'er·y *n.* earthenware

croc'o·dile' *n.* large tropical reptile with massive jaws

cro'cus *n.* small plant of the iris family

crois·sant (krə sänt') *n.* a rich, crescent-shaped bread roll

crone *n.* old hag

cro'ny *n., pl.* **-nies** close friend

crook *n.* **1** a bend or curve **2** [Inf.] swindler

crook'ed *a.* **1** not straight **2** dishonest

croon *v.* sing softly —**croon'er** *n.*

crop *n.* **1** saclike part of a bird's gullet **2** farm product, growing or harvested **3** group **4** riding whip —*v.* **cropped,** **crop'ping** cut or bite off the ends of — **crop out** (or **up**) appear suddenly — **crop'per** *n.*

crop'-dust'ing *n.* spraying of crops with pesticides from an airplane

cro·quet' (-kā') *n.* game with hoops in the ground through which balls are hit

cro·quette' (-ket') *n.* small mass of meat, fish, etc. deep-fried

cross *n.* **1** upright post with another across it **2** figure of this, symbolic of Christianity **3** any affliction **4** mark made by intersecting lines, bars, etc. **5** hybrid —*v.* **1** place, go, or lie across **2** go (*over*) to the other side **3** intersect **4** draw a line across **5** thwart **6** interbreed —*a.* **1** lying or passing across **2** irritable —**cross off** (or **out**) cancel as by drawing lines across — **cross'ing** *n.* —**cross'ness** *n.*

cross'bones' *n.* picture of two crossed bones under a skull, symbolizing death

cross'bow' *n.* bow on a wooden frame for shooting arrows

cross'breed' *n.* hybrid —*v.* to breed as a hybrid

cross'-coun'try *a.* across open country, as a race

cross'cut' *a., n., v.* cut across

cross'-ex·am·ine *v. Law* question (an opposition witness) —**cross'-ex·am·i·**

na'tion *n.*

cross'-eyed' *a.* having the eyes turned toward the nose

cross'fire' *n.* forceful exchange, as of opposing opinions

cross'hatch' *v.* darken (a drawing) with crossing parallel lines

cross'ing *n.* **1** intersection **2** place for crossing

cross'-pur'pose *n.* contrary aim or intent —**at cross-purposes** misunderstanding each other's aim or intent

cross'-ref'er·ence *n.* reference from one part to another

cross'road' *n.* **1** a road that crosses another **2** *pl.* road intersection

cross section *n.* **1** part cut straight across **2** broad sample

cross'town' *a.* running across the main avenues of a city or town

cross'walk' *n.* pedestrians' lane across a street

cross'wise' *adv.* across: also **cross'ways'**

crotch *n.* place where branches or legs fork

crotch'et *n.* whim

crotch'et·y *a.* cantankerous

crouch *v., n.* stoop with legs bent low

croup (krōōp) *n.* disease with coughing and hard breathing

crou·pi·er (krōō'pē ā') *n.* one controlling a gambling table

crou'ton' (krōō'-) *n.* bit of toast served in soup

crow *n.* **1** large, black bird with a harsh call **2** rooster's cry —*v.* **1** make a rooster's cry **2** boast in triumph — **eat crow** admit one's error

crow'bar' *n.* long, metal bar for prying, etc.

crowd *v.* to throng, press, cram, etc. — *n.* a mass of people —**crowd'ed** *a.*

crown *n.* **1** head covering of a monarch **2** power of a monarch **3** top part, position, quality, etc. —*v.* **1** make a monarch of **2** honor **3** be atop **4** climax

crow's'-feet' *pl.n.* wrinkles at outer corners of eyes

crow's'-nest' *n.* lookout platform on a ship's mast

CRT *n.* cathode-ray tube

cru'cial (-shəl) *a.* **1** decisive **2** trying

cru'ci·ble *n.* **1** container for melting metals **2** severe test

cru'ci·fix' *n.* representation of Jesus on the cross

cru'ci·fy' *v.* **-fied', -fy'ing** execute by suspending from a cross —**cru'ci·fix'ion** (-fik'shən) *n.*

crude *a.* **1** raw; unprocessed **2** rough or clumsy —**cru'di·ty, crude'ness** *n.*

cru'el *a.* causing suffering; pitiless —**cru'el·ty** *n.*

cru'et *n.* small bottle for vinegar, oil, etc.

cruise *v.* travel about, as by ship —*n.* voyage

cruis'er 1 police car **2** fast warship

crul'ler *n.* twisted doughnut

crumb (krum) *n.* small piece, as of bread; bit —**crumb'y** *a.*, **-bi·er, -bi·est**

crum'ble *v.* break into crumbs —**crum'bly** *a.*, **-bli·er, -bli·est**

crum'my *a.* **-mi·er, -mi·est** [Sl.] shabby, inferior, etc.

crum'ple *v.* to crush into wrinkles

crunch *v.* chew or crush with a crackling sound —**crunch'y** *a.*, **-i·er, -i·est**

crunch'time' *n.* [Sl.] tense, crucial phase of some activity

cru·sade' *v., n.* (to engage in) united action for some idea or cause —**cru·sad'er** *n.*

crush *v.* **1** press out of shape **2** pound into bits **3** subdue —*n.* **1** a crushing **2** crowded mass **3** [Inf.] infatuation

crush'ing *a.* **1** overwhelming **2** hurtful

crust *n.* hard outer part or surface layer of bread, earth, etc.

crus·ta'cean (-shən) *n.* hard-shelled invertebrate, as a shrimp or crab

crust'y *a.* bad-tempered

crutch *n.* **1** support held under the arm to aid in walking **2** prop

crux *n.* essential point

cry *v.* **cried, cry'ing 1** utter loudly **2** sob; weep —*n., pl.* **cries 1** a shout **2** entreaty **3** call of a bird, etc. —**a far cry** a great difference

cry'ba'by *n., pl.* **-bies** childish complainer

cry'o·gen'ics *n.* science dealing with very low temperatures

crypt (kript) *n.* underground (burial) vault

cryp'tic *a.* secret; mysterious —**cryp'ti·cal·ly** *adv.*

cryp·tog'ra·phy *n.* secret-code writing or deciphering —**cryp·tog'ra·pher** *n.*

crys'tal *n.* **1** clear quartz **2** clear, brilliant glass **3** solidified substance with its molecules arranged symmetrically —**crys'tal·line** (-lin) *a.*

crys'tal·lize' *v.* **1** form crystals **2** take on or give definite form —**crys'tal·li·za'tion** *n.*

C'-sec'tion *n.* cesarean (section)

CST *abbrev.* Central Standard Time

CT *abbrev.* **1** Central Time **2** Connect-

icut

CT scan *n.* computerized X-ray photography used for medical diagnosis

cu *abbrev.* cubic

cub *n.* young bear, lion, etc.

cub'by·hole' *n.* small, enclosed space

cube *n.* **1** a solid with six equal, square sides **2** product obtained by multiplying a number by its square —*v.* **1** get the CUBE (*n.* 2) of **2** cut into cubes —**cu'bic, cu'bi·cal** *a.*

cube root *n.* quantity that when cubed produces another, given quantity

cu'bi·cle *n.* small room

cu'bit *n.* ancient measure of length, about 18-22 inches

cuck'old *n.* man whose wife is unfaithful

cuck·oo (koo'koo') *n.* brown, slender bird —*a.* [Sl.] crazy

cu'cum·ber *n.* long, green-skinned, fleshy vegetable

cud *n.* food regurgitated by cattle and chewed again

cud'dle *v.* hold or lie close and snug —**cud'dle·some, cud'dly** *a.*

cudg'el (kuj'-) *v., n.* (beat with) a short club

cue *n.* **1** signal to begin **2** hint **3** rod for striking a billiard ball —*v.* to signal

cue ball *n.* in billiards, etc., white ball that the cue strikes

cuff *n.* **1** band or fold at the wrist of a sleeve or the bottom of a trouser leg **2** a slap —*v.* to slap

cuff link *n.* clip for closing a shirt cuff

cui·sine' (kwi zēn') *n.* style of cooking

cuke *n.* [Inf.] a cucumber

cul'-de·sac' *n.* road, etc. with only one outlet

cu'li·nar·y (kyōo'lə-, kul'ə-) *a.* of cookery

cull *v.* pick over; select

cul'mi·nate' *v.* reach its highest point —**cul'mi·na'tion** *n.*

cu·lotte' *n.* often *pl.* woman's wide-leg trousers resembling a skirt

cul'pa·ble *a.* deserving blame —**cul'pa·bil'i·ty** *n.*

cul'prit *n.* one guilty of a crime

cult *n.* **1** system of worship or group of worshipers **2** devoted attachment to person, fad, etc.

cul'ti·vate' *v.* **1** prepare (land) for crops **2** grow (plants) **3** develop, as the mind —**cul'ti·va'tion** *n.*

cul'ture *n.* **1** animal or plant breeding **2** improvement of the mind, manners, etc. **3** civilization of a people or period —**cul'tur·al** *a.*

cul'vert *n.* drain or waterway under a road, etc.

cum (kum, koom) *prep.* with

cum'ber·some *a.* unwieldy

cum·in (kum'in, koo'min) *n.* aromatic fruit used for flavoring

cum'mer·bund' *n.* sash worn around the waist by men

cu·mu·la·tive (kyoo'mya-) *a.* increasing by additions

cu'mu·lus *n.* a cloud having rounded masses piled up

cu·ne'i·form' *n.* ancient wedge-shaped writing

cun'ning *a.* 1 skilled in deception; sly; crafty 2 pretty; cute —*n.* skill in deception; craft

cup *n.* small bowl with handle, for beverages —*v.* **cupped, cup'ping** shape like a cup —**cup'ful'** *n.*, *pl.* **-fuls'**

cup'board (kub'ərd) *n.* cabinet for dishes, food, etc.

cup'cake' *n.* small cake

cu'pid (kyoo'-) *n.* naked cherub representing Roman god of love

cu·pid'i·ty *n.* greed

cu'po·la (kyoo'-) *n.* small dome

cu'pro·nick'el (kyoo'-) *n.* alloy of copper and nickel

cur *n.* 1 mongrel dog 2 contemptible person

cu·rate (kyoor'ət) *n.* clergyman helping a vicar or rector

cu'ra·tive *a.* having the power to cure —*n.* a remedy

cu·ra'tor (or kyoor'āt'ər) *n.* one in charge of a museum, etc. —**cu·ra·to'ri·al** *a.*

curb *n.* 1 restraining strap on a horse's bit 2 thing that restrains 3 raised edging along a street —*v.* to restrain

curb'stone' *n.* stones making up a curb: also **curb'ing**

curd *n.* often *pl.* coagulated part of soured milk

cur'dle *v.* form into curd

cure *n.* 1 a healing 2 remedy —*v.* 1 make well; heal 2 remedy 3 preserve (meat) —**cur'a·ble** *a.*

cure'-all' *n.* something supposed to cure everything

cu·ret·tage (kyoo ret'ij) *n.* a cleaning or scraping of the walls of a body cavity

cur'few' *n.* evening deadline for being off the streets

cu'ri·o' *n.*, *pl.* **-os'** odd art object

cu·ri·os'i·ty *n.* 1 desire to know 2 *pl.* **-ties** oddity

cu·ri·ous *a.* 1 eager to know; inquisi-

tive 2 strange

curl *v.* 1 twist (hair, etc.) into ringlets 2 curve around; coil —*n.* 1 ringlet of hair 2 any curling —**curl'er** *n.* — **curl'y** *a.*, **-i·er, -i·est**

cur'lew' *n.* wading bird

curl'i·cue' *n.* fancy curve

curl'ing *n.* game played on ice by sliding a flat stone

cur·mudg'eon (-muj'ən) *n.* cantankerous person

cur'rant *n.* 1 small, seedless raisin 2 sour berry

cur'ren·cy *n.*, *pl.* **-cies** 1 money circulated in a country 2 general use

cur'rent *a.* 1 of this day, week, etc. 2 commonly accepted or known —*n.* flow of air, water, electricity, etc.

cur·ric'u·lum *n.*, *pl.* **-lums** or **-la** course of study

cur'ry *n.* spicy powder or sauce —*v.* **-ried, -ry·ing** brush the coat of (a horse, etc.) —**curry favor** try to win favor, as by flattery

curse *v.* **cursed** or **curst, curs'ing** 1 call or bring evil down on 2 swear (at) — *n.* 1 a cursing 2 evil or injury —**be cursed with** suffer from —**curs'ed** *a.*

cur'sive (-siv) *a.* of writing with joined letters

cur'sor *n.* movable indicator light on a computer screen

cur'so·ry *a.* hastily done —**cur'so·ri·ly** *adv.*

curt *a.* so brief as to be rude —**curt'ly** *adv.* —**curt'ness** *n.*

cur·tail' *v.* cut short —**cur·tail'ment** *n.*

cur'tain *n.* anything that conceals or closes off, esp. a decorative cloth hung at a window —*v.* cover or decorate with a curtain

curt'sy *n.*, *pl.* **-sies** respectful bow with bended knees made by women —*v.* **-sied, -sy·ing** make a curtsy

cur·va'ceous *a.* having a full, rounded body shape: said of a woman

curve *n.* line, surface, etc. having no straight part —*v.* form or move in a curve —**cur'va·ture** *n.*

cush'ion *n.* 1 pillow or pad 2 something absorbing shock —*v.* provide with or act as a cushion

cush'y *a.*, **-i·er, -i·est** [Sl.] easy; comfortable

cusp *n.* arched, pointed end —**on the cusp** just before a major change

cus'pi·dor' *n.* spittoon

cuss *n.*, *v.* [Inf.] curse

cus'tard *n.* pudding made with eggs, milk, and sugar

cus·to'di·an *n.* 1 one having custody

2 janitor

cus'to·dy *n.* 1 guarding; care 2 imprisonment —**cus·to'di·al** *a.*

cus'tom *n.* 1 usual or traditional practice; usage 2 *pl.* duties on imported goods 3 *pl.* [*with sing. v.*] government agency collecting such duties —*a.* made to order: also **cus'tom-built'** or **cus'tom-made'**

cus'tom·ar'y *a.* usual —**cus'tom·ar'i·ly** *adv.*

cus'tom·er *n.* one who buys

cus'tom·ize' *v.* make according to personal specifications

cut *v.* **cut, cut'ting** 1 to gash 2 pierce 3 sever 4 hew 5 reap 6 trim 7 pass across 8 reduce 9 change direction suddenly —*n.* 1 a cutting 2 part cut open or off 3 reduction 4 style 5 picture made by engraving 6 insult 7 [Inf.] a swing at a ball 8 [Inf.] share, as of profits —**cut and dried** dull; boring —**cut down (on)** reduce —**cut out for** suited for

cut'back' *n.* reduction or discontinuing of production, etc.

cute *a.* [Inf.] 1 clever 2 pretty or pleasing

cut'i·cle (kyōōt'i-) *n.* 1 hardened skin, as at the base of a fingernail 2 outer structure as of some insects, etc.

cut'lass *n.* short, thick, curved sword

cut'ler·y *n.* cutting tools, as knives, scissors, etc.

cut'let *n.* small slice of meat

cut'off' *n.* 1 shortcut road, etc. 2 device for shutting off flow of a fluid, etc. 3 *pl.* jeans with knee-length legs

cut'-rate' *a.* selling or on sale at a lower price

cut'ter *n.* small, swift ship

cut'throat' *n.* murderer —*a.* merciless

cut'ting *n.* shoot cut from a plant —*a.* 1 sharp 2 piercing 3 sarcastic

cutting edge *n.* the leading or most advanced position; vanguard

cut'tle·fish' *n.* mollusk with eight arms and large eyes

-cy *suf.* 1 quality or state of being 2 position, rank, or office of

cy'a·nide' (sī'-) *n.* poisonous white compound

cy·ber·net'ics *n.* comparative study of electronic computers and the human nervous system

cy'ber·space' *n.* electronic system of linked computers for information and interaction

cy'cla·mate' *n.* artificial sweetener

cy'cle *n.* 1 complete round of regular events, or period for this 2 bicycle, etc. —*v.* ride a bicycle, etc. —**cy·clic** (sik'lik), **cy'cli·cal** *a.* —**cy'clist** *n.*

cy'clone' *n.* storm with heavy rain and whirling winds

cy'clo·tron' *n.* apparatus that speeds up particles, as to split atomic nuclei

cyg'net (sig'-) *n.* young swan

cyl'in·der *n.* round figure with two flat ends that are parallel circles —**cy·lin'dri·cal** *a.*

cym'bal *n.* round brass plate used as a percussion instrument

cyn'ic *n.* one inclined to question goodness, sincerity, etc. —**cyn'i·cal** *n.* —**cyn'i·cism'** *n.*

cy'no·sure' (sī'nə-, sin'ə-) *n.* center of attention

cy'press *n.* evergreen tree

cyst (sist) *n.* sac containing fluid or hard matter —**cyst'ic** *a.*

cystic fibrosis *n.* children's disease of the pancreas

czar (zär) *n.* Russian emperor

D

d *abbrev.* 1 degree 2 diameter 3 died

DA, D.A. *abbrev.* District Attorney

dab *v.* **dabbed, dab'bing** put on with light, quick strokes —*n.* soft or moist bit —**dab'ber** *n.*

dab'ble *v.* 1 splash in water 2 do something superficially: with *in* or *at* —**dab'bler** *n.*

dace *n.* small freshwater fish

dachs·hund (däks'ənd) *n.* small dog with a long body

Da·cron (dā'krän', dak'rän') *trademark* synthetic fabric or fiber —*n.* [**d-**] this fabric or fiber

dad *n.* [Inf.] father: also **dad'dy**, *pl.* **-dies**

daddy long'legs' *n.*, *pl.* **-legs'** long-legged arachnid

da'do (dā'-) *n.*, *pl.* **-does** 1 groove in a board forming a joint 2 lower part of a wall decorated differently

daf'fo·dil' *n.* yellow flower

daf'fy *a.* **-fi·er, -fi·est** [Inf.] crazy; silly

daft *a.* 1 silly 2 insane

dag'ger *n.* 1 short, sharp-pointed weapon 2 printed reference mark (†)

dahl·ia (dal'yə) *n.* plant with large, showy flowers

dai'ly *a., adv.* (done or happening) every day —*n.* daily newspaper

daily double *n.* bet won by choosing winners in two races on a program

dain'ty *a.* **-ti·er, -ti·est** 1 delicately pretty 2 fastidious —*n., pl.* **-ties** a delicacy **—dain'ti·ly** adv. **—dain'ti·ness** n.

dai·qui·ri (dak'ər ē) n. cocktail with rum, lemon juice, etc.

dair'y n., pl. **-ies** place where milk, butter, etc. are made or sold **—dair'y·man** n., pl. **-men**

da·is (dā'is, dī'-) n. speaker's platform

dai'sy n., pl. **-sies** flower with white rays around a yellow disk

dale n. small valley

dal'ly v. **-lied, -ly·ing 1** to toy or flirt **2** loiter **—dal'li·ance** (or dal'yəns) n.

Dal·ma'tian (-shən) n. large, black-and-white dog

dam n. **1** barrier to hold back flowing water **2** female parent of a horse, cow, etc. —v. **dammed, dam'ming** keep back; confine

dam'age n. **1** injury; harm **2** pl. money paid for harm done —v. do damage to

dam'ask n. fabric with figured weave —a. deep-pink

dame n. **1** lady **2** [D-] woman's title of honor in Britain **3** [Sl.] any woman

damn (dam) v. **damned, damn'ing** condemn; declare bad, doomed, etc. —a., adv. [Inf.] damned **—dam'na·ble** a. **—dam·na'tion** n.

damned a. **1** condemned **2** [Inf.] outrageous —adv. [Inf.] very

damp n. **1** moisture **2** mine gas —a. slightly wet; moist —v. **1** moisten **2** check or deaden Also **damp'en**

damp'-dry' v. **-dried', -dry'ing** dry with some moisture retained

damp'er n. **1** thing that depresses or lessens **2** valve in a flue to control the draft

dam'sel (-zəl) n. girl: old-fashioned

dam'son (-zən, -sən) n. small, purple plum

dance v. move in rhythm to music —n. **1** rhythmic movement to music **2** party or music for dancing **—danc'er** n.

D and C n. medical procedure in which tissue is scraped from uterus

dan·de·li'on n. common weed with yellow flowers

dan'der n. [Inf.] anger

dan'dle v. dance (a child) up and down on the knee

dan'druff n. little scales of dead skin on the scalp

dan'dy n., pl. **-dies** vain man —a. **-di·er, -di·est** [Inf.] very good; first-rate

dan'ger n. **1** liability to injury, loss, etc.; peril **2** thing that may cause injury, etc. **—dan'ger·ous** a.

dan'gle v. hang loosely

Dan'ish (dān'-) a. of the people or language of Denmark —n. **1** language of Denmark **2** [also d-] pastry with a filling

dank a. disagreeably damp **—dank'ness** n.

dap'per a. trim; spruce

dap'ple a. spotted; mottled: also **dap'pled** —v. mottle

dare v. **1** have the courage (to) **2** challenge —n. a challenge **—dare say** think probable **—dar'ing** a., n.

dare'dev'il n., a. (one who is) bold and reckless

dark a. **1** with little or no light **2** not light in color **3** gloomy **4** ignorant —n. a being dark **—dark'en** v. **—dark'ly** adv. **—dark'ness** n.

Dark Ages pl.n. first half of the Middle Ages

dark horse n. one who wins or may win unexpectedly

dark'room' n. dark room for developing photographs

dar'ling n., a. beloved

darn v. mend by sewing

dart n. **1** small pointed weapon for throwing **2** sudden movement —v. to throw or move quickly

dash v. **1** smash **2** strike violently against **3** do hastily: with off **4** rush —n. **1** bit of something **2** short race **3** vigor **4** mark of punctuation (—)

dash'board' n. instrument panel in an automobile

dash'ing a. lively

das'tard·ly a. cowardly

da·ta (dāt'ə, dat'ə) pl.n. [sing. or pl. v.] facts; information

da'ta·base' n. large mass of organized data in a computer: also **data base**

data proc'ess·ing n. handling of data, esp. by computer

date n. **1** time of an event **2** day of the month **3** social engagement **4** fruit of a tall palm —v. **1** mark with a date **2** belong to a particular time

date'book' n. notebook for entering appointments, etc.

date rape n. rape by an acquaintance

daub (dôb) v. **1** smear with sticky stuff **2** paint badly

daugh'ter n. female as she is related to her parents

daugh'ter-in-law' n., pl. **daugh'ters-** wife of one's son

daunt (dônt) v. dishearten

daunt'less a. fearless

dau'phin (dô'-, dô'-) n. [Hist.] eldest son of the French king

dav'en·port' n. large sofa

daw'dle v. waste time; loiter

dawn v. **1** begin to be day **2** begin to be understood —n. **1** daybreak **2** beginning

day n. **1** period from sunrise to sunset **2** period of 24 hours, esp. from midnight to midnight **3** a period; era — **day'light'** n. —**day'time'** n.

day'bed' n. couch usable as a bed

day'break' n. time of the first light in the morning

day care n. daytime care for children or adults —**day'-care'** a.

day'dream' n. pleasant, dreamy thinking or wishing —v. have daydreams

day'light' n. **1** sunlight **2** daytime **3** understanding

daylight saving(s) time n. time one hour later than standard

Day of Atonement n. Yom Kippur

day'time' n. time between dawn and sunset

day'-to-day' a. daily; routine

daze v. **1** stun **2** dazzle —n. dazed condition

daz'zle v. overpower with light or brilliance

dba abbrev. doing business as

DBS abbrev. direct broadcast satellite

DC abbrev. **1** direct current **2** District of Columbia

DD, D.D. abbrev. Doctor of Divinity

DDS, D.D.S. abbrev. Doctor of Dental Surgery

DDT n. powerful insecticide

DE abbrev. Delaware

de- pref. **1** away from; off **2** reverse the action of

dea·con (dē'kən) n. one who assists a minister

de·ac'ti·vate' v. **1** make (an explosive, etc.) inactive **2** disband (troops)

dead (ded) a. **1** not living **2** dull; inactive **3** complete **4** [Inf.] exhausted —n. time of most cold, darkness, etc. —adv. completely

dead'beat' n. [Sl.] **1** one who avoids paying for things **2** lazy, idle person

dead'bolt' n. door lock with a long, square bolt worked by a key

dead'en v. to dull

dead end n. street closed at one end — **dead'-end'** a.

dead heat n. a tie in a race

dead'line' n. time limit

dead'lock' n. standstill with equal forces opposed

dead'ly a. **-li·er, -li·est** fatal —adv. **1** like death **2** extremely

dead'-on' a. [Inf.] accurate; exact

dead'pan' a., adv. without expression

dead'wood' n. useless thing

deaf (def) a. **1** unable to hear **2** unwilling to respond —**deaf'en** v.

deaf'-mute' n. deaf person who has not learned speech

deal v. **dealt** (delt), **deal'ing 1** distribute **2** have to do (with) **3** do business —n. transaction or agreement —a **good** (or **great**) **deal 1** large amount **2** very much —**deal'er** n. —**deal'ing** n.

deal'er·ship' n. a franchise

dean n. **1** church or college official **2** senior member of a group

dean's list n. list of students with highest grades at a college

dear a. **1** much loved **2** esteemed **3** costly **4** earnest —n. darling

dearth (durth) n. scarcity

death n. **1** a dying or being dead **2** cause of death

death'bed' n. used chiefly in **on one's deathbed**, dying

death'less a. immortal

death'ly a. characteristic of death — adv. extremely

de·ba·cle (də bäk'əl) n. complete defeat or failure

de·bar' v. **-barred', -bar'ring** exclude (from)

de·bark' v. leave a ship or aircraft — **de'bar·ka'tion** n.

de·base' v. to lower in quality, etc. — **de·base'ment** n.

de·bate' v. argue in a formal way —n. formal argument —**de·bat'a·ble** a. — **de·bat'er** n.

de·bauch' (-bôch') v. to corrupt —n. orgy —**de·bauch'er·y** n., pl. **-ies**

de·ben'ture n. bond issued by a corporation, etc.

de·bil'i·tate' v. make weak —**de·bil'i·ta'tion** n.

de·bil'i·ty n. weakness

deb'it n. entry in an account of money owed —v. enter as a debt

debit card n. bank card that deducts cost of purchases from one's bank account

deb'o·nair' a. elegant and gracious; urbane: also sp. **deb'o·naire'**

de·brief' v. receive information from about a recent mission

de·bris' (-brē') n. broken, scattered remains; rubbish

debt (det) n. **1** something owed **2** state of owing

debt'or n. one owing a debt

de·bug' v. remove bugs, errors, etc. from

de·bunk' v. to expose the false claims, etc. of

de·but' (-byōō') n. **1** first public appearance, as of an actor **2** a formal introduction into society

deb'u·tante' (-tänt') n. girl making a social debut

dec abbrev. deceased

Dec abbrev. December

dec'ade' n. ten-year period

dec'a·dence n. a declining, as in morals or art —**dec'a·dent** a., n.

de·caf'fein·at'ed (-kaf'ə nāt'-) a. having its caffeine removed

de'cal' n. picture for transfer from prepared paper

Dec'a·logue', Dec'a·log' n. [sometimes d-] Ten Commandments

de·camp' v. leave secretly

de·cant' v. pour off gently

de·cant'er n. decorative bottle for serving wine

de·cap'i·tate' v. behead —**de·cap'i·ta'tion** n.

de·cath'lon' n. contest of ten track and field events

de·cay' v. **1** fall into ruin **2** rot —n. a decaying; rot

de·cease' n. death

de·ceased' a. dead —**the deceased** dead person(s)

de·ceit' (-sēt') n. **1** act of deceiving **2** deceitful quality —**de·ceit'ful** a.

de·ceive' v. make believe what is not true; mislead

de·cel'er·ate' v. to slow down —**de·cel'er·a'tion** n.

De·cem'ber n. 12th month

de'cent a. **1** proper **2** respectable **3** adequate —**de'cen·cy** n.

de·cen'tral·ize' v. shift power from main to local units

de·cep'tion n. **1** a deceiving **2** illusion or fraud —**de·cep'tive** a.

dec'i·bel n. unit for measuring loudness of sound

de·cide' v. **1** settle by passing judgment **2** make up one's mind

de·cid'ed a. definite —**de·cid'ed·ly** adv.

de·cid'u·ous (-sij'ōō-) a. shedding leaves annually

dec'i·mal a. based on the number ten —n. a fraction with a denominator of ten or a power of ten, shown by a point (**decimal point**) before the numerator

dec'i·mate' v. destroy or kill a large part of

de·ci'pher (-sī'-) v. translate from code or illegibility

de·ci'sion (-sizh'ən) n. **1** a deciding **2** judgment **3** determination

de·ci'sive (-sī'siv) a. **1** conclusive **2** showing decision

deck n. **1** floor of a ship **2** pack of playing cards —v. adorn; trim

de·claim' v. speak in a loud, rhetorical way —**dec'la·ma'tion** n. —**de·clam'a·to'ry** a.

de·clare' v. **1** announce formally **2** say emphatically —**dec'la·ra'tion** n. —**de·clar'a·tive** a.

de·clas'si·fy' v. make (secret documents) public and available

de·clen'sion n. grammatical inflection of nouns, etc.

de·cline' v. **1** slope downward **2** lessen, as in force **3** refuse politely **4** Gram. give inflected forms of —n. **1** a failing, decay, etc. **2** downward slope

de·cliv'i·ty n. downward slope

de·code' v. translate (a coded message) into plain language

dé·col·le·té' (dā käl'ə tā') a. cut low so as to bare the neck and shoulders

de·com·pose' v. **1** break up into basic parts **2** rot —**de'com·po·si'tion** n.

de'com·press' v. free from air pressure —**de'com·pres'sion** n.

de'con·gest'ant n. medicine that relieves congestion, as of nasal passages

de·con·tam'i·nate' v. to rid of a harmful substance

dé·cor, de·cor (dā kôr') n. decorative scheme

dec'o·rate' v. **1** adorn; ornament **2** give a medal to —**dec'o·ra·tive** a. —**dec'o·ra·tor** n. —**dec·o·ra'tion** n.

de·co'rum n. proper behavior —**dec'o·rous** a. —**dec'o·rous·ly** adv.

de'coy' n. artificial bird, etc. used as a lure —v. lure

de·crease' (or dē'krēs') v. grow or make less or smaller —n. a decreasing

de·cree' n. official order; edict —v. **-creed', -cree'ing** order by decree

de·crep'it a. old and worn out —**de·crep'it·ly** adv. —**de·crep'i·tude'** n.

de·cre·scen'do (dā'krə shen'-) a., adv. Mus. (getting) gradually louder

de·crim'i·nal·ize' v. eliminate or reduce the penalties for

de·cry' v. **-cried', -cry'ing** to denounce

ded'i·cate' v. **1** set apart formally **2** devote **3** inscribe —**ded'i·ca'tion** n.

de·duce' v. conclude by reasoning; infer —**de·duc'i·ble** a.

de·duct' v. subtract or take away —**de·duct'i·ble** a.

de·duc'tion n. **1** a deducing or deducting **2** amount deducted **3** conclusion

deed n. **1** act **2** feat of courage, etc. **3** legal document transferring property —v. to transfer by deed

deem v. think; believe

de·em'pha·size' v. make less important

deep a. **1** extending far down, in, or back **2** hard to understand **3** involved (in) **4** of low pitch **5** intense —n. deep place or part —adv. far down, etc. —**deep'en** v.

deep'-dish' pie n. pie baked in a deep dish with top crust only

deep'freeze' v. freeze (food) suddenly so as to preserve

deep'-fry' v. fry in deep pan of boiling fat or oil

deep'-seat'ed a. firmly fixed: also **deep'-root'ed**

deep space n. outer space

deer n., pl. **deer** hoofed, cud-chewing animal, the male of which bears antlers

de·es'ca·late' v. reduce in scope

de·face' v. mar

de fac'to a., adv. existing but not officially approved

de·fame' v. slander —**def'a·ma'tion** n. —**de·fam'a·to·ry** a.

de·fang' v. render harmless

de·fault' v., n. fail(ure) to do or pay as required

de·feat' v. **1** win victory over **2** frustrate —n. a defeating or being defeated

de·feat'ist n., a. (one) too readily accepting defeat

def'e·cate' v. excrete waste matter from the bowels

de'fect' (v.: dē fekt') n. imperfection; fault —v. to desert —**de·fec'tion** n. —**de·fec'tive** a.

de·fend' v. **1** protect **2** support by speech or act **3** Law act for (an accused) —**de·fend'er** n.

de·fend'ant n. Law person sued or accused

de·fense' n. **1** a defending against attack **2** something that defends **3** defendant and his counsel —**de·fense'less** a. —**de·fen'sive** a., n.

de·fer' v. **-ferred', -fer'ring 1** postpone **2** to yield in opinion, etc.

def'er·ence n. **1** a yielding in opinion, etc. **2** respect

de·fer'ment n. a deferring or postponing: also **de·fer'ral**

de·fi'ance n. open resistance to authority —**de·fi'ant** a.

de·fi'cien·cy (-fish'ən-) n., pl. **-cies** shortage; lack —**de·fi'cient** a.

deficiency disease n. disease due to lack of vitamins, minerals, etc.

def'i·cit n. amount by which a sum of money is less than expected, etc.

de·file' v. dirty; sully —n. narrow pass

de·fine' v. **1** mark the limits of **2** state the meaning of —**def'i·ni'tion** n.

def'i·nite a. **1** having exact limits **2** explicit **3** certain —**def'i·nite·ly** adv.

de·fin'i·tive a. **1** conclusive **2** most nearly complete

de·flate' v. **1** collapse by letting out air **2** lessen in amount, importance, etc. —**de·fla'tion** n.

de·flect' v. turn to one side

de·fog'ger n. device for clearing moisture from a window in a car, etc.

de·fo'li·ant n. chemical that strips plants of leaves

de·fo'li·ate' v. remove leaves from (trees, etc.)

de·for'est v. clear (land) of trees or forests —**de·for'est·a'tion** n.

de·form' v. mar the form of —**de·form'i·ty** n., pl. **-ties**

de·formed' a. misshapen

de·fraud' v. cheat

de·fray' v. pay (the cost)

de·frost' v. rid or become rid of frost or ice

deft a. quick and skillful

de·funct' a. no longer existing

de·fuse' v. **1** remove the fuse from (a bomb, etc.) **2** make less tense, etc.

de·fy' v. **-fied', -fy'ing 1** resist openly **2** dare

de·gen'er·ate' (-āt'; a., n.: -ət) v. **1** deteriorate **2** to become corrupt morally, etc. —a. **1** deteriorated **2** depraved —n. a degenerate person —**de·gen'er·a·cy** n. —**de·gen'er·a'tion** n.

de·grad'a·ble a. readily decomposed by chemical action

de·grade' v. lower in rank, value, etc. —**deg'ra·da'tion** n.

de·gree' n. **1** successive step in a series **2** intensity, extent, etc. **3** rank given to a college graduate **4** unit of measure for angles, temperature, etc.

de·greed' a. having a college degree

de·hu'man·ize' v. deprive of human qualities —**de·hu'man·i·za'tion** n.

de·hu'mid·i·fy' v. **-fied', -fy'ing** remove moisture from (air, etc.) —**de·hu·mid'i·fi'er** n.

de·hy'drate' v. remove water from —**de·hy·dra'tion** n.

de-ice' v. to melt ice from (something)

—de·ic'er n.

de'i·fy' v. -fied', -fy'ing make a god of —de·i·fi·ca'tion n.

deign (dān) v. condescend

de'ism' n. belief in God on purely rational grounds —de'ist n.

de'i·ty n., pl. -ties god or goddess

dé·jà vu (dā'zhä vōō') n. feeling that one has been in a place or has had an experience before

de·ject'ed a. sad; depressed

de·jec'tion n. depression; sadness

de·lay' v. 1 put off; postpone 2 make late; detain —n. a delaying

de·lec'ta·ble —a. delightful

de'lec·ta'tion n. delight

del'e·gate (-gət; v.: -gāt') n. representative —v. 1 appoint as delegate 2 entrust to another

del'e·ga'tion n. group of delegates

de·lete' v. take out (a word, etc.) —de·le'tion n.

del'e·te'ri·ous (-tir'ē-) a. harmful to health, etc.

del'i n. delicatessen

de·lib'er·ate' (-āt'; a.: -gāt') v. consider carefully —a. 1 done on purpose 2 not rash or hasty 3 unhurried —de·lib'er·a'tion n.

del'i·ca·cy n. 1 delicate quality 2 pl. -cies a choice food; dainty

del'i·cate a. 1 fine and lovely 2 fragile or frail 3 needing care 4 sensitive 5 considerate and tactful —del'i·cate·ly adv. —del'i·cate·ness n.

del'i·ca·tes'sen n. shop selling meats, fish, cheeses, etc.

de·li'cious (-lish'əs) a. very pleasing, esp. to taste or smell

de·light' v. please greatly —n. great pleasure —de·light'ful a.

de·lim'it v. fix the limits of

de·lin'e·ate' v. 1 draw; sketch 2 describe

de·lin'quent a. 1 not obeying duty or law 2 overdue —n. one guilty of minor crimes —de·lin'quen·cy n.

del'i·quesce' (-kwes') v. become liquid by absorbing moisture from the air

de·lir'i·um n. 1 temporary mental state of restlessness, hallucinations, etc. 2 wild excitement —de·lir'i·ous a.

de·liv'er v. 1 set free; rescue 2 assist in birth of 3 utter 4 hand over 5 distribute 6 strike or throw —de·liv'er·ance n.

de·liv'er·y n., pl. -ies a delivering or something delivered

dell n. small valley

del·phin'i·um n. tall plant with flower spikes

del'ta n. 1 letter of Greek alphabet 2 soil deposit at a river mouth

de·lude' v. mislead

del'uge' (-yōōj') n. 1 great flood 2 heavy rainfall —v. 1 to flood 2 overwhelm

de·lu'sion n. false, esp. psychotic, belief —de·lu'sive a.

de·luxe' a. very good; elegant

delve v. investigate

Dem abbrev. Democrat(ic)

dem'a·gogue', dem'a·gog' (-gäg') n. one who appeals to prejudices, etc. to win power —dem'a·gog'y (-gä'jē), dem'a·gogu'er·y (-gäg'ər ē) n.

de·mand' v. 1 ask for boldly 2 require —n. 1 strong request 2 requirement —on demand when presented for payment

de'mar·ca'tion n. boundary line

de·mean' v. degrade

de·mean'or n. behavior

de·ment'ed a. mentally ill; crazy

de·men'tia (-shə) n. loss of mental powers

de·mer'it n. 1 fault 2 mark for poor work, etc.

demi- pref. half

dem'i·god' n. minor deity

de·mil'i·ta·rize' v. to free from military control

de·mise' (-mīz') n. death

dem'i·tasse' (-tas') n. small cup of coffee

dem'o n., pl. -mos recording made to demonstrate a song, etc.

de·mo'bi·lize' v. to disband (troops)

de·moc'ra·cy n., pl. -cies 1 government in which the power is vested in all the people 2 equality of rights, etc. —dem'o·crat' n. —dem'o·crat'ic a. —dem'o·crat'i·cal·ly adv.

de·mog'ra·phy n. statistical study of populations —dem'o·graph'ic a.

de·mol'ish v. destroy; ruin —dem'o·li'tion n.

de'mon n. 1 devil; evil spirit 2 evil, cruel person or thing —de·mon'ic a. —de·mon'i·cal·ly adv.

de'mon·ize' v. make as if a devil, evil person, etc. —de'mon·i·za'tion n.

dem'on·strate' v. 1 prove 2 explain with examples 3 show the working of 4 show feelings publicly —de·mon'stra·ble a. —dem'on·stra'tion n. —dem'on·stra'tor n.

de·mon'stra·tive a. 1 showing clearly 2 giving proof (of) 3 showing feelings openly —de·mon'stra·tive·ly adv.

de·mor'al·ize' v. to lower in morale —

de·mor·al·i·za'tion n.

de·mote' v. reduce in rank —**de·mo'tion** n.

de·mul'cent a., n. soothing (ointment)

de·mur' (-mur') v. -**murred'**, -**mur'ring** to scruple (at) —n. objection

de·mure' (-myoor') a. modest

den n. 1 animal's lair 2 haunt of thieves, etc. 3 small, cozy room

de·na'ture v. to make (alcohol) unfit to drink

de·ni'al n. 1 a denying 2 contradiction

den'i·grate' v. belittle the character of; defame —**den'i·gra'tion** n.

den'im n. coarse, twilled cotton cloth

den'i·zen n. inhabitant

de·nom'i·nate' v. to name

de·nom'i·na'tion n. 1 a name 2 specific class or kind 3 specific religious group —**de·nom'·i·na'tion·al** a.

de·nom'i·na'tor n. term below the line in a fraction

de·note' v. 1 indicate 2 mean explicitly —**de·no·ta'tion** n.

de·noue·ment, dé·noue·ment (dā'nōō·män') n. unraveling of a plot

de·nounce' v. 1 accuse publicly 2 condemn strongly

dense a. 1 packed tightly 2 thick 3 stupid —**dense'ly** adv.

den'si·ty n. 1 number per unit 2 ratio of the mass of an object to its volume

dent n. slight hollow made in a surface by a blow —v. make a dent in

den'tal a. of the teeth

dental floss n. thread for removing food from the teeth

den'ti·frice (-fris) n. substance for cleaning teeth

den'tin (-tin) n. tissue under the enamel of teeth: also **den'tine'** (-tēn', -tin)

den'tist n. one who cares for and repairs teeth —**den'tist·ry** n.

den'ture n. often pl. set of artificial teeth

de·nude' v. make bare; strip

de·nun'ci·a'tion n. a denouncing

de·ny' v. 1 declare untrue 2 refuse to give, accept, etc. —**deny oneself** do without

de·o'dor·ize' v. counteract the odor of —**de·o'dor·ant** a., n. —**de·o'dor·iz'er** n.

de·part' v. 1 leave 2 die 3 deviate (from) —**de·par'ture** n.

de·part'ment n. 1 division 2 field of activity —**de'part·men'tal** a. —**de'part·men'tal·ize'** v.

department store n. large retail store

with goods arranged in departments

de·pend' v. 1 be determined by something else 2 rely, as for support —**de·pend'ence** n. —**de·pend'en·cy** n., pl. **-cies** —**de·pend'ent** a., n.

de·pend'a·ble a. reliable —**de·pend'a·bil'i·ty** n.

de·pict' v. 1 represent by drawing, etc. 2 describe

de·pil'a·to'ry n., pl. **-ries**; a. (substance or device for) removing unwanted hair

de·plane' v. leave an airplane after it lands

de·plete' v. 1 empty (wholly) 2 exhaust —**de·ple'tion** n.

de·plore' v. 1 be sorry about 2 disapprove of —**de·plor'a·ble** a.

de·ploy' v. Mil. to place (troops, etc.)

de·po'nent (-pōn'-) n. Law one who testifies in writing under oath

de·pop'u·late' v. to reduce the population of

de·port' v. 1 behave (oneself) 2 expel (an alien) —**de'por·ta'tion** n.

de·port'ment n. behavior

de·pose' v. 1 remove from office 2 Law obtain a written statement under oath from —**dep'o·si'tion** n.

de·pos'it v. 1 place for safekeeping 2 give as partial payment 3 set down —n. something deposited —**de·pos'i·tor** n.

de·pos'i·to'ry n., pl. **-ries** place to put things for safekeeping

de'pot (-pō) n. 1 warehouse 2 train or bus station

de·prave' v. make morally bad —**de·praved'** a. —**de·prav'i·ty** n.

dep're·cate' v. 1 express disapproval of 2 belittle —**dep're·ca'tion** n. —**dep're·ca·to'ry** a.

de·pre'ci·ate' (-shē-) v. 1 lessen in value 2 belittle —**de·pre'ci·a'tion** n.

dep're·da'tion n. a robbing or looting

de·press' v. 1 press down 2 sadden 3 lower in value, etc. —**de·pres'sant** a., n. —**de·pressed'** a.

de·pres'sion n. 1 a depressing 2 hollow place 3 dejection 4 condition marked by hopelessness, self-doubt, lethargy, etc. 5 period of reduced business and prosperity

de·pres'sur·ize' v. reduce pressure in

de·prive' v. take away or withhold from —**dep'ri·va'tion** n.

de·pro'gram v. undo indoctrination in

dept abbrev. 1 department 2 deputy

depth n. 1 distance from the top or back 2 deepness 3 profundity 4 pl. deepest part —**in depth** comprehensively; thoroughly

dep'u·ta'tion *n.* delegation

de·pute' *v.* 1 authorize as a deputy 2 appoint in one's place

dep'u·tize' *v.* appoint as deputy

dep'u·ty *n., pl.* **-ties** substitute or agent

de·rail' *v.* run off the rails —**de·rail'-ment** *n.*

de·rail'leur (-lər) *n.* device to shift gears on a bicycle

de·range' *v.* 1 upset or disturb 2 make insane —**de·range'ment** *n.*

der'by *n., pl.* **-bies** stiff felt hat with a round crown

de·reg'u·late' *v.* remove regulations governing —**de·reg'u·la'tion** *n.*

der'e·lict' *a.* 1 abandoned 2 negligent —*n.* 1 thing abandoned as worthless 2 destitute person —**der'e·lic'tion** *n.*

de·ride' *v.* to ridicule —**de·ri'sion** (-rizh'ən) *n.* —**de·ri'sive** (-ri'siv) *a.*

de·rive' *v.* 1 take or get (*from*) 2 deduce 3 come (*from*) —**der'i·va'tion** *n.* —**de·riv'a·tive** *a., n.*

der'ma·ti'tis *n.* inflammation of the skin

der'ma·tol'o·gy *n.* study of the skin and its diseases —**der'ma·tol'o·gist** *n.*

der'o·gate' *v.* detract (*from*) —**der'o-ga'tion** *n.*

de·rog'a·to'ry *a.* detracting; disparaging

der'rick *n.* 1 machine for moving heavy objects 2 framework for drilling, as over an oil well

der'ri·ère' (-ē er') *n.* the buttocks

der'vish *n.* Muslim ascetic

de·sal'i·na'tion (-sal'-) *n.* removal of salt from sea water to make it drinkable

de·scend' (-send') *v.* 1 move down 2 come from earlier times 3 derive 4 to make a sudden attack (*on*) —**de·scent'** *n.*

de·scend'ant *n.* offspring of a certain ancestor

de·scribe' *v.* picture in words; tell about —**de·scrip'tion** *n.* —**de·scrip'tive** *a.*

de·scry' *v.* **-scried', -scry'ing** catch sight of

des'e·crate' *v.* violate the sacredness of; profane —**des'e·cra'tion** *n.*

de·seg're·gate' *v.* end racial segregation (in) —**de·seg're·ga'tion** *n.*

de·sen'si·tize' *v.* make less sensitive —**de·sen'si·ti·za'tion** *n.*

de·sert' *v.* abandon —*n. often pl.* reward or punishment —**de·ser'tion** *n.*

des·ert' *n.* arid, sandy region

de·serve' *v.* be worthy of —**de·serv'ing** *a.*

des'ic·cate' *v.* dry up

de·sid'er·a'tum (-ə rät'əm) *n., pl.* **-ta** something needed and wanted

de·sign' *v.* 1 to plan 2 contrive 3 make original patterns, etc. —*n.* 1 plan; scheme 2 purpose 3 a pattern —**by design** purposely —**de·sign'er** *n.*

des'ig·nate' *v.* 1 to point out; specify 2 appoint —**des'ig·na'tion** *n.*

des'ig·nat'ed driver *n.* one of a group at a bar, etc. who refrains from alcohol so as to drive the others

de·sign'ing *a.* scheming; crafty

de·sire' *v.* wish or long for; want —*n.* 1 a wish 2 thing wished for 3 sexual appetite —**de·sir'a·ble** *a.* —**de·sir'ous** *a.*

de·sist' *v.* stop; cease

desk *n.* writing table

des'o·late (-lit; *v.:* -lāt') *a.* 1 lonely; forlorn 2 uninhabited 3 laid waste —*v.* make desolate —**des'o·la'tion** *n.*

de·spair' *v.* lose hope —*n.* loss of hope

des'per·a'do (-ä'-) *n., pl.* **-does** or **-dos** reckless outlaw

des'per·ate *a.* 1 reckless from despair 2 serious —**des'per·a'tion** *n.*

de·spi'ca·ble *a.* deserving scorn; contemptible

de·spise' *v.* 1 to scorn 2 loathe

de·spite' *prep.* in spite of

de·spoil' *v.* rob; plunder

de·spond'en·cy *n.* loss of hope; dejection: also **de·spond'ence** —**de·spond'-ent** *a.*

des'pot *n.* tyrant —**des·pot'ic** *a.* —**des'pot·ism'** *n.*

des·sert' *n.* sweet dish ending a meal

des'ti·na'tion *n.* place to which one is going

des'tine (-tin) *v.* head for, as by fate —**destined for** bound or intended for

des'ti·ny *n., pl.* **-nies** (one's) fate

des'ti·tute' *a.* needy —**destitute of** lacking —**des'ti·tu'tion** *n.*

de·stroy' *v.* 1 tear down; demolish 2 ruin 3 kill

de·stroy'er *n.* fast warship

de·struct' *v.* be automatically destroyed

de·struc'tion *n.* ruin —**de·struc'tive** *a.*

de·sul'to·ry *a.* 1 not methodical 2 random

de·tach' *v.* unfasten and remove —**de·tach'a·ble** *a.*

de·tached' *a.* aloof; impartial

de·tach'ment *n.* 1 separation 2 troops on special task 3 impartiality or aloofness

de·tail' (or dē'tāl') v. **1** tell minutely **2** Mil. choose for a special task —n. **1** minute account **2** small part **3** Mil. those chosen for a special task —**in detail** item by item

de·tain' v. **1** keep in custody **2** delay

de·tect' v. discover (thing hidden, etc.) —**de·tec'tion** n. —**de·tec'tor** n.

de·tec'tive n. one who investigates crimes, etc.

dé·tente, de·tente (dā tänt') n. lessening of tension between nations

de·ten'tion n. a detaining

de·ter' v. **-terred', -ter'ring** keep (a person) from an action —**de·ter'ment** n. —**de·ter'rence** n. —**de·ter'rent** a., n.

de·ter'gent a., n. cleansing (substance)

de·te'ri·o·rate' (-tir'ē-) v. make or become worse —**de·te'ri·o·ra'tion** n.

de·ter'mi·nant n. thing that determines

de·ter'mi·na'tion n. **1** firm intention **2** firmness of purpose

de·ter'mine v. **1** set limits to **2** decide; resolve **3** find out exactly —**de·ter'mined** a.

de·test' v. hate —**de·test'a·ble** a. —**de'tes·ta'tion** n.

de·thatch' v. remove dead grass from (a lawn)

de·throne' v. to depose (a monarch)

det'o·nate' v. explode —**det'o·na'tor** n.

de'tour' v., n. (use) an indirect or alternate road

de·tox' (n.: dē'täks') [Inf.] v. detoxify —n. detoxification

de·tox'i·fy' v. **-fied', -fy'ing** remove a poison or poisonous effect from —**de·tox'i·fi·ca'tion** n.

de·tract' v. take something desirable (from) —**de·trac'tor** n.

det'ri·ment n. damage; harm —**det'ri·men'tal** a.

de·tri'tus (-trī'-) n. **1** debris **2** rock fragments

deuce (dōōs, dyōōs) n. **1** playing card with two spots **2** in tennis, tie score after which one side must score twice in a row to win

de·val'ue v. lessen the value of: also **de·val'u·ate'**

dev'as·tate' v. destroy; ravage —**dev'as·ta'tion** n.

de·vel'op v. **1** grow, improve, expand, etc. **2** work out by degrees **3** treat (film) to make the picture visible —**de·vel'op·ment** n. —**de·vel'op·men'**

tal a.

de'vi·ant n., a. (person) deviating from social norms

de'vi·ate' v. turn aside; diverge —**de'vi·a'tion** n.

de·vice' n. **1** a plan or scheme **2** mechanical contrivance **3** a design

dev'il n. **1** evil spirit **2** [often D-] Satan **3** wicked or reckless person —v. **1** to season (food) highly **2** tease —**dev'il·try** n., pl. **-tries** —**dev'il·ish** a.

dev'il-may-care' a. reckless; careless

dev'il·ment n. mischief

devil's advocate n. one defending an argument but not believing in it

dev'il's-food' cake n. rich chocolate cake

de'vi·ous a. roundabout

de·vise' (-vīz') v. to plan

de·vi'tal·ize' v. weaken

de·void' a. empty (of)

de·volve' v. pass (on) to another: said as of a duty

de·vote' v. **1** dedicate **2** apply to a purpose

de·vot'ed a. **1** dedicated **2** loyal —**de·vot'ed·ly** adv.

dev'o·tee' (-tē', -tā') n. one devoted to something

de·vo'tion n. **1** a devoting **2** pl. prayers **3** loyalty

de·vour' (-vour') v. **1** eat up hungrily **2** take in eagerly

de·vout' a. pious or sincere

dew n. atmospheric moisture condensing on cool surfaces at night —**dew'y** a., **-i·er**, **-i·est**

dew'lap' n. loose skin under the throat of cattle, etc.

dex'ter·ous (-tər əs, -trəs) a. skillful in using one's hands, mind, etc.: also **dex'trous** (-trəs) —**dex·ter'i·ty** n.

dex'trose' (-trōs') n. sugar found in plants and animals

di- pref. twice; double

di·a·be·tes (dī'ə bēt'ēz, -is) n. disease marked by excess sugar in the blood and urine —**di'a·bet'ic** a., n.

di'a·bol'ic a. devilish: also **di'a·bol'i·cal**

di'a·crit'ic n. a mark to show pronunciation —**di'a·crit'i·cal** a.

di'a·dem' n. a crown

di'ag·no'sis n., pl. **-ses'** (-sēz') identifying of a disease —**di'ag·nose'** v. —**di'ag·nos'tic** a. —**di'ag·nos·ti'cian** n.

di·ag'o·nal a. slanting between opposite corners —n. a diagonal line

di'a·gram' n., v. sketch, plan, etc. to help explain

di'al n. **1** face of a clock, meter, etc. for indicating some variable **2** rotating disk, or numbered buttons, on a tele-phone —v. **1** tune in (a station, pro-gram, etc.) **2** call by using a tele-phone dial

di'a·lect' n. form of speech limited to a region, group, etc. —**di'a·lec'tal** a.

di'a·lec'tic n. often pl. logical examina-tion of ideas —**di'a·lec'ti·cal** a.

di'a·logue', di'a·log' n. conversation

di·al'y·sis (-al'ə-) n. separation of impurities in the blood by diffusion through a membrane

di·am'e·ter n. **1** straight line through the center of a circle, etc. **2** its length —**di'a·met'ri·cal** a.

di'a·mond (dī'mənd, dī'ə-) n. **1** pre-cious gem of great brilliance **2** figure shaped like ◇ **3** baseball field

di'a·mond·back' n. large, poisonous rattlesnake

di·a·per (dī'pər, dī'ə-) n. cloth worn around a baby's hips —v. to put a dia-per on

di·aph'a·nous a. gauzy

di'a·phragm' (-fram') n. **1** wall of muscle between chest and abdomen **2** vibrating disk producing sound waves **3** vaginal contraceptive

di'ar·rhe'a (-rē'ə) n. very loose bowel movements

di'a·ry n., pl. **-ries** daily record of per-sonal notes

di·as·to·le (dī as'tə lē') n. usual rhyth-mic expansion of the heart —**di·a·stol'ic** a.

di'a·ther'my n. use of electric current to heat tissues below the skin

di'a·ton'ic a. of any standard musical scale of eight tones

di'a·tribe' n. denunciation

dice pl.n., sing. **die** small, spotted cubes, used in gambling —v. cut into cubes

di·chot'o·my (-kät'-) n., pl. **-mies** divi-sion into two parts

dick n. [Sl.] detective

dick'er v. barter; haggle

dick'ey n. detachable shirt front

di·cot'y·le'don (-kät ə lē'-) n. plant with two seed leaves: also **di'cot'**

dic'tate' v. **1** speak (something) for another to write down **2** command —n. an order —**dic·ta'tion** n.

dic·ta'tor n. an absolute ruler; tyrant —**dic·ta·to'ri·al** a. —**dic·ta'tor·ship'** n.

dic'tion n. **1** choice of words **2** enun-ciation

dic'tion·ar·y n., pl. **-ies** book of words alphabetically listed and defined

dic'tum n. formal opinion

did v. pt. of DO

di·dac'tic (dī-) a. meant to teach

did'dle v. [Inf.] **1** to cheat **2** waste time

did'n't contr. did not

die v. **died, dy'ing 1** stop living **2** to stop functioning **3** fade away **4** [Inf.] wish very much —n. **1** sing. of DICE **2** device for molding, stamping, etc. —**die away** (or **down**) cease gradu-ally —**die off** die one by one until all are gone —**die out** go out of existence

die'-hard', die'hard' n. stubborn, resistant person

die·sel (dē'zəl, -səl) n. [often D-] inter-nal-combustion engine that burns fuel oil

di'et n. **1** one's usual food **2** special food taken as for health —v. follow a diet, as to lose weight —**di'e·tar'y** a.

di'e·tet'ics n. study of food as needed for health —**di'e·tet'ic** a.

di'e·ti'tian (-tish'ən) n. planner of diets

dif'fer v. **1** to be different or unlike **2** disagree

dif'fer·ence n. **1** a being unlike **2** dis-tinguishing characteristic **3** disagree-ment **4** amount by which two quan-tities differ —**dif'fer·en'tial** (-shəl) a., n.

dif'fer·ent a. **1** not alike **2** distinct **3** unusual

differential gear (or **gear'ing**) n. arrangement allowing one axle to turn faster than another

dif'fer·en'ti·ate' (-shē-) v. **1** be or make different **2** distinguish

dif'fi·cult' a. hard to do, learn, deal with, etc. —**dif'fi·cul'ty** n., pl. **-ties**

dif'fi·dent a. shy —**dif'fi·dence** n.

dif·frac'tion n. a breaking up of light as into the colors of the spectrum

dif·fuse' (-fyoos'; v.: -fyooz') a. **1** spread out **2** wordy —v. spread widely —**dif·fu'sion** n.

dig v. **dug, dig'ging 1** turn up (soil), as with a spade **2** make or get by dig-ging —n. [Inf.] sarcastic remark

di·gest' (v.: dī jest') n. summary —v. **1** to change (food) in the stomach, etc. so that it can be absorbed **2** absorb mentally —**di·gest'i·ble** a. —**di·ges'tion** n. —**di·ges'tive** a.

dig'it (dij'-) n. **1** any number from 0 to 9 **2** a finger or toe

dig'i·tal a. **1** of a finger **2** showing time, temperature, etc. in a row of digits **3** designating a recording method in which sounds or images are converted into electronic bits **4** of a computer that processes data by electronic means

dig·i·tal'is n. 1 plant with long spikes of flowers 2 heart medicine made from its leaves

dig'i·tize' v. make digital

dig·ni·fied' a. having or showing dignity

dig'ni·fy' v. -fied', -fy'ing give dignity to

dig'ni·tar'y n., pl. -ies person of high position

dig'ni·ty n. 1 worthiness 2 high repute; honor 3 calm stateliness

di·gress' v. wander from the subject, as in talking —**di·gres'sion** n. —**di·gres'sive** a.

dike n. embankment to hold back the sea, etc.

di·lap'i·dat'ed a. falling to pieces

di'late' (or dī lāt') v. make or become wider —**di·la'tion** n.

dil'a·to'ry a. 1 causing delay 2 slow

di·lem'ma n. perplexing situation

dil'et·tante' (-tänt', -tant') n. dabbler in the arts

dil'i·gent a. careful and industrious —**dil'i·gence** n.

dill n. plant with aromatic seeds

dil'ly-dal'ly v. -lied, -ly·ing waste time

di·lute' v. weaken as by mixing with water —a. diluted —**di·lu'tion** n.

dim a. **dim'mer, dim'mest** not bright or clear —v. **dimmed, dim'ming** make or grow dim

dime n. cupronickel coin equal to ten cents

di·men'sion n. 1 any measurable extent 2 pl. measurements in length, breadth, and, often, height

dime store n. store selling a variety of inexpensive things

di·min'ish v. lessen

di·min'u·en'do a., adv. decrescendo

di·min'u·tive a. tiny

dim'i·ty n. a thin cotton cloth

dim'mer n. device for dimming electric lights

dim'ple n. small, natural hollow, as on the cheek

dim'wit' n. [Sl.] stupid person —**dim'wit'ted** a.

din n. confused clamor —v. **dinned, din'ning** 1 make a din 2 keep repeating

DIN (din) n. German association setting manufacturing standards

din'-din' n. [Inf.] dinner

dine v. 1 eat dinner 2 give dinner to

din'er n. 1 person eating dinner 2 railroad car for serving meals 3 restaurant built like this

di·nette' (-net') n. small dining room

ding n. sound of a bell: also **ding'-dong'**

din·ghy (diŋ'gē) n., pl. -ghies small boat

din'go n., pl. -goes Australian wild dog

din·gy (din'jē) a. -gi·er, -gi·est dirty; shabby

dink'y a. -i·er, -i·est [Inf.] small

din'ner n. chief daily meal

dinner jacket n. tuxedo jacket

din'ner·ware' n. dishes

di'no·saur' (-sôr') n. huge extinct reptile

dint n. force: now chiefly in **by dint of**

di'o·cese (-sis, -sēz') n. district headed by a bishop —**di·oc'e·san** (-äs'ə sən) a.

di'ode' n. device used esp. as a rectifier

di·ox'ide' n. oxide with two oxygen atoms per molecule

di·ox'in n. toxic impurity in some herbicides

dip v. **dipped, dip'ping** 1 plunge into liquid for a moment 2 scoop up 3 sink or slope down —n. 1 a dipping 2 sauce into which food may be dipped 3 downward slope

diph·the·ri·a (dif thir'ē ə, dip-) n. acute infectious disease of the throat

diph'thong n. sound made by gliding from one vowel to another in one syllable

di·plo'ma n. certificate of graduation from a school

di·plo'ma·cy n. 1 the conducting of relations between nations 2 tact —**dip'lo·mat'** n. —**dip'lo·mat'ic** a.

dip'per n. long-handled cup, etc. for dipping

dip·so·ma·ni·a n. excessive desire for alcoholic drink —**dip'so·ma'ni·ac'** n.

dip'stick' n. graduated rod for measuring depth

dir abbrev. director

dire a. 1 dreadful; terrible 2 urgent

di·rect' a. 1 straight 2 frank 3 immediate 4 exact —v. 1 manage; guide 2 order 3 aim —adv. directly —**di·rect'ly** adv. —**di·rec'tor** n.

direct current n. electric current moving in one direction

di·rec'tion n. 1 management; guidance 2 pl. instructions 3 an order 4 the point one faces or moves toward —**di·rec'tion·al** a.

di·rec'tive (-tiv) n. an order

direct object n. word receiving the action of a transitive verb

di·rec'to·ry n., pl. -ries book of names

and addresses of a specific group

dirge (durj) n. song of mourning

dir'i‧gi‧ble (or də rij'ə-) n. airship

dirk n. long dagger

dirt n. **1** dust, filth, etc. **2** earth; soil

dirt'-poor' a. very poor; destitute

dirt'y a. **-i‧er, -i‧est** **1** soiled **2** obscene **3** contemptible **4** unfair —v. **-ied, -y‧ing** to soil —**dirt'i‧ness** n.

dis v. **dissed, dis'sing** [Sl.] **1** insult **2** disapprove of

dis- pref. **1** the opposite of **2** reverse the action of

dis‧a'ble v. make unable or unfit; cripple —**dis‧a‧bil'i‧ty** n., pl. **-ties**

dis‧a'bled pl.n., a. (persons) having a physical or mental handicap

dis‧a‧buse' v. rid of false ideas

dis‧ad‧van'tage n. drawback; handicap; detriment —**dis‧ad‧van‧ta'geous** a.

dis‧ad‧van'taged a. poor

dis‧af‧fect' v. make unfriendly or discontented —**dis‧af‧fec'tion** n.

dis‧a‧gree' v. **1** differ **2** quarrel **3** give distress: with with —**dis‧a‧gree'ment** n.

dis‧a‧gree'a‧ble a. **1** unpleasant **2** quarrelsome

dis‧al‧low' v. reject

dis‧ap‧pear' v. **1** go out of sight **2** cease being —**dis‧ap‧pear'ance** n.

dis‧ap‧point' v. spoil the hopes of —**dis‧ap‧point'ment** n.

dis‧ap‧prove' v. **1** have an unfavorable opinion (of) **2** reject —**dis‧ap‧prov'al** n.

dis‧arm' v. **1** remove weapons from **2** make friendly —**dis‧ar'ma‧ment** n.

dis‧ar‧range' v. to disorder

dis‧ar‧ray' n. disorder

dis‧as‧sem'ble v. take apart

dis‧as‧so'ci‧ate' v. separate

dis‧as'ter n. sudden misfortune; calamity —**dis‧as'trous** a.

dis‧a‧vow' v. deny knowing or approving —**dis‧a‧vow'al** n.

dis‧band' v. break up

dis‧bar' v. **-barred', -bar'ring** deprive of the right to practice law

dis‧be‧lieve' v. refuse to believe (in) —**dis‧be‧lief'** n.

dis‧burse' v. pay out

disc n. **1** disk **2** phonograph record

dis‧card' (n.: dis'kärd') v. throw away —n. thing discarded

disc brake n. brake with two pads that press on a disc

dis‧cern' (di surn', -zurn') v. perceive —**dis‧cern'i‧ble** a. —**dis‧cern'ment** n.

dis‧cern'ing a. astute

dis‧charge' (n.: dis'chärj') v. **1** dismiss **2** unload **3** shoot **4** emit **5** do (a duty) —n. a discharging or thing discharged

dis‧ci‧ple (-sī'-) n. follower; pupil

dis‧ci‧pli‧nar'i‧an n. enforcer of discipline

dis‧ci‧pline (-plin) n. **1** orderly training or conduct **2** punishment —v. **1** train; control **2** punish —**dis‧ci‧pli‧nar'y** a.

disc jockey n. one who plays recordings on the radio, in a nightclub, etc.

dis‧claim' v. disown; deny

dis‧claim'er n. denial or rejection of responsibility

dis‧close' v. to reveal —**dis‧clo'sure** n.

dis‧co n., pl. **-cos** nightclub for dancing to recorded music

dis‧col'or v. to stain; tarnish —**dis‧col‧or‧a'tion** n.

dis‧com'fit v. upset; make uneasy —**dis‧com'fi‧ture** n.

dis‧com'fort n. lack of comfort

dis‧com‧mode' v. to inconvenience

dis‧com‧pose' v. fluster —**dis‧com‧po'sure** n.

dis‧con‧cert' v. confuse

dis‧con‧nect' v. to separate

dis‧con‧nect'ed a. **1** separated **2** incoherent

dis‧con'so‧late a. very unhappy

dis‧con‧tent' n. dissatisfaction: also **dis‧con‧tent'ment** n.

dis‧con‧tent'ed a. not contented

dis‧con‧tin'ue v. to stop —**dis‧con‧tin'u‧ous** a.

dis‧cord' n. **1** disagreement **2** dissonance; harsh sound —**dis‧cord'ant** a.

dis‧co‧thèque' (-tek') n. disco

dis‧count' (v.: also dis kount') v. **1** deduct, as from a price **2** disregard in part or entirely —n. deduction

dis‧coun'te‧nance v. embarrass

dis‧cour'age v. **1** deprive of hope or confidence **2** dissuade **3** work against —**dis‧cour'age‧ment** n.

dis‧course' n. talk or formal lecture —v. to talk

dis‧cour'te‧ous a. impolite —**dis‧cour'te‧sy** n.

dis‧cov'er v. **1** be the first to find, see, etc. **2** find out —**dis‧cov'er‧y** n., pl. **-ies**

dis‧cred'it v. **1** disbelieve **2** cast doubt on **3** disgrace —n. **1** doubt **2** disgrace

dis‧creet' a. careful; prudent —**dis‧creet'ly** adv.

dis‧crep'an‧cy n., pl. **-cies** inconsistency

dis·crete' *a.* separate; distinct

dis·cre·tion (di skresh'ən) *n.* **1** freedom to decide **2** prudence —**dis·cre'tion·ar·y** *a.*

dis·crim'i·nate' *v.* **1** distinguish **2** show partiality —**dis·crim'i·na'tion** *n.* —**dis·crim'i·na·to'ry** *a.*

dis·cur'sive *a.* rambling

dis'cus *n.* heavy disk thrown in a contest

dis·cuss' *v.* talk or write about —**dis·cus'sion** *n.*

dis·dain' *v., n.* scorn —**dis·dain'ful** *a.*

dis·ease' *n.* (an) illness —**dis·eased'** *a.*

dis'em·bark' *v.* go ashore

dis'em·bod'y *v.* to free from bodily existence

dis'en·chant' *v.* disillusion —**dis'en·chant'ment** *n.*

dis'en·fran'chise' *v.* deprive of the right to vote: also **dis·fran'chise'**

dis'en·gage' *v.* disconnect

dis'en·tan'gle *v.* extricate

dis·fa'vor *n.* **1** dislike **2** a being disliked

dis·fig'ure *v.* spoil the looks of; mar —**dis·fig'ure·ment** *n.*

dis·gorge' *v.* **1** relinquish unwillingly **2** pour forth

dis·grace' *n.* shame; dishonor —*v.* to bring shame upon —**dis·grace'ful** *a.*

dis·grun'tle *v.* make discontented

dis·guise' (-gīz') *v.* make unrecognizable —*n.* thing, as clothing or makeup, used for disguising

dis·gust' *n.* sickening dislike; loathing —*v.* cause disgust —**dis·gust'ed** *a.* —**dis·gust'ing** *a.*

dish *n.* **1** plate, etc. for food **2** kind of food

dis·ha·bille (dis'ə bēl') *n.* state of being only partly dressed

dish'cloth' *n.* cloth for washing dishes

dis·heart'en *v.* discourage

di·shev'el *v.* muss up (hair, etc.); rumple

dis·hon'est *a.* not honest —**dis·hon'es·ty** *n.*

dis·hon'or *n., v.* shame; disgrace —**dis·hon'or·a·ble** *a.*

dish'pan' *n.* basin for washing dishes, etc.

dish'wash'er *n.* a person or machine that washes dishes

dis·il·lu'sion *v.* strip of ideals, etc. and make disappointed

dis'in·clined' *a.* unwilling

dis'in·fect' *v.* kill bacteria in —**dis'in·fect'ant** *n.*

dis'in·gen'u·ous (-jen'-) *a.* not candid

dis'in·her'it *v.* to deprive of an inheritance

dis·in'te·grate' *v.* separate into parts; break up —**dis·in'te·gra'tion** *n.*

dis·in'ter·est·ed *a.* **1** impartial **2** indifferent

dis·joint'ed *a.* without unity or coherence

disk *n.* **1** thin, flat, circular thing **2** thin plate for storing computer data **3** disc

disk·ette' *n.* floppy disk

disk jockey *n.* disc jockey

dis·like' *v., n.* (have) a feeling of not liking

dis·lo'cate' *v.* **1** put out of joint **2** disarrange —**dis·lo·ca'tion** *n.*

dis·lodge' *v.* force from its place

dis·loy'al *a.* not loyal —**dis·loy'al·ty** *n.*

dis'mal (diz'-) *a.* dreary

dis·man'tle *v.* take apart

dis·may' *v.* dishearten —*n.* loss of confidence

dis·mem'ber *v.* tear apart —**dis·mem'ber·ment** *n.*

dis·miss' *v.* **1** send away **2** discharge **3** set aside —**dis·miss'al** *n.* —**dis·mis'sive** *a.*

dis·mount' *v.* get off

dis'o·bey' *v.* refuse or fail to obey —**dis'o·be'di·ence** *n.* —**dis'o·be'di·ent** *a.*

dis·or'der *n.* **1** confusion **2** commotion **3** ailment —*v.* to cause disorder in —**dis·or'der·ly** *a.*

dis·or'gan·ize' *v.* throw into confusion —**dis·or'gan·i·za'tion** *n.*

dis'o·ri·ent' *v.* confuse mentally

dis·own' *v.* refuse to acknowledge as one's own

dis·par'age *v.* belittle —**dis·par'age·ment** *n.*

dis'pa·rate *a.* not alike

dis·par'i·ty *n., pl.* **-ties** difference; unlikeness

dis·pas'sion·ate *a.* free from emotion or bias

dis·patch' (*n.* 2, 3: *also* dis'pach') *v.* **1** send **2** finish quickly **3** kill —*n.* **1** speed **2** message **3** news story —**dis·patch'er** *n.*

dis·pel' *v.* **-pelled'**, **-pel'ling** drive away

dis·pen'sa·ble *a.* not important

dis·pen'sa·ry *n., pl.* **-ries** place in a school, etc. for getting medicines or first aid

dis·pense' *v.* **1** distribute **2** prepare and give out —**dispense with** do without —**dis'pen·sa'tion** *n.* —**dis·pens'er** *n.*

dis·perse' *v.* scatter —**dis·per'sal** *n.* —**dis·per'sion** *n.*

dis·pir'it·ed *a.* dejected

dis·place' *v.* **1** move from its usual place **2** replace —**dis·place'ment** *n.*

dis·placed' person *n.* one forced from his or her country, esp. by war

dis·play' *v.* to show; exhibit —*n.* exhibition

dis·please' *v.* annoy; offend —**dis·pleas'ure** *n.*

dis·port' *v.* amuse (oneself)

dis·pos'al *n.* kitchen device for grinding up garbage

dis·pose' *v.* **1** arrange **2** incline mentally —**dispose of 1** settle **2** get rid of —**dis·pos'a·ble** *a.* —**dis·po·si'tion** *n.*

dis·pos·sess' *v.* to force to give up property; oust

dis·pro·por'tion *n.* lack of proportion —**dis'pro·por'tion·ate** *a.*

dis·prove' *v.* prove false

dis·pu·ta'tious *a.* fond of arguing

dis·pute' *v., n.* **1** debate **2** quarrel —**in dispute** not settled —**dis·put'a·ble** *a.* —**dis·pu·ta'tion** *n.*

dis·qual'i·fy' *v.* **-fied'**, **-fy'ing** make ineligible —**dis·qual'i·fi·ca'tion** *n.*

dis·qui'et *v.* make uneasy

dis·qui·si'tion (-zish'ən) *n.* treatise

dis're·gard' *v.* ignore —*n.* lack of attention

dis're·pair' *n.* state of needing repairs

dis're·pute' *n.* bad reputation —**dis·rep'u·ta·ble** *a.*

dis're·spect' *n.* lack of respect —**dis're·spect'ful** *a.*

dis·robe' *v.* undress

dis·rupt' *v.* break up; disorder —**dis·rup'tion** *n.* —**dis·rup'tive** *a.*

dis·sat'is·fy' *v.* **-fied'**, **-fy'ing** make discontented —**dis·sat·is·fac'tion** *n.*

dis·sect' (*or* di'sekt') *v.* **1** cut apart so as to examine **2** analyze closely —**dis·sec'tion** *n.*

dis·sem'ble *v.* to disguise one's feelings, etc.

dis·sem'i·nate' *v.* spread widely —**dis·sem'i·na'tion** *n.*

dis·sen'sion *n.* strife

dis·sent' *v.* disagree —*n.* difference of opinion

dis'ser·ta'tion *n.* formal essay

dis·ser'vice *n.* harmful act

dis'si·dent *a., n.* dissenting (person) —**dis'si·dence** *n.*

dis·sim'i·lar *a.* not alike

dis'si·pate' *v.* **1** vanish or disperse **2** squander **3** indulge in wild, harmful pleasure —**dis'si·pa'tion** *n.*

dis·so'ci·ate' *v.* separate

dis'so·lute' *a.* dissipated and immoral

dis'so·lu'tion *n.* a dissolving or breaking up

dis·solve' *v.* **1** melt **2** pass or make pass into solution **3** break up **4** end

dis'so·nance *n.* lack of harmony, esp. in sound; discord —**dis'so·nant** *a.*

dis·suade' (-swād') *v.* cause to turn from a purpose

dist *abbrev.* **1** distance **2** district

dis'taff' *n.* staff for holding flax, wool, etc. in spinning —*a.* female

dis'tance *n.* **1** length between two points **2** aloofness **3** faraway place

dis'tant *a.* **1** far apart; remote **2** away **3** aloof

dis·taste' *n.* dislike —**dis·taste'ful** *a.*

dis·tem'per *n.* infectious disease of dogs, etc.

dis·tend' *v.* swell; expand —**dis·ten'tion, dis·ten'sion** *n.*

dis·till' *v.* subject to or obtain by distillation

dis·til·la'tion *n.* process of purifying a mixture by heating it and condensing the vapor —**dis'til·late'** *n.*

dis·till'er·y *n., pl.* **-ies** place for distilling liquor —**dis·till'er** *n.*

dis·tinct' *a.* **1** not alike **2** separate **3** definite

dis·tinc'tion *n.* **1** a keeping distinct **2** quality that differentiates **3** fame

dis·tinc'tive *a.* making distinct

dis·tin'guish *v.* **1** perceive or show a difference (*in* or *between* or *among*) **2** classify **3** make famous —**dis·tin'guish·a·ble** *a.* —**dis·tin'guished** *a.*

dis·tort' *v.* **1** twist out of shape **2** misrepresent —**dis·tor'tion** *n.*

dis·tract' *v.* **1** divert (the mind, etc.) **2** confuse —**dis·trac'tion** *n.*

dis·traught' *a.* extremely troubled

dis·tress' *v., n.* pain, trouble, worry, etc.

dis·trib'ute *v.* **1** give out in shares **2** scatter **3** arrange —**dis'tri·bu'tion** *n.*

dis·trib'u·tor *n.* **1** one who distributes, deals in a product, etc. **2** device distributing electricity to spark plugs in a gasoline engine

dis'trict *n.* **1** division of a state, etc. **2** region

district attorney *n.* prosecuting attorney of a district

dis·trust' *n.* lack of trust —*v.* have no trust in —**dis·trust'ful** *a.*

dis·turb' *v.* **1** break up the quiet or settled order of **2** make uneasy **3** interrupt —**dis·turb'ance** *n.*

dis·u'nite *v.* divide; separate

dis·use' *n.* lack of use

ditch *n.* channel dug out for drainage, etc. —*v.* [Sl.] get rid of

dith'er n. excited state

ditto mark n. mark (") in lists showing the item above is to be repeated: also **dit'to**, pl. **-tos**

dit'ty n., pl. **-ties** short, simple song

di·u·ret'ic (-yōo-) n., a. (substance) increasing urine discharge

di·ur'nal (-ur'-) a. daily

div abbrev. division

di'va (dē'-) n. Mus. prima donna

di·van' n. large sofa

dive v. **dived** or **dove**, **dived**, **div'ing** 1 plunge into water 2 plunge suddenly or steeply —n. 1 sudden plunge 2 [Inf.] cheap saloon —**div'er** n.

di·verge' v. 1 branch off 2 deviate — **di·ver'gence** n. —**di·ver'gent** a.

di'vers (-varz) a. various

di·verse' (-vurs') a. 1 different 2 varied

di·ver'si·fy v. **-fied'**, **-fy'ing** vary —**di·ver'si·fi·ca'tion** n.

di·ver'sion n. 1 a diverting 2 pastime; amusement

di·ver'si·ty n. variety

di·vert' v. 1 turn aside from a course, etc. 2 amuse

di·ver·tic·u·li'tis (dī'-) n. inflammation of sac opening out from intestine

di·vest' v. strip or deprive (of)

di·vide' v. 1 separate into parts 2 apportion 3 Math. separate into equal parts by a divisor —n. ridge — **di·vis'i·ble** (-viz'-) a.

div'i·dend n. 1 number to be divided 2 sum divided among stockholders, etc.

di·vine' a. 1 of God or a god 2 supremely good —n. member of the clergy —v. 1 prophesy 2 guess

divining rod n. forked stick believed to dip when held over underground water

di·vin'i·ty n. 1 a being divine 2 pl. **-ties** a god

di·vi'sion n. 1 a dividing 2 thing that divides 3 segment, group, etc. 4 section of an army corps

di·vi'sive a. causing disagreement

di·vi'sor n. number by which the dividend is divided to get the quotient

di·vorce' n. 1 legal dissolution of a marriage 2 separation —v. separate from, as by divorce

di·vor·cée', **di·vor·cee'** (-sā') n. divorced woman —**di·vor·cé'** (-sā') n.masc.

div'ot n. turf dislodged by a golf club

di·vulge' v. make known

Dix'ie·land' n. early jazz for small bands

DIY abbrev. do-it-yourself

diz'zy a. **-zi·er**, **-zi·est** 1 having a whirling feeling 2 confused 3 causing dizziness —**diz'zi·ly** adv. —**diz'zi·ness** n.

DJ n. disc jockey

DNA n. basic material of chromosomes that transmits hereditary pattern

do v. **did**, **done**, **do'ing** 1 perform (an action) 2 finish 3 cause 4 deal with as required 5 have as one's work 6 get along 7 be adequate Do is also an important auxiliary verb —**do in** [Sl.] kill —**do's** (or **dos**) **and don'ts** [Inf.] things permitted and things forbidden —**do without** get along without —**have to do with** relate to — **do'er** n.

DOA abbrev. dead on arrival

Do'ber·man pin'scher (-chər) n. large dog with short, dark hair

doc·ile (däs'əl) a. easy to train —**do·cil'i·ty** n.

dock n. 1 landing pier; wharf 2 water between piers 3 place for the accused in a courtroom —v. 1 bring or come to a dock 2 cut short 3 deduct from

dock'et n. list of cases to be tried by a law court

dock'yard' n. shipyard

doc'tor n. 1 person with the highest degree from a university 2 physician or surgeon —v. [Inf.] 1 try to heal 2 tamper with

doc'tor·ate n. highest degree from a university —**doc'tor·al** a.

doc'tri·naire' (-ner') a. adhering strictly to a doctrine

doc'trine (-trin) n. something taught, as a religious tenet —**doc'tri·nal** a.

doc'u·dra'ma n. TV dramatization of real events

doc'u·ment (-mənt; v.: -ment') n. printed or written record providing information or proof —v. to support by documents

doc'u·men'ta·ry a. 1 of or supported by documents 2 recording or analyzing news events dramatically —n., pl. **-ries** documentary film

doc'u·men·ta'tion n. 1 (the supplying of) documents for use as evidence 2 instructions for computer hardware or software

dod'der v. shake as from old age

dodge v. 1 move quickly aside 2 avoid; evade —n. 1 a dodging 2 a trick

do'do n. 1 large extinct bird 2 [Sl.] stupid person

doe n. female deer, rabbit, etc.

does (duz) v. pres. t. of DO: used with *he, she,* or *it*

doe'skin' n. leather from the skin of a female deer or a lamb

does'n't contr. does not

doff v. take off; remove

dog n. domesticated animal of the wolf family —v. **dogged, dog'ging** follow like a dog

dog'-ear' n. turned-down corner of a page —**dog'-eared'** a.

dog'ged a. stubborn

dog'ger·el n. trivial, monotonous verse

do·gie (dō'gē) n. stray calf

dog'ma n. strict doctrine

dog·mat'ic·a 1 of a dogma 2 positive in stating opinions; arrogant —**dog·mat'i·cal·ly** adv. —**dog'ma·tism'** n.

dog'-tired' a. very tired

dog'wood' n. tree with pink or white flowers

doi'ly n., pl. **-lies** small mat to protect a table, etc.

do'ings pl.n. actions

dol'drums (dōl'-) pl.n. low spirits

dole n. money paid to those in need by the government: with *the* —v. give (*out*) sparingly

dole'ful a. sad; sorrowful

doll n. child's toy made to resemble a person

dol'lar n. U.S. monetary unit, equal to 100 cents

dol'lop n. small quantity of a soft food

dol'ly n., pl. **-lies** 1 [Inf.] doll 2 low, wheeled frame for moving heavy objects

dol'men (dōl'-) n. monument with stone laid across upright stones

do'lor·ous (dōl'ər-) a. sorrowful

dol'phin n. sea mammal with a beak-like snout

dolt n. stupid person —**dolt'ish** a.

-dom suf. 1 rank or domain of 2 state of being

do·main' n. 1 territory under one ruler 2 field of activity

dome n. large, round roof

do·mes'tic a. 1 of one's home or family 2 of one's country 3 tame —n. a maid, cook, etc. —**do·mes'ti·cal·ly** adv. —**do'mes·tic'i·ty** n.

do·mes'ti·cate v. to tame —**do·mes'ti·ca'tion** n.

dom'i·cile' (-sīl') n. home

dom'i·nate' v. 1 rule or control 2 rise high above —**dom'i·nance** n. —**dom'i·nant** a. —**dom'i·na'tion** n.

dom'i·neer' v. rule harshly

do·min'ion n. 1 rule; power 2 governed territory

dom'i·noes', dom'i·nos' n. game with tiles marked with dots

don v. **donned, don'ning** put on (clothes)

don n. Spanish gentleman

do'nate' (or dō nāt') v. give; contribute —**do·na'tion** n.

done (dun) v. pp. of DO

don'key n., pl. **-keys** horse-like animal with long ears

don'ny·brook' n. [Inf.] rowdy fight

do'nor n. one who donates

don't contr. do not

do'nut' n. [Inf.] doughnut

doo'dle v., n. scribble

doo'-doo' n. 1 [Inf.] excrement 2 [Sl.] trouble

doom n. 1 a judgment 2 fate 3 ruin —v. 1 condemn 2 destine to a tragic fate —**doom'y** a.

dooms'day' n. the end of the world

door n. 1 movable panel for closing an entrance 2 entrance, with or without a door: also **door'way'** —**out of doors** outdoors

door'bell' n. bell rung by one wishing to enter

door'man' n., pl. **-men'** one whose work is opening doors, hailing taxicabs, etc.

door'step' n. step from outer door to path, lawn, etc.

dope n. 1 [Inf.] narcotic 2 [Sl.] information 3 [Inf.] stupid person —v. to drug

dor'mant a. quiet; inactive

dor'mer n. an upright window structure in a sloping roof

dor'mi·to'ry n., pl. **-ries** 1 room with many beds 2 building with many bedrooms Also **dorm**

dor'mouse' n., pl. **-mice'** small rodent with a furry tail

dor'sal a. of the back

do'ry n., pl. **-ries** small, flat-bottomed fishing boat

dose n. amount of medicine taken at one time —v. to give doses to —**dos'age** n.

do·sim'e·ter n. device that measures radiation absorbed

dos'si·er' (-ā') n. group of documents about a person

dost (dust) v. [Ar.] do: used with *thou*

dot n. tiny mark or round spot —v. **dot'ted, dot'ting** mark with dots

dot'age (dōt'-) n. senility

dot'ard n. one in his or her dotage

dote v. be too fond: with *on*

doth (duth) v. [Ar.] does

dot'-ma'trix *a.* of computer printing in which characters are formed of tiny dots

dou'ble *a.* **1** of or for two **2** twice as much or as many —*adv.* twofold or twice —*n.* **1** anything twice as much or as many **2** a duplicate **3** *Baseball* hit putting the batter on second —*v.* **1** make or become double **2** fold **3** duplicate **4** turn backward **5** serve two purposes, etc. —**on the double** [Inf.] quickly

double agent *n.* spy working for two rival governments

double bass (bās) *n.* largest, deepest-toned instrument of violin family

dou'ble-breast'ed *a.* overlapping across the chest

dou'ble-cross' *v.* [Inf.] to betray — **dou'ble-cross'er** *n.*

double date [Inf.] *n.* social engagement shared by two couples — **dou'ble-date'** *v.*

dou'ble-deal'ing *n.* deceitful behavior

dou'ble-deck'er *n.* **1** vehicle, etc. with upper deck **2** [Inf.] two-layer sandwich

dou'ble-en-ten'dre (-än tän'drə) *n.* term with two meanings, one risqué

dou'ble-head'er *n.* two games played in succession

dou'ble-joint'ed *a.* having fingers, etc. that bend at unusual angles

dou'ble-park' *v.* to park next to another vehicle parked at a curb

double play *n.* baseball play that puts out two players

double standard *n.* code of behavior stricter for women than for men

dou'blet *n.* [Hist.] man's tight jacket

dou'bly *adv.* twice

doubt (dout) *v.* **1** be uncertain (about) **2** to disbelieve —*n.* **1** wavering of belief **2** uncertainty —**no doubt** certainly —**doubt'ful** *a.*

doubt'less *adv.* certainly

douche (dōōsh) *n.* jet of liquid for cleaning a body part —*v.* use a douche (on)

dough (dō) *n.* **1** thick mixture of flour, liquid, etc. for baking **2** [Sl.] money

dough'nut' *n.* small, fried cake, usually ring-shaped

dour (door, dour) *a.* gloomy

douse (dous) *v.* **1** thrust into liquid **2** drench **3** [Inf.] extinguish (a light)

dove (dŭv) *v.* alt. pt. of DIVE

dove (duv) *n.* kind of pigeon

dove'cote' *n.* cote with compartments for nesting pigeons

dove'tail' (duv'-) *n.* joint formed by fit-ting together wedge-shaped parts —*v.* fit together closely

dow'a-ger *n.* wealthy widow

dow'dy *a.* **-di-er, -di-est** not neat or not stylish

dow'el *n.* peg fitted into holes to join two pieces

dow'er *n.* widow's inheritance

down *adv.* **1** to or in a lower place, state, etc. **2** to a later time **3** in cash **4** in writing —*a.* **1** descending **2** in a lower place **3** gone, brought, etc. down **4** discouraged —*prep.* down toward, into, along, etc. —*v.* put, knock, etc. down —*n.* **1** descent **2** misfortune **3** soft feathers or hair **4** *pl.* high, grassy land —**down with!** overthrow!

down'-and-dirty' *a.* [Sl.] **1** realistic **2** coarse **3** dishonest **4** competitive

down'cast' *a.* **1** directed downward **2** sad

down'er *n.* [Sl.] any sedative

down'fall' *n.* sudden fall, as from power

down'grade' *n.* downward slope — *adv., a.* downward —*v.* to demote

down'heart'ed *a.* sad

down'hill' *adv., a.* down a slope; downward

down'-home' *a.* of rural folk or rural life

down'load' *v.* transfer (information) as from a network or main computer to another computer

down'play' *v.* minimize

down'pour' *n.* a heavy rain

down'right' *adv.* thoroughly —*a.* **1** utter **2** plain

down'scale' *a.* for people who are not affluent or stylish —*v.* make smaller, less, cheaper, etc.

down'size' *v.* **1** make smaller, less, etc. **2** become smaller, as by eliminating employees

down'spout' *n.* pipe for carrying rainwater from roof gutter

down'stairs' *adv., a.* to or on a lower floor —*n.* lower floor or floors

down'stream' *adv., a.* **1** in the direction of a stream's flow **2** toward the end of some process

down'swing' *n.* **1** downward swing of golf club **2** downward trend

Down syndrome *n.* congenital disease marked by mental deficiency: also **Down's syndrome**

down'-to-earth' *a.* sensible

down'town' *n.* city's business district

down'trod'den *a.* oppressed

down'turn' *n.* downward trend

down'ward *adv., a.* toward a lower place, etc.: also **down'wards** *adv.*

down'y *a.* soft and fluffy

dow'ry *n., pl.* **-ries** property a bride brings to her husband at marriage

doz *abbrev.* dozen(s)

doze *v., n.* sleep; nap

doz'en *n.* set of twelve

Dr, Dr. *abbrev.* 1 Doctor 2 Drive

drab *a.* **drab'ber, drab'best** dull — **drab'ness** *n.*

draft *n.* 1 liquid for drinking 2 rough sketch of a writing 3 plan 4 current of air 5 written order for money 6 selection for compulsory military service 7 depth of water a ship displaces —*v.* 1 select to serve 2 make a plan, outline, etc. for —*a.* 1 used for pulling loads 2 drawn from a cask — **on draft** ready to be drawn from a cask

draft'ee' *n.* one drafted for military service

drafts'man *n., pl.* **-men** one who draws plans, as of structures

draft'y *a.* **-i·er, -i·est** open to drafts of air

drag *v.* **dragged, drag'ging** 1 pull or be pulled with effort, esp. along the ground 2 search (a river bottom, etc.) as with a net 3 pass slowly —*n.* 1 hindrance 2 [Sl.] puff of a cigarette, etc. 3 [Sl.] clothing of opposite sex

drag'net' *n.* 1 net dragged along the bottom of a river, etc. 2 system for catching criminals

drag'on *n.* large, mythical reptile that breathes out fire

drag'on·fly' *n., pl.* **-flies'** long insect with four wings

dra·goon' *n.* armed cavalryman —*v.* force to do something

drag race *n.* race between cars accelerating from a standstill on a short, straight course (**drag strip**)

drain *v.* 1 draw off (liquid, etc.) gradually 2 empty 3 exhaust (energy, resources, etc.) 4 flow off —*n.* channel; pipe

drain'age *n.* 1 a draining or system for draining 2 that which is drained off

drain'pipe' *n.* large pipe carrying off water, etc.

drake *n.* male duck

dram *n.* in apothecaries' weight, $\frac{1}{8}$ ounce

dra'ma *n.* 1 a play 2 art of writing and staging plays

dra·mat'ic *a.* 1 of drama 2 vivid, exciting, etc.

dra·mat'ics *n.* performing or producing of plays

dram'a·tist *n.* playwright

dram'a·tize' *v.* 1 make into a drama 2 regard or show in a dramatic manner —**dram'a·ti·za'tion** *n.*

drank *v.* pt. of DRINK

drape *v.* cover or hang as with cloth in loose folds —*n.* curtain

drap'er·y *n., pl.* **-ies** curtain

dras'tic *a.* severe; harsh —**dras'ti·cal·ly** *adv.*

draught (draft) *n., v., a.* chiefly Br. sp. of DRAFT

draughts (drafts) *n.* [Br.] the game of checkers

draw *v.* **drew, drawn, draw'ing** 1 pull 2 attract 3 inhale 4 take out; get 5 come; move 6 write (a check) 7 deduce 8 stretch 9 make (lines, pictures, etc.) as with a pencil —*n.* 1 stalemate 2 thing that attracts

draw'back' *n.* disadvantage

draw'bridge' *n.* bridge that can be raised

drawer (drôr) *n.* 1 sliding box in a table, etc. 2 *pl.* underpants

draw'ing *n.* 1 art of sketching 2 picture sketched

drawing board *n.* board to hold paper for making drawings —**back to the drawing board** [Inf.] back to the start, as to see what went wrong

drawing card *n.* entertainment drawing a large audience

drawing room *n.* parlor

drawl *n.* slow, prolonged manner of speech —*v.* to speak with a drawl

drawn *a.* haggard

draw'string' *n.* cord in a hem as in the waist of a garment, used to tighten it

dray *n.* wagon for heavy loads

dread (dred) *v.* await with fear or distaste —*n.* fear —*a.* inspiring fear — **dread'ful** *a.*

dread'locks' *pl.n.* long, thin braids or twisted locks of hair

dream *n.* 1 images, etc. seen during sleep 2 reverie 3 fond hope —*v.* **dreamed** or **dreamt** (dremt), **dream'ing** have dreams —**dream'y** *a.*

drear'y *a.* **-i·er, -i·est** dismal —**drear'i·ness** *n.*

dredge *n.* apparatus for scooping up mud, etc. as in deepening channels — *v.* 1 enlarge with a dredge 2 gather (*up*) as with a dredge 3 sprinkle with flour

dregs *pl.n.* 1 particles at the bottom in a liquid 2 most worthless part

drench *v.* soak

dress v. 1 clothe 2 adorn 3 treat (a wound, etc.) 4 prepare (a fowl, etc.) by skinning, etc. —n. 1 clothes 2 woman's garment —**dress up** improve the look of, as by decorating —**dress′ mak′er** n.

dres·sage (-säzh′) n. skilled style of horsemanship

dress circle n. theater seats in an arc near the stage

dress code n. set of rules governing clothing to be worn, as in a school

dress′-down′ a. of a policy allowing clothing more informal than usual, as at work

dress′er n. chest of drawers with a mirror

dress′ing n. 1 bandages, etc. 2 salad sauce 3 stuffing for roast fowl

dressing gown n. loose robe for wear when one is not fully clothed

dress rehearsal n. final rehearsal as of a play exactly as it will be presented

dress′y a. -i·er, -i·est elegant

drew v. pt. of DRAW

drib′ble v. 1 flow in drops 2 drool —n. dribbling flow

drib′let n. small amount

dried v. pt. & pp. of DRY

dri′er n. substance that dries

drift v. be carried along, as by a current —n. 1 snow, etc. driven into a heap 2 trend 3 meaning —**drift′er** n.

drift′wood′ n. wood that has drifted ashore

drill n. 1 tool for boring 2 systematic training 3 seeding machine 4 coarse, twilled cloth —v. 1 bore with a drill 2 train systematically —**drill′er** n.

drink v. **drank, drunk, drink′ing** swallow (liquid) —n. 1 liquid for drinking 2 alcoholic liquor

drip v. **dripped, drip′ping** fall or let fall in drops —n. a dripping

drip′-dry′ a. of clothing that needs little or no ironing

drive v. **drove, driv′en** (driv′-), **driv′ing** 1 force to go, do, pierce, etc. 2 operate, or go in, a vehicle —n. 1 trip in a vehicle 2 paved road 3 energy 4 urge 5 campaign 6 Comput. device for accessing data on a disk —**drive at** to mean —**driv′er** n.

drive′-by′ a. of a shooting in which the gun is fired from a car

drive′-in′ n. place for eating, etc. in one's car

driv′el n. silly talk

drive shaft n. shaft carrying power to automobile axle

drive′-through′ a. of a business serv-

ing customers sitting in their cars

drive′way′ n. path for cars

driz′zle v., n. rain in fine, mistlike drops

drogue (drōg) n. device towed behind aircraft to slow it

droll (drōl) a. quaintly amusing

drom′e·dar′y n., pl. **-ies** one-humped camel

drone n. 1 male honeybee 2 constant hum —v. 1 to hum 2 talk monotonously

drool v. drip saliva

droop v. 1 sink or bend down 2 lose vitality —n. a drooping —**droop′y** a., **-i·er, -i·est** —**droop′i·ly** adv.

drop n. 1 small, round mass, as of falling liquid 2 tiny amount 3 sudden fall 4 distance down —v. **dropped, drop′ping** 1 fall or let fall 2 send 3 utter (a hint, etc.) —**drop in** visit —**drop off** [Inf.] take somewhere and leave —**drop out** stop taking part —**drop′per** n.

drop′cloth′ n. large cloth, etc. used as cover when painting

drop′-dead′ [Sl.] a. spectacular; striking —adv. extremely

drop′let n. very small drop

drop′-off′ n. a steep drop or decline

drop′out′ n. student who leaves school before graduating

drop′sy n. edema: old-fashioned term

dross n. rubbish; refuse

drought (drout) n. spell of dry weather

drove v. pt. of DRIVE —n. herd of cattle, etc.

drown v. 1 die or kill by suffocation in water 2 muffle (sound, etc.): with out

drowse v. be sleepy; doze —**drows′y** a., **-i·er, -i·est**

drub v. **drubbed, drub′bing** 1 thrash 2 defeat —**drub′bing** n.

drudge n. one who does hard or dull work —v. do such work —**drudg′er·y** n.

drug n. 1 medicinal substance 2 narcotic —v. **drugged, drug′ging** add or give a drug to

drug′gist n. pharmacist —**drug′store′** n.

dru′id n. member of religious order in ancient British Isles and France

drum n. 1 cylinder covered with a membrane and used as a percussion instrument 2 container, as for oil —v. **drummed, drum′ming** beat as on a drum —**drum up** solicit (business) —**drum′mer** n.

drum′lin n. long ridge or hill

drum major n. one who leads a marching band —**drum ma'jor·ette'** (-et') *n.fem.*

drum'stick' *n.* **1** stick for beating a drum **2** lower leg of a cooked fowl

drunk *v.* pp. of DRINK —*a.* overcome by alcohol —*n.* [Inf.] drunken person — **drunk'ard** *n.*

drunk'en *a.* intoxicated —**drunk'en·ness** *n.*

dry *a.* **dri'er, dri'est** **1** not wet **2** lacking rain **3** thirsty **4** not sweet **5** matter-of-fact **6** dull —*v.* **dried, dry'ing** make or become dry —**dry'ly** *adv.*

dry'ad' *n.* tree nymph

dry cell *n.* voltaic cell using dry electrolyte

dry'-clean' *v.* to clean (garments) with a solvent, as naphtha —**dry cleaner** *n.*

dry dock *n.* dock for building and repairing ships

dry'er *n.* device that dries

dry goods *pl.n.* cloth (products)

dry ice *n.* carbon dioxide in a solid state

dry run *n.* [Inf.] rehearsal

dry'wall' *n.* thin boards of plaster used for interior walls of a house, etc.

DST *abbrev.* daylight saving time

du'al *a.* **1** of two **2** double

du·al'i·ty *n., pl.* **-ties** a being two, or double

dub *v.* **dubbed, dub'bing** **1** confer a title upon **2** insert (dialogue, etc.) in film soundtrack

du'bi·ous *a.* doubtful

du'cal *a.* of a duke

duc·at (duk'ət) *n.* a former European coin

duch'ess *n.* duke's wife

duch'y *n., pl.* **-ies** land ruled by a duke

duck *n.* **1** flat-billed, webfooted swimming bird **2** cloth like canvas but lighter —*v.* **1** dip under water briefly **2** bend suddenly, as to avoid a blow **3** [Inf.] avoid

duck'bill' *n.* platypus

duck'ling *n.* young duck

duck'pins' *n.* bowling game with small pins and balls

duct *n.* tube, channel, or pipe, as for fluid —**duct'less** *a.*

duc'tile (-tal) *a.* **1** that can be drawn thin **2** easily led

duct tape *n.* strong, waterproof adhesive tape for sealing ducts, etc.

duct'work' *n.* system of air ducts in a building

dud *n.* [Inf.] **1** bomb, etc. that fails to explode **2** failure

dude *n.* **1** dandy; fop **2** [Sl.] man or boy

dudg·eon (duj'ən) *n.* now chiefly in **in high dudgeon**, very angry

due *a.* **1** owed **2** suitable **3** expected to arrive —*adv.* exactly —*n.* anything due —**due to** **1** caused by **2** [Inf.] because of

due bill *n.* receipt for money paid, exchangeable for goods, etc. only

du'el *n.* planned formal fight between two armed persons —*v.* fight a duel — **du'el·ist** *n.*

due process (of law) *n.* legal procedures for protecting individual rights

dues *pl.n.* **1** fee or tax **2** money paid for membership

du·et' *n.* musical composition for two performers

duf'fel bag *n.* large canvas bag for clothes, etc.: also **duf'fle bag**

duf'fer *n.* [Inf.] unskilled golfer

dug *v.* pt. & pp. of DIG

dug'out' *n.* **1** boat hollowed out of a log **2** *Baseball* shelter for players when not in the field

DUI *n.* citation for driving under the influence of alcohol, etc.

duke *n.* nobleman next in rank to a prince —**duke'dom** *n.*

dul'cet (-sət) *a.* pleasant to hear

dul'ci·mer (-sə-) *n.* musical instrument with metal strings that are struck or plucked

dull *a.* **1** stupid **2** sluggish **3** boring **4** not sharp **5** not bright —*v.* make or become dull —**dul'ly** *adv.*

dull'ard *n.* stupid person

du'ly *adv.* properly

dumb *a.* **1** unable to talk **2** silent **3** [Inf.] stupid —**dumb down** [Inf.] make less difficult intellectually

dumb'bell' *n.* **1** short bar joining two weights, used in exercising **2** [Sl.] stupid person

dumb'found', dum'found' *v.* make speechless; amaze

dumb'wait'er *n.* small elevator for food, etc.

dum'my *n., pl.* **-mies** **1** humanlike figure for displaying clothes **2** imitation **3** [Sl.] stupid person —*a.* sham

dump *v.* **1** unload in a heap **2** throw away —*n.* a place for dumping rubbish —**(down) in the dumps** [Inf.] dejected

dump'ling *n.* **1** piece of boiled dough **2** crust filled with fruit

Dump'ster *trademark* large, metal trash bin —*n.* **[d-]** such a trash bin

dump truck *n.* truck with tilting container for unloading

dump'y *a.* **-i·er, -i·est** **1** squat; stumpy

2 [Inf.] ugly; run-down

dun *a.* dull grayish-brown —*v.*
dunned, dun'ning to demand money
owed

dunce *n.* stupid person

dune *n.* hill of drifted sand

dung *n.* animal excrement

dun'ga·rees' *pl.n.* work clothes of
coarse cotton

dun'geon (-jən) *n.* dark underground
prison

dunk *v.* **1** dip (food) into coffee, etc. **2**
Basketball thrust (the ball) into the
basket

du'o *n., pl.* **-os** performers of a duet or
any two musicians playing together

du'o·de'num (or doo äd'ə-) *n.* first section of small intestine

dupe *n.* person easily tricked —*v.*
deceive

du'plex' *n.* house with two separate
family units

du'pli·cate (-kət; *v.:* -kāt') *a.* **1** double
2 exactly alike —*n.* exact copy —*v.* **1**
make a copy **2** make happen again —
du'pli·ca'tion *n.* —**du'pli·ca'tor** *n.*

du·plic'i·ty (-plis'-) *n., pl.* **-ties** cunning
deception

du'ra·ble *a.* lasting a long time —**du'**
ra·bil'i·ty *n.*

du·ra'tion *n.* time that a thing continues or lasts

du·ress' *n.* coercion

dur'ing *prep.* **1** throughout **2** in the
course of

du'rum (door'əm) *n.* hard wheat used
for pasta, etc.

dusk *n.* evening twilight

dust *n.* finely powdered matter, esp.
earth —*v.* **1** sprinkle with powder **2**
wipe dust from —**dust'y** *a.*, **-i·er**, **-i·**
est

dust'pan' *n.* pan into which floor dust
is swept

Dutch *a., n.* (of) the people or language
of the Netherlands —**go Dutch** [Inf.]
have each pay own expenses

Dutch door *n.* door with separate
upper and lower halves

Dutch oven *n.* heavy cooking pot

Dutch treat *n.* [Inf.] a date, etc. with
each paying for himself or herself

Dutch uncle *n.* [Inf.] one who scolds
another, often with good intent

du'ti·ful *a.* showing respect; obedient:
also **du'te·ous** —**du'ti·ful·ly** *adv.*

du'ty *n., pl.* **-ies** **1** respect owed, as to
parents **2** sense of obligation, justice,
etc. **3** thing one must do **4** tax, as on
imports

DVD *n.* digital optical disc for storing

images, data, etc.

dwarf *n., pl.* **dwarfs** or **dwarves**
unusually small being or thing —*v.* **1**
stunt in growth **2** make seem small
—*a.* stunted

dweeb *n.* [Sl.] dull, unsophisticated,
etc. person

dwell *v.* **dwelt** or **dwelled, dwell'ing**
make one's home —**dwell on** (or
upon) talk or think about at length

dwelling (place) *n.* residence

DWI *n.* citation for driving while
intoxicated

dwin'dle *v.* decrease

dyb·buk (dib'ək) *n.* dead person's
spirit in Jewish folklore

dye *n.* coloring matter in solution —*v.*
dyed, dye'ing to color with a dye —
dy'er *n.*

dyed'-in-the-wool' *a.* not changing,
as in beliefs

dy'ing *v. prp.* of DIE

dy·nam'ic *a.* **1** of energy **2** energetic;
forceful —**dy·nam'i·cal·ly** *adv.*

dy·nam'ics *n.* science of motions produced by forces

dy'na·mism' *n.* energetic quality

dy'na·mite' *n.* powerful explosive —*v.*
blow up with dynamite

dy'na·mo' *n., pl.* **-mos'** **1** generator;
earlier term **2** dynamic person

dy'nas·ty (-nəs-) *n., pl.* **-ties** family line of
rulers —**dy·nas'tic** *a.*

dys·en·ter·y (dis'-) *n.* disease characterized by bloody diarrhea

dys·func'tion *n.* abnormal functioning
—**dys·func'tion·al** *a.*

dys·lex'i·a *n.* impairment of reading
ability —**dys·lex'ic, dys·lec'tic** *a., n.*

dys·pep'si·a *n.* indigestion

dz *abbrev.* dozen(s)

E

E *abbrev.* **1** east(ern) **2** *Baseball*
error(s) Also **e**

ea *abbrev.* each

each *a., pron.* every one of two or more
—*adv.* apiece

ea'ger *a.* very desirous; anxious to do
or get

ea'gle *n.* large bird of prey with sharp
vision

ea'gle-eyed' *a.* having keen vision

ear *n.* **1** organ of hearing **2** sense of
hearing **3** attention **4** grain-bearing
spike of a cereal plant

ear'drum' *n.* TYMPANUM (*n.* 2)

earl *n.* Br. nobleman

ear'lobe' *n.* soft lower part of the ear

ear'ly *adv., a.* **-li·er, -li·est 1** near the beginning **2** before the expected or usual time

ear'mark' *v.* reserve for a special purpose

ear'muffs' *pl.n.* warm covering for the ears

earn *v.* **1** receive for one's work **2** get as deserved **3** gain as profit

ear'nest *a.* serious or sincere —**in earnest 1** serious **2** with determination

earn'ings *pl.n.* **1** wages **2** profits, interest, etc.

ear'phone' *n.* receiver as for a telephone, held to the ear

ear'ring' *n.* ear ornament

ear'shot' *n.* distance within which a sound can be heard

ear'split'ting *a.* very loud

earth *n.* **1** the planet we live on **2** land **3** soil

earth'en *a.* made of clay

earth'en·ware' *n.* dishes, etc. made of baked clay

earth'ling *n.* human being

earth'ly *a.* **1** terrestrial **2** worldly **3** secular **4** conceivable

earth'quake' *n.* a shaking of the crust of the earth

earth'work' *n.* embankment; fortification

earth'worm' *n.* common worm in soil

earth'y *a.* **-i·er, -i·est 1** of or like earth **2** coarse

ease *n.* **1** comfort **2** poise **3** facility — *v.* **1** to comfort **2** relieve **3** facilitate **4** shift carefully

ea·sel (ē'zəl) *n.* a stand to hold an artist's canvas

ease'ment *n.* right one may have in another's land

eas'i·ly *adv.* **1** with ease **2** without a doubt

east *n.* **1** direction in which sunrise occurs **2** region in this direction **3** [E-] Asia —*a., adv.* in, toward, or from the east —**east'er·ly** *a., adv.* — **east'ern** *a.* —**east'ern·er** *n.* —**east'ward** *a., adv.* —**east'wards** *adv.*

East Asia area in E Asia, including China, Japan, Korea, and Mongolia

Eas'ter *n.* spring Christian festival

Eastern Orthodox Church *n.* Christian church dominant in E Europe, W Asia, and N Africa

eas'y *a.* **-i·er, -i·est 1** not difficult **2** without worry, pain, etc. **3** comfortable **4** not stiff **5** not strict **6** unhurried —*adv.* [Inf.] easily —**take it easy** [Inf.] **1** refrain from anger, etc. **2** relax

eas'y·go·ing *a.* not worried, rushed, or strict

eat *v.* **ate, eat'en, eat'ing 1** chew and swallow (food) **2** wear away, corrode, etc. **3** make by eating

eat'er·y *n.* restaurant

eats *pl.n.* [Inf.] food

eaves *pl.n.* projecting edge of a roof

eaves'drop' *v.* **-dropped', -drop'ping** listen secretly

ebb *n., v.* **1** flow back toward the sea: said of the tide **2** decline

eb'on·y *n., pl.* **-ies** hard, dark, tropical wood —*a.* black

e·bul'lient (i boōl'yənt) *a.* bubbling with joy —**e·bul'lience** *n.*

EC *abbrev.* European Community

ec·cen'tric (ek sen'-) *a.* **1** having its axis off center **2** odd in conduct —*n.* eccentric person —**ec'cen·tric'i·ty** (-tris'-) *n., pl.* **-ties**

ec·cle'si·as'tic *n.* member of the clergy —*a.* ecclesiastical

ec·cle'si·as'ti·cal *a.* of the church or clergy

ech'e·lon' (esh'-) *n.* **1** steplike formation of troops, ships, or planes **2** level of command

ech·o (ek'ō) *n., pl.* **-oes** repetition of a sound by reflection of sound waves — *v.* **1** resound **2** repeat

é·clair' (ā-, i-) *n.* oblong pastry filled with custard, etc.

é·clat (ā klä') *n.* **1** striking effect **2** acclaim **3** fame

ec·lec'tic *a.* using various sources

e·clipse' *n.* the obscuring of the sun by the moon, or of the moon by the earth's shadow —*v.* surpass

e·clip'tic *n.* sun's apparent annual path

e'co·cide' *n.* destruction of the environment

e·col'o·gy *n.* science dealing with organisms in their environment —**e'co·log'i·cal** *a.* —**e·col'o·gist** *n.*

econ *abbrev.* economics

ec·o·nom'ic (or ē'kə-) *a.* **1** of the management of income, expenditures, etc. **2** of economics

ec·o·nom'i·cal *a.* thrifty —**ec·o·nom'i·cal·ly** *adv.*

ec·o·nom'ics *n.* science that deals with the production, distribution, and use of wealth —**e·con'o·mist** *n.*

e·con'o·mize' *v.* be thrifty

e·con'o·my *n., pl.* **-mies 1** management of finances **2** thrift **3** system of producing and consuming wealth

e'co·sys'tem (or ek'ō-) *n.* community of animals, plants, etc.

ec·ru' (-rōō') *a.*, *n.* beige

ec·sta·sy *n.*, *pl.* **-sies** overpowering joy —**ec·stat'ic** *a.* —**ec·stat'i·cal·ly** *adv.*

ec·u·men'i·cal *a.* 1 of the Christian Church as a whole 2 furthering the unity of Christian churches

ec'u·men·ism' *n.* 1 movement to unify Christian churches 2 promoting of cooperation among religions

ec·ze·ma (ek'sə-, eg'zə-) *n.* itchy, scaly skin disease

ed *abbrev.* 1 edited (by) 2 edition 3 editor 4 education

-ed *suf.* 1 having or being 2 pt. and pp. ending of many verbs

E'dam (cheese) *n.* mild yellow cheese

ed'dy *n.*, *pl.* **-dies** little whirlpool or whirlwind —*v.* **-died, -dy·ing** to whirl

e·de'ma *n.* abnormal swelling

E'den *n. Bible* garden where Adam and Eve first lived

edge *n.* 1 blade's cutting side 2 brink 3 border 4 [Inf.] advantage —*v.* 1 put an edge on 2 move sideways —**on edge** tense

edg'ing *n.* trimming on an edge

edg'y *a.* **-i·er, -i·est** tense

ed'i·ble *a.* fit to be eaten

e'dict' *n.* public order

ed'i·fice (-fis) *n.* large, imposing building

ed'i·fy' *v.* **-fied', -fy'ing** instruct or improve —**ed'i·fi·ca'tion** *n.*

ed'it *v.* revise, select, etc. (writing) for publication 2 be in charge of (a newspaper, etc.) 3 prepare (film, etc.) by cutting, etc. —**ed'i·tor** *n.*

e·di'tion *n.* 1 form in which a book is published 2 total copies of a book, etc. published at one time

ed'i·to'ri·al *n.* article in a newspaper, etc. stating the opinions of the editor, publisher, etc. —*a.* of an editor —**ed'i·to'ri·al·ize'** *v.* —**ed'i·to'ri·al·ly** *adv.*

ed'u·cate' *v.* develop the knowledge, skill, etc. of by schooling —**ed·u·ca'tion** *n.* —**ed'u·ca'tor** *n.*

-ee *suf.* 1 recipient of an action 2 one in a specified condition

EEG *abbrev.* electroencephalogram

eel *n.* snakelike fish

e'er (er) *adv.* [Poet.] ever

ee·rie, ee·ry (ir'ē) *a.* **-ri·er, -ri·est** weird; uncanny —**ee'ri·ly** *adv.*

ef·face' *v.* erase; wipe out

ef·fect' *n.* 1 a result 2 influence 3 meaning 4 *pl.* belongings —*v.* bring about —**in effect** 1 actually 2 in operation —**take effect** begin to act

ef·fec'tive *a.* 1 producing a desired result 2 in operation —**ef·fec'tive·ly**

adv. —**ef·fec'tive·ness** *n.*

ef·fec'tu·al (-choō'əl) *a.* EFFECTIVE (*a.* 1) —**ef·fec'tu·al·ly** *adv.*

ef·fec'tu·ate' *v.* effect

ef·fem'i·nate *a.* showing womanly traits; unmanly

ef·fer·vesce' (-ves') *v.* 1 to bubble 2 be lively —**ef·fer·ves'cence** *n.* —**ef·fer·ves'cent** *a.*

ef·fete' (-fēt') *a.* decadent

ef·fi·ca'cious *a.* EFFECTIVE (*a.* 1)

ef·fi'cient (-fish'ənt) *a.* effective with a minimum of effort, expense, etc. —**ef·fi'cien·cy** *n.* —**ef·fi'cient·ly** *adv.*

ef'fi·gy *n.*, *pl.* **-gies** statue or image; esp., a crude figure of a despised person, as for mock hanging

ef'flu·ent *n.* outflow of a sewer, etc.

ef'fort *n.* 1 use of energy to do something 2 attempt

ef·fron'ter·y *n.* impudence

ef·fu'sive (-fyōō'-) *a.* gushing

e.g. *abbrev.* for example

e·gal·i·tar'i·an *a.* advocating full equality for all

egg *n.* 1 oval body from which young of birds, fish, etc. are hatched 2 ovum —*v.* to urge on

egg'head' *n.* [Sl.] an intellectual

egg'nog' *n.* drink made of eggs, milk, sugar, etc.

egg'plant' *n.* large, purple, pear-shaped vegetable

eg'lan·tine' (-tīn', -tēn') *n.* kind of pink rose

e'go *n.* 1 the self 2 conceit 3 the rational part of the mind that controls actions

e'go·cen'tric *a.* self-centered

e'go·ism' *n.* 1 selfishness 2 conceit —**e'go·ist** *n.* —**e'go·is'tic** *a.*

e'go·tism' *n.* 1 excessive reference to oneself 2 conceit —**e'go·tist** *n.* —**e'go·tis'tic, -ti·cal** *a.*

ego trip *n.* [Sl.] egocentric or vain experience

e·gre'gious (-jəs) *a.* flagrant

e'gress' *n.* an exit

e'gret' *n.* heron having long, white plumes

E·gyp'tian (ē jip'shən) *n.*, *a.* (native) of Egypt

eh (ā, e) *int.* sound expressing surprise, doubt, etc.

ei'der (ī'-) *n.* large sea duck with soft, fine down (**ei'der·down'**)

eight *a.*, *n.* one more than seven —**eighth** *a.*, *n.*

eight'een' *a.*, *n.* eight more than ten —**eight'eenth'** *a.*, *n.*

eight'y *a.*, *n.*, *pl.* **-ies** eight times ten

—**eight'i·eth** a., n.

ei'ther (ē'-, ī'-) a., pron. one or the other (of two) —con. correlative used with or —adv. any more than the other

e·jac'u·late' v. **1** eject (esp. semen) **2** exclaim suddenly —**e·jac·u·la'tion** n.

e·ject' v. throw out; expel

eke (ēk) v. barely manage to make (a living): with out

EKG abbrev. electrocardiogram

e·lab'o·rate' (-rāt'; a.: -rət) v. add details —a. in great detail

é·lan (ā län') n. spirited self-assurance

e·lapse' v. pass, as time

e·las'tic a. **1** springing back to shape **2** flexible —n. band, etc. with rubber in it —**e·las·tic'i·ty** (-tis'-) n.

e·las'ti·cize' v. make elastic

e·late' v. make proud, happy, etc. —**e·la'tion** n.

el'bow n. joint between the upper and lower arm —v. push or shove as with the elbows

elbow grease n. [Inf.] hard work

el'bow·room' n. ample space

eld'er a. older —n. **1** older person **2** church official **3** shrub with dark berries

el'der·ber'ry n., pl. –ries **1** the ELDER (n. 3) **2** its berry

eld'er·ly a., pl.n. quite old (people)

eld'est a. oldest

e·lect' v. select, esp. by voting —a. specially chosen —**e·lec'tion** n.

e·lec'tion·eer' v. canvass votes in an election

e·lec'tive a. **1** filled by election **2** optional —n. optional subject in school

e·lec'tor n. **1** qualified voter **2** member of the electoral college

e·lec'tor·al college n. assembly that formally elects the U.S. president

e·lec'tor·ate n. the body of qualified voters

e·lec'tric, e·lec'tri·cal a. of, charged with, or worked by electricity

e·lec·tri'cian (-trish'ən) n. one who installs and repairs electrical apparatus

e·lec·tric'i·ty (-tris'-) n. **1** form of energy with magnetic, chemical, and radiant effects **2** electric current

e·lec'tri·fy' v. **–fied', –fy'ing 1** equip for the use of electricity **2** thrill

e·lec'tro·car'di·o·gram' n. tracing showing electrical changes in the heart

e·lec'tro·car'di·o·graph' n. instrument for making electrocardiograms

e·lec'tro·cute' v. kill by electricity —**e·lec'tro·cu'tion** n.

e·lec'trode' n. terminal of an electric source

e·lec'tro·en·ceph'a·lo·gram' (-sef'-) n. tracing showing electrical activity in brain

e·lec'tro·en·ceph'a·lo·graph' n. instrument for making electroencephalograms

e·lec·trol'y·sis (-träl'ə-) n. breakdown into ions of a chemical compound in solution by electrical current

e·lec'tro·lyte' (-līt') n. substance which in solution conducts electric current —**e·lec·tro·lyt'ic** (-lit'-) a.

e·lec'tro·mag'net n. soft iron core made magnetic by an electric current —**e·lec'tro·mag·net'ic** a. —**e·lec'tro·mag'net·ism'** n.

electromagnetic wave n. wave generated by an oscillating electric charge

e·lec'tro·mo'tive a. producing an electric current

e·lec'tron' n. negatively charged particle in an atom

e·lec·tron'ic a. of or done by the action of electrons

electronic mail n. e-mail

e·lec·tron'ics n. science of electronic action —pl.n. electronic equipment

electron microscope n. instrument using electrons to enlarge the image of an object

electron tube n. electronic device used in radio, etc.

e·lec'tro·plate' v. coat with metal by electrolysis

el'e·gant a. tastefully luxurious —**el'e·gance** n. —**el'e·gant·ly** adv.

el'e·gy (-jē) n., pl. –gies poem lamenting a dead person —**e·le·gi'ac** (-jī'-) a.

elem abbrev. elementary

el'e·ment n. **1** natural environment **2** basic part or feature **3** Chem. substance that cannot be separated into different substances except by nuclear disintegration —**the elements** wind, rain, etc. —**el'e·men'tal** a.

el'e·men'ta·ry a. of fundamentals; introductory

elementary school n. school of the first six (or eight) grades

el'e·phant n. huge, thick-skinned mammal with a long trunk and ivory tusks

el'e·phan'tine' (-tēn') a. huge, clumsy, etc.

el'e·vate' v. **1** raise **2** raise in rank **3** elate

el·e·va'tion n. 1 high place 2 height, as above sea level

el·e·va'tor n. 1 suspended cage for hoisting or lowering goods or people 2 warehouse for grain

e·lev'en a., n. one more than ten —**e·lev'enth** a., n.

elf n., pl. **elves** small fairy —**elf'in** a.

e·lic'it (-lis'-) v. draw forth

e·lide' v. slur over

el'i·gi·ble a. qualified —n. eligible person —**el'i·gi·bil'i·ty** n.

e·lim'i·nate' v. 1 remove 2 excrete —**e·lim'i·na'tion** n.

e·lite' (ā lēt') n. best or most powerful part of a group

e·lit'ism' n. government or control by an elite —**e·lit'ist** a., n.

e·lix'ir (-ər) n. medicine in a sweetened solution

elk n. large deer

ell n. 1 extension at right angles to main part 2 L-shaped joint

el·lipse' n. closed curve that is a symmetrical oval —**el·lip'ti·cal** a.

el·lip'sis n. 1 omission of a word or words 2 mark (...) showing this

elm n. tall shade tree

el'o·cu'tion n. art of public speaking

e·lon'gate' v. lengthen —**e·lon·ga'tion** n.

e·lope' v. run away to marry —**e·lope'ment** n.

el'o·quent a. vivid or forceful in expression —**el'o·quence** n.

else a. 1 different; other 2 in addition —adv. 1 otherwise 2 if not

else'where' adv. in or to some other place

e·lu'ci·date' v. explain

e·lude' v. escape; evade

e·lu'sive a. hard to grasp; baffling

elves n. pl. of ELF

e·ma'ci·ate' (-shē-, -sē-) v. make too thin —**e·ma'ci·a'tion** n.

e-'mail' n. message(s) sent by computer, as through a telephone line

em'a·nate' v. come or issue —**em'a·na'tion** n.

e·man'ci·pate' v. set free —**e·man'ci·pa'tion** n. —**e·man'ci·pa'tor** n.

e·mas'cu·late' v. castrate

em·balm' (-bäm') v. preserve (a dead body)

em·bank'ment n. bank of earth, etc. as to keep back water

em·bar'go n., pl. **-goes** legal restriction of commerce or shipping

em·bark' v. 1 go aboard a ship 2 begin; start —**em'bar·ka'tion** n.

em·bar'rass v. cause to feel self-conscious —**em·bar'rass·ment** n.

em'bas·sy n., pl. **-sies** staff or headquarters of an ambassador

em·bat'tled a. in a conflict

em·bed' v. **-bed'ded, -bed'ding** set firmly (in)

em·bel'lish v. 1 decorate 2 add details, often untrue —**em·bel'lish·ment** n.

em'ber n. glowing piece of coal or wood

em·bez'zle v. steal (money entrusted) —**em·bez'zle·ment** n. —**em·bez'zler** n.

em·bit'ter v. make bitter

em·bla'zon v. 1 decorate 2 display openly

em'blem n. visible symbol; sign —**em'blem·at'ic** a.

em·bod'y v. **-ied, -y·ing** 1 give form to 2 include —**em·bod'i·ment** n.

em·bold'en v. make bold

em'bo·lism' n. obstruction of a blood vessel

em·boss' v. decorate with raised designs

em·bou·chure' (äm'boo shoor') n. way of putting lips on mouthpiece of a wind instrument

em·brace' v. 1 hug lovingly 2 adopt, as an idea 3 include —n. an embracing

em·broi'der v. ornament with needlework —**em·broi'der·y** n., pl. **-ies**

em·broil' v. get involved

em'bry·o' (-brē-) n., pl. **-os'** animal or plant in earliest stages of development —**em'bry·on'ic** a.

em·cee' v. **-ceed', -cee'ing**; n. [Inf.] (act as) master of ceremonies

e·mend' v. correct, as a text —**e'men·da'tion** n.

em'er·ald n. green jewel

e·merge' v. come out; appear —**e·mer'gence** n.

e·mer'gen·cy n., pl. **-cies** sudden occurrence demanding quick action

e·mer'i·tus a. retired, but keeping one's title

em'er·y n. hard corundum used for grinding, etc.

e·met'ic n., a. (substance) causing vomiting

em'i·grate' v. leave one country to settle in another —**em'i·grant** a., n. —**em'i·gra'tion** n.

é·mi·gré, **e·mi·gré** (em'i grā') n. one forced to flee for political reasons

em'i·nent a. prominent or high —**em'i·nence** n.

eminent domain n. right of a govern-

e·mir (e mir') n. Muslim ruler

em'is·sar·y n., pl. **-ies** one sent on a mission

e·mit' v. **e·mit'ted, e·mit'ting 1** send out; discharge **2** utter —**e·mis'sion** n. —**e·mit'ter** n.

e·mol'lient (-yənt) n., a. (medicine) for soothing the skin

e·mol'u·ment (-yŏo-) n. salary

e·mote' v. [Inf.] show emotion dramatically

e·mo'tion n. strong feeling, as of love, fear, anger, etc. —**e·mo'tion·al** a.

e·mo'tion·al·ize' v. deal with in an emotional way

em'pa·thet'ic a. showing empathy

em'pa·thize' v. have empathy (with)

em'pa·thy n. ability to share another's feelings

em'per·or n. ruler of an empire —**em'press** n.fem.

em'pha·sis n., pl. **-ses'** (-sēz') **1** stress; importance **2** stress on a syllable

em'pha·size' v. to stress

em·phat'ic a. **1** using emphasis **2** forcible —**em·phat'i·cal·ly** adv.

em'phy·se'ma (-fə-) n. disease of the lungs

em'pire' n. group of countries under one sovereign

em·pir'i·cal (-pir'-) a. based on experiment or experience

em·place'ment n. prepared position for a large gun

em·ploy' v. **1** to use **2** keep busy **3** hire or have as workers —n. employment

em·ploy·ee, em·ploy'e (-ē) n. person working for another for pay

em·ploy'er n. one who employs others for pay

em·ploy'ment n. **1** an employing or being employed **2** work; occupation

em·po'ri·um n. large store

em·pow'er v. **1** authorize **2** enable

emp'ty a. **-ti·er, -ti·est 1** with nothing or no one in it **2** worthless —v. **-tied, -ty·ing 1** make or become empty **2** pour out —n., pl. **-ties** empty bottle, etc. —**emp'ti·ness** n.

em·py're·an (-pir'ē-) n. **1** highest heaven **2** the sky

EMT abbrev. emergency medical technician

e·mu (ē'myōō') n. ostrichlike bird

em'u·late' v. **1** to try to equal or surpass **2** imitate —**em·u·la'tion** n.

e·mul'si·fy' v. **-fied', -fy'ing** form into an emulsion

e·mul'sion n. oil suspended in watery liquid

en- pref. **1** to put on **2** to make **3** in or into

-en suf. **1** make or become **2** get or give **3** made of

en·a'ble v. make able

en·act' v. **1** pass, as a law **2** act out

en·am'el n. **1** glassy coating fused to metal **2** white coating of teeth **3** hard, glossy paint —v. coat with enamel —**en·am'el·ware'** n.

en·am'or v. fill with love; charm

en bloc' adv. all together

en·camp' v. set up, or put in, a camp —**en·camp'ment** n.

en·cap'su·late' v. **1** enclose in a capsule **2** condense

en·case' v. enclose

-ence suf. act, state, or result: also **-ency**

en·ceph'a·li'tis (-sef'-) n. inflammation of the brain

en·chant' v. charm; delight

en·chi·la·da (-lä'-) n. tortilla rolled with meat inside

en·cir'cle v. surround

encl abbrev. enclosure

en'clave' n. foreign land inside another country

en·close' v. **1** surround; shut in **2** insert in an envelope —**en·clo'sure** n.

en·code' v. put (a message) into code

en·co'mi·um n. high praise

en·com'pass v. **1** surround **2** contain

en'core' (än'-) int. again —n. song, etc. added by demand

en·coun'ter v. **1** meet unexpectedly **2** fight —n. **1** unexpected meeting **2** fight

en·cour'age v. **1** give courage or hope to **2** help —**en·cour'age·ment** n.

en·croach' v. intrude (on) —**en·croach'ment** n.

en·crust' v. to cover with, or form into, a crust —**en·crus·ta'tion** n.

en·cum'ber v. **1** hinder **2** burden —**en·cum'brance** n.

en·cyc'li·cal (-sik'-) n. papal letter to bishops

en·cy·clo·pe'di·a n. book or set of books on one or all branches of knowledge —**en·cy·clo·pe'dic** a.

end n. **1** last part; finish **2** destruction **3** tip **4** purpose —v. finish; stop —a. final —**end'ing** n.

en·dan'ger v. put in danger

en·dear' v. make beloved

en·dear'ment n. affection

en·deav'or (-dev'-) v. try hard —n. earnest attempt

en·dem'ic *a.* prevalent in a place, as a disease

en'dive' *n.* salad plant like lettuce

end'less *a.* 1 eternal; infinite 2 lasting too long 3 with the ends joined to form a ring

end'most' *a.* farthest

en'do·crine' (-krin') *a.* designating or of any gland that produces a hormone —*n.* any such gland or hormone

en·dorse' *v.* 1 sign on the back of (a check) 2 approve —**en·dorse'ment** *n.*

en·dow' *v.* 1 provide with some quality 2 give money to —**en·dow'ment** *n.*

end'point' *n.* point of completion or most progress

en·dur'ance *n.* ability to last, stand pain, etc.

en·dure' *v.* 1 stand (pain, etc.) 2 tolerate 3 to last

end'ways' *adv.* 1 lengthwise 2 end to end Also **end'wise'**

en·e'ma *n.* forcing of a liquid into the colon through the anus as a purgative, etc.

en'e·my *n., pl.* **-mies** person or nation hostile to another; foe

en'er·gize' *v.* give energy to

en'er·gy *n., pl.* **-gies** 1 vigor; power 2 capacity to do work —**en'er·get'ic** *a.*

en'er·vate' *v.* weaken

en·fee'ble *v.* weaken

en·fold' *v.* 1 wrap up 2 embrace

en·force' *v.* 1 impose by force 2 make people obey (a law) —**en·force'ment** *n.* —**en·forc'er** *n.*

en·fran'chise' *v.* 1 free from slavery 2 give the right to vote

Eng *abbrev.* 1 England 2 English

en·gage' *v.* 1 involve oneself 2 hire 3 attract and hold 4 enter into conflict with 5 interlock; mesh —**en·gage'ment** *n.*

en·gaged' *a.* 1 promised in marriage 2 busy

en·gag'ing *a.* charming

en·gen'der *v.* cause

en'gine *n.* 1 a machine using energy to develop mechanical power 2 locomotive

en'gi·neer' *n.* 1 one trained in engineering 2 locomotive driver —*v.* manage skillfully

en'gi·neer'ing *n.* practical use of sciences in industry, building, etc.

Eng'lish *a., n.* 1 (of) the people or language of England

en·gorge' *v.* congest (tissue), as with blood

en·grave' *v.* cut (designs) on (a metal plate, etc.), as for printing —**en·grav'er** *n.* —**en·grav'ing** *n.*

en·gross' (-grōs') *v.* take the full attention of

en·gulf' *v.* swallow up

en·hance' *v.* make greater

e·nig'ma *n.* baffling matter, person, etc. —**en'ig·mat'ic, e·nig·mat'i·cal** *a.*

en·join' *v.* 1 to command 2 prohibit by law

en·joy' *v.* 1 get pleasure from 2 have the use of —**enjoy oneself** have a good time —**en·joy'a·ble** *a.* —**en·joy'ment** *n.*

en·large' *v.* make larger —**enlarge on (or upon)** discuss fully —**en·large'ment** *n.*

en·light'en *v.* free from ignorance, prejudice, etc.

en·list' *v.* 1 enroll in an army, etc. 2 engage in a cause —**en·list'ment** *n.*

en·liv'en *v.* liven up

en masse' *adv.* all together

en·mesh' *v.* entangle

en'mi·ty *n.* ill will

en·no'ble *v.* dignify

en·nui' (än'wē') *n.* boredom

e·nor'mi·ty *n., pl.* **-ties** 1 great wickedness 2 huge size; vastness

e·nor'mous *a.* huge; vast

e·nough' *a., adv.* as much as is needed —*n.* amount needed —*int.* no more

en·plane' *v.* board an airplane

en·quire' *v.* inquire —**en·quir'y** *n., pl.* **-ies**

en·rage' *v.* put into a rage

en·rap'ture *v.* fill with delight

en·rich' *v.* make rich(er) —**en·rich'ment** *n.*

en·roll' *v.* put or be put in a list, as a member, etc. —**en·roll'ment** *n.*

en route (än rōōt') *adv., a.* on the way

en·sconce' *v.* place snugly

en·sem'ble (än säm'-) *n.* 1 total effect 2 costume of matching parts 3 group of musicians playing together

en·shrine' *v.* enclose as in a shrine

en·shroud' *v.* hide

en'sign (-sən) *n.* 1 flag 2 lowest-ranking navy officer

en'si·lage *n.* green fodder in silo

en·slave' *v.* make a slave of

en·snare' *v.* catch as in a snare

en·sue' *v.* follow; result

en·sure' *v.* 1 make sure 2 protect

en·tail' *v.* make necessary

en·tan'gle *v.* trap; confuse

en·tente (än tänt') *n.* agreement between nations

en'ter *v.* 1 come or go in 2 put in a list, etc. 3 join 4 begin —**enter into**

1 take part in **2** form a part of — **enter on** (or **upon**) begin

en·ter·i′tis n. inflammation of the intestine

en′ter·prise′ n. **1** important undertaking **2** energy and boldness

en′ter·pris′ing a. full of energy and boldness

en·ter·tain′ v. **1** amuse **2** act as host to **3** consider, as an idea —**en′ter·tain′er** n. —**en′ter·tain′ment** n.

en·thral(l)′ v. fascinate

en·throne′ v. place on throne

en·thuse′ (-thōōz′) v. [Inf.] act or make enthusiastic

en·thu′si·asm′ n. eager interest —**en·thu′si·ast′** n. —**en·thu′si·as′tic** a.

en·tice′ v. tempt

en·tire′ a. complete; whole —**en·tire′ly** adv. —**en·tire′ty** n.

en·ti·tle v. **1** give a title to **2** give a right to

en·ti·ty n., pl. **-ties** thing having real existence

en·tomb′ v. put in a tomb; bury

en·to·mol′o·gy n. study of insects

en·tou·rage′ (än′tōō räzh′) n. retinue; attendants

en′trails pl.n. inner organs; spec., intestines

en·trance (v.: en trans′) n. **1** act of entering **2** door, gate, etc. **3** permission to enter —v. to delight

en′trant n. one who enters a contest

en·trap′ v. catch in a trap

en·treat′ v. ask earnestly

en·treat′y n., pl. **-ies** earnest request; prayer

en·tree, en·trée (än′trā′) n. main dish

en·trench′ v. set securely —**en·trench′ment** n.

en·tre·pre·neur (än′trə prə nur′) n. one who organizes and operates a business

en′tro·py n. tendency of energy system to run down

en·trust′ v. assign the care of (to)

en′try n., pl. **-tries 1** entrance **2** item in a list, etc. **3** contestant

en′try-lev′el a. **1** of a job with low pay but possible advancement **2** introductory

en·twine′ v. twist together or around

e·nu′mer·ate′ v. name one by one —**e·nu′mer·a′tion** n.

e·nun′ci·ate′ v. **1** to state **2** pronounce (words) clearly —**e·nun′ci·a′tion** n.

en·u·re′sis n. inability to control urination

en·vel′op v. **1** wrap up **2** surround —**en·vel′op·ment** n.

en′ve·lope′ (än′-, en′-) n. covering, esp. for a letter

en·ven′om v. **1** put venom into **2** fill with hate

en·vi′ron·ment n. **1** surroundings **2** conditions of life on earth —**en·vi′ron·men′tal** a.

en·vi′ron·men′tal·ist n. person working to solve environmental problems

en·vi′rons pl.n. suburbs

en·vis′age (-viz′-) v. imagine

en·vi′sion v. imagine

en′voy (än′-, en′-) n. **1** messenger **2** diplomatic official

en′vy n. **1** discontent and ill will over another's advantages, etc. **2** object of such feeling —v. feel envy toward —**en′vi·a·ble** a. —**en′vi·ous** a.

en′zyme′ (-zīm′) n. a catalyst formed in body cells

e′on n. very long time

EPA abbrev. Environmental Protection Agency

ep′au·let′ (ep′ə-) n. shoulder ornament on a uniform

e·pee, é·pée (ā pā′) n. rigid sword for fencing

e·phem′er·al a. short-lived

ep′ic n. long poem about a hero's deeds —a. heroic; grand: also **ep′i·cal**

ep′i·cen′ter n. focal point, as of an earthquake

ep′i·cure′ n. one with a fine taste for foods and liquors —**ep′i·cu·re′an** a.

ep′i·dem′ic n., a. (disease) that spreads rapidly

ep′i·der′mis n. outermost layer of the skin

ep′i·glot′tis n. thin lid of cartilage covering windpipe during swallowing

ep′i·gram′ n. witty saying

ep′i·lep′sy n. disease marked by convulsive fits, etc. —**ep′i·lep′tic** a., n.

ep′i·logue′, ep′i·log′ (-lôg′) n. part added at the end of a novel, play, etc.

e·piph′a·ny n. moment of insight

e·pis′co·pal a. **1** of or governed by bishops **2** [E-] of the U.S. Anglican church —**E·pis′co·pa′li·an** a., n.

ep′i·sode′ n. incident —**ep′i·sod′ic** a.

e·pis′tle (-pis′əl) n. **1** letter **2** [E-] letter in the New Testament

ep′i·taph′ n. inscription on a tomb

ep′i·thet′ n. word or phrase characterizing a person, etc.

e·pit′o·me′ (-mē′) n. **1** typical part or thing **2** summary —**e·pit′o·mize′** v.

ep′och (-ək) n. period marked by certain events —**ep′och·al** a.

ep·ox′y n. resin used in strong glues, enamels, etc.

Ep'som salts (or **salt**) *n.* salt used as a cathartic

eq'ua·ble (ek'wə-) *a.* even; calm —**eq'ua·bly** *adv.*

e'qual *a.* of the same quantity, value, rank, etc. —*n.* person or thing that is equal —*v.* be, or do something, equal to —**equal to** capable of —**e·qual'i·ty** *n.* —**e'qual·ize'** *v.* —**e'qual·ly** *adv.*

e'qual-op'por·tu'ni·ty *a.* not discriminating because of race, sex, etc.

equal sign *n.* sign (=) indicating equality

e'qua·nim'i·ty (ek'wə-, ē'kwə-) *n.* composure

e·quate' *v.* treat, regard, or express as equal

e·qua'tion *n.* **1** an equating **2** *Math.* equality of two quantities as shown by the equal sign

e·qua'tor *n.* imaginary circle around the earth, equidistant from the North and South Poles —**e'qua·to'ri·al** *a.*

e·ques'tri·an *a.* of horses or horsemanship —*n.* a rider or acrobat on horseback

equi- *pref.* equal, equally

e'qui·dis'tant *a.* equally distant

e'qui·lat'er·al *a.* having all sides equal

e'qui·lib'ri·um *n.* state of balance

e'quine' *a.* of a horse

e'qui·nox' *n.* time when the sun crosses the equator, making night and day of equal length everywhere

e·quip' *v.* **-quipped', -quip'ping** fit out, as for an undertaking —**e·quip'ment** *n.*

equi·ui·page (ek'wə pij) *n.* horse and carriage with servants

e·qui·poise' *n.* equilibrium

eq'ui·ta·ble *a.* fair; just

eq'ui·ta'tion *n.* horsemanship

eq'ui·ty *n., pl.* **-ties 1** fairness **2** value of property beyond amount owed on it **3** *pl.* shares of stock

e·quiv'a·lent *a.* equal in quantity, meaning, etc. —*n.* equivalent thing —**e·quiv'a·lence** *n.*

e·quiv'o·cal *a.* **1** purposely ambiguous **2** doubtful —**e·quiv'o·cate'** *v.* —**e·quiv'o·ca'tion** *n.*

ER *abbrev.* emergency room

-er *suf.* one that

e·ra (ir'ə, er'ə) *n.* period of time

ERA *abbrev.* **1** earned run average: also **era 2** Equal Rights Amendment

e·rad'i·cate' *v.* wipe out —**e·rad'i·ca'tion** *n.*

e·rase' *v.* rub out, as writing —**e·ras'er** *n.* —**e·ras'a·ble** *a.*

e·ra'sure (-shər) *n.* **1** erased mark **2**

place where something was erased

ere (er) *con., prep.* [Poet.] before

e·rect' *a.* upright —*v.* **1** construct; build **2** set upright —**e·rec'tion** *n.*

e·rec'tile (-til, -tīl') *a.* that becomes rigid when filled with blood

erg *n.* unit of work

er·go·nom'ics (ur'-) *n.* the science of suitable working conditions —*pl.n.* ergonomic factors —**er·go·nom'ic** *a.*

er·mine (ur'min) *n.* weasel with white fur in winter

e·rode' *v.* wear away —**e·ro'sion** *n.*

e·rog'e·nous (-räj'-) *a.* sensitive to sexual stimulation

e·ros (er'äs') *n.* sexual desire

e·rot'ic *a.* causing sexual feelings or desires

e·rot'i·ca *pl.n.* [*sing.* or *pl.* v.] erotic books, etc.

err (ur, er) *v.* **1** be wrong **2** violate a moral code

er'rand *n.* short trip to do a thing

er'rant *a.* wandering

er·ra'ta (-rät'ə) *pl.n., sing.* **-tum** printing errors

er·rat'ic *a.* irregular; odd

er·ro'ne·ous *a.* wrong

er'ror *n.* **1** mistake; blunder **2** mistaken belief

er'satz' (-zäts') *a.* being an inferior substitute

erst'while' *a.* former

e·ruct' *v.* to belch —**e·ruc·ta'tion** *n.*

er'u·dite' (-yōō-) *a.* learned; scholarly —**er·u·di'tion** *n.*

e·rupt' *v.* **1** burst forth **2** break out in a rash —**e·rup'tion** *n.*

-ery *suf.* **1** a place to or for **2** act or product of **3** condition of

er'y·sip'e·las (er'ī-) *n.* acute skin disease

e·ryth'ro·cyte (e rith'rō sīt') *n.* mature red blood cell containing hemoglobin

es'ca·late' *v.* rise, expand, or increase —**es·ca·la'tion** *n.*

es'ca·la'tor *n.* moving stairway on an endless belt

es·cal'lop, es·cal'op (e skäl'əp, -skal'-) *n., v.* scallop

es'ca·pade' *n.* reckless adventure or prank

es·cape' *v.* **1** get free **2** slip away from —*n.* act or means of escape

es·cap'ee' *n.* one who has escaped

es·cape'ment *n.* notched wheel regulating movement in a clock

es·cap'ism' *n.* tendency to escape reality by fantasy

es·car·got' (-gō') *n.* edible snail

es·ca·role′ n. endive

es·carp′ment n. cliff

es·chew′ v. shun

es′cort′ (v.: i skôrt′) n. person(s) accompanying another, as to protect or honor —v. go with as an escort

es′crow′ n. state of a deed held by a third party until conditions are fulfilled

es·cutch′eon (-ən) n. shield bearing a coat of arms

Es′ki·mo′ n., pl. **-mos′** or **-mo′**; a. (member) of a people living in Greenland, arctic North America, etc.

Eskimo dog n. strong dog used in some arctic regions to pull sleds

ESL abbrev. English as a second language

e·soph′a·gus n., pl. **-gi′** (-jī′) passage between the pharynx and stomach

es·o·ter′ic a. known or understood by few

ESP n. extrasensory perception

esp. abbrev. especially

es′pa·drille′ n. flat canvas shoe with rope sole

es·pal′ier (-yər, -yā′) n. tree growing flat on lattice

es·pe′cial a. special; chief —**es·pe′cial·ly** adv.

Es′pe·ran′to (-rän′-) n. artificial international language

es′pi·o·nage′ (-näzh′) n. a spying

es′pla·nade′ (or -näd′) n. a public walk

es·pouse (e spouz′) v. 1 marry 2 support (an idea or cause) —**es·pous′al** n.

es·pres′so n. coffee made by forcing steam through ground coffee beans

es·py (e spī′) v. **-pied′, -py′ing** catch sight of; see

-esque (esk) suf. having the quality or style of

Es′quire′ n. title of courtesy put after a man's surname, or, in U.S., after a lawyer's name: abbrev. **Esq.**

-ess suf. female

es·say′ (n.: es′ā) v. to try —n. **1** a try **2** short personal writing on one subject —**es′say·ist** n.

es′sence n. **1** basic nature **2** substance in concentrated form **3** perfume

es·sen′tial (-shəl) n., a. (something) necessary

est abbrev. **1** established: also **estab 2** estimate(d)

EST abbrev. Eastern Standard Time

es·tab′lish v. **1** set up; fix **2** to found **3** prove

es·tab′lish·ment n. **1** an establishing **2** a business —**the Establishment**

powerful elite of a nation, etc.

es·tate′ n. **1** one's possessions **2** piece of land with a residence, esp. a large one

es·teem′ v. value highly —n. high regard

es′ter n. organic salt

es′thete′ n. aesthete —**es·thet′ic** a.

es′ti·ma·ble a. worthy of esteem

es′ti·mate′ (-māt′; n.: -mət) v. to figure roughly (size, cost, etc.) —n. **1** rough calculation **2** opinion —**es′ti·ma′tion** n.

es·trange′ v. make unfriendly

es′tro·gen n. female sex hormone

es′tu·ar′y (-tyōō-, -chōō-) n., pl. **-ies** wide mouth of a river

ET abbrev. Eastern Time

ETA abbrev. estimated time of arrival

et al. abbrev. and others

et cet′er·a and so forth: abbrev. **etc.**

etch v. put a design on metal plates or glass with acid, often for making prints —**etch′ing** n.

e·ter′nal a. **1** everlasting **2** forever the same —**e·ter′nal·ly** adv.

e·ter′ni·ty n. **1** a being eternal **2** endless time

eth′ane′ n. gaseous hydrocarbon used as fuel

e′ther n. an anesthetic

e·the′re·al (-thir′ē-) a. **1** light; delicate **2** heavenly

eth′ic n. **1** ethics **2** particular moral standard or value

eth′i·cal a. **1** of ethics **2** proper; right

eth′ics pl.n. [sing. or pl. v.] moral standards; system of morals

eth′nic a. of any of the many peoples of mankind —n. member of a nationality group in a larger community

eth·nic′i·ty (-nis′-) n. ethnic affiliation

eth·nol′o·gy n. comparative study of the cultures of contemporary societies —**eth′no·log′i·cal** a.

e′thos′ (-thäs′) n. characteristic attitudes, beliefs, etc.

eth′yl (-əl) n. carbon-hydrogen radical of common alcohol, etc.

eth′yl·ene′ n. flammable, smelly gaseous hydrocarbon

e·ti·ol′o·gy (ēt′ē-) n., pl. **-gies** cause of a disease, etc.

et′i·quette (-kət) n. social forms; good manners

et seq. abbrev. and the following

é′tude′ (ā′-) n. Mus. instrumental piece stressing a technique

et′y·mol′o·gy n., pl. **-gies** origin of a word **2** study of word origins

EU abbrev. European Union

eu·ca·lyp'tus (yōō'kə lip'-) n. a sub-tropical evergreen

Eu'cha·rist (-kə-) n. Holy Communion

eu'chre (-kər) n. card game played with 32 cards

eu·gen'ics n. movement for improving the human race by heredity control —**eu·gen'ic** a.

eu'lo·gy n., pl. **-gies** praise —**eu'lo·gize'** v.

eu'nuch (-nək) n. castrated man

eu'phe·mism' n. mild word replacing an offensive one —**eu'phe·mis'tic** a.

eu·pho'ni·ous a. pleasant sounding —**eu·pho'ny** n.

eu·pho'ri·a n. feeling of well-being —**eu·phor'ic** a.

eu·re'ka int. cry of triumph

eu'ro n. monetary unit of the European Union

Eu'ro·pe'an n., a. (native) of Europe

European plan n. hotel billing in which rate covers room but not meals

European Union n. economic union of European nations

eu·ryth'mics n. rhythmical body movements to music

eu·sta'chian tube (-shən) n. [also E- t-] tube between middle ear and pharynx

eu·tha·na'sia (-zhə) n. painless death to end suffering

e·vac'u·ate' v. 1 make empty 2 to discharge (excrement) 3 remove 4 withdraw (from) —**e·vac'u·a'tion** n.

e·vac'u·ee' n. person evacuated from area of danger

e·vade' v. avoid by deceit or cleverness —**e·va'sion** n. —**e·va'sive** a.

e·val'u·ate' v. find the value of —**e·val'u·a'tion** n.

ev'a·nes'cent a. fleeting

e'van·gel'i·cal a. of the Gospels or New Testament

e·van'ge·list n. 1 [E-] Gospel writer 2 revivalist preacher —**e·van'ge·lism'** n. —**e·van'ge·lize'** v.

e·vap'o·rate' v. 1 change into vapor 2 condense by heating 3 vanish —**e·vap'o·ra'tion** n.

eve n. 1 [Poet.] evening 2 evening before a holiday 3 time just before

e'ven a. 1 flat; level 2 constant; uniform 3 calm 4 equal 5 divisible by two 6 exact —adv. 1 indeed 2 exactly 3 still —v. make or become even —**even if though** —**e'ven·ly** adv.

e'ven·hand'ed a. fair; just

eve'ning n. end of day and beginning of night

e·vent' n. 1 an occurrence 2 contest in a track meet, etc. —**in any event**

no matter what happens —**in the event of** in case of

e'ven–tem'pered a. not quickly angered or excited

e·vent'ful a. full of events; important

e·ven'tu·al (-chōō-) a. final —**e·ven'tu·al·ly** adv.

e·ven'tu·al'i·ty n., pl. **-ties** possible outcome

ev'er adv. 1 always 2 at any time 3 at all

ev'er·glade' n. swampy land

ev'er·green' n., a. (tree or plant) having green leaves all year

ev'er·last'ing a. eternal

ev'er·more' adv. [Ar.] forever; constantly

ev'er·y (-rē) a. 1 each of a group 2 all possible —**every now and then** occasionally —**every other** each alternate —**ev'er·y·bod'y, ev'er·y·one'** pron. —**ev'er·y·thing'** pron. —**ev'er·y·where'** adv.

ev'er·y·day' a. 1 daily 2 usual; common

e·vict' v. put (a tenant) out by law —**e·vic'tion** n.

ev'i·dence n. 1 sign; indication 2 basis for belief —v. make evident

ev'i·dent a. easy to see; clear —**ev'i·dent'ly** adv.

e·vil a. 1 morally bad 2 harmful —n. wickedness —**e'vil·do'er** n. —**e'vil·ly** adv.

e·vince' v. show plainly (a quality, feeling, etc.)

e·vis'cer·ate' (-vis'ər-) v. remove the entrails from

e·voke' v. call forth; produce —**ev'o·ca'tion** n.

ev'o·lu'tion n. 1 an evolving 2 theory that all species developed from earlier forms —**ev'o·lu'tion·ar'y** a.

e·volve' v. develop gradually; unfold

ewe (yōō) n. female sheep

ew'er (yōō'ər) n. large, wide-mouthed water pitcher

ex abbrev. 1 example 2 exchange

ex- pref. former

ex·ac'er·bate' (eg zas'-) v. aggravate —**ex·ac'er·ba'tion** n.

ex·act' a. strictly correct; precise —v. demand and get —**ex·act'i·tude'** n. —**ex·act'ly** adv.

ex·act'ing a. strict; hard

ex·ag'ger·ate' v. make seem greater than it really is; overstate —**ex·ag'ger·a'tion** n.

ex·alt' v. 1 raise in dignity 2 praise 3 fill with joy —**ex·al·ta'tion** n.

ex·am' n. examination

ex·am'ine v. 1 inspect 2 test by questioning —**ex·am'i·na'tion** n.

ex·am'ple n. 1 sample 2 a warning 3 illustration 4 model

ex·as'per·ate' v. annoy; vex —**ex·as'per·a'tion** n.

ex'ca·vate' v. 1 make a hole in 2 unearth 3 dig out —**ex'ca·va'tion** n. —**ex'ca·va'tor** n.

ex·ceed' v. 1 go beyond (a limit) 2 surpass

ex·ceed'ing a. extreme —**ex·ceed'ing·ly** adv.

ex·cel' v. **-celled', -cel'ling** be better than

Ex'cel·len·cy n., pl. **-cies** title of honor

ex'cel·lent a. unusually good —**ex'cel·lence** n.

ex·cel'si·or n. wood shavings used for packing

ex·cept' prep. leaving out; but —v. exclude —**except for** if it were not for

ex·cept'ing prep. except

ex·cep'tion n. 1 person or thing excluded 2 case to which a rule does not apply 3 objection —**take exception** to object

ex·cep'tion·al a. 1 unusual 2 gifted or handicapped

ex'cerpt' (v.: ek sʉrpt') n. passage selected from a book, etc. —v. select; extract

ex·cess' (a.: ek'ses') n. 1 more than is needed 2 surplus —a. extra —**ex·ces'sive** a.

ex·change' v. 1 to trade; barter 2 to interchange —n. 1 an exchanging 2 thing exchanged 3 place for exchanging —**ex·change'a·ble** a.

ex·cheq'uer (-chek'ər) n. treasury

ex'cise' (v.: ek sīz') n. tax on certain goods within a country: also **excise tax** —v. cut out —**ex·ci'sion** (-sizh'ən) n.

ex·cite' v. 1 make active 2 arouse; stir the feelings of —**ex·cit'a·ble** a. —**ex·cite'ment** n.

ex·claim' v. utter sharply —**ex'cla·ma'tion** n. —**ex·clam'a·to'ry** a.

exclamation point (or **mark**) n. mark of punctuation (!)

ex·clude' v. keep out or shut out —**ex·clu'sion** n.

ex·clu'sive a. 1 not shared 2 snobbish —**exclusive of** not including —**ex·clu'sive·ly** adv.

ex'com·mu'ni·cate' v. expel from communion with a church —**ex'com·mu'ni·ca'tion** n.

ex·co'ri·ate' (-kôr'ē-) v. denounce

ex'cre·ment n. waste material from the bowels

ex·cres'cence n. abnormal outgrowth

ex·crete' v. eliminate (waste) from the body —**ex·cre'tion** n. —**ex'cre·to'ry** a.

ex·cru'ci·at'ing (-shē āt'-) a. very painful; agonizing

ex'cul·pate' v. exonerate —**ex'cul·pa'tion** n.

ex·cur'sion n. short trip, as for pleasure

ex·cuse' (ek skyooz'; n.: ek skyoos') v. 1 overlook (an offense or fault) 2 release from a duty, etc. 3 let leave 4 justify —n. 1 something that excuses 2 pretext —**ex·cus'a·ble** a.

exec abbrev. 1 executive 2 executor

ex'e·cra·ble a. detestable

ex'e·crate' v. 1 denounce 2 loathe; abhor —**ex'e·cra'tion** n.

ex'e·cute' v. 1 carry out; do 2 put to death legally 3 make valid (a will, etc.) —**ex'e·cu'tion** n.

ex'e·cu'tion·er n. official who puts to death legally

ex·ec'u·tive a. 1 having to do with managing 2 administering laws, etc. —n. one who administers affairs

ex·ec'u·tor n. one who carries out the provisions of a legal will

ex·em'plar (-plər, -plär') n. model; pattern

ex·em'pla·ry a. serving as a model or example

ex·em'pli·fy' v. **-fied', -fy'ing** show by example

ex·empt' v., a. free(d) from a rule or obligation —**ex·emp'tion** n.

ex'er·cise' n. 1 active use 2 activity to develop the body, a skill, etc. 3 pl. program, as at a graduation ceremony —v. 1 use 2 do or give exercises 3 exert

ex·ert' v. put into action

ex·er'tion n. 1 act of exerting 2 effort

ex·hale' v. breathe forth —**ex'ha·la'tion** n.

ex·haust' v. 1 use up 2 drain 3 tire out —n. discharge from an engine —**ex·haust'i·ble** a. —**ex·haus'tion** n.

ex·haus'tive a. thorough

ex·hib'it (eg zib'-) v., n. show; display —**ex·hib'i·tor** n.

ex'hi·bi'tion (ek·sə-) n. 1 a (public) showing 2 that which is shown

ex'hi·bi'tion·ist n. one who likes to show off —**ex'hi·bi'tion·ism'** n.

ex·hil'a·rate' (eg zil'-) v. stimulate —**ex·hil'a·ra'tion** n.

ex·hort' (eg zôrt') v. urge earnestly —**ex'hor·ta'tion** n.

ex·hume' (eks hyoom') v. dig out of

the earth

ex·i·gen·cy *n.*, *pl.* **–cies 1** urgency **2** *pl.* pressing needs

ex·ig·u·ous *a.* scanty

ex·ile′ *n.* **1** a prolonged, often enforced, living away from one's country **2** person in exile —*v.* send into exile

ex·ist′ *v.* **1** be **2** occur **3** live —**ex·ist′ ence** *n.*

ex·is·ten′tial *a.* of existence

ex′it *n.* a (way of) leaving

ex′o·dus *n.* departure

ex of·fi·ci·o (ə fish′ē ō′) *adv.* by virtue of one's position

ex·on′er·ate′ *v.* to free from blame

ex·or′bi·tant *a.* excessive —**ex·or′bi·tance** *n.*

ex′or·cise′, ex′or·cize′ *v.* drive out (an evil spirit), as by magic —**ex′or·cism′** *n.*

ex·ot′ic *a.* **1** foreign **2** strangely beautiful, etc.

ex·pand′ *v.* **1** spread out **2** enlarge —**ex·pan′sion** *n.*

ex·panse′ *n.* wide extent

ex·pan′sive *a.* **1** broad **2** warm and open in talk, etc.

ex·pa′ti·ate′ (-pā′shē-) *v.* speak or write at length

ex·pa′tri·ate (-āt′; *n., a.:* -ət) *v., n., a.* exile(d)

ex·pect′ *v.* **1** look for as likely or due **2** [Inf.] suppose —**be expecting** [Inf.] be pregnant —**ex·pect′an·cy** *n.* —**ex·pect′ant** *a.* —**ex·pec·ta′tion** *n.*

ex·pec′to·rant *n.* medicine to bring up phlegm

ex·pec′to·rate′ *v.* to spit

ex·pe′di·ent *a.* **1** useful for the purpose **2** based on self-interest —*n.* a means to an end —**ex·pe′di·en·cy** *n.,* *pl.* **-cies**

ex′pe·dite′ *v.* speed up; facilitate —**ex′pe·dit·er** *n.*

ex·pe·di′tion *n.* **1** a journey, as for exploration **2** those on such a journey

ex·pe·di′tious (-dish′əs) *a.* prompt

ex·pel′ *v.* **-pelled′, -pel′ling 1** force out **2** dismiss by authority

ex·pend′ *v.* spend; use up —**ex·pend′a·ble** *a.*

ex·pend′i·ture *n.* **1** spending of money, time, etc. **2** amount spent

ex·pense′ *n.* **1** cost **2** *pl.* the charges met with in one's work, etc.

ex·pen′sive *a.* high-priced

ex·pe′ri·ence *n.* **1** a living through an event **2** thing one has done or lived through **3** skill gotten by training, work, etc. —*v.* have experience of

ex·per′i·ment *n., v.* test to discover or prove something —**ex·per′i·men′tal** *a.* —**ex·per′i·men·ta′tion** *n.*

ex′pert *a.* very skillful —*n.* one with great skill or knowledge in a field

ex′per·tise′ (-tēz′, -tēs′) *n.* the skill or knowledge of an expert

ex′pi·ate′ *v.* atone for —**ex′pi·a′tion** *n.*

ex·pire′ *v.* **1** die **2** come to an end **3** exhale —**ex′pi·ra′tion** *n.*

ex·plain′ *v.* **1** make plain or understandable **2** account for —**ex′pla·na′tion** *n.* —**ex·plan′a·to′ry** *a.*

ex′ple·tive *n.* oath or exclamation

ex·plic′a·ble *a.* that can be explained

ex′pli·cate′ *v.* explain fully

ex·plic′it *a.* clearly stated; definite

ex·plode′ *v.* **1** burst noisily **2** discredit —**ex·plo′sion** *n.*

ex′ploit′ (*v.:* ek sploit′) *n.* bold deed —*v.* use to advantage —**ex′ploi·ta′tion** *n.*

ex·plore′ *v.* **1** investigate **2** travel in (a region) for discovery —**ex′plo·ra′tion** *n.* —**ex·plor′a·to′ry** *a.*

ex·plo′sive *a.* of or like an explosion —*n.* substance that can explode

ex·po′nent *n.* **1** one who explains or promotes **2** representative **3** *Math.* symbol at upper right showing times as a factor

ex·port′ (*n.:* eks′pôrt′) *v.* send (goods) to another country for sale —*n.* something exported —**ex′por·ta′tion** *n.*

ex·pose′ *v.* **1** lay open, as to danger **2** reveal **3** to subject photographic film to light —**ex·po′sure** *n.*

ex′po·sé′ (-zā′) *n.* disclosure of a scandal

ex′po·si′tion *n.* **1** explanation **2** public exhibition

ex·pos′i·to′ry *a.* explanatory

ex post fac′to *a.* retroactive

ex·pos′tu·late′ (-päs′chə-) *v.* reason with a person in protest

ex·pound′ *v.* explain fully

ex·press′ *v.* **1** put into words **2** reveal; show **3** symbolize —*a.* **1** explicit **2** specific **3** fast and direct —*adv.* by express —*n.* an express train, bus, delivery service, etc.

ex·pres′sion *n.* **1** an expressing **2** certain word or phrase **3** look, etc. that shows how one feels —**ex·pres′sion·less** *a.* —**ex·pres′sive** *a.*

ex·pres′sion·ism′ *n.* art, writing, etc. expressing inner experience

ex·press′way′ *n.* divided highway for high-speed traffic

ex·pro′pri·ate′ *v.* take (land, etc.) for public use —**ex·pro′pri·a′tion** *n.*

117

ex·pul'sion *n.* an expelling or being expelled

ex·punge' *v.* erase

ex'pur·gate' *v.* delete objectionable material from

ex'qui·site *a.* 1 beautiful, delicate, etc. 2 very keen

ext *abbrev.* extension

ex'tant *a.* still existing

ex·tem'po·re (-rē) *adv., a.* without preparation: also **ex·tem'po·ra'ne·ous** *a.*

ex·tem'po·rize' *v.* speak, do, etc. extempore

ex·tend' *v.* 1 prolong 2 expand 3 stretch forth 4 offer

ex·tend'ed family *n.* nuclear family and other relatives living with them or nearby

ex·ten'sion *n.* 1 an extending 2 an addition

ex·ten'sive *a.* vast; far-reaching

ex·tent' *n.* 1 size 2 scope 3 vast area

ex·ten'u·ate' *v.* lessen the seriousness of (an offense)

ex·te'ri·or *a.* on or from the outside — *n.* the outside

ex·ter'mi·nate' *v.* to destroy entirely —**ex·ter'mi·na'tion** *n.* —**ex·ter'mi·na'tor** *n.*

ex·ter'nal *a.* on or from the outside

ex·tinct' *a.* no longer existing or active

ex·tinc'tion *n.* a dying out; annihilation

ex·tin'guish *v.* 1 put out (a fire) 2 destroy

ex'tir·pate' *v.* root out

ex·tol', ex·toll' *v.* -tolled', -tol'ling praise highly

ex·tort' *v.* get (money) by threats, etc. —**ex·tor'tion** *n.* —**ex·tor'tion·ist, ex·tor'tion·er** *n.*

ex'tra *a.* more than expected; additional —*n.* extra person or thing — *adv.* especially

extra– *pref.* outside, besides

ex·tract' (*n.:* eks'trakt') *v.* 1 pull out 2 get by pressing, distilling, etc. 3 select —*n.* something extracted —**ex·trac'tion** *n.*

ex'tra·cur·ric'u·lar *a.* not part of required curriculum

ex'tra·dite' *v.* return (a fugitive) —**ex'tra·di'tion** *n.*

ex·tra'ne·ous *a.* not essential or pertinent

ex·traor'di·nar'y (ek strôr'-) *a.* very unusual

ex·trap'o·late' *v.* to estimate on the basis of known facts —**ex·trap'o·la'tion** *n.*

ex'tra·sen'so·ry *a.* apart from normal sense perception

ex·trav'a·gant *a.* 1 excessive 2 wasteful —**ex·trav'a·gance** *n.*

ex·trav'a·gan'za *n.* spectacular show

ex·treme' *a.* 1 utmost 2 very great 3 excessive or drastic 4 radical —*n.* extreme degree, state, etc. —**ex·treme'ly** *adv.*

ex·trem'ism' (ek strēm'-) *n.* a being extreme, as in politics —**ex·trem'ist** *a., n.*

ex·trem'i·ty (ek strem'-) *n., pl.* -ties 1 end 2 extreme need, danger, etc. 3 *pl.* hands and feet

ex'tri·cate' *v.* set free

ex·trin'sic (-sik, -zik) *a.* 1 not essential 2 external

ex'tro·vert' *n.* active, sociable person —**ex'tro·ver'sion** *n.* —**ex'tro·vert'ed** *a.*

ex·trude' *v.* force out, as through a small opening —**ex·tru'sion** *n.*

ex·u'ber·ant *a.* 1 very healthy and lively 2 luxuriant —**ex·u'ber·ance** *n.*

ex·ude' *v.* 1 discharge 2 radiate

ex·ult' *v.* rejoice greatly —**ex·ult'ant** *a.* —**ex'ul·ta'tion** *n.*

ex·ur'bi·a *n.* communities beyond the suburbs —**ex·ur'ban·ite'** *n., a.*

eye *n.* 1 organ of sight 2 *often pl.* vision 3 a look 4 attention —*v.* **eyed, eye'ing** or **ey'ing** look at

eye'ball' *n.* ball-shaped part of the eye

eye'brow' *n.* bony arch over the eye, or the hair on this

eye'ful' *n.* [Sl.] striking person or thing

eye'glass'es *pl.n.* pair of lenses to help faulty vision

eye'lash' *n.* hair on the edge of the eyelid

eye'let *n.* small hole, as for a hook, cord, etc.

eye'lid' *n.* either of two folds of flesh that cover and uncover the eyeball

eye'-o'pen·er *n.* surprising news, sudden realization, etc.

eye'sight' *n.* power of seeing

eye'sore' *n.* ugly sight

eye'tooth' *n., pl.* -teeth' upper canine tooth

eye'wit'ness *n.* one who has seen something happen

F

F *abbrev.* 1 Fahrenheit 2 female or feminine 3 folio Also, for 2 & 3, **f**

FAA *abbrev.* Federal Aviation Administration

fa'ble n. **1** brief tale having a moral **2** untrue story

fab'ric n. cloth

fab'ri·cate' v. **1** construct **2** make up (a reason, etc.)

fab'u·lous a. **1** fictitious **2** incredible **3** [Inf.] wonderful

fa·cade', fa·çade (fə säd') n. main face of a building

face n. **1** front of the head **2** (main) surface **3** appearance **4** dignity: used chiefly in **lose** (or **save**) **face** —v. **1** turn, or have the face turned, toward **2** confront —**make a face** to grimace —**on the face of it** apparently —**fa'cial** (-shəl) a.

face'down' n. a confrontation

face'less a. without individuality

face-lift n. **1** cosmetic surgery to remove wrinkles from the face **2** altering of an exterior Also **face lift**

face'-off' n. [Inf.] a confrontation

face'-sav'ing a. preserving one's self-respect

fac'et (fas'-) n. **1** a surface of a cut gem **2** aspect

fa·ce·tious (fə sē'shəs) a. joking, esp. at an inappropriate time

face value n. **1** value printed on a bill, bond, etc. **2** seeming value

fa'cial (-shəl) a. of or for the face —n. treatment of the skin of the face with massage, creams, etc.

facial tissue n. soft tissue paper used as a handkerchief, etc.

fac·ile (fas'əl) a. **1** easy **2** superficial

fa·cil'i·tate' v. make easier

fa·cil'i·ty n., pl. **-ties 1** ease or skill **2** pl. things that help do something **3** building, etc. for some activity

fac·sim'i·le (-lē) n. exact copy

fact n. **1** actual happening **2** truth —**in fact** really

fac'tion n. **1** clique **2** dissension —**fac'tion·al** a. —**fac'tious** a.

fac·ti'tious (-tish'əs) a. forced or artificial

fac'toid' n. trivial or useless fact

fac'tor n. **1** causal element **2** Math. any of two or more quantities multiplied together

fac'to·ry n., pl. **-ries** building in which things are manufactured

fac·to'tum n. handyman

fac'tu·al (-chōō-) a. of facts; real

fac'ul·ty n., pl. **-ties 1** natural power or aptitude **2** staff of teachers

fad n. passing fashion —**fad'dish** a.

fade v. **1** (make) lose color or strength **2** die out

fag v. **fagged, fag'ging** make tired

fag'ot, fag'got n. bundle of sticks or twigs

Fahr·en·heit (fer'ən hīt') a. of a thermometer on which the boiling point of water is 212°, the freezing point 32°

fail v. **1** fall short **2** weaken **3** become bankrupt **4** not succeed **5** neglect **6** not pass a test or course

fail'ing n. **1** failure **2** fault —prep. lacking

faille (fīl) n. soft, ribbed fabric of silk or rayon

fail'-safe' a. of a system for preventing accidental operation, as of nuclear weapons

fail'ure n. **1** act of failing **2** one that fails

faint a. **1** weak, dim, etc. **2** weak and dizzy —n. state of temporary unconsciousness —v. fall into a faint —**faint'ness** n.

fair a. **1** beautiful **2** blond **3** clear and sunny **4** just **5** according to the rules **6** average —adv. in a fair way —n. exposition with exhibits, amusements, etc. —**fair'ly** adv. —**fair'ness** n.

fair shake n. [Inf.] fair treatment

fair'y n., pl. **-ies** tiny imaginary being in human form, with magic powers

faith n. **1** unquestioning belief, esp. in religion **2** particular religion **3** loyalty

faith'ful a. **1** loyal **2** exact —**faith'ful·ly** adv.

faith'less a. disloyal

fake v., n., a. sham

fa·kir (fə kir') n. Muslim or Hindu religious mendicant

fa·la'fel (-lä'-) n. deep-fried patty of ground chickpeas

fal'con (fal'-, fôl'-) n. bird of prey trained to hunt —**fal'con·ry** n.

fall v. **fell, fall'en, fall'ing 1** to drop or descend **2** tumble; collapse **3** occur —n. **1** a falling **2** autumn **3** overthrow or ruin **4** amount of what has fallen **5** pl. [often sing. v.] a waterfall —**fall back** retreat —**fall off** lessen or worsen —**fall on** (or **upon**) to attack —**fall out** quarrel —**fall through** fail —**fall** to begin

fal'la·cy n., pl. **-cies 1** false idea; error **2** false reasoning —**fal·la'cious** a.

fall guy n. [Sl.] one set up to take blame, etc.

fal'li·ble a. liable to error —**fal'li·bil'i·ty** n.

fal·lo'pi·an tube n. [also F- t-] either of two tubes carrying ova to the uterus

fall'out' *n.* **1** descent of radioactive particles after a nuclear explosion **2** these particles

fal·low (fal'ō) *a.* **1** plowed but unplanted **2** inactive

false *a.* **1** not true **2** lying **3** unfaithful **4** not real —**fal'si·fy'** *v.*, **-fied'**, **-fy'ing** —**fal'si·ty** *n.*

false'hood' *n.* a lie or lying

fal·set'to *n.* artificial, high-pitched singing

fal'ter *v.* **1** stumble **2** waver

fame *n.* great reputation

fa·mil'iar (-yəl) *a.* of or common to a family

fa·mil'iar (-yər) *a.* **1** friendly; intimate **2** too intimate; presumptuous **3** closely acquainted (*with*) **4** well-known —**fa·mil·i·ar'i·ty** *n.* —**fa·mil'iar·ize'** *v.*

fam'i·ly *n.*, *pl.* **-lies 1** parents and their children **2** relatives **3** lineage **4** group of related things

family practitioner *n.* doctor for the general needs of a family

family tree *n.* diagram of family members

fam'ine (-in) *n.* widespread food shortage

fam'ish *v.* be very hungry

fam'ished *a.* very hungry

fa'mous *a.* having fame

fan *n.* **1** device to move air for cooling, etc. **2** enthusiastic supporter —*v.* **fanned, fan'ning 1** blow air toward **2** stir up **3** spread (*out*)

fa·nat'ic *n.* fanatical person —*a.* fanatical —**fa·nat'i·cism** *n.*

fa·nat'i·cal *a.* too enthusiastic or zealous

fan'ci·er *n.* person with a special interest, esp. in plant or animal breeding

fan'cy *n.*, *pl.* **-cies 1** playful imagination **2** whim **3** a liking —*a.*, **-ci·er, -ci·est 1** extravagant **2** elaborate *3 of superior quality —*v.* **-cied, -cy·ing 1** imagine **2** be fond of **3** suppose —**fan'ci·ful** *a.* —**fan'ci·ness** *n.*

fan'cy-free' *a.* carefree

fan'fare' *n.* **1** blast of trumpets **2** showy display

fang *n.* long, pointed tooth

fan·ta'sia (-zhə) *n. Mus.* improvisational or free-form composition

fan'ta·size' *v.* have fantasies (about)

fan·tas'tic *a.* **1** unreal **2** grotesque **3** extravagant —**fan·tas'ti·cal·ly** *adv.*

fan'ta·sy *n.*, *pl.* **-sies 1** fancy **2** illusion **3** fantastic work of fiction

far *a.* **far'ther, far'thest** distant —*adv.* **1** very distant **2** very much —**by far**

very much — (**in**) **so far as** to the extent that

far'a·way' *a.* distant

Far East East Asia

farce *n.* **1** exaggerated comedy **2** absurd thing —**far'ci·cal** *a.*

fare *v.* get along —*n.* **1** transportation charge **2** paying passenger **3** food

fare'box' *n.* box for collecting fares on a bus, etc.

fare·well' (*a.*: fer'wel') *int.* goodbye —*a.*, *n.* parting (wishes)

far'-fetched' *a.* not reasonable; strained

far'-flung' *a.* extensive

fa·ri'na (-rē'-) *n.* flour or meal eaten as cooked cereal

farm *n.* land used to raise crops or animals —*v.* cultivate (land) —**farm out** let out (work or workers) on contract —**farm'er** *n.* —**farm'house'** *n.* —**farm'ing** *n.*

farm'hand' *n.* hired worker on a farm: also **farm'work'er**

farm'yard' *n.* yard around or enclosed by farm buildings

far'-off' *a.* distant

far'-out' *a.* [Inf.] nonconformist; avant-garde

far'-reach'ing *a.* having wide range, influence, etc.

far'sight'ed *a.* **1** planning ahead **2** seeing far objects best

far'ther *a.* **1** more distant **2** additional —*adv.* at or to a greater distance or extent

far'thest *a.* most distant —*adv.* at or to the greatest distance

fas'ci·nate' *v.* hold spellbound; captivate —**fas'ci·na'tion** *n.*

fas·cism (fash'iz'əm) *n.* militaristic dictatorship —**fas'cist** *n.*, *a.*

fash'ion *n.* **1** manner **2** current style —*v.* make; form

fash'ion·a·ble *a.* stylish

fast *a.* **1** firm **2** loyal **3** unfading **4** rapid; quick **5** of loose morals —*adv.* **1** firmly **2** rapidly —*v.* abstain from food —*n.* period of fasting

fas·ten (fas'ən) *v.* **1** attach **2** make secure; fix —**fas'ten·er** *n.*

fas'ten·ing *n.* thing used to fasten

fast'-food' *a.* of a business serving quickly prepared food

fas·tid'i·ous *a.* not easy to please

fast'-talk' *v.* [Inf.] persuade with fast, smooth talk

fat *n.* **fat'ter, fat'test** plump —*n.* oily animal substance —**fat'ty** *a.*, **-ti·er, -ti·est**

fa'tal *a.* causing death

fa'tal·ism' n. belief that all events are destined by fate —**fa'tal·ist** n. —**fa'tal·is'tic** a.

fa·tal'i·ty n., pl. **-ties** death caused by disaster

fate n. **1** power supposedly making events inevitable **2** one's lot in life **3** outcome **4** death; ruin —**fate'ful** a.

fat'ed a. destined

fa'ther n. **1** male parent **2** founder; creator **3** [often F-] Christian priest **4** [F-] God —v. beget, found, etc. —**fa'ther·hood'** n. —**fa'ther·ly** a.

fa'ther-in-law' n., pl. **fa'thers-** father of one's wife or husband

fa'ther·land' n. one's native land

fath·om (faḵ'əm) n. Naut. six feet —v. understand

fa·tigue' (-tēg') n. weariness —v. to weary

fat'so n., pl. **-sos** or **-soes** [Sl.] fat person

fat'ten v. make or get fat

fatty acid n. lipid in animal and vegetable fats and oils

fat'u·ous (fach'-) a. foolish

fau'cet n. device with valve to draw liquid from a pipe

fault n. **1** flaw **2** error **3** blame —**find fault (with)** criticize —**fault'less** a.

faulty a. **-i·er, -i·est** defective

faun n. Roman deity, half man and half goat

fau'na n. the animals of a certain region

faux pas (fō pä') n., pl. **faux pas'** (-päz') social blunder

fa'vor n. **1** approval **2** partiality **3** kind act **4** small gift —v. **1** show favor toward **2** resemble Also, Br. sp., **fa'vour** —**in favor of** approving —**fa'vor·a·ble** a.

fa'vor·ite a., n. preferred (one) —**fa'vor·it·ism'** n.

fawn v. flatter servilely —n. baby deer

fax n. **1** electronic sending of pictures, print, etc., as over telephone lines **2** device for such sending —v. send by fax

faze v. disturb

FBI abbrev. Federal Bureau of Investigation

FCC abbrev. Federal Communications Commission

FDA abbrev. Food and Drug Administration

FDIC abbrev. Federal Deposit Insurance Corporation

fear n. anxious anticipation of danger, pain, etc. —v. be afraid (of) —**fear'ful** a. —**fear'less** a.

fear'some a. causing fear

fea'si·ble (fē'zə-) a. capable of being done —**fea'si·bil'i·ty** n.

feast n. **1** religious festival **2** banquet —v. **1** have a feast (for) **2** delight

feat n. bold and daring deed

feath'er n. **1** one of the outgrowths covering a bird **2** kind —**feath'er·y** a.

feath'er·bed'ding n. use of extra workers to make more jobs, as by union contract

fea'ture n. **1** pl. form or look of the face **2** part of the face **3** special part, article, etc. **4** main attraction —v. make a feature of

Feb abbrev. February

fe'brile (-brəl) a. having a fever

Feb'ru·ar'y (-rōō-, -yōō-) n., pl. **-ar'ies** or **-ar'ys** second month

fe'ces' (-sēz') pl.n. excrement —**fe'cal** (-kəl) a.

feck'less a. **1** ineffective **2** careless

fe'cund a. fertile —**fe·cun'di·ty** n.

fed v. pt. & pp. of FEED —n. [often F-] [Inf.] U.S. federal agent —**fed up** [Inf.] annoyed or disgusted from too much of something

Fed abbrev. **1** Federal **2** Federation

fed'er·al a. **1** of a union of states under a central government **2** of the central government, esp. [often F-] of the U.S.

fed'er·al·ize' v. **1** unite in a federal union **2** put under federal authority

fed'er·ate' v. unite in a federation

fed'er·a'tion n. union of states or groups; league

fe·do'ra n. man's felt hat

fee n. charge for some service or right

fee'ble a. weak; not strong —**fee'bly** adv.

feed v. fed, feed'ing **1** give food to **2** supply as fuel, material, etc. **3** gratify **4** eat —n. fodder

feed'back' n. **1** transfer of part of the output back to the input, as of electricity or information **2** a response

feel v. felt, feel'ing **1** touch **2** have a feeling (of) **3** be aware of **4** believe **5** be or seem to be **6** grope —n. **1** sense of touch **2** way a thing feels —**feel like** [Inf.] have a desire for

feel'er n. **1** antenna or other organ of touch **2** remark or offer made to elicit opinions

feel'ing n. **1** sense of touch **2** sensation **3** an emotion **4** pl. sensitiveness **5** sympathy **6** opinion

feet n. pl. of FOOT

feign (fān) v. to pretend

feint (fānt) n. pretended attack, as in

boxing —v. make a feint

feist·y (fīs'tē) a. **-i·er, -i·est** [Inf.] **1** lively **2** quarrelsome

feld'spar' n. hard, crystalline mineral

fe·lic'i·tate' (-lis'-) v. congratulate — **fe·lic'i·ta'tion** n.

fe·lic'i·tous a. appropriate

fe·lic'i·ty n. **1** happiness **2** pl. **-ties** apt and pleasant expression

fe'line a. of or like a cat —n. a cat

fell v. **1** pt. of FALL **2** knock down **3** cut down

fel'low n. **1** an associate **2** an equal **3** one of a pair **4** [Inf.] man or boy —a. associated —**fel'low·ship'** n.

fel'on n. criminal

fel'o·ny n., pl. **-nies** major crime —**fe·lo'ni·ous** a.

felt n. fabric made of fibers pressed together

fem abbrev. female or feminine

fe'male' a. **1** designating or of the sex that bears offspring **2** feminine —n. female person or animal

fem'i·nine (-nin) a. of or like women or girls; female —**fem'i·nin'i·ty** n.

fem'i·nism' n. movement to win equal rights for women —**fem'i·nist** n., a.

fe'mur n. thighbone

fen n. swamp; bog

fence n. **1** barrier of posts, wire, etc. **2** dealer in stolen goods —v. **1** enclose with a fence **2** engage in fencing — **fenc'er** n.

fence'-mend'ing n. repairing political, etc. relations

fenc'ing n. sport of fighting with foils or swords

fend v. ward (off) —**fend for oneself** manage by oneself

fend'er n. a guard over an automobile wheel

fen'nel n. an herb used to flavor

fer·ment' (v.: fər ment') n. **1** thing causing fermentation **2** agitation —v. undergo or cause fermentation (in)

fer·men·ta'tion n. chemical change caused by yeast, bacteria, etc.

fern n. nonflowering plant with fronds

fe·ro'cious (-shəs) a. savage; fierce — **fe·roc'i·ty** n.

fer'ret n. kind of weasel —v. search (out)

fer'ric, fer'rous a. of iron

Fer'ris wheel n. large, revolving wheel with hanging seats, as in amusement parks

fer'rule (-əl) n. metal ring or cap around the end of a cane, etc. to strengthen it

fer'ry v. **-ried, -ry·ing** take across a

river, etc. in a boat —n., pl. **-ries** boat used for ferrying: also **fer'ry·boat'**

fer'tile a. **1** producing abundantly **2** able to produce young, fruit, etc. — **fer·til'i·ty** n.

fer'til·ize' v. **1** make fertile **2** spread fertilizer on **3** make fruitful by introducing a male germ cell —**fer·til·i·za'tion** n.

fer'til·iz'er n. manure, chemicals, etc. to enrich the soil

fer'vent a. intense; ardent

fer'vid a. fervent

fer'vor n. ardor; zeal

fes'tal a. joyous; merry

fes'ter v. **1** form pus **2** rankle

fes'ti·val n. time or day of celebration

fes'tive a. joyous; merry

fes·tiv'i·ty n., pl. **-ties** **1** gaiety **2** pl. things done in celebration

fes·toon' n. garland, etc. hanging in loops —v. adorn with festoons

fet'a (cheese) n. soft, white cheese

fetch v. **1** go after and bring back; get **2** sell for

fetch'ing a. attractive

fete, fête (fāt, fet) n. festival; outdoor party —v. honor with a fete

fet'id a. stinking

fet'ish n. **1** object thought to have magic power **2** object of irrational devotion

fet'lock' n. leg joint above a horse's hoof

fet'ter n. ankle shackle —v. restrain as with fetters

fet'tle n. used chiefly in **in fine fettle**, in good condition

fe'tus n. unborn young —**fe'tal** a.

feud (fyood) n. deadly quarrel, as between families —v. engage in a feud

feu'dal·ism' n. medieval system with lords, vassals, and serfs —**feu'dal** a.

fe'ver n. abnormally high body temperature —**fe'ver·ish** a.

few a. not many —pron., n. a small number

fez n., pl. **fez'zes** conical Turkish hat

ff abbrev. **1** folio(s) **2** following (pages, etc.)

FG abbrev. Basketball, Football field goal: sometimes **fg**

fi·an·cé (fē'än sā') n. man to whom one is betrothed —**fi'an·cée'** (-sā') n.fem.

fi·as'co (fē-) n., pl. **-coes** or **-cos** utter failure

fi'at (fē'ät, fī'ät') n. a decree

fib n. trivial lie —v. **fibbed, fib'bing** tell a fib

fi'ber *n.* 1 threadlike part(s) forming organic tissue 2 threadlike part(s) used for weaving, etc. —**fi'brous** *a.*

Fi'ber·glas' *trademark* material made of fine filaments of glass —*n.* [f-] this material: also **fi'ber·glas'**

fi'ber-op'tic, fiber optic *a.* of synthetic fibers for transmitting light

fi'bre *n.* Br. sp. of FIBER

fi·bril·la'tion (fib'ri-) *n.* rapid series of heart contractions, causing weak heartbeats

fi'broid' *a.* like or made of fibrous tissue

fi·bro'sis *n.* abnormal growth of fibrous tissue

fib'u·la (-yōo-) *n., pl.* **-lae'** (-lē') or **-las** thinner bone of lower leg

FICA *abbrev.* Federal Insurance Contributions Act

fick'le *a.* tending to change one's mind

fic'tion *n.* literary work(s) with imaginary characters and events —**fic'tion·al** *a.*

fic·ti'tious (-tish'əs) *a.* imaginary

fic'tive *a.* 1 of fiction 2 imaginary

fi'cus *n., pl.* **-cus** tropical plant with leathery leaves

fid'dle *n.* [Inf.] violin —*v.* 1 [Inf.] play a violin 2 fidget (*with*) —**fid'dler** *n.*

fi·del'i·ty *n.* faithfulness

fidg'et (fij'-) *v.* make nervous movements —**fidg'et·y** *a.*

fie (fī) *int.* [Ar.] shame

field *n.* 1 piece of open land, esp. one for crops, grazing, etc. 2 expanse 3 area for athletic event 4 sphere of knowledge or activity 5 all contestants

field day *n.* an occasion of exciting activity or opportunity

field glasses *pl.n.* portable, telescopic eyeglasses

field goal *n.* 1 *Basketball* basket toss from play, scoring two or three points 2 *Football* goal kicked from the field, scoring three points

field guide *n.* handbook for use in identifying birds, plants, etc.

field hand *n.* hired worker on a farm

fiend (fēnd) *n.* 1 devil 2 [Inf.] addict —**fiend'ish** *a.*

fierce *a.* 1 savage; wild 2 violent —**fierce'ly** *adv.*

fi'er·y *a.* **-i·er, -i·est** 1 flaming, hot, etc. 2 ardent

fi·es'ta (fē-) *n.* festival

fife *n.* small, shrill flute

fif'teen' *a., n.* five more than ten —**fif'teenth'** *a., n.*

fifth *a.* preceded by four others —*n.* 1 one after the fourth 2 one of five equal parts 3 fifth of a gallon

fifth column *n.* subversive group within a country, etc.

fifth wheel *n.* superfluous person or thing

fif'ty *a., n., pl.* **-ties** five times ten —**fif'ti·eth** *a., n.*

fig *n.* sweet, chewy fruit with seed-filled pulp

fig *abbrev.* 1 figurative(ly) 2 figure(s)

fight *n., v.* **fought, fight'ing** struggle; battle; contest —**fight'er** *n.*

fig'ment *n.* thing imagined

fig·ur·a·tive *a.* using metaphors, similes, etc.

fig'ure *n.* 1 outline; shape 2 person 3 likeness of a person or thing 4 illustration 5 design 6 a number 7 sum of money —*v.* 1 compute 2 appear 3 [Inf.] believe —**figure out** solve

fig'ure·head' *n.* leader with no real power

figure of speech *n.* a vivid expression, as a metaphor or simile

figure skating *n.* ice-skating featuring leaps, spins, etc.

fig·u·rine' (-rēn') *n.* small statue

fil'a·ment *n.* threadlike part

filch *v.* steal (something trivial)

file *n.* 1 container for keeping papers in order 2 orderly arrangement of papers, etc. 3 line of persons or things 4 ridged tool for scraping, etc. 5 *Comput.* collection of data —*v.* 1 put papers, etc. in order 2 move in a file 3 smooth or grind with a file 4 register officially

fi·let (fi lā') *n., v.* fillet

filet mi·gnon (min yōn', -yän') *n.* thick cut of beef tenderloin

fil'i·al *a.* of or suitable to a son or daughter

fil'i·bus'ter *n.* obstruction of a bill in a legislature, as by a long speech —*v.* obstruct a bill in this way

fil'i·gree' *n.* lacelike work of fine wire

fil'ings *pl.n.* small pieces scraped off with a file

fill *v.* 1 make or become full 2 put into or hold (a job or office) 3 supply things ordered —*n.* anything that fills —**fill in** 1 make complete 2 substitute —**fill out** 1 make or become larger, etc. 2 complete (a blank form)

fil·let (fi lā') *n.* boneless piece of fish or meat —*v.* to bone (fish, etc.)

fill'ing *n.* thing used to fill something else

filling station *n.* service station

fil'lip *n.* stimulus; tonic

fil'ly *n., pl.* **-lies** young mare

film *n.* **1** thin coating **2** flexible cellulose material used in photography **3** series of pictures flashed on a screen in rapid succession so that things in them seem to move **4** story in the form of a FILM (*n.* 3) —*v.* make a FILM (*n.* 3 & 4) (of)

film'strip' *n.* strip of film with stills of pictures, charts, etc. on some subject

film'y *a.* **-i-er, -i-est** blurred

fil'ter *n.* thing used for straining out particles, etc. from a fluid, etc. —*v.* **1** pass through a filter **2** remove with a filter **3** pass slowly —**fil-tra'tion** *n.*

filter tip *n.* cigarette with a tip of cellulose, etc. to filter the smoke

filth *n.* **1** foul dirt **2** obscenity — **filth'i-ness** *n.* —**filth'y** *a.,* **-i-er, -i-est**

fin *n.* winglike, membranous organ on a fish

fi-na'gle *v.* use, or get by, trickery —**fi-na'gler** *n.*

fi'nal *a.* **1** last **2** conclusive —*n. pl.* last of a series of contests —**fi-nal'i-ty** *n.* —**fi'nal-ly** *adv.* —**fi'nal-ist** *n.* —**fi'nal-ize'** *v.*

fi-na'le (-näl'ē, -nä'lā) *n.* last part of a musical work

fi'nance' (*or* fə nans') *n.* **1** *pl.* funds **2** science of managing money matters —*v.* supply money for —**fi-nan'cial** (-shəl) *a.* —**fin'an-cier'** (-sir') *n.*

finch *n.* small songbird

find *v.* **found, find'ing** **1** come upon; discover **2** learn **3** recover (a thing lost) **4** decide —*n.* something found

fine *a.* **1** excellent **2** not heavy or coarse **3** sharp **4** discriminating — *adv.* [Inf.] very well —*n.* money paid as a penalty —*v.* cause to pay a fine

fine arts *pl.n.* painting, sculpture, music, etc.

fin'er-y *n.* showy clothes

fi-nesse' *n.* skill in handling delicate situations

fin'ger *n.* any of the parts (five with the thumb) at the end of the hand — *v.* to touch with the fingers —**fin'ger-nail'** *n.* —**fin'ger-tip'** *n.*

fin'ger-board' *n.* part of a stringed instrument against which the strings are pressed

fin'ger-point'ing *n.* a blaming others

fin'ger-print' *n.* impression of the lines of a fingertip

fin'ick-y *a.* too particular; fussy

fi-nis (fin'is) *n.* the end; finish

fin'ish *v.* **1** to end **2** complete **3** use up **4** perfect; polish —*n.* **1** last part;

end **2** polish or perfection **3** way a surface is finished

fi'nite' *a.* having limits

Finn *n.* Finnish person

Finn'ish *a., n.* (of) the people or language of Finland

fiord (fyôrd) *n.* sea inlet bordered by steep cliffs

fir *n.* evergreen tree

fire *n.* **1** flame **2** thing burning **3** ardor **4** discharge of guns —*v.* **1** make burn **2** shoot (a gun, etc.) **3** discharge from a job —**on fire** burning —**under fire** under attack

fire'arm' *n.* rifle, pistol, etc.

fire'bomb' *n.* incendiary bomb —*v.* attack, etc. with a firebomb

fire'crack'er *n.* noisy explosive rolled in paper

fire engine *n.* truck equipped for fire-fighting

fire escape *n.* outside stairway to help people escape a burning building

fire'fight'er *n.* one who fights fires — **fire'fight'ing** *n.*

fire'fly' *n.* winged beetle with a glowing abdomen

fire'man *n., pl.* **-men** **1** firefighter **2** stoker

fire'place' *n.* place built in a wall for a fire

fire'plug' *n.* street hydrant

fire'proof' *v., a.* (make) not easily destroyed by fire

fire'trap' *n.* building particularly unsafe in the case of fire

fire'wood' *n.* wood used as fuel

fire'works' *pl.n.* firecrackers, rockets, etc. for noisy or brilliant displays

firm *a.* **1** solid **2** fixed; stable **3** strong and steady —*v.* make firm —*n.* business company —**firm'ness** *n.*

fir'ma-ment *n.* [Poet.] sky

first *a., adv.* before any others —*n.* **1** first one **2** beginning

first aid *n.* emergency care for injuries —**first'-aid'** *a.*

first'-class' *a.* of the highest quality — *adv.* with the best accommodations

first'hand' *a., adv.* from the source; direct(ly)

first lady *n.* [*often* F- L-] wife of the U.S. president

first lieutenant *n.* military officer ranking just above second lieutenant

first'ly *adv.* in the first place

first'-rate' *a.* excellent

firth *n.* narrow inlet of the sea

fis'cal *a.* financial

fish *n., pl.* **fish**; for different kinds, **fish'es** coldblooded animal with gills and fins, living in water —*v*. **1** to catch fish **2** try to get something indirectly —**fish'er·man** *n.*, *pl.* **-men** — **fish'er·y** *n.*, *pl.* **-ies**

fish'hook' *n.* hook for catching fish

fish'y *a.* **-i·er, -i·est 1** like a fish **2** [Inf.] questionable

fis·sion (fish'ən) *n.* **1** a splitting apart **2** nuclear fission

fis·sure (fish'ər) *n.* a cleft or crack

fist *n.* clenched hand

fist'ful *n.* handful

fist'i·cuffs' *pl.n.* boxing: old-fashioned term

fit *v.* **fit'ted** or **fit, fit'ting 1** be suitable to **2** be the proper size, etc. (for) **3** adjust to fit **4** equip —*a.* **fit'ter, fit' test 1** suited **2** proper **3** healthy —*n.* **1** way of fitting **2** seizure, as of coughing **3** outburst —**fit'ness** *n.*

fit'ful *a.* not regular; spasmodic

fit'ting *a.* proper —*n.* **1** adjustment **2** *pl.* fixtures

five *a.*, *n.* one more than four

five'-star' *a.* highly rated; excellent

fix *v.* **1** fasten or set firmly **2** determine **3** adjust or repair **4** prepare (food, etc.) **5** [Inf.] influence by bribery, etc. —*n.* **1** determination of location **2** [Inf.] predicament —**fix up** [Inf.] set in order —**fixed** *a.*

fix·a'tion *n.* obsession

fix'ings *pl.n.* [Inf.] accessories or trimmings

fix'ture *n.* any of the attached furnishings of a house

fizz *v.*, *n.* (make) a hissing, bubbling sound

fiz'zle *v.* **1** to fizz **2** [Inf.] fail

fjord (fyôrd) *n.* fiord

fl *abbrev.* **1** flourished **2** fluid

FL *abbrev.* Florida

flab *n.* [Inf.] sagging flesh

flab'ber·gast' *v.* amaze

flab'by *a.* **-bi·er, -bi·est 1** limp and soft **2** weak

flac·cid (flak'sid, flas'id) *a.* flabby

flag *n.* **1** cloth with colors or designs, used as a national symbol, etc. **2** iris (flower) —*v.* **flagged, flag'ging 1** to signal with flags **2** grow weak

flag'el·late' (flaj'-) *v.* to whip —**flag'el·la'tion** *n.*

flag'on (flag'-) *n.* container for liquids

flag'pole' *n.* pole for flying a flag: also **flag'staff'**

fla'grant *a.* glaringly bad —**fla'gran·cy** *n.*

flag'ship' *n.* **1** commander's ship **2** chief member of a network

flag'stone' *n.* flat paving stone

flail *n.* implement used to thresh grain by hand —*v.* **1** use a flail **2** beat

flair *n.* aptitude; knack

flak *n.* **1** fire of antiaircraft guns **2** [Inf.] criticism

flake *n.* **1** soft, thin mass **2** chip or peeling —*v.* form into flakes

flak'y *a.* **-i·er, -i·est 1** of or producing flakes **2** [Sl.] eccentric

flam·bé (fläm bā') *a.* served with flaming rum, etc.

flam·boy'ant *a.* showy —**flam·boy' ance** *n.*

flame *n.* tongue(s) of fire; blaze —*v.* burst into flame

fla·men'co *n.* Spanish gypsy music or dancing

flame'out' *n.* failure of combustion in jet engine in flight

fla·min'go *n.* pink, long-legged wading bird

flam'ma·ble *a.* easily set on fire

flange (flanj) *n.* projecting rim on a wheel, etc.

flank *n.* **1** side of an animal between the ribs and the hip **2** side of anything —*v.* be at, or go around, the side of

flan'nel *n.* soft, napped cloth of wool, etc.

flan'nel·ette', flan'nel·et' (-et') *n.* soft, fleecy, cotton cloth

flap *n.* **1** flat, loose piece **2** motion or sound of a swinging flap —*v.* **flapped, flap'ping** flutter

flap'jack' *n.* pancake

flare *v.* **1** blaze up **2** spread outward —*n.* **1** bright, unsteady blaze **2** brief, dazzling signal light **3** sudden outburst **4** a spreading outward

flare'-up' *n.* sudden outburst

flash *v.* **1** send out a sudden, brief light **2** sparkle **3** move suddenly **4** [Inf.] show briefly —*n.* **1** sudden, brief light **2** an instant **3** bit of late news

flash'back' *n.* interruption in a story by a return to some earlier episode

flash'bulb' *n.* bulb giving brief, bright light, for taking photographs

flash'card' *n.* one of a set of cards used as an aid to memorizing

flash'cube' *n.* rotating cube with flash-bulbs in four sides

flash'ing *n.* metal roofing for joints, etc.

flash'light' *n.* portable electric light

flash'y *a.* **-i·er, -i·est** gaudy; showy

flask *n.* kind of bottle

flat *a.* **flat'ter, flat'test 1** smooth and level **2** broad and thin **3** lying spread out **4** absolute **5** without taste or sparkle **6** dull; lifeless **7** emptied of air **8** *Mus.* below true pitch —*adv.* in a flat way —*n.* **1** flat surface or part **2** deflated tire **3** *Mus.* note ½ step below another: symbol (♭) **4** [Chiefly Br.] apartment —**flat'ten** v.

flat'bed' n. trailer, etc. having no sides

flat'car' n. railroad car without sides

flat'fish' n. fish with a very broad, flat body

flat'foot' n. condition in which a foot has a flattened arch

flat'i·ron n. iron for pressing clothes

flat'-out' a. [Inf.] **1** at full speed, effort, etc. **2** absolute

flat'ter v. **1** praise insincerely **2** gratify the vanity of —**flat'ter·y** n.

flat·u·lent (flach'ə-) a. having gas in the stomach —**flat'u·lence** n.

flat'ware' n. flat tableware

flaunt (flônt) v. show off

fla'vor n. the taste of a substance —v. give flavor to

fla'vor·ing n. essence, etc. added to food to give it a flavor

flaw n. defect —**flawed** a. —**flaw'less** a.

flax n. plant with fibers that are spun into linen thread

flax'en a. pale yellow

flay v. strip the skin from

flea n. small, bloodsucking insect

fleck n., v. spot

fledg'ling (flej'-) n. young bird just able to fly

flee v. **fled**, **flee'ing** escape swiftly, as from danger

fleece n. wool covering a sheep —v. to swindle —**fleec'y** a., **-i·er**, **-i·est**

fleet n. **1** group of warships under one command **2** any similar group, as of trucks, planes, etc. —a. swift

fleet'ing a. passing swiftly

flesh n. **1** tissue between the skin and the bones **2** pulp of fruits and vegetables **3** the body —**flesh'y** a., **-i·er**, **-i·est**

flesh'-and-blood' a. **1** alive **2** real

fleur-de-lis (flur'də lē') n., pl. **fleurs'-de-lis'** (flur'-) lilylike emblem

flew v. pt. of FLY

flex v. **1** bend, as an arm **2** tense, as a muscle

flex'i·ble a. **1** easily bent; pliable **2** adaptable

flex'time' n. flexible scheduling of work hours

flick n. light, quick stroke —v. strike, throw, etc. with such a stroke

flick'er v. move, burn, or shine

unsteadily —n. dart of flame or light

fli'er n. **1** aviator **2** handbill or leaflet

flight n. **1** act or power of flying **2** distance flown **3** group of things flying together **4** trip by airplane or spacecraft **5** set of stairs **6** a fleeing —**flight'less** a.

flight'y a. **-i·er**, **-i·est** unsettled; frivolous

flim'sy a. **-si·er**, **-si·est 1** easily broken **2** ineffectual —**flim'si·ness** n.

flinch v. draw back, as from a blow

fling v. throw with force —n. **1** a flinging **2** [Inf.] a try **3** [Inf.] brief love affair

flint n. a hard quartz

flip v. **flipped**, **flip'ping** toss with a quick jerk —a. [Inf.] flippant

flip'pant a. frivolous and disrespectful —**flip'pan·cy** n.

flip'per n. flat limb adapted for swimming, as in seals

flip side n. [Inf.] reverse side (of a phonograph record)

flirt v. play at love —n. one who flirts —**flir·ta'tion** n. —**flir·ta'tious** a.

flit v. **flit'ted**, **flit'ting** move lightly and rapidly

float n. **1** thing that stays on the surface of a liquid **2** flat, decorated vehicle in a parade —v. **1** stay on the surface of a liquid **2** drift gently in air, etc. **3** put into circulation (a bond issue, etc.)

flock n. **1** group, esp. of animals **2** tiny fibers put on wallpaper, etc. as a velvetlike surface: also **flock'ing** —v. gather in a flock

floe n. large sheet of floating ice

flog v. **flogged**, **flog'ging** beat, thrash, or whip

flood n. **1** overflowing of water on land **2** great outpouring —v. to overflow

flood'light' n. lamp casting a very bright, broad light

flood tide n. rising tide

floor n. **1** bottom surface of a room, etc. **2** story in a building **3** permission to speak —v. **1** furnish with a floor **2** knock down **3** astound

floor'ing n. material for making a floor

floor show n. show with singers, dancers, etc., as in a nightclub

flop v. **flopped**, **flop'ping 1** move, drop, or flap about clumsily **2** [Inf.] fail —n. a flopping —**flop'py** a.

floppy disk n. small, flexible computer disk: also **flop'py**

flo'ra n. plants of a region

flo'ral *a.* of or like flowers

flor'id *a.* 1 ruddy 2 gaudy

flo'rist *n.* one who grows or sells flowers

floss *n.* 1 soft, silky fibers 2 dental floss —*v.* clean (the teeth) with dental floss

flo·ta'tion *n.* a floating

flo·til'la *n.* small fleet

flot'sam *n.* floating debris or cargo of a shipwreck

flounce *v.* move with quick, flinging motions —*n.* a ruffle

floun'der *v.* struggle or speak clumsily —*n.* kind of edible flatfish

flour *n.* a powdery substance ground from grain

flour'ish (flur'-) *v.* 1 thrive 2 be in one's prime 3 brandish —*n.* 1 sweeping motion or stroke 2 fanfare

flout *v.* mock or scorn

flow *v.* 1 move as water does 2 move smoothly 3 proceed 4 hang loose —*n.* a flowing or thing that flows

flow'chart' *n.* diagram showing steps in a process

flow'er *n.* 1 petals and pistil of a plant 2 a plant grown for its blossoms 3 best part —*v.* 1 to produce blossoms 2 become its best

flow'er·pot' *n.* container with earth for a plant to grow in

flow'er·y *a.* **-i·er, -i·est** showy in expression

flown *v.* pp. of FLY

flu *n.* influenza

flub [Inf.] *v.* **flubbed, flub'bing** bungle —*n.* blunder

fluc'tu·ate' (-chōō-) *v.* keep changing, as prices —**fluc'tu·a'tion** *n.*

flue *n.* shaft in a chimney

flu'ent *a.* speaking or writing easily —**flu'en·cy** *n.* —**flu'ent·ly** *adv.*

fluff *n.* loose, soft mass —*v.* 1 make fluffy 2 bungle

fluff'y *a.* **-i·er, -i·est** soft and light

flu'id *a.* 1 able to flow 2 not fixed —*n.* liquid or gas —**flu·id'i·ty** *n.*

fluke *n.* 1 anchor blade 2 [Inf.] stroke of luck

flung *v.* pt. & pp. of FLING

flunk *v.* [Inf.] to fail

flunk'y *n.*, *pl.* **-ies** low, servile person

fluo·res'cent (flôr es'ənt) *a.* giving off cool light —**fluo·res'cence** *n.*

fluo'ri·date' (flôr'ə-) *v.* add fluoride to (water) —**fluo'ri·da'tion** *n.*

fluo·ride (flôr'īd') *n.* fluorine compound preventing tooth decay

fluo·rine (flôr'ēn') *n.* yellowish gas, a chemical element

fluo'ro·car'bon (flôr'ə-, floor'ə-) *n.* compound containing carbon, fluorine, and, sometimes, hydrogen

fluo'ro·scope' (flôr'ə-) *n.* kind of X-ray machine

flur'ry *n.*, *pl.* **-ries** 1 gust of wind, rain, or snow 2 sudden commotion

flush *v.* 1 to redden in the face 2 drive (*out*) from cover 3 wash out —*n.* a blush; glow —*a.* 1 well-supplied 2 level (*with*)

flus'ter *v.* make confused

flute *n.* tubelike wind instrument —**flut'ist** *n.*

flut'ed *a.* grooved

flut'ter *v.* wave, move, or beat rapidly or irregularly —*n.* 1 a fluttering 2 confusion —**flut'ter·y** *a.*

flux *n.* 1 a flowing 2 constant change 3 substance used to help metals fuse

fly *v.* **flew** or (*v.* 5) **flied, flown** or (*v.* 5) **flied, fly'ing** 1 move through the air by using wings 2 wave or float in the air 3 move swiftly 4 flee 5 hit a fly in baseball 6 travel in or pilot (aircraft) —*n.*, *pl.* **flies** 1 flap concealing a zipper, etc. in a garment 2 baseball batted high 3 winged insect

fly'-by-night' *a.* financially irresponsible

fly'catch'er *n.* small bird that catches flying insects

fly'er *n.* flier

flying colors *n.* notable success

flying fish *n.* fish with winglike fins that glides in the air

flying saucer *n.* unidentified flying object

fly'leaf' *n.* blank leaf at the front or back of a book

fly'pa'per *n.* sticky paper set out to catch flies

fly'wheel' *n.* wheel that regulates a machine's speed

FM *n.* high-fidelity broadcasting by frequency modulation

FM *abbrev.* frequency modulation

foal *n.* young horse

foam *n.* 1 bubbly mass on liquids 2 spongy mass of rubber, plastic, etc. —*v.* to form foam —**foam'y** *a.*, **-i·er, -i·est**

foam rubber *n.* rubber foam

fob *n.* pocket-watch chain or ornament on it

focal point *n.* FOCUS (*n.* 3)

fo'cus *n.*, *pl.* **-cus·es** or **-ci'** (-sī') 1 point where rays of light meet 2 adjustment of lens distance for clear image 3 center of activity —*v.* 1 bring into focus 2 concentrate —**fo'**

cal a.

fod'der n. coarse food for cattle, horses, etc.

foe n. enemy

fog n. 1 thick mist 2 mental confusion —v. fogged, fog'ging make or become foggy —**fog'gy** a., -gi-er, -gi-est —**fog'gi-ness** n.

fog'horn' n. horn blown to warn ships in a fog

fo-gy (fō'gē) n., pl. **-gies** old-fashioned person

foi'ble n. small weakness in character

foil v. thwart —n. 1 thin fencing sword 2 thin sheet of metal 3 one that enhances another by contrast

foist v. impose by fraud

fol. abbrev. following

fold v. 1 double (material) over 2 intertwine 3 wrap up —n. 1 folded layer 2 pen for sheep

-fold suf. times as many

fold'a·way' a. that can be folded together and stored

fold'er n. 1 folded sheet of cardboard to hold papers 2 booklet of folded sheets

fo'li·age n. plant leaves

fol'ic acid n. B vitamin used to treat anemia

fo'li·o' n., pl. **-os'** largest regular size of book

folk n., pl. **folk** or **folks** people —a. of the common people

folk'lore' n. beliefs, legends, etc. of a people

folk song n. song made and handed down among the common people — **folk singer** n.

folk'sy a. -si·er, -si·est [Inf.] friendly or sociable

fol'li·cle n. small sac or gland, as in the skin

fol'low v. 1 come or go after 2 go along 3 take up (a trade) 4 result (from) 5 obey 6 pay attention to 7 understand —**follow out** (or **up**) carry out fully —**fol'low·er** n.

fol'low·ing a. next after —n. group of followers

fol'ly n., pl. **-lies** foolish state, action, belief, etc.

fo·ment' v. incite

fond a. loving; tender —**fond of** liking —**fond'ly** adv.

fon'dle v. to caress

fon·due', fon·du' n. oil, melted cheese, etc. for dipping cubes of meat, bread, etc.

font n. basin for holy water

food n. substance taken in by an animal or plant to enable it to live and grow

food chain n. series of organisms (as grass, rabbit, fox), each feeding on the one before

food poi'son·ing n. sickness caused by eating contaminated food

fool n. 1 silly person 2 dupe —v. 1 be silly or playful 2 trick

fool'har'dy a. -di·er, -di·est foolishly daring; rash

fool'ish a. silly; unwise

fool'proof' a. simple, safe, etc.

foot n., pl. **feet** 1 end part of the leg, on which one stands 2 bottom; base 3 measure of length, 12 inches —v. [Inf.] pay (a bill) —**on foot** walking —**under foot** in the way

foot'age n. length in feet, as of film

foot'ball' n. 1 team game played on a field with an inflated oval-shaped ball 2 this ball

foot'hill' n. low hill at the foot of a mountain

foot'hold' n. place for the feet, as in climbing

foot'ing n. 1 secure placing of the feet 2 basis for relationship

foot'lights' pl.n. lights at the front of a stage floor

foot'lock'er n. small storage trunk

foot'loose' a. free to go or do as one likes

foot'man n., pl. **-men** male servant assisting a butler

foot'note' n. note at the bottom of a page

foot'print' n. mark left by a foot

foot'rest' n. support for foot or feet

foot'step' n. 1 sound of a step 2 footprint

foot'stool' n. stool for a seated person's feet

fop n. vain man fussy about his clothes, etc. —**fop'pish** a.

for prep. 1 in place of 2 in the interest of 3 in favor of 4 with the purpose of 5 in search of 6 meant to be received, used, etc. by 7 with respect to 8 because of 9 to the extent or duration of —con. because

for'age n. fodder —v. to search for food

for'ay n., v. raid

for·bear' v. -bore', -borne', -bear'ing 1 refrain (from) 2 control oneself — **for·bear'ance** n.

for·bid' v. -bade' (-bad') or -bad', -bid'den, -bid'ding not permit; prohibit

for·bid'ding a. frightening

force *n.* **1** strength; power **2** coercion **3** effectiveness **4** organized group, as an army —*v.* **1** make do something; compel **2** break open **3** impose, produce, etc. by force —**force′ful** *a.*

forced *a.* **1** compulsory **2** not natural

for′ceps *n., pl.* **-ceps′** tongs for grasping and pulling, used esp. by surgeons

for′ci·ble *a.* with force —**for′ci·bly** *adv.*

ford *n.* shallow place in a river —*v.* cross at a ford

fore *adv., a., n.* (in or toward) the front part —*int.* used as a warning shout by golfers

fore- *pref.* before; in front

fore′arm′ *n.* arm between the elbow and wrist

fore′bear′ *n.* ancestor

fore·bode′ *v.* foretell

fore′cast′ *v.* **-cast′** or **-cast′ed, -cast′ing** predict —*n.* prediction —**fore′cast′er** *n.*

fore·cas·tle (fōk′səl, fôr′kas′əl) *n.* forward deck or front part of a ship

fore·close′ *v.* take away the right to redeem (a mortgage) —**fore·clo′sure** *a.*

fore′fa′ther *n.* ancestor

fore′fin′ger *n.* finger nearest the thumb

fore′front′ *n.* extreme front

fore·go′ing *a.* preceding

fore·gone′ *a.* previously determined; inevitable

fore′ground′ *n.* part of a scene nearest the viewer

fore′hand′ *n.* racket stroke with palm of hand turned forward

fore′head′ *n.* part of the face above the eyebrows

for′eign (-in) *a.* **1** of or from another country **2** not characteristic —**for′eign-born′** *a.* —**for′eign·er** *n.*

foreign minister *n.* cabinet member in charge of foreign affairs

fore′knowl′edge *n.* knowledge of something beforehand

fore′leg′ *n.* front leg of animal

fore′man *n., pl.* **-men** **1** man in charge of workers **2** chairman of a jury

fore′most′ *a., adv.* first

fore′noon′ *n.* time before noon

fo·ren′sic *a.* **1** of or suitable for public debate **2** of scientific techniques of crime investigation

fore′or·dain′ *v.* predestine

fore′play′ *n.* touching, etc. before sexual intercourse

fore·run′ner *n.* person or thing foretelling another

fore·see′ *v.* **-saw′, -seen′, -see′ing** see or know beforehand

fore·shad′ow *v.* presage

fore·short′en *v.* shorten some lines in drawing to make some parts seem farther away

fore′sight′ *n.* **1** power to foresee **2** prudence

fore′skin′ *n.* fold of skin over the end of the penis

for′est *n.* tract of land covered with trees

fore·stall′ *v.* prevent by acting beforehand

for′est·a′tion *n.* planting or care of forests

for′est·ry *n.* science of the care of forests —**for′est·er** *n.*

fore·tell′ *v.* **-told′, -tell′ing** predict

fore′thought′ *n.* foresight

for·ev′er *adv.* **1** for all time **2** at all times

fore·warn′ *v.* warn beforehand

fore′wom′an *pl.n.* **-wom′en** woman serving as a foreman

fore′word′ *n.* a preface

for′feit (-fit) *n.* thing lost as a penalty —*v.* lose as a penalty —**for′fei·ture** (-fə chər) *n.*

for·gath′er *v.* assemble; meet

forge *n.* **1** furnace for heating metal to be wrought **2** smith's shop —*v.* **1** shape by heating and hammering **2** counterfeit (a signature) **3** advance slowly

for′ger·y *n., pl.* **-ies** **1** crime of forging documents, signatures, etc. **2** anything forged

for·get′ *v.* **-got′, -got′ten** or **-got′, -get′ting** **1** be unable to remember **2** neglect —**for·get′ful** *a.*

for·get′-me-not′ *n.* plant with small, blue flowers

for·give′ *v.* **-gave′, -giv′en, -giv′ing** give up wanting to punish; pardon —**for·give′ness** *n.* —**for·giv′ing** *a.*

for·go′ *v.* **-went′, -gone′, -go′ing** do without

fork *n.* **1** pronged instrument for lifting **2** place of branching —*v.* to branch —**fork over** [Inf.] pay out; hand over —**fork′ful′** *n., pl.* **-fuls′**

fork′lift′ *n.* (device on) a truck for lifting and moving heavy objects

for·lorn′ *a.* **1** abandoned **2** wretched; miserable —**for·lorn′ly** *adv.*

form *n.* **1** shape; figure **2** mold **3** style; customary behavior **4** document to be filled in **5** variation in spelling, etc. of a word due to changes in function —*v.* **1** to shape **2** develop (habits) **3** constitute —**form′less** *a.*

for′mal *a.* **1** according to custom, rule, etc. **2** stiff; prim **3** for use at ceremonies —**for′mal·ize**′ *v.* —**for′mal·ly** *adv.*

form·al′de·hyde′ *n.* disinfectant and preservative

for·mal′i·ty *n.* **1** an observing of customs, rules, etc. **2** *pl.* **-ties** formal act

for′mal-wear′ *n.* formal clothes, as tuxedos or evening gowns

for′mat′ *n.* general arrangement, as of a book

for·ma′tion *n.* **1** a forming **2** thing formed; structure —**form′a·tive** *a.*

for′mer *a.* **1** of the past **2** being the first mentioned —**for′mer·ly** *adv.*

form′-fit′ting *a.* fitting the body closely: also **form′fit′ting**

For·mi′ca *trademark* laminated, heat-resistant plastic for countertops

for·mi′da·ble *a.* **1** hard to overcome **2** awesome —**for′mi·da·bly** *adv.*

for′mu·la *n., pl.* **-las** or **-lae**′ (-lē′) **1** fixed expression or rule **2** set of symbols expressing a mathematical rule, chemical compound, etc. —**for′mu·late**′ *v.* —**for′mu·la′tion** *n.*

for·ni·ca′tion *n.* sexual intercourse between unmarried people —**for′ni·cate**′ *v.*

for·sake′ *v.* **-sook**′, **-sak′en**, **-sak′ing** abandon; desert

for·swear′ *v.* **1** swear to give up **2** commit perjury

for·syth′i·a (-sith′-) *n.* shrub with yellow flowers

fort *n.* fortified place for military defense

for·te (fôr′tā; *n.:* fôrt, fôr′tā) *a., adv. Mus.* loud —*n.* what one does well

forth *adv.* **1** forward **2** out; into view

forth′com′ing *a.* **1** about to appear **2** ready at hand

forth′right′ *a.* frank

forth·with′ *adv.* at once

for·ti·fi·ca′tion *n.* **1** a fortifying **2** a fort

for′ti·fy′ *v.* **-fied**′, **-fy′ing** to strengthen, enrich, etc.

for·tis′si·mo′ *a., adv. Mus.* very loud

for′ti·tude′ *n.* calm courage

fort′night′ *n.* two weeks

for′tress *n.* fortified place

for·tu′i·tous *a.* **1** accidental **2** lucky

for′tu·nate (-chə nət) *a.* lucky —**for′tu·nate·ly** *adv.*

for′tune (-chən) *n.* **1** luck; fate **2** good luck **3** wealth

for′tune·tell′er *n.* one claiming to foretell others′ future —**for′tune·tell′ing** *n., a.*

for′ty *a., n., pl.* **-ties** four times ten — **for′ti·eth** *a., n.*

fo′rum *n.* meeting for public discussion

for′ward *a.* **1** at, to, or of the front **2** advanced **3** bold —*adv.* ahead: also **for′wards** —*v.* **1** promote **2** send on

fos′sil *n.* hardened plant or animal remains, as in rock —*a.* **1** of a fossil **2** taken from the earth —**fos′sil·ize**′ *v.*

fos′ter *v.* **1** bring up **2** promote —*a.* in a family but not by birth or adoption

fought *v.* *pt.* & *pp.* of FIGHT

foul *a.* **1** filthy **2** stormy **3** outside the rules or limits **4** very bad —*n.* foul hit, blow, etc. —*v.* **1** make filthy **2** entangle **3** make a foul

foul′-up′ *n.* [Inf.] mix-up; mess

found *v.* *pt.* & *pp.* of FIND **2** establish —**found′er** *n.*

foun·da′tion *n.* **1** establishment or basis **2** base of a wall, house, etc. **3** philanthropic fund or institution

foun′der *v.* **1** fall or go lame **2** fill and sink, as a ship

found′ling′ *n.* deserted child

found′ry *n., pl.* **-ries** place where metal is cast

fount *n.* source

foun′tain *n.* **1** spring of water **2** sculpture, device, etc. from which jet of water issues **3** source

foun′tain·head′ *n.* source

fountain pen *n.* pen getting ink from its own reservoir

four *a., n.* one more than three

four′score′ *a., n.* eighty

four′some *n.* group of four people

four′square′ *a.* **1** firm **2** frank —*adv.* frankly

four·teen′ *a., n.* four more than ten — **four′teenth**′ *a., n.*

fourth *a.* preceded by three others —*n.* **1** one after the third **2** one of four equal parts

4WD *abbrev.* four-wheel-drive (vehicle)

fowl *n.* **1** any bird **2** domestic bird, as the chicken

fox *n.* **1** small, wild, doglike animal **2** sly person —*v.* to trick —**fox′y** *a.,* **-i·er, -i·est**

fox′glove′ *n.* DIGITALIS

fox′hole′ *n.* hole dug as protection against gunfire

fox terrier *n.* small terrier with smooth or wiry coat

fox trot *n.* ballroom dance

foy′er *n.* entrance hall

Fr *abbrev.* **1** Father **2** French

fra′cas (frā′-) *n.* brawl

frac'tion *n.* **1** part of a whole, as $\frac{3}{4}$, $\frac{1}{2}$, etc. **2** small part

frac'tious *a.* unruly

frac'ture *n.* a break, esp. in a bone —*v.* to break; crack

frag'ile *a.* easily broken —**fra·gil'i·ty** *n.*

frag'ment *n.* **1** part broken away **2** incomplete part —*v.* break up —**frag'men·tar·y** *a.*

fra'grant *a.* sweet-smelling —**fra'grance** *n.*

frail *a.* **1** fragile **2** delicate or weak —**frail'ty** *n., pl.* **-ties**

frame *v.* **1** make, form, build, etc. **2** enclose in a border **3** [Sl.] make seem guilty by a plot —*n.* **1** framework **2** framing border or case **3** condition; state, as of mind

frame'-up' *n.* [Inf.] falsifying of evidence to make seem guilty

frame'work' *n.* supporting or basic structure

franc *n.* Fr. monetary unit

fran'chise' (-chīz') *n.* **1** special right **2** right to vote **3** business with right to provide product or service

fran'gi·ble *a.* breakable

frank *a.* outspoken; candid —*v.* send (mail) free —**frank'ly** *adv.* —**frank'ness** *n.*

Frank'en·stein' *n.* anything that becomes a danger to its creator

frank'furt·er *n.* smoked link sausage; wiener

frank'in·cense' *n.* gum resin burned as incense

fran'tic *a.* wild with anger, worry, etc. —**fran'ti·cal·ly** *adv.*

frap·pé (fra pā') *n.* dessert of partly frozen fruit juices

fra·ter'nal *a.* **1** brotherly **2** of a fellowship society

fra·ter'ni·ty *n., pl.* **-ties 1** brotherliness **2** college social club for men **3** group with like interests

frat'er·nize' *v.* be friendly

frat'ri·cide' *n.* **1** killing of one's brother or sister **2** one who does this —**frat'ri·ci'dal** *a.*

fraud *n.* **1** a cheating or tricking; dishonesty **2** hypocrite; cheat

fraud'u·lent (frô'jə-) *a.* **1** using fraud **2** done or obtained by fraud

fraught *a.* filled (*with*)

fray *n.* quarrel or fight —*v.* make or become ragged

fraz'zle [Inf.] *v.* wear out —*n.* frazzled state

freak *n.* **1** abnormal animal or plant **2** [Sl.] devoted fan —*a.* abnormal

freck'le *n.* small brown spot on the skin —*v.* to spot with freckles

free *a.* **fre'er, fre'est 1** not under another's control **2** loose, clear, unrestricted, etc. **3** without cost —*adv.* **1** without cost **2** in a free way —*v.* **freed, free'ing** make free —**free from** (or of) without —**free up** to release to use —**free'ly** *adv.*

free'boot'er *n.* a pirate

free'dom *n.* **1** independence **2** liberty **3** ease of movement **4** a right

free fall *n.* unchecked fall through the air, esp. part of parachutist's jump before parachute opens

free'-for-all' *n.* a brawl

free'-form' *a.* **1** having an irregular outline **2** spontaneous

free'lance', free'-lance' *a.* selling services to individual buyers

free'load'er *n.* [Inf.] one imposing on others for free food, etc.

free'think'er *n.* religious skeptic

free'way' *n.* multiple-lane highway with interchanges

freeze *v.* **froze, fro'zen, freez'ing 1** to change into, or become covered with, ice **2** make or become very cold **3** preserve (food) by rapid refrigeration **4** make or become fixed **5** fix (prices, etc.) at a set level —*n.* a freezing

freeze'-dry' *v.* **-dried', -dry'ing** preserve (food) by freezing quickly and drying

freez'er *n.* refrigerator for freezing and storing foods

freight (frāt) *n.* **1** goods transported **2** transportation of goods or its cost **3** train for freight

freight'er *n.* ship for freight

French *a., n.* (of) the people or language of France —**French'man** *n., pl.* **-men**

French doors *pl.n.* pair of doors hinged at the sides to open in the middle

French dressing *n.* orange-colored salad dressing

French fried *a.* fried in deep fat

French fries *pl.n.* potatoes cut in strips and fried in deep fat

French horn *n.* brass musical instrument with a coiled tube

French toast *n.* bread dipped in a batter of egg and milk and fried

fre·net'ic *a.* frantic

fren'zy *n., pl.* **-zies** wild excitement —**fren'zied** *a.*

Fre'on' *trademark* gaseous compound used esp. as a refrigerant

fre'quen·cy *n., pl.* **-cies 1** frequent occurrence **2** number of times anything recurs in a given period

frequency modulation n. changing of the frequency of the radio wave according to the signal being broadcast

fre′quent a. **1** occurring often **2** constant —v. go to habitually

fres′co n., pl. **-coes** or **-cos** painting done on wet plaster

fresh a. **1** not spoiled, stale, worn out, etc. **2** new **3** refreshing **4** not salt: said of water —**fresh′en** v. —**fresh′en·er** n.

fresh′et n. overflowing of a stream

fresh′man n., pl. **-men** first-year student in high school or college

fresh′wa′ter a. of or in water that is not salty

fret v. **fret′ted, fret′ting**; n. to worry —n. **1** worry **2** ridge on fingerboard of banjo, guitar, etc. —**fret′ful** a.

fret′work n. ornate openwork

Freud·i·an (froi′dē ən) a. of Sigmund Freud

Fri abbrev. Friday

fri′a·ble (frī′-) a. easily crumbled

fri′ar n. R.C.Ch. member of a religious order

fric′as·see′ n. stewed pieces of meat

fric′tion n. **1** rubbing of one object against another **2** conflict —**fric′tion·al** a. —**fric′tion·less** a.

Fri′day n. sixth day of the week

fried v. pt. & pp. of FRY

friend n. **1** person one knows well and likes **2** ally —**friend′ship′** n.

friend′ly a. **-li·er, -li·est** kindly; helpful

fries pl.n. [Inf.] French fries

frieze (frēz) n. decorative band around a wall, etc.

frig′ate n. fast sailing warship

fright n. sudden fear

fright′en v. **1** make afraid **2** drive (away) with fear

fright′ful a. **1** causing fright **2** disgusting —**fright′ful·ly** adv.

frig′id a. very cold —**fri·gid′i·ty** n.

frill n. **1** ruffle **2** unnecessary ornament —**frill′y** a.

fringe n. border, as of loose threads — v. to edge, as with a fringe

fringe benefit n. payment other than wages, as a pension or insurance

frip′per·y n., pl. **-ies** showy display, clothes, etc.

Fris′bee trademark plastic disk tossed in a game —n. [f-] such a disk

frisk v. to frolic

frisk′y a. **-i·er, -i·est** lively —**frisk′i·ness** n.

frit′ter v. waste (money, etc.) bit by bit —n. small fried cake

friv′o·lous a. **1** trivial **2** silly —**fri·vol′i·ty** n., pl. **-ties**

frizz, friz′zle v. to form tight curls —**friz′zy** a.

fro adv. back: used only in **to and fro,** back and forth

frock n. **1** dress **2** robe

frog n. **1** leaping web-footed animal **2** braided loop —**frog in the throat** hoarseness

frol′ic n. merry time; fun —v. **-icked, -ick·ing** have fun —**frol′ic·some** a.

from prep. **1** beginning at **2** out of **3** originating with **4** out of the possibility, reach, etc. of **5** as not being like **6** because of

frond n. fern or palm leaf

front n. **1** forward part **2** first part **3** land along a street, ocean, etc. **4** outward behavior **5** person or group hiding the activity of another —a. of or at the front —v. to face —**front′age** n. —**fron′tal** a.

fron·tier′ n. **1** border of a country **2** new or unexplored field —**fron·tiers′man** n., pl. **-men**

fron′tis·piece′ n. picture facing the title page

front′man n., pl. **-men′** most prominent member of a musical group

front′-run′ner n. leading candidate, runner, etc.

frost n. **1** temperature causing freezing **2** frozen dew or vapor —v. cover with frost or frosting —**frost′y** a., **-i·er, -i·est**

frost′bite′ n. injury from intense cold —**frost′bit′ten** a.

frost′ing n. **1** icing **2** dull finish on glass

froth n., v. foam —**froth′y** a., **-i·er, -i·est**

fro′ward a. stubborn

frown v. **1** contract the brows **2** look with disapproval (on) —n. a frowning

frow′zy a. slovenly

froze v. pt. of FREEZE

fro′zen v. pp. of FREEZE

fruc′tose′ n. sugar in honey, sweet fruit, etc.

fru′gal a. thrifty or sparing —**fru·gal′i·ty** n.

fruit n. **1** pulpy, edible product of a plant or tree **2** result; product —**fruit′ful** a. —**fruit′less** a.

fruit′cake′ n. rich cake with fruit, nuts, etc.

fru·i′tion (-ish′ən) n. **1** the bearing of fruit **2** fulfillment

frump *n.* dowdy woman —**frump'y** *a.*

frus'trate' *v.* thwart; block —**frus·tra'tion** *n.*

fry *v.* **fried, fry'ing** cook in hot fat or oil —*n.* young fish

fry'er *n.* **1** utensil for deep-frying foods **2** tender chicken for frying

ft *abbrev.* **1** foot **2** feet

Ft *abbrev.* Fort

FT *abbrev.* Basketball free throw

FTC *abbrev.* Federal Trade Commission

fuch'sia (fyōō'shə) *n.* plant with purplish-red flowers —*a.* purplish-red

fudge *n.* soft candy made of butter, sugar, etc.

fu'el *n.* thing burned for heat or power —*v.* supply with or get fuel

fu'gi·tive *a.* **1** fleeing **2** fleeting —*n.* one who has fled from the law, etc.

fugue (fyōōg) *n.* musical work with theme in counterpoint

-ful *suf.* **1** full of **2** having the qualities of **3** apt to **4** quantity that will fill

ful'crum *n.* support on which a lever turns

ful·fill' *v.* **-filled', -fill'ing** carry out or complete (a promise, duty, etc.): Br. sp. **ful·fil'** —**ful·fill'ment, ful·fil'ment** *n.*

full *a.* **1** containing all there is space for **2** having much in it **3** complete **4** ample —*n.* greatest amount, etc. —*adv.* **1** completely **2** exactly —**full'ness** *n.* —**full'y** *adv.*

full'-blown' *a.* matured

full'-bore' *adv.* to the greatest degree —*a.* thorough

full dress *n.* formal dress

full'-fledged' *a.* fully developed; of full status

full'-grown' *a.* fully grown

full house *n.* poker hand with three of a kind and a pair

full'-scale' *a.* **1** to the utmost degree **2** of full size

full'-serv'ice *a.* **1** offering all usual services **2** not self-service

full'-size' *a.* of usual or normal size: also **full'-sized'**

full'-throat'ed *a.* sonorous

full'-time' *a.* of work, etc. using all one's regular working hours

ful'mi·nate' (ful'-) *v.* **1** explode **2** denounce strongly

ful'some (fool'-) *a.* sickeningly insincere

fum'ble *v.* grope or handle clumsily —*n.* a fumbling

fume *n.* offensive smoke or vapor —*v.*

1 give off fumes **2** show anger

fu'mi·gate' *v.* fill with fumes so as to kill vermin, germs, etc.

fun *n.* **1** lively play; merry time **2** source of amusement —**make fun of** ridicule

func'tion *n.* **1** special or typical action, use, duty, etc. **2** formal ceremony or social affair —*v.* do its work —**func'tion·al** *a.*

func'tion·ar'y *n., pl.* **-ies** an official

fund *n.* **1** supply; store **2** money set aside for a purpose **3** *pl.* ready money

fun'da·men'tal *a., n.* basic (thing)

fun'da·men'tal·ism' *n.* [*also* F-] religious beliefs based literally on the Bible —**fun'da·men'tal·ist** *n., a.*

fund'rais'er *n.* person or event that gathers money, as for a charity —**fund'rais'ing** *n.*

fu'ner·al *n.* ceremonies for burial or cremation

funeral director *n.* manager of place (**funeral home** or **parlor**) for funerals

fu·ne're·al (-nir'ē-) *a.* gloomy

fun'gi·cide' (fun'jə-, fuŋ'gə-) *n.* chemical substance that kills fungi

fun'gus *n., pl.* **-gi** (-jī', -gī') or **-gus·es** any of the mildews, molds, mushrooms, etc. —**fun'gal, fun'gous** *a.*

funk *n.* [Inf.] depressed mood

fun'nel *n.* **1** slim tube with a cone-shaped mouth **2** ship's smokestack —*v.* to pour as through a funnel

fun'ny *a.* **-ni·er, -ni·est 1** amusing **2** [Inf.] odd

funny bone *n.* place on the elbow where a sharp impact causes tingling

fur *n.* soft, thick hair on an animal —**fur'ry** *a.*, **-ri·er, -ri·est**

fur·be·low' (-bə lō') *n.* fancy trimming

fu'ri·ous *a.* full of fury

furl *v.* roll up (a flag, sail, etc.) tightly

fur'long *n.* ⅛ of a mile

fur'lough (-lō) *n.* military leave of absence —*v.* grant a furlough to

fur'nace *n.* structure in which heat is produced

fur'nish *v.* **1** put furniture into **2** supply

fur'nish·ings *pl.n.* **1** furniture and fixtures, as for a house **2** things to wear

fur'ni·ture *n.* chairs, beds, etc. in a room, etc.

fu·ror (fyoor'ôr') *n.* **1** widespread enthusiasm **2** fury

fur'ri·er *n.* one who processes, or deals in, furs

fur'ring *n.* thin wood strips put on a wall, floor, etc. before boards or plas-

fur'row n. 1 groove made in the ground by a plow 2 deep wrinkle —v. make furrows in

fur'ther a. 1 additional 2 more distant —adv. 1 to a greater extent 2 in addition 3 at or to a greater distance —v. to promote —**fur'ther·ance** n.

fur'ther·more' adv. besides

fur'thest a. most distant —adv. at or to the greatest distance or extent

fur'tive a. done or acting in a stealthy way

fu'ry n. 1 wild rage 2 violence

fuse v. melt (together) —n. 1 wick that is lighted to set off an explosive 2 safety device that breaks an electric circuit when the current is too strong —**fu'sion** n.

fu'se·lage' (-läzh') n. body of an airplane

fu'sil·lade' (-läd', -lād') n. simultaneous discharge of many guns

fu'sion n. 1 a melting together 2 blending 3 nuclear fusion

fuss n. 1 nervous, excited state 2 a quarrel 3 showy display of delight —v. bustle about or worry over trifles

fuss'budg'et n. [Inf.] one who fusses

fuss'y a. **-i·er, -i·est** 1 hard to please 2 fretting

fus'ty a. **-ti·er, -ti·est** 1 musty 2 old-fashioned

fu·tile (fyōōt'l) a. useless —**fu'tile·ly** adv. —**fu·til'i·ty** n.

fu'ton' (fōō'-) n. thin floor mattress

fu'ture a. that is to be or come —n. 1 time that is to come 2 what is going to be; prospects —**fu'tur·is'tic** a.

fu·tu'ri·ty (-toor'ə-) n. quality of being future

fuzz n. loose, light particles; fine hairs —**fuzz'y** a., **-i·er, -i·est**

FYI abbrev. for your information

G

G trademark film rating indicating content suitable for persons of all ages

G abbrev. 1 goal(s) 2 gram(s) Also **g**

GA abbrev. Georgia

gab n., v. **gabbed, gab'bing** [Inf.] chatter —**gab'by** a., **-bi·er, -bi·est**

gab'ar·dine' (-ər dēn') n. cloth with a diagonal weave

gab'ble v., n. jabber

ga'ble n. triangular wall enclosed by the sloping ends of a roof —**ga'bled** a.

gad v. **gad'ded, gad'ding** roam about restlessly —**gad'a·bout** n.

gad'fly' n. 1 large, stinging fly 2 one who annoys others in stirring them up

gadg'et (gaj'-) n. small mechanical device

Gael·ic (gā'lik) n. traditional language of Ireland or Scotland

gaff n. large hook on a pole for landing fish

gaffe n. a blunder

gaf'fer n. person in charge of lighting on the set of a film

gag v. **gagged, gag'ging** 1 retch or cause to retch 2 keep from speaking, as with a gag —n. 1 something put into the mouth to prevent speech 2 joke

gage n., v. gauge

gag'gle n. 1 flock of geese 2 any group or cluster

gai'e·ty (gā'-) n. 1 cheerfulness 2 merriment

gai'ly adv. 1 merrily 2 brightly

gain n. 1 increase 2 profit —v. 1 earn 2 win 3 get as an addition or advantage 4 reach 5 make progress —**gain on** draw nearer to, as in a race

gain'ful a. profitable

gain'say' v. **-said', -say'ing** deny or contradict

gait n. manner of walking or running

gal n. [Sl.] girl

gal abbrev. gallon(s)

ga'la a. festive —n. festival

gal'ax·y n., pl. **-ies** very large group of stars —**ga·lac'tic** a.

gale n. 1 strong wind 2 outburst, as of laughter

gall (gôl) n. 1 bile 2 tumor on plant tissue 3 impudence —v. annoy

gal'lant a. 1 brave and noble 2 polite to women —**gal'lant·ry** n., pl. **-ries**

gall'blad'der n. sac attached to the liver, in which excess bile is stored

gal'le·on n. large Spanish ship of 15th-16th centuries

gal'le·ri'a n. large arcade or court with a glass roof

gal'ler·y n., pl. **-ies** 1 covered walk 2 outside balcony 3 theater balcony 4 place for art exhibits

gal'ley n., pl. **-leys** 1 ancient sailing ship with oars 2 ship's kitchen

gal'li·vant' v. gad about for pleasure

gal'lon n. four quarts

gal'lop n. fastest gait of a horse —v. go or make go at a gallop

gal'lows n., pl. **-lows** or **-lows·es** structure for hanging condemned persons

gall'stone' *n.* abnormal stony mass in the gallbladder

ga·lore' *adv.* in great plenty

ga·losh'es *pl.n.* high overshoes

gal·van'ic *a.* of electric current, esp. from a battery

gal'va·nize' *v.* 1 stimulate; spur 2 plate (metal) with zinc

gam'bit *n.* opening move in chess

gam'ble *v.* 1 play games of chance for money 2 take a risk 3 bet —*n.* risk; chance —**gam'bler** *n.*

gam'bol *v., n.* frolic

game *n.* 1 amusement or sport with competing players 2 wild animals hunted for sport —*v.* gamble —*a.* 1 plucky 2 ready (*for*) 3 [Inf.] lame — **the game is up** failure is certain

game'keep'er *n.* person who takes care of animals used as game

game plan *n.* long-range strategy

gam·ete (gam'ēt) *n.* reproductive cell

gam'ma ray *n.* electromagnetic radiation with short wavelength

gam'ut *n.* entire range or extent

gam'y (gām'-) *a.* -i·er, -i·est 1 having a strong flavor of game 2 slightly tainted

gan'der *n.* male goose

gang *n.* group working or acting together —**gang up on** [Inf.] attack as a group

gan'gling *a.* thin and tall

gan'gli·on *n.* mass of nerve cells

gang'plank' *n.* movable ramp from a ship to the dock

gan'grene' *n.* decay of body tissue from lack of blood supply —**gan'gre·nous** *a.*

gang'ster *n.* member of a gang of criminals

gang'way' *n.* 1 passageway 2 gangplank

gant'let (gônt'-, gant'-) *n.* former punishment of being beaten as one runs between two rows of men

gan'try *n., pl.* **-tries** wheeled framework with a crane, etc.

gaol (jāl) *n.* Br. sp. of JAIL

gap *n.* 1 opening or break 2 blank space

gape *v.* 1 open wide 2 stare with the mouth open

gar *n.* long fish with a long snout: also **gar'fish'**

ga·rage' (-räzh', -räj') *n.* shelter or repair shop for automobiles, etc.

garb *n.* style of dress —*v.* clothe

gar'bage (-bij) *n.* waste parts of food

gar'ble *v.* distort (a story, etc.)

gar'den *n.* 1 plot for flowers, vegetables, etc. 2 public park —*v.* make, or work in, a garden —**gar'den·er** *n.*

gar·de'ni·a (-dēn'ya) *n.* waxy white flower

gar'den-va·ri'e·ty *a.* ordinary

gar·gan'tu·an (-chōō-) *a.* huge

gar'gle *v.* rinse the throat —*n.* sound as of one gargling

gar'goyle' *n.* gutter spout in the form of a sculptured grotesque creature

gar'ish (gar'-) *a.* gaudy

gar'land *n.* wreath of flowers, leaves, etc.

gar'lic *n.* strong-smelling plant bulb, used as seasoning

gar'ment *n.* piece of clothing

gar'ner *v.* gather and store

gar'net *n.* deep-red gem

gar'nish *v.* 1 decorate (food) 2 attach (a debtor's wages) to pay the debt: also **gar'nish·ee'** —*n.* decoration for food —**gar'nish·ment** *n.*

gar'ret (gar'-) *n.* attic

gar'ri·son *n.* fort or the troops in it — *v.* provide with troops

gar·rote' (-rät', -rōt') *v.* strangle —*n.* device for strangling

gar·ru·lous (gar'-) *a.* talking much — **gar·ru'li·ty** *n.*

gar'ter *n.* elastic band to hold up a stocking

garter belt *n.* wide elastic belt with garters attached

garter snake *n.* small, striped snake

gas *n.* 1 fluid substance that can expand; vapor: some gases are used as fuel 2 [Inf.] gasoline —*v.* **gassed**, **gas'sing** attack with gas —**gas up** [Inf.] to supply with gasoline —**gas'e·ous** *a.*

gash *v.* cut deep into —*n.* deep cut

gas'ket *n.* rubber or metal ring sealing a joint, etc.

gas'o·hol' *n.* fuel mixture of gasoline and alcohol

gas'o·line' (-lēn') *n.* liquid fuel from petroleum

gasp *v.* catch the breath with effort — *n.* a gasping

gas station *n.* service station

gas'sy *a.* -si·er, -si·est flatulent

gas'tric *a.* of the stomach

gas·tri'tis (-trīt'is) *n.* inflammation of the stomach

gas·tron'o·my *n.* art of good eating — **gas'tro·nom'i·cal** *a.*

gas'tro·pod' *n.* kind of mollusk, as a snail or slug

gate *n.* 1 hinged door in a fence or wall 2 number of paid admissions

gate'-crash'er *n.* [Inf.] one who

attends without invitation or payment

gate'fold' *n.* large page of a book, etc., bound for unfolding

gate'way' *n.* entrance with a gate

gath'er *v.* **1** bring or come together; collect **2** infer **3** draw into pleats —*n.* a pleat —**gath'er·ing** *n.*

gauche (gōsh) *a.* tactless

gau'cho (gou'-) *n., pl.* **-chos** South American cowboy

gaud'y *a.* **-i·er, -i·est** showy but tasteless —**gaud'i·ly** *adv.*

gauge (gāj) *n.* **1** standard measure **2** device for measuring —*v.* **1** to measure **2** to estimate

gaunt *a.* haggard; thin

gaunt'let *n.* **1** long glove with a flaring cuff **2** gantlet —**throw down the gauntlet** challenge

gauze *n.* loosely woven material — **gauz'y** *a.*

gave *v.* pt. of GIVE

gav'el *n.* chairman's small mallet

ga·votte' (-vät') *n.* 17th-c. dance like the minuet

gawk *v.* stare stupidly

gawk'y *a.* **-i·er, -i·est** clumsy

gay *a.* **1** joyous and lively **2** bright **3** homosexual

gaze *v.* look steadily —*n.* steady look

ga·ze'bo (-zē'-, -zā'-) *n., pl.* **-bos** or **-boes** small, open, roofed building in garden or park

ga·zelle' *n.* swift antelope

ga·zette' *n.* newspaper

gaz'et·teer' *n.* dictionary of geographical names

ga·zil'lion *n.* [Sl.] very large, indefinite number

gaz·pa'cho (gäs pä'-) *n.* cold Spanish vegetable soup

gear *n.* **1** equipment **2** toothed wheel that meshes with others —*v.* **1** connect by gears **2** adjust

gear'shift' *n.* device for changing transmission gears

geck'o *n., pl.* **-os** or **-oes** tropical lizard

GED *abbrev.* general equivalency diploma

gee (jē) *int.* [Sl.] used to express surprise, etc.: also **gee whiz**

geek *n.* [Sl.] one considered oddly different —**geek'y** *a.*, **-i·er, -i·est**

geese *n.* pl. of GOOSE

gee'zer (gē'-) *n.* [Sl.] eccentric old man

Gei'ger counter (gī'gər) *n.* instrument for measuring radioactivity

gei'sha (gā'-) *n., pl.* **-sha** or **-shas** Japanese woman entertainer

gel (jel) *n.* jellylike substance

gel'a·tin *n.* jellied substance extracted from bones, hoofs, vegetables, etc. — **ge·lat'i·nous** *a.*

geld (geld) *v.* castrate (a horse, etc.) — **geld'ing** *n.*

gel'id (jel'-) *a.* frozen

gem *n.* precious stone

Gem'i·ni' (-nī', -nē') *n.* third sign of the zodiac

gen, genl *abbrev.* general

Gen *abbrev.* General

gen·darme' (zhän-) *n.* armed French police officer

gen'der *n.* **1** classification of words as masculine, feminine, or neuter **2** fact of being male or female

gene *n.* unit of heredity in chromosomes

ge·ne·al'o·gy (jē'nē äl'-) *n.* history of ancestry —**ge·ne·a·log'i·cal** *a.*

gen'er·a *n.* pl. of GENUS

gen'er·al *a.* **1** of or for all **2** widespread **3** usual **4** not specific —*n.* high-ranking army officer —**in general** usually —**gen'er·al·ly** *adv.*

gen'er·al'i·ty *n., pl.* **-ties** nonspecific idea or statement —**gen'er·al·ize'** *v.*

general practitioner *n.* physician who is not a specialist

gen'er·ate' *v.* cause to be; produce — **gen'er·a·tive** *a.*

gen'er·a'tion *n.* **1** production **2** all persons born about the same time **3** average time (30 years) between generations —**gen'er·a'tion·al** *a.*

generation gap *n.* differences between contemporary older and younger generations

Generation X *n.* generation born in 1960s and 1970s

gen'er·a'tor *n.* machine for changing mechanical into electrical energy

ge·ner'ic *a.* **1** inclusive; general **2** of a genus **3** having no special brand name —**gen·er'i·cal·ly** *adv.*

gen'er·ous *a.* **1** giving readily; unselfish **2** ample —**gen·er·os'i·ty** *n.*

gen'e·sis *n.* **1** origin **2** [G-] first book of the Bible

gene therapy *n.* treatment of disease by modifying disease-causing genes, etc.

genetic code *n.* arrangement of chemical substances in DNA molecules transmitting genetic information

ge·net'ics *n.* study of heredity —**ge·net'ic** *a.* —**ge·net'i·cist** *n.*

gen'i·al (jēn'-) *a.* kindly; amiable —**ge'ni·al'i·ty** *n.* —**gen'i·al·ly** *adv.*

ge·nie (jē'nē) *n.* jinni, esp. one in stories, who grants wishes

gen'i·tals *pl.n.* external sex organs: also **gen'i·ta'li·a** —**gen'i·tal** *a.*

gen'i·tive *a., n. Gram.* (in) the case showing possession or origin

gen·ius (-yəs) *n.* **1** great mental or creative ability **2** person having this —**gen'o·ci'dal** *a.*

gen'o·cide' *n.* systematic killing of a whole people —**gen'o·ci'dal** *a.*

gen·re (zhän'rə) *n.* type of art, story, etc.

gen·teel' *a.* (overly) polite, refined, etc.

gen'tian (-shən) *n.* plant with blue, fringed flowers

gen'tile' (-tīl') *a., n. [also* G-*]* non-Jewish (person)

gen·til'i·ty *n.* politeness

gen·tle *a.* **1** mild; moderate **2** kindly; patient —**gen'tly** *adv.*

gen'tle·folk' *pl.n.* well-bred people: also **gen'tle·folks'**

gen'tle·man *n., pl.* -**men 1** well-bred, courteous man **2** any man: polite term —**gen'tle·man·ly** *a.*

gen'tri·fy' *v.* -**fied'**, -**fy'ing** raise to a higher status or condition —**gen'tri·fi·ca'tion** *n.*

gen'try *n.* people just below the nobility

gen·u·flect' *v.* bend the knee, as in worship —**gen'u·flec'tion** *n.*

gen·u·ine (-in) *a.* **1** real; true **2** sincere —**gen'u·ine·ly** *adv.*

ge·nus (jē'-) *n., pl.* **gen'er·a** or sometimes **ge'nus·es** class; kind, esp. in biology

ge'o·cen'tric *a.* with the earth as a center

ge·ode' *n.* a stone having a cavity lined with crystals, etc.

ge'o·des'ic *a.* of a dome with a gridlike framework

ge'o·det'ic *a.* of the measurement of the earth

ge·og'ra·phy *n.* science of the earth's surface, climates, plants, animals, etc. —**ge·og'ra·pher** *n.* —**ge'o·graph'i·cal, ge'o·graph'ic** *a.*

ge·ol'o·gy *n.* science of the earth's crust and of rocks and fossils —**ge'o·log'i·cal** *a.* —**ge·ol'o·gist** *n.*

ge'o·mag·net'ic *a.* of the earth's magnetic properties —**ge'o·mag·ne·tism'** *n.*

ge·om'e·try *n.* branch of mathematics dealing with plane and solid figures —**ge'o·met'ric, ge'o·met'ri·cal** *a.*

ge'o·phys'ics *n.* science of the effects of weather, tides, etc. on the earth —**ge'o·phys'i·cal** *a.*

ge'o·sta'tion·ar'y *a.* of an orbiting satellite staying above same point over earth's surface: also **ge'o·syn'chro·nous**

ge'o·ther'mal *a.* of heat inside the earth: also **ge'o·ther'mic**

Ger *abbrev.* German(y)

ge·ra'ni·um *n.* plant with showy flowers

ger'bil *n.* small rodent

ger'i·at'rics *n.* branch of medicine dealing with diseases of old age

germ *n.* **1** microscopic, disease-causing organism **2** seed, bud, etc. **3** origin —**germ'y** *a.*

Ger'man *n., a.* (native or language) of Germany

ger·mane' *a.* relevant

ger·ma'ni·um *n.* a chemical element used in transistors, semiconductors, etc.

German shepherd *n.* large, wolflike dog

germ cell *n.* cell from which a new organism develops

ger'mi·cide' *n.* anything used to destroy germs —**ger'mi·ci'dal** *a.*

ger'mi·nal *a.* in earliest stage of growth

ger'mi·nate' *v.* sprout, as from a seed —**ger'mi·na'tion** *n.*

ger·on·tol'o·gy *n.* study of aging —**ger·on·tol'o·gist** *n.*

ger'ry·man'der *v.* divide (voting area) to benefit one party

ger'und *n.* verbal noun ending in *-ing*

ges·ta'tion *n.* pregnancy

ges·tic'u·late' *v.* to gesture

ges'ture *n.* movement of part of the body, to express ideas, feelings, etc. —*v.* make gestures

get *v.* **got**, **got** or **got'ten**, **get'ting 1** come to have; obtain **2** come, go, or arrive **3** bring **4** make or become **5** [Inf.] be obliged **6** [Inf.] possess **7** [Inf.] baffle **8** [Inf.] understand —**get along** manage —**get around** circumvent —**get away** escape —**get by** [Inf.] survive; manage —**get over** recover from —**get through 1** finish **2** survive —**get together 1** assemble **2** [Inf.] reach an agreement —**get up** rise (from sleep, etc.)

get'a·way' *n.* **1** a starting, as in a race **2** an escape

get'-go' *n.* [Inf.] beginning

get'-to·geth'er *n.* informal gathering

gew·gaw (gyōo'gô') *n.* trinket

gey·ser (gī'zər) *n.* gushing hot spring

ghast'ly (gast'-) *a.* -**li·er**, -**li·est 1** horrible **2** pale as a ghost

gher′kin (gur′-) *n.* small pickle

ghet·to (get′ō) *n., pl.* **-tos** or **-toes** section of a city lived in by members of a minority group

ghost *n.* supposed disembodied spirit of a dead person —**ghost′ly** *a.*

ghost′writ′er *n.* writer of books, etc. for another claiming authorship —**ghost′write′** *v.*

ghoul (gōōl) *n.* supposed evil spirit that feeds on the dead —**ghoul′ish** *a.*

GI *n., pl.* **GI′s** or **GIs** [Inf.] enlisted soldier

gi′ant *n.* person or thing of great size, strength, etc. —*a.* like a giant

gib′ber (jib′-) *v.* speak incoherently

gib′ber·ish *n.* confused talk

gib′bet (jib′-) *n.* a gallows

gib′bon (gib′-) *n.* small, slender, long-armed ape

gibe (jīb) *v., n.* taunt

gib′let (jib′-) *n.* edible internal part of a fowl

gid′dy *a.* **-di·er, -di·est** 1 dizzy 2 frivolous —**gid′di·ness** *n.*

gift *n.* 1 a present 2 a giving 3 natural ability

gift′ed *a.* talented

gig *n.* [Sl.] job performing music

gi·gan′tic *a.* huge

gig′gle *v.* laugh in a nervous, silly way —*n.* such a laugh

gig′o·lo′ (jig′-) *n., pl.* **-los′** man supported by his female lover

Gi·la monster (hē′lə) *n.* stout, poisonous lizard

gild *v.* **gild′ed** or **gilt, gild′ing** 1 to cover with a layer of gold 2 make better than it is

gill (gil; *n.* 2: jil) *n.* 1 breathing organ of a fish 2 ¼ pint

gilt *n.* surface layer of gold

gilt′-edged′ *a.* of highest value, quality, etc.: said as of securities

gim′bals (gim′-) *pl.n.* pair of pivoted rings that keep ship's compass level

gim′crack′ (jim′-) *n.* object that is showy but useless

gim′let (gim′-) *n.* small tool for making holes

gim′mick *n.* [Inf.] tricky or deceptive device —**gim′mick·y** *a.*

gin *n.* 1 an alcoholic liquor 2 machine for separating cotton from the seeds

gin′ger *n.* spice from the root of a tropical herb

ginger ale *n.* soft drink flavored with ginger

gin′ger·bread′ *n.* cake flavored with ginger

gin′ger·ly *a., adv.* careful(ly) or tim-id(ly)

gin′ger·snap′ *n.* crisp ginger cookie

ging·ham (giŋ′əm) *n.* cotton cloth in stripes or checks

gin·gi·vi·tis (jin′jə vīt′is) *n.* inflammation of gums

gink·go (giŋ′kō) *n., pl.* **-goes** Asian tree with fan-shaped leaves: also **ging′ko**

Gip′sy *n., pl.* **-sies** Gypsy

gi·raffe′ *n.* large African animal with a very long neck

gird *v.* **gird·ed** or **girt, gird′ing** 1 encircle 2 prepare for action

gird′er *n.* large beam for supporting a floor, etc.

gir′dle *n.* 1 [Ar.] a belt 2 light, flexible corset

girl *n.* female child or young woman —**girl′ish** *a.*

girl′friend′ *n.* [Inf.] 1 sweetheart of a boy or man 2 girl who is one's friend 3 woman friend of a woman

Girl Scout *n.* member of the Girl Scouts, girls' club stressing healthful activities

girth *n.* 1 strap around horse's belly 2 circumference

gist (jist) *n.* main point

give *v.* **gave, giv′en, giv′ing** 1 hand over; deliver 2 cause to have 3 produce 4 utter 5 perform 6 bend, etc. from pressure —*n.* a bending, etc. under pressure —**give away** 1 bestow 2 [Inf.] expose — **give forth** (or **off**) emit —**give in** surrender — **give out** 1 make public 2 distribute 3 become worn out —**give up** 1 relinquish 2 cease

give′a·way′ *n.* thing given away or sold cheap

giv′en *a.* 1 bestowed 2 accustomed 3 stated

giz′mo, gis′mo *n., pl.* **-mos** [Sl.] gadget or gimmick

giz′zard *n.* muscular second stomach of a bird

gla·cé (gla sā′) *a.* candied, as fruit

gla′cier (-shər) *n.* large mass of ice that moves slowly down a slope —**gla′cial** (-shəl) *a.*

glad *a.* **glad′der, glad′dest** 1 happy 2 causing joy 3 pleased —**glad′ly** *adv.* —**glad′ness** *n.*

glad′den *v.* make glad

glade *n.* clearing in a forest

glad′i·a·tor *n.* 1 in ancient Rome, a fighter in public shows 2 any fighter

glad′i·o′lus *n., pl.* **-lus·es** or **-li′** plant with tall spikes of funnel-shaped flowers: also **glad′i·o′la,** *pl.* **-las**

glam'or·ize' v. to make glamorous

glam'our, glam'or n. **1** bewitching charm **2** elegance —**glam'or·ous, glam'our·ous** a.

glance v. **1** strike and go off at an angle **2** look briefly —n. a glimpse

gland n. body organ that secretes a substance —**gland'u·lar** (-jə lər) a.

glare v. **1** shine with a dazzling light **2** stare fiercely —n. **1** dazzling light **2** fierce stare **3** glassy surface, as of ice

glar'ing a. flagrant

glass n. **1** hard, brittle substance, usually transparent **2** drinking vessel, mirror, etc. made of this **3** pl. eyeglasses or binoculars

glass ceiling n. policy barring promotion of women or minorities

glass'ware' n. glass articles

glass'y a. **-i·er, -i·est 1** like glass **2** expressionless

glau·co'ma n. an eye disease

glaze v. **1** furnish with glass **2** give a glossy finish to **3** cover with a sugar coating —n. glassy coating

gla'zier (-zhər) n. one who fits glass in windows

gleam n. **1** faint glow of light **2** faint trace, as of hope —v. send out a gleam

glean v. collect (facts, etc.)

glee n. joy —**glee'ful** a.

glee club n. singing group

glen n. secluded valley

glib a. **glib'ber, glib'best** fluent, esp. in a shallow way

glide v. to move or descend smoothly —n. a smooth, easy flow or descent

glid'er n. engineless airplane carried by air currents

glim'mer v., n. (give) a faint, flickering light

glimpse n. brief, quick view —v. catch a glimpse of

glint v., n. gleam

glis·ten (glis'ən) v., n. sparkle

glitch n. [Sl.] mishap, error, etc.

glit'ter v., n. sparkle

glitz n. [Inf.] gaudy showiness —**glitz'y** a., **-i·er, -i·est**

gloam'ing n. twilight

gloat v. feel or show malicious pleasure

glob n. rounded lump

glob'al·ism' n. worldwide outlook

global warm'ing n. increase in the temperature of the lower atmosphere

globe n. **1** ball-shaped thing **2** the earth, or a model of it —**glob'al** a.

globe'-trot'ter n. world traveler

glob'u·lar a. **1** spherical **2** of globules

glob'ule' n. small drop

glock'en·spiel' (-spēl') n. instrument with tuned metal bars played with hammers

gloom n. **1** darkness **2** dark place **3** sadness —**gloom'y** a., **-i·er, -i·est**

glop n. [Inf.] soft, gluey substance

glo'ri·fy' v. **-fied', -fy'ing 1** give glory to; honor **2** make seem greater —**glo'ri·fi·ca'tion** n.

glo'ri·ous a. **1** full of glory **2** splendid

glo'ry n., pl. **-ries 1** great praise or fame **2** splendor **3** heavenly bliss —v. **-ried, -ry·ing** exult (in)

gloss n. **1** surface luster **2** explanation; footnote —v. to smooth over (an error, etc.) —**gloss'y** a., **-i·er, -i·est**

glos'sa·ry n., pl. **-ries** list of difficult terms with definitions, as for a book

glos'so·la'li·a n. utterance of unintelligible sounds in religious ecstasy

glot'tis n. opening between the vocal cords —**glot'tal** a.

glove n. **1** covering for the hand with sheaths for the fingers **2** padded mitt for boxing —**gloved** a.

glow v. **1** give off bright or steady light **2** be elated **3** be bright with color —n. **1** bright or steady light **2** brightness, warmth, etc.

glow'er (glou'-) v., n. stare with sullen anger

glow'worm' n. phosphorescent insect or larva

glu'cose' n. the sugar in fruits and honey

glue n. thick, adhesive liquid —v. make stick as with glue —**glu'ey** a., **-i·er, -i·est**

glum a. **glum'mer, glum'mest** gloomy

glut v. **glut'ted, glut'ting** feed, fill, or supply to excess —n. excess

glu'ten n. sticky protein substance in wheat flour

glu'ti·nous a. sticky

glut'ton n. one who eats too much —**glut'ton·ous** a.

glut'ton·y n. overeating

glyc'er·in (glis'-) n. glycerol: also sp. **glyc'er·ine**

glyc'er·ol' n. colorless, syrupy liquid used in lotions, etc.

gly'co·gen (glī'kə-) n. substance in animal tissues that is changed into glucose

GM abbrev. General Manager

gnarl (närl) n. knot on a tree

gnarled a. knotty and twisted: also **gnarl'y**

gnash (nash) v. grind (the teeth)

together

gnat (nat) *n.* small insect

gnaw (nô) *v.* **1** wear away by biting **2** torment —**gnaw'ing** *n.*

gneiss (nīs) *n.* rock like granite formed in layers

gnome (nōm) *n.* a dwarf

GNP *abbrev.* gross national product

gnu (n⊙⊙, nyⓞⓞ) *n.* African antelope

go *v.* **went, gone, go'ing 1** move along; pass or proceed **2** depart **3** work properly **4** become **5** fit or suit **6** belong in a place —*n.* **1** a success **2** [Inf.] energy **3** [Inf.] a try —**go back on** [Inf.] break (a promise, etc.) —**go in for** [Inf.] engage or indulge in —**go off** explode —**go out 1** be extinguished **2** go to social affairs, etc. —**go over 1** examine **2** do again —**go through 1** endure **2** search —**go under** fail —**let go 1** set free **2** release one's hold

goad *n.* **1** pointed stick **2** stimulus — *v.* urge on

go'-a·head' *n.* permission

goal *n.* **1** place where a race, trip, etc. ends **2** end striven for **3** place to put the ball or puck to score

goal'keep'er *n.* player guarding a goal: also **goal'ie** or **goal'tend'er**

goat *n.* cud-chewing horned animal — **get someone's goat** [Inf.] annoy someone

goat·ee' *n.* pointed beard on a man's chin

goat'herd' *n.* herder of goats

goat'skin' *n.* (leather made from) skin of goat

gob *n.* **1** lump or mass **2** [Sl.] U.S. sailor

gob'ble *n.* cry of a male turkey —*v.* **1** make this cry **2** eat greedily —**gob'bler** *n.*

gob'ble·dy·gook' *n.* [Sl.] pompous, wordy talk or writing with little meaning

go'-be·tween' *n.* one acting between two persons

gob'let *n.* glass with base and stem

gob'lin *n.* evil spirit

God *n.* **1** monotheistic creator and ruler of the universe **2** [g-] any divine being —**god'dess** *n.fem.* —**god'like'** *a.*

god'child' *n., pl.* **-chil'dren** the person (**god'daugh'ter** or **god'son'**) that a godparent sponsors

god'hood' *n.* state of being a god

god'less *a.* irreligious

god'ly *a.* **-li·er, -li·est** pious; devout

god'par'ent *n.* sponsor (**god'fa'ther** or **god'moth'er**) of an infant at baptism

god'send' *n.* something unexpected but much needed

go'fer, go'-fer *n.* [Sl.] employee who does minor tasks

gog'gle *v.* stare with bulging eyes —*n. pl.* large spectacles to protect the eyes against dust, etc.

go'ing *n.* **1** departure **2** degree of ease in traveling —*a.* **1** working **2** current

goi'ter, goi'tre *n.* enlargement of the thyroid gland

gold *n.* **1** yellow precious metal, a chemical element **2** money; wealth **3** bright yellow —*a.* of gold —**gold'en** *a.*

golden ag'er *n.* [Inf.] retired person 65 or older

gold'en·rod' *n.* plant with long, yellow flower clusters

gold'-filled' *a.* of cheap metal overlaid with gold

gold'finch' *n.* small, yellow American songbird

gold'fish' *n.* small, yellowish fish, kept in ponds, etc.

gold'smith' *n.* skilled maker of gold articles

golf *n.* outdoor game in which a small ball is driven, with special clubs, into holes —**golf'er** *n.*

go'nad *n.* ovary or testicle

gon'do·la (*or* gän dō'lə) *n.* boat used on the canals of Venice —**gon'do·lier'** (-lir') *n.*

gone *v.* pp. of GO

gon'er *n.* person sure to die, be ruined, etc.

gong *n.* metal disk that resounds loudly when struck

gon'or·rhe'a, gon'or·rhoe'a (-rē'ə) *n.* a venereal disease

goo *n.* **1** anything sticky **2** sentimentality

goo'ber *n.* peanut

good *a.* **bet'ter, best 1** having proper qualities **2** beneficial **3** of moral excellence **4** enjoyable, happy, etc. **5** considerable —*n.* **1** worth or virtue **2** benefit —**for good** finally; permanently —**good'ness** *n.*

good'bye', good'-bye' *int., n.* farewell: also **good'by'** or **good'-by'**

Good Friday *n.* Friday before Easter

good'-heart'ed *a.* kind

good'-look'ing *a.* beautiful or handsome

good'ly *a.* rather large

good'-na'tured *a.* pleasant

goods *pl.n.* **1** personal property **2** wares **3** fabric

good Sa·mar'i·tan (-mer'-) *n.* person

who helps others unselfishly

good'will' *n.* **1** friendly attitude **2** willingness

good'y *n.*, *pl.* **-ies** [Inf.] thing good to eat

goof [Inf.] *n.* **1** a blunder **2** stupid or silly person —*v.* **1** to blunder **2** waste time: with *off* —**goof'y** *a.*, **-i-er, -i-est**

gook *n.* [Sl.] sticky or slimy substance

goon *n.* [Sl.] **1** hired thug **2** stupid person

goop *n.* [Sl.] sticky, semiliquid substance

goose *n.*, *pl.* **geese 1** long-necked water bird like a large duck **2** silly person —**cook someone's goose** [Inf.] spoil someone's chances

goose'ber'ry *n.*, *pl.* **-ries** sour berry used for jam, etc.

goose bumps *pl.n.* small raised areas on the skin caused by cold, fear, etc.: also **goose pimples** *pl.n.* or **goose flesh** *sing.n.*

goose'liv'er *n.* smoked liver sausage

GOP *abbrev.* Grand Old (Republican) Party

go'pher *n.* burrowing rodent

gore *n.* **1** clotted blood **2** tapered piece of cloth inserted to add width —*v.* pierce as with a tusk —**gor'y** *a.*, **-i-er, -i-est**

Gore'-Tex' *trademark* synthetic material used to make clothing repel water

gorge *n.* deep, narrow pass —*v.* eat or stuff greedily

gor'geous (-jəs) *a.* magnificent

go-ril'la *n.* largest of the apes, native to Africa

gor'mand-ize' *v.* eat like a glutton

go'-round' *n.* one of a series of encounters, etc.

gosh *int.* exclamation of surprise

gos'ling (gäz'-) *n.* young goose

gos'pel *n.* **1** [often **G-**] teachings of Jesus and the Apostles **2** belief proclaimed as true

gos'sa-mer *n.* filmy cobweb or cloth —*a.* filmy

gos'sip *n.* **1** one who spreads rumors about others **2** such rumors —*v.* indulge in gossip —**gos'sip-y** *a.*

got *v.* pt. & alt. pp. of GET

Goth'ic *a.* of a medieval art style of N Europe

got'ten *v.* alt. pp. of GET

Gou'da (cheese) (gōo'-, gou'-) *n.* mild cheese

gouge (gouj) *n.* **1** chisel for cutting grooves **2** any deep groove —*v.* **1**

scoop out as with a gouge **2** [Inf.] overcharge —**goug'er** *n.*

gou-lash (gōo'läsh') *n.* stew seasoned with paprika

gou-ra-mi (gōo rä'mē) *n.* brightly colored fish, often kept in aquariums

gourd (gôrd, goord) *n.* **1** bulb-shaped fruit of a trailing plant **2** its dried shell hollowed out for use

gour-mand (goor mänd', gôr-) *n.* one who likes to eat

gour-met (goor mā', gôr-) *n.* judge of fine foods and drinks

gout *n.* disease with painful swelling of the joints

gov, Gov *abbrev.* **1** government **2** governor

gov'ern *v.* **1** rule; control **2** influence; determine

gov'ern-ess *n.* woman hired to teach children at home

gov'ern-ment *n.* **1** control; rule **2** system of ruling **3** those who rule —**gov'ern-men'tal** *a.*

gov'er-nor *n.* **1** one who governs; esp., head of a U.S. state **2** device to control engine speed automatically

govt, Govt *abbrev.* government

gown *n.* **1** woman's dress **2** long robe, as for a judge

GP, gp *abbrev.* general practitioner

Gr *abbrev.* **1** Greece **2** Greek

grab *v.* **grabbed, grab'bing** snatch suddenly —*n.* a grabbing

grab'by *a.* **-bi-er, -bi-est** [Inf.] avaricious

grace *n.* **1** beauty of form, movement, etc. **2** favor; goodwill **3** delay granted for payment due **4** prayer of thanks at a meal **5** God's unmerited love for man —*v.* dignify or adorn —**in the good graces of** in favor with —**grace'ful** *a.* —**grace'ful-ly** *adv.*

grace'less *a.* **1** ignorant of propriety **2** clumsy

gra'cious (-shəs) *a.* kind, polite, charming, pleasing, etc.

grack'le *n.* small blackbird

grad *n.* [Inf.] a graduate

grad *abbrev.* graduate(d)

gra-da'tion *n.* **1** arrangement in steps **2** a stage in a graded series

grade *n.* **1** degree in a scale of rank or quality **2** slope **3** any of the school years through the 12th **4** mark or rating, as on a test —*v.* **1** classify; sort **2** give a GRADE (n. 4) to **3** make (ground) sloped or level

grade crossing *n.* place where a road crosses a railroad

grade school *n.* elementary school

gra'di·ent n. slope, or degree of slope

grad'u·al (graj'-) a. little by little —**grad'u·al·ly** adv.

grad'u·al·ism' n. principle of gradual social change

grad'u·ate (-at; v. -āt') n. one who has completed a course of study at a school or college —v. **1** give a diploma to (a graduate) **2** become a graduate **3** mark with degrees for measuring —**grad'u·a'tion** n.

graf·fi'ti (-fēt'ē) pl.n., sing. **-to** crude drawings or writing on a public wall, etc.

graft n. **1** shoot, etc. of one plant inserted in another to grow **2** transplanting of skin, etc. **3** dishonest financial gain by public officers —v. insert (a graft)

gra·ham (grā'əm, gram) a. made of whole-wheat flour

Grail n. in legend, cup used by Jesus

grain n. **1** seed of wheat, corn, etc. **2** cereal plants **3** particle, as of salt or sand **4** smallest unit of weight **5** natural markings on wood, etc.

grain'y a. **-i·er, -i·est 1** of wood that shows grain **2** granular —**grain'i·ness** n.

gram n. metric unit of weight (⅒ of an ounce)

gram abbrev. grammar

-gram suf. a writing or drawing

gram'mar n. system of speaking and writing a language —**gram·mar'i·an** (-mer'-) n. —**gram·mat'i·cal** a.

gran'a·ry (gran'-, grān'-) n., pl. **-ries** building for storing grain

grand a. great in size, beauty, importance, etc.; imposing, splendid, etc. —n., pl. **grand** [Sl.] a thousand dollars

grand'child' n. child (**grand'daugh'ter** or **grand'son'**) of one's son or daughter

gran'deur (-jər, -dyoor') n. great size, beauty, etc.; splendor

grandfather clock n. clock in tall, upright case

gran·dil'o·quent a. bombastic

gran'di·ose' (-ōs') a. **1** very grand **2** too grand

grand jury n. jury with power to indict persons for trial

grand'par'ent n. parent (**grand'fa'ther** or **grand'moth'er**) of one's father or mother

grand piano n. large piano with a horizontal case

grand slam n. home run hit with a runner on each base

grand'stand' n. structure for specta-

tors at a sporting event —v. [Inf.] show off to get attention

grange (grānj) n. **1** farm **2** [G-] association of farmers

gran'ite (-it) n. very hard crystalline rock

gran'ny n., pl. **-nies** [Inf.] grandmother

gra·no'la n. breakfast cereal of oats, honey, raisins, nuts, etc.

grant v. **1** consent to or give **2** concede —n. something granted —**take for granted** consider as a fact

grant'-in-aid' n., pl. **grants'-** grant of funds by a foundation, etc. to an artist, scientist, etc.

gran'u·lar a. of, like, or made up of grains or granules

gran'u·late' v. form into granules —**gran'u·la'tion** n.

gran'ule n. small grain

grape n. small, round fruit growing in clusters on a vine

grape'fruit' n. large citrus fruit with a yellow rind

grape hyacinth n. small plant with blue, bell-shaped flowers

grape'vine' n. **1** woody vine that bears grapes **2** means of spreading information or gossip

graph n. a diagram that shows changes in value

-graph suf. **1** that writes **2** thing written

graph'ic a. **1** vivid; in lifelike detail **2** of the arts of drawing, printing, etc. —**graph'i·cal·ly** adv.

graph'ics n. **1** graphic arts **2** design in graphic arts

graph'ite' n. soft, black carbon in pencils, etc.

graph·ol'o·gy n. study of handwriting —**graph·ol'o·gist** n.

grap'nel n. device with hooks or claws for grasping

grap'ple n. grapnel —v. **1** grip and hold **2** struggle

grasp v. **1** grip; seize **2** comprehend —n. **1** a grip **2** control **3** power to grasp **4** comprehension

grasp'ing a. greedy

grass n. **1** green plant grown for lawns **2** pasture —**grass'y** a., **-i·er, -i·est**

grass'hop'per n. leaping insect with long hind legs

grass'land' n. open land with grass; prairie

grass'-roots' a. of common people having basic political opinions

grate v. **1** form into particles by scraping **2** rub with a harsh sound **3** irritate —*n.* **1** frame of bars to hold fuel **2** a grating

grate′ful *a.* thankful

grat′i·fy′ *v.* **-fied′, -fy′ing 1** to please **2** indulge —**grat′i·fi·ca′tion** *n.*

grat′ing *n.* framework of bars over an opening

gra·tis (grat′is, grät′-) *adv., a.* free

grat′i·tude′ *n.* thankful appreciation

gra·tu′i·tous *a.* **1** free of charge **2** uncalled-for

gra·tu′i·ty *n., pl.* **-ties** gift of money for a service

grave *a.* **1** serious **2** solemn —*n.* burial place, esp. a hole in the ground

grav′el *n.* bits of rock

grav′el·ly *a.* hoarse or rasping

grav′en image (grāv′-) *n.* idol of stone or wood

grave′stone′ *n.* tombstone

grave′yard′ *n.* cemetery

grav′id (grav′-) *a.* pregnant

grav′i·tate′ *v.* be attracted

grav′i·ta′tion *n. Physics* force of mutual attraction between masses

grav′i·ty *n.* **1** seriousness **2** weight **3** *Physics* gravitation; esp., the pull on bodies toward earth's center

gra′vy *n., pl.* **-vies** sauce made with juice from cooking meat

gray *n.* mixture of black and white —*a.* **1** of this color **2** dreary —**gray′ish** *a.*

gray′beard′ *n.* old man

gray matter *n.* **1** grayish brain tissue **2** [Inf.] intelligence

graze *v.* **1** feed on growing grass, etc. **2** rub lightly in passing —*n.* a grazing

Gr Brit, Gr Br *abbrev.* Great Britain

grease *n.* **1** melted animal fat **2** thick oily lubricant —*v.* put grease on —**greas′y** *a.,* **-i·er, -i·est**

grease′paint′ *n.* greasy stage makeup

great *a.* much larger, more, or better than average —**great′ly** *adv.*

great- *pref.* older (or younger) by one generation

Great Dane *n.* large, strong dog with short hair

grebe (grēb) *n.* diving bird

Gre′cian (-shən) *a.* Greek

greed *n.* excessive desire, as for wealth —**greed′y** *a.,* **-i·er, -i·est** —**greed′i·ly** *adv.*

Greek *n., a.* (native or language) of Greece

green *n.* **1** color of grass **2** *pl.* leafy vegetables **3** smooth turf —*a.* **1** of the color green **2** unripe **3** inexperienced —**green′ness** *n.*

green′back′ *n.* U.S. paper money

green′belt′ *n.* area around a city, reserved for parks or farms

green′er·y *n.* green foliage

green′-eyed′ *a.* very jealous

green′gro′cer *n.* [Br.] grocer who sells fruits and vegetables

green′horn′ *n.* beginner

green′house′ *n.* heated glass building for growing plants

greenhouse effect *n.* the warming of the earth by trapped solar heat

green light *n.* [Inf.] permission —**green′light′** *v.*

green thumb *n.* knack for growing plants

greet *v.* to address, meet, or receive in a certain way

greet′ing *n.* act or words of one who greets

gre·gar′i·ous (-ger′-) *a.* sociable

gre·nade′ *n.* small bomb usually thrown by hand

gren′a·dier′ (-dir′) *n.* Br. soldier of a special regiment

gren′a·dine′ (-dēn′) *n.* syrup made from pomegranates

grew *v.* pt. of GROW

grey *n., a.* Br. sp. of GRAY

grey′hound′ *n.* swift dog

grid *n.* **1** a grating **2** network of crossed lines, as on a map

grid′dle *n.* flat pan for cooking pancakes, etc.

grid′i′ron *n.* **1** GRILL (*n.* 1) **2** football field

grid′lock′ *n.* traffic jam allowing no movement at all

grief *n.* deep sorrow —**come to grief** fail

griev′ance *n.* complaint or a basis for it

grieve *v.* be or make sad

griev′ous *a.* **1** causing grief **2** deplorable —**griev′ous·ly** *adv.*

grif′fin *n.* mythical beast, part eagle and part lion

grill *n.* **1** framework of bars or wires on which to broil food **2** restaurant serving grilled foods —*v.* **1** broil **2** question relentlessly

grille *n.* open grating forming a screen

grim *a.* **grim′mer, grim′mest 1** fierce; cruel **2** stern **3** repellent —**grim′ly** *adv.*

gri·mace′ (*or* grim′is) *n.* twisting of the facial features —*v.* make grimaces

grime *n.* sooty dirt —**grim′y** *a.,* **-i·er, -i·est**

grin *v.* **grinned, grin′ning** smile broadly —*n.* such a smile

grind v. **ground**, **grind'ing 1** crush into bits **2** sharpen, smooth, etc. by friction **3** rub harshly **4** work by cranking —n. hard task

grind'stone' n. revolving stone for sharpening, etc.

gri·ot (grē'ō) n. traditional W African storyteller

grip n. **1** firm hold **2** handclasp **3** a handle **4** small suitcase —v. **gripped**, **grip'ping** hold firmly

gripe v. **1** cause pain in the bowels of **2** [Sl.] complain —n. [Sl.] complaint

grippe (grip) n. influenza

gris'ly (griz'-) a. **-li·er**, **-li·est** ghastly

grist n. grain to be ground

gris'tle (-əl) n. cartilage

grit n. **1** rough bits of sand, etc. **2** obstinate courage —v. **grit'ted**, **grit'ting** grind (the teeth) —**grit'ty** a., **-ti·er**, **-ti·est**

grits pl.n. coarsely ground grain

griz'zled, **griz'zly** a. grayish

grizzly bear n. large, ferocious North American bear

groan v., n. (utter) a deep sound of pain, etc.

gro'cer n. storekeeper who sells food, etc.

gro'cer·y n., pl. **-ies 1** store of a grocer **2** pl. goods sold by a grocer

grog n. rum and water

grog'gy a. **-gi·er**, **-gi·est** dazed or sluggish

groin n. fold where the abdomen joins either thigh

grom'met n. metal, etc. ring put in an eyelet

groom n. **1** man who tends horses **2** bridegroom —v. **1** make neat **2** train

groove n. **1** narrow furrow **2** channel **3** routine —v. make a groove in

grope v. feel or search about blindly

gross (grōs) a. **1** flagrant **2** coarse **3** total —n. **1** overall total **2** pl. gross twelve dozen —v. earn before deductions —**gross out** [Sl.] disgust, offend, etc.

gross national product n. value of a nation's output of goods and services

gro·tesque' (-tesk') a. **1** bizarre **2** absurd

grot'to n., pl. **-toes** or **-tos 1** cave **2** cavelike shrine, place, etc.

grouch n. [Inf.] **1** one who grumbles **2** sulky mood —**grouch'y** a., **-i·er**, **-i·est**

ground v. **1** pt. & pp. of GRIND **2** set or keep on the ground **3** base **4** instruct (in) —n. **1** land; earth **2** pl. tract of land **3** often pl. cause or basis **4** background **5** pl. dregs —a. of or on

the ground

ground crew n. group of workers who maintain aircraft

ground'er n. batted ball that rolls or bounces along the ground: also **ground ball**

ground'hog' n. woodchuck: also **ground hog**

ground'less a. without reason

ground rule n. any basic rule

ground'swell' n. rapid increase in popular feeling: also **ground swell**

ground'work' n. foundation

group n. persons or things gathered or classed together —v. form a group

group'ie n. [Inf.] fan of rock groups

grouse n., pl. **grouse** game bird

grout n. thin mortar

grove n. small group of trees

grov'el (gräv'-, gruv'-) v. **1** crawl abjectly **2** behave humbly

grow v. **grew**, **grown**, **grow'ing 1** develop **2** increase **3** become **4** raise (crops) —**grow up** to mature

growl n. rumbling sound, as of an angry dog —v. make this sound

grown'-up' (n: -up') a., n. adult

growth n. **1** a growing **2** something that grows or has grown

grub v. **grubbed**, **grub'bing 1** dig or dig up **2** work hard —n. **1** wormlike larva, esp. of a beetle **2** [Sl.] food

grub'by a. **-bi·er**, **-bi·est** dirty; untidy

grub'stake' n. [Inf.] money advanced for an enterprise

grudge v. begrudge —n. resentment or a reason for this

gru'el n. thin porridge

gru'el·ing, **gru'el·ling** a. very trying; exhausting

grue'some a. causing loathing or horror

gruff a. **1** rough and surly **2** hoarse —**gruff'ly** adv.

grum'ble v. mutter in discontent —**grum'bler** n.

grump'y a. **-i·er**, **-i·est** peevish; surly

grunge n. [Sl.] dirt or garbage

grun'gy a. **-gi·er**, **-gi·est** [Sl.] dirty, messy, etc.

grunt v., n. (make) the deep sound of a hog

gua·no (gwä'nō) n. manure of seabirds or bats

guar abbrev. guaranteed

guar·an·tee' (gar'-) n. **1** pledge to replace something sold if faulty **2** assurance **3** pledge or security for another's debt or obligation —v. **1** give a guarantee for **2** assure —**guar'an·tor'** n.

guar·an·ty n., pl. **-ties** a guarantee — v. **-tied, -ty·ing** to guarantee

guard v. **1** protect; defend **2** keep from escape **3** take precautions (*against*) —n. **1** a person or thing that guards **2** careful watch

guard·ed a. **1** kept safe **2** kept from escape **3** cautious

guard'house' n. Mil. jail

guard'i·an n. **1** one legally in charge of a minor, etc. **2** custodian

guard'rail' n. protective railing

gua·va (gwä'-) n. yellow tropical fruit

gu·ber·na·to·ri·al a. of a governor or governor's office

guer·ril'la, gue·ril'la (gə-) n. fighter who makes raids behind enemy lines

guess v. **1** estimate; judge **2** suppose —n. estimate; surmise

guess'work' n. **1** a guessing **2** view based on this

guest n. **1** one entertained at another's home, etc. **2** paying customer, as at a hotel —a. **1** for guests **2** performing by invitation

guf·faw' n., v. laugh in a loud, coarse burst

guide v. **1** show the way to **2** control —n. person or thing that guides — **guid'ance** n.

guide'book' n. book for tourists

guid'ed missile n. war missile guided as by electronic signals

guide'line' n. principle for directing policies, etc.

guild (gild) n. association to promote mutual interests

guile (gīl) n. deceit

guil·lo·tine (gil'ə tēn') n. instrument for beheading

guilt n. **1** fact of having committed an offense **2** painful feeling that one has done a wrong

guilt'y a. **-i·er, -i·est** having or showing guilt —**guilt'i·ly** adv.

guin·ea (gin'ē) n. former English coin, equal to 21 shillings

guinea fowl (or **hen**) n. speckled domestic fowl

guinea pig n. small rodent used in experiments

guise (gīz) n. assumed or false appearance

gui·tar' n. musical instrument usually with six strings plucked or strummed —**gui·tar'ist** n.

gulch n. deep, narrow valley

gulf n. **1** ocean area partly enclosed by land **2** wide chasm **3** vast separation

gull n. **1** gray and white seabird **2** a dupe —v. to cheat

gul'let n. esophagus

gul'li·ble a. easily tricked —**gul'li·bil'i·ty** n.

gul'ly n., pl. **-lies** narrow ravine

gulp v. swallow greedily or hastily —n. a gulping

gum n. **1** sticky substance from some plants **2** an adhesive **3** flesh around the teeth **4** chewing gum —v. **gummed, gum'ming** make or become sticky —**gum'my** a., **-mi·er, -mi·est**

gum'bo n. soup made with okra pods

gum'drop' n. chewy candy

gump'tion n. [Inf.] initiative

gun n. weapon for shooting projectiles —v. **gunned, gun'ning 1** shoot or hunt with a gun **2** [Sl.] increase the speed of (an engine)

gun'fire' n. the firing of guns

gung'-ho' a. [Inf.] enthusiastic

gunk n. [Sl.] thick, messy substance

gun'man n., pl. **-men** armed gangster

gun'ner·y n. the making or firing of large guns —**gun'ner** n.

gun'ny·sack' n. sack made of coarse fabric

gun'play' n. exchange of gunshots

gun'pow'der n. explosive powder used in guns, etc.

gun'ship' n. armed helicopter

gun'shot' n. shot fired from a gun

gun'smith' n. one who makes or repairs small guns

gun·wale (gun'əl) n. upper edge of a boat's side

gup'py n., pl. **-pies** tiny tropical fish

gur'gle n. bubbling sound —v. make this sound

gur'ney n. wheeled stretcher or cot used in hospitals

gu'ru' n. Hindu spiritual advisor or teacher

gush v. **1** flow copiously **2** talk too emotionally —n. a gushing —**gush'er** n.

gus'set n. a triangular piece inserted in a garment

gust n. **1** sudden rush of air **2** sudden outburst

gus·ta·to·ry a. of the sense of taste

gus'to n. zest; relish

gut n. **1** pl. intestines **2** cord made of intestines **3** pl. [Inf.] courage —v. **gut'ted, gut'ting** destroy the interior of

gut'less a. [Inf.] lacking courage

guts'y a. **-i·er, -i·est** [Inf.] courageous, forceful, etc.

gut·ta-per'cha n. rubberlike substance from some trees

gut'ter n. channel to carry off water

gut'tur·al (-ər əl) *a.* sounded in the throat; rasping

guy *n.* 1 guiding rope 2 [Inf.] a man

guz'zle *v.* drink greedily

gym (jim) *n.* [Inf.] gymnasium

gym·na'si·um *n.* place for physical training and sports

gym·nas'tics *n.* sport employing acrobatics, etc. **—gym'nast'** *n.* **—gym·nas'tic** *a.*

GYN *abbrev.* gynecology

gy·ne·col'o·gy (gī'nə-) *n.* branch of medicine dealing with women's diseases **—gy'ne·col'o·gist** *n.*

gyp (jip) *n., v.* **gypped, gyp'ping** [Inf.] swindle

gyp'sum *n.* calcium sulfate, a chalky white mineral

Gyp'sy *n., pl.* **-sies** [*also* g-] member of a wandering people

gy'rate' (jī'-) *v.* to whirl **—gy·ra'tion** *n.*

gy·ro (yir'ō, jir'-; jī'rō) *n., pl.* **-ros** sandwich consisting of slices of lamb, onions, etc. wrapped in a pita

gy'ro·scope' *n.* wheel mounted in a ring and spinning rapidly, used as a stabilizer **—gy·ro·scop'ic** *a.*

H

H *abbrev.* Baseball hit(s): also **h**

ha *int.* exclamation of surprise, triumph, etc.

ha'be·as cor'pus *n.* writ requiring a court to decide the legality of a prisoner's detention

hab'er·dash'er *n.* dealer in men's hats, shirts, etc. **—hab'er·dash'er·y** *n., pl.* **-ies**

ha·bil'i·ments *pl.n.* attire

hab'it *n.* 1 particular costume 2 custom 3 fixed practice

hab'it·a·ble *a.* fit to live in

hab'i·tat' *n.* natural living place

hab'i·ta'tion *n.* dwelling

hab'it-form'ing *a.* resulting in addiction

ha·bit'u·al (-bich'ōō-) *a.* 1 done by habit 2 constant 3 usual **—ha·bit'u·al·ly** *adv.*

ha·bit'u·ate' *v.* accustom

ha·bit·u·é' (-ā') *n.* frequenter of a place

hack *v.* 1 chop roughly 2 cough harshly **—n.** 1 gash 2 harsh cough 3 vehicle for hire 4 old, worn-out horse 5 a literary drudge

hack'er *n.* 1 unskilled golfer 2 computer user who breaks into others' systems

hack'les *pl.n.* hairs on a dog's back that bristle

hack'neyed' (-nēd') *a.* trite; stale

hack'saw' *n.* saw for cutting metal: also **hack saw**

had *v.* pt. & pp. of HAVE

had'dock *n.* small ocean fish used as food

Ha·des (hā'dēz') *n.* hell

had'n't *contr.* had not

haft *n.* handle, as of an ax

hag *n.* ugly old woman

hag'gard *a.* having a wasted, worn look; gaunt

hag'gle *v.* argue about terms, price, etc.

hah (hä) *int.* ha

hai'ku' (hī'-) *n.* three-line Japanese poem

hail *n.* 1 greeting 2 frozen raindrops 3 shower of or like hail **—int.** shout of greeting, etc. **—v.** 1 cheer 2 shout to 3 pour down (like) hail

hail'stone' *n.* piece of hail

hair *n.* 1 threadlike outgrowth from the skin 2 growth of these, as on the head **—split hairs** quibble **—hair'y** *a.*, **-i·er, -i·est**

hair'breadth' *n.* very short distance **—** *a.* very narrow

hair'cut' *n.* act or style of cutting the hair

hair'do' (-dōō') *n., pl.* **-dos'** hairstyle

hair'dress'er *n.* person whose work is arranging hair

hair'line' *n.* 1 thin line 2 outline of hair above the forehead

hair'piece' *n.* wig

hair'pin' *n.* wire for keeping hair in place **—a.** U-shaped

hair'-rais'ing *a.* horrifying

hair'style' *n.* special style of arranging hair

hake *n.* bony food fish

hal'cy·on (-sē ən) *a.* tranquil

hale *a.* healthy; robust **—v.** force to go

half *n., pl.* **halves** either of the two equal parts of a thing **—a.** 1 being a half 2 partial **—adv.** 1 to the extent of a half 2 partially

half'-breed' *n.* one with parents of different races: offensive term

half brother (or **sister**) *n.* brother (or sister) by one parent only

half'heart'ed *a.* with little enthusiasm or interest

half'tone' *n.* semitone

half'track' *n.* army vehicle with a continuous tread instead of rear wheels

half'way' *a.* 1 midway between points 2 partial **—adv.** to the halfway point

half'-wit' *n.* silly or stupid person **—**

half'-wit'ted a.

hal'i·but n. large flounder

hal'i·to'sis n. bad-smelling breath

hall n. **1** public building with offices **2** large room for meetings, shows, etc. **3** vestibule **4** passageway

hal·le·lu'jah, hal·le·lu'iah (-ya) int., n. praise (to) God

hall'mark' n. mark of quality

hal'low v. make or regard as holy — **hal'lowed** a.

Hal'low·een', Hal'low·e'en' n. evening of October 31

hal·lu'ci·na'tion n. apparent perception of sights, etc. not really present —**hal·lu'ci·nate'** v. —**hal·lu'ci·na·to'ry** a.

hal·lu'ci·no·gen n. drug that produces hallucinations

hall'way' n. corridor

ha'lo n. ring of light

halt v., n. stop

hal'ter n. **1** rope for tying an animal **2** woman's backless upper garment

halt'ing a. uncertain; jerky

halve (hav) v. **1** divide into halves **2** reduce to half

halves n. pl. of HALF

hal'yard (-yərd) n. rope for raising a flag, etc.

ham n. **1** meat from upper part of a hog's hind leg **2** [Inf.] amateur radio operator **3** incompetent actor

ham'burg'er n. **1** ground beef **2** cooked patty of such meat, often in a bun Also **ham'burg**

ham'let n. small village

ham'mer n. tool with a metal head for pounding —v. pound, drive, shape, etc. with or as with a hammer

ham'mock n. bed of canvas, etc. swung from ropes

ham'per v. hinder; impede —n. large basket

ham'ster n. small rodent kept as a pet

ham'string' n. tendon back of the knee

hand n. **1** end of the arm beyond the wrist **2** side or direction **3** active part **4** handwriting **5** applause **6** help **7** hired worker **8** pointer on a clock **9** cards held by a player in a card game —a. of, for, or by the hand —v. give as with the hand —**at hand** near — **hand down** bequeath —**hand in hand** together —**hands down** easily —**on hand** available —**hand'ful'** n.

hand'bag' n. woman's purse

hand'ball' n. game in which players hit a ball against a wall with the hand

hand'bill' n. printed notice passed out by hand

hand'book' n. compact book of instructions or facts

hand'clasp' n. handshake

hand'cuff' n. one of a pair of shackles for the wrists —v. put handcuffs on

hand'gun' n. firearm held with one hand, as a pistol

hand'-held' a. of computers, etc. that are very small and portable

hand'i·cap' n. **1** difficulty or advantage given to some contestants to equalize their chances **2** hindrance **3** physical disability —v. **-capped', -cap'ping** hinder

hand'i·capped' a. physically disabled

hand'i·craft' n. work calling for skill with the hands

hand'i·work' n. result of one's actions

hand'ker·chief (haŋ'kər chif') n. small cloth for wiping the nose, etc.

han'dle n. part of tool, etc. by which it is held —v. **1** touch, lift, etc. with the hand **2** manage **3** deal with **4** deal in; sell

han'dle·bar' n. often pl. curved bar for steering a bicycle, etc.

hand'made' adv. made by hand, not by machine

hand'out' n. **1** gift to a beggar, etc. **2** leaflet, etc. handed out

hand'pick' v. choose with care

hand'rail' n. rail along a staircase, etc.

hand'shake' n. a clasping of hands in greeting

hand'some a. **1** good-looking in a manly or impressive way **2** sizable **3** gracious

hand'spring' n. a turning over in mid-air with the hands touching the ground

hand'-to-hand' a. in close contact

hand'-to-mouth' a. with just enough to live on

hand'-wring'ing, hand'wring'ing n. show of distress

hand'writing n. writing done by hand —**hand'writ'ten** a.

hand'y a. **-i·er, -i·est 1** nearby **2** easily used **3** clever with the hands —**hand'i·ly** adv.

hand'y·man' n., pl. **-men'** man who does odd jobs

hang v. **hung** or (v. 3) **hanged, hang'ing 1** to attach or be attached from above **2** attach so as to swing freely **3** kill by suspending from a rope around the neck **4** attach to a wall **5** droop —n. **1** way a thing hangs **2** way a thing is done —**hang around** [Inf.] loiter —**hang back** hesitate, as from shyness —**hang on 1** keep hold **2** persevere —**hang up 1** end a telephone call **2** delay

hang′ar n. aircraft shelter

hang′dog′ a. abject; cowed

hang′er n. that on which something is hung

hang glid′ing n. a gliding through the air using a kitelike device (**hang glider**)

hang′man n., pl. **-men** man who hangs convicted criminals

hang′nail′ n. bit of torn skin next to a fingernail

hang′o′ver n. sickness that is an aftereffect of being drunk

hang′-up′ n. [Sl.] personal problem one finds hard to cope with

hank n. skein of yarn

han′ker v. long (for)

han′ky-pan′ky n. [Inf.] shady activities

Ha·nuk·kah (khä′nŏŏ kä′) n. Jewish festival: also **Ha′nu·ka′**

hap′haz′ard a. not planned; random

hap′less a. unlucky

hap′pen v. **1** take place **2** occur by chance **3** have the luck or occasion

hap′pen·ing n. event

hap′py a. **-pi·er, -pi·est 1** joyous; pleased **2** lucky **3** apt —**hap′pi·ly** adv. —**hap′pi·ness** n.

hap′py-go-luck′y a. easygoing

har·a-ki·ri (här′ə kir′ē) n. Japanese ritual suicide

ha·rangue′ (-raŋ′) v., n. (to address in) a noisy or scolding speech

har·ass (har′əs, hə ras′) v. trouble or attack constantly —**har·ass′ment** n.

har′bin·ger (-jər) n. forerunner

har′bor n. protected inlet for ships — v. **1** to shelter **2** hold in the mind

hard a. **1** firm or solid **2** powerful **3** difficult to do, understand, etc. **4** harsh —adv. **1** with energy **2** with strength **3** firmly —**hard and fast** strict —**hard′en** v.

hard′-bit′ten a. tough; stubborn

hard′-boiled′ a. **1** boiled until solid **2** [Inf.] tough; unfeeling

hard′-core′ adv. **1** absolute **2** portraying sexual acts graphically

hard disk n. rigid computer disk

hard drive n. Comput. drive for hard disks

hard hat n. **1** protective helmet **2** [Sl.] worker wearing a hard hat

hard′head′ed a. **1** shrewd **2** stubborn

hard′heart′ed a. cruel

har′di·hood′ n. boldness, vigor, etc.

hard′-line′ a. politically unyielding

hard′ly adv. **1** barely **2** not likely

hard′-nosed′ a. [Inf.] tough and stubborn

hard′-pressed′ a. confronted with great difficulty, etc.

hard sell n. high-pressure salesmanship

hard′ship′ n. thing hard to bear, as poverty or pain

hard′tack′ n. unleavened bread in hard wafers

hard′ware′ n. **1** metal articles, as tools, nails, etc. **2** electronic equipment

hard′wood′ n. tough timber with a compact texture

har′dy a. **-di·er, -di·est 1** bold and resolute **2** robust —**har′di·ness** n.

hare n. rabbit, esp. one of the larger kind

hare′brained′ a. foolish; silly

hare′lip′ n. congenital cleft of the upper lip

ha·rem (her′əm) n. **1** quarters for the women in a Muslim house **2** these women

hark v. [Poet.] listen

hark′en v. hearken

har′le·quin n. masked clown

har′lot n. prostitute

harm n., v. hurt; damage —**harm′ful** a. —**harm′less** a.

har·mon′i·ca n. small wind instrument with metal reeds

har′mo·nize′ v. **1** be, sing, etc. in harmony **2** bring into harmony

har′mo·ny n. **1** pleasing agreement of parts **2** agreement in ideas, action, etc. **3** pleasing combination of musical tones —**har·mon′ic** a. —**har·mon′i·cal·ly** adv. —**har·mo′ni·ous** a.

har′ness n. straps, etc. for hitching a horse to a wagon, etc. —v. **1** put harness on **2** control for use

harp n. **1** stringed musical instrument played by plucking **2** [Sl.] harmonica —v. keep talking or writing (on) —**harp′ist** n.

har·poon′ n. barbed shaft for spearing whales —v. to strike or catch with a harpoon

harp′si·chord′ n. early keyboard instrument

Har′py n., pl. **-pies** Gr. myth. monster that is part woman and part bird

har′ri·dan (har′-) n. bad-tempered woman

har′row (har′-) n. frame with spikes or disks for breaking up plowed land — v. **1** draw a harrow over **2** distress

har′ry (har′-) v. **-ried, -ry·ing** harass;

torment

harsh *a.* **1** rough to the ear, eye, taste, etc. **2** cruel or severe —**harsh′ly** *adv.* —**harsh′ness** *n.*

hart *n.* male deer; stag

har′vest *n.* **1** a season's crop or the gathering of it **2** season for this —*v.* reap

has *v.* [A.] pres. t. of HAVE: used with *he, she,* or *it*

has′-been′ *n.* [Inf.] one whose popularity is past

hash *n.* a cooked mixture of chopped meat, potatoes, etc.

hash′ish′ (-ēsh′) *n.* narcotic made from Indian hemp

has′n′t *contr.* has not

hasp *n.* clasplike fastening for a door, lid, etc.

has′sle *n.* [Inf.] **1** a squabble **2** troubling situation —*v.* [Sl.] annoy; harass

has′sock *n.* firm cushion used as a footstool, etc.

hast *v.* [A.] have: with *thou*

haste *n.* **1** quickness of motion **2** reckless hurrying

has·ten (hās′ən) *v.* to hurry

hast′y *a.* **-i·er, -i·est** done with haste —**hast′i·ly** *adv.*

hat *n.* head covering, often with a brim

hatch *v.* **1** bring or come forth from (an egg) **2** contrive (a plot) —*n.* hatchway or its lid

hatch′back′ *n.* automobile with rear lid over wide storage area

hatch′er·y *n., pl.* **-ies** place for hatching eggs

hatch′et *n.* short ax

hatch′way′ *n.* opening in a ship's deck, or in a floor

hate *v.* dislike strongly —*n.* strong dislike: also **ha′tred**

hate′ful *a.* deserving hate

hath *v.* [A.] has

haugh·ty (hôt′ē) *a.* **-ti·er, -ti·est** scornfully proud —**haugh′ti·ly** *adv.* —**haugh′ti·ness** *n.*

haul *v.* **1** pull; drag **2** transport by truck, etc. —*n.* **1** amount taken in **2** load or distance transported

haunch *n.* hip, rump, and upper thigh

haunt *v.* **1** visit often **2** recur often to —*n.* place often visited

haunt′ed *a.* supposedly frequented by ghosts

haunt′ing *a.* not easily forgotten

haute cou·ture (ōt′kōō toor′) *n.* high fashion for women

haute cuisine *n.* fine food (preparation)

hau·teur (hō tur′) *n.* scornful pride

have *v.* **had, hav′ing 1** hold; possess **2** experience **3** hold mentally **4** get; take **5** beget **6** engage in **7** cause to do, be, etc. **8** permit **9** be required *Have* is also an important auxiliary verb —*n.* rich person or nation —**have on** be wearing —**have to do with** deal with

ha′ven *n.* shelter; refuge

have′-not′ *n.* poor person or nation

have′n′t *contr.* have not

hav′er·sack′ *n.* bag for provisions, worn over one shoulder

hav′oc *n.* great destruction —**play havoc with** ruin

hawk *n.* bird of prey —*v.* **1** peddle (goods) in the streets **2** clear the throat

hawk′er *n.* peddler

haw′ser (-zər) *n.* cable for anchoring or towing a ship

haw′thorn′ *n.* small tree with red berries

hay *n.* grass, clover, etc. cut and dried —*v.* mow grass, etc. and dry

hay fever *n.* allergy to pollen that affects one like a cold

hay′mow′ (-mou′) *n.* pile of hay in a barn

hay′stack′ *n.* pile of hay outdoors

hay′wire′ *a.* [Inf.] wrong or crazy

haz′ard *n.* **1** chance **2** risk; danger **3** obstacle on a golf course —*v.* to risk —**haz′ard·ous** *a.*

haze *n.* **1** mist of fog, smoke, etc. **2** vagueness —*v.* initiate (someone) in a humiliating way —**ha′zy** *a.*, **-zi·er, -zi·est**

ha′zel *n.* **1** tree bearing small nut (**ha′zel·nut′**) **2** reddish brown

H′-bomb′ *n.* hydrogen bomb

hdqrs *abbrev.* headquarters

HDTV *abbrev.* high-definition television

he *pron.* **1** the male mentioned **2** anyone: some now object to this usage

head *n.* **1** part of the body above or in front of the neck **2** mind **3** top or front part **4** leader —*a.* **1** chief **2** at the head —*v.* **1** to lead **2** set out; go —**head off** intercept —**head over heels** completely —**keep** (or **lose**) **one's head** keep (or lose) one's poise —**not make head or tail of** not understand —**over someone's head** beyond someone's understanding —**turn someone's head** make someone vain

head′ache′ *n.* pain in the head

head′dress′ *n.* decorative head covering

head'first' *adv.* headlong

head'ing *n.* title; caption

head'light' *n.* light at the front of a vehicle

head'line' *n.* title of newspaper article —*v.* feature

head'long' *a., adv.* **1** with the head first **2** rash(ly)

head'-on' *a., adv.* **1** with the head or front foremost **2** directly

head'phones' *pl.n.* device with tiny speakers worn over the ears

head'quar'ters *pl.n.* [*sing.* or *pl.* v.] center of operations; main office

head'room' *n.* space overhead

head start *n.* early start or other competitive advantage

head'stone' *n.* grave marker

head'strong' *a.* obstinate

head'wa'ters *pl.n.* sources of a river

head'way' *n.* progress

head'y *a.* **-i·er, -i·est 1** intoxicating **2** clever

heal *v.* cure or mend

health *n.* **1** soundness of body and mind **2** physical condition —**health'ful** *a.* —**healthy** *a.*, **-i·er, -i·est**

health'care' *n.* medical treatment or the system providing it

heap *n., v.* pile; mass

hear *v.* **heard, hear'ing 1** receive (sounds) through the ear **2** listen to **3** be told —**not hear of** not permit

hear'ing *n.* **1** ability to hear **2** chance to be heard **3** meeting where evidence is presented

hark·en (här'kən) *v.* listen (*to*)

hear'say' *n.* gossip; rumor

hearse (hurs) *n.* vehicle to carry a body to the grave

heart *n.* **1** organ that circulates the blood **2** vital part **3** love, sympathy, courage, etc. **4** figure shaped like ♥ —**by heart** from memory —**take to heart** take (too) seriously

heart'ache' *n.* sorrow

heart'beat' *n.* the throbbing of the heart

heart'break' *n.* great sorrow

heart'break'er *n.* person or thing causing great sorrow

heart'bro'ken *a.* overwhelmed with sorrow —**heart'break'ing** *a.*

heart'burn' *n.* burning sensation in the stomach

heart'en *v.* encourage

heart'felt' *a.* sincere

hearth (härth) *n.* floor of a fireplace

heart'less *a.* unkind

heart'-rend'ing *a.* agonizing

heart'sick' *a.* very sad

heart'-stop'ping *a.* very moving, frightening, etc.

heart'strings' *pl.n.* deepest feelings

heart'-to-heart' *a.* intimate

heart'y *a.* **-i·er, -i·est 1** cordial **2** vigorous **3** strong and healthy **4** nourishing —**heart'i·ly** *adv.*

heat *n.* **1** hotness, or the perception of it **2** strong feeling **3** single race, etc. in a series **4** sexual excitement in animals —*v.* to make or become hot —**heat'ed·ly** *adv.* —**heat'er** *n.*

heath *n.* tract of open wasteland

hea·then (hē'thən) *a., n.* (of) one not a Jew, Christian, or Muslim

heath'er (heth'-) *n.* low plant with purple flowers

heat wave *n.* period of very hot weather

heave *v.* **heaved** or **hove, heav'ing 1** lift, or lift and throw, with effort **2** make (a sigh) with effort **3** rise and fall in rhythm —*n.* act of heaving

heav'en *n.* **1** *pl.* sky **2** state of bliss **3** [*often* H-] *Theol.* the place where God and his angels are —**heav'en·ly** *a.*

heavy *a.* **-i·er, -i·est 1** weighing much **2** very great, intense, etc. **3** sorrowful —*n., pl.* **-ies** stage villain —**heav'i·ly** *adv.* —**heav'i·ness** *n.*

heav'y-du'ty *a.* made to withstand hard use

heav'y-hand'ed *a.* awkward

heav'y-heart'ed *a.* sad

heav'y·set' *a.* stout; stocky

He'brew' *n.* language of ancient and modern Israel —*a.* of the Jews

heck'le *v.* annoy (a speaker) with questions, taunts, etc. —**heck'ler** *n.*

hec'tare' *n.* measure of land, 10,000 square meters

hec'tic *a.* rushed, frenzied, etc. —**hec'ti·cal·ly** *adv.*

hec'tor *v.* to bully

he'd *contr.* **1** he had **2** he would

hedge *n.* dense row of shrubs —*v.* **1** put a hedge around **2** avoid direct answers

hedge'hog' *n.* porcupine

he'don·ist *n.* pleasure-seeker —**he'don·ism** *n.* —**he'do·nis'tic** *a.*

heed *n.* careful attention —*v.* pay heed (to) —**heed'ful** *a.* —**heed'less** *a.*

heel *n.* **1** back part of the foot **2** part of shoe, etc. at the heel —*v.* **1** furnish with heels **2** follow closely **3** lean to one side, as a ship

heft [Inf.] *n.* heaviness —*v.* to lift —**hef'ty** *a.*, **-i·er, -i·est**

he·gem'o·ny (hi jem'-) *n.* dominance of one nation over others

heif′er (hef′-) *n.* young cow

height *n.* 1 highest point or degree 2 distance from bottom to top 3 altitude 4 *often pl.* high place

height′en *v.* make or become higher, greater, etc.

Heim′lich maneuver (hīm′lik) *n.* emergency technique for dislodging an object in the windpipe

hei′nous (hā′-) *a.* shockingly evil

heir (er) *n.* one who inherits another's property, etc. —**heir′ess** *n.fem.*

heir′loom′ *n.* a possession handed down in a family

heist (hīst) [Sl.] *n.* a robbery —*v.* rob

held *v.* pt. & pp. of HOLD

hel′i·cop′ter *n.* aircraft with a horizontal propeller above the fuselage

he′li·o·cen′tric *a.* having the sun as center

he′li·o·trope′ *n.* plant with clusters of purple flowers

hel′i·port′ *n.* airport for helicopters

he′li·um *n.* very light, nonflammable gas, a chemical element

he′lix *n., pl.* **-lix·es** or **hel·i·ces** (hel′ə sēz′) spiral —**hel′i·cal** *a.*

hell *n.* 1 [*often* H-] *Theol.* place of torment for sinners after death 2 state of evil or great suffering —**hell′ish** *a.*

he′ll *contr.* 1 he will 2 he shall

Hel·len′ic *a.* Greek

hell′gram·mite′, hell′gra·mite′ *n.* fly larva used as fish bait

hell′ion (-yən) *n.* [Inf.] person fond of mischief; rascal

hel·lo′ *int.* exclamation of greeting

helm *n.* 1 tiller or wheel to steer a ship or boat 2 control

hel′met *n.* protective head covering of metal, etc.

helms′man *n., pl.* **-men** one who steers a ship or boat

help *v.* 1 give assistance (to); aid 2 to remedy 3 avoid 4 serve —*n.* 1 aid; assistance 2 remedy 3 one that helps 4 hired helper(s) —**help′er** *n.* —**help′ful** *a.*

help′ing *n.* portion of food served to one person

help′less *n.* 1 unable to help oneself 2 unprotected

help′mate′ *n.* helpful companion; spec., a wife: also **help′meet′**

hel′ter-skel′ter *adv., a.* in or showing haste or confusion

hem *v.* hemmed, hem′ming 1 fold the edge of and sew down 2 clear the throat audibly —*n.* hemmed edge —**hem and haw** hesitate in speaking —**hem in** surround or confine

hem′a·tite′ *n.* kind of iron ore

he′ma·tol′o·gy *n.* study of blood and its diseases —**he′ma·tol′o·gist** *n.*

hem′i·sphere′ *n.* 1 half a sphere 2 any of the halves (N or S, E or W) of the earth

hem′lock′ *n.* 1 evergreen tree 2 poisonous weed

hemo- *pref.* blood

he′mo·glo′bin *n.* coloring matter of red blood cells carrying oxygen to body tissues

he′mo·phil′i·a *n.* inherited condition in which the blood fails to clot —**he′mo·phil′i·ac′** *n.*

hem′or·rhage′ (-ər ij′) *n.* heavy bleeding —*v.* bleed heavily

hem′or·rhoids′ (-ər oidz′) *pl.n.* swollen veins near the anus —**hem′or·rhoi′dal** *a.*

hemp *n.* tall plant with fibers used to make rope, etc.

hem′stitch′ *n.* ornamental stitch, used esp. at a hem

hen *n.* female of the chicken or certain other birds

hence *adv.* 1 from this place or time 2 therefore

hence·forth′ *adv.* from now on

hench′man *n., pl.* **-men** helper or follower, esp. of a criminal

hen′na *n.* reddish-brown dye from a tropical shrub

hen′peck′ *v.* domineer over (one's husband) —**hen′pecked′** *a.*

he·pat′ic *a.* of the liver

hep′a·ti′tis *n.* inflammation of the liver

her *pron.* objective case of SHE —*a.* of her

her′ald *n.* 1 messenger 2 forerunner —*v.* announce, foretell, etc.

her′ald·ry *n.* 1 study of coats of arms, etc. 2 pomp —**he·ral′dic** *a.*

herb (urb, hurb) *n.* nonwoody plant, now esp. one used as seasoning or in medicine —**herb′al** (hurb-, urb′-) *a.*

herb′al·ist (hurb′-, urb′-) *n.* one who grows or sells herbs

her′bi·cide′ (hur′-, ur′-) *n.* chemical used to kill plants, esp. weeds

her·biv′o·rous (hər-) *a.* plant-eating —**her′bi·vore′** *n.*

her·cu′le·an *a.* having or involving great strength, courage, etc.

her′cu·les (-lēz′) *n.* very strong man

herd *n.* cattle, etc. feeding or living together —*v.* form into a herd or group

herds′man *n., pl.* **-men** one who tends a herd

here adv. 1 in, at, or to this place 2 at this point; now —n. this place

here'a·bout' adv. near here: also **here'a·bouts'**

here·af'ter adv. from now on —n. state after death

here·by' adv. by this means

he·red'i·tar·y a. of, or passed down by, heredity or inheritance

he·red'i·ty n. passing on of characteristics to offspring or descendants

here·in' adv. in this place, matter, writing, etc.

her'e·sy n., pl. **-sies** unorthodox opinion or religious belief —**her'e·tic** n. —**he·ret'i·cal** a.

here·to·fore' adv. until now

her'it·a·ble a. that can be inherited

her'it·age n. tradition, etc. handed down from the past

her·maph'ro·dite' n. one with both male and female parts —**her·maph'ro·dit'ic** a.

her·met'ic a. airtight: also **her·met'i·cal** —**her·met'i·cal·ly** adv.

her'mit n. one who lives alone in a secluded place

her'ni·a n. rupture, as of the abdominal wall

her'ni·ate' v. form a hernia

he'ro n., pl. **-roes** 1 brave, noble person, esp. a man 2 central male character in a story —**he·ro'ic** a. —**her'o·ine** (-in) n.fem. —**her'o·ism'** n.

her'o·in n. narcotic derived from morphine

her'on n. wading bird

hero sandwich n. meat, cheese, etc. in long, sliced roll

her'pes' (-pēz') n. viral disease causing blisters

her'ring n. food fish of the Atlantic

her'ring·bone' n. pattern of parallel, slanting lines

hers pron. that or those belonging to her

her·self' pron. intensive or reflexive form of SHE

hertz n., pl. **hertz** international unit of frequency, as of electromagnetic waves

he's contr. 1 he is 2 he has

hes'i·tate' v. 1 feel unsure; waver 2 pause —**hes'i·tan·cy** n. —**hes'i·tant** a. —**hes'i·ta'tion** n.

het'er·o·dox' a. unorthodox, as in religious beliefs —**het'er·o·dox'y** n.

het'er·o·ge'ne·ous a. 1 dissimilar 2 varied

het'er·o·sex'u·al a. of or having sexual desire for those of the opposite sex —

n. heterosexual person

heu·ris'tic (hyōō-) a. helping to learn, as by self-teaching

hew v. **hewed, hewed** or **hewn, hew'ing** chop, as with an ax

hex n. spell bringing bad luck; jinx

hex'a·gon' n. figure with 6 angles and 6 sides —**hex·ag'o·nal** a.

hey (hā) int. exclamation to get attention, etc.

hey'day' n. peak period

hgt abbrev. height

hi int. [Inf.] word of greeting

HI abbrev. Hawaii

hi·a'tus n. gap or interruption

hi·ba'chi n. charcoal-burning cooking grill

hi'ber·nate' v. spend the winter in a sleeplike state —**hi'ber·na'tion** n. —**hi'ber·na'tor** n.

hi·bis'cus n. plant with large, colorful flowers

hic'cup' n. muscle spasm that stops the breath, making a loud sound —v. have a hiccup Also **hic'cough'**

hick n. [Inf.] unsophisticated country person: contemptuous term

hick'o·ry n., pl. **-ries** 1 hardwood tree 2 its nut

hide v. **hid, hid'den** or **hid, hid'ing** 1 put, or be, out of sight 2 keep secret —n. animal skin or pelt

hide'a·way' n. [Inf.] secluded place

hide'bound' n. narrow-minded

hid'e·ous a. very ugly

hide'-out' n. [Inf.] hiding place, as for gangsters

hie v. **hied, hie'ing** or **hy'ing** hasten

hi'er·ar'chy (-är'kē) n., pl. **-chies** group of officials in graded ranks —**hi'er·ar'chi·cal** a.

hi'er·o·glyph'ics (hī'ər ə glif'-, hī'rə glif'-) pl.n. picture writing, as of the ancient Egyptians —**hi'er·o·glyph'ic** a., n.

hi'-fi' a. of high fidelity

high a. 1 tall 2 to, at, or from a height 3 above others in rank, size, cost, etc. 4 raised in pitch; shrill 5 elated 6 [Sl.] under the influence of liquor or a drug —adv. in or to a high level, etc. —n. 1 high level, degree, etc. 2 the gear arrangement giving greatest speed —**high'ly** adv.

high'ball' n. liquor mixed with soda water, etc.

high'brow' n., a. intellectual

high'-def'i·ni'tion a. producing extremely clear images and sound

high'-end' a. [Inf.] high-quality

high'fa·lu'tin a. [Inf.] pompous: also

high′fa·lu′ting

high fidelity n. accurate reproduction of sound

high′-flown′ a. too showy

high frequency n. radio frequency between 3 and 30 megahertz

high′hand′ed a. arrogant

high′land n. mountainous region

high′light′ n. brightest or most interesting part, scene, etc. —v. emphasize

high′-mind′ed a. having high ideals or principles

high′ness n. 1 height 2 [H-] title of royalty

high′-pres′sure a. using insistent methods

high′-pro′file a. well-known

high′-rise′ a. having many stories —n. tall building

high roller n. [Sl.] one who spends or risks money freely

high school n. school from grades 9 (or 10) through 12

high seas pl.n. ocean waters not belonging to any nation

high′-spir′it·ed a. lively

high′-strung′ a. excitable

high′-tech′ a. of complex technology

high′-ten′sion a. carrying a high voltage

high′way′ n. main road

high′way·man n., pl. **-men** highway robber

hi′jack′ v. steal (aircraft, goods in transit, etc.) by force

hike v., n. 1 (take) a long walk 2 [Inf.] increase

hi·lar′i·ous a. very funny or merry — **hi·lar′i·ty** n.

hill n. mound of land —**hill′y** a., **-i·er**, **-i·est**

hill′bil′ly n., pl. **-lies** [Inf.] native of mountains or backwoods of southern U.S.: sometimes a contemptuous term

hill′ock n. small hill

hilt n. handle of a sword, dagger, etc.

him pron. objective case of HE

him·self′ pron. intensive or reflexive form of HE

hind a. back; rear —n. female of the red deer

hin′der v. keep back; stop or thwart —**hin′drance** n.

Hin′di n. main language of India

hind′most′ a. farthest back

hind′sight′ n. recognition, after the event, of what one should have done

Hin′du′ n. follower of Hinduism —a. 1 of Hindus 2 of Hinduism

Hin′du·ism′ n. main religion of India

hinge n. joint on which a door, etc.

swings —v. 1 attach by a hinge 2 depend

hint n. slight indication —v. give a hint

hin′ter·land′ n. remote area

hip n. part between the upper thigh and the waist

hip′-hop′ n. style of popular music, dance, etc. that includes rap

hip′pie n. [Sl.] young person, esp. of 1960′s, alienated from conventional society

hip′po·drome′ n. arena

hip′po·pot′a·mus n., pl. **-mus·es** or **-mi′** (-mī′) large, thick-skinned animal of Africa

hire v. pay for the services or use of —n. amount paid in hiring

hire′ling n. one who will do almost anything for pay

hir′sute′ (hur′-) a. hairy

his pron. that or those belonging to him —a. of him

His·pan′ic n. Spanish-speaking Latin American living in U.S.

hiss n. prolonged s sound —v. 1 make this sound 2 show disapproval of by hissing

hist abbrev. history

his′to·ry n., pl. **-ries** study or record of past events —**his·to′ri·an** n. —**his·tor′i·cal, his·tor′ic** a.

his′tri·on′ics (-trē-) pl.n. exaggerated emotional behavior —**his′tri·on′ic** a.

hit v. hit, hit′ting 1 come against with force; bump 2 give a blow (to); strike 3 affect strongly 4 come (on or upon) —n. 1 a blow 2 collision 3 successful song, play, etc. —**hit or miss** haphazard —**hit′ter** n.

hit′-and-run′ a. of a car driver who leaves after hitting a victim: also **hit′-skip′**

hitch v. 1 move with jerks 2 fasten with a hook, knot, etc. —n. 1 a tug; jerk 2 hindrance 3 kind of knot

hitch′hike′ v. travel by asking for rides from motorists —**hitch′hik′er** n.

hith′er adv. to this place

hith′er·to′ adv. until now

HIV n. virus causing AIDS

hive n. 1 colony of bees or its shelter 2 pl. [sing. or pl. v.] skin allergy with raised, itching patches

HMO n. medical insurance plan with enrolled doctors, etc.

HMS abbrev. Her (or His) Majesty's Ship

hoa·gie, hoa·gy (hō′gē) n., pl. **-gies** hero sandwich

hoard n. hidden supply —v. accumu-

late and store away (money, etc.) —
hoard′er n.

hoar′frost′ n. frozen dew

hoarse a. sounding rough and husky

hoar′y a. **-i·er, -i·est 1** white **2** white-haired and old **3** very old

hoax n. a trick; practical joke —v. to fool

hob′ble v. **1** to limp **2** hamper by tying the legs —n. a limp

hob′by n., pl. **-bies** pastime activity — **hob′by·ist** n.

hob′by·horse′ n. stick with horse's head: child's toy

hob′gob′lin n. **1** elf **2** bugbear

hob′nail′ n. broad-headed nail for shoe soles

hob′nob′ v. **-nobbed′, -nob′bing** be friendly (with)

ho′bo n., pl. **-bos** or **-boes** a vagrant; tramp

hock n. hind-leg joint that bends back-ward —v. [Sl.] to pawn

hock′ey n. team game played on ice skates

hock′shop′ n. [Sl.] pawnshop

ho′cus-po′cus n. **1** magic tricks **2** trickery

hod n. **1** trough for carrying bricks, etc. **2** coal scuttle

hodge′podge′ n. a jumble

hoe n. garden tool with a thin blade on a long handle —v. **hoed, hoe′ing** cultivate with a hoe

hoe′down′ n. lively dance

hog n. **1** pig **2** [Inf.] greedy person — v. **hogged, hog′ging** [Sl.] take all of

hogs′head′ n. large barrel

hog′tie′ v. [Inf.] hinder from action

hog′wash′ n. insincere words

hog′-wild′ a. [Inf.] excited, joyful, angry, etc. without restraint

hoi pol·loi (hoi′pə loi′) n. the common people

hoist v. raise, esp. with a crane, etc. — n. apparatus for lifting

hoke v. [Sl.] treat in a sentimental or contrived way: with up —**hok′ey** a.

ho′kum n. [Sl.] nonsense

hold v. **held, hold′ing 1** keep in the hands **2** keep in a certain position **3** keep back **4** occupy **5** have (a meeting, etc.) **6** contain **7** regard **8** remain unyielding —n. **1** grip **2** a strong influence **3** ship's interior below deck —**get hold of** acquire — **hold up 1** delay **2** rob

hold′ings pl.n. property, esp. stocks or bonds, owned

hold′out′ n. one who refuses to perform, join in, etc.

hold′o′ver n. [Inf.] one staying on from former time

hold′up′ n. **1** a delay **2** robbery

hole n. **1** hollow place **2** burrow **3** an opening, tear, etc. —**hole up** [Inf.] hibernate, as in a hole

hol′i·day′ n. **1** religious festival **2** work-free day, usually set aside by law

ho′li·ness n. a being holy

ho·lis′tic a. dealing with whole systems rather than their parts

hol′lan·daise′ sauce (-dāz′) n. creamy sauce of butter, egg yolks, etc.

hol′ler v., n. [Inf.] shout

hol′low a. **1** having a cavity within it **2** concave; sunken **3** insincere **4** deep-toned and dull —n. **1** cavity **2** small valley —v. make or become hollow

hol′ly n. evergreen shrub with red berries

hol′ly·hock′ n. tall plant with large, showy flowers

hol′o·caust′ n. great destruction, esp. of people or animals by fire

hol′o·graph′ n. document handwritten by the author

ho·log′ra·phy n. method of making a three-dimensional image on a thin film —**hol′o·gram′** (häl′ə-, hō′lə-) n. — **ho·lo·graph′ic** a.

hol′ster n. leather pistol case

ho′ly a. **-li·er, -li·est 1** sacred **2** sinless **3** deserving reverence

Holy Communion n. church rite in which bread and wine are received as (symbols of) the body and blood of Jesus

Holy Spirit (or **Ghost**) n. third person of the Trinity

hom′age (häm′-, äm′-) n. anything done to show honor or respect

home n. **1** place where one lives **2** household or life around it —a. **1** domestic **2** central —adv. **1** at or to home **2** to the target —**home′less** a. —**home′made′** a.

home′-care′ a. providing care, at home, as for an aging person

home′land′ n. native land

home′ly a. **-li·er, -li·est 1** simple **2** plain or unattractive

home′mak′er n. person managing a home

ho′me·op′a·thy n. treatment of a disease with drugs that produce similar symptoms

home page n. initial page at a website

home plate n. Baseball last base touched in scoring a run

home run n. *Baseball* hit by which the batter scores a run

home'sick' a. longing for home —**home'sick'ness** n.

home'spun' n. cloth made of yarn spun at home —a. plain or simple

home'stead' (-sted) n. a home and its grounds

home'stretch' n. final part of racetrack, project, etc.

home'ward adv., a. toward home: also **home'wards** adv.

home'work' n. schoolwork done outside the classroom

hom'ey a. **-i·er, -i·est** comfortable, cozy, etc.

hom'i·cide' n. 1 a killing of one person by another 2 one who kills another —**hom'i·ci'dal** a.

hom'i·let'ics n. art of writing and preaching sermons

hom'i·ly n., pl. **-lies** sermon

hom'i·ny n. coarsely ground dry corn

homo- pref. same; equal

ho·mo·ge'ne·ous a. 1 similar 2 made up of similar parts

ho·mog'e·nize' (-mäj'-) v. make uniform throughout —**ho·mog'e·nous** a.

hom'o·graph' n. word with same spelling as another but having a different meaning

hom'o·nym' (-nim·) n. word pronounced like another but having a different meaning and, usually, spelling

Ho·mo sa·pi·ens (hō'mō sā'pē enz') n. mankind; human being

ho'mo·sex'u·al a. of or having sexual desire for those of the same sex —n. homosexual person

Hon abbrev. honorable

hon'cho n., pl. **-chos** [Sl.] person in charge; chief

hone n. fine whetstone —v. sharpen with or as with a hone

hon'est (än'-) a. 1 not cheating, stealing, or lying; upright 2 sincere or genuine 3 frank and open —**hon'es·ty** n.

hon'ey n. sweet, syrupy substance made by bees (**hon'ey·bees'**)

hon'ey·comb' n. structure of wax cells made by bees to hold their honey, etc. —v. fill with holes

hon'ey·dew' melon n. muskmelon with a whitish rind

hon'ey·moon' n. vacation for a newly married couple —v. have a honeymoon

hon'ey·suck'le n. a vine with small, fragrant flowers

honk n. 1 call of a wild goose 2 sound of an auto horn —v. make this sound

hon'ky-tonk' n. [Old Sl.] cheap, noisy nightclub

hon'or (än'-) n. 1 high regard 2 good reputation 3 adherence to right principles 4 glory or credit 5 [H-] title of certain officials 6 something showing respect 7 source of respect and fame —v. 1 treat with respect or high regard 2 confer an honor on 3 accept as valid

hon'or·a·ble a. deserving honor —**hon'or·a·bly** adv.

hon·o·ra'ri·um (-rer'ē-) n. fee paid for professional services

hon'or·ar'y a. done, given, or held as an honor

hon·or·if'ic a. signifying honor, as a title

hon'our n. Br. sp. of HONOR

hood n. 1 covering for the head and neck 2 cover over an automobile engine 3 [Sl.] hoodlum —**hood'ed** a.

-hood suf. 1 state or quality 2 whole group of

hood'lum n. ruffian

hoo'doo' n., pl. **-doos'** [Inf.] bad luck or its cause

hood'wink' v. deceive

hoof n., pl. **hoofs** or **hooves** horny covering on the feet of cattle, horses, etc.

hook n. 1 bent piece of metal used to catch or hold something, spec., one for catching fish 2 sharp curve or curving motion —v. catch, fasten, hit, etc. with a hook —**hook up** connect, as a radio

hook·ah, hook·a (hoo'kə) n. tobacco pipe with a tube for drawing smoke through water

hook'er n. [Sl.] a prostitute

hook'up' n. connection of parts, as in radio

hook'worm' n. a small intestinal roundworm

hook'y n. [Inf.] used only in **play hooky**, be a truant

hoo'li·gan n. [Sl.] ruffian

hoop n. large, circular band

hoop'la' n. [Inf.] excitement

hoop skirt n. woman's skirt worn over hoop framework

hoo·ray' int., n. hurray

hoot n. 1 cry an owl makes 2 shout of scorn —v. utter a hoot or hoots

hop v. hopped, hop'ping leap on one foot, or on both or all feet at once —n. 1 a hopping 2 [Inf.] a dance 3 pl. dried cones of a vine, used to flavor beer, etc.

hope n. **1** trust that what is wanted will happen **2** object of this —v. want and expect —**hope'ful** a. —**hope'less** a.

hop'per n. trough from which material can be emptied slowly

hop'sack'ing n. sturdy fabric used for bags, clothing, etc.: also **hop'sack'**

hop'scotch' n. children's hopping game

horde n. a crowd; throng

hore'hound' n. medicine or candy made from a bitter plant

ho·ri'zon n. line where sky and earth seem to meet

hor·i·zon'tal a. **1** parallel to the horizon **2** level

hor'mone' n. substance that is formed by a gland and stimulates an organ —**hor·mo'nal** a.

horn n. **1** bonelike growth on the head of a cow, etc. **2** brass musical instrument —**horned** a.

hor'net n. large wasp

horn'pipe' n. sailor's dance

horn'y a. **-i·er, -i·est** **1** hard; callous **2** [Sl.] easily aroused sexually

hor'o·scope' n. chart of the zodiac used by astrologers

hor·ren'dous a. horrible

hor'ri·ble a. **1** causing horror **2** [Inf.] very bad, ugly, etc. —**hor'ri·bly** adv.

hor'rid a. horrible

hor'ri·fy' v. **-fied', -fy'ing** **1** make feel horror **2** [Inf.] shock greatly

hor'ror n. **1** strong fear or dislike **2** cause of this

hors d'oeuvre (ôr' durv') n., pl. **hors' d'oeuvres'** appetizer

horse n. **1** large animal domesticated for pulling loads, carrying a rider, etc. **2** supporting frame on legs —**horse around** [Sl.] **1** engage in horseplay **2** waste time —**hors'y** a.

horse'back' adv., n. (on) the back of a horse

horse chestnut n. **1** tree with large brown seeds **2** its seed

horse'hair' n. stiff fabric made from hair of horse's mane or tail

horse'man n., pl. **-men** skilled rider of horses —**horse'man·ship** n. —**horse'wom'an** n., pl. **-wom'en**

horse'play' n. rough play

horse'pow'er n., pl. **-er** unit of power output, as of engines

horse'rad·ish n. plant with a pungent, edible root

horse sense n. [Inf.] common sense

horse'shoe' n. flat, U-shaped, metal

plate nailed to a horse's hoof

hor·ta·to'ry a. exhorting

hor'ti·cul'ture n. art of growing flowers, fruits, etc. —**hor'ti·cul'tur·al** a.

ho·san'na (-zan'-, -zän'-) int., n. shout of praise to God

hose n. **1** pl. **hose** stocking **2** flexible tube to convey liquids

hos'er n. [Cdn. Sl.] lout

ho'sier·y (-zhər-) n. stockings

hos'pice (-pis) n. shelter for travelers, sick, poor, etc.

hos'pi·ta·ble (or häs pit'-) a. friendly to guests —**hos'pi·tal'i·ty** n.

hos'pi·tal n. place of medical care for sick and injured —**hos'pi·tal·ize'** v.

host n. **1** one who entertains guests **2** great number

hos'tage n. person held as a pledge

hos'tel n. lodging place

host'ess n. **1** woman who acts as a host **2** woman in charge of seating in a restaurant

hos'tile (-tal) a. **1** of or like an enemy **2** unfriendly

hos·til'i·ty n., pl. **-ties** **1** enmity **2** pl. warfare

hos'tler (-lər) n. one caring for horses in stable or inn

hot a. **hot'ter, hot'test** **1** high in temperature; very warm **2** spicy; peppery **3** angry, violent, eager, etc. **4** close behind **5** [Inf.] fresh or new —**hot'ly** adv.

hot'bed' n. a place of rapid growth or activity

hot'-blood'ed a. excitable

hot cake n. pancake

hot dog n. [Inf.] wiener

ho·tel' n. place with rooms, food, etc. for travelers

hot flash n. sudden feverish feeling

hot'head'ed a. easily angered —**hot'head'** n.

hot'house' n. greenhouse

hot line n. phone line for emergencies

hot plate n. small, portable stove

hot rod n. [Sl.] car rebuilt for speed —**hot rod'der** n.

hot'shot' n. [Sl.] one thought of as skillful, important, etc.

hot tub n. large, heated tub accommodating several people

hot water n. [Inf.] trouble

hound n. breed of hunting dog —v. keep pursuing

hour n. **1** $\frac{1}{24}$ of a day; 60 minutes **2** a particular time —**hour'ly** a., adv.

hour'glass' n. instrument for measuring time by the flow of sand in it

house (v.: houz) n. **1** building to live in

2 family **3** building for specified use **4** business firm **5** legislative assembly —*v.* cover, shelter, lodge, etc. — **keep house** take care of a home

house'bound' *a.* confined to one's home

house'break'ing *n.* breaking into another's house to steal

house'bro'ken *a.* trained to live in a house, as a dog

house'guest' *n.* one staying at another's home

house'hold' *n.* **1** all those living in one house **2** home and its affairs

house'hold'er *n.* **1** owner of a house **2** head of a household

house'keep'er *n.* one who manages a home, esp. a woman hired to do so

house'warm'ing *n.* party given when someone moves into a new home

house'wife' *n., pl.* **-wives'** woman managing a home

house'work' *n.* work of cleaning, cooking, etc. in a house

hous'ing *n.* **1** shelter or lodging **2** houses **3** enclosing frame, box, etc.

hov'el (huv'-) *n.* small, miserable dwelling

hov'er (huv'-) *v.* **1** flutter in the air near one place **2** linger close by

how *adv.* **1** in what way **2** in what condition **3** why **4** to what extent

how'dah (-də) *n.* seat for riding on the back of an elephant or camel

how·ev'er *adv.* **1** by whatever means **2** to whatever degree **3** nevertheless

how'itz·er *n.* short cannon

howl *v.* **1** long, wailing cry of a wolf, dog, etc. **2** similar cry, as of pain —*v.* **1** utter a howl **2** laugh in scorn, mirth, etc.

howl'er *n.* [Inf., Chiefly Br.] ludicrous blunder

how'so·ev'er *adv.* however

hoy'den *n.* tomboy

HP, hp *abbrev.* horsepower

HQ, hq *abbrev.* headquarters

hr *abbrev.* hour

HR *abbrev.* **1** *Baseball* home run(s) **2** House of Representatives

HS *abbrev.* high school

ht *abbrev.* height

HTML *abbrev.* Hypertext Markup Language

hua·ra·ches (wä rä'chēz, hə-) *pl.n.* flat sandals

hub *n.* **1** center of a wheel **2** center of activity, etc.

hub'bub' *n.* tumult

hu'bris (hyōō'-) *n.* arrogance

huck'le·ber'ry *n., pl.* **-ries** edible dark-

blue berry

huck'ster *n.* peddler

HUD *abbrev.* (Department of) Housing and Urban Development

hud'dle *v.* **1** to crowd close together **2** draw (oneself) up tightly —*n.* confused crowd or heap

hue *n.* color; tint —**hue and cry** loud outcry

huff *v.* to blow; puff —*n.* angry state — **huff'y** *a.,* **-i·er, -i·est**

hug *v.* **hugged, hug'ging 1** embrace **2** keep close to —*n.* embrace

huge *a.* very large; immense

hu'la *n.* native Hawaiian dance

hulk *n.* **1** body of an old, dismantled ship **2** big, clumsy person or thing — **hulk'ing** *a.*

hull *n.* **1** outer covering of a seed or fruit **2** main body of a ship —*v.* remove the hulls from

hul'la·ba·loo' *n.* clamor

hum *v.* **hummed, hum'ming 1** sing with closed lips **2** make a low, steady murmur —*n.* this sound

hu'man *a.* of or like a person or people —*n.* a person: also **human being** — **hu'man·ly** *adv.*

hu·mane' *a.* kind, merciful, etc. —**hu·mane'ly** *adv.*

hu'man·ism *n.* system of thought based on the interests and ideals of humankind —**hu'man·ist** *n.*

hu·man'i·tar'i·an *n.* one devoted to promoting the welfare of humanity — *a.* helping humanity

hu·man'i·ty *n., pl.* **-ties 1** a being human or humane **2** the human race —**the humanities** literature, philosophy, history, etc.

hu'man·ize' *v.* make human or humane

hu'man·kind' *n.* people

hu'man·oid' *a., n.* nearly human (creature)

hum'ble *a.* **1** not proud; modest **2** lowly; unpretentious —*v.* to make humble —**hum'bly** *adv.*

hum'bug' *n.* fraud; sham

hum'drum' *a.* monotonous

hu'mer·us *n.* bone of upper arm

hu'mid *a.* damp; moist

hu·mid'i·fy' *v.* **-fied', -fy'ing** make humid —**hu·mid'i·fi'er** *n.*

hu·mid'i·ty *n.* **1** dampness **2** amount of moisture in the air

hu'mi·dor' *n.* jar, etc. for keeping tobacco moist

hu·mil'i·ate' *v.* lower the pride or dignity of; mortify —**hu·mil'i·a'tion** *n.*

hu·mil'i·ty *n.* humbleness

hum'ming·bird' *n.* tiny bird able to hover

hum'mock (-ək) *n.* low, rounded hill

hu·mon'gous (-mäŋ'-, -muŋ'-) *a.* [Sl.] huge

hu'mor *n.* 1 comical quality, talk, etc. 2 ability to see or express what is funny 3 mood 4 whim —*v.* indulge Also, Br. sp., **hu'mour** —**hu'mor·ist** *n.* —**hu'mor·ous** *a.*

hump *n.* rounded bulge —*v.* to arch

hump'back' *n.* (person having) a back with a hump

hu'mus *n.* dark soil made up of decayed leaves, etc.

hunch *v.* arch into a hump —*n.* feeling not based on facts

hunch'back' *n.* humpback

hun'dred *a., n.* ten times ten —**hun'dredth** *a., n.*

hun'dred-weight' *n.* unit of weight, 100 pounds

hung *v.* pt. & pp. of HANG

Hun·gar'i·an (-ger'-) *n., a.* (native or language) of Hungary

hun'ger *n.* 1 need or craving for food 2 strong desire —*v.* feel hunger (*for*) —**hun'gry** *a.*, **-gri·er**, **-gri·est** —**hun'gri·ly** *adv.*

hung jury *n.* jury unable to agree on a verdict

hunk *n.* [Inf.] large piece

hun'ker *v.* squat: often with *down*

hunt *v.* 1 search out (game) to catch or kill 2 search; seek 3 chase —*n.* a chase or search —**hunt'er** *n.*

hur'dle *n.* 1 frame for jumping over in a race 2 obstacle —*v.* 1 jump over 2 overcome (an obstacle)

hur'dy-gur'dy *n., pl.* **-dies** barrel organ

hurl *v.* throw with force or violence —**hurl'er** *n.*

hurl'y-burl'y *n.* turmoil

hur·rah', **hur·ray'** *int., n.* shout of joy, approval, etc.

hur'ri·cane' *n.* violent storm from the tropics

hur'ry *v.* **-ried**, **-ry·ing** move, act, etc. with haste; rush —*n.* rush; haste —**hur'ried·ly** *adv.*

hurt *v.* hurt, **hurt'ing** 1 cause pain or injury to 2 damage 3 offend 4 have pain —*n.* pain, injury, or harm —**hurt'ful** *a.*

hur'tle *v.* move swiftly or with force

hus'band *n.* married man —*v.* manage thriftily

hus'band·ry *n.* 1 thrifty management 2 farming

hush *v.* make or become silent —*n.* silence; quiet

hush puppy *n.* cornmeal fritter

husk *n.* dry covering of some fruits and seeds —*v.* remove the husk from

husk'y *a.* **-i·er**, **-i·est** 1 hoarse 2 big and strong —*n.* [also H-] arctic dog used for pulling sleds

hus'sy *n., pl.* **-sies** bold or shameless woman

hus'tings *pl.n.* [*usually sing. v.*] (place for) political campaigning

hus'tle (-əl) *v.* 1 shove roughly 2 move, work, etc. quickly or energetically —*n.* a hustling

hus'tler (-lər) *n.* [Sl.] 1 one who gets money dishonestly 2 a prostitute

hut *n.* shedlike cabin

hutch *n.* 1 chest or cupboard 2 pen or coop for small animals

HVAC *abbrev.* heating, ventilating, and air conditioning

hwy *abbrev.* highway

hy'a·cinth' *n.* plant with spikes of flowers

hy'brid *n.* offspring of two animals or plants of different species, etc.

hy'brid·ize' *v.* produce hybrids; crossbreed —**hy'brid·i·za'tion** *n.*

hy'dra *n.* tiny freshwater polyp

hy·dran'gea (-drän'jə) *n.* shrub with large clusters of flowers

hy'drant *n.* large pipe with a valve for drawing water from a water main

hy·drau'lic (-drô'-) *a.* 1 worked by force of a moving liquid 2 of hydraulics

hy·drau'lics *n.* study and use of the mechanical properties of liquids

hydro- *pref.* 1 water 2 hydrogen

hy'dro·car'bon *n.* compound of hydrogen and carbon

hy'dro·chlo'ric acid *n.* acid formed of hydrogen and chlorine

hy'dro·e·lec'tric *a.* of the production of electricity by water power

hy'dro·foil' *n.* (winglike structure on) high-speed watercraft that skims just above water

hy'dro·gen *n.* colorless gas, the lightest chemical element

hy·drog'e·nat'ed (-dräj'-) *a.* treated with hydrogen

hydrogen bomb *n.* very destructive atomic bomb

hydrogen peroxide *n.* liquid bleach and disinfectant

hy·drol'y·sis *n.* chemical reaction of a substance with water that produces another substance

hy'dro·pho'bi·a *n.* rabies

hy'dro·plane' *n.* 1 small, highspeed

motorboat with hydrofoils **2** seaplane

hy'dro·pon'ics *n.* science of growing plants in liquid mineral solutions

hy'dro·ther'a·py *n.* treatment of disease by the use of water

hy·drox'ide' *n.* substance containing the radical OH

hy·e'na *n.* wolflike animal of Africa and Asia

hy'giene' (-jēn') *n.* set of principles for health

hy·gien'ic (-jen'-) *a.* **1** of hygiene or health **2** sanitary

hy·grom'e·ter *n.* device for measuring humidity

hy'men *n.* membrane covering part of the opening of the vagina

hymn (him) *n.* song of praise, esp. a religious one

hym'nal *n.* book of religious hymns; also **hymn'book'**

hype (hīp) [Inf.] *n.* sensational publicity —*v.* promote in a sensational way —**hype up** [Sl.] stimulate

hy'per- [Inf.] *a.* excitable; high-strung

hyper- *pref.* over; excessive

hy·per'bo·le (-bə lē) *n.* exaggeration for effect —**hy'per·bol'ic** *a.*

hy'per·crit'i·cal *a.* too critical

hy'per·ex·tend' *v.* injure (knee, etc.) by bending it too far —**hy'per·ex·ten'sion** *n.*

hy'per·gly·ce'mi·a *n.* condition of too much sugar in the blood

hy'per·link' *n.* hypertext link

hy'per·sen'si·tive *a.* too sensitive

hy'per·ten'sion *n.* abnormally high blood pressure

hy'per·text' *n.* Comput. data linking one document to another

hy'per·thy'roid *a.* of or having excessive activity of the thyroid gland

hy'per·ven'ti·la'tion *n.* extreme rapid breathing, often causing dizziness, etc.

hy'phen *n.* mark (-) used between parts or syllables of a word

hy'phen·ate' *v.* join or write with a hyphen —**hy'phen·a'tion** *n.*

hyp·no'sis (hip-) *n.* sleeplike state in which one responds to the hypnotist's suggestions —**hyp·not'ic** *a.*

hyp'no·tize' *v.* induce hypnosis in —**hyp'no·tism'** *n.* —**hyp'no·tist** *n.*

hypo- *pref.* **1** under **2** less than; deficient in

hy'po·chon'dri·ac' (-kän'-) *n.* one who suffers from abnormal anxiety over his or her health

hy·poc'ri·sy (hi-) *n.,* *pl.* **-sies** pretense of virtue, piety, etc.

hyp'o·crite' (-krit') *n.* one who pretends to have a virtue, feeling, etc. he or she does not have —**hyp'o·crit'i·cal** *a.*

hy'po·der'mic *a.* injected under the skin —*n.* syringe and needle for giving hypodermic injections

hy'po·gly·ce'mi·a *n.* condition of too little sugar in the blood

hy·pot'e·nuse' (-nōōs') *n.* side of right-angled triangle opposite the right angle

hy'po·ther'mi·a *n.* subnormal body temperature —**hy'po·ther'mal** *a.*

hy·poth'e·sis *n.,* *pl.* **-ses'** (-sēz') tentative explanation —**hy·poth'e·size'** *v.*

hy'po·thet'i·cal *a.* based on a hypothesis; supposed

hy'po·thy'roid *a.* of or having deficient activity of the thyroid gland

hys'sop (his'səp) *n.* fragrant plant of mint family

hys·ter·ec'to·my (his'-) *n.,* *pl.* **-mies** surgical removal of the uterus

hys·te'ri·a *n.* outbreak of wild emotion —**hys·ter'i·cal** *a.*

hys·ter'ics *pl.n.* hysteria

Hz *abbrev.* hertz

I

I *pron.* person speaking or writing

IA *abbrev.* Iowa

ib., ibid. *abbrev.* in the same place

i'bex' *n.* wild goat

i'bis *n.* large wading bird

-ible *suf.* **1** that can or should be **2** tending to

i'bu·pro'fen (ī'byōō-) *n.* drug that relieves pain or fever

-ic, -ical *suf.* **1** of or having to do with **2** like **3** produced by **4** containing

ICBM *n.* intercontinental ballistic missile

ICC *abbrev.* Interstate Commerce Commission

ice *n.* **1** water frozen solid by cold **2** frozen dessert of fruit juice, sugar, etc. —*v.* **1** change into ice **2** cool with ice **3** cover with icing —**iced** *a.*

ice'berg' *n.* great mass of ice afloat in the sea

ice'box' *n.* refrigerator, esp. one in which ice is used

ice'break'er *n.* sturdy boat for breaking through ice

ice cream *n.* frozen cream dessert

ice milk *n.* frozen dessert less rich than ice cream

ice skate *n.* shoe with a metal runner

for gliding on ice —**ice′-skate′** v.

ich·thy·ol·o·gy (ik′thē-) n. study of fishes —**ich′thy·ol′o·gist** n.

i′ci·cle n. hanging stick of ice

ic′ing n. sweet, soft coating for cakes; frosting

i′con′ n. **1** sacred image or picture **2** symbol on computer screen for starting a program, etc.

i·con·o·clast′ n. one who attacks venerated institutions or ideas

-ics suf. art or science

ICU abbrev. intensive care unit

i′cy a. **i′ci·er, i′ci·est 1** full of or covered with ice **2** very cold —**i′ci·ly** adv. —**i′ci·ness** n.

id n. part of mind thought to be source of psychic energy

ID n. identification (card, etc.)

ID abbrev. Idaho

id. abbrev. the same

I′d contr. **1** I had **2** I would

i·de′a n. **1** mental conception; a thought or belief **2** a plan or scheme

i·de′al n. **1** conception of something in its perfect form —a. **2** thought of as, or being, an ideal —**i·de′al·ly** adv.

i·de′al·ism′ n. conception of, or striving for, an ideal —**i·de′al·ist** n. —**i·de′al·is′tic** a.

i·de′al·ize′ v. regard or show as perfect —**i·de′al·i·za′tion** n.

i·den′ti·cal a. **1** the same **2** exactly alike —**i·den′ti·cal·ly** adv.

i·den′ti·fy′ v. **-fied′, -fy′ing 1** show to be a certain one **2** associate closely (with) —**i·den′ti·fi·ca′tion** n.

i·den′ti·ty n., pl. **-ties 1** state or fact of being the same **2** individuality

i·de·ol′o·gy (ī′dē-, id′ē-) n., pl. **-gies** system of beliefs, as of a group —**i′de·o·log′i·cal** a.

id′i·om n. **1** set phrase with a special meaning **2** usual way of expression in words —**id′i·o·mat′ic** a.

id′i·o·path′ic a. of a disease with unknown cause

id′i·o·syn′cra·sy (-sin′-) n., pl. **-sies** personal oddity

id′i·ot n. foolish or stupid person —**id′i·o·cy** n. —**id′i·ot′ic** a.

i′dle a. **1** useless **2** baseless **3** not busy or working **4** lazy —v. **1** loaf **2** be or make idle —**i′dler** n. —**i′dly** adv.

i′dol n. image or object worshiped or adored

i·dol′a·try n. worship of idols —**i·dol′a·ter** n. —**i·dol′a·trous** a.

i′dol·ize′ v. adore as an idol

i′dyll, i′dyl (ī′dəl, id′əl) n. short poem

about pleasant rural life —**i·dyl′lic** (ī dil′-) a.

i.e. abbrev. that is (to say)

if con. **1** in case that **2** although **3** whether —as **if** as it would be if

if′fy a. **-fi·er, -fi·est** [Inf.] not definite

ig′loo′ n., pl. **-loos′** Eskimo hut made of snow blocks

ig′ne·ous a. **1** of fire **2** produced by great heat or a volcano

ig·nite′ v. **1** set fire to **2** catch on fire

ig·ni′tion n. **1** an igniting **2** electrical system for igniting the gases in an engine

ig·no′ble a. not noble; base

ig′no·min′y n. shame; disgrace —**ig′no·min′i·ous** a.

ig′no·ra′mus (-rā′məs, -ram′əs) n., pl. **-mus·es** ignorant person

ig′no·rant a. **1** having or showing little or no knowledge **2** unaware —**ig′no·rance** n.

ig·nore′ v. pay no attention to

i·gua′na (i gwä′-) n. large tropical lizard

IL abbrev. Illinois

-ile suf. of or like

ilk n. kind; sort

ill a. **worse, worst 1** bad **2** sick —n. an evil or disease —adv. **worse, worst 1** badly **2** scarcely —**ill at ease** uncomfortable

I′ll contr. **1** I shall **2** I will

ill′-ad·vised′ a. unwise

ill′-bred′ a. rude; impolite

il·le′gal a. against the law —**il·le·gal′i·ty** n., pl. **-ties** —**il·le′gal·ly** adv.

il·leg′i·ble a. hard or impossible to read —**il·leg′i·bil′i·ty** n. —**il·leg′i·bly** adv.

il′le·git′i·mate (-mət) a. **1** born of unwed parents **2** contrary to law, rules, etc. —**il′le·git′i·ma·cy** n.

ill′-fat′ed a. unlucky

ill′-got′ten a. obtained unlawfully or dishonestly

il·lib′er·al a. narrow-minded

il·lic′it a. improper or unlawful

il·lim′it·a·ble a. boundless; vast

il·lit′er·ate (-ət) a. unable to read —n. illiterate person —**il·lit′er·a·cy** n.

ill′-man′nered a. impolite; rude

ill′ness n. sickness; disease

il·log′i·cal a. not logical

ill′-suit′ed a. not appropriate

ill′tem′pered a. irritable

ill′-timed′ a. inappropriate

ill′-treat′ v. to treat unkindly, unfairly, etc. —**ill′-treat′ment** n.

il·lu′mi·nate′ v. **1** light up **2** explain **3** decorate —**il·lu′mi·na′tion** n.

il·lu·mine (-mən) v. light up

illus *abbrev.* **1** illustrated **2** illustration **3** illustrator

ill'-use' (-yōōz'; *n.:* -yōōs') v. abuse —*n.* cruel treatment: also **ill'-us'age**

il·lu'sion n. **1** false idea **2** misleading appearance —**il·lu'sive, il·lu'so·ry** a.

il'lus·trate' v. **1** explain, as by examples **2** furnish (books, etc.) with pictures —**il'lus·tra'tion** n. —**il·lus'tra·tive** a. —**il'lus·tra'tor** n.

il·lus'tri·ous a. famous

ill will n. hate; dislike

im- *pref.* in-: used before *b, m,* or *p*

I'm *contr.* I am

im'age n. **1** a representation, as a statue **2** reflection in a mirror, etc. **3** mental picture; idea **4** likeness —v. reflect

im'age·ry n. **1** mental images **2** figures of speech

i·mag'i·nar'y a. existing only in the imagination

i·mag'i·na'tion n. **1** power to form mental pictures or ideas **2** thing imagined —**i·mag'i·na·tive** a.

i·mag'ine v. **1** conceive in the mind **2** suppose —**i·mag'i·na·ble** a.

im'ag·ing n. creation of an X-ray, radar, etc. image

i·mam' (i mäm') n. [*often* I-] Muslim leader

im·bal'ance n. lack of balance in proportion, force, etc.

im·be·cile' (-səl) a. stupid —n. stupid person —**im·be·cil'ic** a. —**im·be·cil'i·ty** n.

im·bed' v. embed

im·bibe' v. **1** drink (in) **2** absorb into the mind

im·bro'glio (-brōl'yō) n., pl. **-glios** involved misunderstanding or disagreement

im·bue' (-byōō') v. **1** dye **2** fill *with* ideas, emotions, etc.

im'i·tate' v. **1** copy or mimic **2** resemble —**im'i·ta'tion** n., a. —**im'i·ta'tor** n.

im·mac'u·late (-ya lit) a. **1** perfectly clean **2** without a flaw **3** pure

im'ma·nent a. **1** inherent **2** present everywhere: said of God

im'ma·te'ri·al a. **1** unimportant **2** spiritual

im'ma·ture' a. not fully grown or developed —**im'ma·tu'ri·ty** n.

im·meas'ur·a·ble a. boundless; vast —**im·meas'ur·a·bly** adv.

im·me'di·a·cy n. direct relation to present time, place, etc.

im·me'di·ate (-ət) a. **1** closest **2** instant **3** direct —**im·me'di·ate·ly** adv.

im·me·mo'ri·al a. very old

im·mense' a. vast; huge —**im·men'si·ty** n.

im·merse' v. **1** plunge into a liquid **2** engross —**im·mer'sion** n.

im'mi·grant n. one who immigrates —a. immigrating

im'mi·grate' v. enter a country, etc. in order to settle there —**im'mi·gra'tion** n.

im'mi·nent a. likely to happen without delay —**im'mi·nence** n.

im·mo'bile (-bəl) a. **1** not moving **2** not movable —**im·mo·bil'i·ty** n. —**im·mo'bi·lize'** v.

im·mod'er·ate (-ət) a. without restraint; excessive

im·mod'est a. indecent —**im·mod'es·ty** n.

im·mor'al a. not moral; esp., unchaste —**im·mo·ral'i·ty** n.

im·mor'tal a. **1** living forever **2** having lasting fame —n. immortal being —**im·mor·tal'i·ty** n.

im·mov'a·ble a. **1** firmly fixed **2** unyielding

im·mune' a. exempt from or protected against something bad, as a disease —**im·mu'ni·ty** n. —**im'mu·nize'** v. —**im'mu·ni·za'tion** n.

immune system n. system protecting body from disease by producing antibodies

im'mu·nol'o·gy n. study of immunity to disease

im·mure' (-myoor') v. to shut up within walls

im·mu'ta·ble a. unchangeable —**im·mu'ta·bly** adv.

imp n. **1** young demon **2** mischievous child

im'pact' n. (force of) a collision

im·pact'ed a. describing a tooth lodged tightly in jaw

im·pair' v. make worse, less, etc. —**im·pair'ment** n.

im·pa'la (-pä'lə, -pal'ə) n. reddish African antelope

im·pale' v. pierce through with something pointed

im·pal'pa·ble a. that cannot be felt or easily perceived

im·pan'el v. *Law* choose (a jury) from a jury list

im·part' v. **1** give **2** tell

im·par'tial a. fair; just —**im·par·ti·al'i·ty** n.

im·pass'a·ble a. that cannot be traveled over

im'passe' (-pas') n. deadlock

im·pas'sioned a. passionate; fiery

im·pas'sive a. calm

im·pas'to (-päs'-) n. painting with paint laid thickly on the canvas

im·pa'tient a. annoyed because of delay, etc. —**im·pa'tience** n.

im·peach' v. bring (an official) to trial on a charge of wrongdoing —**im·peach'ment** n.

im·pec'ca·ble a. flawless

im·pe·cu'ni·ous a. having no money; poor

im·ped'ance (-pēd'-) n. total resistance in a circuit to the flow of an electric current

im·pede' v. hinder

im·ped'i·ment n. thing that impedes; spec., a speech defect

im·ped'i·men'ta pl.n. encumbrances

im·pel' v. **-pelled', -pel'ling** 1 drive forward 2 force

im·pend' v. be imminent —**im·pend'ing** a.

im·pen'e·tra·ble a. that cannot be penetrated

im·pen'i·tent a. not ashamed

im·per'a·tive a. 1 necessary; urgent 2 of the mood of a verb expressing a command

im·per·cep'ti·ble a. not easily perceived; subtle

im·per'fect a. 1 not complete 2 not perfect

im·per·fec'tion n. 1 a being imperfect 2 fault

im·pe'ri·al (-pir'ē-) a. of an empire, emperor, or empress

imperial gallon n. Br. gallon, equal to 1¼ U.S. gallons

im·pe'ri·al·ism' n. policy of forming and maintaining an empire, as by subjugating territories —**im·pe'ri·al·ist** n., a.

im·per'il v. endanger

im·pe'ri·ous a. domineering

im·per·ish·a·ble a. indestructible

im·per'ma·nent a. not permanent

im·per'son·al a. without reference to any one person

im·per'son·ate' v. 1 assume the role of 2 mimic —**im·per·son·a'tion** n.

im·per'ti·nent a. 1 not relevant 2 insolent —**im·per'ti·nence** n.

im·per·turb'a·ble a. calm; impassive

im·per'vi·ous a. 1 incapable of being penetrated 2 not affected by: with to

im·pe·ti'go (-tī'-) n. skin disease with pustules

im·pet'u·ous (-pech'-) a. impulsive; rash —**im·pet'u·os'i·ty** n.

im·pe·tus n. 1 force of a moving body 2 stimulus

im·pinge' v. 1 strike, hit, etc. (on) 2 encroach (on)

im'pi·ous (-pē-) a. not pious —**im·pi'e·ty** (-pī'-) n.

im·plac'a·ble (-plak'ə-, -plā'kə-) a. not to be appeased

im·plant' (n.: im'plant') v. 1 plant firmly 2 insert surgically —n. implanted organ, etc.

im·plau'si·ble a. not plausible

im'ple·ment (-mənt; v.: -ment') n. tool or instrument —v. put into effect

im'pli·cate' v. show to be a party to a crime, etc.

im'pli·ca'tion n. 1 an implying or implicating 2 something implied

im·plic'it (-plis'-) a. 1 implied 2 absolute

im·plode' v. burst inward —**im·plo'sion** n.

im·plore' v. beseech

im·ply' v. **-plied', -ply'ing** hint; suggest

im·po·lite' a. not polite

im·pol'i·tic a. unwise

im·pon'der·a·ble a. not measurable or explainable —n. anything imponderable

im·port' (n.: im'pôrt') v. 1 bring (goods) into a country 2 signify —n. 1 thing imported 2 meaning 3 importance —**im·por·ta'tion** n.

im·por'tant a. 1 having much significance 2 having power or authority —**im·por'tance** n.

im·por·tune' v. urge repeatedly —**im·por'tu·nate** a.

im·pose' v. put (a burden, tax, etc.) on —**impose on** 1 take advantage of 2 cheat —**im'po·si'tion** n.

im·pos'ing a. impressive

im·pos'si·ble a. that cannot be done, exist, etc. —**im·pos'si·bly** adv. —**im·pos'si·bil'i·ty** n., pl. **-ties**

im·pos'tor n. a cheat pretending to be what he or she is not

im'po·tent (-pə-) a. lacking power; helpless —**im'po·tence** n.

im·pound' v. seize by law

im·pov'er·ish v. make poor

im·prac'ti·ca·ble a. that cannot be put into practice

im·prac'ti·cal a. not practical

im'pre·cate' v. to curse —**im'pre·ca'tion** n.

im·pre·cise' a. not precise; vague

im·preg'na·ble a. that cannot be overcome by force

im·preg'nate' v. 1 make pregnant 2 saturate —**im'preg·na'tion** n.

im·pre·sa'ri·o (-sä'-) *n., pl.* **-os** manager, as of concerts

im·press' (*n.:* im'pres') *v.* **1** to stamp **2** affect the mind or emotions of **3** to fix in the memory —*n.* an imprint —**im·pres'sive** *a.*

im·pres'sion *n.* **1** a mark **2** effect produced on the mind **3** vague notion

im·pres'sion·a·ble *a.* sensitive; easily influenced

im·pres'sion·ism' *n.* style of art, music, etc. reproducing a brief, immediate impression —**im·pres'sion·ist** *n.* —**im·pres'sion·is'tic** *a.*

im·pri·ma'tur (-mät'ər) *n.* permission, esp. to publish

im·print' (*n.:* im'print') *v.* mark or fix as by pressing —*n.* **1** a mark; print **2** characteristic effect

im·pris'on *v.* put in prison

im·prob'a·ble *a.* unlikely

im·promp'tu *a., adv.* without preparation; offhand

im·prop'er *a.* not proper

im·pro·pri'e·ty (-prī'-) *n., pl.* **-ties** improper act

im·prove' *v.* make or become better or more valuable —**im·prove'ment** *n.*

im·prov'i·dent *a.* not thrifty

im·pro·vise' *v.* **1** compose and perform without preparation **2** make or do with whatever is at hand —**im·prov'i·sa'tion** *n.*

im·pru'dent *a.* rash; indiscreet —**im·pru'dence** *n.*

im·pu'dent (-pyōō-) *a.* insolent —**im'pu·dence** *n.*

im·pugn' (-pyōōn') *v.* to challenge as false or questionable

im'pulse' *n.* **1** driving force; impetus **2** sudden inclination to act —**im·pul'sive** *a.*

im·pu'ni·ty *n.* exemption from punishment or harm

im·pure' *a.* **1** dirty **2** immoral **3** adulterated —**im·pu'ri·ty** *n., pl.* **-ties**

im·pute' *v.* to attribute

in *prep.* **1** contained by **2** wearing **3** during **4** at the end of **5** with regard to **6** because of **7** into —*adv.* to or in the inside —*n.* **1** *pl.* those in power **2** [Inf.] special access —**in that** because —**in with** associated with

in *abbrev.* inch(es)

IN *abbrev.* Indiana

in– *pref.* **1** in, into, or toward **2** no, not, or lacking: add *not* or *lack of* to meaning of base word in list below

in·a·bil'i·ty
in·ac·ces'si·ble
in·ac'cu·ra·cy

in·ac'cu·rate
in·ac'tive
in·ad·e·qua·cy
in·ad'e·quate
in'ad·mis'si·ble
in'ad·vis'a·ble
in·an'i·mate
in·ap'pli·ca·ble
in'ap·pro'pri·ate
in·apt'
in·ar·tic'u·late
in·at·ten'tion
in·au'di·ble
in·aus·pi'cious
in·ca'pa·ble
in'ca·pac'i·ty
in·ci·vil'i·ty
in'co·her'ence
in'co·her'ent
in'com·bus'ti·ble
in'com·pat'i·ble
in'com·pre·hen'si·ble
in'con·ceiv'a·ble
in·con·clu'sive
in'con·gru·ous
in·con·sid'er·a·ble
in·con·sid'er·ate
in·con·sis'ten·cy
in·con·sis'tent
in·con'stant
in'con·tro·vert'i·ble
in'cor·rect'
in'cor·rupt'i·ble
in·cur'a·ble
in·de'cent
in·de·ci'sion
in·de·ci'sive
in·dec'o·rous
in·def'i·nite
in'di·gest'i·ble
in'di·rect'
in'dis·cern'i·ble
in'dis·creet'
in'dis·cre'tion
in'dis·pu'ta·ble
in'dis·tinct'
in'dis·tin'guish·a·ble
in'di·vis'i·ble
in·ed'i·ble
in'ef·fec'tive
in'ef·fec'tu·al
in'ef·fi·ca'cious
in·ef'fi·cient
in'e·las'tic
in·el'e·gant
in'e·qual'i·ty
in·eq'ui·ta·ble
in·eq'ui·ty
in·ex·act'
in'ex·cus'a·ble

in·ex·haust′i·ble

in·ex·pe′di·ent

in·ex·pen′sive

in·ex·tin′guish·a·ble

in·fer′tile

in·fre′quent

in·glo′ri·ous

in·grat′i·tude′

in·har·mo′ni·ous

in·hos′pi·ta·ble

in·hu·mane′

in·ju·di′cious

in·of·fen′sive

in·op′er·a·ble

in·op′er·a·tive

in·op·por·tune′

in·sep′a·ra·ble

in·sig·nif′i·cance

in·sig·nif′i·cant

in·sol′u·ble

in·solv′a·ble

in·sta·bil′i·ty

in·suf·fi′cient

in·sur·mount′a·ble

in·tan′gi·ble

in·tol′er·a·ble

in·tol′er·ance

in·tol′er·ant

in·var′i·a·ble

in·vul′ner·a·ble

in ab·sen′tia (-sen′shə) adv. although not present

in·ac′ti·vate′ v. make no longer active

in′ad·vert′ent a. not on purpose; accidental —in′ad·vert′ence n.

in·al′ien·a·ble (-āl′yən-) a. that cannot be taken away

in·ane′ a. lacking sense; silly —in·an′i·ty n.

in′as·much′ as con. because

in·au′gu·rate′ v. 1 formally induct into office 2 begin; open —in·au′gu·ral a. —in·au′gu·ra′tion n.

in′board′ a. inside the hull of a boat

in′born′ a. present at birth; natural

in′bound′ a. going inward

in′breed′ v. breed by continually mating from the same stock

inc abbrev. incorporated: also Inc.

In′ca n. member of Indian people of Peru —In′can a.

in·cal′cu·la·ble a. too great to be calculated

in·can·des′cent a. 1 glowing with heat 2 shining

in′can·ta′tion n. words chanted in magic spells

in·ca·pac′i·tate′ v. make unable or unfit

in·car′cer·ate′ v. imprison —in·car′cer·a′tion n.

in·car′nate a. in human form; personified —in′car·na′tion n.

in·cen′di·ar·y a. 1 causing fires 2 stirring up strife —n. one who willfully sets fire to property or provokes strife

in′cense′ (v.: in sens′) n. 1 substance burned to produce a pleasant odor 2 this odor —v. enrage

in·cen′tive n. motive or stimulus

in·cep′tion n. a beginning; start

in·ces′sant a. constant

in′cest′ n. sexual contact between close relatives —in·ces′tu·ous a.

inch n. measure of length, $\frac{1}{12}$ foot —v. to move very slowly, by degrees —every inch in all respects

in·cho′ate (-kō′it) a. not fully formed

in′ci·dence n. range of occurrence or effect

in′ci·dent n. event

in′ci·den′tal a. 1 happening along with something more important 2 minor —n. 1 something incidental 2 pl. miscellaneous items —in′ci·den′tal·ly adv.

in·cin′er·ate′ v. burn to ashes

in·cin′er·a′tor n. furnace for burning trash

in·cip′i·ent a. just beginning to exist or appear

in·cise′ (-sīz′) v. cut into; engrave

in·ci′sion (-sizh′ən) n. 1 a cutting into 2 a cut; gash

in·ci′sive (-sī′siv) a. piercing; acute

in·ci′sor (-sī′zər) n. any of the front cutting teeth

in·cite′ v. urge to action —in·cite′ment n.

incl abbrev. 1 including 2 inclusive

in·clem′ent a. stormy

in·cline′ (n.: in′klīn′) v. 1 lean; bend; slope 2 tend 3 have a preference 4 influence —n. a slope —in′cli·na′tion n.

in·close′ v. enclose

in·clude′ v. have or take in as part of a whole; contain —in·clu′sion n.

in·clu′sive a. 1 including everything 2 including the limits mentioned

in·cog′ni·to (-nē′-) a., adv. disguised under a false name

in′come′ n. money one gets as wages, salary, rent, etc.

in′com′ing a. coming in

in′com·mu′ni·ca′do (-kä′dō) a., adv. without a means of communicating

in·com′pa·ra·ble a. beyond comparison; matchless

in·com′pe·tent n., a. (one) without adequate skill or knowledge —in·com′pe·tence n.

in·com·plete' *a.* lacking a part or parts; unfinished

in·con·se·quen'tial *a.* unimportant

in·con·sol'a·ble *a.* that cannot be comforted or cheered

in·con·spic'u·ous *a.* attracting little attention

in·con·test'a·ble *a.* certain

in·con'ti·nent *a.* unable to control one's natural functions —in·con'ti·nence *n.*

in·con·ven'ience *n.* 1 lack of comfort, etc. 2 inconvenient thing —*v.* cause bother, etc. —in·con·ven'ient *a.*

in·cor'po·rate' *v.* 1 combine; include 2 merge 3 form (into) a corporation —in·cor'po·ra'tion *n.*

in·cor'ri·gi·ble *a.* too bad to be reformed

in·crease' (*or* in'krēs) *v.* make or become greater, larger, etc. —*n.* 1 an increasing 2 amount of this

in·creas'ing·ly *adv.* more and more

in·cred'i·ble *a.* too unusual to be believed

in·cred'u·lous (-krej'-) *a.* showing doubt —in'cre·du'li·ty (-krə doo'-) *n.*

in·cre'ment *n.* 1 an increasing 2 amount of this

in·crim'i·nate' *v.* involve in, or make appear guilty of, a crime —in·crim'i·na'tion *n.*

in·crust' *v.* to encrust

in'cu·bate' *v.* sit on and hatch (eggs) —in·cu·ba'tion *n.*

in'cu·ba'tor *n.* 1 heated container for hatching eggs 2 similar device in which premature babies are kept

in·cul'cate' *v.* fix in the mind, as by insistent urging

in·cum'bent *a.* resting (*on* or *upon* a person) as a duty —*n.* holder of an office, etc.

in·cur' *v.* -curred', -cur'ring bring upon oneself

in·cur'sion *n.* raid

in·debt'ed *a.* 1 in debt 2 owing gratitude

in·debt'ed·ness *n.* 1 a being indebted 2 amount owed

in·de·ci'pher·a·ble (-sī'fər-) *a.* illegible

in·deed' *adv.* certainly —*int.* exclamation of surprise, doubt, sarcasm, etc.

in·de·fat'i·ga·ble *a.* not tiring; tireless

in·de·fen'si·ble *a.* that cannot be defended or justified

in·del'i·ble *a.* that cannot be erased, washed out, etc. —in·del'i·bly *adv.*

in·del'i·cate (-kət) *a.* lacking propriety; coarse

in·dem'ni·fy' *v.* -fied', -fy'ing repay

for or insure against loss —in·dem'ni·ty *n.*

in·dent' *v.* 1 to notch 2 to move in from the regular margin —in·den·ta'tion *n.*

in·den'ture *v.* bind by a contract to work for another

Independence Day *n.* July 4, a U.S. holiday

in·de·pend'ent *a.* not ruled, controlled, supported, etc. by others —in'de·pend'ence *n.*

in'-depth' *a.* thorough

in·de·scrib'a·ble *a.* beyond the power of description

in·de·struct'i·ble *a.* that cannot be destroyed

in·de·ter'mi·nate (-nət) *a.* not definite; vague

in'dex *n., pl.* -dex'es *or* -di·ces' (-di sēz') 1 indication 2 alphabetical list of names, etc. in a book, showing pages where they can be found 3 number indicating changes in prices, wages, etc. —*v.* make an index of or for

index finger *n.* the forefinger

index fund *n.* mutual fund tied to particular stock-market index

In'di·an *n., a.* 1 (native) of India 2 (member) of any of the aboriginal peoples of the Western Hemisphere

Indian summer *n.* warm weather in late autumn

in'di·cate' *v.* 1 point out; show 2 be a sign of —in'di·ca'tion *n.* —in·dic'a·tive *a.* —in'di·ca'tor *n.*

in·dict' (-dīt') *v.* charge with a crime —in·dict'ment *n.*

in·dif'fer·ent *a.* 1 neutral 2 unconcerned 3 of no importance 4 fair, average, etc. —in·dif'fer·ence *n.*

in·dig'e·nous (-dij'-) *a.* native

in'di·gent *a.* poor; needy —in'di·gence *n.*

in·di·ges'tion *n.* difficulty in digesting food

in·dig'nant *a.* angry at unjust or mean action —in'dig·na'tion *n.*

in·dig'ni·ty *n., pl.* -ties an insult to someone's dignity or self-respect

in'di·go' *n.* 1 blue dye 2 deep violet-blue

in'di·rect' object *n.* word indirectly affected by the action of a verb

in·dis·crim'i·nate (-nət) *a.* making no distinctions

in·dis·pen'sa·ble *a.* absolutely necessary

in'dis·posed' *a.* slightly ill

in'dis·sol'u·ble *a.* that cannot be dissolved or destroyed

in·di·vid·u·al (-vij´-) *n.* single person, thing, or being —*a.* **1** single **2** of, for, or typical of an individual —**in·di·vid·u·al·ly** *adv.*

in·di·vid·u·al·ism *n.* the leading of one's life in one's own way —**in·di·vid·u·al·ist** *n.*

in·di·vid·u·al·i·ty *n.* distinct characteristics

in·doc·tri·nate *v.* teach a doctrine or belief to —**in·doc·tri·na´tion** *n.*

in·do·lent (-də-) *a.* idle; lazy —**in·do·lence** *n.*

in·dom·i·ta·ble *a.* unyielding; unconquerable

in·door *a.* being, belonging, done, etc. in a building

in·doors *adv.* in or into a building

in·du·bi·ta·ble *a.* that cannot be doubted

in·duce´ *v.* **1** persuade **2** bring on; cause —**in·duce´ment** *n.*

in·duct *v.* **1** install in an office, a society, etc. **2** bring into the armed forces —**in·duct·ee´** *n.*

in·duc·tion *n.* **1** an inducting **2** a coming to a general conclusion from particular facts

in·dulge´ *v.* **1** satisfy (a desire) **2** gratify the wishes of —**in·dul´gence** *n.* —**in·dul´gent** *a.*

in·dus·tri·al *a.* having to do with industries or people working in industry

in·dus·tri·al·ist *n.* owner or manager of a large industrial business

in·dus·tri·al·ize *v.* build up industries in

industrial park *n.* area zoned for industry and business

in·dus·tri·ous *a.* working hard and steadily

in·dus·try *n., pl.* **-tries 1** steady effort **2** any branch of manufacture or trade —*ine suf.* of or like

in·e·bri·ate´ (-āt´; *n.:* -ət) *v.* make drunk —*n.* drunkard —**in·e·bri·a´tion** *n.*

in·ef·fa·ble *a.* that cannot be expressed or described

in·e·luc·ta·ble *a.* not to be avoided or escaped

in·ept´ *a.* **1** unfit **2** foolishly wrong **3** awkward —**in·ep´ti·tude**, **in·ept´ness** *n.*

in·ert´ *a.* **1** unable to move or act **2** dull; slow **3** without active properties

in·er·tia (-sha) *n.* tendency of matter to remain at rest, or to continue moving in a fixed direction

in·es·cap´a·ble *a.* that cannot be escaped

in·es´ti·ma·ble *a.* too great to be estimated

in·ev´i·ta·ble *a.* certain to happen —**in·ev·i·ta·bil´i·ty** *n.*

in·ex·o·ra·ble *a.* unrelenting —**in·ex´o·ra·bly** *adv.*

in´ex·pe´ri·enced *a.* lacking experience or skill

in·ex´pert *a.* not skillful

in·ex´pli·ca·ble *a.* that cannot be explained

in·ex·press´i·ble *a.* that cannot be expressed

in·ex´tri·ca·ble *a.* that one cannot get free from

in·fal´li·ble *a.* never wrong

in·fa·my *n.* **1** disgrace **2** great wickedness —**in·fa·mous** *a.*

in·fant *n.* baby —*a.* **1** of infants **2** in an early stage —**in·fan·cy** *n.* —**in´fan·tile´** *a.*

in·fan·try *n.* soldiers trained to fight on foot —**in·fan·try·man** *n., pl.* **-men**

in·farct´ *n.* area of dying tissue: also **in·farc´tion**

in·fat·u·ate´ (-fach´ōō-) *v.* inspire with unreasoning passion —**in·fat´u·a´tion** *n.*

in·fect´ *v.* make diseased —**in·fec´tion** *n.*

in·fec´tious *a.* **1** caused by microorganisms in the body **2** tending to spread to others

in·fer´ *v.* **-ferred´, -fer´ring** conclude by reasoning —**in·fer·ence** *n.*

in·fe´ri·or (-fir´ē-) *a.* **1** lower in space, order, status, etc. **2** poor in quality —**in·fe·ri·or´i·ty** *n.*

in·fer´nal *a.* of hell; hellish

in·fer´no *n., pl.* **-nos** hell

in·fest´ *v.* overrun in large numbers

in·fi·del *n.* one who rejects (a) religion

in·fi·del´i·ty *n.* unfaithfulness

in´field´ *n.* Baseball area enclosed by base lines —**in´field´er** *n.*

in´fight´ing *n.* personal conflict within a group

in·fil´trate (*or* in´fil-) *v.* pass through stealthily —**in·fil·tra´tion** *n.*

in´fi·nite (-nit) *a.* **1** lacking limits; endless **2** vast

in·fin·i·tes´i·mal *a.* too small to be measured

in·fin´i·tive *n.* form of a verb without reference to person, tense, etc.

in·fin´i·ty *n.* unlimited space, time, or quantity

in·firm´ *a.* weak; feeble —**in·fir´mi·ty** *n., pl.* **-ties**

in·fir'ma·ry n. hospital

in·flame' v. 1 excite 2 make red, sore, and swollen —**in·flam·ma'tion** n. —**in·flam'ma·to·ry** a.

in·flam'ma·ble a. flammable

in·flate' v. make swell out, as with gas

in·fla'tion n. 1 an inflating 2 increase in the currency in circulation resulting in a fall in its value and a rise in prices —**in·fla'tion·ar·y** a.

in·flect' v. 1 vary the tone of (the voice) 2 change the form of (a word) to show tense, etc. —**in·flec'tion** n.

in·flex'i·ble a. stiff, fixed, unyielding, etc.

in·flict' v. cause to suffer (a wound, punishment, etc.) —**in·flic'tion** n.

in'-flight' a. done while an aircraft is in flight

in·flo·res'cence n. 1 production of blossoms 2 flowers

in'flu·ence n. 1 power to affect others 2 one with such power —v. have an effect on —**in'flu·en'tial** a.

in'flu·en'za n. acute, contagious viral disease

in'flux' n. a flowing in

in'fo n. [Sl.] information

in'fo·mer'cial n. long TV commercial made to resemble a talk show, interview, etc.

in·form' v. give information (to) —**in·form'er** n.

in·for'mal a. 1 not following fixed rules 2 casual; relaxed —**in'for·mal'i·ty** n., pl. **-ties**

in·form'ant n. person who gives information

in'for·ma'tion n. news or knowledge imparted —**in·form'a·tive** a.

in'fo·tain'ment n. TV programming of information, as about celebrities, in a dramatic style

in·fra- pref. below

in·frac'tion n. violation of a law, etc.

in'fra·red' a. of those invisible rays having a penetrating, heating effect

in'fra·struc'ture n. basic installations and facilities, as roads and schools

in·fringe' v. break (a law, etc.) — **infringe** on encroach on —**in·fringe'ment** n.

in·fu'ri·ate' v. enrage

in·fuse' v. 1 instill 2 inspire 3 to steep —**in·fu'sion** n.

-ing suf. used to form the present participle

in'gath'er·ing n. a gathering together

in·gen'ious (-jēn'-) a. clever; resourceful —**in·ge·nu'i·ty** n.

in·gé·nue (an'zhə nōō', än'-) n. innocent young woman, as in a play

in·gen'u·ous (-jen'-) a. naive; artless

in·gest' v. take (food, drugs, etc.) into the body

in·got (iŋ'gət) n. mass of metal cast as a bar, etc.

in'grained' a. firmly fixed

in'grate' n. ungrateful person

in·gra'ti·ate' (-grā'shē-) v. get (oneself) into another's favor

in·gre'di·ent n. component part of a mixture

in'gress' n. entrance

in'grown' a. grown inward, esp. into the flesh

in·hab'it v. live in

in·hab'it·ant n. person or animal inhabiting a place

in·hal'ant n. medicine, etc. to be inhaled

in'ha·la'tor n. 1 INHALER (n. 2) 2 respirator

in·hale' v. breathe in —**in·ha·la'tion** n.

in·hal'er n. 1 respirator 2 apparatus for inhaling medicine

in·her'ent (-hir'-, -her'-) a. inborn; natural; basic

in·her'it v. 1 receive as an heir 2 have by heredity —**in·her'it·ance** n.

in·hib'it v. restrain; check —**in'hi·bi'tion** n.

in·hu'man a. cruel, brutal, etc. —**in'hu·man'i·ty** n.

i·nim'i·cal a. 1 hostile 2 adverse

in·im'i·ta·ble a. that cannot be imitated

in·iq·ui·ty (i nik'wə tē) n., pl. **-ties** sin or wicked act —**in·iq'ui·tous** a.

in·i·tial (i nish'əl) a. first —n. first letter of a name —v. mark with one's initials —**in·i'tial·ly** adv.

in·i'ti·ate' v. 1 begin to use 2 teach the fundamentals to 3 admit as a new member —**in·i'ti·a'tion** n.

in·i'ti·a·tive n. 1 first step 2 ability to get things started

in·ject' v. 1 force (a fluid) into tissue, etc. with a syringe, etc. 2 throw in; insert —**in·jec'tion** n.

in·junc'tion n. order or command, esp. of a court

in·jure v. do harm to; hurt —**in·ju'ri·ous** a.

in'ju·ry n., pl. **-ries** harm or wrong

in·jus'tice n. 1 a being unjust 2 unjust act

ink n. colored liquid for writing, printing, etc. —v. mark or color with ink —**ink'y** a., **-i·er, -i·est**

ink'blot' n. pattern of blots of ink used in a psychological test

ink'ling *n.* hint or notion

in'land *a., adv.* in or toward a country's interior

in'-law' *n.* [Inf.] a relative by marriage

in'lay' *v.* **-laid', -lay'ing** decorate with (pieces of wood, etc.) set in a surface —*n., pl.* **-lays'** **1** inlaid decoration **2** filling in a tooth

in'let' *n.* narrow strip of water going into land

in'-line' skate *n.* roller skate with wheels in a line from toe to heel

in'mate' *n.* one kept in a prison, hospital, etc.

in'most' *a.* innermost

inn *n.* hotel or restaurant

in'nards *pl.n.* [Inf.] internal organs of the body

in'nate' *a.* inborn; natural

in'ner *a.* **1** farther in **2** more intimate

inner city *n.* crowded or blighted central section of a city

in'ner·most' *a.* **1** farthest in **2** most secret

in'ning *n. Baseball* round of play in which both teams have a turn at bat

in'no·cent *a.* **1** without sin **2** not guilty **3** harmless **4** artless; simple —*n.* innocent person —**in'no·cence** *n.*

in·noc'u·ous *a.* harmless

in'no·va'tion *n.* new method, device, etc. —**in'no·va'tor** *n.*

in·nu·en'do (in'yōō-) *n., pl.* **-does** or **-dos** a hint or sly remark

in·nu'mer·a·ble *a.* too numerous to be counted

in·oc'u·late' *v.* inject a vaccine so as to immunize —**in·oc'u·la'tion** *n.*

in·or'di·nate (-nət) *a.* excessive

in·or·gan'ic *a.* not living; not animal or vegetable

in·pa'tient *n.* patient who stays at a hospital during treatment

in'put' *n.* **1** what is put in, as power into a machine or data into a computer **2** opinion or advice —*v.* feed (data) into a computer —**in'put'ter** *n.*

in'quest' *n.* judicial inquiry, as by a coroner

in·quire' *v.* **1** seek information **2** investigate (*into*) —**in·quir'y** (in'kwə rē, in kwīr'ē) *n., pl.* **-ies**

in·qui·si'tion *n.* **1** investigation **2** strict suppression, as of heretics by a tribunal —**in·quis'i·tor** *n.*

in·quis'i·tive (-kwiz'-) *a.* asking many questions; prying

in'road' *n.* an advance, esp. an encroachment: *usually used in pl.*

ins *abbrev.* insurance

in·sane' *a.* **1** mentally ill; crazy **2** of or for insane people —**in·san'i·ty** *n.*

in·sa'ti·a·ble (-sā'shə bəl) *a.* that cannot be satisfied

in·scribe' *v.* mark or engrave (words, etc.) on —**in·scrip'tion** *n.*

in·scru'ta·ble *a.* that cannot be understood

in'seam' *n.* seam along the inside of a trousers leg

in'sect' *n.* small animal with six legs, as a fly

in·sec'ti·cide' *n.* substance used to kill insects

in·se·cure' *a.* **1** not safe **2** not confident **3** not firm —**in'se·cu'ri·ty** *n.*

in·sem'i·nate' *v.* sow or impregnate —**in·sem'i·na'tion** *n.*

in·sen'sate' *a.* not feeling

in·sen'si·ble *a.* **1** unconscious **2** unaware

in·sen'si·tive *a.* not sensitive or responsive —**in·sen'si·tiv'i·ty** *n.*

in·sert' (*n.:* in'surt') *v.* put into something else —*n.* a thing inserted —**in·ser'tion** *n.*

in'set' *v.* set in —*n.* something inserted

in'shore' *adv., a.* near or in toward the shore

in'side' *n.* inner side or part —*a.* **1** internal **2** secret —*adv.* **1** within **2** indoors —*prep.* in

in·sid'er *n.* one having confidential information

in·sid'i·ous *a.* sly or treacherous

in'sight' *n.* understanding of a thing's true nature

in·sig'ni·a *pl.n.* badges, emblems, etc., as of rank or membership

in·sin·cere' *a.* deceptive or hypocritical —**in·sin·cer'i·ty** *n.*

in·sin'u·ate' *v.* **1** hint; imply **2** to get in artfully —**in·sin·u·a'tion** *n.*

in·sip'id *a.* tasteless; dull

in·sist' *v.* **1** demand strongly **2** maintain a stand —**in·sist'ence** *n.* —**in·sist'ent** *a.*

in'so·far' as' *con.* to the degree that

in'sole' *n.* (removable) inside sole of a shoe

in'so·lent (-sə-) *a.* showing disrespect —**in'so·lence** *n.*

in·sol'vent *a.* bankrupt

in·som'ni·a *n.* abnormal inability to sleep —**in·som'ni·ac'** *n.*

in'so·much' *as con.* inasmuch as

in·sou'ci·ant (-sōō'sē-) *a.* calm; care-free

in·spect' *v.* **1** look at carefully **2** examine officially —**in·spec'tion** *n.* —**in·spec'tor** *n.*

in·spire' v. **1** stimulate, as to a creative effort **2** arouse (a feeling) **3** inhale —**in·spi·ra'tion** n.

inst abbrev. **1** institute **2** institution

in·stall' v. **1** put formally in office **2** establish in a place **3** fix in place for use —**in·stal·la'tion** n.

in·stall'ment n. any of the several parts of a payment, magazine serial, etc.

installment plan n. system by which debts, as for purchases, are paid in installments

in·stance n. **1** example **2** occasion

in·stant a. **1** immediate **2** quick to prepare —n. moment —**in'stant·ly** adv.

in·stan·ta'ne·ous a. done or happening in an instant

in·stead' adv. in place of the other —**instead of** in place of

in'step' n. upper surface of the arch of the foot

in'sti·gate' v. urge on to an action; incite —**in'sti·ga'tion** n. —**in'sti·ga'tor** n.

in·still', in·stil' v. put in gradually; implant

in'stinct' n. **1** inborn tendency to do a certain thing **2** knack —**in·stinc'tive** a.

in'sti·tute' v. establish —n. organization for promoting art, science, etc.

in'sti·tu'tion n. **1** an instituting **2** established law, custom, etc. **3** organization with a public purpose —**in'sti·tu'tion·al** a. —**in'sti·tu'tion·al·ize'** v.

in·struct' v. **1** teach **2** direct —**in·struc'tion** n. —**in·struc'tion·al** a. —**in·struc'tive** a. —**in·struc'tor** n.

in'stru·ment n. **1** means; agent **2** tool or device for doing exact work **3** device producing musical sound

in'stru·men'tal a. **1** serving as a means **2** of, for, or by musical instruments

in'stru·men·tal'i·ty n., pl. **-ties** means; agency

in'sub·or'di·nate (-nət) a. disobedient

in'sub·stan'tial (-shəl) a. **1** unreal **2** weak or flimsy

in·suf'fer·a·ble a. intolerable

in'su·lar (-sə-, -syoo-) a. **1** of an island **2** narrow in outlook

in'su·late' v. **1** protect with a material to prevent the loss of electricity, heat, etc. **2** set apart —**in'su·la'tion** n. —**in'su·la'tor** n.

in'su·lin n. pancreatic hormone used to treat diabetes

in'sult' (v.: in sult') n. act or remark meant to hurt the feelings —v. to subject to an insult

in·su'per·a·ble a. that cannot be overcome

in·sur'ance (-shoor'-) n. **1** an insuring **2** contract whereby a company guarantees payment for a loss, death, etc. **3** amount for which a thing is insured

in·sure' v. **1** ensure **2** get or give insurance on

in·sured' n. person insured against loss

in·sur'er n. company that insures against loss

in·sur'gent a. rising up in revolt; rebelling —n. a rebel —**in·sur'gence** n.

in'sur·rec'tion n. rebellion

int abbrev. **1** interest **2** interjection **3** international

in·tact' a. kept whole

in·ta'glio (-tal'yō') n., pl. **-glios'** design carved below the surface

in'take' n. **1** amount taken in **2** place in a pipe, etc. where fluid is taken in

in'te·ger n. whole number

in'te·gral (or in teg'rəl) a. essential to completeness

in'te·grate' v. **1** form into a whole; unify **2** desegregate —**in'te·gra'tion** n.

in'te·grat'ed circuit n. electronic circuit on a chip of semiconductor material

in·teg'ri·ty n. **1** honesty, sincerity, etc. **2** wholeness

in·teg'u·ment n. skin, rind, shell, etc.

in'tel·lect' n. **1** ability to reason **2** high intelligence

in'tel·lec'tu·al a. **1** of the intellect **2** requiring or showing high intelligence —n. one with intellectual interests

in'tel·lec'tu·al·ize' v. examine rationally, not emotionally

in·tel'li·gence n. **1** ability to learn or to solve problems **2** news; information —**in·tel'li·gent** a.

in·tel'li·gi·ble a. that can be understood; clear

in·tem'per·ate (-ət) a. not moderate; excessive

in·tend' v. **1** to plan; purpose **2** to mean

in·tend'ed n. [Inf.] one's prospective wife or husband

in·tense' a. **1** very strong, great, deep, etc. **2** very emotional —**in·ten'si·fy'** v., **-fied', -fy'ing** —**in·ten'si·fi·ca'tion** n. —**in·ten'si·ty** n.

in·ten'sive *a.* **1** thorough **2** *Gram.* emphasizing

in·tent' *a.* firmly fixed in attention or purpose —*n.* purpose; intention

in·ten'tion *n.* thing intended or planned; purpose —**in·ten'tion·al** *a.*

in·ter' (-tur') *v.* -terred', -ter'ring bury

inter- *pref.* **1** between; among **2** with each other

in·ter·act' *v.* **1** act on one another **2** deal, work, etc. (with) —**in·ter·ac'tion** *n.* —**in·ter·ac'tive** *a.*

in'ter·breed' *v.* -bred', -breed'ing hybridize

in'ter·cede' (-sēd') *v.* **1** plead for another **2** mediate —**in'ter·ces'sion** (-sesh'ən) *n.*

in'ter·cept' *v.* seize or interrupt on the way —**in'ter·cep'tion** *n.*

in'ter·change' (*n.:* in'tər chānj') *v.* **1** exchange **2** alternate —*n.* **1** an interchanging **2** traffic entrance or exit on a freeway —**in'ter·change'a·ble** *a.*

in'ter·col·le'giate (-jət) *a.* between or among colleges

in'ter·com' *n.* communication system, as between rooms

in'ter·con·nect' *v.* connect with one another

in'ter·con'ti·nen'tal *a.* able to travel between continents

in'ter·course' *n.* **1** dealings between people, countries, etc. **2** sexual union

in'ter·de·nom'i·na'tion·al *a.* between or among religious denominations

in'ter·de·pend'ence *n.* mutual dependence —**in'ter·de·pend'ent** *a.*

in'ter·dict' *v.* **1** prohibit **2** hinder (the enemy) or isolate (an area, etc.) —**in'ter·dic'tion** *n.*

in·ter·est (in'trist) *n.* **1** feeling of curiosity or concern **2** thing causing this feeling **3** share in something **4** welfare; benefit **5** *usually pl.* group with a common concern **6** (rate of) payment for the use of money —*v.* have the interest or attention of

in'ter·est·ing *a.* exciting curiosity or attention

in'ter·face' *n.* point or means of interaction —*v.* interact with

in'ter·fere' (-fir') *v.* **1** come between; intervene **2** meddle —**interfere with** hinder —**in'ter·fer'ence** *n.*

in'ter·im *n.* time between; meantime —*a.* temporary

in·te'ri·or (-tir'ē-) *a.* **1** inner **2** inland **3** private —*n.* **1** interior part **2** domestic affairs of a country

in'ter·ject' *v.* throw in between; insert

in'ter·jec'tion *n.* **1** an interjecting **2** thing interjected **3** *Gram.* exclamation

in'ter·lace' *v.* join as by weaving together

in'ter·lard' *v.* intersperse

in'ter·line' *v.* write between the lines of

in'ter·lock' *v.* lock together

in'ter·loc'u·to·ry *a. Law* not final

in'ter·lop'er *n.* intruder

in'ter·lude' *n.* thing that fills time, as music between acts of a play

in'ter·mar'ry *v.* -ried, -ry·ing marry: said of persons of different races, religions, etc. —**in'ter·mar'riage** *n.*

in'ter·me'di·ar'y *a.* intermediate —*n., pl.* -ies go-between

in'ter·me'di·ate (-ət) *a.* in the middle; in between

in·ter'ment *n.* burial

in'ter·mez'zo' (-met'sō') *n., pl.* -zos' or -zi' (-sē') short musical piece

in·ter'mi·na·ble *a.* lasting, or seeming to last, forever

in'ter·min'gle *v.* mix together

in'ter·mis'sion *n.* interval, as between acts of a play

in'ter·mit'tent *a.* periodic; recurring at intervals

in'tern (*v.:* in turn') *n.* doctor in training at a hospital —*v.* **1** serve as an intern **2** confine (foreign persons), as during a war

in·ter'nal *a.* **1** inner **2** within a country —**in·ter'nal·ize'** *v.*

internal medicine *n.* diagnosis and nonsurgical treatment of disease

in'ter·na'tion·al *a.* **1** among nations **2** for all nations —**in'ter·na'tion·al·ize'** *v.*

in'ter·ne'cine (-nē'sin) *a.* destructive to both sides

In'ter·net' *n.* extensive computer network of thousands of smaller networks

in'tern'ist *n.* doctor specializing in internal medicine

in'ter·of'fice *a.* between offices of an organization

in'ter·per'son·al *a.* between persons

in'ter·plan'e·tar'y *a.* between planets

in'ter·play' *n.* action or influence on each other

in·ter'po·late' *v.* to insert (extra words, etc.)

in'ter·pose' *v.* place or come between

in·ter'pret *v.* explain or translate —**in·ter'pre·ta'tion** *n.* —**in·ter'pret·er** *n.*

in'ter·ra'cial *a.* among or for persons of different races

in'ter·re·lat'ed *a.* closely connected

with one another

in·ter·ro·gate' (-ter'-) *v.* question formally —**in·ter·ro·ga'tion** *n.*

in·ter·rog'a·tive *n., a.* (word) asking a question

in·ter·rupt' *v.* **1** break in on (talk, etc.) **2** obstruct —**in·ter·rup'tion** *n.*

in·ter·scho·las'tic *a.* between or among schools

in·ter·sect' *v.* **1** divide by passing across **2** cross each other —**in·ter·sec' tion** *n.*

in·ter·sperse' *v.* scatter among other things

in·ter·state' *a.* between or among states of a country

in·ter·stice (-stis) *n., pl.* **-sti·ces'** (-stə sēz') small space between things

in·ter·twine' *v.* twist together

in·ter·ur·ban *a.* going between towns or cities

in·ter·val *n.* **1** space between things **2** time between events **3** difference in musical pitch —**at intervals** now and then

in·ter·vene' *v.* **1** come or be between **2** come in so as to help settle something —**in·ter·ven'tion** *n.*

in·ter·view' *n.* meeting of people, as to confer or ask questions —*v.* have an interview with

in·tes'tate *a.* not having made a will

in·tes'tine (-tin) *n. usually pl.* alimentary canal from the stomach to the anus —**in·tes'tin·al** *a.*

in·ti·mate' (-māt'; *a., n.:* -mət) *v.* hint —*a.* **1** most personal **2** very familiar —*n.* an intimate friend —**in'ti·ma·cy** *n., pl.* **-cies** —**in'ti·ma'tion** *n.*

in·tim'i·date' *v.* make afraid as with threats —**in·tim'i·da'tion** *n.*

intl, intnl *abbrev.* international

in'to *prep.* **1** from outside to inside of **2** to the form, state, etc. of **3** [Inf.] involved in or concerned with

in·to·na'tion *n.* manner of utterance with regard to rise and fall in pitch

in·tone' *v.* utter in a chant

in to'to *adv.* as a whole

in·tox'i·cate' *v.* **1** make drunk **2** excite greatly —**in·tox'i·cant** *n.* —**in·tox'i·ca'tion** *n.*

intra- *pref.* within; inside

in·trac'ta·ble *a.* hard to manage

in·tra·mu'ral *a.* among members of a school or college

in·tran'si·gent *a.* refusing to compromise —**in·tran'si·gence** *n.*

in·tran'si·tive (-tiv) *a.* designating verbs not taking a direct object

in'tra·ve'nous *a.* into or within a vein

in·trep'id *a.* fearless

in'tri·cate (-kət) *a.* hard to follow because complicated —**in'tri·ca·cy** *n., pl.* **-cies**

in·trigue' (-trēg') *v.* **1** to plot secretly **2** excite the curiosity of —*n.* **1** secret plot **2** secret love affair

in·trin'sic *a.* real; essential —**in·trin'si·cal·ly** *adv.*

in'tro·duce' *v.* **1** insert **2** bring into use **3** make acquainted with **4** give experience of **5** begin —**in'tro·duc' tion** *n.* —**in'tro·duc'to·ry** *a.*

in'tro·spec'tion *n.* a looking into one's own thoughts, feelings, etc.

in'tro·vert' *n.* one more interested in oneself than in external objects or other people —**in'tro·ver'sion** *n.* —**in' tro·vert'ed** *a.*

in·trude' *v.* force oneself upon others without welcome —**in·trud'er** *n.* —**in·tru'sion** *n.* —**in·tru'sive** *a.*

in·tu·i'tion (-ish'ən) *n.* immediate knowledge of something without conscious reasoning —**in·tu'i·tive** *a.*

in·un·date' *v.* to flood —**in'un·da'tion** *n.*

in·ure' (-yoor') *v.* make accustomed to pain, trouble, etc.

in·vade' *v.* enter forcibly, as to conquer —**in·vad'er** *n.* —**in·va'sion** *n.*

in'va·lid *n.* one who is ill or disabled

in·val'id *a.* not valid, sound, etc. —**in·val'i·date'** *v.*

in·val'u·a·ble *a.* priceless

in·va'sive *a.* **1** invading **2** penetrating

in·vec'tive *n.* strong critical or abusive language

in·veigh' (-vā') *v.* talk or write bitterly (*against*)

in·vei'gle (-vā'-) *v.* trick or lure into an action

in·vent' *v.* **1** produce (a new device) **2** think up —**in·ven'tor** *n.*

in·ven'tion *n.* **1** an inventing **2** power of inventing **3** something invented —**in·ven'tive** *a.*

in'ven·to·ry *n., pl.* **-ries** complete list or stock of goods

in·verse' (*or* in'vurs') *a.* inverted; directly opposite —*n.* inverse thing

in·vert' *v.* **1** turn upside down **2** reverse —**in·ver'sion** *n.*

in·ver'te·brate (-brət) *n., a.* (animal) having no backbone

in·vest' *v.* **1** install in office **2** furnish with authority **3** put (money) into business, etc. for profit —**in·vest' ment** *n.* —**in·ves'tor** *n.*

in·ves'ti·gate' *v.* search (into); examine —**in·ves'ti·ga'tion** *n.* —**in·ves'ti·**

ga'tor *n.*

in·ves'ti·ture *n.* formal investing, as with an office

in·vet'er·ate (-ət) *a.* firmly fixed; habitual

in·vid'i·ous *a.* giving offense, as by discriminating unfairly

in·vig'or·ate' *v.* enliven

in·vin'ci·ble *a.* unconquerable —**in·vin'ci·bil'i·ty** *n.*

in·vi'o·la·ble *a.* not to be profaned or injured

in·vi'o·late (-lət) *a.* kept sacred or unbroken

in·vis'i·ble *a.* not visible or not evident —**in·vis·i·bil'i·ty** *n.* —**in·vis'i·bly** *adv.*

in·vi·ta'tion *n.* **1** an inviting **2** message or note used in inviting

in·vi·ta'tion·al *n., a.* (event) only for those invited to take part

in·vite' (*n.:* in'vīt') *v.* **1** ask to come somewhere or to do something **2** request **3** give occasion for —[*Inf.*] invitation

in·vit'ing *a.* alluring; tempting

in vi'tro' (-vē'-) *a.* kept alive apart from the organism, as in a test tube

in·vo·ca'tion *n.* prayer for blessing, help, etc.

in'voice' *n.* itemized list of goods or services provided; bill

in·voke' *v.* call on (God, etc.) for help, etc.

in·vol'un·tar'y *a.* **1** not done by choice **2** not consciously controlled

in·vo·lu'tion *n.* **1** entanglement **2** intricacy

in·volve' *v.* **1** complicate **2** draw into difficulty, etc. **3** include **4** require **5** occupy the attention of —**in·volve'ment** *n.*

in'ward *a.* **1** internal **2** directed toward the inside —*adv.* **1** toward the inside **2** into the mind or soul Also **in'wards** *adv.* —**in'ward·ly** *adv.*

i'o·dine' *n.* chemical element used in medicine, etc.

i'o·dize' *v.* treat with iodine

i'on' *n.* electrically charged atom or group of atoms

-ion *suf.* **1** act or state of **2** result of

i'on·ize' *v.* separate into ions or become electrically charged —**i'on·i·za'tion** *n.*

i·on'o·sphere' *n.* outer part of earth's atmosphere

i·o'ta *n.* a jot

IOU *n.* signed note acknowledging a debt

-ious *suf.* having; characterized by

ip·e·cac (ip'ə kak') *n.* emetic made

from a plant root

IPO *abbrev.* initial public offering

ip'so fac'to [[*L.*]] by that very fact

IQ *n.* number showing one's level of intelligence, based on a test

IRA *n.* individual retirement account

I·ra'ni·an (-rä'-, -rä'-) *n., a.* (native) of Iran

I·ra'qi (i rä'kē, -rak'ē) *n., a.* (native) of Iraq

i·ras'ci·ble (-ras'ə-) *a.* easily angered

i·rate' *a.* very angry

ire *n.* anger; wrath

ir·i·des'cent *a.* showing a play of rainbowlike colors —**ir·i·des'cence** *n.*

i'ris *n.* **1** colored part of the eye, around the pupil **2** plant with sword-shaped leaves and showy flowers

I'rish *a., n.* (of) the people or language of Ireland —**I'rish·man** *n., pl.* **-men**

irk *v.* annoy

irk'some *a.* annoying; tiresome

i·ron (ī'ərn) *n.* **1** strong metal that is a chemical element **2** device used for smoothing wrinkles from cloth **3** *pl.* iron shackles **4** golf club with metal head —*a.* **1** of iron **2** strong —*v.* press with a hot iron —**iron out** smooth away

i'ron·clad' *a.* **1** covered with iron **2** difficult to change or break

i'ron-fist'ed *a.* despotic and brutal

iron lung *n.* large respirator enclosing the body

i'ron·man' *n.* man of great strength and endurance

i·ro·ny (ī'rə nē) *n., pl.* **-nies 1** expression in which what is meant is the opposite of what is said **2** event that is the opposite of what is expected —**i·ron'ic, i·ron'i·cal** *a.*

ir·ra'di·ate' *v.* **1** expose to X-rays, ultraviolet rays, etc. **2** shine; radiate

ir·ra'tion·al *a.* lacking reason or good sense —**ir·ra'tion·al·ly** *adv.*

ir·rec·on·cil'a·ble *a.* that cannot be reconciled or made to agree

ir're·deem'a·ble *a.* that cannot be brought back, changed, etc.

ir·ref'u·ta·ble (*or* ir'i fyōōt'-) *a.* that cannot be disproved —**ir·ref'u·ta·bly** *adv.*

ir·reg'u·lar *a.* **1** not conforming to rule, standard, etc. **2** not straight or uniform —**ir·reg·u·lar'i·ty** *n.*

ir·rel'e·vant *a.* not to the point —**ir·rel'e·vance** *n.*

ir're·li'gious *a.* not religious

ir're·me'di·a·ble *a.* that cannot be remedied or corrected

ir·rep'a·ra·ble *a.* that cannot be

repaired or remedied

ir·re·press'i·ble *a.* that cannot be held back

ir·re·proach'a·ble *a.* blameless; faultless

ir·re·sist'i·ble *a.* that cannot be resisted —**ir·re·sist'ib·ly** *adv.*

ir·res'o·lute *a.* not resolute; wavering

ir·re·spec'tive *a.* regardless (*of*)

ir·re·spon'si·ble *a.* lacking a sense of responsibility

ir·re·triev'a·ble *a.* that cannot be recovered —**ir·re·triev'ab·ly** *adv.*

ir·rev'er·ent *a.* showing disrespect —**ir·rev'er·ence** *n.*

ir·re·vers'i·ble *a.* that cannot be reversed, annulled, etc.

ir·re·vo·ca·ble *a.* that cannot be undone or changed —**ir·rev'o·ca·bly** *adv.*

ir'ri·gate' *v.* 1 supply with water by means of ditches, etc. 2 wash out (a body cavity) —**ir'ri·ga'tion** *n.*

ir'ri·ta·ble *a.* easily irritated or angered —**ir·ri·ta·bil'i·ty** *n.*

ir'ri·tate' *v.* 1 to anger; annoy 2 make sore —**ir'ri·tant** *a., n.* —**ir'ri·ta'tion** *n.*

IRS *abbrev.* Internal Revenue Service

is *v. pres. t. of* BE: used with *he, she,* or *it*

-ise *suf.* chiefly Br. sp. of -IZE

-ish *suf.* 1 like; like that of 2 somewhat

i'sin·glass' (ī'zin-) *n.* 1 gelatin made from fish bladders 2 mica

Is·lam (is'läm, iz'-) *n.* Muslim religion —**Is·lam'ic** *a.*

is'land *n.* land mass surrounded by water —**is'land·er** *n.*

isle (īl) *n.* small island

is·let (ī' lət) *n.* very small island

ism *n.* doctrine, theory, system, etc. whose name ends in *-ism*

-ism *suf.* 1 theory or doctrine of 2 act or result of 3 condition or qualities of 4 an instance of

isn't *contr.* is not

ISO *abbrev.* International Standards Organization

i'so·bar' *n.* line on a map connecting points of equal barometric pressure

i'so·late' *v.* to place alone —**i'so·lat'ed** *a.* —**i'so·la'tion** *n.*

i'so·la'tion·ist *n.* one who believes his or her country should not get involved with other countries

i'so·mer *n.* chemical compound whose molecules have same atoms as another, but differently arranged

i'so·met'ric *a.* 1 of equal measure 2 of exercises in which muscles tense

against each other

i·sos·ce·les (ī säs'ə lēz') *a.* designating a triangle with two equal sides

i'so·tope' *n.* any of two or more forms of an element with different atomic weights

Is·rae·li (iz rā'lē) *n., a.* (native) of Israel

Is·ra·el·ite (iz'rē ə līt) *n.* one of the people of ancient Israel

is'sue *n.* 1 result 2 offspring 3 point under dispute 4 an issuing or amount issued —*v.* 1 emerge 2 to result 3 put out; give out 4 publish —**at issue** disputed —**take issue** disagree —**is'su·ance** *n.* —**is'su·er** *n.*

-ist *suf.* 1 one who practices 2 adherent of

isth·mus (is'məs) *n.* strip of land connecting two larger bodies of land

it *pron., pl.* **they** the animal or thing mentioned: *it* is also used as an indefinite subject or object

It, Ital *abbrev.* 1 Italian 2 Italy

ital *abbrev.* italic type

I·tal'ian *n., a.* (native or language) of Italy

i·tal'ic *a.* of type in which the letters slant upward to the right —*n. also pl.* italic type —**i·tal'i·cize'** *v.*

itch *n.* 1 tingling of the skin, with the desire to scratch 2 restless desire —*v.* have an itch —**itch'y** *a.,* -**i·er,** -**i·est**

-ite *suf.* 1 inhabitant of 2 adherent of

i'tem *n.* 1 article; unit 2 bit of news

i'tem·ize' *v.* list the items of —**i'tem·i·za'tion** *n.*

it'er·ate' *v.* repeat —**it·er·a'tion** *n.*

i·tin'er·ant *a.* traveling —*n.* traveler

i·tin'er·ar·y *n., pl.* -**ies** 1 route 2 plan of a journey

-itis *suf.* inflammation of

its *a.* of it

it's *contr.* 1 it is 2 it has

it·self' *pron.* intensive or reflexive form of IT

-ity *suf.* state or quality

IV *n.* intravenous apparatus

IV *abbrev.* intravenous(ly)

-ive *suf.* 1 of, or having the nature of 2 tending to

I've *contr.* I have

i'vo·ry *n., pl.* -**ries** 1 hard, white substance in elephants' tusks, etc. 2 tusk of elephant, etc. 3 creamy white

ivory tower *n.* academic world, seen as isolated from everyday reality

i'vy *n., pl.* **i'vies** climbing evergreen vine

-ize *suf.* 1 make or become 2 unite with 3 engage in

J

jab v., n. **jabbed, jab'bing** punch or poke

jab'ber v. talk quickly or foolishly —n. chatter

jack n. **1** device to lift something **2** playing card with picture of male royal attendant **3** *Naut.* small flag **4** electric plug-in receptacle —**jack up 1** lift with a jack **2** [Inf.] raise (prices, etc.)

jack'al n. wild dog of Asia or Africa

jack'ass' n. **1** male donkey **2** fool

jack'daw n. European crow

jack'et n. **1** short coat **2** outer covering

jack'ham'mer n. hammering power tool for breaking pavement

jack'-in-the-box' n. toy consisting of a box with a figure springing out

jack'-in-the-pul'pit n. plant with a hooded flower spike

jack'knife n. large pocketknife —v. to bend at the middle

jack'-o'-lan'tern n. hollow pumpkin cut to look like a face and used as a lantern

jack'pot n. cumulative stakes, as in a poker game

jack rabbit n. large hare of W North America

jac·quard (jə kärd') n. fabric with a figured weave

jade n. hard, green stone

jad'ed a. **1** tired **2** satiated

jade plant n. house plant with thick leaves

jag'ged a. having sharp points; notched or ragged

jag'uar' (-wär') n. American leopard

jai alai (hī'lī') n. game like handball, using a basketlike racket

jail n. prison for short-term confinement —v. to put or keep in a jail —**jail'er, jail'or** n.

ja·la·pe·ño (hä'lə pän'yō) n. Mexican hot pepper

ja·lop'y n., pl. **-pies** [Sl.] old, worn-out automobile

jal'ou·sie' (-ə sē') n. window or door made of slats fixed as in a Venetian blind

jam v. **jammed, jam'ming 1** cram; stuff **2** to crush or crowd **3** wedge tight —n. **1** a jamming **2** [Inf.] a difficult situation **3** spread made by boiling fruit and sugar

jamb (jam) n. side post of a doorway

jam'bo·ree' n. noisy revel

Jan *abbrev.* January

jan'gle v., n. (make or cause to make) a harsh, inharmonious sound

jan'i·tor n. one who takes care of a building —**jan'i·to'ri·al** a.

Jan'u·ar'y n., pl. **-ar'ies** first month

Jap'a·nese' n., pl. **-nese'**; a. (native or language) of Japan

jar v. **jarred, jar'ring** to jolt or shock —n. **1** a jolt or shock **2** wide-mouthed container

jar·di·niere' (-nir') n. large flower pot

jar'gon n. special vocabulary of some work, class, etc.

jas'mine, jas'min (-min) n. shrub with fragrant flowers

jas'per n. colored quartz

jaun·dice (jôn'dis) n. disease that turns the skin, eyeballs, etc. yellow —v. make bitter with envy

jaunt n. short pleasure trip

jaun'ty a. **-ti·er, -ti·est** easy and care-free

jav'e·lin n. light spear thrown in contests

jaw n. either of the two bony parts that hold the teeth —v. [Sl.] to talk

jaw'bone' n. lower bone of jaw —v. try to persuade by using one's high position

jaw'break'er n. piece of hard candy

jay n. **1** bird of the crow family **2** blue jay

jay'walk' v. cross a street heedlessly —**jay'walk'er** n.

jazz n. popular American music with strong rhythms —v. [Sl.] make exciting or elaborate: with *up*

jazz'y a. **-i·er, -i·est** [Sl.] lively, flashy, etc.

JD, J.D. *abbrev.* Doctor of Laws

jeal'ous (jel'-) a. **1** resentfully suspicious or envious **2** watchful in guarding —**jeal'ous·y** n., pl. **-ies**

jeans *pl.n.* trousers or overalls of twilled cotton cloth

jeep n. small, rugged, military automobile —[J-] *trademark* similar vehicle for civilian use

jeer v. to ridicule —n. derisive comment

Je·ho'vah n. God

je·june' a. childish

je·ju'num n. middle part of the small intestine

jell v. **1** become, or make into, jelly **2** [Inf.] become definite

jel'ly n., pl. **-lies 1** soft, gelatinous food made from cooked fruit syrup **2** gelatinous substance

jelly bean n. small, bean-shaped candy

jel'ly·fish' n. jellylike sea animal with tentacles

jel'ly·roll' n. thin cake spread with jelly and rolled up

jeop'ard·ize' (jep'-) v. to risk; endanger

jeop'ard·y n. danger; peril

jerk n. **1** sharp pull **2** muscular twitch **3** [Sl.] disagreeable or contemptible person —v. **1** move with a jerk **2** to twitch —**jerk'y** a., -i·er, -i·est

jer'kin n. snug, usually sleeveless jacket

jerk'wa'ter a. [Inf.] small and remote

jer'ky n. dried strips of meat

jer'ry-built' a. poorly built

jer'sey n. **1** soft, knitted cloth **2** pl. -seys pullover shirt, etc. of this

jest v., n. **1** joke **2** ridicule —**jest'er** n.

Je'sus founder of the Christian religion

jet v. **jet'ted**, **jet'ting 1** shoot out in a stream **2** travel by jet airplane —n. **1** liquid or gas in such a stream **2** spout that shoots a jet **3** jet-propelled airplane **4** black mineral —a. **1** jet-propelled **2** black

jet lag n. fatigue, etc. from adjusting to jet travel over great distances

jet'lin'er n. commercial jet passenger plane

jet propulsion n. propulsion by means of gases from a rear vent —**jet'-pro·pelled'** a.

jet'sam n. cargo thrown overboard to lighten a ship

jet'ti·son v. **1** throw (goods) overboard to lighten a ship **2** discard

jet'ty n., pl. -ties **1** wall built into the water **2** landing pier

Jew n. **1** descendant of people of ancient Israel **2** believer in Judaism —**Jew'ish** a.

jew'el n. **1** gem **2** small gem used as a watch bearing

jew'el·er, jew'el·ler n. one who deals in jewelry

jew'el·ry n. jewels, or ornaments with jewels

jib n. triangular sail ahead of all other sails

jibe v. **1** shift a sail, or the course, of a ship **2** [Inf.] be in accord **3** to gibe —n. a gibe

jif'fy n. [Inf.] an instant: also **jiff**

jig n. **1** lively dance **2** device to guide a tool —v. **jigged**, **jig'ging** dance a (jig)

jig'ger n. glass of 1½ ounces for measuring liquor

jig'gle v. move in slight jerks —n. a jiggling —**jig'gly** a.

jig'saw' n. saw with a narrow blade set in a frame: also **jig saw**

jigsaw puzzle n. picture cut into pieces that are to be fitted together again

jilt v. reject (a lover)

jim'my n., pl. -mies short crowbar used by burglars —v. -mied, -my·ing pry open

jim'son weed n. poisonous weed with trumpet-shaped flowers

jin'gle v. make light, ringing sounds —n. **1** jingling sound **2** light verse

jin'go·ism' n. warlike chauvinism —**jin'go·ist** n.

jin·ni' n., pl. **jinn** supernatural being in Muslim folklore

jin·rik'i·sha' (-rik'shô') n. two-wheeled Asian carriage pulled by one or two men

jinx [Inf.] n. person or thing supposed to cause bad luck —v. bring bad luck to

jit'ter·y [Inf.] a. nervous or restless —**the jitters** nervous feeling

jive n. [Sl.] foolish or insincere talk —v. [Inf.] be in accord; jibe

job n. **1** a piece of work **2** employment; work —a. done by the job —v. handle (goods) as a middleman

job action n. refusal by employees to perform duties when forbidden to strike

job'ber n. one who buys goods in quantity and sells them to dealers

job lot n. goods, often of various sorts, for sale as one quantity

jock n. [Sl.] **1** disc jockey **2** male athlete

jock'ey n. race-horse rider —v. maneuver for advantage

jo·cose' a. joking; playful

joc'u·lar a. joking; full of fun —**joc'u·lar'i·ty** n.

joc'und a. cheerful; genial

jodh·purs (jäd'pərz) pl.n. riding breeches

jog v. **jogged**, **jog'ging 1** nudge; shake **2** move at a slow, steady, jolting pace, spec. as exercise —n. **1** nudge **2** jogging pace **3** part that changes direction sharply

jog'ging n. steady trotting as exercise —**jog'ger** n.

jog'gle v., n. jolt; jounce

john n. [Sl.] toilet

join v. **1** to connect; unite **2** become a part or member (of)

join'er *n.* carpenter of interior wood-work

joint *n.* 1 place where two things are joined 2 one of the parts of a jointed whole 3 [Sl.] any building, esp. a cheap bar —*a.* 1 common to two or more 2 sharing with another —*v.* connect by a joint —**out of joint** 1 dislocated 2 disordered —**joint'ly** *adv.*

joist *n.* any of the parallel timbers holding up planks of a floor, etc.

joke *n.* 1 anything said or done to arouse laughter 2 thing not to be taken seriously —*v.* make jokes

jok'er *n.* 1 one who jokes 2 deceptive clause, as in a contract 3 extra playing card used in some games

jol'ly *a.* -**li·er**, -**li·est** merry —**jol'li·ness** *n.* —**jol'li·ty** *n.*

jolt *v., n.* 1 jar; jerk 2 shock or surprise

jon'quil *n.* narcissus with yellow or white flower

josh *v.* [Inf.] tease, fool, etc.

jos'tle (-əl) *v.* shove roughly

jot *n.* very small amount —*v.* **jot'ted, jot'ting** write (*down*) briefly

jounce *v.* jolt or bounce

jour'nal (jur'-) *n.* 1 diary 2 record of proceedings 3 a newspaper or magazine 4 book for business records 5 part of an axle, etc. that turns in a bearing

jour'nal·ism' *n.* newspaper writing and editing —**jour'nal·ist** *n.* —**jour'nal·is'tic** *a.*

jour'ney *n.* a trip —*v.* to travel

jour'ney·man *n., pl.* -**men** worker skilled at a trade

joust (joust) *n., v.* fight with lances on horseback

jo'vi·al *a.* merry; jolly

jowl *n.* 1 cheek 2 *pl.* fleshy, hanging part under the jaw —**jowl'y** *a.*

joy *n.* gladness; delight —**joy'ful** *a.* —**joy'ous** *a.*

joy ride *n.* [Inf.] reckless, speedy ride in a car, just for fun

joy'stick' *n.* 1 [Sl.] control stick of airplane 2 manual control device for video games, etc.

JP *abbrev.* Justice of the Peace

Jpn *abbrev.* Japan(ese)

Jr *abbrev.* junior: also **jr**

ju'bi·lant *a.* rejoicing —**ju'bi·la'tion** *n.*

ju'bi·lee' *n.* 1 a 50th or 25th anniversary 2 time of rejoicing

Ju'da·ism' *n.* Jewish religion

judge *v.* 1 hear and decide cases in a law court 2 determine the winner 3 appraise or criticize 4 think; suppose —*n.* one who judges

judg'ment *n.* 1 a deciding 2 legal decision 3 opinion 4 ability to make wise decisions Also *sp.* **judgement**

judg·men'tal *a.* making judgments, esp. harsh judgments; critical

Judgment Day *n.* time of divine judgment of all people

ju·di'cial (-dish'əl) *a.* 1 of judges, courts, etc. 2 careful in thought

ju·di'ci·ar·y (-dish'ē er'ē, -dish'ər ē) *a.* of judges or courts —*n., pl.* -**ries** 1 part of government that administers justice 2 judges collectively

ju·di'cious (-dish'əs) *a.* showing good judgment —**ju·di'cious·ly** *adv.*

ju'do *n.* kind of jujitsu used for self-defense

jug *n.* container for liquids, with a small opening and a handle

jug'ger·naut' *n.* relentless irresistible force

jug'gle *v.* 1 do tricks with (balls, etc.) 2 handle in a tricky way 3 toss up balls in the air —**jug'gler** *n.*

jug'u·lar (**vein**) *n.* either of two large veins in the neck

juice *n.* liquid from fruit or cooked meat —**juic'y** *a.*, -**i·er**, -**i·est**

ju·jit'su' *n.* Japanese wrestling using leverage

ju'jube' (-jōōb', -jōō bē') *n.* gelatinous, fruit-flavored candy

juke'box' *n.* coin-operated phonograph or CD player: also **juke box**

Jul *abbrev.* July

ju'li·enne' *a.* cut into strips: said of vegetables, etc.

Ju·ly' *n., pl.* -**lies'** seventh month

jum'ble *v., n.* (mix into) a confused heap

jum'bo *a.* very large

jump *v.* 1 spring from the ground, etc. 2 leap or make leap over 3 move or change suddenly 4 rise or raise suddenly, as prices —*n.* 1 a jumping 2 distance jumped 3 sudden move or change —**jump at** accept eagerly —**jump'er** *n.*

jump'er *n.* sleeveless dress worn over a blouse, etc.

jump'-start' *v.* [Inf.] energize, revive, etc. —*n.* [Inf.] quick start, recovery, etc.

jump'suit' *n.* coveralls, worn for work or leisure

jump'y *a.* -**i·er**, -**i·est** 1 moving jerkily 2 nervous

Jun *abbrev.* June

jun'co *n., pl.* -**cos** small bird with gray

or black head

junc'tion n. 1 a joining 2 place where things join

junc'ture n. 1 junction 2 point of time

June n. sixth month

jun'gle n. dense forest in the tropics

jun·ior (jōōn'yər) a. 1 the younger: written *Jr.* 2 of lower rank, etc. —n. high school or college student in the next-to-last year

junior college n. school with courses two years beyond high school

ju'ni·per n. small evergreen with berrylike cones

junk n. 1 old metal, paper, etc. 2 Chinese ship with flat bottom 3 [Inf.] worthless thing(s); rubbish —v. [Inf.] to discard; scrap —**junk'y** a., -i·er, -i·est

junk'er n. [Sl.] old, worn-out car, etc.

junk'et n. 1 milk thickened as curd 2 excursion by an official at public expense

junk food n. snack foods providing little nourishment

junk'ie, junk'y n., pl. -ies [Sl.] narcotics addict

junk mail n. advertisements, etc. mailed widely and cheaply

jun'ta (hoon'-, jun'-) n. military group seizing political power

Ju'pi·ter n. fifth planet from the sun

ju·ris·dic'tion n. (range of) authority, as of a court

ju·ris·pru'dence n. science or philosophy of law

ju'rist n. an expert in law

ju'ror n. member of a jury

ju'ry n., pl. -ries group of people chosen to give a decision in a law case or decide winners in a contest

just a. 1 right or fair 2 righteous 3 well-founded 4 correct; exact —adv. 1 exactly 2 only 3 barely 4 a very short time ago 5 [Inf.] quite; really —**just now** a moment ago —**just the same** [Inf.] nevertheless —**just'ly** adv.

jus'tice (-tis) n. 1 being just 2 reward or penalty as deserved 3 the upholding of what is just 4 a judge

justice of the peace n. local magistrate in minor cases

jus'ti·fy' v. -fied', -fy'ing 1 show to be just, right, etc. 2 free from blame —**jus'ti·fi'a·ble** a. —**jus'ti·fi'a·bly** adv. —**jus'ti·fi·ca'tion** n.

jut v. jut'ted, jut'ting stick out

jute n. strong fiber used to make burlap, rope, etc.

ju've·nile (-nīl', -nəl) a. 1 young; immature 2 of or for juveniles —n.

child or young person

juvenile delinquency n. antisocial or illegal behavior by minors

jux'ta·pose' v. put side by side —**jux'ta·po·si'tion** n.

K

k abbrev. kilogram

K abbrev. 1 karat 2 kilobyte 3 kilometer 4 *Baseball* strikeout Also, for 1 & 3, **k**

Ka·bu'ki n. [also k-] form of Japanese drama

kad'dish (käd'-) n. Jewish mourner's prayer

Kai·ser (kī'zər) n. title of former Austrian and German rulers

kale n. a cabbage with spreading, curled leaves

ka·lei·do·scope' (-lī'-) n. small tube containing bits of colored glass that change patterns as the tube is turned —**ka·lei·do·scop'ic** a.

kan·ga·roo' n. leaping marsupial of Australia

kangaroo court n. [Inf.] unofficial court, ignoring normal legal procedure

ka'o·lin n. white clay, used to make porcelain, etc.

ka'pok' n. silky fibers from tropical trees, used for stuffing pillows, etc.

ka·put' (-poot') a. [Sl.] ruined, destroyed, etc.

kar·a·kul (kar'ə kul') n. curly black fur from the fleece of Asian lambs

ka·ra·o·ke (kar·ē ō'kē) n. entertainment by an amateur singer using prerecorded instrumental music

kar'at n. one 24th part (of pure gold)

ka·ra'te (-rät'ē) n. self-defense by blows with side of open hand

kar'ma n. fate; destiny

ka'ty·did' n. insect resembling the grasshopper

kay'ak (kī'-) n. Eskimo canoe

ka·zoo' n. toy musical instrument into which one hums

KB abbrev. kilobyte(s)

kc abbrev. kilocycle(s)

ke·bab, ke·bob (kə bäb') n. small pieces of meat broiled on a skewer

keel n. center piece along the bottom of a ship —**keel over** turn or fall over

keen a. 1 sharp 2 piercing 3 perceptive; acute 4 eager 5 intense —v. make a mournful, wailing sound —**keen'ly** adv.

keep v. kept, keep'ing 1 fulfill;

observe **2** protect; take care of **3** preserve **4** retain **5** continue **6** hold and not let go **7** refrain —*n.* food and shelter —**keep to oneself 1** avoid others **2** to refrain from telling — **keep'er** *n.*

keep'ing *n.* care or protection —**in keeping** with conformity with

keep'sake' *n.* souvenir

keg *n.* small barrel

kelp *n.* brown seaweed

Kel'vin *a.* of a temperature scale on which 0° equals -273.16°C

ken *n.* range of knowledge

ken'nel *n.* **1** doghouse **2** often *pl.* place where dogs are bred or kept

kerb *n.* Brit. sp. of CURB (*n.* 3)

ker'chief (-chif) *n.* **1** cloth worn around the head or neck **2** handkerchief

ker'nel *n.* **1** grain or seed **2** soft, inner part of a nut or fruit pit

ker'o·sene', ker'o·sine' (-sēn') *n.* oil distilled from petroleum

kes'trel *n.* European falcon

ketch *n.* sailing vessel

ketch'up *n.* thick sauce of tomatoes, spices, etc.

ket'tle *n.* **1** pot used in cooking **2** teakettle

ket'tle·drum' *n.* hemispheric copper drum with an adjustable parchment top

key *n.* **1** device for working a lock **2** lever pressed in operating a piano, typewriter, etc. **3** thing that explains, as a code **4** controlling factor **5** mood or style **6** low island **7** *Mus.* scale based on a certain keynote —*a.* controlling —*v.* bring into harmony — **key in** input (data) with a keyboard — **key up** excite

key'board' *n.* row(s) of keys of a piano, computer terminal, etc. —*v.* to input using a keyboard —**key'board'er** *n.*

key'hole' *n.* opening for key (in a lock)

key'note' *n.* **1** *Mus.* lowest, basic note of a scale **2** basic idea

key'pad' *n.* cluster of keys on telephone, etc.

key'stone' *n.* central, topmost stone of an arch

key'stroke' *n.* single stroke made on a computer keyboard

kg *abbrev.* kilogram(s)

kha·ki (kak'ē) *a., n.* yellowish-brown (uniform)

kHz *abbrev.* kilohertz

kib·butz' (-boōts') *n., pl.* **-but·zim'** (-boō tsēm') Israeli collective farm

kib'itz *v.* [Inf.] act as meddlesome

onlooker —**kib'itz·er** *n.*

ki'bosh' (*or* ki bäsh') *n.* [Sl.] used chiefly in **put the kibosh on**, check, squelch, etc.

kick *v.* **1** strike (out) with the foot **2** recoil, as a gun **3** [Inf.] complain —*n.* **1** a kicking **2** [Inf.] often *pl.* thrill

kick'back' *n.* [Sl.] forced or secret rebate

kick'off' *n.* kick in football that begins play

kick'stand' *n.* metal bar on a bicycle to hold it upright

kick'-start' *v.* [Inf.] energize, revive, etc.

kid *n.* **1** young goat **2** leather from its skin: also **kid'skin'** **3** [Inf.] child —*v.* a kicking **2** [Inf.] often *pl.* tease, fool, etc. —**kid'der** *n.*

kid'die, kid'dy *n., pl.* **-dies** [Inf.] child

kid'nap' *v.* **-napped'**, **-nap'ping** seize and hold a person, esp. for ransom — **kid'nap'per** *n.*

kid'ney *n., pl.* **-neys** the urine-forming gland

kidney bean *n.* seed of common garden bean

kiel·ba·sa (kēl bä'sə) *n., pl.* **-si** (-sē) or **-sas** smoked Polish sausage

kill *v.* **1** make die; slay **2** destroy **3** spend (time) idly —*n.* **1** a killing **2** animal(s) killed —**kill'er** *n.*

kill'ing *n.* **1** murder **2** [Inf.] sudden great profit

kill'joy' *n.* spoiler of pleasure for others

kiln (kil, kiln) *n.* oven for baking bricks, etc.

ki·lo (kē'lō, kil'ō) *n., pl.* **-los** kilogram

kilo- *pref.* one thousand

kil'o·byte' *n.* 1, 024 bytes

kil'o·cy·cle *n.* kilohertz

kil'o·gram' *n.* 1,000 grams

kil'o·hertz' *n.* 1,000 hertz

kil'o·li·ter *n.* 1,000 liters

kil'o·me·ter (*or* ki läm'ət ər) *n.* 1,000 meters

kil'o·watt' *n.* 1,000 watts

kilt *n.* skirt worn by men of Northern Scotland

kil'ter *n.* [Inf.] used chiefly in **out of kilter**, not in working order

ki·mo'no (-nə) *n.* **-nos** Japanese robe

kin *n.* relatives; family

kind *n.* sort; variety —*a.* gentle, generous, etc. —**in kind** in the same way — **kind of** [Inf.] somewhat —**kind'ly** *a., adv.* —**kind'ness** *n.*

kin'der·gar'ten *n.* class or school for children about five years old —**kin'der·gart'ner, kin'der·gar'ten·er** (-gärt' nər) n.

kind·heart'ed a. kind

kin'dle v. **1** set on fire **2** start burning **3** excite

kin'dling n. bits of wood, etc. for starting a fire

kin'dred n. relatives; kin —a. related or similar

kine n. [Ar.] cows; cattle

ki·net'ic a. of motion

kin'folk' pl.n. family; relatives: also **kin'folks'**

king n. **1** male monarch of a state **2** playing card with a king's picture **3** chief chess piece

king'dom n. country ruled by a king or queen

king'fish'er n. fish-eating diving bird

king'pin' n. [Inf.] main person or thing

king'-size' a. larger than usual size

kink n., v. curl or twist

kink'y a. **-i·er, -i·est 1** tightly curled **2** [Sl.] weird, eccentric, etc.; spec., sexually abnormal

kin'ship' n. **1** family relationship **2** close connection

kins'man n., pl. **-men** (male) relative —**kins'wom'an** n.fem., pl. **-wom'en**

ki·osk (kē'äsk') n. small, open structure used as a newsstand, etc.

kip'per n. salted and dried or smoked herring

kirk n. [Scot.] church

kis'met n. fate

kiss v. caress with the lips in affection or greeting —n. **1** act of kissing **2** kind of candy

kit n. **1** set of tools, etc. **2** box or bag for it

kitch'en n. place for preparing and cooking food

kitch'en·ette', kitch'en·et' n. small kitchen

kitch'en·ware' n. kitchen utensils

kite n. **1** kind of hawk **2** light frame covered with paper, tied to a string, and flown in the wind

kith and kin n. friends and relatives

kitsch (kich) n. pretentious but shallow popular art, etc.

kit'ten n. young cat: also [Inf.] **kit'ty**, pl. **-ties**

kit'ten·ish a. coy

kit'ty-cor'nered a., adv. cater-cornered: also **kit'ty·cor'ner**

ki·wi (kē'wē) n., pl. **-wis** flightless bird of New Zealand

KKK abbrev. Ku Klux Klan

Klee'nex trademark soft tissue paper used as a handkerchief, etc. —n. [k-] a piece of such paper

klep'to·ma'ni·a n. persistent impulse to steal —**klep'to·ma'ni·ac'** n.

klutz n. [Sl.] clumsy or stupid person

km abbrev. kilometer(s)

knack n. special ability

knack·wurst (näk'wurst') n. thick, spicy sausage

knap'sack' n. bag to carry supplies on the back

knave n. dishonest person; rogue —**knav'ish** a.

knav'er·y n. dishonesty

knead v. press and squeeze

knee n. joint between thigh and lower leg

knee'cap' n. patella

knee'-deep' a. very much involved

knee'-jerk' a. [Inf.] automatic and predictable

kneel v. **knelt** or **kneeled, kneel'ing** rest on the bent knee or knees

kneel'er n. cushion, etc. to kneel on in a church pew

knell n. slow tolling of a bell, as at a funeral

knew v. pt. of KNOW

knick'ers pl.n. breeches gathered below the knees: also **knick'er·bock'·ers**

knick'knack' n. small, showy article

knife n., pl. **knives** sharp cutting blade set in a handle —v. to stab with a knife

knight n. **1** medieval chivalrous soldier **2** Br. man holding honorary rank **3** chess piece like a horse's head —**knight'hood'** n.

knit v. **knit'ted** or **knit, knit'ting 1** make by looping yarn with needles **2** draw or grow together

knit'wear' n. knitted clothing

knob n. round handle —**knob'by** a., **-bi·er, -bi·est**

knock v. **1** hit; strike; rap **2** make a pounding noise **3** [Inf.] find fault with —n. **1** a hit; blow **2** a pounding noise —**knock down** take apart —**knock off** [Inf.] **1** stop working **2** deduct —**knock out** make unconscious —**knock'er** n.

knock'-kneed' a. having legs that bend inward at the knees

knock'out' n. **1** [Sl.] very attractive person or thing **2** boxing victory when an opponent can no longer fight

knock'wurst' n. knackwurst

knoll (nōl) n. little hill; mound

knot n. **1** lump in tangled thread, etc. **2** a tying together of string, rope, etc. **3** small group **4** hard lump in wood where a branch has grown **5** one nau-

tical mile per hour —v. **knot'ted,
knot'ting** form a knot (in)

knot'ty a. **-ti·er, -ti·est 1** full of knots **2** hard to solve; puzzling

know v. knew, known, know'ing **1** be informed (about) **2** be aware (of) **3** be acquainted with

know'-how' n. [Inf.] technical skill

know'ing a. **1** having knowledge **2** shrewd; cunning —**know'ing·ly** adv.

knowl·edge (nä'lij) n. things known or learned —**knowl'edge·a·ble** a.

knuck'le n. joint of a finger —**knuckle down** work hard —**knuckle under** surrender

KO abbrev. Boxing knockout: also **K.O.** or **k.o.**

ko·a'la (-ä'-) n. tree-dwelling marsupial of Australia

kohl·ra·bi (kōl'rä'bē) n., pl. **-bies** kind of cabbage

kook (kōōk) n. [Sl.] silly, eccentric person —**kook'y, kook'ie** a.

Ko·ran (ka ran', kôr'an') n. sacred book of Muslims

Ko·re'an n., a. (native or language) of Korea

ko'sher a. fit to eat according to Jewish dietary laws

kow'tow' (kou'tou') v. show great deference (to)

Krish'na n. important Hindu god

KS abbrev. Kansas

ku·chen (kōō'kan) n. breadlike cake, with raisins, etc.

ku'dos' (-däs', -dōs') n. credit for achievement

kud·zu (kood'zōō) n. fast-growing vine with large leaves

kum'quat' (-kwät') n. small, oval, orangelike fruit

kung' fu' n. system of self-defense like karate but with circular movements

kvetch n., v. [Sl.] (one who) complain(s) naggingly: also **kvetch'er** n.

kW, kw abbrev. kilowatt(s)

KY abbrev. Kentucky

L

l abbrev. **1** line **2** liter(s): also **L 3** loss(es)

L abbrev. **1** lake **2** Latin

LA abbrev. **1** Los Angeles **2** Louisiana

lab n. [Inf.] laboratory

la'bel n. card, etc. marked and attached to an object to show its contents, etc. —v. **1** attach a label to **2** classify as

la·bi·a pl.n., sing. **-bi·um** liplike folds

of the vulva

la·bi·al a. of the lips

la'bor n. **1** work **2** task **3** all workers **4** process of childbirth —v. **1** work hard **2** move with effort

lab'o·ra·to·ry (lab'ra-) n., pl. **-ries** place for scientific work or research

Labor Day n. first Monday in September, holiday honoring workers

la'bored a. with effort

la'bor·er n. worker; esp., unskilled worker

la·bo'ri·ous a. difficult

labor union n. association of workers to further their interests

la'bour n., v. Br. sp. of LABOR

Lab'ra·dor retriever n. short-haired black or yellow retriever

la·bur'num n. shrub with drooping yellow flowers

lab'y·rinth' (-ə-) n. maze

lac (lak) n. resinous source of shellac

lace n. **1** string used to fasten together parts of a shoe, etc. **2** openwork fabric woven in fancy designs —v. **1** fasten with a lace **2** intertwine **3** add alcohol, etc. to

lac'er·ate' (las'-) v. tear jaggedly —**lac'er·a'tion** n.

lace'work' n. lace, or any openwork like it

lach'ry·mose' (lak'ri-) a. tearful; sad

lack n. state of not having enough or any —v. have little or nothing of

lack'a·dai'si·cal (-dā'zi-) a. showing lack of interest

lack'ey n., pl. **-eys 1** menial servant **2** toady

lack'lus'ter a. dull

la·con'ic a. concise; brief

lac·quer (lak'ər) n. a varnish, often like enamel —v. coat with lacquer

la·crosse' n. ball game using long-handled sticks

lac'tate' v. secrete milk

lac'te·al a. of or like milk

lac'tic a. **1** of milk **2** of an acid in sour milk

lac'tose' n. sugar found in milk

la·cu'na (-kyōō'-) n. gap; space

lac'y a. **-i·er, -i·est** of or like lace —**lac'i·ness** n.

lad n. boy; youth

lad'der n. series of rungs framed by two sidepieces for climbing up or down

lade v. lad'ed, lad'ed or lad'en, lad'ing to load

lad'en a. **1** loaded **2** burdened

lad'ing n. a load; cargo

la'dle n. long-handled, cuplike spoon

for dipping —v. dip out with a ladle

la'dy n., pl. **-dies** 1 well-bred, polite woman 2 any woman —a. [Inf.] female —**la'dy·like'** a.

la'dy·bug' n. small beetle with a spotted back

la'dy·fin'ger n. small, finger-shaped spongecake

la'dy·like' a. refined; well-bred

la'dy·love' n. sweetheart

la'dy-slip'per n. orchid with flowers like slippers

lag v. **lagged, lag'ging** to fall behind —n. 1 a falling behind 2 amount of this

la'ger (beer) (lä'-) n. a beer aged at a low temperature

lag'gard a. backward; slow —n. one who falls behind

la·gniappe, la·gnappe (lan yap') n. gratuity

la·goon' n. 1 shallow lake joined to a larger body of water 2 water inside an atoll

laid v. pt. & pp. of LAY

laid'-back' a. [Sl.] easygoing

lain v. pp. of LIE (recline)

lair n. animal's den

lais·sez faire (les'ā fer') n. noninterference

la'i·ty n. all laymen, as a group

lake n. large inland body of water

lake'front' a., n. (of) land along a lake's shore

lam n. [Sl.] used in **on the lam**, in flight from the police

la'ma (lä'-) n. Buddhist priest or monk in Tibet

la'ma·ser'y n., pl. **-ies** monastery of lamas

La·maze (lə mäz') n. training program in natural childbirth

lamb (lam) n. 1 young sheep 2 its flesh as food

lam·baste' (-bāst', -bast') v. [Inf.] beat or scold soundly

lam'bent a. 1 flickering 2 glowing softly 3 light and graceful

lame a. 1 crippled 2 stiff and painful 3 poor; ineffectual —v. make lame

la·mé (la mā') n. cloth interwoven with metal threads

lame duck n. elected official whose term goes beyond a reelection defeat

la·ment' v. feel or show deep sorrow for —n. 1 a lamenting 2 elegy; dirge —**lam·en·ta·ble** a. —**lam'en·ta'tion** n.

lam'i·nate' v. 1 to form of or into thin layers 2 to coat with plastic —**lam'i·nat'ed** a. —**lam'i·na'tion** n.

lamp n. 1 device for producing light 2

such a device set in a stand

lamp'black' n. fine soot used as a black pigment

lam·poon' n. written satirical attack —v. to attack as in a lampoon

lamp'post' n. post supporting a street lamp

lam'prey (-prē) n., pl. **-preys** eel-like water animal

la·nai (lä nä'ē, -nī') n. veranda

lance n. 1 long spear 2 lancet —v. cut open with a lancet

lanc'er n. cavalry soldier armed with a lance

lan'cet n. surgical knife

land n. 1 solid part of earth's surface 2 country or region 3 ground; soil 4 real estate —v. 1 put or go on shore or land 2 catch 3 [Inf.] get or secure

land'ed a. 1 owning land 2 consisting of land

land'fall' n. sighting of land

land'fill' n. place for burying garbage

land'hold'er n. owner of land

land'ing n. 1 a coming to shore 2 pier; dock 3 platform at the end of stairs 4 an alighting

land'locked' a. 1 surrounded by land 2 confined to fresh water

land'lord' n. one who leases land, houses, rooms, etc. to others —**land'la·dy** n.fem.

land'lub'ber n. one with little experience at sea

land'mark' n. 1 identifying feature of a locality 2 important event

land'mass' n. large area of land

land'-of'fice business n. [Inf.] a booming business

land'scape' n. (picture of) natural scenery —v. to plant lawns, bushes, etc. on —**land'scap'er** n.

land'slide' n. 1 sliding of rocks or earth down a slope 2 overwhelming victory

lane n. narrow path, road, etc.

lan'guage (-gwij) n. 1 speech or writing 2 any means of communicating

lan'guid a. 1 weak 2 listless; sluggish

lan'guish v. 1 become weak 2 yearn; pine —**lan'guish·ing** a.

lan'guor (-gər) n. lack of vigor —**lan'guor·ous** a.

lank a. tall and lean

lank'y a. **-i·er, -i·est** awkwardly tall and lean

lan'o·lin' n. fatty substance obtained from wool

lan'tern n. transparent case holding a light

lan'tern-jawed' a. having long, thin

jaws and sunken cheeks

lan'yard (-yərd) *n. Naut.* short rope

lap *n.* **1** front part from the waist to the knees of a sitting person **2** one circuit of a race track **3** overlapping part —*v.* **lapped, lap'ping 1** fold or wrap **2** lay or extend partly over **3** dip up with the tongue **4** splash lightly

la·pel' *n.* fold-back part at the upper front of a coat

lap'i·dar'y (-der'-) *n., pl.* **-ies** one who cuts and polishes gems

lap'is laz'u·li' (-yōō lī') *n.* azure, opaque semiprecious stone

lap robe *n.* heavy blanket, etc. laid over the lap

lapse *n.* **1** small error **2** a falling into a lower condition **3** passing, as of time —*v.* **1** fall into a certain state **2** deviate from virtue **3** become void

lap'top' *n.* portable microcomputer including a screen, keyboard and battery

lar'board (-bərd) *n.* a. left; port

lar'ce·ny *n., pl.* **-nies** theft —**lar'ce·nous** *a.*

larch *n.* kind of pine tree

lard *n.* melted fat of hogs —*v.* cover with lard

lard'er *n.* (place for keeping) food supplies

large *a.* of great size or amount —*adv.* in a large way —**at large 1** free; not jailed **2** in general —**large'ness** *n.*

large'ly *adv.* mainly

large'-scale' *a.* extensive

lar·gess', lar·gesse' *n.* generous giving

lar·go *a., adv. Mus.* slow and stately

lar'i·at *n.* a rope; esp., a lasso

lark *n.* **1** any of various songbirds **2** merry time —*v.* to play or frolic

lark'spur' *n.* delphinium

lar'va *n., pl.* **-vae'** (-vē') early form of an animal that changes when an adult —**lar'val** *a.*

lar·yn·gi·tis (lar'in jīt'is) *n.* inflammation of the larynx

lar'ynx (-iηks) *n.* upper end of the trachea

la·sa'gna (-zän'yə) *n.* wide noodles baked with layers of cheese, ground meat, tomato sauce, etc.

las·civ'i·ous (lə siv'-) *a.* showing or exciting lust

la'ser *n.* device that concentrates light rays in an intense beam

lash *n.* **1** striking part of a whip **2** a stroke as with a whip **3** eyelash —*v.* **1** strike or drive as with a lash **2** swing sharply **3** to tie with a rope,

etc. —**lash out** speak angrily

lass *n.* young woman

las'si·tude' *n.* weariness

las'so *n., pl.* **-sos** or **-soes** rope with a sliding noose, for catching cattle, etc. —*v.* to catch with a lasso

last *a.* **1** after all others **2** only remaining **3** most recent —*adv.* **1** after all others **2** most recently —*n.* last one —*v.* stay in use, etc. —**at last** finally

last hurrah *n.* final attempt or appearance

last'ly *adv.* in conclusion

last straw *n.* final trouble resulting in breakdown, loss of patience, etc.

lat *abbrev.* latitude

Lat *abbrev.* Latin

latch *n.* fastening for a door, window, etc., esp. a bar that fits into a notch —*v.* fasten with a latch

late *a.* **1** after the expected time **2** near the end of a period **3** recent **4** recently dead —*adv.* **1** after the expected time **2** near the end of a period **3** recently —**of late** recently

late'ly *adv.* recently

la'tent *a.* undeveloped

lat'er *adv.* after some time

lat'er·al *a.* sideways

la'tex' *n.* milky fluid in certain plants and trees

lath (lath) *n.* framework for plaster, as thin strips of wood

lathe (lāth) *n.* machine for shaping wood, metal, etc. with a cutting tool

lath'er *n.* **1** foam formed by soap and water **2** foamy sweat —*v.* cover with or form lather

Lat'in *n.* **1** language of ancient Rome **2** speaker of a Latin language —*a.* of or derived from Latin

Latin A·mer'i·ca countries south of the U.S. where Spanish, Portuguese, and French are official languages

La·ti'no *a.; n., pl.* **-nos** (of) a person in the U.S. of Latin American birth or descent —**La·ti'na** *a.; n.fem., pl.* **-nas**

lat'i·tude' *n.* **1** freedom of opinion, action, etc. **2** distance in degrees from the equator

la·trine' (-trēn') *n.* toilet for the use of many people

lat·te (lä'tā) *n.* espresso coffee mixed with steamed milk

lat'ter *a.* **1** nearer the end **2** last mentioned of two

lat'tice (-is) *n.* a structure of crossed strips of wood, etc.

lat'tice·work' *n.* **1** lattice **2** lattices collectively

laud (lôd) *v.*, *n.* praise —**laud′a·to′ry** *a.*

laud′a·ble *a.* praiseworthy

laud′a·num *n.* solution of opium in alcohol

laugh (laf) *v.* make vocal sounds showing mirth, scorn, etc. —*n.* act of laughing: also **laugh′ter** —**laugh′a·ble** *a.*

laugh′ing·stock′ *n.* object of ridicule

launch *v.* 1 send into space 2 set afloat 3 begin —*n.* large motorboat

launch′pad′, **launch pad** *n.* platform for launching a rocket, etc.

laun′der *v.* wash or wash and iron (clothes, linens, etc.) —**laun′dress** *n.fem.*

laun′dro·mat′ *n.* self-service laundry

laun′dry *n.* 1 *pl.* **-dries** place for laundering 2 things (to be) laundered

lau′rel *n.* 1 evergreen with large, glossy leaves 2 *pl.* fame; victory

la·va (lä′və, lav′ə) *n.* rock from a volcano

lav′a·to′ry *n.*, *pl.* **-ries** 1 washbowl 2 room with toilet and washbowl

lav′en·der *n.* pale purple

lav′ish *a.* very generous —*v.* give or spend freely

law *n.* 1 any of the rules of conduct made by a government 2 obedience to these 3 profession of lawyers 4 fundamental rule 5 series of natural events always happening in the same way —**law′break′er** *n.* —**law′mak′er** *n.*

law′-a·bid′ing *a.* obeying the law

law′ful *a.* LEGAL (*a.* 1)

law′less *a.* disobeying law

law′mak′er *n.* one who makes laws

lawn *n.* (area of) grass, cut short

lawn mower *n.* machine to cut lawn grass

law′suit′ *n.* case before a court for decision

law′yer *n.* person licensed to practice law

lax *a.* 1 not tight 2 not strict —**lax′i·ty** *n.*

lax′a·tive *n.*, *a.* (medicine) making the bowels move

lay *v.* **laid**, **lay′ing** 1 put down on something 2 to set in place 3 put or place 4 to deposit (an egg) 5 settle; allay 6 to bet 7 devise 8 to present or assert —*n.* 1 position; arrangement 2 short poem —*a.* of or for laymen —**lay aside** (or **away** or **by**) save for future use —**lay off** to put out of work

lay *v.* pt. of LIE (recline)

lay′a·way′ *n.* method of buying by making a deposit to hold item until full payment

lay′er *n.* single thickness

lay·ette′ *n.* complete outfit for a newborn baby

lay′man *n.*, *pl.* **-men** one not belonging to the clergy or to a given profession

lay′off′ *n.* temporary unemployment

lay′out′ *n.* arrangement

lay′o′ver *n.* stop in a journey

laze *v.* idle or loaf

la′zy *a.* **-zi·er**, **-zi·est** 1 not willing to work 2 sluggish —**la′zi·ly** *adv.* —**la′zi·ness** *n.*

Lazy Su′san *n.* revolving food tray

lb *abbrev.* pound(s)

lc *abbrev.* lowercase

l.c. *abbrev.* in the place cited

LD *abbrev.* learning disability

leach *v.* 1 extract (a soluble substance) from 2 dissolve and wash away

lead (lēd) *v.* **led**, **lead′ing** 1 direct or guide as by going before 2 be at the head of 3 go or pass 4 bring as a result 5 move first in a game, etc. —*n.* 1 guidance 2 first place 3 distance ahead 4 clue 5 leading role —**lead off** begin —**lead on** lure —**lead up to** prepare the way for —**lead′er** *n.* —**lead′er·ship′** *n.*

lead (led) *n.* 1 heavy, soft metal, a chemical element 2 graphite used in pencils

lead′en (led′-) *a.* 1 of lead 2 heavy 3 gloomy

lead′ing (lēd′-) *a.* chief

leading question *n.* question asked so as to suggest the answer desired

lead time (lēd) *n.* time between deciding on a product and starting production

leaf *n.*, *pl.* **leaves** 1 flat, thin, usually green part growing from a plant stem 2 sheet of paper, etc. —*v.* turn the pages of

leaf′let *n.* 1 small leaf 2 folded printed sheet

leaf′y *a.* **-i·er**, **-i·est** having many leaves

league (lēg) *n.* 1 association of nations, groups, etc. 2 unit of distance, about three miles —*v.* join in a league

leak *v.* 1 pass or let pass out or in accidentally 2 become known gradually 3 allow (secrets) to become known —*n.* accidental crack that allows leaking —**leak′y** *a.*, **-i·er**, **-i·est**

leak′age *n.* 1 a leaking 2 amount that leaks

lean v. **1** to bend or slant **2** rely (*on*) **3** be apt or inclined (*to*) **4** to rest against something —*a.* **1** with little or no fat **2** meager —**lean'ness** n.

lean'ing n. tendency

lean'-to n., pl. **-tos'** structure whose sloping roof abuts a wall, etc.

leap v. **leapt** or **lept** or **leaped**, **leap'ing** jump (over) —n. a jump

leap'frog' n. game in which players leap over the backs of others —v. **-frogged'**, **-frog'ging** leap or skip (*over*)

leap year n. every fourth year, having 29 days in February

learn v. **1** get knowledge or skill by study **2** hear (*of*) **3** memorize —**learn'ing** n.

learn'ed a. having or showing much learning

learning disability n. nervous-system condition interfering with learning of reading, etc. —**learn'ing-dis-a'bled** a.

lease n. contract by which property is rented —v. give or get by a lease

leash n. strap or chain for holding a dog, etc. in check

least a. smallest —adv. in the smallest degree —n. smallest in degree, etc. — **at least** at any rate

leath'er n. animal skin that has been tanned —**leath'er-y** a.

leave v. **left**, **leav'ing 1** let remain **2** to have remaining behind or after one **3** bequeath **4** go away (from) —n. **1** permission **2** permitted absence from duty —**leave out** omit —**take one's leave** depart

leav'en (lev'-) n. **1** yeast, etc. used to make dough rise: also **leav'en-ing 2** permeating influence —v. affect with leaven

leaves n. pl. of LEAF

leav'ings pl.n. remnants

lech'er n. lewd man —**lech'er-ous** a.

lec'i-thin (les'ə-) n. fatty compound in living cells

lec'tern n. reading stand

lec'ture n. **1** informative talk **2** a scolding —v. give a lecture (to) —**lec'tur-er** n.

led v. pt. & pp. of LEAD (guide)

ledge n. **1** shelflike projection **2** projecting ridge of rocks

ledg'er n. book of final entry for transactions

lee a., n. (on) the side away from the wind

leech n. bloodsucking worm

leek n. onionlike vegetable

leer n. malicious or suggestive grin —

v. look with a leer

leer'y a. wary

lees pl.n. dregs; sediment

lee'ward (also Naut. loo'ərd) a. away from the wind —n. lee side —adv. toward the lee

lee'way' n. [Inf.] margin of time, money, etc.

left a. of that side toward the west when one faces north —n. **1** left side **2** liberal or radical party, etc. —adv. toward the left

left v. pt. & pp. of LEAVE

left'-hand'ed a. **1** using the left hand more easily **2** for the left hand **3** insincere —adv. with the left hand

left'ist n., a. liberal or radical

left'o'ver n., a. (something) remaining

left wing n. more liberal or radical part of a group or party —**left'-wing'** a.

leg n. **1** limb used for standing and walking **2** thing like a leg

leg'a-cy n., pl. **-cies** something handed down to one, esp. by a will

le'gal a. **1** of, based upon, or permitted by law **2** of lawyers —**le-gal'i-ty** n. —**le'gal-ize'** v. —**le'gal-ly** adv.

le'gal-ese' (-ēz') n. legal jargon, often thought of as incomprehensible

legal tender n. money legally acceptable for payment

leg'ate (-ət) n. papal envoy

le-ga'tion n. envoy with staff and headquarters

le-ga'to (li gät'ō) a., adv. Mus. in a smooth, even style

leg'end n. **1** traditional tale **2** inscription, title, etc. —**leg'end-ar'y** a.

leg'er-de-main' n. sleight of hand

leg'gings pl.n. coverings for protecting the legs

leg'horn' n. [also L-] kind of small chicken

leg'i-ble a. that can be read —**leg'i-bly** adv.

le'gion (-jən) n. **1** large body of soldiers **2** great number

le'gion-naire' n. member of a legion

leg'is-late' v. **1** make laws **2** bring about by laws —**leg'is-la'tion** n. —**leg'is-la'tive** a. —**leg'is-la'tor** n.

leg'is-la'ture n. group of persons who make laws

le-git'i-mate (-mət) a. **1** born of a married couple **2** lawful **3** reasonable

le-git'i-mize' v. legalize, authorize, justify, etc.

leg'man' n., pl. **-men'** assistant who does routine work outside the office

leg-ume (leg'yoom') n. plant with pods,

as the bean —**le·gu′mi·nous** *a.*

lei (lā) *n., pl.* **leis** garland or wreath with flowers

lei·sure (lē′zhər, lezh′ər) *a., n.* free (time) for rest, play, etc.

lei′sure·ly *a.* slow —*adv.* in an unhurried manner

leit·mo·tif (līt′mō tēf′) *n.* recurring musical theme

lem′ming *n.* small arctic rodent

lem′on *n.* small, sour, yellow citrus fruit

lem·on·ade′ *n.* drink of lemon juice, sugar, and water

le′mur *n.* small mammal related to the monkey

lend *v.* **lent, lend′ing 1** let another use (a thing) temporarily **2** let out (money) at interest **3** impart —**lend′er** *n.*

length *n.* **1** distance from end to end **2** extent in space or time —**at length** finally —**length′wise′** *a., adv.*

length′en *v.* make or become longer

length′y *a.* **-i·er, -i·est** long; esp., too long

le′ni·ent *a.* merciful; gentle —**le′ni·en·cy, le′ni·ence** *n.*

lens *n.* **1** curved piece of glass, plastic, etc. for adjusting light rays passing through it **2** similar part of the eye

lent *v.* pt. & pp. of LEND

Lent *n.* period of 40 weekdays before Easter —**Lent′en** *a.*

len′til *n.* small edible seed of a pealike plant

Le′o *n.* fifth sign of the zodiac

le′o·nine *a.* like a lion

leop′ard (lep′-) *n.* large, black-spotted wildcat of Asia and Africa

le′o·tard′ *n.* dancer's tight-fitting, one-piece garment

lep′er *n.* one having leprosy

lep′re·chaun′ (-kôn′) *n.* Irish fairy in the form of a little man

lep′ro·sy *n.* disease with skin ulcers, scaling, etc.

les′bi·an (lez′-) *a., n.* female homosexual

le′sion (-zhən) *n.* injury of an organ or tissues

less *a.* not so much, so great, etc. —*adv.* to a smaller extent —*n.* a smaller amount —*prep.* minus

-less *suf.* **1** without **2** that does not **3** that cannot be

les·see′ *n.* one to whom property is leased

less′en *v.* make or become less

less′er *a.* smaller, less, etc.

les′son *n.* **1** exercise for a student to

learn **2** something learned by experience

les′sor′ *n.* one giving a lease

lest *con.* for fear that

let *v.* **1** allow; permit **2** leave **3** rent *Let* is also used as an auxiliary verb —**let down 1** lower **2** disappoint —**let on** [Inf.] pretend —**let up 1** relax **2** cease

let′down′ *n.* a disappointment

le′thal *a.* fatal; deadly

leth′ar·gy *n.* lack of energy —**le·thar′gic** *a.*

let′ter *n.* **1** character in an alphabet **2** message sent by mail **3** literal meaning **4** *pl.* literature —*v.* mark with letters —**let′tered** *a.*

let′ter·head′ *n.* **1** name, etc. of a person or firm as a heading on letter paper **2** a sheet of this paper

let′ter-per′fect *a.* entirely correct

let′ter-qual′i·ty *a.* producing printed characters of similar quality to typewritten characters

let′tuce (-əs) *n.* plant with crisp, green leaves used in salads

let′up′ *n.* [Inf.] **1** a slackening **2** stop or pause

leu·ke′mi·a (lōō-) *n.* disease characterized by an abnormal increase in the white blood corpuscles

leu′ko·cyte′ (-sīt′) *n.* colorless blood cell important in body's resistance to infection

lev′ee *n.* river embankment built to prevent flooding

lev′el *n.* **1** instrument for determining the horizontal **2** horizontal plane, line, etc. **3** height **4** position, rank, etc. —*a.* **1** flat and even **2** even in height (*with*) —*v.* **1** make or become level **2** demolish **3** [Sl.] be honest (*with*) —**lev′el·er** *n.*

lev′el·head′ed *a.* sensible

le′ver (or lē′vər) *n.* bar turning on a fulcrum, used to lift or move weights

lev′er·age *n.* action or power of a lever

le·vi′a·than (-vī′-) *n.* huge thing

Le·vi′s (lē′vīz′) *trademark* denim trousers

lev′i·tate′ *v.* (make) rise and float in the air —**lev·i·ta′tion** *n.*

lev′i·ty *n.* improper gaiety; frivolity

lev′y *v.* **-ied, -y·ing 1** impose (a tax, etc.) **2** enlist (troops) **3** wage (war) —*n., pl.* **-ies** a levying or something levied

lewd (lōōd) *a.* indecent

lex·i·cog′ra·phy *n.* work of writing a dictionary —**lex′i·cog′ra·pher** *n.*

lex'i·con' *n.* dictionary

lg *abbrev.* large

li·a·bil'i·ty *n.*, *pl.* **-ties** 1 a being liable 2 debt 3 disadvantage

li'a·ble *a.* 1 legally responsible 2 subject to 3 likely

li·ai·son (lē ā'zän') *n.* 1 communication between military units 2 illicit love affair

li'ar *n.* one who tells lies

lib *n.* liberation

li·ba'tion *n.* 1 wine or oil poured in honor of a god 2 alcoholic drink

li'bel *n.* statement in writing that may unjustly hurt a reputation —*v.* make a libel against —**li'bel·ous, li'bel·lous** *a.*

lib'er·al *a.* 1 generous 2 not strict 3 tolerant 4 favoring reform —*n.* person who favors reform —**lib'er·al·ism'** *n.* —**lib'er·al'i·ty** *n.* —**lib'er·al·ize'** *v.*

liberal arts *pl.n.* literature, philosophy, history, etc.

lib'er·al'i·ty *n.* 1 generosity 2 tolerance

lib'er·ate' *v.* set free; release —**lib'er·a'tion.** —**lib'er·a'tor** *n.*

lib·er·tar'i·an *n.* advocate of full civil liberties

lib'er·tine' (-tēn') *n.* sexually promiscuous person

lib'er·ty *n.*, *pl.* **-ties** 1 freedom from slavery, etc. 2 a particular right 3 *pl.* excessive familiarity —**at liberty** 1 not confined 2 permitted (*to*)

li·bi·do (-bē'-) *n.* sexual urge —**li·bid'i·nous** *a.*

Li'bra (lē'-) *n.* seventh sign of the zodiac

li'brar·y *n.*, *pl.* **-ies** collection of books or a place for it —**li·brar'i·an** *n.*

li·bret'to *n.*, *pl.* **-tos** or **-ti** (-ē) text of an opera, etc. —**li·bret'tist** *n.*

lice *n.* pl. of LOUSE

li'cense *n.* 1 legal permit 2 freedom from rules 3 freedom that is abused —*v.* permit formally Br. sp., **li'cence**

li·cen'tious (-shəs) *a.* morally unrestrained

li·chen (lī'kən) *n.* mosslike plant growing on rocks, trees, etc.

lic'it (lis'-) *a.* lawful

lick *v.* 1 pass the tongue over 2 [Inf.] defeat —*n.* 1 a licking 2 small quantity —**lick up** consume by licking

lic·o·rice (lik'ə rish) *n.* 1 black flavoring from a plant root 2 candy with this flavoring

lid *n.* 1 movable cover 2 eyelid —**lid'ded** *a.*

lie *v.* lay, lain, ly'ing 1 be horizontal or rest horizontally 2 be or exist —*n.* position; lay

lie *v.* lied, ly'ing make a false statement knowingly —*n.* thing said in lying

lie detector *n.* polygraph

liege (lēj) *n.* feudal lord or vassal

lien (lēn) *n.* legal claim on another's property until a debt is paid

lieu (lōō) *n.* used chiefly in **in lieu of,** instead of

Lieut *abbrev.* Lieutenant

lieu·ten'ant *n.* 1 low-ranking commissioned officer 2 deputy —**lieu·ten'an·cy** *n.*, *pl.* **-cies**

lieutenant governor *n.* elected state official who may substitute for a governor

life *n.*, *pl.* **lives** 1 active existence of plants and animals 2 living things 3 time of being alive 4 way of living 5 a biography 6 liveliness —**life'less** *a.* —**life'like** *a.*

life'boat' *n.* small escape boat carried by a ship

life'-form' *n.* specific organism, esp. if unusual or newly found

life'guard' *n.* swimmer employed to prevent drownings

life jacket (or **vest**) *n.* life preserver like a jacket or vest

life'long' *a.* lasting for life

life pre·serv'er *n.* device for keeping the body afloat

life'sav·er *n.* [Inf.] person or thing that gives help in time of need

life'-size' *a.* as big as the thing represented

life'style' *n.* individual's way of life: also **life style**

life'-sup·port' *a.* of a system providing support needed to maintain life

life'time' *a.*, *n.* (lasting for) the length of one's life

lift *v.* 1 bring higher; raise 2 go up; rise 3 [Sl.] steal —*n.* 1 a lifting 2 lifting force 3 raising of one's spirits 4 help; aid 5 ride in the direction one is going 6 [Br.] elevator

lift'off' *n.* vertical takeoff of a spacecraft, etc.

lig'a·ment *n.* connective tissue for bones or organs

lig'a·ture *n.* 1 thing for tying, as surgical thread 2 letters united, as *fl*

light *n.* 1 radiant energy by which one sees 2 brightness 3 lamp, lantern, etc. 4 daylight 5 thing to ignite something 6 aspect 7 knowledge —*a.* 1 bright 2 pale; fair 3 not heavy 4 not important 5 easy to bear or do 6 happy **7** dizzy **8** moderate —*adv.* **1** palely **2** lightly —*v.* **light'ed** or **lit, light'ing 1** ignite **2** furnish with light **3** brighten **4** be lighted: with *up* **5** come to rest **6** happen (*on*) — **in the light of** considering — **make light of** treat as unimportant

light'en *v.* make or become brighter, less heavy, etc.

light'er *n.* **1** thing that ignites something **2** large, open barge

light'-fin'gered *a.* thievish

light'head'ed *a.* **1** dizzy **2** flighty

light'heart'ed *a.* free from care; cheerful

light'house' *n.* tower with a light to guide ships

light'ly *adv.* **1** gently **2** to a small degree **3** cheerfully **4** carelessly

light'-mind'ed *a.* frivolous

light'ning *n.* flash of light in the sky from a discharge of atmospheric electricity

lightning bug *n.* firefly

lightning rod *n.* metal rod to divert lightning

light'-year' *n.* distance that light travels in a year, about 6 trillion miles

lik'a·ble *a.* pleasant, friendly, etc.: also **like'a·ble**

like *a.* similar; equal —*prep.* **1** similar(ly) to **2** typical of **3** in the mood for **4** indicative of —*con.* [Inf.] **1** as **2** as if —*v.* **1** be fond of; enjoy **2** wish —*n.* **1** an equal **2** *pl.* preferences — **like crazy** (or **mad,** etc.) [Inf.] wildly —**lik'ing** *n.*

-like *suf.* like

like'ly *a.* **1** credible **2** probable; expected **3** suitable —*adv.* probably —**like'li·hood'** *n.*

like'-mind'ed *a.* having the same ideas, tastes, etc.

lik'en (līk'-) *v.* compare

like'ness *n.* **1** a being like **2** picture; copy

like'wise' *adv.* **1** in the same way **2** also; too

li'lac' *n.* shrub with tiny, pale-purple flower clusters

lilt *n.* light, graceful rhythm —**lilt'ing** *a.*

lil'y *n., pl.* **-ies** plant with trumpet-shaped flowers

lil'y-liv'ered *a.* cowardly

lily of the valley *n., pl.* **lilies of the valley** plant with a spike of bell-shaped flowers

li'ma bean (lī'-) *n.* large, flat, edible bean in pods

limb (lim) *n.* **1** arm, leg, or wing **2** large tree branch

lim'ber *v., a.* (make or become) flexible

lim'bo *n.* uncertain state or condition

Lim'burg'er (cheese) *n.* white, strong-smelling cheese

lime *n.* **1** white substance obtained from limestone **2** green, lemonlike fruit

lime'light' *n.* prominent position before the public

lim'er·ick *n.* rhymed, funny poem of five lines

lime'stone' *n.* rock used in building, making lime, etc.

lim'it *n.* **1** point where something ends **2** *pl.* bounds —*v.* set a limit to —**lim'i·ta'tion** *n.*

lim'it·ed *a.* restricted

limn (lim) *v.* portray in pictures or words

lim'ou·sine' (-ə zēn') *n.* large luxury automobile: also [Inf.] **lim'o,** *pl.* **-os**

limp *v., n.* (walk with) lameness —*a.* not firm

lim'pet *n.* shellfish that clings to rocks, etc.

lim'pid *a.* transparent

linch'pin' *n.* **1** pin affixing wheel to axle **2** thing holding parts together

lin'den *n.* tree with heart-shaped leaves

line *n.* **1** cord, rope, etc. **2** system of pipes or wires **3** long, thin mark **4** boundary **5** a row or series **6** conformity **7** transportation system **8** route; course **9** stock of goods **10** short letter **11** place where football teams line up —*v.* **1** mark with lines **2** form (into) a line: with *up* **3** put, or serve as, a lining in

lin·e·age (lin'ē ij) *n.* line of descent; ancestry

lin'e·al *a.* **1** directly descended **2** linear

lin'e·a·ment *n.* distinctive facial feature

lin'e·ar *a.* **1** of a line or lines **2** of length

line drive *n.* batted baseball that travels close to the ground

line'man *n., pl.* **-men 1** person who works on power lines, etc. **2** football player at the line who blocks, etc.

lin'en *n.* **1** cloth of flax **2** things of linen or cotton

lin'er *n.* ship or airplane of a LINE (*n.* 7)

line'up' *n.* a row of persons or things

lin'ger *v.* **1** continue to stay **2** delay

lin·ge·rie (län'zhə rā') *n.* women's underwear

lin'go *n., pl.* **-goes** unfamiliar jargon

lin·gui'ne (-gwē'nē) *n.* flat, narrow spaghetti: also **lin·gui'ni**

lin'guist (-gwist) *n.* expert in linguistics

lin·guis'tics *n.* science of (a) language

lin'i·ment *n.* medicated liquid for the skin

lin'ing *n.* material covering an inner surface

link *n.* **1** loop in a chain **2** thing that connects —*v.* join; connect —**link'age** *n.*

links *pl.n.* place where golf is played

link'up' *n.* a joining

li·no'le·um *n.* hard, smooth floor covering

lin'seed' oil *n.* yellow oil from seed of flax

lint *n.* bits of thread, fluff, etc. from cloth —**lint'y** *a.*, **-i·er**, **-i·est**

lin'tel *n.* horizontal piece over a door or window

li'on *n.* **1** large animal of the cat family, found in Africa and SW Asia **2** very strong, brave person **3** a celebrity —**li'on·ess** *n.fem.*

li'on-heart'ed *a.* very brave

li'on·ize' *v.* treat as a celebrity

lip *n.* **1** upper or lower edge of the mouth **2** thing like a lip, as a cup's rim

lip'id *n.* a fat or similar compound in living cells

lip'o·suc'tion (lip'ō-, li'pə-) *n.* surgical removal of fatty tissue by suction

lip reading *n.* recognition of words by watching a speaker's lips —**lip'-read'** *v.*

lip service *n.* insincere words of support, etc.

lip'stick' *n.* small stick of cosmetic paste to color the lips

lip'-sync' (-siŋk) *v.* move the lips in time with (recorded singing, etc.)

liq'ue·fy' (lik'wi-) *v.* **-fied'**, **-fy'ing** change to a liquid: also **liq'ui·fy'**

li·queur' (li kur', -koor') *n.* sweet alcoholic liquor

liq'uid *a.* **1** readily flowing **2** readily changed into cash —*n.* substance that flows easily

liq'ui·date' *v.* **1** settle the accounts of (a business) **2** pay (a debt) **3** change into cash —**liq'ui·da'tion** *n.*

liq'uor (-ər) *n.* alcoholic drink, as whiskey

li·ra (lir'ə) *n., pl.* **-re** (-ā) or **-ras** Italian monetary unit

lisle (līl) *n.* fabric woven of strong cotton thread

lisp *v.* substitute the sounds "th" and "*th*" for the sounds of "s" and "z" —*n.* act or sound of lisping

lis'some, lis'som *a.* lithe and graceful

list *n.* series of names, words, etc. set forth in order —*v.* put in a list

list *v.* tilt to one side, as a ship —*n.* a listing

lis'ten (-ən) *v.* **1** try to hear **2** pay attention

list'ing *n.* **1** making of a list **2** entry in a list

list'less *a.* indifferent because ill, tired, etc.

list price *n.* retail price

lists *pl.n.* area where knights jousted

lit *v.* pt. & pp. of LIGHT

lit *abbrev.* **1** literally **2** literature

lit'a·ny *n., pl.* **-nies** prayer with responses

li'ter (lē'-) *n.* metric unit of capacity (61.0237 cubic inches)

lit'er·al *a.* **1** precise; strict **2** prosaic **3** restricted to fact —**lit'er·al·ly** *adv.*

lit'er·ar'y *a.* having to do with literature

lit'er·ate (-ət) *a.* **1** able to read and write **2** well-educated —**lit'er·a·cy** *n.*

lit·e·ra'ti (-rät'ē) *pl.n.* writers, scholars, etc.

lit'er·a·ture *n.* **1** all the valuable writings of a specific time, nation, etc. **2** all writings on some subject

lithe (līth) *a.* bending easily

lith'i·um *n.* the lightest metal, a chemical element

lith'o·graph' *n.* print made from stone or metal treated with grease and water —**li·thog'ra·phy** *n.*

lit'i·gant *n.* party to a lawsuit

lit'i·gate' *v.* to contest in a lawsuit —**lit'i·ga'tion** *n.*

lit'mus paper *n.* treated paper that turns blue in bases and red in acids

lit'mus test *n.* test whose results depend on a single factor

li'tre *n.* Br. sp. of LITER

lit'ter *n.* **1** portable couch **2** stretcher **3** young borne at one time by a dog, cat, etc. **4** things lying about in disorder —*v.* make untidy

lit'ter·bug' *n.* one who litters public places with rubbish

lit'tle *a.* **1** small in size or amount **2** short; brief **3** not important —*adv.* **1** slightly **2** not at all —*n.* small amount or short time —**little by little** gradually —**not a little** very

Little Dipper *n.* dipper-shaped constellation containing the North Star

lit'to·ral *a.* of or along the shore

lit·ur·gy *n., pl.* **-gies** ritual for public worship —**li·tur'gi·cal** *a.*

liv'a·ble *a.* fit or pleasant to live in

live (liv) *v.* **1** have life **2** stay alive; endure **3** pass one's life in a certain way **4** have a full life **5** feed (*on*) **6** reside

live (līv) *a.* **1** having life **2** of interest now **3** still burning **4** unexploded **5** carrying electrical current **6** broadcast while happening

live'li·hood' *n.* means of supporting oneself

live'long' (liv'-) *a.* whole

live'ly *a.* **-li·er, -li·est 1** full of life **2** exciting **3** cheerful **4** having much bounce —**live'li·ness** *n.*

liv'en (līv'-) *v.* cheer (*up*)

liv'er *n.* organ in vertebrates that makes bile

liv'er·wurst' *n.* sausage made of ground liver

liv'er·y *n., pl.* **-ies 1** uniform as of a servant **2** business of renting horses and carriages

lives *n.* pl. of LIFE

live'stock' *n.* animals kept or raised on a farm

liv'id *a.* **1** grayish-blue **2** enraged

liv'ing *a.* **1** having life **2** in active use **3** of persons alive **4** true; lifelike **5** of life **6** enough to live on —*n.* **1** a being alive **2** livelihood **3** way that one lives

living room *n.* room for lounging, entertaining, etc.

living wage *n.* wage high enough to live on in some comfort

living will *n.* document rejecting the use of any measures to maintain life if one is dying of an incurable condition

liz'ard *n.* reptile with a long tail and four legs

ll *abbrev.* lines

lla'ma (lä'-) *n.* South American cud-chewing animal

LLB, LL.B. *abbrev.* Bachelor of Laws

LLD, LL.D. *abbrev.* Doctor of Laws

lo *int.* look; see

load *n.* **1** amount carried **2** a burden —*v.* **1** put (a load) in or on **2** to burden **3** put ammunition into

load'star' *n.* lodestar

load'stone' *n.* lodestone

loaf *n., pl.* **loaves** bread, etc. baked in one piece —*v.* spend time idly —**loaf'er** *n.*

Loaf'er *trademark* low shoe that slips onto the foot —*n.* [l-] such a shoe

loam *n.* rich soil

loan *n.* **1** act of lending **2** something lent, esp. money at interest —*v.* lend

loan shark *n.* [Inf.] person loaning money at excessive interest

loath (lōth) *a.* reluctant

loathe (lōth) *v.* abhor —**loath'some** *a.*

loath'ing (lōth'-) *n.* intense dislike

lob *v.* **lobbed, lob'bing** toss or hit (a ball) in a high curve —*n.* a toss or hit made this way

lob'by *n., pl.* **-bies 1** entrance hall **2** group of lobbyists —*v.* **-bied, -by·ing** act as a lobbyist

lob'by·ist *n.* one who tries to influence legislators

lobe *n.* rounded projection

lo·bot'o·my *n., pl.* **-mies** surgical incision into a lobe of the cerebrum

lob'ster *n.* edible sea animal with large pincers

lobster tail *n.* edible tail of any of various crayfish

lo'cal *a.* of or for a particular place or area —*n.* **1** bus, etc. making all stops **2** branch, as of a labor union —**lo'cal·ly** *adv.*

lo·cale' (-kal') *n.* a place or setting for events, etc.

lo·cal'i·ty *n., pl.* **-ties** place or district

lo'cal·ize' *v.* limit to a certain place

lo'cate' *v.* **1** establish in a certain place **2** find or show the position of

lo·ca'tion *n.* **1** a locating **2** position; place

loc. cit. *abbrev.* in the place cited

loch (läk) *n.* [Scot.] **1** lake **2** arm of the sea

lock *n.* **1** device for fastening a door, etc. as with a key **2** part of a canal where boats are raised and lowered **3** curl of hair —*v.* **1** fasten with a lock **2** shut (*in* or *out*) **3** jam or link together

lock'er *n.* chest, closet, etc. that can be locked

lock'et *n.* little case worn on a necklace

lock'jaw' *n.* tetanus

lock'out' *n.* a locking out of employees to force agreement to employer's terms

lock'smith' *n.* one who makes or repairs locks and keys

lock'up' *n.* a jail

lo'co *a.* [Sl.] crazy; insane

lo·co·mo'tion *n.* act or power of moving about

lo·co·mo'tive *n.* engine for a railroad train

lo'co·weed' *n.* plant causing a disease in horses, etc.

lo'cust *n.* **1** grasshopper-like insect **2** cicada **3** tree with white flowers

lo·cu'tion (-kyōō'-) *n.* word, phrase, etc.

lode *n.* vein or stratum of metallic ore

lode'star' *n.* star by which one directs one's course

lode'stone' *n.* magnetic iron ore

lodge *n.* **1** a house for special use or chapter of a society —*v.* **1** to house or dwell for a time **2** (cause) to be fixed (*in*) **3** to file (a complaint, etc.) — **lodg'er** *n.*

lodg'ing *n.* **1** place to live **2** *pl.* rented rooms

loft *n.* **1** space below a roof **2** upper story of a warehouse, etc. **3** gallery —*v.* send (a ball) high into the air

loft'y *a.* **-i·er, -i·est 1** very high **2** noble **3** haughty —**loft'i·ness** *n.*

log *n.* **1** section cut from a tree trunk **2** daily record of a ship's, etc. progress **3** logarithm —*v.* **logged, log'ging 1** cut down trees and remove the logs **2** enter in a ship's log —**log on** (or **off**) enter information to begin (or end) activity on a computer terminal

lo'gan·ber'ry *n., pl.* **-ries** purple-red berry

log'a·rithm (-ri*th* əm) *n. Math.* power to which a base number must be raised to get a given number

loge (lōzh) *n.* theater or stadium box

log'ger *n.* one who fells trees for use as lumber, etc.

log'ger·head' *n.* used chiefly in **at loggerheads,** in disagreement; quarreling

log'ic (läj'-) *n.* **1** science of reasoning **2** (correct) reasoning —**lo·gi·cian** (lō jish'ən) *n.*

log'i·cal *a.* **1** using or used in logic **2** expected because of what has gone before —**log'i·cal·ly** *adv.*

lo·gis'tics *n.* military science of moving and supplying troops

log'jam' *n.* obstacle or deadlock

lo'go' *n.* distinctive company symbol, trademark, etc.

log'roll'ing *n.* mutual exchange of favors, esp. among lawmakers

lo'gy (-gē) *a.* **-gi·er, -gi·est** [Inf.] dull or sluggish

-logy *suf.* science or study of

loin *n.* **1** lower back from ribs to hipbone **2** *pl.* hips and lower abdomen

loin'cloth' *n.* cloth worn about the loins, as by some tribes

loi'ter *v.* **1** spend time idly **2** move slowly

loll (läl) *v.* **1** lounge about **2** droop or let hang loosely

lol'li·pop', lol'ly·pop' *n.* piece of candy on a stick

lol'ly·gag' *v.* **-gagged', -gag'ging** [Inf.] waste time aimlessly

lone *a.* by oneself or itself

lone'ly *a.* **-li·er, -li·est 1** alone and unhappy **2** unfrequented —**lone'li·ness** *n.*

lon'er *n.* [Inf.] one who avoids the company of others

lone'some *a.* having or causing a lonely feeling

long *a.* **1** measuring much **2** in length **3** of great length **4** tedious **5** far-reaching **6** well supplied —*adv.* **1** for a long time **2** for the time of **3** at a remote time —*v.* to wish earnestly; yearn —**as** (or **so**) **long as 1** while **2** since **3** provided that —**before long** soon

long *abbrev.* longitude

long'-dis'tance *a.* to or from distant places —*adv.* by long-distance telephone

long distance *n.* telephone service for long-distance calls

lon·gev'i·ty (län jev'-) *n.* **1** long life **2** length of time spent in service, etc.

long'-faced' *a.* glum

long'hand' *n.* ordinary handwriting

long'ing *n.* earnest desire

lon'gi·tude' *n.* distance, in degrees, east or west of a line through Greenwich, England

lon'gi·tu'di·nal *a.* **1** of length **2** of longitude

long jump *n.* a jump for distance

long'-lived' (-līvd', -livd') *a.* having a long life span

long'-range' *a.* covering a long distance or time

long'shore'man *n., pl.* **-men** one whose work is loading and unloading ships

long shot *n.* [Inf.] venture having only a slight chance of success

long'-term' *a.* for a long time

long ton *n.* 2,240 pounds

long'ways' *adv.* lengthwise

long'-wind'ed (-win'dəd) *a.* wordy and tiresome

look *v.* **1** direct the eyes so as to see **2** search **3** seem —*n.* **1** an act of looking **2** appearance **3** [Inf.] *pl.* personal appearance —*int.* **1** see **2** pay attention —**look after** care for —**look into** investigate —**look up to** admire

look'ing glass *n.* glass mirror

look'out' *n.* **1** careful watching **2** guard; sentry

look'-see' n. [Inf.] quick look

loom n. machine for weaving —v. come into sight suddenly

loon n. ducklike bird

loon'ie n. [Cdn.] Canadian one-dollar coin

loon'y a. **-i·er, -i·est** [Sl.] crazy; insane

loop n. line, figure, etc. that curves back to cross itself —v. make a loop

loop'hole' n. means of evading something

loose (lōōs) a. **1** free **2** not firm or tight **3** inexact **4** sexually promiscuous —v. **1** to free **2** make less tight, etc. **3** release —**on the loose** not confined; free —**loose'ly** adv. —**loos'en** v.

loos'ey-goos'ey a. [Sl.] relaxed

loot n., v. plunder —**loot'er** n.

lop v. lopped, **lop'ping** cut off

lope v., n. (move with) a long, swinging stride

lop'sid·ed a. heavier, lower, etc. on one side

lo·qua'cious (-kwā'shəs) a. very talkative

lord n. **1** master **2** Br. nobleman **3** [L-] God **4** [L-] Jesus Christ

lore n. knowledge

lor·gnette' (-nyet') n. eyeglasses on a handle

lor'ry n., pl. **-ries** [Br.] motor truck

lose (lōōz) v. **lost, los'ing 1** become unable to find **2** have taken from one by accident, death, etc. **3** fail to keep **4** fail to win

loss n. **1** a losing, or damage, etc. resulting from losing something **2** person, thing, etc. lost

lost a. **1** ruined **2** missing or mislaid **3** wasted

lot n. **1** deciding of a matter by chance **2** fate **3** piece of land **4** group **5** often pl. [Inf.] great amount or number —**a (whole) lot** very much

lo'tion n. liquid for softening or healing the skin

lots adv. very much

lot'ter·y n., pl. **-ies** game in which numbered chances on prizes are sold

lot'to n. game like bingo

lo'tus n. tropical waterlily

loud a. **1** strong in sound **2** noisy **3** [Inf.] flashy —adv. in a loud way —**loud'ly** adv. —**loud'ness** n.

loud'mouthed' (-mouṯẖd', -mouṯẖt') a. talking in a loud, irritating way

loud'speak'er n. speaker in a radio, etc.

lounge v. **1** sit in a relaxed way **2** to be idle —n. **1** room furnished for lounging **2** couch

lounge'wear' n. loose-fitting casual clothes

louse (lous) n., pl. **lice** small insect parasite —**louse up** [Sl.] botch; ruin

lous·y (lou'zē) a. **-i·er, -i·est 1** infested with lice **2** [Sl.] inferior, contemptible, etc. **3** [Sl.] well supplied (with)

lout n. boor

lou'ver (lōō'-) n. **1** window, etc. with slanted boards that let in air and keep out rain **2** such a board

love n. **1** strong affection **2** object of this **3** in tennis, a score of zero —v. feel love (for) —**in love** feeling love —**make love** kiss, embrace, etc. —**lov'a·ble, love'a·ble** a. —**lov'er** n. —**lov'ing·ly** adv.

love'lorn' a. pining from love

love'ly a. **-li·er, -li·est 1** beautiful **2** [Inf.] very enjoyable —**love'li·ness** n.

love seat n. small sofa for two

lov'ing a. feeling or expressing love

loving cup n. large drinking cup, often given as a trophy

low a. **1** not high **2** below others in rank, size, cost, etc. **3** gloomy **4** deep in pitch **5** vulgar **6** not loud —adv. **1** in or to a low level, etc. —n. **1** low level, degree, etc. **2** gear arrangement giving least speed —v. to moo —**lay low** kill —**lie low** stay hidden

low'brow' n., a. nonintellectual

low'-cal' a. having few calories

low'down' (a.: lō'doun') n. [Sl.] pertinent facts: with the —a. [Inf.] **1** mean or contemptible **2** depressed

low'-end' a. [Inf.] cheap and of low quality

low'er (lō'-) a. below in rank, etc. —v. **1** let or put down **2** make or become less in amount, value, etc.

low'er (lou'-) v. **1** to scowl **2** appear threatening

low·er·case' a., n. (of or in) small, rather than capital, letters

low frequency n. radio frequency between 30 and 300 kilohertz

low'-key' a. subdued; not intense

low'land n. land lower than land around it

low'ly a. **1** of low rank **2** humble —**low'li·ness** n.

low'-mind'ed a. having a coarse, vulgar mind

lox n. smoked salmon

loy'al a. faithful to one's friends, country, etc. —**loy'al·ly** adv. —**loy'al·ty** n., pl. **-ties**

loy'al·ist n. supporter of the government during a revolt

loz'enge n. cough drop, small piece of

hard candy, etc.

LPN *abbrev.* Licensed Practical Nurse

LSD *n.* psychedelic drug

Lt *abbrev.* Lieutenant

Ltd, ltd *abbrev.* limited

lu·au (lōō'ou') *n.* Hawaiian feast

lube *n.* [Inf.] a lubrication or lubricant

lu'bri·cant *a.* that lubricates —*n.* oil, grease, etc.

lu'bri·cate' *v.* apply a substance that reduces friction —**lu'bri·ca'tion** *n.*

lu'cid *a.* 1 clear 2 sane 3 shining — **lu·cid'i·ty** *n.* —**lu'cid·ly** *adv.*

Lu'cite' *trademark* a transparent plastic

luck *n.* 1 chance; fortune 2 good fortune —**luck'less** *a.*

luck'y *a.* **-i·er, -i·est** having, resulting in, or thought to bring good luck — **luck'i·ly** *adv.*

lu'cra·tive *a.* profitable

lu'cre (-kər) *n.* riches; money

lu'cu·brate' (lōō'kə-) *v.* work or study hard, esp. late at night —**lu·cu·bra'tion** *n.*

lu'di·crous (-krəs) *a.* so incongruous as to be funny

lug *v.* **lugged, lug'ging** carry with effort —*n.* 1 earlike handle or support 2 bolt, used with **lug nut**, to mount a wheel

luge (lōōzh) *n.* racing sled

lug'gage *n.* suitcases, trunks, etc.

lu·gu'bri·ous (lə gōō'-) *a.* exaggeratedly mournful

luke'warm' *a.* 1 slightly warm 2 lacking enthusiasm

lull *v.* 1 soothe by gentle sound or motion 2 become calm —*n.* short period of calm

lull'a·by' *n., pl.* **-bies'** song for lulling a baby to sleep

lum·ba'go *n.* pain in the lower back

lum'bar' (-bär', -bər) *a.* of or near the loins

lum'ber *n.* wood sawed into beams, boards, etc. —*v.* move heavily and clumsily —**lum'ber·ing** *a.*

lum'ber·jack' *n.* logger

lum'ber·man *n., pl.* **-men** lumber dealer

lu'mi·nar·y *n., pl.* **-ies** famous person

lu'mi·nes'cence *n.* giving off light without heat —**lu'mi·nes'cent** *a.*

lu'mi·nous *a.* bright; shining —**lu·mi·nos'i·ty** *n.*

lum'mox (-əks) *n.* [Inf.] clumsy person

lump *n.* 1 a mass of something 2 a swelling —*a.* in a lump or lumps —*v.* to group together —**lump'y** *a.*, **-i·er, -i·est**

lump sum *n.* total sum paid at one time

lu'nar (-nər) *a.* of the moon

lu'na·tic *a.* 1 insane 2 utterly foolish —*n.* an insane person —**lu'na·cy** *n.*

lunch *n.* midday meal —*v.* eat lunch

lunch'eon (-ən) *n.* formal lunch

lunch'eon·ette' *n.* small restaurant serving light lunches

luncheon meat *n.* meat processed in loaves, etc., ready to eat

lung *n.* organ in the chest for breathing

lunge *n.* 1 sudden thrust 2 forward plunge —*v.* make a lunge

lung'fish' *n.* fish having lungs as well as gills

lu'pine (-pin) *n.* plant with spikes of rose, white, or blue flowers

lu'pus *n.* disease with skin lesions

lurch *v.* sway suddenly to one side —*n.* lurching movement —**leave in the lurch** leave in a difficult situation

lure (loor) *n.* 1 thing that attracts 2 device to attract fish —*v.* attract; entice

lu·rid (loor'id) *a.* 1 shocking 2 glowing strangely

lurk *v.* stay or be hidden, ready to attack

lus·cious (lush'əs) *a.* 1 delicious 2 pleasing

lush *a.* of or having luxuriant growth

lust *n.* 1 strong sexual desire 2 strong desire, as for power —*v.* feel an intense desire —**lust'ful** *a.*

lus'ter *n.* 1 gloss; brightness 2 fame or distinction —**lus'trous** (-trəs) *a.*

lust'y *a.* **-i·er, -i·est** vigorous; robust — **lust'i·ly** *adv.*

lute *n.* stringed, guitarlike instrument

lu'te·nist *n.* lute player: also **lu'ta·nist, lut'ist**

Lu'ther·an *n., a.* (member) of the Protestant church founded by Martin Luther

lux·u'ri·ant (lug zhoor'-, luk shoor'-) *a.* 1 growing in abundance 2 richly ornamented —**lux·u'ri·ance** *n.*

lux·u'ri·ate' *v.* 1 live in luxury 2 revel (in)

lux·u'ri·ous *a.* 1 giving a feeling of luxury 2 fond of luxury

lux'u·ry *n., pl.* **-ries** costly comfort(s) or pleasure(s) —*a.* characterized by luxury

-ly *suf.* 1 like 2 in a specified way, or at a specified time or place 3 in sequence 4 every

lye (li) *n.* strong alkaline substance

ly'ing *v.* prp. of LIE

ly'ing-in' *a.*, *n.* (of or for) childbirth

lymph (limf) *n.* clear, yellowish body fluid —**lym·phat'ic** *a.*

lym'pho·cyte' (-sīt') *n.* leukocyte producing antibodies

lynch (linch) *v.* kill by mob action, without lawful trial, as by hanging

lynx (links) *n.* North American wildcat

ly·on·naise (lī'ə nāz') *a.* made with fried, sliced onions

lyre (līr) *n.* ancient instrument like a small harp

lyr'ic (lir'-) *a.* **1** suitable for singing **2** expressing the poet's emotions —*n.* **1** lyric poem **2** *pl.* words of a song

lyr'i·cal *a.* **1** lyric **2** very enthusiastic, etc. —**lyr'i·cal·ly** *adv.*

M

m *abbrev.* **1** meter(s) **2** mile(s)

M *abbrev.* **1** male **2** Monsieur

ma *n.* [Inf.] mother

MA *abbrev.* **1** Massachusetts **2** Master of Arts: also **M.A.**

ma'am *n.* [Inf.] madam

ma·ca'bre (-käb'rə, -käb') *a.* grim and horrible

mac·ad'am *n.* **1** small broken stones, used to make some roads **2** such a road

mac·a·ro'ni *n.* tubes of flour paste, cooked for food

mac·a·roon' *n.* cookie made with almonds or coconut

ma·caw' *n.* large parrot

mace *n.* **1** heavy, spiked club **2** official's staff **3** spice made from ground nutmeg shell —[M-] *trademark* combined tear gas and nerve gas

mac'er·ate' (mas'-) *v.* soften by soaking

ma·che'te (-shet'ē) *n.* large, heavy knife

Mach'i·a·vel'li·an (mak'-, mäk'-) *a.* crafty, deceitful, etc.

mach'i·na'tion (mak'-) *n.* wily or evil scheme

ma·chine' (-shēn') *n.* **1** device with moving parts, for doing work **2** group in control of a political party —*a.* of or done by machines —*v.* to shape, etc. by machinery

machine gun *n.* gun firing a stream of bullets

ma·chin'er·y *n.* **1** machines **2** working parts

ma·chin'ist *n.* one who makes or operates machines

ma·chis'mo (-chēz'-) *n.* macho quality

Mach number (mäk) *n.* number that is the ratio of airspeed to the speed of sound

ma'cho *a.* overly virile, domineering, etc.

mack'er·el *n.* edible fish of N Atlantic

mack'i·naw' (coat) *n.* short, heavy coat, often plaid

mack'in·tosh' *n.* raincoat of rubberized cloth

mac·ra·mé' (-mā') *n.* coarse thread or cord knotted in designs

macro- *pref.* large

mac'ro·bi·ot'ics *n.* diet involving whole grains, etc. —**mac'ro·bi·ot'ic** *a.*

mac'ro·cosm' *n.* universe

ma'cron (-krən) *n.* pronunciation mark (¯)

mad *a.* **mad'der**, **mad'dest** **1** insane **2** frantic **3** foolish **4** angry —**mad'ly** *adv.* —**mad'ness** *n.*

mad'am *n.*, *pl.* **mes·dames** (mā däm') polite title for a woman

ma·dame (mə däm') *n.*, *pl.* **mes·dames'** (mā däm') married woman: Fr. for *Mrs.*

mad'cap' *a.* reckless; wild

mad'den *v.* make mad —**mad'den·ing** *a.*

mad'der *n.* **1** vine with berries **2** red dye made from its root

made *v.* pt. & pp. of MAKE

ma·de·moi·selle (mad'ə mə zel') *n.* unmarried woman: Fr. for *Miss*

made'-to-or'der *a.* made to customer's specifications

made'-up' *a.* **1** invented; false **2** with cosmetics applied

mad'house' *n.* **1** insane asylum **2** place of turmoil

mad'man' *n.*, *pl.* **-men'** insane person

Ma·don'na *n.* picture or statue of the Virgin Mary

ma·dras (-drəs) *n.* cotton cloth, usually striped or plaid

mad'ri·gal *n.* part song for small group

mael'strom (māl'-) *n.* **1** violent whirlpool **2** confused state

maes'tro (mīs'-) *n.* great composer or conductor

Ma'fi·a *n.* secret, criminal society

Ma'fi·o'so *n.*, *pl.* **-si** [*also* m-] member of the Mafia

mag'a·zine' (-zēn') *n.* **1** periodical publication **2** storage place, as for military supplies **3** supply chamber, as in a rifle

ma·gen'ta *n.* purplish red

mag'got *n.* wormlike larva —**mag'got·y** *a.*

Ma·gi (mā'jī') *pl.n.* wise men in the

Bible

mag'ic n. **1** use of charms, spells, etc. **2** sleight of hand —a. of or as if by magic: also **mag'i·cal** —**mag'i·cal·ly** adv.

magic bullet n. remedy, spec. for a disease

ma·gi'cian (-jish'ən) n. one who does magic

mag'is·te'ri·al (maj'-) a. authoritative

mag'is·trate' (maj'-) n. official with limited judicial powers —**mag'is·tra·cy** n.

mag'ma n. molten rock

mag·nan'i·mous a. generous in overlooking injury —**mag'na·nim'i·ty** n.

mag'nate' n. influential person in business

mag·ne'sia (-zhə) n. white powder (magnesium oxide) used as a laxative

mag·ne'si·um (-zē əm) n. light, silvery metal, a chemical element

mag'net n. piece of iron, steel, etc. that attracts iron or steel

magnetic tape n. thin plastic tape magnetized for recording

mag'net·ism' n. **1** properties of magnets **2** personal charm —**mag·net'ic** a.

mag'net·ize' v. **1** make a magnet of **2** to charm

mag·ne'to n., pl. **-tos** small electric generator

mag·ne·tom'e·ter n. device for measuring magnetic forces

mag·nif'i·cent a. grand and stately; splendid —**mag·nif'i·cence** n.

mag'ni·fy' v. **-fied', -fy'ing 1** increase the apparent size of, as with a lens **2** exaggerate —**mag'ni·fi·ca'tion** n. —**mag'ni·fi'er** n.

mag'ni·tude' n. greatness of size, extent, or importance

mag·no'li·a n. tree with large, fragrant flowers

mag'pie' n. noisy bird of the crow family

Mag'yar' n. person or language of Hungary

ma·ha·ra'jah, ma·ha·ra'ja n. in India, a prince, formerly the ruler of a native state —**ma·ha·ra'ni, ma·ha·ra'nee** n.fem.

ma·hat'ma (-hät'-, -hät'-) n. in India, a wise and holy person

mah'-jongg', mah'jong' n. Chinese game played with small tiles

ma·hog'a·ny n. reddish-brown wood of a tropical tree

ma·hout' (-hout') n. in India, an elephant driver

maid n. **1** young unmarried woman **2** woman or girl servant

maid'en n. [Now Rare] young unmarried woman —a. **1** of or for a maiden **2** unmarried **3** first; earliest —**maid'en·hood'** n. —**maid'en·ly** a.

maid'en·hair' n. delicate fern

mail n. **1** letters, etc. sent by postal service **2** postal system **3** e-mail **4** armor made of metal mesh —a. of mail —v. send by mail —**mail'box'** n. —**mail'man'** n., pl. **-men'**

mail carrier n. one who carries and delivers mail

maim v. cripple; disable

main a. chief; leading; principal —n. **1** chief pipe in a system **2** [Poet.] ocean —**in the main** mostly —**with might and main** with all one's strength —**main'ly** adv.

main'frame' n. large computer connected to several terminals

main'land' n. main part of a continent

main'spring' n. chief spring in a clock, etc.

main'stay' n. main support

main'stream' n. prevailing trend

main·tain' v. **1** keep up; carry on **2** keep in working condition **3** declare; assert **4** support

main'te·nance n. **1** a maintaining **2** means of support

maî·tre d'hô·tel (me trə dô tel') n. [Fr.] supervisor of waiters: also [Inf.] **maî·tre d'** (mât'ər dē')

maize (māz) n. [Br.] corn

Maj abbrev. Major

maj'es·ty n. **1** grandeur; dignity **2** [M-] title for a sovereign —**ma·jes'tic** a. —**ma·jes'ti·cal·ly** adv.

ma·jol'i·ca n. Italian glazed pottery

ma'jor a. **1** greater in size, rank, etc. **2** Mus. semitone higher than the minor —n. **1** military officer above a captain **2** main field of study —v. specialize (in a subject)

ma'jor-do'mo n. man in charge of a great house

ma'jor·ette' n. girl who leads a marching band

major general n. officer above brigadier general

ma·jor'i·ty n. **1** more than half **2** full legal age

make v. **made, mak'ing 1** bring into being; build, create, etc. **2** cause to be **3** amount to; equal **4** acquire; earn **5** cause success of **6** execute, do, etc. **7** force; compel **8** [Inf.] get a place on (a team) —n. **1** act of making **2** style or build —**make away with** steal —

make believe pretend —make out 1 see 2 succeed —make over change —make up 1 put together 2 invent 3 compensate 4 stop quarreling —mak'er n.

make'-be·lieve' n. pretense —a. pretended

make'shift' a., n. (as) a temporary substitute

make'up', make'-up' n. 1 way a thing is put together 2 cosmetics

mal- pref. bad or badly

mal·ad·just'ed a. badly adjusted, as to one's environment —mal·ad·just'ment n.

mal·a·droit' a. clumsy

mal'a·dy n., pl. -dies illness

ma·laise' (-lāz') n. vague feeling of illness

mal'a·mute' (-myo͞ot') n. breed of sled dog used by Eskimos

mal'a·prop'ism' n. ridiculous misuse of words

ma·lar'i·a (-ler'-) n. disease with chills and fever, carried by mosquitoes

ma·lar'key, ma·lar'ky n. [Sl.] nonsensical talk

mal'a·thi'on' (-thī'än') n. kind of organic insecticide

mal'con·tent' a., n. dissatisfied (person)

male a. 1 of the sex that fertilizes the ovum 2 of, like, or for men or boys —n. a male person, animal, or plant

mal'e·dic'tion n. a curse

mal'e·fac'tor n. evildoer —mal'e·fac'tion n.

ma·lev'o·lent a. wishing harm to others —ma·lev'o·lence n.

mal·fea'sance (-fē'zəns) n. wrongdoing in public office

mal·for·ma'tion n. faulty formation —mal·formed' a.

mal·func'tion v. fail to work as it should —n. failure

mal'ice (-is) n. ill will; wish to harm another —ma·li'cious (-lish'əs) a.

ma·lign' (-līn') v. speak evil of —a. evil; harmful

ma·lig'nan·cy n. 1 malignant quality 2 pl. -cies malignant tumor

ma·lig'nant a. 1 evil 2 very harmful 3 likely to cause death

ma·lin'ger n. feign illness to escape duty —ma·lin'ger·er n.

mall n. 1 shaded public walk 2 enclosed shopping center

mal'lard n. duck with green head

mal'le·a·ble a. that can be hammered or pressed into shape —mal'le·a·bil'i·ty n.

mal'let n. hammer with a wooden head

mal'low n. family of plants including the hollyhock

mal·nour'ished a. improperly nourished

mal·nu·tri'tion n. faulty diet; lack of nourishment

mal·oc·clu'sion n. faulty position of teeth so that they do not meet properly

mal·o'dor·ous a. having a bad smell; stinking

mal·prac'tice n. improper practice, as by a doctor

malt n. barley, etc. soaked and dried for use in brewing and distilling

malt'ed (milk) n. drink of milk, malt, ice cream, etc.

mal·treat' v. to abuse —mal·treat'ment n.

ma'ma, mam'ma n. mother: child's word

mam'mal n. any vertebrate the female of which suckles its offspring

mam'ma·ry a. of milk-secreting glands

mam·mog'ra·phy n. X-ray technique to detect breast tumors

mam'mon n. riches as an object of greed

mam'moth n. huge, extinct elephant —a. huge

man n., pl. men 1 human being; person 2 adult male person 3 human race —v. manned, man'ning furnish with a labor force for work, etc. —to a man with no exception

man'a·cle n., v. handcuff

man'age v. 1 to control or guide 2 have charge of 3 succeed in doing —man'age·ment n. —man'ag·er n.

man'aged care n. medical system using certain doctors and hospitals to reduce costs

man·a·ge'ri·al (-jir'ē-) a. of a manager

ma·ña·na (mä nyä'nä) adv., n. [Sp.] tomorrow

man'a·tee' n. large mammal living in tropical waters

man'da·rin n. 1 high official of former Chinese empire 2 [M-] main Chinese dialect

man'date' n. 1 an order; command 2 the will of voters as expressed in elections 3 [Hist.] commission given to a nation to administer a region 4 [Hist.] such a region —man'da·to'ry a.

man'di·ble n. lower jaw

man'do·lin' n. musical instrument

with 8 to 12 strings

man'drake' *n.* root formerly used in medicine

man'drill (-dril) *n.* large African baboon

mane *n.* long hair on the neck of a horse, lion, etc.

man'-eat'er *n.* animal that eats human flesh

ma·neu'ver (-nōō'-) *n.* **1** a planned movement of troops, warships, etc. **2** scheme —*v.* **1** perform maneuvers **2** get, etc. by some scheme

man'ga·nese' *n.* grayish metal in alloys, a chemical element

mange (mānj) *n.* parasitic skin disease of animals —**man'gy** *a.*, **-gi·er, -gi·est**

man·ger (mān'jər) *n.* box from which livestock feed

man'gle *v.* **1** mutilate by hacking, etc. **2** botch **3** press in a mangle —*n.* machine with rollers for ironing

man'go *n., pl.* **-goes** or **-gos** yellow-red tropical fruit

man'grove *n.* tropical tree with branches that send down roots to form trunks

man'han'dle *v.* handle roughly

man'hole' *n.* hole for entering a sewer, etc.

man'hood' *n.* **1** time of being a man **2** manly qualities

man'-hour' *n.* one hour of work by one person

man'hunt' *n.* hunt for a fugitive

ma'ni·a *n.* **1** wild insanity **2** obsession

ma'ni·ac' *n.* violently insane person —**ma·ni'a·cal** (-nī'-) *a.*

man'ic *a.* [Inf.] very excited, elated, etc. —**man'ic·al·ly** *adv.*

man'ic-de·pres'sive *a.* bipolar

man'i·cure' *v., n.* trim, polish, etc. (of) the fingernails —**man'i·cur'ist** *n.*

man'i·fest' *a.* obvious —*v.* reveal; show —*n.* list of a ship's cargo —**man'i·fes·ta'tion** *n.*

man'i·fes'to *n., pl.* **-toes** or **-tos** public declaration

man'i·fold' *a.* of many parts, sorts, etc. —*n.* pipe with several outlets, as for carrying exhaust from an engine

man'i·kin *n.* mannequin

Ma·nil'a (paper) *n.* tan paper

ma·nip'u·late' *v.* **1** handle skillfully **2** manage unfairly or dishonestly —**ma·nip'u·la'tion** *n.* —**ma·nip'u·la'tive** *a.*

man'kind' *n.* **1** human race **2** all human males

man'ly *a.* **-li·er, -li·est** of, like, or fit for a man —**man'li·ness** *n.*

man'-made' *a.* synthetic; artificial

man'na *n.* thing provided as by a miracle

man'ne·quin (-kin) *n.* model of the human body, as for displaying clothes

man'ner *n.* **1** way; style **2** habit **3** *pl.* (polite) ways of behaving **4** kind; sort

man'ner·ism' *n.* (affected) peculiarity of manner

man'ner·ly *a.* polite

man'nish *a.* masculine

man'-of-war' *n., pl.* **men'-of-war'** warship

man'or *n.* large estate

man'pow'er *n.* **1** human physical strength **2** the collective strength of a nation, etc.

man'sard (roof) (-särd) *n.* roof with two slopes on each side

manse *n.* residence of a minister or clergyman

man'sion *n.* large, imposing house

man'slaugh'ter *n.* unintentional killing of a person

man'tel *n.* frame around or shelf above a fireplace

man·til'la *n.* woman's scarf for the hair and shoulders

man'tis *n.* large, predatory insect

man'tle *n.* **1** sleeveless cloak **2** thing that covers —*v.* to cover

man'-to-man' *a.* frank

man'tra *n.* Hindu hymn or text chanted as a prayer

man'u·al *a.* made or done by hand —*n.* handbook

man'u·fac'ture *n.* making of goods by machinery —*v.* make, esp. by machinery —**man'u·fac'tur·er** *n.*

man'u·mit' *v.* **-mit'ted, -mit'ting** free from slavery —**man'u·mis'sion** *n.*

ma·nure' *n.* animal waste as fertilizer

man'u·script' *n.* written or typed book, article, etc.

man'y *a.* **more, most** numerous —*pl.n., pron.* large number (of persons or things)

map *n.* drawing of the features of a region, the earth's surface, the sky, etc. —*v.* **mapped, map'ping 1** to make a map of **2** to plan

ma'ple *n.* **1** large shade tree **2** its hard wood **3** flavor of syrup or sugar made from its sap

mar *v.* **marred, mar'ring** damage; spoil

Mar *abbrev.* March

mar'a·bou' (-bōō') *n.* (plumes of) a stork of Africa or India

ma·ra'ca *n.* pebble-filled musical rattle

mar'a·schi'no cherry (-shē'-, -skē'-) *n.* cherry in a syrup

mar'a·thon' *n.* **1** foot race of about 26

miles **2** any endurance contest

ma·raud′er n. raider

mar′ble n. hard limestone, white or colored —a. of or like marble

mar′ble·ize′ v. make look like marble

march v. **1** walk with regular steps **2** advance steadily —n. **1** a marching **2** progress **3** distance marched **4** marching music

March n. third month

mar′chion·ess (-shən is) n. wife or widow of a marquess

Mar′di Gras′ (-grä′) n. last day before Lent begins

mare n. female horse, mule, donkey, etc.

mar′ga·rine (-jə rin) n. a spread like butter, of vegetable oil, etc.

mar′gin n. **1** edge, as the blank border of a page **2** extra amount in reserve —**mar′gin·al** a.

mar′gin·al·ize′ v. exclude or ignore

ma·ri·a·chi (mär′ē ä′chē) n. **1** (member of) a strolling band in Mexico **2** its music

mar′i·gold′ n. plant with yellow or orange flowers

mar′i·jua′na, mar·i·hua′na (-wä′nə) n. narcotic from the hemp plant

ma·rim′ba n. kind of xylophone

ma·ri′na (-rē′-) n. small harbor with docks

mar′i·nade′ n. spiced pickling solution for meat, fish, etc.

mar′i·nate′ v. soak in a marinade

ma·rine′ a. of or in the sea, ships, etc. —n. [M-] member of the Marine Corps

mar′i·ner n. sailor

mar′i·o·nette′ n. puppet on strings

mar′i·tal a. of marriage

mar′i·time′ a. **1** on or near the sea **2** of sailing

mar′jo·ram n. plant used for flavoring

mark n. **1** spot, scratch, etc. **2** sign or label **3** sign of quality **4** grade **5** impression **6** target; goal —v. **1** put a mark on **2** show by a mark **3** characterize **4** listen to **5** rate —**mark′er** n.

mark′down′ n. price decrease

marked a. **1** having a mark **2** noticeable

mar′ket n. **1** place where goods are sold **2** store selling food **3** buying and selling **4** demand for (goods, etc.) —v. buy or sell —**mar′ket·a·ble** a. —**mar′ket·er** n.

mar′ket·place′ n. **1** an outdoor market **2** the world of business

market share n. company's percentage of the total sales of some commodity

mark′ing n. arrangement of marks, as on fur

marks′man n., pl. **-men** one who shoots well —**marks′man·ship′** n.

mark′up′ n. price increase

mar′lin n. large, slender deep-sea fish

mar′ma·lade′ n. preserve of oranges or other fruits

mar′mo·set′ (-zet′, -set′) n. small monkey

mar′mot n. thick-bodied burrowing squirrel, as the woodchuck

ma·roon′ n., a. dark brownish red —v. put (a person) ashore in a lonely place

mar·quee′ (-kē′) n. rooflike projection over an entrance

mar′quess (-kwis) n. **1** British nobleman above an earl **2** marquis

mar′que·try (-kə-) n. fancy inlaid work in furniture, etc.

mar′quis (-kwis) n. nobleman above an earl or count —**mar·quise′** (-kēz′) n.fem.

mar·qui·sette′ (-ki zet′) n. thin, netlike cloth

mar′riage (-ij) n. **1** married life **2** wedding —**mar′riage·a·ble** a.

mar′row n. **1** soft core inside bones **2** central part

mar′ry v. **-ried, -ry·ing 1** join as husband and wife **2** take as spouse **3** unite

Mars n. fourth planet from the sun

marsh n. swamp —**marsh′y** a., **-i·er, -i·est**

mar′shal n. **1** highest ranking officer in some armies **2** federal officer like a sheriff **3** head of a police or fire department —v. arrange (troops, ideas, etc.)

marsh′mal′low n. soft, white, spongy candy

mar·su′pi·al n. animal with a pouch for carrying its young

mart n. market

mar′ten n. **1** weasellike animal **2** its fur; sable

mar′tial (-shəl) a. **1** of war **2** military **3** warlike

martial art n. system of self-defense from Japan, etc.: usually used in pl.

martial law n. military rule over civilians

Mar′tian (-shən) n., a. (alien) from Mars

mar′tin n. kind of swallow

mar′ti·net′ n. strict disciplinarian

mar·ti′ni n., pl. **-nis** a cocktail

mar′tyr (-tər) n. one who suffers or dies for his or her beliefs —v. treat as a martyr —**mar′tyr·dom** n.

mar·vel n. wonderful thing —v. be amazed —**mar'vel·ous** a.

Marx'ism' n. doctrine of socialism —**Marx'ist** a., n.

mar'zi·pan' n. candy of ground almonds, sugar, egg white, etc.

masc abbrev. masculine

mas·car'a (-kar'ə) n. cosmetic to color eyelashes

mas'cot' n. animal or thing kept for good luck

mas'cu·line (-kyoo lin) a. of or like men or boys; male —**mas'cu·lin'i·ty** n.

ma'ser (-zər) n. device that emits radiation in a narrow beam

mash n. 1 grain crushed in water for brewing, etc. 2 moist feed mixture for horses, etc. —v. crush into a soft mass

mask n., v. cover to conceal or protect the face

mas'o·chist (-ə kist) n. one who gets pleasure from being hurt —**mas'o·chism'** n. —**mas'o·chis'tic** a.

ma'son n. construction worker in brick, stone, etc.

ma'son·ry n. mason's work

masque (mask) n. 1 MASQUERADE (n. 1) 2 elaborate verse play

mas'quer·ade' (-kər-) n. 1 party with masks and costumes 2 disguise —v. be disguised

mass n. 1 quantity of matter 2 large number 3 size 4 [M—] R.C.Ch. service of the Eucharist —v. gather into a mass —**the masses** the common people

mas'sa·cre (-kər) n. indiscriminate killing —v. kill in large numbers

mas·sage (mə säzh') n. rubbing and kneading of part of the body —v. give a massage to

mas·seur' (mə sur') n. a man whose work is massaging —**mas·seuse'** (-sooz') n.fem.

mas'sive a. big and heavy

mass media pl.n. newspapers, magazines, radio, and TV

mass number n. number of neutrons and protons in the nucleus of an atom

mass production n. production of goods in large quantities

mast n. tall, upright pole on a ship, supporting sails

mas·tec'to·my n., pl. **-mies** surgical removal of a breast

mas'ter n. 1 man who rules others or is in control 2 expert —a. 1 of a master 2 chief; main —v. 1 control 2 become expert in

mas'ter·ful a. 1 domineering 2

expert; skillful: also **mas'ter·ly**

master key n. key that opens every one of a set of locks

mas'ter·mind' v., n. (be) an ingenious planner of (a project)

Master of Arts (or **Science**, etc.) n. advanced college degree

master of ceremonies n. person who presides at an entertainment, banquet, etc.

mas'ter·piece' n. thing made or done with expert skill

mas'ter·y n. 1 control 2 victory 3 expert skill

mast'head' n. part of a newspaper, etc. giving address, publisher, etc.

mas'ti·cate' v. chew up —**mas'ti·ca'tion** n.

mas'tiff n. big, strong dog

mas'to·don' n. extinct animal like the elephant

mas'toid' a., n. (of) a bony projection behind the ear

mas'tur·bate' v. manipulate genitals for sexual pleasure —**mas'tur·ba'tion** n.

mat n. 1 flat piece, as of woven straw, for protecting a floor, etc. 2 thick tangled mass 3 border around a picture —v. **mat'ted, mat'ting** 1 cover with a mat 2 weave or tangle together

mat'a·dor' n. bullfighter

match n. 1 short sliver with a tip that catches fire by friction 2 person or thing like another 3 contest 4 marriage —v. 1 be equal (to) 2 put in opposition 3 get an equivalent to

match'less a. without equal

match'mak'er n. arranger of marriages

mate n. 1 companion, fellow worker, etc. 2 one of a pair 3 husband or wife 4 lower officer on a ship —v. join, as in marriage

ma·te'ri·al n. 1 what a thing is made of 2 fabric —a. 1 physical 2 essential

ma·te'ri·al·ism' n. 1 concern with physical things only 2 belief that everything has a physical cause —**ma·te'ri·al·is'tic** a.

ma·te'ri·al·ize' v. give or take material form

ma·te'ri·al·ly adv. 1 physically 2 considerably

ma·te'ri·el' n. military supplies

ma·ter'nal a. of, like, or from a mother

ma·ter'ni·ty n. motherhood —a. for pregnant women

math n. [Inf.] mathematics

math abbrev. mathematics

math·e·mat·ics *n.* science dealing with quantities and forms, their relationships, etc. —**math·e·mat·i·cal** *a.* —**math·e·ma·ti·cian** (-tish'ən) *n.*

mat·i·nee, mat·i·née (mat''n ā') *n.* afternoon performance of a play, etc.

mat'ins *pl.n.* morning prayer

ma'tri·arch' (-ärk') *n.* woman who rules her family or tribe —**ma'tri·ar'chal** *a.*

mat'ri·cide' *n.* **1** the killing of one's mother **2** a person who does this —**mat'ri·ci'dal** *a.*

ma·tric'u·late' *v.* enroll, as in college —**ma·tric'u·la'tion** *n.*

mat'ri·mo'ny *n.* marriage —**mat'ri·mo'ni·al** *a.*

ma'trix *n.,* pl. **-tri·ces'** (-trə sēz') or **-trix·es** that within which a thing develops

ma'tron *n.* **1** wife or widow **2** woman manager of domestic affairs, as of a prison

matte (mat) *n.* dull surface or finish —*a.* not glossy

mat'ted *a.* closely tangled

mat'ter *n.* **1** physical substance of a thing **2** thing or affair **3** occasion **4** importance **5** trouble —*v.* be of importance —**as a matter of fact** really —**no matter** regardless of

mat'ter-of-fact' *a.* sticking to facts; literal

mat'ting *n.* woven straw, etc. used as for mats

mat'tock (-ək) *n.* kind of pickax

mat'tress *n.* casing filled with cotton, springs, etc., for use on a bed

ma·ture' (-toor', -choor') *a.* **1** fully grown, developed, etc. **2** due for payment —*v.* make or become mature —**ma·tu'ri·ty** *n.*

mat·zo (mät'sə) *n.,* pl. **-zot, -zoth** (-sōt), or **-zos** (piece of) unleavened bread eaten at Passover

maud'lin *a.* foolishly sentimental

maul *v.* handle roughly

maun'der *v.* talk or move aimlessly

mau'so·le'um *n.* large, imposing tomb **2** building with burial vaults above the ground

mauve (mōv, môv) *n.* pale purple

mav'er·ick *n.* **1** lost, unbranded calf **2** [Inf.] political independent

maw *n.* throat, gullet, jaws, etc.

mawk'ish *a.* sentimental in a sickening way

max *abbrev.* maximum

maxi- *pref.* maximum, very large, very long

max·il'la *n.* upper jawbone

max'im *n.* concise saying that is a rule of conduct

max'i·mize' *v.* to increase to the maximum

max'i·mum *a., n.* greatest possible (quantity or degree)

may *v.* pt. **might** auxiliary verb showing: **1** possibility **2** permission

May *n.* fifth month

may'be *adv.* possibly; perhaps

may'flow'er *n.* early spring flower

may'fly' *n.,* pl. **-flies'** delicate winged insect

may'hem *n.* **1** crime of maiming a person intentionally **2** deliberate destruction or violence

may'o *n.* [Inf.] mayonnaise

may'on·naise' (-nāz') *n.* dressing or sauce of emulsified egg yolks and oil

may'or *n.* head of a city —**may'or·al** *a.* —**may'or·al·ty** *n.*

maze *n.* confusing network of paths

maz·el tov (mä'zəl tōv') *n., int.* [Heb.] good luck: used for congratulations

ma·zur'ka *n.* lively Polish dance

MB *abbrev.* **1** Manitoba **2** megabyte(s)

MC *abbrev.* Master of Ceremonies

MD *abbrev.* **1** Doctor of Medicine: also **M.D.** **2** Maryland

mdse *abbrev.* merchandise

me *pron.* objective case of I

ME *abbrev.* Maine

mead *n.* alcoholic liquor made from honey

mead·ow (med'ō) *n.* level field of grass

mea'ger *a.* **1** poor; scanty **2** thin Br. sp. **mea'gre**

meal *n.* **1** any of the times for eating **2** food served then **3** coarsely ground grain, etc. —**meal'y** *a.,* **-i·er, -i·est**

meal'y-mouthed' *a.* not sincere

mean *v.* meant (ment), mean'ing **1** intend **2** intend to express **3** signify **4** have a certain importance —*a.* **1** low in quality or rank **2** poor or shabby **3** ignoble, petty, unkind, etc. **4** stingy **5** halfway between extremes —*n.* **1** middle point **2** pl. [sing. or pl. v.] that by which a thing is gotten or done **3** pl. wealth —**by all** (or **no**) **means** certainly (not) —**by means of** by using —**mean'ly** *adv.* —**mean'ness** *n.*

me·an'der *v.* **1** wind back and forth **2** wander idly

mean'ing *n.* what is meant, signified, etc. —**mean'ing·ful** *a.* —**mean'ing·less** *a.*

mean'time' *adv., n.* (during) the intervening time: also **mean'while'**

mea'sles (-zəlz) *n.* contagious disease,

usually of children

mea'sly *a.* **-sli-er, -sli-est** [Inf.] slight, worthless, etc.

meas'ure (mezh'ər) *v.* **1** find out the extent, dimensions, etc. of **2** mark off (a certain amount) **3** be a thing for measuring **4** be of specified dimensions —*n.* **1** extent, dimensions, capacity, etc. **2** unit of measuring **3** system of measuring **4** instrument for measuring **5** definite quantity **6** course of action **7** a law **8** notes and rests between two bars on a musical staff —**meas'ur-a-ble** *a.* —**meas'ure-less** *a.* —**meas'ure-ment** *n.*

meat *n.* **1** flesh of animals used as food **2** edible part **3** essence —**meat'y** *a.,* **-i-er, -i-est**

meat'-and-po-ta'toes *a.* [Inf.] basic

Mec'ca *n.* [*often* m-] place attracting many visitors

me-chan'ic (-kan'-) *n.* worker who repairs machines

me-chan'i-cal *a.* **1** of or run by machinery **2** machinelike —**me-chan'i-cal-ly** *adv.*

mechanical engineering *n.* engineering dealing with machinery

me-chan'ics *n.* **1** science of motion and the effect of forces on bodies **2** knowledge of machinery **3** technical aspect

mech'a-nism' (mek'-) *n.* **1** working parts of a machine **2** system of interrelated parts

mech'a-nize' *v.* **1** to make mechanical **2** to equip with machinery, trucks, etc. —**mech'a-ni-za'tion** *n.*

med *abbrev.* **1** medical **2** medicine **3** medium

med'al *n.* flat, inscribed piece of metal given as an honor or reward

med'al-ist *n.* one who wins a medal

me-dal'lion (-yən) *n.* **1** large medal **2** a round, medallike design

med'dle *v.* interfere in another's affairs —**med'dler** *n.* —**med'dle-some** *a.*

me'di-a *n.* alt. pl. of MEDIUM —**the media** [*sing.* v.] all the means of providing news, etc., as newspapers, radio, and TV

me'di-an *n., a.* (number, point, etc.) in the middle

me'di-ate' *v.* (try to) settle (differences) between two parties —**me'di-a'tion** *n.* —**me'di-a'tor** *n.*

med'ic *n.* [Inf.] **1** doctor **2** member of an army medical corps

Med'ic-aid' *n.* [*also* m-] state and federal program helping the poor pay

medical bills

med'i-cal *a.* having to do with the practice or study of medicine —**med'i-cal-ly** *adv.*

Med'i-care' *n.* [*also* m-] federal program helping senior citizens pay medical bills

med'i-cate' *v.* treat with medicine —**med'i-ca'tion** *n.*

me-dic'i-nal (-dis'-) *a.* that is or is used as a medicine

med'i-cine (-sən) *n.* **1** science of treating and preventing disease **2** drug, etc. used in treating disease

medicine man *n.* among North American Indians, etc., a man believed to have healing powers

me'di-e'val (mē'dē-, med'ē-) *a.* of or like the Middle Ages

me'di-o'cre (-kər) *a.* ordinary; average —**me'di-oc'ri-ty** (äk'-) *n., pl.* **-ties**

med'i-tate' *v.* **1** think deeply **2** plan —**med'i-ta'tion** *n.* —**med'i-ta'tive** *a.*

Med'i-ter-ra'ne-an *a.* of the Mediterranean Sea or nearby regions

me'di-um *a.* intermediate in amount, degree, etc. —*n., pl.* **-di'ums** or **-di'a** **1** medium thing or state **2** thing through which a force acts **3** means, agency, etc. **4** means of reaching the public **5** surrounding substance

med'ley *n.* **1** mixture of unlike things **2** musical piece made up of several songs

meek *a.* **1** patient and mild **2** easily imposed on

meer'schaum (-shəm) *n.* (tobacco pipe made of) white, claylike mineral

meet *v.* **met, meet'ing 1** come upon **2** be present at the arrival of **3** be introduced (to) **4** come into contact (with) **5** come together **6** satisfy **7** pay —*n.* a meeting —*a.* [Now Rare] suitable

meet'ing *n.* **1** a coming together **2** a gathering of people **3** junction

mega- *pref.* **1** large, great **2** a million of

meg'a-byte' *n.* million bytes

meg'a-hertz' *n., pl.* **-hertz'** million hertz

meg'a-lo-ma'ni-a *n.* delusion of grandeur or power

meg'a-lop'o-lis *n.* vast urban area

meg'a-phone' *n.* funnel-shaped device to increase the volume of the voice

meg'a-ton' *n.* explosive force of a millions tons of TNT

mel'an-cho'li-a (-kō'-) *n.* extreme depression

mel'an-chol'y (-käl'ē) *n.* sadness and

mental depression —a. sad or saddening —**mel'an·chol'ic** a.

mé·lange (mā lönzh') n. mixture or medley

mel'a·nin n. dark pigment of skin, etc.

mel·a·no'ma n., pl. **-mas** or **-ma·ta** skin tumor

Mel'ba toast n. very crisp, thinly sliced toast

meld v. to blend; merge

me·lee, mê·lée (mā'lā') n. brawling group fight

mel'io·rate' (mēl'yə-) v. make or become better

mel·lif'lu·ous a. sounding smooth and sweet: also **mel·lif'lu·ent** —**mel·lif'lu·ence** n.

mel'low a. full, rich, gentle, etc.; not harsh —v. make or become mellow

me·lo'di·ous a. 1 having melody 2 pleasing to hear

mel'o·dra'ma n. sensational, extravagant drama —**mel'o·dra·mat'ic** a.

mel'o·dra·mat'ics pl.n. melodramatic behavior

mel'o·dy n., pl. **-dies** a tune, song, etc. —**me·lod'ic** a. —**me·lod'i·cal·ly** adv.

mel'on n. large, juicy, many-seeded fruit

melt v. 1 change from solid to liquid, as by heat 2 dissolve 3 disappear or merge gradually 4 soften

melt'down' n. dangerous melting of fuel in a nuclear reactor

melting pot n. place in which various immigrants are assimilated

mem'ber n. 1 distinct part, as an arm 2 person in an organization

mem'ber·ship' n. 1 state of being a member 2 all the members

mem'brane' n. thin tissue lining an organ or part —**mem'bra·nous** a.

me·men'to n., pl. **-tos** or **-toes** souvenir

mem'o n., pl. **-os** memorandum

mem'oirs' (-wärz') pl.n. account of one's past life

mem·o·ra·bil'i·a pl.n. things saved or collected, as mementos

mem'o·ra·ble a. worth remembering

mem'o·ran'dum n., pl. **-dums** or **-da** short note to remind one of something

me·mo'ri·al n. anything meant to help people remember a person or event

Memorial Day n. U.S. holiday in May honoring soldiers, etc. killed in wars

me·mo'ri·al·ize' v. commemorate

mem'o·rize' v. to commit to memory

mem'o·ry n., pl. **-ries** 1 power or act of remembering 2 something or everything remembered 3 commemoration 4 device in a computer, etc. that stores information

men n. pl. of MAN

men'ace n. a threat —v. to threaten

mé·nage, me·nage (mā näzh') n. household

me·nag'er·ie (-naj'-, -nazh'-) n. collection of wild animals

mend v. 1 repair 2 make or become better —n. mended place —**on the mend** improving —**mend'er** n.

men·da'cious a. lying or false —**men·da'cious·ly** adv. —**men·dac'i·ty** n.

men'di·cant n. beggar

men'folk pl.n. [Inf.] men

me'ni·al a. servile —n. servant

men·in·gi'tis (-jīt'is) n. inflammation of membranes of the brain and spinal cord

me·nis'cus n. curved upper surface of a column of liquid

men'o·pause' n. permanent cessation of menstruation

me·no'rah n. Jewish candelabrum

men'ses' (-sēz') pl.n. monthly menstrual flow

men'stru·ate' v. have a flow of blood monthly from the uterus —**men'stru·al** a. —**men'stru·a'tion** n.

men·su·ra'tion (-sha-) n. a measuring

-ment suf. 1 result of a means for 3 act of 4 state of being

men'tal a. 1 of or in the mind 2 for the mentally ill —**men'tal·ly** adv.

men·tal'i·ty n. mental power, attitude, outlook, etc.

mental retardation n. congenital below-average intelligence

men'thol' (-thôl') n. derivative of oil of peppermint —**men'tho·lat·ed** a.

men'tion n. brief reference —v. refer to briefly

men'tor n. wise advisor

men'u n., pl. **-us** list of choices, as of meals or computer functions

me·ow', me·ou' v., n. (make) the sound of a cat

mer'can·tile (-tíl', -til) a. of merchants or trade

mer'ce·nar'y a. thinking mainly of money —n., pl. **-ies** soldier paid to serve in a foreign army

mer'cer·ized' a. designating cotton treated for greater strength

mer'chan·dise' (-dīz'; n.: also -dīs') v. buy and sell —n. things bought and sold

mer'chant n. 1 dealer in goods 2 storekeeper

mer'chant·man n., pl. **-men** ship used in commerce

merchant marine n. ships of a nation used in trade

mer·ci (mer sē′) int. [Fr.] thank you

mer·cu′ri·al (-kyoor′ē-) a. changeable, fickle, etc.

mer′cu·ry n. **1** silvery liquid metal, a chemical element **2** [M-] planet nearest the sun

mer′cy n., pl. **-cies 1** kindness; forbearance **2** power to forgive —**at the mercy of** in the power of —**mer′ci·ful** a. —**mer′ci·less** a.

mercy killing n. euthanasia

mere a. **mer′est** no more than; only

mere′ly adv. only; simply

mer·e·tri′cious (-trish′əs) a. flashy; tawdry

mer·gan′ser n. large duck

merge v. unite or combine so as to lose identity

merg′er n. a merging; spec., a combining of companies, corporations, etc.

me·rid′i·an n. **1** circle through the earth's poles **2** line of longitude

me·ringue′ (-raŋ′) n. egg whites and sugar beaten stiff

me·ri′no (-rē′-) n., pl. **-nos** (silky wool of) a hardy breed of sheep

mer′it n. **1** worth; value **2** something deserving praise —v. deserve

mer·i·to′ri·ous a. deserving reward, praise, etc.

mer′maid′ n. imaginary creature like a woman with a fish's tail

mer′ry a. **-ri·er, -ri·est** full of fun —**make merry** have fun —**mer′ri·ly** adv. —**mer′ri·ment** n.

mer′ry-go-round′ n. revolving platform with seats, as in an amusement park

mer′ry·mak′ing n. fun; festivity —**mer′ry·mak·er** n.

me′sa (mā′-) n. high plateau with steep sides

mes·cal′ n. cactus plant: source of mescaline

mes′ca·line (-lin) n. psychedelic drug

mes·dames (mā däm′) n′. pl. of MADAM, MADAME, or MRS.

mesh n. (cord or wire of) a net or network —v. **1** to entangle **2** interlock

mes′mer·ize (mez′-) v. hypnotize —**mes′mer·ism′** n. —**mes′mer·ist** n.

mes·quite′, mes·quit′ (-kēt′) n. spiny shrub

mess n. **1** a jumble **2** trouble **3** untidy condition **4** communal meal as in the army —v. **1** make dirty, jumbled, etc. **2** meddle —**mess′i·ness** n. —**mess′y** a., **-i·er, -i·est**

mes′sage n. **1** a communication **2** important idea

mes′sen·ger n. one who carries a message, etc.

mess hall n. room or building where soldiers, etc. regularly eat

Mes·si′ah (-sī′-) n. **1** Judaism expected deliverer of the Jews **2** Christianity Jesus —n. [m-] expected savior or liberator —**Mes′si·an′ic** a.

Messrs. (mes′ərz) abbrev. pl. of MR.

mes·ti′zo (-tē′-) n., pl. **-zos** or **-zoes** one of American Indian and Spanish parentage

met v. pt. & pp. of MEET

met abbrev. metropolitan

me·tab′o·lism′ n. changing of food by organisms into energy, cells, etc. —**met·a·bol′ic** a. —**me·tab′o·lize′** v.

met·a·car′pus n., pl. **-pi** (-pī) part of the hand between the wrist and the fingers —**met·a·car′pal** a.

met′al n. **1** shiny, usually solid, chemical element **2** an alloy —a. of metal —**me·tal′lic** a.

met′al·lur·gy n. science of refining metals —**met·al·lur′gi·cal** a. —**met′al·lur′gist** n.

met·a·mor′pho·sis n., pl. **-ses** (-sēz) **1** change in form **2** any change —**met·a·mor′phic** a.

met′a·phor′ n. word for one thing used for another —**met·a·phor′ic, met·a·phor′i·cal** a.

met·a·phys′ics n. philosophy that deals with first principles —**met·a·phys′i·cal** a.

me·tas′ta·sis n., pl. **-ses** (-sēz) spread of disease to an unrelated body part, as through the bloodstream —**me·tas′ta·size′** v. —**met·a·stat′ic** a.

met′a·tar′sus n., pl. **-si** (-sī) part of the foot between the ankle and the toes —**met·a·tar′sal** a.

mete (mēt) v. allot; distribute

me′te·or n. fiery meteoroid traveling through the earth's atmosphere —**me′te·or′ic** a.

me′te·or·ite′ n. part of a meteor fallen to earth

me′te·or·oid′ n. small, solid body traveling through outer space at high speed

me′te·or·ol′o·gy n. science of weather, climate, etc. —**me′te·or·o·log′i·cal** a. —**me′te·or·ol′o·gist** n.

me′ter n. **1** rhythmic pattern in verse **2** metric unit of length (39.37 inches) **3** device to measure flow of fluid

meth′a·done′ (-dōn′) n. synthetic narcotic used in treating heroin addicts

meth′ane′ n. colorless, odorless flammable gas

meth'a·nol' (-nôl') *n.* toxic liquid used as fuel, antifreeze, etc.

me·thinks' *v.* [Ar.] it seems to me

meth'od *n.* 1 way; process 2 system

me·thod'i·cal *a.* orderly

meth'od·ol'o·gy *n., pl.* **-gies** system of methods

me·tic'u·lous *a.* very careful about details; fussy

mé·tier' (mā tyā') *n.* work one is suited for

me'tre *n.* Br. sp. of METER

met'ric *a.* 1 of the meter (unit of length) 2 of the metric system 3 metrical

met'ri·cal *a.* 1 of or composed in meter or verse 2 used in measurement — **met'ri·cal·ly** *adv.*

met'ri·ca'tion *n.* a changing to the metric system

metric system *n.* decimal system of weights and measures

met'ro *a.* metropolitan

met'ro·nome' *n.* device that beats time at a set rate

me·trop'o·lis *n.* main or important city —**met'ro·pol'i·tan** *a.*

met'tle *n.* spirit; courage —**on one's mettle** ready to do one's best

met'tle·some *a.* spirited; ardent

mew *v., n.* meow

mewl *v.* to cry weakly, like a baby

mews *pl.n.* [*sing. v.*] [Br.] stables or carriage houses in a court or alley

Mex *abbrev.* 1 Mexican 2 Mexico

Mex'i·can *n., a.* (native) of Mexico

mez'za·nine' (-nēn') *n.* 1 low story built between two main stories 2 first few rows of balcony seats

mez'zo-so·pra'no (met'sō-) *n.* voice or singer between soprano and contralto

MFA, M.F.A. *abbrev.* Master of Fine Arts

mfg *abbrev.* manufacturing

mfr *abbrev.* manufacture(r)

mg *abbrev.* milligram(s)

mgr *abbrev.* manager

MHz *abbrev.* megahertz

mi *abbrev.* mile(s)

MI *abbrev.* Michigan

mi·as'ma (mī az'-) *n.* vapor from swamps, once believed poisonous

mi'ca (mī'-) *n.* mineral that forms into thin, heat-resistant layers

mice *n.* pl. of MOUSE

micro- *pref.* small

mi'crobe' *n.* minute organism, esp. one causing disease

mi'cro·chip' *n.* CHIP (*n.* 5)

mi'cro·com·put'er *n.* small computer

for home use, etc.

mi'cro·cosm' *n.* universe on a small scale

mi'cro·fiche' (-fēsh') *n.* small sheet of microfilm with a number of greatly reduced pages

mi'cro·film' *n.* film on which documents, etc. are recorded in a reduced size

mi·crom'e·ter *n.* instrument for measuring very small distances, angles, etc.

mi'cron' *n.* one millionth of a meter

mi'cro·or'gan·ism' *n.* microscopic organism

mi'cro·phone' *n.* instrument for changing sound waves into electric impulses

mi'cro·proc'es·sor *n.* microchip used as CPU

mi'cro·scope' *n.* device for magnifying minute objects

mi'cro·scop'ic *a.* so small as to be invisible except through a microscope

mi'cro·wave' *n.* radio or infrared wave used in radar, cooking, etc. —*v., a.* (to cook) using microwaves

mid, 'mid *prep.* [Poet.] amid

mid- *pref.* middle of

mid'air' *n.* point not in contact with any surface

mid'course' *a.* happening in the middle of a trip, etc.

mid'day' *n., a.* noon

mid'dle *a.* halfway between two points, etc. —*n.* middle point or part

mid'dle-aged' *a.* in the time between youth and old age

Middle Ages *pl.n.* a period in Europe, A.D. 476 to about A.D. 1450

middle class *n.* social group between the very wealthy and the lower-paid workers —**mid'dle-class'** *a.*

Middle East area from Afghanistan to Libya, including Iran, Iraq, Israel, Saudi Arabia, etc. —**Middle Eastern** *a.*

mid'dle·man' *n., pl.* **-men'** 1 one who buys from a producer and sells at wholesale or retail 2 go-between

mid'dle-of-the-road' *a.* avoiding extremes

middle school *n.* school including grades five or six through eight

mid'dling *a.* of middle size, quality, etc.

mid'dy *n., pl.* **-dies** loose blouse with a sailor collar

Mid·east' Middle East —**Mid·east'ern** *a.*

midge *n.* small gnat

midg′et n. very small person —adv. miniature

mid′land a., n. (of) the middle region of a country

mid′night′ n. twelve o'clock at night

mid′riff n. part of body between abdomen and chest

mid′ship′man n., pl. **-men** naval officer trainee

midst n. the middle —prep. [Poet.] in the midst of

mid′sum′mer n. time of summer solstice, about June 21

mid′town′ a., n. (in or of) the center of a city

mid′way′ a., adv. in the middle; halfway —n. location for side shows, etc. at a fair

mid′wife′ n., pl. **-wives′** woman who helps others in childbirth —mid′wife′ry n.

mid′win′ter n. time of winter solstice, about December 22

mien (mēn) n. one's manner

miff v. [Inf.] offend

might v. pt. of MAY: might is also used to show less possibility or permission than may —n. strength; force

might′y a. **-i-er, -i-est** powerful, great, etc. —adv. [Inf.] very —might′i-ly adv.

mi′graine′ n. periodic headache

mi′grate′ v. move from one place or region to another, as with the change in season —mi′grant a., n. —mi·gra′tion n. —mi′gra·to′ry a.

mi·ka′do (mi kä′-) n., pl. **-dos** emperor of Japan: title no longer used

mike n. [Inf.] microphone

mil n. .001 of an inch **2** [Sl.] million

mil abbrev. military

milch a. kept for milking

mild a. **1** gentle **2** weak in taste — **mild′ly** adv. —**mild′ness** n.

mil′dew′ n. whitish fungus on plants, damp cloth, etc.

mile n. unit of measure, 5,280 feet

mile′age n. **1** total miles traveled **2** allowance per mile for traveling expenses

mil′er n. contestant in mile races

mile′stone′ n. significant event

mi·lieu (mēl yu′) n. surroundings; environment

mil′i·tant a. ready to fight —mil′i·tan·cy n. —mil′i·tant·ly adv.

mil′i·ta·rism′ n. **1** warlike spirit **2** maintenance of strong armed forces —mil′i·ta·rist n. —mil′i·ta·ris′tic a.

mil′i·tar′y a. of soldiers, war, etc. —n. the army: used with the

mil′i·tate′ v. work (for or against)

mi·li′tia (-lish′ə) n. citizens trained for emergency military service

milk n. **1** white liquid secreted by female mammals for suckling their young **2** any liquid like this —v. draw milk from (a mammal) —milk′i·ness n. —milk′y a., -i-er, -i-est

milk′man′ n., pl. **-men′** man who sells or delivers milk

milk of magnesia n. milky-white liquid used as laxative, etc.

milk′shake′ n. frothy drink of milk, flavoring, and ice cream

milk′sop′ n. sissy

milk′weed′ n. plant with a milky juice

mill n. **1** place for grinding grain into flour **2** machine for grinding **3** factory **4** $\frac{1}{10}$ of a cent —v. **1** grind by or in a mill **2** move (around or about) confusedly —mill′er n.

mill′age n. taxation in mills per dollar of valuation

mil·len′ni·um n., pl. **-ni·ums** or **-ni·a 1** period of 1,000 years **2** Theol. 1,000-year period of Christ's future reign on earth **3** period of peace and joy

mil′let n. cereal grass

milli- pref. $\frac{1}{1000}$ part of

mil′li·gram′ n. one thousandth of a gram

mil′li·li′ter n. one thousandth of a liter

mil′li·me′ter n. one thousandth of a meter

mil′li·ner n. one who makes or sells women's hats

mil′li·ner·y n. **1** women's hats **2** business of a milliner

mil′lion n., a. a thousand thousands — **mil′lionth** a., n.

mil′lion·aire′ n. one having at least a million dollars, pounds, etc.

mill′stone′ n. **1** flat, round stone used for grinding grain, etc. **2** heavy burden

mill′wright′ n. worker who installs or repairs heavy machinery

milt n. fish sperm

mime n., v. clown or mimic

mim′e·o·graph′ n. machine for making stenciled copies of typewritten matter —v. make (such copies) of

mim′ic v. **-icked, -ick·ing 1** imitate, as to ridicule **2** to copy closely —n. one who mimics —mim′ic·ry n.

mi·mo′sa n. flowering tree or shrub of warm climates

min abbrev. **1** minimum **2** minute(s)

min′a·ret′ n. mosque tower

mince v. **1** cut into small pieces **2** lessen the force of (words) **3** act with affected daintiness —**minc′ing** *a.*

mince′meat′ *n.* pie filling of raisins, spices, suet, etc., and sometimes meat

mind *n.* **1** center of thought, feeling, etc. **2** intellect **3** sanity **4** memory **5** opinion, intention, etc. —*v.* **1** observe **2** obey **3** take care of **4** be careful about **5** object to —**bear** (or **keep**) **in mind** remember —**have in mind** intend —**make up one's mind** reach a decision —**put in mind** remind

mind′-bog′gling *a.* [Sl.] amazing, perplexing, etc.: also **mind′-blow′ing**

mind′ful *a.* aware (*of*)

mind′s eye *n.* the imagination

mine *pron.* that or those belonging to me —*n.* **1** large excavation from which to extract ores, coal, etc. **2** great source of supply **3** explosive device hidden under land or water —*v.* **1** dig (ores, etc.) from a mine **2** hide mines in —**min′er** *n.*

min′er·al *n.* ore, rock, etc. found naturally in the earth —*a.* of or containing minerals

mineral jelly *n.* petrolatum

min′er·al′o·gy (-äl′-) *n.* science of minerals —**min′er·al′o·gist** *n.*

mineral oil *n.* oil from petroleum used as a laxative

mineral water *n.* water having mineral salts or gases

mi·ne·stro·ne (min′ə strō′nē) *n.* thick vegetable soup

min′gle *v.* **1** mix or become mixed **2** join with others

mini- *pref.* miniature; very small; very short

min′i·a·ture *n.* tiny copy, model, painting, etc. —*a.* minute

min′i·a·tur·ize′ *v.* make in a small, compact form

min′i·bike′ *n.* small motorcycle

min′i·bus′ *n.* very small bus

min′i·cam′ *n.* portable TV camera

min′i·com·put′er *n.* computer between a mainframe and a microcomputer in size, power, etc.

min′i·mize′ *v.* reduce to or estimate at a minimum

min′i·mum *n.* **1** smallest quantity possible **2** lowest degree reached —*a.* lowest or least possible —**min′i·mal** *a.* —**min′i·mal·ize′** *v.*

min′ing *n.* work of removing ores, etc. from a mine

min′ion (-yən) *n.* faithful or servile follower

min′is·cule′ *a.* minuscule: disputed spelling

min′i·skirt′ *n.* skirt ending well above the knee

min′is·ter *n.* **1** head of a governmental department **2** diplomatic official below an ambassador **3** one who conducts religious services —*v.* give help; serve —**min′is·te′ri·al** (-tir′ē-) *a.* —**min′is·tra′tion** *n.*

min′is·try *n., pl.* **-tries 1** office of a member of the clergy **2** clergy **3** government department headed by a minister **4** a ministering

min′i·van′ *n.* small passenger van with windows all around and rear seats

mink *n.* **1** weasellike mammal **2** its valuable fur

min′now (-ō) *n.* very small freshwater fish

mi′nor *a.* **1** lesser in size, rank, etc. **2** *Mus.* semitone lower than the major —*n.* **1** one under full legal age **2** secondary field of study

mi·nor′i·ty *n., pl.* **-ties 1** smaller part or number **2** racial, religious, etc. group that differs from the larger group **3** time of being a minor

min′strel *n.* **1** traveling singer of the Middle Ages **2** entertainer in an old-style U.S. variety show

mint *n.* **1** place where the government makes coins **2** large amount **3** aromatic plant with leaves used for flavoring **4** candy with such flavoring —*v.* coin (money)

min′u·end′ *n.* number from which another is to be subtracted

min′u·et′ *n.* slow, stately 17th-c. dance

mi′nus *prep.* less —*a.* **1** negative **2** less than —*n.* sign (−) showing subtraction or negative quantity

mi·nus′cule′ (or min′ə skyōōl′) *a.* tiny; minute

min·ute (min′it) *n.* **1** sixtieth part of an hour **2** moment **3** *pl.* official record

mi·nute (mī nōōt′, -nyōōt′) *a.* **1** very small **2** exact —**mi·nute′ly** *adv.*

mi·nu·ti·ae (mi nōō′shə, -nyōō′-) *pl.n.* small or unimportant details

minx *n.* bold or saucy girl

mir′a·cle *n.* **1** event that seems to contradict scientific laws **2** remarkable thing —**mi·rac′u·lous** *a.*

mi·rage (mi räzh′) *n.* optical illusion caused by refraction of light

mire *n.* deep mud or slush —*v.* stick or cause to get stuck as in mire

mir′ror *n.* coated glass that reflects images

mirth *n.* gaiety with laughter —**mirth′ful** *a.*

mis- *pref.* wrong(ly); bad(ly)

mis'ad·ven'ture *n.* bad luck

mis'an·thrope' *n.* one who hates all people: also **mis'an'thro·pist** —**mis'an·throp'ic** *a.* —**mis·an'thro·py** *n.*

mis'ap·ply' *v.* **-plied', -ply'ing** apply badly or wrongly

mis'ap·pre·hend' *v.* understand wrongly —**mis'ap·pre·hen'sion** *n.*

mis'ap·pro'pri·ate' *v.* use (funds, etc.) dishonestly —**mis'ap·pro'pri·a'tion** *n.*

mis'be·got'ten *a.* illegitimate

mis'be·have' *v.* behave badly —**mis'be·hav'ior** *n.*

misc *abbrev.* miscellaneous

mis·cal'cu·late' *v.* misjudge —**mis'cal·cu·la'tion** *n.*

mis·car'ry *v.* **1** go wrong **2** lose a fetus before full term —**mis·car'riage** (*or* mis'kar'ij) *n.*

mis·cast' *v.* cast (an actor) in an unsuitable role

mis'ce·ge·na'tion (-sej ə nā'-) *n.* interracial marriage or sex

mis'cel·la'ne·ous *a.* of various kinds; mixed

mis'cel·la'ny *n., pl.* **-nies** collection of various kinds

mis·chance' *n.* bad luck

mis'chief (-chif) *n.* **1** harm or damage **2** prank **3** teasing —**mis'chie·vous** (-chə vəs) *a.*

mis'ci·ble (mis'ə-) *a.* that can be mixed

mis'con·ceive' *v.* misunderstand —**mis'con·cep'tion** *n.*

mis·con'duct *n.* wrong conduct

mis'con·strue' *v.* misinterpret

mis'cre·ant *n.* villain

mis·deal' (*n.:* mis'dēl') *v.* **-dealt', -deal'ing** deal (playing cards) wrongly —*n.* wrong deal

mis·deed' *n.* crime, sin, etc.

mis'de·mean'or *n. Law* minor offense

mis'di·rect' *v.* direct wrongly or badly —**mis'di·rec'tion** *n.*

mi'ser (-zər) *n.* stingy hoarder of money —**mi'ser·ly** *a.*

mis'er·a·ble (miz'-) *a.* **1** in misery **2** causing misery **3** bad, poor, etc. —**mis'er·a·bly** *adv.*

mis'er·y *n., pl.* **-ies** pain, poverty, distress, etc.

mis·file' *v.* file in the wrong place

mis·fire' *v.* fail to go off

mis·fit' *v.* fit improperly —*n.* **1** improper fit **2** maladjusted person

mis·for'tune *n.* **1** bad luck; trouble **2** mishap, calamity, etc.

mis·giv'ings *pl.n.* feelings of fear, doubt, etc.

mis·gov'ern *v.* govern badly —**mis·gov'ern·ment** *n.*

mis·guide' *v.* mislead

mis·han'dle *v.* abuse or mismanage

mis'hap' *n.* unlucky accident

mish'mash' *n.* a jumble

mis'in·form' *v.* give wrong information to —**mis'in·for·ma'tion** *n.*

mis·in·ter'pret *v.* to interpret wrongly —**mis·in·ter·pre·ta'tion** *n.*

mis·judge' *v.* judge wrongly

mis·la'bel *v.* label wrongly

mis·lay' *v.* **-laid', -lay'ing** put in a place later forgotten

mis·lead' *v.* **1** lead astray **2** deceive

mis·man'age *v.* manage badly

mis·match' (*n.:* mis'mach') *v.* match badly —*n.* bad match

mis·name' *v.* give an inappropriate name to

mis·no'mer *n.* name wrongly applied

mi·sog'y·nist (-säj'ə-) *n.* one who hates women —**mi·sog'y·ny** *n.*

mis·place' *v.* put in a wrong place

mis·play' (*n.:* mis'plā') *v.* play wrongly —*n.* wrong play

mis'print' *n.* printing error

mis·pri'sion (-prizh'ən) *n.* misconduct by a public official

mis'pro·nounce' *v.* pronounce wrongly

mis·quote' *v.* quote incorrectly

mis·read' (-rēd') *v.* **-read'** (-red'), **-read'ing** read wrongly and so misunderstand

mis'rep·re·sent' *v.* give a false idea of

mis·rule' *n.* bad government

miss *v.* **1** fail to hit, meet, do, see, hear, etc. **2** avoid **3** note or feel the loss of —*n.* **1** failure to hit, etc. **2** unmarried woman **3** [M-] title used before her name

mis'sal (-əl) *n. R.C.Ch.* prayer book for Mass for the year

mis·shap'en (-shāp'-) *a.* badly shaped; deformed

mis'sile (-əl) *n.* object to be thrown or shot

miss'ing *a.* absent; lost

mis'sion *n.* **1** special task or duty **2** group or station of missionaries **3** diplomatic delegation

mis'sion·ar'y *n., pl.* **-ies** person sent by a church to make converts, esp. abroad

mis'sive *n.* letter or note

mis·spell' *v.* spell incorrectly

mis·spend' *v.* **-spent', -spend'ing** spend improperly or wastefully

mis·state' *v.* state wrongly —**mis·state'ment** *n.*

mis'step' *n.* **1** wrong step **2** mistake in conduct

mist *n.* mass of water vapor; thin fog

mis·take' v. -took', -tak'en, -tak'ing understand or perceive wrongly —n. error

mis·tak'en a. wrong or incorrect

mis'ter n. title before a man's name: usually *Mr.*

mis'tle·toe' (mis'əl-) n. evergreen plant with white berries

mis·treat' v. treat badly —**mis·treat' ment** n.

mis'tress n. **1** woman in charge or control **2** woman in a sexual relationship with, and supported by, a man without marriage

mis·tri'al n. *Law* trial made void by an error, etc.

mis·trust' n. lack of trust —v. have no trust in; doubt

mist'y a. -i·er, -i·est **1** like or covered with mist **2** vague or indistinct

mis'un·der·stand' v. -stood', -stand' ing fail to understand correctly

mis'un·der·stand'ing n. **1** failure to understand **2** a quarrel

mis·use' (-yōōz'; n.: -yōōs') v. **1** use improperly **2** abuse —n. incorrect use

mite n. **1** tiny, parasitic arachnid **2** tiny amount

mi'ter n. **1** tall cap of a bishop **2** corner joint of two pieces cut at an angle

mit'i·gate' v. make or become less severe —**mit'i·ga'tion** n.

mi·to'sis n. process of cell division

mitt n. **1** padded baseball glove **2** [Sl.] hand

mit'ten n. glove without separate finger pouches

mix v. **1** stir or come together in a single mass **2** make by mixing ingredients **3** combine —n. mixture, or its ingredients —**mix up 1** confuse **2** involve (*in*)

mixed a. **1** blended **2** of different kinds **3** of both sexes

mix'er n. **1** person or thing that mixes **2** (dance) party

mix'ture n. **1** a mixing **2** something made by mixing

mix'-up' n. confusion —**mixed'-up'** a.

mkt *abbrev.* market

ml *abbrev.* milliliter(s)

Mlle *abbrev.* Mademoiselle

mm *abbrev.* millimeter(s)

Mme *abbrev.* Madame

MN *abbrev.* Minnesota

mne·mon'ic (nē-) a. of or helping the memory

mo *abbrev.* month

MO *abbrev.* **1** Missouri **2** mode of operation **3** money order

moan n. low, mournful sound —v. **1**

utter (with) a moan **2** complain

moat n. deep, usually water-filled ditch around a castle

mob n. crowd, esp. a disorderly one — v. **mobbed**, **mob'bing** crowd around and attack

mo'bile (-bəl, -bil'; n.: -bēl') a. readily movable or adaptable —n. suspended abstract sculpture with parts that move —**mo·bil'i·ty** n.

mobile home n. large trailer outfitted as a home

mo'bi·lize' v. make or become ready, as for war —**mo'bi·li·za'tion** n.

mob'ster n. [Sl.] gangster

moc'ca·sin n. heelless slipper of soft leather

mo'cha (-kə) n. kind of coffee

mock v. **1** ridicule **2** mimic and deride —a. false; imitation

mock'er·y n., pl. -ies **1** a mocking **2** poor imitation

mock'ing·bird' n. small bird with imitative call

mock'-up' n. full-scale model

mode n. **1** way of acting or doing **2** fashion

mod'el n. **1** small copy of something **2** one to be imitated **3** style **4** one who poses for an artist **5** one who displays clothes by wearing them —a. serving as a model —v. **1** plan or form **2** work as a model

mo'dem n. device converting computer data for transmission, as by telephone

mod'er·ate (-ət; v.: -āt') a. avoiding extremes —n. moderate person —v. **1** to make or become moderate **2** preside over (a debate, etc.) —**mod'er·ate·ly** adv. —**mod·er·a'tion** n. —**mod'er·a'tor** n.

mod'ern a. of recent times; up-to-date —n. modern person —**mod'ern·ize'** v.

mod'ern·ism' n. style of art, etc. of early 20th c. —**mod'ern·ist** n., a. —**mod'ern·is'tic** a.

mod'est a. **1** not conceited **2** decent **3** moderate —**mod'es·ty** n.

mod'i·cum n. small amount

mod'i·fy' v. -fied', -fy'ing change or limit slightly —**mod'i·fi·ca'tion** n. —**mod'i·fi'er** n.

mod'ish (mōd'-) a. fashionable

mod'u·late' (mäj'ə-) v. adjust or vary, as the pitch of the voice —**mod'u·la'tion** n.

mod'ule (mäj'ōōl') n. detachable section with a special function —**mod'u·lar** a.

mo'gul n. important person

mo'hair' *n.* goat-hair fabric

Mo·ham'med·an *a.*, *n.* Muslim —**Mo·ham'med·an·ism'** *n.*

moi'e·ty *n.*, *pl.* **-ties** 1 half 2 indefinite part

moire (mwär) *n.* fabric with a wavy pattern: also **moi·ré** (mwä rā')

moist *a.* slightly wet

mois'ten (-ən) *v.* make moist

mois'ture *n.* slight wetness

mois'tur·ize' *v.* make moist —**mois'tur·iz'er** *n.*

mo'lar *n.* back tooth

mo·las'ses *n.* dark syrup left after sugar is refined

mold *n.* 1 hollow form in which a thing is shaped 2 thing shaped 3 furry, fungous growth —*v.* 1 make in a mold 2 shape 3 become moldy

mold'er *v.* crumble

mold'ing *n.* decorative strip of wood, etc.

mold'y *a.* **-i·er, -i·est** of or covered with MOLD (*n.* 3)

mole *n.* 1 small, dark, congenital spot on the skin 2 small, burrowing animal

mol'e·cule' *n.* smallest particle of a substance that can exist alone —**mo·lec'u·lar** *a.*

mole'hill' *n.* small ridge made by a burrowing mole

mole'skin' *n.* strong cotton fabric with soft nap

mo·lest' *v.* 1 to trouble or harm 2 make improper sexual advances to —**mo'les·ta'tion** *n.*

mol'li·fy' *v.* **-fied', -fy'ing** soothe; make calm

mol'lusk, mol'lusc *n.* invertebrate with soft body in a shell

mol'ly·cod'dle *v.* pamper

molt *v.* shed hair, skin, etc. before getting a new growth

mol'ten (mōl'-) *a.* melted by heat

mom *n.* [Inf.] mother

mo'ment *n.* brief period of, or certain point in, time

mo'men·tar'i·ly *adv.* 1 for a short time 2 at any moment

mo'men·tar'y *a.* lasting for only a moment

mo·men'tous *a.* very important

mo·men'tum *n.* impetus of a moving object

mom'my *n.*, *pl.* **-mies** mother: child's word

Mon *abbrev.* Monday

mon'arch (-ərk, -ärk') *n.* hereditary ruler —**mo·nar'chi·cal** (-när'ki-) *a.*

mon'ar·chy *n.*, *pl.* **-ies** government by

a monarch —**mon'ar·chist** *n.*

mon'as·ter·y *n.*, *pl.* **-ies** residence for monks

mo·nas'tic *a.* of or like monks or nuns —*n.* monk or nun —**mo·nas'ti·cism'** *n.*

mon·au'ral (-ôr'əl) *a.* of sound reproduction using one channel

Mon'day *n.* second day of the week

mon'e·tar'y *a.* 1 of currency 2 of money

mon'ey *n.*, *pl.* **-eys** or **-ies** 1 metal coins or paper notes used as the legal medium of exchange 2 wealth —**make money** to become wealthy

mon'ey·bags' *n.* [Inf.] rich person

mon'eyed (-ēd) *a.* rich

mon'ey·mak'er *n.* something financially profitable —**mon'ey·mak'ing** *a.*, *n.*

money market fund *n.* mutual fund with short-term investments

money order *n.* order for payment of money issued at a bank, etc.

Mon'gol·oid' *n.*, *a.* (member) of the large human group including most of the Asian people

mon'goose' *n.*, *pl.* **-goos'es** ferretlike animal of Africa, Asia, etc.

mon'grel *n.*, *a.* (animal or plant) of mixed breed

mon'i·ker *n.* [Sl.] name or nickname

mon'i·tor *n.* 1 student who helps keep order, etc. 2 TV receiver or computer video screen —*v.* watch, or check on

monk *n.* man who is a member of an ascetic religious order

mon'key *n.*, *pl.* **-keys** small, long-tailed primate —*v.* [Inf.] meddle; trifle

monkey business *n.* [Inf.] foolishness, deceit, etc.

mon'key·shines' *pl.n.* [Inf.] playful tricks or pranks

monkey wrench *n.* wrench with an adjustable jaw

monk's cloth *n.* heavy cloth with a weave like that of a basket

mon·o *n.* mononucleosis

mono- *pref.* one; alone

mon'o·chrome' *n.*, *a.* (photograph, etc.) in one color

mon'o·cle *n.* eyeglass for one eye

mon'o·cot'y·le'don (-kät'ə lē'-) *n.* plant with one seed leaf: also **mon'o·cot'**

mo·nog'a·my *n.* practice of being married to only one person at a time —**mo·nog'a·mous** *a.*

mon'o·gram' *n.* initials of a name, made into a design

mon'o·graph' *n.* book or article on a

single subject

mon'o·lith' *n.* pillar, statue, etc. made of a single, large stone —**mon'o·lith'ic** *a.*

mon'o·logue', mon'o·log' *n.* **1** long speech **2** skit for one actor only

mon'o·ma'ni·a *n.* excessive interest in one thing —**mon'o·ma'ni·ac'** *n., a.*

mon'o·nu'cle·o'sis *n.* acute viral disease with fever, tiredness, etc.

mo·nop'o·ly *n., pl.* **-lies 1** total control of something, esp. of a product or service **2** company having this —**mo·nop'o·lis'tic** *a.* —**mo·nop'o·lize'** *v.*

mon'o·rail' *n.* railway with cars on a single rail

mon'o·so'di·um glu'ta·mate' *n.* kind of food seasoning

mon'o·syl'la·ble *n.* word of one syllable —**mon'o·syl·lab'ic** *a.*

mon'o·the·ism' *n.* belief that there is only one God —**mon'o·the·is'tic** *a.*

mon'o·tone' *n.* sameness of tone, pitch, color, etc.

mo·not'o·ny *n.* **1** lack of variety **2** tiresome sameness —**mo·not'o·nous** *a.*

mon·ox'ide' *n.* oxide with one oxygen atom per molecule

mon·sieur (mə syur') *n., pl.* **mes·sieurs** (mes'ərz) gentleman: Fr. for *Mr.*

Mon·si'gnor (-sēn'yər) *n. R.C.Ch.* title of high rank

mon·soon' *n.* wind bringing rainy season to S Asia

mon'ster *n.* huge or very abnormal plant or animal

mon'strous *a.* **1** horrible **2** huge **3** very abnormal —**mon·stros'i·ty** *n., pl.* **-ties**

mon·tage' (-täzh') *n.* superimposing of images, as in a movie

Mon·tes·so'ri method *n.* method of teaching children, encouraging self-education

month *n.* any of the 12 divisions of the year

month'ly *a.* happening, appearing, etc. every month —*n., pl.* **-lies** monthly periodical —*adv.* every month

mon'u·ment *n.* **1** memorial statue, building, etc. **2** famous work

mon'u·men'tal *a.* **1** serving as a monument **2** important **3** colossal

moo *v., n.* (make) the vocal sound of a cow

mooch [Sl.] *v.* get by begging, etc. —**mooch'er** *n.*

mood *n.* **1** state of mind **2** verb form

to express a fact, wish, or order

mood'y *adv.* **-i·er, -i·est 1** changing in mood **2** gloomy

moon *n.* **1** body that revolves around a planet **2** [*often* **M-**] body that revolves around the earth —*v.* look dreamy or listless

moon'beam' *n.* ray of moonlight

moon'light' *n.* light of the moon —*v.* hold a second job along with a main one

moon'lit' *a.* lighted by the moon

moon'scape' *n.* surface of the moon

moon'shine' *n.* **1** moonlight **2** [Inf.] whiskey made illegally —**moon'shin'er** *n.*

moon'shot' *n.* launching of a spacecraft to the moon

moon'stone' *n.* milky-white gem

moon'struck' *a.* romantically dreamy

moon'walk' *n.* a walking about on the moon's surface

Moor *n.* Muslim of NW Africa —**Moor'ish** *a.*

moor *n.* [Br.] open wasteland —*v.* to secure by cables, ropes, etc.

moor'ings *pl.n.* cables, or place, for mooring a ship

moose *n., pl.* **moose** largest animal of the deer family

moot *a.* debatable

mop *n.* rags, sponge, etc. on a stick, as for washing floors —*v.* **mopped, mop'ping** clean, as with a mop —**mop up** [Inf.] finish (a task)

mope *v.* be gloomy

mo'ped' *n.* bicycle with a small motor

mop'pet *n.* [Inf.] little child

mo·raine' *n.* heap of rocks, etc. left by a glacier

mor'al *a.* **1** of or dealing with right and wrong **2** good; virtuous **3** giving sympathy, but no active help —*n.* **1** moral lesson **2** *pl.* moral rules or standards —**mor'al·ly** *adv.*

mo·rale' (-ral') *n.* degree of courage, discipline, etc.

mo·ral'i·ty *n.* **1** moral quality **2** virtue

mor'al·ize' *v.* discuss moral questions —**mor'al·ist** *n.*

mo·rass' *n.* bog; swamp

mor'a·to'ri·um *n.* authorized delay or stopping of some activity

mo'ray (eel) *n.* voracious eel

mor'bid *a.* **1** diseased **2** gloomy or unwholesome —**mor·bid'i·ty** *n.*

mor'dant *a.* sarcastic

more *a., n.* **1** greater (in) amount or degree **2** (something) additional —*adv.* **1** to a greater degree **2** in addition —**more or less** somewhat

more·o'ver *adv.* besides

mo·res (môr'ēz', -āz') *pl.n.* customs with the force of law

morgue (môrg) *n.* place where bodies of accident victims, etc. are taken, as for identification

mor'i·bund' *a.* dying

morn *n.* [Poet.] morning

morn'ing *n.* first part of the day, till noon

morning glory *n.* vine with trumpet-shaped flowers

morning sickness *n.* nausea during pregnancy

mo·roc'co *n.* fine, soft leather made of goatskin

mo'ron' *n.* foolish or stupid person —**mo·ron'ic** *a.*

mo·rose' (-rōs') *a.* gloomy

mor'phine' (-fēn') *n.* opium-derived drug used to relieve pain

morph'ing *n.* computerized transforming of one video image into another —**morph** *v.*

mor·phol'o·gy *n.* form and structure, as in biology

mor'row *n.* [Ar.] the following day

Morse code *n.* [often **m- c-**] code of dots and dashes used in telegraphy

mor'sel *n.* bit, as of food

mor'tal *a.* **1** that must die **2** causing death **3** [Inf.] very great; extreme — *n.* human being —**mor'tal·ly** *adv.*

mor·tal'i·ty *n.* **1** a being mortal **2** death rate

mor'tar *n.* **1** bowl for pulverizing things with a pestle **2** small cannon **3** cement mixture used between bricks, etc.

mor'tar·board' *n.* **1** square board for carrying mortar **2** academic cap with square, flat top

mort·gage (môr'gij) *n.* deed pledging property as security for a debt —*v.* pledge (property) by a mortgage

mor·ti'cian (-tish'ən) *n.* funeral director

mor'ti·fy' *v.* **-fied'**, **-fy'ing 1** shame; humiliate **2** control by fasting, etc. — **mor'ti·fi·ca'tion** *n.*

mor·tise (môrt'is) *n.* hole cut for a tenon to fit in

mor'tu·ar'y (-chōō-) *n.*, *pl.* **-ies** place to keep dead bodies before burial

mo·sa'ic (-zā'-) *n.* design made of colored stones inlaid in mortar

mo'sey (-zē) *v.* [Sl.] amble along

Mos'lem *n.*, *a.* Muslim

mosque (mäsk) *n.* Muslim place of worship

mos·qui·to (mə skēt'ō) *n.*, *pl.* **-toes** or **-tos** small biting insect that sucks blood

moss *n.* tiny green plant growing in clusters on rocks, etc. —**moss'y** *a.*

moss'back' *n.* [Inf.] conservative person

most *a.* **1** greatest in amount or number **2** almost all —*n.* the greatest amount or number —*adv.* to the greatest degree —**make the most of** take full advantage of

most'ly *adv.* **1** mainly; chiefly **2** usually; generally

mote *n.* speck, as of dust

mo·tel' *n.* roadside hotel for motorists

moth *n.* four-winged insect like a butterfly

moth'ball' *n.* small ball of crystalline substance: its fumes repel moths

moth'er *n.* **1** female parent **2** [often **M-**] mother superior —*a.* **1** of or like a mother **2** native —*v.* be a mother to —**moth'er·hood'** *n.* —**moth'er·ly** *a.*

moth'er-in-law' *n.*, *pl.* **moth'ers-** mother of one's husband or wife

moth'er·land' *n.* one's native land

moth'er-of-pearl' *n.* hard, shiny lining of some shells

mother superior *n.* [often **M- S-**] woman head of a convent

mo·tif' (-tēf') *n.* a main theme of an artistic work

mo'tile (mōt'l) *a.* that can move —**mo·til'i·ty** *n.*

mo'tion *n.* **1** a moving; change of position **2** gesture **3** proposal made at a meeting —*v.* make, or direct by, gestures —**mo'tion·less** *a.*

motion picture *n.* a FILM (*n.* 3 & 4)

mo'ti·vate' *v.* provide with a motive — **mo'ti·va'tion** *n.* —**mo'ti·va'tor** *n.*

mo'tive *n.* reason for doing something —*a.* of motion

mot'ley *a.* of many different or clashing elements; varied

mo'to·cross' *n.* cross-country motorcycle race

mo'tor *n.* **1** machine using electricity to make something work **2** engine; esp., a gasoline engine —*a.* **1** of or run by a motor **2** of or for motor vehicles **3** producing motion **4** of muscular movements —*v.* to travel in an automobile —**mo'tor·ist** *n.*

mo'tor·bike' *n.* [Inf.] **1** bicycle with motor **2** light motorcycle

mo'tor·boat' *n.* boat propelled by a motor

mo'tor·cade' *n.* procession of cars

mo'tor·car' *n.* automobile

mo'tor·cy'cle *n.* two-wheeled, engine-powered vehicle

mo'tor·ize' v. equip with a motor or motor vehicles

motor vehicle n. car, truck, bus, etc.

mot'tle v. to blotch

mot'to n., pl. **-toes** or **-tos** maxim or phrase that shows one's ideals, etc.

moue (mōō) n. pout or grimace

mould (mōld) n., v. chiefly Br. sp. of MOLD —**mould'y** a., **-i·er, -i·est**

moult (mōlt) v. chiefly Br. sp. of MOLT

mound n. heap of earth, etc.

mount v. 1 climb; go up 2 get up on 3 increase in amount 4 fix on or in a mounting —n. 1 act of mounting 2 horse to ride 3 a support, setting, etc. 4 mountain

moun'tain n. very high rise of land on earth's surface

mountain bike n. sturdy bicycle for rough terrain

moun'tain·eer' n. 1 mountain dweller 2 mountain climber

mountain goat n. long-haired goatlike antelope of Rocky Mountains

mountain lion n. cougar

moun'tain·ous a. 1 full of mountains 2 very big

moun'te·bank' n. charlatan

mount'ed a. 1 on or in a mounting 2 on horseback

Mount'ie, Mount'y n., pl. **-ies** [Inf.] member of the Royal Canadian Mounted Police

mount'ing n. a backing, support, setting, etc.

mourn (môrn) v. feel or show grief or sorrow (for) —**mourn'er** n. —**mourn'ful** a.

mourn'ing n. 1 grief at a death 2 mourners' black clothes

mouse (mous) n., pl. **mice** 1 small rodent 2 timid person 3 hand-held device for controlling images on a computer screen —**mous'y, mous'ey** a., **-i·er, -i·est**

mousse (mōōs) n. 1 chilled dessert of egg, gelatin, etc. 2 aerosol foam for styling hair —v. to style (hair) with mousse

mous·tache' n. mustache

mouth (mouth; v.: mouth) n. 1 opening in the face for food 2 any opening —v. form (words) with the mouth soundlessly —**mouth'ful'** n.

mouth organ n. harmonica

mouth'piece' n. 1 part held in or near the mouth 2 spokesman for another

mouth'wash' n. liquid for rinsing the mouth

mouth'wa·ter·ing a. tasty

mouth'y a. **-i·er, -i·est** talkative

mou·ton (mōō'tän') n. lamb fur made to resemble beaver, etc.

move v. 1 change the place of 2 set or keep in motion 3 change one's residence 4 be active or take action 5 cause 6 stir emotionally 7 propose formally —n. 1 movement or action 2 Games one's turn —**mov'a·ble, move'a·ble** a., n. —**mov'er** n.

move'ment n. 1 a moving or way of moving 2 action toward a goal 3 moving parts of a clock, etc. 4 Mus. main division of a composition

mov'ie n. a FILM (n. 3 & 4) —**the movies** 1 film industry 2 a showing of a film

mow (mō) v. **mowed, mowed** or **mown, mow'ing** cut down (grass) — **mow down** kill or knock down — **mow'er** n.

mow (mou) n. heap of hay, esp. in a barn

moz·za·rel'la (mät'sə-) n. soft, white cheese with mild flavor

MP abbrev. 1 Member of Parliament 2 Military Police

mpg abbrev. miles per gallon

mph abbrev. miles per hour

Mr. abbrev. mister: used before a man's name

MRI n. medical imaging using radio waves

Mrs. abbrev. mistress: used before a married woman's name

MS abbrev. 1 manuscript 2 Master of Science: also **M.S.** 3 Mississippi 4 multiple sclerosis

Ms. (miz) abbrev. Miss or Mrs.

MSG abbrev. monosodium glutamate

MST abbrev. Mountain Standard Time

mt abbrev. mountain

Mt abbrev. 1 Mount 2 Mountain

MT abbrev. 1 Montana 2 Mountain Time

mtg abbrev. 1 meeting 2 mortgage: also **mtge**

much a. **more, most** great in quantity, degree, etc. —adv. 1 greatly 2 nearly —n. 1 great amount 2 something great

mu·ci·lage (myōō'si lij') n. gluey or gummy adhesive

muck n. 1 black earth 2 dirt; filth

muck'rake' v. expose corruption in politics or business —**muck'rak·er** n.

mu'cous (myōō'-) a. 1 of or secreting mucus 2 slimy

mucous membrane n. membrane lining body cavities

mu'cus n. slimy secretion of mucous

membranes
mud *n.* soft, wet earth
mud'dle *v.* 1 mix up; confuse 2 act confusedly —*n.* mess, confusion, etc.
mud'dle-head'ed *a.* confused
mud'dy *a.* **-di·er, -di·est** 1 full of or covered with mud 2 clouded or obscure —*v.* **-died, -dy·ing** make or become muddy
mud'sling'ing *n.* unfair verbal attack
mu·ez'zin (myōō-) *n.* crier calling Muslims to prayer
muff *n.* cylindrical covering to warm the hands —*v.* bungle; miss
muf'fin *n.* bread baked in a small cupcake mold
muf'fle *v.* 1 wrap up warmly 2 deaden (sound), as on an automobile
muf'fler *n.* 1 thick scarf 2 device to deaden noise, as on an automobile
muf'ti *n.* civilian clothes
mug *n.* 1 heavy drinking cup 2 [Sl.] face
mug'gy *a.* **-gi·er, -gi·est** hot and humid
mug shot *n.* official photograph of a criminal or suspect
muk'luk' *n.* Eskimo boot
mu·lat·to (mə lät'ō) *n., pl.* **-toes** or **-tos** person with a black parent and a white parent
mul'ber·ry *n., pl.* **-ries** tree with berry-like fruit
mulch *v., n.* (use) a cover of leaves, peat, etc. around plants
mulct (mulkt) *v.* take from by fraud
mule *n.* 1 offspring of a male donkey and a female horse 2 [Inf.] stubborn person 3 lounging slipper
mul'ish (myōōl'-) *a.* stubborn
mull *v.* 1 ponder (*over*) 2 heat and flavor (wine, etc.)
mul'lein (-in) *n.* tall plant with spikes of colorful flowers
mul'let *n.* an edible fish
mul'li·gan stew *n.* meat stew
mul'li·ga·taw'ny *n.* meat soup flavored with curry
mul'lion (-yən) *n.* vertical bar between windowpanes
multi- *pref.* of or having many or several
mul'ti·cul'tur·al *a.* including different cultures —**mul'ti·cul'tur·al·ism'** *n.*
mul'ti·fac'et·ed *a.* manifold; complex
mul'ti·far'i·ous *a.* of many kinds; varied
mul'ti·lat'er·al *a.* involving several parties
mul'ti·me'di·a *n., a.* (presentation, etc.) combining different media

mul'ti·na'tion·al *n., a.* (corporation) with branches in various countries
mul'ti·ple *a.* having many parts, etc. —*n.* product of two numbers, one specified
mul'ti·ple-choice' *a.* listing several answers to choose from
multiple sclerosis *n.* disease of nervous system
mul'ti·plex' *a.* of a system for combining signals sent over one circuit, etc.
mul'ti·pli·cand' *n.* the number to be multiplied by another
mul'ti·plic'i·ty (-plis'-) *n.* great number
mul'ti·ply' *v.* **-plied', -ply'ing** 1 to increase in number, degree, etc. 2 find the product (of) by adding a certain number a certain number of times —**mul'ti·pli·ca'tion** *n.* —**mul'ti·pli'er** *n.*
mul'ti·stage' *a.* operating by successive propulsion systems, as a rocket
mul'ti·tude' *n.* large number
mul'ti·tu'di·nous *a.* many
mum *n.* [Inf.] chrysanthemum —*a.* silent
mum'ble *v.* speak or say indistinctly —*n.* mumbled utterance
mum'bo jum'bo *n.* meaningless ritual or talk
mum'mer *n.* actor, esp. one with a mask or disguise
mum'mer·y *n., pl.* **-ies** [Now Rare] foolish ritual; false show
mum'mi·fy' *v.* **-fied', -fy'ing** make into a mummy
mum'my *n., pl.* **-mies** ancient embalmed body
mumps *n.* disease in which the salivary glands swell
mun *abbrev.* municipal
munch *v.* chew noisily
mun'dane' *a.* of the world
mu·nic'i·pal (-nis'-) *a.* of a city or town
mu·nic'i·pal'i·ty *n., pl.* **-ties** city or town having its own local government
mu·nif'i·cent *a.* very generous —**mu·nif'i·cence** *n.*
mu·ni'tions *pl.n.* weapons and ammunition for war
mu·ral (myoor'əl) *a.* of or on a wall —*n.* picture painted on a wall
mur'der *v.* kill (a person) unlawfully and with malice —*n.* act of murdering —**mur'der·er** *n.*
mur'der·ous *a.* 1 of or like murder 2 guilty of, or ready to, murder
murk *n.* darkness; gloom —**murk'y** *a.,* **-i·er, -i·est**
mur'mur *n.* 1 low, steady sound 2 mumbled complaint —*v.* 1 make a

murmur **2** say in a low voice

mur'rain (-in) *n.* a cattle plague

mus *abbrev.* **1** museum **2** music

mus'ca·tel' *n.* wine made from type of sweet grape (**mus'cat**)

mus'cle (-əl) *n.* **1** tissue forming the fleshy parts that move the body **2** any single part of this tissue **3** strength

mus'cle-bound' *a.* having some muscles enlarged and less elastic

mus'cu·lar *a.* **1** of or done by muscle **2** strong

muscular dys·tro·phy (dis'trə fē) *n.* disease in which muscles waste away

mus'cu·la·ture (-chər) *n.* muscular system of a body, limb, etc.

muse *v.* think deeply —*n.* spirit inspiring an artist

mu·se'um *n.* place for displaying artistic, historical, or scientific objects

mush *n.* **1** thick, soft mass **2** boiled cornmeal **3** [Inf.] maudlin sentimentality —*int.* shout urging on sled dogs —*v.* travel over snow —**mush'y** *a.*, **-i·er**, **-i·est**

mush'room' *n.* fleshy, umbrella-shaped fungus, often edible —*v.* grow or spread rapidly

mu'sic *n.* **1** songs, symphonies, etc. **2** art of composing or performing these

mu'si·cal *a.* of, fond of, or set to music —*n.* a play or film with singing and dancing —**mu'si·cal·ly** *adv.*

mu'si·cale' (-kal') *n.* social affair with musical program

mu·si'cian (-zish'ən) *n.* person skilled in music

mu'si·col'o·gy *n.* study of history and forms of music —**mu'si·col'o·gist** *n.*

musk *n.* strong-smelling animal secretion, used in perfumes —**musk'y** *a.*, **-i·er**, **-i·est**

mus'kel·lunge' *n.* large, edible pike: also **mus'kie**

mus'ket *n.* former long gun —**mus'ket·eer'** *n.*

musk'mel'on *n.* cantaloupe, honeydew melon, etc.

musk'rat' *n.* water rodent

Mus'lim (muz'-, mooz'-) *n.* follower of the religion of Mohammed —*a.* of Islam or Muslims

mus'lin (muz'-) *n.* strong cotton cloth, as for sheets

muss *v.* make messy —*n.* [Inf.] mess —**muss'y** *a.*

mus'sel *n.* bivalve mollusk

must *v.* auxiliary verb showing: **1** obligation **2** probability **3** certainty —*n.* [Inf.] thing that must be done

mus'tache' (-tash') *n.* hair grown out on the upper lip of men

mus'tang' *n.* small, wild horse

mus'tard *n.* yellow, spicy paste, used as a seasoning

mus'ter *v.* **1** to bring or come together, as troops **2** summon —*n.* a mustering

mus'ty *a.* **-ti·er**, **-ti·est** stale and moldy

mu'ta·ble *a.* changeable

mu'tant *n.* abnormal animal or plant

mu·ta'tion *n.* a change, esp. a sudden variation in a plant or animal —**mu'tate'** *v.*

mute *a.* **1** silent **2** not able to speak —*n.* **1** one unable to speak; spec., a deaf-mute **2** device to mute a musical instrument —*v.* soften the sound of

mu'ti·late' *v.* cut off or damage part of

mu'ti·ny *n., pl.* **-nies** revolt, as against one's military superiors —**mu'ti·neer'** *n.* —**mu'ti·nous** *a.*

mutt *n.* [Sl.] mongrel dog

mut'ter *v.* **1** speak or say in low, indistinct tones **2** grumble —*n.* muttered utterance

mut'ton *n.* flesh of grown sheep used as food

mu'tu·al *a.* **1** of or for one another **2** in common —**mu'tu·al·ly** *adv.*

mutual fund *n.* (company managing) diverse investments owned jointly

muu-muu (mōō'mōō') *n.* long, loose Hawaiian dress

Mu'zak' *n.* recorded music played in public places

muz'zle *n.* **1** snout **2** device for an animal's mouth to prevent biting **3** front end of a gun barrel —*v.* **1** put a muzzle on **2** prevent from talking

my *a.* of me

my·col'o·gy *n.* study of fungi —**my·col'o·gist** *n.*

my'e·li'tis (-līt'is) *n.* inflammation of bone marrow or spinal cord

my'na, my'nah *n.* Asian starling

my·o'pi·a *n.* nearsightedness —**my·op'ic** (-äp'-) *a.*

myr'i·ad (mir'-) *n.* great number —*a.* very many

myrrh (mur) *n.* resin used in incense, perfume, etc.

myr'tle *n.* **1** evergreen shrub **2** creeping evergreen plant

my·self' *pron.* intensive or reflexive form of I

mys'ter·y *n., pl.* **-ies** **1** unexplained or unknown thing **2** obscurity or secrecy —**mys·te'ri·ous** *a.*

mys'tic *a.* **1** occult or mysterious **2** mystical —*n.* believer in mysticism

mys′ti·cal *a.* **1** of mysticism **2** spiritually symbolic **3** mystic

mys′ti·cism *n.* belief that God can be known directly

mys′ti·fy′ *v.* **-fied′, -fy′ing** perplex or puzzle —**mys′ti·fi·ca′tion** *n.*

mys·tique′ (-tēk′) *n.* mysterious and fascinating quality of a person, etc.

myth *n.* **1** traditional story explaining some phenomenon **2** fictitious person or thing —**myth′i·cal** *a.*

myth *abbrev.* mythology

my·thol′o·gy *n.*, *pl.* **-gies 1** study of myths **2** myths of a certain people —**myth′o·log′i·cal** *a.*

N

n *abbrev.* noun

N *abbrev.* north(ern)

NA *abbrev.* North America

NAACP *abbrev.* National Association for the Advancement of Colored People

nab *v.* **nabbed, nab′bing** [Inf.] seize or arrest

na·bob (nā′bäb) *n.* very rich or important person

na·cre (nā′kər) *n.* mother-of-pearl

na·dir (nā′dər) *n.* lowest point

nag *v.* **nagged, nag′ging** scold or urge constantly —*n.* **1** one who nags **2** inferior horse

nai·ad (nā′ad, nī′-) *n.* [*also* N-] Gr. & Rom. myth. nymphs living in water

nail *n.* **1** horny layer at the ends of the fingers and toes **2** narrow, pointed piece of metal driven into pieces of wood to hold them together —*v.* fasten as with nails

nail′-bit′er *n.* [Inf.] suspenseful drama, sports event, etc.

na·ive, na·ïve (nä ēv′) *a.* innocent; simple —**na·ive·té′, na·ïve·té′** (-tā′) *n.*

na′ked *a.* **1** without clothing or covering **2** plain

nam′by-pam′by *a.; n., pl.* **-bies** insipid, indecisive (person)

name *n.* **1** word or words for a person, thing, or place **2** reputation —*a.* wellknown —*v.* **1** give a name to **2** mention or identify by name **3** appoint

name′less *a.* without a name **2** obscure; vague

name′ly *adv.* that is to say

name′sake′ *n.* person named after another

nan′ny goat *n.* female goat

na′no·sec′ond (nan′ō-) *n.* one billionth of a second

nap *v.* **napped, nap′ping** sleep briefly —*n.* **1** short sleep **2** fuzzy surface of fibers on cloth

na′palm′ (-päm′) *n.* jellylike gasoline used in bombs, etc.

nape *n.* back of the neck

naph·tha (naf′-, nap′-) *n.* oily liquid used as a solvent, etc.

naph′tha·lene′ *n.* crystalline substance made from coal tar

nap′kin *n.* small piece of paper or cloth for use while eating

narc *n.* [Sl.] police agent enforcing narcotics laws

nar′cis·sism′ (-sə-) *n.* self-love —**nar′cis·sist** *n.*

nar·cis′sus (-sis′-) *n.* flowering bulbous plant

nar·cot′ic *n.* drug that causes deep sleep and lessens pain —*a.* of or like a narcotic

nar′rate′ *v.* tell a story —**nar′ra′tor** *n.*

nar·ra′tion *n.* **1** a narrating **2** a narrative

nar′ra·tive *a.* in story form —*n.* story; account

nar′row *a.* **1** not wide **2** intolerant **3** limited in size, degree, etc. —*v.* lessen in width, extent, etc.

nar′row-mind′ed *a.* bigoted

nar′whal (när′wəl) *n.* small whale with a long tusk

nar′y *a.* [Dial.] used in **nary a**, not any

NASA *abbrev.* National Aeronautics and Space Administration

na′sal (-zəl) *a.* of or through the nose

na′sal·ize′ *v.* speak with nasal sound —**na·sal·i·za′tion** *n.*

nas′cent (*or* nā′sənt) *a.* starting to be or develop

nas·tur′tium (-shəm) *n.* yellowish-red flower

nas′ty *a.* **-ti·er, -ti·est 1** dirty **2** obscene **3** unpleasant; mean —**nas′ti·ly** *adv.* —**nas′ti·ness** *n.*

na′tal *a.* of (one's) birth

na′tion *n.* **1** a people with history, language, etc. in common **2** people under one government

na′tion·al *a.* of a whole nation —*n.*

na′tion·al·ism′ *n.* **1** patriotism **2** advocacy of national independence —**na′tion·al·ist** *a., n.* —**na′tion·al·is′tic** *a.*

na′tion·al′i·ty *n., pl.* **-ties** nation, esp. of one's birth or citizenship

na′tion·al·ize′ *v.* transfer control of to a government —**na′tion·al·i·za′tion** *n.*

na′tion·wide′ *a.* throughout the whole nation

na'tive *a.* **1** belonging to a region or country by birth, growth, etc. **2** being or of the place of one's birth **3** inborn —*n.* native person, animal, or plant

Native American *n., a.* American Indian

na'tive-born' *a.* born in a specified place

na-tiv'i-ty *n.* birth

NATO (nā'tō) *n.* North Atlantic Treaty Organization

nat'ty *a.* **-ti-er, -ti-est** neat and stylish

nat'u-ral (nach'-) *a.* **1** of or dealing with nature **2** not artificial **3** innate **4** lifelike; usual **5** to be expected **6** *Mus.* neither sharp nor flat —**nat'u-ral-ly** *adv.*

natural childbirth *n.* childbirth without anesthesia but with prior training

natural history *n.* study of nature

nat'u-ral-ism' *n.* art or writing about people and things as they really are

nat'u-ral-ist *n.* one who studies plants and animals

nat'u-ral-ize' *v.* confer citizenship upon (an alien) —**nat·u·ral·i·za'tion** *n.*

natural resource *n.* a form of natural wealth, as coal, oil, or water power

natural science *n.* a science dealing with nature, as biology or chemistry

na'ture *n.* **1** basic quality of a thing **2** inborn character **3** kind; sort **4** physical universe or its forces **5** natural scenery

naught (nôt) *n.* **1** nothing **2** zero

naugh'ty *a.* **-ti-er, -ti-est** mischievous **2** not nice or proper —**naugh'ti-ly** *adv.* —**naugh'ti-ness** *n.*

nau'se-a (-shə, -zhə) *n.* **1** feeling of wanting to vomit **2** disgust —**nau'se-ate'** (-shē-, -zē-) *v.* —**nau'seous** *a.*

naut *adj.* nautical

nau'ti-cal *a.* of sailors, ships, or navigation

nautical mile *n.* unit of linear measure used in navigation, equal to about 6,076 feet

nau'ti-lus *n.* tropical mollusk

Nav'a-jo', Nav'a-ho' (-hō') *n.* member of an Indian people of SW U.S.

na'val *a.* of or for a navy, its ships, etc.

nave *n.* main, long part of some churches

na'vel *n.* small, abdominal scar where the umbilical cord was attached

nav'i-ga-ble *a.* wide or deep enough for ship travel

nav'i-gate' *v.* **1** travel through or on (air, sea, etc.) in a ship or aircraft **2** steer or plot the course of (a ship, etc.) —**nav'i-ga'tion** *n.* —**nav'i-ga'tor** *n.*

na'vy *n., pl.* **-vies** entire fleet of warships, etc. of a nation **2** very dark blue: also **navy blue**

navy bean *n.* small, white bean

nay *n.* **1** denial **2** negative vote or voter

Na·zi (nät'sē) *n., a.* (adherent) of the German fascist party (1933-45) —**Na'zism'** *n.*

NB *abbrev.* New Brunswick

n.b. *abbrev.* note well

NC *abbrev.* North Carolina

NCO *abbrev.* noncommissioned officer

NC-17 *trademark* film rating indicating no one under 17 may be admitted

ND *abbrev.* North Dakota

NE *abbrev.* **1** Nebraska **2** northeast **3** northeastern

Ne·an'der·thal' *a., n.* **1** (of) a prehistoric type of human **2** crude, primitive, etc. (person)

neap tide *n.* lowest high tide, occurring twice a month

near *adv.* at a short distance —*a.* **1** close in distance, time, etc. **2** intimate **3** stingy —*v.* to draw near to —*prep.* close to —**near'ness** *n.*

near'by' *a., adv.* near; close at hand

near'ly *adv.* almost

near miss *n.* result that is not quite successful

near'sight'ed *a.* seeing only near objects distinctly

neat *a.* **1** tidy; clean **2** trim in form —**neat'ly** *adv.* —**neat'ness** *n.*

neb'bish *n.* one who is inept, dull, etc.

neb'u-la *n., pl.* **-lae'** (-lē') or **-las** cloud-like patch seen in the night sky —**neb'u-lar** *a.*

neb'u-lous *a.* vague

nec'es-sar'i-ly *adv.* **1** because of necessity **2** as a necessary result

nec'es-sar'y *a.* **1** that must be had or done; essential **2** inevitable —*n., pl.* **-ies** necessary thing

ne-ces'si-tate' *v.* make (something) necessary

ne-ces'si-ty *n., pl.* **-ties 1** great need **2** something necessary **3** poverty

neck *n.* **1** part that joins the head to the body **2** narrow part, as of a bottle —*v.* [Sl.] to hug, kiss, and caress passionately —**neck and neck** very close as to outcome

neck'er·chief (-chif) *n.* kerchief worn around the neck

neck'lace (-ləs) *n.* chain of gold, beads, etc. worn around the neck

neck'tie' *n.* neck band worn under a collar and tied in front

neck'wear *n.* neckties, scarves, etc.

ne·crol'o·gy (ne-) *n., pl.* **-gies** list of people who have died

nec'ro·man'cy *n.* black magic

ne·cro'sis *n.* death or decay of tissue in some body part

nec'tar *n.* sweet liquid in flowers

nec'tar·ine' (-tə rēn') *n.* smooth-skinned peach

nee, née (nā) *a.* having as her unmarried name

need *n.* **1** lack of something required; also, the thing lacking **2** poverty or distress —*v.* **1** have need of **2** to be obliged *Need* is also used as an auxiliary verb —**if need be** if it is required

need'ful *a.* necessary

nee'dle *n.* **1** a very slender, pointed piece, as for sewing, knitting, etc. **2** anything needle-shaped —*v.* [Inf.] goad or tease

nee'dle·point' *n.* embroidery of woolen threads on canvas

need'less *a.* unnecessary

nee'dle·work' *n.* sewing, embroidery, crocheting, etc.

need'y *a.* **-i·er, -i·est** very poor

ne'er (ner) *adv.* [Poet.] never

ne'er-do-well' *a., n.* lazy and irresponsible (person)

ne·far'i·ous (-fer'-) *a.* very wicked

neg *abbrev.* negative(ly)

ne·gate' *v.* deny or nullify —**ne·ga'tion** *n.*

neg'a·tive *a.* **1** saying "no" **2** not positive **3** of electricity with excess electrons **4** being less than zero —*n.* **1** a negative word, reply, etc. **2** battery terminal where electrons flow out **3** photographic plate or film in which light and shadow are reversed

ne·glect' *v.* **1** fail to do **2** fail to care for properly —*n.* a neglecting —**ne·glect'ful** *a.*

neg'li·gee' (-zhā') *n.* woman's dressing gown

neg'li·gent *a.* (habitually) careless —**neg'li·gence** *n.*

neg'li·gi·ble *a.* unimportant

ne·go'ti·ate' (-shē āt') *v.* **1** discuss so as to agree on **2** arrange for (a loan, etc.) **3** transfer or sell **4** move across —**ne·go'ti·a·ble** *a.* —**ne·go'ti·a'tion** *n.* —**ne·go'ti·a'tor** *n.*

Ne'gro *a., n., pl.* **-groes** (of) a member of dark-skinned peoples of Africa, or a person having African ancestors; black —**Ne'groid'** *a.*

neigh (nā) *v., n.* (utter) the cry of a horse

neigh'bor *n.* **1** one that lives or is

near another **2** fellow human being —*a.* nearby —*v.* live or be near

neigh'bor·hood' *n.* **1** one part of a city or the people in it —**in the neighborhood of** [Inf.] near or nearly

neigh'bor·ly *a.* friendly

nei'ther (nē'-, nī'-) *a., pron.* not one or the other (of two) —*con.* correlative used with *nor*

nem'e·sis *n., pl.* **-ses** (-sēz') inevitable cause of one's downfall or defeat

neo- *pref.* [*often* N-] new; recent

ne'o·co·lo'ni·al·ism' *n.* exploitation of a supposedly independent region by a foreign power

ne·ol'o·gism' (-äl'-) *n.* new word

ne'on' *n.* inert gas used in electric signs, a chemical element

ne'o·nate' *n.* newborn baby —**ne'o·na'tal** *a.*

ne'o·phyte' (-fīt') *n.* novice

ne'o·plasm' *n.* abnormal growth of tissue, as a tumor

neph'ew (-yōō) *n.* **1** son of one's brother or sister **2** son of one's brother-in-law or sister-in-law

ne·phri'tis (-frīt'is) *n.* inflammation of the kidneys

nep'o·tism' *n.* a giving of jobs, etc. to relatives

Nep'tune' *n.* eighth planet from the sun

nerd *n.* [Sl.] person who is socially awkward, unsophisticated, etc.

nerve *n.* **1** cordlike fiber carrying impulses to and from the brain **2** courage **3** *pl.* nervousness **4** [Inf.] impudence —**get on someone's nerves** [Inf.] make someone nervous or annoyed

nerve center *n.* **1** group of nerve cells working together **2** headquarters

nerve gas *n.* poisonous liquid that paralyzes: used in warfare

nerve'-rack'ing, nerve'-wrack'ing *a.* very trying to one's composure or patience

nerv'ous *a.* **1** of nerves **2** easily upset; restless **3** fearful —**nerv'ous·ness** *n.*

nervous system *n.* all the nerve cells and nervous tissues of an organism

nerv'y *a.* **-i·er, -i·est 1** bold **2** [Inf.] impudent; brazen

-ness *suf.* quality; state

nest *n.* **1** place where a bird or other animal raises its young **2** cozy place **3** set of things in increasing sizes —*v.* make a nest

nest egg *n.* money put aside

nes'tle (-əl) *v.* **1** settle down snugly **2**

lie sheltered

net *n.* **1** openwork fabric as of string, for snaring fish, etc. **2** fine net to hold the hair **3** netlike cloth **4** net amount **5** NETWORK (*n.* 2) —*a.* left over after deductions, etc. —*v.* **net'ted, net'ting 1** to snare **2** to gain

neth'er *a.* under

net'ting *n.* net fabric or material

net'tle *n.* weed with stinging hairs —*v.* annoy

net'work' *n.* **1** arrangement of wires or threads as in a net **2** system of roads, computers, etc. **3** chain of radio or TV stations —*v.* **1** to form into a network **2** develop business, etc. contacts

neu·ral (noor'əl) *a.* of a nerve or nerves

neu·ral'gi·a (-jə) *n.* pain along a nerve path

neu·ri'tis (-rīt'is) *n.* inflammation of nerves —**neu·rit'ic** *a.*

neuro- *pref.* of nerves

neu·rol'o·gy *n.* branch of medicine dealing with the nervous system —**neu·rol'o·gist** *n.*

neu'ron' *n.* nerve cell and its processes

neu·ro'sis *n.*, *pl.* -**ses'** (-sēz') mental disorder with abnormally intense anxieties, obsessions, etc. —**neu·rot'ic** *a.*, *n.*

neu'ro·sur'ger·y *n.* surgery on the brain or spinal cord —**neu'ro·sur'geon** *n.*

neu'ro·trans'mit·ter *n.* hormone, etc. affecting nerve impulses

neu'ter *a.* neither masculine nor feminine —*v.* castrate or spay (an animal)

neu'tral *a.* **1** supporting neither side in a war or quarrel **2** not one or the other **3** having no decided color —*n.* **1** neutral nation, etc. **2** position of disengaged gears —**neu·tral'i·ty** *n.*

neu'tral·ize' *v.* counteract the effectiveness of

neu·tri'no (-trē'-) *n.*, *pl.* -**nos** uncharged atomic particle smaller than a neutron

neu'tron' *n.* uncharged atomic particle

nev'er *adv.* **1** at no time **2** in no way

nev'er·the·less' *adv.*, *con.* in spite of that; however

new *a.* **1** never existing before **2** unfamiliar or foreign **3** fresh **4** unused **5** modern; recent **6** beginning again —*adv.* recently

New Age *n.* [*often* n- a-] of a movement involving astrology, meditation, etc.

new blood *n.* new people as a source of new ideas, vigor, etc.

new'born' *a.* **1** just born **2** reborn

new'com'er *n.* recent arrival

new'fan'gled *a.* new and strange

new'ly *adv.* recently

new'ly·wed' *n.* recently married person

news *n.* **1** new information **2** (reports of) recent events

news'boy' *n.* boy who sells or delivers newspapers

news'cast' *n.* radio or TV news broadcast —**news'cast'er** *n.*

news'let'ter *n.* special group's news bulletin, issued regularly

news'man' *n.*, *pl.* -**men'** newscaster or reporter, esp. a male —**news'wom'an** *n.*, *pl.* -**wom'en**

news'pa'per *n.* daily or weekly news publication

news'print' *n.* cheap paper used for newspapers, etc.

news'stand' *n.* a stand for the sale of newspapers, etc.

news'wor'thy *a.* timely and important or interesting

news'y *a.* -**i·er, -i·est** [Inf.] containing much news

newt *n.* small salamander

New Testament *n.* second part of the Christian Bible

new wave *n.* experimental trend in music, etc.

New Year's (Day) *n.* January 1

next *a.* nearest; closest —*adv.* in the nearest time, place, etc.

next'-door' *a.* in or at the next house, building, etc.

nex'us *n.*, *pl.* -**us·es** or -**us** connection or link

NF *abbrev.* Newfoundland

NH *abbrev.* New Hampshire

ni'a·cin *n.* nicotinic acid

nib *n.* **1** bird's beak **2** (pen) point

nib'ble *v.* eat with quick, small bites —*n.* small bite

nice *a.* **1** pleasant, kind, good, etc. **2** precise; accurate **3** refined —**nice'ly** *adv.*

ni'ce·ty *n.*, *pl.* -**ties 1** accuracy **2** refinement **3** small detail; fine point

niche (nich) *n.* **1** recess in a wall for a statue, etc. **2** suitable position

nick *v.* make a small cut, chip, etc. in or on —*n.* small cut, chip, etc. —**in the nick of time** exactly when needed

nick'el *n.* **1** rust-resistant metal, a chemical element **2** nickel and copper coin worth 5 cents

nick'name' *n.* **1** a substitute name, as "Slim" **2** familiar form of a proper name, as "Bob" —*v.* give a nickname to

nic·o·tine' (-tēn') *n.* poisonous liquid in tobacco leaves

nic·o·tin'ic acid (-tin'-) *n.* member of the vitamin B complex

niece (nēs) *n.* **1** daughter of one's sister or brother **2** daughter of one's sister-in-law or brother-in-law

nif'ty *a.* [Sl.] very good

nig'gard·ly *a.* stingy; miserly

nigh (nī) *adv., a., prep.* [Dial.] near

night *n.* period of darkness between sunset and sunrise —**night'time'** *n.*

night blindness *n.* poor vision in near darkness or dim light

night'cap' *n.* **1** cap worn in bed **2** [Inf.] alcoholic drink taken just before bedtime

night'clothes' *pl.n.* clothes to be worn in bed, as pajamas: also **night clothes**

night'club' *n.* place for eating, drinking, dancing, etc. at night

night crawl'er *n.* large earthworm that comes to the surface at night

night'fall' *n.* close of the day

night'gown' *n.* long, loose sleeping garment for women

night'ie *n.* [Inf.] nightgown

night'in·gale' *n.* a European thrush that sings at night

night life *n.* pleasure-seeking activity at night, as in nightclubs

night'ly *a., adv.* (done or happening) every night

night'mare' *n.* frightening dream or experience

night owl *n.* one who stays up late

night'shade' *n.* belladonna or related plant

night'shirt' *n.* long shirtlike garment worn to bed

night'spot' *n.* [Inf.] nightclub

night'stand' *n.* small bedside table

night'stick' *n.* long, heavy club carried by a policeman

night'time' *n.* night

ni·hil·ism (nī'ə liz'əm, nē'-) *n.* general rejection of usual beliefs in morality, religion, etc. —**ni'hil·ist** *n.*

nil *n.* nothing

nim'ble *a.* quick in movement or thought —**nim'bly** *adv.*

nim'bus *n.* **1** rain cloud **2** halo

nin'com·poop' *n.* a fool

nine *a., n.* one more than eight —**ninth** *a., n.*

nine'teen' *a., n.* nine more than ten —**nine'teenth'** *a., n.*

nine'ty *a., n., pl.* -**ties** nine times ten —**nine'ti·eth** *a., n.*

nin'ja *n., pl.* -**ja** or -**jas** in former times, a trained Japanese assassin

nin'ny *n., pl.* -**nies** a fool

nip *v.* **nipped, nip'ping 1** pinch or bite **2** pinch off **3** spoil, as by frost —*n.* **1** stinging cold **2** small drink of liquor —**nip and tuck** very close as to outcome

nip'per *n.* **1** *pl.* pliers, pincers, etc. **2** claw of a crab or lobster

nip'ple *n.* **1** protuberance on a breast or udder **2** thing shaped like this

nip'py *a.* -**pi·er, -pi·est** sharp; biting

nir·va'na (-vä'-) *n. Buddhism* state of perfect blessedness

nit *n.* egg of a louse

nite *n.* [Inf.] night

ni'ter *n.* salt used in explosives, fertilizer, etc.: also, Br. sp., **ni'tre**

nit'-pick'ing *a.* fussy —**nit'pick'er** *n.*

ni'trate' *n.* salt of nitric acid

ni'tric acid *n.* corrosive acid containing nitrogen

ni·tro·cel'lu·lose' (-yōō lōs') *n.* pulplike substance, used in making explosives, etc.

ni'tro·gen *n.* colorless, odorless gas, a chemical element —**ni·trog'e·nous** (-träj'-) *a.*

ni·tro·glyc'er·in, ni'tro·glyc'er·ine (-glis'-) *n.* thick, explosive oil, used in dynamite

nit'ty-grit'ty *n.* [Sl.] basic facts, issues, etc.

nit'wit' *n.* stupid person

nix *v.* [Sl.] put a stop to

NJ *abbrev.* New Jersey

NM *abbrev.* New Mexico

no *adv.* **1** not at all **2** not so —*a.* not any; not a —*n., pl.* **noes 1** a refusal **2** negative vote

no *abbrev.* number

no·bil'i·ty *n., pl.* -**ties 1** noble state or rank **2** people of noble rank

no'ble *a.* **1** highly moral **2** grand; splendid **3** of high hereditary rank —*n.* person of high rank —**no'ble·man** *n., pl.* -**men** —**no'bly** *adv.*

no·blesse' o·blige' (-blēzh') *n.* obligation of upper classes to behave kindly toward others

no'bod·y *pron.* no one —*n., pl.* -**ies** unimportant person

no'-brain'er *n.* [Inf.] something so obvious as to need little thought

noc·tur'nal *a.* **1** of the night **2** done, happening, etc. at night

noc'turne' *n.* romantic musical composition

nod *v.* **nod'ded, nod'ding 1** bend the head quickly **2** show (assent) thus **3** let the head fall forward in dozing —

n. a nodding

node *n.* **1** knob; swelling **2** point on a stem from which a leaf grows

nod·ule (näj′ōol) *n.* small knot or rounded lump

No·el, No·ël (nō el′) *n.* Christmas

no′-fault′ *a.* of forms of insurance or divorce, not requiring that fault or blame be determined

nog′gin *n.* [Inf.] the head

no′-good′ *a.* [Sl.] despicable

noise *n.* sound, esp. a loud, unpleasant sound —*v.* spread (a rumor) *around,* etc. —**noise′less** *a.*

noi′some *a.* **1** unhealthful **2** foul-smelling

nois′y *a.* **-i·er, -i·est 1** making noise **2** full of noise —**nois′i·ly** *adv.* —**nois′i·ness** *n.*

no′-load′ *a.* of mutual funds charging no commission

no′mad′ *n.* **1** member of a wandering tribe **2** wanderer —**no·mad′ic** *a.*

no′men·cla·ture (-klā′chər) *n.* system or list of names

nom′i·nal *a.* **1** in name only **2** relatively small —**nom′i·nal·ly** *adv.*

nom′i·nate′ *v.* **1** appoint **2** name as a candidate —**nom′i·na′tion** *n.*

nom′i·na·tive *a., n.* Gram. (in) the case of the subject of a verb

nom′i·nee′ *n.* a person who is nominated

non- *pref.* not: see list below

non·ab·sorb′ent
non·ac′tive
non·ag·gres′sion
non·al·co·hol′ic
non·be·liev′er
non·com·bus′ti·ble
non·com·mer′cial
non·con·form′ist
non·con·ta′gious
non·es·sen′tial
non·ex·ist′ent
non·fac′tu·al
non·fa′tal
non·fic′tion
non·flow′er·ing
non·fly′ing
non·func′tion·al
non·in·ter·fer′ence
non·in·ter·ven′tion
non·ir′ri·tat·ing
non·ma·lig′nant
non·mil′i·tar·y
non·of·fi′cial
non·pay′ment
non·per′ish·a·ble
non·poi′son·ous
non·po·lit′i·cal

non·po′rous
non·pre·scrip′tive
non·pro·duc′tive
non·pro·fes′sion·al
non·re·li′gious
non·res·i·den′tial
non·smok′er
non·sup·port′ing
non·sus·tain′ing
non·tax′a·ble
non·tech′ni·cal
non·tox′ic

non′age (-ij) *n.* state of being under legal age

non′a·ligned′ *a.* not aligned with either side in a conflict

no′-name′ *a.* not famous

non′bind′ing *a.* not holding one to an obligation, promise, etc.

nonce *n.* the present time

non′cha·lant′ (-shə länt′) *a.* casually indifferent —**non′cha·lance′** *n.*

non′com′ *n.* [Inf.] noncommissioned officer

non′com·bat′ant *n.* **1** civilian in wartime **2** soldier not in combat

non′com·mis′sioned officer *n.* corporal or sergeant in the armed forces

non′com·mit′tal *a.* not taking a definite stand

non′con·duc′tor *n.* thing that does not conduct electricity, heat, etc.

non′cus·to′di·al *a.* without custody, as of one's children after divorce

non′dair′y *a.* containing no milk products

non′de·script′ *a.* of no definite class or type

none (nun) *pron.* **1** no one **2** not any —*adv.* not at all

non·en′ti·ty *n., pl.* **-ties** unimportant person

none′the·less′ *adv.* nevertheless: also **none the less**

non′fer′rous *a.* of metals other than iron

non′in·va′sive *a.* not penetrating or spreading

non·met′al *n.* element that is not a metal, as carbon —**non′me·tal′lic** *a.*

non′pa·reil′ (-pə rel′) *a.* without equal; peerless

non′par′ti·san *a.* not of any single party, faction, etc.

non′plus′ *v.* **-plused′** or **-plussed′, -plus′ing** or **-plus′sing** thoroughly bewilder

non′prof′it *a.* not for profit

non′res′i·dent *n., a.* (person) not living in the locality of one's work, etc.

non′sec·tar′i·an *a.* not connected with

a specific religion

non'sense' *n.* absurd or meaningless words or acts —**non·sen'si·cal** *a.*

non seq. *abbrev.* it does not follow

non' se'qui·tur (-sek'wi-) *n.* remark having no relation to something just said

non'stop' *a., adv.* without a stop

non'sup·port' *n.* failure to support a legal dependent

non·un'ion *a.* not belonging to, or done by a labor union

non·vi'o·lent *a.* not using violence — **non·vi'o·lence** *n.*

noo'dle *n.* flat strip of dry dough

nook *n.* **1** corner **2** small secluded spot

noon *n.* twelve o'clock in the daytime; midday: also **noon'day'** or **noon'time'**

no one *pron.* no person

noose *n.* loop with a slipknot for tightening it

nor *con.* and not (either)

Nor'dic *a.* of a physical type like tall, blond Scandinavians

norm *n.* standard or pattern for a group —**norm'a·tive** *a.*

nor'mal *a.* **1** usual; natural **2** average —*n.* what is normal; usual state — **nor'mal·cy, nor·mal'i·ty** *n.* —**nor'mal·ize'** *v.*

nor'mal·ly *adv.* **1** in a normal way **2** usually

Norse *n., a.* (language) of the vikings —**Norse'man** *n., pl.* **-men**

north *n.* direction or region to the right of one facing the sunset —*a., adv.* in, toward, or from the north — **north'er·ly** *a., adv.* —**north'ern** *a.* —**north'ern·er** *n.* —**north'ward** *a., adv.* —**north'wards** *adv.*

north'east' *n.* direction or region between north and east —*a., adv.* in, toward, or from the northeast — **north'east'er·ly** *a., adv.* —**north'east'ern** *a.* —**north'east'ward** *a., adv.* — **north'east'wards** *adv.*

northern lights *pl.n.* aurora borealis

North Pole northern end of the earth's axis

North Star *n.* bright star almost directly above the North Pole

north'west' *n.* direction or region between north and west —*a., adv.* in, toward, or from the northwest — **north'west'er·ly** *a., adv.* —**north'west'ern** *a.* —**north'west'ward** *a., adv.* —**north'west'wards** *adv.*

Nor·we'gian *n., a.* (native or language) of Norway

nose *n.* **1** part of the face with two

openings for breathing and smelling **2** sense of smell **3** thing like a nose — *v.* **1** find, as by smell **2** push with the front forward **3** pry inquisitively — **nose out** defeat narrowly

nose'bleed' *n.* bleeding from the nose

nose cone *n.* foremost part of a rocket or missile

nose dive *n.* **1** swift downward plunge of an airplane, nose first **2** sharp drop, as of prices —**nose'-dive'** *v.*

nose drops *n.* medication put into the nose in drops

nose'gay' *n.* bunch of flowers

nosh *v., n.* [Sl.] (eat) a snack

no'-show' *n.* one not showing up

nos·tal'gia (-jə) *n.* a longing for something past or far away —**nos·tal'gic** *a.*

nos'tril *n.* either of two outer openings of the nose

nos'trum *n.* quack medicine

nos'y, nos'ey (nōz'-) *a.* **-i·er, -i·est** [Inf.] inquisitive

not *adv.* in no manner, degree, etc.

no'ta·ble *a., n.* remarkable or outstanding (person) —**no'ta·bly** *adv.*

no'ta·rize' *v.* certify (a document) as a notary

no'ta·ry *n., pl.* **-ries** one authorized to certify documents, etc.: in full, **notary public**

no·ta'tion *n.* **1** (use of) a system of symbols, as in music **2** a note

notch *n.* **1** a V-shaped cut **2** [Inf.] a step; degree —*v.* to cut notches in

note *n.* **1** brief writing, comment, letter, etc. **2** notice; heed **3** written promise to pay **4** musical tone or its symbol **5** importance —*v.* **1** to notice **2** make a note of —**compare notes** exchange views

note'book' *n.* **1** book for keeping memorandums, etc. **2** small laptop computer

not'ed *a.* renowned; famous

note'wor'thy *a.* outstanding

noth'ing *n.* **1** no thing **2** unimportant person or thing zero —*adv.* not at all —**for nothing 1** free **2** in vain **3** without reason —**noth'ing·ness** *n.*

no'tice *n.* **1** announcement or warning **2** a short review **3** attention —*v.* observe —**take notice** observe

no'tice·a·ble *a.* **1** easily seen **2** significant —**no'tice·a·bly** *adv.*

no'ti·fy' *v.* **-fied', -fy'ing** give notice to; inform —**no'ti·fi·ca'tion** *n.*

no'tion *n.* **1** general idea **2** belief; opinion **3** whim **4** *pl.* small wares

no·to'ri·ous *a.* widely known, esp.

unfavorably —**no'to·ri'e·ty** n.

not'with·stand'ing prep., adv. in spite of (that)

nou'gat (nōō'-) n. candy of sugar paste with nuts

nought (nôt) n. 1 nothing 2 zero

noun n. word that names a person, thing, etc.

nour'ish (nur'-) a. feed to promote life and growth —**nour'ish·ment** n.

Nov abbrev. November

no'va n., pl. **-vas** or **-vae** (-vē) star that brightens intensely and then gradually dims

nov'el a. new and unusual —n. long fictional narrative

nov'el·ist n. writer of novels

nov'el·ty n., pl. **-ties** 1 newness 2 novel thing 3 small, cheap toy, etc.

No·vem'ber n. 11th month

no·ve'na n. R.C.Ch. the saying of special prayers for nine days

nov'ice n. 1 one in a religious order before taking vows 2 beginner

no·vi·ti·ate (nō vish'ē ət) n. period of being a novice

No'vo·cain' trademark procaine

now adv. 1 at this moment; at present 2 at that time; then 3 with things as they are —con. since —n. the present time —**now and then** occasionally: also **now and again**

now'a·days' adv. at the present time

no'where' adv. not in, at, or to any place

no'wise' adv. in no way

nox·ious (näk'shəs) a. harmful to health or morals

noz'zle n. small spout at the end of a hose, etc.

NR abbrev. not rated

NS abbrev. Nova Scotia

NT abbrev. Northwest Territories

nt wt abbrev. net weight

nu'ance' (-äns') n. slight change in color, meaning, etc.

nub n. 1 lump or small piece 2 [Inf.] gist

nub'by a. **-bi·er, -bi·est** rough and knotty, as cloth

nu'bile (-bəl, -bīl') a. sexually attractive: said of a young woman

nu'cle·ar a. of, like, or forming a nucleus or nuclei

nuclear energy n. energy that atoms release in nuclear fission or fusion

nuclear family n. family including parents and their children living in one household

nuclear fission n. splitting of nuclei of atoms, with the release of much energy, as in the atomic bomb

nuclear fusion n. fusion of nuclei of atoms, with the release of much energy, as in the hydrogen bomb

nuclear reactor n. device for creating controlled chain reaction, as for producing energy

nu'cle·us n., pl. **-cle·i** (-klē ī') or **-cle·us·es** central part, spec. of an atom or of a living cell

nude a., n. naked (figure) —**nu'di·ty** n.

nudge v. push gently, as with the elbow to get someone's attention —n. gentle push

nud'ism' n. practice or cult of going nude —**nud'ist** a., n.

nug'get n. lump of gold ore

nui·sance (nōō'-) n. annoying act, person, etc.

nuke v., n. [Sl.] (attack with) nuclear weapon

null a. without legal force: also **null and void**

nul'li·fy v. **-fied', -fy'ing** make null 2 make useless —**nul'li·fi·ca'tion** n.

numb (num) a. not able to feel —v. make numb

num'ber n. 1 symbol or word showing how many or what place in a series 2 total 3 often pl. many 4 quantity 5 one part of a program of entertainment 6 form of a word showing it to be singular or plural —v. 1 to count 2 give a number to 3 include 4 to total or contain

num'ber·less a. countless

nu'mer·al n. figure, letter, or word expressing a number

nu'mer·a'tor n. part above the line in a fraction

nu·mer'i·cal a. 1 of, in, or having to do with number(s) 2 (expressed) by numbers Also **nu·mer'ic** —**nu·mer'i·cal·ly** adv.

nu'mer·ol'o·gy n. divination by numbers

nu'mer·ous a. 1 very many 2 large in number

nu·mis·mat'ics n. study or collecting of coins, etc. —**nu·mis'ma·tist** n.

num'skull' n. stupid person

nun n. woman living in a convent under vows

nun'cio' (-shō', -shē ō') n., pl. **-cios'** papal ambassador

nun'ner·y n., pl. **-ies** [Ar.] convent

nup'tial (-shəl) a. of marriage or a wedding —n. pl. a wedding

nurse n. 1 one trained to care for the sick, help doctors, etc. 2 nursemaid —v. 1 take care of (an invalid, etc.) 2

try to cure; treat **3** suckle **4** protect or conserve **5** nourish

nurse'maid' *n.* woman hired to care for children

nurs'er·y *n., pl.* **-ies 1** room set aside for children **2** place where trees and plants are raised for sale

nursery rhyme *n.* poem for children

nursery school *n.* school for children about three to five years old

nurs'ing home *n.* residence providing care for the infirm, chronically ill, disabled, etc.

nur'ture *n.* training; care —*v.* **1** nourish **2** train; rear

nut *n.* **1** dry fruit with a kernel inside a hard shell **2** the kernel **3** small metal block for screwing onto a bolt, etc. **4** [Sl.] odd or crazy person **5** [Sl.] fan; devotee

nut'crack'er *n.* device for cracking nutshells

nut'hatch' *n.* small songbird

nut'meat' *n.* kernel of a nut

nut'meg' *n.* aromatic seed grated and used as a spice

nu'tri·a (-trē-) *n.* soft, brown fur of a South American rodent

nu'tri·ent *a., n.* nutritious (substance)

nu'tri·ment *n.* food

nu·tri'tion (-trish'ən) *n.* **1** process of taking in and assimilating food **2** food —**nu·tri'tive** (-tiv) *a.*

nu·tri'tious *a.* nourishing

nuts *a.* [Sl.] crazy; silly

nut'shell' *n.* shell of a nut —**in a nutshell** in a few words

nut'ty *a.* **-ti·er, -ti·est 1** containing nuts **2** tasting like nuts **3** [Sl.] crazy, enthusiastic, etc.

nuz'zle *v.* **1** push against with the nose **2** snuggle

NV *abbrev.* Nevada

NW *abbrev.* northwest(ern)

NY *abbrev.* New York

NYC, N.Y.C. *abbrev.* New York City

ny'lon' *n.* **1** synthetic material made into thread, etc. **2** *pl.* stockings of this

nymph (nimf) *n.* minor Greek or Roman nature goddess

nym'pho·ma'ni·a *n.* uncontrollable sexual desire in a woman —**nym'pho·ma'ni·ac'** *a., n.*

O

O *int.* **1** exclamation in direct address **2** oh

O *abbrev. Baseball* out(s)

oaf *n.* stupid, clumsy fellow —**oaf'ish** *a.*

oak *n.* hardwood tree bearing acorns —**oak'en** *a.*

oa'kum *n.* hemp fiber used to caulk seams in boats

oar *n.* pole with a broad blade at one end, for rowing —**oars'man** *n., pl.* **-men**

oar'lock' *n.* device supporting an oar in rowing

o·a'sis *n., pl.* **-ses'** (-sēz') fertile place with water in the desert

oat *n. usually pl.* **1** a cereal grass **2** its grain —**oat'en** *a.*

oath *n.* **1** sworn declaration to tell the truth, etc. **2** word used in cursing

oat'meal' *n.* ground or rolled oats, cooked as porridge

ob'bli·ga'to (-gät'ō) *n., pl.* **-tos** or **-ti** (-ē) musical accompaniment to a piece, usually by a solo instrument

ob'du·rate (-dər ət) *a.* **1** stubborn; unyielding; inflexible **2** not repenting —**ob'du·ra·cy** *n.*

o·be'di·ent *a.* obeying or willing to obey —**o·be'di·ence** *n.* —**o·be'di·ent·ly** *adv.*

o·bei'sance (-bā'-, -bē'-) *n.* **1** bow, curtsy, etc. **2** homage

ob'e·lisk *n.* slender, tapering, four-sided pillar

o·bese' *a.* very fat —**o·be'si·ty** *n.*

o·bey' *v.* **1** carry out orders (of) **2** be guided by

ob·fus'cate' *v.* to obscure; confuse —**ob'fus·ca'tion** *n.*

ob'i·ter dic'tum *n., pl.* **ob'i·ter dic'ta** incidental remark

o·bit'u·ar'y (-bich'ōō-) *n., pl.* **-ies** notice of a person's death, as in a newspaper: also **o'bit**

obj *abbrev.* **1** object **2** objective

ob'ject (*v.:* əb jekt') *n.* **1** thing that can be seen or touched **2** person or thing to which action, etc. is directed **3** purpose; goal **4** *Gram.* word receiving the action of the verb or governed by a preposition —*v.* feel or express opposition or disapproval —**ob·jec'tor** *n.*

ob·jec'tion *n.* **1** expression of disapproval **2** a reason for objecting

ob·jec'tion·a·ble *a.* offensive; disagreeable

ob·jec'tive *a.* **1** real or actual; not subjective **2** without bias **3** *Gram.* of the case of an object of a preposition or verb —*n.* goal —**ob'jec·tiv'i·ty** *n.* —**ob·jec'tive·ly** *a.*

object lesson *n.* practical example of

some principle

ob·jet d'art (äb′zhä där′) n., pl. **ob′jets d'art′** (-zhä-) small object of artistic value

ob′jur·gate′ v. to rebuke; upbraid —**ob·jur·ga′tion** n.

ob·late′ a. Geometry flattened at the poles

ob·la′tion n. sacrifice or offering to God or a god

ob′li·gate′ v. bind by a promise, sense of duty, etc. —**ob′li·ga′tion** n. —**ob·lig′a·to′ry** a.

o·blige′ (-blīj′) v. 1 compel, as by law or duty 2 make indebted; do a favor for

o·blig′ing a. helpful

ob·lique′ (ō blēk′) a. 1 slanting 2 not direct —**ob·liq′ui·ty** n.

ob·lit′er·ate′ v. 1 blot out 2 destroy —**ob·lit′er·a′tion** n.

ob·liv′i·on n. 1 state of being forgotten 2 forgetful state

ob·liv′i·ous a. not aware

ob′long′ a. rectangular and longer than broad —n. oblong figure

ob′lo·quy (-kwē) n. widespread censure or disgrace

ob·nox′ious (-näk′shəs) a. offensive

o′boe n. double-reed woodwind instrument

ob·scene′ (-sēn′) a. offensive to decency —**ob·scen′i·ty** (-sen′-) n., pl. -**ties**

ob·scure′ a. 1 dim 2 not clear or distinct 3 not well-known —v. make obscure —**ob·scu′ri·ty** n.

ob′se·quies (-si kwēz′) pl.n. funeral rites

ob·se′qui·ous (-sē′kwē-) a. servile

ob·serv′ance n. 1 the observing of a law, etc. 2 customary act, rite, etc.

ob·serv′ant a. 1 attentive 2 perceptive; alert

ob·serv′a·to′ry n., pl. -**ries** building for astronomical research

ob·serve′ v. 1 adhere to (a law, etc.) 2 celebrate (a holiday, etc.) 3 notice; watch 4 to remark —**ob·serv′a·ble** a. —**ob′ser·va′tion** n. —**ob·serv′er** n.

ob·sess′ v. haunt in mind; preoccupy or be preoccupied greatly

ob·ses′sion n. idea, etc. that obsesses one

ob·sid′i·an n. hard, dark volcanic glass

ob′so·les′cent a. becoming obsolete —**ob′so·les′cence** n.

ob′so·lete′ a. no longer used

ob·sta·cle n. obstruction

ob·stet′rics n. branch of medicine dealing with childbirth —**ob·stet′ric,**

ob·stet′ri·cal a. —**ob·ste·tri′cian** n.

ob′sti·nate (-nət) a. 1 stubborn 2 hard to treat or cure —**ob′sti·na·cy** n.

ob·strep′er·ous a. unruly

ob·struct′ v. 1 to block 2 hinder —**ob·struc′tion** n. —**ob·struc′tive** a.

ob·tain′ v. 1 get by trying 2 prevail; be in effect

ob·trude′ v. 1 push out 2 force oneself upon others —**ob·tru′sive** a.

ob·tuse′ a. 1 more than 90°: said of an angle 2 blunt 3 slow to understand

ob·verse′ (n.: äb′vurs′) a. facing the observer —n. front or main side of a coin, etc.

ob′vi·ate′ v. prevent, as by proper measures

ob′vi·ous a. easy to understand —**ob′vi·ous·ly** adv.

oc′a·ri′na (-rē′-) n. small, oval wind instrument

oc·ca′sion n. 1 happening 2 special event 3 opportunity 4 a cause —v. to cause —**on occasion** sometimes

oc·ca′sion·al a. 1 for special times 2 infrequent —**oc·ca′sion·al·ly** adv.

Oc′ci·dent (äk′sə-) Europe and the Western Hemisphere —**Oc·ci·den′tal** a., n.

oc·clude′ v. to close or shut

oc·clu′sion n. the way the upper and lower teeth come together

oc·cult′ a. 1 secret 2 mysterious 3 magical

oc′cu·pan·cy n., pl. -**cies** an occupying —**oc′cu·pant** n.

oc′cu·pa′tion n. 1 an occupying 2 work; vocation —**oc′cu·pa′tion·al** a.

oc′cu·py′ v. -**pied′, -py′ing** 1 take possession of 2 dwell in 3 employ

oc·cur′ v. -**curred′, -cur′ring** 1 exist 2 come to mind 3 happen —**oc·cur′rence** n.

o·cean (ō′shən) n. 1 body of salt water covering much of the earth 2 one of its four main divisions —**o′ce·an′ic** (ō′shē-) a.

o′ce·an·og′ra·phy (ō′shə näg′-) n. study of the ocean environment

o′ce·lot (äs′ə-) n. large, spotted wildcat

o·cher, o·chre (ō′kər) n. yellow or red clay pigment

o′clock′ adv. by the clock

Oct abbrev. October

oc′ta·gon′ n. figure with eight sides and eight angles —**oc·tag′o·nal** n.

oc′tane′ number n. number representing efficiency of a gasoline in reducing excessive noise during combustion

oc′tave (-tiv) n. eight full steps of a

musical scale

oc·tet′, oc·tette′ *n.* group of eight, esp. of musical performers

Oc·to′ber *n.* tenth month

oc′to·ge·nar′i·an *n., a.* (person) between 80 and 90 years old

oc′to·pus *n.* mollusk with soft body and eight arms

oc′u·lar (-yōo-) *a.* of, for, or by the eye

oc′u·list *n.* [Ar.] ophthalmologist

OD *n., v.* [Sl.] overdose, esp. fatal(ly)

odd *a.* **1** having a remainder of one when divided by two; not even **2** left over, as from a pair **3** with a few more **4** occasional **5** peculiar; strange —**odd′ly** *adv.*

odd′ball′ *a., n.* [Sl.] peculiar (person)

odd′i·ty *n.* **1** odd quality **2** *pl.* **-ties** odd person or thing

odds *pl.n.* **1** advantage **2** betting ratio based on chances —**at odds** quarreling

odds and ends *pl.n.* remnants

odds′-on′ *a.* having a very good chance of winning

ode *n.* lofty poem in praise

o′di·ous *a.* disgusting

o′di·um *n.* **1** hatred **2** disgrace

o·dom′e·ter *n.* device that measures distance traveled

o′dor *n.* smell; aroma —**o′dor·ous** *a.*

o′dor·if′er·ous *a.* giving off a strong odor

o′dour *n.* Br. sp. of ODOR

od·ys·sey (äd′ə sē) *n.* long journey with adventures

Oed′i·pal (ed′-) *a.* of a child's unconscious attachment (**Oed′i·pus com′plex**) to the opposite-sex parent

o′er (ō′ər) *prep., adv.* [Poet.] over

oeu·vre (u′vr′) *n., pl.* **oeu′vres** [Fr.] all the works of a writer, composer, etc.

of *prep.* **1** being or coming from **2** belonging to **3** having or containing **4** concerning; about **5** during

off *adv.* **1** farther away in space or time **2** so as to be no longer on **3** so as to be less —*prep.* **1** not on **2** dependent on **3** away from **4** below the standard of —*a.* **1** not on **2** on the way **3** away from work; absent **4** below standard **5** in error; wrong —**off and on** now and then

off *abbrev.* **1** office **2** officer **3** official

of·fal (ôf′əl) *n.* refuse; garbage

off′beat′ *a.* [Inf.] unconventional

off′-col′or *a.* not quite proper; risqué

of·fend′ *v.* **1** commit an offense **2** make angry; displease —**of·fend′er** *n.*

of·fense′ (or ô′fens′) *n.* **1** sin or crime **2** an offending **3** an attacking —**give**

offense make angry; insult —**take offense** become offended

of·fen′sive *a.* **1** attacking **2** disgusting —*n.* **1** position of attack **2** an attack —**of·fen′sive·ly** *adv.*

of′fer *v.* **1** to present or give **2** suggest —*n.* thing offered —**of′fer·ing** *n.*

of′fer·to·ry *n., pl.* **-ries** [*often* O-] **1** the offering up of bread and wine to God at Mass **2** collection of money at church service

off′hand′ *adv.* without preparation —*a.* **1** said offhand **2** rude; curt Also **off′hand′ed**

of′fice *n.* **1** a favor **2** post of authority **3** place for doing business **4** rite

of′fice·hold′er *n.* **1** government official

of′fi·cer *n.* **1** one having a position of authority in business, the armed forces, etc. **2** police officer

of·fi′cial (-fish′əl) *a.* **1** authorized **2** formal —*n.* one holding an office —**of·fi′cial·ly** *adv.*

of·fi′ci·ate′ (-fish′ē-) *v.* perform official duties or functions

of·fi′cious (-fish′əs) *a.* meddlesome

off′ing *n.* used chiefly in **in the offing**, at some future time

off′-key′ *a.* not harmonious

off′-lim′its *a.* not to be gone to

off′-line′ *a.* not connected to a computer's CPU

off′-price′ *a.* selling high-quality clothing, etc. at a price lower than the retail price

off′-put′ting *a.* [Chiefly Br.] distracting, annoying, etc.

off′-sea′son *n.* time when usual activity is reduced

off·set′ *v.* **-set′, -set′ting** compensate for

off′shoot′ *n.* anything that comes from a main source

off′shore′ *a., adv.* (moving) away from shore

off′side′ *a.* not in proper position for play

off′spring′ *n.* child or children

off′-the-wall′ *a.* [Sl.] very unusual, eccentric, etc.

off′-white′ *a.* grayish-white or yellowish-white

off year *n.* year of little production

oft *adv.* [Poet.] often

of·ten (ôf′ən, -tən) *adv.* many times: also **of′ten·times′**

o·gle (ō′gəl) *v.* look at in a boldly desirous way —*n.* ogling look

o′gre (-gər) *n.* **1** *Folklore* man-eating giant **2** cruel man

oh (ō) *int., n., pl.* **oh's** or **ohs** exclamation of surprise, fear, pain, etc.

OH *abbrev.* Ohio

ohm (ōm) *n.* unit of electrical resistance

-oid *suf.* like; resembling

oil *n.* 1 any greasy liquid 2 petroleum —*v.* lubricate with oil —*a.* of, from, or like oil —**oil′y** *a.*

oil′cloth′ *n.* cloth waterproofed with oil or paint

oil color *n.* paint made of pigment ground in oil

oil painting *n.* painting in oil colors

oil shale *n.* shale from which oil can be distilled

oil′skin′ *n.* cloth made waterproof with oil

oink *v., n.* (make) the vocal sound of a pig

oint′ment *n.* oily cream for healing the skin

OK, O.K. *a., adv., int.* all right —*n.* approval —*v.* **OK'd, O.K.'d, OK'ing, O.K.'ing** to approve Also *sp.* **o′kay′**

OK *abbrev.* Oklahoma

o′kra *n.* plant with edible green pods

old *a.* 1 having lived or existed for a long time 2 of a specified age 3 not new 4 former —*n.* time long past — **old′ness** *n.*

Old English *n.* English language before A.D. 1100

old′-fash′ioned *a.* of the past; out-of-date

old′-growth′ *a.* of a forest of large, old trees, with great biodiversity

old guard *n.* most conservative part of a group

old hand *n.* experienced person

old hat *a.* [Sl.] 1 old-fashioned 2 trite

old′ie, old′y *n., pl.* **-ies** [Inf.] old joke, song, etc.

old lady *n.* [Sl.] one's mother or wife

old′-line′ *a.* long-established, conservative, etc.

old maid *n.* spinster: mildly disparaging

old man *n.* [Sl.] one's father or husband

old school *n.* people holding to tradition, conservatism, etc.

old′ster *n.* [Inf.] old or elderly person

Old Testament *n.* Bible of Judaism, or the first part of the Christian Bible

old′-tim′er *n.* [Inf.] 1 longtime member, worker, etc. 2 old person

old′-tim′ey *a.* [Inf.] evoking memories of the past

old′-world′ *a.* of customs, etc. associated with European culture

o·lé (ō lā′) *int., n.* [Sp.] shout of approval, etc., as at a bullfight

o′le·ag′i·nous (-aj′-) *a.* oily; unctuous

o′le·an′der *n.* flowering evergreen shrub

o′le·o·mar′ga·rine, o′le·o·mar′ga·rin *n.* margarine: also **o′le·o′**

ol·fac′to·ry *a.* of the sense of smell

ol′i·gar′chy (-gär′kē) *n., pl.* **-chies** 1 state rule by a few people 2 these people

ol′ive (-iv) *n.* 1 evergreen tree 2 its small, oval fruit 3 yellowish green

O·lym′pic games *pl.n.* biennial athletic competition alternating summer and winter sports: also the **O·lym′pics**

om′buds·man *n., pl.* **-men** official who investigates complaints against an organization, etc.

o·me′ga *n.* last letter of the Greek alphabet

om·e·let, om·e·lette (äm′lət) *n.* eggs beaten up and cooked as a pancake

o′men *n.* sign of something to come

om′i·nous *a.* threatening

o·mis′sion *n.* an omitting or thing omitted

o·mit′ *v.* **o·mit′ted, o·mit′ting** 1 leave out 2 fail to do

omni- *pref.* all; everywhere

om′ni·bus *a.* providing for, or including, many things at once

om·nip′o·tent *a.* all-powerful —**om·nip′o·tence** *n.*

om′ni·pres′ent *a.* present in all places at the same time

om·nis′cient (-nish′ənt) *a.* knowing all things —**om·nis′cience** *n.*

om·niv′o·rous *a.* 1 eating both animal and vegetable foods 2 taking in everything —**om′ni·vore′** *n.*

on *prep.* 1 held up by, covering, or attached to 2 near to 3 at the time of 4 connected with 5 in a state of 6 by means of 7 concerning 8 [Inf.] using habitually —*adv.* 1 in a situation of touching, covering, or being held up by 2 toward 3 forward 4 continuously 5 into operation —*a.* in action

ON *abbrev.* Ontario

once *adv.* 1 one time 2 at any time 3 formerly —*n.* one time —**at once** 1 immediately 2 simultaneously

once′-o′ver *n.* [Inf.] quick look, examination, etc.

on·col′o·gy *n.* branch of medicine dealing with tumors —**on·col′o·gist** *n.*

on′com′ing *a.* approaching

one *a.* 1 being a single thing 2 united 3 specific, but unnamed 4 some —*n.* 1 lowest number 2 single person or thing —*pron.* a person or thing —**one by one** individually

one'-di·men'sion·al *a.* having a single quality, concern, etc. and thus narrow, limited, etc.

one'ness *n.* unity; identity

on'er·ous *a.* oppressive

one·self' *pron.* one's own self; himself or herself —**be oneself** function normally —**by oneself** alone

one'-sid'ed *a.* **1** unequal **2** partial

one'-stop' *a.* of or done at a full-service bank, etc.

one'-time' *a.* **1** former **2** done, occurring, etc. once Also, esp. for 1, **one' time'**

one'-track' *a.* [Inf.] limited in scope

one'-way' *a.* in one direction only

on'go'ing *a.* progressing

on·ion (un'yən) *n.* bulblike, sharp-tasting vegetable

on'ion·skin' *n.* tough, thin, translucent, glossy paper

on'-line' *a.* connected to a computer's CPU

on'look'er *n.* spectator

on'ly *a.* **1** alone of its or their kind **2** best —*adv.* **1** and no other **2** merely —*con.* [Inf.] except that —**only too** very

on'o·mat'o·poe'ia (-pē'ə) *n.* formation or use of words whose sound reflects or reinforces their meaning

on'rush' *n.* strong onward rush

on·set' *n.* **1** attack **2** start

on'slaught' *n.* violent attack

on'stream' *adv.* into operation

on'to *prep.* to and upon

o'nus *n.* **1** burden **2** blame

on'ward *adv.* forward: also **on'wards** —*a.* advancing

on'yx (-iks) *n.* kind of agate

ooze *v.* flow out slowly —*n.* **1** something that oozes **2** soft mud or slime

o'pal *n.* iridescent gem

o·paque' (-pāk') *a.* not transparent — **o·pac'i·ty** (-pas'-) *n.*

op. *cit. abbrev.* in the work cited

OPEC (ō'pek') *n.* Organization of Petroleum Exporting Countries

Op'-Ed' *a.* of or on a newspaper page featuring opinion columns, etc.

o'pen *a.* **1** not closed, covered, etc. **2** not enclosed **3** unfolded **4** free to be entered, used, etc. **5** not restricted **6** available **7** frank —*v.* **1** to cause to be or become open **2** begin **3** start operating —**open to** willing to consider —**o'pen·er** *n.* —**o'pen·ly** *adv.*

o'pen-air' *a.* outdoor

o'pen-and-shut' *a.* easily decided

o'pen-end'ed *a.* unlimited

o'pen-eyed' *a.* with the eyes wide open, as in surprise

o'pen-faced' *a.* **1** having a frank, honest face **2** without a top slice of bread

o'pen-hand'ed *a.* generous

open house *n.* **1** informal home reception **2** time when an institution is open to visitors

o'pen·ing *n.* **1** open place **2** beginning **3** favorable chance **4** unfilled job

o'pen-mind'ed *a.* impartial

o'pen·work' *n.* ornamental work with openings in it

op'er·a *n.* play set to music and sung with an orchestra —**op'er·at'ic** *a.*

op'er·a·ble *a.* **1** able to function **2** that can be treated by surgery

opera glass'es *pl.n.* small binoculars

op'er·ate *v.* **1** be or keep in action **2** have an effect **3** perform an operation **4** manage —**op'er·a'tor** *n.*

operating system *n.* software controlling a computer's basic operations

op'er·a'tion *n.* **1** act or way of operating **2** a being in action **3** one process in a series **4** surgical treatment for an illness —**op'er·a'tion·al** *a.*

op'er·a·tive *a.* **1** operating (effectively) **2** most important —*n.* a spy

op'er·et'ta *n.* light opera

oph'thal·mol'o·gy (äf'-) *n.* branch of medicine dealing with diseases of the eye —**oph'thal·mol'o·gist** *n.*

o'pi·ate (-pē ət) *n.* narcotic drug containing opium

o·pine' *v.* think; suppose: usually humorous

o·pin'ion (-yən) *n.* **1** what one thinks true **2** estimation **3** expert judgment

o·pin'ion·at'ed *a.* holding stubbornly to one's own opinion

o'pi·um *n.* narcotic drug made from a certain poppy

o·pos'sum *n.* small, tree-dwelling mammal

op·po'nent *n.* person against one in a fight, debate, etc.

op'por·tune' *adv.* appropriate or timely

op'por·tun'ist *n.* one who adapts actions to circumstances without regard to principles —**op'por·tun'ism'** *n.* —**op'por·tun·is'tic** *a.*

op'por·tu'ni·ty *n.,* pl. **-ties** fit time to do something

op·pose' *v.* **1** to place opposite **2** fight or resist —**op'po·si'tion** (-zish'ən) *n.*

op'po·site (-zit) *a.* **1** entirely different

226

2 opposed to —n. anything opposed — prep. across from

op·press' v. 1 weigh down 2 rule in a cruel way —**op·pres'sion** n. —**op·pres'sor** n.

op·pres'sive a. 1 burdensome 2 cruel and unjust

op·pro'bri·ous a. abusive; disrespectful

op·pro'bri·um n. scolding contempt for something regarded as inferior

opt v. make a choice (*for*) —**opt out** (**of**) choose not to be or continue (in)

op'tic a. of the eye

op'ti·cal a. 1 of vision 2 aiding sight 3 of optics

optical disc (or **disk**) n. disk of data, as computer text or music, recorded so as to be read by a laser

op·ti'cian (-tish'ən) n. maker or seller of eyeglasses

op'tics n. science dealing with light and vision

op'ti·mism' n. tendency to take the most hopeful view of matters —**op'ti·mist** n. —**op'ti·mis'tic** a.

op'ti·mize' v. make the greatest use of

op'ti·mum n., a. (the) best: also **op'ti·mal** a.

op'tion n. choice or right to choose —**op'tion·al** a.

op·tom'e·trist n. one who tests eyes and fits eyeglasses —**op·tom'e·try** n.

op'u·lent a. 1 wealthy 2 abundant —**op'u·lence** n.

o'pus n., pl. **o'pe·ra** or **o'pus·es** a work, esp. of music

or con. word introducing an alternative, synonym, etc.

OR abbrev. 1 Oregon 2 operating room

-or suf. person or thing that

or'a·cle n. ancient Greek or Roman priestess or priest who acted as prophet —**o·rac'u·lar** a.

o·ral (ôr'əl) a. 1 spoken 2 of the mouth —**o'ral·ly** adv.

or'ange n. 1 sweet, round, reddish-yellow citrus fruit 2 reddish yellow

or'ange·ade' n. drink of orange juice, water, and sugar

o·rang'u·tan' n. large, reddish ape

o·rate' v. speak pompously

o·ra'tion n. formal public speech —**or'a·tor** n.

or'a·to'ri·o' n., pl. **-os'** vocal and orchestral composition on a religious theme

or'a·to'ry n. skill in public speaking —**or'a·tor'i·cal** a.

orb n. (celestial) sphere

or'bit n. path of a satellite around a celestial body —v. put or go in an orbit

or'chard n. grove of fruit trees

or'ches·tra (-kis-) n. 1 large group of musicians playing together 2 main floor of a theater —**or·ches'tral** (-kes'-) a.

or'ches·trate' v. arrange music for an orchestra —**or'ches·tra'tion** n.

or'chid (-kid) n. 1 plant having flowers with three petals, one of which is enlarged 2 light bluish red

or·dain' v. 1 to decree 2 admit to the ministry

or·deal' n. difficult or painful experience

or'der n. 1 peaceful, orderly, or proper state 2 monastic or fraternal brotherhood 3 general condition 4 a command 5 (a request for) items to be supplied 6 class; kind —v. 1 arrange 2 command 3 request (supplies) —**in order that** so that —**in short order** quickly —**on the order of** 1 similar to 2 approximately

or'der·ly a. 1 neatly arranged 2 well-behaved —n., pl. **-lies** 1 soldier acting as an officer's servant 2 male hospital attendant —**or'der·li·ness** n.

or'di·nal number n. number used to show order in a series, as *first*, *second*, etc.

or'di·nance n. statute, esp. of a city government

or'di·nar'y a. 1 customary; usual; regular 2 common; average —**or'di·nar'i·ly** adv.

or'di·na'tion n. an ordaining or being ordained

ord'nance n. Mil. heavy guns, ammunition, etc.

ore n. rock or mineral containing metal

o·reg'a·no n. plant with fragrant leaves used as seasoning

or'gan n. 1 keyboard musical instrument using pipes, reeds, or electronic tubes 2 animal or plant part with a special function 3 agency or medium —**or'gan·ist** n.

or'gan·dy, or'gan·die n. sheer, stiff cotton cloth

or·gan'ic a. 1 of a body organ 2 systematically arranged 3 of or from living matter 4 of chemical compounds containing carbon

or'gan·ism' n. living thing

or'gan·i·za'tion n. 1 act of organizing 2 group organized for some purpose

or'gan·ize' v. 1 arrange according to a

system **2** form into a group, union, etc. —**or'gan·iz'er** n.

or·gan'za n. stiff fabric of rayon, silk, etc.

or'gasm' n. climax of a sexual act

or'gy (-jē) n., pl. **-gies 1** wild merry-making, esp. with sexual activity **2** unrestrained indulgence

o'ri·ent v. adjust (oneself) to a specific situation —[O-] E Asia —**O'ri·en'tal** a., n. —**o'ri·en·ta'tion** n.

o'ri·en·teer'ing n. timed cross-country foot race with compass and map

or'i·fice (-fis) n. mouth; opening

orig abbrev. origin(al)(ly)

o'ri·ga'mi (-gä'-) n. Japanese art of folding paper to form flowers, etc.

or'i·gin n. **1** beginning **2** parentage **3** source

o·rig'i·nal a. **1** first **2** new; novel **3** inventive —n. an original work, form, etc. —**o·rig'i·nal'i·ty** n. —**o·rig'i·nal·ly** adv.

o·rig'i·nate' v. **1** create; invent **2** begin; start —**o·rig'i·na'tion** n. —**o·rig'i·na'tor** n.

o'ri·ole n. bird with bright orange and black plumage

Or'lon' trademark synthetic fiber —n. [o-] this fiber

or'mo·lu' n. alloy used to imitate gold

or'na·ment (-mənt; v.: -ment') n. decoration —v. decorate —**or'na·men'tal** a. —**or'na·men·ta'tion** n.

or·nate' a. showy —**or·nate'ly** adv.

or'ner·y a. **-i·er, -i·est** [Inf.] mean; obstinate

or·ni·thol'o·gy n. study of birds —**or'ni·thol'o·gist** n.

o'ro·tund' a. **1** full and deep in sound **2** bombastic

or'phan n. child whose parents are dead —v. cause to be an orphan —**or'phan·age** n.

or'ris n. iris having a root (**or'ris·root'**) pulverized for perfume, etc.

or·tho·don'tics n. dentistry of teeth straightening: also **or'tho·don'tia** (-shə) —**or'tho·don'tist** n.

or·tho·dox' a. **1** holding to the usual or fixed beliefs; conventional **2** [O-] of a large eastern Christian church —**or'tho·dox'y** n.

or·thog'ra·phy n., pl. **-phies** correct spelling

or·tho·pe'dics n. surgery dealing with bones —**or'tho·pe'dic** a. —**or'tho·pe'dist** n.

-ory suf. **1** of or like **2** place or thing for

os'cil·late' (äs'ə-) v. **1** swing to and fro

2 fluctuate —**os'cil·la'tion** n.

os·cil'lo·scope' (ə sil'ə-) n. instrument showing an electrical wave on a fluorescent screen

os'cu·late' (-kyōō-) v. kiss: humorous usage —**os'cu·la'tion** n.

-ose suf. full of; like

-osis suf. **1** condition or action **2** diseased condition

os·mo'sis n. diffusion of fluids through a porous membrane

os'prey (-prē) n., pl. **-preys** large, fish-eating hawk

os'si·fy' v. **-fied', -fy'ing** change into bone

os·ten'si·ble a. seeming; apparent —**os·ten'si·bly** adv.

os·ten·ta'tion n. showiness —**os'ten·ta'tious** a.

os·te·o·ar·thri'tis n. arthritis with cartilage deterioration

os·te·op'a·thy n. school of medicine emphasizing interrelationship of muscles and bones —**os'te·o·path'** n.

os·te·o·po·ro'sis n. a disorder marked by porous, brittle bones

os'tra·cize' v. banish; shut out —**os'tra·cism'** n.

os'trich n. large, nonflying bird

OT abbrev. overtime

oth'er a. **1** being the one(s) remaining **2** different **3** additional —pron. **1** the other one **2** some other one —adv. otherwise

oth'er·wise' adv. **1** differently **2** in all other ways **3** if not; else —a. different

oth'er·world'ly a. apart from earthly interests

o·ti·ose (ō'shē ōs') a. **1** futile **2** useless

ot'ter n. weasellike animal

ot'to·man n. low, cushioned seat or footstool

ouch int. cry of pain

ought v. auxiliary verb showing: **1** duty **2** desirability **3** probability

oui (wē) adv., int. [Fr.] yes

ounce n. **1** unit of weight, $\frac{1}{16}$ pound **2** fluid ounce, $\frac{1}{16}$ pint

our a. of us

ours pron. that or those belonging to us

our·selves' pron. intensive or reflexive form of WE

-ous suf. having; full of; characterized by

oust v. force out; expel

oust'er n. dispossession

out adv. **1** away from a place, etc. **2** outdoors **3** into being or action **4**

thoroughly **5** from a group —*a.* **1** not used, working, etc. **2** having lost —*n.* **1** [Sl.] excuse **2** *Baseball* retirement of a batter or runner from play —*v.* **1** become known **2** [Inf.] identify (a person) publicly as a homosexual —*prep.* out of —**on the outs** [Inf.] quarreling —**out for** trying to get or do —**out of 1** from inside of **2** beyond **3** from (material) **4** because of **5** no longer having **6** so as to deprive —**out of it** [Sl.] **1** unsophisticated **2** mentally impaired

out- *pref.* **1** outside **2** outward **3** better or more than

out′age (-ij) *n.* accidental suspension of operation

out′-and-out′ *a.* thorough

out′back′ *n.* remote, sparsely settled region

out·bal′ance *v.* be greater than in weight, value, etc.

out′bid′ *v.* **-bid′, -bid′ding** bid or offer more than (someone else)

out′board′ *a.* located on the outer surface of a boat

out′bound′ *a.* going outward

out′break′ *n.* a breaking out, as of disease or rioting

out′build′ing *n.* building apart from the main one

out′burst′ *n.* sudden show of feeling, energy, etc.

out′cast′ *a., n.* shunned (person)

out′class′ *v.* surpass

out′come′ *n.* result

out′crop′ *n.* exposed rock layer

out′cry′ *n., pl.* **-cries′ 1** a crying out **2** strong protest

out′dat′ed *a.* out-of-date

out′dis′tance *v.* leave behind, as in a race

out′do′ *v.* do better than

out′door′ *a.* in the open

out′doors′ *adv.* in or into the open; outside —*n.* the outdoor world

out′er *a.* on or closer to the outside

out′er·most′ *a.* farthest out

outer space *n.* space beyond the earth's atmosphere

out′er·wear′ *n.* garments worn over the usual clothing

out′field′ *n. Baseball* the area beyond the infield —**out′field′er** *n.*

out′fit′ *n.* **1** equipment for some activity **2** group; esp., military unit —*v.* **-fit′ted, -fit′ting** equip

out′flank′ *v.* go around and beyond the flank of (troops)

out′fox′ *v.* outwit

out′go′ *n.* expenditure

out′go′ing *a.* **1** leaving or retiring **2** sociable

out′grow′ *v.* grow too large for

out′growth′ *n.* **1** result **2** an offshoot

out′guess′ *v.* outwit

out′house′ *n.* outdoor latrine

out′ing *n.* picnic, trip, etc.

out·land′ish *a.* **1** strange **2** fantastic

out·last′ *v.* endure longer than

out′law′ *n.* notorious criminal —*v.* declare illegal

out′lay′ *n.* money spent

out′let′ *n.* **1** passage or way out **2** market for goods

out′line′ *n.* **1** bounding line **2** sketch showing only outer lines **3** general plan

out·live′ *v.* live longer than

out′look′ *n.* **1** viewpoint **2** prospect

out′ly′ing *a.* remote

out·ma·neu′ver (-nōō′-) *v.* to maneuver with better effect than

out·mod′ed (-mōd′-) *a.* obsolete; old-fashioned

out·num′ber *v.* be greater in number than

out′-of-date′ *a.* no longer used

out′-of-doors′ *a.* outdoor —*n., adv.* outdoors

out′-of-the-way′ *a.* secluded

out′pa′tient *n.* hospital patient treated without lodging or meals

out′post′ *n.* remote settlement or military post

out′put′ *n.* **1** total quantity produced in a given period **2** information from a computer **3** current or power delivered

out′rage′ *n.* **1** extremely vicious act **2** deep insult —*v.* **1** offend, insult, etc. **2** to cause anger in —**out·ra′geous** *a.*

out·rank′ *v.* to exceed in rank

out′reach′ *n.* program for getting help to people in a community

out′rig′ger *n.* **1** canoe with a float at the side **2** the float

out′right′ *a., adv.* complete(ly)

out′set′ *n.* beginning

out′side′ *n.* **1** the exterior **2** area beyond —*a.* **1** outer **2** from some other **3** slight —*adv.* on or to the outside —*prep.* on or to the outside of

out′sid′er *n.* one not of a certain group

out′size′ *a.* unusually large

out′skirts′ *pl.n.* outlying districts of a city, etc.

out′smart′ *v.* outwit

out′source′ *v.* transfer (work) outside a company to reduce costs

out′spo′ken *a.* frank; bold

out′stand′ing *a.* **1** prominent **2**

unpaid

out'stretched' *a.* extended

out'strip' *v.* **-stripped', -strip'ping** excel

out'take' *n.* faulty recording, film scene, etc. not used in the final version

out'ward *a.* **1** outer **2** visible —*adv.* toward the outside Also **out'wards** —**out'ward·ly** *adv.*

out'wear' *v.* **-wore', -worn', -wear'ing** outlast

out·wit' *v.* **-wit'ted, -wit'ting** to overcome by cleverness

o'va *n.* pl. of OVUM

o'val *a., n.* egg-shaped (thing)

o'va·ry *n., pl.* **-ries 1** female gland where ova are formed **2** part of a flower where the seeds form —**o·va'ri·an** (-ver'-) *a.*

o·va'tion *n.* loud and long applause or cheering

ov'en (uv'-) *n.* compartment for baking, drying, etc.

ov'en·proof' *a.* withstanding high temperatures of an oven

o'ver *prep.* **1** above **2** on; upon **3** across **4** during **5** more than **6** about —*adv.* **1** above or across **2** more **3** down **4** other side up **5** again —*a.* **1** finished **2** on the other side

over- *pref.* excessive or excessively: see list below

o'ver·a·bun'dance

o'ver·ac'tive

o'ver·anx'ious

o'ver·bur'den

o'ver·cau'tious

o'ver·con'fi·dent

o'ver·cook'

o'ver·crowd'

o'ver·eat'

o'ver·em'pha·size'

o'ver·es'ti·mate'

o'ver·ex·ert'

o'ver·ex·pose'

o'ver·heat'

o'ver·in·dulge'

o'ver·load'

o'ver·pop'u·late'

o'ver·pro·duc'tion

o'ver·ripe'

o'ver·stim'u·late'

o'ver·stock'

o'ver·sup·ply'

o'ver·a·chieve' *v.* **1** do better in school than expected **2** drive oneself to reach unreasonable goals

o'ver·age (-āj') *a.* above the standard or accepted age

o'ver·age (-ij) *n.* a surplus

o'ver·all' *a.* **1** end to end **2** total —*n. pl.* work trousers with attached bib

o'ver·arch'ing *a.* inclusive

o'ver·awe' *v.* subdue by inspiring awe

o'ver·bear'ing *a.* bossy

o'ver·blown' *a.* **1** excessive **2** pompous

o'ver·board' *adv.* from a ship into the water

o'ver·cast' *a.* cloudy; dark

o'ver·coat' *n.* coat worn over the usual clothing

o'ver·come' *v.* get the better of; master

o'ver·do' *v.* do too much

o'ver·dose' (*n.:* ō'vər dōs') *v., n.* (take) too large a dose

o'ver·draw' *v.* draw on in excess of the amount credited to one —**o'ver·draft'** *n.*

o'ver·drawn' *a.* drawn on in excess of the amount credited to one

o'ver·dress' *v.* dress too warmly, showily, or formally

o'ver·drive' *n.* gear that reduces an engine's power without reducing its speed

o'ver·due' *a.* past the time for payment, arrival, etc.

o'ver·flight' *n.* flight of an aircraft over foreign territory

o'ver·flow' (*n.:* ō'vər flō') *v.* flood; run over —*n.* **1** an overflowing **2** vent for overflowing liquids

o'ver·grow' *v.* **1** grow over all of **2** grow too much

o'ver·hand' *a., adv.* with the hand held higher than the elbow

o'ver·hang' *n.* part of a building projecting over another part

o'ver·haul' *v.* check thoroughly and make needed repairs

o'ver·head' *a., adv.* above the head —*n.* continuing business costs

o'ver·hear' *v.* hear a speaker without his knowledge

o'ver·joyed' *a.* delighted

o'ver·kill' *n.* much more than is needed, suitable, etc.

o'ver·land' *a., adv.* by or across land

o'ver·lap' *v.* lap over

o'ver·lay' *v.* **-laid', -lay'ing** spread over **2** cover with decorative layer

o'ver·look' (*n.:* ō'vər look') *v.* **1** look down on **2** fail to notice **3** neglect **4** excuse —*n.* high place with a view

o'ver·lord' *n.* person with great authority over others

o'ver·ly *adv.* excessively

o'ver·night' (*a.:* ō'vər nīt') *adv.* during the night —*a.* of or for a night

o'ver·pass' *n.* bridge over a railway, road, etc.

o'ver·pow'er *v.* subdue

o'ver·rate' *v.* estimate too highly

o'ver·re·act' *v.* react in an overly emotional way

o'ver·ride' *v.* overrule

o'ver·rule' *v.* set aside or decide against

o'ver·run' *v.* **1** spread out over **2** swarm over

o'ver·seas' *a., adv.* **1** across or beyond the sea **2** foreign

o'ver·see' *v.* supervise —**o'ver·se'er** *n.*

o'ver·shad'ow *v.* be more important than

o'ver·shoe' *n.* waterproof boot worn over a regular shoe

o'ver·sight' *n.* **1** failure to see **2** careless omission

o'ver·sim'pli·fy' *v.* simplify to the point of distortion —**o'ver·sim'pli·fi·ca'tion** *n.*

o'ver·size' *a.* **1** too large **2** larger than usual Also **o'ver·sized'**

o'ver·sleep' *v.* sleep longer than intended

o'ver·step' *v.* go beyond the limits of

o'ver·stuffed' *a.* upholstered with deep stuffing

o·vert' (*or* ō'vurt) *a.* open; public

o'ver·take' *v.* **1** catch up with **2** come upon suddenly

o'ver·tax' *v.* **1** tax too much **2** make excessive demands on

o'ver-the-count'er *a.* **1** sold without prescription **2** traded directly

o'ver-the-top' *a.* outrageously excessive

o'ver·throw' (*n.:* ō'vər thrō') *v.,* *n.* defeat

o'ver·time' *n.* **1** time beyond a set limit **2** pay for overtime work —*a.,* *adv.* of or for overtime

o'ver·tone' *n. Mus.* higher tone heard faintly when a main tone is played

o'ver·ture *n.* **1** *Mus.* introduction **2** introductory proposal

o'ver·turn' *v.* **1** turn over **2** defeat

o'ver·ween'ing *a.* haughty

o'ver·weight' *a.* above the normal or allowed weight

o'ver·whelm' *v.* **1** cover over completely **2** crush

o'ver·work' *v.* work too hard —*n.* too much work

o'ver·wrought' (-rôt') *a.* very nervous or excited

o'vi·duct' (*or* äv'i-) *n.* tube for passage of ova from ovary to uterus

o'void' *a.* egg-shaped

ov'u·late' (äv'yōō-) *v.* make and release ova —**ov'u·la'tion** *n.*

ov·ule *n.* **1** immature ovum **2** part of a plant that develops into a seed

o'vum *n., pl.* **-va** mature female germ cell

owe *v.* **1** be in debt (to) for a certain sum **2** feel obligated to give

ow'ing (ō'-) *a.* due; unpaid —**owing to** because of

owl *n.* night bird of prey with large eyes —**owl'ish** *a.*

owl'et *n.* small or young owl

own *a.* belonging to oneself or itself —*n.* what one owns —*v.* **1** possess **2** confess —**own'er** *n.* —**own'er·ship** *n.*

ox *n., pl.* **ox'en** **1** cud-chewing animal, as a cow, bull, etc. **2** castrated bull

ox'blood' *n.* deep-red color

ox'bow' (-bō') *n.* U-shaped part of an ox yoke

ox'ford (-fərd) *n.* **1** low shoe laced over the instep **2** cotton cloth used for shirts, etc.

ox'i·dant *n.* substance that oxidizes another

ox'ide' *n.* oxygen compound

ox'i·dize' *v.* unite with oxygen —**ox'i·da'tion** *n.*

ox'y·gen *n.* colorless gas, commonest chemical element

ox'y·gen·ate' *v.* treat or combine with oxygen

ox'y·mo'ron *n.* combination of contradictory ideas or terms

oys'ter *n.* edible mollusk with hinged shell

oz *abbrev.* ounce(s)

o'zone' *n.* form of oxygen with a strong odor

P

p *abbrev.* **1** page **2** participle **3** past

pa *n.* [Inf.] father

PA *abbrev.* **1** Pennsylvania **2** public address (system)

pab'lum *n.* simplistic or bland writing, ideas, etc.

PAC (pak) *n.* group raising funds for political campaigns

pace *n.* **1** a step or stride **2** rate of speed **3** gait —*v.* **1** to walk back and forth across **2** measure by paces **3** set the pace for

pace'mak'er *n.* **1** one leading the way: also **pace'set'ter** **2** electronic device placed in the body to regulate heart beat

pach'y·derm' (pak'ə-) *n.* large, thick-skinned animal, as the elephant

pach'y·san'dra *n.* low evergreen plant grown as ground cover

pa·cif'ic *a.* peaceful; calm

pac'i·fism' (pas'ə-) *n.* opposition to all war —**pac'i·fist** *n.*

pac'i·fy' -**fied'**, -**fy'ing** make calm — **pac'i·fi·ca'tion** *n.* —**pac'i·fi'er** *n.*

pack *n.* 1 bundle of things 2 package of a set number 3 a group of animals, etc. —*v.* 1 put (things) in a box, bundle, etc. 2 crowd; cram 3 fill tightly 4 send (*off*)

pack'age *n.* 1 things packed, as in a box 2 container —*v.* make a package of

pack'et *n.* small package

pack'ing-house' *n.* plant where meats, etc. are packed for sale

pack rat *n.* [Inf.] one who hoards miscellaneous items

pack'sad'dle *n.* saddle with fastenings to secure a load

pact *n.* compact; agreement

pad *n.* 1 soft stuffing or cushion 2 sole of an animal's foot 3 water lily leaf 4 paper sheets fastened at one edge —*v.* **pad'ded**, **pad'ding** 1 stuff with material 2 walk softly 3 fill with needless or dishonest material

pad'dle *n.* 1 oar for a canoe 2 thing shaped like this, for games, etc. —*v.* 1 propel with a paddle 2 spank

paddle wheel *n.* wheel with boards around it for propelling a steamboat

pad'dock *n.* small enclosure for horses

pad'dy *n.*, *pl.* -**dies** rice field

pad'lock' *n.* lock with a U-shaped arm —*v.* fasten with a padlock

pa·dre (pä'drā) *n.* father: title for a priest

pae·an (pē'ən) *n.* song of joy

pa'gan *n., a.* heathen —**pa'gan·ism'** *n.*

page *n.* 1 one side of a leaf of a book, etc. 2 the leaf 3 boy attendant 4 Web page —*v.* 1 number the pages of 2 try to find by calling out the name of 3 contact with a pager —**on the same page** [Inf.] in agreement

pag'eant (paj'ənt) *n.* elaborate show, parade, play, etc. —**pag'eant·ry** *n.*

pag'er *n.* small portable device for sending and receiving messages

pag'i·na'tion (paj'-) *n.* numbering of pages

pa·go'da *n.* towerlike temple of the Orient

paid *v.* pt. & pp. of PAY

pail *n.* bucket —**pail'ful'** *n.*

pain *n.* 1 hurt felt in body or mind 2 *pl.* great care —*v.* cause pain to —

pain'ful *a.* —**pain'less** *a.*

pains'tak'ing *a.* careful

paint *n.* pigment mixed with oil, water, etc. —*v.* 1 make pictures (of) with paint 2 cover with paint — **paint'er** *n.* —**paint'ing** *n.*

pair *n.* two things, persons, etc. that match or make a unit —*v.* form pairs (of)

pais'ley (pāz'-) *a.* [*also* P-] of a complex pattern used for fabrics

pa·ja'mas (-jä'məz, -jam'əz) *pl.n.* matching trousers and top for sleeping

pal *n.* [Inf.] close friend

pal'ace (-əs) *n.* 1 monarch's residence 2 magnificent building —**pa·la'tial** (-shəl) *a.*

pal'at·a·ble *a.* pleasing to the taste

pal'ate (-ət) *n.* 1 roof of the mouth 2 taste

pa·lav'er (-ə-) *n.* idle talk —*v.* talk idly

pale *a.* 1 white; colorless 2 not bright or intense —*v.* 1 pointed fence stake 2 boundary —*v.* turn pale

pa'le·on·tol'o·gy *n.* study of fossils — **pa'le·on·tol'o·gist** *n.*

pal·ette (-ət) *n.* thin board on which artists mix paint

pal'frey (pôl'-) *n., pl.* -**freys** [Ar.] saddle horse

pal'i·mo'ny *n.* money paid to support a person one lived with but was not married to

pal'imp·sest' *n.* parchment, etc. with writing on top of previous writing

pal'in·drome' *n.* word, phrase, or sentence that reads the same backward as forward

pal'ing (pāl'-) *n.* fence made of pales

pal'i·sade' *n.* 1 fence of large pointed stakes for fortification 2 *pl.* steep cliffs

pall (pôl) *v.* **palled**, **pall'ing** become boring —*n.* dark covering as for a coffin

pall'bear'er *n.* bearer of a coffin at a funeral

pal'let *n.* 1 straw bed 2 wood platform

pal'li·ate' *v.* 1 relieve; ease 2 make seem less serious —**pal'li·a'tion** *n.* — **pal'li·a'tive** *a., n.*

pal'lid *a.* pale —**pal'lor** *n.*

palm (päm) *n.* 1 tall tropical tree topped with a bunch of huge leaves 2 its leaf: symbol of victory 3 inside of the hand —**palm off** [Inf.] get rid of, sell, etc. by fraud

pal·met'to *n., pl.* -**tos** or -**toes** small palm tree

palm·is·try n. fortunetelling from the lines, etc. on a person's palm —**palm'ist** n.

Palm Sunday n. the Sunday before Easter

palm'y a. **-i·er, -i·est** prosperous

pal·o·mi'no (-mē') n., pl. **-nos** pale-yellow horse with white mane and tail

pal'pa·ble a. 1 that can be touched, felt, etc. 2 obvious —**pal'pa·bly** adv.

pal'pi·tate' v. to throb —**pal'pi·ta'tion** n.

pal·sy (pôl'zē) n. paralysis in part of the body, often with tremors —**pal'sied** a.

pal'try (pôl'trē) a. **-tri·er, -tri·est** trifling; petty

pam·pas (päm'pəs) pl.n. treeless plains of Argentina

pam'per v. to be overindulgent with

pam'phlet (-flət) n. thin, unbound booklet

pan n. broad, shallow container used in cooking, etc. —v. **panned, pan'ning** 1 move (a camera) to view a panorama 2 [Inf.] criticize adversely —**pan out** [Inf.] turn out (well)

pan- pref. all; of all

pan·a·ce'a (-sē'-) n. supposed remedy for all diseases or problems

pa·nache' (-nash') n. dashing, elegant manner or style

Pan·a·ma (**hat**) n. hat woven of straw, etc.

Pan'-A·mer'i·can a. of all the Americas

pan'cake' n. thin cake of batter fried in a pan

pan·chro·mat'ic (-krō-) a. describing film sensitive to all colors

pan'cre·as (-krē əs) n. gland that secretes a digestive juice —**pan'cre·at'ic** a.

pan'da n. white-and-black, bearlike animal of Asia

pan·dem'ic n., a. (disease) that is epidemic in a large area

pan'de·mo'ni·um n. wild disorder or noise

pan'der v. 1 act as a pimp 2 help others satisfy their desires —n. pimp

pane n. sheet of glass

pan'e·gyr'ic (-jir'-) n. speech or writing of praise

pan'el n. 1 flat section set off on a wall, door, etc. 2 group chosen for judging, discussing, etc. —v. provide with panels —**pan'el·ing** n. —**pan'el·ist** n.

pang n. sudden, sharp pain

pan'han'dle v. [Inf.] beg on the streets

pan'ic n. sudden, wild fear —v. **-icked, -ick·ing** fill with panic —**pan'ick·y** a.

pan'ic-strick'en a. badly frightened

pan'nier, pan'ier (-yər) n. basket for carrying loads on the back

pan'o·ply (-plē) n., pl. **-plies** 1 suit of armor 2 splendid display

pan'o·ram'a n. 1 unlimited view 2 constantly changing scene —**pan'o·ram'ic** a.

pan'sy (-zē) n., pl. **-sies** small plant with velvety petals

pant v. 1 breathe in pants 2 long (for) 3 gasp out —n. rapid, heavy breath

pan'ta·loons' pl.n. [Hist.] trousers

pan'the·ism n. doctrine that all forces of the universe are God —**pan'the·ist** n. —**pan'the·is'tic** a.

pan'the·on' n. temple for all the gods

pan'ther n. 1 cougar 2 leopard

pant'ies pl.n. women's or children's short underpants

pan'to·mime' v., n. (make) use of gestures without words to present a play

pan'try n., pl. **-tries** a room for food, pots, etc.

pants pl.n. trousers

pant'suit' n. matched jacket and pants for women

pant'y·hose' n. women's hose joined to form a one-piece garment that extends to the waist: also **panty hose**

pant'y·waist' n. [Sl.] sissy

pap n. soft food

pa'pa n. father: child's word

pa'pa·cy (pā'-) n. position, authority, etc. of the Pope

pa'pal a. of the Pope or the papacy

pa·pa·raz'zi (-rät'tsē) pl.n. photographers who take candid shots of celebrities

pa·paw (pô'pô') n. tree with yellow fruit

pa·pa·ya (pə pī'ə) n. tropical palmlike tree with large, orange fruit

pa'per n. 1 thin material in sheets, used to write or print on, wrap, etc. 2 sheet of this 3 essay 4 newspaper 5 wallpaper 6 pl. credentials —a. of or like paper —v. cover with wallpaper —**pa'per·y** a.

pa'per·back' n. book bound in paper

pa'per·boy' n. boy who sells or delivers newspapers —**pa'per·girl'** n.fem.

paper tiger n. one reputedly dangerous but actually harmless

paper trail n. documents, receipts, etc. providing a record of actions

pa'per·weight' n. object set on papers to hold them down

pa'pier–mâ·ché' (-pər mə shā') *n.* paper-pulp material easily molded into objects when wet

pa·pil'la *n., pl.* **-lae** (-ē) small projection of tissue, as on the tongue

pa·poose' *n.* North American Indian baby

pa·pri'ka (-prē'-) *n.* ground, mild, red seasoning

Pap test *n.* test for uterine cancer

pa·py'rus *n.* **1** paper made by ancient Egyptians from a water plant **2** this plant

par *n.* **1** equal rank **2** average **3** face value of stocks, etc. **4** skillful score in golf

para– *pref.* **1** beside; beyond **2** helping; secondary

par'a·ble *n.* short, simple story with a moral

pa·rab'o·la *n.* curve formed when a cone is sliced parallel to its side

par'a·chute' *n.* umbrellalike device used to slow down a person or thing dropping from an aircraft —*v.* drop by parachute —**par'a·chut'ist** *n.*

pa·rade' *n.* **1** showy display **2** march or procession —*v.* **1** march in a parade **2** show off

par'a·digm' (-dīm') *n.* example

par'a·dise' *n.* **1** place or state of great happiness **2** [P-] heaven

par'a·dox' *n.* contradictory statement that is or seems false —**par'a·dox'i·cal** *a.*

par'af·fin *n.* white, waxy substance used to make candles, seal jars, etc.

par'a·gon' *n.* model of perfection or excellence

par'a·graph' *n.* distinct section of a piece of writing, begun on a new line and often indented

par'a·keet' *n.* small parrot

par'a·le'gal *a., n.* (of) a lawyer's assistant

par'al·lax' *n.* apparent change in object's position resulting from change in viewer's position

par'al·lel' *a.* **1** in the same direction and at a fixed distance apart **2** similar —*n.* **1** parallel line, surface, etc. **2** one like another **3** imaginary line parallel to the equator, representing degrees of latitude —*v.* be parallel with

par'al·lel'o·gram' *n.* four-sided figure with opposite sides parallel and equal

parallel park'ing *n.* way of parking a vehicle near and parallel to the curb

pa·ral'y·sis *n.* **1** loss of power to move any part of the body **2** helpless inactivity —**par'a·lyt'ic** (-lit'-) *a., n.*

par'a·lyze' (-līz') *v.* **1** cause paralysis in **2** make ineffective

par'a·me'ci·um *n., pl.* **-ci·a** a freshwater protozoan

par'a·med'ic *n.* person trained to assist doctors, provide emergency medical services, etc.

par'a·med'i·cal *a.* of medical auxiliaries, as nurses' aides, midwives, etc.

pa·ram'e·ter *n.* boundary or limit

par'a·mil'i·tary *a.* of a private, often secret, military group

par'a·mount' *a.* supreme

par'a·mour' (-moor') *n.* illicit lover

par'a·noi'a *n.* mental illness of feeling persecuted —**par'a·noid'** *a., n.*

par'a·pet' *n.* wall for protection from enemy fire

par'a·pher·na'li·a *pl.n.* [*sing. or pl. v.*] belongings or equipment

par'a·phrase' *n.* a rewording —*v.* reword

par'a·ple'gi·a (-plē'jē ə, -jə) *n.* paralysis of the lower body —**par'a·ple'gic** *a., n.*

par'a·pro·fes'sion·al *n.* worker trained to assist a professional

par'a·psy·chol'o·gy *n.* study of psychic phenomena

par'a·sail'ing *n.* sport of sailing through the air with a special parachute (**par'a·sail'**) while being towed by a boat, etc.

par'a·site' *n.* plant or animal that lives on or in another —**par'a·sit'ic** *a.*

par'a·sol' (-sôl') *n.* light umbrella used as a sunshade

par'a·thi'on' (-thī'än') *n.* a poisonous insecticide

par'a·thy'roid' (-thī'-) *a.* of certain small glands near the thyroid

par'a·troops' *pl.n.* troops trained to parachute into a combat area —**par'a·troop'er** *n.*

par·boil' *v.* boil until partly cooked

par'cel *n.* **1** package **2** piece (of land) —*v.* apportion: with *out*

parcel post *n.* postal branch which delivers parcels

parch *v.* **1** make hot and dry **2** make thirsty

parch'ment *n.* **1** skin of a sheep, etc. prepared as a surface for writing **2** paper resembling this

par'don *v.* **1** to release from punishment **2** excuse; forgive —*n.* act of pardoning —**par'don·a·ble** *a.*

pare *v.* **1** peel **2** reduce gradually

par'e·gor'ic *n.* medicine with opium, for diarrhea, etc.

par·ent *n.* **1** father or mother **2** source —**pa·ren'tal** *a.* —**par'ent·hood'** *n.* —**par'ent·ing** *n.*

par·ent·age *n.* descent from parents or ancestors

pa·ren'the·sis *n., pl.* **-ses'** (-sēz') **1** word, clause, etc. of explanation put into a sentence **2** either of the marks ( ) used to set this off —**par·en·thet'i·cal** *a.*

pa·re'sis *n.* brain disease caused by syphilis

par ex'cel·lence (ek'sə läns') *a.* beyond comparison

par·fait' (-fā') *n.* ice cream dessert in a tall glass

pa·ri'ah (-rī'ə) *n.* outcast

pari·mu'tu·el (-chōō əl) *n.* racetrack betting in which winners share the total amount bet

par'ing (per'-) *n.* strip peeled off

par·ish *n.* **1** part of a diocese under a priest, etc. **2** church congregation

pa·rish'ion·er *n.* member of a parish

par'i·ty *n., pl.* **-ties** equality of value at a given ratio between moneys, commodities, etc.

park *n.* public land for recreation or rest —*v.* leave (a vehicle) temporarily

par'ka *n.* hooded coat

Par'kin·son's disease *n.* disease causing tremors

park'way' *n.* broad road lined with trees

par'lance *n.* mode of speech

par'lay *v.* **1** bet (wager plus winnings from one race, etc.) on another **2** exploit (an asset) successfully —*n.* bet or bets made by parlaying

par·ley (-lē) *v., n.* talk to settle differences, etc.

par'lia·ment (-lə-) *n.* legislative body, spec. [P-] of Great Britain, Canada, etc. —**par'lia·men'ta·ry** *a.*

par'lor *n.* **1** living room **2** business establishment, as a shop where hair is styled

Par'me·san' cheese (-zän', -zhän') *n.* a dry Italian cheese

par·mi·gia'na (-zhä'nə) *a.* made with Parmesan cheese

pa·ro'chi·al (-kē əl) *a.* **1** of a parish **2** designating a school run by a church **3** limited; narrow

par'o·dy *v.* **-died, -dy·ing;** *n., pl.* **-dies** (write) a farcical imitation of a work

pa·role' *v., n.* release from prison on condition of future good behavior

pa·rol·ee' *n.* one on parole

par·ox·ysm (par'ək siz'əm) *n.* spasm or outburst

par·quet' (-kā') *n.* flooring of parquetry

par'quet·ry (-kə trē) *n.* inlaid flooring in geometric forms

par'ri·cide' *n.* **1** act of murdering one's parent **2** one who does this

par'rot *n.* brightly colored bird that can imitate speech —*v.* repeat or copy without full understanding

par'ry *v.* **-ried, -ry·ing 1** ward off **2** evade

parse *v.* analyze (a sentence) grammatically

par'si·mo'ny *n.* stinginess —**par·si·mo'ni·ous** *a.*

pars'ley *n.* plant with leaves used to flavor some foods

pars'nip *n.* sweet white root used as a vegetable

par'son *n.* [Inf.] minister or clergyman

par'son·age *n.* dwelling provided by a church for its minister

part *n.* **1** portion, piece, element, etc. **2** duty **3** role **4** music for a certain voice or instrument in a composition **5** *usually pl.* region **6** dividing line formed in combing the hair —*v.* **1** divide; separate **2** go away from each other —*a.* less than whole —**part with** give up—**take part** participate

par·take' *v.* **-took', -tak'en, -tak'ing 1** participate (*in*) **2** eat or drink (*of*) —**par·tak'er** *n.*

par·the·no·gen'e·sis *n.* sexual reproduction without fertilization

par'tial (-shəl) *a.* **1** favoring one over another **2** not complete —**partial to** fond of —**par·ti·al'i·ty** (-shē al'-) *n.* —**par'tial·ly** *adv.*

par·tic'i·pate' (-tis'-) *v.* have or take a share with others (*in*) —**par·tic'i·pant** *n.* —**par·tic'i·pa'tion** *n.*

par'ti·ci·ple *n.* verb form having the qualities of both verb and adjective —**par'ti·cip'i·al** *a.*

par'ti·cle *n.* **1** tiny fragment **2** preposition, article, or conjunction

par'ti-col'ored *a.* having different colors in different parts

par·tic'u·lar *a.* **1** of one; individual **2** specific **3** hard to please —*n.* a detail —**par·tic'u·lar·ize'** *v.* —**par·tic'u·lar·ly** *adv.*

par·tic'u·late (-lit) *a.* of or formed of tiny, separate particles

part'ing *a., n.* **1** dividing **2** departing

par'ti·san (-zən) *n.* **1** strong supporter **2** guerrilla —*a.* of a partisan

par·ti'tion (-tish'ən) *n.* **1** division into parts **2** thing that divides —*v.* divide into parts

part'ly *adv.* not fully

part′ner n. one who undertakes something with another; associate; mate —**part′ner·ship′** n.

part of speech n. class of word, as noun, verb, etc.

par′tridge n. short-tailed game bird

part song n. song for several voices

part time n. part of the usual time —**part′-time′** a.

part′-tim′er n. part-time employee, etc.

par·tu·ri′tion (-rish′ən) n. childbirth

par′ty n., pl. **-ties** 1 group working together for a political cause, etc. 2 social gathering 3 one involved in a lawsuit, crime, etc. 4 [Inf.] person —v. **-tied, -ty·ing** take part in social activity, esp. boisterously

par′ty·go′er n. one who attends many parties

party line n. single circuit for two or more telephone users

par′ve·nu′ n. upstart

pas′chal (-kəl) a. of the Passover or Easter

pass v. 1 go by, beyond, etc. 2 go or change from one form, place, etc. to another 3 cease; end 4 approve or be approved 5 take a test, etc. successfully 6 cause or allow to go, move, qualify, etc. 7 throw 8 spend (time) 9 happen 10 give as an opinion, judgment, etc. —n. 1 a passing 2 free ticket 3 brief military leave 4 narrow passage —**pass′a·ble** a.

pas′sage n. 1 a passing 2 right to pass 3 voyage 4 path, opening, etc. 5 part of something written

pas′sage·way′ n. narrow way, as a hall, alley, etc.

pass′book′ n. bankbook

pas·sé′ (pa sā′) a. out-of-date

pas′sen·ger n. one traveling in a train, car, etc.

pass′er·by′ n., pl. **pass′ers·by′** one who passes by

pass′ing a. 1 that passes 2 casual —**in passing** incidentally

pas′sion n. 1 strong emotion, as hate, love, etc. 2 an object of strong desire —**pas′sion·ate** a.

pas′sive a. 1 inactive, but acted upon 2 submissive —**pas·siv′i·ty** n.

pas′sive-ag·gres′sive a. resisting others′ demands, as by delaying or procrastinating

passive resistance n. opposition to a law by refusal to comply or by nonviolent acts

pass′key′ n. key that fits a number of locks

Pass′o′ver n. Jewish holiday in the spring

pass′port′ n. government document identifying a citizen traveling abroad

pass′word′ n. secret word given to be allowed to pass a guard

past a. 1 gone by 2 of a former time —n. 1 history 2 time gone by —prep. beyond in time, space, etc. —adv. to and beyond

pas′ta (päs′-) n. spaghetti, macaroni, etc.

paste n. 1 moist, smooth mixture 2 adhesive mixture with flour, water, etc. —v. make adhere, as with paste

paste′board′ n. stiff material made of layers of paper or paper pulp

pas·tel′ a., n. soft and pale (shade)

pas′teur·ize′ (-chər-, -tər-) v. kill bacteria (in milk, etc.) by heating —**pas′teur·i·za′tion** n.

pas·tiche′ (-tēsh′) n. artistic composition made up of bits from several sources

pas′time′ n. way to spend spare time

past master n. an expert

pas′tor n. clergyman in charge of a congregation

pas′to·ral a. 1 of a pastor 2 simple and rustic

past participle n. participle used to indicate a past time

pas·tra′mi (pə strä′-) n. spiced, smoked beef

pas′try (pās′-) n., pl. **-tries** fancy baked goods

pas′ture n. ground for grazing: also **pas′tur·age** or **pas′ture·land′** —v. let (cattle) graze

past′y a. **-i·er, -i·est** of or like paste

pat n. 1 gentle tap with something flat 2 small lump, as of butter —v. **pat′ted, pat′ting** give a gentle pat to —a. 1 apt 2 glib

patch n. 1 piece of material used to mend a hole, etc. 2 spot 3 adhesive pad containing a drug to be absorbed through the skin —v. 1 put a patch on 2 to make crudely

patch′work′ n. quilt made of odd patches of cloth

pate (pāt) n. top of the head

pâ·té (pä tā′) n. meat paste or spread

pa·tel′la n., pl. **-las** or **-lae** (-ē) movable bone at the front of the knee

pat′ent (pat′-; a. 2: pāt′-) n. document granting exclusive rights over an invention —a. 1 protected by patent 2 obvious —v. get a patent for

pat′ent leather (pat′-) n. leather with

a hard, glossy finish

patent medicine *n.* an over-the-counter medicine with a trademark

pa·ter·nal *a.* **1** fatherly **2** on the father's side —**pa·ter·nal·ism**' *n.* —**pa·ter·nal·is'tic** *a.*

pa·ter'ni·ty *n.* fatherhood

path *n.* **1** way worn by footsteps **2** line of movement **3** course of conduct

pa·thet'ic *a.* **1** arousing pity **2** pitifully unsuccessful, ineffective, etc. —**pa·thet'i·cal·ly** *adv.*

path'o·gen'ic (-jen'-) *a.* producing disease —**path'o·gen** *n.*

pa·thol'o·gy *n.* study of the nature and effect of disease —**path'o·log'i·cal** *a.* —**pa·thol'o·gist** *n.*

pa·thos (pā'thäs') *n.* the quality in a thing which arouses pity

path'way' *n.* path

-pathy *suf.* (treatment of) disease

pa'tient (-shənt) *a.* **1** enduring pain, delay, etc. without complaint **2** persevering —*n.* one receiving medical care —**pa'tience** *n.* —**pa'tient·ly** *adv.*

pat'i·na *n.* green oxidized coating on bronze or copper

pa'ti·o' *n., pl.* **-os'** **1** courtyard **2** paved lounging area next to house

pat'ois' (-wä') *n., pl.* **-ois'** (-wäz') dialect of a region

pat pend *abbrev.* patent pending

pa'tri·arch' (-ärk') *n.* **1** father and head of a family or tribe **2** dignified old man —**pa'tri·ar'chal** *a.*

pa·tri'cian (-trish'ən) *a., n.* aristocratic (person)

pat'ri·cide' *n.* **1** the murdering of one's father **2** person doing this —**pat'ri·ci'dal** *a.*

pat'ri·mo'ny *n.* inheritance from one's father

pa'tri·ot·ism' *n.* love of and loyalty to one's country —**pa'tri·ot** *n.* —**pa'tri·ot'ic** *a.*

pa·trol' *v.* **-trolled'**, **-trol'ling** make trips around in guarding —*n.* a patrolling, or a group that patrols

pa·trol'man *n., pl.* **-men** policeman who patrols a certain area

pa'tron *n.* **1** a sponsor **2** regular customer

pa'tron·age *n.* **1** help given by a patron **2** customers, or their trade **3** political favors

pa'tron·ize' *v.* **1** be condescending to **2** be a regular customer of

patron saint *n.* guardian saint of a person, place, etc.

pat'ro·nym'ic (-nim'-) *n.* name showing descent from a given person

pat'sy *n., pl.* **-sies** [Sl.] person easily imposed on

pat'ter *n.* **1** series of rapid taps **2** glib talk —*v.* make or utter (a) patter

pat'tern *n.* **1** one worthy of imitation **2** plan used in making things **3** a design **4** usual behavior, procedure, etc. —*v.* copy as from a pattern

pat'ty *n., pl.* **-ties** flat cake of ground meat, etc.

pau'ci·ty (pô'-) *n.* **1** fewness **2** scarcity

paunch *n.* fat belly

pau'per *n.* very poor person

pause *v., n.* (make a) temporary stop

pave *v.* surface (a road, etc.) as with asphalt

pave'ment *n.* paved surface

pa·vil'ion (-yən) *n.* **1** large tent **2** building for exhibits, etc., as at a fair

paw *n.* foot of an animal with claws —*v.* **1** to touch, etc. with paws or feet **2** handle roughly

pawl *n.* catch for the teeth of a ratchet wheel

pawn *v.* give as security for a loan —*n.* **1** chessman of lowest value **2** person who is subject to another's will

pawn'bro'ker *n.* one licensed to lend money on things pawned —**pawn' shop'** *n.*

pay *v.* **paid**, **pay'ing** **1** give (money) to (one) for goods or services **2** settle, as a debt **3** give, as a compliment **4** make, as a visit **5** be profitable (to) —*n.* wages —*a.* operated by coins, etc. —**pay out** *pt.* **payed out** let out, as a rope —**pay·ee'** *n.* —**pay'er** *n.* —**pay'ment** *n.*

pay'a·ble *a.* due to be paid

pay'check' *n.* check in payment of wages or salary

pay'load' *n.* load carried by an aircraft, missile, etc.

pay'mas'ter *n.* official in charge of paying employees

pay'off' *n.* **1** reckoning or payment **2** [Inf.] climax or culmination

pay'-per-view' *a.* TV of a cable, etc. system charging for each showing of a program

pay'roll' *n.* **1** list of employees to be paid **2** amount due them

pc *abbrev.* piece

PC *n.* personal computer, or microcomputer

pct *abbrev.* percent

pd *abbrev.* paid

PE *abbrev.* **1** physical education **2** Prince Edward Island

pea *n.* plant with pods having round, edible seeds

peace n. **1** freedom from war or strife **2** agreement to end war **3** law and order **4** calm —**peace'a·ble** a.

peace'ful a. **1** not fighting **2** calm **3** of a time of peace —**peace'ful·ly** adv.

peace'mak·er n. one who settles quarrels, etc.

peach n. round, juicy, orange-yellow fruit

pea'cock' n. male of a large bird (**pea' fowl'**), with a long showy tail —**pea' hen'** n.fem.

pea jacket n. short, double-breasted wool coat

peak n. **1** pointed end or top **2** mountain with pointed summit **3** highest point —v. come or bring to a peak

peak'ed a. thin and drawn

peal n. **1** loud ringing of bell(s) **2** loud, prolonged sound —v. to ring; resound

pea'nut' n. **1** vine with underground pods and edible seeds **2** the pod or a seed

peanut butter n. food paste made by grinding peanuts

pear n. soft, juicy fruit

pearl (purl) n. **1** smooth, roundish stone formed in some oysters, used as a gem **2** mother-of-pearl **3** bluish gray —**pearl'y** a., **-i·er**, **-i·est**

peas'ant (pez'-) n. farm worker of Europe, etc. —**peas'ant·ry** n.

peat n. decayed plant matter in bogs, dried for fuel

peat moss n. peat made up of moss residues, used for mulch

peb'ble n. small, smooth stone —**peb' bly** a., **-bli·er**, **-bli·est**

pe·can' (pez'-) n. edible nut with a thin, smooth shell

pec·ca·dil'lo n., pl. **-loes** or **-los** minor or petty sin

pec'ca·ry n., pl. **-ries** wild piglike animal with tusks

peck v. strike as with the beak —n. **1** stroke made as with the beak **2** dry measure equal to 8 quarts

peck'ing order n. hierarchy

pec'tin n. substance in some fruits causing jelly to form

pec'to·ral a. of the chest

pe·cu'liar (-kyōōl'yər) a. **1** of only one; exclusive **2** special **3** odd —**pe·cu'li·ar'i·ty** (-kyōōl'nē-) n., pl. **-ties**

pe·cu'ni·ar·y (-kyōō'nē-) a. of money

ped'a·gogue', ped'a·gog' (-gäg') n. teacher —**ped'a·gog'y** (-gä'jē) n. —**ped'a·gog'ic** a. —**ped'a·gog'i·cal** a.

ped'al n. lever worked by the foot —v. operate by pedals —a. of the foot

ped'ant n. one who stresses trivial points of learning —**pe·dan'tic** a. —**ped'ant·ry** n.

ped'dle v. go from place to place selling —**ped'dler** n.

ped'er·ast'y n. sexual acts by a man with a boy —**ped'er·ast'** n.

ped'es·tal n. base, as of a column, statue, etc.

pe·des'tri·an a. **1** going on foot **2** dull and ordinary —n. one who goes on foot; walker

pe'di·at'rics n. medical care and treatment of babies and children —**pe'di·a·tri'cian** (-trish'ən) n.

ped'i·cab' n. a three-wheeled carriage pedaled by the driver

ped'i·cure' n. a trimming, polishing, etc. of the toenails

ped'i·gree' n. ancestry; descent —**ped'i·greed'** a.

ped'i·ment n. ornamental triangular piece over a doorway

pe·dom'e·ter n. device measuring a distance walked

pe'do·phil'i·a (pedə-, pē'də-) n. sexual attraction to children —**pe'do·phile'** n.

peek v. to glance, often furtively —n. a glance

peel v. **1** cut away (the rind, etc.) of **2** shed skin, bark, etc. **3** come off in layers or flakes —n. rind or skin of fruit

peel'ing n. rind peeled off

peen n. end of hammer head opposite the striking surface

peep v. **1** make the chirping cry of a young bird **2** look through a small opening **3** peek **4** appear partially —n. **1** peeping sound **2** furtive glimpse —**peep'hole'** n.

peer n. **1** an equal **2** British noble —v. look closely —**peer'age** n.

peer'less a. without equal

peeve [Inf.] v. make peevish —n. annoyance

pee'vish a. irritable

pee'wee' n. [Inf.] something very small

peg n. **1** short pin or bolt **2** step or degree —v. **pegged**, **peg'ging** fix or mark as with pegs

peign·oir' (pān wär') n. woman's loose dressing gown

pe·jo'ra·tive a. derogatory

Pe'king·ese' (-kə nēz') n., pl. **-ese'** small dog with pug nose: also **Pe'kin·ese'**

pe'koe n. a black tea

pelf n. mere wealth

pel'i·can *n.* water bird with a pouch in its lower bill

pel·la'gra (-lä'-) *n.* disease caused by vitamin deficiency

pel'let *n.* little ball

pell'-mell' *adv.* in reckless haste: also **pell'mell'**

pel·lu'cid (-l⁻σ⁻-) *a.* clear

pelt *v.* **1** throw things at **2** beat steadily —*n.* skin of a fur-bearing animal

pel'vis *n.* cavity formed by bones of the hip and part of the backbone — **pel'vic** *a.*

pem'mi·can *n.* dried food concentrate

pen *n.* **1** enclosure for animals **2** device for writing with ink **3** [Sl.] penitentiary —*v.* **penned** or (*v.*1) **pent, pen'ning 1** enclose as in a pen **2** write with a pen

pe'nal *a.* of or as punishment

pe'nal·ize (*or* pen'əl-) *v.* punish

pen'al·ty *n.*, *pl.* **-ties 1** punishment **2** disadvantage

pen'ance *n.* voluntary suffering to show repentance

pence *n.* [Br.] *pl.* of PENNY (*n.* 2)

pen'chant *n.* strong liking

pen'cil *n.* device with a core of graphite, etc. for writing, etc. —*v.* write with a pencil

pend *v.* await decision

pend'ant *n.* hanging object used as an ornament

pend'ent *a.* suspended

pend'ing *a.* not decided —*prep.* **1** during **2** until

pen'du·lous (-dy⁻σ⁻-) *a.* hanging freely

pen'du·lum *n.* weight hung so as to swing freely

pen'e·trate' *v.* **1** enter by piercing **2** to affect throughout **3** understand — **pen'e·tra·ble** *a.* —**pen'e·tra'tion** *n.*

pen'guin (-gwin) *n.* flightless bird of the Antarctic

pen·i·cil'lin *n.* antibiotic drug obtained from a mold

pen·in'su·la *n.* land area almost surrounded by water —**pen·in'su·lar** *a.*

pe'nis *n.* male sex organ —**pe'nile** *a.*

pen'i·tent *a.* willing to atone —*n.* a penitent person —**pen'i·tence** *n.*

pen·i·ten'tia·ry (-sha rē) *n.*, *pl.* **-ries** prison

pen'knife' *n.* small pocketknife

pen'man·ship' *n.* quality of handwriting

pen name *n.* pseudonym

pen'nant *n.* long, narrow flag

pen'ne' (-ā') *n.* tubular pasta

pen'ni·less *a.* very poor

pen'non *n.* flag or pennant

pen'ny *n.* **1** *pl.* **-nies** cent **2** *pl.* **pence** Br. coin, $\frac{1}{12}$ pound

penny arcade *n.* public amusement hall with coin-operated games

pe·nol'o·gy *n.* study of prison management and the reform of criminals

pen pal *n.* (foreign) friend with whom one corresponds

pen'sion *n.* regular payment to a retired or disabled person —*v.* pay a pension to

pen'sive (-siv) *a.* thoughtful; reflective

pent *a.* shut in; kept in: often with *up*

pen'ta·gon' *n.* figure with five angles and five sides

pen·tam'e·ter *n.* line of verse of five metrical feet

pen·tath'lon' *n.* athletic contest with five different events

Pen'te·cost' *n.* Christian festival

Pen'te·cos'tal·ism' *n.* Christian fundamentalism stressing divine inspiration —**Pen'te·cos'tal** *a.*

pent'house' *n.* apartment on the roof of a building

pent'-up' *a.* confined; checked

pe·nu·che, pe·nu·chi (pə n⁻σσ'chē) *n.* fudgelike candy

pe·nul'ti·mate *a.* next to last

pe·nu'ri·ous (pe nyoor'ē-) *a.* stingy

pen'u·ry *n.* extreme poverty

pe'on' *n.* landless laborer of Latin America —**pe'on·age** *n.*

pe'o·ny *n.*, *pl.* **-nies** plant with large showy flowers

peo'ple (pē'-) *pl.n.* **1** human beings **2** a populace **3** one's family —*n.*, *pl.* **-ples** a nation, race, etc. —*v.* populate

pep [Inf.] *n.* energy; vigor —*v.* **pepped, pep'ping** fill with pep: with *up* — **pep'py** *a.*, **-pi·er, -pi·est**

pep'per *n.* **1** plant with a red or green, hot or sweet pod **2** the pod **3** spicy seasoning made from berries (**pep'per·corns'**) of a tropical plant —*v.* **1** season with pepper **2** pelt with small objects

pepper mill *n.* hand mill used to grind peppercorns

pep'per·mint' *n.* mint plant yielding an oily flavoring

pep·per·o'ni *n.* highly spiced Italian sausage

pep'per·y *a.* **1** fiery **2** hot-tempered

pep'sin *n.* stomach enzyme that helps digest proteins

pep'tic *a.* of digestion

per *prep.* **1** by means of **2** for each

per·am'bu·late' *v.* walk through or over

per·am'bu·la'tor *n.* [Chiefly Br.] a baby carriage

per an'num *a., adv.* by the year

per·cale' (-kāl') *n.* cotton cloth used for sheets

per cap'i·ta *a., adv.* for each person

per·ceive' (-sēv') *v.* **1** grasp mentally **2** become aware (of) through the senses

per·cent' *adv., a.* out of every hundred: also **per cent** —*n.* [Inf.] percentage

per·cent'age *n.* **1** rate per hundred **2** portion

per·cen'tile' *n.* any of 100 equal parts

per·cep'ti·ble *a.* that can be perceived

per·cep'tion *n.* **1** ability to perceive **2** knowledge got by perceiving —**per·cep'tu·al** (-chōō-) *a.*

per·cep'tive *a.* able to perceive readily

perch *n.* **1** small food fish **2** a pole or branch that birds roost on —*v.* rest on a perch

per·chance' *adv.* [Ar.] perhaps

per'co·late' *v.* **1** filter **2** make in a percolator

per'co·la'tor *n.* pot in which boiling water filters through ground coffee

per·cus'sion (-kush'ən) *n.* **1** hitting of one thing against another **2** musical instruments played by striking, as drums —**per·cus'sion·ist** *n.*

per di·em (dē'əm) *adv.* daily

per·di'tion (-dish'ən) *n.* **1** hell **2** loss of one's soul

per'e·gri·na'tion *n.* a traveling about

per·emp'to·ry *a.* **1** overbearing **2** not to be refused

per·en'ni·al *a.* **1** lasting a year **2** living more than two years —*n.* plant living more than two years

per'fect (*v.:* pər fekt') *a.* **1** complete **2** excellent **3** completely accurate —*v.* make perfect —**per·fect'i·ble** *a.* —**per·fec'tion** *n.* —**per'fect·ly** *adv.*

per·fec'tion·ist *n.* one who strives for perfection

per·fi·dy *n., pl.* **-dies** treachery —**per·fid'i·ous** *a.*

per'fo·rate' *v.* pierce with a hole or holes —**per'fo·ra'tion** *n.*

per·force' *adv.* necessarily

per·form' *v.* **1** do; carry out **2** act a role, play music, etc.

per·form'ance *n.* **1** a doing or thing done **2** display of one's skill or talent

performance art *n.* art form having elements of theater, dance, video, etc.

per·form'ing arts *pl.n.* arts, as drama and dance, performed before an audience

per·fume' (*or* pur'fyōōm) *v.* fill with fragrance or put perfume on —*n.* **1** fragrance **2** liquid with a pleasing odor

per·func'to·ry *a.* done without care or interest

per'go·la *n.* arbor with latticework roof

per·haps' *adv.* possibly; probably

per'i·gee' (-jē') *n.* point nearest earth in a satellite's orbit

per'il *v., n.* (put in) danger or risk —**per'il·ous** *a.*

pe·rim'e·ter *n.* outer boundary of a figure or area

per'i·ne'um *n., pl.* **-ne'a** area between the anus and genitals

pe'ri·od *n.* **1** portion of time **2** mark of punctuation (.)

pe'ri·od'ic *a.* recurring at regular intervals

pe'ri·od'i·cal *n.* magazine published every week, month, etc. —*a.* periodic —**pe'ri·od'i·cal·ly** *adv.*

periodic table *n.* arrangement of elements by number of protons

per'i·o·don'tal *a.* around a tooth and affecting the gums

per'i·pa·tet'ic *a.* moving or walking about; itinerant

pe·riph'er·y (-rif'-) *n., pl.* **-ies** outer boundary or part —**pe·riph'er·al** *a.*

pe·riph'ras'tic *a.* wordy

per'i·scope' *n.* tube with mirrors, etc., for seeing over or around an obstacle

per'ish *v.* be destroyed; die

per'ish·a·ble *n., a.* (food) liable to spoil

per'i·stal'sis (*or* -stôl'-) *n.* action of intestines that moves food onward

per'i·to·ni'tis (-nīt'is) *n.* inflammation of the membrane (**per'i·to·ne'um**) lining the abdominal cavity

per'i·win'kle *n.* creeping evergreen plant

per'jure' *v.* tell a lie while under oath —**per'jur·er** *n.* —**per'ju·ry** *n., pl.* **-ries**

perk *v.* **1** raise or liven (*up*) **2** make stylish or smart: with *up* —*n.* [Inf.] perquisite —**perk'y** *a.*, **-i·er**, **-i·est**

perm [Inf.] *n.* a permanent —*v.* give a permanent to

per'ma·frost' *n.* permanently frozen subsoil

per'ma·nent *a.* lasting indefinitely —*n.* long-lasting hair wave —**per'ma·nence** *n.* —**per'ma·nent·ly** *adv.*

per'me·ate' *v.* diffuse; penetrate (through or among) —**per'me·a·ble** *a.*

per·mis'si·ble *a.* allowable

per·mis'sion *n.* consent

per·mis'sive *a.* tolerant; lenient

per·mit' (n.: pur'mit') v. **-mit'ted, -mit'ting** allow —n. document giving permission

per·mu·ta'tion (-myōō-) n. a change, as in order

per·ni'cious (-nish'əs) a. very harmful or damaging

per·o·ra'tion n. last part or summation of a speech

per·ox'ide n. hydrogen peroxide

per·pen·dic'u·lar a. **1** at right angles to a given line or plane **2** vertical —n. perpendicular line

per'pe·trate' v. do (something evil, wrong, etc.) —**per'pe·tra'tion** n. —**per'pe·tra'tor** n.

per·pet'u·al (-pech'-) a. **1** lasting forever **2** constant

per·pet'u·ate' (-pech'-) v. cause to continue or be remembered —**per·pet'u·a'tion** n.

per'pe·tu'i·ty (-pə tōō'-) n. existence forever

per·plex' v. confuse or puzzle —**per·plex'i·ty** n., pl. **-ties**

per'qui·site (-kwi zit) n. privilege or profit incidental to one's employment

per' se' (-sā') by (or in) itself

per'se·cute' v. torment continuously for one's beliefs, etc. —**per'se·cu'tion** n. —**per'se·cu'tor** n.

per·se·vere' (-vir') v. continue in spite of difficulty —**per·se·ver'ance** n.

Per'sian (-zhən) n. domestic cat with a long, thick coat

Persian lamb n. karakul

per'si·flage' (-fläzh') n. playful or frivolous talk

per·sim'mon n. orange-red, plumlike fruit

per·sist' v. continue insistently or steadily —**per·sist'ent** a. —**per·sist'ence** n.

per·snick'e·ty a. [Inf.] fussy

per'son n. **1** human being **2** the body or self **3** Gram. any of the three classes of pronouns indicating the identity of the subject, as I, you, he, etc.

-person suf. person (without regard to sex)

per'son·a·ble a. pleasing in looks and manner

per'son·age n. (important) person

per'son·al a. **1** private; individual **2** of the body **3** of the character, conduct, etc. of a person **4** indicating person in grammar **5** other than real estate: said of property —**per'son·al·ize'** v. —**per'son·al·ly** adv.

personal computer n. microcomputer

personal effects pl.n. personal belongings worn or carried

per·son·al'i·ty n., pl. **-ties** **1** distinctive or attractive character of a person **2** notable person

per·so'na non gra'ta (grät'ə) n. unwelcome person

per·son'i·fy' v. **-fied', -fy'ing** **1** represent as a person **2** typify —**per·son'i·fi·ca'tion** n.

per·son·nel' n. persons employed in any work, etc.

per·spec'tive n. **1** appearance of objects from their relative distance and positions **2** sense of proportion

per·spi·ca'cious a. having keen insight

per·spire' v. to sweat —**per·spi·ra'tion** n.

per·suade' v. cause to do or believe by urging, etc. —**per·sua'sive** a.

per·sua'sion n. **1** a persuading **2** belief

pert a. saucy; impudent

per·tain' v. **1** belong **2** have reference

per·ti·na'cious (-nā'shəs) a. persistent —**per·ti·nac'i·ty** (-nas'-) n.

per'ti·nent a. relevant; to the point —**per'ti·nence** n.

per·turb' v. alarm; upset

pe·ruse' (-rōōz') v. read —**pe·rus'al** n.

per·vade' v. spread or be prevalent throughout —**per·va'sive** a.

per·verse' a. **1** stubbornly contrary **2** wicked —**per·ver'si·ty** n., pl. **-ties**

per·vert' (n.: pur'vurt') v. **1** lead astray; corrupt —n. one who engages in abnormal sexual acts —**per·ver'sion** n.

pes'ky a. **-ki·er, -ki·est** [Inf.] annoying

pe'so (pā'-) n., pl. **-sos** monetary unit of various Latin American countries

pes'si·mism' n. tendency to expect the worst —**pes'si·mist** n. —**pes'si·mis'tic** a.

pest n. person or thing that causes trouble, etc.

pes'ter v. annoy; vex

pes'ti·cide' n. chemical for killing insects, weeds, etc.

pes·tif'er·ous a. **1** noxious **2** [Inf.] annoying

pes'ti·lence n. virulent or contagious disease —**pes'ti·lent** a.

pes'tle (-əl, -tal) n. tool used to pound or grind substances in a mortar

pes'to n. thick sauce of basil, etc.

pet n. **1** domesticated animal treated fondly **2** favorite —v. **pet'ted, pet'ting** stroke gently

pet'al n. leaflike part of a blossom

pet'cock' n. small valve for draining

pipes, etc.

pe′ter v. [Inf.] be reduced gradually to nothing: with *out*

pe·tit (pet′ē) a. small or lesser

pe·tite′ (-tēt′) a. small and trim in figure

pe·tit four (pet′ē) n. tiny frosted cake

pe·ti′tion n. solemn, earnest request, esp. in writing —v. address a petition to

pet′rel n. small sea bird

pet′ri·fy′ v. **-fied′, -fy′ing 1** change into stony substance **2** stun, as with fear

pet′ro·chem′i·cal n. chemical derived from petroleum

pet′rol n. [Br.] gasoline

pe·tro·la′tum n. greasy, jellylike substance used for ointments: also **petroleum jelly**

pe·tro′le·um n. oily liquid in rock strata: yields gasoline, etc.

pet′ti·coat′ n. skirt worn under an outer skirt

pet′ti·fog′ger n. unethical lawyer handling petty cases

pet′tish a. irritable; petulant

pet′ty a. **-ti·er, -ti·est 1** of little importance **2** narrow-minded **3** low in rank

petty cash n. fund for incidentals

petty officer n. naval enlisted person: noncommissioned officer

pet′u·lant (pech′ə-) a. impatient or irritable —**pet′u·lance** n.

pe·tu′ni·a (-tōōn′yə) n. plant with funnel-shaped flowers

pew (pyōō) n. a long bench in a church

pew′ter n. alloy of tin with lead, copper, etc.

pe·yo′te (pā ō′tē) n. mescal cactus

pf abbrev. preferred

pg abbrev. page

PG trademark film rating indicating some content unsuitable for childern under 17

PG-13 trademark film rating indicating some content especially unsuitable for children under 13

pH n. degree of acidity or alkalinity of a solution

pha′e·ton (fā′-) n. light, four-wheeled carriage

pha′lanx′ n. massed group of individuals

phal′lo·cen′tric a. dominated by men

phal′lus n., pl. **-li′** or **-lus·es** image of the penis —**phal′lic** a.

phan′tasm′ n. figment of the mind

phan·tas·ma·go′ri·a n. rapidly changing series of things seen, as in a dream

phan′tom n. **1** ghost; specter **2** illusion —a. unreal

Phar·aoh (far′ō) n. [sometimes **p-**] title of ancient Egyptian rulers

phar′i·see′ n. self-righteous person

phar′ma·ceu′ti·cal (-sōō′-) a. **1** of pharmacy **2** of or by drugs —n. a drug or medicine

phar′ma·cist n. one whose profession is pharmacy

phar′ma·col′o·gy n. study of drugs —**phar′ma·col′o·gist** n.

phar′ma·co·pe′ia (-pē′ə) n. official book listing drugs and medicines

phar′ma·cy n., pl. **-cies 1** science of preparing drugs and medicines **2** drugstore

phar′yn·gi′tis (far′in jīt′is) n. inflammation of the pharynx; sore throat

phar′ynx (-iŋks) n. cavity between mouth and larynx

phase n. **1** aspect; side **2** one of a series of changes

phase′out′ n. gradual withdrawal

PhD, Ph.D. abbrev. Doctor of Philosophy

pheas′ant (fez′-) n. game bird with a long tail

phe′no·bar′bi·tal′ n. white compound used as a sedative

phe′nol′ (-nōl′, -nôl′) n. carbolic acid

phe′nom′ n. [Sl.] young, very gifted athlete, etc.

phe·nom′e·non n., pl. **-na 1** observable fact or event **2** anything very unusual —**phe·nom′e·nal** a.

pher′o·mone′ n. substance secreted by animals to signal others of the same species

phi′al (fī′-) n. vial

phi·lan′der (fi-) v. make love insincerely —**phi·lan′der·er** n.

phi·lan′thro·py n. **1** desire to help mankind **2** pl. **-pies** thing done to help mankind —**phil′an·throp′ic** a. —**phi·lan′thro·pist** n.

phi·lat′e·ly n. collection and study of postage stamps —**phi·lat′e·list** n.

-phile suf. one that loves or is attracted to

Phil′har·mon′ic n. orchestra

phil′ip·pic′ n. bitter verbal attack

phil′is·tine′ (-tēn′) n. one who is smugly conventional

phil′o·den′dron n. tropical American climbing plant

phi·lol′o·gy n. linguistics: old-fashioned term —**phi·lol′o·gist** n.

phi·los′o·pher n. one learned in philosophy

phi·los·o·phize' v. to reason like a philosopher

phi·los·o·phy n. **1** study of ultimate reality, ethics, etc. **2** pl. **-phies** system of principles **3** mental calmness —**phil'o·soph'ic,** **phil'o·soph'i·cal** a.

phil'ter n. magic potion to arouse love: also [Chiefly Br.] **phil'tre**

phle·bi·tis (fli bīt'is) n. inflammation of a vein

phle·bot'o·my n. therapeutic removal of blood from the body

phlegm (flem) n. mucus in the throat, as during a cold

phleg·mat'ic (fleg-) a. sluggish, unexcitable, etc.

phlo'em' n. plant tissue that carries food to where it is needed

phlox (fläks) n. plant with clusters of flowers

-phobe suf. one that fears or hates

pho'bi·a n. irrational, persistent fear of something —**pho'bic** a.

-phobia suf. fear or hatred of

phoe·be (fē'bē) n. small bird

phoe'nix n. Egyptian myth. immortal bird

phone n., v. telephone

phone card n. CALLING CARD (n. 2)

pho'neme' n. a set of speech sounds heard as one sound

pho·net'ics n. science of speech sounds and the written representation of them —**pho·net'ic** a.

phon'ics n. phonetic method of teaching reading

pho'no·graph' n. device that reproduces sound from grooved discs

pho·nol'o·gy n. (study of) speech sounds in a language —**pho·no·log'i·cal** a. —**pho·nol'o·gist** n.

pho'ny n., pl. **-nies;** a. **-ni·er, -ni·est** [Inf.] fake

phos'phate' n. **1** salt of phosphoric acid **2** fertilizer with phosphates

phos'pho·res'cent a. giving off light without heat —**phos'pho·res'cence** n.

phos'pho·rus n. phosphorescent, waxy chemical element —**phos·phor'ic, phos'pho·rous** a.

pho'to n., pl. **-tos** photograph

pho'to·cop'y n., pl. **-ies** copy made by photographic device —**pho'to·cop'i·er** n.

pho'to·e·lec'tric a. of the electric effects produced by light on some substances

pho'to·en·grav'ing n. reproduction of photographs in relief on printing plates —**pho'to·en·grav'er** n.

photo finish n. finish of a race so close the winner is known only by a photograph of the finish

pho'to·flash' a. using a flashbulb synchronized with camera shutter

pho·to·gen'ic (-jen'-) a. attractive to photograph

pho'to·graph' n. picture made by photography —v. take a photograph of —**pho·tog'ra·pher** n.

pho·tog'ra·phy n. process of producing images on a surface sensitive to light —**pho·to·graph'ic** a.

pho'ton' n. subatomic particle; quantum unit of light

pho'to·stat' n. **1** [often P-] device for making photographic copies on paper **2** copy so made —v. make a photostat of —**pho'to·stat'ic** a.

pho'to·syn'the·sis (-sin'-) n. formation of carbohydrates in plants by the action of sunlight

phrase n. **1** a short, colorful expression **2** group of words, not a sentence or clause, conveying a single idea —v. express in words

phra'se·ol'o·gy n. wording

phy·lac'ter·y (fi-) n., pl. **-ies** tefillin

phy'lum (fī'-) n., pl. **-la** major category in classification of living organisms, esp. animals

phys abbrev. **1** physical **2** physician **3** physics

phys'ic (fiz'-) n. cathartic

phys'i·cal adv. **1** of matter **2** of physics **3** of the body —n. medical examination; checkup —**phys'i·cal·ly** adv.

physical education n. instruction in the exercise and care of the body

physical science n. any science of inanimate matter, as physics or chemistry

physical therapy n. treatment of disease by massage, exercise, etc.

phy·si'cian (-zish'ən) n. doctor of medicine

phys'ics n. science that deals with matter and energy —**phys'i·cist** n.

phys·i·og'no·my n. facial features and expression

phys·i·ol'o·gy n. science of how biological structures work —**phys'i·o·log'i·cal** a. —**phys·i·ol'o·gist** n.

phys·i·o·ther'a·py n. physical therapy

phy·sique' (-zēk') n. form or build of the body

pi (pī) n. symbol (π) for the ratio of circumference to diameter, about 3.1416

pi·a·nis'si·mo' (pē'-) a., adv. Mus. very soft

pi'an·ist (or pē an'ist) n. piano player

pi·a'no (a., adv.: -ä'-) n., pl. **-nos** keyboard instrument with hammers that strike steel wires: also **pi·an'o·forte'** —*a.*, *adv. Mus.* soft

pi·az·za (pē ät'sə; *n.* 2: -az'ə) *n.* 1 in Italy, a public square 2 veranda

pi'ca (pī'-) *n.* size of printing type

pi·can·te (pē kän'tā) *a.* hot and spicy

pic'a·resque' (-resk') *a.* of adventurous vagabonds

pic'a·yune' *a.* trivial

pic'ca·lil'li *n.* relish of vegetables, mustard, etc.

pic'co·lo' *n.*, *pl.* **-los'** small flute

pick *v.* 1 scratch or dig at with something pointed 2 gather, pluck, etc. 3 choose; select 4 provoke (a fight) —*n.* 1 choice 2 the best 3 pointed tool for breaking up soil, etc. 4 plectrum —**pick at** eat sparingly —**pick on** [Inf.] criticize; tease —**pick out** choose —**pick up** 1 lift 2 get, find, etc. 3 gain (speed) 4 improve —**pick'er** *n.*

pick'ax', pick'axe' *n.* pick with one end of the head pointed, the other axlike

pick'er·el *n.* fish with a narrow, pointed snout

pick'et *n.* 1 pointed stake 2 soldier(s) on guard duty 3 striking union member, etc. stationed outside a factory, etc. —*v.* place or be a picket at

picket line *n.* line of people serving as pickets

pick'ings *pl.n.* scraps

pick'le *v.* preserve in vinegar, brine, etc. —*n.* cucumber, etc. so preserved

pick'pock'et *n.* one who steals from pockets

pick'up' *n.* 1 power of speeding up 2 small truck

pick'y *a.* **-i·er, -i·est** [Inf.] very fussy

pic'nic *n.* outing with an outdoor meal —*v.* **-nicked, -nick·ing** to hold a picnic —**pic'nick·er** *n.*

pi·cot (pē'kō) *n.* loop that is part of fancy edge on lace

pic'to·graph' *n.* picturelike symbol used in a system of writing

pic·to'ri·al *a.* of or expressed in pictures

pic'ture *n.* 1 likeness made by painting, photography, etc. 2 description 3 a FILM (*n.* 3 & 4) —*v.* 1 make a picture of 2 describe 3 imagine

pic'ture-per'fect *a.* perfect; flawless

pic'tur·esque' (-esk') *a.* 1 having natural beauty 2 quaint 3 vivid

pid'dle *v.* dawdle; trifle

pid'dling *a.* insignificant

pid·dly *a.* piddling

pidg'in English (pij'-) *n.* mixture of English and Chinese

pie *n.* fruit, meat, etc. baked on or in a crust

pie'bald' *a.* covered with patches of two colors

piece *n.* 1 part broken off or separated 2 part complete in itself 3 single thing —*v.* join (*together*) the pieces of

pièce de ré·sis·tance (pyes de rä zēs täns') *n.* [Fr] main item or event

piece'meal' *a.*, *adv.* (made or done) piece by piece

piece'work' *n.* work which one is paid for by the piece

pied (pīd) *a.* spotted with various colors

pied-à-terre (pyä tä ter') *n.* [Fr] part-time residence

pie'-eyed' *a.* [Sl.] drunk

pier (pir) *n.* 1 landing place built out over water 2 heavy, supporting column

pierce *v.* 1 pass through as a needle does 2 make a hole in 3 sound sharply —**pierc'ing** *a.*

pi'e·ty (pī'-) *n.* devotion to religious duties, etc.

pif'fle *n.* [Inf.] insignificant or nonsensical talk, etc.

pig *n.* 1 fat farm animal; swine 2 greedy or filthy person —**pig'gish** *a.*

pi·geon (pij'ən) *n.* plump bird with a small head

pi'geon·hole' *n.* a compartment, as in a desk, for filing papers —*v.* 1 put in a compartment 2 lay aside 3 classify

pi'geon-toed' *a.* having the toes or feet turned inward

pig'gy·back' *adv.* on the shoulders or back —*a.* (carried) on the back, a train, etc. —*v.* place on top of or in addition to (something)

pig'head'ed *a.* stubborn

pig iron *n.* molten iron

pig'ment *n.* coloring matter

pig·men·ta'tion *n.* coloration in plants or animals

pig'my *a.*, *n.*, *pl.* **-mies** pygmy

pig'pen' *n.* a pen for pigs: also **pig'sty'**, *pl.* **-sties'**

pig'skin' *n.* 1 leather made from the skin of a pig 2 [Inf.] a football

pig'tail' *n.* braid of hair hanging down the back

pike *n.* 1 slender, freshwater fish 2 turnpike 3 metal-tipped spear

pik'er *n.* [Sl.] petty or stingy person

pi·laf, pi·laff (pē'läf') *n.* boiled, seasoned rice with meat, etc.

pi·las'ter *n.* column projecting from a wall

pile *n.* 1 mass of things heaped

together **2** thick nap, as on a rug **3** heavy, vertical beam —*v.* **1** heap up **2** accumulate **3** to crowd

piles *pl.n.* hemorrhoids

pile'up' *n.* **1** accumulation **2** [Inf.] collision of several cars

pil'fer *v.* steal; filch

pil'grim *n.* traveler to a holy place — **pil'grim·age** *n.*

pill *n.* tablet, capsule, etc. of medicine to be swallowed whole —**the pill** (or **Pill**) [Inf.] oral contraceptive for women

pil'lage *v., n.* plunder

pil'lar *n.* upright support; column

pil'lion (-yən) *n.* extra seat on a horse or motorcycle

pil'lo·ry *n., pl.* **-ries** device with holes for head and hands, in which offenders were locked —*v.* **-ried, -ry·ing** expose to public scorn

pil'low *n.* cloth case of soft material, as for supporting the head while sleeping —*v.* rest as on a pillow

pil'low·case' *n.* removable covering for a pillow: also **pil'low·slip'**

pi'lot *n.* **1** one whose job is steering ships in harbors, etc. **2** one who flies aircraft or spacecraft **3** guide —*v.* be pilot of, in, etc.

pi'lot·house' *n.* enclosure for helmsman on a ship

pilot light *n.* small gas jet kept burning to light burners

pi·men'to *n., pl.* **-tos** sweet, bell-shaped red pepper: also **pi·mien'to** (-myen'-)

pimp *v., n.* (act as) a prostitute's agent

pim'ple *n.* small, sore swelling of the skin —**pim'ply** *a.,* **-pli·er, -pli·est**

PIN (pin) *n.* personal identification number, as for use at an ATM

pin *n.* **1** pointed piece of wire to fasten things together **2** thin rod to hold things with **3** thing like a pin **4** ornament with a pin to fasten it **5** bottle-shaped wooden object at which a ball is bowled —*v.* **pinned, pin'ning** fasten as with a pin

pin'a·fore' *n.* apronlike garment for girls

pin'ball' machine *n.* game machine with inclined board and rolling ball that hits objects, etc. to score points

pince-nez (pans'nā') *n., pl.* **-nez'** (-nāz') eyeglasses held in place only by a spring gripping bridge of nose

pin'cers *pl.n.* **1** tool for gripping things **2** claw of a crab, etc. Also **pinch'ers**

pinch *v.* **1** squeeze between two sur-

faces **2** to make look thin, gaunt, etc. **3** be stingy —*n.* **1** a squeeze **2** small amount **3** an emergency: in **in a pinch** —*a.* substitute

pinch'-hit' *v.* **-hit', -hit'ting** substitute (*for* someone) —**pinch hitter** *n.*

pin'cush'ion *n.* small cushion to stick pins in

pine *n.* **1** evergreen tree with cones and needle-shaped leaves **2** its wood —*v.* **1** waste (*away*) through grief, etc. **2** yearn (*for*)

pine'ap'ple *n.* large, juicy tropical fruit

pin'feath'er *n.* an undeveloped feather

ping *n.* sound of a bullet striking something sharply

Ping'-Pong' *trademark* table-tennis equipment —*n.* [*often* p- p-] table tennis

pin'ion (-yən) *n.* **1** small cogwheel **2** wing or wing feather —*v.* bind the wings or arms of

pink *n.* **1** plant with pale-red flowers **2** pale red —*v.* cut a saw-toothed edge on (cloth) —**in the pink** [Inf.] healthy; fit

pink'eye' *n.* acute, contagious conjunctivitis

pink'ie, pink'y *n., pl.* **-ies** smallest finger

pink'ing shears *pl.n.* shears for pinking cloth to prevent fraying

pin money *n.* a little money, as for incidental expenses

pin'na·cle *n.* **1** slender spire **2** mountain peak **3** highest point

pin'nate *a.* having a featherlike structure: said of a leaf

pi'noch'le (pē'nuk'-, -näk'-) *n.* bridge-like card game using 48 cards

pin'point' *v.* show the precise location of

pin'prick' *n.* **1** tiny hole made by a pin **2** minor annoyance

pin'set'ter *n.* person or machine that sets bowling pins: also **pin'spot'ter**

pin'stripe' *n.* fabric pattern of very narrow stripes

pint *n.* ½ quart

pin'to *a., n.* piebald (horse)

pinto bean *n.* mottled kidney bean

pin'up' *n.* [Inf.] picture of a sexually attractive person

pin'wheel' *n.* **1** small plastic wheel that turns in the wind **2** similar wheel of fireworks

Pin'yin' *n.* system for converting Chinese symbols into the W alphabet

pi'o·neer' *n.* early settler, first investigator, etc. —*v.* be a pioneer

pi'ous *a.* having, showing, or pretending religious devotion —**pi'ous·ly** *adv.*

pip *n.* 1 seed of an apple, etc. 2 [Old Sl.] one much admired

pipe *n.* 1 long tube for conveying water, gas, etc. 2 tube with a bowl at one end, for smoking tobacco 3 tube for making musical sounds —*v.* 1 utter in a shrill voice 2 convey (water, etc.) by pipes 3 play (a tune) on a pipe —**pip'er** *n.*

pipe dream *n.* [Inf.] fantastic plan, vain hope, etc.

pipe'line' *n.* 1 line of pipes for water, gas, etc. 2 any means of conveying something

pip'ing *n.* 1 music made by pipes 2 shrill sound 3 pipelike cloth trimming

pip'it *n.* small songbird

pip'pin *n.* kind of apple

pip'squeak' *n.* [Inf.] insignificant person or thing

pi·quant (pē'kənt) *a.* 1 agreeably pungent 2 stimulating —**pi'quan·cy** *n.*

pi·qué, pi·que (pē kā') *n.* cotton fabric with vertical cords

pique (pēk) *n.* resentment at being slighted —*v.* 1 offend 2 excite

pi·ra·nha (pə rän'ə) *n., pl.* **-nhas** or **-nha** small fish that hunts in schools

pi'rate (-rət) *n.* 1 one who robs ships at sea 2 one who uses a copyrighted or patented work without authorization —*v.* take, use, etc. by piracy —**pi'ra·cy** *n.*

pi·ro·gi (pi rō'gē) *n., pl.* **-gi** or **-gies** a small pastry filled with meat, etc.

pir·ou·ette' (-ōō-) *n.* a whirling on the toes —*v.* **-et'ted, -et'ting** do a pirouette

pis·ca·to'ri·al *a.* of fishing

Pis·ces (pī'sēz') *n.* 12th sign of the zodiac

pis'mire (*or* piz'-) *n.* [Ar.] ant

piss'ant' *a., n,* [Sl.] insignificant and contemptible (person)

pis·tach·i·o (pi stash'ē ō') *n., pl.* **-os'** greenish nut

pis'til *n.* seed-bearing organ of a flower

pis'tol *n.* small firearm held with one hand

pis'tol-whip' *v.* beat with a pistol

pis'ton *n.* part that moves back and forth in a hollow cylinder from pressure caused by combustion, etc.

pit *n.* 1 stone of a plum, peach, etc. 2 hole in the ground 3 small hollow in a surface 4 section for the orchestra in front of the stage —*v.* **pit'ted, pit'ting** 1 remove the pit from (a fruit) 2 mark with pits 3 set in competition (*against*)

pi'ta (pē'-) *n.* round, flat bread of Middle East: also **pita bread**

pit'a·pat' *adv.* with rapid, strong beating

pitch *v.* 1 set up (tents) 2 throw 3 plunge forward 4 set at some level, key, etc. 5 rise and fall, as a ship —*n.* 1 throw 2 point or degree 3 degree of slope 4 highness or lowness of a musical sound 5 black, sticky substance from coal tar, etc. —**pitch in** [Inf.] begin working hard

pitch'-black' *a.* very black

pitch'blende' *n.* dark, uranium-bearing mineral

pitch'-dark' *a.* very dark

pitch'er *n.* 1 container for holding and pouring liquids 2 baseball player who pitches to the batters

pitch'fork' *n.* large fork for lifting and tossing hay

pitch pipe *n.* small musical pipe making a fixed tone as a standard of pitch for singers, etc.

pit'e·ous *a.* deserving pity —**pit'e·ous·ly** *adv.*

pit'fall' *n.* 1 covered pit as a trap 2 hidden danger

pith *n.* 1 soft, spongy tissue in the center of plant stems 2 essential part

pith'y *a.* **-i·er, -i·est** full of meaning or force

pit'i·a·ble *a.* 1 deserving pity 2 deserving contempt —**pit'i·a·bly** *adv.*

pit'i·ful *a.* 1 arousing or deserving pity 2 contemptible —**pit'i·ful·ly** *adv.*

pit'i·less *a.* without pity

pit'tance *n.* small amount, esp. of money

pit'ter-pat'ter *n.* rapid series of tapping sounds

pi·tu'i·tar'y *a.* of a small endocrine gland (**pituitary gland**) attached to the brain

pit'y *n.* 1 sorrow for another's misfortune 2 cause for sorrow or regret —*v.* **-ied, -y·ing** feel pity (for)

piv'ot *n.* 1 person or thing on which something turns or depends 2 pivoting motion —*v.* provide with or turn on a pivot —**piv'ot·al** *a.*

pix'el *n.* any of the dots making up an image on a video screen

pix'ie, pix'y *n., pl.* **-ies** puckish elf

pi·zazz', piz·zazz' *n.* [Inf.] 1 vitality 2 style, flair, etc.

piz·za (pēt'sə) *n.* baked dish of thin dough topped with cheese, tomato sauce, etc.

piz·ze·ri'a *n.* a place where pizzas are made and sold

piz·zi·ca·to (pit'si kät'ō) *adv., a. Mus.* with the strings plucked

pj's *pl.n.* [Inf.] pajamas

pk *abbrev.* 1 pack 2 park 3 peck

pkg *abbrev.* package(s)

pl *abbrev.* 1 place: also **Pl** 2 plate 3 plural

plac'ard *v., n.* (put up) a sign in a public place

pla'cate' *v.* appease

place *n.* 1 space 2 region 3 city or town 4 residence 5 particular building, site, part, position, etc. 6 job or its duties —*v.* 1 put in a certain place 2 identify by some relationship —**in place of** rather than —**take place** occur

pla·ce'bo *n., pl.* -**bos** or -**boes** harmless preparation without medicine given to humor a patient

place mat *n.* table mat of cloth, etc. for one place setting

place'ment *n.* a placing, esp. in a job

pla·cen'ta *n., pl.* -**tas** or -**tae** (-tē) organ in the uterus to nourish the fetus

plac'er (plas'-) *n.* gravel with gold, etc.

place setting *n.* dish, utensils, etc. set for one who is eating

plac'id (plas'-) *a.* calm

plack'et *n.* slit at the waist of a skirt or dress

pla'gia·rize' (-jə rīz') *v.* present another's writings as one's own —**pla'gia·rism'** *n.* —**pla'gia·rist** *n.*

plague (plāg) *n.* 1 affliction 2 deadly epidemic disease —*v.* vex; trouble

plaice *n.* kind of flatfish

plaid (plad) *n., a.* (cloth) with crisscross pattern

plain *a.* 1 clear 2 outspoken 3 obvious 4 simple 5 homely 6 not fancy 7 common —*n.* an extent of flat land —*adv.* clearly —**plain'ly** *adv.* —**plain'ness** *n.*

plain'clothes' man *n.* policeman who does not wear a uniform

plain'song' *n.* very old church music chanted in unison

plaint *n.* complaint

plain'tiff *n.* one who brings a suit into a court of law

plain'tive (-tiv) *a.* sad; mournful

plait *v., n.* 1 braid 2 pleat

plan *n.* 1 outline; map 2 way of doing; scheme —*v.* planned, plan'ning 1 make a plan of or for 2 intend —**plan'ner** *n.*

plane *a.* flat —*n.* 1 flat surface 2 level

or stage 3 airplane 4 carpenter's tool for leveling or smoothing —*v.* smooth or level with a plane

plan'et *n.* a large mass that revolves around a star, esp. one revolving around the sun —**plan'e·tar'y** *a.*

plan·e·tar'i·um (-ter'-) *n.* large domed room for projecting images of the night sky

plane tree *n.* American sycamore

plank *n.* 1 long, broad, thick board 2 a principle in a political platform —*v.* cover with planks

plank'ton *n.* tiny animals and plants floating in bodies of water

plant *n.* 1 living thing that cannot move and makes it own food, as a tree, flower, etc. 2 factory —*v.* 1 to put in the ground to grow 2 set firmly in place

plan'tain (-tin) *n.* 1 weed with broad leaves 2 banana plant with coarse fruit

plan'tar (-tər) *a.* of the sole of the foot

plan·ta'tion *n.* estate with its workers living on it

plant'er *n.* container for plants

plant'ing *n.* 1 act of putting seeds, etc. into soil 2 something planted

plaque (plak) *n.* 1 flat, inscribed piece of wood or metal, used to commemorate an event, etc. 2 thin film of bacteria on teeth

plas'ma (plaz'-) *n.* fluid part of blood, lymph, etc.

plas'ter *n.* lime, sand, and water, mixed as a coating that hardens on walls —*v.* cover as with plaster

plaster of Paris *n.* paste of gypsum and water that hardens quickly

plas'tic *a.* 1 that shapes or can be shaped 2 of plastic —*n.* substance that can be molded and hardened —**plas·tic'i·ty** (-tis'-) *n.*

plas'ti·cize' *v.* make or become plastic

plastic surgery *n.* surgical grafting of skin or bone

plat *n.* 1 map 2 PLOT (*n.* 1)

plate *n.* 1 shallow dish 2 plated dinnerware 3 cast of molded type 4 engraved illustration 5 denture 6 home plate —*v.* coat with metal

pla·teau' (pla tō') *n.* 1 tract of high, level land 2 period of no progress

plat'en *n.* 1 plate that presses paper against printing type 2 typewriter roller on which keys strike

plat'form' *n.* 1 raised horizontal surface 2 political party's stated aims

plat'i·num *n.* silvery, precious metal, a chemical element

plat'i·tude' n. trite remark

pla·ton'ic a. spiritual or intellectual, not sexual

pla·toon' n. small group, as of soldiers

plat'ter n. large serving dish

plat'y·pus n., pl. **-pus·es** or **-pi'** (-pī') small, egg-laying water mammal

plau'dits (plô'-) pl.n. applause

plau'si·ble (-zə-) a. credible —**plau'si·bil'i·ty** n.

play v. 1 have fun 2 do in fun 3 take part in a game or sport 4 perform on a musical instrument 5 make a tape or disc machine give out sounds or images 6 trifle 7 cause 8 act in a certain way 9 act the part of —n. 1 recreation 2 fun 3 motion or freedom for motion 4 move in a game 5 drama —**play up** [Inf.] emphasize —**play'er** n.

play'act' v. 1 pretend 2 act in dramatic way

play'back' n. playing of tape, disc, etc. that has been recorded

play'bill' n. program, poster, etc. for a play

play'boy' n. man, often rich, given to pleasure-seeking —**play'girl'** n.fem.

play'ful a. full of fun; frisky —**play'ful·ly** adv. —**play'ful·ness** n.

play'go'er n. one who attends plays frequently

play'ground' n. outdoor place for games and play

play'house' n. 1 theater 2 small house for children to play in

playing cards pl.n. cards in four suits for playing poker, bridge, etc.

play'mate' n. companion in recreation

play'off' n. contest played to break a tie or decide a championship

play on words n. pun

play'pen' n. enclosure for infant to play in

play'thing' n. toy

play'wright' (-rīt') n. one who writes plays

pla·za (plä'zə, plaz'ə) n. public square

PLC abbrev. [Br.] public limited company

plea n. 1 appeal; request 2 statement in defense

plea bar'gain·ing n. legal negotiations before a trial to reduce charges —**plea bargain** n. —**plea'-bar'gain** v.

plead v. 1 beg; entreat 2 argue (a law case) 3 offer as an excuse

pleas'ant (plez'-) a. pleasing; agreeable —**pleas'ant·ly** adv.

pleas'ant·ry n., pl. **-ries** 1 jocular remark 2 a polite social remark

please v. 1 satisfy 2 be the wish of 3 be obliging enough to: used in polite requests —**pleased** a.

pleas'ing a. giving pleasure —**pleas'ing·ly** adv.

pleas'ure (plezh'-) n. 1 delight or satisfaction 2 one's choice —**pleas'ur·a·ble** a.

pleat n. fold made by doubling cloth —v. make pleats in

ple·be'ian (-bē'ən) a., n. common (person)

pleb'i·scite' (-sīt') n. direct popular vote on an issue

plec'trum n., pl. **-trums** or **-tra** small device for plucking a banjo, etc.

pledge n. 1 thing given as security for a contract, etc. 2 promise —v. 1 give as security 2 promise

ple'na·ry a. full or fully attended

plen'i·po·ten'ti·ar'y (-shē er'ē) n., pl. **-ies**; a. (a diplomat) having full authority

plen'i·tude' n. 1 fullness 2 abundance

plen'ti·ful a. abundant: also **plen'te·ous**

plen'ty n. 1 prosperity 2 ample amount

pleth'o·ra n. overabundance

pleu·ri·sy (ploor'ə sē) n. inflammation of membrane lining the chest cavity

Plex'i·glas' trademark transparent plastic

plex'i-glass' n. material like Plexiglas

pli'a·ble a. easily bent; flexible —**pli'a·bil'i·ty** n.

pli'ant a. 1 flexible 2 compliant —**pli'an·cy** n.

pli'ers pl.n. small tool for gripping

plight n. condition, esp. a bad or dangerous one —v. 1 pledge 2 betroth

plinth n. block at base of column, pedestal, etc.

plod v. **plod'ded**, **plod'ding** 1 trudge 2 work steadily —**plod'der** n.

plop n. sound of object falling into water —v. **plopped**, **plop'ping** fall with a plop

plot n. 1 piece of ground 2 diagram, plan, etc. 3 plan of action of a play, etc.: also **plot'line'** 4 secret, esp. evil, scheme —v. **plot'ted**, **plot'ting** 1 make a map, plan, etc. of 2 scheme —**plot'ter** n.

plov'er (pluv'-) n. shorebird with long, pointed wings

plow (plou) n. 1 implement for cutting and turning up soil 2 machine for removing snow —v. 1 use a plow (on) 2 make one's way Also [Chiefly Br.]

plough —**plow'man** n., pl. **-men**

plow'share' n. blade of a plow

ploy n. ruse; trick

pluck v. **1** pull off or out **2** pull at and release quickly —n. **1** a pull **2** courage

pluck'y a. **-i·er, -i·est** brave; spirited

plug n. **1** stopper **2** device for making electrical contact **3** [Inf.] insinuated advertisement **4** [Sl.] worn-out horse —v. **plugged, plug'ging 1** stop up with a plug **2** [Inf.] advertise with a plug **3** [Inf.] work doggedly **4** [Sl.] hit with a bullet

plum n. **1** smooth-skinned, juicy fruit **2** choice thing

plum'age (plōōm'-) n. a bird's feathers

plumb (plum) n. weight on a line for checking a vertical wall or sounding a depth —a. perpendicular —adv. v. **1** straight down **2** [Inf.] entirely —v. **1** test with a plumb **2** solve

plumb'er n. one who fits and repairs water pipes, etc. —**plumb'ing** n.

plume n. feather or tuft of feathers — v. **1** adorn with plumes **2** preen

plum'met v. fall straight downward — n. plumb

plump a. full and rounded —v. drop heavily —adv. suddenly; heavily

plun'der v. rob by force —n. goods plundered

plunge v. **1** thrust suddenly (into) **2** dive or rush —n. dive or fall

plung'er n. **1** rubber suction cup to open drains **2** part that moves with a plunging motion, as a piston

plunk v. **1** strum (a banjo, etc.) **2** put down heavily —n. sound of plunking

plu'ral (ploor'əl) a. more than one —n. Gram. word form designating more than one —**plu'ral·ize'** v.

plu'ral·ism' n. various ethnic, etc. groups existing together in a nation or society —**plu'ral·ist, plu'ral·is'tic** a.

plu·ral'i·ty n. **1** majority **2** excess of winner's votes over nearest rival's

plus prep. added to —a. **1** designating a sign (+) showing addition **2** positive **3** more than —n. something added

plush n. fabric with a long pile —a. [Inf.] luxurious

Plu'to n. ninth planet from the sun

plu·toc'ra·cy n., pl. **-cies** (government by) wealthy people —**plu'to·crat'** n. —**plu'to·crat'ic** a.

plu·to'ni·um n. radioactive chemical element

ply n., pl. **plies** one layer in plywood, folded cloth, etc. —v. **plied, ply'ing 1** work at (a trade) with (a tool) **2**

keep supplying (with) **3** travel back and forth (between)

ply'wood' n. board made of glued layers of wood

PM abbrev. **1** after noon: also **P.M., p.m., pm 2** Postmaster **3** Prime Minister

PMS abbrev. premenstrual syndrome

pneu·mat'ic (nōō-) a. **1** of or containing air or gases **2** worked by compressed air

pneu·mo'ni·a n. infection in the lungs

PO abbrev. **1** Post Office **2** post office box

poach v. **1** cook (an egg without its shell) in water **2** hunt or fish illegally —**poach'er** n.

pock'et n. **1** little bag or pouch, esp. when sewn into clothing **2** pouchlike cavity or hollow —a. that can be carried in a pocket —v. **1** put into a pocket **2** take dishonestly; appropriate —**pock'et·ful'** n.

pock'et·book' n. purse

pock'et·knife' n., pl. **-knives'** small knife with folding blades

pock'mark' n. scar left by a pustule: also **pock**

pod n. shell of peas, beans, etc. containing the seeds

po·di'a·try (-dī'-) n. treatment of foot ailments —**po·di'a·trist** n.

po'di·um n. **1** platform for an orchestra conductor **2** lectern

po'em n. piece of imaginative writing in rhythm, rhyme, etc.

po'et n. writer of poems —**po'et·ess** n.fem.

poetic justice n. justice, as in stories, applied in an especially fitting way

poetic license n. deviation from strict fact, as for artistic effect

poet lau·re·ate (lôr'ē it) n. official poet of a country, etc.

po'et·ry n. **1** writing of poems **2** poems **3** rhythms, deep feelings, etc. of poems —**po·et'ic, po·et'i·cal** a.

po'grom n. [Hist.] organized persecution, as of Russian Jews

poi n. Hawaiian dish of taro paste

poign·ant (poin'yənt) a. **1** painful to the feelings **2** emotionally touching **3** keen —**poign'an·cy** n.

poin·set'ti·a (-set'ə, -set'ē ə) n. plant with petal-like red leaves

point n. **1** a dot **2** specific place or time **3** a stage or degree reached **4** item; detail **5** special feature **6** unit, as of a game score **7** sharp end **8** cape (land) **9** purpose; object **10** essential idea **11** mark showing direction on a compass —v. **1** sharpen to a point **2** call attention (to) **3** show **4** aim —**at the point of** very close to —**beside the point** irrelevant —**to the point** pertinent

point'-blank' a., adv. **1** (aimed) straight at a mark **2** direct(ly)

point'ed a. **1** sharp **2** aimed at someone, as a remark

point'er n. **1** long, tapered rod for pointing **2** indicator **3** large hunting dog **4** [Inf.] hint; suggestion

poin'til·lism' (pwan'-) n. painting done in tiny points of color —**poin'til·list** n., a. —**poin'til·lis'tic** a.

point'less a. without meaning —**point'less·ly** adv.

point of view n. way something is viewed or thought of

poise (poiz) n. **1** balance **2** ease and dignity of manner —v. balance

poised a. **1** calm **2** ready

poi'son n. substance which can cause illness or death —v. **1** harm or kill with poison **2** put poison into **3** corrupt —**poi'son·ous** a.

poison ivy n. plant that can cause severe skin rash

poke v. **1** prod, as with a stick **2** search (about or around) **3** move slowly (along) —n. jab; thrust —**poke fun (at)** ridicule

pok'er n. **1** gambling game with cards **2** iron bar for stirring a fire

poker face n. expressionless face

pok'y a. **-i·er, -i·est** slow; dull: also **pok'ey**

po'lar a. **1** having opposite magnetic poles **2** opposite in character, nature, etc. —**po·lar'i·ty** n., pl. **-ties** —**po'lar·i·za'tion** n. —**po'lar·ize'** v.

polar bear n. large white bear of arctic regions

Po'lar·oid' trademark a camera that produces a print within seconds

Pole n. Polish person

pole n. **1** long, slender piece of wood, metal, etc. **2** end of an axis, as of the earth **3** either of two opposed forces, as the ends of a magnet —v. propel (a boat) with a pole

pole'cat' n. **1** kind of European weasel **2** skunk

po·lem'ics n. [sometimes pl. v.] art or practice of disputation —**po·lem'ic** a., n. —**po·lem'i·cist** n. —**po·lem'i·cize'** v.

pole vault n. a leap for height by vaulting with aid of a pole —**pole'-vault'** v.

po·lice' n. **1** department of a city, etc. for keeping law and order **2** [pl. v.]

members of such a department —v. control, etc. with police

po·lice'man n., pl. **-men** member of a police force —**po·lice'wom'an** n.fem., pl. **-wom'en**

police officer n. member of a police force

pol'i·cy n., pl. **-cies 1** governing principle, plan, etc. **2** insurance contract

po'li·o·my'e·li'tis (-lit'is) n. virus disease often resulting in paralysis: also **po'li·o'**

Pol'ish (pōl'-) n., a. (language) of Poland

pol'ish (päl'-) v. **1** smooth and brighten, as by rubbing **2** refine (manners, etc.) —n. **1** surface gloss **2** elegance **3** substance used to polish

po·lite' a. **1** showing good manners; courteous **2** refined —**po·lite'ly** adv.

pol'i·tic a. wise or shrewd

po·lit'i·cal a. of government, politics, etc. —**po·lit'i·cize'** v.

po·lit'i·cal·ly correct a. holding orthodox liberal views: usually disparaging

political science n. study of political institutions, government, etc.

pol'i·ti'cian (-tish'ən) n. one active in politics

pol'i·tick'ing n. political activity

po·lit'i·co' n., pl. **-cos'** a politician

pol'i·tics pl.n. [sing. or pl. v.] **1** science of government **2** political affairs; methods, opinions, scheming, etc.

pol'i·ty n., pl. **-ties 1** system of government **2** a state

pol'ka (pōl'-) n. fast dance for couples

pol'ka dot (pō'-) n. any of a pattern of dots on cloth

poll (pōl) n. **1** a counting or listing as of voters **2** number of votes recorded **3** pl. voting place **4** survey of opinion —v. **1** take the votes or opinions of **2** receive, as votes

pol'len n. powderlike sex cells from anthers of a flower

pol'li·nate' v. put pollen on the pistil of —**pol'li·na'tion** n.

pol'li·wog' n. tadpole

poll'ster n. taker of opinion polls

pol·lute' v. make unclean or impure —**pol·lu'tant** n. —**pol·lu'tion** n.

Pol'ly·an'na n. excessively optimistic person

po'lo n. team game played on horseback

pol'ter·geist' (-gīst') n. ghost believed to cause mysterious noises

pol·troon' n. coward

poly- pref. much; many

pol'y·clin'ic n. clinic for treatment of

various kinds of diseases

pol'y·es'ter *n.* synthetic substance used in plastics, fibers, etc.

pol'y·eth'yl·ene' *n.* polymer of ethylene used in plastics, film, etc.

po·lyg'a·my (-lig'-) *n.* a being married to more than one person at one time —**po·lyg'a·mist** *n.* —**po·lyg'a·mous** *a.*

pol'y·gon' *n.* closed plane figure, as a hexagon

pol'y·graph' *n.* device measuring bodily changes, used on one suspected of lying

pol'y·he'dron *n.* solid figure with usually more than six plane surfaces

pol'y·math' *n.* person of great and varied learning

pol'y·mer *n.* substance of giant molecules formed by linking one or more kinds of smaller molecules

pol'yp (-ip) *n.* **1** tubular water animal with tentacles **2** growth on a mucous membrane

pol'y·sty'rene' *n.* clear polymer used in making containers, etc.

pol'y·syl'la·ble *n.* word of more than three syllables —**pol'y·syl·lab'ic** *a.*

pol'y·tech'nic (-tek'-) *a.* instructing in many scientific and technical subjects

pol'y·the·ism' (-thē-) *n.* belief in more than one god —**pol'y·the·is'tic** *a.*

pol'y·un·sat'u·rat'ed *a.* of fats or oils with a low cholesterol content

pol'y·vi'nyl *a.* of any of a group of polymer vinyl compounds

po·made' (pä-) *n.* perfumed ointment for the hair

pome'gran'ate (päm'-, päm'ə-) *n.* hard, round, red fruit with red, juicy seeds

pom'mel (pum'-) *n.* rounded, upward-projecting front part of a saddle —*v.* pummel

pomp *n.* stately or ostentatious display

pom'pa·dour' (-dôr') *n.* hair style with the hair brushed up high from the forehead

pom·pa·no' *n.*, *pl.* **-no'** or **-nos'** food fish of the West Indies, etc.

pom'pom' *n.* tuft of fabric decorating hats, waved by cheerleaders, etc.: also **pom'pon'**

pom'pous *a.* pretentious —**pom·pos'i·ty** *n.*

pon'cho *n.*, *pl.* **-chos** cloak like a blanket

pond *n.* small lake

pon'der *v.* think deeply (about)

pon'der·o·sa (**pine**) *n.* yellow pine of western North America

pon'der·ous *a.* heavy; clumsy

pone *n.* [Chiefly South] cornmeal bread

pon·gee' *n.* soft, silk cloth

pon'iard (-yard) *n.* dagger

pon'tiff *n.* **1** bishop **2** [P-] the Pope —**pon·tif'i·cal** *a.*

pon·tif'i·cate' *v.* be dogmatic or pompous

pon·toon' *n.* one of the floats supporting a bridge or airplane on water

po'ny *n.*, *pl.* **-nies** small horse

po'ny·tail' *n.* hairstyle in which hair is tied to hang in back

poo'dle *n.* curly-haired dog

pooh *int.* exclamation of contempt, disbelief, etc.

pool *n.* **1** small pond **2** puddle **3** tank for swimming **4** billiards on a table with pockets **5** common fund of money, etc. **6** shared equipment, task, etc. or the group sharing it —*v.* put into a common fund

poop *n.* raised deck at the stern of a sailing ship

poor *a.* **1** having little money **2** below average; inferior **3** worthy of pity —**poor'ly** *adv.*

poor'-mouth' *v.* [Inf.] complain about one's lack of money

pop *n.* **1** light, explosive sound **2** flavored soda water **3** pop music, etc. —*v.* **popped, pop'ping 1** make, or burst with, a pop **2** cause to pop **3** move, go, etc. suddenly **4** bulge —*adv.* like a pop —*a.* **1** of music popular with many people **2** intended for popular taste **3** of a realistic art style influenced by commercial art

pop *abbrev.* **1** popularly **2** population

pop'corn' *n.* corn with kernels that pop open when heated

pope *n.* [often P-] head of the Roman Catholic Church

pop'gun' *n.* toy gun that shoots pellets by compressed air

pop'lar *n.* tall tree

pop'lin *n.* ribbed cloth

pop'o'ver *n.* hollow muffin

pop'py *n.*, *pl.* **-pies** plant with showy flowers

pop'py·cock' *n.* [Inf.] nonsense

pop'u·lace (-ləs) *n.* the common people

pop'u·lar *a.* **1** of, by, or for people generally **2** very well liked —**pop'u·lar'i·ty** *n.* —**pop'u·lar·ize'** *v.*

pop'u·late' *v.* inhabit

pop'u·la'tion *n.* total number of inhabitants

pop'u·list *a.*, *n.* (of) one, often a demagogue, who claims to represent the common people —**pop'u·lism'** *n.*

pop'u·lous *a.* full of people

por'ce·lain (-lin) *n.* hard, white, ceramic material

porch *n.* open or screen-enclosed room on the outside of a building

por'cine' (-sīn') *a.* of or like pigs

por'cu·pine' *n.* gnawing animal with long, sharp spines in its coat

pore *v.* study or ponder (*over*) —*n.* tiny opening, as in the skin, for absorbing or discharging fluids

pork *n.* flesh of a pig used as food

pork barrel *n.* [Inf.] government grants for political favors

por·nog'ra·phy *n.* writings, pictures, etc. intended to arouse sexual desire: also [Sl.] **por'no** or **porn** —**por'no·graph'ic** *a.* —**por·nog'ra·pher** *n.*

po'rous *a.* full of pores or tiny holes —**po·ros'i·ty** *n.*

por'poise (-pəs) *n.* **1** sea mammal with a blunt snout **2** dolphin

por'ridge *n.* cereal or meal boiled in water or milk

por'rin·ger (-jər) *n.* bowl for porridge, etc.

port *n.* **1** harbor **2** city with a harbor **3** sweet, dark-red wine **4** left side of a ship as one faces the bow **5** porthole **6** opening or outlet for water, electronic data, etc.

port'a·ble *a.* that can be carried — **port·a·bil'i·ty** *n.*

por'tage *n.* **1** carrying of boats and supplies overland between waterways **2** route so used

por'tal *n.* doorway; gate

por·tend' *v.* be an omen or warning of —**por'tent** *n.* —**por·ten'tous** *a.*

por'ter *n.* **1** doorman **2** attendant who carries luggage, sweeps up, etc.

por'ter·house' (**steak**) *n.* choice cut of beef from the loin

port·fo'li·o *n.*, *pl.* **-os'** **1** briefcase **2** list of investments or securities **3** collected samples of an artist's work

port'hole' *n.* window in a ship's side

por'ti·co *n.*, *pl.* **-coes** or **-cos** porch consisting of a roof supported by columns

por·tiere', por·tière' (-tyer') *n.* curtain hung in a doorway

por'tion *n.* part; share —*v.* divide or give out in portions

port'ly *a.* **-li·er, -li·est** stout and stately

port·man'teau (-tō) *n.*, *pl.* **-teaus** or **-teaux** (-tōz) kind of suitcase

por·to·bel'lo mushroom *n.* large, flavorful brown mushroom

por'trait (-trit) *n.* a painting, photograph, etc. of a person

por·tray' *v.* **1** make a portrait of **2** describe **3** represent on the stage — **por·tray'al** *n.*

Por'tu·guese' (-chə gēz') *n.*, *pl.* **-guese**; *a.* (native or language) of Portugal

por·tu·lac'a (-chə lak'ə) *n.* plant with small flowers

pos *abbrev.* positive

pose *v.* **1** present, as a question **2** assume a bodily posture, a false role, etc. —*n.* assumed posture, etc. — **pos'er** *n.*

po·seur' (-zur') *n.* one who assumes attitudes for their effect

posh *a.* [Inf.] luxurious and fashionable

pos'it *v.* postulate

po·si'tion *n.* **1** way of being placed **2** opinion **3** place; location **4** status **5** job —*v.* to place

pos'i·tive *a.* **1** explicit; definite **2** sure or too sure **3** affirmative **4** real; absolute **5** of electricity with a lack of electrons **6** *Gram.* of an adjective, etc. in its uncompared degree **7** *Math.* greater than zero —*n.* **1** anything positive **2** battery terminal where electrons flow in —**pos'i·tive·ly** *adv.*

pos'i·tron' *n.* positive antimatter particle of an electron

pos'se (-ē) *n.* [Hist.] body of men called to help a sheriff

pos·sess' *v.* **1** own **2** have as a quality, etc. **3** control —**pos·ses'sor** *n.*

pos·ses'sion *n.* **1** a possessing **2** thing possessed

pos·ses'sive *a.* **1** showing or desiring possession **2** *Gram.* of a form, etc. indicating possession

pos'si·ble *a.* that can be, can happen, etc. —**pos'si·bil'i·ty** *n.*, *pl.* **-ties** —**pos'si·bly** *adv.*

pos'sum *n.* [Inf.] opossum —**play possum** feign sleep, ignorance, etc.

post *n.* **1** piece of wood, etc. set upright as a support **2** place where a soldier or soldiers are stationed **3** job; position **4** mail —*v.* **1** put up (a notice, etc.) **2** assign to a post **3** to mail **4** inform

post- *pref.* after; following

post'age *n.* amount charged for mailing a letter, etc.

post'al *a.* of (the) mail

postal code *n.* [Cdn.] group of routing numbers and letters in an address

post·bel'lum *a.* after the war

post'card' *n.* card, often a picture card, sent by mail

post·date' *v.* **1** mark with a later date **2** be later than

post'er *n.* large sign or notice posted publicly

pos·te'ri·or (-tir'ē-) *a.* **1** at the back **2** later —*n.* buttocks

pos·ter'i·ty *n.* all future generations

post·grad'u·ate *a.* of study after graduation

post'haste' *adv.* speedily

post'hole' *n.* hole dug for bottom of a post

post'hu·mous (päs'chōo-) *a.* after one's death

Post'-it' *trademark* small sheets of adhesive-backed paper for attaching notes —*n.* a sheet of this

post'lude' *n.* concluding musical piece

post'man *n., pl.* **-men** mail carrier

post'mark' *v., n.* mark to show the date and place of mailing at the post office

post'mas'ter *n.* person in charge of a post office

postmaster general *n.* head of a government's postal system

post'me·rid'i·an *a.* after noon

post me·rid'i·em *a.* after noon

post'mod'ern·ism' *n.* eclectic cultural and artistic trend in art, etc. of late 20th c. —**post'mod'ern** *a.* —**post'mod'ern·ist** *a., n.*

post'–mor'tem *a.* after death —*n.* autopsy

post·na'tal *a.* after birth

post office *n.* place where mail is sorted, etc.

post·op'er·a·tive *a.* after surgery

post'paid' *a.* with the sender paying the postage

post'par'tum *a.* of the time after childbirth

post·pone' *v.* put off; delay —**post'pone'ment** *n.*

post'script' *n.* note added at the end of a letter, etc.

pos·tu·late (päs'chə lāt'; *n.:* -lət) *v.* assume to be true, real, etc. —*n.* something postulated

pos'ture *n.* way one holds the body —*v.* pose

post'war' *a.* after war

po'sy (-zē) *n., pl.* **-sies** flower or bouquet: old-fashioned

pot *n.* round container for cooking, etc. —*v.* **pot'ted, pot'ting** to put into a pot —**go to pot** go to ruin

po'ta·ble (pōt'ə-) *a.* drinkable

pot'ash' *n.* white substance obtained from wood ashes

po·tas'si·um *n.* soft, white, metallic chemical element

po·ta'to *n., pl.* **-toes** starchy tuber of a common plant, used as a vegetable

potato chip *n.* thin slice of potato fried crisp

pot'bel'ly *n., pl.* **-lies** belly that sticks out

pot'–bound' *a.* having outgrown its pot: said of a plant

po'tent *a.* **1** powerful **2** effective —**po'ten·cy** *n.*

po'ten·tate' *n.* person having great power; ruler; etc.

po·ten'tial (-shəl) *a.* that can be; possible; latent —*n.* **1** something potential **2** voltage at a given point in a circuit —**po·ten'ti·al'i·ty** (-shē al'-) *n., pl.* **-ties** —**po·ten'tial·ly** *adv.*

pot'hold'er *n.* small pad for handling hot pots, etc.

po'tion *n.* a drink, esp. of medicine or poison

pot'luck' *n.* whatever is available

potluck dinner (or **supper**) *n.* dinner in which everyone brings a dish of food to share

pot'pie' *n.* meat pie

pot·pour·ri (pō'pŏo rē') *n.* mixture

pot'sherd' *n.* piece of broken pottery

pot'shot' *n.* random shot, attack, etc.

pot'ter *n.* one who makes pots, dishes, etc. of clay

potter's field *n.* graveyard for paupers or unknown persons

potter's wheel *n.* rotating disk upon which bowls, etc. are made from clay

pot'ter·y *n.* earthenware

pot'ty *n., pl.* **-ties** (child's) toilet

pouch *n.* **1** small sack or bag **2** baglike part

poul·tice (pōl'tis) *n.* hot, soft mass applied to a sore part of the body

poul'try *n.* domestic fowls

pounce *v.* leap or swoop down, as if to seize —*n.* a pouncing

pound *n.* **1** unit of weight, 16 ounces **2** British monetary unit **3** enclosure for stray animals —*v.* **1** hit hard **2** beat to pulp, powder, etc. **3** throb

pound'cake' *n.* rich, buttery cake

pound sign *n.* symbol (#) on a telephone key, etc.

pour (pôr) *v.* **1** flow or make flow steadily **2** rain heavily

pout *v.* **1** push out the lips, as in displeasure **2** sulk —*n.* a pouting

pov'er·ty *n.* **1** a being poor; need **2** inadequacy

pov'er·ty-strick'en *a.* very poor

POW *n., pl.* **POW's** prisoner of war

pow'der *n.* dry substance of fine particles —*v.* 1 put powder on 2 make into powder —**pow'der·y** *a.*

pow'er *n.* 1 ability to do or act 2 strength or energy 3 authority 4 powerful person, nation, etc. 5 result of multiplying a number by itself —*a.* operated by electricity, fuel engine, etc. —**pow'er·less** *a.*

pow'er·ful *a.* strong; mighty —**pow'er·ful·ly** *adv.*

power of attorney *n.* written authority to act for another

pow'wow' *n.* conference of or with North American Indians

pox *n.* disease with skin eruptions

pp *abbrev.* 1 pages 2 past participle

PP, pp *abbrev.* parcel post

ppd *abbrev.* 1 postpaid 2 prepaid

PPO *n.* medical insurance plan with enrolled doctors, etc.

pr *abbrev.* 1 pair(s) 2 price

PR *abbrev.* 1 public relations: also **P.R.** 2 Puerto Rico

prac'ti·ca·ble (-kə-) *a.* that can be done —**prac'ti·ca·bil'i·ty** *n.*

prac'ti·cal *a.* 1 of or obtained through practice 2 useful 3 sensible 4 virtual —**prac'ti·cal'i·ty** *n.* —**prac'ti·cal·ly** *adv.*

practical joke *n.* trick played on someone in fun

prac'tice (-tis) *v.* 1 do repeatedly so as to gain skill 2 make a habit of 3 work at as a profession —*n.* 1 a practicing 2 habit or custom 3 work or business of a professional Also, chiefly Br. sp., **prac'tise**

prac'ticed *a.* skilled

prac·ti'tion·er (-tish'ən-) *n.* one who practices a profession, etc.

prag·mat'ic *a.* practical

prag'ma·tism' *n.* 1 a being pragmatic 2 system using practical results to determine truth —**prag'ma·tist** *n.*

prai·rie (prer'ē) *n.* large area of grassy land

prairie dog *n.* small, squirrellike animal

prairie schooner *n.* large covered wagon

praise *v.* 1 say good things about 2 show reverence for —*n.* a praising —**praise'wor·thy** *a.*

pra'line' (-lēn') *n.* candy of (brown) sugar, nuts, etc.

prance *v.* 1 move along on the hind legs, as a horse 2 strut —**pranc'er** *n.*

prank *v.* mischievous trick —**prank'ster** *n.*

prate *v.* talk foolishly

prat'tle *v., n.* chatter or babble

prawn *n.* shellfish like a shrimp but larger

pray *v.* 1 implore 2 ask for by prayer 3 say prayers

prayer (prer) *n.* 1 a praying 2 words of worship or entreaty to God 3 thing prayed for —**prayer'ful** *a.*

pray'ing mantis *n.* mantis

pre- *pref.* before

preach *v.* 1 give (a sermon) 2 urge or advise as by preaching —**preach'er** *n.*

pre·am'ble *n.* introduction

pre·ap·prove' *v.* authorize before an application is submitted

pre·ar·range' *v.* arrange beforehand

prec *abbrev.* preceding

pre·can'cer·ous *a.* that may become cancerous

pre·car'i·ous *a.* not safe or sure; risky

pre·cau'tion *n.* care taken beforehand, as against danger —**pre·cau'tion·ar'y** *a.*

pre·cede' *v.* go or come before —**prec'e·dence** (pres'-) *n.*

prec'e·dent *n.* earlier case that sets an example

pre'cept *n.* rule of ethics

pre·cep'tor *n.* teacher

pre'cinct' (-siŋkt') *n.* 1 subdivision of a city, ward, etc. 2 *pl.* grounds

pre'cious (presh'əs) *a.* 1 of great value 2 beloved 3 too refined —**pre'ci·os'i·ty** (presh'ē-, pres'-) *n.* —**pre'cious·ly** *adv.*

prec'i·pice (-pis) *n.* steep cliff

pre·cip'i·tant *a.* precipitate

pre·cip'i·tate' *v.* 1 bring on; hasten 2 hurl down 3 separate out as a solid from solution —*a.* hasty; rash —*n.* precipitated substance

pre·cip'i·ta'tion *n.* 1 a precipitating 2 (amount of) rain, snow, etc.

pre·cip'i·tous *a.* 1 steep; sheer 2 hasty; rash

pré·cis' (prā sē') *n.* summary

pre·cise' *a.* 1 exact; definite; accurate 2 strict; scrupulous —**pre·cise'ly** *adv.* —**pre·ci'sion** (-sizh'ən) *n.*

pre·clude' *v.* make impossible, esp. in advance

pre·co'cious (-shəs) *a.* advanced beyond one's age —**pre·coc'i·ty** (-käs'-) *n.*

pre'cog·ni'tion *n.* perception of a future event

pre'-Co·lum'bi·an *a.* of any period in the Americas before 1492

pre'con·ceive' *v.* form (an opinion) beforehand —**pre'con·cep'tion** *n.*

pre'con·di'tion *v.* prepare (one) to

react in a certain way under certain conditions —*n.* something required before something else can occur

pre·cur'sor *n.* forerunner

pred'a·tor *n.* **1** animal that takes prey **2** one that plunders or exploits others —**pred'a·to'ry** *a.*

pre·de·cease' *v.* die before someone else

pred'e·ces'sor *n.* one preceding another, as in office

pre·des'tine (-tin) *v.* determine beforehand —**pre·des'ti·na'tion** *n.*

pre·de·ter'mine *v.* set or decide beforehand

pre·dic'a·ment *n.* difficult situation

pred'i·cate (-kāt'; *a., n.:* -kət) *v.* base upon facts, conditions, etc. —*a., n. Gram.* (of) the word or words that make a statement about the subject

pre·dict' *v.* tell about in advance —**pre·dict'a·ble** *a.* —**pre·dic'tion** *n.*

pre·di·gest' *v.* treat (food) with enzymes for easier digestion

pred'i·lec'tion *n.* special liking; partiality

pre·dis·pose' *v.* make likely to get, etc.; incline —**pre·dis·po·si'tion** *n.*

pre·dom'i·nate *v.* be greater in amount, power, etc.; prevail —**pre·dom'i·nance** *n.* —**pre·dom'i·nant** *a.*

pre·em'i·nent, pre-em'i·nent *a.* most outstanding —**pre·em'i·nence, pre-em'i·nence** *n.*

pre·empt', pre-empt' *v.* **1** seize before anyone else can **2** replace (a scheduled radio or TV program) —**pre·emp'tive, pre-emp'tive** *a.*

preen *v.* groom (the feathers): said of a bird

pref *abbrev.* **1** preferred **2** prefix

pre'fab' *n.* [Inf.] prefabricated building

pre·fab'ri·cat'ed *a.* made in sections ready for quick assembly, as a house

pref'ace (-əs) *n.* introduction to a book, speech, etc. —*v.* give or be a preface to —**pref'a·to'ry** *a.*

pre'fect' *n.* administrator

pre·fer' *v.* **-ferred', -fer'ring 1** like better **2** bring (charges) before a court —**pref'er·a·ble** *a.*

pref'er·ence *n.* **1** a preferring **2** thing preferred **3** advantage given to one over others —**pref'er·en'tial** *a.*

pre·fer'ment *n.* promotion

pre'fix' *n.* syllable(s) added to the beginning of a word to alter its meaning

preg'nant *a.* **1** bearing a fetus in the uterus **2** filled (*with*) —**preg'nan·cy**

n., pl. **-cies**

pre·hen'sile (-səl) *a.* adapted for grasping, as a monkey's tail

pre'his·tor'ic *a.* of times before recorded history

pre·judge' *v.* judge beforehand

prej'u·dice (-dis) *n.* **1** unreasonable bias **2** hatred or intolerance of other races, etc. —*v.* **1** to harm **2** fill with prejudice —**prej'u·di'cial** *a.*

prel'ate (-ət) *n.* high-ranking clergyman

prelim *abbrev.* preliminary

pre·lim'i·nar'y *a.* leading up to the main action —*n., pl.* **-ies** preliminary step

pre·lit'er·ate (-it) *a.* of a society lacking a written language

prel'ude (prel'yo̅o̅d', prā'lo̅o̅d') *n.* preliminary part, as of a musical piece

pre·mar'i·tal *a.* before marriage

pre'ma·ture' *a.* before the proper or usual time

pre·med'i·tate' *v.* think out or plan beforehand —**pre·med'i·ta'tion** *n.*

pre·men'stru·al (-strəl) *a.* before a menstrual period

pre·mier' (-mir') *a.* foremost —*n.* prime minister

pre·mière', pre·miere' (-mir') *n.* first performance of a play, etc.

prem'ise (-is) *n.* **1** a basic assumption **2** *pl.* piece of real estate

pre'mi·um *n.* **1** bonus **2** extra charge **3** a payment **4** high value

prem'o·ni'tion *n.* feeling of imminent evil

pre·na'tal *a.* before birth

pre·nup'tial (-shəl) *a.* before marriage

pre·oc'cu·py' *v.* **-pied', -py'ing** engross; absorb —**pre·oc'cu·pa'tion** *n.*

pre-owned' *a.* not new; used

prep *v.* preparatory —*v.* **prepped, prep'ping** prepare (a patient) for surgery

prep *abbrev.* **1** preparatory **2** preposition

preparatory school *n.* private school preparing students for college

pre·pare' *v.* **1** make or get ready **2** put together —**prep'a·ra'tion** *n.* —**pre·par'a·to'ry** *a.* —**pre·par'ed·ness** *n.*

pre·pay' *v.* pay in advance —**pre·pay'ment** *n.*

pre·plan' *v.* to plan in advance

pre·pon'der·ate' *v.* predominate —**pre·pon'der·ance** *n.* —**pre·pon'der·ant** *a.*

prep'o·si'tion (-zish'ən) *n.* word that connects a noun or pronoun to another word —**prep'o·si'tion·al** *a.*

pre'pos·sess'ing a. making a good impression

pre·pos'ter·ous a. absurd

prep'py, prep'pie n., pl. **-pies** (former) student at a preparatory school

pre'puce' n. foreskin

pre're·cord' v. record (a TV or radio program) for later use

pre·re·cord'ed a. of a magnetic tape on which sound, etc. has been recorded before its sale

pre·req'ui·site (-rek'wə zit) n., a. (something) required beforehand

pre·rog'a·tive n. exclusive privilege

pres abbrev. present

Pres abbrev. President

pres'age (v.: prē sāj') n. 1 omen 2 foreboding —v. 1 portend 2 predict

Pres'by·te'ri·an n., a. (member) of a Protestant church governed by elders

pre'school' a. of or for children three to five years old —n. school for such children

pres'cience (presh'əns) n. foresight —**pres'cient** a.

pre·scribe' v. 1 to order 2 order to take a certain medicine or treatment

pre'script' n. prescribed rule —**pre·scrip'tive** a.

pre·scrip'tion n. 1 a prescribing, esp. by a doctor 2 medicine prescribed

pre'se·lect' v. select in advance

pres'ence n. 1 a being present 2 vicinity 3 impressive personality, etc.

presence of mind n. ability to think and act quickly in an emergency

pres'ent (v.: prē zent') a. 1 being at a certain place 2 of or at this time —n. 1 present time 2 gift —v. 1 introduce 2 display 3 offer for consideration 4 give (to)

pre·sent'a·ble a. 1 fit to present 2 properly dressed

pres'en·ta'tion n. 1 a presenting 2 thing presented

pre·sen'ti·ment n. premonition

pres'ent·ly adv. 1 soon 2 now

pre·sent'ment n. presentation

present participle n. participle expressing present or continuing action

pres'er·va'tion·ist n. one working to preserve something, as old buildings

pre·serve' v. 1 keep from harm, spoiling, etc. 2 maintain —pl.n. fruit cooked with sugar —**pre·serv'a·tive** a., n. —**pres'er·va'tion** n.

pre·set' v. set (controls) beforehand

pre·shrunk' a. shrunk to minimize shrinkage in laundering

pre·side' (-zīd') v. 1 act as chairman 2 have control

pres'i·dent n. chief executive of a republic, firm, etc. —**pres'i·den·cy** n., pl. **-cies** —**pres'i·den'tial** (-shəl) a.

pre'-soak' v. soak (laundry) with detergent before washing

press v. 1 push against; squeeze 2 iron, as clothes 3 force 4 entreat 5 urge on 6 keep moving 7 crowd —n. 1 pressure 2 crowd 3 machine for crushing, printing, etc. 4 journalism or journalists

press conference n. group interview of a celebrity by journalists

press'ing a. urgent

pres'sure (presh'ər) n. 1 a pressing 2 distress 3 strong influence 4 urgency 5 force of weight —v. try to influence

pressure cook'er n. metal pot for cooking with steam under pressure

pressure group n. group trying to influence government through lobbying, publicity, etc.

pres'sur·ize' v. keep nearly normal air pressure inside (aircraft, etc.) at high altitude

pres'ti·dig'i·ta'tion (-dij'-) n. sleight of hand

pres·tige' (-tēzh') n. impressive reputation

pres·ti'gious (-tij'əs) a. having prestige or distinction

pres'to int. (see it) change suddenly: magician's command

pres'to adv., a. fast

pre·sume' v. 1 dare 2 suppose 3 take liberties —**pre·sump'tion** n. —**pre·sump'tive** a.

pre·sump'tu·ous (-chōō əs) a. too bold or daring

pre·sup·pose' v. assume beforehand

pre'teen' n. child nearly a teenager

pre·tend' v. 1 claim falsely 2 make believe 3 lay claim: with to

pre·tense' (or prē'tens') n. 1 false claim or show 2 a making believe

pre·ten'sion n. 1 a claim 2 ostentation

pre·ten'tious a. showy; flashy

pre'term' a., n. (of premature birth or) a premature baby

pre'ter·nat'u·ral a. supernatural

pre'text' n. false reason used to hide the real one

pret'ty (prit'ē) a. **-ti·er, -ti·est** attractive and dainty —adv. somewhat —**pret'ti·ly** adv. —**pret'ti·ness** n.

pret'zel n. hard, salted biscuit, twisted in a knot

pre·vail' v. 1 win out or be successful

2 become more common

pre·vail'ing *a.* 1 superior 2 prevalent

prev'a·lent *a.* common; general —**prev'a·lence** *n.*

pre·var'i·cate' *v.* evade the truth; lie —**pre·var'i·ca'tion** *n.* —**pre·var'i·ca'tor** *n.*

pre·vent' *v.* stop or keep from doing or happening —**pre·vent'a·ble, pre·vent'i·ble** *a.* —**pre·ven'tion** *n.*

pre·ven'tive *n., a.* (something) that prevents: also **pre·vent'a·tive**

pre'view' *n.* advance showing of (scenes from) a movie

pre'vi·ous *a.* coming before; prior —**pre'vi·ous·ly** *adv.*

pre'war' *a.* before the war

prey (prā) *n.* 1 animal seized by another for food 2 victim —*v.* 1 hunt other animals for food as prey 2 victimize others 3 have a harmful effect Used with *on* or *upon*

price *n.* sum asked or paid for a thing —*v.* get or put a price on

price'less *a.* beyond price

pric'ey *a.* [Inf.] expensive

prick *v.* 1 pierce with a sharp point 2 pain sharply 3 raise (the ears) —*n.* 1 a pricking 2 sharp pain —**prick up one's ears** listen closely

prick'le *n.* thorn or spiny point —*v.* tingle —**prick'ly** *a.*, **-li·er, -li·est**

prickly heat *n.* skin rash, as from exposure to heat

pride *n.* 1 too high opinion of oneself 2 self-respect 3 satisfaction in one's achievements 4 person or thing one is proud of —**pride oneself on** be proud of

priest *n.* one who conducts religious rites —**priest'ess** *n.fem.* —**priest'hood** *n.* —**priest'ly** *a.*

prig *n.* smug, moralistic person —**prig'gish** *a.*

prim *a.* **prim'mer, prim'mest** stiffly proper —**prim'ly** *adv.*

prim *abbrev.* primary

pri'ma·cy *n.* supremacy

pri'ma don'na (prē'-) *n.* 1 chief woman singer in an opera 2 [Inf.] temperamental, vain, etc. person

pri·ma fa·cie (prī'mə fā'shə) *a. Law* adequate to prove a fact unless refuted: said of evidence

pri'mal *a.* 1 original 2 chief

pri'mar·y *a.* 1 most important 2 basic 3 first in order —*n., pl.* **-ies** preliminary election —**pri·mar'i·ly** *adv.*

pri'mate' *n.* 1 archbishop 2 member of the order of mammals having hands and feet with five digits, including humans, apes, etc.

prime *a.* first in rank, importance, or quality —*n.* best period or part —*v.* make ready

prime meridian *n.* meridian through Greenwich, England, at 0° longitude

prime minister *n.* chief official in some countries

prim'er (prim'-) *n.* 1 explosive used to set off a larger explosive 2 preliminary coat of paint, etc.

prim'er (prim'-) *n.* elementary textbook, esp. for reading

prime rate *n.* favorable interest rate a bank charges large corporations

prime time *n.* hours when radio or TV have the largest audience available

pri·me'val *a.* of the first age or ages

prim'i·tive *a.* 1 of earliest times 2 crude, simple, etc. —*n.* primitive person or thing

pri·mo·gen'i·ture (-jen'-) *n.* eldest son's exclusive right of inheritance

pri·mor'di·al (-dē-) *a.* primitive

primp *v.* groom oneself fussily

prim'rose' *n.* plant with tubelike flowers in clusters

prince *n.* 1 monarch's son 2 ruler of a principality —**prince'ly** *a.* —**prin'cess** *n.fem.*

prin'ci·pal *a.* chief; main —*n.* 1 principal person or thing 2 head of a school 3 amount on which interest is computed —**prin'ci·pal·ly** *adv.*

prin·ci·pal'i·ty *n., pl.* **-ties** land ruled by a prince

principal parts *pl.n.* main inflected forms of a verb

prin'ci·ple *n.* 1 basic truth, law, etc. 2 rule of conduct 3 integrity

print *n.* 1 cloth stamped with a design 2 impression made by inked type, plates, etc. 3 photograph —*v.* 1 to impress inked type, etc. on paper 2 publish in print 3 write in letters like printed ones —**print'er** *n.* —**print'ing** *n., a.*

print'ed circuit *n.* electrical circuit in fine lines on an insulating sheet

print'out' *n.* printed or typed computer output

pri'or *a.* preceding in time, order, or importance —*n.* head of a monastery or order —**pri'or·ess** *n.fem.*

pri·or'i·tize' *v.* arrange in order of importance

pri·or'i·ty *n., pl.* **-ties** 1 precedence 2 prior right

pri'o·ry *n., pl.* **-ries** monastery headed by a prior or convent headed by a prioress

prism n. clear glass, etc. of angular form, for dispersing light into the spectrum —**pris·mat'ic** a.

pris'on n. place of confinement —**pris'on·er** n.

pris'sy a. **-i·er, -i·est** [Inf.] very prim or prudish

pris·tine' (-tēn') n. fresh and untouched

pri'vate a. **1** of or for a particular person or group; not public **2** secret —n. Mil. soldier of the lowest rank —**pri'va·cy** n. —**pri'vate·ly** adv.

pri·va·teer' n. private ship commissioned to attack enemy ships

private eye n. [Sl.] private detective

pri·va'tion n. lack of necessities

pri'va·tize' v. turn over (public property, etc.) to private interests

priv'et n. evergreen shrub

priv'i·lege (-lij) n. special right, favor, etc. —v. grant a privilege to

priv'y n., pl. **-ies** outhouse —**privy to** privately informed about

privy council n. group of advisors to a monarch

prize v. value highly —n. **1** thing given to the winner of a contest, etc. **2** valued possession

prize'fight' n. professional boxing match —**prize'fight'er** n.

pro adv. on the affirmative side —n., pl. **pros** **1** reason or vote for **2** professional

pro- pref. in favor of

pro'-am' n. sports event for amateurs and professionals

prob abbrev. **1** probably **2** problem

prob'a·ble a. likely to occur or to be so —**prob'a·bil'i·ty** n., pl. **-ties** —**prob'a·bly** adv.

pro'bate' v. establish the validity of (a will) —a. of such action —n. a probating

pro·ba'tion n. **1** a trial of ability, etc. **2** conditional suspension of a jail sentence —**pro·ba'tion·ar·y** a.

probation officer n. official who watches over persons on probation

probe n. **1** a slender surgical instrument for exploring a wound **2** investigation **3** spacecraft, etc. used to get information about an environment —v. **1** explore with a probe **2** investigate —**prob'er** n.

pro'bi·ty n. honesty

prob'lem n. **1** question to be solved **2** difficult matter, etc.

prob'lem·at'ic a. **1** hard to solve or deal with **2** uncertain Also **prob'lem·at·i·cal**

pro·bos'cis n. elephant's trunk, or similar snout

pro'caine' n. drug used as a local anesthetic

pro·ce'dure (-jər) n. act or way of doing something

pro·ceed' v. **1** go on after stopping **2** carry on an action **3** come forth (from)

pro·ceed'ing n. **1** course of action **2** pl. transactions **3** pl. legal action

pro'ceeds' pl.n. money from a business deal

proc'ess' n. **1** series of changes in developing **2** act or way of doing something **3** court summons **4** projecting part —v. prepare for a special process

pro·ces'sion n. group moving forward in an orderly way

pro·ces'sion·al n. hymn or music for a procession

pro'-choice' a. supporting the legal right to have a medical abortion

pro·claim' v. announce officially —**proc·la·ma'tion** n.

pro·cliv'i·ty n., pl. **-ties** inclination

pro·cras'ti·nate' v. put off; delay —**pro·cras·ti·na'tion** n. —**pro·cras'ti·na'tor** n.

pro·cre·ate' v. produce (young) —**pro'cre·a'tion** n.

proc'tor n. one supervising students, as during a test

pro·cure' v. get; obtain —**pro·cur'a·ble** a. —**pro·cure'ment** n. —**pro·cur'er** n.

prod n., v. **prod'ded, prod'ding** goad or poke

prod'i·gal a. very wasteful or generous —n. spendthrift —**prod'i·gal'i·ty** n.

pro·di'gious (-dij'əs) a. **1** amazing **2** enormous —**pro·di'gious·ly** adv.

prod'i·gy n., pl. **-gies** **1** remarkable person or thing **2** young genius

pro·duce' (n.: prō'dōōs) v. **1** show **2** bring forth **3** manufacture **4** cause **5** get (a play, etc.) ready for the public —n. fresh fruits and vegetables —**pro·duc'er** n. —**pro·duc'tion** n.

prod'uct' n. **1** thing produced **2** result **3** result of multiplying numbers

pro·duc'tive a. **1** producing much **2** causing: with of —**pro·duc·tiv'i·ty** n.

Prof abbrev. Professor

pro·fane' a. **1** not religious **2** scornful of sacred things —v. treat irreverently —**pro·fane'ly** adv.

pro·fan'i·ty n., pl. **-ties** swearing

pro·fess' v. **1** openly declare **2** claim to have or be **3** declare one's belief in

pro·fes'sion n. **1** occupation requiring

special study **2** its members **3** avowal

pro·fes′sion·al n., a. (one) of a profession, or (one) paid to play in games, etc. —**pro·fes′sion·al·ly** adv.

pro·fes′sor n. college teacher —**pro′fes·so′ri·al** a.

prof′fer v., n. offer

pro·fi′cient (-fish′ənt) a. skilled —**pro·fi′cien·cy** n.

pro′file′ n. **1** side view of the face **2** short biographical sketch

prof′it n. **1** gain; benefit **2** net income from business —v. benefit —**prof′it·a·ble** a. —**prof′it·a·bil′i·ty** n. —**prof′it·a·bly** adv. —**prof′it·less** a.

prof·it·eer′ n. one who makes excessive profits

prof′li·gate a. **1** dissolute **2** wasteful —**prof′li·ga·cy** n.

pro for′ma a. done for the sake of form or custom

pro·found′ a. **1** very deep **2** complete —**pro·fun′di·ty** n., pl. **-ties**

pro·fuse′ (-fyōōs′) a. abundant —**pro·fuse′ly** adv. —**pro·fu′sion** n.

pro·gen′i·tor n. ancestor

prog′e·ny (präj′-) n. offspring

pro·ges′ter·one′ n. hormone secreted in the ovary

prog·no′sis n., pl. **-ses** (-sēz′) prediction

prog·nos′ti·cate′ v. predict —**prog·nos′ti·ca′tion** n. —**prog·nos′ti·ca′tor** n.

pro′gram′ n. **1** list of things to be performed **2** plan of procedure **3** scheduled radio or TV broadcast **4** logical sequence of operations for electronic computer —v. **1** schedule in a program **2** plan a computer program for **3** furnish with a program Br. sp. **pro′gramme′** —**pro·gram′ma·ble** a.

prog·ress′ (prō gres′; n.: präg′res) v. advance, develop, or improve —n. a progressing —**pro·gres′sion** n.

pro·gres′sive a. **1** progressing **2** favoring progress, reform, etc. —n. progressive person —**pro·gres′sive·ly** adv.

pro·hib′it v. **1** forbid, as by law **2** prevent —**pro·hib′i·tive, pro·hib′i·to′ry** a.

pro′hi·bi′tion (-bish′ən) n. a forbidding, esp. of the manufacture and sale of liquor —**pro′hi·bi′tion·ist** n.

proj·ect′ (v.: prō jekt′) n. **1** scheme **2** undertaking —v. **1** propose **2** stick out **3** cause (a light, etc.) to fall upon a surface —**pro·jec′tion** n. —**pro·jec′tor** n.

pro·jec′tile (-təl, -tīl′) n. object to be

shot forth, as a bullet

pro·jec′tion·ist n. operator of a film or slide projector

pro·lapse′ (n.: prō′laps′) v. fall or slip out of place: said of the uterus, etc. —n. prolapsed condition

pro′le·tar′i·at n. the working class —**pro′le·tar′i·an** a., n.

pro′-life′ a. opposing the legal right to have a medical abortion

pro·lif′er·ate′ v. increase rapidly —**pro·lif′er·a′tion** n.

pro·lif′ic a. producing much

pro·lix′ a. wordy —**pro·lix′i·ty** n.

pro′logue′ (-lôg′) n. introduction to a poem, play, etc.

pro·long′ v. lengthen —**pro′lon·ga′tion** n.

prom n. formal dance at a college, etc.

prom′e·nade′ (-nād′, -näd′) n. **1** walk for pleasure **2** public place for walking —v. take a promenade

prom′i·nent a. **1** projecting **2** conspicuous; very noticeable **3** famous —**prom′i·nence** n.

pro·mis′cu·ous (-kyōō-) a. engaging in casual sexual relations with many people —**prom′is·cu′i·ty** n.

prom′ise n. **1** agreement to do or not do something **2** sign as of future success —v. **1** to make a promise of or to **2** to cause to expect

prom′is·ing a. showing signs of future success

prom′is·so′ry a. containing or being a promise

pro′mo a., n. [Inf.] (of) an advertising promotion

prom′on·to′ry n., pl. **-ries** peak of high land jutting out into the sea

pro·mote′ v. **1** raise in rank **2** further the growth or sale of —**pro·mot′er** n. —**pro·mo′tion** n. —**pro·mo′tion·al** a.

prompt a. ready; quick —v. **1** help with a cue **2** inspire or urge —**prompt′er** n. —**prompt′ly** adv.

prompt′i·tude′ n. quality of being prompt

prom′ul·gate′ v. proclaim; publish —**prom′ul·ga′tion** n.

pron abbrev. **1** pronoun **2** pronunciation

prone a. **1** lying face downward **2** apt or likely (to)

prong n. projecting point, as of a fork —**pronged** a.

prong′horn′ n. deer having curved horns

pro′noun′ n. word used in place of a noun —**pro·nom′i·nal** a.

pro·nounce′ v. **1** declare officially **2**

utter the sounds of —**pro·nounce′a·ble** a. —**pro·nounce′ment** n.

pro·nounced′ a. definite; unmistakable

pron′to adv. [Sl.] at once; quickly

pro·nun′ci·a′tion n. act or way of pronouncing words

proof n. 1 convincing evidence 2 a test 3 strength of a liquor —a. strong enough to resist: with *against*

-proof suf. impervious to

proof′read′ v. to read in order to correct errors

prop abbrev. 1 proper(ly) 2 property 3 proprietor

prop′a·gan′da n. 1 systematic spreading of ideas 2 ideas so spread —**prop′a·gan′dist** a., n. —**prop′a·gan′dize′** v.

prop′a·gate′ v. 1 produce offspring 2 raise; breed 3 spread (ideas) —**prop·a·ga′tion** n.

pro′pane′ n. a gas used as a fuel

pro·pel′ v. **-pelled′, -pel′ling** drive forward

pro·pel′lant, pro·pel′lent n. fuel for a rocket

pro·pel′ler n. blades on end of a revolving shaft for propelling a ship or aircraft

pro·pen′si·ty n., pl. **-ties** natural tendency

prop′er a. 1 suitable; fit 2 correct 3 genteel; respectable 4 belonging (to) 5 actual —**prop′er·ly** adv.

prop′er·ty n., pl. **-ties** 1 thing owned 2 characteristic

proph′e·cy (-sē) n., pl. **-cies** prediction

proph′e·sy′ (-sī′) v. **-sied′, -sy′ing** to predict; foretell —**pro·phet′ic** a.

proph′et n. 1 leader regarded as divinely inspired 2 one who predicts

pro·phy·lac′tic (-fə-) n., a. (medicine, device, etc.) that prevents disease, etc.

pro′phy·lax′is n., pl. **-lax′es′** (-ēz′) cleaning of the teeth

pro·pin′qui·ty n. nearness

pro·pi′ti·ate′ (-pish′ē-) v. to appease

pro·pi′tious a. favorable

prop′jet′ n. turboprop

pro·po′nent n. supporter

pro·por′tion n. 1 part in relation to the whole 2 ratio 3 symmetry 4 pl. dimensions —v. 1 make symmetrical 2 make fit —**pro·por′tion·al, pro·por′tion·ate** a.

pro·pose′ v. 1 suggest for considering

2 plan 3 offer marriage —**pro·pos′al** n.

prop′o·si′tion (-zish′ən) n. 1 a plan 2 subject for debate

pro·pound′ v. suggest for consideration

pro·pri′e·tar′y a. held under a patent, etc.

pro·pri′e·tor n. owner

pro·pri′e·ty n. fitness; correctness

pro·pul′sion n. a propelling or a force that propels —**pro·pul′sive** a.

pro·rate′ v. divide or assess proportionally

pro·sa′ic (-zā′-) a. commonplace

pro·sce′ni·um (-sē′-) n., pl. **-ni·ums** or **-ni·a** arch framing a conventional stage

pro·scribe′ v. forbid

prose n. nonpoetic language

pros′e·cute′ v. 1 engage in 2 take legal action against —**pros′e·cu′tion** n. —**pros′e·cu′tor** n.

pros′e·lyte′ (-līt′) n. convert

pros′e·lyt·ize′ v. try to convert or persuade

pros′pect′ n. 1 outlook 2 likely customer, etc. 3 pl. apparent chance for success —v. search (*for*) —**pros′pec′tor** n.

pro·spec′tive a. expected

pro·spec′tus n. report outlining a new work, etc.

pros′per v. thrive

pros·per′i·ty n. wealth —**pros′per·ous** a. —**pros′per·ous·ly** adv.

pros′tate′ a. of a gland at the base of the bladder in males

pros·the′sis n., pl. **-ses′** (-sēz′) (use of) artificial body part(s) —**pros·thet′ic** a.

pros′ti·tute′ n. one who engages in sexual intercourse for pay —v. sell (one's talents, etc.) for base purposes —**pros′ti·tu′tion** n.

pros′trate′ a. 1 lying flat, esp. face downward 2 overcome —v. 1 lay flat 2 overcome —**pros·tra′tion** n.

pro·tag′o·nist n. main character or leading figure

pro′te·an a. readily taking on many forms

pro·tect′ v. shield from harm —**pro·tec′tion** n. —**pro·tec′tive** a. —**pro·tec′tor** n.

pro·tec′tor·ate n. territory controlled and protected by a strong state

pro·te·gé (prōt′ə zhā′) n. one under another's patronage —**pro′té·gée′** (-zhā′) n.fem.

pro′tein (-tēn′) n. nitrogenous substance essential to diet

pro tem *a.* temporary

pro·test' (*n.:* prō'test') *v.* **1** to object **2** assert —*n.* objection —**prot'es·ta'tion** *n.* —**pro·test'er, pro·tes'tor** *n.*

Prot'es·tant *n.* Christian not of the Roman Catholic or Eastern Orthodox Church —**Prot'es·tant·ism'** *n.*

proto- *pref.* original

pro'to·col' (-kôl') *n.* set of rules and procedures controlling an action, as among diplomats, in data transmission, etc.

pro'ton' *n.* positive particle in the nucleus of an atom

pro'to·plasm' *n.* essential matter in all living cells —**pro'to·plas'mic** *a.*

pro'to·type' *n.* first thing of its kind

pro'to·zo'an *n., pl.* **-zo'a** one-celled animal

pro·tract' *v.* draw out; prolong —**pro·trac'tion** *n.*

pro·trac'tor *n.* device for drawing and measuring angles

pro·trude' *v.* jut out —**pro·tru'sion** *n.*

pro·tu'ber·ance *n.* bulge —**pro·tu'ber·ant** *a.*

proud *a.* **1** haughty **2** feeling or causing pride **3** splendid —**proud of** highly pleased with —**proud'ly** *adv.*

proud flesh *n.* excessive growth of flesh around a healing wound

prove (prōōv) *v.* **proved, proved or prov'en, prov'ing 1** test by experiment **2** establish as true

prov'e·nance *n.* origin; source

prov'en·der *n.* fodder

prov'erb *n.* wise saying

pro·ver'bi·al *a.* well-known

pro·vide' *v.* **1** supply; furnish (with) **2** prepare (*for* or *against*) **3** stipulate —**pro·vid'er** *n.*

pro·vid'ed *con.* on condition (*that*): also **pro·vid'ing**

prov'i·dence *n.* **1** prudent foresight **2** guidance of God or Nature **3** [P-] God —**prov'i·dent** *a.* —**prov'i·den'tial** (-shəl) *a.*

prov'ince *n.* **1** division of a country **2** *pl.* parts of a country outside major cities **3** sphere; field

pro·vin'cial (-shəl) *a.* **1** of a province **2** narrow-minded —**pro·vin'cial·ism'** *n.*

proving ground *n.* place for testing new equipment, etc.

pro·vi'sion (-vizh'ən) *n.* **1** a providing **2** *pl.* stock of food **3** stipulation —*v.* supply with provisions

pro·vi'sion·al *a.* temporary

pro·vi'so' (-vī'zō') *n., pl.* **-sos'** or **-soes'** stipulation

prov'o·ca'tion *n.* **1** a provoking **2**

thing that provokes —**pro·voc'a·tive** *a.*

pro·voke' *v.* **1** anger **2** stir up or evoke

pro'vost' (-vōst') *n.* high executive official, as in some colleges

prow (prou) *n.* forward part of a ship

prow'ess *n.* **1** bravery; valor **2** superior skill, etc.

prowl *v.* roam or stalk furtively

prox·im'i·ty *n.* nearness

prox'y *n., pl.* **-ies** (one with) authority to act for another

Pro'zac' *trademark* drug used to treat depression, etc.

prude *n.* one overly modest or proper —**prud'er·y** *n.* —**prud'ish** *a.*

pru'dent *a.* wisely careful —**pru'dence** *n.* —**pru·den'tial** (-shəl) *a.*

prune *n.* dried plum —*v.* trim twigs, etc. from

pru'ri·ent (proor'ē-) *a.* lustful —**pru'ri·ence** *n.*

pry *n., pl.* **pries** lever —*v.* **pried, pry'ing 1** raise with a lever **2** look closely or inquisitively

P.S., p.s., PS *abbrev.* postscript

psalm (säm) *n.* sacred song or poem

psalm'ist *n.* composer of psalms

pseu·do (sōō'dō) *a.* false

pseudo- *pref.* sham; counterfeit

pseu'do·nym' (-nim') *n.* fictitious name assumed by an author, etc.

pshaw (shô) *int., n.* exclamation of disgust, etc.

psi (sī) *a.* psychic

pso·ri'a·sis (sə rī'ə-) *n.* skin disease with scaly, reddish patches

PST *abbrev.* Pacific Standard Time

psych (sīk) *v.* [Sl.] **1** probe behavior psychologically so as to outwit or control: often with *out* **2** prepare (oneself) psychologically: with *up*

psy·che (sī'kē) *n.* **1** soul **2** mind

psy·che·del'ic *a.* of or causing extreme changes in the conscious mind

psy·chi'a·try (-kī'-) *n.* branch of medicine dealing with mental disorders —**psy·chi·at'ric** (-kē-) *a.* —**psy·chi'a·trist** *n.*

psy'chic (-kik) *a.* **1** of the mind **2** supernatural Also **psy'chi·cal** *a.* **3** one sensitive to psychic phenomena

psy'cho (-kō) [Inf.] *n., pl.* **-chos** psychopath —*a.* psychopathic

psycho- *pref.* mind; mental processes: also **psych-**

psy'cho·ac'tive *a.* affecting the mind: said of a drug

psy'cho·a·nal'y·sis *n.* method of treating neuroses —**psy'cho·an'a·lyst** *n.* —

psy·cho·an′a·lyze′ v.

psy·cho·gen′ic a. mental in origin

psy·chol′o·gy n. science dealing with the mind and behavior —**psy′cho·log′i·cal** a. —**psy′cho·log′i·cal·ly** adv. —**psy·chol′o·gist** n.

psy·cho·path′ic a. of mental disorder —**psy′cho·path′** n.

psy·cho′sis n., pl. **-ses** (-sēz′) severe mental disorder —**psy·chot′ic** a., n.

psy·cho·so·mat′ic a. of a physical disorder caused by emotional disturbance

psy·cho·ther′a·py n. treatment of mental disorder —**psy′cho·ther′a·pist** n.

psy·cho·trop′ic n., a. (drug) affecting the mind

pt abbrev. **1** part **2** past tense **3** pint(s) **4** point

PT abbrev. Pacific Time

PTA abbrev. Parent-Teacher Association

ptar′mi·gan (tär′-) n. northern grouse

pter·o·dac′tyl (ter′ə dak′təl) n. extinct flying reptile

pto′maine′ (tō′-) n. substance in decaying matter: sometimes poisonous

pub n. [Br. Inf.] bar; tavern: in full, **public house**

pub abbrev. **1** public **2** published **3** publisher

pu′ber·ty (pyōō′-) n. time of maturing sexually

pu·bes′cent a. of or in puberty

pu′bic a. of or in the region of the groin

pub′lic a. **1** of people as a whole **2** for everyone **3** known by all —n. the people —**in public** in open view —**pub′lic·ly** adv.

pub′li·ca′tion n. **1** printing and selling of books, etc. **2** thing published

public defender n. court-appointed lawyer, as for a poor person

public domain n. condition of being free from copyright or patent

pub′li·cist n. publicity agent

pub·lic′i·ty (-lis′-) n. **1** public attention **2** information meant to bring one this —**pub′li·cize′** v.

public relations n. [sing. or pl. v.] functions of an organization for creating favorable public opinion

public servant n. government official or employee

pub′lish v. **1** issue (a printed work) for sale **2** announce —**pub′lish·er** n.

puce n. brownish purple

puck n. hard rubber disk used in ice hockey

puck′er n., v. wrinkle

puck′ish a. mischievous

pud′ding (pood′-) n. soft food of flour, milk, eggs, etc.

pud′dle n. small pool of water

pudg′y a. **-i·er, -i·est** short and fat

pueb′lo (pweb′-) n., pl. **-los** American Indian village of SW U.S.

pu·er·ile (pyōō′ər əl) a. childish —**pu′er·il′i·ty** n.

puff n. **1** brief burst of wind, etc. **2** draw at a cigarette **3** light pastry shell **4** soft pad —v. **1** blow in puffs **2** breathe rapidly **3** smoke **4** swell —**puff′i·ness** n. —**puff′y** a., **-i·er, -i·est**

puff′ball′ n. round, white fungus

puff′in n. northern seabird

pug n. small dog

pu·gil·ism (pyōō′jə liz′əm) n. sport of boxing —**pu′gil·ist** n. —**pu′gil·is′tic** a.

pug·na′cious a. quarrelsome —**pug·na′cious·ly** adv. —**pug·nac′i·ty** (-nas′-) n.

pug nose n. short, thick nose turned up at the end —**pug′-nosed′** a.

puke v., n. [Inf.] vomit

puk′ka a. **1** [Br.] first-rate **2** genuine

pul′chri·tude′ (-krə-) n. beauty

pull v. **1** to make (something) move toward one **2** pluck out **3** rip **4** strain **5** [Inf.] do; perform **6** move (away, ahead, etc.) —n. **1** act or effort of pulling **2** handle, etc. **3** [Inf.] influence —**pull for** [Inf.] cheer on —**pull off** accomplish —**pull out 1** depart **2** quit or withdraw —**pull over** drive toward, and stop at, the curb —**pull through** [Inf.] get over (an illness, etc.)

pul′let (pool′-) n. young hen

pul′ley n., pl. **-leys** wheel with a grooved rim in which a rope runs, for raising weights

Pull′man (car) n. railroad car with berths for sleeping

pull′-on′ a. easily put on

pull′out′ n. removal, withdrawal, etc.

pull′o·ver n. sweater, etc. to be pulled over the head

pul′mo·nar·y a. of the lungs

pulp n. **1** soft, inside part, as of fruit **2** moist wood fiber, ground to make paper —**pulp′y** a., **-i·er, -i·est**

pul′pit n. clergyman′s platform for preaching

pul′sar′ n. celestial object emitting pulses of radiation

pul′sate′ v. throb —**pul·sa′tion** n.

pulse n. regular beat, as of blood in the arteries

pul'ver·ize' v. grind or crush into powder

pu'ma (pyōō'-, pōō'-) n. cougar

pum'ice n. light, spongy rock, used for cleaning, etc.

pum'mel v. hit with repeated blows

pump n. **1** machine that forces fluids in or out **2** low-cut, strapless shoe —v. **1** move or empty (fluids) with a pump **2** move like a pump **3** [Inf.] question (one) persistently for

pumped a. [Sl.] very enthusiastic

pum'per·nick'el n. coarse, dark rye bread

pump'kin n. large, round, orange-yellow gourd

pun n. humorous use of different words that sound alike —v. **punned, pun'ning** make puns

punch n. **1** tool for piercing, etc. **2** fruit drink **3** blow with the fist —v. **1** pierce, etc. with a punch **3** hit with the fist

punch'-drunk' a. [Inf.] dazed

punch line n. the surprise line carrying the point of a joke

punch'y a. **-i·er, -i·est** [Inf.] **1** forceful **2** dazed

punc·til'i·ous a. **1** careful in behavior **2** precise

punc'tu·al (-chōō əl) a. on time —**punc'tu·al'i·ty** n.

punc'tu·ate' v. use periods, commas, etc. in (writing) —**punc'tu·a'tion** n.

punc'ture n. hole made by a sharp point —v. pierce as with a point

pun'dit n. very learned person

pun'gent a. **1** sharp in taste or smell **2** keen and direct —**pun'gen·cy** n.

pun'ish v. make suffer pain, loss, etc. as for a crime or offense —**pun'ish·a·ble** a. —**pun'ish·ment** n.

pu'ni·tive a. of or inflicting punishment —**pu'ni·tive·ly** adv.

punk n. **1** substance that smolders, used to light fireworks **2** [Sl.] inexperienced young person **3** [Sl.] young hoodlum

pun'ster n. one who makes puns: also **pun'ner**

punt v. **1** kick a dropped football before it touches the ground **2** move (a boat) using a long pole —n. **1** a punting **2** square, flat-bottomed boat

pu'ny a. **-ni·er, -ni·est** small or weak

pup n. young dog, wolf, etc.

pu'pa (pyōō'-) n., pl. **-pae** (-pē) or **-pas** insect just before the adult stage

pu'pil n. **1** person being taught **2** contracting opening in iris of the eye

pup'pet n. **1** doll moved manually by

strings, etc. **2** person controlled by another —**pup'pet·eer'** n.

pup'py n., pl. **-pies** young dog

pup tent n. small, portable tent

pur'chase (-chəs) v. buy —n. **1** thing bought **2** act of buying —**pur'chas·er** n.

pure a. **1** unmixed **2** clean **3** mere **4** faultless **5** chaste **6** abstract —**pure'ly** adv. —**pu'ri·fy** v. —**pu·ri·fi·ca'tion** n. —**pu'ri·ty** n.

pure'bred' a. belonging to a breed of unmixed descent

pu·rée, pu·ree (pyoo rā') n. **1** mashed, strained food **2** thick soup —v. **-rééd'** or **-reed', -rée'ing** or **-ree'ing** make a purée of

pur'ga·tive (-gə-) a. purging —n. a laxative

pur'ga·to'ry n. R.C.Ch. state or place for expiating sins after death

purge v. **1** cleanse; make pure **2** move (the bowels) **3** get rid of —n. **1** a purging **2** a laxative

pur'ist n. person who insists on observing precise usage or formal rules in art, etc.

pu'ri·tan (pyoor'ə-) n. one very strict in morals and religion —**pu·ri·tan'i·cal, pu'ri·tan'ic** a.

purl v. invert (stitches) in knitting to form ribbing

pur·lieu (purl'yōō) n. outlying part

pur·loin' v. steal

pur'ple n., a. bluish red

pur·port' (n.: pur'pôrt) v. seem or claim to mean or be —n. meaning

pur'pose (-pəs) n. **1** intention; aim **2** determination —**on purpose** intentionally —**pur'pose·ful** a. —**pur'pose·less** a. —**pur'pose·ly** adv.

purr v., n. (make) the sound of a cat at ease

purse n. **1** small bag for money **2** woman's handbag **3** prize money —v. **1** to pucker (the lips)

purs'er n. ship's officer in charge of accounts, etc.

pur·su'ant a. following —**pursuant to** according to

pur·sue' v. **1** try to overtake; chase **2** go on with **3** seek —**pur·su'ance** n.

pur·suit' n. **1** a pursuing **2** occupation

pu'ru·lent (pyoor'ə-) a. of or discharging pus —**pu'ru·lence** n.

pur·vey' (-vā') v. supply, as food —**pur·vey'or** n.

pur'view' n. scope or extent of control, activity, etc.

pus n. yellowish matter forming in infections

push v. **1** to move by pressing against **2** urge on —n. **1** a pushing **2** an advance

push'er n. [Sl.] one who sells drugs illegally

push'o'ver n. [Sl.] **1** anything easy to do **2** one easily persuaded, defeated, etc.

push'-up', **push'up'** n. exercise of raising one's prone body by pushing down on the palms

push'y a. **-i·er**, **-i·est** [Inf.] annoyingly aggressive

pu'sil·lan'i·mous a. cowardly; timid

puss (poos) n. **1** cat: also **puss'y**, **puss'y·cat'** **2** [Sl.] face or mouth

puss'y·foot' v. [Inf.] **1** move cautiously **2** avoid taking a stand

pussy willow n. willow with soft, silvery catkins

pus'tule' (-chōōl', -tyōōl') n. inflamed, pus-filled pimple

put v. **put**, **put'ting 1** make be in some place, state, relation, etc. **2** impose or assign **3** express **4** go (in, out, etc.) —**put down 1** repress **2** [Sl.] belittle or humiliate —**put in for** apply for —**put off 1** postpone **2** perturb —**put on 1** pretend **2** [Sl.] to hoax —**put out 1** extinguish **2** inconvenience —**put up 1** preserve (fruits, etc.) **2** give lodgings to **3** provide (money) —**put upon** impose on —**put up with** tolerate

pu'ta·tive a. supposed

put'-down' n. [Sl.] belittling remark

put'-on' n. [Sl.] hoax

pu'tre·fy' v. **-fied'**, **-fy'ing** rot —**pu'tre·fac'tion** n.

pu'trid a. rotten; stinking

putt v., n. Golf (make) a stroke to roll the ball into the hole

putt'er v. busy oneself aimlessly —n. Golf club for putting

put'ty n. pliable substance to fill cracks, etc. —v. **-tied**, **-ty'ing** fill with putty

puz'zle v. perplex —n. **1** thing that puzzles **2** problem to test cleverness

PVC n. polyvinyl chloride: plastic used for pipes, etc.

Pvt abbrev. Private

PX service mark general store at an army post

pyg'my (pig'-) n., pl. **-mies** dwarf

py·ja'mas pl.n. Br. sp. of PAJAMAS

py'lon' (pī'-) n. towerlike shaft

py·lo'rus n., pl. **-ri** (-rī') opening from stomach into intestines —**py·lor'ic** a.

py·or·rhe·a, py·or·rhoe·a (pī'ə rē'ə) n. infection of gums and tooth sockets

pyr'a·mid (pir'-) n. solid figure or

structure with triangular sides meeting at a point —v. build up in a pyramid —**py·ram'i·dal** a.

pyre (pīr) n. pile of wood for burning a dead body

py'ro·ma'ni·a n. compulsion to start fires —**py·ro·ma'ni·ac'** n.

py·ro·tech'nics pl.n. **1** display of fireworks **2** dazzling display

py'thon' n. large snake that crushes its prey to death

Q

q abbrev. question

QB abbrev. Football quarterback: sometimes **qb**

QC abbrev. Quebec

Q.E.D., q.e.d. abbrev. which was to be demonstrated

qt abbrev. quart(s)

qty abbrev. quantity

quack v. utter the cry of a duck —n. **1** this cry **2** one who practices medicine fraudulently —**quack'er·y** n.

quad'ran'gle n. **1** plane figure with four angles and four sides **2** four-sided area surrounded by buildings: also **quad**

quad'rant n. quarter section of a circle

quad'ra·phon'ic a. using four channels to record and reproduce sound

quad·ren'ni·al a. lasting or occurring every four years

quad'ri·ceps' n. large front muscle of the thigh

quad'ri·lat'er·al a., n. four-sided (figure)

qua·drille' n. dance in which four couples form a square, etc.

quad'ri·ple'gi·a n. paralysis of the body from the neck down —**quad'ri·ple'gic** a., n.

quad'ru·ped' n. four-footed animal

quad·ru'ple a., adv. four times as much —v. make or become quadruple

quad·ru'plet n. any of four offspring from the same pregnancy

quad·ru'pli·cate' (-kāt'; a., n. -kət) v. make four copies of —a. made in four identical copies —n. one of these copies

quaff (kwäf) v. drink deeply —n. a quaffing

quag'mire' n. a bog

qua·hog, qua'haug' (kō'häg', kwô'-) n. edible, hard-shelled clam

quail v. draw back in fear —n. game bird

quaint a. pleasingly odd or old-fashioned —**quaint'ly** adv. —**quaint'ness** n.

quake v. shake —n. **1** a quaking **2** earthquake

Quak'er n. member of Society of Friends

qual'i-fied' a. **1** skilled; able **2** limited

qual'i-fy' v. **-fied'**, **-fy'ing 1** make or be fit for a job, etc. **2** modify; restrict **3** moderate —**qual'i-fi-ca'tion** n. —**qual'i-fi'er** n.

qual'i-ty n., pl. **-ties 1** characteristic **2** kind **3** degree of (excellence) —**qual'i-ta'tive** a.

qualm (kwäm) n. scruple; misgiving

quan'da-ry n., pl. **-ries** state of perplexity; dilemma

quan'ti-ty n., pl. **-ties 1** amount **2** large amount **3** number or symbol expressing measure —**quan'ti-ta'tive** a.

quan'tum n., pl. **-ta** Physics basic unit of energy, etc.

quar'an-tine' (-tēn') n. isolation to keep contagious disease from spreading —v. place under quarantine

quark n. basic unit of matter

quar'rel v., n. (have) an argument or disagreement —**quar'rel-some** a.

quar'ry n., pl. **-ries 1** animal, etc. being hunted down **2** place where stone is excavated —v. **-ried**, **-ry-ing** excavate from a quarry

quart n. ¼ gallon

quar'ter n. **1** any of four equal parts; ¼ **2** 25-cent coin **3** district **4** pl. lodgings **5** mercy —v. **1** divide into quarters **2** provide lodgings for —**at close quarters** at close range

quar'ter-back' n. Football back who calls signals and passes the ball

quar'ter-deck' n. after part of a ship's top deck

quar'ter-ly a. occurring regularly four times a year —adv. once every quarter of the year —n., pl. **-lies** publication issued quarterly

quar'ter-mas'ter n. army officer in charge of supplies

quar-tet' n. **1** musical composition for four performers **2** group of four performers

quar'to n. book-page size about 9 × 12 inches

quartz n. bright mineral

quartz crystal n. Electronics piece of quartz that vibrates at a particular frequency

qua'sar' n. a distant celestial object that emits immense quantities of light and radio waves

quash (kwäsh) v. **1** annul **2** suppress

qua-si (kwā'zī', kwä'zē') a., adv. seeming(ly)

quat'rain n. stanza of four lines

qua'ver v. **1** tremble **2** be tremulous: said of the voice —n. tremulous tone

quay (kē) n. wharf

quea'sy (kwē'-) a. **-si-er**, **-si-est** feeling nausea

queen n. **1** wife of a king **2** woman monarch **3** female in an insect colony **4** playing card with a queen's picture **5** most powerful chess piece

queen'-size' a. large, but smaller than king-size

queer a. **1** odd **2** [Inf.] eccentric —**queer'ly** adv.

quell v. subdue or quiet

quench v. **1** extinguish **2** satisfy —**quench'less** a.

quer'u-lous (kwer'-) a. **1** fretful **2** complaining

que'ry (kwir'-) n., pl. **-ries**; v. **-ried**, **-ry-ing** question

quest n. a seeking —v. seek

ques'tion n. **1** inquiry **2** thing asked **3** doubt **4** problem **5** point being debated —v. **1** inquire **2** doubt **3** challenge —**out of the question** impossible —**ques'tion-er** n.

ques'tion-a-ble a. **1** doubtful **2** not well thought of

question mark n. mark of punctuation (?) indicating direct question

ques'tion-naire' n. list of questions for gathering information

queue (kyōō) n. **1** pigtail **2** line of persons

quib'ble v. evade a point by carping

quiche (kēsh) n. hot custard pie made with cheese, spinach, etc.

quiche Lor-raine (lô ren') n. custard pie made with cheese and bacon

quick a. **1** swift **2** prompt —adv. rapidly —n. **1** the living **2** one's deepest feelings —**quick'ly** adv.

quick'en v. **1** enliven **2** hasten

quick'-freeze' v. freeze (food) suddenly for storage

quick'ie n. [Inf.] anything done or made quickly

quick'lime' n. unslaked lime

quick'sand' n. wet, deep sand that engulfs heavy things

quick'sil'ver n. mercury

quick'-tem'pered a. easily angered

quick'-wit'ted a. alert

quid n. **1** piece of tobacco to be chewed **2** [Br. Inf.] one pound sterling

quid pro quo n. one thing in return for another

qui·es'cent (kwī-) *a.* quiet; inactive

qui'et *a.* **1** still **2** silent **3** gentle —*n.* **1** stillness **2** silence —*v.* make or become quiet —**qui'et·ly** *adv.* —**qui'et·ness** *n.*

qui'e·tude' *n.* calmness

quill *n.* **1** large feather **2** pen made from this **3** spine of a porcupine

quilt *v., n.* (make) a bedcover stitched in layers

quince *n.* yellowish fruit

qui'nine' *n.* alkaloid used in treating malaria

quin·tes'sence *n.* **1** pure essence **2** perfect example

quin·tet', quin·tette' *n.* **1** musical composition for five performers **2** group of five performers

quin·tu'plet (-tup'lət) *n.* any of five offspring from the same pregnancy

quip *v., n.* **quipped, quip'ping** (make) a witty remark

quire *n.* set of 24 or 25 sheets of the same paper

quirk *n.* peculiarity —**quirk'y** *a.*

quirt *n.* riding whip with braided leather lash

quis'ling (kwiz'-) *n.* traitor

quit *v.* **quit** or **quit'ted, quit'ting 1** give up **2** leave **3** stop —*a.* free

quit'claim' *n.* deed resigning a claim, as to property

quite *adv.* **1** completely **2** really **3** very or fairly —**quite a few** [Inf.] many

quits *a.* on even terms —**call it quits** [Inf.] stop working, being friendly, etc.

quit'tance *n.* **1** discharge of a debt **2** recompense

quit'ter *n.* [Inf.] one who gives up easily

quiv'er *v.* tremble —*n.* **1** tremor **2** case for arrows

quix·ot'ic *a.* idealistic but impractical

quiz *n., pl.* **quiz'zes** test of knowledge —*v.* **quizzed, quiz'zing** give a quiz to

quiz'zi·cal *a.* **1** comical **2** perplexed —**quiz'zi·cal·ly** *adv.*

quoit *n.* **1** ring thrown to encircle an upright peg **2** *pl.* [*sing. v.*] game so played

quon'dam *a.* former

Quon'set hut *n.* metal shelter with a curved roof

quo'rum *n.* minimum number needed to transact business at an assembly

quot *abbrev.* quotation

quo'ta *n.* share assigned to each one

quo·ta'tion *n.* **1** a quoting **2** words quoted **3** current price of a stock or bond

quotation marks *n.* marks ("...") around quoted words

quote *v.* **1** repeat (the words of) **2** state (the price of) —*n.* [Inf.] **1** quotation **2** quotation mark —**quot'a·ble** *a.*

quoth (kwōth) *v.* [Ar.] said

quo·tid'i·an *a.* **1** daily **2** usual

quo'tient (-shənt) *n.* number gotten by dividing one number into another

q.v. *abbrev.* which see

R

R *trademark* film rating indicating anyone under 17 admitted only with a parent or guardian

R, r *abbrev. Baseball* run(s)

rab'bi (-ī) *n., pl.* **-bis** ordained teacher of the Jewish law —**rab·bin'i·cal** *a.*

rab'bin·ate (-it, -āt') *n.* **1** position of rabbi **2** rabbis as a group

rab'bit *n.* burrowing rodent with soft fur and long ears

rab'ble *n.* a mob

rab'ble-rous'er *n.* one who tries to incite others to anger or violence

rab'id *a.* **1** fanatical **2** of or having rabies

ra'bies *n.* disease of dogs, etc., transmitted by biting

rac·coon' *n.* small, furry mammal with black-ringed tail

race *n.* **1** a competition, esp. of speed **2** swift current **3** division of mankind, based on skin color, etc. **4** any group or class —*v.* **1** be in a race **2** move swiftly —**rac'er** *n.* —**ra'cial** (-shəl) *a.*

race'horse' *n.* horse bred and trained for racing

ra·ceme' (-sēm') *n.* flower cluster

race'track' *n.* course for racing

race'way' *n.* race track for harness races or one for drag races, etc.

rac'ism' *n.* racial discrimination or persecution —**rac'ist** *a., n.*

rack *n.* **1** framework for holding things **2** torture device **3** toothed bar meshing with a gearwheel —*v.* to torture —**rack one's brain** think hard

rack'et *n.* **1** noisy confusion **2** dishonest scheme **3** netted frame used as a bat in tennis: also sp. **rac'quet**

rack'et·eer' *n.* one who gets money by fraud, etc. —**rack'et·eer'ing** *n.*

rac'on·teur' (-tur') *n.* one clever at telling stories

rac'quet·ball' *n.* game like handball

rac·y (rā′sē) *a.* **-i·er, -i·est 1** lively **2** risqué

ra′dar′ *n.* device for locating objects by their reflection of radio waves

ra′di·al (ply) tire *n.* tire with ply cords at right angles to the center line of tread

ra′di·al *a.* of or like a ray or rays

ra′di·ant *a.* **1** shining brightly **2** showing pleasure, etc. **3** issuing in rays —**ra′di·ance** *n.* —**ra′di·ant·ly** *adv.*

ra′di·ate′ *v.* **1** send out rays, as of heat or light **2** branch out as from a center

ra′di·a′tion *n.* **1** a radiating **2** rays sent out **3** nuclear rays or particles

ra′di·a′tor *n.* device for radiating heat

rad′i·cal *a.* **1** basic **2** favoring extreme change —*n.* **1** one with radical views **2** *Chem.* group of atoms acting as one —**rad′i·cal·ism′** *n.* —**rad′i·cal·ly** *adv.*

ra′di·o′ *n.* **1** way of sending sounds through space by electromagnetic waves **2** *pl.* **-os′** set for receiving radio waves **3** broadcasting by radio —*a.* of radio —*v.* **-oed′, -o′ing** send by radio

ra′di·o·ac′tive *a.* emitting radiant energy by the disintegration of atomic nuclei —**ra′di·o·ac·tiv′i·ty** *n.*

ra′di·o·gram′ *n.* message sent by radio

ra′di·ol′o·gy *n.* medical use of X-rays, etc. —**ra′di·ol′o·gist** *n.*

ra′di·o·ther′a·py *n.* treatment of disease by X-rays or rays from radioactive substance

rad′ish *n.* edible pungent root of certain plant

ra′di·um *n.* radioactive metallic chemical element

ra′di·us *n., pl.* **-di·i′** (-dē ī′) *or* **-di·us·es 1** straight line from the center to the outside of a circle or sphere **2** shorter bone of the forearm

ra′don′ *n.* radioactive gas, a chemical element

RAF *abbrev.* Royal Air Force

raf′fi·a *n.* fiber from leaves of a palm, used in weaving

raff′ish *a.* **1** carelessly unconventional **2** tawdry

raf′fle *n.* lottery —*v.* offer as a prize in a raffle

raft *n.* floating platform of logs fastened together

raft′er *n.* beam in a roof

rag *n.* **1** piece of torn or waste cloth **2** *pl.* tattered clothes —**rag′ged** *a.*

ra′ga (rä′gə) *n.* traditional melody pattern used by musicians of India

rag′a·muf′fin *n.* dirty, ragged child

rage *n.* **1** furious anger **2** craze; fad —*v.* **1** show violent anger **2** be unchecked

ragg *a.* (made) of sturdy yarn having a speckled pattern

rag′lan *n.* designating a sleeve that continues in one piece to the collar

ra·gout (ra gōō′) *n.* stew

rag′time′ *n.* syncopated music popular about 1890 to 1920

rag′weed′ *n.* common weed whose pollen causes hay fever

raid *n.* sudden attack or invasion —*v.* make a raid on

rail *n.* **1** bar put between posts as a guard or support **2** either of the bars of a railroad track **3** railroad **4** small wading bird —*v.* speak bitterly

rail′ing *n.* fence made of rails and posts

rail′ler·y *n.* light, pleasant ridicule

rail′road′ *n.* **1** road with steel rails for trains **2** system of such roads —*v.* [Inf.] rush through unfairly

rail′way′ *n.* **1** railroad **2** track with rails for cars

rai′ment (rā′-) *n.* [Ar.] attire

rain *n.* water falling in drops from the clouds —*v.* fall as or like rain —**rain′y** *a.,* **-i·er, -i·est**

rain′bow′ *n.* arc of colors formed by sunshine on rain

rain check *n.* ticket for admission to event replacing one canceled due to rain

rain′coat′ *n.* waterproof coat

rain′drop′ *n.* single drop of rain

rain′fall′ *n.* **1** fall of rain **2** amount of rain over an area during a given time

rain forest *n.* dense, evergreen forest in a rainy area

rain′mak′er *n.* [Sl.] powerful person who brings new energy, attracts new clients, etc., as to a business

rain′storm′ *n.* storm with heavy rain

raise *v.* **1** lift up **2** increase in amount, degree, etc. **3** build or put up **4** bring up **5** collect **6** make grow —*n.* a pay increase

rai′sin *n.* sweet, dried grape

rai·son d'être (rā′zōn det′) *n.* reason for existing

ra·jah, ra·ja (rä′jə) *n.* prince in India

rake *n.* **1** long-handled tool with teeth at one end **2** debauched man —*v.* **1** gather (leaves, etc.) with a rake **2** search carefully **3** sweep with gunfire

rake′-off′ *n.* [Sl.] illegal commission or share

rak′ish (rāk′-) *a.* smartly trim and casual; jaunty

ral′ly *v.* **-lied, -ly·ing 1** regroup **2** gather for a common aim **3** revive — *n., pl.* **-lies 1** a rallying **2** mass meeting

ram *n.* **1** male sheep **2** battering ram —*v.* **rammed, ram′ming 1** strike against with force **2** force into place

RAM (ram) *n.* computer memory allowing direct access of data: also **ran′dom-ac′cess memory**

ram′ble *v.* **1** stroll; roam **2** talk or write aimlessly **3** spread, as vines — *n.* a stroll —**ram′bler** *n.*

ram·bunc′tious (-shəs) *a.* disorderly; unruly

ram′e·kin, ram′e·quin *n.* small baking dish

ra′men (rä′-) *pl.n.* Japanese noodles

ram′i·fy *v.* **-fied′, -fy′ing** spread out into branches —**ram′i·fi·ca′tion** *n.*

ramp *n.* sloping passage joining different levels

ram′page *v.* rush wildly about —*n.* wild, angry action: usually in **on the** (or **a**) **rampage**

ramp′ant *a.* spreading widely

ram′part *n.* fortified embankment

ram′rod′ *n.* rod for ramming down a charge in a gun

ram′shack′le *a.* rickety

ran *v.* pt. of RUN

ranch *n.* large farm for raising livestock —**ranch′er** *n.*

ranch dressing *n.* creamy buttermilk salad dressing

ran′cid *a.* like stale oil or fat; spoiled

ran′cor *n.* bitter hate or ill will —**ran′cor·ous** *a.* —**ran′cor·ous·ly** *adv.*

rand *n., pl.* **rand** South African monetary unit

ran′dom *a.* haphazard —**at random** haphazardly

ran′dy *a.* **-di·er, -di·est** lustful

rang *v.* pt. of RING

range *v.* **1** set in rows **2** roam about **3** extend —*n.* **1** row or line, esp. of mountains **2** effective distance **3** extent **4** open land **5** place for shooting practice **6** cooking stove

rang′er *n.* **1** trooper who patrols a region **2** warden who patrols forests

rang·y (rān′jē) *a.* **-i·er, -i·est** long-limbed and thin

rank *n.* **1** row; line **2** class or grade **3** *pl.* enlisted soldiers —*v.* **1** to place in, or hold, a certain rank **2** outrank —*a.* **1** growing wildly **2** bad in taste or smell **3** utter

rank and file *n.* [*sing. or pl. v.*] **1** enlisted men and women **2** common people

rank′ing *a.* **1** of highest rank **2** prominent

ran′kle *v.* cause mental pain, resentment, etc.

ran′sack′ *v.* **1** search thoroughly **2** plunder; loot

ran′som *n.* **1** the freeing of a captive by paying money **2** price asked —*v.* buy a captive's freedom

rant *v.* talk wildly; rave

rap *v.* **rapped, rap′ping 1** strike or knock sharply **2** [Sl.] to chat; talk — *n.* quick, sharp knock

ra·pa′cious (-shəs) *a.* greedy; voracious —**ra·pac′i·ty** *n.*

rape *n.* **1** crime of attacking sexually **2** plant whose leaves are used for fodder —*v.* commit rape (on) —**rap′ist** *n.*

rap′id *a.* swift —**ra·pid′i·ty** *n.* —**rap′id·ly** *adv.*

rap′ids *pl.n.* part of a river with very swift current

ra′pi·er *n.* light, sharp sword

rap·ine (rap′in) *n.* plunder

rap (music) *n.* popular music with rhymed lyrics spoken over repeated rhythms

rap·port′ (-pôr′) *n.* sympathetic relationship; harmony

rap·proche·ment (ra prôsh mäN′) *n.* an establishing of friendly relations

rap·scal′lion (-yən) *n.* rascal

rap sheet *n.* [Sl.] a person's criminal record

rapt *a.* engrossed (*in*)

rap′ture *n.* ecstasy

rare *a.* **1** scarce; uncommon **2** very good **3** not dense **4** partly raw —*v.* be eager: used in prp. with infinitive —**rare′ness** *n.* —**rar′i·ty** *n., pl.* **-ties**

rare′bit *n.* Welsh rabbit

rar′e·fy′ *v.* **-fied′, -fy′ing** make or become less dense

rare′ly *adv.* seldom

ras′cal *n.* **1** rogue **2** mischievous child —**ras·cal′i·ty** *n.* —**ras′cal·ly** *adv.*

rash *a.* too hasty; reckless —*n.* red spots on the skin —**rash′ly** *adv.*

rash′er *n.* slice(s) of bacon

rasp *v.* **1** scrape harshly **2** irritate — *n.* **1** rough file **2** grating sound

rasp′ber′ry *n., pl.* **-ries 1** shrub with red or black berries **2** the berry

rat *n.* long-tailed rodent, larger than a mouse —*v.* **rat′ted, rat′ting** [Sl.] inform on others

ratch′et *n.* wheel or bar with slanted teeth that catch on a pawl

rate *n.* **1** relative amount or degree **2**

price per unit 3 rank —v. **1** appraise **2** rank **3** [Inf.] deserve

rath'er adv. **1** preferably **2** with more reason **3** more truly **4** on the contrary **5** somewhat

raths'kel'ler n. restaurant below street level

rat'i·fy' v. **-fied', -fy'ing** approve formally —**rat'i·fi·ca'tion** n.

rat'ing n. **1** rank **2** appraisal

ra'tio (-shō, -shē ō') n., pl. **-tios** relation of one thing to another in size, etc.

ra·ti·o'ci·na'tion (rash'ē äs'ə-) n. reasoning by logic

ra·tion (rash'ən, rā'shən) n. fixed share, as of food —v. to give in rations —**ra'tion·ing** n.

ra'tion·al (rash'-) a. **1** able to reason **2** reasonable —**ra'tion·al'i·ty** n. —**ra'tion·al·ly** adv.

ra·tion·ale (rash'ə nal') n. reasons or explanation

ra'tion·al·ism' n. belief in reason as the only authority

ra'tion·al·ize' v. give plausible explanations for —**ra'tion·al·i·za'tion** n.

rat race n. [Sl.] intense stressful competition, as in business

rat·tan' n. palm stems used in wickerwork, etc.

rat'tle v. **1** make or cause to make a series of sharp, short sounds **2** chatter **3** upset —n. **1** a rattling **2** baby's toy that rattles

rat'tle·snake' n. snake with a tail that rattles: also **rat'tler**

rau·cous (rô'kəs) a. loud or rowdy

raun'chy a. **-chi·er, -chi·est** [Sl.] risqué, vulgar, etc.

rav'age v., n. ruin

rave v. **1** talk wildly **2** praise greatly —n. [Sl.] enthusiastic praise

rav'el v. untwist; fray

ra'ven n. large black crow —a. black and shiny

rav'en·ing (rav'-) a. greedily seeking prey

rav'e·nous a. greedily hungry —**rav'e·nous·ly** adv.

ra·vine' (-vēn') n. long, deep hollow in the earth

rav'ing a. **1** frenzied **2** [Inf.] remarkable

ra·vi·o'li (rav'ē-) n. dough casings holding meat, cheese, etc.

rav'ish v. **1** fill with great joy **2** rape

rav'ish·ing a. delightful

raw a. **1** uncooked **2** unprocessed **3** inexperienced **4** sore and inflamed **5** cold and damp —**raw'ness** n.

raw'boned' a. lean; gaunt

raw'hide' n. untanned cattle hide

ray n. **1** thin beam of light **2** stream of radiant energy **3** tiny amount **4** broad, flat fish

ray'on n. fabric made from cellulose

raze v. demolish

ra'zor n. sharp-edged instrument for shaving

razz v. [Sl.] make fun of

raz'zle-daz'zle n. [Sl.] flashy display

RBI n., pl. **RBIs** or **RBI** Baseball run batted in: also **rbi**

RC abbrev. Roman Catholic

Rd abbrev. Road

re (rē) prep. regarding

re- pref. **1** back **2** again: add again to meaning of base word in list below

re'ad·just'
re'af·firm'
re'ap·pear'
re'ap·point'
re·arm'
re'as·sem'ble
re'as·sign'
re'a·wak'en
re·boot'
re·born'
re·build'
re·cap'ture
re'con·sid'er
re'con·struct'
re'dis·cov'er
re·dou'ble
re·ed'u·cate'
re'e·lect'
re'en·act'
re'en·list'
re·en'ter
re'ex·am'ine
re·fill'
re·fu'el
re·heat'
re'in·vest'
re·load'
re'lo·cate'
re·make'
re·mar'ry
re·mix'
re·o'pen
re·or'der
re·phrase'
re·play'
re·print'
re'proc·ess'
re·read'
re're·lease'
re·tell'
re'u·nite'

reach v. **1** extend the hand, etc. **2** touch **3** get to **4** to influence **5** get in touch with **6** try to get —*n.* act or extent of reaching

re·act' *v.* **1** respond to stimulus **2** return to an earlier state **3** act with another substance in a chemical change —**re·ac'tion** *n.*

re·act'ant *n.* any substance involved in a chemical reaction

re·ac'tion·ar·y *a.; n., pl.* **-ies** ultraconservative

re·ac'ti·vate' *v.* make or become active again

re·ac'tor *n.* device for producing atomic energy

read (rēd) *v.* **read** (red), **read'ing** **1** understand or utter (written or printed matter) **2** to study **3** to register, as a gauge **4** access computer data —**read'er** *n.*

read'er·ship' *n.* all the readers of a magazine, etc.

read'ing *n.* **1** act of one that reads **2** thing to be read **3** interpretation **4** amount measured

read'out' *n.* displayed information

read'y *a.* **-i·er, -i·est** **1** prepared to act **2** willing **3** available —*v.* **-ied, -y·ing** prepare —**at the ready** prepared for immediate use —**read'i·ly** *adv.* —**read'i·ness** *n.*

read'y-made' *a.* ready for use or sale at once

re·a'gent *n.* chemical used to detect or convert another

re·al' *a.* **1** actual; true **2** genuine —*adv.* [Inf.] very —**re·al'ly** *adv.*

real estate *n.* land, including buildings, etc., on it

re·al'ism' *n.* awareness of things as they really are —**re·al'ist** *n.* —**re·al'is'tic** *a.* —**re·al'is'ti·cal·ly** *adv.*

re·al'i·ty *n., pl.* **-ties** **1** state of being real **2** real thing; fact

re·al'ize' *v.* **1** achieve **2** understand fully **3** make real **4** gain —**re·al·i·za'tion** *n.*

real'-life' *a.* actual

realm (relm) *n.* **1** kingdom **2** region; sphere

Re·al'tor *trademark* certified real estate broker —*n.* [r-] real estate agent

re·al'ty *n.* real estate

ream *n.* quantity of 480 to 516 sheets of paper —*v.* enlarge (a hole) —**ream'er** *n.*

re·an'i·mate' *v.* give new life or vigor to —**re·an'i·ma'tion** *n.*

reap *v.* cut and gather (grain, etc.) —**reap'er** *n.*

re·ap·por'tion *v.* adjust the represen-

tation pattern of (a legislature) —**re'ap·por'tion·ment** *n.*

rear *n.* back part or place —*a.* of or at the rear —*v.* **1** bring up; raise **2** rise on the hind legs

rear admiral *n.* naval officer above a captain

re·ar·range' *v.* arrange in a different way —**re·ar·range'ment** *n.*

rea'son *n.* **1** explanation **2** cause **3** power to think **4** good sense —*v.* think or argue with logic —**rea'son·ing** *n.*

rea'son·a·ble *a.* **1** fair **2** sensible **3** not expensive —**rea'son·a·bly** *adv.*

re·as·sure' *v.* restore to confidence —**re·as·sur'ance** *n.*

re'bate' *v., n.* return (of) part of a payment

reb'el (*v.:* rē bel') *n.* one who openly resists authority —*a.* rebellious —*v.* **re·bel', -belled', -bel'ling** resist authority —**re·bel'lion** *n.* —**re·bel'lious** *a.*

re·bound' (*n.:* rē'bound') *v., n.* recoil

re·buff' *v., n.* snub

re·buke' ('-byōōk') *v.* to scold sharply —*n.* sharp scolding

re'bus *n.* puzzle in which pictures stand for words

re·but' *v.* **-but'ted, -but'ting** contradict formally —**re·but'tal** *n.*

re·cal'ci·trant *a.* refusing to obey —**re·cal'ci·trance** *n.*

re·call' (*n.:* rē'kôl') *v.* **1** call back **2** remember **3** revoke —*n.* a recalling

re·cant' *v.* to renounce (one's beliefs)

re·cap' (*n.:* rē'kap') *v.* **-capped', -cap'ping** **1** put new tread on (worn tire) **2** recapitulate —*n.* **1** a recapped tire **2** recapitulation

re'ca·pit'u·late' ('-pich'ə-) *v.* summarize —**re'ca·pit'u·la'tion** *n.*

recd, rec'd *abbrev.* received

re·cede' *v.* **1** move or slope backward **2** diminish

re·ceipt' ('-sēt') *n.* **1** a receiving **2** written acknowledgment of sum received **3** *pl.* amount received

re·ceiv'a·ble *a.* due

re·ceive' *v.* **1** get; be given **2** greet (guests) **3** react to

re·ceiv'er *n.* **1** one who receives **2** one holding in trust property in bankruptcy, etc. **3** apparatus that converts electrical signals into sound or images, as in radio and TV

re'cent *a.* of a short time ago —**re'cent·ly** *adv.*

re·cep'ta·cle *n.* container

re·cep'tion *n.* **1** a receiving or being

received **2** social function **3** the receiving of signals on radio or TV

re·cep'tion·ist *n.* employee who receives callers, etc.

re·cep'tive *a.* ready to receive suggestions

re·cep'tor *n.* nerve ending that feels heat, pressure, pain, etc.

re'cess (*or* rē ses') *n.* **1** hollow in a wall **2** break from work —*v.* **1** take a recess **2** set back

re·ces'sion *n.* temporary falling off of business activity

re·ces'sion·al *n.* hymn at end of church service when clergy and choir march out

re·ces'sive *a.* tending to recede

re·cher·ché (rə sher'shā') *a.* **1** rare **2** too refined

rec'i·pe (res'ə pē') *n.* directions for preparing dish or drink

re·cip'i·ent *n.* one that receives

re·cip'ro·cal *a.* **1** done, etc. in return **2** mutual —**re·cip'ro·cal·ly** *adv.* —**re·cip'ro·cate'** *v.* —**rec'i·proc'i·ty** (-präs'-) *n.*

re·cit'al (-sīt'-) *n.* **1** account told **2** musical program

re·cite' *v.* **1** repeat something memorized **2** narrate —**rec'i·ta'tion** *n.*

reck'less *a.* heedless; rash —**reck'less·ly** *adv.* —**reck'less·ness** *n.*

reck'on *v.* **1** to count **2** to estimate **3** [Inf.] suppose —**reckon with** to deal with

reck'on·ing *n.* **1** a figuring out **2** settlement of accounts

re·claim' *v.* restore for use —**rec'la·ma'tion** *n.*

re·cline' *v.* lie down or lean back

rec'luse *n.* one who lives a secluded, solitary life

rec'og·nize' *v.* **1** to identify as known before **2** to perceive **3** acknowledge; notice formally —**rec'og·ni'tion** *n.* —**rec'og·niz'a·ble** *a.*

re·coil' (*n.:* rē'koil') *v.* pull back —*n.* a recoiling

rec'ol·lect' *v.* remember —**rec'ol·lec'tion** *n.*

rec'om·mend' *v.* suggest (as fit or worthy) —**rec'om·men·da'tion** *n.*

rec'om·pense' *v.* pay or pay back —*n.* compensation

rec'on·cile' (-sīl') *v.* **1** make friendly again **2** settle (a quarrel) **3** to make agree or fit **4** to make acquiescent (*to*) —**rec'on·cil'a·ble** *a.* —**rec'on·cil'i·a'tion** (-sil'-) *n.*

rec'on·dite' *a.* abstruse

re'con·di'tion *v.* put back in good condition

re·con'nais·sance (-kän'ə səns) *n.* a spying on an area

re'con·noi'ter *v.* examine or spy on an area

re·cord' (*n., a.:* rek'ərd) *v.* **1** keep a written account of **2** show on a dial, etc. **3** put (sound, images, etc.) on a disc, tape, etc. —*n.* **1** official account **2** known facts **3** a disc with recorded sound **4** the best yet done —*a.* best

re·cord'er *n.* **1** person or machine that records **2** early form of flute

re·cord'ing *n.* **1** what is recorded on a disc, tape, etc. **2** the record itself

re·count' (*n.:* rē'kount) *v.* count again —*n.* a second count

re·coup' (-kōōp') *v.* make up for, as a loss

re·course' *n.* **1** a turning for aid **2** source of aid

re·cov'er (-kuv'-) *v.* **1** get back; regain **2** become normal **3** keep from a fall **4** reclaim —**re·cov'er·y** *n., pl.* **-ies**

recovery room *n.* hospital room where patients are first cared for after surgery

rec're·ant [Ar.] *a.* **1** cowardly **2** disloyal —*n.* **1** coward **2** traitor

rec're·a'tion *n.* refreshing play —**rec're·a'tion·al** *a.*

re·crim'i·nate' *v.* accuse one's accuser —**re·crim'i·na'tion** *n.*

re'cru·des'cence *n.* a breaking out again, esp. of something bad —**re'cru·des'cent** *a.*

re·cruit' *n.* new member, soldier, etc. —*v.* enlist (recruits) —**re·cruit'er** *n.* —**re·cruit'ment** *n.*

rec'tal *a.* of, for, or near the rectum

rec'tan·gle *n.* four-sided figure with four right angles —**rec·tan'gu·lar** *a.*

rec'ti·fy' *v.* **-fied', -fy'ing** **1** to correct **2** convert (alternating current) to direct current —**rec'ti·fi·ca'tion** *n.* —**rec'ti·fi'er** *n.*

rec'ti·lin'e·ar *a.* bounded or formed by straight lines

rec'ti·tude' *n.* honesty

rec'tor *n.* head of some schools or parishes

rec'to·ry *n., pl.* **-ries** rector's residence

rec'tum *n.* lowest part of the intestine

re·cum'bent *a.* lying down

re·cu'per·ate' *v.* recover health, losses, etc. —**re·cu'per·a'tion** *n.*

re·cur' *v.* **-curred', -cur'ring** **1** occur again **2** return in talk, etc. —**re·cur'rence** *n.* —**re·cur'rent** *a.*

re·cy'cle *v.* **1** pass through a cycle again **2** use (metal, paper, etc.) again

(and again)

red n. 1 color of blood 2 [R-] communist —a. **red'der, red'dest** of the color red —**in the red** losing money —**red'dish** a. —**red'ness** n.

red blood cell (or corpuscle) n. blood cell containing hemoglobin

red'cap' n. porter in a railroad or bus station

red carpet n. very grand or impressive welcome: with the —**red'-car'pet** a.

red'coat' n. British soldier in a uniform with a red coat

red'den v. make or become red

re·deem' v. 1 buy back 2 pay off 3 turn in for a prize 4 free, as from sin 5 atone for —**re·deem'a·ble** a. —**re·deem'er** n. —**re·demp'tion** n.

red'-flag' v. to mark with a warning

red'-hand'ed a. while committing a crime

red'head' n. person with red hair —**red'head'ed** a.

red herring n. something used to divert attention from the basic issue

red'-hot' a. 1 glowing hot 2 very excited 3 very new

red'-let'ter a. memorable

re·do' v. 1 do again 2 redecorate

re·do'lent a. 1 fragrant 2 smelling (of) 3 suggesting —**red'o·lence** n.

re·doubt' (-dout') n. stronghold

re·doubt'a·ble a. 1 formidable 2 deserving respect

re·dound' v. have a result

re·dress' (n.: rē'dres') v. correct and make up for —n. a redressing

red snapper n. ocean food fish

red tape n. rules and details that waste time and effort

re·duce' v. 1 lessen; decrease 2 change the form of 3 lower 4 lose weight —**re·duc'tion** n.

re·dun'dant a. 1 excess; superfluous 2 wordy —**re·dun'dan·cy** n., pl. **-cies**

red'wood' n. 1 giant evergreen 2 its reddish wood

reed n. 1 a hollow-stemmed grass 2 musical pipe made of this 3 vibrating strip in some musical instruments —**reed'y** a., **-i·er, -i·est**

reef n. ridge of land near the surface of water —v. take in part of a sail

reek v., n. (emit) a strong, offensive smell

reel n. 1 spool or frame on which thread, film, etc. is wound 2 amount wound on it 3 lively dance —v. 1 to wind (in or out) on a reel 2 tell fluently: with off 3 stagger

re-en'try, re-en'try n., pl. **-tries** a

coming back, as of a spacecraft into the earth's atmosphere

ref n., v. [Inf.] referee

ref abbrev. 1 referee 2 reference 3 reformed 4 refund

re·fec'to·ry n., pl. **-ries** dining hall, as in a monastery or college

re·fer' v. **-ferred', -fer'ring** 1 go to, or direct someone to, for aid, information, etc. 2 allude (to)

ref·er·ee' n. 1 one chosen to decide something 2 a judge in sports —v. act as referee in

ref'er·ence n. 1 a referring 2 relation or connection 3 mention of a source of information 4 recommendation, or person giving it —**make reference to** mention

ref'er·en'dum n. submission of a law to direct popular vote

re·fer'ral n. 1 a referring or being referred 2 person referred to another person

re·fine' v. to free from impurities, coarseness, etc. —**re·fine'ment** n.

re·fined' a. 1 purified 2 cultivated or elegant

re·fin'er·y n., pl. **-ies** plant for purifying materials, as oil

re·flect' v. 1 throw back, as (an image, sound, etc.) 2 to express or show —**reflect on (or upon)** 1 ponder 2 cast blame —**re·flec'tion** n. —**re·flec'tive** a. —**re·flec'tor** n.

re'flex a., n. (designating or of) an involuntary reaction to a stimulus

re·flex'ive a. 1 designating a verb whose subject and object are the same 2 designating a pronoun used as object of such a verb

re·form' v. 1 improve 2 behave or make behave better —n. improvement —**re·form'er** n.

ref'or·ma'tion n. a reforming —**the Reformation** 16th-c. movement establishing Protestant churches

re·form'a·to'ry n., pl. **-ries** institution for reforming young lawbreakers

re·fract' v. bend (a light ray, etc.) —**re·frac'tion** n.

re·frac'to·ry a. obstinate

re·frain' v. hold back (from) —n. repeated verse of a song

re·fresh' v. make fresh or stronger; renew or revive —**re·fresh'er** n.

re·fresh'ing a. 1 that refreshes 2 pleasingly new or different

re·fresh'ment n. 1 a refreshing 2 pl. food or drink

re·frig'er·ate' (-frij'-) v. make cold, as to preserve —**re·frig·er·a'tion** n. —**re-**

frig′er·ant *a.*, *n.*

re·frig′er·a′tor *n.* box or room for refrigerating

ref′uge (-yōōj) *n.* protection from danger or pursuit

ref′u·gee′ *n.* one who flees to seek refuge

re·ful′gent (-ful′jənt) *a.* shining; radiant

re·fund′ (*n.*: rē′fund) *v.* give back (money, etc.) —*n.* amount refunded

re·fur′bish *v.* renovate

re·fuse (rē fyōōz′; *n.*: ref′yōōs) *v.* 1 reject 2 decline (*to* do, etc.) —*n.* rubbish —**re·fus′al** *n.*

re·fute′ *v.* prove wrong —**ref·u·ta′tion** *n.*

reg *abbrev.* 1 registered 2 regular 3 regulation

re·gain′ *v.* get back; recover

re′gal *a.* royal

re·gale′ *v.* entertain, as with a feast

re·ga′li·a *pl.n.* insignia or decorations, as of a rank

re·gard′ *n.* 1 concern 2 affection and respect 3 reference 4 *pl.* good wishes —*v.* 1 to gaze upon 2 think of; consider 3 concern; pertain to —**as regards** concerning —**re·gard′ful** *a.* —**re·gard′less** *a.*, *adv.*

re·gat′ta (-gät′-) *n.* boat race

re·gen′er·ate *v.* 1 give new life to; renew 2 improve —**re·gen′er·a′tion** *n.*

re′gent *n.* interim ruler in place of a monarch —**re′gen·cy** *n.*, *pl.* -**cies**

reg·gae (reg′ā) *n.* type of popular Jamaican music

reg′i·cide′ *n.* killer or killing of a king

re·gime (rā zhēm′) *n.* political or ruling system

reg′i·men *n.* system of diet, exercise, etc.

reg′i·ment *n.* section of an army division —*v.* to control and discipline strictly —**reg′i·men′tal** *a.* —**reg′i·men·ta′tion** *n.*

re′gion *n.* 1 large surface area 2 place, division, or part —**re′gion·al** *a.*

re′gion·al·ism′ *n.* regional quality, character, custom, etc.

reg′is·ter *n.* 1 list of names, etc. 2 recording device, as for cash transactions 3 a device for adjusting passage of air 4 musical range —*v.* 1 enter in a list 2 indicate 3 make an impression —**reg′is·trant** (-trənt) *n.* —**reg′is·tra′tion** *n.*

reg′is·tered nurse *n.* trained nurse who has passed a U.S. state examination

reg′is·trar′ (-trär′) *n.* keeper of records, as in a college

re·gress′ *v.* go backward —**re·gres′sion** *n.* —**re·gres′sive** *a.*

re·gret′ *v.* -**gret′ted**, -**gret′ting** be sorry for (a mistake, etc.) —*n.* a being sorry —**re·gret′ful** *a.* —**re·gret′ta·ble** *a.*

re·group′ *v.* 1 reorganize 2 collect oneself

reg′u·lar *a.* 1 according to rule; orderly 2 usual 3 unchanging —**reg′u·lar′i·ty** *n.* —**reg′u·lar·ize′** *v.* —**reg′u·lar·ly** *adv.*

reg′u·late′ *v.* 1 control 2 adjust to a standard, etc. —**reg′u·la′tor** *n.* —**reg′u·la·to′ry** *a.*

reg′u·la′tion *n.* 1 a regulating 2 a rule —*a.* usual

re·gur′gi·tate′ (-jə-) *v.* bring up from the stomach —**re·gur′gi·ta′tion** *n.*

re·hab′ *n.* [Inf.] rehabilitation —*vt.* -**habbed′**, -**hab′bing** rehabilitate

re·ha·bil′i·tate′ *v.* restore to earlier state —**re·ha·bil′i·ta′tion** *n.*

re·hash′ *v.* repeat; go over again —*n.* a rehashing

re·hearse′ (-hurs′) *v.* 1 recite 2 practice for a performance —**re·hears′al** *n.*

reign (rān) *n.* (period of) a sovereign's rule —*v.* rule as sovereign

re′im·burse′ *v.* pay back —**re′im·burse′ment** *n.*

rein (rān) *n.* 1 strap hooked to a bit for controlling a horse 2 *pl.* means of controlling —**give (free) rein to** to free from restraint

re′in·car·na′tion *n.* rebirth (of the soul) —**re′in·car′nate** *v.*

rein′deer′ *n.*, *pl.* -**deer′** large northern deer

re′in·force′ *v.* strengthen —**re′in·force′ment** *n.*

re′in·state′ *v.* restore —**re′in·state′ment** *n.*

re·it′er·ate′ *v.* to repeat —**re·it′er·a′tion** *n.*

re·ject′ (*n.*: rē′jekt) *v.* 1 refuse to accept 2 discard —*n.* thing rejected —**re·jec′tion** *n.*

re·joice′ *v.* be or make happy —**re·joic′ing** *n.*

re·join′ *v.* 1 join again 2 answer

re·join′der *n.* an answer to a reply

re·ju′ve·nate′ *v.* make young again —**re·ju′ve·na′tion** *n.*

rel *abbrev.* 1 relative(ly) 2 religion

re·lapse′ (*n.*: rē′laps) *v.*, *n.* fall back into a past state

re·late′ *v.* 1 narrate 2 connect, as in

meaning **3** have reference (*to*)

re·lat'ed *a.* of the same family or kind

re·la'tion *n.* **1** a relating or being related **2** kinship **3** a relative **4** *pl.* dealings, as between people —**re·la'·tion·ship'** *n.*

rel'a·tive *a.* **1** related **2** comparative —*n.* related person

relative humidity *n.* ratio of humidity to the most possible humidity at a certain temperature, given as a percentage

rel'a·tiv'i·ty *n.* **1** a being relative **2** modern theory of the universe

re·lax' *v.* **1** loosen up **2** rest, as from work —**re·lax'ant** *a.* —**re·lax·a'tion** *n.*

re'lay' *n.* fresh group of workers, runners, etc. —*v.* get and pass on

relay race *n.* a race between teams, each member of which goes part of the distance

re·lease' *v.* **1** set free **2** allow to be issued —*n.* **1** a releasing **2** device to release a catch

rel'e·gate' *v.* **1** put into a lower position **2** assign —**rel'e·ga'tion** *n.*

re·lent' *v.* become less stern

re·lent'less *a.* **1** pitiless **2** persistent

rel'e·vant *a.* pertinent —**rel'e·vance, rel'e·van·cy** *n.*

re·li'a·ble *a.* that can be relied on —**re·li'a·bil'i·ty** *n.* —**re·li'a·bly** *adv.*

re·li'ance *n.* trust or confidence —**re·li'ant** *a.*

rel'ic *n.* something from the past, spec., a sacred object

re·lief' *n.* **1** a relieving **2** thing that relieves **3** public aid, as to the poor **4** sculpted figures projecting from a flat surface

re·lieve' *v.* **1** to ease; comfort **2** give aid to **3** to free by replacing **4** bring a pleasant change to

re·li'gion *n.* **1** belief in God or gods **2** system of worship —**re·li'gious** *a.*

re·lin'quish *v.* to let go

rel'ish *n.* **1** pleasing flavor **2** enjoyment **3** (chopped) pickles, etc. served with a meal —*v.* enjoy

re·live' *v.* experience again

re·luc'tant *a.* unwilling —**re·luc'tance** *n.* —**re·luc'tant·ly** *adv.*

re·ly' *v.* **-lied', -ly'ing** to trust; depend *on* or *upon*

rem *n.*, *pl.* **rem** standard unit of absorbed radiation

re·main' *v.* **1** be left when part is gone **2** stay **3** continue —**re·main'der** *n.*

re·mains' *pl.n.* **1** part left **2** dead body

re·mand' *v.* send back

re·mark' *v.*, *n.* (make) a brief comment

or observation

re·mark'a·ble *a.* unusual —**re·mark'a·bly** *adv.*

re·me'di·al *a.* corrective

re·me'di·ate' *v.* to remedy

rem'e·dy *n.*, *pl.* **-dies** thing that corrects, etc. —*v.* **-died, -dy·ing** to cure, correct, etc.

re·mem'ber *v.* **1** think of again **2** to bear in mind —**re·mem'brance** *n.*

re·mind' *v.* to cause to remember —**re·mind'er** *n.*

rem'i·nis'cence *n.* **1** memory **2** *pl.* an account of remembered events —**rem'i·nisce'** (-nis') *v.* —**rem'i·nis'cent** *a.*

re·miss' *a.* careless; negligent

re·mit' *v.* **-mit'ted, -mit'ting 1** forgive **2** refrain from exacting **3** slacken **4** send money —**re·mis'sion** *n.* —**re·mit'tance** *n.*

rem'nant *n.* part left over

re·mod'el *v.* make over; rebuild

re·mon'strate' *v.* say in protest —**re·mon'strance** *n.*

re·morse' *n.* deep sense of guilt —**re·morse'ful** *a.* —**re·morse'less** *a.*

re·mote' *a.* **1** distant **2** slight —**re·mote'ly** *adv.*

remote control *n.* **1** control from a distance **2** hand-held device for controlling TV, etc.

re·move' *v.* **1** take away **2** dismiss **3** get rid of —**re·mov'a·ble** *a.* —**re·mov'al** *n.*

re·mu'ner·ate' (-myoo'-) *v.* pay for; reward —**re·mu'ner·a'tion** *n.* —**re·mu'ner·a'tive** *a.*

ren'ais·sance' (-ə säns') *n.* rebirth; revival: also **re·nas'cence** —**the Renaissance** period in Europe, 14th-16th c.

Renaissance man (or **woman**) *n.* man (or woman) educated and skilled in many things

re'nal *a.* of the kidneys

rend *v.* **rent, rend'ing** tear; split apart

ren'der *v.* **1** submit **2** give in return **3** cause to be **4** perform **5** translate **6** melt (fat) —**ren·di'tion** *n.*

ren·dez·vous (rän'dā vōō') *n.* appointed meeting (place) —*v.* meet as agreed

ren'e·gade' *n.* traitor

re·nege' (-nig') *v.* go back on a promise

re·new' *v.* **1** make new again **2** begin again **3** replenish (a supply) —**re·new'al** *n.*

ren'net *n.* bovine extract for curdling milk

re·nounce' *v.* **1** give up (a claim, etc.) **2** disown —**re·nounce'ment** *n.*

ren'o·vate' v. make like new; restore —**ren'o·va'tion** n. —**ren'o·va'tor** n.

re·nown' n. fame —**re·nowned'** a.

rent n. 1 payment for the use of property 2 a rip —v. get or give rent (for)

rent'al n. 1 rate of rent 2 thing for rent —a. of or for rent

re·nun'ci·a'tion n. a renouncing, as of a right

rep n. [Inf.] a representative

rep abbrev. 1 report(ed) 2 reporter

Rep abbrev. 1 Representative 2 Republic(an)

re·pair' v. 1 fix; mend 2 make amends for 3 go (to) —n. a repairing or being repaired

rep'a·ra'tion n. 1 a making of amends 2 often pl. compensation, as for war damage

rep'ar·tee' (-tē', -tā') n. quick, witty reply or conversation

re·past' n. a meal

re·pa'tri·ate' v. return to country of birth, etc. —**re·pa'tri·a'tion** n.

re·pay' v. pay back —**re·pay'ment** n.

re·peal' v. revoke; annul (a law) —n. revocation

re·peat' v. say or do again —n. 1 a repeating 2 thing repeated —**re·peat'ed·ly** adv. —**re·peat'er** n.

re·pel' v. **-pelled'**, **-pel'ling** 1 force back 2 disgust —**re·pel'lent** a., n.

re·pent' v. feel sorry for (a sin, etc.) —**re·pent'ance** n. —**re·pent'ant** a.

re'per·cus'sion (-kush'ən) n. 1 echo 2 effect, often an indirect one

rep'er·toire' (-twär') n. stock of plays, songs, etc. one is prepared to perform: also **rep'er·to'ry**, pl. **-ries**

rep'e·ti'tion (-tish'ən) n. 1 a repeating 2 thing repeated —**rep'e·ti'tious** a. —**re·pet'i·tive** a.

re·pine' v. complain

re·place' v. 1 put back 2 take the place of 3 put another in place of —**re·place'ment** n.

re·plen'ish v. fill again —**re·plen'ish·ment** n.

re·plete' a. filled —**re·ple'tion** n.

rep'li·ca n. exact copy —**rep'li·cate'** v.

re·ply' v. **-plied'**, **-ply'ing**; n., pl. **-plies'** answer

re·port' v. 1 give an account of 2 tell as news; announce 3 denounce (an offender, etc.) to someone in authority 4 present oneself —n. 1 statement or account 2 rumor 3 explosive noise —**re·port'ed·ly** adv.

report card n. periodic written report on a student's progress

re·port'er n. one who gathers and reports news

re·pose' v., n. rest

re·pos'i·to'ry n., pl. **-ries** a place where things may be put for safekeeping

re'pos·sess' v. take back from a defaulting buyer

rep're·hen'si·ble a. deserving scolding or blame

rep're·sent' v. 1 portray or describe 2 symbolize 3 act in place of 4 be an example of —**rep're·sen·ta'tion** n.

rep're·sent'a·tive a. 1 representing 2 typical —n. 1 typical example 2 one chosen to act for others 3 [R-] Congressional or state legislator

re·press' v. 1 hold back 2 subdue 3 force (painful ideas, etc.) into the unconscious —**re·pres'sion** n. —**re·pres'sive** a.

re·prieve' n., v. delay (in) the execution of (one sentenced to die)

rep'ri·mand' n., v. rebuke

re·pris'al (-prī'zəl) n. injury done for injury received

re·proach' v. blame; rebuke —n. 1 disgrace 2 a scolding or blaming —**re·proach'ful** a.

rep'ro·bate' a., n. depraved (person)

re'pro·duce' v. produce copies, offspring, etc. —**re'pro·duc'tion** n. —**re'pro·duc'tive** a.

re·proof' n. a reproving; rebuke: also **re·prov'al**

re·prove' v. find fault with

rept abbrev. report

rep'tile' n. coldblooded, creeping vertebrate, as a snake, lizard, etc.

rep·til'i·an a. 1 of reptiles 2 sneaky, groveling, etc.

re·pub'lic n. government by elected representatives —**re·pub'li·can** a., n.

re·pu'di·ate' v. disown; cast off —**re·pu'di·a'tion** n.

re·pug'nant a. 1 opposed 2 distasteful; offensive —**re·pug'nance** n.

re·pulse' v. 1 repel 2 rebuff —**re·pul'sion** n.

re·pul'sive a. disgusting

rep'u·ta·ble a. having a good reputation

rep'u·ta'tion n. 1 others' opinion of one 2 good character 3 fame

re·pute' v. consider to be —n. reputation —**re·put'ed** a. —**re·put'ed·ly** adv.

re·quest' n. 1 an asking for 2 thing asked for —v. ask for

Re'qui·em (rek'wē-, rā'kwē-) n. R.C.Ch. [also r-] Mass for the dead

re·quire' v. 1 to demand 2 to need —**re·quire'ment** n.

req·ui·site (rek'wə zit) *n.*, *a.* (something) necessary

req·ui·si'tion *n.* written order or request —*v.* **1** to demand or take **2** submit a requisition for

re·quite' *v.* repay for —**re·quit'al** *n.*

re·route' *v.* send by a different route

re·run' *n.* showing of a film, etc. after the first showing

res *abbrev.* **1** reserve **2** residence **3** resigned

re·scind' (-sind') *v.* cancel; repeal —**re·scis'sion** *n.*

res·cue *v.* to free or save —*n.* a rescuing —**res'cu·er** *n.*

re·search' (*or* rē surch') *v.*, *n.* (do) careful study in a subject

re·sec'tion *n.* surgical removal of part of an organ, etc.

re·sem'ble *v.* be like —**re·sem'blance** *n.*

re·sent' *v.* feel anger at —**re·sent'ful** *a.* —**re·sent'ment** *n.*

res·er·va'tion *n.* **1** a reserving, as of a hotel room **2** public land set aside, as for North American Indians

re·serve' *v.* keep back; set aside —*n.* **1** thing reserved **2** limitation **3** reticence **4** *pl.* troops subject to call —**re·served'** *a.*

res·er·voir (-vwär', -vôr') *n.* **1** place for storing water **2** large supply

re·side' *v.* **1** live (*in* or *at*) **2** be present (*in*)

res'i·dence *n.* **1** a residing **2** home —**res'i·dent** *a.*, *n.* —**res·i·den'tial** (-shəl) *a.*

res·i·den·cy *n.*, *pl.* **-cies** period of advanced medical training

res'i·due *n.* part that is left —**re·sid'u·al** (-zij'-) *a.*

re·sign' *v.* **1** give up, as a claim, position, etc. **2** be submissive —**resign oneself** (*to*) accept (something) passively —**res'ig·na'tion** *n.* —**re·signed'** *a.*

re·sil'ient *a.* bouncing back; elastic —**re·sil'ience, re·sil'ien·cy** *n.*

res'in *n.* **1** substance from trees used in varnish, etc. **2** rosin —**res'in·ous** *a.*

re·sist' *v.* **1** withstand **2** to fight against

re·sist'ance *n.* **1** power to resist **2** opposition to another force —**re·sist'ant** *a.*

re·sis'tor *n.* device in electrical circuit providing resistance

re·sole' *v.* put a new sole on (a shoe, etc.)

res'o·lute' *a.* firm; determined —**res'o·lute·ly** *adv.*

res'o·lu'tion *n.* **1** a resolving **2** formal statement **3** determination

re·solve' *v.* **1** decide **2** solve **3** to change —*n.* fixed purpose —**re·solved'** *a.*

res'o·nant *a.* **1** resounding **2** intensifying sound —**res'o·nance** *n.*

res'o·na'tor *n.* device that produces resonance

re·sort' *v.* **1** go often **2** turn for help (*to*) —*n.* **1** place for a vacation, etc. **2** source of help

re·sound' (-zound') *v.* make an echoing sound

re·sound'ing *a.* **1** reverberating **2** complete

re·source' (*or* ri sôrs') *n.* **1** emergency supply **2** *pl.* assets **3** resourcefulness

re·source'ful *a.* able to handle problems, etc. effectively

re·spect' *v.* **1** think highly of **2** show concern for —*n.* **1** honor **2** concern **3** *pl.* regards **4** reference **5** detail —**re·spect'ful** *a.* —**re·spect'ful·ly** *adv.*

re·spect'a·ble *a.* **1** of good reputation **2** good enough —**re·spect·a·bil'i·ty** *n.*

re·spect'ing *prep.* concerning; about

re·spec'tive *a.* of or for each separately —**re·spec'tive·ly** *adv.*

res'pi·ra'tion *n.* act or process of breathing —**res'pi·ra·to'ry** *a.*

res'pi·ra'tor *n.* device to aid breathing artificially

res'pite (-pit) *n.* **1** a delay **2** period of relief or rest

re·splend'ent *a.* dazzling

re·spond' *v.* **1** to answer **2** react —**re·spond'ent** *n.*

re·sponse' *n.* **1** a reply **2** reaction —**re·spon'sive** *a.*

re·spon'si·ble *a.* **1** obliged to do or answer for **2** involving duties **3** dependable —**re·spon·si·bil'i·ty** *n.*, *pl.* **-ties**

rest *n.* **1** ease or inactivity **2** peace **3** a support **4** a pause **5** remainder —*v.* **1** get, or be at, ease **2** become still **3** lie or lay **4** depend —**rest'ful** *a.*

res'tau·rant' (-tə ränt', -tränt') *n.* place for buying and eating meals

res·tau·ra·teur (res'tə rə tur') *n.* restaurant owner or operator: also **res'tau·ran·teur'** (-rän-)

res'ti·tu'tion *n.* **1** a giving back **2** reimbursement

res'tive *a.* restless

rest'less *a.* **1** uneasy **2** disturbed **3** never still; always active

re·store' *v.* **1** give back **2** return to a former position, condition, etc. —**res'to·ra'tion** *n.* —**re·stor'a·tive** *a.*, *n.*

re·strain' v. 1 to hold back from action; check 2 to limit; restrict

re·straint' n. 1 a restraining 2 thing that restrains 3 self-control

re·strict' v. to limit; confine —**re·stric'tion** n. —**re·stric'tive** a.

rest'room' n. public room with toilets and washbowls: also **rest room**

re·struc'ture v. plan or provide a new structure, etc. for

re·sult' v. 1 happen as an effect 2 to end (in) —n. 1 what is caused; outcome 2 mathematical answer —**re·sult'ant** a.

re·sume' v. 1 take again 2 continue after interrupting —**re·sump'tion** n.

ré·su·mé (rez'ə mā') n. summary, esp. of one's employment history

re·sur'face v. 1 put a new surface on 2 come to the surface again

re·sur'gent a. rising again —**re·sur'gence** n.

res·ur·rect' v. bring back to life, use, etc. —**res'ur·rec'tion** n.

re·sus·ci·tate (-sus'ə-) v. revive, as one almost dead —**re·sus'ci·ta'tion** n.

ret abbrev. 1 retired 2 return(ed)

re'tail' n. sale of goods in small amounts to consumers —a. of such a sale —v. sell at retail —**re'tail'er** n.

re·tain' v. 1 keep in possession, use, etc. 2 keep in mind 3 hire (a lawyer)

re·tain'er n. 1 servant to a rich person or family 2 fee paid to hire a lawyer

re·take' (n.: rē'tāk') v. take again —n. scene photographed again

re·tal'i·ate' v. return injury for injury —**re·tal'i·a'tion** n. —**re·tal'i·a·to'ry** a.

re·tard' v. slow down; delay —**re'tar·da'tion** n.

re·tard'ant n. substance delaying chemical reaction

re·tard'ed a. slowed in development, esp. mentally

retch v. strain to vomit

re·ten'tion n. 1 a retaining 2 ability to retain —**re·ten'tive** a.

ret'i·cent a. disinclined to speak —**ret'i·cence** n.

ret'i·na n. layer of cells lining the interior of the eyeball, on which images are formed

ret'i·nue' n. attendants on a person of rank

re·tire' v. 1 withdraw or retreat 2 withdraw from one's career, etc. 3 go to bed —**re·tire'ment** n.

re·tired' a. no longer working because of age, etc.

re·tir·ee' n. one who has retired from work, business, etc.

re·tir'ing a. shy; modest

re·tool' v. adapt (factory machinery) for different use

re·tort' v. reply sharply or cleverly —n. 1 sharp or clever reply 2 container for distilling, etc.

re·touch' v. touch up

re·trace' v. go back over

re·tract' v. 1 draw back or in 2 withdraw (a charge, etc.) —**re·trac'tion** n.

re'tread' n. recapped tire

re·treat' n. 1 withdrawal, esp. under attack 2 quiet place 3 period of contemplation by a group —v. withdraw

re·trench' v. economize —**re·trench'ment** n.

ret'ri·bu'tion n. deserved punishment

re·trieve' v. 1 get back or bring back 2 make good (a loss or error) 3 Comput. get (data) from memory, disk, etc. —**re·triev'al** n.

re·triev'er n. dog trained to retrieve game

ret'ro·ac'tive a. effective as of a prior date

ret'ro·fire' v. fire a retrorocket

ret'ro·grade' a. 1 moving backward 2 getting worse

ret'ro·gress' v. move backward into a worse state —**ret'ro·gres'sion** n.

ret'ro·rock'et n. small rocket on spacecraft fired opposite to flight direction to reduce landing speed

ret'ro·spect' n. contemplation of the past —**ret'ro·spec'tive** a.

ret·si'na (-sē'-) n. Greek wine flavored with pine resin

re·turn' v. 1 go or come back 2 bring or send back 3 repay (a visit, etc.) 4 yield (profit) —n. 1 a going or coming back 2 something returned 3 recurrence 4 requital 5 often pl. yield or profit 6 official report —a. of or for a return —**in return** as a return

Reu·ben (sandwich) n. sandwich of corned beef, sauerkraut, etc.

re·u'ni·fy' v. unify again —**re·u'ni·fi·ca'tion** n.

re·un'ion n. a coming together again

rev v. revved, rev'ving [Inf.] increase speed of (an engine): with up

rev abbrev. 1 revenue 2 revise(d) 3 revolution

Rev abbrev. Reverend

re·vamp' v. renovate; redo

re·veal' v. 1 make known (a secret, etc.) 2 show

rev·eil·le (rev'ə lē) n. Mil. morning signal to wake up

rev'el v. 1 make merry 2 take pleasure (in) —n. lively celebration —**rev'**

el·ry *n., pl.* -ries

rev·e·la'tion *n.* 1 a revealing 2 striking disclosure

re·venge' *v., n.* (do) harm in retaliation (for) —re·venge'ful *a.*

rev·e·nue' *n.* a government's income from taxes, etc.

re·ver'ber·ate' *v.* 1 echo again; resound 2 have repercussions —re·ver'ber·a'tion *n.*

re·vere' *v.* show deep respect or love for —rev'er·ence *n.* —rev'er·ent *a.*

rev'er·end *a.* respected: [R-] used with *the* for a member of the clergy

rev'er·ie (-ē) *n.* daydream(ing)

re·vers' (-vir') *n., pl.* -vers' (-virz') lapel

re·verse' *a.* opposite —*n.* 1 the opposite 2 the back of a coin, etc. 3 change for the worse 4 gear for reversing —*v.* 1 turn about or inside out 2 revoke 3 go or make go in the opposite direction —re·ver'sal *n.* —re·vers'i·ble *a.*

re·vert' *v.* go back to a former state, owner, etc. —re·ver'sion *n.*

re·view' *n.* 1 general survey 2 reexamination 3 critique of a book, play, etc. 4 formal inspection —*v.* 1 to survey 2 study again 3 to inspect formally 4 write a review of (a book, etc.) —re·view'er *n.*

re·vile' *v.* use abusive language to or about

re·vise' *v.* change, esp. after reading —re·vi'sion *n.*

re·vi'sion·ist *a., n.* (of) one who revises an accepted theory —re·vi'sion·ism' *n.*

re·vis'it *v.* 1 visit again 2 reconsider

re·viv'al *n.* 1 a reviving 2 meeting to arouse religious feeling —re·viv'al·ist *n.*

re·vive' *v.* return to life, use, etc.

re·voke' *v.* put an end to; cancel —rev'o·ca·ble *a.* —rev'o·ca'tion *n.*

re·volt' *v.* 1 to rebel 2 disgust or be disgusted —*n.* a rebellion —re·volt'ing *a.* —re·volt'ing·ly *adv.*

rev·o·lu'tion *n.* 1 movement in an orbit 2 complete cycle 3 complete change 4 overthrow of a government, etc. —rev·o·lu'tion·ar·y *a.; n., pl.* -ies —rev·o·lu'tion·ist *n.*

rev·o·lu'tion·ize' *v.* make a drastic change in

re·volve' *v.* 1 rotate 2 move in an orbit 3 to be pondered

re·volv'er *n.* pistol with a revolving cylinder for bullets

re·vue' *n.* musical show

re·vul'sion *n.* disgust

re·ward' *n.* thing given in return for something done —*v.* give a reward to or for

re·wind' *v.* -wound', -wind'ing wind (film or tape) back onto the reel

re·word' *v.* put into other words

re·write' *v.* revise

rhap'so·dize' (rap'-) *v.* speak or write ecstatically

rhap'so·dy *n., pl.* -dies 1 extravagantly enthusiastic speech or writing 2 a musical piece of free form —rhap·sod'ic, rhap·sod'i·cal *a.*

rhe·a (rē'ə) *n.* large, ostrichlike bird

rhe'o·stat' *n.* device for regulating electric current

rhe'sus (monkey) *n.* small, brownish monkey of India

rhet'o·ric *n.* effective or showy use of words —rhe·tor'i·cal *a.* —rhet'o·ri'cian (-rish'ən) *n.*

rhetorical question *n.* question with an obvious answer

rheum (rōōm) *n.* watery discharge from nose, eyes, etc.

rheumatic fever *n.* disease with fever, aching joints, etc.

rheu'ma·tism' (rōō'-) *n.* painful condition of the joints, etc. —rheu·mat'ic *a., n.* —rheu'ma·toid' *a.*

rheumatoid arthritis *n.* chronic disease with swollen joints

Rh factor *n.* antigen group in some human blood

rhine'stone' (rīn'-) *n.* artificial gem of hard glass

rhi·ni'tis (rī-) *n.* inflammation in the nose

rhi'no *n., pl.* -nos rhinoceros

rhi·noc'er·os (-näs'-) *n.* large mammal with one or two horns on the snout

rhi'zome' *n.* creeping stem with leaves near its tips and roots growing underneath

rho·do·den'dron (rō'-) *n.* shrub with showy flowers

rhom'boid' (räm'-) *n.* a parallelogram with oblique angles and only the opposite sides equal

rhom'bus *n., pl.* -bus·es or -bi' (-bī') equilateral parallelogram, esp. with oblique angles

rhu'barb' (rōō'-) *n.* 1 plant with edible leafstalks 2 [Sl.] heated argument

rhyme (rīm) *n.* 1 likeness of end sounds in words or lines of poetry 2 verse having rhyme —*v.* 1 form a rhyme 2 have rhyme

rhythm (riŧh'əm) *n.* pattern of regular beat, accent, etc. —rhyth'mic, rhyth'mi·cal *a.* —rhyth'mi·cal·ly *adv.*

RI *abbrev.* Rhode Island

rib *n.* **1** any of the curved bones around the chest **2** anything riblike —*v.* **ribbed, rib'bing 1** form with ribs **2** [Sl.] tease

rib'ald *a.* coarsely joking —**rib'ald·ry** *n.*

rib'bon *n.* **1** narrow strip, as of silk **2** *pl.* shreds

rib'bon-cut'ting *n.* ceremony to officially open a new building, construction site, etc.

rib'-eye' (steak) *n.* boneless beefsteak from the rib section

ri'bo·fla'vin *n.* a vitamin in milk, eggs, etc.

rice *n.* food grain grown in warm climates

rich *a.* **1** wealthy **2** well-supplied **3** costly **4** full of fats or sugar **5** full and deep **6** producing much —**the rich** wealthy people —**rich'ly** *adv.* —**rich'ness** *n.*

rich'es *pl.n.* wealth

Rich'ter scale (rik'-) *n.* scale for measuring earthquake severity

rick *n.* stack of hay, straw, etc.

rick'ets *n.* disease causing a softening of the bones

rick'et·y *a.* weak; shaky

rick'rack' *n.* flat, zigzag cloth strip for trimming dresses, etc.

rick'shaw', rick'sha *n.* jinrikisha

ri·co·chet' (-shā') *n.*, *v.* **-cheted'** (-shād') **-chet'ing** (-shā'iŋ) skip off at an angle

ri·cot'ta *n.* soft Italian cheese

rid *v.* **rid** or **rid'ded, rid'ding** to free or relieve of —**get rid of** dispose of —**rid'dance** *n.*

rid'den *a.* dominated: used in compounds

rid'dle *n.* puzzling question, thing, etc. —*v.* perforate

ride *v.* **rode, rid'den, rid'ing 1** sit on and make go **2** move along, as in a car **3** be carried along on or by **4** [Inf.] tease —*n.* **1** a riding **2** thing to ride in at an amusement park

rid'er *n.* **1** one who rides **2** addition to a contract or legislative bill

rid'er·ship' *n.* passengers using a transportation system

ridge *n.* **1** crest **2** narrow, raised strip —*v.* form into ridges

ridge'pole' *n.* beam at the ridge of a roof, to which rafters are attached

rid'i·cule' *n.* remarks meant to make fun of another —*v.* make fun of

ri·dic'u·lous *a.* foolish; absurd —**ri·dic'u·lous·ly** *adv.*

rife *a.* **1** widespread **2** abounding

riff *n.* constantly repeated musical phrase as in jazz

rif'fle *n.* ripple in a stream

riff'raff' *n.* people thought of as low, common, etc.

ri'fle *n.* gun with spiral grooves in the barrel —*v.* ransack and rob —**ri'fle·man** *n.*, *pl.* **-men**

rift *n.*, *v.* crack; split

rig *v.* **rigged, rig'ging 1** equip **2** arrange dishonestly —*n.* **1** equipment **2** arrangement of sails

rig'ging *n.* ropes, etc. to work the sails of a ship

right *a.* **1** just and good **2** correct **3** suitable **4** normal **5** of that side toward the east when one faces north —*n.* **1** what is right **2** right side **3** power or privilege **4** conservative or reactionary party, etc. —*adv.* **1** directly **2** properly **3** completely **4** toward the right —*v.* **1** restore to upright position **2** correct —**right away** at once —**right'ful** *a.* —**right'ly** *adv.*

right angle *n.* 90-degree angle

right·eous (rī'chəs) *a.* **1** virtuous **2** morally right —**right'eous·ly** *adv.* —**right'eous·ness** *n.*

right'-hand'ed *a.* **1** using the right hand more easily **2** for the right hand

right'ist *n.*, *a.* conservative or reactionary

right'-mind'ed *a.* having sound principles

right of way *n.* legal right to proceed, pass over, etc.

right wing *n.* more conservative or reactionary part of a group or party —**right'-wing'** *a.*

rig'id (rij'-) *a.* **1** stiff and firm **2** severe; strict —**ri·gid'i·ty** *n.*

rig'ma·role' *n.* **1** rambling talk **2** involved procedure

rig'or *n.* strictness or hardship —**rig'or·ous** *a.*

rig'or mor'tis *n.* stiffening of muscles after death

rile *v.* [Inf.] to anger

rill *n.* little brook

rim *n.* edge, esp. of something round —*v.* **rimmed, rim'ming** form a rim around

rime *n.*, *v.* rhyme

rime *n.* white frost

rind *n.* firm outer layer

ring *v.* **rang, rung 1** make, or cause to make, the sound of a bell **2** seem **3** resound **4** encircle —*n.* **1** sound of a bell **2** band for the finger **3** any similar band **4** group with questionable goals **5** enclosed area —**ring'er** n.

ring'lead·er n. leader of a group, as of lawbreakers

ring'let n. long curl

ring'mas·ter n. director of circus performances

ring'side' n. space just outside the ring at boxing match, etc.

ring'worm' n. skin disease

rink n. smooth area for skating

rinse v. **1** wash lightly **2** wash out soap from —n. a rinsing or liquid for this

ri'ot v., n. (take part in) mob violence —**ri'ot·er** n. —**ri'ot·ous** a.

rip v., n. ripped, rip'ping **1** tear apart roughly **2** become torn —n. torn place

R.I.P., RIP abbrev. may he (she) rest in peace

rip cord n. cord pulled to open parachute during descent

ripe a. **1** ready to be harvested, eaten, etc. **2** ready —**rip'en** v. —**ripe'ness** n.

rip'-off' n. [Sl.] a stealing, cheating, etc.

ri·poste', ri·post' n. sharp retort

rip'ple v. to form small surface waves —n. small wave

rip'saw' n. saw for cutting wood along the grain

rise v. rose, ris'en, ris'ing **1** stand up **2** come or go up **3** increase **4** begin **5** revolt —n. **1** ascent **2** upward slope **3** an increase **4** origin

ris·er (rī'zər) n. vertical piece between steps

ris'i·ble (riz'-) a. laughable; funny

risk n. chance of harm, loss, etc. —v. **1** put in danger **2** take the chance of —**risk'y** a., -i·er, -i·est

ris·qué' (-kā') a. almost indecent

rite n. ceremonial act

rite of passage n. (ceremony marking) key event in one's life

rit'u·al (rich'-) a. of a rite —n. system of rites

ri'val n. competitor —a. competing —v. compete with —**ri'val·rous** a. —**ri'val·ry** n., pl. -ries

riv'en a. split

riv·er n. large stream —**riv'er·side'** n., a.

river basin n. area drained by a river and its tributaries

riv'et n. metal bolt used to fasten by hammering the plain end into a head —v. fasten firmly —**riv'et·er** n.

riv'u·let (-yōō-) n. little stream

RN abbrev. Registered Nurse

roach n. cockroach

road n. way made for traveling —**road'side'** n., a.

road'bed' n. foundation for railroad tracks or highway

road'block' n., v. blockade

road'kill' n. [Sl.] carcass of animal killed on a road by a vehicle

road'run'ner n. desert bird of SW U.S.: also **road runner**

road'show' n. touring theatrical show

roam v. wander about; rove

roan a. reddish-brown, etc. thickly sprinkled with white —n. roan horse

roar v., n. **1** (make) a loud, deep, rumbling sound **2** (burst out in) loud laughter

roast v. cook (meat, etc.) in an oven or over an open fire —n. roasted meat —a. roasted —**roast'er** n.

rob v. robbed, rob'bing take property from unlawfully by force —**rob'ber** n. —**rob'ber·y** n., pl. -ies

robe n. long, loose outer garment —v. dress as in a robe

rob'in n. red-breasted North American thrush

ro'bot n. automatic manlike device —**ro·bot'ic** a. —**ro·bot'ics** n.

ro·bust' a. strong and healthy —**ro·bust'ness** n.

rock n. **1** mass or pieces of stone **2** popular music based on jazz, folk music, etc. —v. move back and forth —**on the rocks** [Inf.] **1** in serious trouble **2** served with ice cubes —**rock'i·ness** n. —**rock'y** a., -i·er, -i·est

rock'-and-roll' n. popular music with a strong rhythm

rock bottom n. lowest level

rock'bound' a. covered with rocks

rock'er panel n. panel below automobile door

rock'et n. projectile propelled by the thrust of escaping gases

rock'et·ry n. building and launching of rockets

rocking chair n. chair mounted on curved pieces for rocking: also **rock'er**

rock salt n. common salt in masses

rock wool n. fibrous insulation made from molten rock

ro·co'co a. full of elaborate decoration

rod n. **1** straight stick or bar **2** measure of length, 5½ yards

rode v. pt. of RIDE

ro'dent n. gnawing mammal, as a rat or squirrel

ro'de·o' n., pl. -os' public exhibition of the skills of cowboys

roe n. **1** fish eggs **2** pl. roe or roes small deer

roent·gen (rent′gən) *n.* unit for measuring radiation

Rog′er *int.* [*also* **r-**] OK

rogue (rōg) *n.* **1** scoundrel **2** mischievous person —**ro′guish** (-gish) *a.*

rogues′ gallery *n.* police collection of pictures of criminals

roil *v.* make muddy or cloudy

roist′er *v.* revel; carouse —**roist′er·er** *n.*

role, rôle *n.* **1** part played by an actor **2** function taken on by someone

role model *n.* one serving as a model for others

roll *v.* **1** move by turning **2** move on wheels **3** wind into a ball or cylinder **4** flatten with a rolling cylinder **5** rock **6** trill —*n.* **1** a rolling **2** scroll **3** list of names **4** small cake of bread **5** a swaying motion **6** loud, echoing sound —**roll′er** *n.*

Roll′er·blade′ *trademark* kind of in-line skate

roller coaster *n.* ride with cars on tracks that dip and curve sharply

roller skate *n.* frame or shoe with four small wheels, for gliding on a floor, sidewalk, etc. —**roll′er-skate′** *v.*

rol′lick·ing (räl′-) *a.* lively and carefree

roll′ing pin *n.* cylinder for rolling out dough

roll′-top′ *a.* of a desk having a flexible, sliding top

ro′ly-po′ly *a.* pudgy

Rom *abbrev.* Roman

ROM (räm) *n.* computer memory that can be read but not altered

ro·maine′ *n.* type of lettuce having long head and leaves

Ro′man *a.* of Rome —*n.* **1** a native of Rome **2** [**r-**] type with non-slanting letters

Roman candle *n.* tubular firework

Roman Catholic *n.*, *a.* (member) of Christian church headed by the Pope

ro·mance′ *a.* [**R-**] of any language derived from Latin —*n.* **1** tale of love, adventure, etc. **2** exciting quality **3** love affair —*v.* [Inf.] woo

Roman numerals *pl.n.* Roman letters used as numerals: I=1, V=5, X=10, L=50, C=100, D=500, M=1,000

ro·man′tic *a.* **1** of romance **2** visionary **3** full of feelings of romance —*n.* a romantic person —**ro·man′ti·cal·ly** *adv.* —**ro·man′ti·cism′** *n.*

ro·man′ti·cize′ *v.* treat in a romantic way

romp *v.* play boisterously —*n.* a romping

romp′ers *pl.n.* loose, one-piece outer garment for a small child

rood (rood) *n.* crucifix

roof *n.*, *pl.* **roofs** outside top covering of a building —*v.* cover with a roof

roof′ing *n.* material for roofs

roof′top′ *n.* roof of building

rook *n.* **1** European crow **2** chess piece moving horizontally or vertically

rook′ie [Inf.] beginner

room *n.* **1** enough space **2** space set off by walls **3** *pl.* living quarters; apartment —*v.* to lodge —**room′er** *n.* —**room′ful′** *n.* —**room′mate′** *n.* —**room′y** *a.*, **-i·er**, **-i·est**

roost *n.* perch for birds —*v.* perch on a roost

roost′er *n.* male chicken

root (root, root) *n.* **1** underground part of a plant **2** embedded part, as of a tooth **3** cause **4** quantity to be multiplied by itself —*v.* **1** take root **2** place firmly **3** dig (*up* or *out*) with snout **4** rummage about **5** [Inf.] show support (*for*) —**take root 1** grow by putting out roots **2** become fixed

root beer *n.* carbonated drink made of root extracts

root canal *n.* (procedure involving) channel in a tooth's root

rope *n.* strong cord of twisted strands —*v.* **1** mark off with a rope **2** catch with a lasso

Roque′fort (rōk′-) *trademark* strong cheese with bluish mold

ro′sa·ry *n.*, *pl.* **-ries** string of beads used when praying

rose *n.* **1** sweet-smelling flower that has a prickly stem **2** pinkish red —**rose′bud′** *n.* —**rose′bush′** *n.* —**rose′-col′ored** *a.*

ro·sé′ (-zā′) *n.* a pink wine

ro′se·ate (-zē-) *a.* rose-colored

rose′mar′y *n.* fragrant herb used in cooking

ro·sette′ *n.* roselike ornament

rose′wood′ *n.* a reddish wood

Rosh Ha·sha·na (rōsh′ hə shô′nə, -shä′-) *n.* holiday beginning the Jewish year

ros′in (räz′-) *n.* hard resin

ros′ter *n.* list; roll

ros′trum *n.* speakers' platform

ros′y *a.*, **-i·er**, **-i·est 1** rose-red or pink **2** bright or promising —**ros′i·ly** *adv.* —**ros′i·ness** *n.*

rot *v.* **rot′ted**, **rot′ting** decay; spoil —*n.* **1** a rotting **2** plant disease

ro′ta·ry *a.* **1** rotating **2** having rotating parts

ro·tate' *v.* **1** turn around an axis **2** alternate —**ro·ta'tion** *n.*

ROTC *abbrev.* Reserve Officers' Training Corps

rote *n.* fixed routine —**by rote** by memory alone

ro·tis·ser·ie (-ē) *n.* electric grill with a turning spit

ro'tor *n.* rotating blades on a helicopter, etc.

ro'to·till'er *n.* machine for tilling soil —**ro'to·till'** *v.*

rot'ten *a.* **1** decayed **2** corrupt —**rot'ten·ness** *n.*

ro·tund' *a.* round; plump —**ro·tun'di·ty** *n.*

ro·tun'da *n.* round building with a dome

rouge (roozh) *n.* **1** cosmetic to redden cheeks and lips **2** red polish for jewelry —*v.* put rouge on

rough *a.* **1** not smooth; uneven **2** disorderly **3** harsh **4** not perfected **5** [Inf.] difficult —*adv.* in a rough way —*n.* rough part —*v.* **1** treat roughly: with *up* **2** shape roughly —**rough it** live without comforts —**rough'en** *v.*

rough'age *n.* coarse food

rough'house' *v.* [Inf.] play or fight boisterously

rough'neck' *n.* [Inf.] a rowdy

rou·lette' (roo let') *n.* gambling game played with a ball in a whirling bowl

round *a.* **1** that forms a circle or curve **2** complete **3** expressed in tens, hundreds, etc. rather than exactly —*n.* **1** thigh of beef **2** a course or series **3** *often pl.* regular circuit **4** single gun shot **5** outburst **6** period of action or time **7** simple song for three or four voices —*v.* make round: often with *off* **2** express as a round number: with *off* **3** finish: with *out* or *off* **4** pass around —*adv.* around —*prep.* around —**round up** collect in a herd, etc.

round'a·bout' *a.* indirect

round'house' *n.* round building for repairing and storing locomotives

round'-shoul'dered *a.* having the shoulders stooped

round steak *n.* a cut from a round of beef

round table *n.* group discussion

round'-the-clock' *a., adv.* without interruption

round trip *n.* trip to a place and back

round'up' *n.* a bringing together, esp. of cattle

round'worm' *n.* unsegmented worm

rouse (rouz) *v.* **1** excite **2** wake

roust'a·bout' *n.* unskilled or transient worker

rout *n.* **1** confused flight **2** crushing defeat —*v.* **1** make flee **2** defeat

route (root, rout) *n.* course traveled, as to make deliveries —*v.* send by a certain route

rou·tine' (roo tēn') *n.* regular procedure —*a.* regular; customary —**rou·tine'ly** *adv.*

rove *v.* roam —**rov'er** *n.*

row (rō) *n.* **1** line of people, seats, etc. **2** a trip by rowboat —*v.* move (a boat) with oars

row (rou) *n., v.* quarrel; brawl

row'boat' *n.* boat made to be rowed

row'dy *a.* **-di·er, -di·est** rough, disorderly, etc. —*n., pl.* **-dies** rowdy person —**row'di·ly** *adv.* —**row'di·ness** *n.*

row'el (rou'-) *n.* small wheel with points, as on a spur

roy'al *a.* of a monarch, kingdom, etc. —**roy·al·ist** *a., n.* —**roy'al·ly** *adv.*

roy'al·ty *n.* **1** royal rank, person, or persons **2** *pl.* **-ties** set payment for use of copyright or patent

rpm *abbrev.* revolutions per minute

RR *abbrev.* **1** railroad **2** rural route: also **R.R.**

R.S.V.P., r.s.v.p. *abbrev.* please reply: also **RSVP, rsvp**

rte *abbrev.* route

rub *v.* **rubbed, rub'bing 1** move over a surface with pressure and friction **2** spread on, erase, injure, etc. by rubbing —*n.* **1** a rubbing **2** difficulty; trouble —**rub down** to massage

ru·ba'to (-bät'ō) *a., adv. Mus.* not in strict tempo

rub'ber *n.* **1** elastic substance **2** overshoe —**rub'ber·ize'** *v.* —**rub'ber·y** *a.*

rubber band *n.* elastic loop for bundling things

rubber cement *n.* glue made of rubber

rubber stamp *n.* **1** printing stamp made of rubber **2** [Inf.] routine approval —**rub'ber-stamp'** *v.*

rub'bish *n.* **1** trash; worthless material **2** nonsense

rub'ble *n.* broken stones, bricks, etc.

rub'down' *n.* a massage

ru·bel'la *n.* contagious disease with red skin spots

ru'bi·cund' *a.* reddish

ru'ble *n.* monetary unit of Russia

ru'bric *n.* title or heading of a chapter, section, etc.

ru'by *n., pl.* **-bies** deep-red precious stone

ruck'sack' *n.* knapsack

ruck'us *n.* [Inf.] uproar; disturbance

rud'der n. steering piece at ship's stern or aircraft's tail

rud'dy a. **-di·er, -di·est** 1 healthily red 2 reddish —**rud'di·ness** n.

rude a. 1 coarse; crude 2 impolite —**rude'ly** adv. —**rude'ness** n.

ru'di·ment n. 1 first principle of a subject 2 undeveloped form of something —**ru·di·men'ta·ry** a.

rue v. regret —**rue'ful** a.

ruff n. 1 high, frilled collar 2 raised ring of feathers or fur around a bird's or beast's neck

ruf'fi·an n. brutal, lawless person

ruf'fle v. 1 to ripple 2 make ruffles in or on 3 make (feathers, etc.) stand up 4 disturb —n. narrow, pleated cloth strip used for trimming

rug n. floor covering of thick fabric in one piece

rug'by n. English game like football

rug'ged a. 1 uneven; rough 2 harsh; severe 3 strong

ru'in n. 1 anything destroyed, etc. 2 pl. remains of this 3 downfall; destruction —v. bring or come to ruin —**ru·in·a'tion** n. —**ru'in·ous** a.

rule n. 1 a set guide for conduct, etc. 2 custom; usage 3 government 4 RULER (n. 2) —v. 1 govern 2 decide officially —**as a rule** usually —**rule out** exclude —**rul'ing** a., n.

rule of thumb n. crude but practical method

rul'er n. 1 one who governs 2 straight-edged strip for drawing lines, measuring, etc.

rum n. alcoholic liquor made from molasses, etc.

rum'ba n. Cuban dance

rum'ble v., n. (make) a deep rolling sound

ru'mi·nant a. cud-chewing —n. cud-chewing mammal

ru'mi·nate v. 1 chew the cud 2 meditate —**ru'mi·na'tion** n.

rum'mage v. search thoroughly

rummage sale n. sale of miscellaneous articles

rum'my n. card game

ru'mor n. unconfirmed report or story —v. spread as a rumor

rump n. 1 animal's hind part 2 buttocks

rum'ple n., v. wrinkle

rum'pus n. [Inf.] uproar

run v. **ran, run, run'ning** 1 go by moving the legs fast 2 make a quick trip 3 compete (in) 4 unravel 5 spread (over) 6 continue 7 operate 8 follow (a course) 9 undergo 10 cause to run —n. 1 act or period of running 2 journey; trip 3 continuous series 4 brook 5 a kind 6 freedom 7 unraveled part in a fabric 8 Baseball point scored by a circuit of the bases —**run across** to encounter —**run down** 1 cease operating 2 knock down 3 pursue and capture or kill 4 disparage —**run out** expire —**run out of** use up —**run over** 1 ride over 2 overflow

run'a·round' n. [Inf.] series of evasions

run'a·way' n. person or animal that has run away or fled —a. 1 running away 2 uncontrolled

run'down' n. quick summary

run'-down' a. in poor condition

rung v. pp. of RING —n. rodlike step of a ladder, etc.

run'-in' n. [Inf.] a quarrel

run'ner n. 1 one that runs 2 long, narrow rug 3 unraveled part 4 either of the pieces on which a sled slides

run'ner-up' n. the second to finish in a contest

run'ning a. 1 that runs 2 measured straight 3 continuous —adv. in succession —n. act of one that runs —**in (or out of) the running** in (or out of) the competition

running mate n. lesser candidate, as for vice-president

run'ny a. **-ni·er, -ni·est** 1 flowing too freely 2 discharging mucus

run'off' n. a deciding contest

run'-of-the-mill' a. ordinary

run'-through' n. a complete rehearsal

run'way' n. a landing strip

ru'pee n. monetary unit of India, Pakistan, etc.

rup'ture n. 1 a breaking apart 2 hernia —v. 1 break 2 induce a hernia in

ru'ral (roor'əl) a. of or living in the country

ruse (rooz) n. artful trick

rush v. 1 move, push, attack, etc. swiftly 2 hurry —n. 1 a rushing 2 busyness 3 grassy marsh plant

rush hour n. time when traffic is heavy

rusk n. sweet bread toasted brown

rus'set n., a. yellowish (or reddish) brown

Rus'sian n., a. (native or language) of Russia

rust n. 1 reddish-brown coating formed on iron, etc. 2 plant disease —v. 1 form rust on 2 deteriorate, as through disuse —**rust'y** a., **-i·er, -i·est**

rus'tic a. **1** rural **2** plain or rough —n. country person

rus'tle (-əl) v. **1** make soft sounds **2** [Inf.] steal (cattle, etc.) —n. series of soft sounds —**rus'tler** n.

rut n. **1** groove as made by wheels **2** fixed routine **3** sexual excitement in animals —v. **rut'ted, rut'ting** make ruts in

ru·ta·ba·ga n. yellow turnip

ruth'less a. without pity

RV n., pl. **RVs** recreational vehicle for camping trips, etc.

Rx abbrev. prescription

-ry suf. -ERY

rye (rī) n. **1** cereal grass **2** its grain, used for flour

S

S abbrev. south(ern)

Sab'bath (-əth) n. day of rest and worship; Saturday for Jews, Sunday for many Christians

sab·bat'i·cal (leave) n. period of absence, with pay, for study, travel, etc., as for teachers

sa'ber, sa'bre n. cavalry sword

sa'ble n. **1** weasel-like animal **2** its valuable fur

sab'o·tage (-täzh') n. destruction of factories, etc. by enemy agents, strikers, etc. —v. destroy by sabotage

sab'o·teur' (-tʉr') n. one who commits sabotage

sac n. pouchlike part

sac·cha·rin (sak'ə rin) n. sugar substitute

sac'cha·rine' (-rin') a. very sweet —n. saccharin

sac'er·do'tal (sas'-) a. of priests

sa·chet (sa shā') n. small bag of perfumed powder

sack n. **1** bag **2** large bag of coarse cloth **3** a plundering **4** [Sl.] bed —v. **1** put in sacks **2** plunder **3** [Sl.] dismiss from a job —**hit the sack** [Sl.] go to sleep

sack'cloth' n. coarse cloth worn to show sorrow

sack'ing n. coarse cloth for making sacks

sac'ra·ment n. sacred Christian rite, as Communion —**sac'ra·men'tal** a.

sa'cred a. **1** consecrated to a god or God **2** venerated **3** inviolate —**sa'cred·ly** adv. —**sa'cred·ness** n.

sac'ri·fice' n. **1** offer (something) to a deity **2** give up something for another **3** take a loss in selling —n. a

sacrificing —**sac'ri·fi'cial** (-fish'əl) a.

sac'ri·lege (-lij) n. desecration of something sacred —**sac·ri·le'gious** (-lij'əs) a.

sac'ris·ty n., pl. **-ties** room in a church for storing sacred vessels, etc.

sac'ro·il'i·ac' n. joint at lower end of the spine

sac'ro·sanct' a. very holy

sad a. **sad'der, sad'dest** showing or causing sorrow; unhappy —**sad'den** v. —**sad'ly** adv. —**sad'ness** n.

sad'dle n. seat for a rider on a horse, etc. —v. **1** put a saddle on **2** burden

sad'dle·bag' n. **1** bag hung behind a horse's saddle **2** similar bag on a bicycle, etc.

saddle shoe n. white oxford with dark band over the instep

sad'ist (sā'-, sa'-) n. one who gets pleasure from hurting others —**sad'ism'** n. —**sa·dis'tic** a.

sad'o·mas'o·chist (-kist) n. one who gets pleasure from sadism or masochism, or both —**sad'o·mas'o·chism'** n. —**sad'o·mas'o·chis'tic** a.

sa·fa'ri n. hunting trip, esp. in Africa

safe a. **1** free from danger **2** unharmed **3** trustworthy **4** cautious —n. metal box with a lock —**safe'ly** adv. —**safe'ty** n.

safe'-con'duct n. permission to travel safely

safe'-de·pos'it a. of a bank box, etc. for storing valuables: also **safe'ty-de·pos'it**

safe'guard' n. protection; precaution —v. protect

safe'keep'ing n. protection

safe sex n. sex in which a condom, etc., is used to avoid infection

safety glass n. glass that resists shattering

safety match n. match that strikes only on a prepared surface

safety pin n. bent pin with the point held in a guard

safety razor n. razor with a detachable blade held between guards

safety valve n. outlet to release excess pressure, emotion, etc.

saf'flow'er n. plant whose seeds yield an edible oil

saf'fron n. orange-yellow seasoning from a plant

sag v. **sagged, sag'ging** **1** sink in the middle **2** hang unevenly **3** lose strength —n. place that sags

sa'ga (sä'-) n. long story of heroic deeds

sa·ga'cious (-gā'shəs) a. very wise or

shrewd —**sa·gac'i·ty** (-gas'-) *n.*

sage *a.* very wise —*n.* **1** very wise old man **2** green leaves used as seasoning **3** sagebrush

sage'brush' *n.* shrub of the western plains of the U.S.

Sag·it·tar'i·us (saj'-) *n.* ninth sign of the zodiac

sa'go (sā'-) *n.* (starch from) a palm tree

sa·hib (sä'ib', -ēb') *n.* title for a European, once used in India

said *v.* pt. & pp. of SAY —*a.* aforesaid

sail *n.* **1** canvas sheet to catch the wind and move a boat **2** boat trip —*v.* **1** move by means of sails **2** travel on water **3** glide —**set sail** begin a trip by water —**sail'boat'** *n.*

sail'board' *n.* board used in windsurfing

sail'cloth' *n.* canvas

sail'fish' *n.* ocean fish with a tall dorsal fin

sail'or *n.* **1** enlisted man in the navy **2** one who sails

saint *n.* holy person —**saint'li·ness** *n.* —**saint'ly** *a.*, **-li·er**, **-li·est**

saith (seth) *v.* [Ar.] says

sake *n.* **1** motive; cause **2** advantage

sa·ke (sä'kē) *n.* Japanese alcoholic beverage

sa·laam (sə läm') *n.* Muslim, Indian, etc. greeting of bowing low

sal'a·ble, sale'a·ble *a.* that can be sold

sa·la'cious (-lā'shəs) *a.* obscene

sal'ad *n.* mixture of vegetables, fruit, etc., with salad dressing

salad bar *n.* restaurant counter where customers assemble their own salad

salad dressing *n.* oil, vinegar, spices, etc. put on a salad

sal'a·man'der *n.* amphibian resembling a lizard

sa·la'mi *n.* spiced, salted sausage

sal'a·ry *n.*, *pl.* **-ries** fixed payment at regular intervals for work —**sal'a·ried** *a.*

sale *n.* **1** a selling **2** special selling of goods at reduced prices —**for sale** to be sold —**on sale** for sale at a reduced price

sales'clerk' *n.* one employed to sell goods in a store

sales'man *n.*, *pl.* **-men** man employed to sell goods or services —**sales'man·ship'** *n.* —**sales'wom·an** *n.fem.*, **-wom·en**

sales'per'son *n.* one employed to sell goods or services

sales slip *n.* bill of sale

sal'i·cyl'ic acid (-sil'-) *n.* pain-relieving compound, used as in aspirin

sa·lient (sāl'yənt) *a.* **1** prominent; conspicuous **2** projecting —**sa'lience** *n.*

sa'line (-lēn, -līn) *a.* salty

sa·li'va *n.* watery fluid secreted by glands in the mouth —**sal'i·var·y** *a.*

sal'low *a.* sickly yellow

sal'ly *n.*, *pl.* **-lies** **1** sudden rush forward **2** quip **3** short trip —*v.* **-lied**, **-ly·ing** start out briskly

salm'on (sam'-) *n.* large, edible ocean fish

sal'mo·nel'la (sal'mə-) *n.* bacillus causing food poisoning and typhoid

sa·lon' *n.* special room or shop

sa·loon' *n.* **1** public place where liquor is sold and drunk **2** large public room

sal'sa (säl'-) *n.* sauce made with chilies, tomatoes, etc.

salt *n.* **1** white substance found in the earth, sea water, etc., used to flavor food **2** a compound formed from an acid **3** [Inf.] sailor —*a.* containing salt —*v.* add salt to —**salt of the earth** finest or noblest person(s) —**salt'i·ness** *n.* —**salt'y** *a.*, **-i·er**, **-i·est**

salt'cel'lar *n.* **1** small dish for salt **2** saltshaker

salt·ine' (-ēn') *n.* flat, salted cracker

salt lick *n.* rock salt for animals to lick

salt'pe'ter *n.* niter

salt'shak'er *n.* salt container with holes on top

salt'wa'ter *a.* of salt water, or of the sea

sa·lu'bri·ous *a.* healthful

sal'u·tar'y (-yoo-) *a.* **1** healthful **2** beneficial

sal'u·ta'tion *n.* act or form of greeting

sa·lute' *n.* formal gesture, act, etc. expressing respect —*v.* to greet with a salute

sal'vage (-vij) *n.* **1** rescue of a ship, etc. from shipwreck **2** reclaimed property or goods —*v.* save from shipwreck, etc. —**sal'vage·a·ble** *a.*

sal·va'tion *n.* **1** a saving or being saved **2** one that saves **3** saving of the soul

salve (sav) *n.* soothing ointment —*v.* soothe

sal'ver *n.* tray

sal'vo *n.*, *pl.* **-vos** or **-voes** discharge of a number of guns together

sam'ba *n.* Brazilian dance, or music for it

same *a.* **1** being the very one **2** alike **3** unchanged **4** before-mentioned —*pron.* the same person or thing —*adv.* in like manner —**same'ness** *n.*

sam'o·var' *n.* metal urn to heat water

for tea

sam'pan' *n.* small Asian boat, propelled with a scull

sam'ple *n.* **1** part typical of a whole **2** example —*v.* take a sample of

sam'pler *n.* cloth embroidered with designs, mottoes, etc.

sam'u·rai' (-ə rī') *n.*, *pl.* **-rai'** member of a military class in feudal Japan

san'a·to'ri·um *n.* [Chiefly Br.] sanitarium

sanc'ti·fy' *v.* **-fied', -fy'ing** to make holy or free from sin —**sanc'ti·fi·ca'tion** *n.*

sanc'ti·mo'ni·ous *a.* pretending to be pious —**sanc'ti·mo'ny** *n.*

sanc'tion *n.* **1** authorization **2** approval **3** punitive measure against a nation: *often used in pl.* —*v.* **1** authorize **2** approve

sanc'ti·ty *n.* **1** holiness **2** sacredness

sanc'tu·ar·y (-chōo-) *n.*, *pl.* **-ies 1** holy place, as a church **2** place of refuge

sanc'tum *n.* sacred or private place

sand *n.* loose grains of disintegrated rock —*v.* to sandpaper —**sand'er** *n.*

san'dal *n.* open shoe with sole tied to the foot by straps

san'dal·wood' *n.* tree with sweet-smelling wood

sand'bag' *n.* sand-filled bag for ballast, etc. —*v.* **-bagged', -bag'ging 1** put sandbags around **2** [Inf.] force into doing something

sand'bar' *n.* ridge of sand along a shore: also **sand'bank'**

sand'blast' *v.* clean with a blast of air and sand

sand'box' *n.* box with sand, for children to play in

sand dollar *n.* disk-shaped sea animal

sand'hog' *n.* laborer in underground or underwater construction

sand'lot' *a.* of baseball played by amateurs

sand'man' *n.* mythical bringer of sleep to children

sand'pa'per *n.* paper coated with sand —*v.* to smooth with sandpaper

sand'pip'er *n.* shorebird with a long bill

sand'stone' *n.* kind of rock much used in building

sand'storm' *n.* windstorm with clouds of blown sand

sand'wich' *n.* slices of bread with meat, etc. between them —*v.* squeeze in between two others

sand'y *a.* **-i·er, -i·est 1** of or like sand **2** dull yellow

sane *a.* **1** mentally healthy **2** sensible

—**sane'ly** *adv.*

sang *v.* pt. of SING

sang-froid' (säɴ frwä') *n.* cool composure

san·gri'a *n.* punch made with red wine

san'gui·nar'y (-gwi-) *a.* **1** of or with bloodshed **2** bloodthirsty

san'guine (-gwin) *a.* **1** blood-red **2** cheerful or optimistic

san'i·tar'i·um *n.* institution for invalids or convalescents

san'i·tar·y *a.* **1** of health **2** clean and healthful —**san'i·tize'** *v.*

sanitary napkin *n.* absorbent pad worn during menstruation

san'i·ta'tion *n.* **1** hygienic conditions **2** sewage disposal

san'i·ty *n.* soundness of mind or judgment

sank *v.* pt. of SINK

sans *prep.* without

San'skrit' *n.* language of ancient India

San'ta Claus' *n.* *Folklore* fat, bearded man who brings gifts at Christmas

sap *n.* **1** juice of a plant **2** vigor **3** [Sl.] a fool —*v.* **1** undermine **2** weaken —**sap'py** *a.*, **-pi·er, -pi·est**

sa'pi·ent *a.* wise —**sa'pi·ence** *n.*

sap'ling *n.* young tree

sap·phire (saf'īr) *n.* deep-blue precious stone

sap'suck'er *n.* small woodpecker

sa·ran' *n.* plastic used in making wrapping material, fabrics, etc.

sar'casm *n.* taunting, ironic remark(s) —**sar·cas'tic** *a.*

sar·co'ma *n.*, *pl.* **-mas** or **-ma·ta** malignant tumor

sar·coph'a·gus (-käf'-) *n.*, *pl.* **-gi'** (-jī') or **-gus·es** stone coffin

sar·dine' (-dēn') *n.* small herring preserved in tightly packed cans

sar·don'ic *a.* bitterly sarcastic

sa·ri (sä'rē) *n.* long, draped outer garment of Hindu women

sa·rong' *n.* skirtlike garment of East Indies

sar'sa·pa·ril'la (sas'pə-) *n.* drink flavored with a root extract

sar·to'ri·al *a.* **1** of tailors **2** of (men's) clothing

SASE *abbrev.* self-addressed, stamped envelope

sash *n.* **1** band worn over the shoulder or around the waist **2** sliding frame for glass in a window

sass *v.*, *n.* [Inf.] (address with) impudent words

sas'sa·fras' *n.* tree whose root bark is used for flavoring

sass'y *a.* **-i·er, -i·est** [Inf.] impudent

sat v. pt. & pp. of SIT

Sat abbrev. Saturday

Sa'tan n. the Devil —**sa·tan'ic** a.

Sa'tan·ism' n. worship of Satan —**Sa'tan·ist** n.

satch'el n. small traveling bag

sate v. **1** satisfy fully **2** satiate

sa·teen' n. satinlike cotton cloth

sat'el·lite' n. **1** small planet revolving around a larger one **2** man-made object orbiting in space **3** small state dependent on a larger one

sa'ti·ate' (sā'shē-) v. give too much to, causing disgust —**sa·ti'e·ty** (sa tī'-) n.

sat'in n. smooth and glossy silk, nylon, or rayon cloth

sat'in·wood' n. tree yielding smooth wood used in fine furniture

sat'ire n. **1** use of ridicule, irony, etc. to attack vice or folly **2** literary work in which this is done —**sa·tir'i·cal** (-tir'-), **sa·tir'ic** a. —**sat'i·rist** n.

sat'i·rize' v. attack with satire

sat'is·fy' v. **-fied', -fy'ing 1** fulfill the needs and desires of **2** fulfill the requirements of **3** convince **4** pay in full —**sat'is·fac'tion** n. —**sat'is·fac'to·ry** a.

sa·to'ri (sä tôr'ē) n. Buddhism spiritual enlightenment

sa'trap (sā'-, sa'-) n. petty tyrant

sat'u·rate' (sach'-) v. **1** soak thoroughly **2** fill completely —**sat'u·rat'ed** a. —**sat'u·ra'tion** n.

Sat'ur·day' n. seventh day of the week

Sat'urn n. sixth planet from the sun

sat'ur·nine' a. gloomy

sa·tyr (sāt'ər) n. Gr. myth. woodland god with goat's legs

sauce n. **1** tasty, soft or liquid dressing for food **2** stewed fruit **3** flavored syrup

sauce'pan' n. metal cooking pot with a long handle

sau'cer n. shallow dish, esp. one for holding a cup

sau'cy a. **-ci·er, -ci·est 1** impudent **2** lively and bold —**sau'ci·ly** adv. —**sau'ci·ness** n.

sau·er·bra·ten (sou'ər brät'n) n. beef marinated before cooking

sau'er·kraut' (-krout'-) n. chopped, fermented cabbage

sau'na n. bath with exposure to hot, dry air

saun'ter v., n. stroll

sau'sage n. chopped, seasoned pork, etc., often stuffed into a casing

sau·té (sō tā') v. **-téed', -té'ing** fry quickly in a little fat

Sau·ternes (sō turn') n. a sweet white wine: also **Sau·terne'**

sav'age a. **1** fierce; untamed **2** primitive; barbarous —n. an uncivilized or brutal person —**sav'age·ly** adv. —**sav'age·ry** n.

sa·van'na, sa·van'nah n. treeless, grassy plain

sa·vant' (sa vänt') n. scholar

save v. **1** rescue; keep safe **2** keep or store for future use **3** avoid waste (of) —prep., con. except; but

sav'ing a. that saves —n. **1** reduction in time, cost, etc. **2** pl. money saved

sav'ior, sav'iour (-yər) n. **1** one who saves or rescues **2** [S-] Jesus Christ

sa·voir-faire (sav'wär fer') n. social poise; tact

sa'vor v., n. (have) a special taste, smell, or quality

sa'vor·y a. **-i·er, -i·est** tasting or smelling good

sav'vy [Inf.] n. shrewdness —a. shrewd

saw n. **1** thin, metal blade with sharp teeth, for cutting **2** proverb —v. **1** pt. of SEE **2** cut with a saw —**saw'yer** n.

saw'dust n. fine bits of wood formed in sawing wood

sawed'-off' a. short or shortened

saw'horse' n. rack to hold wood while sawing it: also **saw'buck'**

sax'o·phone' n. single-reed, metal wind instrument

say v. **said, say'ing 1** utter **2** state **3** estimate —n. **1** chance to speak **2** power to decide —**that is to say** that means

say'ing n. proverb

say'-so' n. [Inf.] **1** (one's) word, assurance, etc. **2** power to decide

SC abbrev. South Carolina

scab n. **1** crust over a healing sore **2** worker who takes the place of a striking worker —v. **scabbed, scab'bing** form a scab

scab'bard (-ərd) n. sheath for a sword, dagger, etc.

sca'bies (skā'-) n. itch caused by mites

scab'rous a. **1** scaly **2** indecent, shocking, etc.

scads pl.n. [Inf.] very large number or amount

scaf'fold n. **1** framework to hold workmen, painters, etc. **2** platform on which criminals are executed

scald (skôld) v. **1** burn with hot liquid or steam **2** heat almost to a boil —n. burn caused by scalding

scale n. **1** series of gradations or degrees **2** ratio of a map, etc. to the thing represented **3** any of the thin, hard plates on a fish, snake, etc. **4** flake **5** either pan of a balance **6** *often pl.* balance or weighing machine **7** *Mus.* series of consecutive tones — *v.* **1** climb up **2** set according to a scale **3** scrape scales from **4** flake off in scales —**scale back** scale down —**scale down** (or **up**) reduce (or increase) —**scal'y** *a.*, **-i·er, -i·est** —**scal'i·ness** *n.*

scal'lion (-yən) *n.* green onion

scal'lop *n.* **1** edible mollusk **2** any of the curves forming a fancy edge —*v.* **1** to edge in scallops **2** to bake with a milk sauce, etc.

scalp *n.* skin on top of the head —*v.* **1** cut the scalp from **2** [Inf.] sell (tickets, etc.) above the regular price —**scalp'er** *n.*

scal'pel *n.* sharp knife used in surgery, etc.

scam *n.* [Sl.] a trick or swindle

scamp *n.* rascal

scam'per *v.* run quickly —*n.* quick dash

scam'pi *n., pl.* **-pi** or **-pies** large, edible prawn

scan *v.* **scanned, scan'ning 1** look at quickly **2** examine **3** analyze the meter of (verse)

scan'dal *n.* **1** disgrace or thing that disgraces **2** gossip —**scan'dal·ous** *a.*

scan'dal·ize' *v.* outrage the moral feelings of

scan'dal·mon'ger (-muŋ'-, -mäŋ'-) *n.* one who spreads gossip

Scan'di·na'vi·an *n., a.* (person) of N Europe

scan'sion *n.* the scanning of poetry

scant *a.* not enough —**scant'y** *a.*, **-i·er, -i·est** —**scant'i·ly** *adv.* —**scant'i·ness** *n.*

scape'goat' *n.* one who is blamed for others' mistakes

scape'grace' *n.* rogue

scap'u·la *n.,* **-lae'** (-lē') or **-las** shoulder bone

scar *n.* mark left after a wound has healed —*v.* **scarred, scar'ring** to mark with or form a scar

scar'ab (skar'-) *n.* a beetle

scarce *a.* **1** not common **2** hard to get —*adv.* scarcely: a literary usage —**scarce'ness** *n.* —**scar'ci·ty** *n.*

scarce'ly *adv.* hardly

scare *v.* frighten —*n.* sudden fear — [Inf.] **scar'y** *a.*, **-i·er, -i·est**

scare'crow' *n.* human figure set up to scare away birds from crops

scarf *n., pl.* **scarves** or **scarfs** long or broad cloth piece for the neck, etc.

scar'i·fy' *v.* **-fied', -fy'ing 1** criticize sharply **2** loosen (topsoil)

scar'let *n.* bright red

scarlet fever *n.* contagious disease with fever and a rash

scat *int.* [Inf.] go away

scath'ing (skāth'-) *a.* harsh; bitter — **scath'ing·ly** *adv.*

scat·o·log'i·cal *a.* obscene

scat'ter *v.* **1** throw about **2** move in several directions

scat'ter·brain' *n.* one incapable of clear thinking —**scat'ter·brained'** *a.*

scatter rug *n.* small rug

scav'en·ger *n.* **1** one who collects refuse **2** animal that eats decaying matter —**scav'enge** *v.*

sce·nar'i·o' (sə nar'-, -när'-) *n., pl.* **-os'** **1** movie script **2** outline for proposed action

scene (sēn) *n.* **1** place; setting **2** view **3** division of a play, film, etc. **4** display of strong emotion

scen'er·y *n., pl.* **-ies 1** painted backdrops for a stage play **2** outdoor views

sce'nic *a.* **1** of scenery **2** picturesque

scent (sent) *v.* **1** to suspect **2** to perfume —*n.* **1** odor **2** perfume **3** sense of smell

scep'ter (sep'-) *n.* a staff as symbol of a ruler's power: also [Chiefly Br.] **scep'tre**

scep'tic (skep'-) *n.* chiefly Br. sp. of SKEPTIC

sched·ule (ske'jool) *n.* **1** timetable **2** timed plan **3** list of details —*v.* to place in a schedule

scheme (skēm) *n.* **1** plan; system **2** plot; intrigue **3** diagram —*v.* to plot —**sche·mat'ic** *a.* —**schem'er** *n.*

scher·zo (sker'tsō) *n., pl.* **-zos** or **-zi** (-tsē) lively musical movement in 3/4 time

schil'ling (shil'-) *n.* Austrian monetary unit

schism (siz'əm) *n.* split, esp. in a church, over doctrine —**schis·mat'ic** *a.*

schist (shist) *n.* glassy rock easily split into layers

schiz·o·phre'ni·a (skits'ə frē'-) *n.* severe mental illness —**schiz'o·phren'ic** (-fren'-) *a., n.*

schle·miel' (shlə mēl') *n.* [Sl.] bungling person who habitually fails

schlep, schlepp *v.* [Sl.] carry, haul, drag, etc.

schlock *a., n.* [Sl.] cheap or inferior (thing)

schmaltz *n.* [Sl.] very sentimental music, writing, etc.

schnapps (shnäps) *n., pl.* **schnapps** flavored gin

schnau′zer (shnou′-) *n.* small terrier

schol·ar (skä′lər) *n.* **1** learned person **2** student —**schol′ar·ly** *a.*

schol′ar·ship *n.* **1** academic knowledge; learning **2** money given to help a student

scho·las′tic *a.* of schools, students, teachers, etc.

school *n.* **1** place for teaching and learning **2** its students and teachers **3** education **4** group with the same beliefs **5** group of fish —*v.* train; teach —*a.* of, in, or for school — **school′mate′** *n.* —**school′teach′er** *n.*

school board *n.* group in charge of a local school or a system of schools

school′ing *n.* training or education

schoon′er *n.* ship with two or more masts

schwa (shwä) *n.* vowel sound in an unaccented syllable: symbol (ə)

sci·at′ic (sī-) *a.* of or in the hip or its nerves

sci·at′i·ca *n.* neuritis in the hip and thigh

sci′ence *n.* systematized knowledge or a branch of it —**sci·en·tif′ic** *a.* —**sci′en·tif′i·cal·ly** *adv.*

science fiction *n.* imaginative fiction involving scientific phenomena

sci′en·tist *n.* expert in science

sci′-fi′ *n.* [Inf.] science fiction

scim′i·tar (sim′-) *n.* curved sword

scin·til′la (sin-) *n.* tiny bit

scin′til·late′ *v.* **1** sparkle **2** be clever and witty —**scin′til·la′tion** *n.*

sci′on (sī′-) *n.* **1** a bud or shoot **2** descendant

scis′sors (siz′-) *n.* [*also pl. v.*] cutting tool with two opposing blades that move on a pivot

scle·ro′sis (skli-) *n.* a hardening of body tissues —**scle·rot′ic** *a.*

scoff *n.* scornful remark —*v.* mock or jeer (at)

scoff′law′ *n.* [Inf.] habitual violator of traffic laws, etc.

scold *v.* find fault with angrily —*n.* one who scolds

sconce *n.* wall bracket for candles

scone *n.* small tea cake

scooch (skōōch) *v.* **1** scrunch (*down,* etc.) **2** slide (*over*) in a series of jerks Also **scootch**

scoop *n.* **1** small, shovel-like utensil **2** bucket of a dredge, etc. **3** a scooping —*v.* **1** take up with a scoop **2** hollow out

scoot *v.* [Inf.] scurry off

scoot′er *n.* **1** child's two-wheeled vehicle **2** small motorcycle

scope *n.* **1** range of understanding, action, etc. **2** chance

-scope *suf.* instrument, etc. for seeing

scorch *v.* **1** burn slightly **2** parch —*n.* surface burn

score *n.* **1** points made in a game, etc. **2** grade on a test **3** piece of music showing all parts **4** scratch or mark **5** twenty **6** *pl.* very many **7** debt —*v.* **1** make a score or scores **2** evaluate **3** achieve **4** keep score **5** [Sl.] to get or steal —**scor′er** *n.*

score′board′ *n.* large board or screen posting scores, etc., as in a stadium

score′less *a.* having scored no points

scorn *n.* contempt; disdain —*v.* **1** treat with scorn **2** refuse —**scorn′ful** *a.* — **scorn′ful·ly** *adv.*

Scor·pi·o′ *n.* eighth sign of the zodiac

scor′pi·on *n.* arachnid with a poisonous sting

Scot *n.* native or inhabitant of Scotland

Scotch *n.* [*often* s-] whiskey made in Scotland —*a.* Scottish —*v.* [s-] put an end to

Scotch tape *n.* a thin, transparent adhesive tape

scot′-free′ *adv., a.* without being punished

Scot′tie, Scot′ty *n., pl.* **-ties** Scottish terrier

Scot′tish *a., n.* (of) the people or language of Scotland

Scottish terrier *n.* short-legged terrier with wiry hair

scoun′drel *n.* villain

scour *v.* **1** to clean by rubbing with abrasives **2** go through thoroughly, as in search or pursuit

scourge (skurj) *n., v.* **1** whip **2** torment; plague

scout *n., v.* (one sent ahead) to spy, search, etc.

scout′mas′ter *n.* adult leader of a troop of Boy Scouts

scow *n.* flat-bottomed boat

scowl *v., n.* (to have) an angry frown

scrag′gly *a.* **-gli·er, -gli·est** sparse, rough, jagged, etc.

scram *v.* scrammed, scram′ming [Sl.] get out

scram′ble *v.* **1** climb, crawl, etc. hurriedly **2** struggle for something **3** to mix; jumble **4** stir and cook (eggs) **5** make (signals) unclear —*n.* a scrambling

scrap *n.* **1** fragment **2** discarded material **3** *pl.* bits of food **4** [Inf.] a

fight —a. 1 in fragments 2 discarded
—v. scrapped, scrap'ping 1 discard 2
[Inf.] to fight —scrap'py a., -pi·er,
-pi·est

scrap'book' n. book in which to paste
pictures, etc.

scrape v. 1 rub smooth or rub away 2
scratch 3 gather bit by bit —n. 1 a
scratch or abrasion 2 harsh sound 3
predicament —scrap'er n.

scrap'heap' n. pile of discarded
material or things

scratch v. 1 cut the surface 2 scrape
or dig with one's nails 3 scrape
noisily 4 cross out —n. mark from
scratching —a. for hasty notes, etc. —
from scratch from nothing —
scratch'y a., -i·er, -i·est

scratch'pad' n. pad of paper for jotting
notes

scrawl v. write carelessly —n. poor
handwriting

scraw'ny a. -ni·er, -ni·est lean; thin

scream v., n. (make) a loud, shrill cry
or noise

screech v., n. (give) a harsh, high
shriek

screen n. 1 thing used to shield, conceal, etc. 2 wire mesh in a frame 3
surface for showing video images,
films, etc. —v. 1 conceal or shelter 2
sift or sift out

screen'play' n. script for a FILM (n. 3 &
4)

screw n. 1 nail-like fastener with a
spiral groove 2 propeller —v. 1 to
turn; twist 2 fasten, as with a screw
—screw up [Inf.] bungle

screw'ball' a., n. [Sl.] erratic or unconventional (person)

screw'driv'er n. tool for turning
screws

screw'y a. -i·er, -i·est [Sl.] 1 crazy 2
peculiar or eccentric

scrib'ble v. 1 write carelessly 2 draw
marks —n. scribbled writing

scribe n. writer; author

scrim'mage (-ij) n. practice game of
football, etc. —v. take part in a scrimmage

scrimp v. spend or use as little as possible

scrip n. certificate redeemable for
stocks, money, etc.

script n. 1 handwriting 2 copy of the
text of a play, film, TV show, etc.

scrip'ture n. 1 any sacred writing 2
[S-] often pl. sacred writings of the
Jews: Old Testament 3 [S-] often pl.
Christian Bible; Old and New Testa-
ments —scrip'tur·al a.

scrod n. young cod, haddock, etc.

scrof'u·la n. tuberculosis of the lym-
phatic glands

scroll n. 1 roll of paper, etc. with writing on it 2 coiled or spiral design

scro'tum n. skin pouch containing the
testicles

scrounge v. [Inf.] hunt around for and
take; pilfer

scrub v. scrubbed, scrub'bing rub
hard, as in washing —n. 1 a scrub-
bing 2 a growth of stunted trees or
bushes —a. 1 inferior 2 undersized
—scrub'by a., -bi·er, -bi·est

scruff n. back of the neck; nape

scruff'y a. -i·er, -i·est shabby or
unkempt

scrump'tious a. [Inf.] delicious

scrunch v. 1 crumple or crunch 2
huddle, squeeze, etc.

scru'ple n. a doubt as to what is right,
proper, etc. —v. hesitate from doubt

scru'pu·lous a. 1 showing or having
scruples 2 precise

scru'ti·nize' v. examine closely —scru'
ti·ny n.

scu'ba n. equipment, as an air tank,
for breathing underwater

scud v. scud'ded, scud'ding move
swiftly

scuff v. 1 scrape with the feet 2 wear
a rough place on —n. worn spot

scuf'fle n. rough, confused fight —v.
be in a scuffle

scull n. 1 large oar at the stern of a
boat 2 light rowboat for racing —v.
propel with a scull

scul'ler·y n., pl. -ies [Now Rare] room
for rough kitchen work

sculp'ture v. carve wood, stone, etc.
into statues, etc. —n. art of sculptur-
ing or work sculptured —sculp'tor n.
—sculp'tur·al a.

scum n. 1 surface impurities on a
liquid 2 [Inf.] vile person or people —
scum'my a., -mi·er, -mi·est

scup'per n. side opening for water to
run off a deck, building, roof, etc.

scurf n. scales shed by skin

scur'ri·lous a. vulgarly abusive —scur-
ril'i·ty n., pl. -ties

scur'ry v., n. -ried, -ry·ing scamper

scur'vy a. -vi·er, -vi·est low; mean —n.
disease due to vitamin C deficiency

scut'tle n. bucket for coal —v. -tled,
-tling 1 scamper 2 cut holes in (a
ship) to sink it 3 abandon (a plan,
etc.)

scut'tle·butt' n. [Inf.] rumor

scythe (sīth) n. long-bladed tool to cut
grass, etc.

SD *abbrev.* South Dakota

SE *abbrev.* southeast(ern)

sea *n.* **1** the ocean **2** a smaller body of salt water **3** large body of fresh water **4** heavy wave

sea anemone *n.* sea polyp with gelatinous body

sea bass *n.* edible ocean fish

sea′bed′ *n.* ocean floor

sea′bird′ *n.* bird that lives near the sea, as a gull

sea′board′ *n.* land along the sea: also **sea′coast′**

sea′far′ing (-fer′-) *a., n.* (of) sea travel or a sailor's work —**sea′far′er** *n.*

sea′food′ *n.* ocean fish or shellfish used as food

sea′go′ing *a.* **1** made for use on the open sea **2** seafaring

sea gull *n.* a gull (bird)

sea horse *n.* small fish with a head like that of a horse

seal *n.* **1** sea mammal with flippers **2** official design stamped on a letter, etc. **3** thing that seals —*v.* **1** certify as with a seal **2** close tight **3** settle finally

seal′ant *n.* substance, as wax, plastic, etc. used for sealing

sea level *n.* mean level of the sea's surface

sea lion *n.* seal of N Pacific

seam *n.* **1** line where two pieces are sewn or welded together **2** layer of ore or coal —*v.* join with a seam

sea′man *n., pl.* **-men** **1** sailor **2** navy enlisted man

seam′stress *n.* woman whose work is sewing

seam′y *a.* **-i·er, -i·est** unpleasant or sordid

sé·ance (sā′äns) *n.* spiritualists' meeting

sea′plane′ *n.* airplane which can land on water

sea′port′ *n.* a port for ocean ships

sear *a.* alt. sp. of SERE —*v.* **1** wither **2** burn the surface of

search *v.* look through or examine to find something —*n.* a searching

search′light′ *n.* **1** strong light **2** device to project it

search warrant *n.* writ authorizing a police search

sea′shell′ *n.* mollusk shell

sea′shore′ *n.* land along the sea

sea′sick′ness *n.* nausea caused by a ship's rolling —**sea′sick′** *a.*

sea′son *n.* **1** any of the four divisions of the year **2** special time —*v.* **1** to flavor **2** make more usable, as by

aging —**sea′son·al** *a.*

sea′son·a·ble *a.* timely

sea′son·ing *n.* flavoring for food

seat *n.* **1** place to sit **2** thing or part one sits on **3** right to sit as a member **4** chief location —*v.* **1** set on a seat **2** have seats for

seat belt *n.* strap across the hips to protect a seated passenger

sea urchin *n.* small sea animal with a spiny shell

sea′way′ *n.* inland waterway for ocean-going ships

sea′weed′ *n.* any sea plant(s)

sea′wor·thy *a.* fit for travel on the sea: said of a ship

se·ba′ceous (-shəs) *a.* of a gland secreting a greasy substance (**se′bum**)

seb′or·rhe′a, seb′or·rhoe′a (-rē′ə) *n.* oily skin condition

sec *abbrev.* **1** second(s) **2** secondary **3** secretary **4** section(s)

se·cede′ (-sēd′) *v.* withdraw formally from a group, etc. —**se·ces′sion** (-sesh′ən) *n.*

se·clude′ *v.* isolate —**se·clu′sion** *n.*

sec′ond *a.* **1** next after the first **2** another, like the first —*n.* **1** one that is second **2** thing not of the first quality **3** assistant **4** $\frac{1}{60}$ of a minute —*v.* support (a suggestion, motion, etc.) —*adv.* in the second place, etc. —**sec′ond·ly** *adv.*

sec′ond·ar·y *a.* **1** second in order **2** less important **3** derivative

secondary school *n.* high school

sec′ond-class′ *a.* **1** of the class, rank, etc. next below the highest **2** inferior

sec′ond-guess′ *v.* [Inf.] use hindsight in judging

sec′ond·hand′ *a.* **1** not from the original source **2** used before

second lieutenant *n. Mil.* commissioned officer of the lowest rank

second nature *n.* deeply fixed, acquired habit

sec′ond-rate′ *a.* inferior

sec′ond-string′ *a.* [Inf.] playing as a substitute at a specified position, as in sports

second thought *n.* change in thought after reconsidering

se′cret *a.* **1** kept from being known by others **2** hidden —*n.* secret fact, etc. —**se′cre·cy** *n.* —**se′cret·ly** *adv.*

sec′re·tar′i·at (-ter′-) *n.* staff headed by a secretary

sec′re·tar′y *n., pl.* **-ies** **1** one who keeps records, writes letters, etc. for a person or group **2** [*often* S-] head of a department of government **3** tall desk —**sec're·tar'i·al** a.

se·crete' v. 1 to hide 2 make (a body substance), as a gland —**se·cre'tion** n.

se'cre·tive a. not frank or open —**se'cre·tive·ly** adv.

sect n. group having the same beliefs, esp. in religion

sect abbrev. section(s)

sec·tar'i·an (-ter'-) a. 1 of or like a sect 2 narrow-minded

sec'tion n. distinct part —v. divide into sections —**sec'tion·al** a.

sec'tor n. 1 part of a circle like a pie slice 2 district for military operations

sec'u·lar a. not connected with church or religion

sec'u·lar·ize' v. to change from religious to civil control

se·cure' a. 1 free from danger, care, etc. 2 firm; stable 3 sure —v. 1 make secure 2 get —**se·cure'ly** adv.

se·cu'ri·ty n., pl. **-ties** 1 secure state or feeling 2 protection 3 thing given as a pledge of repayment, etc. 4 pl. stocks, bonds, etc.

secy, sec'y abbrev. secretary

se·dan' n. closed automobile with front and rear seats

se·date' a. quiet and dignified —v. make calm or sleepy —**se·date'ly** adv.

sed'a·tive (-tiv) a. making one calmer —n. sedative medicine —**se·da'tion** n.

sed'en·tar'y a. characterized by much sitting

Se·der (sā'dər) n. [also s-] feast on the eve of Passover

sedge n. coarse, grasslike plant of marshes

sed'i·ment n. matter that settles from a liquid —**sed'i·men'ta·ry** a.

se·di'tion (-dish'ən) n. stirring up a rebellion —**se·di'tious** a.

se·duce' v. 1 to lead astray 2 entice into sexual intercourse, esp. for the first time —**se·duc'er** n. —**se·duc'tion** n. —**se·duc'tive** a.

sed'u·lous (sej'-) a. diligent

see v. **saw, seen, see'ing** 1 look at 2 understand 3 find out 4 make sure 5 escort 6 meet; visit with 7 consult 8 have the power of sight —n. office or district of a bishop —**see to** attend to

seed n., pl. **seeds** or **seed** 1 the part of a plant from which a new one will grow 2 source 3 sperm —v. 1 plant with seeds 2 take the seeds from —**seed'less** a.

seed'ling n. young plant grown from a seed

seed money n. money to begin a project or attract more funds for it

seed'y a. **-i·er, -i·est** 1 full of seeds 2 shabby; untidy

see'ing con. considering

seek v. **sought, seek'ing** 1 search for 2 try to get

seem v. look, feel, etc. (to be)

seem'ing a. not actual —**seem'ing·ly** adv.

seem'ly a. **-li·er, -li·est** suitable, proper, etc.

seep v. leak through; ooze —**seep'age** n.

seer n. prophet

seer'suck'er n. crinkled fabric

see'saw' n. balanced plank ridden at the ends for swinging up and down —v. to move up and down or back and forth

seethe (sēth) v. boil

seg'ment (-mənt; v.: -ment) n. section —v. divide into segments

seg're·gate' v. set apart —**seg're·ga'tion** n.

seine (sān) n. fishing net

seis'mic (sīz'-) a. of an earthquake

seis'mo·graph' n. instrument to record earthquakes

seize (sēz) v. 1 take suddenly or by force 2 attack 3 capture

sei'zure n. 1 act or instance of seizing 2 sudden attack, esp. of epilepsy, etc.

sel'dom adv. rarely

se·lect' a. 1 chosen with care 2 exclusive —v. choose; pick out —**se·lec'tion** n. —**se·lec'tive** a. —**se·lec'tive·ly** adv.

selective service n. compulsory military training

se·lect'man n., pl. **-men** New England town official

self n., pl. **selves** one's own person, welfare, etc.

self- pref. of, by, in, to, or with oneself or itself: see list below

self'-ad·dressed'
self'-ap·point'ed
self'-crit'i·cism'
self'-de·ni'al
self'-de·scribed'
self'-de·struc'tive
self'-dis'ci·pline
self'-ed'u·cat'ed
self'-es·teem'
self'-ex·plan'a·to'ry
self'-ex·pres'sion
self'-in·dul'gence
self'-pit'y
self'-pres'er·va'tion
self'-pro·pelled'
self'-re·li'ance
self'-re·spect'
self'-sat'is·fied'

self´-sup·port´ing

self´-taught´

self´-ad·he´sive *a.* made to stick without moistening

self´-as·ser´tion *n.* a demanding to be recognized or of one's rights, etc.

self´-as·sur´ance *n.* self-confidence

self´-cen´tered *a.* selfish

self´-con´fi·dent *a.* sure of oneself — **self´-con´fi·dence** *n.*

self´-con´scious *a.* ill at ease

self´-con·tained´ *a.* 1 self-controlled 2 reserved 3 self-sufficient

self´-con´tra·dic´to·ry *a.* having elements that contradict each other

self´-con·trol´ *n.* control of one's emotions, actions, etc.

self´-de·fense´ *n.* defense of oneself or of one's rights, etc.

self´-de·struct´ *v.* 1 destroy itself automatically 2 greatly harm oneself

self´-de·ter´mi·na´tion *n.* 1 free will 2 right to choose one's government

self´-ef·fac´ing *a.* modest; retiring — **self´-ef·face´ment** *n.*

self´-em·ployed´ *a.* working for oneself, with direct control over work

self´-ev´i·dent *a.* evident without proof

self´-ful·fill´ing *a.* occurring because expected

self´-gov´ern·ment *n.* government of a group by its own members — **self´-gov´ern·ing** *a.*

self´-im´age *n.* one's idea of oneself, one's worth, etc.

self´-im·por´tance *n.* pompous conceit — **self´-im·por´tant** *a.*

self´-in´ter·est *n.* (selfish) interest in one's own welfare

self´ish *a.* caring too much about oneself — **self´ish·ly** *adv.* — **self´ish·ness** *n.*

self´less *a.* unselfish

self´-love´ *n.* excessive regard for oneself, one's own interests, etc.

self´-made´ *a.* successful, rich, etc. through one's own efforts

self´-pos·ses´sion *n.* full control over one's actions, etc. — **self´-pos·sessed´** *a.*

self´-re·crim´i·na´tion *n.* a blaming of oneself

self´-re·straint´ *n.* self-control — **self´-re·strained´** *a.*

self´-right´eous *a.* feeling more righteous than others

self´-sac´ri·fice´ *n.* sacrifice of oneself for another's benefit

self´same´ *a.* identical

self´-seek´ing *n., a.* (a) seeking to further one's own interests

self´-serv´ice *a., n.* (of) practice of serving oneself in a store, cafeteria, etc.

self´-serv´ing *a.* serving one's selfish interests

self´-styled´ *a.* so called by oneself

self´-suf·fi´cient *a.* independent — **self´-suf·fi´cien·cy** *n.*

self´-sus·tain´ing *a.* 1 supporting oneself 2 able to continue once begun

self´-willed´ *a.* stubborn

self´-wind´ing *a.* wound automatically, as some watches

sell *v.* **sold, sell´ing** 1 exchange for money 2 offer for sale 3 be sold (*for*) — **sell out** 1 sell completely 2 [Inf.] betray

sell´out´ *n.* [Inf.] show, game, etc. for which all seats have been sold

selt´zer *n.* carbonated water

sel´vage, sel´vedge (-vij) *n.* edge woven to prevent raveling

se·man´tics *n.* study of words — **se·man´tic** *a.*

sem´a·phore *n.* flags or lights for signaling

sem´blance *n.* outward show

se´men *n.* reproductive fluid of the male

se·mes´ter *n.* either of the terms in a school year

sem´i (-ī´) *n.* [Inf.] semitrailer and its attached TRACTOR (*n.* 2)

semi- *pref.* 1 half 2 partly 3 twice in some period (sem´i·an´nu·al, sem´i·month´ly, sem´i·week´ly)

sem´i·cir·cle *n.* half circle

sem´i·co´lon *n.* mark of punctuation (;)

sem´i·con·duc´tor *n.* substance, as silicon, used in transistors, etc. to control current flow

sem´i·fi´nal *n., a.* (contest) just before the finals

sem´i·nal *a.* primary or crucial

sem´i·nar´ (-när´) *n.* (course for) group of supervised students doing research

sem´i·nar´y (-ner´-) *n., pl.* **-ies** school to train ministers, etc.

Sem´i·nole´ *n.* member of Indian people now in Florida

sem´i·pre´cious *a.* less valuable than precious gems

sem´i·pri´vate *a.* of a hospital room with two, three, or sometimes four beds

sem´i·skilled´ *a.* of manual work requiring little training

Se·mit´ic *n.* language group including Hebrew — *a.* of these languages or those who speak them

sem'i·tone' *n. Mus.* half of a whole tone

sem'i·trail'er *n.* detachable trailer attached to a TRACTOR (*n.* 2)

sem·o·li·na (-lē'-) *n.* coarse flour from hard wheat

Sen *abbrev.* **1** Senate **2** Senator

sen'ate *n.* **1** lawmaking assembly **2** [S-] upper branch of Congress or a state legislature —**sen'a·tor** *n.* —**sen·a·to'ri·al** *a.*

send *v.* **sent, send'ing 1** cause to go or be carried **2** impel; drive —**send for** summon —**send'er** *n.*

send'-off' *n.* [Inf.] friendly farewell for someone leaving

se·nile' *a.* **1** of old age **2** weak in mind and body —**se·nil'i·ty** *n.*

sen'ior (-yər) *a.* **1** the older: written *Sr.* **2** of higher rank, etc. —*n.* high school or college student in the last year

senior citizen *n.* elderly person, esp. one retired

sen·ior'i·ty (-yôr'-) *n.* status gained by length of service

sen'na *n.* laxative derived from a cassia plant

se·ñor (se nyôr') *n.*, *pl.* **-ño'res** [Sp.] Mr.

se·ño'ra *n.* [Sp.] Mrs.

se·ño·ri'ta *n.* [Sp.] Miss

sen·sa'tion *n.* **1** sense impression or the power to receive it **2** exciting thing

sen·sa'tion·al *a.* exciting or shocking —**sen·sa'tion·al·ism** *n.*

sense *n.* **1** power to see, hear, taste, feel, etc. **2** sound judgment **3** meaning —*v.* perceive or understand —**in a sense** to some extent —**make sense** be intelligible

sense'less *a.* **1** unconscious **2** foolish or stupid

sen'si·bil'i·ty *n.*, *pl.* **-ties 1** power of feeling **2** *often pl.* delicate feelings

sen'si·ble *a.* **1** reasonable; wise **2** aware **3** noticeable —**sen'si·bly** *adv.*

sen'si·tive (-tiv') *a.* **1** quick to feel, notice, etc. **2** susceptible to stimuli **3** tender or sore **4** easily offended, irritated, etc. —**sen'si·tiv'i·ty** *n.*

sen'si·tize' *v.* make sensitive

sen'sor *n.* device for detecting heat, light, etc.

sen'so·ry *a.* of the senses

sen'su·al (-shōō-) *a.* of or enjoying the pleasures of the body —**sen'su·al·ly** *adv.* —**sen·su·al'i·ty** *n.*

sen'su·ous *a.* having to do with the senses

sent *v.* pt. & pp. of SEND

sen'tence *n.* **1** word(s) stating (asking, etc.) something **2** court decision **3** punishment —*v.* pronounce punishment on

sen·ten'tious *a.* **1** pithy **2** pompously boring

sen'tient (-shənt) *a.* conscious

sen'ti·ment *n.* **1** a feeling **2** opinion: *often used in pl.* **3** tender feelings **4** maudlin emotion —**sen'ti·men'tal** *a.* —**sen'ti·men'tal·ist** *n.* —**sen'ti·men·tal'i·ty** *n.* —**sen'ti·men'tal·ly** *adv.*

sen'ti·men'tal·ize' *v.* treat or think of in a sentimental way

sen'ti·nel *n.* guard; sentry

sen'try *n.*, *pl.* **-tries** guard posted to protect a group

se'pal *n.* leaflike part at the base of a flower

sep'a·rate' (-rāt', *a.*: -rət) *v.* **1** divide; set apart **2** keep apart **3** go apart —*a.* set apart; distinct —**sep'a·ra·ble** *a.* —**sep'a·rate·ly** *adv.* —**sep'a·ra'tion** *n.* —**sep'a·ra'tor** *n.*

sep'a·ra·tism' *n.* advocacy of separation, racially, politically, etc.

se'pi·a *n.*, *a.* reddish brown

sep'sis *n.* blood infection —**sep'tic** *a.*

Sept *abbrev.* September

Sep·tem'ber *n.* ninth month

sep·tet', sep·tette' *n.* group of seven, esp. of musical performers

sep'ti·ce'mi·a *n.* infection of the blood

septic tank *n.* tank into which house waste drains

sep'tu·a·ge·nar'i·an *n.*, *a.* (person) between 70 and 80 years old

sep'tum *n.*, *pl.* **-tums** or **-ta** *Biol.* partition, as in the nose

sep'ul·cher (-kər) *n.* tomb: also, Br. sp., **sep'ul·chre** —**se·pul'chral** *a.*

se'quel *n.* **1** result **2** book, etc. that continues an earlier one

se'quence *n.* **1** succession or the order of this **2** series **3** scene; episode

se·ques'ter *v.* separate; isolate —**se'ques·tra'tion** *n.*

se'quin *n.* small, shiny disk for decorating cloth

se·quoi'a (-kwoi'-) *n.* giant evergreen tree

se·rag'lio (-ral'yō) *n.*, *pl.* **-lios** HAREM (sense 1)

se·ra·pe (sə ra'pē) *n.* blanket worn over the shoulders

ser'aph (-əf) *n.*, *pl.* **-aphs** or **-a·phim'** angel of the highest rank —**se·raph'ic** *a.*

sere (sir) *a.* [Poet.] withered

ser·e·nade' *v., n.* (perform) music sung or played at night, esp. by a lover

ser·en·dip'i·ty *n.* the making of lucky discoveries by chance

se·rene' (-rēn') *a.* undisturbed; calm —**se·rene'ly** *adv.* —**se·ren'i·ty** (-ren'-) *n.*

serf *n.* feudal farmer, almost a slave —**serf'dom** *n.*

serge *n.* strong, twilled fabric

ser·geant (sär'jənt) *n.* 1 police officer ranking below captain or lieutenant 2 noncommissioned officer above a corporal, etc.

ser'geant-at-arms' *n., pl.* **ser'geants-at-arms'** one who keeps order, as in a court

se'ri·al (sir'ē-) *a.* of, in, or published in a series —*n.* serial story —**se'ri·al·i·za'tion** *n.* —**se'ri·al·ize'** *v.*

serial number *n.* one of a series of numbers given for identification

se'ries *n., pl.* **se'ries** number of similar things coming one after another

se'ri·ous *a.* 1 earnest 2 important 3 dangerous

ser'mon *n.* 1 religious speech by a clergyman 2 serious talk on duty, etc.

ser'pent *n.* snake

ser'pen·tine' (-tēn', -tīn') *a.* winding

ser'rate' *a.* edged like a saw: also **ser'rat·ed**

ser'ried (-ēd) *a.* placed close together

se·rum (sir'əm) *n., pl.* **-rums** or **-ra** (-ə) 1 clear, yellowish fluid in blood 2 antitoxin from the blood of an immune animal —**se'rous** *a.*

serv'ant *n.* one hired to perform household duties for another, by a government, etc.

serve *v.* 1 be a servant to 2 aid 3 do official service 4 spend a prison term 5 offer (food, etc.) to 6 be used by 7 deliver 8 hit a ball to start play —*n.* a hitting of a ball in tennis, etc. —**serv'er** *n.*

serv'ice *n.* 1 a serving 2 governmental work 3 armed forces 4 religious ceremony 5 set of silverware, etc. 6 aid —*v.* 1 supply 2 repair —**of service** helpful —**serv'ice·a·ble** *a.*

serv'ice·man' *n., pl.* **-men'** member of the armed forces

service mark *n.* mark used like a trademark by supplier of services

service station *n.* place selling gasoline, oil, etc.

ser'vile (-vəl, vīl') *a.* humbly submissive —**ser·vil'i·ty** *n.*

ser'vi·tude' *n.* slavery

ser'vo·mech'a·nism' *n.* automatic remote control system

ses'a·me' *n.* (a plant with) oily, edible seeds

ses'qui·cen·ten'ni·al (ses'kwi-') *n.* 150th anniversary

ses'sion *n.* meeting of a court, legislature, class, etc.

set *v.* **set, set'ting** 1 put; place 2 put in the proper condition, position, etc. 3 make or become firm or fixed 4 establish; fix 5 sit on eggs, as a hen 6 start 7 mount (gems) 8 furnish (an example) 9 sink below the horizon 10 fit (words) to music —*a.* 1 fixed 2 obstinate 3 ready —*n.* 1 way in which a thing is set 2 scenery for a play, film, etc. 3 group of like persons or things 4 assembled parts, as of a TV —**set about** (or **in** or **to**) begin —**set forth** state —**set off** 1 show by contrast 2 explode —**set on** (or **upon**) attack —**set up** 1 erect 2 establish

set'back' *n.* relapse

set·tee' *n.* small sofa

set'ter *n.* long-haired hunting dog

set'ting *n.* 1 that in which a thing is set 2 time, place, etc., as of a story 3 surroundings

set·tle *v.* 1 put in order 2 set in place firmly or comfortably 3 go to live in 4 deposit sediment, etc. 5 calm 6 decide 7 pay, as a debt 8 come to rest 9 sink —**set'tler** *n.*

set'tle·ment *n.* 1 a settling 2 a colonizing of new land 3 colony 4 village 5 an agreement 6 payment

set'-to' *n., pl.* **-tos'** [Inf.] fight or argument

set'up' *n.* details or makeup of organization, equipment, plan, etc.

sev'en *a., n.* one more than six —**sev'enth** *a., n.*

sev·en·teen' *a., n.* seven more than ten —**sev'en·teenth'** *a., n.*

sev'en·ty *a.; n., pl.* **-ties** seven times ten —**sev'en·ti·eth** *a., n.*

sev'er *v.* cut off; separate —**sev'er·ance** *n.*

sev'er·al *a.* 1 more than two but not many 2 separate —*n.* several persons or things —**sev'er·al·ly** *adv.*

se·vere' *a.* 1 harsh; strict 2 grave 3 very plain 4 intense —**se·vere'ly** *adv.* —**se·ver'i·ty** *n.*

sew (sō) *v.* **sewed, sewn** or **sewed, sew'ing** fasten, make, etc. by means of needle and thread —**sew'er** *n.* —**sew'ing** *n.*

sew'age (sōō'-) *n.* waste matter carried off by sewers

sew'er *n.* underground drain for water and waste matter

sex n. 1 either of the two divisions of organisms, male or female 2 character of being male or female 3 attraction between the sexes 4 sexual intercourse —**sex'u·al** a. —**sex'u·al·ly** adv.

sex'a·ge·nar'i·an n., a. (person) between 60 and 70 years old

sex'ism' n. unfair treatment of one sex by the other, esp. of women by men —**sex'ist** a.

sex'tant n. ship's instrument for navigation

sex·tet', sex·tette' n. group of six, esp. of musical performers

sex'ton n. official who maintains church property

sexual intercourse n. sexual union

sex'y a. **-i·er, -i·est** [Inf.] exciting sexual desire

sf, SF abbrev. science fiction

Sgt abbrev. Sergeant

shab'by a. **-bi·er, -bi·est** 1 worn out 2 clothed poorly 3 shameful —**shab'bi·ly** adv. —**shab'bi·ness** n.

shack n. shanty

shack'le n. metal fastening for a prisoner's wrist or ankle —v. 1 put shackles on 2 restrain

shad n. edible saltwater or freshwater fish

shade n. 1 partial darkness caused by cutting off light rays 2 device to cut off light 3 degree of darkness of a color 4 small difference —v. 1 to screen from light 2 change slightly 3 represent shade in (a painting, etc.) —**shad'y** a., **-i·er, -i·est**

shad'ing n. 1 a shielding against light 2 slight variation

shad'ow n. 1 shade cast by a body blocking light rays 2 sadness 3 small amount —v. follow in secret —**shad'ow·y** a.

shad'ow·box' v. spar with imaginary boxing opponent

shaft n. 1 arrow or spear, or its stem 2 long, slender part or thing 3 vertical opening 4 bar that transmits motion to a mechanical part

shag n. long nap on cloth

shag'gy a. **-gi·er, -gi·est** 1 having long, coarse hair 2 unkempt

shah (shä) n. title of former rulers of Iran

shake v. **shook, shak'en, shak'ing** 1 move quickly up and down, back and forth, etc. 2 tremble 3 weaken, disturb, upset, etc. 4 clasp (another's hand), as in greeting —n. a shaking —**shake off** get rid of —**shake up** 1

mix by shaking 2 jar 3 reorganize —**shak'y** a., **-i·er, -i·est**

shake'down' n. [Sl.] extortion of money

shak'er n. 1 device used in shaking 2 [S-] member of celibate religious sect

Shake·spear'e·an, Shake·spear'i·an a. of William Shakespeare's works

shake'-up' n. extensive reorganization

shak'o (shak'-) n., pl. **-os** high, stiff military dress hat

shale n. rock of hard clay

shall v. pt. **should** auxiliary verb showing: 1 future time 2 determination or obligation

shal·lot' n. onionlike plant

shal'low a. not deep

shallows pl.n. [often sing. v.] shoal

shalt v. [Ar.] used with thou

sham n., a. (something) false or fake —v. **shammed, sham'ming** pretend

sham'ble v. walk clumsily

sham'bles n. scene of great destruction

shame n. 1 guilt, embarrassment, etc. felt for a wrong act 2 dishonor 3 a misfortune —v. 1 make ashamed 2 dishonor 3 force by a sense of shame —**shame'ful** a. —**shame'ful·ly** adv.

shame'faced' a. ashamed

shame'less a. showing no shame or modesty —**shame'less·ly** adv.

sham·poo' v. wash (the hair, etc.) —n. a shampooing, or soap, etc. for this

sham'rock' n. plant, esp. a clover, with three leaflets

shang·hai' (-hī') v. **-haied', -hai'ing** to kidnap for service aboard ship

shank n. the leg, esp. between the knee and ankle

shan't contr. shall not

Shan'tung' n. fabric of silk, etc.

shan'ty n., pl. **-ties** small, shabby dwelling

shape n. 1 outer form 2 definite form 3 condition; state —v. form or adapt —**shape up** [Inf.] 1 come to definite form 2 behave as one should —**take shape** become definite —**shape'less** a.

shape'ly a. **-li·er, -li·est** having a full, rounded figure

shard n. broken piece

share n. 1 part each gets or has 2 equal part of stock in a corporation —v. 1 give in shares 2 have a share (in) 3 use in common with

share'crop' v. **-cropped', -crop'ping** work (land) for a share of the crop —**share'crop'per** n.

share'hold'er n. an owner of share(s) of corporation stock

shark *n.* a large, fierce fish

shark'skin *n.* smooth, silky cloth

sharp *a.* 1 having a fine point or cutting edge 2 abrupt 3 distinct 4 clever or shrewd 5 vigilant 6 harsh or intense 7 *Mus.* above the true pitch —*n. Mus.* a note one half step above another: symbol (♯) —*adv.* 1 in a sharp way 2 precisely —**sharp'en** *v.* —**sharp'en·er** *n.* —**sharp'ly** *adv.* —**sharp'ness** *n.*

sharp'er *n.* swindler; cheat

sharp'-eyed' *a.* having keen sight or perception

sharp'shoot'er *n.* good marksman

sharp'-tongued' *a.* sarcastic; highly critical

sharp'-wit'ted *a.* thinking quickly

shat'ter *v.* 1 break into pieces 2 damage badly —**shat'ter·proof** *a.*

shave *v.* **shaved, shaved** or **shav'en, shav'ing** 1 cut thin slices from 2 cut the hair or beard (of) to the skin —*n.* act of shaving —**close shave** [Inf.] narrow escape —**shav'er** *n.*

shav'ing *n.* 1 act of one who shaves 2 thin piece shaved off

shawl *n.* cloth covering for the head and shoulders

she *pron.* the female mentioned

s/he *pron.* she or he

sheaf *n., pl.* **sheaves** bundle of stalks, papers, etc.

shear *v.* **sheared, sheared** or **shorn, shear'ing** 1 cut or cut off as with shears 2 clip hair from

shears *pl.n.* large scissors

sheath (shēth) *n.* 1 case for a knife blade, etc. 2 any covering like this

sheathe (shēth) *v.* put into or cover with a sheath

she-bang' *n.* [Inf.] affair, thing, contrivance, etc.

shed *n.* small shelter or storage place —*v.* **shed, shed'ding** 1 make flow 2 radiate 3 throw or cast off

she'd *contr.* 1 she had 2 she would

sheen *n.* luster; gloss

sheep *n., pl.* **sheep** cud-chewing animal with heavy wool —**sheep'skin** *n.*

sheep'ish *a.* bashful or embarrassed

sheer *v.* to swerve —*a.* 1 very thin 2 absolute 3 very steep —*adv.* completely

sheet *n.* 1 large cloth of cotton, etc. used on beds 2 piece of paper 3 broad, thin piece of glass, etc.

sheet'ing *n.* cloth material for sheets

sheet music *n.* music printed on sheet(s) of paper

sheik, sheikh (shēk, shāk) *n.* Arab chief

shek'el *n.* ancient Hebrew coin

shelf *n., pl.* **shelves** 1 thin, flat board for holding things 2 ledge or reef

shelf life *n.* time a packaged product will stay fresh

shell *n.* 1 hard outer covering, as of an egg 2 narrow rowboat for racing 3 missile from a large gun 4 cartridge —*v.* 1 remove the shell from 2 bombard

she'll *contr.* 1 she will 2 she shall

shel·lac', shel·lack' *n.* thin varnish of resin and alcohol —*v.* **-lacked', -lack'ing** 1 put shellac on 2 [Sl.] to beat 3 [Sl.] defeat decisively

shell'fish' *n.* aquatic animal with a shell

shell shock *n.* anxiety, etc. resulting from combat

shel'ter *n.* something that covers or protects —*v.* give shelter to

shelve *v.* 1 put on a shelf 2 lay aside

shelv'ing *n.* 1 material for shelves 2 shelves

she·nan'i·gans *pl.n.* [Inf.] mischief; trickery

shep'herd (-ərd) *n.* 1 one who herds sheep 2 religious leader —*v.* be a shepherd —**shep'herd·ess** *n.fem.*

sher'bet *n.* frozen dessert of fruit juice, milk, etc.

sher'iff *n.* chief law officer of a county

sher'ry *n., pl.* **-ries** a strong wine

she's *contr.* 1 she is 2 she has

shib'bo·leth' *n.* password

shield *n.* 1 flat, wide armor carried in the hand or on the arm 2 thing that protects —*v.* protect

shift *v.* 1 move or change from one person, place, direction, etc. to another 2 get along —*n.* 1 a shifting 2 time at work 3 trick

shift'less *a.* lazy

shift'y *a.* **-i·er, -i·est** tricky; evasive

shill *n.* [Sl.] one who pretends to buy, bet, etc. to lure others

shil·le·lagh (shi lā'lē) *n.* Irish cudgel

shil'ling *n.* former British coin, $\frac{1}{20}$ of a pound

shil'ly-shal'ly *v.* **-lied, -ly·ing** hesitate

shim *n.* wedge for filling space

shim'mer *v., n.* (shine with) a wavering light

shim'my *n., v.* **-mied, -my·ing** shake or wobble

shin *n.* front of the leg between knee and ankle —*v.* **shinned, shin'ning** climb, as a rope, with hands and legs: also **shin'ny, -nied, -ny·ing**

shin'bone' *n.* tibia

shin'dig' n. [Inf.] informal party, dance, etc.

shine v. **shone** or (esp. for v. 3) **shined, shin'ing 1** be or make be bright **2** excel **3** make shiny by polishing —n. **1** brightness **2** polish

shin'gle n. **1** piece of wood, slate, etc. for roofing **2** [Inf.] small signboard —v. put shingles on (a roof)

shin'gles n. form of herpes infecting nerves, causing pain and blisters

shin'guard' n. padded guard for the shin, worn in sports

shin'splints' pl.n. [sing. or pl. v.] muscle strain of lower leg

Shin'to n. Japanese religion: also **Shin' to-ism'**

shin'y a. **-i-er, -i-est** bright; shining

ship n. **1** large water vehicle with an engine or sails **2** aircraft —v. **shipped, ship'ping 1** put or go in a ship **2** transport —**on shipboard** on a ship —**ship'load'** n. —**ship'ment** n. — **ship'per** n.

-ship suf. **1** state of **2** rank of **3** skill as

ship'mate' n. fellow sailor

ship'shape' a. neat; trim

ship'wreck' v., n. (cause) loss or ruin of a ship

ship'yard' n. place where ships are built and repaired

shire n. county in England

shirk v. to neglect (a duty) —**shirk'er** n.

shirr v. **1** pull stitches tight in rows **2** bake (eggs) with crumbs

shirt n. **1** garment for upper body **2** undershirt

shirt'waist' n. **1** [Ar.] woman's blouse tailored like a shirt **2** dress with shirtlike bodice

shish kebab n. small chunks of meat and vegetables broiled on a skewer

shiv'er v. **1** shake or tremble **2** shatter —n. **1** a trembling **2** sliver

shoal n. **1** school of fish **2** shallow place in water

shock n. **1** sudden blow or jar **2** sudden emotional upset **3** effect of electric current on the body **4** bundle of grain **5** thick mass of hair —v. **1** astonish; horrify **2** give an electric shock to

shock ab-sorb'er n. cushioning device on motor vehicle that absorbs bumps

shock'proof' a. able to stand shock without damage

shock therapy n. treatment of mental disorders, using electric current

shod'dy a. **-di-er, -di-est** inferior — **shod'di-ness** n.

shoe n. **1** outer covering for the foot **2** horseshoe **3** part of a brake that presses on the wheel —v. **shod, shoe' ing** put shoes on

shoe'horn' n. device to help slip a shoe on the foot

shoe'lace' n. LACE (n. 1)

shoe'string' n. **1** shoelace **2** small amount of capital

shoe tree n. form put in a shoe to hold shoe's shape

sho'gun' n. hereditary governor of Japan: absolute rulers until 1867

shone v. pt. & pp. of SHINE

shoo int. go away —v. to drive away abruptly

shoo'-in' n. [Inf.] one expected to win easily

shook v. pt. of SHAKE

shoot v. **shot, shoot'ing 1** send out, or move, with force, speed, etc. **2** send a bullet, etc. from **3** wound or kill with a bullet, etc. **4** to photograph **5** to score (a point, etc.) in sports **6** grow rapidly **7** to mark in spots, etc. (with color) —n. new growth; sprout — **shoot'er** n.

shooting star n. meteor

shop n. **1** place where things are sold **2** manufacturing place —v. **shopped, shop'ping** look at or buy goods in shops —**shop'per** n.

shop'lift'er n. one who steals from a store during shopping hours —**shop' lift** v.

shopping center n. complex of stores with common parking area

shop'talk' n. talk about work after hours

shore n. **1** land next to water **2** prop; support —v. prop (up)

shore'bird' n. bird living or feeding near the shore

short a. **1** not measuring much **2** not tall **3** brief **4** brusque **5** less than enough —n. **1** short movie **2** pl. short pants **3** short circuit —adv. abruptly or briefly —v. short-circuit —**in short** briefly —**short'en** v. —**short'ness** n.

short'age n. lack, deficit, etc.

short'cake' n. light biscuit or sweet cake

short'change' v. [Inf.] give less change than is due

short circuit n. side circuit of low resistance that disrupts an electric circuit —**short'-cir'cuit** v.

short'com'ing n. defect

short'cut' n. **1** shorter route **2** way of saving time, etc.

short'en·ing n. fat used to make

baked goods flaky

short'hand' n. system of symbols for writing fast

short'-hand'ed a. short of workers or helpers

short'horn' n. kind of cattle with short, curved horns

short'-lived' (-līvd', -livd') a. lasting only a short time

short'ly adv. 1 briefly 2 soon 3 curtly

short shrift n. little attention

short'sight'ed a. lacking in foresight

short'stop' n. Baseball infielder between second and third basemen

short subject n. short FILM (n. 3 & 4)

short'-tem'pered a. easily angered

short'-term' a. for a short time

short'wave' n. radio wave 60 meters or less in length

short'-wind'ed (-win'dəd) a. easily put out of breath

shot v. pt. & pp. of SHOOT —n. 1 act of shooting 2 range; scope 3 attempt 4 throw, etc., as of a ball 5 projectile(s) for a gun 6 marksman 7 photograph 8 dose or drink —a. worn out —**shot' gun'** n.

shot put n. track event in which a heavy metal ball is thrown

should (shood) v. pt. of SHALL: should is used to express obligation, probability, etc.

shoul'der (shōl'-) n. 1 part of the body to which an arm or foreleg is connected 2 edge of a road —v. 1 push with the shoulder 2 assume the burden of

shoulder harness n. strap across chest to protect a seated passenger

shout v., n. (utter) a loud, sudden cry or call

shove (shuv) v. 1 push along a surface 2 push roughly —n. a push

shov'el n. tool with a broad scoop and a handle —v. move or dig with a shovel —**shov'el·ful'** n.

show v. showed, shown or showed, show'ing 1 bring into sight; reveal 2 appear 3 be noticeable 4 guide 5 point out 6 prove; explain —n. 1 a display, performance, etc. 2 pompous display 3 pretense —**show off** make a display of, spec. of oneself —**show up** 1 expose 2 arrive

show'boat' n. boat with theater and actors who play river towns

show business n. theater, movies, TV, etc. as an industry: also [Inf.] **show' biz'**

show'case' n. glass case for things on display —v. to display to good advan-

tage

show'down' n. [Inf.] disclosure of facts to force a settlement

show'er n. 1 brief fall of rain 2 any sudden fall or flow 3 party with gifts for a bride, etc. 4 (bathing under) a fine water spray from an overhead nozzle —v. 1 to spray with water 2 give, or fall, abundantly 3 bathe under a SHOWER (n. 4) —**show'er·y** a.

show'man n., pl. -men one who produces shows skillfully —**show'man· ship'** n.

show'off' n. one who shows off

show'piece' n. a fine example

show'place' n. beautiful place (on display)

show'room' n. room for displaying merchandise for sale, etc.

show'time' n. time when a show starts

show'y a. -i·er, -i·est 1 of striking appearance 2 gaudy; flashy —**show'i· ly** adv. —**show'i·ness** n.

shpt abbrev. shipment

shrap'nel n. fragments of an exploded artillery shell

shred n. 1 torn strip 2 fragment —v. **shred'ded** or **shred, shred'ding** cut or tear into shreds

shrew n. 1 small, mouselike mammal 2 nagging woman —**shrew'ish** a.

shrewd a. clever or sharp in practical affairs —**shrewd'ly** adv. —**shrewd' ness** n.

shriek (shrēk) v., n. (utter) a loud, piercing cry

shrike n. shrill-voiced bird of prey

shrill a. high-pitched and piercing in sound —**shrill'ness** n. —**shril'ly** adv.

shrimp n. 1 small, long-tailed, edible shellfish 2 [Inf.] small person

shrine n. saint's tomb or other sacred place

shrink v. shrank or shrunk, shrunk or shrunk'en, shrink'ing 1 lessen in size; contract 2 draw back —**shrink' age** n.

shrink'-wrap' v., n. (to seal in) clear plastic wrapping

shriv'el v. dry up; wither

shroud n. 1 cloth used to wrap a corpse 2 cover; veil —v. hide; cover

shrub n. bush —**shrub'ber·y** n.

shrug v., n. shrugged, shrug'ging (draw up the shoulders in) a gesture of doubt, indifference, etc.

shtick n. [Sl.] 1 comic act 2 attention-getting device

shuck v., n. husk; shell

shud'der v. shake, as in horror —n. a

shuddering

shuf′fle v. **1** walk with feet dragging **2** mix or jumble together —n. a shuffling

shuf′fle·board′ n. game in which disks are pushed toward numbered squares

shun v. **shunned, shun′ning** keep away from

shunt v. **1** move to one side **2** switch or shift

shush int. be quiet —v. say "shush" to

shut v. **shut, shut′ting 1** close (a door, etc.) **2** prevent entrance to —a. closed —**shut down** cease operating —**shut off** prevent passage of or through —**shut out** prevent from scoring —**shut up 1** enclose **2** [Inf.] stop talking

shut′·eye′ n. [Sl.] sleep

shut′-in′ a. confined indoors by illness —n. invalid

shut′out′ n. game in which a team is kept from scoring

shut′ter n. **1** movable window cover **2** light-controlling device on a camera lens

shut′tle n. **1** device to carry thread back and forth in weaving **2** bus, airplane, etc. traveling back and forth regularly —v. move rapidly to and fro

shut′tle·cock′ n. feathered cork ball in badminton

shy a. **shy′er** or **shi′er, shy′est** or **shi′est 1** timid **2** bashful **3** distrustful **4** [Sl.] lacking —v. **shied, shy′ing 1** be startled **2** hesitate **3** fling sideways —**shy′ly** adv. —**shy′ness** n.

shy′ster (shī′-) n. [Sl.] dishonest lawyer

Si′a·mese′ twins n. pair of twins born joined

sib′i·lant a., n. hissing (sound) —**sib′i·lance** n.

sib′ling n. a brother or sister

sib′yl (-əl) n. prophetess of ancient Greece or Rome

sic v. **sicced** or **sicked, sic′cing** or **sick′ing** to urge to attack

sick a. **1** having disease; ill **2** nauseated **3** of or for sick people **4** disgusted **5** [Inf.] morbid —v. sic —**the sick** sick people —**sick′ness** n.

sick bay n. ship's hospital

sick′bed′ n. sick person's bed

sick′en v. make or become sick —**sick′en·ing** a.

sick′le n. curved blade with a short handle, for cutting tall grass

sick′ly a. **-li·er, -li·est 1** in poor health **2** faint or weak

side n. **1** right or left half **2** a bounding line **3** a surface **4** aspect **5** relative position **6** party; faction —a. **1** of, at, or to a side **2** secondary —**side with** support —**take sides** support one faction

side′arm′ a., adv. with the arm from the side, below the shoulder

side arm n. weapon worn at the side

side′bar′ n. short, accompanying news story

side′board′ n. dining-room cabinet for linen, etc.

side′burns′ pl.n. hair on the cheeks, beside the ears

side dish n. separate dish along with the main course of food

side effect n. incidental effect, as of a drug

side′kick′ n. [Sl.] **1** close friend **2** partner

side′light′ n. bit of incidental information

side′line′ n. **1** secondary line of merchandise, work, etc. **2** line marking the side of an athletic field, court, etc. —v. remove from active participation —**on the sidelines** not actively participating

side′long′ adv., a. to the side

si·de′re·al (-dir′ē-) a. of or measured by the stars

side′sad′dle adv., n. (on) a saddle so designed that the rider does not straddle the animal

side′show′ n. small show associated with a main show

side′split′ting a. very funny

side′step′ v. avoid as by stepping aside

side′swipe′ v. hit along the side in passing —n. such a glancing blow

side′track′ v. turn aside from a course, subject, etc.

side′walk′ n. path for pedestrians alongside a street

side′wall′ n. side of a tire

side′ways′ a., adv. **1** to or from one side **2** side first Also **side′wise′**

sid′ing (sīd′-) n. **1** outside boards, etc. on a building **2** short railroad track off the main track

si′dle v. move sideways cautiously

SIDS (sidz) abbrev. sudden infant death syndrome

siege (sēj) n. **1** encircling of a place to effect its capture **2** persistent attack

si·en′na (sē-) n. yellowish brown or reddish brown

si·er′ra (sē-) n. serrate mountain range

si·es′ta (sē-) n. brief rest or nap, esp. in the afternoon

sieve (siv) n. strainer with many small holes

sift v. 1 pass through a sieve, as to separate 2 examine with care

sigh (sī) v. 1 let out a deep breath, as in sorrow 2 long (for) —n. a sighing

sight n. 1 something seen 2 act or power of seeing 3 range of vision 4 aiming device —v. 1 to see 2 aim (a gun, etc.) —at (or on) **sight** as soon as seen —**sight′less** a.

sight′ed a. not blind

sight′ly a. **-li·er, -li·est** pleasing to look at

sight′see′ing n. the visiting of places of interest

sign n. 1 mark or symbol 2 meaningful gesture 3 signboard, road marker, etc. 4 trace; vestige —v. write one's name (on) —**sign off** stop broadcasting —**sign′er** n.

sig′nal n. 1 gesture, device, etc. to warn, order, etc. 2 radio wave —a. notable —v. make signals (to)

sig′nal·ize′ v. make noteworthy

sig′na·to′ry n., pl. **-ries** nation signing a pact, etc.

sig′na·ture n. one's name written by oneself

sign′board′ n. board bearing advertising

sig′net n. small official seal

sig·nif′i·cance n. 1 meaning 2 importance —**sig·nif′i·cant** a.

sig′ni·fy′ v. **-fied′, -fy′ing** 1 to mean 2 make known, as by a sign —**sig′ni·fi·ca′tion** n.

Sikh (sēk, sik) n. member of a religion of Asia

si′lage n. green fodder preserved in a silo

si′lence n. absence of sound —v. 1 make silent 2 repress —int. be silent

si′lent a. 1 not speaking 2 still; quiet 3 inactive —**si′lent·ly** adv.

sil′hou·ette′ (-ōō-) v., n. (make) a dark shape against a light background

sil′i·ca n. glassy mineral found in the form of quartz, etc.

sil′i·con′ n. chemical element forming silica, etc.

sil′i·cone′ n. silicon compound resistant to heat, water, etc.

sil′i·co′sis n. chronic lung disease from inhaling silica dust

silk n. thread or fabric of soft fiber made by silkworms —**silk′en** a. — **silk′y** a., **-i·er, -i·est**

silk′worm′ n. moth caterpillar that spins silk fiber

sill n. bottom of a door frame or window frame

sil′ly a. **-li·er, -li·est** foolish; absurd —

sil′li·ness n.

si′lo n., pl. **-los** tower for storing green fodder

silt n. fine particles of soil floating in or left by water —v. fill with silt

sil′ver n. 1 white, precious metal, a chemical element 2 silver coins 3 silverware 4 grayish white —a. of silver —v. cover as with silver —**sil′ver·y** a.

sil′ver·fish′ n. wingless insect found in damp places

silver lining n. hope or comfort in the midst of despair

sil′ver·smith′ n. one who makes things of silver

sil′ver·tongued′ a. eloquent

sil′ver·ware′ n. tableware of or plated with silver

sim′i·an n. ape or monkey

sim′i·lar a. nearly alike —**sim′i·lar′i·ty** n., pl. **-ties** —**sim′i·lar·ly** adv.

sim′i·le′ (-lē′) n. figure of speech using like or as

si·mil′i·tude′ n. likeness

sim′mer v., n. (keep or be at or near) a gentle boiling

si′mon-pure′ a. genuine

si′mo·ny (or sim′ə-) n. buying or selling of sacred things

sim·pa′ti·co (-pä′-) a. compatible or congenial

sim′per v. smile in a silly way —n. silly smile

sim′ple a. 1 having only one or a few parts 2 easy to do or understand 3 plain 4 natural 5 common 6 foolish —**sim·plic′i·ty** n., pl. **-ties**

simple interest n. interest computed on principal alone

sim′ple-mind′ed a. 1 naive 2 foolish 3 mentally retarded

sim′ple·ton n. fool

sim′pli·fy′ v. **-fied′, -fy′ing** make easier —**sim′pli·fi·ca′tion** n.

sim·plis′tic a. oversimplifying or oversimplified

sim′ply adv. 1 in a simple way 2 merely 3 completely

sim′u·late′ v. 1 pretend 2 create an imitation or model, as with a computer —**sim′u·la′tion** n.

si′mul·cast′ n., v. (a program) broadcast simultaneously over radio and TV

si′mul·ta′ne·ous a. done, etc. at the same time —**si′mul·ta′ne·ous·ly** adv.

sin n. offense against God, good morals, etc. —v. sinned, sin′ning commit a sin —**sin′ful** a. —**sin′ner** n.

since adv., prep. 1 from then until

now **2** at some time between then and now —*con.* **1** after the time that **2** because

sin·cere' (-sir') *a.* **1** without deceit **2** genuine —**sin·cere'ly** *adv.* —**sin·cer'i·ty** (-ser'-) *n.*

si'ne·cure' *n.* well-paid job with little work

si'ne qua non' (sī'nē, -nä) something indispensable

sin'ew (-yōō) *n.* **1** tendon **2** strength —**sin'ew·y** *a.*

sing *v.* **sang, sung, sing'ing 1** make musical sounds with the voice, etc. **2** perform by singing —*n.* [Inf.] group singing —**sing'er** *n.*

sing *abbrev.* singular

singe *v.* **singed, singe'ing** burn superficially —*n.* a singeing

sin'gle *a.* **1** one only **2** of or for one person or family **3** unmarried —*v.* select from others: with *out* —*n.* **1** single person or thing **2** *pl.* tennis game with one player on each side **3** *Baseball* hit on which the batter reaches first base —**sin'gle·ness** *n.*

single file *n.* column of persons one behind the other

sin'gle-hand'ed *a.* without help

sin'gle-mind'ed *a.* with only one purpose

sin'gly *adv.* **1** alone **2** one by one

sing'song' *a., n.* (having) a monotonous rise and fall of tone

sin'gu·lar *a.* **1** unique **2** separate **3** exceptional **4** unusual —*n. Gram.* word form designating only one —**sin'gu·lar'i·ty** *n.* —**sin'gu·lar·ly** *adv.*

sin'is·ter *a.* **1** ominous **2** evil

sink *v.* **sank** or **sunk, sunk, sink'ing 1** go or put beneath the surface of water, etc. **2** go down slowly **3** become lower **4** pass gradually (*into* sleep, etc.) **5** invest **6** defeat —*n.* basin with a drain pipe —**sink** in [Inf.] be understood fully

sink'er *n.* lead weight used on a fishing line

sinking fund *n.* fund built up to pay off a debt

sin'u·ous *a.* winding in and out

si'nus *n.* any air cavity in the skull opening into the nasal cavities

si'nus·i'tis *n.* inflammation of the sinuses

Sioux (sōō) *n., pl.* **Sioux;** *a.* (member) of a North American Indian people of the C plains

sip *v.* **sipped, sip'ping** drink a little at a time —*n.* a small amount sipped

si'phon *n.* tube for carrying liquid from one container to another below it —*v.* drain through a siphon

sir *n.* **1** polite title for a man **2** [S-] title for a knight or baronet

sire *n.* male parent —*v.* be the male parent of

si'ren *n.* **1** warning device with a wailing sound **2** a seductive woman

sir'loin' *n.* choice cut of beef from the loin

si·roc'co *n., pl.* **-cos** hot wind blowing from N Africa into S Europe

sir'up *n.* syrup —**sir'up·y** *a.*

sis *n.* [Inf.] sister

si'sal *n.* strong fiber used for making rope, etc.

sis'sy *n., pl.* **-sies** [Inf.] unmanly boy or man —**sis'si·fied'** *a.*

sis'ter *n.* **1** female related to one by having the same parents **2** female fellow member **3** [*often* S-] nun —**sis'ter·hood'** *n.* —**sis'ter·ly** *a.*

sis'ter-in-law' *n., pl.* **sis'ters-in-law' 1** sister of one's spouse **2** brother's wife

sit *v.* **sat, sit'ting 1** rest on one's buttocks or haunches **2** perch **3** be in session **4** pose, as for a portrait **5** be located **6** baby-sit —**sit down** take a seat —**sit in** take part —**sit out** take no part in —**sit'ter** *n.*

si·tar' (or si·tär') *n.* lutelike instrument of India

sit'com' *n.* TV comedy show

sit'-down' strike *n.* strike in which strikers refuse to leave their factory, etc.

site *n.* location; scene

sit'-in' *n.* demonstration in which those protesting against a policy refuse to leave a place

sit'ting *n.* **1** session, as of court **2** time of being seated

sitting duck *n.* [Inf.] easy target

sit'u·ate' (sich'ōō-) *v.* put or place; locate

sit'u·a'tion *n.* **1** location **2** condition **3** job

six *a., n.* one more than five —**sixth** *a., n.*

six'teen' *a., n.* six more than ten —**six' teenth'** *a., n.*

sixth sense *n.* intuitive power

six'ty *a., n., pl.* **-ties** six times ten —**six'ti·eth** *a., n.*

siz'a·ble, size'a·ble *a.* fairly large

size *n.* **1** dimensions **2** any of a series of measures, often numbered **3** pasty glaze: also **siz'ing** —*v.* **1** arrange by SIZE (*n.* 2) **2** apply SIZE (*n.* 3) —**size up** [Inf.] **1** to estimate **2** meet requirements

siz'zle v. to hiss when hot —n. such a sound

SK abbrev. Saskatchewan

skate n. **1** ice skate **2** roller skate **3** in-line skate —v. move along on skates

skate'board' n. short board on wheels, for gliding on sidewalks, etc.

skeet n. trapshooting from different angles

skein (skān) n. coil of yarn or thread

skel'e·ton n. framework, as of the bones of a body —**skel·e'tal** a.

skeleton key n. key used to open various locks

skep'tic n. one who questions matters generally accepted —**skep'ti·cal** a. —**skep'ti·cism'** n.

sketch n. **1** rough drawing or design **2** outline —v. make a sketch (of) —**sketch'y** a., -i·er, -i·est

skew (skyōō) v. distort

skew'er n. long pin to hold meat together as it cooks

ski (skē) n., pl. **skis** long, flat runner fastened to the shoe for gliding over snow —v. use skis —**ski'er** n.

skid n. **1** plank, log, etc. on which to support or slide something heavy **2** act of skidding —v. **skid'ded, skid' ding** slide sideways

skid row n. run-down section of a city where vagrants gather

skiff n. small, open boat

skill n. **1** great ability **2** art or craft involving use of the hands or body —**skilled** a. —**skill'ful, skil'ful** a.

skil'let n. frying pan

skim v. **skimmed, skim'ming 1** take floating matter from a liquid **2** read quickly **3** glide swiftly

skim milk n. milk with the cream removed

skimp v. [Inf.] scrimp

skimp'y a. -i·er, -i·est [Inf.] barely enough; scanty

skin n. **1** tissue covering the body **2** pelt **3** covering like skin, as fruit rind —v. **skinned, skin'ning** remove the skin from

skin diving n. underwater swimming with special equipment —**skin'-dive'** v.

skin'flint' n. miser

skin'ny a. -ni·er, -ni·est very thin —**skin'ni·ness** n.

skin'ny-dip' n., v. -**dipped'**, -**dip'ping** [Inf.] swim in the nude

skip v. **skipped, skip'ping 1** move by hopping on alternate feet **2** leap lightly (over) **3** bounce **4** omit —n. act of skipping

skip'per n. ship's captain

skir'mish v., n. (take part in) a small, brief battle

skirt n. **1** part of a dress, coat, etc. below the waist **2** woman's garment that hangs from the waist —v. go along the edge of

skit n. short, funny play

skit'tish a. **1** lively; playful **2** very nervous

skiv'vies pl.n. [Sl.] men's underwear

skul·dug'ger·y, skull·dug'ger·y n. [Inf.] mean trickery

skulk v. to move or lurk in a stealthy way

skull n. bony framework of the head

skunk n. small mammal that ejects a smelly liquid when frightened, etc.

sky n., pl. **skies** often pl. upper atmosphere or space around the earth

sky'box' n. stadium loge

sky'cap' n. porter at an air terminal

sky diving n. parachute jumping

sky'jack' v. hijack (an aircraft)

sky'lark' n. lark of Europe and Asia, famous for its song

sky'light' n. window in a roof or ceiling

sky'line' n. outline of a city, etc. seen against the sky

sky'rock'et n. fireworks rocket —v. rise fast

sky'scrap'er n. very tall building

sky'ward a., adv. toward the sky: also **sky'wards** adv.

slab n. flat, thick piece

slack a. **1** loose **2** not busy **3** slow; sluggish —n. slack part —**cut some- one some slack** [Sl.] demand less of someone — **slack off (or up)** slacken

slack'en v. **1** slow down **2** loosen

slack'er n. one who shirks

slacks pl.n. trousers

slag n. refuse from smelting

slain v. pp. of SLAY

slake v. **1** satisfy (thirst) **2** mix (lime) with water

sla'lom (slä'-) n. downhill ski race over a zigzag course

slam v. **slammed, slam'ming** shut, hit, etc. with force —n. heavy impact

slan'der n. spoken falsehood harmful to another —v. speak slander against —**slan'der·ous** a.

slang n. vigorous, short-lived, informal language

slant v., n. **1** incline; slope **2** (show) a special attitude or bias

slap n. a blow with something flat —v. **slapped, slap'ping** strike with a slap

slap'dash' *a., adv.* hurried(ly) or careless(ly)

slap'-hap'py *a.* [Sl.] **1** dazed or silly or giddy

slap'stick' *n.* crude comedy

slash *v.* **1** cut at with a knife **2** cut slits in **3** reduce —*n.* a slashing; cut

slat *n.* narrow strip of wood, etc.

slate *n.* **1** bluish-gray rock in thin layers **2** tile, etc. of slate **3** list of candidates —*v.* designate

slat'tern *n.* untidy woman —**slat'tern·ly** *a., adv.*

slaugh'ter (slô'-) *v.* **1** kill (animals) for food **2** kill (people) brutally —*n.* a slaughtering

slaugh'ter·house' *n.* place for butchering animals

slave *n.* human being owned by another —*v.* to toil —**slav'ish** *a.*

slave driver *n.* merciless taskmaster

slav'er (slav'-) *v.* drool

slav'er·y *n.* **1** condition of slaves **2** ownership of slaves **3** drudgery

Slav'ic (släv'-) *a.* of the Russians, Poles, Slovaks, etc.

slaw *n.* coleslaw

slay *v.* **slew, slain, slay'ing** kill by violent means —**slay'er** *n.*

sleaze *n.* [Sl.] **1** sleaziness **2** something or someone sleazy

slea'zy *a.* **-zi·er, -zi·est** shabby, shoddy, morally low, etc. —**slea'zi·ness** *n.*

sled *n.* vehicle with runners, used on snow —*v.* **sled'ded, sled'ding** ride a sled

sledge *n.* **1** sledgehammer **2** heavy sled

sledge'ham'mer *n.* long, heavy hammer

sleek *a.* smooth and shiny —*v.* make sleek

sleep *n.* natural regular rest, as at night —*v.* **slept, sleep'ing** to be in a state of sleep —**sleep'less** *a.*

sleep'er *n.* **1** one who sleeps **2** railway car with berths

sleeping bag *n.* warmly lined bag for sleeping outdoors

sleep'y *a.* **-i·er, -i·est 1** drowsy **2** dull; quiet

sleet *n.* partly frozen rain —*v.* fall as sleet

sleeve *n.* **1** part of a garment covering the arm **2** protective cover —**sleeve'less** *a.*

sleigh (slā) *n.* horse-drawn vehicle on runners

sleight of hand (slīt) *n.* **1** skill in doing tricks with the hands **2** such tricks

slen'der *a.* **1** long and thin **2** small in size or force

slen'der·ize' *v.* make or become slender

slept *v.* pt. & pp. of SLEEP

sleuth (slooth) *n.* detective

slew *v.* pt. of SLAY —*n.* [Inf.] large number or amount

slice *n.* **1** thin, broad piece cut off **2** share —*v.* cut into slices or as a slice —**slic'er** *n.*

slick *v.* make smooth —*a.* **1** smooth **2** slippery **3** [Inf.] clever —*n.* smooth area, as of oil on water

slick'er *n.* loose, waterproof coat

slide *v.* **slid, slid'ing 1** move along a smooth surface **2** glide **3** slip —*n.* **1** a sliding **2** inclined surface to slide on **3** picture for projection on a screen —**let slide** fail to take proper action

slide fastener *n.* fastener with interlocking tabs worked by a sliding part

slid'er *n. Baseball* fast pitch that curves

slide rule *n.* device for calculating that looks like a ruler

sliding scale *n.* schedule of costs, etc. that varies with given conditions

slight *a.* **1** slender **2** unimportant **3** small or weak —*v., n.* neglect or snub —**slight'ly** *adv.*

slim *a.* **slim'mer, slim'mest 1** long and thin **2** small —*v.* **slimmed, slim'ming** make or become slim

slime *n.* soft, wet, sticky matter —**slim'y** *a.*, **-i·er, -i·est**

sling *n.* **1** device for hurling stones **2** looped band or piece of cloth for raising or supporting —*v.* **slung, sling'ing** throw; hurl

sling'shot' *n.* Y-shaped device with elastic band for shooting stones, etc.

slink *v.* **slunk, slink'ing** move in a sneaking way

slink'y *a.* **-i·er, -i·est** [Sl.] **1** furtive **2** sinuous and graceful

slip *v.* **slipped, slip'ping 1** go quietly **2** put or pass smoothly or quickly **3** slide accidentally **4** escape from **5** become worse **6** err —*n.* **1** DOCK (*n.* 2) for ships **2** woman's long, sleeveless undergarment **3** a falling down **4** error: also [Inf.] **slip'-up' 5** plant stem or root, for planting, etc. **6** small piece of paper

slip'knot' *n.* knot that can slip along a rope

slip'page (-ij) *n.* a slipping

slipped disk *n.* ruptured disk between

vertebrae

slip'per *n.* light, low shoe

slip'per·y *a.* **-i·er, -i·est** 1 that can cause slipping 2 tending to slip 3 tricky

slip'shod' *a.* careless

slit *v.* **slit, slit'ting** cut or split open — *n.* a straight, narrow opening

slith'er (slith'-) *v.* slide or glide along

sliv'er *n.* thin, pointed piece cut or split off

slob *n.* [Inf.] sloppy or coarse person

slob'ber *v., n.* drool

sloe *n.* dark-blue fruit

slog *v.* **slogged, slog'ging** plod

slo'gan *n.* motto or phrase, as for advertising purposes

sloop *n.* boat with one mast

slop *n.* 1 spilled liquid 2 slush 3 watery food 4 *often pl.* liquid waste —*v.* slopped, slop'ping splash

slope *n.* 1 rising or falling surface, line, etc. 2 amount of such rise or fall —*v.* have a slope

slop'py *a.* **-pi·er, -pi·est** 1 slushy 2 careless

slosh *v.* to splash

slot *n.* narrow opening

sloth (slôth) *n.* 1 laziness 2 South American mammal living in trees — **sloth'ful** *a.*

slouch *n.* 1 [Inf.] incompetent person 2 drooping posture —*v.* have a drooping posture

slough (sluf; *n.:* sloō) *v.* to shed; discard —*n.* swamp

slov'en (sluv'-) *n.* slovenly person

slov'en·ly *a.* careless or untidy

slow *a.* 1 taking longer than usual 2 low in speed 3 behind the right time 4 stupid 5 sluggish —*v.* make or become slow —*adv.* in a slow way— **slow'ly** *adv.* —**slow'ness** *n.*

slow'-mo'tion *a.* of a film or video showing action slowed down

slow'poke' *n.* [Sl.] one who acts slowly

slow'-wit'ted *a.* mentally slow; dull

sludge *n.* 1 mud or mire 2 slimy waste

slue *n., v.* turn or swerve

slug *n.* 1 small mollusk 2 bullet 3 false coin —*v.* slugged, slug'ging [Inf.] hit hard —**slug'ger** *n.*

slug'gard *n.* lazy person

slug'gish *a.* slow-moving

sluice (sloōs) *n.* water channel or a gate to control it

slum *n.* populous area with very poor living conditions

slum'ber *v., n.* sleep

slump *v.* 1 sink or decline suddenly 2

to slouch —*n.* sudden decline, etc.

slur *v.* slurred, slur'ring 1 pronounce indistinctly 2 insult —*n.* 1 a slurring 2 insult

slurp [Sl.] *v.* drink or eat noisily —*n.* loud sipping or sucking sound

slush *n.* partly melted snow —**slush'y** *a.*

slut *n.* promiscuous woman

sly *a.* **sli'er** or **sly'er, sli'est** or **sly'est** 1 cunning; crafty 2 playfully mischievous —**on the sly** secretly —**sly'ly** *adv.*

smack *n.* 1 slight taste 2 sharp noise made by parting the lips suddenly 3 sharp slap 4 loud kiss 5 fishing boat —*v.* 1 have a trace 2 make a smack with one's lips 3 slap loudly —*adv.* directly

small *a.* 1 little in size, extent, etc. 2 trivial 3 mean; petty —*n.* small part —**small'ish** *a.*

small arms *pl.n.* guns of small caliber, as pistols or rifles

small'pox' *n.* contagious viral disease with fever and sores

small talk *n.* light, informal conversation

small'-time' *a.* [Inf.] minor; petty

smarm'y *a.* [Brit. Inf.] praising in an unctuous way

smart *v.* 1 cause or feel stinging pain 2 suffer —*a.* 1 that smarts 2 brisk; lively 3 bright; clever 4 neat 5 stylish 6 *Comput.* programmed in advance —**smart'ly** *adv.*

smart' al'eck, smart' al'ec *n.* [Inf.] conceited, insolent person

smart bomb *n.* [Sl.] bomb guided to a target electronically

smart'en *v.* make or become smarter

smash *v.* 1 break or hit violently 2 crash 3 to destroy —*n.* a smashing

smash'up' *n.* very damaging collision

smat'ter·ing *n.* 1 slight knowledge 2 small number or amount

smear *v.* 1 make greasy, dirty, etc. 2 spread 3 slander —*n.* a smearing

smell *v.* smelled or [Chiefly Br.] smelt, smell'ing 1 catch the odor of 2 sniff 3 have an odor —*n.* 1 power to smell 2 thing smelled; odor

smell'y *a.* **-i·er, -i·est** having a bad smell

smelt *n.* small, silvery food fish —*v.* melt (ore or metal) so as to remove the impurities —**smelt'er** *n.*

smidg'en *n.* [Inf.] tiny amount: also **smidge**

smile *v.* 1 to show pleasure, amusement, etc. by curving the corners of

305smirch / snore

the mouth upward **2** regard with
approval: with *on* or *upon* —*n.* act of
smiling

smirch *v., n.* smear

smirk *v.* to smile in a conceited or
annoyingly complacent way —*n.* such
a smile

smite *v.* **smote, smit′ten, smit′ing 1**
hit or strike hard **2** affect strongly

smith *n.* one who makes or repairs
metal objects

smith′er·eens′ *pl.n.* [Inf.] bits; fragments

smith′y *n., pl.* **-ies** blacksmith's shop

smock *n.* loose, protective outer garment

smog *n.* fog and smoke —**smog′gy** *a.,*
-gi·er, -gi·est

smoke *n.* vaporous matter rising from
something burning —*v.* **1** give off
smoke **2** use cigarettes, a pipe, etc. **3**
cure (meats, etc.) with smoke —
smoke′less *a.* —**smok′er** *n.* —**smok′y**
a., **-i·er, -i·est**

smoke′house′ *n.* building for smoking
meats, etc.

smoke screen *n.* something intended
to conceal or mislead

smoke′stack′ *n.* tall chimney

smol′der *v.* **1** burn without flame **2**
exist in a suppressed state Br. sp.
smoul′der

smooch *n., v.* [Sl.] kiss

smoosh (smoosh) *v.* [Inf.] smush

smooth *a.* **1** having no roughness or
bumps; even **2** with no trouble **3**
ingratiating —*v.* to make smooth —
adv. in a smooth way —**smooth′ness**
n.

smor′gas·bord′ (-gəs-) *n.* variety of
tasty foods served buffet style

smoth′er (smuth′-) *v.* **1** suffocate **2**
cover thickly

smudge *n.* **1** dirty spot **2** fire with
dense smoke —*v.* to smear —**smudg′y**
a.

smug *a.* **smug′ger, smug′gest** too self-
satisfied —**smug′ly** *adv.*

smug′gle *v.* bring in or take out
secretly or illegally —**smug′gler** *n.*

smush (smoosh) *v.* [Inf.] to press,
smash, etc.

smut *n.* **1** sooty matter **2** obscene
matter **3** plant disease —**smut′ty** *a.,*
-ti·er, -ti·est

snack *v., n.* (eat) a light meal

snag *n.* **1** sharp projection **2** tear
made by this **3** hidden difficulty —*v.*
snagged, snag′ging 1 tear on a snag
2 hinder

snail *n.* mollusk with a spiral shell

snake *n.* long, legless reptile —*v.* move
like a snake —**snak′y** *a.,* **-i·er, -i·est**

snap *v.* **snapped, snap′ping 1** bite or
grasp suddenly **2** shout (*at*) **3** break
suddenly **4** make a cracking sound —
n. **1** sharp sound **2** fastening that
clicks shut **3** [Sl.] easy job —*a.* impulsive —**snap′per** *n.* —**snap′pish** *a.*

snap′drag′on *n.* plant with showy,
saclike flowers

snap′py *a.* **-pi·er, -pi·est** [Inf.] **1**
lively; brisk **2** stylish; smart

snap′shot′ *n.* informal picture taken
with a small camera

snare *n.* **1** trap for small animals **2**
dangerous lure —*v.* to trap

snarl *v.* **1** growl, baring the teeth **2**
speak sharply **3** tangle —*n.* **1** a
snarling **2** tangle; disorder

snatch *v.* seize; grab —*n.* **1** a grab **2**
brief time **3** fragment

sneak *v.* move, do, etc. secretly —*n.*
one who sneaks —**sneak′y** *a.,* **-i·er, -i·**
est

sneak′er *n.* canvas shoe with a rubber
sole

sneer *v.* show scorn —*n.* sneering look
or remark

sneeze *v.* expel breath from the nose
and mouth in a sudden, uncontrolled
way —*n.* act of sneezing

snick′er *v., n.* (give) a silly, partly sti-
fled laugh

snide *a.* slyly malicious

sniff *v.* inhale forcibly through the
nose, as in smelling —*n.* act of snif-
fing

snif′fle *v., n.* sniff to check mucus flow
—**the sniffles** [Inf.] a head cold

snif′ter *n.* goblet with a small opening,
as for brandy

snig′ger *v., n.* snicker

snip *v.* **snipped, snip′ping** cut in a
quick stroke —*n.* small piece cut off

snipe *n.* wading bird —*v.* shoot at from
a hidden place —**snip′er** *n.*

snip′pet *n.* small piece; bit

snip′py *a.* **-pi·er, -pi·est** [Inf.] inso-
lently curt

snitch [Sl.] *v.* inform; tattle (*on*) —*n.*
informer; tattler

sniv′el *v.* **1** cry and sniffle **2** whine

snob *n.* one who disdains supposed
inferiors —**snob′bish** *a.* —**snob′ber·y**
n.

snood *n.* kind of hair net

snoop [Inf.] *v.* pry in a sneaky way —
n. one who snoops: also **snoop′er**

snoot′y *a.* **-i·er, -i·est** [Inf.] snobbish

snooze *v., n.* [Inf.] (take) a nap

snore *v.* breathe noisily while asleep

—*n.* a snoring

snor'kel *v., n.* (use) a breathing tube for swimming underwater

snort *v.* force breath audibly from the nose —*n.* a snoring

snot *n.* [Sl.] 1 nasal mucus 2 insolent person —**snot'ty** *a.*, **-ti-er, -ti-est**

snout *n.* projecting nose and jaws of an animal

snow *n.* flakes of frozen water vapor that fall from the sky —*v.* 1 fall as snow 2 cover with snow 3 [Sl.] mislead with glib talk —**snow under** overwhelm —**snow'y** *a.*, **-i-er, -i-est**

snow'ball' *n.* mass of snow squeezed into a ball —*v.* increase rapidly

snow'board' *n.* board like a surfboard, for sliding on snow

snow'bound' *a.* confined by snow

snow'drift' *n.* pile of snow heaped up by the wind

snow'fall' *n.* fall of snow or the amount of this

snow'flake' *n.* single snow crystal

snow'man' *n., pl.* **-men'** crude human figure made of compressed snow

snow'mo-bile' *n.* motor vehicle for snow travel, with runners and tractor treads

snow'plow' *n.* machine for removing snow

snow'shoe' *n.* racketlike footgear for walking on snow

snow'storm' *n.* storm with a heavy snowfall

snow'suit' *n.* child's lined garment, often with a hood

snow tire *n.* tire with a deep tread for added traction

snub *v.* **snubbed, snub'bing** treat with scorn —*n.* a slight —*a.* short and turned up, as a nose

snuff *v.* put out (a candle, etc.) —*n.* powdered tobacco —**up to snuff** [Inf.] up to the usual standard

snug *a.* **snug'ger, snug'gest** 1 cozy 2 compact 3 tight in fit

snug'gle *v.* cuddle; nestle

so *adv.* 1 in such a way 2 to such a degree 3 very 4 therefore 5 more or less 6 also 7 [Inf.] very much —*con.* 1 in order (*that*) 2 with the result (*that*) —*int.* word showing surprise —**and so on** (or **forth**) and the rest

soak *v.* 1 make wet 2 stay in liquid 3 absorb: usually with *up*

soap *n.* substance that makes suds in water for washing —*v.* rub with soap —**soap'y** *a.*, **-i-er, -i-est**

soap'box' *n.* improvised platform for public speaking

soap opera *n.* [Inf.] melodramatic TV serial drama

soap'stone' *n.* compact variety of talc

soar *v.* fly high in the air

sob *v.* **sobbed, sob'bing** weep aloud with short gasps —*n.* act of sobbing

so'ber *a.* 1 not drunk 2 serious; sedate 3 plain —*v.* make or become sober —**so-bri'e-ty** *n.*

so'bri-quet' (-kā', -ket') *n.* nickname

soc *abbrev.* 1 social 2 society

so'-called' *a.* called thus, but usually inaccurately

soc'cer *n.* team game based on kicking a round ball into a goal

so'cia-ble (-sha-) *a.* friendly; agreeable —**so'cia-bil'i-ty** *n.* —**so'cia-bly** *adv.*

so'cial *a.* 1 of society 2 living in groups 3 sociable 4 of social work —*n.* a party —**so'cial-ly** *adv.*

so'cial-ism' *n.* public ownership of the means of production —**so'cial-ist** *n., a.* —**so'cial-is'tic** *a.*

so'cial-ite' *n.* person prominent in fashionable society

so'cial-ize' *v.* 1 put under public ownership 2 take part in social affairs

social science *n.* field of study dealing with society

Social Security *n.* federal insurance for old age, unemployment, etc.

social work *n.* work of clinics, agencies, etc. to improve living conditions

so-ci'e-ty *n., pl.* **-ties** 1 community of people 2 all people 3 companionship 4 organized group 5 the fashionable class —**so-ci'e-tal** *a.*

Society of Friends *n.* Christian denomination that rejects violence

so'ci-o-ec'o-nom'ic (sō'sē-, -shē-) *a.* of social and economic factors

so'ci-ol'o-gy (-sē-) *n.* study of the organization, problems, etc. of society —**so'ci-o-log'i-cal** *a.* —**so'ci-ol'o-gist** *n.*

sock *n.* 1 *pl.* **socks** or **sox** short stocking 2 [Sl.] a blow —*v.* [Sl.] hit with force

sock'et *n.* hollow part into which something fits

sock'eye' *n.* reddish salmon

sod *n.* surface layer of earth with grass —*v.* **sod'ded, sod'ding** cover with sod

so'da *n.* 1 substance containing sodium 2 soda water 3 ice cream mixed with soda water and flavoring

soda cracker *n.* crisp cracker

soda fountain *n.* counter for serving sodas, sundaes, etc.

soda pop *n.* flavored, carbonated soft

drink

soda water *n.* carbonated water

sod'den *a.* soaked or soggy

so'di·um *n.* silver-white metallic chemical element

sodium bi·car·bon·ate (-ət) *n.* baking soda

sodium chloride *n.* common salt

sodium hydroxide *n.* lye

sodium nitrate *n.* a clear salt used in explosives, etc.

sod'om·y *n.* any type of sexual intercourse held to be abnormal

so'fa *n.* couch with back and arms

sofa bed *n.* sofa that can be opened into a bed

soft *a.* 1 not hard; easy to crush, cut etc. 2 not harsh; mild, gentle, etc. 3 without minerals that hinder lathering 4 weak 5 nonalcoholic —*adv.* gently —**soft'ly** *adv.* —**soft'ness** *n.*

soft'ball' *n.* 1 kind of baseball played with a larger ball 2 this ball

soft'-boiled' *a.* boiled briefly to keep the egg's yolk soft

soft'-core' *a.* portraying sexual acts in a suggestive way rather than graphically

soft drink *n.* nonalcoholic drink, esp. one that is carbonated

soft'en (sôf'-) *v.* make or become soft —**soft'en·er** *n.*

soft'heart'ed *a.* 1 compassionate 2 lenient

soft landing *n.* a landing of a spacecraft without damage to the craft

soft money *n.* money donated to a party, not a candidate

soft'-ped'al *v.* [Inf.] make less emphatic; tone down

soft sell *n.* subtle salesmanship

soft soap *n.* [Inf.] smooth talk or flattery —**soft'-soap'** *v.*

soft'ware' *n.* programs, etc. for a computer or other electronic equipment

soft'y *n.*, *pl.* **-ies** [Inf.] overly sentimental or trusting person

sog'gy *a.* **-gi·er, -gi·est** very wet and heavy; soaked

soil *n.* earth or ground, esp. the surface layer —*v.* make or become dirty

soi·ree, soi·rée (swä rā') *n.* an evening party

so'journ (-jurn) *n.*, *v.* visit, as in a foreign land

sol'ace *n.* relief or comfort —*v.* comfort

so'lar *a.* of or having to do with the sun

so·lar'i·um *n.* glassed-in room for sunning

solar plex'us *n.* [Inf.] belly area just below sternum

solar system *n.* the sun and all its planets

sold *v.* pt. & pp. of SELL

sol'der (säd'ər) *n.* metal alloy for joining metal parts —*v.* join with solder

sol'dier (sōl'jər) *n.* member of an army, esp. one who is not an officer —*v.* be a soldier

sole *n.* 1 bottom of the foot, or of a shoe 2 edible flatfish —*v.* put a sole on (a shoe) —*a.* one and only

sole'ly *adv.* 1 alone 2 only

sol'emn (-əm) *a.* 1 formal 2 serious —**sol'emn·ly** *adv.*

so·lem'ni·ty *n.*, *pl.* **-ties** 1 solemn ritual 2 seriousness

sol'em·nize *v.* celebrate or perform formally

so'le·noid *n.* coil of wire used as an electromagnetic switch

so·lic'it (-lis'-) *v.* ask for —**so·lic'i·ta'tion** *n.*

so·lic'i·tor *n.* 1 one who solicits trade, etc. 2 in England, lawyer not a barrister 3 in U.S., lawyer for a city, etc.

so·lic'i·tous *a.* 1 showing concern 2 anxious —**so·lic'i·tude'** *n.*

sol'id *a.* 1 firm or hard 2 not hollow 3 three-dimensional 4 of one piece, color, etc. —*n.* 1 firm or hard substance 2 three-dimensional object —**so·lid'i·fy'** *v.*, **-fied', -fy'ing** —**so·lid'i·ty** *n.*

sol·i·dar'i·ty *n.* firm unity

so·lil'o·quy (-kwē) *n.*, *pl.* **-quies** a talking to oneself —**so·lil'o·quize'** *v.*

sol'i·taire' (-ter') *n.* 1 gem set by itself 2 card game for one person

sol'i·tar'y *a.* 1 alone; lonely 2 single

sol'i·tude' *n.* state of being alone

so'lo *n.*, *a.* (piece of music) for one performer —**so'lo·ist** *n.*

sol'stice (-stis) *n.* date when the sun reaches its highest or lowest point in the sky

sol'u·ble *a.* 1 that can be dissolved 2 solvable —**sol·u·bil'i·ty** *n.*

sol'ute' (-yōōt) *n.* substance dissolved

so·lu'tion *n.* 1 the solving of a problem 2 explanation or answer 3 liquid with something dissolved in it

solve *v.* find the answer to —**solv'a·ble** *a.*

sol'vent *a.* 1 able to pay one's debts 2 able to dissolve a substance —*n.* substance used to dissolve another —**sol'ven·cy** *n.*

som'ber *a.* 1 dark and gloomy 2 sad Chiefly Br. sp. **som'bre**

som·bre'ro (-brer'ō) *n.*, *pl.* **-ros** broad-brimmed hat

some *a.* **1** certain but unspecified **2** of indefinite quantity **3** about —*pron.* indefinite quantity —*adv.* **1** approximately **2** [Inf.] to some extent

-some *suf.* tending to (be)

some'bod'y *n.*, *pl.* **-ies** important person —*pron.* person not named or known

some'day' *adv.* sometime

some'how' *adv.* in some way

some'one' *pron.* somebody

som·er·sault (sum'ər sôlt') *v.*, *n.* (perform) a rotation of the body, feet over head

some'thing *pron.* thing not named or known

some'time' *adv.* at some unspecified time —*a.* former

some'times' *adv.* at times

some'what' *pron.* some part, amount, etc. —*adv.* a little

some'where' *adv.* in, to, or at some unnamed place

som·nam'bu·lism' *n.* act of walking while asleep

som'no·lent *a.* sleepy —**som'no·lence** *n.*

son *n.* male in relation to his parents

so·na'ta *n.* piece of music for one or two instruments

song *n.* **1** music, or poem, to be sung **2** singing sound

song'bird' *n.* bird that makes vocal sounds like music

song'ster *n.* singer —**song'stress** *n.fem.*

son'ic *a.* of or having to do with sound

sonic barrier *n.* large increase of air resistance as an aircraft nears the speed of sound

sonic boom *n.* explosive sound produced by a supersonic aircraft

son'-in-law' *n.*, *pl.* **sons'-** husband of one's daughter

son'net *n.* 14-line poem

so·no'rous *a.* resonant —**so·nor'i·ty** *n.*

soon *adv.* **1** in a short time **2** early **3** readily

soot *n.* black particles in smoke —**soot'y** *a.*, **-i-er**, **-i-est**

soothe (sōōth) *v.* **1** make calm, as by kindness **2** ease (pain, etc.) —**sooth'ing·ly** *adv.*

sooth'say'er (sōōth'-) *n.* [Hist.] one who professes to prophesy

sop *n.* bribe —*v.* **sopped, sop'ping 1** soak **2** absorb: with *up*

so·phis'ti·cat·ed *a.* **1** knowledgeable, subtle, etc. **2** highly complex;

advanced —**so·phis'ti·cate** (-kət) *n.* —**so·phis'ti·ca'tion** *n.*

soph'ist·ry, soph'ism' *n.* clever but misleading reasoning —**soph'ist** *n.*

soph'o·more' *n.* second-year student in high school or college

soph'o·mor'ic *a.* immature

sop'o·rif'ic *n.*, *a.* (drug) causing sleep

sop'ping *a.* very wet: also **sop'py, -pi-er, -pi-est**

so·pra'no (-pran'ō, -prä'nō) *n.*, *pl.* **-nos** highest female voice

sor'bet (-bā') *n.* tart ice, as of fruit juice

sor'cer·y *n.* black magic —**sor'cer·er** *n.* —**sor'cer·ess** *n.fem.*

sor'did *a.* **1** dirty; filthy **2** morally low

sore *a.* **1** painful **2** sad **3** [Inf.] angry —*n.* sore spot on the body —**sore'ness** *n.*

sore'ly *adv.* greatly

sor'ghum (-gam) *n.* grass grown for grain, syrup, etc.

so·ror'i·ty *n.*, *pl.* **-ties** social club for women

sor'rel *n.* **1** reddish brown **2** horse of this color

sor'row *v.*, *n.* (feel) sadness —**sor'row·ful** *a.*

sor'ry *a.* **-ri·er, -ri·est 1** full of sorrow, regret, etc. **2** pitiful; wretched

sort *n.* kind; class —*v.* arrange according to kind —**of sorts** or **of a sort** an inferior kind —**out of sorts** [Inf.] slightly ill —**sort of** [Inf.] somewhat

sor'tie (-tē) *n.* **1** raid by besieged troops **2** mission by a single military plane

SOS *n.* signal of distress

so'-so' *a.*, *adv.* fair or fairly well: also **so so**

sot *n.* habitual drunkard

sot·to vo·ce (sät'ō vō'chē) *adv.* in a soft voice

souf·flé (sōō flā') *n.* a dish made light and puffy by being baked with beaten egg whites

sought *v.* pt. & pp. of SEEK

soul *n.* **1** spiritual part of a person **2** vital part **3** person —**soul'ful** *a.*

sound *n.* **1** that which is heard **2** strait or inlet of the sea —*v.* **1** (cause) to make a sound **2** seem **3** measure the depth of water **4** seek the opinion of: often with *out* —*a.* **1** free from defect; healthy, secure, wise, etc. **2** deep or thorough —*adv.* in a sound way —**sound'ly** *adv.* —**sound'ness** *n.*

sound barrier *n.* sonic barrier

sound bite *n.* brief, quotable remark as by a politician

sound'ing board *n.* person used to test ideas on

sound'proof' *v., a.* (make) impervious to sound

sound'stage' *n.* soundproof studio for making movies, etc.

sound'track' *n.* band along one side of a film, carrying its recorded sound

soup (sōōp) *n.* a liquid food with meat, vegetables, etc. in it

soup'-to-nuts' *a.* [Inf.] complete

soup'y *a.* **-i·er, -i·est** 1 like soup 2 [Inf.] foggy

sour *a.* 1 having an acid taste 2 fermented 3 unpleasant —*v.* make or become sour —**sour'ness** *n.*

source (sôrs) *n.* 1 starting point 2 place of origin

sour grapes *n.* a scorning of something one cannot get or do

souse *n.* 1 pickled food 2 [Sl.] drunkard —*v.* make very wet

south *n.* direction or region to the left of one facing the sunset —*a., adv.* in, toward, or from the south —**go south** [Inf.] to decline, fail, etc. —**south'er·ly** (su*th*'-) *a., adv.* —**south'ern** (su*th*'-) *a.* —**south'ern·er** *n.* —**south'ward** *a., adv.* —**south'wards** *adv.*

south'east' *n.* direction or region between south and east —*a., adv.* in, toward, or from the southeast —**south'east'er·ly** *a., adv.* —**south'east'ern** *a.* —**south'east'ward** *a., adv.* —**south'east'wards** *adv.*

south'paw' *n.* [Sl.] left-handed person, esp. a baseball pitcher

South Pole southern end of the earth's axis

south'west' *n.* direction or region between south and west —*a., adv.* in, toward, or from the southwest —**south'west'er·ly** *a., adv.* —**south'west'ern** *a.* —**south'west'ward** *a., adv.* —**south'west'wards** *adv.*

sou·ve·nir (sōō'və nir') *n.* thing kept as a reminder

sov·er·eign (säv'rən) *a.* 1 chief; supreme 2 independent —*n.* 1 monarch 2 former Br. gold coin —**sov'er·eign·ty** *n., pl.* **-ties**

so'vi·et *n.* elected governing council, as in the Soviet Union

sow (sou) *n.* adult female pig

sow (sō) *v.* **sowed, sown** or **sowed, sow'ing** scatter, or plant with, seed for growing

soy *n.* soybean seeds

soy'bean' *n.* (seed of) a plant of the pea family

soy sauce *n.* sauce from fermented

soybeans

sp *abbrev.* 1 special 2 spelling

Sp *abbrev.* 1 Spain 2 Spanish

spa *n.* resort having a mineral spring

space *n.* 1 limitless expanse containing all things 2 distance or area 3 interval of time —*v.* divide by spaces

space'craft' *n., pl.* **-craft'** vehicle or satellite for outer-space travel, exploration, etc.

spaced'-out' *a.* [Sl.] under the influence of a drug, etc.: also **spaced**

space heater *n.* small heating unit for a room

space'man' *n., pl.* **-men'** astronaut

space'ship' *n.* spacecraft, esp. if manned

space'suit' *n.* garment pressurized for use by astronauts

spac'y, spac'ey *a.* **-i·er, -i·est** [Sl.] flighty, irresponsible, etc. —**spac'i·ness** *n.*

spa'cious (-shəs) *a.* having much space; vast

Spack'le *trademark* paste that dries hard, used to fill holes in wood, etc. —*n.* [s-] this substance

spade *n.* 1 flat-bladed digging tool 2 playing card marked with a ♠ —*v.* dig with a spade

spade'work' *n.* preparatory work, esp. when tiresome

spa·ghet'ti (-get'-) *n.* (cooked) strings of dried flour paste

span *n.* 1 nine inches 2 extent 3 period of time —*v.* extend over

span'gle *n.* shiny decoration, as a sequin —*v.* to decorate with spangles

span'iel (-yəl) *n.* dog with large, drooping ears

Span'ish *a., n.* (of) the people or language of Spain

spank *v., n.* slap on the buttocks

spank'ing *a.* brisk

spar *n.* pole supporting a ship's sail —*v.* **sparred, spar'ring** box cautiously

spare *v.* 1 save or free from something 2 avoid using 3 give up, as time or money —*a.* 1 extra 2 lean; meager —*n.* extra thing

spare'ribs' *pl.n.* thin end of pork ribs

spar'ing *a.* frugal

spark *n.* 1 small glowing piece from a fire 2 a trace 3 flash from an electrical discharge across a gap —*v.* 1 make sparks 2 activate

spar'kle *v.* 1 give off sparks 2 glitter 3 effervesce —*n.* 1 a sparkling 2 brilliance —**spar'kler** *n.*

spark plug *n.* electrical device in an engine cylinder, that ignites the fuel mixture

spar'row n. small songbird

sparse a. thinly spread —**sparse'ly** adv. —**spar'si·ty**, **sparse'ness** n.

Spar'tan a. brave; hardy

spasm (spaz'əm) n. **1** involuntary muscular contraction **2** short, sudden burst of activity —**spas·mod'ic** a.

spas'tic n., a. (one) having muscular spasms

spat v. pt. & pp. of SPIT —n. **1** [Inf.] a brief quarrel **2** cloth ankle covering

spate n. unusually large outpouring, as of words

spa'tial (-shəl) a. of, or existing in, space

spat'ter v. **1** spurt out in drops **2** splash —n. mark made by spattering

spat'u·la (spach'ə-) n. tool with a broad, flat, flexible blade

spawn n. **1** eggs of fishes, etc. **2** offspring —v. produce (spawn)

spay v. sterilize (a female animal)

speak v. **spoke**, **spo'ken**, **speak'ing 1** utter words **2** tell; express **3** make a speech **4** use (a language) in speaking **5** make a request (for)

speak'er n. **1** one who speaks **2** device, as in a radio, for changing electrical signals into sound

spear n. long, slender sharp-pointed weapon —v. pierce or stab as with a spear

spear'head' n. leading person or group, as in an attack

spear'mint' n. fragrant plant of the mint family

spec abbrev. **1** special **2** specifically: also **specif**

spe·cial (spesh'əl) a. **1** distinctive **2** exceptional **3** highly regarded **4** for a certain use —n. special thing —**spe'cial·ly** adv.

spe'cial·ize' v. concentrate on a certain type of study, work, etc. —**spe'cial·ist** n. —**spe'cial·i·za'tion** n.

spe'cial·ty n., pl. **-ties** special feature, interest, etc.

spe'cie (-shē, -sē) n. metal money

spe'cies n., pl. **-cies** distinct kind of plant or animal

spe·cif'ic a. definite; explicit —**spe·cif'i·cal·ly** adv.

spec'i·fi·ca'tion n. **1** a specifying **2** pl. detailed description

spec'i·fy' v. **-fied'**, **-fy'ing** state explicitly

spec'i·men n. sample

spe'cious (-shəs) a. plausible but not genuine

speck n. small spot or bit —v. mark

with specks

speck'le n., v. speck

specs pl.n. [Inf.] specifications

spec'ta·cle n. **1** unusual sight **2** public show **3** pl. eyeglasses: old-fashioned

spec·tac'u·lar a. showy; striking

spec'tate' v. watch a sports event, etc.

spec'ta·tor n. one who watches

spec'ter n. ghost: Br. sp. **spec'tre** —**spec'tral** a.

spec'tro·scope' n. instrument that forms spectra for study

spec'trum n., pl. **-tra** or **-trums** row of colors formed by diffraction

spec'u·late' v. **1** ponder **2** take risky chances in business —**spec'u·la'tion** n. —**spec'u·la'tor** n.

speech n. **1** act or way of speaking **2** power to speak **3** a public talk —**speech'less** a.

speed n. **1** rapid motion **2** rate of movement —v. **sped** or **speed'ed**, **speed'ing 1** move fast **2** aid —**speed'y** a., **-i·er**, **-i·est**

speed'boat' n. fast motorboat

speed·om'e·ter n. device to indicate speed

speed'ster n. very fast driver, runner, etc.

speed'way' n. track for racing automobiles or motorcycles

spe·le·ol'o·gy (spē'lē-) n. scientific study of caves

spell n. **1** supposedly magic words **2** fascination; charm **3** period of work, duty, etc. —v. **1** give in order the letters of (a word) **2** mean **3** [Inf.] relieve (another)

spell'bind' v. **-bound'**, **-bind'ing** cause to be spellbound —**spell'bind'er** n.

spell'bound' a. fascinated

spell'-check'er n. computer program that checks for misspellings —**spell check** n.

spell'er n. **1** one who spells words **2** spelling textbook

spell'ing n. **1** a forming words from letters **2** way a word is spelled

spelling bee n. spelling contest: also **spell'down'**

spe·lunk'er n. cave explorer

spend v. **spent**, **spend'ing 1** use up **2** pay out (money) **3** pass (time)

spend'thrift' n. one who wastes money —a. wasteful

sperm n. **1** semen **2** any of the germ cells in it: also **sper'ma·to·zo'on'**, pl. **-zo'a**

sperm'i·cide' n. substance that kills spermatozoa

sperm whale n. large, toothed whale

spew v. (make) flow plentifully; gush

sphere (sfir) n. **1** globe; ball **2** place or range of action —**spher'i·cal** (sfer'-, sfir'-) a.

sphe·roid (sfir'oid) n. almost spherical body

sphinc'ter (sfiŋk'-) n. ring-shaped muscle for closing a body opening

sphinx (sfiŋks) n. **1** [S-] statue in Egypt with a lion's body and man's head **2** one difficult to understand

spice n. **1** any aromatic seasoning **2** stimulating quality —v. add spice to —**spic'y** a., **-i·er**, **-i·est**

spick'-and-span' a. fresh or tidy

spi'der n. arachnid that spins webs

spiel (spēl) v., n. [Sl.] (give) a speech

spiff'y a. **-i·er**, **-i·est** [Sl.] stylish

spig'ot n. faucet or tap

spike n. **1** sharp-pointed projection **2** long, heavy nail **3** long flower cluster —v. fasten or pierce as with a spike

spill v. **spilled** or **spilt**, **spill'ing 1** let run over **2** overflow **3** shed (blood) **4** make fall —n. **1** a spilling **2** a fall

spill'way' n. channel for excess water

spin v. **spun**, **spin'ning 1** twist fibers into thread **2** make a web, cocoon, etc. **3** tell (a story) **4** to whirl **5** move fast —n. **1** a whirling movement **2** fast ride **3** special emphasis or slant

spin'ach (-ich) n. plant with dark-green, edible leaves

spi'nal a. of the spine —n. a spinal anesthetic

spinal column n. long row of connected bones in the back

spinal cord n. cord of nerve tissue in the spinal column

spin'dle n. **1** rod used in spinning thread **2** rod that acts as an axis

spin'dly a. **-dli·er**, **-dli·est** long and thin: also **spin'dling**

spin doctor n. [Sl.] publicist using SPIN (n. 3), as for a politician

spine n. **1** thorn, quill, etc. **2** spinal column —**spin'y** a., **-i·er**, **-i·est**

spine'less a. **1** having no spine **2** weak or cowardly

spin'et n. small upright piano

spine'-tin'gling a. thrilling, terrifying, etc.

spinning wheel n. simple spinning machine driven by a large wheel

spin'off' n. secondary benefit, product, etc.

spin'ster n. unmarried, older woman

spi'ral a. circling around a center —n. spiral curve or coil —v. move in a spiral

spire n. tapering, pointed part, as of a steeple

spi·re'a (spī-) n. shrub of rose family

spir'it n. **1** soul **2** ghost, angel, etc. **3** pl. mood **4** courage **5** loyalty **6** essential quality **7** pl. alcoholic liquor —v. carry away secretly

spir'it·ed a. lively

spir'it·u·al a. **1** of the soul **2** religious; sacred —n. American folk hymn of 18th and 19th c. U.S. blacks —**spir'it·u·al'i·ty** n.

spir'it·u·al·ism' n. communication with the dead —**spir'it·u·al·ist** n.

spit n. **1** thin rod to roast meat on **2** shoreline narrowed to a point **3** saliva —v. **spit'ted** or (v. 2) **spit** or **spat**, **spit'ting 1** fix as on a spit **2** eject (saliva, etc.) from the mouth

spite n. malice —v. annoy; hurt —**in spite of** regardless of —**spite'ful** a.

spit'tle n. spit; saliva

spit·toon' n. container to spit into

splash v. dash liquid, etc. (on) —n. **1** a splashing **2** a spot made by splashing —**make a splash** [Inf.] attract great attention

splash'down' n. landing of a spacecraft on water

splash'y a. **-i·er**, **-i·est** [Inf.] spectacular

splat'ter n., v. splash

splay v., a. spread out

spleen n. **1** large abdominal organ **2** malice; spite —**sple·net'ic** a.

splen'did a. magnificent; grand —**splen'did·ly** adv. —**splen'dor** n.

splice v., n. (make) a joint with ends overlapped —**splic'er** n.

splint n. stiff strip to hold a broken bone in place

splin'ter n. thin, sharp piece —v. split into splinters or fragments

split v. **split**, **split'ting** separate into parts —n. a break; crack —a. divided

split'-lev'el a. having adjacent floor levels staggered about a half story apart

split'ting a. severe

splotch n., v. spot; stain —**splotch'y** a., **-i·er**, **-i·est**

splurge v., n. [Inf.] (indulge in) extravagant spending spree

splut'ter v. **1** make spitting sounds **2** speak confusedly —n. a spluttering

spoil v. **spoiled** or [Br.] **spoilt**, **spoil'ing** to damage, ruin, decay, etc. —pl.n. plunder —**spoil'age** n.

spoil'sport' n. one who ruins the fun of others

spoke v. pt. of SPEAK —n. rod from

hub to rim

spo'ken v. pp. of SPEAK —a. oral; voiced

spokes'man n., pl. **-men** one who speaks for another —**spokes'per·son** n. —**spokes'wom'an** n.fem., pl. **-wom'en**

sponge (spunj) n. 1 (piece of) absorbent substance made from a sea animal, plastic, etc. 2 the sea animal —v. 1 clean, etc. with a sponge 2 [Inf.] live off others —**spon'gy** a., **-gi·er, -gi·est**

sponge bath n. bath taken by using a wet sponge or cloth without getting into water

sponge'cake' n. light, spongy cake without shortening

spon'sor n. 1 promoter; supporter 2 advertiser who pays for a radio or TV program —v. be sponsor for

spon·ta'ne·ous a. 1 without effort 2 within or by itself 3 unplanned —**spon'ta·ne'i·ty** (-nē'-, -nā'-) n.

spoof n. light satire —v. satirize playfully

spook n. [Inf.] ghost —v. startle, frighten, etc.

spook'y a. **-i·er, -i·est** 1 eerie 2 nervous

spool n. cylinder upon which thread, etc. is wound

spoon n. small bowl with a handle, used in eating —**spoon'ful** n., pl. **-fuls**

spoon'-feed' v. pamper

spoor n. wild animal's trail or track

spo·rad'ic a. not regular —**spo·rad'i·cal·ly** adv.

spore n. tiny reproductive cell of mosses, fern, etc.

sport n. 1 athletic game 2 fun 3 abnormal plant or animal 4 [Inf.] sportsmanlike or sporty person —v. 1 [Inf.] to display 2 to play —a. for play or leisure —**spor'tive** a.

sport'ing a. 1 of sports 2 fair

sports a. sport

sports car n. small, expensive car with powerful engine

sports'man n., pl. **-men** 1 participant in sports 2 one who plays fair —**sports'man·like'** a.

sport utility vehicle n. station wagon on a small truck chassis

sport'y a. **-i·er, -i·est** [Inf.] flashy or showy —**sport'i·ness** n.

spot n. 1 stain; mark 2 place —v. **spot'ted, spot'ting** 1 mark with spots 2 see —a. made at random —**spot'less** a. **spot'less·ly** adv.

spot'-check' v. check at random —n. such a checking

spot'light' n. 1 strong beam of light, or lamp that throws it 2 public notice

spot'ty a. **-ti·er, -ti·est** 1 spotted 2 not uniform —**spot'ti·ly** adv.

spouse n. husband or wife —**spous·al** (spou'zəl) a.

spout n. 1 pipe, etc. by which a liquid pours 2 stream of liquid —v. 1 shoot out with force 2 talk loudly on and on

sprain v. twist a muscle or ligament in a joint —n. injury caused by this

sprang v. pt. of SPRING

sprat n. small herring

sprawl v. sit or spread out in a relaxed or awkward way —n. sprawling position

spray n. 1 mist or stream of tiny liquid drops 2 branch with leaves, flowers, etc. 3 spray gun —v. apply, or emit in, a spray

spray can n. aerosol can

spray gun n. device that sprays a liquid, as paint

spread v. **spread, spread'ing** 1 open out 2 extend in time or space 3 make known 4 to cover 5 go or make go —n. 1 act or extent of spreading 2 a cloth cover 3 butter, jam, etc.

spread'-ea'gled a. with the arms and legs stretched out

spread'sheet' n. computer program organizing data into rows and columns

spree n. 1 lively time 2 drinking bout 3 unrestrained period

sprig n. little twig

spright'ly a. **-li·er, -li·est** brisk; lively —adv. briskly

spring v. **sprang** or **sprung, sprung, spring'ing** 1 to leap 2 grow; develop 3 snap back or shut 4 make or become warped, bent, split, etc. 5 make known —n. 1 a leap 2 resilience 3 resilient coil of wire, etc. 4 flow of water from the ground 5 source 6 season after winter —a. of, for, or in the season of spring —**spring'y** a., **-i·er, -i·est**

spring'board' n. springy board, as to dive from

sprin'kle v. 1 scatter drops of or on 2 rain lightly —n. a sprinkling

sprint v., n. race at full speed for a short distance

sprite n. elf, fairy, etc.

sprock'et n. any tooth in a series on a wheel made to fit the links of a chain

sprout v. begin to grow —n. new growth; shoot

spruce *n.* evergreen tree —*v.*, *a.* (make) neat or trim

sprung *v.* pp. & alt. pt. of SPRING

spry *a.* **spri'er** or **spry'er, spri'est** or **spry'est** lively

spud *n.* [Inf.] potato

spume *n.* foam; froth

spu·mo'ni *n.* Italian ice cream

spun *v.* pt. & pp. of SPIN

spunk *n.* [Inf.] courage —**spunk'y** *a.*, **-i·er, -i·est**

spur *n.* **1** pointed device on a shoe to prick a horse **2** stimulus **3** projecting part —*v.* **spurred, spur'ring 1** to prick with spurs **2** urge on

spu'ri·ous (spyoor'-, spur'-) *a.* false; not genuine

spurn *v.* reject in scorn

spurt *v.* **1** shoot forth; squirt **2** to show a sudden, brief burst of energy, etc. —*n.* a spurting

sput'nik *n.* Russian man-made satellite

sput'ter *v.* **1** speak in a fast, confused way **2** spit out bits **3** make hissing sounds —*n.* a sputtering

spu'tum (spyoo'-) *n.* saliva

spy *v.* **spied, spy'ing 1** watch closely and secretly **2** see —*n.*, *pl.* **spies** one who spies, esp. to get another country's secrets

spy'glass' *n.* small telescope

sq *abbrev.* square

squab (skwäb) *n.* young pigeon

squab'ble *v.*, *n.* quarrel over a small matter

squad *n.* small group

squad'ron *n.* unit of warships, aircraft, etc.

squal'id *a.* **1** foul; unclean **2** wretched —**squal'or** *n.*

squall *n.* **1** brief, violent windstorm **2** harsh, loud cry —*v.* cry loudly

squan'der *v.* spend or use wastefully

square *n.* **1** rectangle with all sides equal **2** area with streets on four sides **3** tool for making right angles **4** product of a number multiplied by itself **5** [Sl.] person who is SQUARE (*a.* 6) —*v.* **1** make square **2** make straight, even, etc. **3** settle; adjust **4** multiply by itself —*a.* **1** shaped like a square **2** forming a right angle **3** straight, level, or even **4** just; fair **5** [Inf.] filling, as a meal **6** [Sl.] old-fashioned, unsophisticated, etc. —*adv.* in a square way —**square'ly** *adv.* —**square'ness** *n.*

square dance *n.* lively dance with couples grouped in a square, etc.

square root *n.* quantity that when

squared produces another, given quantity

squash *v.* **1** press into a soft, flat mass **2** suppress —*n.* **1** a squashing **2** game played with rackets in a walled court **3** fleshy fruit eaten as a vegetable

squat *v.* **squat'ted, squat'ting 1** crouch **2** settle on land without title to it —*a.* short and heavy —*n.* position of squatting —**squat'ter** *n.*

squaw *n.* a North American Indian woman or wife: now rare but considered offensive

squawk *v.* **1** utter a loud, harsh cry **2** [Inf.] complain —*n.* a squawking —**squawk'er** *n.*

squeak *v.* make a sharp, high-pitched sound —*n.* such a sound —**squeak'y** *a.*, **-i·er, -i·est**

squeal *v.*, *n.* (utter) a long, shrill cry

squeam'ish *a.* **1** easily nauseated **2** easily shocked

squee'gee (-jē) *n.* rubber-edged tool used in washing windows

squeeze *v.* **1** press hard **2** extract by pressure **3** force by pressing **4** to hug —*n.* a squeezing —**squeez'er** *n.*

squelch *v.* suppress or silence completely

squib *n.* short news item

squid *n.* long, slender sea mollusk with eight arms and two tentacles

squig'gle *n.* short, wavy line —**squig'gly** *a.*

squint *v.* **1** peer with eyes partly closed **2** be cross-eyed —*n.* a squinting

squire *n.* English country gentleman —*v.* to escort

squirm *v.* twist and turn

squir'rel *n.* tree-dwelling rodent with a bushy tail

squirt *v.*, *n.* (shoot out in) a jet or spurt

squish *v.*, *n.* **1** (make) a soft, splashing sound when squeezed **2** [Inf.] SQUASH (*v.* 1, *n.* 1) —**squish'y** *a.*, **-i·er, -i·est**

Sr *abbrev.* **1** Senior **2** Sister

SRO *abbrev.* **1** single room occupancy **2** standing room only

SS *n.* Nazi party police division

SST *abbrev.* supersonic transport

St *abbrev.* **1** Saint **2** Strait **3** Street

stab *v.* **stabbed, stab'bing** pierce or wound as with a knife —*n.* **1** a thrust, as with a knife **2** [Inf.] a try

sta'bi·lize' *v.* make stable —**sta'bi·li·za'tion** *n.* —**sta'bi·liz'er** *n.*

sta'ble *a.* not apt to slip, change, etc.; firm —*n.* building for horses or cattle —*v.* keep in a stable —**sta·bil'i·ty** *n.*

stac·ca·to (stə kät′ō) *a., adv. Mus.* with distinct breaks between tones

stack *n.* 1 orderly pile 2 smokestack 3 *pl.* series of bookshelves —*v.* to pile in a stack

sta'di·um *n.* place for outdoor games, surrounded by tiers of seats

staff *n., pl.* (*n.* 1, 2, 3) **staffs** or (*n.* 1 & 3) **staves** 1 stick or rod used for support, etc. 2 group of people assisting a leader 3 the five lines on and between which music is written —*v.* provide with workers

stag *n.* full-grown male deer —*a.* for men only

stage *n.* 1 platform, esp. one on which plays are presented 2 the theater 3 part of a journey 4 period in growth or development —*v.* 1 to present as on a stage 2 carry out

stage'coach' *n.* horse-drawn public coach for long trips

stage fright *n.* nervousness felt as a speaker or performer before an audience

stage'hand' *n.* one who sets up scenery, etc. for a play

stage'-struck' *a.* eager to become an actor or actress

stag'ger *v.* 1 (cause to) totter, reel, etc. 2 to shock 3 arrange alternately —*n.* a staggering

stag'ger·ing *a.* astonishing

stag'nant *a.* 1 not flowing, therefore foul 2 sluggish

stag'nate' *v.* become stagnant —**stag·na'tion** *n.*

staid *a.* sober; sedate

stain *v.* 1 discolor; spot 2 dishonor 3 color (wood, etc.) with a dye —*n.* 1 a spot; mark 2 dishonor 3 dye for wood, etc. —**stain'less** *a.*

stainless steel *n.* alloyed steel almost immune to rust and corrosion

stair *n.* 1 one of a series of steps between levels 2 *usually pl.* flight of stairs: also **stair'case'** or **stair'way'**

stair'well' *n.* shaft containing a staircase

stake *n.* 1 pointed stick to be driven into the ground 2 *often pl.* money risked as a wager —*v.* 1 mark the boundaries of 2 to wager —**at stake** being risked

sta·lac'tite *n.* stick of lime hanging from a cave roof

sta·lag'mite *n.* stick of lime built up on a cave floor

stale *a.* 1 no longer fresh 2 trite

stale'mate' *n.* deadlock or tie

stalk *v.* 1 stride haughtily 2 track

secretly 3 follow obsessively —*n.* 1 a stalking 2 plant stem —**stalk'er** *n.*

stall *n.* 1 section for one animal in a stable 2 market booth —*v.* 1 put in a stall 2 to stop 3 delay by evading

stal'lion (-yən) *n.* uncastrated male horse

stal'wart (stôl′-) *a.* strong or brave — *n.* stalwart person

sta'men *n.* pollen-bearing part of a flower

stam'i·na *n.* endurance

stam'mer *v., n.* pause or halt in speaking

stamp *v.* 1 put the foot down hard 2 pound with the foot 3 cut out with a die 4 impress a design on 5 put a stamp on —*n.* 1 a stamping 2 gummed piece of paper, as for postage 3 a stamped mark 4 stamping device —**stamp out** 1 crush or put out by treading on 2 suppress or put down

stam·pede' *n.* sudden, headlong rush, as of a herd —*v.* move in a stampede

stamp'ing ground *n.* [Inf.] favorite gathering place

stance *n.* way one stands

stanch (stänch, stanch) *v.* check the flow of blood from a wound —*a.* staunch

stan·chion (stan'chən) *n.* upright support

stand *v.* **stood, stand'ing** 1 be or get in an upright position 2 place or be placed 3 hold a certain opinion 4 halt 5 endure or resist —*n.* 1 a halt 2 a position 3 platform, rack, counter, etc. 4 a growth (of trees) — **stand by** be ready to help —**stand for** 1 represent 2 [Inf.] tolerate —**stand in for** be a substitute for —**stand out** to project, be prominent, etc. —**stand up** 1 prove valid, durable, etc. 2 [Sl.] fail to keep a date with

stand'ard *n.* 1 flag, banner, etc. 2 thing set up as a rule or model 3 upright support —*a.* 1 that is a standard or rule 2 proper

stand'ard·ize' *v.* make standard or uniform

standard time *n.* official civil time for a region: the 24 time zones are one hour apart

stand'by' *n., pl.* **-bys'** person or thing that is dependable, a possible substitute, etc.

stand'-in' *n.* a substitute

stand'ing *n.* 1 status or rank 2 duration —*a.* 1 upright 2 continuing

stand'off' *n.* tie in a contest

stand'off'ish a. aloof

stand'point' n. viewpoint

stand'still' n. a stop or halt

stank v. alt. pt. of STINK

stan'za n. group of lines making a section of a poem

staph'y·lo·coc'cus (-käk'əs) n., pl. **-coc'ci·** (-käk'sī') kind of spherical bacteria

sta'ple n. **1** main product, part, etc. **2** basic trade item, as flour **3** U-shaped metal fastener —v. fasten with a staple —a. regular or principal —**sta'pler** n.

star n. **1** celestial body seen as a point of light at night **2** flat figure with five or more points **3** asterisk **4** one who excels or plays a leading role, as in acting —v. **starred, star'ring 1** to mark with stars **2** to present in, or play, a leading role —**star'ry** a., **-ri·er, -ri·est**

star'board (-bərd) n. right side of a ship, etc. as one faces the bow

starch n. **1** white food substance in potatoes, etc. **2** powdered form of this —v. stiffen (laundry) with starch —**starch'y** a., **-i·er, -i·est**

star'dom n. status of a STAR (n. 4)

stare v. gaze steadily —n. long, steady look

star'fish' n. small, star-shaped sea animal

star'gaze' v. **1** gaze at the stars **2** to daydream —**star'gaz'er** n.

stark a. **1** bleak **2** complete; utter —adv. entirely —**stark'ly** adv.

stark'-na'ked a. entirely naked

star'let n. young actress promoted as future star

star'ling n. bird with shiny, black feathers

star'ry-eyed' a. **1** glowing with happiness, dreams, etc. **2** overly optimistic, impractical, etc.

star'-span'gled a. studded with stars

star'struck' a. drawn to famous people, esp. in films, etc.

start v. **1** begin to go, do, etc. **2** set in motion **3** to jump or jerk —n. **1** a starting **2** a jump or jerk **3** place or time of beginning **4** a lead; advantage —**start in** begin to do —**start out** (or **off**) begin a trip, etc. —**start'er** n.

star'tle v. **1** frighten suddenly **2** surprise —**star'tling** a.

start'-up' a., n. (of) a new business venture

starve v. **1** suffer or die from lack of food **2** cause to starve —**star·va'tion** n.

stash [Inf.] v. hide away —n. **1** a place for hiding **2** something hidden

stat n. [Inf.] statistic

state n. **1** the way a person or thing is **2** formal style **3** nation **4** [often S-] (a unit of) a federal government —v. to express in words

stat'ed a. fixed; set

state'house' n. building where a U.S. state legislature meets

state'less a. having no state or nationality

state'ly a. **-li·er, -li·est** grand or dignified

state'ment n. **1** a stating **2** something stated **3** report, as of money owed

state of the art n. current level of sophistication of a developing technology

state'room' n. private room in a ship or railroad car

states'man n., pl. **-men** person skillful in government

stat'ic a. **1** not moving; at rest **2** of electricity caused by friction —n. **1** electrical disturbances in radio or TV reception

sta'tion n. **1** assigned place **2** stopping place **3** place for radio or TV transmission **4** social rank —v. assign to a station

sta'tion·ar'y a. not moving or changing

sta'tion·er'y n. writing materials

station wagon n. automobile with a back end that opens

sta·tis'tics n. analysis of numerical data —pl.n. the data —**sta·tis'ti·cal** a. —**stat'is·ti'cian** (-tish'ən) n.

stat'u·ar'y n. statues

stat·ue (stach'oo) n. likeness done in stone, metal, etc.

stat'u·esque' (-esk') a. tall and stately

stat'u·ette' n. small statue

stat·ure (stach'ər) n. **1** person's height **2** level of attainment or esteem

sta'tus n. **1** rank **2** condition

status quo n. existing state of affairs

status symbol n. a possession regarded as a sign of (high) social status

stat'ute (stach'-) n. a law

stat'u·to'ry a. established or punishable by statute

staunch (stônch, stänch) a. firm, loyal, etc. —v. stanch

stave n. **1** any of the wooden side strips of a barrel **2** staff **3** stanza —v. **staved** or **stove, stav'ing** smash (in) —**stave off** ward off, keep back, etc.

staves n. **1** alt. pl. of STAFF (n. 1 & 3) **2** pl. of STAVE

stay v. **1** remain **2** dwell **3** to stop or delay **4** to support —n. **1** a staying **2** a prop **3** guy rope **4** stiffening strip —stay put [Inf.] remain; stay

stay'ing power n. endurance

STD abbrev. sexually transmitted disease

stead (sted) n. place for a substitute

stead'fast' a. constant; firm

stead'y a. -i-er, -i-est **1** firm **2** regular **3** calm **4** reliable —v. -ied, -y-ing make or become steady

steak n. thick slice of meat or fish

steal v. stole, stol'en, steal'ing **1** take dishonestly and secretly **2** move stealthily

stealth (stelth) n. secret action — **stealth'i-ly** adv. —**stealth'y** a., -i-er, -i-est

steam n. water changed to a vapor by boiling: source of heat and power —a. using steam —v. **1** expose to steam **2** cook with steam **3** give off steam — **steam'boat', steam'ship'** n. —**steam'y** a., -i-er, -i-est

steam'er n. thing run by steam

steam'roll'er n. construction machine or vehicle with heavy roller —v. move, crush, override, etc. as (with) a steamroller: also **steam'roll'**

steed n. [Poet.] riding horse

steel n. hard alloy of iron with carbon —a. of steel —v. make hard, tough, etc. —**steel'y** a.

steel wool n. pad of steel shavings, used for cleaning, etc.

steel'yard' n. weighing scale

steep a. having a sharp rise or slope — v. soak or saturate

stee'ple n. high tower

stee'ple-chase' n. horse race over a course with obstacles

steer v. to guide; direct —n. male of beef cattle; ox

steer'age n. part of a ship for passengers paying least

stein (stīn) n. beer mug

stel'lar a. **1** of or like a star **2** excellent **3** most important

stem n. **1** stalk of a plant, flower, etc. **2** stemlike part **3** prow of a ship **4** root of a word —v. stemmed, stem'ming **1** remove the stem of **2** advance against **3** to stop **4** derive

stem'ware' n. glassware with stems

stench n. offensive smell

sten'cil n. sheet cut with letters, etc. to print when inked over —v. to mark with a stencil

ste·nog'ra·phy n. transcription of dictation in shorthand —**ste·nog'ra·pher** n. —**sten'o·graph'ic** a.

sten·to'ri·an (-tôr'ē-) a. very loud

step n. **1** one foot movement, as in walking **2** footstep **3** way of stepping **4** stair tread **5** degree; rank **6** an act in a series —v. **1** move with a step **2** press the foot down (on) —**in** (or **out of**) **step** (not) in rhythm with others —**step up 1** to advance **2** increase in rate

step'broth'er n. stepparent's son by another marriage

step'child' n. spouse's child (**step' daugh'ter** or **step'son'**) by a former marriage

step'-down' n. decrease, as in amount or intensity

step'lad'der n. four-legged ladder with flat steps

step'par'ent n. the spouse (**step' fa'ther** or **step'moth'er**) of one's remarried parent

steppe (step) n. great plain

step'ping-stone' n. **1** stone to step on, as in crossing a stream **2** means of bettering oneself

step'sis'ter n. stepparent's daughter by another marriage

step'-up' n. increase, as in amount, intensity, etc.

ster'e·o' n., pl. **-os'** stereophonic system, etc. —a. stereophonic

ster'e·o·phon'ic a. of a blend of sounds reproduced through separate speakers

ster'e·o·scop'ic a. appearing three-dimensional

ster'e·o·type' v., n. (express or conceive in) a set, trite form —**ster'e·o· typ'i·cal, ster'e·o·typ'ic** a.

ster'ile (-əl) a. **1** unable to reproduce itself or oneself **2** free of germs —**ste· ril'i·ty** n.

ster'i·lize' v. to make sterile —**ster'i·li· za'tion** n.

ster'ling a. **1** (made) of silver at least 92.5% pure **2** of British money **3** excellent

stern a. severe; unyielding —n. rear end of a ship, etc.

ster'num n. front chest bone to which ribs are joined

ster'oid' n. any of a group of compounds including cholesterol, sex hormones, etc.

steth'o·scope' n. medical instrument for hearing chest sounds

ste've·dore' n. one hired to load and

unload ships

stew v. cook by boiling slowly —n. meat with vegetables, cooked in this way

stew'ard n. **1** one put in charge of funds, supplies, etc. **2** attendant on a ship, airplane, etc. —**stew'ard·ess** n.fem.

stick n. **1** dry twig **2** long, thin piece, esp. of wood —v. stuck, stick'ing **1** pierce **2** attach or be attached as by pinning or gluing **3** extend **4** become fixed, jammed, etc. **5** persevere **6** hesitate

stick'er n. gummed label

stick'-in-the-mud' n. [Inf.] one who resists change, etc.

stick'le·back' n. small fish with sharp spines on its back

stick'ler n. one who is stubbornly fussy

stick'pin' n. ornamental pin worn in a necktie, etc.

stick shift n. car gearshift, operated manually by a lever

stick'up' n. [Sl.] robbery

stick'y a. -i·er, -i·est adhesive —**stick'i·ness** n.

stiff a. **1** hard to bend or move **2** thick; dense **3** strong, as a wind **4** harsh **5** difficult **6** tense **7** [Inf.] high —v. stiffed, stiff'ing [Sl.] cheat —**stiff'en** v. —**stiff'ly** adv.

stiff'-necked' a. stubborn

sti'fle v. **1** suffocate **2** suppress

stig'ma n., pl. -mas or -ma·ta **1** sign of disgrace **2** upper tip of a pistil

stig'ma·tize' v. to mark as disgraceful

stile n. step(s) for climbing over a fence or wall

sti·let'to n., pl. -tos or -toes small, thin dagger

still a. **1** quiet **2** motionless **3** calm —n. device to distill liquor —adv. **1** until then or now **2** even; yet **3** nevertheless —v. make or become still —**still'ness** n.

still'born' a. dead at birth —**still'birth'** n.

still life n. painting of inanimate objects, as fruit or flowers

stilt n. supporting pole, esp. one of a pair for walking high off the ground

stilt'ed a. pompous

stim'u·lant n. thing that stimulates, as a drug

stim'u·late' v. make (more) active —**stim·u·la'tion** n.

stim'u·lus n., pl. -li' (-lī') anything causing activity

sting v. stung, sting'ing **1** to hurt with a sting **2** cause or feel sharp pain —

n. **1** a stinging, or pain from it **2** sharp part in some plants, bees, etc. that pricks: also **sting'er**

sting'ray' n. ray fish with poisonous barbs on its tail

stin'gy (-jē) a. -gi·er, -gi·est miserly; grudging

stink v. stank or stunk, stunk, stink'ing; n. (have) a strong, unpleasant smell —**stink'er** n. —**stink'y** a., -i·er, -i·est

stint v. restrict to a small amount —n. **1** a limit **2** period of time doing

sti'pend n. regular payment

stip'ple v. paint or draw in small dots

stip'u·late' v. specify as an essential condition

stir v. stirred, stir'ring **1** move, esp. slightly **2** move around as with a spoon **3** excite —n. **1** a stirring **2** commotion

stir'-cra'zy a. [Sl.] mentally affected by long confinement

stir-fry' v. fry (sliced vegetables, meat, etc.) quickly while stirring

stir'rup n. ring hung from a saddle as a footrest

stirrup pants pl.n. closefitting pants with stirruplike foot straps

stitch n. **1** single movement or loop made by a needle in sewing, knitting, etc. **2** sudden pain —v. sew

stock n. **1** tree trunk **2** ancestry **3** biological breed **4** rifle part holding the barrel **5** pl. frame with holes for feet and hands, once used for punishment **6** broth from meat or fish **7** livestock **8** goods on hand **9** shares in a business —v. supply or keep in stock —a. **1** kept in stock **2** common —in (or out of) stock (not) available

stock·ade' n. defensive wall of tall stakes

stock'bro'ker n. a broker for stocks and bonds

stock car n. standard automobile, modified for racing

stock company n. company of actors presenting a repertoire of plays

stock exchange, stock market n. place of sale for stocks and bonds

stock'hold'er n. one owning stock in a company

Stock'holm' syndrome n. condition of hostage sympathizing with captors

stock'ing n. covering for the leg and foot

stocking cap n. long, tapered, knitted cap

stock'pile' v., n. (accumulate) a reserve supply

stock'-still' *a.* motionless

stock'tak'ing *n.* (self-)evaluation, esp. with regard to progress

stock'y *a.* **-i·er, -i·est** short and heavy

stock'yard' *n.* place to pen livestock till slaughtered

stodg·y (stä'jē) *a.* **-i·er, -i·est 1** dull; uninteresting **2** stubbornly conventional

sto'gie, sto'gy *n.*, *pl.* **-gies** long cigar

sto'ic *a.*, *n.* stoical (person)

sto'i·cal *a.* indifference to grief, pain, etc. —**sto'i·cism** *n.*

stoke *v.* stir up and feed fuel to (a fire) —**stok'er** *n.*

stole *v.* pt. of STEAL —*n.* long fur piece worn by women around the shoulders

stol'en *v.* pp. of STEAL

stol'id (stäl'-) *a.* unexcitable

sto'lon *n.* creeping, leaf-bearing aboveground stem

stom·ach (stum'ək) *n.* **1** digestive organ into which food passes **2** abdomen **3** appetite —*v.* tolerate

stom'ach·ache' *n.* pain in the stomach or abdomen

stomp *v.* STAMP (*v.* 1 & 2)

stomp'ing ground *n.* [Inf.] stamping ground

stone *n.* **1** solid nonmetallic mineral matter **2** piece of this **3** seed of certain fruits **4** abnormal stony mass in the kidney, etc. **5** *pl.* **stone** [Br.] **14** pounds —*v.* throw stones at

stoned *a.* [Sl.] under the influence of liquor, a drug, etc.

stone's throw *n.* short distance

stone'wall' *v.* [Inf.] impede by refusing to comply, cooperate, etc.

ston'y *a.* **-i·er, -i·est 1** full of stones **2** unfeeling

stood *v.* pt. & pp. of STAND

stooge (stōōj) *n.* [Inf.] lackey

stool *n.* **1** single seat with no back or arms **2** feces

stool pigeon *n.* [Inf.] one who betrays by informing

stoop *v.* **1** bend the body forward **2** lower one's dignity —*n.* **1** position of stooping **2** small porch

stop *v.* **stopped, stop'ping 1** close by filling, shutting off, etc. **2** cease; end; halt **3** to block; obstruct **4** stay —*n.* **1** a stopping **2** a place stopped at **3** obstruction, plug, etc. —**stop off** stop for a while —**stop'page** *n.*

stop'cock' *n.* valve to regulate the flow of a liquid

stop'gap' *n.* temporary substitute

stop'light' *n.* **1** traffic light, esp. when red **2** rear light on a vehicle that

lights up when the brakes are applied

stop'o·ver *n.* brief stop at a place during a journey

stop'per *n.* something inserted to close an opening

stop'watch' *n.* watch that can be started and stopped instantly, as to time races

stor'age *n.* **1** a storing **2** place for, or cost of, storing goods

storage battery *n.* battery capable of being recharged

store *v.* **1** supply; stock **2** establishment where goods are sold —*v.* put aside for future use —**in store** to be in the future

store'front' *n.* front room or ground floor, for use as retail store

store'house' *n.* warehouse

store'keep'er *n.* a person in charge of a store

store'room' *n.* a room where things are stored

stork *n.* large, long-legged wading bird

storm *n.* **1** strong wind with rain, snow, etc. **2** any strong disturbance **3** strong attack —*v.* **1** blow violently, rain, etc. **2** to rage **3** rush or attack violently —**storm'y** *a.*, **-i·er, -i·est**

storm door (or window) *n.* door (or window) put outside the regular one as added protection

sto'ry *n.*, *pl.* **-ries 1** a telling of an event **2** fictitious narrative **3** one level of a building **4** [Inf.] a falsehood **5** [Inf.] relevant or accumulated facts —**sto'ried** *a.*

sto'ry·book' *n.* book of stories, esp. one for children

sto'ry·tell'er *n.* one who narrates stories

stout *a.* **1** brave **2** firm; strong **3** fat —*n.* strong, dark beer —**stout'ly** *adv.*

stove *n.* apparatus for heating, cooking, etc. —*v.* alt. pt. & pp. of STAVE

stove'pipe' *n.* metal pipe to carry off stove smoke

stow (stō) *v.* pack or store away —**stow away** hide aboard a ship, etc. for a free ride —**stow'a·way** *n.*

strad'dle *v.* **1** sit or stand astride **2** take both sides of (an issue)

strafe *v.* attack with machine guns from aircraft

strag'gle *v.* **1** wander from the group **2** spread out unevenly —**strag'gler** *n.*

straight *a.* **1** not crooked, not bent, etc. **2** direct **3** in order **4** honest or frank **5** undiluted **6** [Sl.] conventional **7** [Sl.] heterosexual —*adv.* **1** in a straight line **2** directly **3** without delay —**straight away** (or **off**) without delay —**straight'en** v.

straight'-ar'row a. [Inf.] proper, conscientious, etc. and thus considered conservative, stodgy, etc.

straight'a·way' (adv.: strāt'ə wā') a. straight part of a track, road, etc. —adv. at once

straight'edge' n. straight strip of wood, etc. for drawing straight lines

straight face n. facial expression showing no emotion —**straight'-faced'** a.

straight'for'ward a. 1 direct 2 honest

straight man n. actor whose remarks a comedian answers with a quip

straight shooter n. [Inf.] an honest, sincere, etc. person

straight ticket n. ballot cast for candidates of only one party

strain v. 1 stretch tight or to the utmost 2 strive hard 3 sprain 4 filter —n. 1 a straining or being strained 2 excessive demand on one's emotions, etc. 3 ancestry 4 inherited tendency 5 trace; streak 6 often pl. tune —**strain'er** n.

strait n. often pl. 1 narrow waterway 2 distress

strait'ened a. impoverished

strait'jack'et n. coatlike device for restraining a person

strait'-laced' a. narrowly strict or severe, as in moral views

strand n. 1 any of the threads, wires, etc. that form a string, cable, etc. 2 string, as of pearls 3 shore —v. put into a helpless position

strange a. 1 unfamiliar 2 unusual 3 peculiar; odd —**strange'ly** adv.

stran'ger n. 1 newcomer 2 person not known to one

stran'gle v. 1 choke to death 2 stifle Also **stran'gu·late** —**stran'gler** n. —**stran'gu·la'tion** n.

strap n. narrow strip of leather, etc., as for binding things —v. fasten with a strap —**strap'ping** —**strap'less** a.

strapped a. [Inf.] in need of money

strap'ping a. [Inf.] robust

strat'a·gem (-jəm) n. tricky ruse or move to gain an end

strat'e·gy n., pl. **-gies** 1 science of military operations 2 artful managing 3 plan —**stra·te'gic** a. —**stra·te'gi·cal·ly** adv. —**strat'e·gist** n.

strat'i·fy' v. form in layers or levels —**strat'i·fi·ca'tion** n.

strat'o·sphere' n. upper atmosphere

from 12 to 31 miles in altitude

stra'tum n., pl. **-ta** or **-tums** any of a series of layers or levels

stra'tus n., pl. **-ti** long, low, gray cloud layer

straw n. 1 grain stalk or stalks after threshing 2 tube for sucking a drink

straw'ber'ry n., pl. **-ries** small, red, juicy fruit of a vinelike plant

straw boss n. [Inf.] person having subordinate authority

straw vote (or **poll**) n. unofficial poll of public opinion

stray v. 1 wander; roam 2 deviate —a. 1 lost 2 isolated —n. lost domestic animal

streak n. 1 long, thin mark 2 layer 3 tendency in behavior 4 spell, as of luck —v. 1 mark with streaks 2 go fast

stream n. 1 small river 2 steady flow, as of air —v. 1 flow in a stream 2 move swiftly

stream'er n. long, narrow flag or strip

stream'line' v., a. (to make) streamlined

stream'lined' a. 1 shaped to move easily in air, etc. 2 made more efficient

street n. road in a city

street'car' n. passenger car on rails along streets

street'light' n. lamp on a post for lighting a street

street'walk'er n. prostitute

street'wise' a. [Inf.] shrewd from experience in poor, dangerous, etc. urban areas: also **street'-smart'**

strength n. 1 force; power; vigor 2 durability 3 intensity 4 potency —**on the strength of** based upon or relying on —**strength'en** v.

stren'u·ous a. 1 needing or showing much energy 2 vigorous

strep n. streptococcus

strep throat n. [Inf.] sore throat caused by a streptococcus

strep'to·coc'cus (-käk'əs) n., pl. **-coc'ci** (-käk'sī') kind of spherical bacteria

strep'to·my'cin (-mī'sin) n. antibiotic drug

stress n. 1 strain; pressure 2 importance; emphasis 3 special force on a syllable, etc. —v. 1 to strain 2 to accent 3 emphasize —**stress'ful** a.

stretch v. 1 reach out 2 draw out to full extent 3 to strain 4 exaggerate —n. 1 a stretching 2 ability to be stretched 3 extent

stretch'er n. 1 canvas-covered frame to carry the sick 2 one that stretches

strew v. **strewed, strewed** or **strewn, strew'ing 1** scatter **2** cover as by scattering

stri'at·ed a. striped

strick'en a. struck, wounded, afflicted, etc.

strict a. **1** exact or absolute **2** rigidly enforced or enforcing —**strict'ly** adv. —**strict'ness** n.

stric'ture n. strong criticism

stride v. **strode, strid'den, strid'ing** walk with long steps —n. **1** long step **2** pl. progress

stri'dent a. shrill; grating

strife n. a quarrel(ing)

strike v. **struck, struck** or **strick'en, strik'ing 1** to hit **2** sound by hitting some part **3** ignite (a match) **4** make by stamping **5** to attack **6** reach or find **7** occur to **8** assume (a pose) **9** take down or apart **10** stop working until demands are met —n. **1** a striking **2** Baseball pitched ball over home plate or missed by the batter **3** Bowling a knocking down of all the pins at once —**strike out 1** erase **2** Baseball put or go out on three strikes —**strike up** begin —**strik'er** n.

strik'ing a. very attractive, impressive, etc.

string n. **1** thick thread, etc. used as for tying **2** numbers of things on a string or in a row **3** thin cord bowed, etc. to make music, as on a violin **4** Mus. instrument giving tones from vibrating strings **5** [Inf.] pl. conditions attached to a plan, offer, etc. — v. **strung, string'ing 1** provide with strings **2** put on a string **3** extend — **pull strings** use influence to gain advantage —**string'y** a., **-i·er, -i·est**

string bean n. thick bean pod, eaten as a vegetable

strin'gent (-jont) a. strict

strip v. **stripped, strip'ping 1** take off clothing, covering, etc. (of) **2** make bare **3** break the teeth of (a gear, etc.) —n. long, narrow piece

stripe n. **1** narrow band of different color or material **2** a type; sort —v. to mark with stripes

strip'ling n. a youth

strip mall n. shopping center of connected storefronts with common parking in front

strip mining n. mining for coal, etc. by removing minerals near the earth's surface

stripped'-down' a. reduced to essentials

strip'tease' n. act of a performer

undressing slowly in rhythm to music

strive v. **strove** or **strived, striv'en** or **strived, striv'ing 1** try very hard **2** to struggle

strobe (light) n. electronic tube emitting rapid, bright flashes of light

strode v. pt. of STRIDE

stroke n. **1** sudden blow, attack, action, etc. **2** a single movement of the arm, a tool, etc. **3** striking sound **4** vascular injury to the brain causing impaired speech, paralysis, etc. —v. draw one's hand, etc. gently over

stroll n. leisurely walk —v. **1** take a stroll **2** wander

stroll'er n. chairlike cart for a baby

strong a. **1** powerful **2** healthy **3** durable **4** intense —**strong'ly** adv.

strong'-arm' [Inf.] a. using physical force —v. use force upon

strong'box' n. heavily made box or safe for valuables

strong'hold' n. fortress

stron'tium (-sham) n. chemical element with radioactive isotope

strove v. pt. of STRIVE

struck v. pt. & pp. of STRIKE

struc'ture n. **1** thing built **2** plan, design, etc. —**struc'tur·al** a.

stru'del n. pastry of thin dough and filling, rolled up and baked

strug'gle v. **1** to fight **2** strive —n. a struggling

strum v. **strummed, strum'ming** play (a guitar, etc.) with long strokes, often casually

strum'pet n. prostitute

strung v. pt. & pp. of STRING

strut v. **strut'ted, strut'ting** walk arrogantly —n. **1** strutting walk **2** rod used as a support

strych'nine (strik'nin, -nīn') n. poisonous alkaloid

stub n. short, leftover, or blunt part — v. **stubbed, stub'bing** bump (one's toe)

stub'ble n. short, bristly growth

stub'born a. obstinate —**stub'bornness** n.

stub'by a. **-bi·er, -bi·est** short and thick

stuc'co v., **-coed, -co·ing;** n. (cover with) rough plaster

stuck v. pt. & pp. of STICK

stuck'-up' a. [Inf.] snobbish

stud n. **1** decorative nail **2** removable button **3** upright support in a wall **4** breeding stallion **5** [Sl.] virile man — v. **stud'ded, stud'ding** be set thickly on

stu'dent n. one who studies

stud'ied a. done on purpose

stu'di·o' n., pl. **-os'** 1 artist's work area 2 place for producing movies, radio or TV programs, etc.

studio apartment n. one-room apartment including kitchen and separate bathroom

studio couch n. couch that opens into a full-sized bed

stu'di·ous a. 1 fond of study 2 attentive

stud'y v. **-ied, -y'ing** 1 learn by reading, thinking, etc. 2 investigate —n., pl. **-ies** 1 act or product of studying 2 pl. education 3 deep thought 4 place to study

stuff n. 1 material; substance 2 (worthless) objects —v. 1 fill 2 cram —**stuff'ing** n.

stuffed shirt n. [Sl.] pompous, pretentious person

stuff'y a. **-i·er, -i·est** 1 poorly ventilated 2 stopped up 3 [Inf.] dull

stul'ti·fy' v. **-fied', -fy'ing** 1 make seem foolish, etc. 2 make dull, futile, etc.

stum'ble v. 1 walk unsteadily; trip 2 speak confusedly 3 come by chance —n. a stumbling

stum'bling block n. difficulty or obstacle

stump n. part left after cutting off the rest —v. 1 make a speaking tour 2 walk heavily 3 [Inf.] to baffle

stun v. **stunned, stun'ning** 1 make unconscious, as by a blow 2 shock deeply

stung v. pt. & pp. of STING

stunk v. pp. & alt. pt. of STINK

stun'ning a. [Inf.] very attractive

stunt v. keep from growing —n. daring show of skill

stu'pe·fy' v. **-fied', -fy'ing** stun —**stu'pe·fac'tion** n.

stu·pen'dous a. overwhelming

stu'pid a. 1 not intelligent 2 foolish 3 dull —**stu·pid'i·ty** n., pl. **-ties**

stu'por n. dazed condition

stur'dy a. **-di·er, -di·est** 1 firm 2 strong

stur'geon (-jən) n. food fish

stut'ter n., v. stammer

sty n., pl. **sties** pigpen

sty, stye n., pl. **sties** or **styes** swelling on the rim of the eyelid

style n. 1 way of making, writing, etc. 2 fine style 3 fashion —v. 1 to name 2 design the style of 3 to cut, etc. (hair) in a fashionable way

styl'ish a. fashionable

styl'ist n. one who styles hair

styl'ize' v. design or depict in a style rather than naturally

sty'lus n. 1 pointed writing tool 2 phonograph needle

sty'mie v. **-mied, -mie·ing** to hinder

styp'tic (stip'-) a. that halts bleeding by being astringent

styptic pencil n. piece of a styptic substance to stop minor bleeding

Sty'ro·foam' trademark rigid, light, porous plastic —n. **[s-]** substance like this

suave (swäv) a. smoothly polite —**suave'ly** adv. —**suav'i·ty** n.

sub- pref. 1 under; below 2 somewhat 3 being a division

sub'a·tom'ic a. smaller than an atom

sub'com·mit'tee n. subdivision of a committee, with special tasks, etc.

sub·con'scious a., n. (of) one's feelings, wishes, etc. of which one is unaware

sub'con·ti·nent n. large land mass smaller than a continent; often, subdivision of a continent

sub'con·trac·tor n. person(s) assuming obligations from a main contractor

sub'cul'ture n. particular social group within a society

sub'cu·ta'ne·ous (-kyoo-) a. beneath the skin

sub'di·vide' v. 1 divide again 2 divide (land) into small sections for sale —**sub'di·vi'sion** n.

sub·due' v. 1 get control over 2 make less intense

sub·ject (v.: səb jekt') a. 1 that is a subject 2 liable 3 contingent upon —n. 1 one controlled by another 2 topic of discussion or study 3 Gram. word or words about which something is said —v. 1 bring under the control of 2 make undergo —**sub·jec'tion** n.

sub·jec'tive a. from one's feelings rather than from facts —**sub'jec·tiv'i·ty** n.

sub'ju·gate' v. conquer

sub·junc'tive a. of the mood of a verb expressing supposition, desire, etc.

sub·lease' (v.: sub lēs') n. lease granted by a lessee —v. grant or hold a sublease of —also **sub·let'**

sub'li·mate' v. express (unacceptable impulses) in acceptable forms —**sub'li·ma'tion** n.

sub·lime' a. 1 noble 2 inspiring awe through beauty 3 [Inf.] supremely such —v. purify (a solid) by heating and then condensing —**sub·lim'i·ty** n.

sub·lim'i·nal a. below the threshold of awareness

sub·ma·chine′ gun *n.* portable, automatic firearm

sub·mar′gin·al *a.* below minimum standards

sub·ma·rine′ *n.* watercraft operating under water

submarine sandwich *n.* hero sandwich

sub·merge′ *v.* put or go under water —**sub·mer′gence** *n.*

sub·merse′ *v.* submerge —**sub·mer′sion** *n.*

sub·mis′sion *n.* **1** a submitting **2** obedience —**sub·mis′sive** *a.*

sub·mit′ *v.* **-mit′ted, -mit′ting 1** to present for consideration, etc. **2** surrender

sub·nor′mal *a.* below normal, as in intelligence

sub·or′di·nate (-nət; *v.:* -nāt′) *a.* lower in rank; secondary —*n.* subordinate person —*v.* to make subordinate

sub·orn′ *v.* induce (another) to commit perjury

sub′plot′ *n.* secondary plot in a novel, etc.

sub·poe·na (sə pē′nə) *n.* legal paper ordering one to appear in court —*v.* to order or summon with a subpoena Also sp. **sub·pe′na**

sub ro′sa *adv.* secretly

sub·scribe′ *v.* **1** give support or consent (to) **2** promise to contribute (money) **3** agree to take and pay for a periodical, etc.: with *to* —**sub·scrib′er** *n.* —**sub·scrip′tion** *n.*

sub′se·quent′ *a.* following

sub·ser′vi·ent *a.* servile

sub′set′ *n.* subdivision of a mathematical set

sub·side′ *v.* **1** to sink lower **2** become quieter

sub·sid′i·ar·y *a.* helping in a lesser way —*n., pl.* **-ies** company controlled by another

sub′si·dize′ *v.* support with a subsidy

sub′si·dy *n., pl.* **-dies** (government) grant of money

sub·sist′ *v.* continue to live or exist

sub·sist′ence *n.* **1** a subsisting **2** barest means of food, shelter, etc. needed to sustain life

sub′soil′ *n.* layer of soil beneath the surface soil

sub·son′ic *a.* moving at a speed less than sound

sub′stance *n.* **1** essence **2** physical matter **3** central meaning **4** wealth

sub·stand′ard *a.* below standard

sub·stan′tial (-shəl) *a.* **1** material **2** strong **3** large **4** wealthy **5** in essentials

sub·stan′ti·ate′ (-shē-) *v.* prove to be true or real

sub′sti·tute′ *a., n.* (being) one that takes the place of another —*v.* be or use as a substitute —**sub′sti·tu′tion** *n.*

sub′ter·fuge′ *n.* scheme used to evade something

sub′ter·ra′ne·an *a.* **1** underground **2** secret

sub′text′ *n.* underlying meaning, theme, etc.

sub′ti·tle *n.* **1** secondary title **2** line translating dialogue, etc. as at the bottom of a film image

sub·tle (sut′'l) *a.* **1** keen; acute **2** crafty **3** delicate **4** not obvious —**sub′tle·ty** *n., pl.* **-ties** —**sub′tly** *adv.*

sub·to′tal *n.* total forming part of a final total

sub·tract′ *v.* take away, as one number from another —**sub·trac′tion** *n.*

sub′tra·hend′ *n.* quantity to be subtracted from another

sub′urb *n.* district, town, etc. on the outskirts of a city —**sub·ur′ban** *a.* —**sub·ur′ban·ite′** *n.*

sub·ur′bi·a *n.* suburbs or suburbanites collectively

sub·vert′ *v.* overthrow (something established) —**sub·ver′sion** *n.* —**sub·ver′sive** *a., n.*

sub′way′ *n.* underground electric railroad in a city

sub′woof′er *n.* woofer for lowest sounds

suc·ceed′ (sak sēd′) *v.* **1** come next after **2** have success

suc·cess′ (sak ses′) *n.* **1** favorable result **2** the gaining of wealth, fame, etc. **3** successful one —**suc·cess′ful** *a.* —**suc·cess′ful·ly** *adv.*

suc·ces′sion *n.* **1** a coming after another **2** series —**suc·ces′sive** *a.*

suc·ces′sor *n.* one who succeeds another, as in office

suc·cinct′ (sak sinkt′) *a.* terse

suc′cor (-ər) *v., n.* help

suc′co·tash′ *n.* lima beans and corn cooked together

suc′cu·lent *a.* juicy

suc·cumb′ (-kum′) *v.* **1** give in; yield **2** die

such *a.* **1** of this or that kind **2** whatever **3** so much —*pron.* such a one —**such as** for example

suck *v.* **1** draw into the mouth **2** suck liquid from **3** dissolve in the mouth —*n.* act of sucking

suck′er *n.* **1** one that sucks or clings **2** part used for holding by suction **3** lollipop **4** [Sl.] a dupe

suck'le v. give or get milk from the breast or udder

suck'ling n. unweaned child or young animal

su'crose' n. sugar found in sugar cane, sugar beets, etc.

suc'tion n. creation of a vacuum that sucks in fluid, etc. —a. worked by suction

sud'den a. **1** unexpected **2** hasty —**sud'den·ly** adv.

suds pl.n. foam on soapy water —**suds'y** a., **-i·er**, **-i·est**

sue v. **1** begin a lawsuit against **2** petition

suede (swād) n. **1** leather with one side buffed into a nap **2** cloth like this

su'et n. hard animal fat

suf, suff abbrev. suffix

suf'fer v. **1** undergo or endure (pain, loss, etc.) **2** tolerate —**suf'fer·ance** n.

suf·fice' v. be enough

suf·fi'cient (-fish'ənt) a. enough —**suf·fi'cien·cy** n. —**suf·fi'cient·ly** adv.

suf'fix n. syllable(s) added at the end of a word to alter its meaning, etc.

suf'fo·cate' v. **1** kill by cutting off air **2** die from lack of air —**suf'fo·ca'tion** n.

suf'frage n. right to vote

suf·fuse' v. spread over

sug·ar (shoog'ər) n. sweet carbohydrate found in sugar cane, etc.

sugar beet n. beet with a white root having a high sugar content

sugar cane n. tall tropical grass grown for its sugar

sug'ar·coat' v. make seem less unpleasant

sug·gest' (səg jest') v. **1** bring to mind **2** propose as a possibility **3** imply —**sug·ges'tion** n.

sug·gest'i·ble a. readily influenced by suggestion

sug·ges'tive a. suggesting ideas, esp. indecent ideas

su'i·cide' n. **1** act of killing oneself intentionally **2** one who commits suicide —**su'i·ci'dal** a.

su·i ge·ne·ris (soo'ē jen'ə ris) a. unique

suit n. **1** coat and trousers (or skirt) **2** any of the four sets of playing cards **3** lawsuit **4** a suing, pleading, etc. —v. **1** be suitable for **2** make suitable **3** please —**follow suit** follow the example set

suit'a·ble a. appropriate; fitting —**suit'a·bly** adv.

suit'case' n. traveling bag

suite (swēt; 2: also soot) n. **1** group of connected rooms **2** set of matched furniture

suit'or n. man who courts a woman

su·ki·ya'ki (-yä'-) n. Japanese dish of thinly sliced meat and vegetables

sul'fa a. of a family of drugs used in combating certain bacterial infections

sul'fate' n. salt of sulfuric acid

sul'fide' n. compound of sulfur

sul'fur n. yellow, solid substance, a chemical element —**sul·fu'ric** (-fyoor'ik), **sul'fu·rous** a.

sulfuric acid n. acid formed of hydrogen, sulfur, and oxygen

sulk v. be sulky —n. sulky mood: also **the sulks**

sulk'y a., **-i·er**, **-i·est** sullen; glum —n., pl. **-ies** light, two-wheeled carriage —**sulk'i·ly** adv. —**sulk'i·ness** n.

sul'len a. **1** showing ill-humor by morose withdrawal **2** gloomy —**sul'len·ly** adv.

sul'ly v. **-lied**, **-ly·ing** soil, stain, defile, etc.

sul'phur n. chiefly Br. sp. of SULFUR

sul'tan n. Muslim ruler

sul'try a. **-tri·er**, **-tri·est 1** hot and humid **2** suggesting smoldering passion

sum n. **1** amount of money **2** total —v. **summed**, **sum'ming** summarize: with up

su·mac, su·mach (soo'mak', shoo'-) n. plant with lance-shaped leaves and red fruit

sum'ma·rize' v. make or be a summary of

sum'ma·ry n., pl. **-ries** brief report; digest —a. **1** concise **2** prompt —**sum·mar'i·ly** adv.

sum·ma'tion n. summarizing of arguments, as in a trial

sum'mer n. warmest season of the year —a. of or for summer —v. pass the summer —**sum'mer·y** a.

sum'mer·house' n. small, open structure in a garden, etc.

summer sausage n. hard, dried sausage that does not spoil easily

sum'mit n. highest point

sum'mon v. **1** call together **2** send for

sum'mons n. official order to appear in court

su'mo (wrestling) n. Japanese wrestling by large, extremely heavy men

sump n. hole for collecting excess water

sump pump n. pump for draining a sump

sump'tu·ous (-choo əs) a. costly; lav-ish

sun *n.* **1** incandescent body about which (the) planets revolve **2** heat or light of the sun —*v.* **sunned, sun'ning** to expose to sunlight

Sun *abbrev.* Sunday

sun'bathe' *v.* expose the body to sunlight or a sunlamp —**sun bath** *n.* —**sun'bath'er** *n.*

sun'beam' *n.* beam of sunlight

sun'block' *n.* chemical used in creams, etc. to block ultraviolet rays and reduce sunburn

sun'bon'net *n.* bonnet for shading the face, neck, etc. from the sun

sun'burn' *n.* inflammation of the skin from exposure to the sun —*v.* give or get sunburn

sun'burst' *n.* **1** sudden sunlight **2** decoration representing the sun's rays

sun'dae *n.* ice cream covered with syrup, nuts, etc.

Sun'day *n.* first day of the week

sun'der *v.* break apart

sun'di'al *n.* instrument that shows time by the shadow cast by the sun

sun'down' *n.* sunset

sun'dries *pl.n.* sundry items

sun'dry *a.* various

sun'fish' *n.* **1** small freshwater fish **2** large sea fish

sun'flow'er *n.* tall plant with big, daisylike flowers

sung *v.* pp. of SING

sun'glass'es *pl.n.* eyeglasses with tinted lenses

sunk *v.* pp. & alt. pt. of SINK

sunk'en *a.* **1** sunk in liquid **2** fallen in; hollow

sun'lamp' *n.* an ultraviolet-ray lamp, used for tanning the body, etc.

sun'light' *n.* light of the sun

sun'lit' *a.* lighted by the sun

sun'ny *a.* **-ni-er, -ni-est 1** full of sunshine **2** cheerful

sun'rise' *n.* daily rising of the sun in the east

sun'roof' *n.* car roof with a panel to let in air and light

sun'room' *n.* room with large windows to let sunlight in

sun'screen' *n.* chemical used in creams, etc. to block ultraviolet rays and reduce sunburn

sun'set' *n.* daily setting of the sun in the west

sun'shine' *n.* **1** shining of the sun **2** light from the sun —**sun'shin'y** *a.*

sun'spot' *n.* temporary dark spot on sun

sun'stroke' *n.* illness from overexposure to the sun

sun'suit' *n.* short pants with a bib and shoulder straps, worn by babies

sun'tan' *n.* darkening of skin by exposure to the sun

sup *v.* **supped, sup'ping** have supper

su'per *a.* [Inf.] outstanding

super- *pref.* **1** over; above **2** very; very much **3** greater than others **4** extra

su'per·an'nu·at'ed *a.* **1** retired on a pension **2** too old to work or use

su·perb' *a.* excellent

su'per·charge' *v.* increase the power of (an engine)

su·per·cil'i·ous (-sil'-) *a.* disdainful; haughty

su'per·con·duc·tiv'i·ty *n.* lack of electrical resistance in some metals at low temperatures —**su'per·con·duc'tor** *n.*

su·per·e'go *n.* part of mind thought to enforce moral standards

su'per·fi'cial (-fish'əl) *a.* **1** of or on the surface **2** shallow **3** hasty —**su'per·fi'cial·ly** *adv.*

su'per·flu'ous *a.* unnecessary —**su'per·flu'i·ty** *n.*

su'per·he'ro *n.* all-powerful hero, as in comics

su'per·high'way' *n.* expressway

su'per·hu'man *a.* **1** divine **2** greater than normal

su'per·im·pose' *v.* put on top of something else

su'per·in·tend' *v.* direct or manage —**su'per·in·tend'ent** *n.*

su·pe·ri·or *a.* **1** higher in rank, etc. **2** above average **3** haughty —*n.* one that is superior —**superior to** unaffected by —**su·pe'ri·or'i·ty** *n.*

su·per'la·tive *a.* of the highest degree; supreme —*n.* **1** highest degree **2** third degree in the comparison of adjectives and adverbs

su'per·ma·jor'i·ty *n.* quantity of votes above a majority that is needed to pass certain laws, etc.

su'per·man' *n., pl.* **-men'** seemingly superhuman man

su'per·mar'ket *n.* large, self-service food store

su'per·nat'u·ral *a.* beyond known laws of nature —**the supernatural** supernatural beings, forces, etc.

su'per·no'va *n., pl.* **-vas** or **-vae** (-vē) rare, very bright nova

su'per·nu'mer·ar'y *a.; n., pl.* **-ies** extra (person or thing)

su'per·pow'er *n.* extremely powerful,

influential nation

su'per·script' *n.* figure, letter, etc. written above and to the side of another

su'per·sede' *v.* replace, succeed, or supplant

su'per·son'ic *a.* **1** traveling faster than sound **2** ultrasonic

su'per·star' *n.* famous athlete, entertainer, etc.

su'per·sti'tion *n.* belief or practice based on fear or ignorance —**su'per·sti'tious** *a.*

su'per·store' *n.* very large store with a wide variety of goods

su'per·struc'ture *n.* **1** part above a ship's deck **2** upper part of a building

su'per·tank'er *n.* extremely large oil tanker

su'per·vene' *v.* come unexpectedly

su'per·vise' *v.* oversee or direct —**su'per·vi'sion** *n.* —**su'per·vi'sor** *n.* —**su'per·vi'so·ry** *a.*

su·pine' *a.* **1** lying on the back **2** listless

sup'per *n.* evening meal

sup·plant' *v.* take the place of, esp. by force

sup'ple *a.* flexible

sup'ple·ment (-mənt; *v.:* -ment') *n.* something added —*v.* add to —**sup'ple·men'tal, sup'ple·men'ta·ry** *a.*

sup'pli·cate' *v.* implore —**sup'pli·ant, sup'pli·cant** *n., a.* —**sup'pli·ca'tion** *n.*

sup·ply' *v.* -**plied', -ply'ing 1** furnish; provide **2** make up for —*n., pl.* -**plies' 1** amount available **2** *pl.* materials —**sup·pli'er** *n.*

sup·port' *v.* **1** hold up **2** help **3** provide for **4** help prove —*n.* **1** a supporting **2** one that supports

sup·port'ive *a.* giving support, help, or approval

sup·pose' *v.* **1** take as true; assume **2** guess; think **3** expect —**sup·posed'** *a.* —**sup·pos'ing** *n.*

sup·pos'i·to'ry *n., pl.* -**ries** medicated substance put in the rectum or vagina

sup·press' *v.* **1** put down by force **2** keep back; conceal —**sup·pres'sion** *n.*

sup'pu·rate' (sup'yōō-) *v.* form or discharge pus

su'pra·na'tion·al *a.* of, for, or above all or a number of nations

su·prem'a·cist *n.* person advocating the supremacy of a certain group

su·prem'a·cy *n.* supreme power or authority

su·preme' *a.* highest in rank, power, or degree

Supt *abbrev.* Superintendent

sur·cease' *n.* end or cessation

sur·charge' *n.* **1** extra charge **2** overload —*v.* put a surcharge in or on

sure (shoor) *a.* **1** reliable; certain **2** without doubt **3** bound to happen or do —*adv.* [Inf.] surely —**for sure** certainly —**sure enough** [Inf.] without doubt

sure'fire', sure'-fire' *a.* [Inf.] sure to be successful

sure'-foot'ed *a.* not likely to stumble, err, etc.

sure'ly *adv.* **1** with confidence **2** without doubt

sure'ty *n., pl.* -**ties 1** security **2** guarantor of another's debts

surf *n.* ocean waves breaking on a shore or reef —*v.* ride on a surfboard **2** [Inf.] sample (channels, files, etc.) on (a TV, computer, etc.) —**surf'er** *n.*

sur·face *n.* **1** outside of a thing **2** any face of a solid **3** outward appearance —*a.* superficial —*v.* **1** give a surface to **2** rise to the surface

surf'board' *n.* long board used in riding the surf

sur·feit (-fit) *n.* **1** excess, as of food **2** discomfort, disgust, etc. caused by this —*v.* overindulge

surf'ing *n.* sport of riding the surf on a surfboard

surge *v., n.* (move in) a large wave or sudden rush

sur'geon *n.* doctor who practices surgery

sur'ger·y *n.* **1** treatment of disease or injury by operations **2** a room for this —**sur'gi·cal** *a.*

sur'gi·cen'ter *n.* place for performing minor outpatient surgery

sur'ly *a.* -**li·er, -li·est** bad-tempered; uncivil

sur·mise' (-mīz') *n., v.* guess

sur·mount' *v.* **1** to overcome **2** climb over **3** top —**sur·mount'a·ble** *a.*

sur'name' *n.* family name

sur·pass' *v.* **1** excel **2** go beyond the limit of

sur'plice (-plis) *n.* clergyman's loose, white tunic

sur'plus' *n., a.* (quantity) over what is needed or used

sur·prise' *v.* **1** come upon unexpectedly **2** astonish —*n.* **1** a surprising or being surprised **2** thing that surprises —**sur·pris'ing** *a.*

sur·re'al *a.* fantastic or bizarre

sur·re'al·ism' *n.* art depicting the unconscious mind —**sur·re'al·ist** *a., n.*

sur·ren'der *v.* **1** give oneself up **2** give

sur·rep·ti·tious (-tish'əs) *a.* secret; stealthy

sur'rey *n.*, *pl.* **-reys** light, four-wheeled carriage

sur'ro·gate (-gət) *n.*, *a.* (a) substitute

sur·round' *v.* encircle on all sides

sur·round'ings *pl.n.* things, conditions, etc. around a person or thing

sur'tax' *n.* extra tax on top of the regular tax

sur·veil'lance (-vā'-) *n.* watch kept over a person

sur·vey' (*n.:* sur'vā') *v.* **1** examine in detail **2** determine the form, boundaries, etc. of (a piece of land) —*n.* **1** general or comprehensive study **2** act of surveying an area —**sur·vey'or** *n.*

sur·vey'ing *n.* science or work of making land surveys

sur·vive' *v.* **1** outlive **2** continue to live —**sur·viv'al** *n.* —**sur·vi'vor** *n.*

sus·cep'ti·ble (sə sep'-) *a.* easily affected; sensitive

su'shi *n.* Japanese dish of rice cakes with raw fish, etc.

sus·pect' (*n.:* sus'pekt') *v.* **1** believe to be guilty on little evidence **2** distrust **3** surmise —*n.* one suspected

sus·pend' *v.* **1** exclude, stop, etc. for a time **2** hold back (judgment, etc.) **3** hang —**sus·pen'sion** *n.*

sus·pend'ers *pl.n.* shoulder straps to hold up trousers

sus·pense' *n.* tense uncertainty

suspension bridge *n.* bridge suspended by anchored cables from supporting towers

sus·pi·cion (sə spish'ən) *n.* **1** act of suspecting **2** feeling of one who suspects **3** trace —**sus·pi'cious** *a.*

sus·tain' *v.* **1** maintain; prolong **2** provide for **3** support **4** undergo **5** uphold as valid **6** confirm

sus'te·nance *n.* **1** means of livelihood **2** food

su'ture (-chər) *n.* the stitching up of a wound, or material used for this

SUV *abbrev.* sport utility vehicle

su'ze·rain' (-rin', -rān') *n.* state having some control over another state

svelte *a.* **1** slender and graceful **2** suave

SW *abbrev.* southwest(ern)

swab *n.* **1** a mop **2** piece of cotton, etc. used to medicate or clean the throat, etc. —*v.* **swabbed**, **swab'bing** clean with a swab

swad'dle *v.* wrap (a baby) in narrow bands of cloth, a blanket, etc.

swage (swāj) *n.* tool for shaping or bending metal

swag'ger *v.* walk with an arrogant stride —*n.* swaggering walk

Swa·hi'li (-hē'-) *n.* language of an E African people

swain *n.* [Ar.] lover

swal'low *v.* **1** pass (food, etc.) from the mouth into the stomach **2** take in; absorb **3** tolerate **4** suppress —*n.* **1** act of swallowing **2** amount swallowed **3** small, swift-flying bird

swam *v.* pt. of SWIM

swa'mi *n.* Hindu religious teacher

swamp *n.* piece of wet, spongy ground —*v.* **1** flood with water **2** overwhelm —**swamp'y** *a.*, **-i·er**, **-i·est**

swamp buggy *n.* vehicle for traveling over swampy ground

swan *n.* large water bird with a long, graceful neck

swank *a.* [Inf.] ostentatiously stylish: also **swank'y**, **-i·er**, **-i·est**

swan song *n.* last act, final work, etc. of a person

swap *n.*, *v.* **swapped**, **swap'ping** [Inf.] trade

swarm *n.* **1** colony of bees **2** moving crowd or throng —*v.* move in a swarm

swarth·y (swôr'thē) *a.* **-i·er**, **-i·est** dark-skinned

swash'buck'ler *n.* swaggering fighting man

swas'ti·ka *n.* cross with bent arms: Nazi emblem

swat *v.*, *n.* **swat'ted**, **swat'ting** (hit with) a sharp blow —**swat'ter** *n.*

swatch *n.* small sample of cloth

swath *n.* a strip cut by a scythe, mower, etc.

swathe (swāth, swäth) *v.* **1** wrap up in a bandage **2** envelop

SWAT team *n.* police unit trained to deal with riots, terrorism, etc.

sway *v.* **1** swing from side to side or to and fro **2** to influence —*n.* **1** a swaying **2** influence

swear *v.* **swore**, **sworn**, **swear'ing** **1** make a solemn declaration or promise **2** curse **3** make take an oath

swear'word' *n.* profane or obscene word or phrase

sweat *n.* **1** salty liquid given off through the skin **2** moisture collected on a surface —*v.* **sweat** or **sweat'ed**, **sweat'ing** **1** give forth sweat **2** work so hard as to cause sweating —**sweat'y** *a.*, **-i·er**, **-i·est**

sweat'er *n.* knitted garment for the upper body

sweat shirt *n.* heavy jersey pullover worn to absorb sweat

sweat'shop' n. shop where employees work long hours at low wages

sweat suit n. sweat shirt worn together with loose trousers made of jersey (**sweat pants**)

Swed'ish a., n. (of) the people or language of Sweden

sweep v. **swept, sweep'ing** 1 clean, or clear away, with a broom 2 carry away or pass over swiftly 3 extend in a long line —n. 1 a sweeping 2 range or extent —**sweep'ing** a.

sweep'ings pl.n. things swept up

sweep'stakes' n., pl. **-stakes'** lottery whose participants put up the money given as the prize(s)

sweet a. 1 tasting of sugar 2 pleasant 3 fresh —n. [Chiefly Br.] a candy —**sweet'en** v. —**sweet'ly** adv.

sweet'bread' n. calf's pancreas or thymus, used as food

sweet'bri'er, sweet'bri'ar n. kind of rose

sweet corn n. kind of corn cooked and eaten before it is ripe

sweet'en·er n. sugar substitute

sweet'meat' n. a candy

sweet pea n. climbing plant with fragrant flowers

sweet pepper n. 1 plant with large, mild, red pod 2 the pod

sweet potato n. thick, yellow root of a tropical vine

sweet'-talk' v. [Inf.] to flatter

sweet tooth n. [Inf.] fondness for sweet foods

swell v. **swelled, swelled** or **swol'len, swell'ing** 1 bulge 2 increase in size, force, etc. 3 fill, as with pride —n. 1 a swelling 2 large wave —a. [Sl.] excellent

swell'ing n. 1 swollen part 2 increase

swel'ter v. feel oppressed with great heat

swel'ter·ing a. very hot

swept v. pt. & pp. of SWEEP

swerve v., n. (make) a quick turn aside

swift a. 1 moving fast 2 prompt —n. swallowlike bird —**swift'ly** adv.

swig [Inf.] v. **swigged, swig'ging** drink in large gulps —n. large gulp

swill v. drink greedily —n. garbage fed to pigs

swim v. **swam, swum, swim'ming** 1 move through water by moving the limbs, fins, etc. 2 float on a liquid 3 overflow 4 be dizzy —n. act of swimming —**swim'mer** n.

swimming hole n. deep place in a creek, etc. used for swimming

swim'suit' n. garment worn for swimming

swin'dle v. defraud; cheat —n. a swindling

swine n., pl. **swine** pig or hog —**swin'ish** a.

swing v. **swung, swing'ing** 1 sway back and forth 2 turn, as on a hinge 3 [Inf.] manage to make, do, etc. 4 to strike (at) —n. 1 a swinging 2 a sweeping blow 3 rhythm 4 seat hanging from ropes

swing'er n. [Sl.] uninhibited, sophisticated, pleasure-seeking person

swing shift n. [Inf.] work period between 4:00 P.M. and midnight

swipe n. [Inf.] hard, sweeping blow —v. 1 [Inf.] hit with a swipe 2 [Sl.] steal

swirl v., n. whirl; twist

swish v., n. (move with) a hissing or rustling sound

Swiss a., n. (of) the people of Switzerland

Swiss chard n. chard

Swiss cheese n. pale-yellow cheese with large holes

Swiss steak n. round steak pounded with flour and braised

switch n. 1 thin stick used for whipping 2 control device for an electric circuit 3 movable section of railroad track 4 shift; change —v. 1 to whip 2 jerk 3 turn a light, etc. (on or off) 4 move a train to another track 5 shift

switch'blade' (knife) n. jackknife opened by a spring release

switch'board' n. control panel for electric switches

switch'-hit'ter n. baseball player who bats left-handed and right-handed

swiv'el n. a fastening with free-turning parts —v. turn as on a swivel

swiz'zle stick n. small rod for stirring mixed drinks

swol·len (swō'lən) v. alt. pp. of SWELL —a. bulging

swoon v., n. faint

swoop v. sweep down or pounce upon —n. a swooping

sword (sôrd) n. weapon with a handle and a long blade

sword'fish' n. large ocean fish with a swordlike upper jaw

sword'play' n. the act or skill of using a sword

swore v. pt. of SWEAR

sworn v. pp. of SWEAR —a. bound by an oath

swum v. pp. of SWIM

syb'a·rite' (sib'-) n. self-indulgent, pleasure-loving person

syc'a·more' (sik'-) n. shade tree that sheds its bark

syc·o·phant (sik'ə fənt) n. flatterer

syl·lab'i·fy' v. **-fied', -fy'ing** divide into syllables: also **syl·lab'i·cate'** —**syl·lab'i·fi·ca'tion** n.

syl'la·ble n. **1** unit of pronunciation with a single vocal sound **2** written form of this —**syl·lab'ic** a.

syl'la·bus n., pl. **-bus·es** or **-bi'** (-bī') summary or outline

syl'lo·gism' (-jiz'əm) n. two premises and a conclusion

sylph (silf) n. slender, graceful woman

syl'van a. of, living in, or covered with trees

sym·bi·ot'ic (-bī-, -bē-) a. mutually dependent

sym'bol n. object, mark, etc. that represents another object, an idea, etc. —**sym·bol'ic** a. —**sym'bol·ize'** v.

sym'bol·ism' n. use of symbols

sym'me·try n. balance of opposite parts in position or size —**sym·met'ri·cal** a.

sym'pa·thet'ic a. of, in, or feeling sympathy —**sym'pa·thet'i·cal·ly** adv.

sym'pa·thize' v. feel or show sympathy

sym'pa·thy n., pl. **-thies 1** sameness of feeling **2** agreement **3** compassion

sym'pho·ny n., pl. **-nies** full orchestra or composition for it —**sym·phon'ic** a.

sym·po'si·um n., pl. **-ums** or **-a** meeting for discussion

symp'tom n. indication or sign, as of disease —**symp'to·mat'ic** a.

syn'a·gogue' (-gäg') n. building where Jews worship

sync, synch (siŋk) v. **synced** or **synched, sync'ing** or **synch'ing** synchronize —n. synchronization

syn'chro·nize' v. **1** move or occur at the same time or rate **2** make agree in time or rate —**syn'chro·ni·za'tion** n.

syn'co·pate' v. Mus. shift the beat to notes normally not accented —**syn'co·pa'tion** n.

syn'di·cate (-kət; v.: -kāt') n. **1** business association of bankers, corporations, etc. **2** organization selling news stories, etc. —v. publish through a syndicate —**syn'di·ca'tion** n.

syn'drome' n. set of symptoms characterizing a disease or condition

syn'er·gism' n. an interaction of things that results in a greater effect

than the sum of the things' individual effects

syn'od n. council of churches or church officials

syn'o·nym (-nim) n. word meaning the same as another —**syn·on'y·mous** a.

syn·op'sis n., pl. **-ses'** (-sēz') summary

syn'tax' n. the way words are arranged in a sentence —**syn·tac'tic** a.

syn'the·sis n., pl. **-ses'** (-sēz') combining of parts into a whole —**syn'the·size'** v.

syn'the·siz'er n. an electronic device for producing musical sounds without instruments

syn·thet'ic a. **1** of or using synthesis **2** artificial; not natural —n. synthetic thing —**syn·thet'i·cal·ly** adv.

syph'i·lis (sif'-) n. infectious venereal disease —**syph'i·lit'ic** a., n.

sy·ringe' (sə rinj') n. tube with a ball or a piston at one end, for drawing in and then ejecting liquids

syr'up n. sweet, thick liquid, as sugar boiled in water —**syr'up·y** a.

sys'tem n. **1** whole formed of related things **2** set of organized facts, rules, etc. **3** orderly way of doing things —**sys'tem·a·tize'** v.

sys'tem·at'ic a. orderly; methodical —**sys'tem·at'i·cal·ly** adv.

sys·tem'ic a. of or affecting the body as a whole

sys'to·le' (-tə lē') n. usual rhythmic contraction of the heart, esp. of the ventricles —**sys·tol'ic** a.

T

t abbrev. **1** teaspoon(s) **2** tense **3** ton(s)

T abbrev. tablespoon(s)

tab n. small flap or tag —**keep tabs** (or **a tab**) **on** [Inf.] keep informed about

Ta·bas'co trademark a very hot, spicy sauce

tab'by n., pl. **-bies** pet cat

tab'er·nac'le (-nak'əl) n. large place of worship

ta'ble n. **1** flat surface set on legs **2** table set with food **3** orderly list or arrangement —v. postpone consideration of

tab'leau' (-lō') n., pl. **-leaux'** (-lōz') or **-leaus'** striking, dramatic scene

ta'ble·cloth' n. cloth for covering a table at meals

ta·ble d'hôte (tä'bəl dōt') n. complete meal for a set price

ta'ble-hop' v. **-hopped', -hop'ping** leave one's table and visit about at other tables

ta'ble-land' n. plateau

ta'ble-spoon' n. 1 large spoon for eating soup, etc. 2 spoon for measuring ½ fluid ounce —**ta'ble-spoon'ful** n., pl. **-fuls**

tab'let n. 1 flat, inscribed piece of stone, metal, etc. 2 writing pad 3 flat, hard cake of medicine

table tennis n. game somewhat like tennis, played on a table

ta'ble-ware' n. dishes, forks, etc. used for eating

tab'loid' n. small newspaper with often sensational news stories

ta-boo', ta-bu' n. sacred or social prohibition —v. prohibit

tab'u-lar a. of or arranged in a table or list

tab'u-late' v. put in tabular form —**tab-u-la'tion** n.

ta-chom'e-ter (ta käm'-) n. a device showing rate of rotation of a shaft

tach'y-car'di-a (tak'i-) n. abnormally rapid heartbeat

tac'it (tas'-) a. not expressed openly, but implied

tac'i-turn' (tas'-) a. usually silent —**tac'i-tur'ni-ty** n.

tack n. 1 short, flat-headed nail 2 a course of action 3 ship's direction relative to position of sails —v. 1 fasten with tacks 2 add 3 change course

tack'le n. 1 equipment 2 set of ropes and pulleys 3 a tackling —v. 1 undertake 2 *Football* bring down (the ball carrier)

tack'y a. **-i-er, -i-est** 1 slightly sticky 2 [Inf.] in poor taste —**tack'i-ness** n.

ta'co (tä'-) n., pl. **-cos** folded, fried tortilla, filled with meat, etc.

tact n. skill in dealing with people —**tact'ful** a. —**tact'less** a.

tac'tic n. skillful method

tac'tics n. science of battle maneuvers —**tac'ti-cal** a. —**tac-ti'cian** (-tish'ən) n.

tac'tile a. of the sense of touch

tad n. small amount

tad'pole' n. frog or toad in an early stage

taf-fe'ta n. stiff, glossy silk cloth

taff'rail' n. rail around a ship's stern

taf'fy n. a chewy candy

tag n. 1 hanging end 2 card, etc. attached as a label 3 children's chasing game —v. 1 provide with a tag 2 touch as in game of tag 3 [Inf.] follow closely: with *along, after*, etc.

tai chi (tī' jē', -chē') n. Chinese exercises used as in self-defense

tail n. 1 appendage at rear end of an animal's body 2 hind or end part —v. [Inf.] follow closely —a. at or from the rear —**tail'less** a.

tail'bone' n. coccyx

tail'coat' n. man's formal coat with two taillike parts at the back

tail'gate' n. hinged door or gate at the back of a truck, etc. —v. to drive too closely behind (another vehicle)

tail'light' n. red light at the back of a vehicle

tai'lor n. one who makes or alters clothes —v. 1 make by a tailor's work 2 form, alter, etc. to suit requirements

tail'pipe' n. exhaust pipe at the rear of a car or truck

tail'spin' n. sharp downward plunge of a plane with tail spinning in circles

taint v. 1 spoil; rot 2 make morally corrupt —n. trace of contamination

take v. **took, tak'en, tak'ing** 1 grasp 2 capture, seize, win, etc. 3 obtain, select, assume, etc. 4 use, consume, etc. 5 buy; rent 6 travel by 7 deal with 8 occupy 9 derive from 10 write down 11 make (a photograph) 12 require 13 engage in 14 understand 15 have or feel 16 carry, lead, etc. 17 remove 18 subtract —n. amount taken —**take after** act or look like —**take in** 1 admit; receive 2 make smaller 3 understand 4 trick —**take over** begin managing —**take up** 1 make tighter or shorter 2 absorb 3 engage in

take'off' n. 1 a leaving the ground, as for flight 2 [Inf.] mocking imitation; caricature Also **take'-off'**

take'out' a., n. (of) prepared food bought to be eaten at home, etc.

take'o'ver n. act of taking control

tak'ing a. attractive; charming —n. pl. profits

tal'cum (powder) n. powder for the body and face made from a soft mineral (**talc**)

tale n. 1 story 2 lie

tale'bear'er n. a gossip

tal'ent n. special natural ability —**tal'ent-ed** a.

tal'is-man n., pl. **-mans** anything supposed to have magic power

talk v. 1 say words; speak 2 gossip 3 confer 4 discuss —n. 1 a talking 2 conversation 3 a speech 4 conference 5 gossip —**talk back** answer impertinently —**talk'er** n.

talk'a-tive a. talking a great deal: also

talk'y

talk'ing-to' *n.* [Inf.] a scolding

talk show *n. Radio & TV* program featuring informal conversation

tall *a.* high, as in stature

tal'low *n.* hard animal fat used in candles and soap

tall ship *n.* large sailing ship

tal'ly *n., pl.* **-lies** record, account, etc. —*v.* **1** record; score **2** add **3** agree

tal'ly-ho' *int.* fox hunter's cry —*n., pl.* **-hos'** coach drawn by four horses

Tal·mud (täl'mood) *n.* body of early Jewish law

tal'on *n.* claw of a bird of prey

tam *n.* tam-o'-shanter

ta·ma'le (-mä'lē) *n.* spicy chopped meat wrapped in dough of corn meal

tam'a·rack' *n.* larch found in swamps

tam'a·rind' *n.* tropical tree and its brown fruit

tam'bou·rine' (-bə rēn') *n.* small, shallow drum with metal disks around it

tame *a.* **1** trained from a wild state **2** gentle **3** not lively; dull —*v.* make tame —**tame'ly** *adv.* —**tam'er** *n.*

tam'-o'-shan'ter *n.* flat, round Scottish cap

tamp *v.* pack down by tapping —**tamp'er** *n.*

tam'per *v.* interfere (*with*)

tam'pon' *n.* plug of cotton for absorbing blood, etc.

tan *n.* yellowish brown —*a.* **tan'ner, tan'nest** yellowish-brown —*v.* **tanned, tan'ning 1** make (hide) into leather by soaking in tannic acid **2** brown by sun's rays

tan'a·ger *n.* American songbird

tan'bark' *n.* tree bark containing tannic acid

tan'dem *adv.* one behind another

tang *n.* strong taste or odor —**tang'y** *a.,* **-i·er, -i·est**

tan·ge·lo' (-jə-) *n., pl.* **-los'** fruit that is a hybrid of tangerine and grapefruit

tan'gent *a.* touching a curve at one point —*n.* a tangent curve, line, etc. —**go off at** (or **on**) **a tangent** change suddenly to another line of action —**tan·gen'tial** (-jen'shal) *a.*

tan·ge·rine' (-jə rēn') *n.* small, loose-skinned orange

tan'gi·ble *a.* **1** real or solid **2** definite

tan'gle *v.* make or become knotted, confused, etc. —*n.* tangled mass

tan'go *n., pl.* **-gos** South American dance —*v.* dance the tango

tank *n.* **1** large container for liquid or gas **2** armored vehicle carrying guns

tank'ard *n.* large drinking cup with a hinged lid

tank'er *n.* ship for transporting liquids, esp. oil

tank top *n.* casual shirt with shoulder straps

tank truck *n.* motor truck for transporting gasoline, etc.

tan'ner·y *n., pl.* **-ies** place where leather is made by tanning hides —**tan'ner** *n.*

tan'nic acid *n.* acid used in tanning, dyeing, etc.: also **tan'nin**

tan'sy (-zē) *n., pl.* **-sies** plant with small, yellow flowers

tan'ta·lize' *v.* tease by promising something but withholding it

tan'ta·mount *a.* equal (*to*)

tan'trum *n.* fit of rage

tap *v.* **tapped, tap'ping 1** hit lightly **2** draw off (liquid) **3** connect into —*n.* **1** light blow **2** faucet or spigot

tap dance *n.* dance done with sharp taps of the foot, toe, or heel —**tap'-dance'** *v.*

tape *n.* narrow strip of cloth, paper, etc. —*v.* **1** to bind with a tape **2** record on magnetic tape

tape measure *n.* tape having marks for measuring

ta'per *v.* decrease or lessen gradually in thickness, loudness, etc. —*n.* **1** a tapering **2** slender candle

tape recorder *n.* recording device using magnetic tape

tap'es·try *n., pl.* **-tries** cloth with woven designs

tape'worm' *n.* tapelike worm found in the intestines

tap·i·o'ca *n.* starchy substance from cassava roots

ta'pir (-pər) *n.* hoglike tropical animal

tapped out *a.* [Sl.] **1** having no money **2** exhausted

tap'room' *n.* barroom

tap'root' *n.* main root

taps *n.* bugle call for funerals and the end of the day

tar *n.* **1** black liquid distilled from wood or coal **2** [Inf.] sailor —*v.* **tarred, tar'ring** put tar on —**tar'ry** *a.*

ta·ran'tu·la (-chə lə) *n.* large, hairy spider

tar'dy *a.* **-di·er, -di·est** late

tare *n.* a weed

tar'get *n.* thing aimed at, shot at, or attacked

tar'iff *n.* **1** tax on exports or imports **2** list or system of such taxes

tar'mac' *n.* [Chiefly Br.] airport runway

tar'nish *v.* make or become dull or discolored —n. discolored film on metal

ta·ro (ter′ō) n. tropical plant with edible root

tar·ot (tar′ō) n. [*often* T-] any of a set of fortunetelling cards

tar·pau·lin (-pô′-) n. waterproofed canvas

tar′pon n. large ocean fish

tar′ra·gon′ (tar′ə-) n. fragrant leaves of wormwood used for seasoning

tar·ry (tar′ē) v. **-ried, -ry·ing** linger, delay, etc.

tart a. **1** sour; acid **2** sharp in meaning —n. pastry filled with jam, etc. — **tart′ly** adv. —**tart′ness** n.

tar′tan n. plaid cloth

tar′tar n. hard deposit that forms on the teeth

tartar sauce n. sauce of mayonnaise with chopped pickles, olives, etc.

task n. work that must be done —v. burden; strain —**take to task** scold

task force n. group, esp. a military unit, assigned a task

task′mas′ter n. one who assigns severe tasks

tas′sel n. **1** bunch of threads hanging from a knot **2** tuft of corn silk

taste v. **1** notice or test the flavor of in one's mouth **2** eat or drink sparingly **3** have a certain flavor —n. **1** sense for telling flavor **2** flavor **3** small amount **4** ability to know what is beautiful, proper, etc. **5** liking — **taste′ful** a. —**taste′less** a.

taste bud n. taste organ in the tongue

tast′y a. **-i·er, -i·est** that tastes good

tat v. **tat′ted, tat′ting** make lace with a hand shuttle

tat′ter n. **1** rag; shred **2** pl. ragged clothes —**tat′tered** a.

tat′ting n. fine lace made by looping and knotting thread

tat′tle v. **1** tell secrets **2** gossip —n. gossip —**tat′tler** n.

tat′tle·tale′ n. informer

tat·too′ v. **-tooed′, -too′ing** make (designs) on the skin of —n., pl. **-toos′** **1** tattooed design **2** steady beating, as on a drum

taught v. pt. & pp. of TEACH

taunt v. mock; tease —n. scornful remark

taupe (tōp) n. dark, brownish gray

Tau′rus n. second sign of the zodiac

taut a. **1** tightly stretched **2** tense

tau·tol′o·gy n. statement that is true by definition —**tau·to·log′i·cal** a.

tav′ern n. saloon or inn

taw′dry a. **-dri·er, -dri·est** gaudy and cheap

taw′ny a. **-ni·er, -ni·est** brownish-yellow or tan

tax n. **1** compulsory payment to a government **2** burden; strain —v. **1** levy, or make pay, a tax **2** burden **3** accuse; charge —**tax′a·ble** a. —**tax·a′tion** n. —**tax′pay·er** n.

tax′i n., pl. **-is** taxicab —v. **-ied, -i·ing** or **-y·ing 1** go in a taxicab **2** move along the ground or water: said of an airplane

tax′i·cab′ n. automobile for passengers who pay

tax′i·der′my n. art of stuffing animal skins —**tax′i·der′mist** n.

tax·on′o·my n. classification of animals and plants

tax shelter n. investment used to reduce one's income tax

TB n. tuberculosis

TBA abbrev. to be announced

T′-ball′ n. children's baseball game, with the ball batted from a tall tee

T′-bone′ steak n. beefsteak with a T-shaped bone

tbs abbrev. tablespoon(s)

TD abbrev. Football touchdown: sometimes **td**

TDD abbrev. telecommunications device for the deaf

tea n. **1** leaves of an Asian shrub **2** drink made from these **3** similar drink made from other plants, etc. **4** afternoon party with tea —**tea′cup′** n.

tea′ber·ry n., pl. **-ries** wintergreen

teach v. **taught, teach′ing** give lessons (in) —**teach′er** n.

teak n. East Indian tree

tea′ket·tle n. kettle with a spout, used to heat water

teal n. **1** wild duck **2** grayish or greenish blue

team n. **1** two or more animals harnessed together **2** group working or playing together —v. join in a team — **team′mate′** n. —**team′work′** n.

team′ster n. truck driver

tea′pot′ n. pot with spout and handle for brewing tea

tear (ter) v. **tore, torn, tear′ing 1** pull apart, up, etc. by force **2** make by tearing **3** move fast —n. **1** a tearing **2** torn place —**tear down** wreck

tear (tir) n. drop of liquid from the eye: also **tear′drop′** —**in tears** weeping — **tear′ful** a. —**tear·y** a., **-i·er, -i·est**

tear gas n. gas that blinds the eyes with tears: used in warfare

tear′-jerk′er n. [Sl.] sad, overly sentimental film, etc.

tea′room′ n. restaurant that serves

tea, light lunches, etc.

tease v. 1 annoy as by poking fun at 2 fluff up: said as of hair —n. one who teases

tea'sel (-zəl) n. bristly plant with prickly flowers

tea'spoon' n. 1 small spoon as for stirring tea 2 spoon for measuring ⅓ tablespoon —**tea'spoon·ful'** n., pl. **-fuls'**

teat n. nipple on a breast or udder

tech abbrev. 1 technical 2 technology

tech'ie n. [Inf.] expert in computer technology

tech'ni·cal (tek'-) a. 1 dealing with industrial skills or arts 2 of a specific art, science, etc. 3 of technique — **tech'ni·cal·ly** adv.

tech·ni·cal'i·ty n., pl. **-ties** 1 technical detail 2 minute formal point

tech·ni'cian (-nish'ən) n. one skilled in a technique or in a technical area

tech·nique' (-nēk') n. method of procedure, as in art

tech'no·crat' n. one who believes in government by scientists, etc. —**tech·noc'ra·cy** n.

tech·nol'o·gy n. science used to solve practical problems —**tech'no·log'i·cal** a.

tech'no·phile' n. person enthusiastic about advanced technology

tech'no·pho'bi·a n. dislike or fear of advanced technology

ted'dy bear n. child's stuffed toy that looks like a bear

te'di·ous a. tiresome; boring

te'di·um n. a being tedious

tee Golf n. 1 small peg on which the ball is placed to be hit 2 starting place for each hole —v. teed, tee'ing hit a ball from a tee: with off

teem v. abound; swarm

teen n. 1 pl. numbers or years from 13 through 19 2 teenager —a. teenage

teen'age' a. 1 in one's teens 2 of or for those in their teens —**teen'ag·er** n.

tee'ny a. **-ni·er, -ni·est** [Inf.] tiny: also **teen'sy, -si·er, -si·est,** or **tee'ny-wee'ny**

tee'pee n. tepee

tee shirt n. T-shirt

tee'ter v. seesaw

tee'ter-tot'ter n., v. seesaw

teeth n. pl. of TOOTH

teethe (tēth) v. grow teeth

tee'to'tal·er, tee'to'tal·ler n. one who never drinks liquor

te·fil'lin n., pl. **-lin** small leather case holding Jewish Scripture text

Tef'lon' trademark nonsticking coating for cookware, etc. —n. [t-] this finish

tel abbrev. 1 telegram 2 telephone

tel'e·cast' v. **-cast'** or **-cast'ed, -cast'ing;** n. broadcast over television

tel'e·com·mu·ni·ca'tion n. [also pl. with sing. or pl. v.] electronic communication using radio, computers, etc.: also **tel'e·com'**

tel'e·com·mute' v. use a computer to do one's work at home

tel'e·con'fer·ence n. conference among persons linked by telephone or TV

tel'e·gram' n. message sent by telegraph

tel'e·graph' n. device or system for sending messages by electric signals through a wire —v. send a message by telegraph —**te·leg'ra·pher** n. —**tel'e·graph'ic** a. —**te·leg'ra·phy** n.

tel'e·mar'ket·ing n. selling, opinion surveys, etc. done by telephone

tel'e·me'ter n. device for transmitting data about temperature, etc. from a remote point —**te·lem'e·try** n.

te·lep'a·thy n. hypothetical communication between minds without help of speech, sight, etc. —**tel'e·path'ic** a.

tel'e·phone' n. device or system for talking over distances through wires —v. talk (to) by telephone

tel'e·pho'to a. of a camera lens producing a large image of a distant object

tel'e·promp'ter n. electronic device showing a speaker the text of his or her speech line by line

tel'e·scope' n. device with lenses that magnify distant objects —v. slide one into another —**tel'e·scop'ic** a.

tel'e·thon' n. televised campaign seeking donations

tel'e·vise' v. transmit by television

tel'e·vi'sion n. 1 way of sending pictures through space by radio waves to a receiving set 2 such a set

tell v. told, tell'ing 1 report; narrate 2 put into words 3 show 4 inform 5 recognize 6 order —**tell off** [Inf.] criticize sharply

tell'-all' a. of a book, etc. revealing often scandalous facts

tell'er n. 1 one who tells 2 cashier at a bank

tell'ing a. forceful

tell'tale' a. revealing what is meant to be secret

te·mer'i·ty n. rashness; boldness

temp n. one hired for temporary work —v. work as a temp

temp abbrev. 1 temperature 2 temporary

tem'per v. 1 make less intense 2 make (steel) hard —n. 1 state of mind 2 self-control 3 rage 4 tendency to become angry

tem'per·a n. painting with pigments mixed with egg, etc.

tem'per·a·ment (or -prə mənt) n. (moody or excitable) disposition — **tem'per·a·men'tal** a.

tem'per·ance (or -prəns) n. 1 self-restraint; moderation 2 abstinence from liquor

tem'per·ate (or -prət) a. 1 moderate; self-restrained 2 neither very hot nor very cold

tem'per·a·ture (or -prə chər) n. 1 degree of hotness or coldness 2 fever

tem'pered a. having a certain kind of temper

tem'pest n. wild storm —**tem·pes'tu·ous** (-chōo-) a.

tem'plate (-plit) n. pattern for making an exact copy

tem'ple n. 1 a building for worship services or for some special purpose 2 area between the eye and ear

tem'po n., pl. **-pos** or **-pi** (-pē) rate of speed, esp. for playing music

tem'po·ral a. 1 worldly 2 of time

tem'po·rar'y a. lasting only a while — **tem'po·rar'i·ly** adv.

tempt v. 1 entice, esp. to an immoral act 2 provoke 3 to incline strongly — **temp·ta'tion** n.

tempt'ress n. woman who tempts sexually

tem·pu·ra' (or tem poor'ə) n. Japanese dish of deep-fried fish, vegetables, etc.

ten a., n. one more than nine —**tenth** a., n.

ten'a·ble a. that can be defended or believed

te·na'cious (-shəs) a. 1 holding firmly 2 retentive —**te·nac'i·ty** (-nas'-) n.

ten'ant n. occupant (who pays rent) — **ten'an·cy** n.

tend v. 1 take care of 2 be apt; incline 3 lead

tend'en·cy n., pl. **-cies** being likely to move or act in a certain way

ten·den'tious a. expressing a certain point of view

ten'der a. 1 soft or delicate 2 sensitive 3 loving 4 young —n. 1 thing offered, as in payment 2 car with locomotive's coal 3 one who tends —

v. offer to someone —**ten'der·ly** adv.

ten'der·foot' n., pl. **-foots'** or **-feet'** newcomer, esp. one not used to hardships

ten'der·heart'ed a. quick to feel compassion

ten'der·ize' v. make tender

ten'der·loin' n. tenderest part of a loin of meat

ten·di·nit'is n. inflammation of a tendon

ten'don n. cord of tissue binding a muscle to a bone

ten'dril n. threadlike, clinging part of a climbing plant

ten'e·ment n. run-down apartment house

ten'et n. opinion or belief

ten'nis n. game played by hitting a ball over a net with a racket

tennis shoe n. sneaker

ten'on n. projecting part to fit in a mortise

ten'or n. 1 highest male voice 2 general tendency or meaning

tense a. 1 taut 2 anxious —v. make or become tense —n. verb form showing time

ten'sile (-səl) a. of or under tension

ten'sion n. 1 a stretching 2 stress from this 3 nervous strain 4 voltage

tent n. shelter of canvas, nylon, etc. supported by poles and stakes

ten'ta·cle n. slender growth on an animal's head, for feeling, grasping, etc.

ten'ta·tive a. not final

ten'ter·hook' n. hooked nail —**on tenterhooks** in anxious suspense

ten'u·ous (-yōō-) a. 1 thin; fine 2 not dense 3 flimsy

ten'ure (-yər) n. right or duration of holding a position, etc.

te'pee n. cone-shaped tent

tep'id a. lukewarm

te·qui'la (-kē'-) n. strong alcoholic liquor of Mexico

term n. 1 fixed time period 2 pl. conditions of a contract, etc. 3 pl. personal relationship 4 word or phrase 5 either part of a fraction, etc. —v. name —**come to terms** arrive at an agreement —**in terms of** regarding

ter'ma·gant n. nagging woman

ter'mi·nal a. 1 of or at the end 2 final —n. 1 main station, as for buses 2 keyboard and video screen connected to a computer

ter'mi·nate' v. 1 stop; end 2 form the end of —**ter·mi·na'tion** n.

ter·mi·nol'o·gy n., pl. **-gies** special

words or phrases

term insurance *n.* life insurance that expires after a specified period

ter·mi·nus *n., pl.* **-ni'** (-nī') or **-nus·es** an end, limit, etc.

ter'mite' *n.* antlike insect that eats wood

tern *n.* gull-like seabird

ter'race (-əs) *n.* 1 patio 2 flat mound with sloping side 3 row of houses on this —*v.* make a terrace of

ter'ra cot'ta *n.* brownish-red earthenware or its color

ter'ra fir'ma *n.* solid ground

ter·rain' *n.* area of land with regard to its fitness for use

ter'ra·pin *n.* freshwater turtle

ter·rar'i·um (-rer'-) *n., pl.* **-i·ums** or **-i·a** glass enclosure for small plants, etc.

ter·raz'zo (-raz'ō, -rät'sō) *n.* polished flooring of small marble chips in cement

ter·res'tri·al *a.* 1 worldly 2 of the earth 3 of, or living on, land

ter'ri·ble *a.* 1 terrifying 2 severe 3 [Inf.] very bad —**ter'ri·bly** *adv.*

ter'ri·er *n.* breed of small, lively dog

ter·rif'ic *a.* 1 terrifying 2 [Inf.] very intense, enjoyable, etc.

ter'ri·fy' *v.* **-fied'**, **-fy'ing** fill with terror

ter'ri·to'ry *n., pl.* **-ries** 1 land ruled by a nation 2 national region not yet a state 3 region —**ter'ri·to'ri·al** *a.*

ter'ror *n.* great fear, or cause of this

ter'ror·ism' *n.* use of force and threats to intimidate —**ter'ror·ist** *n., a.*

ter'ror·ize' *v.* 1 terrify 2 coerce by terrorism

ter'ry (cloth) *n.* cloth having a pile of uncut loops

terse *a.* concise —**terse'ly** *adv.*

ter'ti·ar·y (-shē-) *a.* third

test *n.* examination or trial to determine a thing's value, a person's knowledge, etc. —*v.* subject to a test

tes'ta·ment *n.* 1 [T-] either part of the Bible 2 legal will

tes'ta·tor *n.* one who has made a will

tes'ti·cle *n.* either of the two male sex glands

tes'ti·fy' *v.* **-fied'**, **-fy'ing** 1 give evidence in court 2 be an indication

tes'ti·mo'ni·al *n.* 1 statement of recommendation 2 thing given as a tribute

tes'ti·mo'ny *n., pl.* **-nies** 1 statement of one who testifies in court 2 proof

tes'tis *n., pl.* **-tes'** (-tēz') testicle

tes·tos'ter·one' (-ōn') *n.* male sex hormone

test tube *n.* tubelike glass container

tes'ty *a.* **-ti·er, -ti·est** irritable; touchy

tet·a·nus (tet'ʼn əs) *n.* acute infectious disease

tête-à-tête (tāt'ə tāt') *a., n.* (of a) private talk between two people

teth'er (teth'-) *n.* rope or chain tied to an animal to confine it —*v.* tie as with this

tet'ra *n.* tropical fish

text *n.* 1 author's words 2 main part of a printed page 3 textbook 4 Biblical passage 5 topic —**tex'tu·al** (-chōō-) *a.*

text'book' *n.* book used in teaching a subject

tex'tile (-til', -təl) *n.* woven fabric —*a.* 1 of weaving 2 woven

tex'ture *n.* look and feel of a fabric or other material —**tex'tur·al** *a.*

tex'tured *a.* having a certain, esp. uneven, texture

thal'a·mus *n., pl.* **-mi'** (-mī') gray matter at the base of the brain

than *con. Than* introduces the second element in a comparison

thank *v.* give thanks to —**thank you** I thank you

thank'ful *a.* showing thanks —**thank'ful·ly** *adv.*

thank'less *a.* 1 ungrateful 2 unappreciated

thanks *pl.n.* expression of gratitude —*int.* I thank you —**thanks to** 1 thanks be given to 2 because of

thanks·giv'ing *n.* 1 thanks to God 2 [T-] U.S. holiday: fourth Thursday in November

that *pron., pl.* **those** 1 the one mentioned 2 the farther one or other one 3 who, whom, or which 4 when —*a., pl.* **those** being that one —*con. That* is used to introduce certain dependent clauses —*adv.* to that extent —**all that** [Inf.] so very —**that is** 1 to be specific 2 in other words

thatch *v., n.* (cover with) a roof of straw, etc.

thaw *v.* 1 melt 2 become so warm that ice melts —*n.* period of thawing weather

the *a., definite article* that or this one in particular or of a certain kind —*adv.* that much or by that much

the'a·ter, the'a·tre *n.* 1 place where plays, movies, etc. are shown 2 scene of events 3 dramatic art —**the·at'ri·cal** *a.*

thee *pron.* [Ar.] objective case of THOU

theft *n.* act of stealing

their *a.* of them

theirs *pron.* that or those belonging to them

the·ism' *n.* belief in a god or gods —**the'ist** *n., a.*

them *pron.* objective case of THEY

theme *n.* **1** topic **2** short essay **3** main melody

them·selves' *pron.* intensive or reflexive form of THEY

then *adv.* **1** at that time **2** next **3** in that case **4** besides —*n.* that time

thence *adv.* from that place

thence·forth' *adv.* from that time on: also **thence·for'ward**

the·oc'ra·cy *n., pl.* **-cies** government by a religious group

theol *abbrev.* theology

the·ol'o·gy *n.* study of God and of religious beliefs —**the'o·lo'gian** (-lō'jən) *n.* —**the'o·log'i·cal** *a.*

the'o·rem *n.* *Math.* statement (to be) proved

the'o·ret'i·cal *a.* based on theory, not on practice —**the'o·ret'i·cal·ly** *adv.*

the'o·ry *n., pl.* **-ries 1** explanation based on scientific study and reasoning **2** principles of an art or science **3** guess, conjecture, etc. —**the'o·rize'** *v.*

ther'a·peu'tic (-pyōō'-) *a.* serving to cure or heal

ther'a·peu'tics *n.* therapy

ther'a·py *n., pl.* **-pies 1** physical method of treating disease or disorders **2** psychotherapy —**ther'a·pist** *n.*

there *adv.* **1** at, in, or to that place **2** at that point **3** in that respect —*n.* that place

there'a·bouts' *adv.* near that place, time, amount, etc.: also **there'a·bout'**

there·af'ter *adv.* after that

there·by' *adv.* by that

there'fore' *adv.* for this or that reason

there·in' *adv.* in that place, matter, writing, etc.

there·of' *adv.* **1** of that **2** from that as a cause

there·on' *adv.* **1** on that **2** thereupon

there·to' *adv.* to that place, thing, etc.

there'to·fore' *adv.* up to that time

there·up·on' *adv.* **1** just after that **2** because of that

there·with' *adv.* **1** with that **2** just after that

ther'mal *a.* of heat

thermal pollution *n.* harmful discharge of heated liquids into lakes, rivers, etc.

ther'mo·dy·nam'ics *n.* science of changing heat into other forms of energy

ther·mom'e·ter *n.* device for measur-

ing temperature

ther'mo·nu'cle·ar *a.* of or using the heat energy released in nuclear fusion

ther'mo·plas'tic *a.* soft and moldable when heated —*n.* thermoplastic substance

Ther'mos *trademark* container for keeping liquids at the same temperature

ther'mo·stat' *n.* device for regulating temperature

the·sau'rus *n.* book containing lists of synonyms or related words

these *pron., a.* pl. of THIS

the'sis *n., pl.* **-ses' (-sēz') 1** statement to be defended **2** essay written to obtain an academic degree

Thes'pi·an *n.* [*often* t-] actor

thews *pl.n.* muscles or sinews

they *pron.* **1** the ones mentioned **2** people

they'd *contr.* **1** they had **2** they would

they'll *contr.* **1** they will **2** they shall

they're *contr.* they are

they've *contr.* they have

thi·a·mine (thī'ə min) *n.* vitamin B_1, found in liver, etc.

thick *a.* **1** great in extent from side to side **2** as measured from side to side **3** dense **4** not clear —*n.* the most active part —**thick'en** *v.* —**thick'ly** *adv.* —**thick'ness** *n.*

thick'et *n.* thick growth of shrubs or small trees

thick'set' *a.* thick and stout

thick'-skinned' *a.* unfeeling

thief *n., pl.* **thieves** one who steals

thieve *v.* steal —**thiev'er·y** *n., pl.* **-ies** —**thiev'ish** *a.*

thigh *n.* the part of the leg between the knee and the hip

thigh'bone' *n.* femur

thim'ble *n.* protective cap worn on the finger in sewing

thin *a.* **thin'ner, thin'nest 1** small in extent from side to side **2** lean; slender **3** sparse **4** watery **5** weak **6** transparent; flimsy —*v.* **thinned, thin'ning** make or become thin —**thin'ness** *n.*

thine [Ar.] *pron.* yours —*a.* [Ar.] your Sing. form

thing *n.* **1** real object or substance **2** a happening, act, event, etc. **3** matter or affair **4** *pl.* belongings

think *v.* **thought, think'ing 1** form in or use the mind **2** consider **3** believe **4** remember: with *of* or *about* **5** have an opinion of: with *of* or *about* **6** consider: with *about* **7** conceive (*of*) —

think better of reconsider —**think up** invent, plan, etc.

think tank *n.* group organized for intensive research

thin'ner *n.* substance added to paint, etc. for thinning

thin'-skinned' *a.* sensitive

Thin'su·late' *trademark* synthetic material for heat insulation, esp. in clothing

third *a.* preceded by two others —*n.* **1** third one **2** one of three equal parts

third'-class' *a.* of the class, etc. next below the second

third degree *n.* [Inf.] cruel treatment to force confession

third dimension *n.* **1** depth **2** quality of seeming real

third party *n.* **1** political party competing with the two major parties **2** person other than the principals in a matter

third'-rate' *a.* very inferior

Third World *n.* [*also* **t- w-**] underdeveloped countries

thirst *n.* **1** need or craving for water **2** strong desire —*v.* feel thirst —**thirst'y** *a.*, **-i·er, -i·est**

thir'teen' *a.*, *n.* three more than ten —**thir'teenth'** *a.*, *n.*

thir'ty *a.*, *n.*, *pl.* **-ties** three times ten —**thir'ti·eth** *a.*, *n.*

this *a.*, *pron.*, *pl.* **these** (being) the one mentioned or nearer —*adv.* to this extent

this'tle (-əl) *n.* prickly plant

thith'er (*thith*'-, *thith*'-) *adv.* to that place

tho, tho' *con.*, *adv.* though

thong *n.* strip of leather used as a lace, strap, etc.

tho'rax' *n.* **1** CHEST (*n.* 3) **2** middle segment of an insect

thorn *n.* short, sharp point on a plant stem —**thorn'y** *a.*, **-i·er, -i·est**

thor'ough (thur'ō) *a.* **1** complete **2** very exact —**thor'ough·ly** *adv.* —**thor'ough·ness** *n.*

thor'ough·bred' *a.* **1** purebred **2** well-bred —*n.* [T-] breed of racehorse

thor'ough·fare' *n.* main highway

thor'ough·go·ing *a.* very thorough

those *pron.*, *a.* pl. of THAT

thou *pron.* [Ar.] you (sing. subject of v.)

though (thō) *con.* **1** although **2** yet **3** even if —*adv.* however

thought *v.* pt. & pp. of THINK —*n.* **1** act or way of thinking **2** idea, plan, etc.

thought'ful *a.* **1** full of thought **2** considerate

thought'less *a.* **1** careless **2** inconsiderate

thou'sand *a.*, *n.* ten hundred —**thou'sandth** *a.*, *n.*

thrall *n.* used chiefly in **hold in thrall,** to dominate psychologically

thrash *v.* **1** thresh **2** beat **3** toss about violently

thrash'er *n.* thrushlike songbird

thread *n.* **1** fine cord of spun cotton, silk, etc. **2** spiral ridge of a screw, etc. —*v.* **1** put a thread through (a needle) **2** make one's way

thread'bare' *a.* shabby

threat *n.* **1** warning of plan to harm **2** sign of danger

threat'en *v.* make or be a threat

three *a.*, *n.* one more than two

three'-di·men'sion·al *a.* having depth or thickness

three'fold' *a.* **1** having three parts **2** having three times as much or as many —*adv.* three times as much or as many

three'score' *a.* sixty

thresh *v.* beat out (grain) from its husk —**thresh'er** *n.*

thresh'old' *n.* **1** sill of a door **2** beginning point

threw *v.* pt. of THROW

thrice *adv.* three times

thrift *n.* careful managing of money, etc. —**thrift'i·ly** *adv.* —**thrift'less** *a.* —**thrift'y** *a.*, **-i·er, -i·est**

thrift shop *n.* store selling used goods

thrill *v.*, *n.* (feel or make feel) great excitement

thrill'er *n.* suspenseful novel, film, etc.

thrive *v.* **thrived** or **throve, thrived** or **thriv'en, thriv'ing 1** be successful **2** grow luxuriantly

throat *n.* **1** front of the neck **2** upper passage from mouth to stomach and lungs

throb *v.* **throbbed, throb'bing** beat or vibrate strongly —*n.* a throbbing

throe (thrō) *n.* spasm or pang of pain: *used in pl.* —**in the throes of** in the act of struggling with

throm'bose' (-bōs', -bōz') *v.* make (into) a clot (**throm'bus**)

throm·bo'sis *n.* a clotting in the circulatory system

throne *n.* **1** official chair, as of a king **2** the power of a king, etc.

throng *n.*, *v.* crowd

throt'tle *n.* valve to control fuel mixture —*v.* choke

through (thrōō) *prep.* **1** from end to end of **2** by way of **3** to places in **4**

throughout 5 by means of **6** because of —*adv.* **1** in and out **2** all the way **3** entirely —*a.* **1** open; free **2** to the end without stops **3** finished

through·out' *adv., prep.* in every part (of)

through'way' *n.* expressway

throw *v.* **threw, thrown, throw'ing 1** send through the air from the hand **2** make fall **3** put suddenly into **4** move (a switch, etc.) **5** direct, cast, etc. —*n.* **1** a throwing **2** distance thrown —**throw off** get rid of, expel, etc. —**throw together** to assemble hastily —**throw up 1** give up **2** vomit

throw'a·way' *a.* designed to be discarded after use

throw'back' *n.* (a) return to an earlier type

throw rug *n.* small rug

thru *prep., adv., a.* [Inf.] through

thrush *n.* any of a large group of songbirds

thrust *v.* **thrust, thrust'ing** push with sudden force —*n.* **1** sudden push **2** stab **3** forward force

thru'way' *n.* expressway

thud *v., n.* **thud'ded, thud'ding** (hit with) a dull sound

thug *n.* rough criminal

thumb *n.* short, thick finger nearest the wrist

thumb'nail' *n.* nail of the thumb —*a.* brief

thumb'tack' *n.* tack with wide, flat head

thump *n.* **1** a blow with a heavy, blunt thing **2** its dull sound —*v.* hit or pound with a thump

thump'ing *a.* [Inf.] very large

thun'der *n.* loud noise after lightning —*v.* **1** cause thunder **2** shout loudly —**thun'der·ous** *a.*

thun'der·bolt' *n.* flash of lightning and its thunder

thun'der·cloud' *n.* storm cloud producing thunder

thun'der·show'er *n.* shower with thunder and lightning

thun'der·storm' *n.* storm with thunder and lightning

thun'der·struck' *a.* amazed

Thur, Thurs *abbrev.* Thursday

Thurs'day *n.* fifth day of the week

thus *adv.* **1** in this way **2** to this or that degree **3** therefore

thwack *v., n.* whack

thwart *v.* block; hinder

thy (*thi*) *a.* [Ar.] your: sing. form

thyme (tīm) *n.* plant of the mint family

thy'mus (thī'-) *n.* small gland in the upper thorax or neck

thy'roid' (thī'-) *a., n.* (of) a gland secreting a growth hormone

thy·self' (*thī'*-) *pron.* [Ar.] yourself: sing. form

ti·a·ra (tē är'ə, -är'-) *n.* woman's crownlike headdress

tib'i·a *n.* thicker bone of the lower leg

tic *n.* involuntary, repeated muscle spasm

tick *n.* **1** light clicking sound **2** blood-sucking insect —*v.* make a ticking sound

ticked *a.* [Sl.] angry

tick'er *n.* **1** one that ticks **2** device for displaying stock prices

tick'et *n.* **1** printed card entitling one to a theater seat, etc. **2** tag, label, etc. **3** list of a party's candidates **4** [Inf.] summons for a traffic violation —*v.* put a ticket on

tick'ing *n.* cloth holding a pillow's contents

tick'le *v.* **1** stroke lightly and make twitch or laugh **2** feel tickled **3** amuse; delight —*n.* a tickling

tick'ler *n.* file for noting items to be remembered

tick'lish *a.* **1** sensitive to tickling **2** touchy

tick'-tack-toe' *n.* game for two people writing an X or O in a nine-square block to complete a row first

tid'al *a.* of, having, or caused by a tide

tidal wave *n.* very large, destructive wave caused by an earthquake or strong wind

tid'bit' *n.* choice morsel

tid'dly·winks' *n.* game of popping small disks into a cup using another disk

tide *n.* **1** rise and fall of the ocean twice a day **2** trend —*v.* chiefly in **tide over,** help through a difficulty

tide'land' *n.* land covered by high tide

tide'wa'ter *n.* **1** water affected by tide **2** seaboard

ti'dings *pl.n.* news

ti'dy *a.* **-di·er, -di·est 1** neat; orderly **2** [Inf.] quite large —*v.* **-died, -dy·ing** make tidy

tie *v.* **tied, ty'ing 1** fasten with string, rope, etc. **2** make (a knot) **3** bind in any way **4** to equal, as in a score —*n.* **1** thing that ties or joins **2** necktie **3** contest with equal scores

tie'-dye' *n.* dyeing method affecting only exposed areas —*v.* dye in this way

tie'-in' *n.* connection

tier (tir) *n.* any of a series of rows, one above another

tie'-up' *n.* **1** temporary stoppage, as of traffic **2** connection

tiff *n.* slight quarrel

ti'ger *n.* large, striped jungle cat —**ti'gress** *n.fem.*

tiger lily *n.* lily with orange flowers

tight *a.* **1** made to keep water, air, etc. out or in **2** fitting closely or too closely **3** taut **4** difficult **5** [Inf.] stingy —*adv.* closely —**tight'en** *v.* —**tight'ly** *adv.*

tight'fist'ed *a.* stingy

tight'-lipped' *a.* secretive

tight'rope' *n.* taut rope on which acrobats perform

tights *pl.n.* tightly fitting garment from the waist to the feet

tight'wad' *n.* [Sl.] miser

til'de (-də) *n.* diacritical mark (~)

tile *n.* thin piece of baked clay, stone, plastic, etc. for roofing, flooring, etc. —*v.* cover with tiles

til'ing *n.* a covering of tiles

till *prep., con.* until —*v.* cultivate (land) for crops —*n.* drawer for money

till'er *n.* bar or handle to turn a boat's rudder

tilt *v., n.* **1** slope; slant **2** joust —**at full tilt** at full speed

tim'ber *n.* **1** wood for building houses, etc. **2** wooden beam **3** trees

tim'ber-line' *n.* farthest point of tree growth, as on a mountain

tim'bre (tam'bər) *n.* the distinctive sound of a voice or musical instrument

time *n.* **1** period; duration **2** the right instant, hour, etc. **3** the passing hours, day, etc.; or, system of measuring them **4** an occasion **5** set period of work, or pay for this **6** tempo or rhythm —*v.* **1** choose a right time for **2** measure the speed of —*a.* **1** of time **2** set to work at a given time —**at times** sometimes —**in time 1** eventually **2** before it is too late —**on time 1** not late **2** by installment payments —**tim'er** *n.*

time'-hon'ored *a.* honored because of long existence

time'keep'er *n.* one who records time played, as in games, or hours worked

time'less *a.* eternal

time'line' *n.* chronological chart or list of events, dates, plans, etc.

time'ly *a.* **-li-er, -li-est** at the right time

time'out' *n.* temporary suspension of play in sports

time'piece' *n.* clock or watch

time'-re-lease' *a.* releasing active ingredients gradually

times *prep.* multiplied by

time sharing *n.* a sharing of a vacation home, etc., each owner using it for a specified period

time'ta'ble *n.* schedule of arrivals and departures

time'worn' *a.* **1** worn out **2** trite

time zone *n.* ZONE (*n.* 1)

tim'id *a.* shy; easily frightened —**ti-mid'i-ty** *n.*

tim'ing *n.* regulation of speed, etc. to improve performance

tim'or-ous *a.* timid

tim'o-thy *n.* a tall grass used for fodder

tim'pa-ni (-nē) *pl.n.* kettledrums

tin *n.* soft, silvery metal, a chemical element —**tin'ny** *a.*, **-ni-er, -ni-est**

tinc'ture *n.* solution of medicine in alcohol —*v.* tinge

tin'der *n.* any dry, easily ignited material

tin'der-box' *n.* **1** flammable object, etc. **2** place, etc. likely to have trouble or war

tine *n.* prong, as of a fork

tin'foil' *n.* **1** thin sheet of tin **2** thin sheet of aluminum

tinge *n.* **1** tint **2** slight trace —*v.* give a tinge to

tin'gle *v.* sting slightly; prickle —*n.* a tingling

tin'ker *n.* mender of pots and pans —*v.* **1** make clumsy attempts to mend something **2** to putter

tin'kle *n.* ring of a small bell —*v.* make a tinkle

tin plate *n.* thin sheets of iron or steel plated with tin

tin'pot' *a.* [Inf.] petty, inferior, etc.

tin'sel *n.* **1** thin strips of metal foil, for decorating **2** showy, cheap thing

tin'smith' *n.* one who works with tin: also **tin'ner**

tint *n.* **1** light color **2** a shading of a color —*v.* give a tint to

ti'ny *a.* **-ni-er, -ni-est** very small

-tion *suf.* **1** act of **2** condition of being **3** thing that is

tip *n.* **1** a point or end **2** thing fitted to an end **3** light blow; tap **4** secret information **5** a warning **6** gratuity **7** slant —*v.* **tipped, tip'ping 1** make or put a tip on **2** give a tip (to) **3** overturn **4** slant —**tip one's hand** [Sl.] reveal a secret, etc.

tip'-off' *n.* a TIP (*n.* 4 & 5)

tip'ple v. drink liquor habitually

tip'sheet' n. publication giving up-to-date information as for betting on a horse race

tip'ster n. [Inf.] one who sells tips, as on horse races

tip'sy a. **-si·er, -si·est** 1 unsteady 2 drunk

tip'toe' n. tip(s) of the toe(s) —v. **-toed', -toe'ing** walk stealthily on one's toes

tip'top' a., adv., n. (at) the highest point

ti'rade' n. long, angry speech

tire v. make or become weary, bored, etc. —n. hoop or rubber tube around a wheel —**tire'less** a.

tired a. weary; exhausted

tire'some a. tiring

tis·sue (tish'oo) n. 1 tissue paper 2 cellular material of organisms 3 thin cloth

tissue paper n. thin, soft paper

ti'tan n. giant

ti·tan'ic a. of great size, etc.

ti·ta'ni·um n. lustrous, metallic chemical element

tit for tat n. this for that

tithe (tīth) v., n. (pay) a tenth part of one's income

ti·tian (tish'ən) n., a. reddish gold

tit'il·late' v. excite pleasurably, often erotically —**tit'il·la'tion** n.

ti'tle n. 1 name of a book, picture, etc. 2 word showing rank or occupation 3 legal right 4 championship —v. name

ti'tlist n. champion in some sport or competition

tit'mouse' n., pl. **-mice'** small, dull-colored bird

tit'ter v., n. giggle

tit'u·lar (tich'-) a. 1 in name only 2 of or having a title

tiz'zy n., pl. **-zies** [Inf.] frenzied excitement

TKO n. Boxing technical knockout

TLC abbrev. tender, loving care

TM abbrev. trademark

TN abbrev. Tennessee

TNT n. an explosive

to prep. 1 toward 2 as far as 3 on, onto, or against 4 until 5 causing 6 with 7 in each To may indicate an infinitive or a receiver of action —adv. 1 forward 2 shut

toad n. froglike land animal

toad'stool' n. poisonous mushroom

toad'y n., pl. **-ies** servile flatterer —v. **-ied, -y·ing** be a toady (to)

toast v. 1 brown (bread, etc.) by heating 2 warm 3 drink in honor of —n.

1 toasted bread 2 a toasting

toast'mas·ter n. one who presides at a banquet

toast'y a. **-i·er, -i·est** warm and cozy

to·bac'co n. plant with leaves dried for smoking, chewing, etc.

to·bac'co·nist n. [Chiefly Br.] dealer in tobacco, etc.

to·bog'gan v., n. (coast on) a flat, runnerless sled

toc'sin n. alarm bell

to·day' adv. 1 during this day 2 nowadays —n. this day or time

tod'dle v. walk unsteadily, as a young child does —**tod'dler** n.

tod'dy n., pl. **-dies** whiskey, etc. mixed with hot water, sugar, etc.

to-do' n. [Inf.] a fuss

toe n. any of five end parts of the foot —v. toed, toe'ing touch with the toes —**on one's toes** [Inf.] alert — **toe the line** (or **mark**) follow orders, etc. strictly —**toe'nail'** n.

toe dance n. dance performed on the tips of the toes

toe'hold' n. slight footing or advantage

toe'shoe' n. ballet slipper

toe'-to-toe' adv., a. directly confronting or competing

tof'fee, tof'fy n. type of taffy

to'fu n. Japanese cheeselike food made from soybeans

to'ga n. loose garment worn in ancient Rome

to·geth'er adv. 1 in one group or place 2 at the same time 3 so as to meet, agree, etc. —**to·geth'er·ness** n.

tog'gle switch n. switch with a lever to open or close an electric circuit

togs pl.n. [Inf.] clothes

toil v. work hard —n. hard work

toi'let n. 1 fixture to receive body waste 2 bathroom 3 one's grooming: also **toi-lette'** (twä-, toi-)

toilet paper n. soft paper for cleaning oneself after evacuation

toi'let·ry n., pl. **-ries** soap, cosmetics, etc.

toilet water n. cologne

toils pl.n. snare or net

toil'some a. laborious

To·kay' n. a sweet wine

to'ken n. 1 sign or symbol 2 keepsake 3 metal disk, as for fare —a. 1 pretended 2 serving merely to fill a symbolic role, a quota, etc.

to'ken·ism' n. use of token concessions, etc.

told v. pt. & pp. of TELL

tole n. lacquered or enameled metalware, as for lamps

tol′er·a·ble a. 1 bearable 2 fairly good —**tol′er·a·bly** adv.

tol′er·ance n. 1 a tolerating, as of another's ways 2 power to resist a drug's effect 3 deviation allowed —**tol′er·ant** a.

tol′er·ate′ v. 1 to put up with; endure 2 permit

toll n. 1 charge on a turnpike, for a long-distance phone call, etc. 2 the number lost, etc. —v. ring (a bell, etc.) with slow, regular strokes

toll′booth′ n. booth at which tolls are collected

toll′gate′ n. gate where tolls are paid

toll road n. road on which tolls must be paid

tom′a·hawk′ n. light ax used by North American Indians

to·ma′to n., pl. **-toes** red, round, juicy vegetable

tomb (tōōm) n. vault or grave for the dead

tom′boy′ n. girl who behaves like an active boy

tomb′stone′ n. stone marking a tomb or grave

tom′cat′ n. male cat

tome n. large book

tom·fool′er·y n., pl. **-ies** foolish behavior; silliness

to·mor′row adv., n. (on) the day after today

tom′-tom′ n. drum beaten with the hands

ton n. 2,000 pounds

to·nal′i·ty n. 1 KEY (n. 7) 2 tonal character

tone n. 1 vocal or musical sound; spec., a full interval of a diatonic scale 2 style, character, feeling, etc. 3 shade or tint 4 healthy condition, as of muscles —**tone down** give a less intense tone to —**ton′al** a.

tone′-deaf′ a. poor at distinguishing musical tones

tongs pl.n. device for seizing, lifting, etc., made of two long, hinged arms

tongue (tuŋ) n. 1 movable muscle in the mouth, used in eating and speaking 2 act or manner of speaking 3 a language 4 tonguelike part —(with) **tongue in cheek** jokingly; ironically

tongue′-lash′ing n. [Inf.] harsh scolding

tongue′-tied′ a. speechless

tongue twister n. phrase or sentence hard to say fast

ton′ic n. medicine, etc. that invigorates

to·night′ adv., n. (on) this night

ton′nage (-ij) n. 1 amount, in tons, of shipping, etc. 2 carrying capacity of a ship

ton′sil n. either of two oval masses of tissue at the back of the mouth

ton′sil·lec′to·my n., pl. **-mies** surgical removal of the tonsils

ton′sil·li′tis (-līt′is) n. inflammation of the tonsils

ton·so′ri·al (-sôr′ē-) a. of a barber or barbering

ton′sure n. shaven crown of a priest's or monk's head

ton′y a. **-i·er, -i·est** [Sl.] fancy, stylish, etc.

too adv. 1 also 2 more than enough 3 very

took v. pt. of TAKE

tool n. 1 instrument, implement, etc. used for some work 2 dupe, lackey, etc. —v. shape or work with a tool

toot v., n. (make) a short blast on a horn, etc.

tooth n., pl. **teeth** 1 any of a set of bony structures in the jaws, used for biting and chewing 2 toothlike part, as of a saw or gear —**tooth and nail** with all one's strength —**tooth′ache′** n. —**tooth′brush′** n.

toothed (tōōtht, tōōthd) a. having teeth

tooth′paste′ n. paste for brushing the teeth

tooth′pick′ n. pointed stick for picking food from between the teeth

tooth′some a. tasty

tooth′y a. **-i·er, -i·est** having prominent teeth

top n. 1 highest point or surface 2 uppermost part or covering 3 highest degree or rank 4 toy that spins round —a. of, at, or being the top —v. **topped, top′ping** 1 provide with a top 2 be at the top of 3 surpass; exceed —**on top of** 1 resting upon 2 besides —**top off** to complete

to′paz′ n. yellow gem

top′coat′ n. light overcoat

top′-draw′er a. of first importance

top′-flight′ a. [Inf.] first-rate

top hat n. man's tall black hat

top′-heav′y a. too heavy at the top and, thus, unstable

top′ic n. subject of an essay, speech, etc.

top′i·cal a. of current or local interest

top′knot′ n. tuft of hair or feathers on top of the head

top′less a. 1 without a top 2 wearing a costume, etc. leaving breasts exposed

top'-lev'el _a._ of or by persons of the highest rank

top'mast' _n._ second mast above the deck of a ship

top'most' _a._ uppermost

top'-notch' _a._ [Inf.] first-rate

to·pog'ra·phy _n._ 1 surface features of a region 2 science of showing these, as on maps —**top'o·graph'ic, top'o·graph'i·cal** _a._

top'ple _v._ (make) fall over

top'sail' _n._ sail next above the lowest sail on a mast

top'-se'cret _a._ designating or of the most secret information

top'side' _adv._ on or to an upper deck or the main deck of a ship

top'soil' _n._ upper layer of soil, usually richer

top'sy-tur'vy _adv., a._ 1 upside down 2 in disorder

To'rah (-ra) _n._ all Jewish religious literature; spec. first five books of the Bible

torch _n._ 1 portable flaming light 2 device that makes a very hot flame, as in welding —**torch'light'** _n._

torch song _n._ sentimental song of unrequited love —**torch singer** _n._

tore _v._ pt. of TEAR (pull apart)

tor'e·a·dor (-ē ə-) _n._ bullfighter

tor'ment (_v._: tôr ment') _n._ great pain —_v._ make suffer —**tor·men'tor** _n._

torn _v._ pp. of TEAR (pull apart)

tor·na'do _n., pl._ **-does** or **-dos** violent wind with a whirling, funnel-shaped cloud

tor·pe'do _n., pl._ **-does** large, cigar-shaped underwater projectile —_v._ **-doed, -do·ing** to destroy or damage

tor'pid _a._ dull; sluggish —**tor'por** _n._

torque (tôrk) _n._ force that gives a twisting motion

tor'rent _n._ swift, violent stream —**tor·ren'tial** (-shal) _a._

tor'rid _a._ very hot

tor'sion _n._ a twisting or being twisted

torsion bar _n._ metal bar having resilience under torsion

tor'so _n., pl._ **-sos** human body minus head and limbs

tort _n._ _Law_ wrongful act, injury, etc.

torte _n._ rich cake

tor'tel·li'ni _n._ tiny, ring-shaped pasta

tor·til'la (-tē'ə) _n._ flat, unleavened cornmeal cake

tor'toise (-təs) _n._ turtle, esp. one living on land

tor'toise-shell' _n._ a mottled, yellow-and-brown substance

tor'tu·ous (-chōō-) _a._ full of twists and turns

tor'ture _n._ 1 inflicting of great pain 2 great pain —_v._ 1 subject to torture 2 twist

To·ry (tôr'ē) _n., pl._ **-ries** 1 Br. loyalist in American Revolution 2 [_often_ t-] a conservative

toss _v._ **tossed, toss'ing** 1 throw lightly from the hand 2 fling or be flung about 3 jerk upward —_n._ a tossing

toss'up' _n._ 1 flipping of a coin to decide something 2 even chance

tot _n._ young child

to'tal _n._ the whole amount; sum —_a._ 1 entire; whole 2 complete —_v._ add (up to) —**to·tal'i·ty** _n._ —**to'tal·ly** _adv._

to·tal'i·tar'i·an _a._ of a dictatorship

tote _v._ [Inf.] carry; haul —_n._ 1 large, open handbag: also **tote bag** 2 small piece of luggage

to'tem _n._ (animal) symbol associated with a family, etc.

to'tem pole _n._ pole with animal symbol(s), made by Indians of NW North America

tot'ter _v._ 1 rock as if about to fall 2 stagger

tou'can' (tōō'-) _n._ tropical bird with a large beak

touch _v._ 1 put the hand, etc. on so as to feel 2 bring or come into contact 3 tap lightly 4 handle; use 5 concern 6 arouse pity, etc. in 7 treat in passing: with _on_ or _upon_ —_n._ 1 a touching 2 way things feel 3 sense of this 4 small bit 5 contact —**in touch** in contact —**touch on** mention —**touch up** improve by additions

touch'-and-go' _a._ uncertain, risky, etc.

touch'down' _n._ 1 goal scored in football, for six points 2 moment when an aircraft lands

tou·ché (tōō shā') _int._ clever reply

touched _a._ 1 emotionally affected 2 slightly demented

touch'ing _a._ arousing tender emotions; moving

touch'stone' _n._ criterion

touch'y _a._ **-i·er, -i·est** 1 irritable 2 difficult

touch'y-feel'y _a._ [Inf.] overly affectionate, sentimental, etc.

tough _a._ 1 hard to chew, cut, break, etc. 2 strong or rough 3 very difficult —_n._ ruffian —**tough'en** _v._

tou·pee (tōō pā') _n._ small wig for a bald spot

tour _n._ long trip, as to see sights or put on plays —_v._ go on a tour (through) —

tour′ist *n.*, *a.*

tour de force *n.*, *pl.* **tours de force** unusually skillful performance, etc.

tour′ism′ *n.* tourist travel

tour′na·ment *n.* **1** series of contests for a championship **2** knights' jousting contest

tour′ney *n.*, *pl.* **-neys** tournament

tour′ni·quet (-kət) *n.* device for compressing a blood vessel to stop bleeding

tou·sle (tou′zəl) *v.* muss

tout (tout) [Inf.] *v.* **1** praise highly **2** sell tips on (race horses) —*n.* one who touts

tow *v.* pull by a rope or chain —*n.* a towing

toward (tôrd, twôrd) *prep.* **1** in the direction of **2** concerning **3** near **4** for Also **towards**

tow′el *n.* piece of cloth or paper to wipe things dry

tow′el·ing, tow′el·ling *n.* material for making towels

tow′er *n.* high structure, often part of another building —*v.* rise high

tow′head′ (tō′-) *n.* person with light yellow hair

tow′hee′ (tō′-) *n.* small North American sparrow

tow′line′ *n.* rope, etc. for towing

town *n.* **1** small city **2** business center —**towns′folk′, towns′peo′ple** *pl.n.*

town crier *n.* one who formerly shouted public announcements through the streets

town hall *n.* town building housing offices of officials, etc.

town house *n.* two-story dwelling in a complex of such houses

town meeting *n.* meeting of the voters of a town

town′ship *n.* **1** part of a county **2** U.S. land unit 6 miles square

towns′man *n.*, *pl.* **-men** one who lives in a town

tow′path′ *n.* path by a canal

tow′rope′ *n.* rope for towing

tox·e′mi·a *a.* condition of toxins or poisons spread throughout the blood

tox′ic *a.* **1** of or caused by a toxin **2** poisonous

tox′i·col′o·gy *n.* science of poisons and their effects —**tox′i·col′o·gist** *n.*

tox′in *n.* poison, esp. from bacteria, viruses, etc.

toy *n.* thing to play with —*a.* small —*v.* play (*with*)

tr *abbrev.* **1** translated **2** translation **3** translator **4** transpose

trace *n.* **1** mark or track left **2** small

bit **3** harness strap connecting to vehicle —*v.* **1** follow (the trail or course of) **2** draw, outline, etc. —**trac′er** *n.*

trac′er·y *n.*, *pl.* **-ies** design of interlacing lines

tra′che·a (-kē-) *n.* air passage from the larynx to the bronchial tubes

tra′che·ot′o·my *n.*, *pl.* **-mies** emergency incision of the trachea, as to allow breathing

trac′ing *n.* something traced

track *n.* **1** footprint, wheel rut, etc. **2** path, trail, or course **3** running sports, etc. **4** pair of rails a train runs on —*v.* **1** follow the track of **2** leave footprints on —**keep** (or **lose**) **track of** keep (or fail to keep) informed about

track′ball′ *n.* ball on a computer for moving the cursor

track record *n.* [Inf.] past performance

tract *n.* **1** large stretch of land **2** system of bodily organs **3** booklet

trac′ta·ble *a.* manageable

tract house *n.* one of a series of houses of the same design

trac′tion *n.* **1** power to grip a surface **2** a pulling

trac′tor *n.* **1** motor vehicle to pull farm machines, etc. **2** truck to haul a trailer

trac′tor-trail′er *n.* coupled TRACTOR (*n.* 2) and trailer or semitrailer

trade *n.* **1** skilled work **2** buying and selling **3** an exchange —*v.* **1** buy and sell **2** exchange

trade′-in′ *n.* thing used as part payment

trade′mark′ *n.* special mark or name (**trade name**) put on a product

trade′-off′ *n.* exchange of a benefit for one more desirable

trades′man *n.*, *pl.* **-men** [Chiefly Br.] storekeeper

trade union *n.* labor union

trade wind *n.* wind that blows toward the equator

trad′ing post *n.* store in an outpost, where trading is done

tra·di′tion *n.* **1** custom, etc. handed down from the past **2** such handing down —**tra·di′tion·al** *a.*

tra·duce′ *v.* to slander

traf′fic *n.* **1** vehicles moving along streets, etc. **2** amount of business done **3** TRADE (*n.* 2) —*v.* **-ficked, -fick·ing** do business, esp. illegally

traffic circle *n.* circular road at the intersection of several streets

traffic light (or **signal**) *n.* set of signal lights to regulate traffic

tra·ge·di·an (trə jē'-) *n.* actor of tragedy —**tra·ge·di·enne'** *n.fem.*

trag'e·dy *n., pl.* **–dies 1** serious play with a sad ending **2** tragic event

trag'ic *a.* **1** of or like tragedy **2** very sad —**trag'i·cal·ly** *adv.*

trail *v.* **1** drag or lag behind **2** follow or drift behind **3** dwindle —*n.* **1** thing trailing behind **2** beaten path

trail bike *n.* small motorcycle as for trails

trail'blaz'er *n.* **1** one who blazes a trail **2** pioneer in any field

trail'er *n.* wagon or van pulled by a car or truck, sometimes used as a home

trailer park *n.* area designed for trailers, esp. mobile homes

trail mix *n.* mixture of nuts, seeds, etc. for snacking

train *n.* **1** a thing that drags behind **2** procession **3** connected series **4** locomotive with cars —*v.* **1** guide the development of **2** instruct or prepare **3** aim —**train·ee'** *n.*

traipse *v.* [Inf. or Dial.] to walk, tramp, etc.

trait *n.* characteristic

trai'tor *n.* disloyal person —**trai'tor·ous** *a.*

tra·jec'to·ry *n., pl.* **–ries** curved path of a missile

tram *n.* [Br.] streetcar

tram'mel *n., v.* (thing) to hinder or restrain

tramp *v.* **1** walk, or step, heavily **2** roam about —*n.* **1** vagrant **2** a tramping

tram'ple *v.* step hard on or crush underfoot

tram'po·line' (-lēn') *n.* apparatus with springs and taut canvas, used for acrobatic tumbling

trance *n.* state of shock, hypnosis, or deep thought

tran'quil *a.* calm; quiet —**tran·quil'li·ty, tran·quil'i·ty** *n.*

tran'quil·ize', tran'quil·lize' *v.* make tranquil —**tran'quil·iz'er, tran'quil·liz'er** *n.*

trans *abbrev.* **1** translated **2** translation **3** translator **4** transportation

trans– *pref.* over, across, beyond

trans·act' *v.* do; complete —**trans·ac'tion** *n.*

trans·at·lan'tic *a.* crossing the Atlantic

tran·scend' (-send') *v.* exceed —**tran·scend'ent** *a.*

tran·scen·den'tal *a.* **1** transcendent **2** supernatural

trans·con·ti·nen'tal *a.* crossing or spanning a continent

tran·scribe' *v.* **1** write or type out **2** to record —**tran·scrip'tion** *n.*

tran'script' *n.* **1** written or printed copy **2** official copy, as of student record

tran'sept' *n.* shorter part of a cross-shaped church

trans·fer' *v.* **-ferred', -fer'ring** move or change from one person, place, etc. to another —*n.* **1** a transferring **2** ticket letting one change to another bus, etc. —**trans·fer'a·ble** *a.* —**trans'fer·ence** *n.*

trans·fig'ure *v.* **1** transform **2** make seem glorious —**trans·fig'u·ra'tion** *n.*

trans·fix' *v.* **1** pierce through **2** make motionless

trans·form' *v.* change the form or condition of —**trans'for·ma'tion** *n.*

trans·form'er *n.* device that changes voltage

trans·fuse' *v.* **1** imbue; fill **2** transfer (blood) to another —**trans·fu'sion** *n.*

trans·gress' *v.* **1** break (a law) **2** do wrong **3** go beyond —**trans·gres'sion** *n.* —**trans·gres'sor** *n.*

tran'si·ent (-shənt, -sē ənt) *a.* temporary —*n.* one that stays only a short time

tran·sis'tor *n.* small electronic device that controls current flow

trans'it *n.* **1** passage across **2** a conveying

tran·si'tion *n.* a passing from one condition, place, etc. to another

tran'si·tive *a.* designating verbs taking a direct object

tran'si·to'ry *a.* temporary

trans·late' *v.* put into another language, form, etc. —**trans·la'tion** *n.* —**trans·la'tor** *n.*

trans·lit'er·ate' *v.* write (words) in characters of another alphabet —**trans·lit'er·a'tion** *n.*

trans·lu'cent *a.* letting light pass through but not transparent

trans'mi·gra'tion *n.* a passing into another body: said of a soul

trans·mis'si·ble *a.* capable of being transmitted

trans·mis'sion *n.* **1** a transmitting **2** car part sending power to wheels

trans·mit' *v.* **-mit'ted, -mit'ting 1** transfer **2** pass or convey **3** send out (radio or TV signals) —**trans·mit'tal** *n.* —**trans·mit'ter** *n.*

trans·mute' *v.* change from one form, nature, etc. into another

trans·na'tion·al *a.* involving more than one nation

trans'o·ce·an'ic (-ō'shē-) *a.* crossing or

tran·som *n.* small window above a door or window

spanning an ocean

trans·par·ent *a.* 1 that can be seen through 2 very clear 3 obvious —**trans·par'en·cy** *n., pl.* **-cies**

tran·spire' *v.* 1 become known 2 happen

trans·plant' (*n.:* trans'plant') *v.* 1 dig up and plant in another place 2 to transfer (tissue or organ) from one to another; graft —*n.* something transplanted

tran·spon'der *n.* radio transmitter and receiver that automatically transmits signals

trans·port' (*n.:* trans'pôrt) *v.* 1 carry from one place to another 2 carry away with emotion —*n.* thing for transporting —**trans'por·ta'tion** *n.*

trans·pose' *v.* 1 to interchange 2 *Mus.* change the key of

trans·sex'u·al *n.* one who identifies with the opposite sex, sometimes so strongly as to undergo sex-change surgery

trans·ship' *v.* to transfer from one ship, train, etc. to another —**trans·ship'ment** *n.*

trans·verse' *a.* situated, placed, etc. across

trans·ves'tite *n.* one who gets sexual pleasure from wearing clothes of the opposite sex

trap *n.* 1 device for catching animals 2 tricky ruse 3 bend in a drainpipe —*v.* **trapped, trap'ping** 1 catch in a trap 2 set traps for animals —**trap'per** *n.*

trap'door' *n.* hinged or sliding door in a roof or floor

tra·peze' *n.* swinglike bar for acrobats

trap'e·zoid' *n.* figure with two of four sides parallel

trap'pings *pl.n.* adornments

trap'shoot'ing *n.* sport of shooting clay disks sprung into the air from throwing devices (**traps**)

trash *n.* rubbish —*v.* 1 destroy (property) 2 criticize or insult —**trash'y** *a.*, **-i·er, -i·est**

trau'ma *n.* 1 emotional shock with lasting psychic effects 2 bodily injury —**trau·mat'ic** *a.* —**trau'ma·tize'** *v.*

trav·ail (tra väl') *n.* 1 labor 2 agony

trav·el *v.* 1 make a journey (through) 2 move or pass —*n.* 1 a traveling 2 *pl.* journeys —**trav'el·er** *n.*

traveler's check *n.* a kind of bank check sold to a traveler, who cashes it later

trav'e·logue', trav'e·log' *n.* illustrated lecture or movie of travels

tra·verse' (*a.:* trav'ərs) *v.* to cross —*a.* of drapes drawn by pulling cords

trav'es·ty *n., pl.* **-ties** farcical imitation —*v.* **-tied, -ty·ing** to make a travesty of

trawl *v., n.* (fish with) a large dragnet —**trawl'er** *n.*

tray *n.* flat, low-sided server to carry things

treach'er·ous (trech'-) *a.* 1 disloyal 2 not safe or reliable —**treach'er·y** *n.*

trea'cle (trē'-) *n.* [Br.] molasses

tread (tred) *v.* **trod, trod'den** or **trod, tread'ing** 1 walk on, along, over, etc. 2 trample —*n.* 1 way or sound of treading 2 part for treading or moving on

trea·dle (tred''l) *n.* foot pedal to operate a wheel, etc.

tread'mill' *n.* device worked by treading an endless belt

treas *abbrev.* 1 treasurer 2 treasury

trea·son (trē'zən) *n.* betrayal of one's country —**trea'son·a·ble, trea'son·ous** *a.*

treas·ure (trezh'-) *n.* 1 accumulated money, jewels, etc. 2 valued person or thing —*v.* 1 save up 2 cherish

treas'ure-trove' *n.* 1 treasure found hidden 2 valuable discovery

treas'ur·y *n., pl.* **-ies** place where money is kept 2 funds of a state, corporation, etc. —**treas'ur·er** *n.*

treat *v.* 1 deal with or act toward 2 pay for the food, etc. of 3 subject to a process, medical care, etc. —*n.* 1 food, etc. paid for by another 2 thing giving pleasure —**treat'ment** *n.*

trea·tise (trēt'is) *n.* a formal writing on a subject

trea'ty *n., pl.* **-ties** agreement between nations

tre·ble (treb'əl) *a.* 1 triple 2 of or for the treble —*n.* 1 *Mus.* highest part 2 high-pitched voice or sound —*v.* to triple

tree *n.* large, woody plant with one main trunk and many branches —*v.* **treed, tree'ing** to chase up a tree

tre'foil' *n.* 1 plant with three-part leaves 2 design like such a leaf

trek *v.* **trekked, trek'king**; *n.* (make) a slow, hard journey

trel'lis *n.* lattice on which vines, etc. are grown

trem'ble *v.* 1 shake from cold, fear, etc. 2 quiver or vibrate —*n.* act or fit of trembling

tre·men'dous *a.* 1 very large 2 [Inf.]

wonderful

trem'o·lo' n., pl. **-los'** Mus. tremulous effect of repeating the same tone

trem'or n. a trembling, shaking, etc.

trem'u·lous (-yŏŏ-) a. trembling

trench n. ditch, esp. one dug for cover in battle

trench'ant a. incisive

trench coat n. belted raincoat in a military style

trench foot n. foot disorder from exposure to wet and cold

trench mouth n. infectious disease of the mouth

trend v., n. (have) a general direction or tendency

trend'y a. **-i·er, -i·est** [Inf.] of or in the latest style

trep'i·da'tion n. fearful uncertainty

tres'pass v. **1** enter another's property unlawfully **2** sin —n. a trespassing —**tres'pass·er** n.

tress n. lock of hair

tres'tle (-əl) n. **1** framework support, as for a bridge **2** sawhorse

trey (trā) n. playing card with three spots

tri- pref. three

tri'ad' n. group of three

tri·age (trē äzh') n., v. (system) to prioritize (emergency patients, etc.)

tri'al n. **1** hearing and deciding of a case in a law court **2** attempt **3** test **4** pain, trouble, etc.

trial and error n. the making of repeated tests or trials, as to find a solution

trial balloon n. something done to test public opinion

tri'an·gle n. three-sided figure with three angles —**tri·an'gu·lar** a.

tribe n. **1** group of people living together under a chief **2** group or class —**trib'al** a. —**tribes'man** n., pl. **-men**

trib·u·la'tion (-yŏŏ-) n. great misery or distress

tri·bu'nal n. law court

trib'une' n. defender of the people

trib'u·tar'y (-ter'-) n., pl. **-ies** river that flows into a larger one

trib'ute' n. **1** forced payment, as by a weak nation to a stronger **2** gift, speech, etc. showing respect

tri·cen·ten'ni·al n. 300th anniversary

tri'ceps n., pl. **-ceps** large back muscle of the upper arm

tri·cer'a·tops' n. dinosaur with bony crest and three horns

trich'i·no'sis (trik'i-) n. disease caused by worms in the intestines, etc.

trick n. **1** something done to fool, cheat, etc. **2** prank **3** clever act or skillful way **4** turn at work **5** personal habit **6** cards played in one round —v. fool or cheat —**trick'er·y** n.

trick'le v. **1** flow in drops or a thin stream **2** move slowly —n. slow flow

trick'ster n. one who tricks; cheat

trick'y a. **-i·er, -i·est 1** deceitful **2** difficult

tri'col'or n. flag having three colors

tri'cy·cle n. three-wheeled vehicle

tri'dent n. three-pronged spear

tried v. pt. & pp. of TRY —a. tested or trustworthy

tri'fle n. **1** thing of little value **2** small amount —v. **1** act jokingly **2** play

tri'fling a. unimportant

trig n. [Inf.] trigonometry

trig'ger n. lever pressed in firing a gun

trig·o·nom'e·try n. mathematics dealing with relations between sides and angles of triangles —**trig·o·no·met'ric** a.

trill v., n. (sing or play with) a rapid alternation of two close notes

tril'lion n. thousand billions —**tril'lionth** a., n.

tril'o·gy n., pl. **-gies** set of three novels, plays, etc.

trim v. **trimmed, trim'ming 1** clip, lop, etc. **2** decorate **3** put (sails) in order —n. **1** good condition **2** decoration —a. **trim'mer, trim'mest 1** orderly; neat **2** in good condition —**trim'mer** n.

tri·mes'ter n. three-month period

trim'ming n. **1** decoration **2** pl. parts trimmed off

Trin'i·ty n. Father, Son, and Holy Spirit as one God

trin'ket n. small ornament

tri·o (trē'ō) n., pl. **-os 1** musical composition for three performers **2** group of three performers

trip v. **tripped, trip'ping 1** move with light, rapid steps **2** stumble or make stumble **3** err or cause to err —n. a journey

tri·par'tite a. **1** having three parts **2** between three parties

tripe n. stomach of a cow, etc. used as food

trip'ham'mer n. heavy power-driven hammer, alternately raised and dropped

tri·ple (trip'əl) a. **1** of or for three **2** three times as much or as many —n. Baseball hit putting the batter on third base —v. to make or become triple —**tri'ply** adv.

trip'let n. any of three offspring from

the same pregnancy

trip′li·cate (-kət) *a.* triple —*n.* one of three exact copies

tri′pod′ *n.* three-legged stool, support, etc.

trip′tych (-tik) *n.* painting, etc. on three hinged panels

trite *a.* trit′er, trit′est worn-out; stale

tri′umph *n.* victory; success —*v.* gain victory or success —**tri·um′phal, tri·um′phant** *a.*

tri·um′phal·ism′ *n.* arrogant confidence in beliefs

tri·um′vi·rate (-və rit) *n.* government by three persons

triv′et *n.* three-legged stand for holding pots

triv′i·a *pl.n.* trifles

triv′i·al *a.* unimportant —**triv′i·al′i·ty** *n., pl.* **-ties**

trod *v.* pt. & alt. pp. of TREAD

trod′den *v.* alt. pp. of TREAD

trog′lo·dyte′ (-dīt′) *n.* **1** cave dweller **2** hermit

troi′ka *n.* **1** Russian three-horse sleigh **2** group of three (leaders)

troll (trōl) *v.* **1** fish with a moving line **2** sing loudly —*n.* Folklore cave-dwelling giant

trol′ley *n., pl.* **-leys 1** overhead device that sends electric current to a streetcar **2** electric streetcar: also **trolley car**

trol′lop *n.* prostitute

trom′bone′ *n.* brass musical instrument with a sliding tube

troop *n.* **1** group of persons **2** *pl.* soldiers **3** cavalry unit —*v.* move in a group

troop′er *n.* **1** cavalryman **2** mounted policeman

tro′phy *n., pl.* **-phies** souvenir of victory, etc.

trop′ic *n.* **1** either of two parallels of latitude (**Tropic of Cancer** and **Tropic of Capricorn**) north and south of the equator **2** [*also* T-] *pl.* hot region between these latitudes. —**trop′i·cal** *a.*

tro′pism′ *n.* tendency to grow or turn in response to a stimulus such as light

tro′po·sphere′ *n.* atmosphere from the earth's surface to about 6 miles above

trot *v.* **trot′ted, trot′ting** go at a trot —*n.* **1** running gait of a horse **2** slow, jogging run —**trot′ter** *n.*

troth (trōth, trôth) *n.* [Ar.] **1** a promise, esp. to marry **2** truth

trou·ba·dour (trōō′bə dôr′) *n.* medieval lyric poet and musician

trou·ble (trub′əl) *n.* **1** worry, distress,

bother, etc. **2** disturbance **3** difficulty —*v.* be or give trouble to —**trou′ble·some** *a.*

trou′bled *a.* **1** worried or disturbed **2** restless or discontented

trou′ble·mak′er *n.* one who makes trouble for others

trou′ble·shoot′er *n.* one who finds and fixes what is out of order

trough (trôf) *n.* **1** long, narrow, open container, as for feeding animals **2** long, narrow hollow

trounce *v.* beat; flog

troupe (trōōp) *n.* troupe of actors, etc. —**troup′er** *n.*

trou′sers *pl.n.* man's two-legged outer garment

trous·seau (trōō sō′) *n., pl.* **-seaux′** or **-seaus′** (-sōz′) bride's outfit of clothes, linen, etc.

trout *n.* freshwater food fish related to the salmon

trow′el (trou′-) *n.* **1** flat tool for smoothing **2** scooplike tool for digging

troy weight *n.* system of weights for gold, silver, etc. in which 12 ounces = 1 pound

tru′ant *n.* **1** pupil who stays away from school without leave **2** one who shirks his or her duties —**tru′an·cy** *n.*

truce *n.* cessation of fighting by mutual agreement

truck *n.* **1** large motor vehicle for carrying loads **2** wheeled frame **3** vegetables raised for market **4** [Inf.] dealings —*v.* carry on a truck —**truck′er** *n.*

truck farm *n.* farm where vegetables are grown for market

truck′le *v.* be servile

truc′u·lent (-yōō-) *a.* fierce —**truc′u·lence** *n.*

trudge *v.* walk wearily

true *a.* **1** loyal **2** not false **3** accurate **4** lawful **5** real; genuine —*adv.* exactly —*n.* that which is true —**tru′ly** *adv.*

true′-blue′ *a.* very loyal

truf′fle *n.* fleshy, edible underground fungus

tru′ism′ *n.* an obvious truth

trump *n.* (playing card of) a suit ranked highest —*v.* take with a trump —**trump up** devise deceitfully

trump′er·y *n., pl.* **-ies** showy but worthless thing

trum′pet *n.* brass instrument with a flared end —*v.* proclaim loudly

trun′cate *v.* cut off a part of —**trun·ca′tion** *n.*

trun'cheon (-chən) *n.* staff or club

trun'dle *v.* roll along

trundle bed *n.* low bed on small wheels

trunk *n.* **1** main stem of a tree **2** body, not including the head and limbs **3** long snout of an elephant **4** large box for clothes, etc. **5** main line **6** *pl.* very short pants worn for sports **7** rear compartment in car for luggage, etc.

trunk line *n.* main line of a railroad, telephone system, etc.

truss *v.* tie, fasten, or tighten —*n.* supporting framework or device

trust *n.* **1** belief in the honesty, reliability, etc. of another **2** one trusted **3** responsibility **4** custody **5** CREDIT (*n.* 4) **6** property managed for another **7** a monopolistic group of corporations —*v.* **1** have trust in **2** put in the care of **3** believe **4** hope **5** let buy on credit —**trust'ful** *a.* —**trust'wor'thy** *a.*

trust·ee' *n.* **1** one put in charge of another's property **2** member of a controlling board —**trust·ee'ship** *n.*

trust fund *n.* money, stock, etc. held in trust

trust'y *a.* **-i·er, -i·est** dependable —*n., pl.* **-ies** a convict with privileges

truth *n., pl.* **truths** (trŏঁthz, trŏঁths) **1** a being true, honest, etc. **2** that which is true **3** established fact —**truth'ful** *a.*

try *v.* **tried, try'ing 1** conduct the trial of **2** test **3** afflict **4** attempt —*n., pl.* **tries** attempt; effort

try'ing *a.* hard to bear

try'out' *n.* [Inf.] test of fitness

tryst (trist) *n.* **1** appointment to meet secretly made by lovers **2** such a meeting

tsar (tsär, zär) *n.* czar

tset·se fly (tset'sē) *n.* African fly that carries disease

T'-shirt' *n.* short-sleeved, pull-over undershirt or sport shirt

tsp *abbrev.* teaspoon(s)

T square *n.* T-shaped ruler

tsu·na·mi (tsŏঁ nä'mē) *n., pl.* **-mis** or **-mi** huge sea wave

tub *n.* **1** large, open container **2** bathtub

tu'ba *n.* large, deep-toned brass instrument

tub'al *a.* of the fallopian tubes

tub'by (-ē) *a.* **-bi·er, -bi·est** fat and short

tube *n.* **1** slender pipe for fluids **2** tubelike, sealed container **3** electron

tube —**the tube** [Inf.] television —**tu'bu·lar** *a.*

tu'ber *n.* thickened part of an underground stem —**tu'ber·ous** *a.*

tu'ber·cle *n.* **1** small, round projection **2** hard growth

tu·ber·cu·lo'sis *n.* infectious bacterial disease, esp. of the lungs —**tu·ber'cu·lar, tu·ber'cu·lous** *a.*

tube'rose' *n.* Mexican plant with a bulblike root and white flowers

tube sock *n.* sock without a shaped heel

tuck *v.* **1** gather up in folds **2** push the edges of something under **3** cover snugly **4** press into a small space —*n.* sewn fold

tuck'er *v.* [Inf.] tire (*out*)

-tude *suf.* quality; state

Tue, Tues *abbrev.* Tuesday

Tues'day *n.* third day of the week

tuft *n.* bunch of hairs, grass. etc. growing or tied together —*v.* form in tufts

tug *v.* **tugged, tug'ging** pull; drag —*n.* **1** hard pull **2** tugboat

tug'boat' *n.* small boat for towing or pushing ships

tug of war *n.* contest with teams pulling at opposite ends of a rope

tu·i'tion (-ish'ən) *n.* charge for instruction, as at a college

tu'lip *n.* bulb plant with cup-shaped flower

tulle (tŏঁl) *n.* fine netting for veils, etc., made of silk, etc.

tum'ble *v.* **1** fall or move suddenly or clumsily **2** toss about **3** do acrobatics —*n.* **1** a fall **2** confused heap

tum'ble-down' *a.* dilapidated

tum'bler *n.* **1** drinking glass **2** acrobat **3** part of a lock moved by a key

tum'ble·weed' *n.* plant that breaks off and is blown about

tu'mid *a.* **1** swollen; bulging **2** inflated; pompous

tum'my *n., pl.* **-mies** [Inf.] stomach

tu'mor *n.* abnormal growth in or on the body

tu'mult' *n.* **1** uproar **2** confusion —**tu·mul'tu·ous** (-chŏঁ əs) *a.*

tun *n.* large cask

tu'na (fish) *n.* large, edible ocean fish

tun'dra *n.* large arctic plain without trees

tune *n.* **1** melody **2** *Mus.* right pitch **3** agreement —*v.* **1** put in TUNE (*n.* 2) **2** adjust to proper performance —**tune** in adjust radio or TV set to receive (a station, program, etc.) —**tun'er** *n.*

tune'ful *a.* full of melody

tune'up', tune'-up' *n.* an adjusting, as

of an engine, to proper condition

tung'sten *n.* hard metal used in alloys, a chemical element

tu'nic *n.* **1** loose gown worn in ancient Greece and Rome **2** long, belted blouse

tun'ing fork *n.* two-pronged steel device struck to sound a tone in perfect pitch

tun'nel *n.* underground passageway — *v.* make a tunnel

tun'ny *n., pl.* **-nies** tuna

tur'ban *n.* scarf wound around the head, as in the Middle East

tur'bid *a.* **1** muddy or cloudy **2** confused

tur'bine (-bin, -bīn') *n.* engine driven by the pressure of air, steam, or water on the vanes of a wheel

tur'bo-charge' *v.* enhance with a jet-driven turbine

tur'bo-jet' *n.* airplane engine providing thrust by means of a jet of hot, exhaust gases

tur'bo-prop' *n.* turbojet engine that drives a propeller

tur'bot (-bot) *n.* kind of flounder

tur'bu·lent *a.* **1** disorderly **2** agitated —**tur'bu·lence** *n.*

tu·reen' (too-) *n.* large, deep dish with a lid, for soup, etc.

turf *n.* top layer of earth with grass — **the turf** (track for) horse racing

tur'gid (-jid) *a.* **1** swollen **2** pompous —**tur·gid'i·ty** *n.*

Turk *n.* native of Turkey

tur'key *n.* **1** large bird with a spreading tail **2** its flesh, used as food

turkey vulture *n.* dark-colored American vulture: also **turkey buzzard**

Turk'ish *n., a.* (language) of Turkey

tur'mer·ic *n.* plant whose powdered root is used for seasoning, etc.

tur'moil' *n.* noisy, excited condition

turn *v.* **1** revolve or rotate **2** change in position or direction **3** make or perform **4** reverse **5** change in feelings, etc. **6** change in form, etc. **7** drive, set, etc. **8** to wrench or twist **9** divert; deflect **10** upset **11** depend **12** reach or pass **13** become **14** become sour —*n.* **1** a turning around **2** change in position or direction **3** short walk, ride, etc. **4** bend; twist **5** chance; try **6** deed **7** turning point **8** style; form **9** sudden shock —**in** (or **out of**) **turn** in (or not in) proper order —**turn down** to reject —**turn in 1** hand in **2** [Inf.] go to bed —**turn off 1** shut off **2** [Sl.] cause to be bored, etc. —**turn on 1** make go on **2** [Sl.]

make or become elated, etc. —**turn out 1** shut off **2** assemble **3** make **4** result —**turn to** rely on —**turn up** happen, appear, etc.

turn'a·bout' *n.* reversal

turn'a·round' *n.* **1** wide area for turning a vehicle around **2** time taken by a business to complete a job

turn'buck'le *n.* metal loop used as a coupling

turn'coat' *n.* traitor

turning point *n.* point in time when a decisive change occurs

tur'nip *n.* plant with an edible, round root

turn'key *n., pl.* **-keys'** jailer

turn'off' *n.* place to turn off a highway, etc.

turn'out' *n.* gathering of people

turn'o'ver *n.* **1** small filled pastry with crust folded over **2** rate of replacement of workers, goods, etc.

turn'pike' *n.* highway, esp. one on which a toll is paid

turn'stile' *n.* gate admitting only one at a time

turn'ta'ble *n.* round, revolving platform

tur'pen·tine' *n.* oil from trees, used in paints, etc.

tur'pi·tude' *n.* vileness

tur'quoise' (-kwoiz', -koiz') *n.* **1** greenish-blue gem **2** greenish blue

tur'ret *n.* **1** small tower on a building **2** armored dome, as on a tank **3** lathe part holding cutting tools

tur'tle *n.* hard-shelled land and water reptile

tur'tle-dove' *n.* wild dove

tur'tle-neck' *n.* high, snug, turned-down collar

tusk *n.* long, projecting tooth, as of an elephant

tus'sle *n., v.* struggle; fight

tus'sock (-ək) *n.* thick tuft or clump of grass, etc.

tu·te·lage (tōōt′'l ij) *n.* **1** instruction **2** protection

tu'tor *n.* private teacher —*v.* teach — **tu·to'ri·al** (-tôr'ē-) *a.*

tut·ti-frut·ti (tōōt′ē frōōt′ē) *n., a.* (ice cream, etc.) made with mixed fruits

tu'tu' *n.* short, projecting ballet skirt

tux·e'do *n., pl.* **-dos** man's semiformal suit: also **tux**

TV *n.* **1** television **2** *pl.* **TVs** or **TV's** television set

TV dinner *n.* precooked frozen dinner packaged in a tray

twad·dle (twäd′'l) *n.* nonsense

twain *n., a.* [Ar.] two

twang *n.* **1** sharp, vibrating sound **2** nasal sound —*v.* to make, or utter with, a twang

'twas *contr.* [Poet.] it was

tweak *v., n.* (give) a sudden, twisting pinch

tweed *n.* **1** rough wool fabric **2** *pl.* clothes of tweed

tweet *v., n.* chirp

tweet'er *n.* small speaker for high-frequency sounds

tweez'ers *pl.n.* [*also with sing. v.*] small pincers for plucking hairs

twelve *a., n.* two more than ten —**twelfth** *a., n.*

12-step *a.* of any rehabilitation program modeled on AA

twen'ty *a.; n., pl.* **-ties** two times ten —**twen'ti·eth** *a., n.*

twerp *n.* [Sl.] insignificant or contemptible person

twice *adv.* **1** two times **2** two times as much

twid'dle *v.* twirl idly

twig *n.* small branch

twi'light' *n.* **1** dim light after sunset **2** gradual decline

twill *n.* cloth woven with parallel diagonal lines

twin *n.* **1** either of two offspring from the same pregnancy **2** either of two very much alike —*a.* being a twin or twins

twin bed *n.* either of a pair of single beds

twine *n.* strong cord made of twisted strands —*v.* **1** interweave **2** wind around

twinge *v., n.* (have) a sudden pain or a qualm

twin'kle *v.* **1** sparkle **2** light up, as with amusement —*n.* a twinkling

twin'-size' *a.* of the size of a twin bed

twirl *v., n.* spin; twist

twist *v.* **1** to wind together or around something **2** force out of shape **3** pervert meaning of **4** sprain **5** rotate **6** curve —*n.* **1** something twisted **2** a twisting

twist'er *n.* [Inf.] tornado or cyclone

twit *n.* [Inf.] foolish or annoying person

twitch *v.* pull or move with a sudden jerk —*n.* sudden, spasmodic motion

twit'ter *v.* **1** chirp rapidly **2** tremble excitedly —*n.* a twittering

two *a., n.* one more than one —**in two** in two parts

two'-bit' *a.* [Sl.] cheap, inferior, etc.

two'-faced' *a.* deceitful

two'-fist'ed *a.* [Inf.] virile

two'fold' *a.* **1** having two parts **2** having twice as much or as many —*adv.* twice as much or as many

two'-ply' *a.* having two layers, strands, etc.

two'some *n.* a couple

two'-time' *v.* [Sl.] be unfaithful to

two'-way' *a.* allowing passage in two directions

Twp *abbrev.* township

TX *abbrev.* Texas

-ty *suf.* quality or condition of

ty·coon' *n.* powerful industrialist

ty'ing *v.* prp. of TIE

tyke (tīk) *n.* [Inf.] small child

tym·pan'ic membrane (tim-) *n.* thin membrane inside the ear

tym'pa·num *n.* **1** cavity beyond tympanic membrane **2** tympanic membrane

type (tīp) *n.* **1** kind or sort **2** model; example **3** metal piece or pieces for printing —*v.* **1** classify **2** use the keyboard of a computer, typewriter, etc.

type'cast' *v.* to cast (an actor) repeatedly in similar role

type'script' *n.* typewritten matter

type'set' *v.* set in type —**type'set'ter** *n.*

type'write' *v.* write with a typewriter

type'writ'er *n.* a keyboard machine for making printed letters on paper

ty'phoid' *n.* infectious bacterial disease with fever, intestinal disorders, etc.: also **typhoid fever**

ty·phoon' *n.* cyclonic storm, esp. in the W Pacific

ty'phus *n.* infectious bacterial disease with fever, skin rash, etc.: also **typhus fever**

typ'i·cal *a.* **1** being a true example of its kind **2** characteristic —**typ'i·cal·ly** *adv.*

typ'i·fy (tip'-) *v.* **-fied', -fy'ing** be typical of; exemplify

typ'ist (tip'-) *n.* one who operates a typewriter

ty'po *n., pl.* **-pos** [Inf.] typographical error; mistake in typing or typesetting

ty·pog'ra·phy *n.* **1** setting of, and printing with, type **2** style, design, etc. of matter printed from type —**ty·pog'ra·pher** *n.* —**ty'po·graph'i·cal** *a.*

ty·ran'no·saur' (-sôr') *n.* huge, two-footed dinosaur

tyr'an·ny (tir'-) *n.* cruel and unjust use of power —**ty·ran'ni·cal** *a.* —**tyr'an·nize'** *v.*

ty'rant (tī'-) *n.* cruel, unjust ruler or

master

ty'ro *n., pl.* **-ros** novice

tzar (tsär, zär) *n.* czar

U

U *abbrev.* **1** Union **2** United **3** University

u·biq·ui·tous (yōō bik'wə təs) *a.* everywhere at the same time —**u·biq'ui·ty** *n.*

U'-boat *n.* German submarine

uc *abbrev.* uppercase

ud'der *n.* large, baglike organ containing milk-secreting glands, as in cows

UFO *n., pl.* **UFOs** or **UFO's** unidentified flying object

ugh *int.* exclamation of disgust, horror, etc.

ug'ly *a.* **-li·er, -li·est** **1** unpleasant to see **2** bad **3** dangerous —**ug'li·ness** *n.*

UHF, uhf *abbrev.* ultrahigh frequency

UK *abbrev.* United Kingdom

u'kase' (yōō'-) *n.* official decree

u·ku·le·le (yōō'kə lā'lē) *n.* small, four-stringed guitar

UL *trademark* Underwriters Laboratories

ul'cer *n.* open sore, as on the skin —**ul'cer·ate'** *v.* —**ul'cer·ous** *a.*

ul'na *n., pl.* **-nae** (-nē) or **-nas** larger bone of the forearm

ul·te'ri·or (-tir'ē-) *a.* beyond what is expressed

ul'ti·mate (-mət) *a.* **1** farthest **2** final **3** basic —*n.* final point or result —**ul'ti·mate·ly** *adv.*

ul·ti·ma'tum *n.* final offer or demand

ultra- *pref.* **1** beyond **2** extremely

ul'tra·ma·rine' *a.* deep-blue

ul'tra·son'ic *a.* above the range of humanly audible sound

ul'tra·sound' *n.* ultrasonic waves used in medical diagnosis, therapy, etc.

ul'tra·vi'o·let *a.* of the invisible rays just beyond the violet end of the spectrum

um'bel *n.* cluster of flowers with stalks of equal length

um'ber *n.* reddish brown

um·bil'i·cal cord *n.* cord connecting a fetus to the placenta

um'brage (-brij) *n.* resentment and displeasure

um·brel'la *n.* cloth screen on a folding frame, carried for protection against rain

um'pire *n.* **1** one who judges a dispute **2** one who supervises baseball games, etc. —*v.* act as umpire Also [Inf.]

ump

ump·teen' *a.* [Sl.] very many —**ump'teenth'** *a.*

UN *abbrev.* United Nations

un- *pref.* **1** not, lack of **2** back: reversal of action   See list below

un·a'ble
un'a·fraid'
un·aid'ed
un'a·shamed'
un'at·tain'a·ble
un·au'thor·ized'
un'a·void'a·ble
un·bear'a·ble
un'be·liev'a·ble
un·bi'ased
un·bro'ken
un·but'ton
un·changed'
un·com'fort·a·ble
un'con·strained'
un'con·tam'i·nat·ed
un·con·trol'la·ble
un'con·tro·ver'sial
un'con·ven'tion·al
un·cooked'
un'co·op'er·a·tive
un'co·or'di·nat·ed
un·de·mon'stra·tive
un·de·served'
un'de·sir'a·ble
un'de·vel'oped
un'dis·cov'ered
un'em·ployed'
un'em·ploy'ment
un·e'ven
un·e'vent'ful
un'ex·cep'tion·al
un'ex·plained'
un'ex·plored'
un·fair'
un·fas'ten
un·fa'vor·a·ble
un·fit'
un·fo'cused
un'fore·seen'
un·for'tu·nate
un·gra'cious
un·harmed'
un·heed'ed
un·hurt'
un'i·den'ti·fied'
un'im·por'tant
un'in·hab'it·ed
un·in'jured
un'in·spir'ing
un'in·ter·est·ing
un'in·vit'ed
un·just'
un·kind'
un·lace'

un·leav'ened

un·man'ly

un·mar'ried

un·named'

un·nec'es·sar·y

un·no'ticed

un·ob·tain'a·ble

un·ob·tru'sive

un·of·fi'cial

un·o'pened

un·or'gan·ized'

un·paid'

un·pop'u·lar

un·pre·pared'

un·pro·fes'sion·al

un·prof'it·a·ble

un·pro·tect'ed

un·proved'

un·prov'en

un·pro·voked'

un·qual'i·fied'

un·re·li'a·ble

un·ripe'

un·san'i·tar·y

un·sat·is·fac'to·ry

un·scram'ble

un·seen'

un·self'ish

un·sight'ly

un·skilled'

un·skill'ful

un·sound'

un·spoiled'

un·suit'a·ble

un·ten'a·ble

un·ti'dy

un·tir'ing

un·tried'

un·trou'bled

un·true'

un·want'ed

un·war'rant·ed

un·war'y

un·wa'ver·ing

un·whole'some

un·will'ing

un·wise'

un·wor'thy

un·wrap'

un·yield'ing

un·a·bridged' a. not abridged; complete

un·ac·count'a·ble a. **1** inexplicable **2** not responsible

un·ac·cus'tomed a. **1** not accustomed (to) **2** unusual

un·a·nim'i·ous (yōō-) a. without dissent —**un·a·nim'i·ty** n. —**un·a·nim'i·mous·ly** adv.

un·ap·proach'a·ble a. **1** aloof **2** without equal

un·armed' a. having no weapon

un·as·sum'ing a. modest

un·at·tached' a. **1** not attached **2** not engaged or married

un·a·vail'ing a. useless

un·a·ware' a. not aware —adv. unawares

un·a·wares' adv. **1** unintentionally **2** by surprise

un·bal'anced a. **1** not in balance **2** mentally ill

un·bar' v. unbolt; open

un·be·com'ing a. **1** not suited **2** not proper

un·be·known' a. unknown (to): also **un'be·knownst'**

un·be·lief' n. lack of belief, esp. in religion —**un'be·liev'er** n.

un·bend' v. **1** relax **2** straighten

un·bend'ing a. **1** rigid; stiff **2** firm; unyielding

un·blush'ing a. shameless

un·bolt' v. withdraw the bolt of (a door, etc.); open

un·born' a. **1** not born **2** not yet born; future

un·bos'om (-booz'-) v. to tell (secrets)

un·bound'ed a. not restrained

un·bowed' (-boud') a. not yielding

un·bri'dled a. uncontrolled

un·bur'den v. relieve (oneself) by disclosing (guilt, etc.)

un·called'-for a. unnecessary and out of place

un·can'ny a. **1** weird **2** unusually good, acute, etc.

un·cer·e·mo'ni·ous a. rudely abrupt

un·cer'tain a. **1** not sure or certain **2** vague **3** not steady or constant —**un·cer'tain·ty** n., pl. **-ties**

un·char'i·ta·ble a. severe or harsh

un·cle' n. **1** brother of one's father or mother **2** husband of one's aunt

Uncle Sam n. [Inf.] (personification of) the U.S.

un·coil' v. unwind

un·com·mit'ted a. not pledged or taking a stand

un·com'mon a. **1** not usual **2** extraordinary

un·com'pro·mis'ing a. unyielding; firm

un·con·cern' n. lack of interest or worry —**un'con·cerned'** a.

un·con·di'tion·al a. without conditions or limits

un·con'scion·a·ble (-shən-) a. **1** unscrupulous **2** unreasonable

un·con'scious (-shəs) a. **1** not conscious **2** not aware (of) **3** unintentional —**the unconscious** part of the mind storing feelings, desires, etc. of which one is unaware

un·cool' a. [Sl.] not cool; excitable, unfashionable, etc.

un·count'ed a. **1** not counted **2** innumerable

un·couth' (-kōōth') a. rude; crude

un·cov'er v. **1** to disclose **2** remove the cover from

unc'tion n. **1** an anointing **2** pretended earnestness

unc'tu·ous (-choo-) a. **1** oily **2** insincerely earnest

un·cut' a. **1** not shaped: said of a gem **2** not abridged

un·daunt'ed a. not hesitating because of fear

un·de·cid'ed a. not (having) decided

un·de·ni'a·ble a. that cannot be denied

un'der prep. **1** lower than; below; beneath **2** covered by **3** less than **4** below and to the other side of **5** subject to **6** undergoing —adv. **1** in or to a lower position **2** so as to be covered —a. lower

under- pref. **1** below **2** less than usual or proper

un·der·a·chieve' v. fail to do as well as expected

un'der·age' a. below the legal age

un'der·arm' a. **1** of or for the armpit **2** UNDERHAND (a. 1)

un'der·brush' n. small trees, bushes, etc. in a forest

un'der·car'riage n. supporting frame

un'der·class'man n., pl. -men freshman or sophomore

un'der·clothes' pl.n. underwear: also **un'der·cloth'ing**

un'der·cov'er a. secret

un'der·cur'rent n. underlying tendency, opinion, etc.

un'der·cut' v. weaken or undermine

un'der·de·vel'oped a. inadequately developed, esp. economically

un'der·dog' n. one that is expected to lose

un'der·done' a. not cooked enough

un'der·es'ti·mate' v. make too low an estimate on or for

un'der·ex·pose' v. expose (photographic film) inadequately to light

un'der·foot' adv., a. **1** under the feet **2** in the way

un'der·gar'ment n. piece of underwear

un'der·go' v. experience; endure

un'der·grad'u·ate n. college student who does not yet have a degree

un'der·ground' a., adv. **1** beneath the earth's surface **2** secret **3** unconventional, radical, etc. —n. secret revolutionary movement

un'der·growth' n. underbrush

un'der·hand' a. **1** with the hand held below the elbow **2** underhanded; sly —adv. with an underhand motion

un'der·hand'ed a. sly, deceitful, etc.

un'der·lie' v. **1** lie beneath **2** to support

un'der·line' v. **1** draw a line under **2** to stress

un'der·ling n. a subordinate

un'der·ly'ing a. basic

un'der·mine' v. **1** dig beneath **2** weaken gradually

un'der·neath' adv., prep. under; below

un'der·pants' pl.n. undergarment of short pants

un'der·pass' n. road under a railway or highway

un'der·pin'ning n. prop or foundation

un'der·priv'i·leged a. needy; poor

un'der·rate' v. rate too low

un'der·score' v. underline

un'der·sea' a., adv. beneath the surface of the sea: also **un'der·seas'**

un'der·sec're·tar'y n. assistant secretary

un'der·sell' v. sell for less than

un'der·shirt' n. undergarment worn under a shirt

un'der·shorts' pl.n. men's or boys' short underpants

un'der·shot' a. with the lower part extending past the upper

un'der·staffed' a. not having enough workers

un'der·stand' v. **-stood'**, **-stand'ing 1** get the meaning (of) **2** take as a fact **3** know or perceive the nature, etc. of **4** sympathize with —**un'der·stand'a·ble** a.

un'der·stand'ing n. **1** comprehension **2** intelligence **3** mutual agreement

un'der·state' v. say with little or no emphasis

un'der·stud'y v. (be ready to) substitute for an actor

un'der·take' v. **1** begin (a task, etc.) **2** promise —**un'der·tak'ing** n.

un'der·tak'er n. funeral director

un'der·the·ta'ble a. [Inf.] done secretly because illegal, etc.

un'der·things' pl.n. women's or girls' underwear

un'der·tone' n. subdued tone, color, etc.

un'der·tow' (-tō') n. strong flow of water back under breaking waves

un'der·wa'ter a., adv. beneath the surface of the water

un·der·wear *n.* clothes worn next to the skin

un·der·weight *a.* weighing too little

un·der·world *n.* **1** the world of criminals **2** Hades

un·der·write *v.* **1** agree to finance or write insurance for —**un·der·writ·er** *n.*

un·do *v.* **1** open, untie, etc. **2** cancel or destroy

un·do·ing *n.* **1** a bringing to ruin **2** cause of ruin

un·done *a.* **1** not done **2** ruined

un·doubt·ed *a.* certain

un·dress *v.* **1** take off the clothes of **2** take off one's clothes

un·due *a.* more than is proper —**un·du·ly** *adv.*

un·du·late (-jə-, -dyə-) *v.* **1** move in waves **2** have or give a wavy form —**un·du·la·tion** *n.*

un·dy·ing *a.* eternal

un·earned *a.* **1** obtained as a return on an investment **2** not deserved

un·earth *v.* **1** dig up from the earth **2** find

un·earth·ly *a.* **1** supernatural **2** weird

un·eas·y *a.* uncomfortable —**un·eas·i·ness** *n.*

un·e·qual *a.* **1** not equal in size, value, etc. **2** not adequate (*to*)

un·e·qualed *a.* without equal

un·e·quiv·o·cal *a.* straightforward; clear

un·ex·pect·ed *a.* not expected; unforeseen —**un·ex·pect·ed·ly** *adv.*

un·fail·ing *a.* always dependable

un·faith·ful *a.* **1** not faithful **2** adulterous

un·fa·mil·iar *a.* **1** not well-known **2** not acquainted (*with*)

un·feel·ing *a.* **1** insensible **2** hardhearted; cruel

un·feigned (-fānd') *a.* real; genuine

un·fin·ished *a.* **1** incomplete **2** not painted, etc.

un·flap·pa·ble *a.* [Inf.] not easily excited

un·flinch·ing *a.* steadfast

un·fold *v.* **1** spread out **2** make or become known

un·found·ed *a.* not based on fact or reason

un·friend·ly *a.* not friendly, kind, or favorable

un·furl *v.* unfold

un·gain·ly *a.* awkward

un·gov·ern·a·ble *a.* unruly

un·guard·ed *a.* **1** unprotected **2** frank; candid **3** careless

un·guent (-gwənt) *n.* salve

un·gu·late (-gyōō lit, -lāt') *a.* having hoofs —*n.* ungulate mammal

un·hand *v.* let go of

un·hap·py *a.* **1** unlucky **2** sad; wretched

un·health·y *a.* **1** not well **2** harmful to health

un·heard *a.* not heard or listened to

un·heard·-of *a.* never known or done before

un·hinge *v.* **1** remove from the hinges **2** unbalance (the mind)

un·ho·ly *a.* **1** not sacred **2** wicked; sinful

un·horse *v.* make fall from a horse

uni- *pref.* having only one

u·ni·bod·y *a.* with structural parts welded together into a single unit

u·ni·corn (yōōn'ə-) *n.* mythical horse with a horn in its forehead

u·ni·cy·cle *n.* one-wheeled vehicle with pedals

u·ni·form *a.* **1** never changing **2** all alike —*n.* special clothes for some group —*v.* dress in a uniform —**u·ni·form'i·ty** *n.*

u·ni·fy *v.* **-fied', -fy'ing** make into one —**u·ni·fi·ca'tion** *n.*

u·ni·lat·er·al *a.* **1** of one side only **2** involving only one of several parties

un·im·peach·a·ble *a.* without fault

un·in·hib·it·ed *a.* free in behavior

un·in·ter·est·ed *a.* not interested; indifferent

un·ion (yōōn'yən) *n.* **1** a uniting **2** group of nations or states united **3** marriage **4** a labor union

un·ion·ize *v.* organize into a labor union

Union Jack *n.* flag of the United Kingdom

u·nique (yōō nēk') *a.* **1** one and only **2** without equal **3** unusual

u·ni·sex *a.* not differentiated for the sexes

u·ni·son *n.* **1** *Mus.* sameness of pitch **2** agreement

u·nit *n.* **1** single part of a whole **2** a special part **3** a standard measure **4** one

U·ni·tar·i·an *n., a.* (member) of a Christian church not believing in Christ's divinity

u·nite *v.* **1** put together as one; combine **2** join together (*in*)

United Nations *n.* international council of nations

u·ni·ty *n.* **1** a being united **2** harmony; agreement

univ *abbrev.* university

u·ni·ver·sal *a.* **1** of or for all **2** present

everywhere —**u·ni·ver·sal·i·ty** n.

u·ni·ver·sal·ly adv. **1** in every case **2** everywhere

Universal Product Code n. bar code on consumer goods

u'ni·verse' n. **1** space and all things in it **2** the world

u'ni·ver·si·ty n., pl. **-ties** school made up of colleges and, often, graduate schools

un·kempt' a. untidy; messy

un·known' a., n. unfamiliar or unidentified (person or thing)

un·law'ful a. against the law —**un·law'ful·ly** adv.

un·lead'ed a. not containing lead compounds, as gasoline

un'leash' v. release as from a leash

un·less' con. except if

un·let'tered a. **1** ignorant **2** illiterate

un·like' a. not alike —prep. not like

un·like'ly a. not likely to happen, be true, succeed, etc.

un·lim'it·ed a. without limits or bounds

un·load' v. **1** remove (a load) **2** take a load from **3** get rid of

un·lock' v. open by undoing a lock

un·luck'y a. having or bringing bad luck

un·make' v. **1** undo **2** ruin **3** depose

un·man' v. deprive of manly courage —**un·man'ly** a.

un·manned' a. without people aboard and operated remotely

un·mask' v. **1** remove a mask (from) **2** expose

un·men'tion·a·ble a. not fit to be spoken of

un'mis·tak'a·ble a. that cannot be mistaken; clear —**un'mis·tak'a·bly** adv.

un·mit'i·gat·ed a. **1** not lessened **2** absolute

un·nat'u·ral a. **1** abnormal **2** artificial

un·nerve' v. to make (someone) lose nerve, courage, etc.

un·num'bered a. **1** countless **2** not numbered

un·pack' v. take things out of a trunk, box, etc.

un·par'al·leled' a. that has no equal or counterpart

un·pleas'ant a. offensive; disagreeable

un·plumbed' (-plumd') a. not fully comprehended

un·prec'e·dent·ed a. having no precedent; unique

un·prin'ci·pled a. without moral principles

un·print'a·ble a. not fit to be printed

un·ques'tion·a·ble a. certain —**un·ques'tion·a·bly** adv.

un'quote' int. that ends the quotation

un·rav'el v. **1** undo the threads of **2** make clear; solve

un·read' (-red') a. **1** not having been read **2** having read little

un·re'al a. fantastic

un·re'al·ized' a. not having been achieved

un·rea'son·a·ble a. **1** not reasonable **2** excessive

un·re·gen'er·ate (-it) a. stubbornly defiant

un·re·lent'ing a. **1** refusing to relent **2** cruel

un·re·mit'ting a. constant; persistent

un·re·quit'ed a. not reciprocated

un·rest' n. restlessness **2** angry discontent

un·ri'valed a. having no rival or equal

un·roll' v. to open (something rolled up)

un·ruf'fled a. calm; smooth

un·rul'y (-rōōl'lē) a. **-i·er, -i·est** not obedient or orderly

un·sa'vor·y a. **1** tasting or smelling bad **2** disgusting

un·scathed' (-skāthd') a. uninjured

un·screw' v. detach or loosen by removing screws

un·scru'pu·lous a. without scruples; dishonest

un·seal' v. to open

un·sea'son·a·ble a. not usual for the season

un·seat' v. **1** throw from a seat **2** remove from office

un·seem'ly a. improper

un·set'tle v. disturb, displace, etc.

un'so·phis'ti·cat·ed a. simple, naive, etc.

un·spar'ing a. showing no mercy

un·speak'a·ble a. so bad, evil, etc. that description is impossible

un·sta'ble a. **1** not fixed, firm, etc. **2** changeable **3** emotionally unsettled

un·stead'y a. unstable

un·struc'tured a. not strictly organized; loose, free, open, etc.

un·strung' a. nervous; upset

un·stuck' a. loosened or freed from being stuck

un·stud'ied a. spontaneous; natural

un'sub·stan'tial a. **1** flimsy **2** unreal

un·sung' a. not honored

un·tan'gle v. free from tangles; straighten out

un·taught' a. **1** uneducated **2** acquired without being taught

un·think'a·ble a. not fit to be considered

un·think′ing a. thoughtless

un·tie′ v. unfasten (something tied or knotted)

un·til′ prep. **1** up to the time of **2** before —con. **1** to the point, degree, etc. that **2** before

un·time·ly a. **1** premature **2** at the wrong time —adv. too soon —**un·time′li·ness** n.

un′to prep. [Poet.] to

un·told′ a. **1** not told or revealed **2** very great

un·touch′a·ble n. member of lowest caste in India

un·to′ward (-tô′ərd) a. **1** inappropriate **2** not favorable

un·truth′ n. lie; falsehood —**un·truth′ful** a.

un·tu′tored a. uneducated

un·used′ a. **1** not in use **2** unaccustomed (to) **3** never used before

un·u′su·al a. not usual; rare —**un·u′su·al·ly** adv.

un·ut′ter·a·ble a. that cannot be spoken or described —**un·ut′ter·a·bly** adv.

un·var′nished a. **1** plain; simple **2** not varnished

un·veil′ v. remove a veil from; disclose

un·well′ a. not well; sick

un·wield′y a. **-i·er, -i·est** hard to handle or deal with because of size, etc. —**un·wield′i·ness** n.

un·wind′ v. **1** make or become uncoiled **2** relax

un·wit′ting a. not intentional —**un·wit′ting·ly** adv.

un·wont′ed a. unusual; rare

un·writ′ten a. **1** not in writing **2** observed only through custom

up adv. **1** to, in, or on a higher place, level, etc. **2** to a later time **3** upright **4** into action, discussion, etc. **5** aside; away **6** so as to be even **7** completely **8** apiece —prep. up along, on, in, etc. —a. **1** put, brought, going, or gone up **2** at an end —v. upped, up′ping [Inf.] increase —ups and downs changes in fortune —up to **1** doing or devising **2** capable of **3** as many as **4** as far as **5** dependent upon

up′-and-com′ing a. **1** promising **2** gaining prominence

up·beat′ a. [Inf.] cheerful or optimistic

up·braid′ v. scold

up·bring′ing n. training received as a child

UPC abbrev. Universal Product Code

up·com′ing a. coming soon

up·coun′try a., adv. inland

up·date′ (n.: up′dāt′) v. make conform to most recent facts, etc. —n. **1** an updating **2** updated report, etc.

up·end′ v. **1** set on end **2** topple

up′front′ a. [Inf.] **1** forthright **2** in advance

up′grade′ n. upward slope —v. raise in grade or rank

up·heav′al n. quick, violent change

up′hill′ a., adv. **1** upward **2** laboriously

up·hold′ v. **1** support **2** confirm; sustain

up·hol′ster v. fit out (furniture) with coverings, etc. —**up·hol′ster·y** n.

up′keep′ n. **1** maintenance **2** cost of maintenance

up′land n. elevated land

up·lift′ v. (n.: up′lift′) **1** lift up **2** raise to a better level —n. a lifting up

up·load′ v. transfer (information) as from a PC to a main computer

up·on′ prep., adv. on; up and on

up′per a. higher in place, rank, etc. —n. part of a shoe above the sole

up′per·case′ a., n. (of or in) capital letters

upper class n. social group of the very wealthy —**up′per-class′** a.

up′per·class′man n., pl. **-men** student who is a junior or senior

up′per·cut′ n. upward blow in boxing

upper hand n. a position of advantage or control

up′per·most′ a. highest in place, power, etc. —adv. in the highest place; first

up·raise′ v. raise up; lift

up′right′ a. **1** standing up; erect **2** honest; just —adv. in an upright position —n. upright pole, beam, etc.

upright bass n. double bass

up·ris′ing n. a revolt

up′roar′ n. loud, confused noise or condition

up·roar′i·ous a. **1** making an uproar **2** boisterous

up·root′ v. **1** pull up by the roots **2** remove entirely

UPS service mark United Parcel Service

up′scale′ a. for affluent or stylish people —v. make suitable for such people

up·set′ (n.: up′set′) v. **1** overturn **2** disturb or distress **3** defeat unexpectedly —n. an upsetting —a. **1** overturned **2** disturbed

up′shot′ n. result; outcome

up′side′ down adv. **1** with the top part underneath **2** in disorder —**up′side′-down′** a.

up·stage' v. draw attention away from

up·stairs' adv., a. to or on an upper floor —n. upper floor or floors

up·stand'ing a. honorable

up·start' n. presumptuous newcomer

up·stream' adv., a. against the current of a stream

up·swing' n. upward trend

up·take' n. a taking up —**quick** (or **slow**) **on the uptake** [Inf.] quick (or slow) to understand

up·tight' a. [Sl.] very tense, nervous, etc.: also **up'·tight'**

up-to-date' a. 1 having the latest facts, ideas, etc. 2 of the newest or latest kind

up'town' n. part of city away from the business district

up'turn' n. upward trend

up'ward adv., a. toward a higher place, position, etc.: also **up'wards** adv. —**upward(s) of** more than

u·ra'ni·um n. radioactive metallic chemical element

U·ra'nus (yoor'-) n. seventh planet from the sun

ur'ban a. of or in a city —**ur'ban·ize'** v.

ur·bane' a. suave; refined —**ur·ban'i·ty** n.

ur'chin n. small, mischievous child

-ure suf. 1 act, result, or means of 2 state of being

u·re'a n. substance found in urine

u·re'mi·a n. toxic condition caused by kidney failure —**u·re'mic** a.

u·re'ter n. duct from a kidney to the bladder

u·re'thra n. duct for discharge of urine from bladder

urge v. 1 insist on 2 to force onward 3 plead with 4 incite —n. impulse

ur'gent a. needing quick action 2 insistent —**ur'gen·cy** n.

u·ric (yoor'ik) a. of or from urine

u'ri·nal (yoor'ə-) n. receptacle or fixture in which to urinate

u'ri·nar'y a. of the organs that secrete or discharge urine

u'ri·nate' v. discharge urine from the body

u·rine (yoor'in) n. waste fluid from the kidneys that passes through the bladder

urn n. 1 vase with a foot 2 metal container for serving coffee, etc.

u·rol'o·gy n. branch of medicine dealing with urinary and genital organs

us pron. objective case of WE

US, U.S. abbrev. United States

USA abbrev. 1 United States of America: also **U.S.A.** 2 United States Army

us'a·ble, use'a·ble a. that can be used

USAF abbrev. United States Air Force

us'age n. 1 treatment 2 custom; habit

USCG abbrev. United States Coast Guard

USDA abbrev. United States Department of Agriculture

use (yōōz; n.: yōōs) v. 1 put into action 2 treat 3 consume —n. 1 a using or being used 2 power or right to use 3 need to use 4 utility or function — **used to** 1 did once 2 familiar with

used a. not new; secondhand

use'ful a. that can be used; helpful — **use'ful·ness** n.

use'less a. worthless

us'er n. one that uses something, esp. narcotic drugs or a computer

us'er-friend'ly a. easy to use or understand, as a computer program

ush'er v. 1 conduct to seats, etc. 2 bring (in) —n. one who ushers

USMC abbrev. United States Marine Corps

USN abbrev. United States Navy

USPS abbrev. United States Postal Service

USSR, U.S.S.R. abbrev. Union of Soviet Socialist Republics

u'su·al a. in common use; ordinary — **u'su·al·ly** adv.

u·surp' v. take by force and without right —**u·sur·pa'tion** n. —**u·surp'er** n.

u·su·ry (yōō'zhə rē) n. lending of money at an excessive interest rate — **u'su·rer** n. —**u·su'ri·ous** a.

UT abbrev. Utah

u·ten'sil n. container or tool for a special purpose

u'ter·ine (-in) a. of the uterus

u'ter·us n. hollow female organ in which a fetus grows

u·til'i·tar'i·an a. useful or practical

u·til'i·ty n., pl. **-ties** 1 usefulness 2 water, gas, etc. for public use 3 company providing this

utility room n. room containing laundry appliances, etc.

u'ti·lize' v. put to use —**u·ti·li·za'tion** n.

ut'most' a. 1 most distant 2 greatest or highest —n. the most possible

U·to'pi·a n. any imaginary place where all things are perfect — **U·to'pi·an, u·to'pi·an** a., n.

ut'ter a. complete; absolute —v. express with the voice —**ut'ter·ly** adv.

ut'ter·ance n. 1 an uttering 2 something said

ut'ter·most' a., n. utmost

U'-turn' n. 180° turn

u·vu·la (yōō′vyə lə) *n., pl.* **-las** or **-lae′** (-lē′) small part hanging down above the back of the tongue

V

v *abbrev.* **1** verb **2** verse **3** versus **4** very

V, v *abbrev.* volt(s)

VA *abbrev.* **1** Veterans Administration (Department of Veterans Affairs) **2** Virginia

va′cant *a.* **1** empty; unoccupied **2** stupid —**va′can·cy** *n., pl.* **-cies**

va′cate′ *v.* **1** make vacant **2** *Law* annul

va·ca′tion *v., n.* period of rest from work, study, etc. —**va·ca′tion·er, va·ca′tion·ist** *n.*

vac·cine′ (-sēn′) *n.* preparation introduced into the body to produce immunity to a disease —**vac′ci·nate′** *v.* —**vac′ci·na′tion** *n.*

vac′il·late′ (vas′-) *v.* **1** waver **2** show indecision —**vac′il·la′tion** *n.*

vac′u·ous *a.* **1** empty **2** stupid; senseless —**va·cu′i·ty** *n., pl.* **-ties**

vac′uum (-yōōm) *n.* **1** completely empty space **2** space with most of the air or gas taken out —*a.* of, having, or working by a vacuum —*v.* clean with a vacuum cleaner

vacuum cleaner *n.* machine that cleans by means of suction

vac′uum-packed′ *a.* packed in airtight container to keep fresh

vacuum tube *n.* electron tube

vag′a·bond′ *a., n.* vagrant

va′gar·y *n., pl.* **-ies** odd action or idea

va·gi′na (-jī′-) *n.* canal leading to the uterus —**vag′i·nal** *a.*

va′grant *n.* homeless wanderer; tramp —*a.* **1** nomadic **2** wayward —**va′gran·cy** *n.*

vague (vāg) *a.* indefinite; unclear —**vague′ly** *adv.* —**vague′ness** *n.*

vain *a.* **1** conceited **2** futile **3** worthless —**in vain** without success **2** profanely

vain′glo′ry *n.* boastful pride —**vain′glo′ri·ous** *a.*

val′ance (val′-) *n.* short drapery forming a border

vale *n.* [Poet.] valley

val′e·dic′to·ry *n., pl.* **-ries** farewell speech, as at graduation —**val′e·dic·to′ri·an** *n.*

va′lence (vā′-) *n. Chem.* combining capacity of an element

val′en·tine′ *n.* **1** sweetheart on Saint Valentine's Day **2** greeting card or gift on this day

val·et (va lā′) *n.* male servant to another man

val′iant (-yant) *a.* brave

val′id *a.* **1** true or sound **2** having legal force —**val′i·date′** *v.* —**va·lid′i·ty** *n.*

va·lise′ (-lēs′) *n.* suitcase

val′ley *n., pl.* **-leys 1** low land between hills **2** land drained by a river system

val′or *n.* courage; bravery —**val′or·ous** *a.*

val′u·a·ble *a.* **1** having value **2** worth much money —*n.* valuable thing: *usually used in pl.*

val′u·a′tion *n.* **1** the fixing of a thing's value **2** value set on a thing

val′ue *n.* **1** importance, desirability, utility, etc. **2** worth in money **3** buying power **4** *pl.* standards —*v.* **1** set the value of **2** think highly of —**val′ue·less** *a.*

valve *n.* **1** device in a pipe, etc. to control the flow of a gas or liquid **2** body membrane like this

vamp *n.* part of a shoe over the instep

vam′pire *n.* **1** *Folklore* person who lives by sucking the blood of others **2** bat that lives on other animals' blood: also **vampire bat**

van *n.* **1** vanguard **2** large closed truck

van′dal *n.* one who destroys another's property on purpose

van′dal·ize′ *v.* destroy maliciously —**van′dal·ism′** *n.*

Van·dyke′ (beard) (-dīk′) *n.* short, pointed beard

vane *n.* **1** device that swings to show wind direction **2** blade of a windmill, etc.

van′guard′ *n.* **1** front part of an army **2** leading group or position in a movement

va·nil′la *n.* flavoring made from the pods of an orchid

van′ish *v.* disappear

van′i·ty *n., pl.* **-ties 1** a being vain, or conceited **2** futility **3** low table with mirror

van′quish *v.* conquer

van′tage *n.* **1** advantage **2** position allowing a clear view, etc.: also **vantage point**

vap′id *a.* tasteless; dull

va′por *n.* **1** thick mist, as fog or steam **2** gas formed by heating a liquid or solid —**va′por·ous** *a.*

va′por·ize′ *v.* change into vapor —**va′por·i·za′tion** *n.* —**va′por·iz′er** *n.*

var·i·a·ble *a.* that varies or can be varied —*n.* variable thing

var·i·ance *n.* **1** a varying **2** degree of difference **3** authorization to bypass legal regulations —**at variance** disagreeing

var·i·ant *a.* slightly different —*n.* variant form

var·i·a·tion *n.* **1** change in form, etc. **2** amount of change

var·i·col·ored *a.* of several or many colors

var·ied *a.* of different kinds

var·i·e·gat·ed *a.* **1** marked with different colors **2** varied

va·ri·e·ty *n., pl.* **-ties 1** state of being varied **2** kind; sort **3** number of different kinds

var·i·ous *a.* **1** of several kinds **2** several or many

var·mint, var·ment *n.* [Inf. or Dial.] objectionable animal or person

var·nish *n.* resinous liquid forming a hard, glossy surface —*v.* cover with this

var·si·ty *n., pl.* **-ties** school's main team in contests, esp. in athletic ones

var·y *v.* **-ied, -y·ing 1** make or become different; change **2** differ

vas·cu·lar *a.* of vessels carrying blood, etc.

vase *n.* open container for flowers, etc.

vas·ec·to·my *n., pl.* **-mies** surgical removal or tying of sperm ducts

Vas·e·line (-lēn´) *trademark* petrolatum —*n.* [**v-**] petrolatum

vas·sal *n.* **1** feudal tenant **2** subject, servant, etc.

vast *a.* very great in size, degree, etc. —**vast´ly** *adv.* —**vast´ness** *n.*

vat *n.* large tank or cask

Vat·i·can *n.* papal government, in an enclave in Rome (**Vatican City**)

vaude·ville (vôd´vil) *n.* stage show with song and dance acts, skits, etc.

vault *n.* **1** arched roof or ceiling **2** arched room **3** burial chamber **4** room for keeping money, etc. as in a bank **5** a vaulting or leap —*v.* **1** provide with a vault **2** leap over, balancing on a pole or the hands —**vault´er** *n.*

vaunt *n., v.* boast

VCR *n.* videocassette recorder

VD *abbrev.* venereal disease

VDT *n.* video display terminal

veal *n.* meat from a calf

vec·tor *n.* *Math.* (line segment used as) a representation of a combination of size or quantity with direction

veep *n.* [Inf.] vice-president

veer *v., n.* shift; turn

veg·e·ta·ble (vej´tə-) *n.* **1** plant eaten raw or cooked **2** any plant

veg·e·tar·i·an *n.* one who eats no meat —*a.* **1** of vegetarians **2** of vegetables only

veg·e·tate *v.* live or grow like a plant

veg·e·ta´tion *n.* plant life

ve·he·ment (-ə-) *a.* **1** showing strong feeling **2** violent —**ve´he·mence** *n.*

ve·hi·cle (-ə-) *n.* means of conveying, esp. a device on wheels —**ve·hic´u·lar** *a.*

veil (vāl) *n.* **1** piece of thin fabric worn by women over the face or head **2** thing that conceals —*v.* **1** cover with a veil **2** conceal

veiled *a.* **1** wearing a veil **2** hidden **3** not openly expressed

vein (vān) *n.* **1** blood vessel going to the heart **2** vascular or supportive tissue in a leaf, insect's wing, etc. **3** body of minerals in a fissure or zone of rock **4** colored streak **5** trace or quality —*v.* mark as with veins

Vel·cro *trademark* nylon material for fastenings, with opposing strips of tiny hooks and clinging pile —*n.* [**v-**] this material

veld, veldt (velt) *n.* South African grassy land

vel·lum *n.* fine parchment

ve·loc·i·ty *n.* speed

ve·lour, ve·lours (-loor´) *n., pl.* **-lours** (-loorz´, -loor´) fabric with a velvety nap

vel·vet *n.* fabric of silk, rayon, etc. with a soft, thick pile —**vel´vet·y** *a.*

vel·vet·een´ *n.* cotton cloth with a nap like velvet

ve·nal *a.* open to bribery —**ve·nal´i·ty** *n.*

vend *v.* sell —**ven´dor, vend´er** *n.*

ven·det´ta *n.* feud, esp. vengeful one between families

vend´ing machine *n.* a coin-operated machine for selling small articles

ve·neer´ *n.* thin, covering layer, as of fine wood —*v.* cover with a veneer

ven´er·a·ble *a.* worthy of respect because of age, etc. —**ven´er·a·bil´i·ty** *n.*

ven´er·ate *v.* show deep respect for —**ven´er·a´tion** *n.*

ve·ne´re·al (-nir´ē-) *a.* of or passed on by sexual intercourse

Ve·ne´tian blind (-shən) *n.* [*also* **v- b-**] window blind of thin, adjustable slats

venge´ance *n.* revenge —**with a vengeance 1** with great force **2** very much

venge'ful a. seeking revenge

ve'ni·al a. pardonable

ven'i·son n. flesh of deer

ven'om n. 1 poison of some snakes, spiders, etc. 2 malice —**ven'om·ous** a.

ve'nous a. of veins or blood in them

vent n. 1 expression 2 opening to let gas out, air in, etc. 3 slit —v. 1 express 2 let out 3 make a vent in

ven'ti·late' v. circulate fresh air in —**ven'ti·la'tion** n. —**ven'ti·la'tor** n.

ven'tral a. of, near, or on the belly

ven'tri·cle n. either lower chamber of the heart

ven·tril'o·quism' n. art of making one's voice seem to come from another point —**ven·tril'o·quist** n.

ven'ture n. risky undertaking —v. 1 place in danger 2 dare to do, say, etc.

ven'ture·some a. 1 daring; bold 2 risky Also **ven'tur·ous**

ven'ue' (-yō̄o') n. 1 locality of a crime, trial, etc. 2 locale of a large gathering

Ve'nus n. second planet from the sun

ve·ra'cious (-shəs) a. truthful or true —**ve·rac'i·ty** (-ras'-) n.

ve·ran'da(h) n. open, roofed porch

verb n. word expressing action or being

ver'bal a. 1 of or in words 2 in speech 3 like or derived from a verb —n. verbal derivative, as a gerund —**ver'bal·ly** adv.

ver'bal·ize' v. 1 use words for communication 2 express in words

verbal noun n. noun derived from a verb, as a gerund or infinitive

ver·ba'tim adv., a. word for word

ver·be'na n. ornamental plant with showy flowers

ver'bi·age (-bē ij) n. wordiness

ver·bose' a. wordy —**ver·bos'i·ty** (-bäs'-) n.

ver'dant a. covered with green vegetation

ver'dict n. decision, as of a jury in a law case

ver'di·gris' (-grēs') n. greenish coating on brass, copper, or bronze

ver'dure (-jər) n. 1 green vegetation 2 color of this

verge v., n. (be on) the edge or border

ver'i·fy' v. -**fied'**, -**fy'ing** 1 prove to be true 2 test the accuracy of —**ver'i·fi'a·ble** a. —**ver'i·fi·ca'tion** n.

ver'i·ly adv. [Ar.] really

ver'i·si·mil'i·tude' n. appearance of being real

ver'i·ta·ble a. true; real

ver'i·ty n., pl. -**ties** (a) truth

ver·mi·cel'li (-sel'-, -chel'-) n. pasta that is like thin spaghetti

ver·mil'ion n. bright red

ver'min n., pl. -**min** small, destructive animal, as a fly or rat

ver·mouth' (-mōōth') n. a white wine

ver·nac'u·lar a., n. (of) the everyday speech of a country or place

ver'nal a. 1 of or in the spring 2 springlike

ver'sa·tile (-təl) a. able to do many things well —**ver·sa·til'i·ty** n.

verse n. 1 poetry 2 stanza 3 short division of a Bible chapter

versed a. skilled

ver'si·fy' v. -**fied'**, -**fy'ing** 1 write poetry 2 tell in verse —**ver·si·fi·ca'tion** n. —**ver'si·fi'er** n.

ver'sion n. 1 translation 2 an account; report

ver'sus prep. against

ver'te·bra n., pl. -**brae** (-brē', -brā') or -**bras** any single bone of the spinal column

ver'te·brate (-brət) n., a. (animal) having a spinal column

ver'tex' n., pl. -**tex·es** or -**ti·ces'** (-tə sēz') highest or lowest point

ver'ti·cal n., a. (line, plane, etc.) that is straight up and down

ver·ti'go' n. dizzy feeling —**ver·tig'i·nous** a.

verve n. vigor; enthusiasm

ver'y a. 1 complete; absolute 2 same; identical 3 actual —adv. 1 extremely 2 truly

ves'i·cle n. small, membranous cavity, sac, etc. —**ve·sic'u·lar** a.

ves'pers n. [often V-] [usually sing. v.] evening prayer or service

ves'sel n. 1 container 2 ship or boat 3 tube of the body, as a vein

vest n. 1 sleeveless garment 2 undershirt —v. 1 to clothe 2 give power, rights, etc. to a person or group

vest'ed a. Law not contingent; fixed

vested interest n. 1 involvement in promoting personal advantage 2 pl. groups using controlling influence to pursue selfish goals

ves'ti·bule' (-byōōl') n. 1 small entrance hall 2 enclosed passage

ves'tige (-tij) n. a trace or mark, esp. of something gone —**ves·tig'i·al** a.

vest'ing n. retention by an employee of pension rights, etc., when changing jobs, etc.

vest'ment n. garment, esp. one for a clergyman

vest'-pock'et a. very small

ves′try *n., pl.* **-tries 1** church meeting room **2** lay financial church group

vet *n.* **1** veteran **2** veterinarian

vet *abbrev.* **1** veteran **2** veterinarian **3** veterinary

vetch *n.* plant grown for fodder

vet′er·an *a.* experienced —*n.* **1** former member of the armed forces **2** long-time employee, etc.

Veterans Day *n.* November 11, U.S. holiday honoring war veterans

vet′er·i·nar′i·an *n.* doctor for animals

vet′er·i·nar′y *a.* of the medical care of animals —*n., pl.* **-ies** veterinarian

ve′to *n., pl.* **-toes 1** power, or right, to prohibit or reject **2** use of this —*v.* **-toed, -to·ing** use a veto on

vex *v.* annoy; disturb —**vex·a′tion** *n.* —**vex·a′tious** *a.*

VHF, vhf *abbrev.* very high frequency

VHS *trademark* electronic system for recording videocassettes

vi·a (vī′ə, vē′ə) *prep.* by way of

vi′a·ble *a.* able to exist

vi′a·duct′ *n.* bridge held up by a series of towers

vi′al *n.* small bottle

vi′and *n.* **1** article of food **2** *pl.* fine food

vibes *n.* vibraphone —*pl.n.* [Sl.] qualities producing emotional reaction

vi′brant *a.* **1** quivering **2** resonant **3** energetic

vi′bra·phone′ *n.* musical instrument like a xylophone, with electrically enhanced sound

vi′brate′ *v.* **1** move rapidly back and forth; quiver **2** thrill —**vi·bra′tion** *n.* —**vi′bra′tor** *n.*

vi·bra′to (-brä′-) *n., pl.* **-tos** *Mus.* pulsating effect made by slight wavering of a tone

vi·bur′num *n.* shrub or small tree with white flowers

vic′ar *n.* **1** Church of England priest **2** *R.C.Ch.* deputy of a bishop, etc.

vic′ar·age *n.* vicar's residence

vi·car′i·ous (-ker′-) *a.* **1** felt by imagined participation **2** taking another's place —**vi·car′i·ous·ly** *adv.*

vice *n.* bad or evil conduct or habit

vice- *pref.* substitute or subordinate

vice′-pres′i·dent *n.* officer next in rank to a president

vice′roy′ *n.* deputy ruler for a sovereign

vi′ce ver′sa (vī′sə, vīs′) *adv.* the other way around

vi·chys·soise (vē′shē swäz′) *n.* cold puréed potato soup

vi·cin′i·ty *n., pl.* **-ties 1** nearness **2** nearby area

vi·cious (vish′əs) *a.* **1** evil **2** unruly **3** malicious —**vi′cious·ly** *adv.* —**vi′cious·ness** *n.*

vi·cis′si·tude′ (-sis′ə-) *n.* any of one's ups and downs; change

vic′tim *n.* **1** one killed, hurt, etc. **2** one cheated, tricked, etc. —**vic′tim·ize′** *v.*

vic′tor *n.* winner

Vic·to′ri·an *a.* prudish, proper, etc.

vic·to′ri·ous *a.* having won a victory

vic′to·ry *n., pl.* **-ries** success in war or any struggle

vict·uals (vit′'lz) *pl.n.* [Inf. or Dial.] food

vi·cu′ña (-kyōō′nyə) *n.* **1** small llama **2** its soft, shaggy wool

vid·e·o′ *a., n.* **1** (of) television **2** (of) performance on videocassette, etc.

vid′e·o′cas·sette′ *n.* cassette containing videotape, recorded on and played back esp. by using a **videocassette recorder**

vid′e·o·disc′ *n.* disc of recorded images and sounds to be reproduced on a TV

vid′e·o·tape′ *n.* magnetic tape for recording and playing back images and sounds —*v.* to record on a videotape

vie *v.* **vied, vy′ing** to compete as in a contest

view *n.* **1** a looking **2** range of vision **3** idea or thought **4** scene **5** opinion **6** aim; goal —*v.* **1** look at or see **2** consider —**in view of** because of

view′er *n.* **1** one who views **2** device for looking at slides, etc.

view′find′er *n.* camera device showing what will be in the photograph

view′point′ *n.* attitude; point of view

vig′il *n.* **1** watchful staying awake **2** watch kept **3** eve of a religious festival

vig′i·lant *a.* watchful —**vig′i·lance** *n.*

vig′i·lan′te (-tē) *n.* one of a group illegally organized to punish crime

vi·gnette (vin yet′) *n.* **1** short literary sketch, scene in a film, etc. **2** picture that shades off at the edges

vig′or *n.* active force; strength and energy —**vig′or·ous** *a.* —**vig′or·ous·ly** *adv.*

vik′ing *n.* [*also* V-] Scandinavian pirate of the Middle Ages

vile *a.* **1** evil; wicked **2** disgusting **3** lowly and bad

vil′i·fy′ *v.* **-fied′, -fy′ing** defame or slander

vil′la *n.* showy country house

vil′lage *n.* small town

vil′lain (-ən) *n.* evil or wicked person —

vil·lain·ess n.fem. —**vil'lain·ous** a. —**vil'lain·y** n., pl. **-ies'**

vim n. energy; vigor

vin'ai·grette' (-ə-) n. dressing of vinegar, oil, herbs, etc.

vin'di·cate' v. **1** clear from criticism, blame, etc. **2** justify —**vin'di·ca'tion** n.

vin·dic'tive a. **1** revengeful in spirit **2** done in revenge

vine n. plant with a stem that grows along the ground or climbs a support

vin'e·gar n. sour liquid made by fermenting cider, wine, etc. —**vin'e·gar·y** a.

vine'yard (vin'yərd) n. land where grapevines are grown

vi'no (vē'-) n. [It. & Sp.] wine

vin'tage (-tij) n. wine of a certain region and year

vint'ner n. **1** wine merchant **2** one who makes wine

vi'nyl (-nəl) n. of a group of chemical compounds used in making plastics

vi·o'la (vē-) n. instrument like, but larger than, the violin —**vi·ol'ist** n.

vi'o·late' v. **1** break (a law, etc.) **2** rape **3** desecrate **4** disturb —**vi'o·la'tion** n. —**vi'o·la·tor** n.

vi'o·lent a. **1** showing or acting with great force or strong feeling **2** intense —**vi'o·lence** n.

vi'o·let n. delicate spring flower, usually bluish-purple

vi'o·lin' n. four-stringed instrument played with a bow —**vi'o·lin'ist** n.

vi·o·lon·cel'lo (vē'-) n., pl. **-los** cello

VIP (vē'ī'pē') n. [Inf.] very important person

vi'per n. **1** venomous snake **2** treacherous person

vi·ra'go (vi rä'-) n., pl. **-goes** or **-gos** shrewish woman

vir'gin n. person, esp. a woman, who has not had sexual intercourse —a. chaste, untouched, pure, etc. —**vir·gin'i·ty** n.

vir'gi·nal a. virgin

Vir·gin'ia creeper n. woodbine

Virginia reel n. American reel danced by couples facing in two lines

Vir'go n. sixth sign of the zodiac

vir'gule' (-gyōōl') n. mark (/) used in place of "or" or "per"

vir·ile (-əl) a. **1** masculine **2** strong, vigorous, etc. —**vi·ril'i·ty** n.

vi·rol'o·gy n. study of viruses

vir'tu·al (-chōō-) a. being so in effect if not in fact —**vir'tu·al·ly** adv.

virtual reality n. realistic computer simulation that one seemingly inter-

acts with using special equipment

vir'tue n. **1** moral excellence **2** good quality, esp. a moral one **3** chastity —**by** (or **in**) **virtue of** because of —**vir'tu·ous** a.

vir·tu·o'so n., pl. **-sos** musician, etc. having great skill —**vir·tu·os'i·ty** (-äs'-) n.

vir'u·lent (-yoo-) a. **1** deadly **2** full of hate —**vir'u·lence** n.

vi'rus n. **1** infective agent that causes disease **2** harmful influence **3** unauthorized computer program instructions added as a joke or to sabotage —**vi'ral** a.

vi'sa (vē'zə) n. endorsement on a passport, granting entry into a country

vis'age (viz'ij) n. the face

vis-à-vis (vēz'ə vē') prep. in relation to

vis'cer·a (-ər ə) pl.n. internal organs of the body —**vis'cer·al** a.

vis'cid (-id) a. viscous

vis'count' (vī'-) n. nobleman above a baron

vis'cous (-kəs) a. thick, syrupy, and sticky —**vis·cos'i·ty** n., pl. **-ties**

vise n. device with adjustable jaws for holding an object firmly

vis·i·bil'i·ty n. distance within which things can be seen

vis'i·ble a. that can be seen; evident —**vis'i·bly** adv.

vis'ion n. **1** power of seeing **2** something seen in a dream, trance, etc. **3** mental image **4** foresight

vis'ion·ar'y a.; n., pl. **-ies** idealistic and impractical (person)

vis'it v. **1** go or come to see **2** stay with as a guest **3** afflict —n. a visiting —**vis'i·tor** n.

vis·it·a'tion n. **1** visit, esp. to inspect **2** punishment sent by God **3** visit with divorced parent, mourning family, etc.

vi'sor n. **1** movable part of a helmet, covering the face **2** brim on a cap for shading the eyes

vis'ta n. view; scene

vis'u·al (vizh'-) a. **1** of or used in seeing **2** visible

vis'u·al·ize' v. form a mental image of

vi'tal a. **1** of life **2** essential to life **3** very important **4** full of life —**vi'tal·ly** adv.

vi·tal'i·ty n. **1** energy; vigor **2** power to survive

vi'tal·ize' v. give life or vigor to

vital signs pl.n. pulse, respiration, and body temperature

vital statistics pl.n. data on births,

deaths, etc.

vi·ta·min *n.* any of certain substances vital to good health: vitamins A and D are found in fish-liver oil, eggs, etc.; vitamin B (complex), in liver, yeast, etc.; vitamin C, in citrus fruits

vi·ti·ate (vish′ē-) *v.* make bad; spoil —**vi·ti·a·tion** *n.*

vit·re·ous *a.* of or like glass

vit·ri·fy *v.* **-fied′, -fy′ing** change into glass by heating

vit·ri·ol′ (-ôl′) *n.* caustic remarks —**vit′ri·ol′ic** (-äl′-) *a.*

vi·tu·per·ate′ *v.* berate

vi·va·cious (-shəs) *a.* spirited; lively —**vi·vac′i·ty** *n.*

viv′id *a.* **1** full of life **2** bright; intense **3** strong; active —**viv′id·ly** *adv.*

viv′i·fy *v.* **-fied′, -fy′ing** give life to

vi·vip′a·rous *a.* bearing living young, as most mammals

vivi·sec′tion *n.* surgery on living animals for medical research

vix′en *n.* **1** female fox **2** shrewish woman

viz., viz *abbrev.* namely

vi·zier (vi zir′) *n.* in Muslim countries, a high government official

vo·cab′u·lar′y *n., pl.* **-ies** all the words used by a person, group, etc. or listed in a dictionary, etc.

vo′cal *a.* **1** of or by the voice **2** speaking freely —**vo′cal·ly** *adv.*

vocal cords *pl.n.* membranes in the larynx that vibrate to make voice sounds

vo·cal′ic *a.* of or like a vowel or vowels

vo′cal·ist *n.* singer

vo′cal·ize′ *v.* speak or sing

vo·ca′tion *n.* one's profession, trade, or career —**vo·ca′tion·al** *a.*

vo·cif′er·ous (-sif′-) *a.* loud; clamorous —**vo·cif′er·ate′** *v.*

vod′ka *n.* Russian alcoholic liquor made from grain

vo′-ed′ *a., n.* [Inf.] (of) vocational education

vogue (vōg) *n.* **1** current fashion **2** popularity

voice *n.* **1** sound made through the mouth **2** ability to make such sound **3** sound like this **4** right to express one's opinion, etc. **5** expression —*v.* utter or express

voice box *n.* larynx

voice mail *n.* electronic storage and delivery of telephone messages

voice′-o′ver *n.* voice of an unseen speaker, as on TV

void *a.* **1** empty; vacant **2** lacking **3** of no legal force —*n.* empty space —*v.*

1 to empty **2** cancel

voi·là (vwä lä′) *int.* [[Fr.]] there is it

voile (voil) *n.* thin fabric

vol *abbrev.* volume

vol′a·tile (-tal) *a.* **1** quickly evaporating **2** changeable; unstable —**vol′a·til′i·ty** *n.*

vol·ca′no *n., pl.* **-noes** or **-nos** mountain formed by erupting molten rock —**vol·can′ic** *a.*

vo·li′tion (-lish′ən) *n.* WILL (*n.* 3)

vol′ley *n., pl.* **-leys;** *v.* **1** discharge (of) a number of weapons together **2** return (of) a tennis ball before it hits the ground

vol′ley·ball′ *n.* **1** game between teams hitting a large, inflated ball back and forth over a net **2** this ball

volt *n.* unit of electromotive force

volt′age *n.* electromotive force, shown in volts

vol·ta′ic *a.* of or producing electricity by chemical action

volt′me′ter *n.* instrument for measuring voltage

vol′u·ble *a.* talkative

vol′ume *n.* **1** a book **2** cubic measure **3** amount **4** loudness of sound

vo·lu′mi·nous *a.* **1** filling or producing volumes **2** large; full

vol′un·tar′y *a.* **1** by choice; of one's own free will **2** controlled by the will —**vol′un·tar′i·ly** *adv.*

vol′un·teer′ *v.* offer, give, etc. of one's own free will —*n.* one who volunteers

vo·lup′tu·ous (-choo əs) *a.* sensual

vom′it *v., n.* (have) matter from the stomach ejected through the mouth

voo′doo′ *n.* religion of the West Indies, based on magic, charms, etc.

vo·ra′cious (-shəs) *a.* **1** greedy or ravenous **2** very eager

vor′tex *n., pl.* **-tex′es** or **-ti·ces′** (-tə sēz′) **1** whirlpool **2** whirlwind

vo′ta·ry *n., pl.* **-ries** worshiper; devotee

vote *n.* **1** a decision or choice shown on a ballot, etc. **2** all the votes **3** the right to vote —*v.* **1** cast a vote **2** decide by vote —**vot′er** *n.*

vo′tive *a.* given or done to fulfill a vow or promise

vouch *v.* give or be a guarantee (*for*)

vouch′er *n.* a paper serving as proof of payment, etc.

vouch·safe′ *v.* be kind enough to grant

vow *v., n.* (make) a solemn promise or statement —**take vows** enter a religious order

vow′el *n.* letter representing a speech sound of air in a continuous stream, as *a, e, i, o,* or *u*

voy·age *n., v.* journey by ship

voy·eur' (-ʉr') *n.* one having very strong interest in viewing sexual activities, etc.

VP *abbrev.* Vice-President

vs., vs *abbrev.* versus

VT *abbrev.* Vermont

vul'can·ize' *v.* treat rubber to make it stronger and more elastic

vul'gar *a.* 1 popular 2 lacking culture; crude 3 obscene —**vul'gar·ly** *adv.*

vul'gar·ism' *n.* coarse word or phrase that is considered improper

vul·gar'i·ty (-ger'-) *n.* 1 vulgar state or quality 2 *pl.* **-ties** vulgar act, etc.

vul'ner·a·ble *a.* 1 that can be hurt, attacked, etc. 2 easily hurt; sensitive —**vul'ner·a·bil'i·ty** *n.*

vul'ture *n.* 1 large bird of prey 2 greedy, ruthless person

vul'va *n.* external female sex organs

vy'ing *a.* that competes

W

w, W *abbrev.* 1 watt(s) 2 west(ern) 3 win(s)

WA *abbrev.* Washington

wack'y *a.* **-i·er, -i·est** [Sl.] erratic, eccentric, or irrational

wad (wäd) *n.* 1 small, soft mass 2 small lump —*v.* **wad'ded, wad'ding** 1 roll into a wad 2 stuff as with padding

wad'ding *n.* any soft material used in padding, packing, etc.

wad'dle *v., n.* walk with short steps, swaying from side to side

wade *v.* 1 walk through water, mud, etc. 2 proceed with difficulty 3 cross by wading 4 [Inf.] attack vigorously: with *in* or *into*

wad'er *n.* 1 one who wades 2 *pl.* high, waterproof boots, often with trousers

wad'ing bird *n.* long-legged bird that wades in shallows, marshes, etc.

wa'fer *n.* 1 thin, crisp cracker 2 disklike thing

waf'fle (wäf'-) *n.* crisp cake baked between two flat, studded plates (**waffle iron**)

waft (wäft) *v.* carry or move lightly over water or through the air —*n.* 1 odor, sound, etc. carried through the air 2 wafting motion

wag *v.* **wagged, wag'ging** move rapidly back and forth or up and down —*n.* 1 a wagging 2 a wit; comic

wage *v.* take part in —*n. often pl.* money paid for work done

wa'ger *n., v.* bet

wag'gish *a.* 1 roguishly merry 2 said, done, etc. in jest

wag'gle *v.* wag abruptly

wag'on *n.* four-wheeled vehicle, esp. for hauling heavy loads

wagon train *n.* line of (covered) wagons traveling together

waif *n.* homeless child, etc.

wail *v., n.* 1 (make a) loud, sad cry 2 lament

wain'scot *n.* wall paneling of wood —*v.* panel with wood

waist *n.* 1 body part between the ribs and the hips 2 waistline

waist'band' *n.* band fitting around the waist on slacks, a skirt, etc.

waist'coat (wes'kət) *n.* [Br.] man's vest

waist'line' *n.* middle or narrow part of the waist

wait *v.* 1 remain until something occurs 2 remain undone 3 serve food at 4 await —*n.* act or time of waiting —**wait on** (or **upon**) 1 be a servant to 2 serve

wait'er *n.* man who serves food at table —**wait'ress** *n.fem.*

wait'ing *a.* 1 that waits 2 of or for a wait —*n.* 1 act of one that waits 2 period of waiting

waiting list *n.* list of applicants, as for a vacancy

waiting room *n.* room where people wait, as in a doctor's office

wait'per'son *n.* waiter or waitress

waive *v.* give up, as a right

waiv'er *n. Law* waiving of a right, claim, etc.

wake *v.* **woke** or **waked, waked** or **wok'en, wak'ing** 1 come or bring out of a sleep 2 become alert (*to*) 3 stir up —*n.* 1 all-night vigil over a corpse 2 track or trail left behind

wake'ful *a.* 1 watchful 2 unable to sleep

wak'en *v.* to wake

wale *n.* 1 welt 2 ridge, as on corduroy

walk *v.* 1 go on foot at moderate speed 2 walk along, over, with, etc. 3 *Baseball* advance to first base by a walk —*n.* 1 way of walking 2 stroll; hike 3 path for walking 4 *Baseball* advancement by batter to first base on four pitches not strikes —**walk of life** way of living

walk'ie-talk'ie *n.* portable radio for sending and receiving

walk'ing stick *n.* stick carried when walking; cane

walk'out' n. 1 labor strike 2 abrupt departure in protest

walk'-up' n. apartment house without an elevator

wall n. upright structure that encloses, divides, etc. —v. 1 to divide, enclose, etc. with a wall 2 to close up: with *up*

wal'la·by (wäl'-) n., pl. **-bies** or **-by** small marsupial like a kangaroo

wall'board' n. paper-covered plaster in thin slabs for making or covering walls

wal'let n. flat case for carrying money, credit cards, etc.

wall'eye' n. North American freshwater food fish

wall'flow'er n. [Inf.] shy or unpopular person

wal'lop (wäl'-) [Inf.] v. 1 hit hard 2 defeat completely —n. a hard blow

wal'low (wäl'-) v. 1 roll around in mud or filth, as pigs do 2 indulge oneself excessively (*in*)

wall'pa'per v., n. (apply) decorative paper for covering walls, etc.

wall'-to-wall' a. covering a floor completely

wal'nut' n. 1 tree bearing an edible nut in a hard shell 2 its nut 3 its wood

wal'rus n. large animal like a seal, with two tusks

waltz n. ballroom dance in 3/4 time —v. dance a waltz

wam'pum (wäm'-) n. beads used as money, etc. by North American Indians

wan (wän) a. sickly pale

wand n. slender rod, as one regarded as having magical powers

wan'der v. 1 roam idly about 2 go astray; stray —**wan'der·er** n.

wan'der·lust' n. strong urge to wander or travel

wane v. 1 get smaller, weaker, etc. 2 approach the end —n. a waning

wan'gle v. [Inf.] get by sly or tricky means

wan'na·be' n. [Sl.] person wanting to be like someone else or gain some status

want v. 1 wish for; desire 2 need 3 lack —n. 1 lack; need 2 poverty 3 desire

want ad n. [Inf.] advertisement for something wanted

want'ing a. 1 lacking 2 inadequate —prep. minus

wan'ton a. 1 senseless and cruel 2 irresponsible 3 immoral —n. wanton person

wap·i·ti (wäp'ət ē) n. North American elk

war n. 1 armed conflict, as between nations 2 any fight —v. warred, war'ring carry on war —war'like' a.

war'ble v. sing with trills, runs, etc. —n. a warbling —war'bler n.

ward n. 1 one under the care of a guardian 2 division of a hospital 3 voting district of a city —ward off turn aside

-ward suf. in a (specified) direction: also **-wards**

war'den n. 1 one who takes care of something 2 head official of a prison

ward'er n. watchman; guard

ward'robe' n. 1 a closet for clothes 2 all one's clothes

ware n. 1 thing for sale: *usually used in pl.* 2 pottery

ware'house' n. building where goods are stored

war'fare' n. war or any conflict

war'head' n. front part of a bomb, etc., with the explosive

war'horse' n. [Inf.] veteran of many struggles

war'lock' n. wizard; male witch

warm a. 1 moderately hot 2 enthusiastic 3 kind and loving —v. make or become warm —warm'ly adv.

warm'blood'ed a. 1 having a relatively constant body temperature 2 ardent

warmed'-o'ver a. 1 reheated 2 presented again, without significant change

warm'heart'ed a. kind; loving

war'mon'ger (-muŋ'-, -mäŋ'-) n. one who tries to cause war

warmth n. 1 a being warm 2 strong feeling

warn v. 1 tell of danger; advise to be careful 2 inform; let know —warn'ing n., a.

warp v. 1 bend or twist out of shape 2 distort —n. 1 a warping or twist 2 long threads in a loom

war'rant n. 1 justification 2 legal writ authorizing an arrest, search, etc. —v. 1 authorize 2 justify

warrant officer n. officer just above a noncommissioned officer

war'ran·ty n., pl. **-ties** GUARANTEE (n. 1)

war'ren n. (limited) area in which rabbits are raised

war'ri·or n. soldier

war'ship' n. ship for combat use

wart n. small, hard growth on the skin

—**wart'y** *a.*

war·y (wer'ē) *a.* **-i·er, -i·est** on guard; cautious —**wary of** careful of —**war'i·ly** *adv.*

was *v.* pt. of BE: used with *I, he, she,* or *it*

wash *v.* **1** clean with water **2** wash clothes **3** flow over or against **4** remove by washing **5** coat thinly —*n.* **1** a washing **2** clothes (to be) washed **3** rush of water **4** eddy from propeller, oars, etc. —*a.* that can be washed —**wash'a·ble** *a.*

wash'-and-wear' *a.* needing little or no ironing after washing

wash'board' *n.* ridged board to scrub clothes on

wash'bowl' *n.* bowl for washing the hands and face: also **wash'ba'sin**

wash'cloth' *n.* small cloth to wash the face or body

washed'-out' *a.* [Inf.] **1** tired **2** pale

washed'-up' *a.* **1** [Inf.] tired **2** [Sl.] having failed

wash'er *n.* **1** machine for washing **2** flat ring used to make a bolt, nut, etc. fit tight **3** one who washes

wash'ing *n.* **1** act of one that washes **2** clothes, etc. to be washed

washing machine *n.* machine for washing clothes, etc.

wash'out' *n.* **1** washing away of soil, etc. **2** [Sl.] a failure

wash'room' *n.* restroom

wash'stand' *n.* plumbing fixture with a washbowl

wash'tub' *n.* tub, often with faucets and a drain, to wash clothes, etc.

was'n't *contr.* was not

wasp *n.* flying insect: some have a sharp sting

wasp'ish *a.* bad-tempered

was·sail (wäs'əl, -āl') *n.* toast (drink)

waste *v.* **1** use up needlessly **2** fail to take advantage of **3** wear away **4** lose strength or weaken **5** destroy —*a.* **1** barren or wild, as land **2** left over —*n.* **1** a wasting **2** wasted matter; refuse; etc. **3** wasteland —**go to waste** be wasted —**lay waste (to)** devastate —**wast'age** *n.* —**waste'ful** *a.*

waste'bas'ket *n.* container for discarded paper, etc.

waste'land' *n.* barren land

waste'pa'per *n.* paper thrown away after use

waste'wa'ter *n.* water that has been used and released as sewage

wast·rel (wās'trəl) *n.* **1** spendthrift **2** useless or worthless person

watch *n.* **1** act of guarding or observing **2** guard(s), or period of guard duty **3** small clock for wrist or pocket **4** *Naut.* period of duty, or crew on duty —*v.* **1** keep vigil **2** observe **3** guard or tend **4** be alert (for) —**watch out** be alert or careful —**watch'ful** *a.*

watch'band' *n.* band for holding a watch on the wrist

watch'dog' *n.* **1** dog kept to guard property **2** one that watches to prevent waste, etc.

watch'man *n.,* pl. **-men** person hired to guard

watch'tow'er *n.* high tower from which a sentinel watches for enemies, etc.

watch'word' *n.* slogan

wa'ter *n.* **1** colorless liquid of rivers, lakes, etc. **2** water solution **3** body secretion, as urine —*v.* **1** to supply with water **2** dilute with water **3** fill with tears **4** secrete saliva —*a.* of, for, in, or by water

water bed *n.* water-filled bag used as a mattress

water buffalo *n.* oxlike work animal of Asia and Africa

water closet *n.* a toilet

wa'ter·col'or *n.* **1** paint made by mixing pigment and water **2** picture painted with such paints

wa'ter-cooled' *a.* cooled by circulating water

wa'ter·course' *n.* river, brook, canal, etc.

wa'ter·craft' *n.,* pl. **-craft'** boat, ship, or other water vehicle

wa'ter·cress' *n.* water plant with leaves used in salads

wa'ter·fall' *n.* steep fall of water, as from a cliff

wa'ter·fowl' *n.* ducks, geese, etc.

wa'ter·front' *n.* land or docks at the edge of a river, harbor, etc.

wa'ter·lil'y *n.,* pl. **-ies** water plant with large, showy flowers

wa'ter·line' *n.* line where water surface touches the side of a boat

wa'ter·logged' *a.* soaked or filled with water

wa'ter·mark' *n.* **1** mark showing how high water has risen **2** design pressed into paper —*v.* to mark (paper) with a watermark

wa'ter·mel'on *n.* large melon with juicy, red pulp

water moccasin *n.* large, poisonous snake of southern U.S.

wa'ter·proof' *v., a.* (to make) impervious to water

wa'ter·re·pel'lent a. keeping water out, but not waterproof

wa'ter·shed' n. 1 area a river system drains 2 ridge between two such areas 3 crucial turning point

wa'ter·ski' v. to be towed over water on a kind of ski

wa'ter·spout' n. whirling water funnel rising from sea

water table n. level below which the ground is saturated with water

wa'ter·tight' a. so tight no water can get through

water tower n. elevated tank for water storage, etc.

wa'ter·way' n. navigable river, lake, canal, etc.

wa'ter·works' pl.n. [often sing. v.] system of reservoirs, pumps, etc. supplying water to a city

wa'ter·y a. 1 of, like, or full of water 2 diluted

watt n. unit of electric power —**watt'age** n.

wat'tle (wät'l) n. 1 sticks woven with twigs 2 flap of skin hanging at the throat of a chicken, etc.

wave v. 1 move to and fro 2 wave the hand, etc., or signal thus 3 arrange or form in curves —n. 1 curving swell moving along on the ocean, etc. 2 wavelike vibration 3 curve(s), as in the hair 4 a waving, as of the hand —**wav'y** a., **-i·er**, **-i·est**

wave'length' n. distance between any point in a wave, as of light or sound, to the same point in the next wave

wa'ver v. 1 flutter, falter, flicker, etc. 2 show indecision —n. a wavering —**wa'ver·y** a.

wax n. 1 plastic substance secreted by bees 2 substance like this, as paraffin —v. 1 put polish or wax on 2 get larger, stronger, etc. 3 to become —**wax'y** a., **-i·er**, **-i·est** —**wax'en** a.

wax bean n. bean with long, edible yellow pods

wax museum n. exhibit of wax figures of famous people: also **wax'works'**

wax paper n. paper made moisture-proof by a wax coating: also **waxed paper**

way n. 1 road or route 2 direction of movement or action 3 method, manner, etc. 4 distance 5 course of action 6 particular 7 wish; will 8 pl. framework on which a ship is built —adv. [Inf.] far —**by the way** incidentally —**by way of** 1 passing through 2 as a means of —**give way** 1 yield 2 break

down —**under way** moving ahead

way'far·er (-fer'-) n. traveler, esp. on foot —**way'far·ing** a., n.

way'lay' v. **-laid'**, **-lay'ing** to ambush

way'-out' a. [Inf.] very unusual or unconventional

ways and means pl.n. methods of raising money

way'side' a., n. (at or along) the edge of a road

way'ward a. 1 willful; disobedient 2 irregular —**way'ward·ness** n.

we pron. the persons speaking or writing

weak a. lacking strength, power, etc.; not strong, effective, etc. —**weak'en** v.

weak'-kneed' a. timid; cowardly

weak'ling n. weak person

weak'ly a. **-li·er**, **-li·est** sickly —adv. in a weak way

weak'ness n. 1 a being weak 2 fault 3 special liking

weal n. skin welt

wealth (welth) n. 1 riches 2 large amount —**wealth'y** a., **-i·er**, **-i·est**

wean v. 1 stop suckling 2 withdraw from a certain habit, etc.

weap'on (wep'-) n. 1 thing used for fighting 2 means of attack or defense

weap'on·ry n. weapons

wear v. **wore**, **worn**, **wear'ing** 1 have on the body as clothes 2 make or become damaged by use 3 endure in use 4 to tire or exhaust —n. 1 clothing 2 gradual impairment from use, etc.

wear and tear (ter) n. loss and damage resulting from use

wea·ry (wir'ē) a. **-ri·er**, **-ri·est** 1 tired 2 bored —v. **-ried**, **-ry·ing** make or become weary —**wea'ri·ness** n. —**wea'ri·some** a.

wea·sel (wē'zəl) n. small mammal that feeds on mice, etc. —v. [Inf.] avoid or evade a commitment: with out

weath'er (weth'-) n. condition outside as to temperature, humidity, etc. —v. 1 to pass through safely 2 wear, discolor, etc. by exposure to sun, rain, etc.

weath'er-beat'en a. roughened, etc. by the weather

weath'er·ize' v. insulate (a building) to conserve heat

weath'er·man' n., pl. **-men'** weather forecaster

weath'er·proof' v., a. (make) able to withstand exposure to the weather

weath'er·strip' n. strip of metal, felt,

etc. for covering joints to keep out drafts, etc.: also **weath'er·strip'ping** —*v.* provide with weatherstrips

weather vane *n.* VANE (*n.* 1)

weave *v.* **wove, wo'ven, weav'ing 1** make cloth by interlacing threads, as on a loom **2** twist or move from side to side or in and out —*n.* pattern of weaving

web *n.* **1** network, esp. one spun by a spider **2** skin joining the toes of a duck, frog, etc.

web'bing *n.* strong fabric woven in strips

web'foot' *n.* foot with a WEB (*n.* 2) — **web'-foot'ed** *a.*

web'site' *n.* World Wide Web location with one or more files (**Web pages**)

wed *v.* **wed'ded, wed'ded** or **wed, wed'ding 1** marry **2** unite

Wed *abbrev.* Wednesday

we'd *contr.* **1** we had **2** we should **3** we would

wed'ding *n.* ceremony of marrying

wedge *n.* piece of wood, etc. tapering to a thin edge —*v.* **1** fix in place with a wedge **2** pack tightly

wed'lock' *n.* matrimony

Wednes'day (wenz'-) *n.* fourth day of the week

wee *a.* very small; tiny

weed *n.* unwanted plant, as in a lawn —*v.* **1** remove weeds **2** take (*out*) as useless, etc.

weeds *pl.n.* black mourning clothes

weed'y *a.* **-i·er, -i·est 1** full of weeds **2** like a weed

week *n.* **1** period of seven days, esp. Sunday through Saturday **2** the hours or days one works each week

week'day' *n.* any day of the week except Sunday and, often, Saturday

week'end', week'-end' *n.* Saturday and Sunday —*v.* spend the weekend

week'ly *a.* **1** lasting a week **2** done, etc. once a week —*adv.* once a week —*n., pl.* **-lies** periodical coming out weekly

weep *v.* **wept, weep'ing 1** shed tears **2** mourn (*for*)

weep'ing *n.* act of one who weeps —*a.* having drooping branches

weep'y *a.* **-i·er, -i·est** weeping or inclined to weep

wee'vil *n.* beetle, usually in its larval stage, that destroys cotton, grain, etc.

weft *n.* threads woven across the warp in a loom

weigh (wā) *v.* **1** determine the heaviness of, as on a scale **2** have a certain weight **3** consider well **4** burden

with *down* **5** hoist (an anchor)

weight *n.* **1** (amount of) heaviness **2** unit of heaviness **3** solid mass **4** burden **5** importance or influence —*v.* to burden —**weight'y** *a.,* **-i·er, -i·est**

weight'less *a.* having little or no apparent weight

weight lift'ing *n.* athletic exercise or sport of lifting barbells

weir (wir) *n.* **1** low dam in a river, etc. **2** fencelike barrier in a stream, etc. for catching fish

weird (wird) *a.* **1** mysterious **2** bizarre

weird'o *n., pl.* **-os** [Sl.] bizarre person or thing

wel'come *a.* **1** gladly received **2** freely permitted **3** under no obligation —*n.* a welcoming —*v.* greet with pleasure

weld *v.* unite by melting together —*n.* welded joint

wel'fare' *n.* health, happiness, and comfort —**on welfare** receiving government aid because of poverty, etc.

well *n.* **1** natural spring **2** hole dug in the earth to get water, oil, etc. **3** hollow shaft **4** source —*v.* gush or flow —*adv.* **bet'ter, best 1** in a pleasing, good, or right way **2** prosperously **3** much **4** thoroughly —*a.* in good health —*int.* expression of surprise, etc. —**as well (as) 1** in addition (to) **2** equally (with)

we'll *contr.* **1** we shall **2** we will

well'-ad·vised' *a.* prudent; wise

well'-ap·point'ed *a.* excellently furnished

well'-be'ing *n.* welfare

well'-bred' *a.* showing good manners

well'-dis·posed' *a.* friendly or receptive

well'-done' *a.* **1** done with skill **2** thoroughly cooked

well'-fixed' *a.* [Inf.] rich

well'-found'ed *a.* based on facts or good judgment

well'-ground'ed *a.* having good basic knowledge of a subject

well'-heeled' *a.* [Sl.] rich; prosperous

well'-in·formed' *a.* having extensive knowledge of a subject or many subjects

well'-known' *a.* famous or familiar

well'-man'nered *a.* polite

well'-mean'ing *a.* with good intentions —**well'-meant'** *a.*

well'-nigh' *adv.* almost

well'-off' *a.* **1** fortunate **2** prosperous

well'-read' (-red') *a.* having read much

well'–round'ed *a.* **1** properly balanced **2** showing diverse talents **3** shapely

well'spring' *n.* source of a stream, continual supply, etc.

well'–to–do' *a.* wealthy

well'–wish'er *n.* one who desires success, luck, etc. for another

well'–worn' *a.* much worn or used

Welsh *a.*, *n.* (of) the people or language of Wales

Welsh rabbit (or rarebit) *n.* melted cheese on toast

welt *n.* **1** leather strip in the seam between shoe sole and upper **2** ridge raised on the skin by a blow

wel'ter *v.* wallow —*n.* confusion

wen *n.* skin cyst

wench *n.* young woman: derogatory or humorous

wend *v.* proceed or go on (one's way)

went *v.* pt. of GO

wept *v.* pt. & pp. of WEEP

were *v.* pt. of BE: used with *you, we*, or *they*

we're *contr.* we are

weren't *contr.* were not

were'wolf' (wer'-) *n.* *Folklore* a person changed into a wolf

west *n.* **1** direction in which sunset occurs **2** region in this direction **3** [W-] Europe and North and South America —*a.*, *adv.* in, toward, or from the west —**west'er·ly** *a.*, *adv.* —**west'ern** *a.* —**west'ern·er** *n.* —**west'ward** *a.*, *adv.* —**west'wards** *adv.*

wet *a.* **wet'ter, wet'test 1** covered or soaked with water **2** rainy **3** not dry yet —*n.* water, rain, etc. —*v.* **wet** or **wet'ted, wet'ting** make or become wet

wet blanket *n.* one who lessens the enthusiasm or joy of others

wet nurse *n.* woman who suckles another's child —**wet'–nurse'** *v.*

wet suit *n.* closefitting rubber suit worn by divers

we've *contr.* we have

whack *v.*, *n.* hit or slap with a sharp sound

whacked'–out' *a.* [Sl.] exhausted

whack'y *a.* **-i·er, -i·est** [Sl.] wacky

whale *n.* huge, fishlike sea mammal —*v.* **1** hunt for whales **2** [Inf.] beat

whale'bone' *n.* horny substance from a whale's jaw

whal'er *n.* a person or ship engaged in hunting whales

wham *int.* sound imitating a heavy blow —*n.* heavy blow

wham'my *n.*, *pl.* **-mies** [Sl.] a jinx

wharf *n.*, *pl.* **wharves** or **wharfs** platform at which ships dock to load, etc.

what *pron.* **1** which thing, event, etc.? **2** that which —*a.* **1** which or which kind of **2** as much or as many as **3** how great! —*adv.* **1** how **2** partly —*int.* exclamation of surprise, etc. — **what for?** why? —**what if** suppose

what·ev'er *pron.* **1** anything that **2** no matter what **3** what —*a.* **1** of any kind **2** no matter what

what'not' *n.* set of open shelves, as for bric-a-brac

what'so·ev'er *pron.*, *a.* whatever

wheal *n.* weal

wheat *n.* cereal grass with seed ground for flour, etc.

whee'dle *v.* coax

wheel *n.* round disk turning on an axle —*v.* **1** move on wheels **2** turn, revolve, etc.

wheel'bar'row *n.* single-wheeled cart with handles

wheel'base' *n.* distance from front to rear axle

wheel'chair' *n.* chair mounted on wheels, as for an invalid

wheeze *v.*, *n.* (make) a whistling, breathy sound

whelk *n.* large sea snail with a spiral shell

whelp *n.* puppy or cub —*v.* give birth to whelps

when *adv.* at what time? —*con.* **1** at what time **2** at which **3** at the time that **4** if —*pron.* what or which time

whence *adv.* from where?

when·ev'er *adv.* [Inf.] when —*con.* at whatever time

where *adv.* **1** in or to what place? **2** in what way? **3** from what source? — *con.* **1** in or at what place **2** in or at which place **3** to the place that — *pron.* **1** what place? **2** the place at which

where'a·bouts' *adv.* at what place? — *pl.n.* [*sing.* or *pl. v.*] location

where·as' *con.* **1** because **2** while on the contrary

where·by' *con.* by which

where'fore' *adv.* [Ar.] why? —*con.* [Ar.] therefore —*n.* the reason

where·in' *con.* in which

where·of' *adv.*, *con.* of what, which, or whom

where·on' *con.* [Ar.] on which

where·up·on' *con.* at or after which

wher·ev'er *adv.* [Inf.] where? —*con.* in or to whatever place

where·with' *con.* [Ar.] with which

where'with·al' (-ôl') *n.* necessary

means, esp. money

whet v. **whet'ted, whet'ting 1** sharpen, as by grinding **2** to stimulate

wheth'er con. **1** if it is true or likely that **2** in either case that

whet'stone' n. abrasive stone for sharpening knives

whew int. exclamation of relief, surprise, etc.

whey (hwā) n. watery part of curdled milk

which pron. **1** what one or ones of several **2** the one or ones that **3** that —a. **1** what one or ones **2** whatever

which·ev'er pron., a. any one that; no matter which

whiff n. **1** light puff of air **2** slight odor

while n. period of time —con. **1** during the time that **2** although —v. to spend (time) pleasantly: often with *away*

whim n. sudden notion

whim'per v., n. (make) a low, broken cry

whim'sy (-zē) n., pl. **-sies 1** whim **2** fanciful humor —**whim'si·cal** a.

whine v., n. (make) a long, high cry, as in complaining

whin'ny v. **-nied, -ny·ing;** n., pl. **-nies** (make) a low, neighing sound

whip v. **whipped** or **whipt, whip'ping 1** move suddenly **2** strike, as with a strap **3** beat (cream, etc.) into a froth **4** [Inf.] defeat —n. **1** rod with a lash at one end **2** dessert of whipped cream, fruit, etc. —**whip up 1** rouse (interest, etc.) **2** [Inf.] to prepare quickly

whip'cord' n. strong worsted cloth with diagonal ribs

whip'lash' n. severe jolting of the neck, as in a car accident

whip'per·snap'per n. impertinent youngster

whip'pet n. small, swift dog

whip'poor·will' n. North American bird active at night

whip'py a. springy; flexible

whir, whirr v. **whirred, whir'ring** fly or revolve with a buzzing sound —n. this sound

whirl v. **1** move or spin rapidly **2** seem to spin —n. **1** a whirling **2** confused condition

whirl'i·gig' n. child's toy that whirls or spins

whirl'pool' n. water in violent, whirling motion

whirl'wind' n. air whirling violently and moving forward

whisk v. move, pull, etc. with a quick, sweeping motion —n. this motion

whisk broom n. small broom

whisk'er n. **1** pl. the hair on a man's face **2** a long hair, as on a cat's upper lip

whis'key n., pl. **-keys** or **-kies** strong liquor made from grain: also sp. **whis'ky,** pl. **-kies**

whis'per v. **1** say very softly **2** tell as a secret —n. a whispering

whist n. card game like bridge

whis'tle (-əl) v. **1** make, or move with, a high, shrill sound **2** blow a whistle —n. **1** device for making whistling sounds **2** a whistling

whis'tle-blow'er n. person who reports wrongdoing

whis'tle-stop' n. small town

whit n. least bit; jot

white a. **1** of the color of snow **2** pale **3** pure; innocent **4** having light skin —n. **1** color of pure snow **2** a white thing, as egg albumen —**white'ness** n.

white ant n. termite

white blood cell (or **corpuscle**) n. colorless blood cell defending against infection

white'-bread' a. [Inf.] bland, conventional, etc.

white'cap' n. wave with its crest broken into foam

white'-col'lar a. of clerical or professional workers

white elephant n. useless thing expensive to maintain

white'fish' n. white, freshwater fish in cool Northern lakes

white flag n. white banner, a signal of truce or surrender

white gold n. silver-gray alloy of gold

white goods n. household linens, as sheets, towels, etc.

white lead n. poisonous lead compound, used in paint

white lie n. lie about a trivial matter

whit'en v. make or become white

white'wall' n. tire with a white band on the side

white'wash' n. mixture of lime, water, etc. as for whitening walls —v. **1** cover with whitewash **2** conceal the faults of

white'-wa'ter a. of boating, etc. in rivers with rapids

whith'er (hwith'-) adv. where?

whit'ing (hwīt'-) n. any of various edible sea fishes

whit'ish a. somewhat white

whit′tle v. 1 cut shavings from wood with a knife 2 reduce gradually

whiz, whizz v. **whizzed, whiz′zing;** n. (make) the hissing sound of a thing rushing through air

who pron. 1 what person? 2 which person? 3 that

whoa int. stop: command to a horse

who·dun′it n. [Inf.] novel, etc. about a crime, gradually giving clues to its solution

who·ev′er pron. 1 any person that 2 no matter who

whole a. 1 not broken, damaged, etc. 2 complete 3 not divided up 4 healthy —n. 1 entire amount 2 thing complete in itself —**on the whole** in general —**whole′ness** n.

whole′heart′ed a. sincere

whole milk n. milk from which no butterfat has been removed

whole′sale′ n. sale of goods in large amounts, as to retailers —a. 1 of such sale 2 extensive —v. to sell at wholesale —**whole′sal′er** n.

whole′some a. 1 healthful 2 improving one's morals 3 healthy —**whole′some·ness** n.

whole′-wheat′ a. (made of flour) ground from whole kernels of wheat

whol′ly adv. completely

whom pron. objective case of WHO

whoop v., n. (to utter) a loud shout, cry, etc.

whoop′ing cough n. infectious bacterial disease, esp. of children

whop′per n. [Inf.] 1 any large thing 2 big lie

whop′ping a. [Inf.] very large or great

whore (hôr) n. prostitute

whorl (hwôrl, hwurl) n. design of circular ridges

who's contr. 1 who is 2 who has

whose pron. that or those belonging to whom —a. of whom or of which

who′so·ev′er pron. whoever

why adv. for what reason? —con. 1 because of which 2 reason for which —n., pl. **whys** the reason —int. expression of surprise, etc.

WI abbrev. Wisconsin

wick n. piece of cord, etc. for burning, as in a candle

wick′ed a. 1 evil 2 unpleasant 3 naughty

wick′er n. 1 long, thin twigs or strips 2 wickerwork —a. made of wicker

wick′er·work′ n. baskets, etc. made of wicker

wick′et n. 1 small door, gate, or window 2 wire arch used in croquet

wide a. 1 great in width, amount, degree, etc. 2 of a specified width 3 far from the goal —adv. 1 over or to a large extent 2 so as to be wide —**wide′ly** adv. —**wid′en** v.

wide′-a-wake′ a. 1 completely awake 2 alert

wide′-eyed′ a. surprised, fearful, or naive

wide′spread′ a. occurring over a wide area

wid′ow n. woman whose husband has died —v. make a widow of —**wid′ow·hood′** n.

wid′ow·er n. man whose wife has died

width n. 1 distance side to side 2 a piece so wide

wield (wēld) v. 1 handle with skill 2 use (power, etc.)

wie′ner n. frankfurter

wife n., pl. **wives** married woman —**wife′ly** a.

wig n. false covering of hair for the head

wig′gle v., n. twist and turn from side to side —**wig′gly** a., **-gli·er, -gli·est**

wig′wag′ v. 1 wag 2 send messages by visible code

wig′wam′ n. cone-shaped tent of North American Indians

wild a. 1 in its natural state 2 not civilized 3 unruly 4 stormy 5 enthusiastic 6 reckless 7 missing the target —adv. in a wild way —n. pl. wilderness

wild′cat′ n. fierce cat of medium size, as the bobcat —a. 1 risky 2 unauthorized

wil′der·ness n. region not cultivated or inhabited

wild′-eyed′ a. 1 staring wildly 2 very foolish

wild′fire′ n. rapidly spreading fire, hard to put out

wild′fowl′ n. wild bird, esp. a game bird: also **wild fowl**

wild′-goose′ chase n. futile pursuit, search, or endeavor

wild′life′ n. wild animals

wild rice n. 1 a tall aquatic grass 2 its edible grain

wile n., v. trick; lure

will v. 1 wish; desire 2 strong purpose 3 power of choice 4 attitude 5 legal document disposing of one's property after death —v. 1 decide 2 control by the will 3 bequeath —**at will** when one wishes

will v. pt. **would** auxiliary verb showing: 1 future time 2 determination or obligation 3 ability or capacity

will'ful *a.* **1** done deliberately **2** stubborn Also sp. **wil'ful** —**will'ful·ly** *adv.* —**will'ful·ness** *n.*

wil'lies *pl.n.* [Sl.] nervous feeling: used with *the*

will'ing *a.* **1** consenting **2** doing or done gladly —**will'ing·ly** *adv.* —**will'ing·ness** *n.*

will'-o'-the-wisp' *n.* anything elusive

wil'low *n.* a tree with narrow leaves

wil'low·y *a.* slender

will'pow'er *n.* self-control

wil'ly-nil'ly *a., adv.* (happening) whether one wishes it or not

wilt *v.* **1** make or become limp **2** make or become weak

wil·y (wī'lē) *a.* **-li·er, -li·est** crafty; sly —**wil'i·ness** *n.*

wimp *n.* [Sl.] weak, dull person — **wimp'y** *a.,* **-i·er, -i·est** —**wimp'ish** *a.*

win *v.* **won, win'ning 1** gain a victory **2** get by work, effort, etc. **3** persuade —*n.* victory

wince *v.* draw back; flinch

winch *n.* machine for hoisting, etc. by a cable or rope wound on a drum

wind (wīnd) *v.* **wound, wind'ing 1** turn, coil, or twine around **2** cover, or tighten, by winding **3** move or go indirectly —*n.* a turn —**wind up** bring to an end; finish

wind (wind) *n.* **1** air in motion **2** gales **3** breath **4** smell **5** *Mus.* instrument played by blowing air, esp. breath, through it —*v.* put out of breath

wind'bag' *n.* [Inf.] one who talks much but says little of importance

wind'break' *n.* fence, trees, etc. protecting a place from the wind

wind'chill' factor *n.* estimated measure of the cooling effect of air and wind on exposed skin

wind'ed *a.* out of breath

wind'fall' *n.* unexpected gain, as of money

wind farm *n.* network of windmills for generating electricity

wind'lass (-ləs) *n.* winch

wind'mill' *n.* machine operated by the wind's rotation of a wheel of vanes

win'dow (-dō) *n.* **1** opening for light and air in a building, car, etc. **2** glass in a frame set in this

window dressing *n.* **1** store-window display **2** what is used to make something seem better

win'dow·pane' *n.* pane of glass in a window

win'dow-shop' *v.* look at goods in store windows without buying

win'dow·sill' *n.* sill of a window

wind'pipe' *n.* trachea

wind'shield' *n.* in cars, etc. glass shield in front of the driver, etc.

wind'surf' *v.* ride standing on a surfboard with a sail —**wind'surf'ing** *n.*

wind'up' (wīnd'-) *n.* end

wind'ward *a., adv., n.* (in or toward) the direction from which the wind blows

wind'y *a.* **-i·er, -i·est 1** with much wind; breezy **2** long-winded, pompous, etc.

wine *n.* fermented juice of grapes or of other fruits —*v.* usually in phrase **wine and dine,** entertain lavishly with food, drink, etc.

wing *n.* **1** organ used by a bird, insect, etc. in flying **2** thing like a wing in use or position **3** political faction **4** extension of a building —*v.* **1** to fly **2** send swiftly **3** wound in the wing or arm —**on the wing** in flight —**take wing** fly away —**under one's wing** under one's protection, etc. —**wing it** [Inf.] act without preparation; improvise —**winged** *a.* —**wing'less** *a.*

wing'ding' *n.* [Sl.] very lively party, event, etc.

wing'span' *n.* distance between tips of an airplane's wings

wing'spread' *n.* distance between tips of fully spread wings

wink *v.* **1** close and open the eyelids quickly **2** do this with one eye, as a signal **3** twinkle —*n.* **1** a winking **2** an instant

win'ner *n.* one that wins

win'ning *a.* **1** victorious **2** charming —*n.* **1** a victory **2** *pl.* something won

win'now (-ō) *v.* **1** blow the chaff from grain **2** sort out

wino *n., pl.* **-os** [Sl.] alcoholic who drinks cheap wine

win'some (-səm) *a.* charming

win'ter *n.* coldest season of the year — *a.* of or for winter —*v.* spend the winter

win'ter·green' *n.* **1** small shrub with evergreen leaves and red berries **2** oil from the leaves, used for flavoring

win'ter·ize' *v.* put into condition for winter

win'try *a.* **-tri·er, -tri·est** of or like winter

wipe *v.* **1** clean or dry by rubbing **2** rub (a cloth, etc.) over something —*n.* a wiping —**wipe out 1** remove **2** kill —**wip'er** *n.*

wiped'-out' *a.* [Sl.] exhausted

wire *n.* **1** metal drawn into a long thread **2** telegraph **3** telegram —*a.*

made of wire —v. **1** furnish or fasten with wire(s) **2** telegraph

wire′hair′ n. fox terrier with a wiry coat

wire′less a. operating by electric waves, not with conducting wire —n. **1** wireless telegraph or telephone **2** [Chiefly Br.] radio

wire service n. agency sending news electronically to subscribers

wire′tap′ v. tap (telephone wire) to get information secretly —n. **1** act of wiretapping **2** device for wiretapping

wir′ing n. system of wires, as for carrying electricity

wir′y a. **-i·er, -i·est 1** like wire; stiff **2** lean and strong —**wir′i·ness** n.

wis′dom n. **1** a being wise; good judgment **2** knowledge

wisdom tooth n. back tooth on each side of each jaw

wise a. **1** having good judgment **2** informed or learned —n. manner — **wise′ly** adv.

-wise suf. **1** in a certain direction, position, or manner **2** with regard to

wise′a·cre n. one annoyingly conceited in claiming knowledge

wise′crack′ v., n. [Sl.] (make) a flippant remark

wish v. **1** to want; desire **2** express a desire concerning **3** request —n. **1** a wishing **2** something wished for **3** request

wish′bone′ n. forked bone in front of a bird's breastbone

wish′ful a. showing a wish

wish′y-wash′y a. [Inf.] **1** weak **2** not decisive

wisp n. slight thing or bit —**wisp′y** a., **-i·er, -i·est**

wis·te′ri·a (-tir′ē-) n. twining shrub with clusters of flowers

wist′ful a. yearning —**wist′ful·ly** adv.

wit n. **1** (one with) the ability to make clever remarks **2** pl. powers of thinking —**to wit** namely

witch n. woman supposed to have evil, supernatural power

witch′craft′ n. power or practices of witches

witch doctor n. one thought to have magical power in curing disease, etc.

witch′er·y n. **1** witchcraft **2** bewitching charm

witch hazel n. lotion made from a plant extract, used as an astringent

with prep. **1** against **2** near to; in the care or company of **3** into **4** as a member of **5** concerning **6** compared to **7** as well as **8** in the opinion of **9**

as a result of **10** by means of **11** having or showing **12** to; onto **13** from **14** after

with·draw′ v. **1** take back **2** move back **3** leave —**with·draw′al** n.

with·drawn′ a. shy, reserved, etc.

with′er (with′-) v. wilt

with′ers (with′-) pl.n. highest part of the back of a horse, dog, etc.

with·hold′ v. **1** keep back; restrain **2** refrain from granting

withholding tax n. income tax kept in advance from workers' pay

with·in′ adv. in or to the inside —prep. **1** inside **2** not beyond

with·out′ adv. on the outside —prep. **1** outside **2** lacking **3** avoiding

with·stand′ v. resist; endure

wit′less a. stupid; foolish

wit′ness n. **1** one who saw and can testify to a thing **2** testimony; evidence **3** an attesting signer —v. **1** see **2** act as a witness of **3** be proof of —**bear witness** testify

wit′ti·cism′ n. witty remark

wit′ty a. **-ti·er, -ti·est** cleverly amusing

wives n. pl. of WIFE

wiz′ard n. magician

wiz′ard·ry n. magic

wiz′ened (-ənd) a. dried up and wrinkled

wk abbrev. week

w/o abbrev. without

wob′ble v. move unsteadily from side to side —n. a wobbling —**wob′bly** a., **-bli·er, -bli·est**

woe n. grief or trouble —**woe′ful** a. — **woe′ful·ly** adv.

woe′be·gone′ a. looking sorrowful or wretched

wok n. bowl-shaped frying pan

woke v. pt. of WAKE

wolf n., pl. **wolves** wild, doglike animal **2** cruel or greedy person —v. eat greedily —**cry wolf** give a false alarm —**wolf′ish** a.

wolf′hound′ n. breed of large dog

wol′ver·ine′ (-ēn′) n. strong animal like a small bear

wom′an n., pl. **wom′en** adult female person —**wom′an·hood′** n. —**wom′-an·ly** a.

wom′an·ish a. like a woman

wom′an·kind′ n. women in general

womb (woom) n. uterus

wom′bat′ (wäm′-) n. burrowing marsupial like a small bear

wom′en·folk′ pl.n. [Inf. or Dial.] women

won v. pt. & pp. of WIN

won'der n. 1 amazing thing; marvel 2 feeling caused by this —v. 1 feel wonder 2 be curious about

won'der·ful a. 1 causing wonder 2 excellent

won'der·land' n. place of wonders, great beauty, etc.

won'der·ment n. amazement

won'drous a. wonderful: a literary usage

wont (wônt, wōnt) a. accustomed —n. habit —**wont'ed** a.

won't contr. will not

woo v. seek to win, esp. as one's spouse

wood n. 1 hard substance under a tree's bark 2 lumber 3 [usually pl., with sing. or pl. v.] forest —a. 1 of wood 2 of the woods —**wood'ed** a.

wood alcohol n. poisonous alcohol used as fuel, etc.; methanol

wood'bine' n. climbing plant

wood'chuck' n. North American burrowing rodent; groundhog

wood'cut' n. print made from a wood engraving

wood'en a. 1 made of wood 2 lifeless, dull, etc.

wood'land' n., a. forest

wood'lot' n. land where trees are raised

wood'peck'er n. bird that pecks holes in bark

wood'shed' n. shed for firewood

wood'wind' a., n. (of) any of the wind instruments, esp. of wood, as the clarinet, oboe, flute, etc.

wood'work' n. wooden doors, frames, moldings, etc.

wood'work'ing n. art or work of making wooden items

wood'y a. **-i·er, -i·est** 1 tree-covered 2 of or like wood

woof (wōōf) n. weft

woof'er (wōōf'-) n. large speaker for low-frequency sounds

wool n. 1 soft, curly hair of sheep, goats, etc. 2 yarn or cloth made of this

wool'en a. of wool —n. pl. woolen goods

wool'gath'er·ing n. daydreaming

wool'ly a. **-li·er, -li·est** of, like, or covered with wool: also sp. **wool'y**

woo'zy a. **-i·er, -i·est** [Inf.] dizzy or dazed, as from drink

word n. 1 a sound or sounds as a speech unit 2 letter or letters standing for this 3 brief remark 4 news 5 promise 6 pl. quarrel —v. put into words

word'ing n. choice and arrangement of words

word of mouth n. speech, as opposed to writing

word'play' n. repartee or punning

word proc'ess·ing n. production, editing, etc. of documents with a computerized device (**word proc'es·sor**)

word'y a. **-i·er, -i·est** using too many words —**word'i·ness** n.

wore v. pt. of WEAR

work n. 1 effort of doing or making; labor 2 occupation, trade, etc. 3 task; duty 4 thing made, done, etc. 5 [pl., with sing. v.] factory 6 pl. engineering structures, as bridges 7 workmanship —v. worked, work'ing 1 do work; toil 2 to function 3 cause to work 4 be employed 5 bring about 6 come or bring to some condition 7 solve (a problem) —**at work** working —**the works** 1 working parts (of) 2 [Inf.] everything: also **the whole works** —**work off** get rid of —**work on** 1 influence 2 try to persuade —**work out** 1 develop or result 2 to exercise —**work up** 1 advance 2 develop 3 excite; arouse —**work'a·ble** a. —**work'er** n. —**work'man** n., pl. **-men**

work'a·day' a. ordinary

work'a·hol'ic n. person having an uncontrollable need to work

work'book' n. book of exercises, etc. for students

work'day' n. day or part of a day during which work is done

work'horse' n. reliable worker

work'house' n. jail where prisoners are put to work

work'ing a. 1 that works 2 of or used in work 3 enough to get work done

working class n. social group of those who do manual work

work'ing·man' n., pl. **-men'** worker, esp. in industry

work'man·like' a. done well

work'man·ship' n. 1 worker's skill 2 quality of work done

work'out' n. strenuous exercise, practice, etc.

work'shop' n. room or building where work is done

work'sta'tion n. person's work area, esp. including a computer terminal

work'ta'ble n. table at which work is done

work'-up' n. complete medical evaluation

world n. 1 the earth 2 the universe 3 all people 4 any sphere or domain 5 secular life **6** *often pl.* great deal

world'-class' *a.* highest-quality

world'ly *a.* **-li·er, -li·est 1** of the world; secular **2** sophisticated

world'ly-wise' *a.* wise in the ways of the world

world'-wea'ry *a.* bored with living

world'wide' *a., adv.* (extending) throughout the world

World Wide Web *n.* group of Internet sources giving access to text, images, sound, etc.

worm *n.* **1** long, slender creeping animal **2** thing like a worm **3** *pl.* disease caused by worms —*v.* **1** move like a worm **2** get in a sneaky way **3** purge of worms —**worm'y** *a.*, **-i·er, -i·est**

worm'wood' *n.* strong-smelling plant with a bitter-tasting oil

worn *v.* pp. of WEAR

worn'-out' *a.* **1** no longer usable **2** very tired

wor'ry *v.* **-ried, -ry·ing 1** make, or be, troubled or uneasy **2** annoy **3** bite at —*n., pl.* **-ries 1** troubled feeling **2** cause of this —**wor'ri·er** *n.* —**wor'ri·some** *a.*

wor'ry·wart' *n.* [Inf.] one who worries too much

worse *a.* **1** more evil, bad, etc. **2** more ill —*adv.* in a worse way —*n.* that which is worse

wors'en *v.* make or become worse

wor'ship *n.* **1** prayer, service, etc. in reverence to a deity **2** intense love or admiration —*v.* **1** show reverence for **2** take part in worship service

worst *a.* most evil, bad, etc. —*adv.* in the worst way —*n.* that which is worst

wor·sted (woos'tid, wur'stid) *n.* smooth wool fabric

worth *n.* **1** value or merit **2** equivalent in money —*prep.* **1** deserving **2** equal in value to —**worth'less** *a.*

worth'while' *a.* worth the time or effort spent

wor'thy *a.* **-thi·er, -thi·est 1** having worth or value **2** deserving —*n., pl.* **-thies** worthy person —**wor'thi·ness** *n.*

would *v.* pt. of WILL: *would* is used to express a condition, a wish, a request, etc.

would'-be' *a.* wishing, pretending, or intended to be

wound (woond) *n.* **1** injury to the body tissue **2** scar **3** injury to the feelings, etc. —*v.* injure; hurt

wound (wound) *v.* pt. & pp. of WIND (turn)

wove *v.* pt. of WEAVE

wo'ven *v.* pp. of WEAVE

wow *int.* expression of surprise, pleasure, etc.

wrack *n.* destruction

wraith *n.* ghost

wran'gle *v., n.* quarrel; dispute

wrap *v.* **wrapped, wrap'ping 1** wind or fold (a covering) around **2** enclose in paper, etc. —*n.* outer garment —**wrap'per** *n.*

wrap'ping *n. often pl.* material for wrapping something

wrap'-up' *n.* [Inf.] concluding, summarizing report, etc.

wrath *n.* great anger —**wrath'ful** *a.*

wreak (rēk) *v.* inflict (vengeance, etc.)

wreath (rēth) *n., pl.* **wreaths** (rēthz, rēths) twisted ring of leaves, etc.

wreathe (rēth) *v.* **1** encircle **2** decorate with wreaths

wreck *n.* **1** remains of a thing destroyed **2** rundown person **3** a wrecking —*v.* **1** destroy or ruin **2** tear down —**wreck'age** (-ij) *n.* —**wreck'er** *n.*

wren *n.* small songbird

wrench *n.* **1** sudden, sharp twist or injury caused by a twist **2** tool for turning nuts, bolts, etc. —*v.* **1** twist or jerk sharply **2** injure with a twist

wrest *v.* take by force

wres'tle (-al) *v.* **1** struggle with (an opponent) trying to throw him **2** contend (*with*) —*n.* a struggle —**wres'tler** *n.* —**wres'tling** *n.*

wretch *n.* **1** very unhappy person **2** person despised

wretch'ed *a.* **1** very unhappy **2** distressing **3** unsatisfactory —**wretch'ed·ness** *n.*

wrig'gle *v.* twist and turn, or move along thus —*n.* a wriggling —**wrig'gler** *n.*

wring *v.* **wrung, wring'ing 1** squeeze and twist **2** force out by this means **3** get by force —**wring'er** *n.*

wrin'kle *n.* **1** small crease or fold **2** [Inf.] clever idea, etc. —*v.* form wrinkles (in)

wrist *n.* joint between the hand and forearm

writ *n.* formal court order

write *v.* **wrote, writ'ten, writ'ing 1** form (words, letters, etc.) **2** produce (writing, music, etc.) **3** write a letter —**write off** cancel, as a debt —**writ'er** *n.*

write'-in' *n.* (a vote for) a person not listed on the ballot

write'-off' *n.* a canceled debt, amortized expense, etc.

write'-up *n.* [Inf.] written report

writhe (rīth) *v.* twist and turn, as in pain

wrong *a.* **1** not right or just **2** not true or correct **3** not suitable **4** mistaken **5** out of order **6** not meant to be seen —*adv.* incorrectly —*n.* something wrong —*v.* treat unjustly

wrong'do'ing *n.* unlawful or bad behavior —**wrong'do'er** *n.*

wrong'ful *a.* unjust, unlawful, etc. — **wrong'ful·ly** *adv.*

wrong'head'ed *a.* stubbornly holding to false ideas, etc.

wrought (rôt) *a.* **1** made **2** shaped by hammering

wrought iron *n.* tough, malleable iron used for fences, etc.

wrought'-up' *a.* very disturbed or excited

wrung *v.* pt. & pp. of WRING

wry (rī) *a.* **wri'er** or **wry'er, wri'est** or **wry'est 1** twisted or distorted **2** ironic —**wry'ly** *adv.* —**wry'ness** *n.*

wt *abbrev.* weight

wuss (woos) *n.* [Sl.] a wimp

WV *abbrev.* West Virginia

WWI *abbrev.* World War I

WWII *abbrev.* World War II

WY *abbrev.* Wyoming

WYSIWYG (wiz'ē wig') *n.* computer screen format showing text as it will be printed

X

xen'o·pho'bi·a (zen'ə-) *n.* fear or hatred of foreigners

xe·rog'ra·phy (zi-) *n.* process for copying printed material electrically

Xe·rox (zir'äks') *trademark* device for copying printed material by xerography —*v.* [x-] to copy by xerography — *n.* [x-] a copy made by xerography

X'mas *n.* [Inf.] Christmas

X'-rat'ed *a.* having graphically portrayed sexual, or obscene, content

X'-ray' *n.* **1** type of electromagnetic wave that can penetrate solid matter **2** photograph made with X-rays —*a.* of or by X-rays —*v.* photograph, treat, or examine with X-rays   Also sp. **X ray, x-ray,** or **x ray**

xy'lem (zī'-) *n.* woody vascular tissue of a plant

xy'lo·phone' (zī'-) *n.* musical instrument consisting of a row of wooden bars struck with hammers

Y

-y *suf.* **1** full of or like **2** rather **3** apt to **4** state of being **5** act of

yacht (yät) *n.* small ship for recreation —*v.* sail in a yacht —**yachts'man** *n.,* *pl.* **-men**

ya'hoo' *n.* person thought of as vulgar, uneducated, etc.

yak [Sl.] *v.* **yakked, yak'king** talk much or idly —*n.* a yakking

yak *n.* wild ox of Asia

yam *n.* **1** starchy, edible root of a tropical plant **2** type of sweet potato

yam'mer *v.* whine or complain

yank *v., n.* [Inf.] jerk

Yan'kee *n.* **1** U.S. citizen **2** native of a northern state

yap *v.* **yapped, yap'ping;** *n.* (make) a sharp, shrill bark

yard *n.* **1** measure of length, three feet **2** ground around a building **3** enclosed place **4** slender spar fastened across a mast

yard'age (-ij) *n.* distance or length in yards

yard'stick' *n.* **1** measuring stick one yard long **2** standard for judging

yar'mul·ke (-məl kə) *n.* small, round cap worn by Jewish men

yarn *n.* **1** spun strand of wool, cotton, etc. **2** [Inf.] tale or story

yaw *v., n.* swing erratically off course

yawl *n.* kind of sailboat

yawn *v.* open the mouth widely, as when one is sleepy —*n.* a yawning

yaws *n.* tropical, infectious skin disease

yd *abbrev.* yard(s)

ye (yē; *a.:* thə) [Ar.] *pron.* you —*a.* the

yea (yā) *adv.* **1** yes **2** truly —*n.* vote of "yes"

yeah (ya) *adv., int.* [Inf.] yes

year *n.* **1** period of 365 days (366 in leap year) or 12 months **2** *pl.* age **3** *pl.* a long time

year'book' *n.* book with data of the preceding year

year'ling *n.* animal in its second year

year'ly *a.* **1** every year **2** of a year — *adv.* every year

yearn (yurn) *v.* feel longing —**yearn'ing** *n.*

year'-round' *a.* open, in use, etc. throughout the year

yeast *n.* single-celled fungus causing fermentation, esp. such a fungus used to make dough rise

yell *v., n.* scream; shout

yel'low a. **1** of the color of ripe lemons **2** [Inf.] cowardly —n. yellow color —v. to make or become yellow —**yel'low-ish** a.

yellow fever n. tropical disease carried by a mosquito

yellow jacket n. bright-yellow wasp or hornet

yelp v., n. (utter) a short, sharp cry or bark

yen n. [Inf.] strong desire

yeo'man (yō'-) n., pl. **-men** U.S. Navy clerk

yes adv. it is so —n., pl. **yes'es** **1** consent **2** affirmative vote

ye·shi'va (-shē'-) n. Jewish seminary

yes man n. [Sl.] one who always approves what his superior says

yes'ter·day' n. **1** day before today **2** recent time —adv. on the day before today

yet adv. **1** up to now **2** now **3** still; even now **4** nevertheless —con. nevertheless

yew n. evergreen tree or shrub

Yid'dish n. language derived from German using the Hebrew alphabet

yield v. **1** produce; give **2** surrender **3** concede; grant **4** give way to force —n. amount produced

yield'ing a. flexible; submissive

yip v. yipped, yip'ping; n. [Inf.] yelp or bark

YMCA abbrev. Young Men's Christian Association

yo'del v. sing with abrupt, alternating changes to the falsetto —n. a yodeling

yo'ga n. Hindu discipline for uniting self with supreme spirit through meditation and various exercises

yo'gi (-gē) n., pl. **-gis** one who practices yoga

yo'gurt, yo'ghurt n. thick, semisolid food made from fermented milk

yoke n. **1** frame for harnessing together a pair of oxen, etc. **2** thing that binds or unites **3** servitude **4** part of a garment at the shoulders —v. **1** harness to **2** join together

yo'kel n. person living in rural area: contemptuous term

yolk (yōk) n. yellow part of an egg

Yom Kip·pur (kip'ər) n. Jewish holiday and day of fasting

yon a., adv. [Dial.] yonder

yon'der a., adv. over there

yore n. time long past

you pron., pl. **you 1** the person spoken to **2** any person

you'd contr. **1** you had **2** you would

you'll contr. **1** you will **2** you shall

young a. **1** in an early stage of life or growth **2** fresh —n. young offspring —**with young** pregnant —**young'ish** a.

young adult n. age group of readers 12 to 18 years old

young'ster n. child

your a. of you

you're contr. you are

yours pron. that or those belonging to you

your·self' pron., pl. **-selves'** intensive or reflexive form of YOU

yours truly pron. [Inf.] I or me

youth n. **1** state or quality of being young **2** adolescence **3** young people **4** young man —**youth'ful** a.

you've contr. you have

yowl v., n. howl; wail

yo'-yo' n., pl. **-yos'** spool-like toy on a string on which it is made to spin up and down

yr abbrev. year(s)

YT abbrev. Yukon Territory

Y2K abbrev. the year 2000

yuc'ca n. desert plant with white flowers

yuck [Sl.] n. something disgusting — int. an expression of disgust —**yuck'y** a., **-i·er**, **-i·est**

yule n. [often Y-] Christmas

yule'tide' n. [often Y-] Christmas time

yum'my a. **-mi·er**, **-mi·est** [Inf.] very tasty; delicious

yup'pie n. [Inf.] affluent, ambitious young professional

YWCA abbrev. Young Women's Christian Association

Z

zaf'tig (zäf'-) a. [Sl.] having a full, shapely figure

za'ny n., pl. **-nies** a silly or foolish person —a. **-ni·er**, **-ni·est** of or like a zany —**za'ni·ness** n.

zap v. zapped, zap'ping [Sl.] move, strike, kill, etc. suddenly and with great speed —int. exclamation used to express such action

zeal n. eager endeavor or devotion

zeal'ot (zel'-) n. one showing zeal, esp. fanatic zeal

zeal'ous (zel'-) a. full of zeal —**zeal'ous·ly** adv.

ze'bra n. striped African animal similar to the horse

ze'bu' n. oxlike animal with a hump

Zen n. form of Buddhism seeking wisdom through meditation

ze'nith *n.* **1** point in the sky directly overhead **2** the highest point

zeph·yr (zef'ər) *n.* breeze

zep'pe·lin *n.* [*often* Z-] dirigible

ze'ro *n., pl.* **-ros** *or* **-roes 1** the symbol 0 **2** point marked 0 on a scale **3** nothing —*a.* of or at zero

zero hour *n.* **1** the time an attack is to begin **2** crucial point

zero population growth *n.* condition in which the birth rate equals the death rate

ze'ro-sum' *a.* of a situation in which a gain for one means a loss for another

zest *n.* **1** stimulating quality **2** keen enjoyment —**zest'ful** *a.*

zig'zag' *n.* line with sharp turns back and forth —*a., adv.* in a zigzag —*v.* **-zagged', -zag'ging** to move or form in a zigzag

zilch *n.* [Sl.] nothing; zero

zil'lion (-yən) *n.* [Inf.] very large, indefinite number

zinc *n.* bluish-white metal, a chemical element

zing *n.* [Sl.] shrill, whizzing sound

zin'ni·a *n.* plant with colorful flowers

Zi'on·ism' (zī'-) *n.* movement supporting the state of Israel

zip *v.* **zipped, zip'ping 1** make a short, sharp hissing sound **2** [Inf.] move fast **3** fasten with a zipper —*n.* **1** a zipping sound **2** [Inf.] energy; vigor —**zip'py** *a.*, **-pi·er, -pi·est**

ZIP Code *service mark* mail delivery system using code numbers for zones —*n.* [*usually* **zip c-**] such a code number

zip'per *n.* fastener with interlocking tabs worked by a sliding part

zir'con' *n.* hard, brownish mineral, used as a gem when transparent

zit *n.* [Sl.] pimple, esp. on face

zith'er *n.* stringed instrument, played by plucking

zo'di·ac' *n.* imaginary belt along the sun's apparent path divided into 12 parts, each named for a different constellation

zom'bie *n.* **1** animated corpse in folklore **2** [Sl.] person who is listless, machine-like, etc.

zone *n.* **1** any of the five areas into which the earth is divided according to climate **2** area set apart in some way —*v.* mark off into zones —**zoned** *a.*

zonked *a.* [Sl.] **1** drunk or under the influence of a drug **2** exhausted

zoo *n.* place with wild animals on exhibition

zo'o·log'i·cal garden (zō'-) *n.* zoo

zo·ol'o·gy (zō-) *n.* science of animal life —**zo'o·log'i·cal** *a.* —**zo·ol'o·gist** *n.*

zoom *v.* **1** make a loud, humming sound **2** speed upward or forward —*n.* a zooming

zoom lens *n.* system of lenses adjustable for close or distant shots while keeping the image always in focus

zuc·chi·ni (zoo kē'nē) *n.* cucumberlike squash

zwie·back (swē'bak', swī'-) *n.* dried, toasted slices of a kind of biscuit

zy'gote *n.* fertilized egg cell before it divides

RULES FOR SPELLING

Words that end in a silent e usually drop the e when a suffix beginning with a vowel is added [*file—filing*]. However, before the suffixes *-able* and *-ous*, the e is usually kept if it follows a soft c or g [*outrage—outrageous*]. The e is usually kept when a suffix beginning with a consonant is added [*time—timely*].

Words that end in a single consonant preceded by a single vowel usually double that consonant when a suffix beginning with a vowel is added, if: a) the word is a single syllable [*sin—sinning*] or b) the word has more than one syllable but is stressed on the last syllable [*refer—referring*]. If the final consonant is *not* preceded by a single vowel or, in American usage, if the last syllable is *not* stressed, the final consonant is usually not doubled [*hurl—hurling, travel—traveling*].

Words that end in a double letter usually drop one letter when a suffix beginning with the same letter is added [*free—freest*].

Words that end in y preceded by a consonant usually change the y to an i when a suffix that does not begin with i is added [*marry—married*]. If the y is preceded by a vowel, the y is usually kept [*play—played*].

Words that end in ie change the ie to a y when the suffix *-ing* is added [*lie—lying*].

Words that end in c usually take on a k when a suffix beginning with i or e is added [*picnic—picnicker*].

Words containing ie or ei: In most native English words, *ie* is used. Two main exceptions are: 1) following the letter c, *ei* is usually used; 2) when the sound (ā) is represented, *ei* is used.

Note that the suffix -ful, unlike the adjective *full,* has only one l [*cupful*].

Verbs ending in -cede and -ceed: Three common verbs (*exceed, proceed,* and *succeed*) end in *-ceed.* Most others end in *-cede.*

RULES FOR FORMING PLURALS

Most nouns in English form the plural by adding *-s* or *-es*. When the singular noun ends in a sound that allows the sound (s) to be added and pronounced without the formation of a new syllable, *-s* is used [*book—books*]. When the singular noun ends in a sound such that (s) cannot be joined to it and pronounced without the formation of another syllable, *-es* is used [*kiss—kisses, torch—torches*].

The chief exceptions to this basic rule are listed below.

Words that end in o usually form the plural by adding *-es* [*hero—heroes*]. However, some of them do so by adding *-s* [*solo—solos*]. There is no absolute rule dealing with this group of words.

Some words that end in f form the plural by changing the f to v and adding *-es* [*wolf—wolves*].

Words that end in y preceded by a consonant usually form the plural by changing the y to i and adding *-es* [*lady—ladies*]. If the y is preceded by a vowel, they form the plural regularly, by adding *-s* [*day—days*].

Some words form the plural by a vowel change. Among the commonest examples are *foot—feet, man—men, tooth—teeth, woman—women.*

Some words have special plurals to which none of the above general statements apply. Among them are words such as *alumna—alumnae, child—children, phenomenon—phenomena, radius—radii, sheep—sheep.*

RULES FOR PUNCTUATION

The **Period** (.) is used: 1) at the end of a sentence; 2) after many abbreviations; 3) in a decimal fraction; 4) as one of a series (usually three spaced periods) to indicate an omission, an interruption, or a break in continuity.

The **Comma** (,) is used: 1) between short independent clauses in parallel construction and between clauses joined by conjunctions such as *and, but, or, nor, yet,* and *for;* 2) after a fairly long dependent clause that precedes an independent clause; 3) before and after a dependent clause that comes in the middle of a sentence; 4) to set off a nonrestrictive word, phrase, or clause; 5) to set off transitional words and phrases; 6) to separate words, phrases, or clauses in series; 7) to set off the word indicating the one spoken to in direct address; 8) to set off a direct quotation; 9) to set off a title, an address, a place name, a date, etc.; 10) after the salutation of an informal letter; 11) after the complimentary close of any letter; 12) in a numeral of five or more digits.

The **Semicolon** (;) is used: 1) in a compound sentence between independent clauses that are not joined by connectives, or between such clauses joined by a conjunctive adverb (such as *thus*); 2) between phrases or clauses that contain internal punctuation.

The **Colon** (:) is used: 1) before a long series; 2) before a lengthy quotation; 3) between chapter and verse, volume and page, hour and minute, etc.; 4) after the salutation of a business letter.

The **Question Mark** (?) is used: 1) after a direct question; 2) as an indication of uncertainty or doubt.

The **Exclamation Point** (!) is used after a word, phrase, or sentence to indicate strong emotion, surprise, etc.

The **Hyphen** (-) is used: 1) between the parts of a compound word or numeral; 2) between the parts of a divided word, as at the end of a line.

The **Dash** (—) is used: 1) between sentence parts, to show a break in continuity; 2) to set off a parenthetical expression.

Quotation Marks: *Double* ("") are used: 1) to enclose a direct quotation; 2) to enclose the titles of articles, short stories, short poems, etc., or the divisions or chapters of books, periodicals, long poems, etc. *Single* ('') are used to enclose a quotation within a quotation.

Italic Type is used: 1) to set off the titles of books, periodicals, newspapers, etc.; 2) to indicate foreign words or phrases; 3) to emphasize a word within a sentence.

The **Apostrophe** (') is used: 1) in place of an omitted letter or letters in a word or contraction; 2) with an added *s* to form the possessive case of all nouns that do not end in the sound (s) or (z); 3) with an optional *s* to form the possessive of singular nouns that end in (s) or (z); 4) without an added *s* to form the possessive of plural nouns that end in (s) or (z); 5) in inflected forms of verbs formed from abbreviations.

Parentheses, ( ), are used: 1) to enclose nonessential material in a sentence; 2) to enclose letters or numbers of reference, as in an outline.

Brackets, [ ], are used to indicate: 1) an insertion, a comment, a correction, etc., made by a person other than the original author of the material; 2) parentheses within parentheses.

A **Capital Letter** is used: 1) to begin a sentence, or a quotation or direct question within a sentence; 2) to begin every word, except conjunctions, articles, and short prepositions that are not the first word, in the name of a book, magazine, work of music or art, business, agency, religion, holiday, etc.; 3) to begin every main word in a proper noun; 4) to begin every main word in the name of a day, month, era, etc.; 5) to begin many abbreviations; 6) to begin a noun or a pronoun referring to the Deity; 7) to begin the salutation and the complimentary close of a letter.

WEIGHTS AND MEASURES

Linear

12 inches	= 1 foot
3 feet	= 1 yard
5.5 yards	= 1 rod
40 rods	= 1 furlong
8 furlongs	= 1 mile

Liquid

16 ounces	= 1 pint
2 pints	= 1 quart
4 quarts	= 1 gallon
31.5 gallons	= 1 barrel (liquid)
2 barrels	= 1 hogshead

Metric Equivalents

1 inch	= 2.5400 centimeters	1 kilometer	= 0.6214 mile
1 foot	= 0.3048 meter	1 quart (dry)	= 1.1012 liters
1 yard	= 0.9144 meter	1 quart (liquid)	= 0.9464 liter
1 mile	= 1.6093 kilometers	1 gallon	= 3.7854 liters
1 centimeter	= 0.3937 inch	1 liter	= 0.9081 dry quart
1 decimeter	= 3.9370 inches	1 liter	= 1.0567 liquid quarts
1 meter	= 39.3701 inches		

Square

144 sq. inches	= 1 sq. foot
9 sq. feet	= 1 sq. yard
30.25 sq. yards	= 1 sq. rod
160 sq. rods	= 1 acre
640 acres	= 1 sq. mile

Circular

60 seconds	= 1 minute
60 minutes	= 1 degree
90 degrees	= 1 quadrant
180 degrees	= 1 semicircle
360 degrees	= 1 circle

Metric Equivalents

1 sq. inch	= 6.4516 sq. centimeters
1 sq. foot	= 929.0304 sq. centimeters
1 sq. mile	= 2.590 sq. kilometers
1 sq. centimeter	= 0.155 sq. inch
1 sq. meter	= 1.196 sq. yards
1 sq. kilometer	= 0.3861 sq. mile

Cubic

1,728 cu. inches	= 1 cu. foot
27 cu. feet	= 1 cu. yard
128 cu. feet	= 1 cord (wood)

Dry

2 pints	= 1 quart
8 quarts	= 1 peck
4 pecks	= 1 bushel

Metric Equivalents

1 cu. inch	= 16.3871 cu. centimeters
1 cu. inch	= 0.0164 liter
1 cu. foot	= 0.0283 cu. meter
1 cu. foot	= 28.3169 liters
1 cu. meter	= 35.3147 cu. feet
1 ounce (avdp.)	= 28.3495 grams
1 pound	= 0.4536 kilogram
1 gram	= 0.0353 ounce
1 kilogram	= 2.2046 pounds
1 (short) ton (2000 pounds)	= 907.1847 kilograms

Longitude and Time

1 second of longitude	= 1/15 second of time
1 minute of longitude	= 4 seconds of time
1 degree of longitude	= 4 minutes of time
15 degrees of longitude	= 1 hour
360 degrees of longitude	= 24 hours